FLEET RENEGADE

The Under Jurisdiction Series

BOOKS IN THIS SERIES

Fleet Inquisitor
Fleet Renegade
Fleet Insurgent (forthcoming)
Blood Enemies (forthcoming)

FLEET RENEGADE

The Under Jurisdiction Series

SUSAN R. MATTHEWS

Hour of Judgement copyright © 1999 by Susan R. Matthews
The Devil and Deep Space copyright © 2002 by Susan R. Matthews
Warring States copyright © 2006 by Susan R. Matthews

A Baen Books Original

Baen Publishing Enterprises
P.O. Box 1403
Riverdale, NY 10471
www.baen.com

ISBN: 978-1-4767-8209-6

Cover art by Kurt Miller

First Baen printing, February 2017

Distributed by Simon & Schuster
1230 Avenue of the Americas
New York, NY 10020

Printed in the United States of America

10 9 8 7 6 5 4 3 2 1

CONTENTS

INTRODUCTION

Twenty Years Under Jurisdiction

Hello, and welcome to *Fleet Renegade*—the second omnibus of my Under Jurisdiction novels, comprising the fourth through sixth in the series. This'll get you caught up for *Blood Enemies*, which is a new novel in the Under Jurisdiction series. I want to say a few words about the over-all series, which is coming up on its twenty-year mark; but first let's talk about these three novels.

The first Baen omnibus (*Fleet Inquisitor*) started with *An Exchange of Hostages*, in which my protagonist Andrej Koscuisko begins his Fleet career as the chief medical officer of a Jurisdiction Fleet warship—Ship's Surgeon; Ship's Inquisitor. His dual role results from the Jurisdiction government's adoption of institutionalized torture as an instrument of state: not in the interests of truth, but in the service of social control and deterrent terror.

The reluctant Andrej discovers that not only is he very good at inflicting horrifying tortures on prisoners, but that he quite enjoys it. He'll be spending the rest of the series grappling with what that means for him as well as for prisoners referred for Inquiry, and trying to find justice—if not honor—in the face of overwhelming odds.

In *Prisoner of Conscience* a shattering personal loss blinds him to the realization of the horrors of the Domitt Prison until it is almost too late to act against them.

Andrej's system of origin is the Dolgorukij Combine. The "Malcontent" secret agent with whom Bench specialists Garol Vogel

1

and Jils Ivers find themselves working in *Angel of Destruction* is Dolgorukij; the Angel of Destruction itself—a savagely racist terrorist organization long thought destroyed—is Dolgorukij as well. Andrej's role is brief but pivotal, and the action of the novel will cast a very long shadow over books to come; you'll be glad you brushed up on it. Trust me.

Fast forward, now, to the novels in *Fleet Renegade*. There are two primary threads in play: one is Andrej's continuing, more and more desperate, search through a rapidly dwindling pool of coping mechanisms and rationalizations for an answer that will help him survive.

The other main thread focuses on the increasingly urgent signs of fundamental fractures in the rule of Law, and on the Bench specialists whose life's work is to preserve Jurisdiction space from the horrors that will come if the Bench collapses, drawing all of known Space into a cataclysmic state of civil war unmitigated by the Judicial order.

When we first met Andrej in *An Exchange of Hostages*, he had eight years of active duty to serve in Fleet before his obligation would be fulfilled and he could leave. At the beginning of *Hour of Judgement* those years are up, and Andrej's ready to go home; though he hates leaving his Security behind, because he owes his life to them many times over.

He's been four years assigned to the Jurisdiction Fleet Ship *Ragnarok*, a warship built to evaluate the newly developed "black hull" technology. Its commander, the sadistic and corrupt Captain Lowden, has a sideline in black-market torture tapes, and an appetite for testing Inquisitors to destruction. After all, the *Ragnarok* is a test bed, isn't it?

Lowden has gone easy on Andrej for several reasons—first and foremost being his own rational self-interested concerns for the health and welfare of his illegal revenue stream. Even so, after four years with Captain Lowden, Andrej is closer to complete collapse into psychosis than he has ever been.

He might not have made it this long, had it not been for his bond-involuntaries: Security slaves, criminals condemned to carry a "governor" in their brains that punishes the slightest infraction with suffering sufficiently extreme to enforce absolute obedience. Fleet assigns them to Inquisitors to serve as instruments of torture, constrained to inflict whatever atrocious torment their officer of assignment should direct.

From the beginning Andrej has treated bond-involuntaries as though they were his family house-guards; spoken to them as though they were human beings, worked around their governors as much as possible. Many of them in turn have given him the only thing they have—their trust; out of self-interest, out of gratitude, even through a peculiar sort of fellow-feeling. Security Chief Stildyne, on the other hand, while not a bond-involuntary, has his own personal reasons for wanting Andrej to win his struggle to stay alive and sane.

Andrej's a man of strong character. He's had to be, to survive. One might have thought that the news he gets at the beginning of *Hour of Judgment*—that he's to be forced to serve another term of duty, working for the man he blames for the horrors of the Domitt Prison and the death of a man he loved as he has few others—would be the last straw; and that he would not survive to be of any use to anybody, ever again.

Andrej surprises them all, Lowden, First Secretary Verlaine, Bench intelligence specialists Ivers and Vogel; Stildyne surprises him. The surprise that the bond-involuntary Robert St. Clare has for him, however, is the one that finally sends Andrej over the edge headlong into the final solution—as he sees it—to the entire problem of his life as a Judicial torturer. (There will be blood.)

Then in *The Devil and Deep Space* Andrej, knowing himself to be as good as dead if the truth of *Hour of Judgment* ever comes out, goes home to settle his affairs. He gets a break: there's to be a new First Judge, selected by consensus among the nine Judiciaries; the Bench is officially distracted.

As the inheriting son of the Koscuisko familial corporation, an influential part of the Dolgorukij Combine, Andrej's political importance is enough to ensure that the *Ragnarok*'s flamboyant resistance to a Fleet frame-up is interpreted—for the time being—as the relatively benign "mutiny in form" rather than "mutiny in intent."

As a result, in *Warring States*, Andrej takes advantage of the opportunity to free his bond-involuntary Security from their governors, sending them to the safety of Gonebeyond Space. So far, so good; but while Andrej is working on his personal priorities, our Bench Specialist friends Ivers and Vogel are facing unprecedented challenges in the selection of the new First Judge. If that process fails, it will be the end of Jurisdiction Space as we know it.

This is a book of astonishments: for Joslire's brother Shona, meeting the man who holds Joslire's knives. For Jils Ivers, treachery and betrayal beyond imagination. For Andrej, the realization that the Security chief in his bedroom is Caleigh Samons from *Scylla*, come to kidnap him on his former captain Irshah Parmin's authority; and the startling discovery that leaves him with the most important apology of his life to make, and Gonebeyond space the place he has to go to make it.

And then there's my latest Under Jurisdiction novel, *Blood Enemies*. As the book opens, Andrej has been in Gonebeyond for a year; he and the *Ragnarok* aren't on speaking terms; and he hasn't seen the bond-involuntaries he stole from the Bench, because they've been fully absorbed in the therapeutic deployment of a main battle cannon on a Kospodar thula on loan from the Malcontent, under general Langsarik direction.

But it's not all fun and games. In significant ways *Blood Enemies* is the roughest Jurisdiction novel since *An Exchange of Hostages*. To solve the problem of the novel Andrej has to unleash the wolf within, and commit an act of profound betrayal that is also an act of absolute trust and loyalty to people he loves. He doesn't know why, but he knows what must be done, and he knows—to his cost—that he's the only man who can do it.

Blood Enemies arrives twenty years after *An Exchange of Hostages* first came out. By the end of *Blood Enemies* Andrej will have either at last solved the problems I put in front of him twenty years ago, or have gone down trying his best to do so. I can't ask him for anything more than that.

I'm proud of these novels. I'm grateful to Baen for bringing these first six back into print, and for publishing *Blood Enemies*. I'm grateful to you guys, you book-reading people, you, for taking an interest in my story and the people who are in it, and for sticking with it all this time.

Thank you all for coming. I hope that you enjoy these novels.

HOUR OF JUDGEMENT

A Novel Under Jurisdiction

Burkhayden is a subject colony, leased by the Bench to a Dolgorukij familial corporation for economic exploitation. When a Nurail woman from the service house is brutally raped and beaten, Andrej Koscuisko—Ship's Inquisitor on board the Jurisdiction Fleet Ship *Ragnarok*—is called upon to render services under contract.

One of Koscuisko's bond-involuntary Security slaves recognizes the tortured woman. And murder is done in Port Burkhayden. The only way Andrej can protect a man he loves is to condemn a guiltless man to atrocious torment. Will he commit the ultimate crime?

Before one fateful night is out Andrej Koscuisko will put himself under sentence of death by doing what he realizes at last he should have done from the beginning.

And Port Burkhayden will burn.

Dedication

This book is dedicated with love to my mother (than whom I could not have chosen a better, had it been mine to choose) because Two has always been her favorite character in the story. My mother's children have always been her favorite characters in their lives, and between her and my daddy they raised all six of us with astounding tolerance and grace.

Acknowledgments

I would like to gratefully acknowledge a "random act of kindness" committed by a gentleman on a plane last October who, when we arrived at SeaTac Airport, chased me half the length of the concourse to bring me my manuscript book, which I'd been writing in during the flight and had left on the seat. There were forty pages of manuscript that I hadn't typed up in that book, and if it hadn't been for him I would have lost it all. Thank you again, sir, and may your tribe increase.

CHAPTER ONE

It was early evening in Port Burkhayden. The air currents that blew toward the bay in the morning hours had stilled and reversed themselves, and the breeze grew colder by the day; but it was warm on the back steps still, sheltered from the wind by the bulk of the great house behind them.

"All right, then," the gardener said, his tone light and challenging. Almost Sylphe wanted to call it affectionate; but that wouldn't be proper, not with the distance between them. Skelern Hanner was a good gardener. But that was all he was.

Plucking a bit of black-twigged greenery out of the little pile that lay between them on the steps, Hanner continued to quiz. "You're solid on the sdotz, one and all. Sdotz are good for color, but delicate tones need background, don't they now?"

It was Hanner's game to tease her, when all she'd ever done was ask him questions about his gardening. He didn't take her seriously. Why should he? Because she had been to school, and he had not—but there was no question that he knew much more about his garden than she did.

"Markept-branch?" she guessed, eagerly, frowning at the twig of evergreen Hanner held out to her. "Or—no, it's markept-branch. Surely. Oh, tell, Skelern."

He laughed at her eagerness, and Sylphe blushed, wishing the breeze would turn and carry the prickling heat of her own gaucherie away from her face. She hated to see herself blush. She blushed in splotches, obvious and awkward, and it always made her blush when Skelern laughed. She wasn't certain why. She only suspected that it had to do with the suddenness of the sight of his white teeth, when the rest of him was ruddy-brown with sun or sweat.

"Perfect marks, little maistress, markept-branch it is, and from the far reaches. From Perkipsie, in fact, come across the Senterif vector to Burkhayden before the Bench came down upon us."

If she was right, why had he laughed? He teased her too often. It was unkind of him. She didn't know why she tolerated his impudence; and yet she'd had nobody else to talk to, not these six months gone past. Standard.

"The Danzilar fleet is only four weeks out, they say." The Senterif vector, somewhere past Burkhayden's pale new moon this time of year. Sylyphe frowned into the darkening sky, wondering where to place the space-lane's terminus. "There will be an end to the Bench, Skelern, in a sense at least. That will be good, won't it?"

The Danzilar fleet was what had brought her mother here six months ago, to position Iaccary Cordage and Textile among the industries eager to enter into partnership with prince Paval I'shenko Danzilar to exploit his newly indentured world. The Bench had been sending Nurail into exile here for longer than that; but Skelern Hanner himself was a native, bred and born in Burkhayden.

And bitter about what had become of Nurail under Jurisdiction, for all that he did not seem to blame her for it. Not personally. "Sold is sold, sweet Sylyphe. I wasn't born cattle. And I had a mother and a father, once."

It was hard to blame him. He had suffered loss and privation under Jurisdiction. It had all been for the preservation of the Judicial order, she was sure of that; though it was hard to understand what threat a gardener could have posed the Bench.

"All the same." She didn't like to argue with him, especially when she felt he might have good cause to feel resentful. But she wished he wouldn't sulk. There was nothing either of them could do about it, after all. "The first step toward citizenship, Skelern. They're odd people, from what I've heard, but practical."

Well, perhaps that was a little overgenerous of her. Dolgorukij were practical, yes. But more than that, Dolgorukij were ferocious competitors, notorious for milking any commercial exchange for everything it might be worth. Not people one would chose as one's employer, if one had the choice; and it would only depress Skelern to remind him that he had none.

Why had she tried to say anything?

Sylyphe hugged her knees to her bosom and frowned at the back of the garden, disgusted at herself.

Hanner spent some moments picking out pieces of grass and fern with a great show of concentration on his dark sharp-chinned face. "The Danzilar fleet. Well. There'll be parties, little maistress, you'll want for a corsage."

The suggestion startled her into turning her head, meeting his black eyes over the posy he offered. It was a perfect little bouquet, wrapped in a leaf and pinned into a tidy bundle with a thorn. Beautiful. Sylyphe took the delicate favor with confused delight, admiring it in the failing light as Hanner spoke on.

"And with the fleet. An escort ship, the *Ragnarok*, have you heard of the Jurisdiction Fleet Ship *Ragnarok*, Sylyphe? It's a man with the blood of Nurail souls on his hands that carries the surgery there, him from the Domitt Prison. Black Andrej."

Sylyphe frowned.

The Domitt Prison . . . it had been years ago, five years; she'd been much younger. The Judicial briefings had mesmerized her mother, and Sylyphe hadn't ever quite understood what the fuss had been about; and still—

"Andrej Koscuisko, do you mean, Skelern?" And still she could recall one image among many, one image that sprang up readily before her mind's eye. A slim young officer, blond, and wearing the black of a Ship's Prime officer—the Ship's Inquisitor, Jurisdiction Fleet Ship *Scylla*. Andrej Koscuisko. *I have cried Failure of Writ against the administration of the Domitt Prison, and I will hazard my life against the justice of my plea.*

"The same." Skelern was looking at her with rather an odd expression on his face. She blushed once more, without knowing quite why. "And there's more than several here in Burkhayden in these days to remember him from Rudistal, but he's got nothing to fear from us. Not after the Domitt. Unlike young Skelern, now—"

Tumbling the pile of flowers into her lap with one swift gesture

Hanner rose to his feet, talking as he went. "—who's much to fear from my respected maistress your lady mither, if I don't get the turves trimmed up in the tea-garden before the morning comes. I'm off."

And in a bit of a hurry all of a sudden, as well. What was on his mind? Sylyphe gathered the cuttings into a loose bunch, careful to keep her posy from being crushed. "Black" Andrej Koscuisko. It had a wicked sort of resonance to it.

The Court had awarded him execution of the sentences passed down at the conclusion of the hearings; he had killed men, and at the Tenth Level of the Question. Taken vengeance for the Bench against the criminals judged responsible for the Domitt Prison. There was a measure of attractiveness to the idea of such a man—an indistinct figure of glittering menace, irresistible with the demonic allure of all of one's darkest nightmares . . . an Inquisitor. Torturer. Executioner.

Perhaps she would meet him at a party, since there were to be so many when the Fleet arrived at last. She would be presented, he would bow; she would return the courtesy with calm—self-possessed— fearless maturity, and he would check himself and look more closely at her, struck by her unusual poise, her womanly grace. . . .

The sun was going down. The breeze from the hills behind Port Burkhayden worried at the leaf-laden branches of the trees at the back of the garden, and the summer's growth of climbing-rose canes bowed anxiously down before the wind's whisper of ice as if in supplication. Sylyphe tucked her armful of cuttings under her arm and stood up, putting her idle fantasies away from her with a mixture of regret and childish guilt.

Enough was enough.

She went into the house to set the cuttings in a vase, to wait for her mother to come and arrange them.

Captain Griers Verigson Lowden—tall and thin, big bones, brown mustache—strolled down the halls towards the senior mess area with all deliberate speed, fuming. The news from the Bench was not at all satisfactory: no Inquisitor to be assigned, not any time soon. No Inquisitor was even identified for assignment yet, since the latest class at Fleet Orientation Station Medical wasn't scheduled to begin for several weeks yet. If he'd convinced Koscuisko to commit to an additional term of service . . . but he hadn't; and the Bench meant him to suffer the lack accordingly.

Nor was he so naive as to believe that the two Bench intelligence specialists who were visiting from the Danzilar fleet had no ulterior motives. He knew all about Koscuisko's appeals to the Bench. He had connections, and paid well for information pertinent to his survival and prosperity. Koscuisko had been trying to get the *Ragnarok* declassified for Writ for years now: to no effect.

What would Koscuisko do, Lowden wondered, if Koscuisko ever realized that the money that thwarted his purpose at every turn, the money that did such a good job of protecting Captain Lowden against the best of Koscuisko's arguments, the secret influence that baffled Koscuisko time and again was funded directly out of Koscuisko's own handiwork?

Copies of the Record, copies of interrogation cubes, were the property of the Bench, and were to be strictly controlled and accounted for at all times.

That only made them more valuable.

And whether or not torture at Koscuisko's level of expertise was functionally restricted to the Protocols—there being no law to interfere with religious practice under Jurisdiction, should religion demand frightful contrition rituals—there was no question but that Koscuisko was a genuine artist in his field. Captain Lowden had never seen anything quite like Andrej Koscuisko in Inquiry. The man was phenomenal. His tapes had proved phenomenally lucrative in turn, over the years.

Now Koscuisko was leaving, and that would be an end to new material. And though Lowden knew he could live quite comfortably off his banked proceeds, he couldn't help but resent the fact that Andrej Koscuisko was to leave him alone on the *Ragnarok* with not so much as a replacement Inquisitor to remember him by.

Sour as his mood was, Lowden almost looked forward to staff meeting. There were good odds that he'd find an outlet for his irritation before the eight was up; and in that hope Captain Lowden went into the room.

They were waiting for him, of course. His senior officers were already rising to their feet as the lowest-ranking officer in the room—Jennet ap Rhiannon, newly assigned—called the formal alert.

"Stand to attention for the Captain, Lowden, commanding."

Command and Ship's Primes, Jurisdiction Fleet Ship *Ragnarok*. Here were Ralph Mendez, the *Ragnarok*'s First Officer, to whom the bulk of the daily tasks involving the operation of a ship of war—or even an experimental ship on its proving-cruise—devolved, by Lowden's own benign neglect and implicit order.

The Ship's Engineer, Serge of Wheatfields, the over-tall Chigan responsible for moving the ship from place to place and keeping the cyclers up.

Ship's Intelligence, the Desmodontae known as Two, one of the few non-hominids with senior Fleet rank under Jurisdiction; two strangers with her, male and female, wearing unmarked uniforms of the peculiar shade of charcoal gray that identified them as Bench intelligence specialists.

His Lieutenants, and finally his Ship's Inquisitor, Andrej Ulexeievitch Koscuisko, the youngest of his senior officers and by far the most valuable—as well as most high-maintenance.

"Well, let's be started," Lowden suggested, pausing on his way into the room to draw a flask of vellme. Plenty of shredded ciraby on top. "You've all got work to do. I don't want to keep you from your tasks. First Officer, report."

Mendez was a tall, long, green-eyed sort of Santone, his face tanned and deeply lined from youth spent under the dry glare of the Gohander desert sun. "Ship's Mast and staffing, Captain. Ship's Mast. Violation of critical safety protocol cried by Ship's Engineer against technician second class Hixson. Adjudication of penalty recommended at three and thirty. Your endorsement, your Excellency."

Passing the record cube across the table, Mendez recited the Charges drily, sounding bored. Lowden turned the cube in his fingers for a moment or two. Should he press Mendez on this? It would be perceived as merely petty, to squeeze Koscuisko for an extra ration of punishment so close to Koscuisko's departure date. Koscuisko would enjoy it, but he would hate enjoying it. No. Too obvious. Lowden coded his counter-seal on the record cube and tossed it back without comment.

Nor did Mendez insult him by looking surprised. Mendez knew better. His First Officer had been part of the *Ragnarok*'s original proving crew, a good First Officer, a competent officer, but one who had stood on principle one too many times for there to be any real chance of a Command in his future. "Very good, Captain. Staffing, a new requirement just in, Chief Warrant Officer Brachi Stildyne has been offered a First Officer's berth on the JFS *Sceppan*."

Had he indeed? Lowden glanced quickly at his Ship's Surgeon out of the corner of his eye. The four-year association between Andrej Koscuisko and his Chief of Security had been marked by conflict, misunderstanding, even a species of power struggle—great fun, all in all. If Koscuisko were not leaving he might be glad to replace Stildyne or he might be reluctant to face the breaking-in of a new Chief of Security. But Koscuisko was leaving. Koscuisko didn't care. Or Mendez had tipped Koscuisko off; or both.

What a bore.

"Well, congratulations are in order for Stildyne. Please pass them on to him from me. He's done good work for us." *And we're sure that Koscuisko has no cause to complain of him*, Lowden wanted to add, but restrained himself. Once again the provocation would be too obvious. "Very well. Serge? No? Two, then."

Desmodontae were newly integrated under Jurisdiction, an intelligent species of night-gliding mammals that subsisted on the protein-rich blood of a species of cattle they nurtured for that purpose. Very short compared to most hominids, Two stood in chairs rather than sitting in them; as far as Lowden had ever been able to tell she couldn't sit at all, in the conventional sense.

Standing in her chair now, Two dipped her velvety black head sharply in token of having heard and commenced to respond, clashing the sharp white teeth in her delicate black muzzle in his direction rapidly, her pink-and-black tongue flickering back and forth in a disconcertingly random manner.

In a moment her translator began to process. By that time Two had finished speaking; and rested her primary wing-joint with its little clawed three-fingered hand against the table's surface, waiting patiently for the translator to catch up.

"I have here some guests for us, to tell us all the gossip, what it is. Bench intelligence specialists Ivers and Vogel; and this means I do not need to give my report after all, because you are distracted by their information. Yes? Of course yes. I admire this cunning, in myself."

Lowden never decided how much of the personality in Two's language was actually hers, and how much an artifact of her translator. They had to have a translator; whether or not Two was capable of speaking Standard—and there was no particular reason why she should not be, when other non-hominid species had learned to manage—few of them were capable of hearing her, since her voice's natural range dropped down into the upper limits of audible tones Standard only occasionally.

"Specialist Vogel, then," Lowden suggested. "We've been expecting you?" He had no clue as to which was which, Vogel and Ivers. The woman—black eyes, black hair, a little shorter than her partner—betrayed no sign of Iversness or Vogelicity, any more than the man looked Iversish or Vogellic. Two's descriptive statements frequently lacked precision, in translation. Lowden had decided years ago that she planned it that way.

"Transfer of preliminary defense locks to your shuttle." Of the two of them at the end of the table it was the man who spoke. Middling tall, middling bald, with a voice that gave neither cause for offense nor any other information—younger than his hairline, Lowden guessed. So he was Vogel. "For transport ahead of the Danzilar fleet, to be ready when prince Paval I'shenko arrives. You're sending?"

Bench intelligence specialists didn't observe rank, didn't conform to the norms of military titles or respectful address. They didn't have to. They were Bench-level operatives chartered on an individual basis by the Bench itself and accountable not to any given Judge, but only to the Jurisdiction's Bench in formal convocation,

"My First Lieutenant. G'herm Wyrlann." Who fortunately had the good sense to rise to his feet and salute when his name was called. Whatever unspecified rank a Bench intelligence specialist might hold it was good odds Vogel outranked a mere Command Branch First Lieutenant. "The shuttle's loaded and waiting for immediate dispatch, Specialist, ready bay five down three over? Serge? Yes."

They needed to get Wyrlann to Burkhayden as soon as possible. It was to be Wyrlann's formal responsibility to complete the final inventory that would be incorporated into the formal contract between Danzilar and the Bench. "If you'd care to accompany Lieutenant Wyrlann, Specialist."

Bench Indentured World, Burkhayden, Meghilder space. Danzilar to be planetary governor, and responsible to the Bench for tax revenues; to be left to himself to exploit Burkhayden as he saw fit as long as the cash continued to flow. Lowden wished Danzilar luck with his enterprise. There was nothing left worth taking off Burkhayden that the Bench hadn't taken—and nobody there but Nurail, resettled from the dregs and scrapings of the Nurail worlds in the bloody aftermath of the promulgation of the Political Stabilization Acts.

Vogel bowed and cocked an eyebrow at Wyrlann, who took his cue and started for the door. Just as they reached the doorway Lowden remembered the advice he had meant to give; important advice, in light of Wyrlann's history on ground detach.

"Lieutenant. Let's be prudent this time around. There are still Bench resources at Burkhayden." *And you don't want to go breaking anything while Fleet still has to pay for it.* Lowden hoped and trusted that the point would be taken, even implicit as it was. Wyrlann had a heavy hand at times. He had to learn prudence in the timing of his little exercises of authority.

Wyrlann didn't like being reminded.

But there was nothing he could do but accept the rebuke and go.

Once the door closed again Lowden turned his attention to the remaining Bench specialist, who by process of elimination could only be Jils Ivers. "And your role in this convoy would be . . . ?"

Convoy was perhaps not the right word. There were eights of ships in the Danzilar fleet, and its flagship—prince Paval I'shenko's *Lady Gechutrian*—displaced space at twice the volume of a mere cruiser-killer in the *Ragnarok*'s class. One Fleet ship in escort was a mere token, its ceremonial nature emphasized by the fact that the *Ragnarok* was not a chartered warship but an experimental test bed sized and shaped like one.

"In this instance to pay my respects to your Chief Medical Officer." Ivers' voice was level and uninflected. Unrevealing. Unimpressed. "And to present the First Secretary's compliments. You may recall having cleared the interview, Captain?"

Well. Perhaps. If he thought about it. He'd wondered at the time why Chilleau Judiciary bothered to send an envoy to Koscuisko. They could hardly hope to succeed where Lowden himself had failed, and persuade Koscuisko to renew his term.

Koscuisko himself had half-turned in his place to frown at Ivers skeptically, ignoring for once the unwisdom of turning one's back on Serge of Wheatfields if one was Ship's Inquisitor. Wheatfields only glared down at the back of Koscuisko's bared neck in turn. Maybe Wheatfields was mellowing. Maybe not.

"I, er, may have neglected to forward the appointment through to Andrej's scheduler, now that you mention it." His turn to come under that mirror-silver glare of Koscuisko's, but Koscuisko was too well trained to let any real displeasure show. Koscuisko was autocrat, surgeon and Inquisitor. But Captain Lowden was his master, and Koscuisko knew it. "Sorry, Andrej. Recent excitement and all, I suppose. Do you have time for Specialist Ivers this shift? Now, for instance."

Koscuisko hadn't had a prisoner in Secured Medical for upwards of two weeks. All Koscuisko had on his scheduler was running his Infirmary. Koscuisko could make time. Koscuisko would.

"Of course, Captain." Koscuisko's clear tenor matched Ivers's own tone for inscrutability. Being irritated about it would get Koscuisko precisely nowhere. It only amused Captain Lowden to see how easily Koscuisko could be annoyed. "If you like, Specialist. My office?"

Koscuisko almost didn't even pretend to wait for an answer, rising as he spoke. "If the Captain will excuse us, of course."

Lowden nodded in reply to Koscuisko's perfunctory bow, secretly delighted. He had not thought to have this much amusement at staff. He was going to genuinely miss Koscuisko when Koscuisko was gone. "Quite so. Good-greeting, Specialist Ivers. Andrej, ward report, my office, second and six."

Could he get rid of the rest of his staff in time to have Two open a channel into Koscuisko's office?

Or should he rather let this staff play out, and pump Koscuisko for the details afterward?

He hadn't heard anything from his Lieutenants. And he was supposed to be paying attention.

"Lieutenant Brem. There's an inventory shortage on the Wolnadi line, I understand, and you were to have a report for me this morning."

Resigning himself to an indulgence postponed, Lowden set his concentration on analyzing cargo loads, and put Andrej Koscuisko to the back of his mind for later.

⊕ ⊕ ⊕

If he thought about it, Andrej believed he might remember this woman. She was shorter than he was, and many women weren't, since he himself was to the short side of the Jurisdiction Standard. Chilleau Judiciary had sent two Bench specialists to the Domitt Prison at port Rudistal, these five years past; they'd arrived in time to assist the inquiry into the Administration's crimes, but Andrej had never managed to convince himself that they hadn't been originally dispatched to cover things up.

"So, then, Specialist. You travel with my cousin Danzilar's fleet to Burkhayden."

Strolling through the corridors of great *Ragnarok*, on the way to Infirmary and his office. There was no sense in being gratuitously unpleasant. He was going home, after all. He was to be free from all this within a very few weeks' time. He could afford to let bygones be bygones, just this once. Justice had been done at the Domitt Prison at last, whether with the help of or despite these Bench specialists. He should be at least polite.

"Audit authority, your Excellency. One last check on inventory before everything goes to Danzilar. Your cousin? Don't tell me, sir, Dolgorukij aristocratic genealogies make my head hurt."

As a matter of fact they did his, as well. "It is either third cousin four times removed or fourth cousin three times removed. I do not know which. It is safest to call them all cousin and forget about it."

He was to go home because eight years had passed since he had sworn his oath to Fleet, and eight years was all Fleet and his father could demand of him. Well, Fleet would have kept him on, because there were not enough Ship's Inquisitors to go around; but eight years had been agreed upon and eight years had been suffered and eight years were passed.

He was never going to be able to forget them.

"The Danzilar prince sends his regards, sir. And said something about cortac brandy. An armful, I think he said."

Had Shiki brought liquor? Well, of course Shiki had. "A crook of liquor, Specialist, four bottles, three under one's arm and one in one's fist. Very promising of Shiki. It is through here; sit down, do you take rhyti?"

Hearing himself engaged for an interview with a Bench specialist had not been a very welcome piece of news, just now. But his office was his own territory. He felt more comfortable just stepping across the threshold, and more inclined to be hospitable accordingly.

"Thank you, your Excellency, no. With respect, sir, I'll come straight out with what I have to say."

He did remember her from the Domitt Prison. Surely he was being paranoid to blame either Ivers or Vogel for crimes that Chilleau Judiciary should have noted and prevented long before his own arrival. Bench specialists were not partisan players. They would have done the same as he, had they found themselves in the same position. Surely.

"Excuse me that I draw a flask, then, I am thirsty. Out with what, yes, I listen."

Once he'd had a moment or two to think about it he didn't even feel she'd changed. That hint of a frown was something that Andrej could remember having found rather fetching, before, for no particular reason.

"Very well." She waited for him to join her in the conference zone of his office, watching him set his flask of rhyti down on the low table between them with an air of concentrating on her thought. "Your Excellency. The term of your initial tour of duty is due to expire very shortly. It is understood that you have not been very satisfied with your placement here on *Ragnarok*, in recent years."

No, he had been critically dissatisfied with his tour of duty on the *Ragnarok* from the moment he'd first set foot to decking. Andrej settled back in the slatwood chair, templing his fingers in front of him, suspicious. What did she mean, his "initial" tour of duty?

"Captain Lowden is not fit to direct my Writ, or any other. So I have pled. I am sure the documentation has been made available for your review."

Captain Lowden was not a support to the rule of Law. It was precisely abuses of power of the sort that Captain Lowden indulged so shamelessly that gave subversion its ever-increasing numbers of champions under Jurisdiction. The Bench had heard his cry against the Domitt Prison; why did the Bench not hear his complaint against his Captain?

But Andrej knew the answer to that question already. It was Fleet and the Bench, this time. "You have not come all this way to give me a going-away present related to this issue, Specialist Ivers?"

Not likely. He was a Bench officer, to the extent that he held the Writ. He was also a Fleet officer under Captain Lowden's authority. Fleet resisted the Bench on principle, regardless of the merits of the case.

Ivers smiled politely, but her smile ended well short of her eyes. "To the extent of assuring his Excellency that no Inquisitor has been identified for immediate assignment, yes." She sat carefully at the edge of her seat, and her back was as straight as an abbess's. "His Excellency has declined to renew his term with Fleet and the Bench."

Indeed he had. And it was in the poorest possible taste to have even expected otherwise. There was a shortage of Ship's Inquisitors? Very well. There should properly be a shortage of Ship's Inquisitors. There should properly be no Ship's Inquisitors at all, especially under Lowden's direction; but Andrej wasn't going to say as much out loud. There were limits.

"Fleet does nothing to protect the bond-involuntaries, Specialist. Tell me that they are all to be reassigned and I will be well satisfied. What is your point?" Because after all they both already knew that he'd refused the offer of a second term. And if she had no news but for the denial of yet another appeal against Griers Verigson Lowden she need not have wasted time and effort telling him how carefully the Bench had considered the merits of his plea.

"The Bench cannot afford the loss of critical skills, your Excellency. The Free Government grows more persuasive daily. Sabotage takes the lives of increasing numbers of loyal citizens, and the Bench must have the weapons it needs to fight the battle against this—one could hardly dignify the Free Government by the name of 'enemy.'"

Ivers's hatred and contempt was clear in her words, regardless of how calm and level her voice was. Andrej could empathize to an extent: terrorism was terrorism, and never to be condoned. It was just that the Bench itself also practiced terrorism, and against its own, against the self-same loyal citizens it claimed to be protecting. Torture was terrorism. Andrej set his hands to the armrests and straightened his spine, decisively.

"Then the Bench must criticize its moral self, Specialist Ivers. Fearlessly." When would the Bench realize that the practice of institutionalized torture as an instrument of statecraft and the maintenance of civil order had just the opposite effect from that intended? "It is by the health and contentment of the body politic that one is to evaluate the rectitude of the State."

Skating perhaps a little close to politically questionable discourse, but nothing actionable. Ivers seemed annoyed.

"Resources must be carefully husbanded in unsettled times, your Excellency. As you may be aware the Bench can exercise the power of annexation of critical resources. According to the provisions of the Political Stabilization Acts the Writ to Inquire is a Bench-critical resource."

Now of a sudden the flooring fell away from underneath his chair, and Andrej knew he dared not so much as glance into the bottomless chasm that gaped open at his feet or else he would fall in. He gripped the armrests of his chair desperately. He could feel the suction of the moiling vortex of black Hell: he had to hang on.

"Annex critical. Resources. Name of all Saints, Specialist, what are you saying?" It had been eight years, eight years, eight years, he was done with this, he had fulfilled his term, he was free to go—

"His Excellency declines to continue service in Fleet. That is understandable in light of his Excellency's stated convictions and dissatisfaction with his post. The Bench cannot afford to lose your skills, sir." She could not see the abyss that yawned hugely between them. She could not have spoken so calmly had she done. "First Secretary Verlaine offers you pride of place at Chilleau Judiciary, command of the sector's medical resources and all the rights and emoluments accruing thereunto. The need is too great, your Excellency. The Bench must make difficult decisions for the greater good of all under the rule of Law."

Chilleau Judiciary.

No.

Andrej swallowed hard, focusing on the talk-alert on the far wall to anchor himself in the world. He had to control himself. He could not panic. There was no reason to panic. She could not mean what she seemed to be saying. It was intolerable.

"Specialist, no one could wish me to this work a single day the longer, Judicial Order or no. Not even for my sins should it be wished on me, and you must know that they are many, and grievous."

Her expression was pained, almost irritated. Andrej didn't care. The rule of Law was no excuse for torture. He had to press what advantage he had, while he could still feel that he had the advantage—

"Say therefore to First Secretary Verlaine that I would rather sell myself to a Chigan brothel and suckle at fish than have anything to do with Chilleau Judiciary. Or the Protocols. Not one day the longer, Specialist Ivers. It has been eight years."

Irritation had shaded over into stubbornness in her face, somehow. Andrej wasn't quite sure how that had happened.

"You've earned a rest, sir. No one dreams of disputing that. You have three eighths of a years' worth of accumulated leave, and I have the privilege of bringing word from the prince your father"—reaching into her over-tunic, as Andrej stared in horror—"with a personal message. Your Excellency."

Holding out a heavy square of folded paper she waited. Andrej was afraid of that message, suddenly. He didn't want to disgrace himself by showing his fear in front of the Bench specialist. It was an effort, but he forced himself to reach out his hand in turn to receive the note, his hand almost absolutely steady. There was his name on the note, in script so black against the clotted fabric of the writing-cloth that it was almost red. And bled as Andrej stared at it, the blood draining from the letter to stain his hand and overflow his fist down to the floor.

Son Andrej.
It will be good to see you again, child. We are glad of the First Secretary's charitable gesture, in letting the past forget itself. Come home and kneel for your mother's blessing before you go to Chilleau Judiciary.

His father's hand, his father's voice, more loving than it had been these past eight years, and as much as Andrej ached for his father's blessing he could not force himself to accept that he would have to pay so high a price to purchase it.

"I cannot go." He whispered it half to himself, half to the room, transfixed with horror. "Oh, it is too much. I cannot be made to go, Specialist Ivers, surely. And my family. I owe duty there that I have much neglected."

Ivers sat unmoving in her chair, straight-backed, formal.

Unyielding. "And the First Secretary understands, sir. There need be no impediment to a long and well-earned duty leave to see to personal business. The facilities at Chilleau Judiciary will be awaiting your arrival upon the conclusion of your leave. I'm sorry, sir—"

She hesitated, but she said it anyway. What, did she see the roiling pit at last, and hear the tortured screams of damned souls in horrific torment? "I'm sorry, your Excellency. Secretary Verlaine has communicated with your family, and has taken great pains to explain the value of your technical qualifications to your father. How much Chilleau Judiciary needs your skills. And it is a Bench prerogative to annex, sir."

He had known that he could not escape his dead, he had known it all along. He almost didn't want to escape them—they had a natural right to be revenged. That was right. It was proper. It was decent and moral. But he had been certain that there would be no more of them once eight years were finally over, finished, done.

The enormity of this disaster left him without the capacity for coherent thought.

"It is intolerable to suggest that I should be punished in this manner. I have done my duty and upheld my Writ, and if the Bench has not heard me to disenfranchise Captain Lowden of my Bonds nor has the Bench any complaint to make of my performance—"

Except. Except, that he had cried to Heaven at the Domitt Prison, and been heard. And Chilleau Judiciary had held the responsibility for the Domitt Prison. Was it for the pride of Secretary Verlaine that this carefully planned torture had been prepared for him?

"Indeed no such thing is contemplated, your Excellency." It seemed that he had genuinely startled her; Ivers spoke slowly, as if putting her thoughts together with care. "The First Secretary holds no grudge of whatever sort associated with the unpleasantness at the Domitt Prison."

He could not sit here for a moment longer.

This horror was too huge and terrible for him.

"Very well, Specialist Ivers." Reaching for his rhyti flask he drained it in one half-convulsive draught, letting the sharpness of the heat in his throat pull his energies into one solid and protective core within him. "You have come to me, and told me. I am not to be permitted to go home to my child."

Why had he ever imagined anything different? He could not go home. How could a man so much as look on his child, with such a stain on him? "Very well, I have of this understanding, and you have delivered your message."

Rising to his feet, Andrej reached out his hand to help Ivers up, politely. There was a peculiar ring of chafed skin around her wrist beneath her sleeve, showing for a brief moment as she moved. Chafed from cold? Or had she recently been in manacles?

"Now it remains only for you to explain how it is that I am to get around it. I do not believe that I can go to Chilleau Judiciary and live, Specialist Ivers. I have only this long survived because the longer it was, the nearer to the end it became."

Was that grammatical? Did it make any sense? Did it matter?

Andrej hardly knew what he was saying. It surprised him to realize that he was trembling; but whether it was fury or horror or a combination of the two Andrej could not begin to guess. "Tell me the way out of this, Specialist Ivers, or I am lost."

"I'm sorry, sir," Ivers repeated. She sounded as though she was surprised at the evident sincerity in her own voice. "In my professional opinion the First Secretary has covered all vectors of approach. I have no advice for you except to enjoy the perks, because as far as I can see you're to be genuinely stuck with the duty whether you enjoy the perks or not."

Polite of her, to gloss over that issue of enjoyment so delicately. She was a Bench intelligence specialist. She probably knew as much as his own gentlemen about what Andrej enjoyed, and how, and when. Or where. And yet her reference was utterly innocent: oh, yes, very delicately done indeed.

"Good-greeting, then, Specialist Ivers. You will excuse me. I must to someone go speak, to understand the meaning of what you have just told me."

Nodding gravely in acceptance of her dismissal, Ivers gave him the bow without another word. Just as well. Too much had been said already. Andrej accepted Ivers's salute in turn with a nod of his head, and she left the room with swift silent dispatch.

He was alone, and the enormity of the disaster that had just overtaken him weighted him down until he could hardly so much as breathe. A sleep-shirt made of lead. An atmosphere of viscous fluid of some sort, that sat in a man's lungs and gave no air, but could not be coughed loose.

He could not stand here in his office. He would choke.

Possessed with dread and driven by horror Andrej fled the room for the one place on board of all *Ragnarok* where hope could be found—if there was any hope, any hope for him at all.

It was a quiet morning, all in all, now that Lowden's staff meeting was out of the way. Convoy duty was not very challenging; things were quiet in Section. Ralph Mendez was treating himself to a little inconsequential talk with Ship's Intelligence when Koscuisko—as blue in the face as a man near-dead of cold—staggered through the open door into Two's office, palming the secure on his way past with so much force that Mendez half-expected he'd put a dent in it.

"I cannot endure it," Koscuisko said. "I will not be asked to tolerate. Your pardon, First Officer, Two, you will tell me, if there is to be no way out of this?"

Straightening in his seat, Mendez waved Koscuisko's apology off, interested. He didn't usually see Koscuisko so exercised in spirit. Angry, yes, and from time to time in an ugly sort of state of savage amusement—when Lowden was working him particularly hard.

This didn't look like angry, or frustrated, or hostile, or otherwise distracted. This looked like somebody's mother was due to be sold to the tinkers for a drab, and no seven-hundred-thousand tinkers Mendez could imagine could possibly begin to afford the mother of the prince inheritor to the Koscuisko familial corporation. Not even if they pooled all their resources.

Two rearranged herself in a rustling of wings from her anchor-perch in the ceiling, and her translator sounded—its calm precise Standard diction at odds with the peculiar idiom of Two's speech. "To you I will certainly tell, Andrej; but a hint would be much appreciated, what 'this' is it?" No telling whether she could catch Koscuisko's state of mind or not. As difficult as it was to decipher Two's expression when she was on the ground, it was next to impossible when she was at her ease hanging upside down in her office.

Koscuisko paced the floor between them, gesturing with his small white hands raised beside his face as if what he really wanted to do was tear his own head off. "This woman that Verlaine has sent, Two, she claims that I can be requisitioned to the Bench, if my father permits. And I cannot trust my father to understand, so you must tell me."

What Koscuisko's father had to do with things Mendez had never quite understood. He'd loved his father too, as far as it went—which didn't go anything like as far as it seemed to go with Koscuisko. No accounting for culture.

Two reached a wing out casually to the far wall to code up a display on her speakers. Mendez knew she couldn't actually see that far; it only made the unerring precision with which she found her target all the more unnerving—that, and the fact that her wings spanned the entire room when she stretched them.

"Well. There is a plot in motion, Andrej. I have not discussed it with our Captain because he is cross enough about the issue of your replacement."

Didn't that call for a question? Ralph wondered. If she had known of plots in motion—

"Two, if there were things of which I needed to be apprised—I cannot understand, why was I not warned. Surely you could not have thought of it as of no interest—"

Koscuisko was still pacing, visibly tense with unexpressed conflict. But at least the level of the body language had toned down a bit.

"I am uncommonly clever, Andrej, it is true, but I cannot see more than three days into tomorrow," Two scolded. "And it is not established that the draft would be approved. So Specialist Ivers has been just a little forward, if she told you that it was done."

Finally Koscuisko stopped, and sat. Threw himself into a seat, pushing the fine fringe of blond hair up from off his forehead with one hand as he did so. Mendez was just as glad that the cup of konghu that he had on the side-table was half-empty, the way it shook.

"She did not say that it was done." Koscuisko needed a haircut; Koscuisko usually did. Nothing to do with actual length, and everything to do with straying from its place. "She said that it would be accomplished, if Verlaine had anything to say about it. Is there nothing to be done, except be damned?"

"It is metaphorical, this 'damned'?" Two demanded. Not unreasonably. "If you are not pleased to be desired you are certainly in a bad place, Andrej."

Mendez felt it was high time he found out exactly what was going on between his officers. Between Two and Koscuisko, that was to say. Nothing went on between Koscuisko and Wheatfields except for bad language, and the occasional physical assault.

"Somebody fill in the First Officer?"

"The maddening thing is that it was not even anything that I did, in the beginning at least," Koscuisko replied. As if he was explaining. "There was a student in orientation with me. She puffed me up to her Patron out of spite, and Fleet gave me the choice to wait for him to requisition me or leave for *Scylla* before the Term was ended."

Which in turn had meant that Koscuisko had had to perform his final exercise, his benchmark Tenth Level Command Termination exercise, when he was already on active duty. Mendez had heard about Koscuisko's Tenth Level even before Koscuisko had been posted to the *Ragnarok*. He'd wondered what kind of psychopathic maniac Koscuisko was at the time; but now that he knew Koscuisko a little better—after four years of breathing the same air—he was regretfully aware of the fact that the question was a little more complicated than that. "You went to *Scylla*, he took it personally, and that business with the Domitt didn't sweeten him on you?"

Koscuisko shuddered. "I cannot go back to the Domitt, First Officer, I swear it. Not in one lifetime. And to submit to the First Secretary would mean the same, even if the name of the place itself were to be different."

No need to ask whether Koscuisko had believed the testimony presented to the Bench about poor decisions made by subordinates, errors concealed from the audit branch, abuses not sanctioned.

"But Verlaine's set up to draft his Writ." Now that he felt he understood the background maybe Two's information would benefit both of them. She cocked her head at one corner of her room, listening to the speaker—he assumed, since he couldn't hear a damned thing. Then she nodded, which always gave him the chuckles, when she was upside down.

"It is confirmed, yes. Very much does Verlaine want Andrej Koscuisko. He has spent many favors which I am not at liberty to divulge, many of them irreplaceable. Once our Andrej leaves this ship—there are several months of accumulated leave, you could go

and visit my children, the cave is large. It would perhaps be possible
for you to become lost."

The humor did not appear to penetrate far enough to touch
Koscuisko in the state of mind that he was in. "If I could have known.
It might have been better to have gone to the Bench in the first place.
I did not understand that such a place was even possible, as the Domitt
Prison."

"So tell me, Two, if Andrej is too depressed to ask." Moral support.
"Is there a way out of Verlaine's draft?"

It was of only abstract interest to him, of course. Koscuisko wasn't
a bad sort as a Chief Medical Officer, once one got past his personal
quirks in the Secured Medical area. But Mendez wasn't sure he really
cared one way or the other.

"It is a problem for Andrej. No one can decide it for him." Two
had learned to shrug as an old woman, she had told him, and he was
to treat her accomplishment with the respect due to the aged instead
of asking her if she needed her back scratched between the shoulder-
blades. "If the Combine protested there would be difficulty, and
perhaps Verlaine would not be able to accomplish his goal. But the
Combine has received many benefits from Chilleau Judiciary.
Especially recently."

"My father wrote to me, after the trials." Koscuisko's sudden
interruption startled Mendez, since Koscuisko had seemed well sunk
in silent gloom a moment ago. "He said that I had done well, that he
was proud. That I should also behave with more humility, in future,
because when all was said and sung a man should have respect for
authority, and it did not present a pleasingly filial appearance for me
to have appealed to the First Judge in so public a manner."

Mendez winced. If Koscuisko's people could say something like
that to him, after those trials, then they simply didn't live in the same
world as that in which the Domitt Prison had existed, and that was all
there was to it.

Respect for authority, yes.

Complicity of silence in atrocities of that nature—well, no.

Nai.

Never.

"Well, there." Two let so long a pause develop that Mendez
wondered if her translator had failed; but no. She seemed to be

expecting a response of some sort, her beautiful brilliant little black eyes fixed on Koscuisko's face. Koscuisko made a gesture with his hands of either helplessness or confusion, and that seemed to clue Two in that she hadn't made her point.

"You are clever, Andrej, you can see. There are four things that you can do, and one of them is to go to work for the very influential First Secretary—who wants you very badly—of the woman who will quite possibly be First Judge someday. You could make your practice in the border worlds, but there are people out there who might recognize you, and you are not much qualified for such a life of crime."

So Two didn't think that voluntary self-imposed exile was a viable option. "Of course you could also go to your home, and—what is the phrase—slide on the ice into fruit-butter, because your life has no more astringent seedlings. Is this the Standard? I am not sure I translate the idiom correctly."

For himself Mendez was almost certain that she hadn't, but her meaning was clear enough. Still, she'd said four things, and Koscuisko was waiting.

"Or there is only one other thing. I must come down to you for this so as to gauge my effect. It will be one moment."

Walking across the ceiling like an impossibly large stalking insect, shifting her weight easily between her strong little feet and the steely three-fingered hands at the first joint of her great leathery wings. Reaching the ground with a final hop from her ladder on the wall. Crawling up onto the surface of the table beneath her anchor-perch, sweeping it clear of its litter of bits of document-cubes and the stray container of fruit that had been dropped onto it from the ceiling with a gesture of one wing as she settled herself once more.

"Because it will be a joke, and it is good to share humor with others, it helps one to remember not to harvest from them. The joke is about the shortage of replacements for our Andrej. It is a thin joke, because the shortage is very short."

"No." Koscuisko stared at her, his face full of blank horror and disbelief. Two stretched out her wings and put her tertiary flanges over Koscuisko's shoulders where he sat; a curiously tender gesture, a Desmodontae embrace, of sorts.

"It is of course not funny, as a joke, but such is the way of things. And it could be that there would be a transfer away from here, since you would volunteer, and you would be more useful on an active-duty craft."

Mendez decided that he didn't want to look at Koscuisko, just at present. Inspecting his manicure instead, he found the point that Two was making all too obvious, even if written in a scant thumbnail's space.

Koscuisko had put Fleet between himself and Secretary Verlaine, at the beginning.

Fleet had loaned him out only grudgingly over the years, because a good battle surgeon was almost as hard to find as people who could live with themselves as Inquisitors, if what Koscuisko's life had come down to could be called living.

And now, just at the point when Koscuisko had thought that he was clear, just at the moment when Koscuisko had believed he could get away— Verlaine blocked his path.

And only Fleet could stand between Andrej Koscuisko and First Secretary Verlaine.

"What must I do?" The voice sounded more than half-strangled, but it was not Two's voice, so it had to be Koscuisko. "First Officer?"

"You'll be obliged to write a statement explaining why you changed your mind about renewing." He still didn't want to look at the man, because his sympathies were engaged. That annoyed him. Koscuisko was smarter than he was, richer than he was, better educated, even better dressed, within the constraints of uniform.

Koscuisko was also put to it more brutally than any bond-involuntary by this turn. Well, more brutally than any bond-involuntary on the *Ragnarok* since Koscuisko's arrival, at any rate, Koscuisko being a little odd about his people.

Stildyne was going to need to know about this.

"Oh, holy Mother."

Now that he had to look—now that the naked despair in Koscuisko's strangled voice demanded attention—he couldn't see, because Two had Koscuisko covered over with her wings, sheltered within a matte-black cocoon of rustling skin.

"I will never get away from here."

A pause, and Koscuisko's voice strengthened, leveled out. "Thank you, First Officer. I would . . . rather . . . even whore for Captain

Lowden than for the man who should have known about the Domitt Prison."

Stildyne needed to know because Stildyne wasn't going to want to leave the *Ragnarok* with Koscuisko still on it. Stildyne needed to know because Koscuisko was clearly in desperate need of moral support, and Mendez was not in a position to provide it. Koscuisko was closer to his Security than anyone else on board of *Ragnarok*.

Though whether or not Stildyne himself had ever been admitted to that intimacy was something that Koscuisko and Stildyne were apparently still negotiating, and none of Mendez's business either way.

"I'll send Stildyne with the documentation, Andrej. Soonest. Two, send a stop order on the termination payments, tell Fleet Medical we're processing a variance in lieu of replacement."

Koscuisko would get a significant increase in pay for renewing his term. It probably wasn't a good time to mention that. As if an increase in pay meant anything to a man like Koscuisko, who had once offered the Bench to buy his bond-involuntaries out—all nine of them, two hundred and fifty thousand Standard each.

Too bad, Mendez told himself, with fleeting regret.

Too bad he couldn't just arrange to have the signing bonus and the longevity increase credited against his own pay records, as long as Koscuisko was not paying attention.

Unfolding her wings slowly, Two kept one delicate little claw on Koscuisko's shoulder, either following him as he stood up or steadying him. Mendez couldn't tell which.

"I will go back to my place, then, and wait."

He'd best be started himself, and call for Stildyne.

He was almost certain that Captain Lowden would be too surprised to even gloat.

Garol Vogel pushed his duty cap up off of his forehead irritably, rubbing the little tuft of hair that was all that remained to cover the dome of his balding head. "One more seal on the dead-box, and Burkhayden will be out of our hands. That Lieutenant's got a dirty reputation."

Their quarters on the *Lady Gechutrian* were ornate and luxurious in proportion with their Bench status. It annoyed him, all the padding and carving. Jils came out of the washroom in her towel-wrap and sat down on one of the heavy wooden chairs to comb out her hair, cocking an eyebrow at him. "That whole ship. The Lieutenant's small game. Problem?"

He had claimed the least padded chair as his from the moment they'd joined the Danzilar fleet. He tilted the chair back against the liquor cabinet, now, trying to ignore the clinking of bottles as he did so. Bottles. Glass, actual breakable silica-based crystal for drinking out of. Wooden furniture. Thick napped carpeting made out of animal hair, hand-loomed by virgins dedicate, for all he knew. These people had too much money for their own good, and they disgusted him deeply, in an abstract sort of way.

"No problem. No new problem." It was an old problem. She was probably as bored with it as he was. "How'd it go on your end?"

Jils declined to look at him, working on a tangle. "He's unstable. We knew that. But he's not stupid, and Verlaine's got him pretty much locked this time."

"Listen. Jils." That was another problem, though she didn't know the extent of it yet. And he had to be careful. "Are you sure it's all to the good of the Judicial order? Koscuisko, I mean. Uncharacteristically petty of Verlaine."

They'd known each other too long for him to risk an overt deception. They understood each other too well. Intimately, if not sexually so, but as far as Garol was concerned once you'd been stuck with the same person in a burrow on Sillpogie for a week sex could only be a letdown.

Jils didn't answer him immediately, concentrating on her plait. She was still getting used to having to deal with the traditional Arakcheek-style working-braid that she'd selected for propriety's sake. Dolgorukij women of rank wore their hair long, so Jils had gone for a quick forced-patch before she'd reported. The more they looked like Dolgorukij the less notice would be taken of them; and that could be one of the most valuable weapons in the inventory. "Koscuisko's got the juice, Garol, you know it. One of the few Inquisitors in the inventory you can count on when you have to get actual answers, and not trash."

She wasn't answering his question, but he couldn't push it. He was unhappy about what he thought might be happening at Chilleau Judiciary, but he couldn't really explain all of the details without compromising his Brief. If it was a Brief. If the Warrant he carried for the life of Andrej Koscuisko was a true Warrant. Things just didn't add up. Or what they seemed to add up to was not an issue he was willing to face just yet.

"So he's good." An argument would cover any hesitation she might detect in his manner. "He should be rewarded, not punished for it. We should let him go home."

Why would Chilleau Judiciary have issued a Warrant on Koscuisko's life if the First Secretary was to have what he wanted from the man?

"Personal sacrifices are sometimes required in support of the greater good. You know that." No, Jils wasn't quite convinced, but she'd get stubborn if he pushed her.

"And if you think this has anything to do with the Judicial order instead of Verlaine's pride you're wrong."

This was working to distract her—a bit too well. He was picking a fight, again. Why shouldn't he? Wasn't conflict just a part of that constant honing of wit and interplay that made Bench intelligence specialists so good at what they did? Yeah. Right.

"One way or the other." Jils, being charitable, was ignoring his best attempts to be irritating. "We can't afford to let a resource of that magnitude escape us, Garol."

Resource his ass. But that was the problem, right there. Koscuisko had the potential to be a resource; and Koscuisko was unquestionably the inheriting son of a very influential family within a respectably powerful bloc in Sant-Dasidar Judiciary.

People like Andrej Koscuisko couldn't be quietly assassinated without someone noticing; and there was the Malcontent—the secret service of the Aznir church, the slaves of St. Andrej Malcontent—to consider.

"Crazy people, she means. A man with his surgical qualifications, and all Lowden ever uses him for is taking people apart. There's intelligence out on Lowden. You know it."

She'd finished dressing, now, and threw his exercise uniform at him from across the room. "Crazy is as crazy does. Four years with Captain Lowden, and he's still alive, and that's more than can be said of the last three. Where there's survival there's got to be a species of sanity. Come on."

It was a point, about Lowden. Unfortunately part of the point could as easily be that Koscuisko had opted to survive by forgetting that he'd ever wanted to be a doctor. "You got a mind-sifter on it that you haven't told me about?"

"Garol—"

Oh. He'd pushed too hard, then. Finally. He was in for it now, and only himself to blame. Yes, he knew that he and Jils trained well together, and that was eighty-seven parts of an intel spec's survival in an uncertain world. The Danzilar prince was going to wonder about the bruises, even so.

"Okay. Okay. I'm coming. Don't hurt me. I take back what I said about the mind-sifter, you're a good psychotech. You don't need a mind-sifter. I'm coming."

Vogel knew how good Jils really was at what she did. His respect for her professional ability was deep and sincere, and she had saved his life—not to speak of what he laughingly referred to as his career—on more than one occasion. So he didn't really want to push her too far on this.

And the last thing he wanted to do to a friend was bring her in on a bad Warrant, if bad it turned out to be.

CHAPTER TWO

It got dark early at this time of the year, but the curfew for Nurail hadn't been shifted yet. Hanner had plenty of time to have his payday treat and get back to his garden before the Port Authority would be patrolling. The Port Authority was generally just as willing to beat a Nurail as look at him, and they didn't need to justify their actions as long as there were no bones broken.

Hanner was prudent.

He would be back to his garden in good time.

The Tavart had got a residence-chit for him, and had suffered him to make a modest habitable place in one of the garden's outbuildings so that he could live there without charge to lodgings and save his wage. The Tavart was a good maistress. She always paid full earnings on the contracted day, and there'd been a nice bit of extra this time, too, that had come into his hand with a vague mention of the winter coming on. He had a new coat of the extra. A new coat, a secure lodging, leave to take his prunings and trimmings in and out as he wished: life was not half bad, just at the present, as long as a man could manage not to mind about Danzilar and the Judicial order.

He had it better than Megh did, for a fact. And here she was, coming through the back way from the service-house into this little hire-kitchen, where even a Nurail could sit and have a bit of meat and not be molested.

Megh.

Taller than he was, shaped very becomingly, and if her lip had got set a little thin over the years of slavery she'd served her eyes were dark and glittering with life and even laughter sometimes yet.

"Hullo, there, cousin Hanner, I was afraid that I'd mistook the day. How do you go?"

She slid into the booth beside him, setting a bottle of ale down between them on the table as she did. Criminal Megh was in the eyes of the Bench, sentenced to thirty years of involuntary servitude for supposed crimes against the Judicial order. But still she was allowed a surplus ration, now that she had passed the first third of her sentence.

Service bond-involuntaries past their first third got a surplus ration of food and drink and more administrative than personal chores assigned. Security bond-involuntaries were issued a more serviceable grade of boots and better fabric for their uniforms.

"I'm a rising young man in the affairs of state, here, Megh, I'll have you know. My maistress has called up a whole field of botanicals, I'm to discover how they thrive in the salt air, see?"

He was not a slave in the same sense as Megh; he wore no implanted governor to monitor his internal states and punish an infraction. He could think treason all he liked, so long as he did none.

He set his little posy to the Megh side of the bottle, keeping his eyes on his plate. It gave her pleasure to have a little bit of flowering straw, and a bloom that was not too unlike a golden ice-flower. Skelern felt it prudent nonetheless to wait until she had had a moment to master the pain that it also brought her before he could evaluate the success of his gift.

"Skelern, I've heard something."

Startled, he looked up at her before time. She sat very still, very quiet, turning the stem of a piece of sheep-fern between her fingers. It had been for a joke, the sheep-fern; it was fodder for the animals, nothing more, but Maistress Tavart had seemed to find it rare and exotic.

"What's the matter, Megh, nothing to grieve you?"

He should have known better than to make such a joke. He was a gardener's son, a gardener. He knew little about the high windy, nor cared to. But Megh had come from the high windy, on her own world. Megh was a herder's daughter.

"Nothing to grieve over, no, cousin. Maybe nothing at all but just the accident of a name." There was a little frown between her honest eyes, an uncertainty between pleasure and fear. "There was a patron, here, these few days past. I served her her meal. And she wanted to ask about the pattern-weave."

Megh put her hand up to the shawl across her right shoulder, a little uncomfortably. It was a cruelty to make her wear it at all, even if it was no honest weave. They liked to remind people that they could do anything they wanted, *and you'll accept it and be grateful, my girl.*

"But she was polite, Skelern, thoughtful-like. As if she really cared to know. And she kept looking at me as though I reminded her."

She was an exotic in a public house, was Megh. The most part of her job was parrying the constant curious questions of customers eager to be titillated with a bit of genuine Nurail folklore. Skelern opened the bottle, pouring two glasses full without comment. It was Megh expected to keep quiet, and let other people talk. He wasn't about to stop her words in the small space of time that she had in which she could speak at her will. He was a gardener. He knew the value of letting well enough alone.

"She seemed kind enough. I'm not forbidden to say only so much as where and from whom. And so I told. The truth, not this rag of lies I wear, and I'm from Marleborne, you know that, Skelern."

And her father's people had once held a famous war-weave. The Narrow Pass, he thought it had been, though he had always tried hard not to brood upon the matter, keeping his mind on his own garden for prudence's sake. If it hadn't been for the war-weaves and the warlike fury they aroused in Nurail hearts the Bench might not have seen them for a threat, all of those years ago. He might have been a free man, then, and his family yet living in decent comfort here in Burkhayden.

"And she interrupted me, Skelern, startled-like. And your mother's people hold the Ice Traverse, she said. As if she knew, cousin, but how could she know the weave, and still say my mother's people?"

The faint hint of outraged modesty made him want to smile. "Most improper it is, cousin. Surely she meant no harm."

Picking up her glass Megh stared at the surface of the beer, tilted back as it was, as though to see her reflection in its surface. Skelern realized with a mild concerned shock that she was blushing. "Skelern, you'll grant me your sweet pardon, but I have to say this. My . . . my father's wife . . . my brothers' mother, her people, they—"

Oh. Skelern made a smoothing gesture, fearful that she would say the taboo thing. "So how did she know of the weave in Marleborne, do you think? And yet not know the rest of it?"

"I asked her that, I did." There was the swallowed sob of anguished hope in Megh's quiet voice; it made him want to weep. "I couldn't help it." Nor would he have been able to resist the same impulse if he'd been the one ripped from his native place, with no news ever of his family. "She couldn't think of why she thought of it, and we spoke no further on that reckoning. But she sent word a day or so after that, and it was a Security chit, so they let it through to me still as it left her."

Else everyone would know what Megh had learned. Whatever that was. No Nurail had a right to privacy, not here in Port Burkhayden.

The glass was empty, now, but Megh hadn't set it back down for a refill in friendship and in courtesy. She held the glass to her instead with both hands wrapped fiercely around it at its middle.

"She had met once a Security troop, and had some cause or another to have remembered him. Bond-involuntary, Nurail. And she didn't remember what his slave-name was." Not as if that would have told Megh anything. Other bond-involuntaries took slave-names from the Judiciary where they'd been condemned, and carried the identification of the place that defined their shame until their Day was past. To Nurail alone even that much identity was denied.

"But what she had called to her mind was a trial that she was at, a talking-drug, something. I don't know. Being tested on a Nurail bond-involuntary. It's what she remembered him telling, that his name was Robin, from Marleborne. And that his mother's people held the Ice Traverse."

There was no missing the significance. Skelern chewed on a bit of the meat from his stew-bowl thoughtfully, not wanting to intrude on the intensity of her feeling. She worried at the fringe of the shawl that she wore; after a moment he felt it might be safe to speak to her. "Your brother, then, Maistress Megh. Do you think it could be?"

Megh had thought that problem up one side of the hill and down the next, so much was obvious. "I saw him last taken away by Jurisdiction, and they were merciful to us, cousin, they let us see each other alive and whole before we were to be parted. Wanted to fight, he did, but it was kindness to let me kiss my brother, with the rest of us— all dead—"

"Hush, now," Skelern warned, hastily, alarmed. "Hush, now, Megh, you'll give yourself such a headache, please, be gentle."

She turned her head and wiped her face with his napkin, crumpling it in her hand. "Look you aren't late for curfew, young Skelern," she said, with a certain weight of tears to drape her admonitory tone. "I believe you are the same age that my brother would be, of course not so tall. It is to hope, that's all."

Little enough to hope for, surely. Bond-involuntary Security had thirty years to serve at labor that was both hard and hazardous. And to be forced to put the tortures forward, at the order of an Inquisitor—

"I'll dream on it with you, then, if you'll permit." There were Nurail here in Burkhayden who had come through the camps at Rudistal, and one of the staff at Center House who had survived the Domitt Prison itself. They said that Koscuisko for one had used his Bonds tenderly, with respect. But Skelern knew that it would never have been remarked upon unless that was unusual.

"I'm glad for all the good you care to hope me," Megh said with plain simplicity, kissing him on the cheek as she rose to go. "Come and see me again, cousin, I'll tell you all about our new maisters, and whether they are any different than the old ones were."

He watched her move gracefully to the back of the shop and through, her shoulders straight beneath the mockery of the weave that Jurisdiction put to her to wear, dignity and suffering alike in the gentle movement of her head.

If it were up to him there would be an entire army of brothers for her, if only they could give her comfort.

But it wasn't up to him.

And he had to mind the curfew.

He finished his meal and went out while he still had time to get back to his garden before curfew fell over the Port and prisoned Nurail behind doors.

Skelern Hanner leaned against his grubbing-hoe and rested himself, the cool still air very pleasant next to his bare skin. His shirt hung on a nail outside the shed for the saving of the garment from the sweat; which made things a little awkward, of a sudden, because here was sweet little Sylphe come running across the blue-turves to seek him.

He watched her come with embarrassment, with fondness, and with dread. A man would prefer to be decently covered in the presence of a lady, especially when a man knew he was too skinny by half to be judged beautiful. He was fond of Sylyphe. She had a good nature. He fervently hoped that she did not want to talk to him about politics.

"Skelern, Skelern, Mother has news for you, there's a job—the Danzilar prince's garden, for his party, there's a Fleet Lieutenant here, and—"

He'd had ample moments of warning, but he hadn't stirred himself, busy watching her come scurrying over the grass. It was a pleasure to watch her, child though she was. She stopped abruptly and drew back when she saw him, the back of her hand coming up to cover her little mouth as if she'd never seen a man without his smock on before, ever.

"Oh, Skelern, this is—surely most improper, please, go and dress yourself."

He wanted to laugh. But he went to fetch his shirt, instead. "If my little maistress doesn't think it seemly, I would suggest she not come looking for her mother's gardener come spring. A man likes to work in his hip-wrap when it's hot, sweet Sylyphe."

She was blushing as deep as a vine-ripened acid-plum, and she did it very prettily, too. Well, perhaps not; her cheeks were blotched and blighted with embarrassment. It looked pretty enough to him.

"I shall carry bells. And call out warning. What are you doing, Skelern?"

She was interested in gardening, that was true. "I'm heading the late starchies. If you don't trim them to the ground they waste themselves away in the winter light as though it was spring, and you lose the spring blossom." Bending down for a clump of leaves, he shook it free of dirt to offer it to her, half-joking. "Flowers, for the little maistress of the house?"

"Oh, don't be ridiculous. Imagine, wearing a vegetable." And yet she tucked the base of the leaf-bundle into her bodice, and arrayed the green leaves carefully in a symmetrical pattern upon her bosom. "There, how do I look?"

"As if you were wearing a vegetable. Of course. What were you calling to me, on your way out? A party for me, is it?"

"Um." She was distracted by her corsage still, making further adjustments. There had been a year when such rubbish as Sylyphe's corsage would have been his dinner. They'd eaten less likely things not so very long ago. "Gardeners for the Danzilar prince's garden, to make ready for his party. Mother's offered you, but you're to be paid, of course, and to have a holiday after."

He wasn't quite sure that he liked being "offered," as if he were a bundle of packaging. Still, the Tavart treated him well enough to take the sting out of any real resentment on his part. Surely the Tavart had earned the right to lend him out, with pay and bonuses. There was a good deal to be said for the contractual value of a new coat before winter, and a warm dry room safe from the weather for his bed. "Tell me about the party, Sylyphe. Am I to have a day to finish up my starchies, here?" He wasn't going to want to let the tubers go. He needed a day or two yet in the late sun to be ready for the ice that was to come.

She dimpled at him, seeming grateful for a chance to talk about it. "It's to be three weeks yet before the Fleet arrives. The master-gardener says a week's worth of work, but a month's pay is offered, Skelern, say that you aren't cross? I mean—"

She meant that he was prickly with her on the issue of being told where to go and how to go when he got there. "Na, there's good to it, then. Plenty of time to finish up what's needful."

It was a little selfish of him to be so self-absorbed when she was all alone here and aching with the excitement of it all. Once the Danzilar arrived there would be more doing in Port Burkhayden, and probably more company for Sylyphe—company more suited than his to her high place.

"And your Lieutenant, Sylyphe, tell me about him, do." No doubt he'd go back to being "Gardener Hanner" then, if she had time to speak to him at all. It was probably just as well.

He could not bear to think of Sylyphe trying to cope with the life of a Nurail gardener with one small room in a gardener's shed of a wintertime, and that was the sum of the best he could ever hope to offer her.

"G'herm Wyrlann. Fleet First Lieutenant, Jurisdiction Fleet Ship *Ragnarok*." She spoke the uncouth name with careful precision, as if testing the contours of it in her mouth with studious attention. "Command Branch, and he looks very stern. The uniform! And

Security, they all move perfectly, Skelern, perfectly, you should just see them."

She'd been with her mother to some public function, no doubt. As prepared as Sylyphe was to be excited they could have sent a maintenance crew, and Sylyphe would have taken them for splendid.

"The Danzilar in four weeks. Oh, your mother's to be busy." Parties all over town, no doubt. He'd want to see about forcing some of his second flat of ice-blooms; the Tavart liked the ice-blooms, and she made good capital of them as well. The Danzilar wanted to exploit the specifically Nurailian nature of its newly indentured world. Ice-blooms were apparently a useful token of Iaccary Textile and Cordage's commitment to the Danzilar's goals.

And on the tail end of his musing, a random thought, come strolling forward from his mouth before he saw it. "Shan't be having much time to chat with you, Sylyphe."

She bridled at the idea, seeming as surprised as he was to have heard it. "Why, whatever can you suppose that to mean, Skelern ?"

There was a silence for a moment, each staring at each, she and he confused alike by why the thought had come and why it had seemed so objectionable. Then Sylyphe recovered herself, to an extent. It was her breeding.

"There will be plenty of time to talk. Later. There's winter gardening, I've read about it, I want to hear all that you can teach me."

But her reassurance, gracious as it was, came too late for either of them. The point had been made, and there was no recalling it. Gardener Hanner it was to be. There was no way it could be otherwise.

"Later, of course." He could only agree, or else give offense. He said it with a certain heaviness of heart all the same. "You'll want to go into the house, before your mother catches you with a tuber in your bosom."

"Oh, Skelern, don't be silly. As if Mother would care."

There was no longer any conviction in her protest.

She removed the now-wilting greens with grave decorous grief, and handed them back to him without meeting his eyes.

Standing in the empty echoing foyer of the Center House, G'herm Wyrlann eyed the overgrown garden through the unwashed panes of the old-fashioned clear-walls with distaste. Captain Lowden's promises aside, he was not enjoying his brief taste of absolute power; there was so little to have power over—so little privilege to abrogate or enjoy.

Fleet's provisioners had done their job too well, down to the very last. There was precious little left to beguile a man in Port Burkhayden, and there would be no one to carpet these bare dirty floors—to hang the high walls with insulating fabric as a barrier to the damp falling dark—to stock the kitchen with anything more than survival rations; not until Danzilar came.

"Oh, yes, very well done indeed," he snarled, at no one in particular. He'd been all over the port inside of the past few hours— what there was left of the port. "Nothing left in the armory, nothing. Nothing left in Administrative Quarters. Nothing left here, and I swear that it would not surprise me if the local Bench itself had been carted off to Stores."

His contact, the Fleet Liaison Officer, merely bowed as if in receipt of a compliment. And Wyrlann hadn't meant it as a compliment. The local Fleet Liaison had gone disgustingly native, from what Wyrlann could gather. He'd received the mildest of the comments Wyrlann had felt called upon to make about Nurail, about Meghilder, about Port Burkhayden itself in particular with a blank stare of disapproval that Wyrlann hadn't cared for, not at all.

No doubt the Fleet Liaison was already on Danzilar's payroll behind Fleet's back. The Danzilar's local majordomo certainly seemed comfortable enough with him; and the Danzilar's majordomo was Nurail, probably Free Government. There was no getting away from Nurail at Burkhayden. The place was filthy with them.

Nor had the welcoming party been so much as properly coached in the expected expressions of respect and gratitude; it had instead been apparently assembled more or less by accident, through mere word of mouth.

Four weeks until the *Ragnarok* arrived, and he was stuck here until then. If he'd realized that it was going to be like this, he would have suggested Lowden send ap Rhiannon instead of him. It would have been a good experience for the crèche-bred junior officer to be isolated in the middle of a derelict port for four weeks with only a suspicious— and suspiciously reserved—Fleet Liaison Officer for company.

Wyrlann sighed. The sun was going down, and if the draft was any indication the wind was picking up as well. "I've seen all I need to see of this, for now. Which isn't saying much." He had no intention of spending the night here, with the heating systems all turned off and no liquor to be had.

He hadn't any doubt that the majordomo's personal quarters were comfortable and luxurious enough, but Artigen was just the sort of icicle-up-his-ass administrative officer to take exception to any suggestions on Wyrlann's part that they go find out. "There's a service house here, isn't there? Or have you had that shipped out as well?"

Now the majordomo answered, and he hadn't been spoken to. Wyrlann wondered that Danzilar's people would put a Nurail in a position of such influence and authority. On the other hand it was Danzilar's lookout if the Nurail robbed him blind. "There is indeed, Fleet Lieutenant. It's part of the contracted package, still in place for the Danzilar prince's use."

Which probably meant that it wasn't very profitable, which in turn probably meant that it wasn't much of a service house. As if anything different could be expected in this stinking Nurail port full of stinking Nurail. Still, as a Command Branch officer he didn't have to pay at service centers.

He could have anything he wanted for the asking. And for now what he really wanted was a little entertainment. The service house would be adequately heated, if nothing else. "Well, let's go, then."

"Yes, Lieutenant." Artigen, once more; Wyrlann was glad to see that at least the Nurail hadn't forgotten his place to the extent of presuming himself to be included. "Your Security as well? Of course."

Captain Lowden would expect him to evaluate what amenities remained in Port Burkhayden.

Good subordinate officers were quick to anticipate and execute the wishes of their senior officers.

She'd told young Hanner that she would tell him all about their new maisters. That she had. So Megh examined this *Ragnarok*'s First Lieutenant covertly as she set his meal to table, mindful of the necessity to keep the inner elbow-point of her patterned shawl out of the food.

Not a sound. Not a single clink or bell-like ting or muffled thud; she knew the trick of it, setting the place without a single stray bit of noise to distract the officer. Tallish. Stoutish, but like it was all muscle and bone, no hint of any easy living, any fat. Mouth that seemed always in a sneer, even drinking his liquor, which should make a man at least stop frowning if it didn't make him smile.

She glanced over at the officer one too many times and met his cold sarcastic gaze, which quite unnerved her. Startled, she let the silence stretch too far for a graceful recovery, and the realization unbalanced her even more. She bent her head to stare at the napery still in her hands, thinking hard and fast.

"The Lieutenant is but half a day in Burkhayden, yet?" she asked with studied timidity in her voice, falling back into the exaggerated Nurail lilt expected of her for camouflage. "How does the officer take to our salt sea, and our proud new sky-starport?"

Burkhayden had been a seaport, once, but the marsh had gotten too far into the bay, and the Jurisdiction had not cared to dredge for navigability when higher tolls could be taken in other channels.

"Can't say that I like it at all." The voice was harsh, amused. She knew that voice; it meant that she'd become a target, once again. That was what she was here for, of course, her primary function; one wretched Nurail slave to mock at, so that the Jurisdiction could forget the menace that it had once felt from the war-weaves.

"Well, it's a poor mean place, compared to what the officer—"

He interrupted her without the slightest hint of discomfort. "You're Nurail, aren't you? I know the accent."

Of course the Lieutenant knew the accent. It was the Jurisdiction Standard accent for a Nurail slave, one she had learned early on. The fact that it had nothing to do with any honest Nurail lilt that she had ever heard was just another part of the point that they were making about Nurail.

"I wonder that you caught it, sir, it takes a keen ear—"

Interrupting again, with obvious relish this time, the Lieutenant— Megh realized—was enjoying the fact that he was being rude. That he could be as rude as he liked with impunity. "Don't try any of that whore-pap on me. I know better. That's not a Nurail pattern, either, so what was your weave? Tell me about it."

Yes, the old question, the old chore. Swallowing a sigh of resignation Megh lifted the shawl down from her right shoulder, and began to count the callings that defined her life.

"Seven tones in a Nurail scale, and four half-tones to each. This color of green's the chord called Dogwood Blossom. These notes together in this set, these chords, it's the defining phrase for the tune of Dancing Meggins, which has been a treaty-record tune once of a time. So this space of threads gives you the Nurail Conventions at Berrine, before the Political Stabilization Acts, and here—"

He'd risen from the cradle-chair he had been resting in and come to stand near her. The house's best room it was, separate bath, no sound from the outside, bed big enough for five to sport in. She'd spent her time in a room like this, but not recently. She was beginning to show too much of her history, and was only bidden to smaller, more utilitarian rooms when she was bidden to provide sexual services at all.

"I thought I told you. I already know that's not a Nurail weave."

She couldn't decide on his tone of voice, whether gentle or threatening. She did know that it made her uncomfortable.

"With the officer's permission, it's the only weave the Bench will have me speak of—"

"Not good enough." Draining his glass, he sat down on the table so forcefully that the cutlery jumped. "I told your proprietor that I wanted amusement. I don't need to hear the damn fake weave, I want to hear your weave. The one you used to have. Before you got what's coming to any insurrectionary, you filthy little traitor."

And she wasn't an insurrectionary except by default, and she wasn't any kind of a traitor, not to her weave and kind. The weave she wore was the only one she was allowed to tell over in public. It was the only one that people were permitted to demand of her.

"Begging the officer's pardon, but it is my weave, it has been so for going on ten years . . . "

Eyes respectfully lowered, she didn't see the hand coming across her face, and the shock almost as much as the blow itself made her stagger back half-collapsing to the ground.

"*Your* weave." Crouching over her, now, and the smell of his breath was heavy with malice and liquor. "Tell your other customers whatever damn lies you please. But to me you tell the truth, understand?"

Well, it seemed clear enough. But she could not speak of her weave even to please a difficult patron, even if it might save her a beating. Her father's people had held the Narrow Pass. She was strictly prohibited to rehearse it, and her governor made sure she would not do the forbidden thing.

"The Fleet Lieutenant surely understands better than anyone else. The weave, it's proscribed, I may not—"

This time she saw the blow coming, but she couldn't avoid it, even so. Back against the heavy base of the sideboard she went, and fetched her head sharply up against it.

"I've had just about enough of this. Do you have any idea who I am?"

Oh, yes. She knew exactly who he was. He was a bully who beat up women, but there wasn't much she could do about that. Influential patrons were left more or less to do as they pleased, as long as the house got its money.

Still, his musical entertainment would be coming, she could get away from him when the musicians came. And the establishment husbanded its livestock responsibly. They would not let her suffer too much pain after an undeserved beating.

"His Excellency is the First Lieutenant of the *Ragnarok*, Command Branch—"

He dragged her away from the sideboard and hit her yet again, keeping a good grip on her arm so that she couldn't put any distance between them. "Wrong. Dear me. The little whore thinks I'm an Excellency. Is that what you think, little whore? Do you think that I'm an Excellency?"

He wouldn't stop hitting her face, and her thoughts rattled against each other into incoherence with each blow. The inside of her cheek was cut against her teeth. It was difficult to speak distinctly.

"The officer is Command Branch, surely."

"But not an Excellency. Maybe it's Koscuisko you have in mind. He spent a lot of time getting to know you Nurail, remember? At the Domitt Prison?"

She kept on trying to get away. She knew he hadn't cleared this with the housemaster, and she couldn't help but try to escape pain. She tried, but his grip was like iron, and it only seemed to make him angrier.

"Everyone knows about Black Andrej. And the Domitt Prison." Keeping her voice low on instinct, Megh kept testing for the right approach to appease him, to get him to stop for long enough for her to get away. Once she could get away she would be safe, the house staff would surely intervene to protect her. She couldn't be beaten for not singing her weave, even had her governor permitted it. It was a killing offense to sing any weave, let alone a war-weave like the Narrow Pass.

"Oh, well, perhaps you're disappointed, then. You'd sing the weave for him, soon enough, but not for me, is that it?"

He shook her and let her go, but she couldn't get to the door, because her legs came out from underneath her as soon as he released her upper arm. And he was still talking. It was important to pay attention to what he was saying; she had to find a way to placate him.

"I'll tell you something, though. I've seen him work. There's really nothing very complicated to it. Anything he can do, I can do, and better."

It was his boot this time, and not a fist at all. A boot sudden and brutal put to her stomach, making her cry out loud of it. And yet another boot, to take the wind out of her belly, so that she rolled her arms around her middle and curled onto her side, trying to find her breath.

"There's his tapes, you know? I watch them sometimes, with the Captain. And if Koscuisko was here I know just what he'd do. Here, we'll pretend I'm your precious 'Black Andrej,' shall we? And when we're done you can sing me your weave like an obedient little slut. Whether you want to or not."

Stooping down to her on the floor he grabbed her wrist, and pulled her flat at length on the carpet. She tried to smooth her breathing out, to be ready for the next blow. It helped sometimes to try to guess the course of a beating, to concentrate on whatever one could use to create an illusion of control.

"And if Koscuisko were here he'd probably start with . . . well. He'd use the butt end of his driver to fuck you wide open, he does amazing things with that whip. Haven't got a whip. This'll do, though, just as well. I'm sure."

He seemed minded to rape her with his boots, never minding the other ugly things he said. There didn't seem to be anywhere that she could get to, to hide from him. He drove her across the carpet to the far wall with his blows; and when she could flee no further he stuffed her shawl deep down into her throat and raped her horribly with the wine-flask. She thought it was the wine-flask, he'd had a wine-flask, but whatever it was forced her belly up into her throat with agony.

"Damn thing's broken, well, if you think I'm going into your stinking cunt after that, you can just think again. Not to disappoint you, I know how much you crave it."

Where were the musicians? Hadn't it been an hour, two hours, half a day since she had come up here to set the table, and she still left here all alone at the mercy of this monster's brutal whims?

"Of course in the end the simple things are best. Traditional. You Nurail like tradition? You'll like this."

She was choking on her own screams, trying to breathe.

And she could not stop screaming even so.

The Port Authority had come and gone, the emergency aid team had left with the injured woman, and the word went out into the silent whispering streets of Port Burkhayden.

The Ragnarok's *First Lieutenant, in the service house.*

There were menials on night shifts, ready to provide hot food to comfort the patrols coming in off the streets for their warming-periods, and the message followed each mobile vendor from station to station as the night deepened.

One of the women, making his meal ready. He tried to make her sing her father's weave.

The city's communications nets were old and poorly maintained, and now that the Jurisdiction had pulled its resources out there were chronic problems with lapses in the net. Strictly licensed Nurail maintenance crews were on call to respond at any hour of the day or night. There was a steady stream of emergency restore orders, and the news was left at nexus after nexus as the hours wore on.

Support staff, not a bed-partner, only setting the table out. Beat her with his fists, put his boots to her. Cut her with broken glass, you can guess where, because nobody wants to have to say.

During the coldest hour, the oldest hour, the least respected of the city's servants rose up out of their meager beds to see that all was waiting, nothing wanting, when the city's maisters rose. Fuel for furnaces, water-heaters brought up in time for them as had the luxury of showers, baths. Fresh sweet milk from outside the port's boundaries, the morning's fresh-picked flowers for the fast-meal table.

A bite to eat for the Nurail that lived in lodgings, that had to be up and doing before the kitchen would be open to provide for them: and the sorry tale came whispering to Skelern Hanner as he stood in the darkness of his gardener's shed and washed his hands and face in icy water, getting dressed.

The woman Megh, the Nurail, at the service house. Raped by the First Lieutenant, and with a flask, a piece of broken furniture, nobody knows what else. Taken off to charity ward, but there's no healer there for such wounds as she's taken. She may be dead already.

Skelern stood in the dark silence of his shed, half-dressed, his face still dripping with the cold water of his early morning wash, frantic phrases rushing through his mind. Megh, poor Megh, he had to go and see her.

He couldn't hope to go see her, not on his own, they wouldn't let him in.

He could wake Sylyphe, that he could, she was pitiful if misguided, she could take him to the hospital.

He could not possibly involve Sylyphe.

She was young and privileged. She did not understand the cruel truths in life, and the cruel truth was that a Command Branch officer in any civil port could do such crimes without reproach. Without reprisals.

If he even told Sylyphe she might make a scene in public, and her mother could be compromised by implication. He owed the Tavart for too many favors to want to see her compromised, nor her daughter permitted to make a fool of herself in public. He couldn't see Sylyphe.

He could ask permission to ask the Tavart, but the Tavart was out of town on business, and by the time he could make his request—the day after tomorrow, sometime, and he'd need a chit from her, too, to give him authorization from his employer to go where he'd no business being otherwise—poor Megh could be dead by then, if she wasn't already.

But he was Nurail as well as Megh was, and she would not thank him for courting a beating by risking it on his own just to see her corpse. Nurail, and a slave, and if the Port Authority did not have the legal right to use his body at its pleasure as the *Ragnarok*'s First Lieutenant had done Megh's there was no lack of reasonable pretexts to torture a Nurail gardener for stepping outside of his place, for involving himself uninvited in the affairs of his betters. And no one watching to see that the punishment was restricted to the Jurisdiction Standard, either.

He washed his face again, to rinse the tears away. He would have to wait. The Tavart would grant him leave to go, he was sure of that.

And maybe Megh would not be dead before he could come to grieve for her in hospital.

CHAPTER THREE

Lights were dimmed and room was quiet, but Garol woke with immediate certainty that he'd heard something. He kept his breathing slow and regular, his eyes still shut, listening hard. There was only Jils in the room with him, Jils in the bed beside him as companionable as a sister. It wasn't Jils who'd awakened him, then; not unless it had been her signal.

Garol opened his eyes and sat up in the dim hush, cautiously, and the tone came at the outer door, the door at the end of the room outside the bedroom. Someone in the corridor.

Jils was awake now too, and he could trust Jils's judgment better than his own. She hadn't signaled danger: not yet. Very well. They'd see.

Pushing his feet into the slew-socks that Dohan Dolgorukij wore for bed-slippers, Garol belted his heavy blue brocade bed-robe—a present from the Danzilar prince—around his waist as he made for the door. The signal was tuned to its lowest intensity, but it was persistent.

He keyed the admit and opened the door, and found himself face to face with the Danzilar prince Paval I'shenko himself, standing in the corridor with a household technical officer and some Security behind him. Bowing, Garol wondered; the Danzilar prince had never come to him in quarters, and had never interrupted his sleep-shift, either.

Danzilar himself seemed to have just gotten up, if the butter-yellow jacket he had on over his thin white silk bed-suit and the tousled condition of his nondescript brown hair was any indication.

"Do not waken the lady, I beg it of you," Danzilar said, softly. "No woman should have to hear of such a thing. There is a problem, Garol Aphon, and I believe that I must insist on an immediate response."

Jils was listening in the other room, Garol knew. She would pretend she was still asleep, then.

"At your disposal, your Excellency, of course. At any time." The "Excellency" had been a little distracting to Vogel, because the same title that translated for the respectful language due a Dolgorukij aristocrat applied to Fleet superior officers in Standard as well. Andrej Koscuisko was an Excellency twice over, even as the Danzilar prince was. And neither the Danzilar prince nor Jils Ivers knew what Garol held in his keeping for Andrej Koscuisko. "Is there a place where we can go to talk?"

Danzilar nodded grimly. "Come, and we will discuss. We can use a side room, here—"

Not far from his quarters, and servants already standing by with service tables. As far as Garol had been able to tell, fresh beverage and hot bread was next to godliness for Danzilar's Dolgorukij. Jils would probably remind him that people whose body temperature ran high usually did need to eat a little more frequently to keep themselves going.

"Here is the master of communications, who has brought me this. You will oblige me by reading it for yourself, Garol Aphon. We have had it done into Standard, and I am unwilling to go into the details."

The Danzilar prince habitually called him by two of his names in the formal Dolgorukij manner. Garol had a hard time really resenting it, even though he had never liked his second name. The Danzilar prince looked so young. But looks were deceiving; the Danzilar prince was forty-seven years old, Standard. Older than Garol himself was.

Garol took the report slate that the watch-master offered him and sat down.

From Burkhayden, not too surprisingly. A protest against damage to property specifically included in the terms of the Contract, more or less predictable. Except that the property was a woman, not a public building or a farm utility vehicle. The whole issue of bond-involuntaries had always given Garol a raging case of the toe-cramps.

And the report was brutally precise on the important issue of exactly what was meant in this case by the "damage."

There didn't seem to be anything for him to say. Garol passed the report slate back to the officer.

"Yes, your Excellency?"

"There is nothing to be done about the vandal, I know that." Danzilar had seated himself in a well-padded chair as Garol read; now he smoothed the broad band at his wrap-jacket's hem carefully over his crossed knees, frowning. He meant Wyrlann, Garol guessed.

Danzilar was right.

There wasn't anything that anyone could do about Wyrlann, except what Garol had been sent to do about Koscuisko. And he had yet to exercise his authority to revise a Bench warrant, regardless of the provocation. He wasn't about to start with a warrant he could not even decide was legitimate.

Danzilar was still talking. "But the staff of a service house is not of small importance, because comfort must be had. And the contract has been signed."

What was Danzilar getting at? "His Excellency will of course be compensated, once the review board has validated loss of function." It didn't make sense for Danzilar to be as upset about this as he seemed to be. The price of any sixteen bond-involuntaries could be easily lost in even the smallest detail of the contract's fiscal stipulations. Yet Danzilar was not only visibly upset, he seemed not far from actually furious, rising to his feet with a ferocious if controlled gesture of rejection.

"I do not want her price, Garol Aphon. I want her worth, as I have been promised in the contract. Her symbolic function at this point is of paramount importance. She belongs to me, Garol Aphon, and I demand her rights."

Of which she had none, whoever she was. Apart from the obvious, of course. "I'm afraid I don't quite understand, your Excellency."

"Aah, it is the middle of the night. I am only—very angry."

Why?

It was perhaps not inappropriate to indulge oneself in a certain degree of moral outrage, under the circumstances. But Danzilar was not a child, no matter how much like a twenty-five-year-old he looked to Garol. The Dolgorukij had defined atrocity, at least as far as the

Sarvaw were concerned; and Danzilar's second cousin thrice removed—or fourth cousin five times distant, or whatever the hell the relation was—was the self-same Andrej Koscuisko who held a Writ which authorized him to practice very much the same sorts of things that Wyrlann appeared to have done to the poor whore at his will and good pleasure, in support of the Judicial order.

So it couldn't be that Danzilar had simply never run into this sort of thing before.

What was going on in Danzilar's mind?

Garol kept silent, and after a moment Danzilar continued. "To do this thing so casually, it shows a lack of respect. For me as well as for the holy Mother. I cannot afford to discard this woman as a piece of spoiled goods. What kind of treatment would any other expect from me, if I did that? These people are to be my people, Garol Aphon. I am responsible for their well-being."

Well, it was true that Dolgorukij were peculiar in that respect. As with Danzilar's cousin Koscuisko, again; and nobody touched Koscuisko's Security, not after what Koscuisko had done to the people he had decided to consider responsible for the death of that bond-involuntary Emandisan of his at Port Rudistal.

"No disrespect is intended, your Excellency. I'm simply not sure what you want me to do about it."

Danzilar glanced at the report slate in the watch-captain's hands with what seemed to be a shudder of horror, or of barely suppressed disgust. "Four pieces of glass, it says, Garol Aphon. And the wounds as long as my hand is broad. There is no surgeon in Burkhayden to address such injuries effectively. My medical administrator says that we will not have a trauma surgeon on site before it cannot but be too late for this poor woman."

Garol started to shrug in involuntary perplexity; but smoothed his shrug out, thinking quickly. He was beginning to think that he knew what the Danzilar had in mind.

"You want Fleet to send a trauma team to Burkhayden. Possibly when Jils and I leave." They were scheduled to depart inside of ten eights, and a ship of the *Ragnarok*'s size carried modular units for just such requirements—although they were usually used to bring newly repossessed or liberated facilities on line.

If there was a hospital building still standing in Burkhayden the

Ragnarok could furnish a surgery and a surgeon, up and running in—how long? Garol did some calculations, concentrating hard. The report was already ten eights old. They had a day and a half or more in transit time, ahead of them; maybe if they left a few hours early—

"I want Fleet to send the best surgeon at its disposal here and now. The Chief Medical Officer's personal involvement would send the strongest possible signal to my people in Burkhayden. That is what I wish you to have done."

"Koscuisko?"

The name escaped Garol in an involuntary yelp of disbelief.

Send Koscuisko to minister to a woman raped? Send the single most notorious pain-master in the entire inventory to tend to a woman brutalized by his own ship's First Lieutenant?

Koscuisko.

It made a certain amount of sense, once he thought about it.

"There are two things that the most uneducated of rabble knows about my cousin Drusha," Danzilar replied, with utter seriousness. It took Garol a moment to make sense of the name: Drusha, from the intimate form of Andrej. "No, perhaps three things. First, there is of course the obvious. Second, that he is the Chief Medical Officer on board the *Ragnarok*. And finally, that there are none better at what he does, irrespective of the capacity in which one invokes his expertise. Is it not so?"

Well, maybe not really. Once the first point had been raised and controverted the rest faded a bit in significance. Still, Koscuisko was recognized as a senior officer by token of the Inquisitorial function that he performed, if nothing else. Koscuisko's symbolic subordination to a Service bond-involuntary was probably a pretty damn solid way for Danzilar to make his point, if that was what Danzilar was after.

"I'll send an emergency override, your Excellency." It was within his authority to demand that Lowden comply with any measures he deemed necessary to complete the transfer of function. Garol decided that he might very well enjoy making a point of that. "The ship's Chief Medical Officer to travel to Burkhayden with me, and to treat the traumatic injuries this woman has sustained to the maximum extent of his professional ability. Shall I report to his Excellency when the requirement has been communicated to Captain Lowden?"

"Four pieces of glass, Garol Aphon." Danzilar stared at the closed door, clearly distracted. "Please, yes, let me know. This must be addressed, and it cannot be done too soon, you understand."

Maybe there was some cultural peculiarity that made Wyrlann's particular crime especially horrible to Danzilar.

Or maybe Danzilar was simply a decent sort at heart, with decent instincts.

"I understand. If you'll excuse me, your Excellency, I'll go to communications right away."

Nodding, Danzilar put his hand out to Garol's shoulder, walking with him toward the door and talking with evident intent to lighten the atmosphere somewhat. "Yes, thank you, Garol Aphon. Excuse me to my cousin that I do not greet him before you leave, beg for me his forgiveness. And remind him. There is to be a party. There will be dancing."

The more Garol thought about it the better he liked the idea of Captain Lowden forced to make good the senseless damage his First Lieutenant had done.

Captain Lowden usually enjoyed disciplinary events on a number of levels, but today was different.

Today his secret knowledge of the joke he planned to play on Koscuisko distracted him to such an extent that he almost wished Koscuisko would just get it over with, and Koscuisko wasn't off his game, no, nor was the guilty technician unresponsive to the impact of Koscuisko's whip. Koscuisko's performance was, as always, a thing of abstract beauty; as great passion and great control were always beautiful, perfect in form and in execution.

Discipline administered as adjudicated, Technician Hixson, if Lowden remembered correctly. Three-and-thirty. Hixson, bound by the wrists to the wall, two Security troops standing facing the room on either side at several pace's remove so as to be out of danger of any stray blow.

Ship's Engineer, the aggrieved party, present as much to keep an eye on Koscuisko as to provide witness that the penalty had been administered and the grievance satisfied. Jennet ap Rhiannon, counting the strokes, because Lowden felt it was important to involve junior lieutenants in the full range of their duties as Command Branch officers.

The room was crowded. All the better. Koscuisko would swallow down questions he might otherwise ask, to spare listening ears the unpleasantness; and that would help the joke forward.

"Twenty-six, twenty-six, twenty-seven," the Lieutenant counted, her voice flat and free from any inflection that might betray any emotion she felt. Did crèche-bred have emotions? Lowden wondered. Neither Fleet nor the Bench had much use for emotions, so why would crèche-bred have been issued any? Apart from the Standard, of course.

Whether it was her dispassionate demeanor or something else that Lowden hadn't noticed, Koscuisko apparently objected to the Lieutenant. Or to something she had done. "Twenty-eight, Lieutenant, the count is twenty-eight. Twenty-nine. Thirty."

Yes, right, now that Lowden thought about it she'd counted twenty-six two times over, just now. Lowden had thought the stroke a hair on the light side himself, but there were good reasons not to challenge Koscuisko on it.

For one thing Lowden was serenely convinced that Koscuisko wouldn't dare actually muddle his count with his Captain in the room. It was the officer's mess, not Secured Medical, so there were no record tapes to review to determine a true count. But Koscuisko was too well trained.

"With respect, sir, the Standard calls for—"

The Standard called for blood to be let on every stroke or the stroke repeated. Koscuisko knew that. Koscuisko was the Judicial officer on board. It wasn't very appropriate for the Lieutenant to challenge him on his count.

"Thirty-one, thirty-two, thirty-three," Koscuisko called firmly, ignoring the Lieutenant. "Three-and-thirty. Gentlemen. Release the technician. Wheatfields, your man."

Ap Rhiannon stifled well; yes, Koscuisko had interrupted, but Koscuisko was the senior officer. Lowden rose from his observation post and stepped down from the Captain's Bar to examine the evidence and decide the issue for himself.

Koscuisko had handed the whip off to one of his Security already, and was drinking a flask of rhyti in his shirtsleeves. Discipline was warm work. Koscuisko always took his over-blouse off. It had only been three-and-thirty, though. Apart from his loosened collar and rolled-back cuffs Koscuisko seemed unaffected by the exertion: he wasn't even breathing hard.

There were medical people standing by to take Hixson to Infirmary, because though Koscuisko had called Wheatfields to take custody of Hixson—as per standard operating procedure—in reality Hixson was to go to Medical to have the welts on his naked back salved. The orderlies and Security stood away for Captain Lowden's approach, of course.

Lowden counted the welts, one ear to the conversation taking place behind him. Koscuisko was apparently in a mood.

"Lieutenant. While I appreciate your concern for the letter of the Law I must say that your behavior surprises me."

Koscuisko had every reason to be in a mood. He'd had that fateful interview with Jils Ivers days ago, and Ivers had accomplished miracles. Lowden was in her debt without being in the least actually obligated to her, which was the best of both.

Koscuisko had been drinking ever since, almost as heavily as though he'd had an assignment in Secured Medical. If Koscuisko hadn't been Dolgorukij—Lowden thought to himself, walking his fingers from welt to welt, counting as Hixson trembled—Koscuisko's body would never have been able to support the demands he made of it.

"I apologize, your Excellency." Ap Rhiannon meant no such thing. It was the approved formula, no more than that. "It was an error on my part. I felt his Excellency would think less of me if I failed to note the . . . what seemed to me to have been a mis-stroke."

Thirty, thirty-one, thirty-two bloodied tracks, and one mere bruise, purple and weeping clear fluid. Well. Either Koscuisko had missed or the final stroke was laid too exactly over an earlier one to be called out as such. Koscuisko could have missed. But if Koscuisko had dared to try a cheat in his Captain's presence—and Lowden really didn't think it had been deliberate—the joke he was going to play would be entirely adequate punishment.

And junior officers should not controvert with their superiors on principle.

"Three-and-thirty," Lowden said firmly, turning away from Hixson with a gesture for the medical people to come forward. "I call it good. Lieutenant. I shouldn't have to remind you that Koscuisko's count is the true count here. If he says three-and-thirty the only person on board this ship who can say differently is me."

Koscuisko bowed in formal appreciation of this endorsement, but he didn't look surprised or relieved. It had been as Lowden had thought. If Koscuisko had made a mistake it had been a genuine mistake, one of which he was genuinely unaware.

Koscuisko could be excused a mistake, just this once. The joke Lowden had in mind would be that much more effective if it was unlooked for.

Ap Rhiannon could only swallow the rebuke. He'd left her no room to cry an honest error. "Of course, Captain. My apologies, your Excellency, no disrespect was intended. It was a failure of good judgment on my part."

Not that Koscuisko cared. "It is forgotten, Lieutenant," Koscuisko assured her, fastening his cuffs before he allowed his Security to help him into his over-blouse. Unlike portions of the uniform that were visible from the outside there was no Jurisdiction Standard for under-blouses; some classes of hominid—the particularly hairy ones—weren't even required to wear an under-blouse in uniform.

The under-blouses that Koscuisko wore had a short little collar that stood straight up from its seam, and very full sleeves, a good deal of fabric gathered into the yoke of it, and fastened with ties slightly to the left of center. Lowden had often wondered what it would look like with blood soaking through it from the other side. "Captain?"

Nobody could leave the room until Lowden as ranking officer had, with the exception of the medical team and their patient. Lowden had no intention of depriving himself of an audience for this.

"Andrej, something's come up. It's difficult." Something had come up during the early eights of first-shift, as a matter of fact. He'd been asleep. But Bench intelligence specialists were allowed global override on privacy channels, any time, any place. "I'm really sorry to have to do this to you. There's been a draft on services, your services. At Burkhayden."

And there *was* a draft on Koscuisko's services, too—Vogel had made that quite clear. Andrej Koscuisko—no other—and the surgical unit. And immediately. Two eights into third shift, actually, and only an eight left to second shift now—Koscuisko would have no time to think twice about it. Perfect.

Koscuisko looked pale, but then Koscuisko had looked pale from early on. He wasn't well. He drank.

"Services, your Excellency." Koscuisko's tone of voice made it quite clear that he thought he knew precisely what Lowden had meant in selecting that word. "Forgive me for asking, but can it not wait? We will at Burkhayden arrive soon enough."

Quite so. For himself Captain Lowden tried to give Koscuisko adequate anticipation time; it sharpened Koscuisko's appetite and improved Koscuisko's performance. Koscuisko was a resource of very significant value . . . not only to the rule of Law, but to Lowden himself, personally, intimately. Monetarily.

"I regret, Andrej. But Vogel was very insistent. Nothing will do for him but that you travel to Burkhayden immediately to support his requirement."

And now he was to have Koscuisko for another period of time— who knew how long? He had connections. Chilleau Judiciary was going to be in no mood to endorse any request for reassignment; quite the contrary, he could rely on Chilleau Judiciary to come up with good reasons why Koscuisko could not be spared from *Ragnarok*, even though Standard procedure was to rotate every four years. *Ragnarok* had demonstrated its ability to make full use of Koscuisko in his Judicial function. It was Koscuisko's experience on the *Ragnarok* that had finally convinced Koscuisko to renew his Term. Yes.

"According to his Excellency's good pleasure." Koscuisko knew better than to press it any further. "Name the time and the place, if you will, sir."

And what would Koscuisko not do, to protect his assigned troops from sanctions?

Could it be that Lowden was to find a way to have his wish, and watch the blood flow from fresh livid weals on Koscuisko's own smooth-skinned and aristocratic back?

"Docking bay down-forward three, and at third and two. First Officer is sending one of your senior Security as acting Chief, I understand. The documentation surrounding Chief Stildyne's refusal of that promotion to First Officer on JFS *Sceppan* isn't complete, and he has to answer to the evaluation board for it. Reasons for declining, and so forth."

Koscuisko hadn't heard about that, either. The pupils of

Koscuisko's eyes had shrunk to small angry smoldering coals surrounded by ice. Oh, it was very gratifying, very gratifying indeed.

The only person who wasn't getting the joke was ap Rhiannon, too new to have heard all about Stildyne's personal predilections, and how he had used to treat the Bonds, and how that had changed with Koscuisko's arrival. And why. And why, and why, and why, and why. She'd get an earful soon enough. Lowden knew he could rely upon his other officers to see to that.

"Very good, sir. Down-forward three. Captain."

He'd done everything he'd wanted; his joke was set, primed, and ready.

"And we'll see you in a week or two. Thank you, gentles, well done all 'round."

It was only a matter of time before his joke went off in Garol Vogel's face; and that would serve Vogel right, for shaking a senior Fleet officer out of bed in the middle of his sleep for no better reason than that Wyrlann had beaten some Nurail whore.

Again.

Jils Ivers watched the *Ragnarok*'s loaders position the surgical unit beneath the courier ship's waiting cargo area, soothed as she always was to see a task done quickly and done well. The Security that was to travel with them to Burkhayden stood waiting for their officer near the passenger loading ramp; Jils thought she could put names to some of them, after all these years of watching Koscuisko for Verlaine.

The tall Nurail would logically be Robert St. Clare, whose lapse had almost ruined Koscuisko for them before he'd even reported to his first duty. Godsalt, whose precise role in the riots at Arnulf had yet to be determined, whether or not there had been Evidence enough to convict him—and impose his Bond.

One man she didn't recognize, but since he was Pitere to look at him, he was probably Garrity.

And the smiling man with the light brown curls might be Hirsel, who had escaped a full Eighth Level inquiry so narrowly in his previous command. They hadn't been able to prove enough to pursue the offense on such a terminal level. But they had sent him to the *Ragnarok*, right enough, and before Koscuisko had come that had been almost as bad where bond-involuntaries were concerned.

Brachi Stildyne she knew: there was no mistaking that wreckage of a face. Stildyne had come from mean streets, and his face showed his history; one eyebrow off center and lined through with scar tissue, one cheekbone noticeably higher than the other, and his nose had been broken so many times it hardly even mattered any more.

Stildyne was talking to the big black Scaltskarmell who would logically be Pyotr Micmac, or Micmac Pyotr, whichever; but that made six in total. There were one too many. Not only that, but there was an officer's duty-case with the Security that Jils thought she recognized—and found out of place.

What would Koscuisko be wanting a field interrogations kit for?

"Garol, give me an eye or two here."

"Um." Garol had been in a bit of a mood since early this morning, and she wasn't exactly sure what the matter was, because it seemed to run deeper than any combination of perfectly reasonable explanations for Garol's being on the brood. "Whatcha got, Jils?"

She pointed. "What does that look like, to you?"

There was a pharmacy tech down there now, and a little genial frisking seemed to be taking place between St. Clare and the woman with her issue-pouch while the senior troops' backs were obligingly turned. "Looks like a date to me, Jils, has it been that long? Really?"

"No, you idiot. The box on the deck." The tech was leaving, but St. Clare had the issue-pouch. Garol crunched in closer to the view-port, frowning.

"What the . . . ? Stinking three-days-rotten ftah." Well, it wasn't just her suspicious nature, then. "What does he want to travel with that thing for? Jils, I'm not having it on board this ship."

The surgical unit contained the surgical machine, the sterile unit, supplies to address gross trauma and delicate microsurgery alike. That box down on the decking with Koscuisko's Security contained other things, the things that a Chief Medical Officer might need if he was being sent to the field for another reason entirely—field interrogation. Instruments of field-expedient Inquiry, Confirmation, and Execution.

"Listen, Garol." Jils had an uneasy feeling that she just might have guessed at what was going on. Lowden was a master manipulator. She'd known that about Koscuisko's superior officer for years. "You didn't talk to Koscuisko, did you? Just to the Captain?"

"Damn it, Jils, I'm not having it, we're not on a search-and-mutilate, not this time—"

Overreacting a bit. Garol didn't usually get emotional about the Judicial function, and it was a little funny to see him bouncing around so far outside of his normal operating mode of depressed disgust. "So we don't know what Lowden told Koscuisko." And it was just the sort of thing that would appeal to Lowden's sense of humor, too.

Garol had his eyes fixed on the scene outside. Trying to identify what it was that he found so fascinating, Jils followed his line of sight and discovered Andrej Koscuisko just entering the loading bay from the far end.

"Well, I'm going to find out."

Garol was halfway across the room before she could say anything, but his intent was screamingly obvious. Jils hurried to follow him. She wanted to know how Koscuisko was holding up after what she'd told him about his new post with Verlaine.

And she had a good notion that Koscuisko wasn't about to chat with her over a friendly game of relki, not even if it was to take a month and a half to get to Port Burkhayden rather than a day and a half or so.

Security might have heard Garol coming, or they might just have been quick to respond to Garol's surely unexpected entrance. They were at attention one way or the other; Jils didn't think Stildyne had seen Koscuisko yet, he was still talking with Pyotr. Garol was just intercepting Koscuisko when she caught up with him, well short of Koscuisko's waiting people.

"Your Excellency." The formal address always sounded disconcertingly casual coming from Garol. Koscuisko had stopped where he stood, looking past them to where his Security detachment waited for him. "I'm Vogel, your Excellency, Bench intelligence specialist second sub seven Garol Vogel. We've met once before, but only briefly. His Excellency may not remember. We'll be traveling together to Burkhayden, sir."

Koscuisko looked at Garol with suspicion and hostility evident in his pale eyes. He didn't look well. "The Captain has told me that you require my professional services. Specialist Ivers."

Acknowledging his nod in her direction with a careful salute, Jils realized just how good Lowden really was. Garol did in fact have a job for Koscuisko that required Koscuisko's "professional services," and Lowden need only have said that much and no more to create the absolutely opposite impression of what was to be asked of him in Koscuisko's mind.

"Well, actually, it's the Danzilar prince who insisted upon his Excellency in person. Because the woman was very badly treated, and Paval I'shenko feels very strongly that the best surgeon Lowden's got should be the one to put her right."

Nor was there anything explicit in Garol's statement to make his question too obvious or his suspicion too clear. It was just the kind of thing that anybody could have said, offering further information about a mission that had—of course—been fully explained to Koscuisko already up front. Lowden had done no such thing: Jils knew it from Koscuisko's face.

"Mister Stildyne." Koscuisko's Chief of Security had joined them, posted behind Garol and Jils and waiting for Koscuisko's word. "I shall have a word for you, Chief, in a moment. Specialist Vogel. Be very careful what you say. Captain Lowden has given me to understand that I am needed for an interrogation, and I can only take your meaning as to the contrary."

"There may have been a bit of confusion on Lowden's part, sir. But Wyrlann isn't denying it, and the Bench doesn't Inquire into cases like this anyway, since the woman's just a service bond-involuntary." Carefully, carefully. Garol put his words simply and succinctly, as respectful of rank as Garol could be when nobody had given him any reason yet why he should not. "His Excellency is needed to perform reconstructive and restorative surgery. Nothing more."

Koscuisko grimaced suddenly in ferocious pain and turned his head to one side, down and away, the white of his under-blouse gleaming unexpectedly between his neck and the dark of his duty blouse. Garol took a half-step closer with his hands held quiet at his sides. "Are you all right, sir?"

Stildyne stepped forward three paces, as though he would have got between them if he could have managed it. "Give us a few eighths, Specialist," Stildyne suggested, the deference due Garol's unspecified rank as evident as Stildyne's determination to be rid of the two of them. "His Excellency will be along presently."

Retreating a full step, Garol bowed politely to the silent figure of

Andrej Koscuisko. "Take your time," Garol agreed. "The sooner we leave the sooner we get there, though." There was nothing more either of them could possibly say. She and Garol returned to the courier ship, leaving Koscuisko to sort things out with Stildyne. Garol was swearing under his breath; she could guess at what he was probably saying to himself, because of long experience of Garol's moods.

Needs a wire, he does. Needs a full energy charge, about gut-level. Needs the Sisprayan plague. Yeah. Needs a bullet.

So was he talking about Lowden, or Koscuisko? Lowden for deliberately creating the certainty of an abhorrent duty in Koscuisko's mind when quite the opposite was in fact intended? Or Koscuisko himself, since Garol's stated opinion was that there wasn't anything to choose between the two of them?

"Hey." She didn't need him in this mood, especially not at the beginning of a trip. "So it's all right, now, okay? Come on."

Safely inside the ship, now, Garol turned toward her suddenly and put his fist to the wall the way he did when he was so unhappy that only inflicting gratuitous physical pain on himself could make him feel any better. It was a problem that Garol had; they'd been living with it for years. "All right nothing, Jils, you've got to know better than that. You saw the look on that sorry jack's face—it's not all right at all. What a cheap trick, jerking on a man's chain like that—"

This was almost funny. "That's good, coming from you, Garol. Just the day before yesterday, was it, that Koscuisko was a deeply disturbed sicko who wasn't worth the consideration you'd give the average asswipe? Remember?"

Being reminded of his own excesses always drove him wild. Garol rolled his eyes in utter exasperation. "He's a man, and any man deserves a little basic decency. You saw his face, Jils, come on, you saw it, the same as I did."

"Yeah, right, sure, and he's probably kind to children and small animals, too. As if that means squat. I don't believe you." He was letting things get a little out of control, if anybody asked her. Which they hadn't. "Ready to promote him to human being just because Lowden didn't give him all the facts?"

"There's more to it than that." He was calmer now, but stubborn still. "I don't like the way that Stildyne tiptoes around him.

Something's going on that no one's telling us, and that could be dangerous, Jils, when it's somebody like Koscuisko that we're talking about."

Whatever it was that had upset him so deeply he wasn't able to quite put his finger on it. At least not yet, or he'd tell her. "We've got company, Garol. Go start the shutdowns. I'll make nice with our guests for you."

Garol stomped off ungraciously toward the control room, and Jils sighed to herself, arranging her face even as she did so.

Even Koscuisko—hostile and resentful as he was bound to be—was company to be preferred to Garol, when Garol was in a mood.

This was not good. Stildyne knew how much pleasure Captain Lowden took in setting up his little pranks; before Koscuisko's arrival and subsequent agreement with the Captain had put an end to it, many of Lowden's best gags had resulted in assessment of two-and-twenty on up for whichever bond-involuntary happened to be closest at time of occurrence.

"Your Excellency, I'm—"

Sorry, Stildyne started to say. *Sorry you had to stay. Sorry I'm not going with you to Port Burkhayden, but we both know that Pyotr would be Chief of Security if he weren't under Bond. I'm not sure he doesn't outrank me even with his Bond. You'll be fine with Pyotr.*

Unfortunately Koscuisko wasn't having any of it. Stildyne wondered, just that fraction of a moment too late, what other humorous trap Captain Lowden might have set recently.

"Tell me then that this nonsense of refusing *Sceppan* is also a lie." Koscuisko challenged him directly, his voice flat and cold and wickedly cutting. "And I will say no more about it. I am waiting to hear, Mister Stildyne."

Koscuisko wouldn't hear what he was waiting to hear. Because that much was true. Why hadn't he said anything to Koscuisko before? Koscuisko had been drunk, that was why. Koscuisko had had problems of his own.

"Very well. If you want to hear more lies." It wasn't going to be pleasant any way he looked at it. Maybe it would be just as well to get it done and over with here and now. Koscuisko was leaving for Port Burkhayden; Stildyne wouldn't see him for more than a week. That could give Koscuisko time to accept the idea and become reconciled to it. One way or the other Stildyne wasn't about to back down.

"You are offered the post of First Officer. It is the culmination of your career," Koscuisko noted; quite calmly, really. "And you know as well as I do that such slots are created only by attrition or new commission, and there are precious few new commissions in these troubled times. How long will it be before there is another chance for you?"

So far, so good. "If his Excellency wishes to state that he finds my performance unacceptable, then do so to my face. Because otherwise I'm not going. I have responsibilities here."

That concept was still as new and alien to him as when he had first realized that he was going to refuse *Sceppan*, and why. Responsibilities. He, himself, Brachi Stildyne, every man for himself and the devil take the hindmost. Koscuisko was at fault. Koscuisko was at fault for so much.

"Stildyne, we have to go, I do not have time to dance with you. You must know how things are. You do not imagine they will change. Why will you not go to *Sceppan*?"

Yes, he knew how things were. On *Sceppan* he would have respect, responsibilities, the safety of a crew and the effectiveness of its fighting troops as his to nurture and protect. On *Ragnarok* he had—what?

"I knew that I was going to decline the promotion when First Officer put it in front of me, your Excellency. And that was before anything changed your plans." On *Ragnarok* he had nothing but grief, No perks left to being Chief Warrant Officer over bond-involuntary Security when Koscuisko disapproved so strongly of anyone taking advantage of sexual access to them.

No particular degree of rapport with Koscuisko himself, who was not inclined to admire other men and who emphatically resented being openly admired himself. Nothing. "You were going home. There would be nobody to look after Godsalt and the others."

Nothing but grief and worry. Koscuisko had tricked him over the years, somehow. Lured him into feeling responsible for the Bonds, while he wasn't looking. Into wanting to do what he could do to protect them from Lowden's sense of humor for no other reason than that they were not permitted to protect themselves.

"For the gentlemen you have made this decision?" He'd caught Koscuisko off guard, startled him. That was funny. Andrej Koscuisko, caught off guard. "Mister Stildyne. I am astonished at you. I had thought—"

He knew what Koscuisko had thought.

Am I never to be forgiven for having once desired you?

Stildyne knew better than to say the words, though.

Koscuisko turned the phrase away, and continued.

"And yet they will not be unshielded here now, because I have the bargain arranged with Captain Lowden. Therefore you need not turn away from the opportunity."

"Yes, right, and you can do it all yourself. You've done it all yourself these years past, haven't you?" A man could get exasperated. "Sorry, sir, it's not negotiable. If you want to get rid of me you'll have to bring a complaint before First Officer. Why don't you load the courier, sir, and leave me to do my job."

He wasn't staying just because he liked short lithe intransigent blonds. If he liked Dolgorukij he knew where he could buy them, at least for a few hours, even if they did run a little high to market— Dolgorukij men in service houses were relatively uncommon, but not impossible to find. Stildyne had hired his share of them over the course of the past four years. It never seemed to make dealing with Koscuisko any easier: so obviously whatever it was about Koscuisko wasn't just wanting him.

Stildyne wasn't interested in thinking it through more thoroughly than that. He had enough problems.

"As long as we are clear, you and I," Koscuisko said thoughtfully. "Because you are quite right, I am not proof against Captain Lowden, and to the extent to which I have implied that you have not protected these gentlemen beyond my ability to do so I apologize to you, Mister Stildyne, from my heart. I am a very great sinner. It was not my intent to attempt to deny respect to you."

That probably meant something, and he would probably figure it out. Sooner or later. For now he had to get Koscuisko on board the courier and away.

"Don't think twice about it." *And whatever you do don't try to explain anything.* Koscuisko's explanations never seemed to explain. They only made things worse. "You're wanted on courier, sir."

For a moment Stildyne thought that Koscuisko was going to open his mouth, say something. For a moment.

Then Koscuisko apparently decided that it would be not only expedient but appropriate to yield the last word, because he only nodded.

Stildyne stepped aside.

Koscuisko crossed the decking toward the courier and climbed the ramp into its waiting belly, and never once looked back.

That's the way to do it, Stildyne me lad, Stildyne told himself.

Never look back.

You've bought these boots now well and truly, and paid cash money, too.

It's up to you to break them in and wear them.

CHAPTER FOUR

So this was Port Burkhayden, in Meghilder space.

Andrej chafed the palms of his hands together irritably in the bleak bare prep room of the loosely-to-be-described-as hospital. It was cold, and the light was thin, when it managed to clear the heavy dark clouds that seemed to be blanketing most of this local geographic. Cold made Andrej uncomfortable. He snapped at the thin young man at the doorway without taking thought for the intruder's clothing.

"Yes, what is it now? Has the heating system also been repossessed? What?"

Security appeared from the other room as soon as he spoke, and Andrej could hear other people in the corridor outside. The intruder himself looked much more frightened than apologetic; he could hardly be on staff, Andrej realized, not dressed like that. Unfeeling of him to threaten so, when he knew perfectly well that the news of his identity had reached the hospital well before he had.

"His Excellency's pardon." So purely parochial an accent Andrej hadn't heard in a long time. He had a particular weakness for Nurail all the same, because of Robert, because of the mettle of the victims of the Domitt Prison, because of too many miscellaneous instances to be remembered. "It's a mistake I've made, my maistress gave me leave to see a woman, if the officer will excuse."

Staff Security was outside, behind the young man. His own Security were standing between Andrej and the intruder now,

74

looking very stern indeed. Unfriendly hands reached through the open doorway to pull the young man out into the hall with rough efficiency. Andrej frowned to see it; he could smell a beating in the making.

"We're very sorry, your Excellency. Some sort of a mistake, we'll be sure his Excellency isn't disturbed any further."

And a raised voice, outside, the same accent. "Disturbed, you with the collar on, what do you mean disturbed, he's nothing to do with my Megh—"

It was so easy to lose control of situations like this. Sighing in resignation—not unmixed with amusement—Andrej waved his Security away from him, beckoning to the staff security. "No, there is no problem. Bring to me this person, I will talk to him."

"Well—"

Andrej could all but read the scan in the staff security's mind. First, an embarrassing incursion, unexpected, makes us look bad, we'll just see about that. Second, strong language, shows disrespect—he's earned it for himself, now. Third, on the other hand, he hasn't really done anything so very wrong, and who knows what Uncle Andrej means when he says "talk?"

"And see if you can obtain for me a glass of rhyti, from the kitchen. If you would. My gentlemen and I have not had a chance to take a meal since we made planetfall. Do you think it can be managed?"

Torture seemed incompatible with fast-meal from one end of the Bench to the other. An appeal for physical comforts on his people's behalf frequently had the positive effect of both reassuring host Security and recruiting their sympathies at the same time. It was a natural impulse of the sentient mind, one that Andrej knew and appreciated.

"Of course, sir, right away." Once again it worked for him; and the chill in the air was diminishing, so the facilities staff had got some warmth redirected at last. All to the good. "This person does have clearance for a visit, your Excellency, but his Excellency's best judgment takes precedence, of course."

The young man reappeared at the doorway, escorted almost benignly by the staff security. Looking confused, as well he might.

"Thank you, shift leader." He had an hour's wait, maybe more, while the surgery was prepared. He was scheduled for pre-op, but he had nothing in particular to do until then; the hospital administration had to be given time to round up all the requisite staff.

The patient document was waiting for him in the reader at the window, but Andrej thought that there was time to see what the matter was with this young man. He had already studied all the information that Vogel had been able to provide. He was fairly secure that he knew what was needed in that area.

"Come and tell me, you, what is your name. What woman did you come to see, and why?"

Speaking as gently, as reassuringly as he could, still Andrej wondered why he bothered. A man with a reputation like his could try all he liked and still be incapable of convincing that there was nothing to fear from him.

"Skelern. Hanner. Your Excellency." Scale-airn. Not an uncommon name, he'd seen it before, if the Standard script spelling of it did not quite describe the sound of it to Andrej's ear. "It's just a woman that I came to see, she lies here somewhere. Not to go in where I'm not wanted, your Excellency."

There was a delicate balance there between the native distrust of all Nurail for authority and the young man's quite sensible awareness of his vulnerability within the unequal power structure of Port Burkhayden. "Of course not, nor was any such thing suggested. Do you work at the service house?"

Oh, the affront, so quickly hidden away out of embarrassment. "No, if it please the officer." And be damned before he would; that was the unspoken part. "A gardener—the Tavart is my maistress. Iaccary Textile and Cordage, it is. I only bring Megh the trimmings, when they're of a sort to remind her. It gives her a little joy to remember the hill country."

"Is she from the hill country? I hadn't thought there were Borderers, at Burkhayden."

Hanner had an honest face, open. Obvious. It showed his thoughts quite clearly: surprise that Andrej connected hill-stations with Borderers; speedy self-reminder that—as everybody knew—what Black Andrej didn't know about Nurail after the Domitt Prison was not worth knowing.

Andrej had never quite understood why he was "black" Andrej, since he was as blond as any of the fairer run of Nurail—or more so.

There was a descriptive element to the word that had nothing to do with hue—black for something that was destructive, something that was powerful.

Nurail had black uncles and other uncles, depending on which had been their mothers' favorite or oldest brother, the one with the most influence over their lives. Andrej had been Uncle Andrej, and he had been Black Andrej, but to the best of his knowledge he'd never been honored with the title of "black uncle," and perhaps that was just as well. For his ego.

"Not from Burkhayden, your Excellency. She's from Marleborne, but she's all alone in the service house—she's the only service Bond imprisoned there. And any Nurail could be my sister, his Excellency knows that."

Or my brother, or my uncle, or my niece. A Nurail proverb of recent coinage, a response to the Bench's determined dispersion of the Nurail nations and the destruction of so many of them.

So Hanner brought Megh flowers, and tried to be a brother to her. "Come back later, Hanner, you don't want to see her now. I'll send a chit to your employer." Especially if he was fond of the woman, he didn't want to see her now.

Hanner frowned and pursed his lips. "Please let me see her, your Excellency, such frightful things I've heard, I'll not be able to get leave again with the Danzilar to be coming. And I'm afraid for her."

Well, it was a reasonable point, and good marks in Hanner's favor as well. Andrej had known enough other reasonable, sensible Nurail who had not quite found the courage within themselves to challenge a torturer on anything. The weather. The brod-toast. Anything. Still—

"She's not to be gaped at for a curiosity. If she had next of kin—but I must insist. You may not see her now. Wait until she is somewhat recovered, and can speak to you."

On the other hand maybe Hanner wasn't a sensible Nurail at all, merely a stubborn one. The color mounted in his brown face, and his dark eyes flashed with a species of sudden unexpected defiance. "Then I claim her by the Narrow Pass and by the Ice Traverse, your Excellency. By her father's weave and her mother's weave I claim her. And you'll let me see my sister."

Andrej could hear the choking sound that St. Clare made behind Andrej's back in shock at this display. He was a little taken aback himself; but not so much as Hanner seemed to be dismayed by his own rash demand, to judge by the way that the color fled his cheeks.

This did change things.

If Hanner knew her family, her father's weave and her mother's weave, then he had a right—in Nurail terms—to be considered as her brother, even if only in a limited sense. He could have made them up, true. But under other circumstances he might be in considerable trouble with the Port Authority for so much as stating them.

And there was a significantly powerful prejudice among Nurail against citing both at once. As if it were equivalent to displaying a sexual act in public, more or less. They could be such prudish people, for all the blunt cheerful explicitness of the language.

"Very well." Vogel's report had only discussed the worst of her injuries; there was no particular reason for Andrej to suspect that she was badly marked, as well as injured. Except that when bullies like the *Ragnarok*'s First Lieutenant beat a woman they generally made an horrific mess of her face, and Andrej couldn't help but feel that no brother could easily bear sight of the evidence to what a sister had suffered from such a brute.

It was hard enough when one was not related, and had the benefit of having seen it all before. One never became inured to brutality. If one was lucky. "Robert, you take Hanner here into the next room for a bit; keep him out of staff security's way. Don't worry, we'll give a shout when fast-meal comes, and if there is fried cold-meal mush you shall sort it out between the two of you."

He would have a look at the patient's documents, he would have a look at the patient. He would do the best he could for her, poor woman. Poor anonymous woman, poor slave, with only a thin—dirty—and incautious gardener to take her part against the misfortunes and the injustices that had befallen her.

"Come along, then, Hanner, you heard the officer." St. Clare's voice was surprisingly harsh from behind him, and Hanner swallowed nervously, but came meekly enough. Good man; Andrej approved. St. Clare had a sister somewhere, Andrej knew. That was why Robert was so painfully sensitive about the abuse that service bond-involuntaries suffered.

Other bond-involuntaries that Andrej had been privileged to know treated service Bonds as members of one family in token of their mutual slavery, calling them all "cousin." Robert's pain was a little more personal and immediate than that. Any given service bond-involuntary could very well be somebody's sister. But somewhere out there was his.

His sister Megh?

No, Andrej told himself, a little embarrassed at his romanticizing. He was imagining things. It was a common name, whether or not he was misremembering something he'd heard from Robert eight years ago and more. But any coincidence of names would only make St. Clare even moodier. Best to get the two of them out of anybody's way until the gardener could be sent safely home.

And then he would see whether a public-funded hospital in a Nurail port could find decent healing work for a Dolgorukij torturer: and keep himself too busy to think about his future, about Captain Lowden, about the Fleet that had created G'herm Wyrlann and would protect him for as long as he held rank.

Center House, Port Burkhayden. The place was swarming with Danzilar's advance party, even at this late hour of the evening. The grand foyer looked very much like a theatrical stage in mid-shift, to Jils Ivers. Garol had been in a state ever since he'd first heard about the Lieutenant's little escapade; and for herself Jils had already decided that Wyrlann deserved everything that Garol was likely to say to him.

The *Ragnarok*'s First Lieutenant had sent his own Security to meet the courier—a gesture possibly calculated to ingratiate himself with them. It hadn't worked, Garol's ingratiation threshold being as high as it was. Now it was time for Wyrlann—waiting for them amid the ladders and the carpet-layers, the glaziers and the technicians—to face that uncomfortable fact.

"Good greeting. Ivers, isn't it? Right. And Vogel. Welcome to Port Burkhayden. Had a nice transit?"

One thing was immediately obvious from Wyrlann's self-satisfied expression, his easy—if somewhat condescending— banter. He didn't think he had anything to apologize for.

"Yeah, well, not too bad. Lieutenant." Garol even in his foulest moods did try to stay away from provoking confrontation. It wasn't out of respect or diffidence, no. He just hated to waste energy. "Have you got the survey forms completed? Let's go, get it out of the way and all that."

Wyrlann coughed, as if embarrassed. "There's been a bit of an unexpected problem. A little local unrest."

She'd just bet there'd been unrest. Garol wasn't taking the hint, though, which meant that Garol was ignoring it, just to be difficult. "To be expected, when a port's in transit. Well, we'll just sign off on the survey, and we can be out of each other's way."

There was a third party involved in the transaction, though he hadn't said anything one way or the other until now: Fleet Liaison Officer Artigen, a well-respected career man, good to have on site in an unsettled environment. "With the Lieutenant's permission. I felt it best to advise the Lieutenant not to complete the survey until the arrival of additional Security, Specialist Vogel. We've had a predictable upswing in anti-Fleet sentiment these last few days."

"Predictable when ranking officers make like eight-to-the Standard bruisers? That the kind of 'predictable' you mean?"

Garol made no effort to keep his voice down, and there was no mistaking the sentiment among the local workmen. Wyrlann evidently felt the hostility as personally directed, for whatever reason.

"Listen, Vogel, I'll thank you to stick to your agenda, and keep yourself out of things that don't concern you. 'Bench intelligence specialist' is all very well, but I have to tell you, I don't like your attitude."

Jils sighed. If she'd had a marker she could have tossed it. Wyrlann had done it, now.

"And I don't like your face, Lieutenant. Your face, your voice, your behavior, your Captain. You disgust me, you disgust them, and Artigen was right to keep your sorry ass off the street, because you deserve a wire, and the only reason I hope you don't get one soon is that nobody deserves to have to pay for it, transmit received?"

And all of it in a perfectly reasonable tone of voice, not raised, not lowered, no hint of anger or even much emotion. Of course Garol sounded just as if he was merely stating a few facts. Because that was exactly what he was doing, no more, no less.

"Ah, if I could make a suggestion, Specialist Vogel—" Fleet Liaison Officer Artigen offered, tactfully. "The Lieutenant had completed the primary surveys prior to the, ah, controversial event. In light of the fact that it was due to my advice that it's incomplete, I'm sure Captain Lowden will accept your best judgment on the balance."

Wyrlann had been about to make an issue of Garol's lack of professional courtesy, so much was obvious. But Artigen had said the magic word. The magic name, rather; as soon as Artigen mentioned Captain Lowden, Wyrlann paled and shut his mouth, transferring his attention to the new parquetry underfoot. Interesting.

"Yeah, I guess. Anybody going to want to shoot at me? What do we have left to do?"

"Perhaps best if we simply went alone, Specialist Vogel. They don't know who you are, or Specialist Ivers, of course. And I'm expected to make the tour on a regular basis. There's the hospital, the service facility, the Port Authority, the civil holding facility. That sort."

"Whattaya say, Jils? Take a walk? Fun-filled excursion to all the attractions, beautiful exotic port like Burkhayden? Naked maidens, dancing boys? Damn. It's starting to rain again, isn't it?"

Maybe if he went out in the rain for an hour or two it would take the gain down a couple of notches. Cool things off all around. "No, I'll just have to stay behind and do the administrative work while you run off to the service house under the transparent pretext of an inspection. Let me know if they've got a bone-bender on staff."

It was a particular weakness of hers. She got her spine worked by a bone-bender every chance she had, whether or not Garol and the Jurisdiction Standard alike believed it did any good. There was plenty for her to do here, though. She needed to inspect the quarters assigned to them.

She needed to trail in to the house-net, to see what it could tell her about the last few days. She needed to assess the snoopers, and make sure that if there were any left that the Danzilar prince's Security didn't already know about they were hidden well enough that they would never be found.

But as Karol turned to leave with Artigen, Wyrlann raised his voice. "If you see Koscuisko at the hospital." There was a note of nasty gloating there, as if Wyrlann felt he was paying Karol off on exponential margins. "Tell him there's been a priority transmit—we received it two eights ago. His extension's been approved. But Fleet won't reassign him in the foreseeable future, in light of Captain Lowden's critical requirement for the resource."

Extension?

Koscuisko, on extension?

Garol was waiting for her cue, but Jils couldn't think of anything to say. Wyrlann turned around and sauntered off, smiling, content that he'd brought bad news and enjoying the impact it made. Jils met Garol's eyes, helpless to respond. What could make Koscuisko desperate enough to extend his contract with the Fleet, even knowing as he must have done that he had no hope of getting clear from Lowden if he did so?

Verlaine.

"Less effort all around if he'd just cut his throat and be done with it." Garol commented, to cover for her confusion, she guessed. "I'll tell him, Jils."

And Garol had to know how hollow the jest really was, the number of times Koscuisko had tried to simply cut his throat and be done with it. Except that he had never quite succeeded; partly because he had been prevented, but also at least partly because he wanted to be free but not to die. Too desperate, in his mind, to be able to accept what he could not change, what he was not permitted to change.

Too clear-eyed and well-grounded to be able to ignore the fact that it was his own actual—permanent—death that he was essaying. Too sane to want to die enough to make it work, not while there was a slim chance or hope of escape, somewhere.

"Thanks, Garol, I'll be doing."

An extension was the only thing that could keep him from Verlaine, though it was so extreme a step that she had honestly not thought of it until now.

It was an irrational impulse on her part, an unreasonable conviction.

But suddenly Jils Ivers knew that if Koscuisko finally succeeded in taking the final escape after this news it would be herself that she would blame.

For murder.

Andrej stood at the inside of a conference-oval in the hospital surgery's prep room, looking around him. "Who have we got, then? Gentles, if you would be so kind, bearing in mind that I'm the hired man from out of town."

It was a short staff, but it would have to do. Half of them were Nurail: that was a plus, if he could rely on them to know how hill-people differed from other folk. Their biggest problem was that it was the middle of the night, well past third-meal. People would be prepared to sleep, not to operate.

And yet the sooner they were started the better chance they had. The woman had been waiting for them too long already. Nobody dared wait a moment longer.

"Orthopedics, your Excellency. Heron Jamoch." One of the weaves was Heron Black-pelt, Andrej remembered. But he had no right to the knowledge. Though he had not taken it by force it had come to him as the last desperate gasp of a dying man, unwilling to let his mother's voice be silenced forever.

"Soft tissue displacement. Sonders Connlin."

Orthopedics had work, but not too much work; soft tissue displacement had the uglier task. "Thank you, Sonders Connlin, you and I have our work cut out for us. Yes?"

"Internal, sir, renal trauma and respiratory malfunction. Aan Jardle. Some experience with smooth muscle tearing, but not enough."

Wyrlann had kicked the woman when she'd been down. In the belly. There was smooth muscle damage, on top of the gross insult to her womb. The sacred cradle. Andrej shook himself just a bit, to try to get centered.

"We are lucky to have any smooth muscle experience at all, Jardle. I'm a beginner in that field, I'm afraid. We haven't heard from everyone yet, though. Who is left?" Probably sensory and micromovement. Or perhaps merely gross trauma.

"Gynecological, as the officer please."

There was more of a surprise there than just the specialty. Andrej hadn't hoped for gynecology; it would make things much easier on them all—well, easier on him, at any rate. But that wasn't the sum of it. The phrase was familiar, but underneath it—what did he think he recognized?

"And your name, sir," Andrej prompted. Gynecology was the oldest person here, quite possibly pushing sixty years Standard to look at him. That meant something. What was it?

"Barit Howe. His Excellency won't remember me. Administrative staff at Fleet Orientation Station Medical, sir. Pending the dawning of the Day."

Reborn.

Barit Howe had been a bond-involuntary, and had lived to see the Day dawn at last. It was no wonder that Andrej's subconscious mind had insisted he knew something quite important about that man—

Bowing, Andrej fumbled for words with which to express the respect due a man who could survive for so long the life to which the Bonds had been condemned. "A very great honor, Master Howe. I am in your presence humbled and silent." Though of course he couldn't afford to be, not literally. He was senior in rank; he was expected to coordinate the surgical attack.

"Very good. I have, heard your names; and it may be arrogance on my part, but I believe that you already know who I am. Neurosurgical. Andrej Koscuisko. And a baseline competence in general practice, which we do not for this exercise particularly need. Shall we to the problem at hand turn attention?"

The woman Megh, Wyrlann's victim. Her injuries had been stabilized, but the hospital had waited to encourage aggressive healing for the arrival of someone who knew how to repair the nerve damage before it scarred over. Four days ago. Not quite five. It could not wait for very much longer.

"If his Excellency will review the material onscreen," Barit Howe suggested. Respectfully: but Howe was a reborn man. The suggestion was not very far from the mark as an order. "We had taken the liberty of preparing a proposed approach. We didn't know we were going to get a surgeon with your qualifications. We need to fine-tune this a bit."

No, they hadn't expected him. His being here was his cousin Danzilar's idea, and very sound reasoning on his cousin's part too, as far as Andrej could tell. "Of course. With the lower body cavity let us be started."

The sooner they finished review of the problem the sooner they could be started to work.

And there was a good deal of work to be done here.

Unfortunately the first tasks fell to Andrej.

It was an offense to approach such a woman in the surgical

machine rather than on his knees in reverence. Andrej could only hope that the holy Mother would forgive the impertinence, because there was no other way in which he could approach the injured bond-involuntary, if he hoped to do her any help instead of further injury.

Secure within the all-embracing environment of the surgical machine, safely insulated from the pitiful reality of her damaged body, Andrej began his calibration exercises, a litany from his childhood uninvited—stubborn—in his distracted mind.

Forgive us, Saint Polaka, that was raped with the fencepost of the impious. That was raped by the company of the impious in violation of all decency. That was raped by the member of a horse at the hands of the impious.

Polaka was a Sarvaw saint, and her litany didn't represent her literal martyrdom—which had actually been a fairly mundane gang-rape if he remembered his religious history correctly.

The litany was more global than just young Saint Polaka, though. Collected into it were all of the atrocities committed against a captive Sarvaw population by its Dolgorukij overlords less than three hundred years ago.

Andrej had learned it in his childhood as part of the observances during the days of contrition, when it was considered to be pious to pretend that one felt guilty for the sins of one's ancestors while continuing to enjoy the fruits of their crimes.

There had been a joke to the litany in the cheerful days of his innocence, an adolescent speculation on what the martyr would look like if represented with all of the purported agents of her glorious death. He had not then believed that such things had been done.

He had not then believed that such things could be done.

He had not then believed that such things were still done, and in the same sweet breathing world that he looked on. He knew better, now, and hoped that the saint would accept this Nurail Megh for her own cherished daughter and grant him grace to salve her wounds in shamed humility.

It was time to begin.

He had no faith. He had so offended the holy Mother over the years that it made no sense to even try to pray any more. Perhaps this once, though, she would listen, because it was not for himself that he petitioned, and there was no understanding of her mercy to be had. Andrej closed his eyes within the waiting stillness of the surgical machine and stood a supplicant in the presence of a deity in whom he no longer quite believed, making his prayer.

Asking for the privilege of being used as the instrument of blessing. Asking for a good exercise without flaw or fault, because there was no room for fault or flaw.

Asking for the holy Mother's blessing on the work of his hands, and that of the rest of the surgical team. Asking for a good recovery, health of body and of spirit, because nothing that they could do to heal her body would avail them if her spirit would not accept contrition on her behalf. Asking for full functionality for the woman's sake, for the sake of the thin young gardener who claimed a brother's right to care what became of her.

Then he put it all out of his mind: Saint Polaka, the sacred cradle, the holy Mother's mysteries, all. He set his mind to the simple certitudes of blood and sinew, nerve and bone, and dissolved himself into the surgical machine to suspend his very existence for as long as she should need for him to be the mind of the machine and do his surgery.

The gray filament wires slipped gently, without injury, between cells around the lidded eye of the unconscious woman, to seek the optic nerve-bundle at the back of her eye and massage a range of sensors there back into alignment.

Andrej forgot his life and went to work.

Robert St. Clare stood for hours in mute misery behind the officer where he sat in the by-room of the operating theater.

It was his sister. It was Megh.

As much as he dreaded the sight of what the Lieutenant had done to her he could not keep himself from straining to see, all of his love and all of his grief focussed hungrily on the pitiful limbs of her, naked and helpless, bruised and bloodied and broken, in the operating theater below. Days and days it had been; they had cleaned her up carefully, but the evidence was still so terrible that he could curse his own eyesight for the keenness of it.

And still he could not bear to turn away. His sister. His Megh. The only one of his family that yet lived, but there was an end to his father's weave, because what the Lieutenant had done to her could not be made right.

Not after three days.

What the Lieutenant had done to her he had done to her father, to her father's mother, to the father of their father's mother, to the whole family lineage of the Narrow Pass. She would be whole, if she could be made so, but she could never bear a child of her body.

What the Lieutenant had done to her . . .

"Your Excellency." The query from the theater sounded, one of the doctors below asking for advice. "Not quite happy with respiration, sir. Can an increased dose of elam be risked at this point?"

Oh, if only she wore the mask, he would not have to look on her. But she could breathe on her own, so her face was uncovered and ghastly in the bright light. The officer shifted.

"How much longer need we maintain her on cynerdahl? Well. It will be safe to increase to nine parts. But let's try not to go ten, if it can be managed."

The officer's subspecialty, in pharmacology. Psycho-pharmacology, but the basics were the same. Settling back in the hammock-slung seat, Koscuisko chanced to glance up at him; what, had he been too quiet, too still?

"Robert. You are suffering. What is the matter, please?" He was suffering. Yes. It was true. He could not look at Megh without rage in his heart for the beast that had fouled her. And the beast was an officer, against whom he could rage all he liked in the quiet of his mind but in whose presence he was a slave.

"It's hard to look at." Choking the words out, Robert could only hope Koscuisko understood. And then hoped Koscuisko didn't understand too much. "Sir. With respect. It's something about just the fact that she's Nurail."

And my sister. He wanted to say it, and he could not. He had no claim to Megh while he was still Bonded. He could not say. He could not claim her. He could only make generalizations—

"And no one to avenge her, because after all it's the Lieutenant. Sir. But it cries out for revenge. If it please the officer."

He knew the uneasy prickling at the back of his neck, the tingling tension in his skull as his governor tried to decide if what he was saying violated his orders and whether he should be punished. But he was speaking to Andrej Koscuisko, and in the presence of Andrej Koscuisko he was safe from the governor. Even from that.

Koscuisko was watching him, wary and measuring; but Koscuisko did not send him away. "Talk to me, Robert. Tell me how it is that she should be avenged. And I will tell you how it would be, on Azanry."

Pretending that it was an abstract sort of issue, a discussion initiated to pass the time. For the officer's amusement. Making the words that ached in his heart an obedient answer, nothing treasonous there.

The governor quieted.

"Well. When a man's done a crime, it's for him to make up the loss, in the hill country." Emboldened, he came forward to stand next to the officer, closer to the clear-wall. Where he could watch Megh. Where he could see her. "And killing is one thing, but this . . . It's another. A killing can be made right with a child. But how can it be made right if a man has murdered a woman's children, in such a way?"

He wasn't sure he made sense. He knew what he was saying. A killing robbed the weave, and a man could make up for it by making the weave whole with a child of his body. What was more precious to a man than his own childer?

"Robert, you seem to say that if I killed her brother I would make amends by—engaging with her?"

That was it precisely, though to hear the sound of the officer's voice he could not quite believe it. Robert could only nod, eyes fixed in misery on the scene below. His sister. His Megh. Oh, his poor darling, and naked in front of all of these people, with no one to care that she would feel shamed by it . . .

"Practical, really. Sir. If you think on it. You've got to convince her that you're really sorry, first." Children were the wealth of the weave, after all. And that was the bottom of what killing meant, a killing robbed the weave. A weave could be made whole. "But a rape means an injury, if the officer please. And I heard you say. To Doctor Howe, there."

Oh, careful, careful. How could he say it, and not reproach his officer? Koscuisko, who had been a good maister to him, though neither of them had chosen their roles. Koscuisko would understand. Koscuisko would not reproach him. The officer frowned, watching below.

"I admit I am not hopeful." Because of the rape, because of the manner of it. Robert could not think. He could barely breathe. "And still it may come out right. It seems odd to me, Robert, that any crime would be worse than a killing, is it indeed so?"

Oh, it was so. It was so exactly. A killing took one life. This thing took the lives that Megh might have had in her, and showed disrespect for a mother's womb. "In the hill country, your Excellency. Yes. There is no way to make such a crime right."

Except by killing. Except by killing the man who had done it, and killing his children, and killing his women lest they carried life that had sprung from a man who could do such a crime. And even then killing could not make it right. Killing solved nothing. Killing was a waste.

Killing the Lieutenant—

Robert waited long moments for the governor's rebuke to punish the thought, unbidden though it was.

There was no rebuke. The governor was silent.

Was it because Robert knew he was right?

"Hill-country Nurail," the officer said, in a musing sort of voice. "Robert. I wonder. Do you believe he is in blood her brother? Oh, well, never mind. He'll do as well as any, I suppose. When this is over we to the gardener should go and speak. I have an idea. Because he is a gardener."

Down in the operating theater the orderlies were moving pieces of surgical equipment back toward the wall. One of the physicians was leaving the room, stripping off the sterile layer of her garment as she went. Two of the orderlies came to the side of the operating level, one to each side, and shook a sterile covering over her naked body, covering her at last. Megh, poor Megh. His sister. His own.

The officer spoke on. "And I have also promised that he could see her, once we were finished. Come along then, Robert. Let us go see Hanner home to his garden. And hope for a greenhouse."

Whatever that meant.

He had seen his sister. He had spoken his mind, and to Koscuisko who received it with care and respect. He could do nothing about the Lieutenant.

He wasn't sorry he'd thought it, even so.

⊕ ⊕ ⊕

It was very early in the morning, scarcely sunrise. Sylyphe Tavart stood half-asleep, half in shock at her mother's side in the front business room, staring at the visitors that had come upon them so suddenly. Security, four of them, all of them tall, and green-sleeves— green piping on their sleeves, bond-involuntaries. So straight, so still, so perfect; and with them was their master.

"I must beg to be forgiven for this untimely intrusion."

Andrej Koscuisko.

The language was so stiff as to almost be insincere. Coming from any other man, it might have been; but Sylyphe could not imagine anything more perfect than the way in which Koscuisko chose his words. And how he spoke them. "I had not marked the time. And it is my fault to have kept your garden-master, may one hope he could be excused his morning's work? Because I have kept him up all night."

Andrej Koscuisko. Slim and elegant in his black uniform, with the dew glittering in his blond hair. He was so fair it was almost unnatural, and if he was not beautiful he was important—more important than any man she'd ever seen so close up.

Her mother stirred in her seat. "It shall be so, your Excellency, since you wish it. But I hardly think you came all of this way simply to make excuses for my gardener. You'll pardon my saying so."

Skelern looked white in the face as well, but he was in the sun all day and was not so pale as Koscuisko. Skelern looked tired and worn. He'd been to see his friend in hospital, and Sylyphe had wanted to know all about his friend, but hadn't been able to quite puzzle out how to ask without giving the wrong impression.

"You are quite right." Koscuisko smiled a little with his ruddy mouth, tilting his head a bit back on his shoulder. A little to one side. He had a perfect smile. Perfect. "It's because the young man is a gardener, and our patient is Nurail. I hoped to beg some medication from you. And here I have come at too early an hour. I shall go away."

It *was* early. Her mother was in her fast-meal wrap and Sylyphe had only put a smock on over her night-dress. It was a very decent smock. But she knew that she was in her night-dress. If Skelern should guess she would die of humiliation: and still she could not bear to leave the room.

"No sense in running an errand twice, your Excellency, and an honor to receive you at any time. Can I offer you something to eat?

What could there be in my house for medication that isn't in hospital stores?"

Sylyphe could hardly stand still, she was so embarrassed. Her mother. Short and plain, and no cosmetics to disguise the pallor of her cheeks, the thin line of her mouth, the weathering of her face. Thin brown hair tied up in the single most unbecoming knot in known Space. And Andrej Koscuisko, dark and dangerous, with an aura that scintillated with the glamour of his craft. Those Bonds. Bound body and soul to the Inquisitor, to do his bidding at his word or suffer the consequences . . .

"If you will permit, Dame Tavart." The housemaster had come in with the beverage set, but Koscuisko paid no attention. How could her mother be so gauche as to offer an Inquisitor his fast-meal, in the first place? As if he was a salesman or a business partner, and not a senior Judicial officer with custody of a Writ to Inquire?

"There is an ointment in the pharmaceutical inventory that originated amongst the Nurail hill-people as a simple fatty salve infused with jellericia flowers. I have asked Gardener Hanner, and he says there may be jellericia flowers in your hand to grant, but more than that he very properly declines to say."

Why would that be? This was confusing. If Skelern had flowers . . . because they were her mother's flowers, perhaps. And Skelern didn't want them simply taken. That was odd of Skelern, why would he be protective of her mother's property, when he so much resented being made near-property himself? Why would Skelern care?

"I still don't understand. The flowers are yours, of course, with all of my goodwill." Sylyphe thought she knew which flowers, now. They were small and very red. The fragrance was subtle if distinct, and the blooms were difficult to force under artificial light. Skelern had worked very hard on the jellericia flowers. Would Koscuisko appreciate the effort? "If it's in the inventory there must be near-naturals to substitute, surely."

It was Andrej Koscuisko who asked for them. An Inquisitor could not easily be denied. "It's only because the patient is Nurail hill-station, Dame Tavart. Her subconscious mind will recognize the fragrance. It's very difficult to match with near-naturals. That is the particular reason that I ask. She will know the fragrance and be glad of it, and it will speed her healing."

It was true that there were fragrances that continued to deny the perfumer's art. It was a comfort item, then. Sylyphe couldn't help but wonder why a man of Koscuisko's rank should stir himself to such an extent for any patient, let alone a woman from the service house.

Sylyphe's mother nodded one final time, in acceptance or agreement—Sylyphe couldn't tell which. Rising to her feet, Sylyphe's mother made her decision known.

"What you have requested shall be yours, your Excellency. I can't promise you the use of my gardener to assist you, though. I'm sorry, but his labor has been committed to other tasks. Is there someone at the hospital who can make up this ointment for you?"

Koscuisko didn't answer, not right away. Skelern cleared his throat, and when Koscuisko—raising one eyebrow, and looking as though he was amused at something—looked back over his shoulder toward where Skelern stood in the back of the room, Skelern spoke.

"The Tavart's lady-daughter knows how to handle the blooms, with the Tavart's permission. She could do it as well as I, your Excellency, or maybe better; she's mindful in such matters."

Sylyphe's mother stared. Sylyphe could see the color rise in Skelern's face even from where she stood. She would have blushed herself in sheer vexation to have her intimacy with a mere gardener exposed in so compromising a light before the Inquisitor, except that part of her was glowing with pleasure to hear Skelern' s praise.

"If the daughter of the house would be graciously pleased to oblige, then," Koscuisko said, to her, to her directly. "I will be very much obliged to you both. For my patient's sake. And for your courtesy in receiving me at this early hour."

"Hanner will give you instruction, then, Sylyphe," her mother agreed. "And see to it that the kitchen gives him a good hot meal, since he's been up all night. Gardener Hanner, speak to my daughter, and then go rest yourself. You're needed at Center House tomorrow in the morning."

Dismissing her. In front of Andrej Koscuisko, dismissing her, and Hanner with her. But she was to have a job to do that would support the prestige and put forward the agenda of Iaccary Cordage and Textile at least as much as anything Hanner did. It was the first useful thing she'd had to do in a long time.

Andrej Koscuisko bowed to her as she went past him to go out of the room, bowed to her almost as if she had been a grown woman and not just her mother's daughter. The daughter of the house.

It made up for her smock and her mother's thin brown hair.

Out of the room and down to the kitchens with Hanner in tow, to be sure that he got a good meal; and walking on air, every step of the way.

CHAPTER FIVE

The power was off again tonight as it had been last night. Port Burkhayden ran on hydroelectric power drawn from the tides in the Worrical Bay several eights to the south; but since the Bench had decided to sell the world to the Danzilar prince no maintenance on the saltwater cylinders and the water-gates had been done. The city was subject to brownout and blackout every night: that was what Garol had been told.

It suited Garol's purpose well enough.

The sky was overcast, and the clouds picked up what little light there was and diffused it over the port. It didn't make it easier to see where one was going, but it made it very obvious where one's goal was to be found if one was headed for an area with auxiliary power.

The public-funded. Then the service house.

Garol found his way into the public-funded through an open door at the back of its great silent kitchen. There were orderlies on staff, right enough, nursing a brewer and some trays of hot-breads under makeshift warmers rigged on temporary circuits; Garol went like a shadow or a stray thought, letting a breath of wind catch the half-open door and swing it wide, waiting patiently just beside a sheltering stack of produce-boxes as the orderly swore and cursed and pulled the door more firmly to.

The kitchen was an industrial one, built to serve round-the-clock for a hospital population fully one-half the size of all Burkhayden. The

Bench had built up Port Burkhayden for a major commercial center, and relocated a significant population of Nurail to fill out its infrastructure.

It hadn't quite worked.

The Nurail that could find their way out of Port Burkhayden did, fleeing in small craft across the great dead reaches of the Baltrune vector to Gonebeyond space. Some of them made it, and some of them didn't, but it made little difference in Port Burkhayden. The result was the same. The port had never prospered since the Bench had made Meghilder a Bench concern.

So the hospital was larger than would be needed for twice Burkhayden's actual population, and less than the eighth part of its capacity had ever actually been used. The Bench had built the public-funded but lost interest in staffing it once it became clear that the Nurail at Burkhayden were not going to bide quietly and turn to trade. Huge, and stripped now of everything but the most basic equipment, so that the night-kitchen had to use laboratory ovens to warm midnight meals.

The service house was a little less ravaged; a service house had to at least seem well-stocked. But the linen was old, and there was only just enough of it, and nobody had rotated staff for more than a year now. That was hell on morale at a service house. People liked variety.

Garol had reviewed the inventory with the housemaster: all of the standard luxury items, but the Bench had gutted the surveillance systems. The house grid was useless, its coordinator ripped out by some overzealous hand salvaging the chemos from the fire suppression systems, leaving the whole house to rely on the most primitive defenses imaginable.

Firewalls.

Some parts of the system had been recharged, true, but with plain water.

And the fire alarms still worked; or at least Garol had seen no reason why they should not. Maybe it hadn't even been the Bench; maybe it had been some enterprising Nurail, taking advantage of an opportunity. Fire suppression chemos could be sold. They could be used, too, for fuel if need be, to power an escape across the Baltrune vector.

Now Garol strolled quietly through the silent halls of the hospital, using the light from the emergency exits to navigate. Koscuisko's people had set up camp in a ward three corridors removed from what portion of the clinic area was in use—to Lieutenant Wyrlann's clear if unspoken disgust, and Garol's own unspoken amusement. Wyrlann was at Center House under guard, for his own protection. Garol wasn't the least surprised that no one wanted to keep him company.

And Koscuisko, having claimed hospital duty as his excuse for staying well clear of Center House and Lieutenant Wyrlann, had followed through with a will. Garol needed to have a word with Koscuisko about that. But just at present he was curious about arrangements. He held a Bench warrant. It was second nature to find out about arrangements.

Garol didn't know exactly where Koscuisko's sleeping quarters were. He didn't need to search long, as it happened. Someone was on watch. And whoever was on watch had company. The sound of voices told Garol where to look.

"It's only natural to wonder. And I drew the frayed end."

One of the voices was female, coming from within a bay that ran three open doors along the corridor. The voices were at the far end of the bay. Garol had checked into another such bay on his way here; he knew the layout. Cautiously, he angled his body through the door to see what there was to see.

"I'm not the man to cry you shame for it. But look Chief Stildyne doesn't catch us gossiping; he's tender about the officer's dignity."

The Nurail troop. Robert St. Clare. There was an inner bay to this ward, and a long hall that paralleled the corridor; St. Clare sat at the doorway to the inner bay. Quite correctly, too. Controlling access.

But Garol wanted in.

"And is it really so simple as that? A man of his nature. One would have thought, surely."

The woman's voice faded as Garol retreated down the hall. The ventilation system on these wards was not quarantined; these had originally, been intended for day-clinic areas. Climbing the service stairs to the floor above Garol found the flue-vent, but he didn't break the vapor seal. Retracing his steps he counted paces till he was as close to his goal as he needed to be. Then he looked around.

"—shoulders." There was the intake, and once Garol had got well inside the capacious vent he could hear St. Clare's voice from below.

He could even hear that St. Clare was teasing, just a bit. "But it's his lady to take the lap-seat, maistress. That's the way of it when they aren't Dolgorukij women. Elsewise there's fear of doing an injury, whilst a man isn't paying the attention that he naturally ought."

Wedging himself shoulder and hip in the cross-shaft Garol worked his way down to the room behind St. Clare's back, where Andrej Koscuisko's bed was made up. The Security post was through the doorway to Koscuisko's private room, and the door was only half-open. There was no reason for it to be otherwise. It was no failing on Security's part; no one could stop a Bench intelligence specialist from getting to where he wanted to go.

And at the same time Garol had particular reasons for wanting Koscuisko's Security to be alert.

He popped the secure on the vent-screen with a click so subtle that it would not carry across the room, let alone through the door and outside into the hall. As far as he could tell St. Clare had as yet heard nothing; listening to the lady, perhaps. Whoever she was.

"It's ungallant, surely, to make the woman labor at such work. And still if that is all—there's nothing to be feared from him, then?"

Free to move around inside the room, now, Garol found the thing he wanted and flipped the lid. The dose-packet that St. Clare had gotten from the orderly, shortly before they'd finished loading the courier. Garol needed some way to signal to Security to step up their surveillance; and at the same time he was curious.

What doses?

Why?

Why carried separately? Why separately delivered?

It was a standard dose-pouch, the preloads registering system integrity on display. Garol tipped a handful of the styli out of the pouch and held them up in the palm of his hand to be close to his face so that he would be able to read the encodes in the dim light.

Not narcotics; and yet under normal circumstances only narcotics or other Controlled List drugs warranted such special handling.

A hypnotic, yes.

Specific for Dolgorukij.

Hypnotics and stimulants and two doses of an antipsychotic psychoactor—the hypnotic was specific, it said so, and if the other drugs were not uniquely prescribed for an Aznir autocrat the dosage

levels clearly pointed at some class of hominid whose weight or
metabolism exceeded the average index—

Drugs for a sick man, for a man half-mad with conflict and self-
loathing. Garol remembered the scene in the loading bay.
Psychoactive drugs for a man who was perhaps insane, if only
periodically sociopathic.

Exercising his Bench warrant would be an act of kindness, then.
Euthanasia. Putting Koscuisko out of his evident suffering.

If only he could be sure about the source—

Carefully, Garol returned the doses to their pouch, making sure to
transpose two doses as he did so. The dust should catch someone's
attention. It didn't need to be anything as obvious as leaving the
ventilator's grid unsecured. Security would sense a discrepancy, and
then they would notice the dust Garol had carried into the room from
the vent-shaft. Then they would search, and when they searched they
would find that the seal of the vent-shaft had been broken, and that
someone had been looking at the dose-pouch.

This part of Garol's mission was accomplished. A quick check of
the clinic and a stroll through the shabby halls of the less-than-
recently-renovated service house, and he would be ready to go to
bed.

To the extent that he'd done what he'd come to do—alert
Koscuisko's security to the potential existence of a hitherto
unsuspected problem—he was satisfied.

But the more he learned about Andrej Koscuisko the less he was
inclined to credit his Bench warrant.

Well past sunset, and the clinic was finally clearing out—not so
much because everything that could be done had been done as that it
was three eights past curfew and people could no longer safely travel
to arrive. Andrej Koscuisko leaned back against the cool edge of an
examining table and folded his arms across his duty-smock with a
deep sigh of satisfaction and weariness.

He wasn't used to being worked so hard, so long.

He enjoyed it.

And with any luck it would be the same for him tomorrow. It
seemed clear that his name and his Judicial function was not, after all,
enough to prevent pragmatic Nurail souls from taking advantage of

the opportunity that an extra physician on duty represented for obtaining free medical care.

A knock at the door, and through the long high narrow windows of the examining room Andrej could just make out the balding head of Garol Vogel with a Security escort. What was Vogel doing here? The door swung open; well, he'd find out, then. Or he wouldn't. Vogel was a Bench intelligence specialist. There was no telling about his ilk.

"Good-greeting, your Excellency, and the evening finds you?"

Polite. Neutral; Vogel only cared to the extent that any ordinary person would care about the health and welfare of a casual acquaintance. Fine as far as Andrej was concerned.

"Very well, thank you, Specialist. The same for you, I hope, and where is Specialist Ivers this evening?"

Vogel stepped into the room and closed the door, leaving it ajar. So that if Andrej was needed he could be got at, Andrej supposed. Good protocol for hospital receiving areas: Bench intelligence specialists were expected to know what the appropriate behavior was under almost any circumstances. It wasn't a matter of memorizing rites and practices. It was a simple question of common sense, and the intelligence to grasp what was needful.

"Center House, sir. The woman will recover? I heard the technical report but I'm not much good at interpreting it. If you'd summarize for me, your Excellency, I'd appreciate it."

Fair enough. "The short answer is yes. The long answer is that physical therapy will be required, she may or may not become infertile, and I hope before Heaven that the guesses I had to make about the nature and intensity of her sensory response to sexual stimulus are close to correct. I am favorably impressed with Paval I'shenko, in pulling rank the way that he did. Gardener Hanner for one will be sure to defend my cousin henceforward."

Vogel grinned, a gesture which suddenly squared his otherwise somewhat round face. "What I like is that that was only part of his reasoning. The rest of it was good old-fashioned decent moral outrage. There isn't enough of that around, these days."

No indeed. "And speaking of moral outrage. I believe you may wish to re-inventory pharmacy stores before the rest of Fleet arrives, Specialist. Someone has broken into stores and made very free with some quite expensive medication, and I am sure that Paval I'shenko would regret having to make an issue of the discrepancy."

Vogel's expression somehow lacked much of an element of surprise. "I'm shocked, your Excellency. Shocked. This person, you wouldn't happen to have an idea of who he was or where I might find him, would you?"

As a matter of fact Andrej was tolerably certain that both he and Vogel knew exactly what was going on. "Quite a good notion, actually. Enough of one to know that regrettably the villain cannot be prosecuted. There is no reason why he should not be identified, however. I hardly know what worse Fleet could do to me than it already has."

Because it was he, himself, Andrej Koscuisko, who had forced the secures and issued the stores. Under the Privilege of the Writ he could not be brought to account for misappropriation of Fleet or Bench stores; nor could any of the subordinate physicians to whom Andrej had released the materials be faulted for simply receiving normal stores in personal ignorance of the exact manner in which release had been authorized.

"Ah," Vogel said, with an odd little gesture of his chin that was supportive and admonitory at once. "Oddly enough that reminds me. News from Fleet, extension approved, no transfer in the foreseeable."

Well. It was only as much as he had expected. There was no sense in noticing the voice in his mind that still raged in protest. He was tired: and Vogel was still talking.

"Hoping the news isn't all bad. Good-night, I'll be on my—oh. Almost forgot."

What kind of trick or trap was this, then?

Andrej waited, deeply suspicious.

"The Danzilar prince. I was to tell you particularly. He apologizes for, let me see, what was it, for not greeting you prior to departure. And promises that there is to be dancing at Center House."

The message was unexpected, and took Andrej by surprise.

Dancing?

Had he even thought about dancing, at any time that he could call to mind, over the past eight years?

And Shiki—his cousin Paval I'shenko—and he had been widely

acknowledged as quite good dancers, when they'd been younger. Before Andrej had gone off to school. Paval I'shenko had always been on the lookout for opportunities to test himself against Andrej, and see who would clear the floor in triumph this time.

He was doomed.

"I have not danced so much as a miletta since I came to Fleet." And Paval I'shenko would know that. Andrej could trust his cousin to be thinking, every moment. "Still less anything more strenuous. I have only two chances."

One, he had not danced, but he had learned to fight; and perhaps some part of the two skill-sets would prove to be more closely related than he would have thought them.

Or, two, that his cousin the prince Paval I'shenko Danzilar might sprain his ankle, and it would not be an issue.

"Sir?" Vogel was waiting, politely. But Andrej was tired. If Vogel wanted to know he could just bring his own special Bench intelligence specialist skill-set to bear on the issue. Though—it suddenly occurred to Andrej—if he could enlist Vogel's help, might Vogel not find a way to engineer the spraining of an ankle, to the preservation of the dignity of a Judicial officer?

No.

Perhaps not.

"Earthquake or flood, Specialist Vogel, because nothing less will keep my cousin from his darshan. I am going to bed. You will excuse me. I do not invite you, it is nothing personal."

He needed to get to bed, because he wanted to be able to open the clinic as soon as curfew lifted in the morning, which was about an eight before sunrise. Vogel bowed.

"Of course. Good rest, your Excellency. I'll see you at the party, if not before."

There was no reason to suppose otherwise. Was there? There was something in Vogel's voice, something in Vogel's bow that half-convinced Andrej of the existence of some secret.

Well, if it was a secret, then that was what it would have to remain.

"And you, Specialist. If you would call for my gentlemen on your way out, please."

Alone in the room now Andrej unfastened his smock and bundled it into the laundry-drawer. The laundry-drawer already contained a discarded smock; it made Andrej wonder whether the hospital was in a position to be able to afford to keep a decent linen schedule.

Robert came in with Andrej's over-blouse and a load of toweling over one arm. If there were towels, didn't that mean that the laundry was running?

"Thank you, Robert." Andrej didn't need help to get dressed. But accepting help was part of accepting the fact that Robert elected to offer it, since Robert knew that body-service was something Andrej considered strictly optional for bond-involuntaries. "I don't know if I have the energy to wash. Perhaps I will rather bathe in the morning. Is there of rhyti a flask for me in quarters?"

Holding the door open for Andrej as he went out Robert shook his head, with great determination. "Na, the officer is mistaken. You want your wash in now, sir. Truly. And quarters are being shifted."

Years ago when they had all been much younger, Robert St. Clare had suffered through the ordeal of the prisoner-surrogate exercise at Fleet Orientation Station Medical to win a reduction of his Bond. Robert had not failed; but the trial had failed, and over the space of several days Robert had lived in an agony both physical and spiritual awaiting the formal declaration of the sentence of his punishment— which was clearly understood by all as amounting to a sentence of death by slow torture.

During that time, the ferocious stress levels Robert had endured had forced the calibration of his governor to one side in some manner. Robert's governor had never been quite right in all of the time that Andrej had known him since. But as long as it was wrong in the right direction Andrej didn't care.

Now as always Robert spoke to him more freely than any of the other Bonds, quite clearly and distinctly telling him what to do.

Andrej would comply with Robert's instructions, of course. Instruction received was instruction implemented, for bond-involuntaries at least, and since it was that way for bond-involuntaries Andrej saw no reason why he should refuse to grant obedience as he was given obedience.

The obedience he was owed by his Bonds could be said to be a simple question of the fact that the governor forced it, on the face of it. Andrej knew better. The obedience he was granted by his bond-involuntaries was given him as freely as even a man enslaved could choose to make a gift instead of paying a debt.

"Shifted, Robert? What was wrong with quarters, that we should shift?"

They were dark and depressing, true. As vacant and empty as any abandoned ward. But wasn't one abandoned ward much the same as any other?

Robert sounded serious now—for perhaps so long as three eighths. "Security issue, your Excellency. We think we had a visitor while quarters were empty. The ventilation system can be compromised. Pyotr's shifting for prudence's sake—"

Robert had led him down a long hall that led into a communal showers. Only a portion of the showers were apparently in use: the majority of the walls and floors and drains were bone-dry, with the powdery fragrance of concrete on a humid day.

"—and here's a sauna for you. I've taken the liberty. I'll take your boots, sir."

And rest-dress by implication would be waiting in the warmth of the dry sauna, with clean linen. Capitulating, Andrej sat down on the changing-bench and started to strip. A man was slave to his servants from one end of the Bench to the other, Andrej mused to himself. There was no sense in arguing with people who had gone to such lengths for one's benefit.

How had Robert managed a sauna, with Burkhayden so starved for power?

Perhaps it was just as well if he did not wonder about that.

A sauna was an intrinsic good, after all, and he would enjoy it just as much as if its warmth had not been thieved from sources unknown.

Andrej Koscuisko came into the day-clinic with a flask of rhyti in one hand and a wrap of bread and meat-paste in the other. He was late. He'd been up well past midnight last night, because it was not to be imagined that anyone should be turned away from day-clinic, and some of them had been waiting all day. He'd been up late the night before, for the same reason, and slept past the mark this morning, so that it was already past the lifting of curfew.

And the clinic's waiting-room already full. People were lined up all down the corridor, women with children in arms, children with younger siblings, men with aged parents. Andrej bowed to the waiting room, keenly aware of the lack of respect inadvertently implied by greeting his patients with his fast-meal in both hands.

"Good-greeting, gentles all, I hope that you will forgive my tardiness. But we will turn none of you away, my oath upon it."

The on-site staff were used to this. There were too few of them, and none with the generalist's skills Andrej had gained in eight years as a Ship's Surgeon. None with his peculiar specialty skills, and they had ceded seniority to him almost without his noticing, as glad as these waiting folk to have his help to accomplish their task. He was in charge of day-clinic here and now.

His gentlemen broke away from post behind him as Andrej crossed the room, going to their own stations. They'd been requisitioned early on to help the physician's aides; they had good triage skills. He was going to owe them a holiday when this was over—but not at the service-house. That was unthinkable.

At an off-license house, perhaps, which would mean scavenging in Port Burkhayden for food and drink to make a party. He would see if he could find a skilled provisioner to the task.

There was a signal for him from the records-desk, the keeper on duty coughing into his hand politely as a young woman rose to her feet from a chair near the desk. Quite a young woman, and the look on her face was so appealing—open and vulnerable. Something in her hands, what had she brought him, and why did she gaze at him with so much tense reluctant longing?

"His Excellency asked after this preparation," she said; and Andrej recognized her at last, the little girl from the gardener's house. The daughter of the house, the young lady Tavart, bearing for him a pot of ointment. Of salve. "I hope that this may serve? It's the first time I've tried it, I'm not sure it's quite right but I didn't want to delay any longer."

She held the ointment-pot out to him, her hands shaking almost imperceptibly. Andrej raised his hands in turn to receive her gift, but his hands were full, and he gestured helplessly, feeling as awkward as if he had been so young as she was all over again. Had he ever been so young? In his life, ever?

"Oh, but my apologies, Miss Tavart." He thought she was a "miss" yet, an unmarried woman in her mother's household. "If you would be so good as to come through. I find myself at a disadvantage."

Through to the treatment room, where he could disembarrass himself of his fast-meal and take the ointment-pot into his hand, tipping the lid off with a careful twist. The creamy fat inside was rosy with the pale ghost of the color of jellericia flowers, and the fragrance—though subtle—was distinct.

It was unusual, so soft, and yet so penetrating—strong enough for all its delicacy to penetrate the insulted brain of a beaten woman and carry its message of comfort, its memory of home, to her dreaming mind. Something to encourage her to return to the world, if only for the fact of such a perfume.

"It is precisely the thing, Miss Tavart. Is it that I shall call you 'miss'?"

She blushed, and Andrej wondered if he was being irresponsible. He was flirting. No. He was not. A man had no business flirting with such a young woman. Let her cleave to her gardener. They were not suited in station, but neither were she and Andrej suited in station, and at least her gardener was of an age. And seemed to be a decent hardworking young man, while for himself though just at present Andrej was hardworking he could not in honesty believe that "decent" could describe him.

"My name is Sylyphe, sir. I've brought these other things, as well—"

She had a carrying-sack with her, and opened it now, setting it on the level to draw her treasures forth. They were alone together in the treatment room, though the door was open. Andrej stood beside her to see what she had brought, straightening up as he noticed himself leaning rather more closely than he ought.

"Hanner has been called away, and I don't have his . . . his knowledge. He said to wash the spent blooms in alcohol to take the last of the scent."

A flask of rose-pale water, but when she unstoppered it a delicious fragrance of jellericia filled the room. It addled him, all of a sudden. The fragrance was as clean and as pure as a maiden's first love; and she was a maiden, clean and pure, who carried within her the awesome divinity of her still-only-potential womanhood. To be the man to dance with her, to lead her across the threshold between childhood and grown age, to be the man to see her first come into the pride and power that was her birthright as a woman—

She passed the vial to him, and their hands touched. Her fingers were cool, as delicate as the spear-shaped leaves that clustered around winter-blooming yellow-trumpets in the snow. She seemed to recoil back from the contact, startled; the same touch grounded Andrej, in some sense, recalled him to the understanding of who and where he was. This was a child that stared at him with such dark lustrous eyes, her blushing mouth half-open. She was perfect, tempting, all points delicious, but she was a child—or at least too young to be a woman to him.

Andrej capped the flask. "Very well done indeed, Miss Sylyphe. And what else is it that you have brought us? I am overwhelmed with this surfeit of bounty."

Miss Sylyphe, yes, that was the way to do it. She dropped her gaze to her carry-pouch, confused, but composing herself with admirable poise. She was to be a formidable woman, when she came into her majority. Was the gardener man enough to partner her?

Why should he wonder about the gardener, when this child of privilege would surely find her match amongst men as privileged as she?

"There was half-a-flat of jellericia coming into bloom already, your Excellency. The flowers lose their fragrance; it was too late to use them for the ointment, but they do still smell a bit, don't they? And they look nice. I thought—"

Call me Andrej, Andrej thought. *You are not angry with me, surely, why should you be so cold as to say "Excellency?" No, you must call me Andrej, all of my friends do.* As if he had any. As if anyone had called him Andrej in the past eight years. *Call me Andrej, come back later, we can talk more freely when the day is done and we can be alone together.*

She held out a lush bouquet of jellericia, its dark green foliage begemmed with tiny crimson flowers. He could see what she meant, if he looked carefully. The blossoms were a little worn, in fact, and the fragrance scarce discernible.

"I applaud your instinct, Miss Sylyphe." And he could do so honestly, without ulterior motives. "This will indeed make a pleasing decoration. Of those out there it may be there is more than one, that remembers what these look like."

When she smiled she was all child, and he was safe from himself. "If the ointment is all right I can have more of it in three days' time, your Excellency. Hanner showed me what needs to be done to force the next flat."

Andrej hefted the pot of ointment, now all adult once again. There was enough here for several days' treatment of the woman from the service house. "If you could let me have as much again in so much time, yes, that would do very well. Thank you, Miss Sylyphe. I am to you indebted, and still now I must ask that you excuse me to the work of the day."

Now he could take her arm and turn her toward the door, and cosset her like an uncle his favorite niece. Now he could be an uncle to her, and not a man of whom her mother would be right to be suspicious. It was a relief. Because he had been so tempted.

"Of course, your Excellency. Thank you, sir." And once he was well settled as an uncle she found her own voice as a niece. Was it his imagination, or was there a suspicion of regret in her tone? "And a very good day to you, your Excellency."

"The best of good days," Andrej agreed heartily. He was not a man. He was the adult male relative of her mother, and that was something else entirely. "My respects to your lady mother, Miss Sylyphe, and my very great appreciation for your hard work. Perhaps I will see you again in three days' time."

And perhaps he would be very sure to have people with him when he did so. There was only so much a man could be expected to take.

She nodded, blushing, and walked away through the wait-room without more words. Andrej watched her go, trying not to notice what a sweet soft cushion there was to her hips, nor how nicely she carried her back and shoulders.

Well.

"My apologies for the delay, gentles, if I might have the first patient. Please."

That had been a pleasant start to a man's morning, and by the grace of the Holy Mother he had neither disgraced himself nor soiled the innocence of that woman-child by taking advantage.

Now he had better concentrate on work.

Fleet Captain Lowden stepped across the cracked flooring that paved the threshold to the hospital's wait-room with precision born of distaste. What a depressing place this was, this public-funded; and yet his errant Ship's Surgeon took to even so pathetic a clinic like debris to an intake pump. Drawn in so strongly that a man could almost hear the suction.

"Captain Lowden. A surprise, sir."

Alerted by the orderlies Koscuisko came out of a treatment room to greet him. Koscuisko's smock was soiled and his face was haggard, but there was amusement in his expression that Lowden could identify—if not appreciate. "Just in to port, your Excellency?"

Wiping his hands on a bit of sterile toweling. The orderlies were showing Koscuisko's patient out of the treatment room; a young woman, infant in arms. She only glanced in their direction. Her eyes were all on Koscuisko's back when she did.

"Oh, it's been the odd hour, Andrej. We weren't expected for another day or two, yes, I know."

Or else Danzilar would be all ready for his party, and they could get that over with and leave. Yes. But also Koscuisko should have been at the landing field to greet his superior officer, and Koscuisko hadn't been. Lowden could excuse that, but he wasn't going to let it pass unremarked upon.

"Were we not." Koscuisko was tired; it took him that extra fraction of an eighth to realize that he was being called to account. And still it was clear to Lowden at least that Koscuisko had genuinely lost track of the time. "I must then beg your pardon, Captain, not to have joined the welcoming party. No disrespect was intended."

Once he did realize, however, Koscuisko accepted the rebuke with grace and dignity, not stooping to insist on tiresome details that would explain and excuse his failure. On the one hand it was appropriate that Koscuisko bend his neck in submission to his superior officer. On the other hand Koscuisko's very humility only emphasized how little Koscuisko cared.

That was all right.

Lowden had never required Koscuisko to care. Merely to obey.

"I've been reviewing the discrepancy lists with the Danzilar prince's people, Andrej, and there seems to be a problem with drugs-stores. And I wonder if that problem has your name on it." He had time. He had four more years to break Koscuisko to his will.

Koscuisko was well humbled already. Inside of a few months Koscuisko would be his, body and soul; and all it would take was enough bodies for the torture, and no time in between.

Koscuisko bowed, only barely not grinning. "I felt it my right and due prerogative, Captain. Have I my authority exceeded? Because I the Lieutenant outrank, after all."

And Lieutenant Wyrlann's self-indulgence, also noted in the discrepancies lists, cost the Bench almost as much as what the allowance for the medication Koscuisko had issued over the past few days amounted to. It was an interesting approach. Lowden smiled in acknowledgement of the creativity it displayed.

"I'll take that into consideration, Andrej. Now that we are here I'll expect you to return to your Command, of course." And stop playing doctor with this roomful of stinking unwashed Nurail. He would provide Koscuisko with other playthings soon enough.

"Of course, Captain. But. If I may be permitted. I have these gentlemen been working hard, I owe them—and myself, with your permission—a holiday. Perhaps I may have your leave to the service-house to go, before this team which has been so overburdened is relieved."

Lowden thought about it.

Koscuisko was tired.

Koscuisko had few opportunities to go to service houses, and Lowden liked it that way, because the less frequently Koscuisko enjoyed human intimacies in a perfectly bland and pathetically mundane manner the keener the tension Koscuisko had stored up within him to focus on his work in Secured Medical. But a man could not be kept from women too strictly; a certain degree of access was required to maintain Koscuisko's bodily health. Captain Lowden was a firm believer in preventive medicine.

"Very well, Andrej. You'll have to take your kit with you, of course." Lowden called up one of his Security with a beckoning gesture of his hand. "I'm not sure how it happened, exactly, but you seem to have left the ship without it."

Koscuisko's field interrogations kit. Had he known Koscuisko would be asking leave to go to the service house he would have left it under guard at Center House, but that was academic now. Koscuisko had not gotten the full benefit of the joke Lowden had set up for him, after all. Vogel had mined the punch line. Koscuisko could just hang on to his field interrogations kit.

Koscuisko grimaced, but bowed. Koscuisko knew perfectly well that Lowden was his master. "Of course, Captain. Even as you say. And to report in the morning, then?"

It always gratified Lowden to see how clearly Koscuisko understood his position. Koscuisko's submissiveness sweetened Lowden's mood now.

"Mid-meal, Andrej," he corrected genially, extending Koscuisko's holiday to midday. "I'll see you at table."

Koscuisko could go to the service house, but Koscuisko would brood; and carry the field interrogations kit with him, to serve as a constant, unwelcome, reminder of what his duty was.

There would be some salvage value to his joke after all, and Lowden carried that pleasing knowledge with him as he left the hospital for Center House.

It was cold in the curfew-darkened streets of Port Burkhayden, a cold that chilled to the bone even in the absence of wind. There was a little rain, but only a little one, so that Andrej could not decide whether it was soft mist or a very low cloud—or the spume from the sea-spray, come up from the marsh to plaster itself greedily against glass and window and leach as much warmth as it could suck from frame and sash.

Captain Lowden doubtless expected them to go to the service house, but what Captain Lowden didn't know wouldn't harm Andrej—at least not tonight. He had not so much as told the Port Authority where he was going, though he had no doubt they could find him if they had to. Stildyne was going to be angry with him about that. He would work it out with Stildyne somehow. In the morning. Later.

The local escort Andrej had recruited at the hospital brought them through black narrow streets to a secret part of town, hidden away behind warehouse walls and traffic diverters, to a dark house standing in the middle of a lot that seemed surprisingly large to Andrej for the middle of the city. Dark house, narrow gate, overgrown path, overgrown garden; and though there was no wind, the trees in the half-wild garden seemed to creak and clatter at him in a manner that Andrej did not find in the least welcoming.

Once inside, though, once through the heavy weathered wooden door cracked reluctantly open only so far as necessary to let them in, once safely within the house it was quite different. Dark, yes, because most of Port Burkhayden was without power yet again tonight, and only a few public utilities—the public-funded hospital, the service house, Center House itself—were on auxiliary power. Dark but welcoming even so, because it was warm inside, friendly with occasional lights powered on reservoir and candles.

Andrej stood bemused in the great foyer while their guide, one of the physician's assistants from the hospital, went forward to complete final arrangements with the management. Candlelight. Candlelight was more practical than not in any service-house, but especially in an off-license house, where the women were by and large of a wider range in age and looks than one might find at the more elite establishments. At an off-license house at least they were all volunteers, or as much volunteer as a man could fantasize any woman to be whom necessity had forced to tender the privilege of her flesh as a commodity for lease.

A girl came out of a side door with a hand-held beam and invited them to follow her with a wordless gesture and a very pretty bow for Andrej himself. She was a pretty little thing all in all, and would be a woman some year doubtless, though she was surely no older than the daughter of the House Tavart—and he was not even going to speculate about that. A man did not have to do with children. No matter how prettily their petals trembled on the border between innocence and experience. No.

They sat all together in a common dining hall and took their meal: Andrej, his Security, their guide, the lady of the house, some girls. Well, some of the house's women. It was a species of pleasure in and of itself to sit in near-darkness and have his supper, while his gentlemen—knowing that it was a holiday, having been strictly instructed that they were on holiday and not on duty—relaxed by degrees, to disport themselves with ladies.

And Pyotr, being black, was very exotic, and liked two at a time, and could give good account of himself as well—at least from report. And Hirsel was generally open to affectionate play from any direction, and the female direction was fully as enticing to him as any other.

Godsalt could usually be prevailed upon to make a woman with dark hair feel appreciated, which was just as well since there were more dark-haired ladies present than otherwise. Garrity was celibate, within the requirements of the community of bond-involuntaries, and would happily sleep alone, which only left all the more for Robert.

Robert liked ladies in more than a casual sense. He really liked women, and from all Andrej had been able to determine women by and large returned his genial if impertinent interest with charitable forbearance—

When Godsalt threw a pinch of bread at his senior fellow Pyotr, and Pyotr in retaliation sent an only half-cleaned fruit-pit into Godsalt's glass of drinking-spirit to splash half of the liquid into Godsalt's plate, Andrej decided it was time he went upstairs.

The lady of the house rose and withdrew at the same time, pausing only to nominate one of the girls to show "the officer" up to his room. It was one of the girls who carried serving-dishes back and forth; she did not mean for Andrej to take his guide to partner—Andrej was secure in that. But it was clearly high time he withdrew and left his gentlemen to their holiday.

He was not going to be the least bit sorry to have a bit of a holiday himself. Even if only a few hours' worth.

Up the stairs, then, and to the wing of the house furthest away from the dining-room. The girl let him in to a large well-warmed room with an actual fire, a wood fire, burning in a grate against the wall; charming, if anachronistic. She wished him the best of his bath, and asked if anything seemed lacking, and made sure he knew how to summon her up should anything be found so; and then while Andrej stood on the threshold of the bathing-room, toying with the concept of asking for her help to scrub his back, trying to determine whether or not he had designs on her—she excused herself, and went away.

Probably just as well, Andrej admitted to himself. And no denying that he took particular pleasure in being left to himself for a little while. On board ship there was always the officer's orderly, always, whoever's turn it was to pull the duty. And whenever he was not on board ship he lived in the middle of a Security squad. A man could hardly so much as urinate in private.

Andrej had been raised in public, in a sense, because he had been raised by body-servants in his father's household. Even as a child Andrej had realized that there was something wonderful about being alone, quite alone, hiding in the closet or riding perversely in an unexpected direction to disappear into the winter forest before anyone could stay him.

But never for long. And never long enough.

It was not decent to hide for long. A person's servants got anxious, and it was not in the least bit thoughtful or respectful to play tricks on them.

Andrej took a good long hot soak in the old-fashioned water tub, concentrating on shutting everything out of his mind except the soothing comfort of the bath and the to-be-anticipated company of a lady. His reenlistment, his ruined hopes of freedom, his despair in facing the future—shutting it all out of his mind. Sylyphe Tavart, with breath so sweet a man all but had to taste that pretty little mouth, so young—and so willing to be charmed with him—

Shutting that out as well. She was a child. A man did not insult the innocence of children, no matter if they thought that they were ripe to be enjoyed. He knew; Sylyphe did not; it was not for him to be the one to teach her. That was all.

When he was washed and dried and belted into the wrap that lay warming on the rod for his use Andrej went out into the bedroom. Someone had come and gone, so quietly—in the manner of servants in such places—that Andrej hadn't noticed; the fire was refreshed, the table laid with snacks and wodac. Also some rhyti. The bed was large, but the mattress was uneven; sitting down at the edge Andrej noticed that a book had been laid open on the bedside table, the bright colors of its illustrations catching his eye. He picked it up, curious.

A fishing-book.

A book of fish-stories.

A fishing-book in the old sense of the term, or in the Dolgorukij sense of the term, a book of natural history, of pictures designed to educate. That was the excuse, at least; to educate—and to beguile, interest, arouse . . .

He was leafing through the fishing-book when the knock came at the door, and the lady of the house came in. Distracted, Andrej did not stand when she crossed the threshold; and gestured toward the book that lay now open in his lap by way of an excuse, apologizing.

"Do you know, I had one of these, or one like it." Well, not exactly like it, of course. One found in a corner of the library where historical curiosities were kept, an antique. Really. Antiquarian interest. Yes.

"There is a gallery at Chelatring Side, where we went in the late part of the summers. My cousin Stanoczk to be bribed consented, to let me in, and Marana with me."

There had been endless vigils to keep in penance afterward, when it had all come out. The vigils had done no good. They only gave him time, private time, quiet time, to meditate on the pictures he had seen in the Malcontent's secret gallery at Chelatring Side, and Marana hand in hand with him, exploring. Experimenting.

The lady of the house had poured herself a dainty cup of rhyti, carrying it over to sit down beside him on the bed. She had changed her garments for bed-dress, and her robe was but loosely knotted around her waist.

Well.

He had not quite expected such an honor, and still it could be that he was mistaken to assume that she was to be his partner. She was the house-mistress, and engaged only for her own recreation, or to pay special honor to a patron. It was only that his fish was as beguiled by the pictures as by his passing memories of that afternoon with Marana in the Malcontent's gallery, so long ago.

His fish would disgrace him, if he was not careful.

With luck she would not want to take the book.

"Let me see, young Anders," the house-mistress suggested, reaching up her left hand to pull out a pin from the damp cloud of hair that lay loosely gathered against the nape of her neck. "Which is your favorite, here? I'll show you mine. But you must show me yours, first."

There was no mistaking the implication of that. She was mistress here; no need for delicate language, surely. "This is an outland fishing-book, not a Dolgorukij fishing-book. Else there would be much more of this sort of recreation to examine."

He found the place where the couple who shared their transports for the pleasure of the beholders did so with the lady in her lover's lap. It was not strictly true that there were more like that in a traditional Dolgorukij fishing-book. But absolutely true that a man who was Aznir did well to take a woman into his lap, if she was not herself also Dolgorukij.

"I've heard rumors of the sort." Her exclamation was so calm as to almost be no exclamation at all. "About Dolgorukij men. My girls all wanted to know, but I'm their mother, I take precedence."

Their figurative mother, needless to say. Or perhaps not. She was not a young woman; perhaps so old as he was, and that meant that it was not impossible that some of the girls—the younger ones especially—actually were children of her body.

Which in turn implied . . .

"I am honored." Andrej acknowledged it with all humility. "And can only trust to live up to what rumors you may have heard. If it can be done."

She supped her rhyti demurely. Her hair was falling out of its damp knot, slowly, slowly tumbling down her back. She was Nurail, to look at her; she might well have borne her children under wretchedly primitive conditions. If no lover's tuck had been taken after the birth of any one . . . there were those who found a woman more desirable, rather than less, for the evidence of motherhood, but the point was that it might yet be that he could pillow himself upon her bosom as though she had been Dolgorukij after all, without fear of causing her an injury in an excess of enthusiasm.

"Fishing, you say." Setting her cup aside; leaning over the look, leaning close beside him. Letting him feel the soft round of her shoulders, beneath her robe. "How is this 'fishing?' Explain yourself to me."

Yes, he had called it by a Dolgorukij name, used a Dolgorukij phrase. Andrej blushed without being able to quite decide why. "In the language of my childhood a fish is as to say that part of a man which shows he is not female, and yet is not his beard. If he has a beard. I mean to say a chin-beard." Because he did have that other kind of beard, though many Dolgorukij did not grow facial hair. He was getting fuddled. Had there been something in the bath-water?

Or was it simply that she smelled of the ocean, subtly so, faintly so, but sweetly and irresistibly so, so that his fish half-raised itself to listen for the glad sound of the surf?

"A fish." She stared at him very frankly, and made no secret of her amusement. "A codling, then. Or perhaps a brook-trout. Bring you to me a salmon-fish, young Andrej? No, a tunny, yes, perhaps."

He didn't know what she was talking about—except in the general sense, of course. Which it was better to ignore, or he would not complete his explanation.

He put the book aside.

"There is in the life of a man a fish, which is rude and inconstant, but which knows one great piece of true wisdom." Putting an arm around her Andrej helped her hair down, letting the tendrils curl around his fingers. Loving the smell of her. "And that is to seek the ocean, which is where all fish come from, to which therefore it is only natural for fish to wish to return."

If he stroked the far side of her face very gently there was the chance that she could be persuaded to turn her face toward his, so that he could provide proper punctuation for his explanation as he spoke on. Explaining himself with kisses. She had a pleasant if somewhat cool taste to her mouth, flavored with rhyti. "It is the ocean we were all rocked in as infants yet unborn. Madame, my fish desires thy ocean."

She wound her arms around his neck and considered his proposal for long moments as he kissed her mouth. It seemed to Andrej that there was the suspicion of a blush beginning to rise into her cheek, but it could just as well have been a shadow from the fireplace. There was no way to be sure.

Sighing—as if she were letting go of some anxiety—she let her hands fall away from his neck and shoulders.

Into his lap.

She slid one cool slim hand beneath the hem of his sleep-shirt and up his thigh with such an air of professional detachment that Andrej almost didn't notice the gesture until she seized upon his fish, which had caused no trouble yet this evening for which it should be reproached in such a manner, and tugged at him indelicately.

"Is this then the terrible weapon from which all off-world women must flee in fear? Surely it cannot be so."

That had been her point about codlings and tunny-fishes, then. In point of fact he was neither remarkable for size and girth or lack of either. At home it didn't matter. A fish was a fish, and a burden no matter its particular rudeness or strength in leaping.

Only when he had left home for the surgical college on Mayon had Andrej discovered that there was an entire world of insult and one-upmanship that could be draped around the fins of a man's fish.

He had never had complaints from the ladies.

He would have nothing of the house-mistress's impertinence now.

"Oh, let us by all means discuss this issue." Her caress had not been sweet or tender, but it was still arousing in its utterly frank focus on what she could expect to concern her most immediately. Andrej didn't really mind. "And when morning comes you will do me the kindness of declaring whether it is an honest fish or whether you have been disappointed in its vigor. Let us seal a bargain on it."

"Well." She had released her grip, but rested still with her hands laid flat atop his thighs beneath the sleep-shirt. "Far be it from me to deny your fish a chance to show himself a, well, a fish. And perhaps he only needs encouragement, shall I give him a kiss for an apology?"

Andrej's fish stiffened and raised its head at the suggestion, greedy for affection as it always was. But Andrej would be stern. "We will have no apologies." His fish was eager for a kiss, but more than one sort of a caress would soothe a fish. Fish had so little true discrimination. Such favors as she proposed were available to him at any time, whether or not he had ever indulged himself. "Favor me with your name, Madame. May I not call thee something other than the lady of the house?"

She had one great mystery to offer him that he could only share at intervals. She was the ocean to his fish. He would make his way to the sea, and lose himself in the salt depths of her, and drown there.

If he slipped one hand beneath the neckline of her robe he could put the robe down from her shoulders, on one side. She had very adequate shoulders, and Andrej sat and admired her nakedness shamelessly, stroking that smooth round curve with his left hand. Foreign women did not know what bared shoulders did to Dolgorukij. And the best of it was that their ignorance did not diminish the impact of their beauty.

"Fallon, then." She'd put her head back, her eyes half-closed. Suffering herself to be caressed. But not pretending she did not enjoy it. "You may call me Fallon, since I've said Anders before this. Just for tonight. Give me your mouth when you do that, you make me as nervous as a cat."

Yes, willingly.

The sound of the surf was in his ears. He could smell the ocean.

There was nothing in his mind but where he was and what he was to do, no reality beyond the simple truth of the joy of his body and the kindness of her hands.

For this eternity of an evening he could even forget he was Inquisitor.

CHAPTER SIX

So this was what a Dohan Dolgorukij made of a Center House, Captain Lowden mused appreciatively, looking all around him. Normally standing in reception lines was not among his favorite occupations, but this time it was almost worth it—just to get an eyeful of the Danzilar prince's decor.

"Who did you say?" Captain Lowden prompted, turning the gift-flask in his hands with the expected expression of impressed respect and gratitude. "Bermeled's distillers? Of course. The pleasure is mine, I assure you."

Clear-wall doors to the garden full two stories tall and more. Lighting fixtures made of spun glass and fractured crystal hanging in great glittering ice-blooms from long chains in the ceiling. Painted walls papered over with figured silk, and the pattern showing through from behind with jewel-like intensity and unnerving depth. Dance floors, three of them, laid on raised squares of resilient wood, and as many different octets of musicians playing the same tunes in variation in perfect synchronization so that the combined effect—coming at one from several different directions at once—was almost overwhelming.

That was it right there, in summary, Lowden decided.

Almost overwhelming. And just that necessary touch of restraint sufficient to keep it all coherent and splendid at once.

"You're very kind. Permit me to introduce my First Officer,

Mendez. Ralph, these are Sarif Pelar and her partner Chons, local representatives from Bermeled's distillery."

Center House was roaring with people, staff, servants, Security. Griers Verigson Lowden stood with the Danzilar prince at the front of the great foyer doing his duty, lending his presence and that of his officers to the reception line as Danzilar greeted his subject people and the hangers-on who hoped to make a profit under the new administration.

Lowden wished them luck of the attempt. Dolgorukij in trade were as ferociously efficient as his favorite little Aznir in torture, as if the thirst for mastery and the habit of dominion were a genetic determinant of the ethnicity. Maybe they were, Lowden mused, watching a senior businesswoman work her way up the long line to Danzilar's position, a wide-eyed youngster in tow. Maybe if you reached the age of discretion without having demonstrated an instinctive grasp of the profit equation you were sold off as Sarvaw, or some similarly disgraceful fate.

"Dame Ranzil Tavart," the majordomo whispered near Lowden's ear, at his back. Just in case Lowden had missed the Danzilar prince's cue. Lowden bowed, his mind half-distracted by the pleasingly substantial pile of booty that the majordomo was accumulating for him on a table against the wall. "Cordage and Textile" didn't sound very promising from that angle, though; what little treats could a textile manufactory offer?

"Oh, and I understand you've had great success with recovering seed-stocks. Weren't we told that those beautiful flowers in front of the House came from your greenhouses?" The polite phrases were automatic, and nobody really expected him to mean a bit of what he said. He didn't have to think, just smile and speak a word, and smile again. Sickening.

"Ralph Mendez—my First Officer, here—is Santone, not much by way of flowers of any sort where he comes from, I'm afraid. What do you say, Ralph?"

Not as if Lowden cared one way or the other; no, of course not. But a man was expected to demonstrate his skill at managing the flow of traffic in a reception line. He certainly wasn't going to be shown up by Danzilar, of all people.

Glancing around him at the crush, Lowden knew that he was

genuinely impressed at what Danzilar had done with a few hours and a very great deal of money. There was no way in which Vogel would have overlooked the beautiful parquetry floor or the fine rich wood wainscoting in his final audit. Paval I'shenko had to have brought them. Bought them, brought them, laid the floor and hung the chandeliers, painted the walls and then papered over them, and all in the few hours between the final signatures on the formalization documents and the opening of the Center House for this reception.

"Well, no, I'm actually not. In fact I haven't any relatives in that Sector. An orphan, sorry." Two in a row with no presents. He could hear Chief Medical further down the line, talking with the textile people; and cocked an ear, curious.

"Very expertly done, Dame Tavart," Koscuisko was saying. "If I may say so, the young lady has done us proud. Perhaps I may be permitted to impose further and dance with the daughter of the house, later on in the evening."

In all, three of Lowden's officers stood in the reception line, beside Lowden himself. Mendez, Two, and Andrej, who ranked lowest out of the Ship's Primes on the scale of things. Lieutenant Wyrlann wasn't required, since Lowden was here to represent Command Branch. The Engineer was back on *Ragnarok* with the Ship's Second Lieutenant.

Lieutenant Wyrlann was in trouble, and Lowden meant to be sure that Wyrlann understood that.

This was going to be a spectacular party before it was finished; a real work-out. A reception, dinner, dancing, late supper, until finally the guests were dismissed to their homes over fast-meal. A man wanted for companionship to share such an event. Especially if a man was expected to uphold the Bench presence and be on his best behavior. Especially when a man was expected to make good the poor impression created by his miserable excuse for a First Lieutenant.

And it was going to cost Wyrlann at performance review time; but meanwhile—as a result of Wyrlann's little lapse—relaxing, truly enjoying himself at the service center was all but out of the question. He'd have to mind his manners. There was little amusement to be found in that.

"What an unusual decoration. Is it an heirloom? No? A personal award? Sir, my very sincere congratulations. It's also quite elegant, you know. And your respected companion as well, if I may say so."

Oh, he'd end up at the service house before the evening was over. There was no question about that. But he'd have to restrict himself to a boring menu of basic exchanges. No spice, no heat to speak of.

Lowden turned the next in line over to Mendez, a question fighting its way up into his consciousness through the layer upon layer of polite social inanities in which he was so thoroughly submerged.

Where was Wyrlann?

The Lieutenant had successfully avoided him since they'd arrived, not that Lowden had been the least bit interested in seeking him out. There had been too much to do between making one last review with an eye to concessions, executing the final security transfer, and calling Koscuisko back from amusing himself with Paval I'shenko's people— and Fleet's pharmaceuticals, a minor irritation but a real one—at the charity hospital.

"Lowden. Jurisdiction Fleet Ship *Ragnarok*, commanding. No, we're still on proving-cruise; it's quite an experimental craft. Black hull technology."

His joke on Koscuisko had gone flat before Koscuisko had even left the *Ragnarok*. So Wyrlann was going to have to fill the void left by the failure of Lowden's prank.

"That's the Intelligence Officer. We just call her Two because that's her staff section, and no one can pronounce her name. We just insult her, trying. No, really, she's almost perfectly harmless, it's Koscuisko you've got to watch out for. Oh? No, trying to make a joke, I do apologize if I've given any offense."

There were Security on display here, on loan as a symbol of Fleet's power. But he was going to leave the bond-involuntaries alone. He had an arrangement with Koscuisko, and as long as Koscuisko continued to conform there was no percentage in violating his agreement; it would only destabilize his relationship with Chief Medical. Who was unstable enough already.

Lowden had called out Koscuisko's bond-involuntaries particularly for duty at Danzilar's party, as a gesture of goodwill toward Koscuisko. Bond-involuntaries were exotic and interesting. Much more liable than the run-of-the-mill Security to be beckoned into a dark corner by some curious and experimentally minded young woman, and no violation committed either, the requirements for ceremonial event Security being as liberally defined as they were.

He wouldn't be surprised—Lowden told himself, cynically, picking out the straight and somber bodies posted around the far walls at precise intervals—if Security didn't get as much exercise at parties like this as he planned to have at the service house. And free, too.

"Not at all, I would be delighted. You're very kind." This was more like it. The best way to meet new masters was with a gift in one's hand, after all. It was Danzilar who was to be their new master; but Lowden appreciated tokens of respect for the Fleet and Bench every bit as much as the next man. It wasn't as though any actual advantage would accrue to the donors, after all. "I understand that the best quality cortac brandy isn't even available for purchase. It's a distinct privilege to have a bottle."

He was taller than most of Danzilar's people; he could see over the heads of most of the crowd. He thought he saw Wyrlann at the drinks table, tossing back a thimbleful of wodac, holding out his glass for a refill. Lowden frowned. It was an impropriety for junior officers to approach food, let alone drink, while their seniors were still on reception line.

On one level, though, Lowden could understand why Wyrlann might wish to be drinking. It could well be that Wyrlann was still trying to decide what excuse he could provide for having done just as he'd been warned not to do, and breaking something while the Bench still had to pay to have it fixed.

"Well, there are always opportunities, and service in Fleet only rarely sets a career back. On balance, though, you might advise the Combine fleet. There is the Free Government problem to be considered. No, of course not, I didn't mean to imply any such thing."

The line seemed of people still waiting to be introduced seemed to stretch on forever.

When this was over he was going to want to have a drink. And then he had a word or two to say to his First Lieutenant.

Skelern Hanner climbed the shallow white stone stairs from the now-dark garden lawn to the veranda that ran the length of the outside of the Danzilar prince's great dancing-hall. The lights that they'd placed at the lawn's perimeter were each of them worth the sum of eight years' pay, and it wouldn't do to embarrass the Danzilar prince by failing to use them to their best effect. Soft yellow glimmerers, glowing in the darkness, beautiful and welcoming in the night . . . it was full dark, but it wasn't cold yet. Not too cold. Not yet.

Scanning the arc of golden light with a critical eye Hanner tested the curve against the measure in his mind's eye and found no fault. It was beautifully done. It was beautiful.

Full clear-wall behind him, and the party going on. White stone veranda extending five, seven paces between the clear-walls and the steps; a series of shallow white steps, like a beach, like the shore of the sea sloping down to the water, an ocean of lawn.

The light at the back of the cove of new grass shimmered like the lights that shone from the far shores of Carrick Sound. The delicate blooms frothed up like spume in waves against the lights, which not only showed their luxurious profusion but drew out the sweet scent of young marbat blossoms in the early dark.

The lamps would keep the garden warm, at least at their level. With luck the frost would not come hard tonight and the blossom would live to set fruit, and bloom again next year.

Three weeks of hard labor, well used, well fed, well housed—and well worked. Three weeks, all leading up to tonight, and all of the money and all of the labor just to show a pleasant vista from inside, looking out.

And they couldn't even see out, not clearly. Could they? It was light inside, brilliant, white light glittering from faceted hanging-lights and reflected in glassware and mirrors. Surely they would not even know that the garden was there, but by the same token Skelern Hanner could see into the room clearly from outside where he stood on the broad veranda.

He had to get to the back of the house. His tools lay ready, waiting, cleaned and assembled, on the path going back. There was to be a party for them as well tonight, a party for them as had broken their backs for the Danzilar's garden. Plenty to eat and drink, and a three days' paid holiday afterward on top of their bonuses. The Danzilar was generous, and labor was cheap, but a party was nice.

Still Skelern stood.

No one would see him from inside, standing there; they would see only their own reflections. It was too dark outside. Nobody would take offense at him watching the privileged folk, not just for a minute.

And then he saw Sylyphe.

Dancing with the torturer, with Black Andrej, a man with so much Nurail blood on his hands—and yet the same man who had helped to make it right for poor Megh, the only man who had been able to make it right with her. And had cried vengeance on behalf of murdered Nurail against the Domitt Prison, but dancing with the little daughter of the Tavart, his Sylyphe—

Mute with misery Skelern stood and stared. It was the black of the officer's uniform that had caught his eye at first, and now he couldn't take his eyes off the two of them, following them as the figures of the dance carried them into clear space and then concealed them behind the bodies of the lookers-on once again.

His Sylyphe?

Never his.

A man like Koscuisko could well mate with Sylyphe. Buy her from her mother in the manner of a great prince, pay the bride-price. Take her to his home and into his bed, and breed children of his body within her sweet little belly, sons and daughters with blond hair and pale eyes that had no color to them to suckle at her breast and call her "lady Mother."

A man like Koscuisko had a natural right to take such as Sylyphe to be his bride. It was the way of things. People should keep to their own place. It made life much simpler and more bearable; so why did his flesh crawl at the sight of Koscuisko's hand around her narrow waist, why did the sight of Koscuisko's beautiful smile and Sylyphe's rapt admiring gaze make his blood boil?

His Sylyphe.

His.

Perhaps it was true after all, and he'd done what he ought not to have done, and lost his head over a woman that could never share in his life. But she was a gardener her own self. She could not consort with Anders Koscuisko. The mere sight of the torturer would turn milk in the breast of the nursing mother, and if he even spoke to a woman who carried a child in womb the babe yet unborn would wither and die, blasted, destroyed, derelict in the mere presence of a Ship's Inquisitor.

Andrej Koscuisko was not a proper man for Sylyphe.

He was a blight, a smut, a rust, a mold, a canker of worms, a creeping plague of parasites boring into the honey-heartwood in

Sylyphe's breast to destroy her from the inside out. Andrej Koscuisko would kill Sylyphe Tavart—not in body, but how could he but kill her in her heart?

She would be honored, she would be transported to be taken by the hand as his consort, but within weeks the life would start to ebb within her, she would fade, she would fail, her pretty little fingers would crumble into dust and the dimple in her sweet ruddy cheek would dry up and crack into a gaping gray-fleshed wound.

And he couldn't stop watching his Sylyphe dance.

Fleet First Lieutenant G'herm Wyrlann was drunk, but for once liquor wasn't helping, didn't make him feel better. He obtained none of the sense of effortless power from Danzilar's wodac that he usually found in wine: for once he had too much on his mind. That was unfair. He was a Fleet First Lieutenant. That anything external should have attained so much weight and importance as to interfere with his enjoyment of life was an offense—but there he was.

Captain was going to want to talk to him.

Captain was not going to be cordial and friendly.

He'd put the problem aside for as long as possible; but it was not going to be possible to put it aside any longer.

Captain had told him after the last time that he was to exercise more restraint.

Go to an unlicensed house if you have to, Captain had told him. *You don't have the rank to do as you please in a service house without Bench Audit noticing. You have to wait. You have to wait your turn. There are claims against Fleet to reimburse the Bench for damages. Sooner or later it's going to start counting against your career potential unless you're careful.*

Wyrlann remembered every word; all too clearly, really.

What was he going to do?

What was he going to say?

There was no problem with the Port Authority, of course. They didn't dare look crosswise at a Command Branch officer. It wasn't that.

His mind was fuddled with alcohol. He had to think. He couldn't face the Captain in this condition.

Stumbling a little, Fleet Lieutenant G'herm Wyrlann made his way unsteadily across the crowded room toward the great clear-walls that let out to the side garden. It would be quieter outside. It would be cold, but the coolness would help him to clear his head. He could see the white steps, gleaming in the nightlights, falling away from the terrace in shallow tiers toward the dark lawn, and the necklace of warming-lights that seemed to float at the outermost edge of the lawn, illuminating the ghostly gaiety of flower-blossom in the night.

One of the doors was cracked halfway open, and the fragrance of the cool garden night was calming. Fumbling with the catch, almost tripping over the threshold, Fleet First Lieutenant G'herm Wyrlann stumbled out into the cold dark night air.

And then he saw that he was not alone.

From where he stood on post Robert St. Clare, keeping his eye out for officers, saw the dark mass of the Fleet Lieutenant's Command Branch uniform moving through the crowd. The intensity and hue of Command Branch uniform black could not be mistaken for anything else: That was precisely why the color had been chosen, with its peculiar intensity and particular hue. Regardless of how one's class of hominid perceived color or tone Command Branch black could be consistently identified for what it was.

Robert watched the Fleet Lieutenant go with mixed feelings, personal and conditioned instincts warring in his heart and mind.

This was the beast who had brutalized his sister. His poor sister, his sweet sister, his darling Megh. She'd been like a mother to him . . . and to see her like that. After all of these years of not even knowing. His sister.

But this was also a superior commissioned officer, and Wyrlann was going out into the garden. Command Branch officers were not expected to go anywhere without a Security escort.

No one else seemed to have noticed, and it was in Robert's area of responsibility, after all.

His sister. . . .

But Wyrlann was Command Branch. Robert St. Clare was a bond-involuntary. He was expected to behave like one. His governor knew what he was supposed to do. His governor wouldn't let him stand and permit the Fleet Lieutenant to go out into the garden alone, not when he knew quite well what was expected, not when he knew that to stand would comprise a violation.

It was a profound violation, an extreme violation, a violation of all that was right and decent and moral to let such a man walk free to enjoy a party, after what Wyrlann had done to his sister—

Robert could sense the conflict building within himself. Conflict was dangerous for bond-involuntaries. Conflict confused the governor. He had to control his own internal state, or fall prey to the punishment his governor would assess; not for doing something wrong—his governor didn't know what was right and what was wrong—but for doing something that Robert had been carefully taught Fleet meant him to take to be a violation.

And it was a violation to permit a senior Command Branch officer go out without an escort. The governor didn't have to know right from wrong. It only had to pay attention to the conflict created in Robert's heart that arose when he did something he'd been conditioned not to do, or failed in some task that he'd been taught he must always complete.

Robert stepped back from his post, back into the shadows, back into the service corridor that surrounded the great hall. There was a door out to the side of the house. They'd had their briefing. They were expected to know all of the ways to get into and out of the special event location.

Out through the service corridors to the side of the great hall. Down the leafy avenue of trees. They were still losing their foliage, but the turf had been swept free of debris not two eights gone and there were no dead leaves to make a sound as he passed over. Nothing to betray his foot.

There was a work-bundle sitting in the pathway, and Robert reached down for the nearest object without thinking. A trowel, that was what it was, but one with a good edge to it. Robert tried the edge against the side of his thumb, absentmindedly, as he went deeper into the garden, down the long avenue of trees that bordered the lawn. It was careless to leave tools unattended.

Where was the Fleet Lieutenant?

Robert came around the side of the steps to the wide stone veranda, and saw the damned bastard. Standing as smug as anyone could please, free and easy and secure in his rank. If there was any justice—if there was any right—Wyrlann would die. He deserved to die.

His body knew what had to be done, if his mind dared not think of it. Almost not noticing, Robert loosened the trowel-blade from its handle, staring at the Fleet Lieutenant from the shadows at the foot of the stairs.

She could have been anyone's sister, even that cheeky young Skelern Hanner's sister. She wasn't just anybody's sister. She was his sister. It was his to punish the man who had hurt her. It was his right. It was his duty. It was more right that he avenge his sister's near-murder than anything Robert had ever known.

He raised the blade.

He knew.

One step, two steps, and he stood on a level with the Fleet Lieutenant, who turned toward him even as he came.

Was there someone else there, with his back to the decorative support-pillar?

What did it matter if there was someone there?

He had no doubt; he was secure, serene, utterly certain at his task. He had to do this. It was right. He didn't have to think, and if he thought—

But no. He knew what he had to do.

Fleet Lieutenant Wyrlann raised his arm and pointed, started to shout, angrily. Robert didn't hear him shout. He saw that hateful face convulsed with angry spite and threw the trowel, absolutely sure of what he was to do. He threw the trowel, he engaged the crozer-hinge in his shoulder to add enough force to the flight of the weapon to separate a man's head from his shoulders.

He was out of practice.

He threw, and the weapon found its target, and it was finished. He'd done what he had been supposed to do.

That was all.

Now he should get back to his duty post.

Someone would see the movement of the Lieutenant's body as it fell, if nothing else. There would be an alarm. He had to be back before he was missed.

He went as quickly as he had come, as quietly, his mind utterly empty of triumph or concern. It had been necessary, and he had done it. He hadn't really thought about it; he was a little surprised at himself. Should he have been able to?

His governor had never been quite right. They'd told him.

Even so, should he have been able to—

To what?

He couldn't afford to think about it. He wasn't even going to think about why he couldn't think about it. That was a trap.

Slipping back quietly into the crowded room, Robert returned to his post. No one seemed to have missed him; it had taken him only a short period of time. He smoothed his face into its mask of professional readiness and stood at his post.

What had he done?

He couldn't think about it.

But it was too immense, and too unimaginable, and he couldn't not think around the edges of it, no matter how desperately he tried.

The First Lieutenant was unhappy to begin with, and the sight of a Nurail workman staring greedily through the clearwall at his masters and their women within was intrinsically offensive. "You!" Wyrlann shouted, meaning to call Security from within doors, raising his arm and pointing. "You, you scabby piece of Nurail trash, what do you think you're doing?"

The workman seemed to jump, as if startled, turning a pale anxious—guilty—face toward the Lieutenant, backing away. Opening his mouth to speak, but Wyrlann wasn't interested in anything any Nurail had to say to him.

"Lurking around out-of-doors, you've no business here. Free Government, is it?"

Advancing on the workman where the Nurail stood with his back to a tall while pillar. Security had better be here quickly, or they'd look foolish in front of the Danzilar's house-staff. There would be penalties assessed for embarrassing Captain Lowden in front of the Danzilar prince.

"I'll have Security on you before you can—"

Something hit him.

Something struck him in the throat, he couldn't breathe.

Cast down into a black unreasoning world of blind bewilderment Wyrlann tried to fix his mind on what had happened, but could not.

And died.

A door in the clear-wall of the great assembly room had been left halfway open, because of all the people that were inside, Hanner supposed. There was a man come out into the night; and Hanner didn't see him, didn't so much as notice he was there, until the harsh shout of confrontation shook him from his anguished focus on Sylyphe and the Inquisitor at last.

"You!"

The First Lieutenant, Wyrlann. It had to be. He had heard the man described to him, and there was the uniform, Command Branch markings—this was the man who had hurt Megh that way, the black beast, the obscene monster, it was him.

"You, you scabby piece of Nurail trash, what do you think you're doing?"

The dreadful image of his friend's abused body rose up white and red in Hanner's mind's-eye to overlay the figure of the Lieutenant as he stood like a chipped piece of semi-opaque layer-rock stuck in a hole in his gardener's shed to let a little bit of light in. Skelern could not focus on the man. He could scarcely even stir, for the horror of it. To see the Lieutenant, and not so much as spit on him, after what he had done—to see him standing on his feet, in his fine uniform, and Megh helpless and naked in the white light of the recovery room, with just a hospital blanket to cover her over from the casual gaze of any stranger—

The Lieutenant stalked toward him imperiously, and Hanner shrank back against the roof-pillar but could not seem to move himself further than that to flee. There was too much conflict in his heart between hatred and self-preservation.

"Lurking around out-of-doors, you've no business here. Free Government, is it?"

In the extremity of his surprise and shock Skelern's senses seemed preternaturally sharp. The Lieutenant's voice sounded as if it was a very long away. He could hear himself breathing. He could hear his heart beat. He could hear the little sounds all around him, behind him, as if of something or someone with them on the veranda. An animal in the shrubbery, or a little breeze.

Except that there was no breeze, no little wind, no animal free to move about within the Danzilar's garden. This was too large an animal. What Skelern heard was footsteps.

A sudden and irrational panic paralyzed him, held him to his place without a single movement. There was another sound now, a sound like the swift passage of a diving-bird, or the drop of a heavy piece of ripe fruit from the highest branches of a tree. A knife, a thrown knife, passing swift and sure over Hanner's right shoulder to strike the First Lieutenant with such force that the blood shot upward like a fountain, clean and bright, and Wyrlann's head reeled sideways from his neck to hang at the tether-end of a narrow scrap of flesh as Wyrlann's body collapsed from the blow.

It was a frightful thing, gut-wrenching, and Hanner's face worked without any sound, trying to call out. Trying to shout. Trying to warn the Lieutenant by sheer reflex, but it wouldn't do the Lieutenant any good, because the Lieutenant lay crumpled across the wide white steps that led down to the garden, with the blood running down into the earth and his head hanging from his carcass by a thread.

Trembling, Hanner took step forward, desperate to give the alarm. But an entire ocean of people was coming toward him now, rushing out of the great hall onto the veranda steps like the water in a tidal bore. Security. And they had seized Skelern and bound him, carried him down into the garden toward the grisly thing and forced him to his knees on the blood-sodden lawn next to the still-twitching body on the stairs before he could so much as catch his breath.

Sylyphe Tavart was awake, and at the same time dreaming.

She had never seen so grand a dancing hall in all of her life. It outshone even the great ceremonial cathedral at Saldona, where her mother had been chief of accounts.

She was wearing the traditional colored scarf of a marriageable woman for the first time in her life, and before she had left the house her mother had examined the folds of fabric over Sylyphe's modest bosom and sighed—but declined to rearrange the folds, a habit of her mother's that Sylyphe had been dreading.

And then walking down the reception line Andrej Koscuisko had called her out, spoken to her, kissed her hand with flattering courtesy and released her fingers from his grasp with something that seemed very like reluctance to Sylyphe. *Dance with the daughter of the house,* he had said, and Sylphe had loved him then and there for treating her like the grown girl that she was, if her mother only realized.

Had loved him for suggesting it, yes, and had not dared to put any more weight on it than that; so when Andrej Koscuisko—the reception line broken up, the dances about to begin—had sought them out and presented himself to her mother once more to "request the pleasure of your daughter's company" it was almost more than Sylphe could believe.

It was a sallbrey, the first dance. She had studied the Dolgorukij folk-dances diligently in order to be able to be a credit to her mother and to Iaccary Cordage and Textile when the time came to demonstrate their desire to participate in all of the Danzilar prince's goals. She knew the steps in a sallbrey, they were among the easiest to learn and to perform, and she could concentrate all of her energies on fixing this moment in her mind forever and ever after this.

He was the inheriting son of the Koscuisko prince, and in the Dolgorukij Combine he outranked the Danzilar prince himself. The wealth of the Koscuisko familial corporation was staggering, but more than that, he was the Ship's Inquisitor, a man with the power of life and death—sweet easeful healing or atrocious torment—both under his authority.

Dancing with her.

A little taller than she was, but not too much so; she felt perfectly at ease with him—or at least she didn't feel awkward. Taller, and all in duty black, for everyone to see—the warmth of his body, the feel of the supple muscle of his fore-arm, the elegance of his small white hands, the effortless grace with which he danced, the strength held in reserve . . .

The figure of the dance carried them across the dance floor and back again. She could catch glimpses of their reflection in the clear-walls at the side of the room, the bright lights reflecting off the glass like a mirror. He was her lord, and she was his princess—at least while they danced the sallbrey.

She was beautiful.

Partnered by the son of the Koscuisko prince, a grown girl now even in her mother's conservative estimation, she was a princess in his arms, and he smiled and chatted with her with unaffected simplicity and candor while they danced.

*How does the daughter of the Tavart this evening? The medication
you prepared is very good indeed, it works quite well. And kind of you
to take thought for the leavings. I saw a man for an arthritis of the joints
who sat and wept as we our interview conducted, and all to be back at
his home for so long as he could smell the flowers.*

He carried a faint perfume with him for his own part, a musky-
peppery scent that seemed to be a thing of soap and skin rather than
a grooming-fragrance. She could not analyze it into its component
parts, but she dizzied herself trying to fix the exact taste of it within her
heart and mind forever. Oh, if she could only make it last, if she could
fold the fabric of time back upon itself and keep this instant of
transcendent joy forever she would not grudge the price. Whatever it
might be.

The dance could not last forever.

But they were interrupted even before the last few measures of the
tune signaled an end to bliss and fantasy.

One of the Danzilar's house-men stood at the front of the ranks of
observers, and as Sylphe passed by in the arms of the Koscuisko
prince she noticed one of the *Ragnarok*'s Security was there as well—
a very tall man, and ugly, with a ruined face so flattened by nature or
by accident it looked as though his features had been razed flat from
forehead to chin. She saw them there, and knew that the Koscuisko
prince could see them too; maybe they had only come to watch?

She knew as soon as she caught sight of them that she was not to
be so lucky. Koscuisko turned his head away when they passed, but
almost at once turned back and gave a nod. So it was over.

"Oh, this is—very unfortunate indeed," Koscuisko said. "Come,
we must escape. Follow with me."

He danced her out of the figure of the dance, off of the dance floor,
so gracefully it seemed part of the dance itself. The Security were
waiting for them; how had Koscuisko brought them so precisely to
the place? She could spare little of her mind to wonder at that. She
was to be deprived of her lord, who had never been her lord, who had
been hers only so long as she could dance with him. She was bereft.
She was her mother's daughter all the same, and knew she could not
show her disappointment.

No words passed between Koscuisko and his man, who only
bowed. His fingers seemed to twitch, was it just nerves? Or was it a

message? Because Koscuisko sighed, and spoke to the Danzilar's house-man.

"Escort the daughter of the house Tavart back to her mother, then, with my profound apologies. Sylyphe. Miss Tavart. I must beg that you excuse me. I am asked for."

He was not just asked for but desired. Profoundly. Passionately. Fiercely. Couldn't he tell how much she wanted him?

Or could he tell, and saved her face as best he could?

She cast about for some polite response, but Koscuisko didn't wait.

Koscuisko bowed and kissed her hand, and it seemed to Sylyphe that he almost touched her fingers to his cheek as he straightened from his bow.

She could not be sure.

And he was gone.

The house-man bowed in turn and gestured with his hand for her to precede him through the crowd. To go back to her mother. To sit alone for the rest of the evening, for how could she countenance another partner, who had danced with the Koscuisko prince?

CHAPTER SEVEN

"*This* piece of trash." Hanner knelt low on the ground beside the now-covered corpse with someone's boot planted firmly between his shoulder-blades to ensure he wouldn't be tempted to try to run away. He couldn't see a thing except for blood, and the boots. What he could hear was hard for him to understand, stunned as he was by the shock of the event and Security's rough handling. "Andrej. Is there anything to be done? Anything at all?"

"No, nothing, Captain." He'd heard that voice before, not long before, cold and moderate in pitch, with an accent. Dolgorukij accent. "Traumatic amputation, there's complete severance for spinal, and the brain is more than six-eighths gone already. It would be a very slim chance even if we had the resources and had caught it sooner. And the resources are not here, and we did not catch it soon enough by half. There's nothing I can do."

He didn't know what a Dolgorukij accent might be, but Koscuisko was Dolgorukij, and he had heard Koscuisko in hospital. And in the Tavart's parlor, of course, later on.

"Were you able to actually see anything, Captain Lowden?" Maybe that voice was familiar, too. But Hanner was still too confused in his mind to put a name to it.

"Unfortunately not, Specialist Vogel." Captain Lowden, again? That would make sense. The dominant voice one way or the other, or so it seemed. Skelern felt sick to his stomach, and hoped he wasn't going to vomit. It would be such a mess. And there was such a mess already . . . "All I really saw was Wyrlann turn and point. And then his head jumped off his shoulders. Quite a sight."

The Captain's voice came closer; the foot moved off his back. "And this is the man poor Wyrlann was pointing at. Hadn't expected to be caught about his dirty business, obviously. I'm surprised he had the nerve to go through with the assassination, what with Wyrlann looking right at him."

What man was that? There'd been someone on the veranda, moving as quietly as a small breeze in the bushes?

"You're quite sure there was nothing else, sir," the second voice urged. Someone kicked Hanner in the stomach, suddenly and very hard, and laid him flat on the ground, gasping for breath. The lawn held the blood like a sponge, and yet somebody put his foot to the side of Hanner's face and pressed down hard.

"Vogel, I as good as saw him throw the knife. We need to move quickly on this."

Hanner couldn't breathe for tasting blood. The knowledge that it wasn't even his own blood sickened him, and the pressure of the foot against his face filled him with irrational fear. He tried to breathe as best he could through one nostril, shuddering at the stink of the fluid that he could not help but draw into his lungs.

Shuddering was a mistake.

The Captain stepped down harder on his face, and Hanner stilled himself as best he could in desperate horror. Captain Lowden was still talking; and though Hanner couldn't quite grasp the meaning of the words, he knew with sickening certainty they meant that something terrible was going to happen to him.

"I don't doubt but that there's Free Government behind this, in light of the recent intelligence reports. We can't leave the port to the Danzilar prince with a potential cell of insurrectionaries unaccounted for."

The horrid pressure of the booted foot shifted at last, and Hanner gulped his breath in great gasping sobs. There were people at him again, pulling him to his feet, straining his arms painfully against the restraints that they latched around his wrists behind his back. He was having a hard time keeping his balance, but fortunately for him Security still held him fast.

"I'll want you to get started right away, Andrej, bring me confession before fast-meal and I won't ask First Officer where Security were when all this happened. Though come to think of it—"

Things began to come back into focus as he finally caught his breath, now that he was no longer doubled over to the ground. The body. Andrej Koscuisko, his rival in a contest for Sylphe's attention that could be no real contest at all. Security, and some other people, important people he'd no business even looking at. Why had they shackled him?

Captain Lowden was looking past Koscuisko at one of the few Security troops here that Hanner had met before. "I don't think I saw you on post, where were you? No. Never mind." The Captain of the *Ragnarok*. Hanner stared up at him in awe. "We have more important issues to address. I'll let it go for now. Confession in due form, Koscuisko, and go as lightly as you can, we wouldn't want to cheat the Bench of its lawful revenge."

Koscuisko bowed; and Hanner could not see the expression on his face, shadowed as it was by the light from the great room within. There hadn't been an alarm. Had there been? He could hear music, laughter, as if the party was continuing, oblivious. Why hadn't there been an alarm? Shouldn't they raise the hue and cry, to track the murderer?

"Instruction received is instruction implemented. Stildyne," Koscuisko said. "If you would go relieve the other gentlemen. Specialist Vogel. There is a Record still at the Port Authority, one presumes? And come to think of it, will the courthouse have power?"

The Captain clearly had other ideas. "Take my Security one-point-three rather, Andrej. Your people have been worked too hard, too long. You told me so yourself, as I remember. I'll see you in the morning."

Then Captain Lowden moved away back toward the lights, back toward the warmth, back toward the music.

"What was that all about?" The voice was the one that had been identified as Specialist Vogel; the man wore a different uniform, one without rank-markings. "Captains interfering in the First Officer's business?"

"A game." Koscuisko's response was savage. Hanner wondered what Koscuisko was so angry about. "Captain Lowden likes to play games. In this one he reminds me that if I don't do as he has instructed me he has a complaint to cry against my Security. Just in case I had had any ideas about consulting my own judgment in how quickly a lawful confession was to be obtained."

"I'd say he made it pretty clear what he expected." Vogel's agreement was not an entirely approving one. "Makes a man a little uncomfortable, if you don't mind my saying so. He didn't actually see the murder."

Hanner had. Hanner had seen the murder. But no one had asked him about the murder. Why hadn't anyone asked him about it? Maybe they had, and he didn't remember. His head was spinning. He could hardly keep his balance, and his stomach was going to pitch at any moment. Just as well he hadn't had his supper.

"What does it matter?" Koscuisko asked. Hanner knew it mattered. Hanner knew it mattered critically—but Koscuisko was still speaking. "If he's guilty he will confess. If he is not guilty there will be no confession."

Only . . .

"As you say, sir." Even to Hanner Vogel sounded dubious enough to strike a spark from Koscuisko, who exploded in challenge quick and sharp almost before Vogel had finished.

"Do you suggest otherwise, Specialist?"

For a moment it seemed to Hanner that Vogel might do just that. But the moment passed. Was that a good thing? Vogel bowed. "Of course not, your Excellency. You'll excuse me, sir, getting back to the party, and all."

Koscuisko glared after the retreating man until Vogel reached the steps; then abruptly transferred his attention back to the grotesque gory scene in the garden.

"Very well." Koscuisko glanced at him now; met his eyes, and let his gaze travel down the length of Hanner's body, soiled from kneeling in the blood that pooled at the foot of the stairs. "Young Hanner. I am heartily sorry to see you here. The Bench makes no provision for family feeling where its officers are concerned."

There hadn't been an alarm, and there would be no alarm. Because they thought that they had found the murderer. That he was the murderer.

"I've done no murder!" Skelern protested, so horrified by his realization of what he was accused of that he nearly stuttered in his frantic need to speak out. "Only watching Sylyphe, for a little moment, there's no harm in watching Sylyphe dance, is there?"

But Koscuisko only snapped his fingers. Rough hands began to drag him away, across the lawn toward the maintenance-track beyond the screening trees. Maybe it was a killing offense to have desired the consort of an Inquisitor. But Uncle Andrej dealt honestly with a man, and Skelern had not realized until he'd seen them dance that Sylyphe was to be soul and flesh of Anders Koscuisko. Surely he could not be put to death for having offended in error.

"What does his Excellency think, a crozer-lance?"

He could hear the words behind him as Koscuisko followed after. Koscuisko. But it was all right then, after all. Wasn't it?

"No, it seems to have been a trowel-blade, Robert. Perhaps a hoe. We'll have the details soon enough."

"It—must have been—the crozer-hinge, the force, the height—"

He knew the voice. St. Clare. Robert St. Clare, a Nurail, but not one like himself. The reproach Koscuisko made grew fainter, in its volume, as Koscuisko stopped while Hanner was hurried off.

"Yes, of course, Robert. What is your point, exactly? You are to go back to your duty post. Captain Lowden will be watching for you. You are to go now. I do not want to be angry with you."

Anybody else, and he would only have been able to despair. But this was Andrej Koscuisko, the bloody butcher, Koscuisko, Black Andrej. And everybody knew that if you were guilty there was no hope, no chance to escape punishment.

But every Nurail also knew that Andrej Koscuisko had the truth-sense on him, the curse of the blood was upon him, and he knew when a man was telling the truth.

It didn't mean a great deal, since Koscuisko was required to test, and the test itself was terrible; but it meant enough. Koscuisko did not condemn the innocent for crimes that they had had no action in.

And Hanner was innocent in word or deed of the murder of the man who had tortured his poor friend. Koscuisko would know.

He would have to bear the testing of it, yes.

But Koscuisko would know.

Robert St. Clare stood in his place. He was safe and secure as long as he was in his place, and at attention-rest as he was expected to be.

Safe and secure, but far from serene. What had he done? And why hadn't he stopped to think that someone would be taken for it? He should have known. Someone had to be taken for it, and there were Nurail all over Port Burkhayden; it was a Nurail port. They had taken that gardener away, and he knew that Hanner hadn't done it. He knew that Hanner couldn't have done it, but did Koscuisko know?

He'd tried to tell Koscuisko, once he'd realized. He'd tried to tell him, and he hadn't been able to. Why had his governor let him do the deed and then prohibited him from speaking of it? He'd known that he was right to do it when he'd done it, and he could even guess that that was why he'd been able to do it at all. But he was wrong to keep silent and let Hanner go to torture. Why wouldn't his governor let him confess himself now?

Because—even though she was his sister, his beloved sister, his sweet sister that he hadn't seen for so many years—even though she was his sister, *his* sister, not that Skelern Hanner's sister, he would not have done the thing if he had been thinking and had realized that someone would have to be taken for it.

He knew what a Tenth Level Command Termination meant, and at his maister's hands particularly.

And if the gardener had not done the murder, as Robert knew quite well that he had not, still Hanner might well prove guilty of enough besides; and Captain Lowden forced such compromises on a man. Trades. If Captain Lowden were to tell Koscuisko to either execute the Tenth Level or keep after other prisoners from Danzilar's people until someone confessed, would not his maister be forced to bend his neck and do the horrible and unjust thing?

It had never been so blatant, so horrible, ever yet, but had Koscuisko not agreed before to execute at a more advanced Level in order to keep as many still-unaccused souls from the torture as he could?

Why had his governor let him do the thing, the thing which until it had been well done he had not known for certain that he could do, and then not let him do the smaller task, confess himself to keep an innocent man from coming beneath his maister's hand?

If only, if only Koscuisko could have heard him, if only Koscuisko could remember. But Robert was too confused now in his mind between his private torment and the stress on his governor to be sure of whether he'd even really managed to say, about the crozer-hinge. If Koscuisko had heard him, Koscuisko would remember, but would his poor maister be too deeply sunk into his passion to call the point to mind before it was too late for Skelern Hanner?

Closing his eyes as tightly as he knew how, Robert tried to set a governor on his mind, since the one the Fleet had given him was not helping. He could do nothing now for Skelern Hanner. He had not stopped to realize what would have to happen, if he did it right, if he could do it at all. Perhaps in another little while he would be able to speak to Chief Stildyne, and Hanner not more than a few hours the worse for it. Not that he cared about Hanner, he didn't know Hanner; although the man seemed to be fond of his sister.

Oh, his sister, after so many years, and then to see her so unkindly served, knowing exactly what the Lieutenant had done . . .

He blinked his eyes open hastily, feeling his balance beginning to erode.

He could not move from his place. He did not have permission. His governor was that much more strict with him now, it seemed, now that the damage was already done, now that he only wanted to surrender himself to punishment—because he could get away with it, he had gotten away with it, but an innocent man was to suffer if he could not confess.

He could not move from his place. His governor protected him from punishment, would not permit him to speak the word that would put himself in jeopardy. It was intended to help him censor his incautious tongue, to ensure that he would not challenge an officer or speak an actionable violation of some sort,

It protected him too well.

He trembled with the fearful frustration of it all, and stood at attention-rest in his place.

It wasn't far enough to the local Bench offices by half, and transport got there entirely too soon. Captain Lowden's Security handled the gardener with the exaggerated roughness typical of people who were not accustomed to the task, and overdoing things accordingly; but what difference could it make?

Andrej said nothing, absorbed in his own gloomy meditations. He knew Skelern Hanner, at least in a manner of speaking. He almost thought that if he knew Hanner any better he'd like the man. But Lowden had said the word. There was to be no help for it.

There was a night watchman. Andrej sent two Security with him to bring the auxiliary power on line. It was true that he didn't need the Record to obtain a lawful confession; he held the Writ, which was necessary and sufficient of itself for that function.

But he had to be able to see to do it.

He went through to the courtroom while he waited. It was empty, of course, but Miss Janisib—the senior Security on this team—had already found a chair for him from somewhere; and as Andrej was trying to decide whether she'd had rhyti leaf on her—or had simply borrowed some in a hurry from Center House—she came back into the room with one of her fellows, carrying a table sturdy enough to be used for his purpose if he elected it.

Janisib knew.

She wasn't bond-involuntary, but there weren't enough bond-involuntaries to go around, and she'd been on one of his Security teams when he'd got to *Ragnarok*. She'd transferred soon after, but the fact remained that she knew enough of what went on around an Inquiry to direct the other members of her team.

By the time the power came on to reveal the depressing extent to which the courtroom was stripped, Miss Janisib had things arranged quite creditably, all things considered.

A heavy armchair for him to sit down in when he got tired of standing or wanted to catch his breath.

A table, long enough to stretch a prisoner at length upon, sturdy enough to take the various stresses of weight and blows and the tensions to which it might be subjected. Rhyti in an open pan with a cracked flask to sup it from, but it was good rhyti. It was not to be imagined that Jan simply carried rhyti about on her person, for such an eventuality. "Thank you, Miss Janisib. If I could see my prisoner, now."

Hanner himself they had left under guard in a closet outside while Security did what could be done to make a workspace out of an abandoned courtroom. Andrej stared at his interrogations kit while he waited, brooding about things.

Confession for breakfast, the Captain had said. Lowden was sure to seek recreation at the service house; it was an unfailing habit.

Andrej could only hope that his Captain wouldn't be so insensitive as to beat up another Service bond-involuntary.

Now Security was marching Hanner in through the double doors at the foot of the room; and it occurred to Andrej that there wasn't any place in particular he wanted them to put Hanner. Looking around for a secure chain from the ceiling or a post or hook in the wall Andrej thought hard and fast, aware all the while of how ridiculous this was.

If he took up his trefold shackles and used the interconnecting chain he could pass it beneath the surface of the table they'd brought him, and shackle Hanner's wrists one to a side. Hanner couldn't possibly work the chain down to one end of the table and under the table-legs to free himself; or if he could he wasn't going to be able to manage the trick without Andrej noticing. So that would do.

But there was something that Andrej needed before Hanner was chained. He could have Hanner stripped just as easily after as before; but the gardener was probably not well paid. His clothing was probably all he possessed that was worth handing on to someone who might want it to remember him by: his sister, perhaps, and how could Andrej hope to check on her recovery after this, knowing what he was about to do to her brother?

"You'll want to undress, Hanner," Andrej suggested, holding his hand up in a sudden sharp gesture of warning to Security to let Hanner alone. "Or your clothing will be damaged, as well as soiled. We'll see to it that Megh gets your things, at least."

It was hard for the gardener to strip himself naked with so many unfriendly eyes watching him. Yet Andrej knew better than to even think of dismissing Security to leave him alone with an unbound prisoner: inquisitors died that way. It was a form of suicide, one that masqueraded as a lapse in judgment. Andrej Koscuisko had not come this far to die of an accident, however deliberately courted. Security would stay.

Had he survived so long for this to come to him, then?

Was it not better to die if to live meant to ruin a decent young man who had avenged his sister, and draw Hanner's death out for seven to ten days in vengeance for a man who tortured helpless women?

But *he* was a man who tortured helpless women.

And something inside of him was focused on a quite different issue. *Eight to eleven,* the voice of his appetite whispered to him, encouragingly. *Eight to eleven. You can do better than you did at the Domitt. This man is fit and strong, and inured to hard labor and to privation. He'll last much better. You could get twelve.*

Andrej shut the seductive meditation off with an effort. It was not time. All too soon he would yield to his own thirst for Hanner's pain because he would not be able to do his work without consenting to take pleasure in it. But he didn't have to start that this early. Captain Lowden wanted a clean confession. He could do it without succumbing to his own beast; there would be need enough—pain enough—grim red atrocity sufficient to slake Andrej's fiendish appetite, later. Tenth Level. Command Termination.

Eight to eleven, you could go twelve . . .

No, Andrej told himself firmly. He'd have none of it. Hanner unclothed himself to the skin and folded his garments into a stack; Miss Janisib carried the clothing away to wrap up in a bundle and stood by the door as the rest of Captain Lowden's Security followed instruction and chained Hanner over the table.

"Thank you, gentles. Now you are excused." Andrej lifted his field interrogations kit onto the table and opened it in front of Hanner, so that Hanner could see what he was doing. "I will call, if I want you. Yes? Go away."

They seemed a little startled at his blunt language, but Andrej didn't care. He was accustomed to being blunt in torture room.

The door at the far end of the room closed behind them; Andrej and Hanner remained alone in the center of the room. One of them clothed. One of them chained. Andrej found what he wanted, and loaded the osmo-stylus with the dose.

"This is the way of it, Skelern." No need at this point for the formal introduction, *My name is Andrej Koscuisko, and I hold the Writ to which you must answer.* So much was understood. "You are taken under accusation for the murder of Fleet First Lieutenant G'herm Wyrlann, Jurisdiction Fleet Ship *Ragnarok.* It is the Captain who cries you guilty, and has also laid it on me that you confess before sunrise tomorrow."

Hanner's face was dirty, stained with mud and dried blood. Dried filth: the blood of the man who had savaged his sister. And very pale, underneath it all, but resolute of spirit for all that. "Or else what, your Excellency?"

Which was a good sign; or a bad sign. And Andrej wasn't going to indulge himself even so far as to try to guess which. "Or else I will be hard pressed to protect my Security, but that's not your problem. Now. This is commonly called extract of allock, class five speak-serum, from the Controlled List."

Setting the loaded stylus down on the table where Hanner could watch it for him, Andrej started to unpack his kit. Showing the instruments of torture was one of the oldest traditions of the craft. It was also one of the most useful and least hurtful of the persuasions Andrej had at his hand; if Hanner could be persuaded to speak freely, they would both be the better for it. For the time being.

"There is circumstantial evidence that places you at the murder site when it happened. The Captain's cry against you is very serious, because of his rank, but it is still hearsay of a sort and not direct evidence. Your confession is absolutely required to find you subject to the penalty for this shocking crime."

Why was he telling Hanner this? Why should he waste his time being honest or candid? Wouldn't it be the same in the end if he forced a confession and lied about how he'd obtained it? The Bench didn't care, not when it came down to it. As long as what could be made to pass for justice was done the Bench overlooked any number of merely procedural irregularities,

"You have two choices before you now. You can confess to me the murder, I will confirm it with an appropriate speak-serum, and we will be done until the time arrives for the penalty to be assessed." *Eight to eleven days*, the voice whispered, eagerly. *You could go twelve.* Andrej frowned, concentrating.

"Or I will administer this dose, which encourages but will not compel truthful utterance. It is still only circumstantial evidence. My authority is to test you with this drug and a degree of coercive persuasion until you say truth."

Hanner looked relieved. He had no cause to be, but Andrej knew what was on his mind even before Hanner spoke. "Then there's no need, your Excellency, and I'll get dressed, it's cold in here. Give me the speak-serum, your Excellency, I'll tell you the truth here and now, drug or no drug. It was only watching you dance with the little maistress. I had neither word nor deed in the murder of the Fleet Lieutenant, though I can't deny that I'm not sorry for it."

Watching him dance? Oh, watching Sylyphe Tavart, rather. If only it was so easy as that. "I appreciate your willingness to cooperate. But I cannot take your word at face value, not with the charges that my Captain has cried. If you confessed to the murder—but since you do not you must be ready to ask yourself, very urgently indeed, whether you had better not do so."

Andrej picked up the dose and pressed it through the browned skin at Hanner's shoulder as he spoke. Hanner was right. It was cold in here. Hanner had goose-bumps; but the dose went through all the same.

"I can't say I've killed the Fleet Lieutenant." Hanner was frightened, and rightly so. But Hanner was firm. "Because I'd no hand in it. And you'll know it, soon enough I hope. I'm innocent. Even if you're to beat me for being so rude as to contradict such a man as the Fleet Captain, Lowden."

Andrej had no respect for Fleet Captain Lowden for his own part, but that didn't mean Andrej lacked respect and sound understanding of what Captain Lowden could do, with his rank. What things Captain Lowden was lawfully entitled to say, or plead, or demand by virtue of his rank.

"Thank you, but it is not good enough." Andrej didn't have the drugs that it would take to elicit a confession at the Fifth Level with speak-sera alone. Results were required. More direct forms of physical coercion were authorized for use in tandem with a speak-serum, Andrej picked up his favorite whip. "We have some hours ahead of us to test, then. Why should you deny the deed? You had the motive. You were there. What could be more natural than to have revenged your sister?"

Once he had laid the soles of Hanner's bare feet open with his whip he would not need to take quite so many precautions against Hanner running away. There were important psychological issues there as well. It would be very awkward for Hanner, chained to the table as he was, if he could not put his weight on his own two feet. It might help him toward an appropriately submissive state of mind.

"I had no weapon, sir, and had I done I'd still have no knowledge of how to use it—your Excellency—"

Hanner spoke on as Andrej moved around the table and behind him. But Hanner's nerves betrayed him to himself. He could not help looking back over his shoulder, his words trailing off as Andrej ran the length of the lash through his lightly clenched fist to straighten it of any stray kinks.

"Face front, if you please."

Oh, Andrej knew the hunger for it, now. Even though he thought that he liked Hanner. Even though Andrej felt sorry for him. Hanner was meat to the knife, nothing more. Andrej Koscuisko was come into his dominion, and rejoiced to recognize it for his own.

"Yes, sir, but I'm innocent, I didn't—"

Swinging the whip around in a long, almost lazy arc, Andrej made his first mark on living canvas. Skelern Hanner shouted with surprise and pain, and stumbled to regain his footing where he stood chained to the table. That wouldn't do. That wouldn't do at all. Andrej moved more quickly, this time, and brought the snapper-end of the stout whip down brutally hard against the bottom of Hanner's foot. The left foot. Just below the ball of the foot, nestled in to the tender place above one arch of muscle and beside another.

Hanner was not so much surprised, this time.

It was a good beginning.

Andrej knew he could have confession before morning. One way or another: and he no longer cared which.

Mendez liked the fancy pattern-dancing, the men and women of all ages in different traditional modes of dress representing different Dolgorukij ethnicities, each of them cheerful and energetic and all apparently having a good time. He tried to picture the Chief Medical Officer on the dance floor, unable to make sense of the projected image. Still, it looked like fun. Under other circumstances he might have been tempted to join in the demonstration, and see if he couldn't interest one or two of the ladies in a Santone sawelling.

"I had thought to tempt your Chief Medical Officer with the fanshaw." The Danzilar prince, beside him, sounded nothing short of gloomy; and Mendez didn't blame him. "I wonder if you know, First Officer. My cousin is a very pretty dancer, especially in fanshaw; because after all his family is Koscuisko."

Quite right, too. He wouldn't have guessed Koscuisko even could dance, which made him regret not having seen it all the more. Stildyne gave the Chief Medical Officer good marks for a sufficient degree of athleticism, true enough, but Stildyne was notoriously prejudiced, and combat drill was not an infallible index of how well a man could dance.

"If his Excellency would care to explain, about a 'fanshaw?' Can't say that there are many opportunities for such as this, on board ship."

The Danzilar prince was a little taller than Koscuisko, and his hair was brown. Blue eyes, though. There were people out there on the dance floor who looked so much like Koscuisko and Danzilar put together that it was easy to imagine a blood relationship.

Now Danzilar smiled a little sadly, gesturing politely with his cupped hand palm-uppermost at the demonstration dance. "Fanshaw is a challenge-piece, by nature. Here they are dancing mixed fanshaw, a courting dance, although the relationships that one dances to obtain are courtships of very short duration. Little permanence."

Or week-long wedlock, Mendez guessed. "Is that why they're all tricked out so bright?" He'd never seen Andrej in a ruffled shirt, much less a brilliant blue embroidered vest. He'd never seen Koscuisko wearing bright green leggings or a painted leather skirt. In fact the only color he'd ever associated with Koscuisko was the little bit of crimson in the cording on his sleeves that identified his area of service. Oh, and the bar of matching crimson that lined through his rank-plaquet, in token of his custody of the Writ to Inquire.

"Well, one wishes to impress the ladies. He has unfair advantage there, because one need not wear one's land-holdings for everyone to be impressed by them."

Andrej was rich, was that what Danzilar was saying? Hard to tell, with Dolgorukij. He already knew that Andrej was rich. The comment gave him an idea, though. There were probably questions he could ask his host, with Koscuisko gone, about all the things he didn't know about the Chief Medical Officer; he might well learn something interesting. About Koscuisko's children, for instance, since Two dropped maddeningly vague hints about their number and situation from time to time.

If a man couldn't pry into the private lives of his fellow Primes then there was no reason to keep on living; gossip was the spice of life.

For Intelligence Officers and Ship's Executives gossip sometimes provided information that came in very handily at the most unexpected points. But the dance was breaking up, and he had already seen Lowden signaling for him; he could not see his way clear to pretending that he hadn't noticed, not since Danzilar had apparently seen it too.

"I hope we get a chance to watch some more of that. It's interesting. With your permission, your Excellency, Captain Lowden seems to need me, if you will excuse the interruption."

It probably wasn't strictly necessary to excuse himself formally. He didn't really need Danzilar's permission. But somebody should probably be at least polite to their host, especially after having soiled his clean white garden steps with blood and an ugly corpse. And if anybody was going to be polite it would have to be him, because Lowden wasn't even pretending very hard any longer.

Nodding, Danzilar frowned a little. "Naturally I do not dream of impeding. Come back to me when the music starts, I will have the dancing-master tell to you about the time when the son of the Koscuisko prince took out nine of his cousins in one set."

Which sounded ever so much more interesting than whatever Lowden could have on his mind. The Captain had been all but publicly gloating about getting a Tenth Level from Koscuisko ever since they'd taken the gardener away. Mendez bowed out of courtesy and retreated; Lowden was visibly impatient, and the sooner he got whatever it was out of the way the sooner Mendez would be free again to pump that dancing-master for juicy tidbits about Koscuisko's other life. His real life. Well, maybe he should just think of it as "other," after all.

Lowden had started for the front entrance, once he had apparently assured himself that Mendez was following. Ralph only just caught up with him on his way out.

"I've had enough of this," Lowden said firmly, his voice sufficiently emphatic to get the attention of everyone within wire range. "I'm going to the service house to take some healthful recreation. I'll need Security, of course, and you'll cover for me if Danzilar notices that I've gone."

Predictable. But very impolite. "Choice of Security, your Excellency? Double teams, perhaps." Apart from it being rude to leave their host's welcoming party without so much as telling Danzilar about it, there was a safety issue to consider. There were Free Government agents in Burkhayden, by Intelligence report—Two had said so. Well, she'd said that there were reports. And then of course a person might want to be a little prudent, when it was Lowden's Lieutenant whose assault had set things in such an uproar. Wyrlann was dead, and maybe that would turn out to be all there was to be to that. Still, Captain Griers Verigson Lowden was an unpopular man even in quiet ports, among people who'd had a chance to get to know him.

"Where's that bunch of Andrej's? The slaves. He'll be distracted; I might just have myself some fun with them. Not that I care. But it makes him so edgy when he doesn't know."

If Koscuisko was going to be distracted—and who would know better than Lowden, about that? —then what real difference could it make whether Lowden took Koscuisko's bond-involuntaries or not?

Mendez didn't feel like playing. "His Excellency has relieved the advance party, but Koscuisko's people have been on line for almost as long. And Koscuisko takes more energy out of a person. Take another of Koscuisko's teams, if you want to make a point of it."

At the rate Koscuisko was going one more worry, one more uncertainty, one more outrage was going to send him off on a hard oblique so sharp that they'd never find his mind to stuff back into his skull again.

"Forget Koscuisko's people, he's going to be giving them enough of a workout." Lowden seemed to have changed his mind anyway, but whether it was because he'd accepted Mendez's point was anybody's guess. "Give me, oh, who've you got? All right, one-point-four. I'll take one-point-four."

Mendez lifted an eyebrow at the senior man on one-point-four, Anji Ghaf; and, bowing, she went to collect the rest of her team. Security one-point-four it was. "Will the Captain be returning to Center House, or shall we send for you in the morning?"

"I'll let you know." And why not? Mendez asked himself rhetorically. Why shouldn't a ship of war with a crew of more than seven hundred souls hang impotent in neutral orbit while its Captain slept off an evening's sensual indulgence in the service house that no one else had been granted leave to visit? Command Branch had its prerogatives, after all. And that was one of them.

"Captain Lowden will be needing you for the rest of the shift. Carry on, Miss Ghaf."

And now that Lowden had reminded him about Koscuisko's Security, one of Andrej's bond-involuntaries had been looking a little less than eight in eighty. He was going to have to ask Chief Stildyne to check on St. Clare, just in case there was something more than usually wrong with that damned defective governor of his.

Then maybe everybody would just leave him alone, and he could go back to ferreting out the deep dark secrets of his Chief Medical Officer's youthful days of cheerful frolic.

Eights passed.

The table had proved itself more useful than Andrej had hoped. Hanner's chains had caught beneath its surface on a rod or brace of some sort, and prevented Hanner's weight from pulling him by the shackled arms painfully down to the end of the table to the floor. No, Hanner was caught there, as efficiently as though Andrej were at home in Secured Medical and Hanner lying across the whipping-block.

Hanner wept, half-strapped onto the table, wept with pain and with the fear of more pain. He could see the whip when Andrej came from his left side, and he was quite properly apprehensive of it. Andrej had worked him hard in the past eights: and yet something wasn't right.

The dose he'd administered and refreshed was a solid performer even at the next Level, one Andrej could rely upon to eat away at a man's will to keep his truth still to himself. Hanner had had two doses of it, one even moderately increased in consideration of Hanner's wiry muscular frame—it could well be that Hanner was heavier than he looked.

More than two doses in a space of four eights Andrej could not see his way clear to administer, and still there was the fact that the first dose should have been enough. It was not to be expected that a man yield to confess himself of such a crime on the persuasion of the whip alone, no matter how thrilling the sound of its impact against helpless quivering flesh, no matter how honestly Hanner reported the pain that the whip granted him. But there had been the drug.

Andrej strolled forward to stand at the middle of the table. Here was where Hanner lay face-down on the table's surface, one cheek flat against the sweat-damp wood. Trembling. Trying to catch his breath.

Andrej wiped tears of pain from Hanner's cheeks carefully with the gathered coils of his whip, and waited, caressing Hanner's cheek with bloodied leather while Hanner settled down.

"What is the matter with you, Skelern Hanner?"

Hanner winced, and closed his eyes tightly. Andrej tried to explain. "I am at a loss to explain your stubborn behavior. One would almost think you had no desire to confess. Is that the problem, Hanner? Have I failed to inspire the correct sense of urgency? Do you lack motivation to make your confession?"

Hanner was polite; it was one of the things that made his intransigence confusing. "No, thank you. Sir. I wish. Very heartily. That I could confess, and be done with this. Your Excellency."

That was all to the good. "Is it that you do not wish to confess to the murder of our Fleet Lieutenant? Because that is the only confession that is of interest, you know that."

Eights, and Hanner was marked from neck to foot, bleeding and bruised. Andrej knew. It had been hard work, if not without its satisfactions. Now he was becoming bored and a little anxious, and he had rather liked young Skelern Hanner; he wanted to make as clean a confession of it as possible. It would mean less to be suffered in the long run, if that could truly be considered when there was the Tenth Level—

"I. I would like. To confess." For a moment Andrej was hopeful, resting his hand against Hanner's back encouragingly. "But must not. To a crime. Which I have not committed."

"You must not want it hard enough." In truth that was the only conclusion to be drawn. Since Hanner had committed murder—and Andrej had no reason, no real reason, to doubt but that he had—the only thing Andrej could think of to explain Hanner's stubbornness was a failure of motivation. Not even the half-choked cry of desperation with which Hanner answered him was good enough.

"Your Excellency—"

"I am sorry to have to say it. But you are simply not adequately engaged in the process. I wonder how I am to be sure of your attention?"

Whether or not he liked Hanner had nothing to do with what he craved from him. And what Andrej knew he was working toward was a good confession; Lowden had required it. But in the mean time he could make Hanner cry; and Andrej's fish sought each whimper of anguish as eagerly as it might seek the blue ocean. His body ached with it. Hanner would pay him back for the aggravation.

Reaching beneath the table, Andrej unfastened the shackles that bound Hanner wrist to wrist at opposite ends of the table's width. Trefold shackles. Hanner didn't move, being freed; Andrej wrapped the chain around Hanner's throat and tightened it snugly. Then snugged it a little more tightly.

"Come, let us discuss this once more in detail." Hanner made a gesture as though he wanted to raise his hands to his throat, to catch at the cord. Hanner didn't dare. Andrej cinched it more sharply yet, just to enjoy the choking sounds Hanner made in his throat. "Onto the floor with you, my young friend. Onto the floor—"

Andrej pulled, and Hanner fell, putting out his hands as he tumbled over the edge to try to break his fall. What a bore. Should he have Hanner back up to the table again, and fasten his wrists behind his back, watch to see how Hanner took the impact then?

He was getting drunk. But his fish would not rule him.

"Here is a thing that I learned long ago." Crouching down to the floor over Hanner's prone body Andrej knelt, with his left knee squarely planted in Hanner's back and his foot flattened sideways against weeping flesh. "It is about Nurail and stubborn-headedness. That is perhaps redundant. And yet the trick was a useful one."

He'd had Security to help him, that once long ago. He was much more practiced in atrocity now than he had been. He could do this himself. One hand flat to the shoulder to keep it in place. One hand at the elbow, to draw it around, to twist it up behind and pop the crozer-hinge—

Then, as before, his prisoner had screamed.

But now, shockingly, there was no slipping of a joint out of socket, but the ugly grinding snap of a bone fractured brutally. A compound fracture. Not a disjoint.

Andrej stared at the shoulder, the undeformed shoulder, the shoulder that showed no hint of the crozer-hinge; stared at the shoulder, and at Hanner's arm, still gripped firmly in hand.

Holy Mother.

In the name of all Saints.

Hanner had called the woman Megh his sister, and she was hill-country Nurail. Andrej realized with all-consuming horror that he had assumed—

But the evidence could be interpreted no other way. Skelern Hanner was from Burkhayden. He was not hill-people. He had no crozer-hinge.

Hanner was Burkhayden Nurail, not hill-station, but there was no way in which a Nurail without a crozer-joint could have thrown something that hard and that fast. The Lieutenant's neck had been all but completely cut through. There was spinal bone, and the trachea was tough, and a good deal of muscle was always required to hold a man's head up upon his shoulders—

"Please, Uncle, please, I didn't mean harm by it, just watching. She's such a pretty thing. I can't confess a thing that isn't true—"

Andrej pushed himself away from Hanner's wracked body and backed away a pace, afraid. Two paces. Three. What could this mean, if Hanner had no crozer-hinge, if Hanner had no crozer-joint, if Hanner could no more throw a crozer-lance than he could?

"Please, Uncle, please Uncle . . . it was only Sylyphe, I couldn't stop watching. I can't bear longer, maybe it's better—oh, take me to death—"

Hanner was not thinking. To confess now would be to be relieved of pain, but only temporarily. And for Andrej to permit Hanner to confess at all would be a sin, as well as an error: because Hanner was innocent.

Andrej knew that now.

What had Captain Lowden said to him, about confession?

It had been important.

Crossing the room to the door at an unsteady jog Andrej shouldered it open to hail the Security who stood on watch outside. Or sat on watch, but he wasn't going to be difficult about it, it had to have been difficult enough to keep watch at all outside the courtroom, empty as it was. Sound would carry.

"His Excellency requires?"

It was Janisib, his Jan. All to the good. "A medical team, and immediately, Jan. Also to the Port Authority call for an escort, but to the hospital first. There is no brief. This prisoner is innocent."

He didn't wait for an answer. He wasn't interested in discussing the issue. Turning back into the wide cold room Andrej closed the door again with a decisive clicking of the latch; and made his way across the floor to where Skelern Hanner lay. Hanner cried out to himself when he saw Andrej coming; Andrej didn't know how much more of Hanner's anguished fear he could abide, not now, not now that he knew that Hanner was not for him.

His fish didn't know.

His fish thirsted for the caress of Hanner's cries.

And fish had the power to cloud men's minds with the thought of the ocean. How else was he to understand how he had spent these hours with Hanner, and never once asked himself the obvious question?

There were painkillers in his field interrogations kit, but hardly enough of them. Andrej approached Hanner with a dose, but Hanner was afraid of the dose, and the persuasiveness of Hanner's terror was almost more than Andrej could stand.

"Sh, there is nothing, not any more." Could Hanner hear him? Could Hanner understand? "It is an anodyne. We are well past the time of testing, Hanner, the drug has not failed. You will be released, and you will go to hospital, but for now you must try very hard for me. To be quiet."

The ocean was made of salt water, and to drink in the imagination only made a man more desperate for the draught. His gentlemen understood. But his gentlemen were not here.

"Ex. Len. Sie," Hanner sobbed aloud, through obediently clenched teeth. "I. Don't under. Stand."

Loose the cord around Hanner's throat. Loose the manacles around Hanner's wrists. The medical team would take—how long? There were not very many mobile units. And there was a party going on in one form or another across the greater part of Port Burkhayden tonight. He needed a blanket to cover Hanner, to keep him safe from cold and shock until the medical team arrived.

"Hush. Rest yourself. It has been a mistake. You were right all along." There was no chance of an apology, no. But under the circumstances the fact that the error had been discovered in time would have to do. It had been a close thing. Hanner had been close to confessing a fault that he had not committed, and—Andrej asked himself—would he have understood the difference? As urgent as his fish was for its playground?

Hanner was naked, Hanner would get cold. Andrej fetched his over-blouse from the back of the chair they'd set out for him and draped it carefully over the worst of the whipping. "I am only going to see about a cover for you, Hanner. I'll be back. Don't try to move. You will be safe now."

Once Andrej had but spoken to the Port Authority Hanner would be safe. And not before: but Hanner need not know that.

"I can't fault you for wanting her, but please." Hanner's voice arrested Andrej in mid-flight, halfway across the room. Hanner spoke in a lisping sing-song characteristic of the euphoria that pain-ease could create. "She'll pine if she's to go from her garden. Oh, please."

Whatever that meant.

He would have to carry the news to Captain Lowden—

But first.

There was something that Andrej had to do, first.

If only he could remember what it had been before it was too late.

CHAPTER EIGHT

Ordinarily the staff gynecologist was not an emergency services physician, and wouldn't be found pulling duty past midnight. But the public-funded here at Port Burkhayden was still too grossly understaffed for such considerations to be honored, and Barit Howe had more of a general grounding in trauma than many in his specialty. It came from the years he'd spent assisting Inquisitors in Secured Medical, inflicting trauma at the direction of a superior officer.

Also since he had those years behind him Howe figured himself for the natural choice, if someone was to go speak to Andrej Koscuisko.

"All right," he said, low-voiced, to his transport team. "Safe to load. I'll just speak to the officer, carry on." Or carry out. Out of this room, Koscuisko's ad-hoc torture chamber, what had once been Judicial chambers. Away from Koscuisko.

The officer himself sat with his back to the wall, well apart, a bottle of overproof wodac in one hand and an unreadable expression on his face. Barit knew it was overproof wodac, which made him a little concerned about the fact that Koscuisko was nearly halfway into it already. Overproof wodac was poisonous. But Koscuisko was Dolgorukij.

"Your Excellency," Howe called out, firmly, and approached Koscuisko where he sat. "You're to come to hospital, sir? We're ready to transport."

He wasn't quite sure whether he was asking Koscuisko or telling him. That would be funny in a little while. Right know he didn't yet know whether he had a problem.

Koscuisko started a bit, as if surprised to be spoken to. Koscuisko was drunk, or Koscuisko should be well on his way, with half a bottle of overproof wodac under his belt. Or waistband. Whatever. Koscuisko didn't sound particularly tipsy, for all that.

"I must to the Port Authority rather go," Koscuisko said. No slurring. No halting; no particular lack of control over the pitch or pacing of his speech. "How is Hanner? I fear for his future, if the shoulder has been too badly compromised."

From another Inquisitor this might have been a plea for reassurance, a petition for kind soothing words about how the prisoner really wasn't all that badly hurt, or had only gotten exactly what he deserved. Barit couldn't read anything of the sort, coming from Koscuisko. Koscuisko was talking to him plainly, man to man, without excuse or apology: one professional to another, and no pretense between them.

"Looks as though the officer meant to go for a fracture?" Barit asked, carefully. It would help if they knew how Koscuisko had approached the traumatic event. All in all Koscuisko had been remarkably careful with his prisoner, in light of the charges and the amount of time Koscuisko had been working on the man. Barit was impressed. Koscuisko knew what he was doing.

"No, I thought to put the crozer-hinge out of joint." Koscuisko's explanation sounded perfectly rational, but Barit was worried about it regardless. Hanner was Burkhayden Nurail. Hadn't Koscuisko known? "And splintered the bone rather. I am an idiot, Mister Howe. I should have realized hours ago."

All right, Koscuisko had made a mistake. Koscuisko was not perfect. The fathomless depths of self-disgust and loathing that seethed beneath the surface of Koscuisko's calm recitation were frightening to behold. Above all else Barit didn't want to fall in. And Koscuisko had done less to harm his prisoner, these hours past, than a lesser torturer might have done in half the time; Koscuisko could afford the error. He had ample margin.

"Better late than never, sir." Wait, that wasn't a particularly graceful thing to say, was it? Fortunately Koscuisko had lifted the wodac bottle to take a pull at its narrow mouth, and did not seem to have noticed the clumsiness of the attempted reassurance. "The Port Authority, you said, sir."

"Yes, absolutely." Koscuisko lowered the bottle, and frowned. "This is a defective flask. See, it is near empty . . . Yes, I must to the Port Authority go, Mister Howe. The Captain has cried the offense against Skelern Hanner, I must be sure the gardener is protected under law before I tell Captain Lowden of the disappointment. He is to be very displeased with me, I'm afraid. I do not look forward to it."

Unfortunately, Koscuisko's nonsensical phrasing made sense. Barit Howe had heard rumors about Fleet Captain Lowden that made Andrej Koscuisko look like a paragon of ethical behavior. The officer wanted to go on Record about Hanner's innocence before Captain Lowden found out, and for that the officer had to go to the Port Authority. Barit wondered what it was that made Koscuisko so certain of Hanner's innocence.

"We're away, then, sir. If his Excellency will excuse me."

"Have I said extract of allock?" Koscuisko asked suddenly. "Nine units per body weight. Based on estimation I went eleven and three, with another ten and six to follow up after the first two eights had elapsed. It is a sizable dose, and you know how stubborn extract of allock is to metabolize. Have you sufficient sansanerie for his pain?"

Because with that much allock in his system the standard anodyne would be close to useless. Barit bowed. "We'll find enough, sir, I promise. Is there anything else?"

Koscuisko held the bottle up to the light, squinting suspiciously at the fluid in the bottom quarter of the flask. "Tell them to bring wodac." Barit couldn't decide whether Koscuisko was actually answering him or not. "I need to go to the Port Authority. And I want a bottle of wodac. This one is not working, someone has adulterated it."

They were lucky to have gotten the word on the speak-serum. He wouldn't have guessed allock. Koscuisko had clearly been determined to give his prisoner a fighting chance of standing the test and living through it: he hadn't cheated with the speak-serum.

It had been well done of Koscuisko, in a sense, even if the pressure Koscuisko had brought to bear had more than made up for the relatively benign action of the speak-serum. Hanner would not be crippled. And Hanner would not be put to death, either, or at least not for the murder of the Fleet Lieutenant.

His emergency team had already cleared the room; Koscuisko's people were waiting a little uncertainly at the door. None of them were green-sleeves. Barit had wondered what they were doing there.

"He says he wants wodac," Barit advised the senior man, a tall Shikender woman whose fine clear features were set now in a grimace of concern. Barit could only suppose they knew how to handle Koscuisko on a drunk; they were his people, after all, whether or not they were bond-involuntaries. Weren't they?

What he didn't know was how aware they might be of what else seemed to be going on in Koscuisko's mind. "If you don't mind my saying so. I'd keep a careful eye out. Not as though I think I need to teach you your job, mind you."

He didn't want to insult anybody. He would have been much happier about leaving Koscuisko to get to the Port Authority had these Security been bond-involuntary. But he had a patient. And Koscuisko was not his officer, after all.

"Thanks." The senior Security troop was frowning through the open doorway at the dark slumped figure of Andrej Koscuisko in his chair, emptying a bottle of overproof wodac. Koscuisko had put his over-blouse back on, but he hadn't fastened it. And his over-blouse had been soaked with blood from Hanner's back. Koscuisko hadn't seemed to notice. "We'll keep it in mind."

With a patient waiting, and with a keen appreciation for the fact that these people knew Koscuisko as he could not pretend to, Barit Howe knew he had to be content with that. That was all he could do. The limit of his authority. The extent of his influence.

That, and to get a call in to the Port Authority, and let the people on staff there know that Koscuisko's people might need some assistance in dealing with their officer.

Assistance: and if it could be managed, a bottle or two of overproof wodac.

Stildyne worked his way through the shadows and the service corridors around the periphery of Danzilar's great glittering dancing-arena collecting people one by one, alerting others. If he was going to have a problem he needed for it to be well contained; and well concealed, of course. Robert would have seen him coming: Robert knew how to watch, and what to watch for.

Mendez had been right about the man. Even from across the room Stildyne had been able to tell that Robert wasn't in top form immediately, while Robert for his part had reacted to making eye contact with an expression that seemed almost one of fear.

Robert surely had no reason to be afraid of him, no serious reason, not as long as Andrej Koscuisko stood between them both; and in point of fact the only thing Stildyne had against Robert St. Clare was Andrej Koscuisko. There was no reason why the man should be so white in the face on his account.

As Stildyne came up quietly from the safe dim passageway behind Robert he could see that Robert was actually shaking as he stood. Robert's light gray duty blouse was black between his shoulders, stained with sweat. Worse than he had guessed. Not good at all.

"Robert. Would you come with me for just a moment, please."

He knew Robert had seen him coming, and had heard him approaching through the corridor behind his back. Yet Robert gave a start, as if surprised; and stamped one foot hard, flat upon the floor, as if he'd been a nervous yearling racer. Turning slowly, without speaking, Robert followed Stildyne's pointing hand into the small as-yet-unfurnished private room at the opposite side of the service corridor, and waited there—facing the wall—while Stildyne checked to ensure that the others were in place before he followed in his turn, closing the door. He had the corridor sealed as far as necessary. He wanted to be sure that there would be no interruptions.

The door-latch clicked, and Robert started again, his trembling more evident now than before. Robert was bond-involuntary, and his governor had never been quite right. There was a distinct possibility that it chosen this particular time and place to slip out of tolerance; which was a very unpleasant thing to happen to a man, even in return for the years of relative freedom Robert had enjoyed as a result of its diminished function.

"Turn around and talk to me, Robert; you don't look well. Are you all right?"

He had to be careful, because he didn't know for certain what was going on. He had to be compassionate, because sometimes

Robert could not bear up under disapproval, and there was nothing to be gained from tormenting a man who was at the mercy of imposed constraint. But mostly he had to take good care of Robert because of Koscuisko. He took good care of all of them; Koscuisko did not play favorites. But Koscuisko had favorites. There was nothing anyone could do about that, and nothing in particular wrong with it, either.

Robert had not yet moved, had not yet spoken. Stildyne went up to him, to take his shoulders in what he hoped would be a reassuring gesture. "Can you tell me what is happening to you, Robert?"

But the moment Stildyne touched him, Robert cried out. Not loud, but high-pitched and hoarse and desolate, falling down heavily onto his hands and knees on the floor. Crouching swiftly down beside him Stildyne tried to see how bad it was; he wasn't going to be able to help unless he could get an idea of what was going on. "Talk to me, please, Robert, what's hurting you so much?"

Because that was the expression on Robert's face, his eyes closed tightly against the sight of something terrible, his teeth clenched behind drawn lips that were white with tension. He could not keep his balance even on all fours, apparently. Collapsing slowly, Robert rolled onto his back, half-leaning against the freshly covered wall.

And then he spoke.

"Give me a knife, oh, if you ever loved him. Please. I couldn't stand, for him—to have to—"

A knife? Robert went under arms; they all did, all of the Security who had come down here with Koscuisko days ago. What did Robert need a knife for that he couldn't do as well or better with his sidearm?

"Can you tell me what is happening to you? Do you need a doctor?"

Robert pulled his knees up to his belly, in an apparent spasm of ferocious pain. "It's not a thing that I'm allowed to say. But it's my only chance, you've got to see."

Physical pain, yes. But something more than that was going on, because if Robert could speak at all he should—all else being equal—be capable of making much more sense than he was making just at present. Asking for help, at the very least. That was the natural thing to do, the first thing most people did when they started to hurt as badly as Robert seemed to be.

"All right. We'd better get you to hospital, something's gone wrong with your governor. We'll get sedation there, hang on, for just a while longer—"

Speaking as soothingly as he could Stildyne started to move away. They needed to get a dose into Robert, first off. Then they could start to try to understand what he was on about. Robert surprised him, though, clutching at his sleeve in a clearly desperate attempt to call him back.

"No dose, no doctor. He's going to know. He's got to. And he'll realize. And then what comes next, it's not for myself that I'm asking, but him, what will it do. To him. You can guess—as well as I—"

"Who? His Excellency?"

Maybe he did need to try harder to understand.

Because what he was beginning to think that he almost imagined Robert might be interpreted as hinting indirectly at was too potentially terrible for him to be able to afford to take any chances.

"I tried to tell him, oh, I tried, I swear it. And the—damned thing— wouldn't let me. He'll remember. And after he's looked after me—for years."

The phrases were beginning to break up, but not enough. Stildyne began to believe that he knew what Robert was saying.

"You. Are worrying about Koscuisko."

Why?

What crime could Robert, of all people, possibly have committed, that he should go in fear of Andrej Koscuisko?

What crime had been committed recently—

Robert caught his breath, as if even thinking about it gave him pain. If Stildyne was right about what was on Robert's mind, then it should cause him pain to even think of it.

No, his governor wouldn't let him speak unless questioned, because he was supposed to be protected against self-incriminating utterances to a limited extent.

But the governor would punish a violation as well. It had access to pain linkages.

A carefully moderated access, at least when the governor was working properly; but if Robert had managed what Stildyne thought Robert was trying to tell him that he'd done, the governor could hardly be said to be working at all. Except now, when it was too late to prevent a violation. Now it was being very thorough about punishment, from all indications.

"If I'd even tried to think . . . it would have stopped. Stopped me."

Indeed. It should have stopped him anyway. Robert was right to beg for a knife, to kill himself. Stildyne realized that deep down at the innermost core of his constantly compromised moral self he really didn't care what happened to the man they'd taken for the murder, one way or the other. But if Koscuisko was to be required to execute the Protocols against Robert St. Clare it would destroy him. Completely. Irrevocably. Past any hope of self-forgiveness or recovery.

He was going to have to shut Robert up, because if he could grasp the problem there was the danger that someone else could do the same more quickly. First Officer, for one. He needed to keep Robert safely silent until he had a chance to find out how it was going with Koscuisko's interrogation. If there was going to be a problem then he would take Robert out before Koscuisko could begin, no matter what the consequences. Koscuisko would understand, Koscuisko would not blame him; not then.

But he couldn't risk preemptive action, dared not silence Robert forever—yet. It was too soon. There was a chance that it would be all right, if he could just keep Robert under wraps until he had more information.

"He loves you. You know that, don't you?" That meant that he was going to have to play a dirty trick on Robert. Stildyne regretted the necessity, because all else aside he did respect the man and hadn't ever actually disliked him.

It was the only way he could think of, on such short notice, to ensure that Robert would be still and not say anything potentially compromising on their way to the hospital. He chose his challenges with care accordingly, confident that at the least he knew what was going to hurt.

Robert folded himself into a compact and defensive huddle, lying on his side now on the carpeted floor. "I did not think. About." The anguish in his voice was deep and genuine, but Stildyne was jealous for Koscuisko's interest, and refused to let himself be deterred from his purpose.

"Loves you, and you know he has the dreams, you know how bad they are. Just think. If it hurts him the way we've seen it hurt him in a dream. Just think, Robert, imagine how much worse it's going to be when it's all real. Tenth Level—"

The sweat ran down Robert's colorless cheeks in little rivulets, his eyes gone wide and staring. "I saw my sister. And. I had to, like." But he could still speak. Stildyne could not afford to let him speak.

"It will kill him. Kill him. But not all at once. You've got to know he won't be able to live, with that in his dreams. Because of you. You've murdered him. How could you do that to him, after all these years?"

Brutal, but effective. Robert moved his lips as if he were trying for a word; but no sound came, just a strained wheezing noise of air passing through the constricted passageway of his windpipe. Crouched down beside Robert on the floor, Stildyne waited until he felt that it was safe to bring the others in on this—until he could be sure that Robert could no longer speak, because of pain.

And now he had to hurry, to get Robert to hospital. Where he could get painease for Robert, and as soon as possible.

Because the pain was clearly terrible.

But silence was of paramount importance.

Jils Ivers watched the Danzilar prince lift his dance partner down from the dance floor with perfect and chaste gallantry, and suppressed a grimace of rueful jealousy. Yes, she was very much the senior of that very young woman, and she didn't regret more than half of the years she'd spent attaining that status.

It was still true that a woman's knees stopped flexing quite so nimbly somewhere between knowledge and wisdom. She hadn't had the bounce that characterized that young woman's step since she'd been . . . since she'd been how old?

"Oh, fine," Garol snarled at her under his breath, standing beside her with his arms folded hermetically over his chest. "And it's little Sylphe Tavart, none other, wouldn't you know. It's her gardener. At least it's her mother's gardener, and what do you suppose she's been talking to our host about? Four guesses, Jils, and the first three are tax due the Bench."

Garol had been in a filthy mood all evening, ever since prince Paval I'shenko's party had gotten off to such a hideously disastrous start. A completely contained and controlled disaster, she'd grant them that.

The news had started to trickle out, of course, but only in bits and threads, so that no five people heard it all at once, and no one would be able to quite credit it at all until some magical psychological mass was attained beyond which everyone would know but no one would be able to remember quite how they'd heard. It was delicately done. It was beautifully done. It was impressive.

It made her wonder whether Garol was right about the threat he claimed the Dolgorukij Combine would ultimately pose to the rule of Law.

Their host paused halfway between the dance floor and where she and Garol were posted to kiss the young Tavart's hand with formal courtesy, and then slip his arm around her waist and kiss her again, very cordially indeed, upon the cheek, with every appearance of having been overcome by a spontaneous impulse.

Jils didn't believe it.

But she wasn't about to ruin the girl-child's dance by even thinking about her skepticism too loudly. The Danzilar's people came up around him; laughing and panting, fanning himself with a white-square and stumbling a bit in apparent tipsiness, prince Paval I'shenko made his way across the crowded room to rejoin them and continue the discussion he had interrupted to go dance. Danzilar had been working hard and steadily all evening. Jils was sure he'd danced with half the women there. He knew his business, did the Danzilar prince.

"Yes, now," Paval I'shenko greeted them, waving his white-square. Someone plucked it out of Danzilar's hand and replaced it with one delicately scented with jessamine and clovax. The Danzilar prince took no apparent notice, leaning up against two of his house Security and opening his collar; smiling all the while as though being out of breath was an enormous joke. "We were talking. Garol Aphon, you are not drinking, how can this be so? Jils Tarocca, I upon your kind offices fling myself, as for mercy. Garol Aphon is not having a good time."

"It's against his religion, your Excellency." This brisk bantering came as second nature to her. She never felt she was particularly good at it, but she enjoyed it regardless. The genius of the Dolgorukij autocrat-entrepreneur lay in making a person feel as though they were masterful in repartee even as they stumbled. "Or if not, then perhaps our standard operating procedure. I haven't checked lately."

Paval I'shenko had gestured to someone over the heads of the house staff that surrounded them. Taking a break from his host duties, he stood alone in the middle of the bustle and to-do of a very brilliant evening; alone, with only herself and Garol for company. "As long as you are not in a mood which I am in danger of violence to gaiety doing, Garol Aphon, I would like to talk. There is a problem."

Security parted ranks to admit three servers. One with a huge platter of all sorts of sweetmeats and savories; it looked to Jils as though everything Danzilar had laid out for his guests was represented on that great wheel, in miniature, of course. One with a tray and a napkin. One to pour glasses of liquor or rhyti from the flasks on the tray, and sweeten it before it was presented.

"Problem, your Excellency?" Garol prompted, as Paval I'shenko accepted a tumbler full of clear liquid so cold that the glass frosted immediately. Jils fervently hoped it wasn't alcoholic, whatever it was. She couldn't imagine working as hard as the Danzilar prince was working tonight, and drinking at the same time.

Danzilar drained half the flask at one draught and handed the tumbler back to the server. "Indeed, and I wonder if, now that Captain Lowden has removed himself. First Officer. You are not drinking. I am offended, deeply, personally. I am a liar. "

What was he saying? Garol wasn't First Officer of anything; but she was distracted by the sight of all the nibbles on the savory-tray.

The house staff had melted away to either side, opening up an avenue of approach that excluded everyone except for Mendez without seeming to exclude anyone. That was what Danzilar had meant. He'd seen the *Ragnarok*'s First Officer, who was approaching with a Security troop in tow and a very reserved expression on his face.

"Your Excellency." Mendez glanced from Danzilar to Garol to Jils herself, but whatever it was that he had to say it was either too important or not important enough to object to them sharing in the conversation. "Here we've already bled all over your nice white steps once tonight, sir, and I've got bad news. We don't have the murderer."

The Security troop was as tall as Mendez, with the golden complexion of a Shikender hominid. Her looks were distinctive, but Jils didn't think she'd seen the woman recently. Which could very well mean that this particular Security troop had left with Captain Lowden—or with Andrej Koscuisko.

"Indeed? Have a drink, First Officer, tell to me your news. I don't think this is bad. Please."

Mendez declined the offered refreshment with a reluctant bow. "Your Excellency, if I tried to swallow one. More. Bite. I'd explode, and that would be two of the *Ragnarok*'s officers in one night. Our Ship's Inquisitor sent word from the Port Authority. The man who was taken for the killing can't have done it."

And why did she have such a sharp suspicion that Paval I'shenko was not surprised? "One wondered, First Officer, from the very start. And did not like to challenge the Captain, but was it not odd? The gardener and I, we are of a height. And yet such a blow. It was very level."

If Paval I'shenko had had reservations why hadn't he voiced them before now? Jils reconsidered. The circumstances were very delicate. He was only just now come into possession of his Port, and Lowden was a senior Fleet officer—the most senior officer in Burkhayden. The murdered man had been Lowden's subordinate.

"Crozer-hinge, she says," Mendez agreed, betraying no sign of entertaining the confusion Jils felt. "Gardener hasn't got one, and Koscuisko says it can only have been done by a man with a crozer-hinge. Or an engine that mimics one. He's at the Port Authority clearing the documentation, and sent the gardener to hospital."

Paval I'shenko frowned, but so briefly that Jils wasn't sure she'd even seen it right. "They are busy, then. What is it that we can do, First Officer? It has been these hours. Is there hope of good finding, if we mounted a search?"

Shaking his head, Mendez declined the offer of bodies to perform a function that Mendez wasn't expected to direct any more. It was Danzilar's Port. "As you think best, sir, absent strong feelings on the Captain's part. And speaking of whom. I'll need to be notifying my commanding officer."

And Captain Lowden was not going to be pleased. That was the unspoken subtext of this conversation, whether or not Paval I'shenko was in on it. She and Garol both knew what was on the First Officer's mind. And Garol was fidgeting, absentmindedly, drumming the fingers of his left hand against the fabric of his over-blouse, arms still folded across his chest. Left hand, right portion of his over-blouse, and as Garol tapped his fingers in sequence against the fabric Jils thought she heard something.

"Let me suggest this, First Officer," Garol said, suddenly. Paval I'shenko looked moderately startled to hear Garol's voice. "You've had experience with your Ship's Surgeon. Maybe you'd better go to the Port Authority and see how he's doing. Can't have a senior officer off alone at the Port Authority, and I can tell Lowden just as well as you. If you don't mind my saying so."

"Garol Aphon offers himself as the person who bears the bad news," Paval I'shenko announced, to the ceiling. "In this way he demonstrates his charity and accumulates merit, for will the Captain not vent his frustration on a man he does not know, saving the First Officer the unpleasantness? I am impressed, Garol Aphon. Have a drink."

What was Garol tapping at there?

Mendez seemed skeptical. "Thanks all the same, Vogel, but I'd better—"

"Excuse me, First Officer," Garol interrupted, but so cheerfully that there was no offense in it. "But you'd better go police up Koscuisko. Pardon the blunt language, Paval I'shenko. I know you're related, but Jils and I came from the Fleet to here with him. It was a small craft. I think someone who knows that there could be a problem should go and make sure things are settled. And I was just about to excuse myself for the service house anyway," Garol admitted, unfolding his arms finally to give his over-blouse a sharp tug at the hem to straighten the lines. "Hadn't mentioned it, didn't want to be obvious about leaving the party. Apologies all around."

Paval I'shenko shrugged. "It seems efficient, First Officer, what do you say? Bring my cousin back to Center House if he is fatigued, or wishes privacy in which to drink. After all, a guest suite has already been prepared for him, as for the rest of Captain Lowden's party."

All of the *Ragnarok*'s officers were to have been the Danzilar prince's guests for the night. Danzilar had a point. And there was something about the way the fabric pulled at the seams of the inner lining when Garol pulled the hem of his over-blouse level at the bottom . . .

"Better you than me," Mendez admitted candidly, giving Garol the nod. "I'm beholden to you, Specialist Vogel."

Garol shook it off. "Not a bit. But I should go soon, if I want to brief Captain Lowden while he's still available. If you'll excuse me, your Excellency, First Officer. Night, Jils."

In his pocket.

Garol bowed to take leave, and as if unconsciously he raised his left hand an pressed it to his chest. Right side. A courtly gesture: but Jils understood, now.

Garol had a warrant.

He was carrying it in the inner pocket of his over-blouse, and whatever it was for, it distracted his subconscious mind when he wasn't thinking about it. So that he kept checking, absentmindedly, to make sure it was there.

"I will give you an escort," Paval I'shenko started to say; but Garol was already almost out of range, moving quickly to the door. Whether or not Danzilar believed Garol had heard him, Garol's intent was clear enough. What did he need an escort for? Port Burkhayden was on holiday; nobody knew who he was. And he was a Bench intelligence specialist. Bench intelligence specialists didn't take escorts from anybody.

Garol had a warrant?

For what?

Or on whom?

Why hadn't he said anything to her about it?

Wasn't it obvious?

Fleet Captain Lowden.

The man was notorious for his corruption, and yet the Fleet refused to give him up to the Bench for trial and punishment. Lowden's corruption was echoed throughout the Fleet at too many levels. He had protection.

Now, having failed to remove an unfit officer through normal channels, someone on the Bench had decided to effect removal in a more direct, if covert, manner.

A Bench warrant.

For the death of the Fleet Captain.

"I'll go check in with the Port Authority, then, your Excellency." Now that it was out of his hands Mendez was clearly not unwilling to accept Garol's offer. "Specialist Ivers, I owe your partner. Later. Your Excellency."

Paval I'shenko waved his white-square, and Mendez excused himself, taking the Security troop with him.

On reflection Jils didn't think that the troop was one of Koscuisko's, though.

Was that a problem?

Did the idea of Andrej Koscuisko in company with Security other than people who really knew him make her uneasy? And if it did, why did it?

"The band-master is playing choice-of-partner," Paval I'shenko said suddenly. He'd left off leaning against his Security some time earlier. His collar was fastened, again. "Specialist Ivers. Do you perhaps in a meuner wish to join me, it is a much quieter dance, I assure you."

She'd sort it out later.

Paval I'shenko wouldn't ask her to dance a second time unless he felt that his guests might have noted their conversation, and the departure of two senior people; and might be wondering. There was nothing to wonder about; everything was under control.

And she'd dance with the Danzilar prince to prove it.

Andrej Koscuisko stood in near-darkness in an empty room on the fifth level of the Port Authority's main administrative building drinking the last of a bottle of wodac and gazing out of the unshaded window toward where the lights from the service house shone brightly amid a Port that was blacked out.

The power had failed, of course, again. The Judicial offices he had come from an eight ago were doubtless dark once more, and here at the Port Authority power was dear enough that the portalume was all that was granted him to light the room.

It didn't matter.

The less light in the room the less obvious its depressing bareness. The less light in the room the more easily he could see the differences in the dark outside the window where the buildings stood back from a street that cut through ranks of warehouses, or whatever stood between the Port Authority and the service house.

Something bothered him, had been bothering him since his

experiment with Skelern Hanner had broken Hanner's arm. Now that the formalities were all completed—now that the Port Authority had opened its Record, and transmitted Andrej's findings, and closed its Record once more—he was at leisure again to ponder on what it was.

Captain Lowden had said something. And it had to do with a crozer-hinge, or why else would he have thought he caught the tail end of the thought just at the moment he'd realized that Hanner hadn't got one?

Captain Lowden wouldn't know about a crozer-hinge one way or the other. He was going to be in trouble with Captain Lowden. He'd had his instructions. And Lowden was going to be almost equally happy with losing his victim as with being exposed in front of the people who'd been there as a bit too quick to condemn a man as guilty of a crime which it was physically impossible for him to have committed. Captain Lowden's self-love would smart at the idea.

The Bench specialist, Garol Vogel, he was no great problem; because they would probably never see him again. But there had been Security.

Bond-involuntary Security.

Lowden was exposed in front of Security, and Lowden would want to soothe his frustrated peevishness by giving Security good reason to forget all about the garden. By reminding Security to live in fear of him. Hadn't Lowden threatened as much already? If Andrej thought of it—

The bottle was empty. There was another. Andrej stripped the seals and checked the first mouthful for quality and consistency. Yes, it was wodac all right, and if his judgment did not fail him it was overproof as well. Wodac warmed the blood, and Andrej was hot, even though he still wore his over-blouse open.

The room was too stuffy, close and confined—that was it. It was the portalume's fault, undoubtedly, the generator was clearly throwing off too much heat. He could go and tell Security just outside the room, though he wasn't quite sure if they were there to guard or to prison him. Security were hard to fathom sometimes. It was just the way things were.

If he tried to go to the door he would know, and he didn't want to. Andrej opened the window instead, forcing the pane up through rusty tracks to the uttermost reach of his outstretched arms. There. Cool air. Cold air. It was better. There was a very great deal of it, all of a sudden, and Andrej shuddered in the cold, taking a drink of wodac. Wodac would warm him up. What had he been thinking?

About the garden. Captain Lowden's humiliation, to have ordered an innocent man to the torture. Lowden's certain displeasure when he learned how Andrej had put Hanner out of his reach; his probable instinct to punish the Security who had been there to witness the embarrassing lapse.

Who had been there?

Vogel, yes, but Vogel was nothing to do with Andrej. Paval I'shenko's house Security. Some of his Bonds, no, one of his Bonds, and Mister Stildyne?

One of his Bonds.

Robert St. Clare.

The man on whom he had first tried his trick with the crozer-hinge, all those years ago, when Robert had played prisoner-surrogate at Fleet Orientation Station Medical, and Andrej had thought he was a true prisoner.

Robert St. Clare, and Captain Lowden had made his point very clearly—that Robert had not been at his post when Captain Lowden went out into the garden. Robert, who was hill-country Nurail, who could engage his crozer-hinge to hurl objects with surprising speed and astonishing force. Andrej had seen him. Robert, and the woman was named Megh. Robert had a sister.

The enormity of the conclusion that presented itself stunned Andrej into half-staggered immobility for a long moment. He almost fell against the sill of the open window; but he caught himself, looking out over the sill to the ground far below. It was a long way. A man wouldn't like to lose his balance. If he should go through by accident he would have very little chance of catching at the grid of the fire-track to break his fall, and there would be no telling whether a man would even survive.

Andrej took a drink, shaken at the narrowness of his escape.

Robert.

Did the Captain know?

Was that what the Captain had been saying to him?

Had Lowden known all along that Skelern Hanner had no part in the crime, and expected that Andrej would take a false confession to protect Robert from the penalty for such a murder?

Such a thing was horrible. It was unthinkable. But it was Fleet Captain Lowden, to the life.

Time and again Captain Lowden had pressed him to go back to prisoners who had confessed. Time and again Captain Lowden had pretended to find cause for suspicion where no real cause lay, in order to generate another few eights' worth of entertainment for himself. Time and again Andrej had bent his neck to the falsehood, and done the deed, and sworn to himself that each was the last time that he would torment some poor creature who should have been allowed to go quickly to death. Time and again. And he whored for Captain Lowden again, every time, and here was where his self-compromise had led him.

Captain Lowden believed that Andrej would condemn an innocent man to a Tenth Level to spare the life of the guilty man, when the guilty man was one of his people.

Could he be sure Captain Lowden was wrong, to have made that assumption?

How could he hope to protect his gentlemen once Captain Lowden heard that Hanner was cleared of all suspicion?

He would cut Robert's throat with his own hand, rather than let Robert face such a death. He would murder his man, even though Andrej loved him, or perhaps because Andrej loved him. He could see St. Clare safe from such sanctions, now and forever after, and take such consequences to himself as might be assessed. He could make Robert free.

But Robert was not the only bond-involuntary on the *Ragnarok*.

How could he protect them all?

Was he to be forced to murder each of them, all of them, every one of them, to put them out of Captain Lowden's power? Did they all have to die?

A knock on the door, someone calling out to him. He could make no sense of what they were saying; he called something back by way of reply, and he had no idea what he'd just said, but whatever it was seemed to work for an answer. There was no further inquiry from the other side of the door, one way or the other. Andrej took a drink. This flask was much lighter than the other had been. It was nearly half-empty.

Trying to murder nine bond-involuntaries would be inefficient.
All he really needed was one death.

One murder would do it. One murder—and one particular murder alone—would ensure that Captain Lowden presented no further threat to either Security or to hapless prisoners unlucky enough to be imprisoned pending Charges when the *Ragnarok* arrived in local space. Only one murder. Obvious.

And if he did the only-one-murder they could have him for it, and that would be only what he deserved, and not enough of it. He should have known. He had had no right to trade the prolongation of suffering of guilty parties for the security of his gentlemen. It hadn't been his bargain to make, because the people who paid the price were not even asked for their thoughts in the matter.

Only one murder.

Setting the wodac-flask down on the floor Andrej leaned carefully out of the window, trying to decide if the fire-track went all the way down to the alley below.

Only one murder.

He had killed so many, and this would be one of the few he had a real right to, even if it would be much more clean and quick than his victim deserved. That didn't matter.

All that mattered was to get the man dead, and for that Andrej had to go to the service house. That was where to find his prey. Andrej knew his habits.

Fortunately—he told himself, with utmost gravity—he was much too drunk to remember that he didn't like climbing down from high places.

Carefully Andrej swung his weight over the windowsill. Carefully Andrej found his foothold on the fire-track to climb down out of the building.

He couldn't possibly take Security with him.

They were supposed to see that murder didn't happen, and that meant that they could only be in his way.

The fire-track was old, but it held his weight.

Only one murder.

It was past time.

He should have killed Fleet Captain Lowden four years ago, when he'd first realized what Lowden meant to the world.

CHAPTER NINE

Stildyne had meant to shut Robert up, and he had, well and truly. The closer they got to the hospital the more anxious Stildyne was to arrive. Robert wasn't just suffering. He wasn't only in agony. Robert was wrapped six atmospheres deep in frightful torment, unable to move. Unable to speak.

Stildyne didn't dare simply cuff him across the back of the head hard enough to deprive him of consciousness. Governors were delicate at times, and making so abrupt a transition from fathomless anguish to the painease of oblivion could do Robert damage. Stildyne dare not risk it.

He'd seen a bond-involuntary die in overload, once, only once, before Andrej Koscuisko had come to *Ragnarok*. Captain Lowden had forced Lipkie Bederico into overload. It had been three days before Medical convinced the Captain that there would be no sound or speech from the man ever again.

Only then had Lowden authorized termination. Only once Captain Lowden had realized that he would have no sport out of pain that extreme.

Why hadn't he just knifed the man?

What had he been thinking?

No, he knew what he'd been thinking. He'd been thinking that he needed to keep Robert quiet until he could determine whether or not the gardener confessed. If the gardener confessed Robert was safe, except from his governor. If the gardener didn't, then Koscuisko would want to kill Robert himself.

Emergency admitting was surprisingly busy. The man who brought the tech team out onto the loading apron to greet them was someone Stildyne had seen before, when he'd come to the hospital looking for Koscuisko and his people. Barit Howe. A man reborn. Garrity and Pyotr got Robert loaded on his back on the mover; and Howe took one look deep into the pupil of Robert's staring eye and said something surprising.

"Should have just pulled it way back when," Doctor Howe swore to the world. "And us not so well equipped. All right, you lot. Through there. Emergency, gross cranial. Damn the officer for being drunk."

Whatever this meant to Barit Howe it meant nothing to Stildyne, who followed the mover into emergency and through to the treatment room with Security trailing. "Hey. Wait. Come on." Doctor Howe had to talk to him, let him know what was happening. Didn't he? Shouldn't he?

The tech snapped the neural cradle into place, and Robert's body began to relax. But the registers on the diagnostics fluctuated so wildly that they looked random and meaningless. Stildyne tried again. Robert had friends who had a right to know. "Doctor Howe. What's going on? What's the matter? Talk to me."

Doctor Howe ignored him for long moments, watching diagnostics. Registers rising, and slowly stabilizing. An orderly came in with a fistful of styli, and Doctor Howe put them through one by one. At the throat. At the groin. At the back of Robert's neck, lifting Robert's head from the neural cradle.

Some of the registers started to fall.

Stildyne could hear Robert breathing now, or half-sobbing, and Robert had been so quiet that Stildyne was glad to hear even the sound of Robert suffering. But Robert shouldn't be permitted to suffer. Koscuisko wouldn't like it.

"Primary failure on governor," Doctor Howe said, finally, staring out through the open door of the room at Pyotr and the rest of Robert's team. "Going to terminal. We're going to have to try for a disconnect. It's all we can do."

The Devil Howe said. "This place rated a neurosurgeon with the specs?" Stildyne demanded. It was up to him to defend Robert's interest. "I don't think so, Doctor. You'll stabilize. And wait for the officer. We'll pull him out of Inquiry if we have to. He wouldn't tolerate anyone messing with Robert's governor but him, if it has to be done."

The cold stare Stildyne got from Doctor Howe in response was more than adequate reminder that Howe was a man reborn, and had little use for Chief Warrant Officers. Little cause to consider their words or advice. "Your officer's out of Inquiry already," Doctor Howe claimed. Stated flatly. "And under the influence of overproof wodac. I've just left the team that's repairing the man who was being questioned. Koscuisko's gone to the Port Authority to make things straight, but he's drinking. He's unfit. And if we botch it he can blame us."

Instead of himself?

What did Howe mean, out of Inquiry?

"We can't let him bide like this; Koscuisko wouldn't want us to." Doctor Howe was speaking almost gently, now. "There isn't a Safe in Burkhayden. We've no choice."

Stildyne stepped up to the head of the level on which Robert lay, stunned by the magnitude of this disaster. Of his crime. He'd known Robert would suffer. He'd meant to overload Robert's governor and put him out of the range of coherent communication. He'd never imagined that it would go terminal. What was he to do?

"And we can't let Koscuisko try to operate, even if Koscuisko wanted to. Because if the man dies Koscuisko would blame himself, and there's history between them, in case you didn't know."

Drugs or no drugs Robert's suffering was terrible to look upon. Stildyne didn't want to hear about history. He didn't care about Robert's history. He'd wanted to save Robert's life if he could, if he could keep Robert safe. But it wasn't going to work. He'd made a mistake. He'd killed Robert, wanting to preserve his life. That was what Barit Howe was telling him.

"You've got to make it stop." Stildyne had no choice but to submit, after all. Doctor Howe had made that clear enough. "I don't know about history. I only know that Koscuisko loves him." In Koscuisko's fashion. And Andrej Koscuisko was a passionate man who loved passionately, even while the affection Koscuisko bore his bond-involuntary troops never seemed to connect with Koscuisko's sexuality.

But Stildyne had known all along that Koscuisko loved Robert, and would never love *him*, so that was nothing new. "And he's a good troop. And nothing he could ever have done would deserve this. When will we know?"

If Robert would live.

Doctor Howe put his hand to Stildyne's shoulder and pushed him gently out of the room.

"See to this one," Doctor Howe advised Pyotr, giving Stildyne a little push—to move him out into the center of the room, Stildyne supposed. "We'll get started. We'll know in two eights. Think positive."

Koscuisko at the Port Authority, Doctor Howe had said. Stildyne didn't dare go to the Port Authority now. And he didn't have the heart to send Security; these were Robert's team. If the Day dawned for Robert St. Clare in the middle of the night in Port Burkhayden, they should be here when it happened.

He was to blame for this, and it was a heavier burden than he'd expected. The fact that he'd only meant to hurt Robert, and not to kill him, and for his own good and Koscuisko's comfort, meant less than nothing.

Stildyne's courage failed, and he lacked the strength to send Robert's teammates away while Robert lay dying, waiting for the knife.

They would wait together.

What was he going to tell Andrej Koscuisko?

By the time Andrej Koscuisko got to the service house he was almost sober, which he took to be a bad sign. He had completed an Inquiry, he remembered that very clearly; and the only safe thing to be under such circumstances was as drunk as possible, for as long as possible. Mister Stildyne was nowhere to be seen. It could even be that he would find enough wodac to end it all, finally.

The doors to the service house had been forced open by crowds of revelers in the street, intent on alcohol and fearless of the Port Authority. If the Port Authority had any sense they would stay well clear of the service house, and Andrej certainly saw no Security he could recognize as such.

The lights from the service house were brilliant compared to the greater blackout in Port Burkhayden, but not all so very bright except in relative terms; auxiliary power was limited by definition. Andrej made his way through the streets that were increasingly crowded as he neared his goal, pausing only when invited to take a swallow from someone's flask. Polite people, the Burkhayden Nurail. Hospitable. Generous. He wondered if they would be as inclined to share their liquor with him had they recognized him for who—and what—he was.

Nobody did. It was unnerving, being out under sky, let alone without Security; but in the dark obscurity of the streets his uniform, blouse undone and collar loosened, went unremarked upon, and Andrej felt truly anonymous. It was tremendously liberating. But he was still drunk.

Struggling up the shallow flight of stairs he shouldered his way into the service house, his mind fixed on his goal. Ignoring the indignant shoves of people he displaced. Not hearing jeers from men more drunk than he, about young gentlemen who were in too much hurry to match threads in a weave to take a neighborly sup with honest men. It was less crowded inside the service house, but hardly less chaotic, and Andrej wandered toward the back of the house for some moments, looking for the housemaster.

Nowhere to be seen.

There was a floor manager within reach, though, hurrying from the kitchen out toward one main salon with a box of panlin tucked under one arm and a crisp white linen towel flung over his shoulder. A floor manager would do in the absence of the house-master. Andrej didn't need to keep him for very long.

Reaching out for the floor manager's arm as he hurried past, Andrej caught him at the crook of the elbow. The floor manager spun round to face Andrej, coming near full circle of his own momentum, stopping himself from knocking headlong into Andrej just barely in time. "Ah—"

A muted cry of frustration and surprise. Andrej wasn't interested in making conversation with the man. It was dark in the main hall with only the auxiliary lights to go by, and in the uncertain shadows the expression on the floor manager's face was unpleasantly haughty.

So Andrej spoke first.

He was the senior officer.

People were expected to listen for his word and perform his will without sneering at him, no matter how disarranged his clothing might have become in shimmying down a fire-track five stories to the alley, no matter if his face had got dirty when he'd taken a fall. No matter if his under-blouse was soiled with dried blood. Hanner's dried blood. Andrej didn't want to think about Hanner; he'd probably brutalized the man. No. Where was to drink?

"I need to see Captain Lowden," he said, and loosened his grip on the floor manager's elbow as he read a change in attention in the man's body-language. Because there was no reading the expression on the man's face. It was too dim, and too deeply shadowed. "I have important information which must be set before him. Immediately."

And so much was only true. The floor manager passed the box of panlin and the towel to a woman as she went by.

"Clarie. Take these in, I'll be right there. Sir. Captain Lowden. It's got to be the back lift, sir, the vig-lift's, I mean to say the reserved lift's out of order, sir. Power out and all."

Vig-lift. That tickled Andrej. Very important guest lift. Had he ever heard it called a vig-lift before? But to get to the vig-lift one transferred at a nexus in which a senior officer customarily left his Security to recreate themselves and secure access to privileged suites at the same time. So it was just as well. If he'd gone up the normal way Security would have wanted to accompany him to the next floor to see Captain Lowden. And Security would likely have tried to prevent him from doing what he'd come for. He hadn't even thought.

He was thinking too much now. "Quite all right, floor manager, but let's go now. If you please." Further toward the back of the house, through to the kitchen. Very lucky for him. There were liquor bottles stacked in careful pyramids along the wall. Andrej plucked the nearest bottle off the top of one stack as he passed. It wasn't wodac. But it would do.

The floor manager keyed the security admit on the service lift, and it opened before them. Andrej was reluctant to step into the darkness.

With a half-swallowed curse of distressed frustration the floor manager reached into the lift, and there were lights there. They'd just been turned off. Not very bright, but enough, enough to prove that

there was a lift there, and not just an empty lift-shaft waiting to
swallow him up.

"You'll excuse me, sir," the floor manager said, "if I don't
accompany. Trying to maintain some control. Sir."

It occurred to Andrej that he was as deep into the lift as he could
get; he'd run into the back wall. He hadn't noticed. It was a surprise.
"Quite all right," he repeated. "Carry on." As long as the service lift
would get him to where he was going he didn't need the floor manager
any longer.

By the time Andrej turned around the lift doors were all but
completely closed, and the lift started moving before he could take
half a pace forward to see if he could understand the floor codings in
the near-dark.

Oh.

Good.

The floor-manager must have done that for him, already. The lift
moved slowly, under auxiliary power; Andrej had plenty of time to
sample the bottle of drink he had borrowed from the kitchen. Very
ordinary sort of liquor, distilled from rotten grain rather than honest
tubers, of a sort a Nurail would call "drinkable" but barely even that
to a Dolgorukij. It was far from optimal. But it would do. Andrej
leaned up against the back wall of the service lift and drank as the lift
labored up to the floor where the *Ragnarok*'s Captain would be
waiting for supper.

The lift stopped, and for a panic-stricken moment Andrej was
certain he was trapped between floors.

But then the doors opened, and he realized that he was only
arrived. That was all.

It was much brighter, on the luxury floor. So that was where all the
auxiliary power went, Andrej mused—to the luxury floor. It was a
moment before he was comfortable standing in the little service area
on the landing, it was so bright. Then his eyes adjusted. He knew
where he was. The floor-plans for luxury floors in service houses did
not vary much across Bench installations.

He needed privacy.

It was a shame to waste the liquor, but he could rely on the bar in
the guest quarters to be well stocked. So—much as it grieved him to
spill the drink—Andrej smashed the flask into the control-panel, to

open a port into which he could poke with drink-clumsy fingers till he found the communications module that the lift used to talk with its motivator.

And pulled it through the holes in the wall that he'd broken with the bottle, displacing baseboards and chip-frames and nodes as he did so.

Not neatly done.

But it would do the trick.

Now he would go and see if he could talk Captain Lowden into giving him a drink.

Port Burkhayden was full of Nurail, natives and non-natives, and it was very poor. These things together combined to very satisfying effect for Captain Lowden. There was a certain degree of commonality between one run of Nurail and some Dolgorukij: and this service house had an employee on staff who could almost pass for Aznir. In the dark. If he kept his mouth shut, and why would he speak, if not spoken to?

Two housemen to assist, and the one to comprise Captain Lowden's entertainment—he could play out some favorite fantasies, to while away the hours before he would hear from Koscuisko himself. Had the gardener done it? Lowden didn't care. It didn't matter. Koscuisko would bring him the confession, or Koscuisko knew who would suffer for it, and it would be an additional point of interest— Lowden decided—if he were to keep the blond houseman with him, all through the night and into the morning, and take Koscuisko's report even as Lowden performed certain select of his morning ablutions with the assistance—no, with the enforced assistance—of someone who looked at least enough like Koscuisko for Koscuisko to get the idea.

There was no knock, but the door to the suite opened anyway. So unexpected was the appearance of the man who stood in the open doorway that Lowden almost thought for a moment he'd made his choice known to the housemaster already, and the houseman had come dressed up in costume to play his role.

Surprise lasted a moment, but no more than that. It was Andrej Koscuisko. And Koscuisko was drunk: so much was clear by the stumbling of his feet as he crossed the threshold.

"Andrej. A surprise. Had I asked for you?"

Because Koscuisko was uninvited, unexpected, and would be unwelcome unless he had very good reason to have come this soon. Koscuisko turned his back on his Captain, back toward the door, locking it and throwing the privacy-bolt with sudden single—mindedness. Drunk. Yes, absolutely.

"I need a drink, Captain, one moment. What have they got for us? Oh, good. Here's wodac."

Drunk, and no keepers. All of Koscuisko's Security were back at Center House. The Security that Koscuisko had to have brought here with him, and left downstairs with the others, were Lowden's Security. They didn't know. In all of these years Chief Stildyne had never once let Koscuisko be seen out of quarters when he was drunk.

What was Stildyne afraid of?

"Excuse me, here, Andrej, you're forgetting. I'm the Captain. You're the Chief Medical officer. You answer my questions. What are you doing here? I thought you had work to do."

The suite had a dining table as the central feature of its outer room, with the bedroom and an exercise room through chastely half-opened doors at either end. Pulling a chair clear from the table, Koscuisko sat down. "Oh, we are finished. Yes. I need to talk to you about that. A disappointment."

Took the lip-seal off the bottle of liquor with a casual gesture and drank, slumped in his chair at the table. Leaning well back. Koscuisko's blouse wasn't fastened properly. The neckband of his under-blouse was undone, and all in all the effect was unprofessional in the extreme.

All right. Captain Lowden had never seen Koscuisko drunk. So he'd never had this experience before, of being ignored by Koscuisko, of having to work to extract meaning from what Koscuisko said. Lowden sat down at the table facing his inebriated Ship's Inquisitor. The houseman he would order up could be made to sit there, later on—an agreeable juxtaposition. Not too much later on, though, or the administration would hear about it. Lowden already knew that the port was busy. That was no excuse for keeping Command Branch waiting.

"Explain yourself, Andrej," Lowden suggested, in a carefully genial tone of voice. Koscuisko didn't seem to have remembered that an explanation was owing. "Why aren't you at Bench offices?"

Shaking his head, Koscuisko all but interrupted, gesturing with the bottle. Which had already lost a noticeable amount of weight. "A mistake, Captain Lowden, and that is the charitable explanation. Were I a suspicious man I could think much worse of you. But out of charity I must insist that you actually believed that the gardener might have done it."

What did that have to do with anything?

"Charges are preferred, Andrej," Lowden warned. Had he made too quick an assumption? How else could the situation have been interpreted? "And that means Inquiry and Confirmation. You're good, but you're not that good, no one is. It's only been—how long?"

Charges were charges. And Koscuisko would answer to him for any failure to obey his master's instructions. That man of Koscuisko's, that Nurail, St. Clare . . .

Koscuisko shuddered, and took a drink. "Oh, eights and eights, Captain. And he was very obedient to me. And I wanted him, Captain, I wanted him a very great deal. It was difficult."

Had Koscuisko made a mistake, and killed the man?

Why else would he be speaking of the Inquiry in the past tense?

If Koscuisko had—Koscuisko knew better than to stage any "accidents" —

"Frank language, Andrej." Much more frank, or even coarse, than Lowden was accustomed to hearing from Chief Medical. Lowden began to wonder whether his longstanding suspicions—about what Koscuisko got up to in quarters with his Bonds when he was drunk— were true after all. There would be a good joke in there if so; Lowden could pretend to misunderstand the precise nature of Koscuisko's mission. "You don't want him any longer, I take it? Why is that? Is it—"

Captain Lowden rose to his feet and leaned well over the table, bringing his face closer to Koscuisko's. He could smell the alcohol on Koscuisko's breath. If the joke came off it would be worth enduring the stink of wodac, for the leverage it would give him with Koscuisko ever after. "Is it something I can help with? Perhaps?"

Had this been the key to managing Koscuisko all along, and him in ignorance for all of these years?

Koscuisko just stared.

Then Koscuisko started to laugh.

"Holy Saints, Saints and sinners. Holy Mother. Captain. I would say that I am flattered. But already I am a sinner, without adding so obvious a lie to the list of faults for which I must answer."

Koscuisko's reaction was too pure and immediate to be feigned. But that didn't mean Captain Lowden had to let go of the joke. In fact it only made the joke better. Lowden moved around the table to insinuate himself between it and Koscuisko, who pushed his chair back, frowning. The chair-legs snagged on a fold in the too-worn carpet. Koscuisko couldn't push it back any further than it was.

"Andrej. After all these years. Why didn't you just tell me? There was no need for you to have suffered. Come to bed. You can tell me all about your gardener, in the morning."

"Suppose I tell you all about the gardener now."

No reaction to the invitation. That was rude. He could make Koscuisko regret having rejected him. It wasn't that he had any particular overwhelming interest. It was a matter of principle, now.

"The gardener is innocent. The Lieutenant was killed by a sharp-edged object thrown with more force than most hominids can muster. It takes a crozer-hinge. And Hanner hasn't got one. I checked, Captain."

The more obvious it was that Koscuisko didn't want to play the more Lowden was enjoying pretending he believed Koscuisko did. "Well. If you say so, Andrej. It's all right. You can have another. You look tired, Andrej, you're half-dressed. Why don't you just get out of these dirty clothes—"

Koscuisko's clothing was soiled, now that Lowden got a closer look at it. Reaching out one hand for the front of Koscuisko's blouse Lowden began to play with one of the fastenings in the most obviously seductive manner he knew how—"and we can talk. If it's not Hanner. Who else? What about—"

Koscuisko simply knocked Lowden's hand away, but with the bottle, so Lowden couldn't be sure Koscuisko had meant to make an overt gesture or had merely been raising the bottle for a drink. Lowden was getting a little tired of Koscuisko's studied obtuseness. Time to get Koscuisko's attention. And one thing never failed.

"—what about Robert St. Clare?"

Koscuisko stopped his drinking in mid-draw, and lowered the bottle slowly. Lowden couldn't decide whether Koscuisko looked more startled than sick. Afraid, perhaps; now to press his advantage. Lowden reached out for the open front of Koscuisko's blouse once more, hooking two fingers between the under-blouse and skin this time. Koscuisko stood up.

"What difference does it make? It could have been my Robert, I suppose."

This surpassed all expectation. Koscuisko's stubborn resistance to suggestion was shading fast into out-and-out insubordination. Providing sexual services was not among the duties of any ordinary Ship's Prime, true enough. But Koscuisko had a weak spot. And that weak spot was his Bonds.

"A very great difference to St. Clare, I think, Andrej. There's a death owing. I wouldn't have thought you wanted it to be St. Clare's." He kept his grip on Koscuisko's under-blouse. Lowden could be as stubborn as Koscuisko when it came to that. Koscuisko seemed to have forgotten that Lowden had a hold on him: in more than one way.

"Quite right," Koscuisko agreed. Too readily. "I should very much regret having to kill Robert, though it may come to that. If he has done murder, and there is no other way around it."

Crazy.

That was it.

Koscuisko had gone out of his mind.

There could be no other explanation for the matter-of-fact way in which Koscuisko seemed to have swallowed the suggestion that had kept him to heel all of these years. Captain Lowden wondered where the emergency call was, in this part of the suite. Under the table?

"If he has done murder? Tenth Level," Captain Lowden reminded Koscuisko. Thinking fast. "Command Termination. Are you sure about the gardener? It's a very unpleasant way to die."

Koscuisko stared again, stupidly. At least he wasn't violent, just a bore. "Nothing like that, Captain, for either of you. If Robert has to die I will kill him. But that isn't what I came about."

What had Koscuisko come about?

Koscuisko hit him so suddenly that Lowden almost didn't even see it coming, a swift powerful punch to the middle of his torso just beneath his ribcage. The breath went out of Lowden in a huge violent exhalation, propelled by the force behind Koscuisko's fist. Lowden fell back across the table, gasping impotently for breath. Not finding any.

"I came to deal with you."

Koscuisko moved on him, leaning over Lowden where he lay with his head and shoulders on the table. It was a very awkward position. But Lowden couldn't move. He recognized the experience of paralysis from report: but this had never happened to him before, ever in his life. Nobody had ever hit him in the stomach. He couldn't catch his breath. His chest wouldn't move to draw breath.

"I am as much at fault as you, Captain, I grant you that freely. I should have known from the beginning that a man could not shield one at such expense to another. And yet I have a duty to protect them; they are my people, they belong to me. It is a solution so obvious now that I have finally realized, and after so long."

Koscuisko put his hands around Lowden's throat, wrapped his hands around Lowden's neck as Lowden struggled for air. Thumbs overlapping. Pressing to either side of the trachea. Panic combined with paralysis now; Koscuisko was trying to kill him. Koscuisko had lost his senses. If he couldn't throw Koscuisko off Koscuisko was going to do him serious injury.

He had to throw Koscuisko off.

He couldn't move.

"You have helped me clarify my choices, Captain." Koscuisko was leaning very close to him. The pressure from Koscuisko's grip was increasing steadily, and through the rushing sound in Lowden's ears that threatened to drown out Koscuisko's voice Lowden could hear whispers and promises. Cries, and gleeful laughter; they were waiting for him. But who were they?

"It is either murder them or murder you. And there are fewer of you. And you deserve to die, Captain, perhaps as much as I do, perhaps—more."

The room had gone black; Koscuisko's face disappearing behind a firestorm of ebon sparks. Captain Lowden struggled frantically to flee from the spirits he sensed gathering around him, but though he could finally move his arms and his legs he could get nowhere with them. Flailing wildly at the table, Captain Lowden fought to take a breath.

"And I'll not whore for you or anybody else. Again. Ever."

Koscuisko said something; but Lowden couldn't tell what it was.

Hands reached out of the dark and seized him, hands like claws. Spirits and shadows, they tore him from his body. He could look down from above the table, down on Koscuisko's bent head, and see his own face discolored crimson and white, his eyes staring up at himself as he floated in the air above his body. He reached out for his body, if he could touch his body he could get back to his body, and if he could only get back to his body he would not die. He couldn't die, not here, not now, not with the room full of harpies bent on revenge. He reached out, but he could not touch. His hand would not reach to his body. He could not make contact.

Then the spirits bound him with chains and drove him on before him with whips and blows.

His body stilled where it lay, and moved no more.

Well.

Andrej loosened his grip, finally, surprised at how much hatred he had had for Captain Lowden, surprised at how hard he had had to grip to kill him. Of course Lowden was vermin. And vermin were resilient by nature.

It wasn't any good just killing an insect; one had to make sure it stayed dead. If you put evil into the earth it bred more evil and rose up again, stronger than before—like twining-weed. That was one of the holy Mother's mysteries. Putting evil into the earth was sacrilege, and would be punished.

Only after it was purified in flame could evil be truly laid to rest and confidently expected to stay there.

Only once it was burned. . . .

He couldn't risk the chance that Lowden wasn't dead, that Lowden would rise and walk. He needed fire to cleanse the hatred from his body. Hatred was poison. Andrej wanted to be as whole as he could be; because he was going to die for the murder of his commanding officer. The cleaner he could go to death the better fit he would be to plead his case before the Canopy, and hope to obtain some small measure of mercy.

Fire.

The body lay on the table. It would move in a fire; he had seen the furnaces at the Domitt Prison. He needed to tie the body down, and the toweling wouldn't do, it was too short. The bed-linen tore in strips, though, and the surplus linen piled very nicely beneath the table. He broke up the chairs and laid them on the linen, and soaked the lot with overproof liquor from the stores. Once the fire was well lit it would feed itself. The problem was getting it well lit.

Andrej found a firepoint laid ready in the washroom, in case a patron desired to smoke. The toweling draped over the body quite well. That was dampened with alcohol, as well, though of lesser proof; Andrej had a few anxious moments, when he touched the pyre off, but after a moment or two of uncertainty the sheeting caught fire with an explosive rush of flame that reached the ceiling and set fire to the lacquered plaster there.

Very satisfying.

The fire ran across the ceiling and down the wall, igniting the wallpaper, setting off the wainscoting very cleverly. And in the middle of the room the fire grew and gained in confidence, reaching up to embrace the body, consuming the sin-offering with grateful greed.

Fire.

There was a sudden shuddering sound from outside in the corridor; the firewalls, Andrej supposed. Why hadn't the fire-suppression systems gone off? Was it because they were on auxiliary power? Or was the sudden additional drain simply too much for even the auxiliary power to handle?

It was just as well, one way or the other. This way the body would burn. It needed to burn. Captain Lowden himself would burn as well, in a manner of speaking; but that was none of Andrej's business, any more.

He'd done his business.

He'd finished what he'd come for.

Now he should probably leave the room.

It was very hot, and the thick black smoke from the body as it began to roast was stifling. It would be best to leave quickly. The fire alarms had gone off. Everyone was to evacuate the building, when that happened.

There was a fire on the wall, fire around him, but the fire-door itself did not burn. It was cool to the touch. Andrej knew there was no fire outside the room. Nothing to worry about.

The door closed behind him, flames reaching through the door as he left to snatch at his clothing and try to play. It was a young fire, and very earnest—but easily distracted by the carpet in the hall and the furnishings. Andrej left it all behind him.

The service lift would be out of order.

There was a fire-path toward the emergency exit, the only thing still lit in the rapidly dimming hall as the service house lost all of its power. Andrej opened the emergency exit and got out onto the fire-track, climbing down carefully, hearing people all around him doing the same thing. Joining a steady stream of people struggling down the fire-tracks in the dark.

Hadn't he climbed down a fire-track once already this evening?

He couldn't remember.

Andrej reached the street level, and went to see if he could find some Security. The Captain was dead. He had killed the Captain. Security should be told.

Whatever happened after that, at least Lowden was dead, and would never demand that Andrej exchange one prisoner's pain for a bond-involuntary's safety again.

Ever.

By the time Garol Vogel drew near to the service house the alarm had gone up, and the streets were filled with people and with smoke. It was a clear cold night, with a steady breeze that blew from the bay through the city; so the smoke didn't linger—but there was a lot of it.

The service house grumbled furiously in the night and held its great gouts of black smoke to itself as jealously as it could, so that when a cloud of smoke escaped it was pursued by a shriek of rushing air and the house's utmost ill-will.

The Port Authority was there in force, what there was of one. The fire-machines were there, but the pressure in the firefighting web was low and there were only manual pumps to draw the water through long lengths of pipes from the bay into the city to the sprayers.

Hopeless.

The firefighters weren't giving up, and they had enough willing help with manual pumps to keep the nearby buildings dampened down. But the service house itself was going to burn. The firefighters could either struggle with the fire in the service house and hope to slow it down, or they could keep the fire from spreading; and they knew their business, and their responsibility to the city.

The fire would not spread.

But it would burn out in the service house. It could not be put out.

There was no hope of making sense of the chaos without plunging into it. No hope of crowd control; that could work in his favor, Garol told himself. He was already familiar with the area. That would help too. Locking off the little two-man transter he'd borrowed from Center House to get here, Garol left the vehicle ten blocks out from the service house and jogged the rest of the way. To see what was going on. To find Captain Lowden.

The nearer he got to the service house the more crowded the streets, but they were all onlookers, curious people, everyone pointing and staring and nobody badly hurt. The service house had clearly been packed to capacity when the alarm had gone off—at its lower levels, at least, and a good crowd making a party in the streets as well from what Garol gathered. Nearer Garol went, closer he came, and still there were no burn injuries; still it was a party, and the burning of the service house—while not a cause for celebration in and of itself—was a spectacle worthy of attention.

No one crying in panic for a friend, though there were some concerns voiced about finding people here and there. Garol wondered if the fire alarms went off more frequently in ports with problems with a power supply. He wouldn't have thought it, but it seemed some of these people at least had had practice with fire alarms, practice that had stood them in good stead.

He hadn't found any officials yet.

Garol pressed on to the front lines, within two blocks of the burning building. The night seemed to glow: the firewalls within the building kept the blaze contained, and it was only by accident that a tongue of flame escaped to illuminate the black smoke that boiled furiously now out of every seam and aperture in the building.

He found some officials.

Port Authority.

Joining a huddled group of senior officers Garol introduced himself, to establish his credentials.

"Evening, gentles. Bench intelligence specialist Garol Aphon Vogel, here. If there's anything I can do to help."

The senior man was too occupied with a schematic to more than nod in Garol's direction; but Garol could wait. He was in no hurry.

There were people in this gather from the Port Authority, from the service house, from Center House; but Garol saw no Security. No representative from the *Ragnarok*.

One of the people bowed to him formally, as though the man recognized him; Garol couldn't quite place the man himself, but cheerfully responded in like kind. There was a fire on. No sense in standing on formalities. He was informal enough in his dress and demeanor; but jogging was warm work. Garol intended to apologize to no man for his unbuttoned over-blouse and open collar. Where was the sense in rank distinctions with everyone's face equally smudged by flying soot?

"All right. Everybody. Hear me and heed me," the senior firefighter said. Garol waited for the noise to die down: the noise from the crowd, not so far distant; the noise from the fire. Which was not going to die down. "We're asking you to establish a cordon on a three-block perimeter. You'll be spread thin, but at least we can channel people. Find out if anyone's missing. We haven't heard any confirmed reports of people trapped inside yet; we could be lucky."

Or they could just not have heard any confirmed reports yet. And Garol hadn't seen either Captain Lowden or Lowden's Security. If Lowden were in the area at all he'd be here, with the senior people at this command post. Or he'd have given the whole thing up as a bore and returned to Center House. Which was it?

"With only the auxiliary power we can keep the triage pumps on line. But that's it. Seven eights till sunrise. This place'll smoke for three days."

Maybe next time he was in a port being transferred like this, and the fire suppression systems in the service house were stripped out as they had been in this service house, he would close the service house for the duration. It wouldn't be a popular move. But so few people were hurt so far in this fire that to count on it happening so gently ever again would be irresponsible.

Garol stepped back into the shadows and melted away, wondering where Captain Lowden's Security were.

In a few blocks he found them.

They'd married up with the Port Authority, and were providing assistance with relay communications. But Captain Lowden was nowhere to be seen. Garol considered just asking one of them, but they were busy. And he was beginning to make up his mind that if he hadn't found Captain Lowden yet, Captain Lowden was simply not going to be found. For three days yet. If ever.

Within the circuit of two or three blocks Garol encountered the first of the Port Authority's triage stations, comprised of two people. One to write. One to talk. Interviewing the man who had bowed to Garol earlier; while a small crowd of people waited patiently for their turn, as though it was part of the game.

"—Fleet Captain," the man was saying. "I showed him to the service lift, since the other one was out. I saw the officer around here not too long ago. Name of Vogel, I believe."

This was a surprise. And clearly a mistake. Garol kept to the crowd, anonymous and invisible. Listening hard. It wasn't difficult to get close and still stay hidden; not in the dark, with the smoke and the chaos.

"Bench intelligence specialist, he said. Just now, that is. But I haven't seen the Fleet Captain. I haven't seen anyone who has. And the alarm went off on the preferred suite level, so I'm pretty concerned."

Had it indeed?

The preferred suites, where Captain Lowden would have been quartered.

But Garol knew he hadn't been shown to any service lift. It made a man wonder. Who had?

Who had the service house employee mistaken him for, who had obviously gone up to see Captain Lowden not long before the fire alarm had gone off on the floor where Lowden was staying?

It made no sense. But that was what Bench intelligence specialists were for. Problems that made no sense.

Methodically now Garol worked his way out from the innermost line of defense against the fire through the crowds of gawkers and the people working out to the far edge of the excitement, where people coming in to see the sight traded places with others who'd had enough and were ready to go home.

Looking for Captain Lowden.

Listening for anyone who had seen Captain Lowden.

Not finding anybody.

But there, out on the periphery of the fire's excitement, weaving a bit and strolling quite casually toward an alley, Garol Vogel saw a man he recognized.

About his size.

With a dark uniform, and no real telling the crucial differences, not in the dark.

The over-blouse hanging open all down the front.

The collar of the under-blouse loosened, bare skin showing through.

And the blond hair smudged and darkened with soot, with smoke, with whatever else Garol did not care to guess.

Andrej Koscuisko.

Drunk. Not disorderly, no, but clearly six measures into a five-measure flagon, and where would a man have picked up a bottle of cortac brandy of that vintage if not in the bar of a luxury suite in the preferred quarters of a service house?

Koscuisko hadn't gotten it from Center House.

Because Koscuisko hadn't had it with him when he'd left. Garol had watched him go. And Koscuisko hadn't been back to Center House since. Garol had come straight from Center House. Koscuisko bad been reported at the Port Authority.

It all came together; and when it did it all added up.

Breaking into a quick jog Garol pulled away from the loosely grouped crowd he'd been hiding among to chase after Koscuisko. Garol caught up to him within the sixth block from the service house fire, and greeted him politely.

"Good-greeting, your Excellency. I trust the evening finds you well?"

Koscuisko close up was much more clearly drunk than Koscuisko from a distance had been. There was no response. As far as Garol could tell Koscuisko didn't so much as hear him. Garol tried again.

"Nice night for a walk, sir. Taking any particular route? May I join you?"

This seemed to give Koscuisko pause; but no, he was only steadying himself against a warehouse wall for as long as it took him to take a drink. There was still no way to tell if Koscuisko had heard him.

Where was Koscuisko going?

Where had he been?

"Well, in that case." Andrej Koscuisko was the son of one of the oldest, most influential, trading-houses in the Dolgorukij Combine. The inheriting son. Men with rank and influence couldn't be allowed to wander around strange ports in the middle of the night. It wasn't done.

"In that case I'll show you to the door, your Excellency. If you'll permit. It's this way, sir, I've got a mover."

Particularly when men who by virtue of their birth or position had political importance were also Ship's Inquisitors, and unpopular as a class, and there was already at least one unsolved murder in Port Burkhayden. Garol had no desire to go for two.

Where were Koscuisko's Security?

Had Koscuisko left them at the service house? At the Port Authority? Where had Koscuisko been? What had Koscuisko done?

Garol knew better than to discount his gut conviction that he already knew.

First things first.

He'd get Koscuisko back to Center House, where the Danzilar prince's staff would put him to bed and watch over him.

And then, and then, and then—

And then he needed some more information.

"Yes, sir, this way. Careful. You'll break the bottle, and it's not empty yet."

If Koscuisko had done what Garol thought he'd done the potential political consequences were staggering.

It was best for them all—and for the Judicial order—to keep this anomalous encounter with Koscuisko as quiet as could be, while they found out whether what Garol suspected could be proved.

CHAPTER TEN

Andrej Koscuisko rose slowly into consciousness from the depths of his alcoholic stupor.

There were people in the room: and they were arguing.

Dare lay a hand on him. He's a guest under this roof. The Danzilar prince's hospitality. It's a blood crime.

And arguing back, *not going to hurt a hair on his precious head, relax. Beauty. Come on.*

Nurail voices, by the accent. But why speaking Standard? Because Andrej didn't have any Nurail vocabulary, beyond a few words here and there that he'd learned from Robert over the years. It was odd. He could think of no reason why two Nurail would speak Standard with each other when they were alone.

Someone was coming, and for some reason it was only on hearing someone approach that Andrej realized his eyes were closed. And he was in bed. Divorced from his body, strangely clearheaded, he took stock of his surroundings untroubled by the panic that usually accompanied such midnight wakings.

His body felt sore, but there was no pain. The smell of clean linen: and another fragrance, a perfume. A flower. Danzilar poppies. Beneath that, a stale taint, a sour hint, the smell of soot and street-dirt; and a taste in his mouth. Drugs prescribed Dolgorukij for a surfeit of alcohol, mixed with the peculiar tang of a Nurail remedy for body-wrack.

"Uncle," someone said, very close, very near, as if crouching down by the side of the bed. "Come on, Uncle, don't sleep, we've waited for so long. Open your eyes. Speak to me."

What was the matter of such urgency? Andrej did as he was so forcefully bid; he opened his eyes to look around. Where was his Security?

"Yes. Uncle. Now. Look at me, do you remember, we've met before."

Some Nurail or another, sitting on his heels at the side of the bed. A young man by the looks of him, beardless, his forehead furrowed with concentration in the dim light. It was a very furrowy forehead. Andrej's stomach threatened to pitch, and he raised his head, looking for the flask of medication that was sure to be nearby. Trying to sit up. Failing miserably.

"Beauty, give us a hand—"

Two of them now, helping him sit up, handling him as carefully as if he were made of glass. Spun angel's-hair glass, as brittle as the ice from a single night's freezing. One of them held him, and one fed him a drink of medicine from a flask, and after a moment or two Andrej leaned back. Gazing with mild curiosity at the man called Beauty as he did so. Closing his eyes with an involuntary spasm of horror to see a man so disfigured, the terrible scar that ran the full diagonal of the man's face pulling eye and mouth and chin into grotesque misalignment.

"Remembers me, doesn't you, Uncle." Beauty seemed amused, if bitterly so. "Dressed me as daintily as never-you-mind. And all the while there was our Chonniskot."

Once awakened not even this odd conversation could stop Andrej's mind from returning to its troubles, and he began to wonder about how he'd come to be here. He was at Center House, that seemed clear enough. Someone had brought him, because he certainly didn't remember coming on his own. But if he was at Center House, washed and undressed and put to bed, where were his Security?

Where were any Security?

Were these Nurail here to serve as Security?

"No, open your eyes, please, Uncle. Don't pass out on me, I've been waiting for years for a chance like this, don't ruin it now."

He had no intention of opening his eyes. His eyes were burning. He couldn't keep them open. But the young Nurail sounded desperate, so Andrej blinked twice, squinting in the dim lights at the man at the doorway. Who were these people?

"You're Andrej Koscuisko. You were at Rudistal. At the Domitt Prison. Surely you remember."

He was not interested. "I cannot forget." His voice sounded rusty; he waved for another swallow from the flask, just to moisten his mouth this time. "I am dreaming, yes? Mostly I cannot forget when I dream. Do not speak of it." The Domitt Prison. He would never be free of the Domitt Prison.

"Just this small bit, Uncle. You can give me just this small bit." Wheedling. Persuasive. Andrej turned his head, and met the young man's keen concentrated gaze in the dim light from the night-glims and what made its way around the man in the doorway from the room beyond. Something about the Nurail was familiar. Something about the eyes.

The young man's voice was low and soothing, but even so vibrant with some unexpressed tension. "And I'll never ask you more, but Uncle, I've heard stories. You're the only one alive who knows the truth."

There had been no truth at the Domitt Prison. It had all been a lie, from start to finish.

"You are giving me a headache. Go away." He had more than enough to think about without being distracted by a dream. And he was dreaming. Andrej had no question in his mind about that.

"Only the weave, Uncle, and we'll go. I swear you'll never even see us again, but Uncle, please Uncle, try to remember. My father's weave. The Shallow Draft."

It meant something. Things in a man's dream almost always did. "You've no business with your father's weave. How dare you? Have you no shame? Insolent puppy." And yet if this young Nurail's father was dead . . .

"I beg your sweet forgiveness." And the Nurail sounded sincere. "But it's lawful if there are none other. And I'm the only one survived. The Shallow Draft, surely you remember. He was my father, and you killed him in the Domitt Prison. The war-leader of Darmon."

Now Andrej was there, again, imprisoned in the stinking cell of his dreams, and a tortured man before him. Trying to tell him something before it was too late.

"Have you no charity in your heart." He heard the dread in his own voice, but knew that it would do no good to beg. He was dreaming. This young Nurail was only his own self; it was a dream. He could never get away from the Domitt Prison at night. "It has been so long. Holy Mother. To be away from there."

"There was no charity for my father, why should I have a care for you?" But the Nurail sounded only reasonable, not accusing. "And I have followed you as closely as we dared forever since. Hoping for this chance. Do you remember?"

Oh, he remembered. It had something to do with a clinker-built hull, a warship with so shallow a draft that it could skim over the chains that zig-zagged the mouth of the harbor and tied into a net of mines to destroy any ship that tried to escape. There was a very great deal more to it than that, of course. There always was.

"No, please, you're fading out on me, give it to me again. You must remember."

Well, he didn't.

Not any more than that.

"You expect too much." Always he demanded so much more of himself than anyone else. Why couldn't he just forget about it, and forgive himself?

There was certainly no sense in looking for forgiveness from a Nurail—

But the young man was weeping. "Oh. Is there no more? Is there no more that you remember, Uncle? Please."

The Nurail was in pain, whoever he was, whatever he was doing in Andrej's dream. And Andrej felt sorry for him. He could do nothing. "No. No more. How could you expect me to remember? Why else do you think I had to write them down?"

The arms of the man who was holding him—"Beauty"—tightened around him suddenly, as if in shock. Surprise. Whatever for? Beauty knew perfectly well about the books. Because Beauty was just Andrej, a splintered piece of Andrej, a dream-piece of Andrej Koscuisko with a scarred face.

"Wrote them down," the young Nurail choked. "What did you say, wrote them down?"

This was becoming tedious. Andrej was beginning to feel exasperated with this dream. "There were too many of them. I couldn't be expected to learn one, let alone so many, and in so short a time. Of course I wrote them down. Five. Six. Maybe eight pocket-manuscript's worth, I lost count, I've never so much as looked at them since."

In fact he'd all but forgotten that they were even there, tucked at the back of a records-box. The Bench had not taken them into evidence, because all he'd written in those books was the weaves. It was illegal for any Nurail to possess such material. He'd had a vague thought about transcribing them for posterity. The Nurail would not be the Jurisdiction's whipping-people forever, after all.

Transcribing them, when he went home. He wasn't going home.

Eight years—

But when he stood within the Domitt Prison in his dreams he knew, he'd known all along, that he was never to be permitted to go home.

And he was dreaming.

It was entirely up to him if he wished to wallow in self-pity for a while.

"Holy God," the young Nurail said. "Beauty. Beauty. We have to get on board of *Ragnarok*. Did you hear him? He's written them down."

Yes, that was what he'd said—

Andrej turned his head and closed his eyes. And wept.

Never to go home.

Never again.

And as he wept he fell back through the layers of this perplexing dream experience and deep into profound un-dreaming sleep once more.

Stildyne sat and stared at the wall for two thousand years, trying to understand what had happened. Why it had happened. He'd meant well. He'd meant to hurt Robert, but not to kill him, and he'd done it without malice or pleasure in what he did. To save Robert's life.

Robert had asked to die.

It made no difference, or not enough.

What was he going to tell Koscuisko?

Someone jostled him from behind; people were moving around him. Startled. Concerned. Stildyne looked up. Pyotr was staring across the room, at the door to the place where Robert lay. Pyotr was black, and when he paled the deep color of his skin grayed to sooty ashes. Pyotr was pale now.

"No, it's all right," Doctor Howe called. "Had some trouble with that thick Nurail skull. Doctor Orklen's a genius."

People were leaving the room. Looking tired. But only that. Not looking disgusted, or angry, depressed or accusing.

So it was all right?

"Send in your chief, I want a word with him."

Maybe not.

Maybe they were just putting a good face on it for the troops' sake.

Stildyne rose unsteadily to his feet and stumbled across the floor toward the treatment room, cursing his body for not being as resilient as it used to be. He was getting old. He'd never been beautiful. Life was unjust.

How was Robert?

It was dark in the treatment room, and the ventilators' hushed vibration generated so much white noise that it almost drowned out the sound of Robert's breathing. But Robert snored. It had tripped him up more than once. He was still learning how to sleep on his feet and not give himself away by snoring while he was about it.

"Wanted to show you," Doctor Howe confided. "Didn't like to show the others, not this. They've seen one already. They show it to you before they implant it." The last of the techs left. Nobody had drawn a sheet up over Robert's face. And he was snoring. Stildyne wanted to weep; but he didn't know how. "Have you ever actually seen a governor?"

Having no practice in weeping Stildyne merely held out his hand, numb and silent, to receive the object that Doctor Howe presented to him. It was almost too light to register in the palm of his hand as being there at all.

A governor.

A tiny bit of dull gray metal, with a glittering eye like that of a malevolent spider.

Whisper-thin filaments like gossamer legs, too thin to bear the weight of so much as an idle thought, and yet capable of invoking such ferocious pain that a man could be governed with absolute rigor by fear of it.

This was the thing that had dealt Robert such horror. This was the thing that had put Lipkie Bederico to death by torture, that ruled the lives of bond-involuntaries, that had the power to make a man execute atrocity rather than disobey a lawful order.

If Stildyne had had any religion he would have wanted to exorcise the thing. But he had no religion. So he decided that he simply wanted to crush it underfoot, instead.

"Interesting." Words seemed inadequate. "Take it back. I don't want anyone seeing it. Save it for the officer. How's Robert?"

Doctor Howe sobered. And he hadn't been particularly giddy to start out with. "We were lucky. The governor was half-dead already, or it would have done some damage coming out—it's got a self-defense mechanism, naturally. Can't have people doing surgery to pull governors. Might contribute to the loss of bond-involuntary troops before the completion of their terms."

Doctor Howe was reborn. There was language behind his words that Stildyne did not want to hear. And fortunately for him Doctor Howe continued smoothly.

"One thing, though, and your officer will expect this. He's not going to remember coming to hospital. He's not going to remember much about the few hours immediately preceding arrival, especially any incident that might have been stressful. Extreme stress condition, traumatic amnesia, you know. Now, usually traumatic amnesia will recover over time."

Doctor Howe was wrapping the governor in a bit of bandaging as he talked. And Stildyne was even halfway familiar with what Doctor Howe was talking about. "But in most cases a person will never recover some portion of his life immediately preceding. And with a governor gone terminal I'll be surprised if he can remember anything after his mid-meal, when he wakes up. Fast-meal for sure, yes. Third-meal for certain no. If he had one."

Was Doctor Howe actually giving him absolution, all unawares?

Was Doctor Howe telling him that what he'd done to Robert had actually protected Robert so well that not only was Robert safe from immediate horror, but Robert would not remember anything that might put his life at risk in the future?

"So tell me." Stildyne struggled for words, overwhelmed with gratitude. "When does he wake up? The others. They'll be anxious." Not him, of course. No. He cared only so much for Robert as for any troop, and not so much as for the next troop either, because Robert annoyed him. For himself he would just as soon Robert St. Clare had never come into his life. Complicated.

"You could wake him up now." Doctor Howe sounded a little thoughtful. "Or you could let him rest. The scans are all good. That kind of pain, he'll be exhausted, even with good drugs in him. Send the rest in. You can all sleep in here, if you'd like. But he's snoring. We could put you all on ward with the diagnostics; they'll move. I expect he'll wake up before midday, sometime."

Or sooner.

Robert liked his fast-meal.

It would be all right.

He could face Koscuisko with a clear mind, secure that he'd done what he could to protect Robert, knowing that Robert was safe from himself.

And he'd tackle everything else there was to deal with, in the morning.

Someone came into the room with fresh rhyti and hot bread, setting the tray down beside the head of the bed before leaning over to kiss the back of Andrej's hand where it lay on the coverlet. Andrej woke so easily and naturally as to be unable to make the distinction between waking and sleeping; the habit of the first twenty-odd years of his life still ran strong in him. At least when he was asleep.

Opening his eyes he looked up at a ceiling gaily decorated with a motif called beard-of-grain. Very pleasant. Traditional. The man who had waked him was standing quiet and patient at his left, waiting to be noticed. One of Paval I'shenko's house staff; one of the Danzilar Dolgorukij house staff, that was to say. He'd been on active duty for more than eight years now. He'd never met a Security troop who waked a man in so old-fashioned a manner.

"Holy Mother, bless this child to your work," Andrej said. Half-unthinking. The houseman smiled and bowed in apparent appreciation.

"And prosper all Saints under Canopy this day. Good-greeting, your Excellency, you are anxiously awaited, if you would care to rise and take bread."

Anxiously awaited was probably an understatement. He had

several missions he needed to accomplish himself, but first things first. Sitting up in the bed Andrej took note of the fact that he was wearing someone else's nightshirt; not his, anyway. Reedstalk-work. Very respectable. But all of his linen was worked in lapped-duckwings.

"Thank you. I will wish to dress. There are Security waiting for me?"

He was a little surprised none were here, in the room with him. He just hadn't decided exactly which Security he'd expected to see, or for what precise purpose.

"The prince's majordomo waits upon your will, sir. I'll send someone to see to the towels."

That meant that Security was not waiting outside. He would have to get past the house-master before he got more information, perhaps. Nodding without bothering to probe further Andrej lifted the covers aside and stood up. He was a little shaky. Shouldn't he be sick? Shouldn't he be crawling to the basin, after the drinking that he'd done last night?

Maybe whomever had brought him here had drugged him as well. There stood a glass of water at the bedside with a stack of appropriate dose-powders beside it, right enough. And the dregs of a dose in the glass as well. All right. That explained that. He couldn't remember having been fed medicine, but that didn't surprise him. He was lucky—he supposed—to remember as much as he did, about what he had accomplished during the past sixteen eights.

By the time he was washed and combed and had changed back into his own linen—freshly laundered, of course, and laid out waiting—there was fast-meal laid out, and the housemaster waiting. That could be a good sign, Andrej told himself; to be waited on by so exalted a personage as the majordomo was a mark of significant respect. So he probably wasn't under arrest. Yet.

"His Excellency may wish for a brief summary of what has taken place in Port Burkhayden since yestreen," the house-master suggested, nodding to the houseman to pour Andrej's rhyti. This was different rhyti than that he had taken with him into the washroom. A guest could not be permitted to drink rhyti from a flask that had stood for so long. Certainly not. Shocking idea. "As his Excellency was, with respect, very drunk last night. When the Bench specialist Vogel brought him to Center House."

All right, so that was how he'd got here. He wasn't certain he remembered. Andrej had a quick sip of rhyti, and gestured for the morning-meat tray. He was hungry. Whatever doses whomever had used on him last night had been good meds; but the body still knew that it had been worked beyond the limits of its tolerance, and demanded he make it up in extra sustenance. Morning-meat. And hot bread. And quite possibly several slices of ripe melon.

"Captain Lowden had cried Charges against a gardener. Skelern Hanner. He and I had gone to Bench offices." Andrej insisted on buttering his own brod-toast; anyone else used either too much or too little. There was a precise ratio to be preserved between melted butter and marmalade. "But the gardener was quite guiltless. I sent him to hospital. And went to the Port Authority to make him clear with the Record."

Updates went more quickly when they could start from a mutually understood jumping-off place. The majordomo smiled. "Yes, your Excellency." The majordomo was Nurail, one of the tall broad-shouldered run of Nurail. Fair skin, light-colored eyes, brown hair. Not the sort of Nurail that Andrej Koscuisko would ever be mistaken for.

"As for his Excellency's personal movements nothing is known, sir, after that. You were reported missing from the Port Authority when First Officer Mendez arrived there. And located some time later near the Port Authority by the Bench specialist, if his Excellency will excuse, seven points before the gale, with all sheets flying. Several additional elements should be placed before you, though. It was a busy night."

Had he been somewhere near the Port Authority? Had he got that far once he'd left the service house? It was possible. The other alternative would seem to be that Vogel was glossing the actual location a bit. And why would he do that?

"One wonders in particular where one's Security have got to," Andrej agreed. Reaching for a dish of egg-pie. He wondered whether the majordomo was Nurail enough to flout tradition and sit down with him; or majordomo enough to stand on his dignity and decline absolutely to sit down with a guest of the house.

On the other hand since the house-master was Nurail, there was no reason to expect him to be willing to sit down with a Judicial officer of whatever sort, guest or no guest. Andrej abandoned the whole idea as a bad lead.

"His Excellency's Security troop St. Clare experienced a medical emergency last night."

This startled Andrej; he stopped where he was in mid-bite, and set his fork down. Carefully. The house-master was still talking. Never before had Andrej been quite so sensitive to the number of extra words that politeness was held to demand, when a house-master was speaking to a guest.

"The warrant officer, Chief Stildyne, went to the hospital with the man and the rest of the team. Security five point three? Thank you, sir, Security five point three. An emergency surgery was successfully performed. They're all still at hospital, sir."

Emergency surgery. Did he have to ask what kind? He'd forgotten what he'd decided about who had killed Wyrlann. He'd been distracted by problems of his own. Now Andrej was as sure as though he'd been told that he knew that the medical emergency had been a governor on overload, a governor which should have prevented the murder from ever taking place. Which would have prevented it, had it not been defective from the very beginning. He knew that Robert's governor had gone critical. He believed he knew why.

"I'll want to go to hospital first thing. Soon, too."

"Yes, sir. So much was in fact anticipated. The Bench specialist requests a few eighths of his Excellency's time be made available this afternoon or after third-meal, with specific provision that you were to feel no need to send excuses for seeing to other business first if you slept later in the day."

He might be Nurail. But he was damnably good at the language of a majordomo. At the same time his conversation was redeemed from the very purest form of mind-numbingly indirect discourse by his persistent tendency to use a second person singular pronoun rather than a noun phrase in the third person. Someone would probably take him gently aside and speak to him about that, before too long.

"For the rest of it the port is under quarantine, and all movement is under escort. There was a fire at the service house last night that may or may not have claimed the life of Fleet Captain Lowden. There are apparently some indications that the fire was set to conceal a crime, but the officer is either dead or missing and presumed dead.

The Bench specialists are conducting the investigation, with the Danzilar prince's permission."

Well, of course Lowden was dead. Or at least Andrej hoped and expected that Lowden was dead. He had very carefully killed Lowden himself, with his own two hands. Which were fortunately free from embarrassing scratches. But he hadn't set the fire to cover the crime. He'd set the fire to be sure that Lowden went to Hell and stayed there.

"Other casualties?"

There was a problem with having set a fire at all, now that he was sober enough to consider the potential consequences of such an act. But service houses had fire suppression systems to protect their patrons. Didn't they?

The sprinklers hadn't gone off in the suite where he'd burned the body, had they?

"Surprisingly few," the housemaster assured him. "All in all there seems to have been an orderly evacuation. There are injuries, but none of them very severe. Sprains and bruises mostly, from people being in too much of a hurry. But portions of the service house are apparently still burning."

Fire suppression systems had been as completely stripped out as the hospital had been, then. He should have stopped to think. Andrej stared at the sweet rolls, stricken with horror. Oh, what he had almost done. What he had done. That it had not become a disaster was clearly better luck than he deserved, and certainly no reflection on any merit of his.

Or was it?

Couldn't he say that to have killed Captain Lowden and set the whole service house on fire, and nobody else killed, meant a species of approval for the act, from the Canopy of Heaven?

It had been fairly early yet in the night.

People had been drunk, but not too drunk to find their way out of a burning building.

He was a sinner, but perhaps—just perhaps—the holy Mother had put out her hand to shelter and protect him, whether or not he was unreconciled still to her Church.

"House-master. I am astonished. Almost I would say that I was sorry to have missed it. But my First Officer has probably been up all night, and would know this for a lie."

Wait. Should he say such a flippant thing about the event that was presumed to have taken the life of his commanding officer?

Certainly he should.

Nobody in Port Burkhayden, nobody on the *Ragnarok*, nobody in Fleet, nobody on the Bench would be the least bit astonished at an indication that the death of Fleet Captain Lowden did not afflict him with an excess of grief.

"His Excellency's First Officer has in fact just gone to bed two eights ago. And leaves expressed concern for your health and well being, sir. I'm directed to advise you that he's been to hospital and everyone's asleep. And that he will expect to see you at some time, but that you're to satisfy the Bench specialists first on any issue."

Probably not quite as Mendez had said it, but Andrej took the meaning. It had been four years. He could speak Mendez.

"Very well, then. I will go to the hospital, and then to see Vogel. But in the meantime I will have some more rhyti."

There was no telling what he was to confront, today.

It only made sense to be sure he was well-fortified to face whatever might come.

Security Chief Stildyne lay on a thin padded mat on the floor with a rolled-up wad of sterile wrapping under his head and a doubled thickness of toweling over his face to shut out the bright light from the unshaded window. He'd had a long night. He'd slept through fast-meal, and he had every intention of sleeping through mid-meal as well. Why not? There was nothing to do, and nowhere to go. He'd spoken to First Officer. He didn't want to see Koscuisko.

He heard voices, coming down the hallway toward the front room of the ward his troops occupied. Robert in the inside room with the diagnostics, sleeping off the exhaustion of having experienced the extreme pain that he'd endured. Despite Stildyne's expectations to the contrary, Robert had slept through fast-meal and mid-meal as well. If he didn't wake in time for third meal they would have to call in a resurrectionist, Stildyne supposed.

"Through here." Stildyne recognized the voice. "Couldn't leave them cluttering up the emergency treatment areas. Security being on the large side."

Who would Doctor Howe be speaking to like that? Respectful and restrained, to an extent. Quite unlike the way Howe talked to Stildyne himself. Someone come to see about Robert, obviously, and that meant—

"Indeed I have always noticed that for large people they are capable of dealing with surprisingly confined spaces." The officer. Andrej Koscuisko. Stildyne rolled off his floor-mat and staggered to his feet in one swift if ungraceful motion. Koscuisko. He wasn't ready for this.

"One of the tricks of the trade, sir, disappearing in place. So your Chief doesn't notice you. Good-greeting, Chief, slept at all, did you?"

Yes, coming into the room. Doctor Barit Howe and Andrej Koscuisko. Stildyne bowed, still clutching the towel that he'd been using as an eye-shade in the fist of one hand. "Tolerably, Doctor Howe. Your Excellency."

Doctor Howe wasn't more than slowing down on his way through. Stildyne stood aside to follow behind Koscuisko, but Koscuisko paused, putting one hand to Stildyne's arm and looking up into his face with a very measuring sort of an expression in his eyes—which looked almost white to Stildyne in the bright room, but he was used to that.

"Have you had a bad night of it, Chief?" Oh, Koscuisko didn't know the half of it. "I should apologize for being drunk, and not here to help out. Tell me what happened."

Damned if he would. Not here. Not now. There was no telling whether they were on monitor, somewhere. "Robert may have been upset that the murder had happened while he was nearby. I don't know, your Excellency. All I really know is that he was suffering, and we assumed his governor was cooking off. We nearly lost him."

Sir, I'm sorry. I'm sorry I did it. I didn't realize how much it was going to hurt him. I'm sorry you weren't here. But Stildyne knew that those were words he'd never say.

"We'd met the gardener," Koscuisko said, as if he was agreeing with Stildyne on something. "Before, I mean. I knew Robert was unhappy about the Captain's accusation. I cannot say I was pleased myself. It may have been enough to push things over."

Yes, that made sense. And it didn't have to. All it really needed was for Koscuisko to say that it made sense. That was what senior officers were for.

"Let us go in," Koscuisko suggested, and started forward. *Let us go in* was not a suggestion from a senior officer. Not really. So there were drawbacks in having senior officers available to one, as well as advantages.

Doctor Howe was standing by the cot where Robert had been sleeping. Robert was sitting up on the edge of the cot in his hip-wrap, with his naked feet splayed firm on the floor and his knees every which way. It was a low cot.

"Name of the Mother," Koscuisko said, as Robert started to stand up. "Sit as you are, Robert. For the love of all Saints."

It couldn't be that Robert was undressed, because he did have some clothing on. Koscuisko was just responding to how white in the face and generally unhealthy Robert still looked. Joining Doctor Howe at the bedside Koscuisko leaned forward to peer into one of Robert's eyes, pulling against the lower lid of the eye with a touch of his thumb; Robert suffered the examination in stoic silence, apparently resigned to letting Koscuisko express his anxiety that way. "How do you go?"

For his own part Stildyne hung back, unwilling to present himself where Robert could see him. Afraid, after all, that Robert would remember at least enough to blame Stildyne for what he'd done.

"Well, thank you. Sir. Your Excellency." Robert's voice was strong, but hesitant. Stildyne realized he'd half-expected Robert to sound different. "Confused, though, with respect. I don't know what's happened. Except—something's missing—I think—your Excellency."

"Indeed, something is missing," Koscuisko agreed, and put his hand to the back of Robert's neck in an affectionate gesture that Stildyne had envied Koscuisko's Bonds on more than one occasion. "There is a soreness, here? It is as it should be."

Robert bent his head in apparent response to some gentle pressure from Koscuisko's hand; Koscuisko examined the back of Robert's neck, carefully, in the light from the un-shaded overhead fixture. "I wish someone would tell me what's going on," Robert grumbled. And then seemed to hear himself talking, and find himself startled by what he had said. "I mean. With respect. Sir. I'm confused."

"A beautiful mark, here," Koscuisko said to Doctor Howe. And it was Doctor Howe who came to Robert's rescue, as Koscuisko continued to consider the site where the surgeon had gone in with whatever he'd used.

"Your governor went critical on us, Mister St. Clare. We had to go for emergency disconnect. I have to remind you, now, don't get used to it. Fleet will see to it that you're Bonded again in double-quick time."

That was a point, Stildyne realized, though he wouldn't have thought of it. Not right away. Koscuisko stepped back from Robert, lifting his hand, apparently happy with his examination; Robert reached out and snagged Koscuisko's hand on its way past.

"Sir. I've got to tell you. If I could have a word. Please."

Stildyne shot Doctor Howe an angry glance, betrayed. Oh, this was bad. Doctor Howe had promised. Hadn't he? "Now, Robert, it's nothing that won't wait, I'm sure—" Stildyne started to say. In the best, most convincing, *shut up now or I'll shut you up myself* tone of voice that he could muster. But it never did him any good with Andrej Koscuisko around.

"Chief. Be still."

And Stildyne shut up. Seething in internal torment: but Koscuisko was the senior man here. And nobody argued with Andrej Koscuisko. It wasn't done.

"Robert, be easy. What is it? Of course."

Robert looked up past Koscuisko to Stildyne where he stood, to Doctor Howe on Koscuisko's left. As if he was trying to decide on something.

"Sir. You might not remember. But Megh. It's my own sister, sir. *My* Megh."

Koscuisko raised his free hand in an abrupt gesture of warning. "Be careful of what you say, Robert. Someone has murdered the Fleet Lieutenant. Do you not remember? Last night? At the party, at Center House?"

This was the meat of the problem, just so. Yes. Stildyne hadn't thought to be hitting it so soon: but maybe it would work out better this way. Get it all over with. Finished. Complete.

Robert looked confused. "Murdered. The Lieutenant? No, sir. Don't remember. I'm sure it'll come to me, though. If you say so."

Too clear and too open, too honest. Too real. Stildyne was convinced, but he wasn't the expert. Nor was he the person whose judgment mattered in things of this nature.

"Doctor Howe?" Koscuisko looked back over his shoulder; and Doctor Howe stepped up to the bedside.

"Going by what the Chief could tell us the governor was probably dying all day, your Excellency. It was already out of maximum tolerance when they reached the hospital last night."

A long moment, as Koscuisko considered this. And during that moment Stildyne imagined that he could see Robert realize what the issue was; but Robert didn't flinch from it.

Why should he?

Everyone knew that a bond-involuntary was ruled both by conditioning and by the governor.

The last thing a bond-involuntary was supposed to be able to do was to assault a superior commanding officer. They knew it was wrong, by the rules they'd been taught. And knowing that it was a violation rendered them incapable of executing it without invoking sanctions from their governor well before any actual act of violence.

In a manner of speaking Robert was protected by the fact that he was a bond-involuntary . . . except in the eyes of people who knew that his governor was faulty. And who could guess that what Robert had done had been overwhelmingly right, in his own mind: right enough to overpower even his conditioning.

"The authorities will want a statement, Robert. You were on duty at the time of the murder. As part of the rest of the special event security. It will have to be a speak-serum, I suppose." Koscuisko was thinking out loud. Not revealing, but seemingly unable to quite accept what Doctor Howe had told him, nonetheless. "Robert, it would be better, I think, if you did not tell anyone else, unless of course the Bench specialists ask, and there is no reason for them to . . . that she is your sister."

And as much sense as this made to Stildyne at least, Robert seemed incapable of accepting it. The pain in Robert's voice was too much like the pain that had been there yesterday evening. Stildyne didn't like hearing it.

"But to know that she's here, sir, and not see her. So many years. Please. Stildyne, speak for me. Couldn't I be allowed to just sit with her?"

If Robert could appeal to him, of all people, then Robert truly did not remember. Stildyne thought fast.

"Sir, if there's evidence, speak-sera will bring it out." Unless the searing agony of a governor gone critical had well and truly erased the slate. "So it'll clear him. Why not, sir? No harm done."

And Robert might never see her again. That was the unspoken subtext, here. Either because he would not live to see the Day, and come back to Burkhayden—Security troops suffered a much diminished life expectancy, by definition. Or else because the Bench would decide that sufficient circumstantial evidence existed to take Robert for the crime, and he would be executed. Which wouldn't happen. Robert would be killed first. Stildyne was sure of that.

Was Koscuisko trying to read some special meaning from his words, trying to fathom some looked-for secret message in his face?

It seemed to Stildyne that the moment stretched.

But neither Doctor Howe nor Robert apparently noticed any such thing.

"It would be very difficult to deny the justice of your claim. Very well. Doctor Howe, there is the orderly's duty, the salve for her bruises. Perhaps Robert could be put to work on ward."

Robert turned his head away, and rubbed at his forehead with one hand. Covering his eyes.

"Settled, then," Doctor Howe agreed.

"Mister Stildyne. I must to the Bench specialist Vogel go and speak. Do you care to come with me?"

So Stildyne would know if there was to be a problem, perhaps?

Or so Koscuisko could pump him in transit for any additional details?

He could leave Pyotr in charge. Pyotr had been in charge, right enough. Stildyne hadn't been doing much chiefing over the last few hours. "Very good, sir. Robert. Get rested. Your orderly, Doctor Howe."

Maybe Robert had done the crime, and maybe Robert would be put to death for it—one way or another.

At least he could see his sister once or twice before he died.

Andrej meant to take Chief Stildyne out of doors and walk the secret out with him, as soon as he had satisfied Bench intelligence specialist Vogel. There was a secret, he could tell. He and Stildyne had known each other for too long, and while their intimacy had not approached the sort that would satisfy his Chief, it had developed over time into a true relationship of sorts.

Stildyne would confess himself, Andrej was certain of it. Stildyne always did. Because as painful as it was to him to suffer diminishment in Andrej's eyes, it was more painful yet to enjoy a false regard founded on concealment.

Andrej meant to have it out of Stildyne, and he had to speak to Specialist Vogel.

But he wanted to see how last night's victim fared, before he did a thing else.

He knew the hospital well enough after his brief tenure here; he didn't need a guide to get from here to there, and no one seemed to think twice to see him in the halls. Well, perhaps they did think twice—they would all have heard of his disgraceful behavior last night.

Though they had known him to be Inquisitor before, the near reminder could not but create some consternation. He only appreciated their courtesy in simply greeting him and going on their way all the more deeply for that.

On his way in to the intensive care wards Andrej heard a commotion of a sort in corridors ahead, and quickened his pace. Commotion was not allowed in hospital. There were too many unavoidable emergencies to countenance the raising of voices for any other reason than great grief or agony, and since he thought he recognized the voice Andrej felt sure it was not so dire a cause as that.

Great grief, yes, perhaps, but not for a loved one's death. Great agony, but of spirit and heart alone. A woman was expected to rule her temper better than that, especially in hospital. If Sylyphe Tavart was not a woman yet, it was still time that she learned better how to be reticent.

"You must let me at least see him. He's our own gardener—I have a right—"

Sylyphe Tavart. As pale as she could be in the unkind light of the bright day, her face scrubbed clean of cosmetics and her eyes ringed with deep bruise-purple shadows born of sleeplessness. Very unbecoming. Arguing with the orderly at the record-station, she had not heard him approach.

"That will do, Miss Tavart, you are making a scene on ward, and that is not seemly of you. Come with me."

The orderly was grateful to be rescued from her insistent pleading, but Andrej kept a straight face. He knew something about Sylyphe Tavart he hadn't known at this hour yesterday. Since she was here there were some things that he could tell her, if she could but be made to hear.

"Indeed I will not, take your hand away—"

But she was too young to make her indignant protest stick, and to her credit she didn't raise her voice. Andrej escorted her firmly to the duty physician's station and nodded at Stildyne to shut the door that separated the small room from the rest of the ward.

The admissions report was in the scroller; it took him a moment to find what he was after. He searched the record with grim concentration, conscious of Sylyphe standing in the middle of the room staring at him. She could not break away and flee from him. Stildyne was at the door, and Stildyne could do one of the best impressions of an immovable object that it had ever been Andrej's pleasure to behold.

Here was the admissions report, Doctor Howe's notes as to the status of his patient Skelern Hanner. Very precise. And very detailed too; it was not for nothing that Howe had survived his years under Bond, and lived to be reborn.

Sylyphe spoke at last, unbidden and unasked but not unexpectedly. Her voice was quiet and calm in the hush of the small room; very cool and formal. "You know, I thought that it was wonderful that Andrej Koscuisko should come to Burkhayden. Such a man, with such a reputation. And now I wish you had never come at all."

She was to be a formidable woman, when she came into her majority. There was no scorn in her words, and that only made the implicit rebuke more telling.

"Oh, don't be tedious. You cannot imagine I have never heard that before."

As seductive as her interest had been, as tempting as he had found her innocent desire for him, it was time to make a proper separation. She was not for him, nor he for her. Andrej meant to leave no traitorous hint of wistful longing in her heart, and if that meant that he would be a brute—so would he be.

"No, I am sure it is all old to you." Very plain she spoke, and wrung her hands. "I didn't know. How you must have laughed at me. . . . How is . . . ? What did you . . . ? Skelern." She offered up her self-pride with a contrite humility that nearly staggered Andrej where he stood. It only made him the more sure of his purpose.

"It's not for me to say, Miss Tavart. That would entail a violation of his privacy, and that would not be lawful. Now. Not since."

Hanner had suffered horribly. Andrej knew his craft, he knew his own skill. Captain Lowden had insisted Hanner be harmed as little as possible, and Andrej had obeyed that order too. It would still be days before Hanner could walk, days longer yet before he could be released to light labor. It wasn't Sylphe's business unless Hanner himself acknowledged it to her.

"They will not let me see him. May I see him? I only want to tell him. There's a message. From the Danzilar prince."

The strain was too much for her; she began to fail beneath the enormity of her self-appointed task. The tears were all too clearly audible in her now-trembling voice. She wrung her white-square with shaking hands, and as much as Andrej wanted to take her into his arms to comfort her he knew that it would not be welcomed if he tried.

"You may not see him now. Nor would you be able to deliver any sort of message; he's asleep." Asleep or still unconscious, under the influence of pain-relief drugs. It didn't matter. "You must trust the doctors to act in Hanner's best interest, Sylphe. I do not ask you to trust me. Only to believe that I am telling you the truth."

Wait, wasn't that the same?

She untwisted her white-square with deliberate determination. Folding it flat, she creased its folds against the soft curve of her young stomach with an unselfconscious childlike gesture and put the thing away. "You won't let me see him. I can't know what you did to him. I will go home, now. Only. Please."

That you had never come to Burkhayden. Yes. Andrej knew. Another woman might have cursed him, struck out at him, spat in his face. Sylphe merely announced that he was unwelcome, now, as unwelcome as if he had only come to Burkhayden to torture her friend and break her heart.

"You have asked me nothing of what I may in fairness tell you." Andrej shut the scroller off at last and leaned his back against the wall, folding his arms across his chest, facing her. "Such things as what excuse he had to make for being where he was. And yet it may well be that you should know."

In an odd and indirect way it was his own fault Hanner had been put to torture for the crime. Andrej's fault. He had not put Sylphe in her place, beguiled by her sweet innocence. Because he had indulged himself in her adoration Hanner had seen them and assumed the worst. It was his fault. He had to make it up somehow, or part of it, at least.

"Very well." Rolling her underlip between her teeth she took a deep breath. Waiting for the blow. "I am listening, your Excellency."

Torturer. Your Excellency, which was to say *criminal*. And so he was. Straightening up, Andrej pushed himself away from the wall; Stildyne caught the gesture Andrej made and moved to one side of the door. Ready to leave. Because Andrej had no intention of staying here for a moment longer once he'd had his say.

"Watching us dance. You and I." He had to select his words carefully. He knew it was his fault: he did not meant for her to conclude that she was the one who was to blame. "He imagined that you . . . Well. I hardly know how to say it. Did you know that he is in love with you, Miss Tavart?"

There was a moment, there, an instant of pure vibrant energy, a shimmering in the air as the sound of Andrej's voice fell away. The space between one breath and the next. Forever. Forever, an eternity of time in which to realize not only that what Andrej had said was true but that she had herself somehow become in love with Skelern Hanner while she'd not been looking.

She only looked at Andrej now, her eyes like great luminous gems. Glittering with tears. He could not stay a moment longer, because if he did he would kiss her quivering mouth, and that was for Hanner to do. Not for him.

So Andrej took her trembling hand and kissed the air above her fingertips, instead. And left the room with her still in it, pure and chaste and suddenly aware. A word or two with the physician's assistant made it right, and they would let her in to see her mother's gardener after all; and now Andrej could leave the area entirely. Not only could, but had to, or risk setting a blight on an uncertain romance by some awkward gesture.

Had he ever been so young as that?

Could he remember how it had felt, when he had first known that he loved Marana?

And now he was in a filthy mood, tired and hung over, and sorry for himself.

There was no time like the present to visit Specialist Vogel.

CHAPTER ELEVEN

Bench intelligence specialist Garol Aphon Vogel sat over a shuffle of documentation laid out on a lab table, the lab stool drawn well up to the work surface, his feet tucked behind the lowest forward rung. Not so much puzzling over his conclusions as weighing their implications. Andrej Koscuisko stopped in the corridor, declining to step into the doorway, taking a deep draw at the smoldering lefrol he carried and releasing the greater part of its thick gray-white smoke into the hall. Rather than into the room. Garol wondered why Koscuisko was smoking at all, in a hospital—deserted wards or no. Koscuisko knew better than that. Surely.

"Your Excellency." Tired and depressed and unsure of the best route to take out of the mess that murder had made of Port Burkhayden, Garol didn't bother to straighten up. "Good of you to stop in. Doing rounds?"

The person who thought he'd seen Garol himself go up to Lowden's suite had turned out to be the floor manager at the service house. Once the floor manager had gotten it into his head that it was Garol he'd shown through, his tentative identification had hardened into rock-solid certainty. Memory was like that. Played tricks on a man.

A Bench intelligence specialist was clearly an appropriate person for a harried floor manager to have shown straight through. If the man to whom the floor manager had given access to luxury quarters was an assassin, though, then the floor manager was potentially to blame for a murder—if that was what it would turn out to be. So it was much safer for the floor manager to be convinced that he'd seen Garol Vogel, and as long as Garol didn't contradict him they could all be happy.

"I came to see my man, and also to check on the gardener. You left word, Specialist Vogel. You wanted to see me."

Reaching into the front-plaquet of his over-blouse, Koscuisko drew out a smooth silvery tube, matte-dull with age and use as only an antique of rhinsillery alloy weathered: a lefrol-keeper. Tucking his lefrol into the container Koscuisko put it away and then stepped across the threshold, but stopped just inside the open doorway.

"How's the gardener doing?" Garol asked, mildly curious. What was the etiquette observed between a man who had been unjustly tortured, and the very much senior-ranking man who had tortured him? "Does he remember anything about the event that might help to identify an assassin?"

Koscuisko frowned, as if as much annoyed at Garol for asking embarrassing questions as out of shame or diffidence. "Hanner is unconscious. Sleeping. Well drugged. Surely you do not imagine that I would have the face to confront him. After what I did."

What Koscuisko had done was only what Koscuisko had been ordered to do. But Garol thought he understood. Koscuisko believed that he should have caught the anomaly with the crozer-hinge right away. Koscuisko was probably right, on one level at least.

"You don't have to make any excuses for doing your lawful duty, not even with the gardener. We all heard the Captain." And though Koscuisko's private passion was fearful sadism, it wasn't Koscuisko who used and indulged it. It had been Captain Lowden who had been responsible for Koscuisko's extravagances.

Koscuisko swore. "Holy Mother. As if there was any excuse to be made for the time that it took to discover. I will not be patronized, Garol Vogel."

Only two names. Did Koscuisko know all three? Koscuisko's point was unarguable. If Koscuisko would not accept rationalization to cover the gardener's ordeal then Koscuisko would not—and was a better man for it than otherwise.

Garol set it all aside as a bent pin and took up the threads of his problem. "All right. The gardener. I'll need a statement. He may have heard something. Seen something. From your man St. Clare, as well."

Koscuisko hadn't stirred to come near or sit down. Koscuisko stood still now. "On a speak-serum, in the presence of a Judicial officer—of course, Specialist Vogel. But Hanner will not remember. Still less will my Robert remember anything. I have just come from having a word with him, and he has lost most of yesterday. Amnesia can be transient when its cause is trauma to the brain itself, but in this instance it is the processing which has been disrupted. I am convinced that any information Robert might have had will be unrecoverable."

Calm; not the least concerned. Garol Vogel was not a Ship's Inquisitor; but his survival depended upon his ability to read people and situations, which was as a consequence fairly well developed. Koscuisko was not worried. So neither man would be able to incriminate anybody. If Koscuisko was that sure that Garol would get no evidence, even under a speak-serum, then there was really no point in even trying; though it would have to be done, of course.

"I'll schedule the interviews for once the gardener's awake and strong enough for it. For the Record. Two or three days?"

He had to complete the investigation, or risk leaving a hole that might arouse suspicion simply by virtue of the fact that he had discarded suspicion without comment. Koscuisko merely nodded. Garol spoke on.

"That's about all I had, sir. Except to ask if you happened to remember what you were doing in the streets last night, when I found you."

"And took me to bed," Koscuisko agreed, with a little smile. "Excuse me, the phrase is not what it was to have said. Conveyed me to Center House. I was drunk, I think."

And wasn't about to tell Garol if he did remember anything. Why should he? Because if Koscuisko wouldn't talk the whole matter would either go forward on a supposition or be allowed to lapse for lack of evidence. Risking the chance that Koscuisko would let slip something incriminating some year; while he slept, for instance.

"We won't know how many are dead in the fire until the Port Authority can get people in to what's left at the site of the service house." Garol had no real doubt in his own mind about it. He knew he wasn't the one who had asked for the Captain at the service house. He hadn't gotten there till the place was already on fire.

But he could see where an over-stressed floor manager might

mistake Andrej Koscuisko in the dark of a house on auxiliary power, and convince himself later that the man he had seen was Garol and none other. Koscuisko had been there. Koscuisko had gone up. And shortly thereafter the fire alarms had gone off, and the service house had been evacuated; all except Captain Lowden.

As nearly as the Port Authority had been able to determine so far, only one person who had been in the service house had failed to get clear with his life. That was powerful evidence for the supposition that Lowden had been dead when the fire had started.

Koscuisko was waiting for him to finish his thought. Garol took a deep breath. "But we know that Lowden was in there. So he's dead. Can't say I'm sorry."

"As long as no innocent man must be taken," Koscuisko agreed. "I'm not sorry myself."

No, Koscuisko knew. Koscuisko remembered. Koscuisko would say something if he had to. But if he didn't have to, why should he say anything?

Captain Lowden had needed to die.

They both understood that.

Garol rubbed at the front of his over-blouse idly, feeling the crackling of the folded document in the inner pocket. Bench warrant. He'd got Jils thinking it was on Lowden. Why shouldn't it have been?

"Yeah, well. Once we find the body maybe we'll know more." But probably not. Probably no more than that it was Lowden's body, or at least verifiable as such from a gene-scan on whatever was left of it. The chances that the body was undamaged enough to prove so much as that a murder had even happened were almost nonexistent. Circumstantial evidence was all they would ever have, in the absence of a confession.

Who had killed the Fleet Lieutenant?

Had it been St. Clare?

How could a bond-involuntary have done such thing?

And what did Garol care, one way or the other?

Wyrlann was dead. The gardener hadn't killed him. Wyrlann had been a bully with a developing reputation as a man who needed killing. He was better dead. The Judicial order was better served by Wyrlann dead than alive, and Captain Lowden as well.

"Call for me when you wish the Record to complete, Specialist

Vogel," Koscuisko said, bringing an end to the interview. As if it had been his interview. As if it were Koscuisko who had sent for Garol, and not the other way around. That was the way of it, with people who held rank.

Garol had dealt with people like Koscuisko for all of his adult life.

He still couldn't quite manage the absolute self-assurance.

"And I will for you the speak-sera administer. To the upholding of the Judicial order in completion of the Record. Though neither man will have any words for you."

That wasn't the point.

Both of them knew that.

The point was that all avenues had to be laid out on Record, drawn out, described, then decisively cancelled. Or someone might follow one of the avenues back to a problem, someday in the future.

"Very good, sir."

And get out.

Why should Koscuisko get away with murder?

What difference did one more murder make, whether the Bench had ordained it or not?

Koscuisko went away with a nod; and left Garol to brood over life and injustice, alone by himself in the deserted lab, with a shuffle of depositions for company.

Megh heard them coming down the hallway toward the half-closed door to her room, and grimaced in irritation. She didn't mind the hospital very bitterly; she hadn't had so much time to herself since she could remember. But that the orderlies came to her to touch her was an irritation. She had to bear it; it was her life to be handled at the will of another, not at her will.

And still she was in hospital, not in the service house.

Which had burned down.

Somehow it seemed more distasteful to her that she should be outside the service house and yet still be subject to someone else's judgment as to where and how she was to suffer being touched.

She closed her eyes and turned her head away from the door, toward the window. It was Doctor Barit Howe. She recognized his voice. And to listen to him he was bringing yet another unfamiliar face, a new orderly, to lift the bedding carefully away from her legs to salve the bruises or to take the bed-wrap down from her shoulders to daub an ointment on the still-healing skin of her arms and shoulders.

"—your fifth-week," Doctor Howe was saying. "You know how to treat a patient. Only take a little more care, we're not a ship of war. This is a civilian hospital. My patients aren't to be told what to do, not like your shipmates. Clear?"

Yes, someone new. Megh looked across the room, out of the window, at the clear light beyond. There was nothing to see, of course; the window let out onto a courtyard. Sometimes looking out the window helped her to take herself away until she was alone again.

She didn't like being handled by anybody, let alone unfamiliar hands. She wasn't supposed to like it. It was the punishment that the Bench had put her to; and still she resented the treatment she got as a patient. Why wouldn't they just let her alone?

But then the orderly spoke.

"Clear, Doctor Howe. You'll not have cause to complain of me to my maister, nor to my Chief either. I can promise you that."

The small hairs at the nape of Megh's neck rose in a swift rush of prickly apprehension. Apprehension that was not fear.

Where had she heard that voice, before?

"Good-greeting, Maistress Megh." Doctor Howe stood at a pace's remove from her bedside, in respect for her privacy. He knew she didn't like being confined to bed in such a public place as a hospital. "Here's company for you. His Excellency has loaned him out for the duration, since the *Ragnarok* will be on site until the investigations are all closed. You can throw him out when you like, but please permit him to apply the ointment before you do."

Oh, she had no call to be rude to Doctor Howe. But no one was making her speak peace to him either. It was only that she had conditioning. She would be lowly and submissive. It was her role. "Thank you, Doctor Howe. I'll bear whomever, as best I can."

Turning her head, she spoke to the doctor.

Turning her head, she saw the other man, who stood beside the doctor staring at her as though his heart could travel through his eyes into her bosom.

She knew that man.

She had never seen him before—and she knew him. "Thank you for your gentle courtesy. I'll be on my way."

Doctor Howe nodded to her and to the orderly, and left.

And shut the door.

Megh stared; and the orderly stared back.

Who was this man?

He had grown tall.

His uniform said that he was a bond-involuntary, like her, only different.

It was their uncle's ghost, risen from the dead and wearing boots.

It was their father's brother Fipps, the one who lived nine days' walk down the coast and fished in a boat for his living.

"Oh, say a word, Megh, darling," the ghost said. "Else I'll explode. It would make such a mess."

It was Robin.

It was her own brother.

"You are grown." He knew that, probably, but she could not but marvel it out loud. "And gotten handsome. Robin. It is you. But can it be?"

He stepped forward to her bedside, falling to his knees. Taking her outstretched hand to numb it with kisses that spoke of the years of loneliness. "Wondered myself, I have, Megh. To have seen you, when my maister came here. I thought that I would die."

His maister, and Doctor Howe had said Excellency. She had heard. The orderlies had told her.

"Robin, you belong to Koscuisko?"

It was beyond belief. It could not be true. She was dreaming this.

But as long as she was dreaming it she would make as much of it as she could. She would stare at him until her eyes turned solid stone and dropped from their sockets, and not see enough to fill the void within. She would hold to him until her hands dried into willow-twigs and turned to dust, and still not get enough of his existence.

Robin.

And alive.

And grown, grown to a man, and such a man, tall and so good to look upon. They had always warned her family that Robin was sure to be a beauty, and was to be carefully nurtured that he not bring some too-trusting soul to grief before he knew the meaning of his actions.

"Anders Koscuisko. Yes. His Excellency. I wouldn't have known it was you, Megh, the Lieutenant used you so foully. But Skelern Hanner said the weaves. I knew."

So it was Anders from the Domitt Prison who tortured Nurail for Jurisdiction, but had brought her Robin safe to her side. *Ragnarok* that had sent the Fleet Lieutenant who had beaten her, but *Ragnarok* that had sent healing to her as well, and had brought her brother to be with her here besides. Jurisdiction had taught Nurail how to lament, but Jurisdiction was teaching Nurail how to believe in miracles of coincidence. It was her brother. It was Robin. He was here.

If only for a while.

But he was here.

"Now." Robin wiped the salt tears of his face with the back of his hand, and it nearly broke her heart to see him do it, it was their daddy to the life. She could endure it. She could live. Her fate had brought her brother living to her. She could brew beer out of spring water and three grains of last year's wild-grass. She could make cheese out of ram's-milk. She could do anything.

"Now. Megh. Oh, darling. There's an ointment to be laid on bruises, my maister went particularly to beg jellericia blooms from a garden here in town, your Hanner's garden. Because he knew the fragrance of it would be a comfort to a woman from the hill-stations, and never even guessed until I said to him."

She'd wondered about the ointment. She'd even wondered whether the materials had come from Skelern's garden. "I haven't seen Skelern, Robin, and I would have thought that he might come see me. Do you know if all is well with him? He's been kind to me, cousin-like."

Something was wrong. Robin ducked his head. "All's right now, Megh, but there's been trouble on the path from then till now. For him to tell you, really. But everything is all right now. Everything's well."

He wasn't only talking about Skelern, but about himself.

About her. About them.

For as long as Fleet would grant them time to speak in each other's company, all unwittingly, by accident—for so long, everything was well with the world. Everything was all right.

Robin opened up his jar of salve and commenced to daub it at her bruised shoulder, working it up gradually into a gentle massaging sort of a caress.

She'd never hoped to see Robin alive.

She would happily forgive the Bench another six such beatings, in return for the joy she had now in seeing her brother.

Five days. Hanner was not to be permitted to leave the hospital, not yet, but he had leave to move around a bit. It hurt to walk, although his feet were healing; if he was careful he could take three steps at a time before he had to sit. It ate upon him more to be idle, and to lie in a bed all day when the sun was out and there was work to be done.

Of course he wasn't to even think about worrying that the gardening would go to ruin. Sylphe had told him so; and so sternly that he could have wept at her solemn dignity, poor thing. The Danzilar prince had sent word to the Tavart to excuse him, and the Tavart had been sent gardeners in the Danzilar prince's pay to keep things up in his absence. He was not to lose his place, though he was to feel free to accept a better offer should one come—as the Tavart apparently felt was likely. It was all but too much for a man.

It wasn't as though he'd never been beaten before in his life, and more than once badly, and had mended bones and scars to show for it. There was no comparing to his most recent experience, there was that, but still for all his life he'd been expected to suffer a beating and lose his day's pay until he could work again, and all for the crime of having been born Nurail. Nothing like this.

Sylphe had come to see him on an embassy from her mother, carrying her errand as tenderly as if it had been a newborn infant. She'd done well. But then when she'd done with her errand Sylphe wept to look at him, tender-hearted as she was. And how was he to comfort her? Him in bed, and in bandages, and hating that she should look at his uncovered skin.

Though he had done the best he could Hanner still felt the lack of it. He could never dream to comfort Sylphe properly, with kisses and love-words. She was too far above him. And she deserved so much better than an under-fed gardener who trimmed her mother's turves for his wages.

Five days, and he had leave to dress himself and walk around the hospital with crutches and a mover. Someone had cleaned his clothing, and he remembered that Koscuisko had let him strip himself at his own pace, and stayed the security from handling him too roughly. That had been kindly intentioned, in its way. He'd been wearing the best shirt that he owned, in token of respect for the Danzilar prince—or for the Danzilar prince's gardens, at any rate.

The hospital staff said that he might go and see Megh. There was to be someone with her, but Hanner could deal with that; it wasn't like there was intimacy between them. He came to the place and signaled at the door, and the door opened, and the tall broad-shouldered person whose body blocked the doorway gave him pause and made him fearful. One of Koscuisko's people. Hanner recognized the troop.

The troop recognized him as well, luckily, and stepped aside; and having petitioned for entry Hanner felt that he could hardly not go in. Even if there was one of Koscuisko's people here. Even if the last person in the world that Skelern Hanner was interested in seeing was anyone with anything to do with Andrej Koscuisko. His Uncle had dealt fairly with him, in the end, but it was too terrible in Hanner's mind for him to find any charity in his heart to spare for Black Andrej.

"Here to look in on Megh," Hanner explained. Surely unnecessarily—wasn't so much obvious by the fact that he was here? "How does she go? Is she awake to greet me?"

The troop closed the door behind them, and Hanner crossed the room to look. Megh, in the bed, the covers drawn up very prettily over her shoulders, and someone had done her hair into a braid. The troop? Surely not. But it wasn't the kind of braid a woman did on her own, not easily.

And if Skelern thought about it that one troop was Nurail.

He knew the man.

He'd met him before.

Hanner had thought he looked familiar, from the start.

"Asleep, the poor darling," the Security troop said; and it was unlike anything that Hanner would have expected to hear from a bond-involuntary troop, surprising him into a fresh stare at the man. And then once he started staring there was something he could not stop staring at.

The last time he'd seen Megh she'd been marked in the face, blue and black, bruised and swollen. But her face was more familiar to him, now, and there was no mistaking the similarity when the Security troop glanced over at her with transparent fondness.

Hanner checked the sleeves of the troop's uniform with a quick sidewise glance. Just to make sure of it. Green piping, bright green, like wet-moss or the bloom-canker on the sweet-starchie flowers that ruined the crop.

Bond-involuntary.

And had spoken so to Koscuisko in the garden till Koscuisko, not understanding the point, had sent him sternly away—the thing he did not have, not him, not Hanner, but Megh's brother had to be from Marleborne—

He didn't know what to say. He had no right to be here with her brother, no right to be between them for the short time they would have before the *Ragnarok* left Burkhayden space.

"She, does she know you're here?" he asked, his voice hushed in the surprise of it all.

Robert St. Clare, that was his name. Megh's Robin. He grinned, and rubbed a spot at the back of his neck behind his ear in a gesture that was familiar to Hanner. "We talk when she's awake, but the pain-meds make her drowsy will-she nill-she. She's mostly sleeping. They let me look after her, to see that she gets her meals and lacks for nothing."

Hanner could understand the love, the longing in those words. He was so glad, for Megh; but her brother pulled himself away from staring at her, as if he was distracted.

"How did it go with you, man, and my maister?"

Koscuisko. Hanner shook his head. "Oh, let's not speak of it. I was so feared of him."

St. Clare nodded, as if he understood. Well, of course he'd know, from observation; but no, it didn't seem to be that he was talking about something that he'd only just watched. "I came under his hand, once, at the beginning. Before he knew that I was to be bound to him. Before it was decided."

There was nothing Hanner could say about that surprising idea. Perhaps Megh's brother had just wanted to offer comfort to him? Because he was still talking.

"And I was feared of him. I still am when the mood is on him, even though he's my good maister. I mean to tell him so, if I can catch him right before they put my governor back in. He'd not believe me, otherwise."

Hanner could only look at Megh's brother with wonder, not understanding why the man should say these things to him. But Megh's brother nodded yet again, and as if it had been a question asked, this time.

"It's malfunctioned, you see, and the doctor had to pull it. So I can speak to Anders Koscuisko like a man, and he'll know there isn't any constraint to the telling of it. So I can tell you what you need to know, young Hanner."

Young Hanner? Oh, no younger than St. Clare's own self, from what Megh had told him. What did he mean, tell what was needful to know?

"The doctor's to come in an eight, there's not much time. You'll want to concentrate. The first thing that you need to know is the traveling. From the corn-field stock. To the brook foot-path. To the post at the edge, with the shelf and the dipper-cup."

Quite suddenly Hanner was chilled to the bone with an icy shock of unimaginable power that stunned him. He could hardly think, but he had to think, he had to hang on, and he reached for the words like an anchor to steady himself with.

"From the edge-post shelf to the left of the break, to the ridge of the roof."

To the Ice Traverse.

He'd claimed the name to claim the right to see her, never dreaming. Never meaning to lay his hand on what was not of his, ready to steal the name of the weave to get his way and nothing further meant by it. Not to pretend that he had a right to it. Not to pretend he knew.

"Talk it to me, cousin, state you your claim, and call my Megh your sister like an honest man."

There was no more profound a gift in all the Nurail tongues than to give a weave. And him a gardener, not from the hill-people, but to stand from now on with the proud folk, and equal with any—

Hanner closed his eyes, thinking hard, steadying himself with one hand against the wall. "The Ice Traverse stems from the ridge of the mountain-roof. To the right from the break, where the valley parts. To the pitch of the roof of the way-shed rest, to the post at the edge and the brook foot-path. To the corn-field stack, in the field, with the reapers."

St. Clare was smiling at him approvingly when he opened his eyes from his concentration. "And the next things that are needful to know are the callings of it, see, these kinds—"

He had the Nurail right, then, if St. Clare approved his Standard of it. He could not stop to congratulate himself; St. Clare was telling out the pattern with his fingers, and Hanner recognized the first part of a lullaby, the mid part of a drinking song, the fifth part of a workingman's chant, all recombined, all reunited to form the background that upheld the weave.

That held the power.

A unity too perfect to be challenged or forgotten, once it was but recognized in whole—

And the power frightened him, but it had to be borne, because the gift of a weave was beyond any fear, and this could be the only chance that Megh's enslaved brother would have to recite it for years. Or forever.

"The first part of the second thing is conny-towing, seabird-tumbling, sense and pease and coin. Right?"

The pattern was there. And, oh, but it moved him. "So, the second part of the second thing must be dark tan leaf and water blowing, blue clouds in the half-sun sky, and barge turned over on the shore-sand." He hoped, he thought, it was so strong within him. It was so right. St. Clare alarmed him, grasping him at the back of his neck suddenly, and kissing his mouth in the fashion of the hill-folk with tears in his eyes. But smiling.

"Thou art a man, and a very clever man, to have caught this— caught this—caught this, thing. And the third thing, third thing, what would be the third thing, can you tell me the third thing, cleverness, my cousin?"

The Ice Traverse, a gift, a weave. It still could not be sung, but it was passed, and it would not be lost. He was its keeper. His to see the pattern would survive, to hold a piece of the great heart of his scattered nation.

"Oh, I. Could hardly say. If it were not. To say the fourth."

The pattern led to the tune, and the tune led to the telling, and the telling and the tune and the pattern all together held power that even the Jurisdiction's Bench had feared.

Would fear again?

No, he was a gardener. He never would have dared to claim the weave, not even to see Megh, if he had known that there might be a man who knew the weave, with him having no right to it.

"Then there would be such mockery that kites could not collect the air, if salmon ran in podge-meal, while the sisters pondered."

He had to mind the gift, to take it perfect from the only man who lived who had preserved it.

And he had to concentrate.

Governor or no governor Megh's brother was taking a significant risk, speaking his weave. Hanner had to learn it as quickly as he could, and give it back whole and entire, complete and correct.

Before Megh chanced to wake.

A woman was not to hear her mother's weave. It was indecent.

He had to hold it carefully, for Megh's children.

CHAPTER TWELVE

The Danzilar prince's business meeting room was in a library at Center House, middling in size, luxuriously appointed to the tastes of a Danzilar Dolgorukij with rugs and printed texts. The Record stood out as an anomaly in this place, and somehow Jils felt out of place as well, although the number of people in the room who were in uniform outnumbered the single man in civilian dress by four to one.

The Record was under Andrej Koscuisko's Writ, and had been removed from Secured Medical on the *Ragnarok* and ferried here by the custodial officer himself under careful escort. Now it stood on the table, nothing more than a flat square frame only as large as a printed text in quarto with a holographic projector in its base. Square, but shallow. Koscuisko had carried it on his person, in his over-blouse.

The murdered officers had been assigned to the *Ragnarok*. It was appropriate that the Writ under Andrej Koscuisko record and report their findings. And although a Record was a Record, the one from the *Ragnarok* had more transmit authority than the one the Bench had left here in Port Burkhayden, the one that she and Vogel would remove as the final step in ceding the port to the Danzilar prince.

Once the Record was removed the Bench would have no further claim on Port Burkhayden absent a request for intervention from the Danzilar prince. Or absent Fleet intervention at the Bench's direction if collection of fees began to lag or collusion with Free Government agencies was suspected.

"I've never seen one," Paval I'shenko was confiding to Koscuisko, who sat at the Danzilar prince's left. "Andrej Ulexeievitch. This is the Record of which we speak?"

Seeing the two of them so close together was instructive. The secondary sub-racial characteristics of the Dolgorukij contributed to a substantial degree of likeness between them; but more than that, they were related to one another, if a little distantly. The resemblance was unmistakable.

Nurail subspecies ethnicity could be invoked to explain why Robert St. Clare and the woman from the service house that Wyrlann had abused looked like they were related, as well. In a pinch.

"This is the piece of the Record that belongs to *Ragnarok*, Paval I'shenko. Yes." Like many things that could be abstract and concrete at once a person had to know context before understanding what was meant by the word "record." "To this Record I make my case and through this Record I record my findings. Secure encodes and access to the validation matrices at Camberlin Judiciary, and so forth, but this Record need only know me, it saves in transmit time."

The Record at Port Burkhayden was a more restricted instrument, that had to transmit for verification and then return with evidence. It had taken two days for the Record at Port Burkhayden to return acceptance validation for Koscuisko's clearing the gardener of the murder. Koscuisko's own Record would transmit direct to Bench offices once Koscuisko declared the Record complete. Quicker. More efficient. And they could all go home.

"Gentles, shall we begin," Jils suggested. Garol was getting impatient, sitting beside her, worrying at the cuticle of his thumb. He had something on his mind, and Jils thought she knew what it was. "Your Excellency. If you would, sir."

There were three Excellencies here, Koscuisko, the Danzilar prince, the First Officer; but only one of them could open the Record. Koscuisko nodded, rising to his feet. "Very well. For the Record. Andrej Ulexeievitch Koscuisko, Jurisdiction Fleet Ship *Ragnarok*, the following parties also present. Please state your names—"

And the crimes of which you have been accused. It was formula. Koscuisko stopped himself just in time, and grinned a little sheepishly at the near-misstep. One by one the people at the table named themselves, starting with the Danzilar prince, and going around the table. Ralph Mendez, the *Ragnarok*'s First Officer, as the representative of his Command. Garol Vogel and Jils Ivers, Bench intelligence specialists, investigating office.

Andrej Ulexeievitch Koscuisko held the Writ, and attended in his capacity as a Bench officer. Once the circuit of identification was complete he spoke once more. "And no others are here present. Presentation and discussion of findings follows for adjudication and decision by parties here present. Suspend Record until further notice."

No recording of discussion, because there was no sense in taking up valuable storage space on recapitulation or controversy. Once they decided what the evidence meant their decision would go on Record. Once that happened it was final.

"Specialist Ivers, Specialist Vogel. Your meeting, gentles."

Koscuisko sat down. Jils rose to her feet. "Thank you, your Excellency. Prince Danzilar. We have two issues here before us."

Two murders. The Danzilar prince had a report already of the actual findings, transcripts of interviews, all of the evidence that she and Garol had taken over the course of the last ten days. Well, not all of it. But all of it that belonged on Record. It saved time. She could get right to the point.

"As to the first, the assassination of Fleet First Lieutenant G'herm Wyrlann. If it wasn't the gardener, who was it? Several considerations, here. The Captain identified Skelern Hanner as guilty, so detail search for physical evidence in the garden itself was delayed until much later that evening."

Because there was no call to search for physical evidence with an accused in custody. With an accused in custody the presumption was that any physical evidence would stay put until whenever, as long as the garden was quarantined—as it had been. To have initiated a search at that point could have been taken as accusing Captain Lowden of bearing false witness, by implication.

"By which time there was none to be found," the Danzilar prince agreed. "Whoever did the murder had a chance to get away. And remove any evidence with him, or her."

Or else third parties, sympathetic to the murderer's cause for whatever reason, had tidied up the garden well before then. No use in suggesting that, though they all knew the possibility existed. The Danzilar prince's house staff was full of Nurail. The Nurail community of Port Burkhayden—by far the majority of the people here—had been quite reasonably outraged at the abuse the bondswoman had suffered at the hands of the Fleet Lieutenant. It was only natural that they might endorse any measures taken in retaliation by shielding the murderer. By destroying evidence.

Jils continued. "There's no weapon, and the accused has been cleared. We have two choices. One is an anonymous Free Government assassin. The other has to do with the fact that the woman is the sister of the bond-involuntary, Robert St. Clare."

Nobody was surprised. That didn't surprise her. It was only reasonable for Koscuisko to have told his First Officer, since Koscuisko knew quite well that St. Clare was protected from accusation by the evidence he'd given.

And as for the Danzilar prince, well, the Danzilar prince knew a great deal more about what was happening at his port than he shared with them. He had good people. Jils suspected some of them were Malcontents, under cover, and the slaves of Saint Andrej Malcontent were intelligence agents that even—or especially—a Bench intelligence specialist had to respect.

"Your report's got the talk you two had with St. Clare. Here," the *Ragnarok*'s First Officer pointed out, tapping the document in front of him. "Speak-serum trial, proved for truthful utterance at the Execution levels. Did you have anything to do with the murder, you asked. St. Clare said he had no knowledge of it. He couldn't have lied. He's clear."

Actually Garol had asked, but Mendez was right. Koscuisko had used the most powerful such drug on the Controlled List, one usually reserved for confirming confession to a capital crime. Absolutely sure of himself, absolutely sure that St. Clare remembered nothing, one way or the other.

"The issue is one of memory, First Officer." Koscuisko's polite qualification rather startled Jils. It was clear to her now—if it had not been before—that Koscuisko was willing to go to great lengths to protect his troops. She hadn't anticipated his participation in this, but she had to admit that it was more convincing coming from the medical professional than from her. "He can state absolutely that he does not remember, because it is true. He cannot say that he had no hand in it, because he doesn't remember."

"So—" Mendez's voice was thoughtful. "If he starts to remember, some year, and turns out to have had something to do with it . . . "

Such as committing the crime, to avenge his sister. Koscuisko looked unruffled, serene. Confident. "He will be under governor, and will have to report the recovered information or suffer the consequences. There will be confession at that time. But without evidence, and with a legally supported claim to have no knowledge, he cannot be pressed further."

And he had been under governor in the first place, technically incapable of the act as far as the Bench knew. No sense in belaboring that point any further.

"All we're left with is that Hanner heard something behind him on the veranda. There's no evidence." She was only saying what they all knew. And they needed a way to close the case and move on. "The rule of Law is not well served by unsolved murders. If it was a Free Government agent the explanation satisfies our responsibility to uphold the rule of Law, even though the criminal goes undetected and unpunished."

Free Government agents could be anybody, but the point was that no one would be put at risk. Everybody knew about Free Government political terrorism. A Free Government assassin could be safely supposed to be far away from Burkhayden, and nothing to do with anyone who lived here. If it was a Free Government assassin the Bench had no brief to continue to search for a murderer amongst the Danzilar prince's people, Dolgorukij and Nurail alike.

"A Free Government assassin." The Danzilar prince sounded a little dubious. "If you say so. It could well be."

"We so recommend." Garol spoke up for the first time. He'd been abstracted lately. No, he'd been abstracted since the beginning of this whole enterprise, from the moment they'd started to Meghilder space with the Danzilar prince's fleet. He just kept getting moodier by the day, was all. "There's absolutely nothing to be gained by leaving it open."

Once Jils had realized that Garol was carrying a Bench warrant, of course, she'd understood. Garol was opposed to Bench warrants on principle. The system should be able to take care of its problems through normal channels, Garol said, and when the Bench had to resort to secret execution it was a failure in the system. But he did his job. He always did his job. And he was good at it.

"Do you know, my Security felt that we were being stalked, when I first to Burkhayden came," Koscuisko said suddenly. "Someone came into quarters when they were unoccupied, and rearranged the doses in a drugs-pouch. Nothing more than that. And yet Pyotr insisted on shifting to more secure quarters, and I had not thought of it to mention this, before."

No reason for Koscuisko to have made it up to convince his cousin Danzilar. Jils was glad he'd said it. The Danzilar prince looked much more comfortable than he had before, and said as much.

"So there has been activity. Very well. We do not cover up for the crime, we merely select the most likely of several unprovable possibilities. I am content. Let us go on."

Not as if it rested with the Danzilar prince, but as the planetary governor he did have a great deal to say about the disposition of the case. It was under his jurisdiction, not that of the Bench—or very nearly so. Jils picked up the thread.

"All right. Next. Captain Lowden. Positive identification of the body." Lying across the table, what was left of one. The floor had held but everything within the room had burned. The fact that Lowden's body lay amid the ashes of the table and traces of napery told them less than nothing, except that he hadn't been in bed.

From all the evidence showed he might have just collapsed over his meal, and died of heart failure—except of course that there was no trace of a meal, which hadn't been sent up yet by report, and that the body lay face up and not face down. Captain Lowden had been murdered. Jils was sure of it.

"The floor-manager's given evidence that Specialist Vogel came to see the Captain shortly before the fire. This evidence is on record, but may plausibly be discounted."

Koscuisko raised an eyebrow at that. Garol hadn't told Koscuisko, then. Odd. She would have expected Garol to level with the Judicial officer. On the other hand she and Garol were a species of judicial officer, themselves.

Garol made a face that Jils recognized, lips pursed together and rolled toward his teeth, raised eyebrows drawn together in the middle of his forehead. Embarrassment. Disclosure of some mildly shocking secret.

"Go ahead, Jils, blow my cover. Prince Danzilar. This is very awkward. I'd owe you an apology, if it wasn't Bench business."

The Danzilar prince looked confused, so Garol had to continue. Had Koscuisko guessed, Jils wondered? Something about the phrase "Bench business" seemed to mean something to him.

"It feels like a violation of your hospitality. Which has been very gracious. Here's what we mean. Someone's given evidence that I went up to see Captain Lowden. Now, this is a Bench warrant."

Drawing the document out of the inside pocket of his over-blouse, Garol gazed at it thoughtfully for a long moment. Giving the implications of the statement a chance to sink in. Giving them time to consider what it meant.

"A Bench warrant, or, specifically, a termination order. It's not very good guest behavior to murder VIPs during Port accession celebrations, your Excellency. But it is my job. At least from time to time."

Garol's Bench warrant meant that though there was evidence connecting him with the murder on record, there would be no challenge from the Bench to a finding of Free Government assassination. Why he'd set fire to the service house to cover the job she didn't understand, but maybe he hadn't. Maybe that had been an accident. Or unrelated. There was no reason to cover up the crime, after all. All he was expected to do was to make it look good enough that the Free Government could be blamed.

"And personally. I'll say this in light of what we all know. Lowden deserved to die. I believe he gave false witness. I was there. I don't think he believed the gardener did it. The gardener was just a convenient victim."

Koscuisko turned his face down and away from her; the Danzilar prince—half-rising—put his hand out to Koscuisko's shoulder, his concern clearly evident.

"You could not know, Drusha," Danzilar said. "Please. You must forgive yourself. You had orders."

The *Ragnarok*'s First Officer, Ralph Mendez, had been quiet for the duration, obviously content to sit and absorb. Now Mendez turned his attention to his hands, clasped before him on the table's surface. It was awkward to be witness to this. Jils could sympathize.

"Orders can never justify." Koscuisko's voice sounded choked. "Oh, Shiki. There is always someone who must do the thing, and that man has a choice, Shiki, truly. I am ashamed."

That it took him so long to realized that Hanner hadn't done it, could not have done it. Garol had told her about Koscuisko's conflict. She honored it; but Koscuisko was wrong. Lawful orders upheld the rule of Law. Obedience to lawful orders was the duty of every responsible citizen under Jurisdiction. Only unlawful orders brought shame on the head of the one who executed them. And as soon as Koscuisko had realized that the gardener was innocent Koscuisko had taken appropriate measures.

"One way or the other," Garol said, in a voice that struck Jils as being curiously soft. "Captain Lowden's death was required by the Bench under warrant. That's all there is to it. We recommend a finding of Free Government activity, targeting officers of the Jurisdiction Fleet Ship *Ragnarok*. Unless there are any questions."

Koscuisko covered his face with his hands. But after a moment Koscuisko straightened up. The Danzilar prince, still watching Koscuisko with concern clearly written on his face, shook his head.

"No. I am content. As long as the Bench will have no expectation of launching a hunt for any such assassins here. I will not have a Fleet interrogations group at Port Burkhayden."

Quite right of him, too. Fleet interrogations groups were very efficient at identifying and locating Free Government operatives. The problem was that a Fleet interrogations group was perfectly capable of finding such activity where there wasn't any. It made no difference to a Fleet interrogations group. Someone could always be brought to confess to the crime, and from there things escalated.

"We'll sign up to that, sir, and go so far as to promise that no further action will be taken." Jils could make that claim honestly, with confidence. Garol would declare his Bench warrant. That would be that. "I think we can go on Record, your Excellency."

Koscuisko stood up, and looked around the table at each of them. Mendez nodded. "Go for it, Andrej."

Koscuisko decided.

"Terminate suspension of Record, conclusion of discussion of evidence and findings. Let the Record show that the death of Fleet First Lieutenant G'herm Wyrlann was accomplished by a person or persons unknown, but presumed to be associated with Free Government terrorists. Let the Record further show a similar finding in the matter of the death of Fleet Captain Griers Verigson Lowden, presumed murdered in the absence of evidence. Let all here now state their concurrence with these findings."

Koscuisko recited the legal formula without inflection, dispassionately. It took a moment for the Danzilar prince to take his cue. Once he did, however, the Danzilar prince spoke his piece clearly and calmly as well.

"Paval I'shenko Danzilar, Bench-proxy governor of Burkhayden in Meghilder space. In the matter of the death of Fleet First Lieutenant G'herm Wyrlann by an assassin of unknown identity, I concur. In the matter of the death of Fleet Captain Lowden by an assassin of unknown identity, I also concur."

Formula. But they all had to say it. Mendez made his statement, and when it came to Garol—next, going around the table—he put the crucial piece of information on Record.

"In the matter of the death of Fleet Captain Lowden by an assassin of unknown identity, I concur. I report the cancellation of an outstanding Bench warrant received."

Because he had exercised it. Port Burkhayden was safe from Fleet interrogations groups. Nobody who reviewed the Record could entertain any doubt about what had really happened. That was one of the reasons that access to the Record was so strictly controlled. Not even Koscuisko—who held the Writ—could invoke the Record to recall information; he could only supply it.

"Bench intelligence specialist Jils Ivers, on assignment. In the matter of the death of Fleet First Lieutenant G'herm Wyrlann."

Done. Finished.

"The decision is unanimous," Koscuisko said. "It is so found. No further action. The Record is complete. Close the Record."

Now they could get on with their lives, to the extent that Bench intelligence specialists had lives.

Whether or not the bond-involuntary would ever remember the murder Jils didn't know, and she didn't really care. What was important was the rule of Law. Nothing more. Sometimes that meant that the innocent were sacrificed to the public order; that had almost happened with Skelern Hanner. It was well worth one man getting away—for now—with the murder, which he might not have committed, of a bully who disgraced his Fleet rank, rather than risk a mistake in the other direction.

"Thank, you, gentles." The Danzilar prince rose to his feet, and spoke their dismissal. "Shall we go to mid-meal. There is Nurail meat-pudding. We do not have to eat any of it."

The Danzilar prince would be much happier when they were all out of Port Burkhayden.

And now there was no longer anything to keep them.

Andrej Koscuisko got out of the transport half-a-block from the wreck of the service house. "Wait for me," he warned Security, to forestall Chief Stildyne. "I will go alone. There is something that is between just the two of us."

Himself, and Specialist Vogel, who stood with his back turned in the middle of the street at the end of the block. By himself. All alone. Andrej had been told that Vogel could be found here.

He had a word or two to say to Vogel before they all went their separate ways.

The burning of the service house had left a gap in the long row of buildings in this part of the port; the walls still stood, and several of the floors had not collapsed, but there was sunlight shining through blackened window-openings from within empty rooms. There was soot everywhere. Vogel heard him coming, but Vogel didn't move, and Andrej stood for a moment and looked at the destroyed hull before he found anything to say.

"They will have to rebuild." Well, obviously. He was just making conversation. "But that no lives were lost, it is a cheap price to pay for such a blessing. Perhaps I am not the man who can say that. Because I am not the man who must pay for the rebuilding."

The Danzilar prince would rebuild the service house. The woman Megh would have to go back, but only in an administrative capacity. She would not be called upon to provide any services more personal than balancing a tally-sheet in the laundry. He could feel good about that. It would be a great comfort to Robert to know that his sister was safe, even if not free.

"Yeah. Well." Vogel squinted up at the top surviving level of the building, the floor where the fire had started. "Shouldn't have left it open, with so little by way of fire suppression. What do you want. Your Excellency."

Because Andrej hadn't tracked Vogel down to the scene of someone's crime in order to talk about casualties. They both knew it. Andrej was convinced they both knew what the crime had been: and who had committed it.

"I wondered, Specialist. I do hold the Writ. And I am a Bench officer accordingly, as well as a Fleet officer on board the *Ragnarok*. Why didn't you tell me."

He had a right to know, in his capacity as a Bench officer. In a sense. But more than that. If the murder was under Bench warrant, and Vogel intended to declare it as such, why had Vogel kept it a secret for so long?

Vogel sighed. As if only now making up his mind to an irreversible step of some kind. "Fair enough. I'll tell you. There's something wrong with the warrant. I don't like it. I hadn't decided whether I was going to execute it or not."

Something wrong? With a Bench warrant?

What did that mean?

"But once it was done." Vogel hadn't executed the Bench warrant, but Lowden was dead. "There have been these ten days past."

Vogel shook his head. "No, not really. Here. You may as well have this."

May as well have what?

Vogel reached into the inside pocket of his over-blouse, and plucked the Bench warrant out of its place there. Handing it to Andrej, who took it eagerly. He'd never seen a termination order. He was interested. Bench codings. Counter-secures. Marks and sigils he'd never seen, at whose meaning Andrej could only guess. Formal Judicial language, *as regards the person of the following named soul the bearer is to exercise the solemn ruling of the Bench in support of the Judicial order.* The name.

Which was not Lowden.

The document trembled in Andrej's hand. Was it only the breeze? This was his life, that he was looking at.

An order for his own execution.

What could this mean?

"I've declared it exercised," Vogel said, as if that could explain.

"Somebody knows. Somebody knows it was issued for you, and not for Lowden. You know what I think? I think it's bogus. And whoever made it up isn't going to stop at a faked warrant, Koscuisko, so be advised."

The words meant nothing. "Why do you tell me this?" Andrej asked, in a horrified whisper. "When we both know . . . " That he'd killed the Captain, and was vulnerable to the most extreme penalty under Jurisdiction. That Vogel had just covered up. Andrej couldn't stop staring at his own name on the warrant. Someone wanted him dead.

But who?

And why?

Was Chilleau Judiciary so intent on revenge on him that it was willing that he should die rather than go free?

Vogel shrugged. "It's academic now. The only people who even care are you and me and whoever wants you dead. And I don't care that Lowden's dead. I meant what I said. I think he gave false witness. I think he knew."

"You're a Bench specialist. You cannot stand by and let murder go unpunished." Andrej held the Bench warrant out for Vogel to take back; but Vogel didn't move. "Where does this come from?"

"I am a Bench specialist," Vogel agreed. "That means I decide what best serves the Judicial order, and I consult my own good reason when I do so. On site. No revisits. No reversals. And I think it's best that they both died by Free Government assassination. I don't have to explain myself to you."

Nor was Vogel doing any explaining, not really. So at least he was consistent.

"And where does it come from, well, that's the big question. Bench warrants are issued by the First Judge or a delegated authority. In reality they can come from any Bench under Jurisdiction. And they do."

Andrej had an abstract sort of knowledge that Vogel was talking to him. And talking sense. He must be in shock, he told himself. All he could think about was his name on the warrant.

"What am I to make of this? What am I to do?"

He hadn't felt so helplessly at a loss since—since he wanted to remember. There were no real answers to questions like that, Andrej knew. Yet Vogel answered him.

"You've got enemies. You know that. But the rule of Law is not to

be subverted for anyone's personal vendetta, Koscuisko. If I were you
I'd put the Malcontent on it. As for the rest nobody knows which
eight's their last, so deal with it accordingly."

Vogel had had enough of Andrej's shocked incomprehension; that
seemed clear enough. Vogel turned his back, and walked away; Andrej
stood where he was with the Bench warrant in hand, staring at the
blackened vaults of the once-service house.

Enemies.

And no man knew which eight would be his last. That was true.

The thought was somehow calming. Andrej folded the warrant up
into the front-plaquet of his own over-blouse, conscious of Chief
Stildyne coming up behind him.

"I need home leave, Chief." He'd have to tell Stildyne; it was in
Stildyne's professional interest to know. "Let us go home. Well, to my
home. Let us take Security five point three." It would be fun to take his
people home to the Matredonat, and spoil them thoroughly. They
could meet his child. He could meet his child, for that matter.

He had not wanted to go home with the taint of torture
contaminating everything he touched. But if he was to die there were
things he needed to do first; and whether or not Specialist Vogel was
right about the Bench warrant it was a useful reminder.

No man knew the hour of his death.

It was prudent to leave no crucial thing undone to be accomplished
in a future that might never be granted one.

"Yes, sir. The shuttle's waiting, your Excellency."

To go on home leave it was necessary to first return to the ship.
That was all right. There were probably not assassins on board
Ragnarok. He would go home. Perhaps he would seek out the
Malcontent.

Had he not suspected for some time that Saint Andrej Malcontent,
rather than Filial Piety, was his true name-saint?

"Let us by all means go." Andrej turned his back on the service
house and everything it stood for. "We have had altogether too much
excitement, Chief. We need a rest."

Ten days of wondering what Vogel would do, whether there was
evidence to link him to the murder, whether he would have to speak
up and accuse himself in order to prevent some other—innocent—
man from the penalty. Ten days of considering a Tenth Level

Command Termination and finding himself unable to regret what he had done, even if he should have to pay so high a price. Ten days of holding his breath. He was exhausted.

"To the contrary. With respect." Security was waiting for him, and Robert in his place. It would be hard on Robert to leave his sister. At least they'd had ten days together. "His Excellency has not participated in combat drill for upwards of twenty days now. We have some serious catching up to do. Sir."

Well, Andrej decided.

He was going to be demanding quite a bit out of Stildyne, if what Vogel had said was true.

He could afford to let Stildyne have the last word. This once.

Therefore he merely nodded; and stepped into the transport, to go back to the *Ragnarok*.

THE
DEVIL AND DEEP
SPACE

A Novel Under Jurisdiction

Andrej Koscuisko, the *Ragnarok*'s Ship's Inquisitor, is going home on leave. His ship of assignment is participating in training exercises, and when an observer station unexpectedly explodes—killing the *Ragnarok*'s captain—Pesadie Training Command has to come up with a cover story in a hurry or risk exposure of its black-market profiteering.

There is a conveniently obvious explanation: the *Ragnarok* did it on purpose. All Pesadie needs are a few confessions—obtained by judicial torture, which creates its own truth. And a bitter enemy from Andrej's earliest days in Fleet has been waiting for just such an opportunity to set a trap and bait it with the lives of people Andrej loves.

Andrej will have to fight Fleet itself to bring the *Ragnarok* the only thing that can save the ship and crew from destruction—a single piece of evidence with the potential to change the course of the history of Jurisdiction Space forever.

Dedication

Dedicated to the Intemperate Muse
according to his Excellency's good pleasure

CHAPTER ONE

An Unfortunate Combination of Circumstances

"I have your report from Burkhayden, Specialist Ivers," the First Secretary said, looking out the great clear-wall window over the tops of the fan-leaf trees in the park below. "I apologize for taking so long to get to it. I find it rather strongly worded in places."

Rather strongly felt, Jils told herself, wryly. But Burkhayden and everything that had happened there were months behind her now; except one thing. "Yes."

The First Secretary looked tired, even from behind. Jils didn't think she'd ever seen him lean against anything in all of her years of working with him. She could understand his fatigue, though; with the recent and unexpected death of the First Judge, Sindha Verlaine was at the defining moment of his entire career.

If the Second Judge at Chilleau—Verlaine's Judge—became First Judge, Verlaine would become the most powerful civil servant under Jurisdiction; Chambers here at Chilleau, with their beautiful gardens and their tall whitewashed walls, would become the center of known Space, since whatever might be in Gonebeyond was not worth consideration.

If the Second Judge failed to negotiate the Judicial support that she needed in order for her claim to prevail, however, it would be all over. Second Judge Sem Porr Har would remain one among eight equally powerful Judges for the rest of her life, and First Secretary Verlaine would still be nothing more than the senior administrative officer at Chilleau Judiciary.

Good enough for most men.

Not good enough for Sindha Verlaine, who had been working toward this moment for his entire adult life—twenty-plus years by the Jurisdiction standard, in service to the Judicial order.

Verlaine turned from the window, his expression open and candid. In the bright morning light his normally pale complexion was an unflattering claylike color, and it was clear from the drawn contours of his face that he had not been getting enough rest for some time. "Please. Sit down, if you will, Bench specialist. I mean to be very frank with you."

He almost always had been. The relationship between a Bench intelligence specialist and the administrative staff of any given Judiciary could become adversarial, because men like Verlaine weren't accustomed to being told no—and only Bench specialists and Judges could do it. Bench intelligence specialists answered to no single Judge, but to the Bench itself.

Some Secretaries that Jils had coordinated with had tried to wheedle, threaten, influence. Verlaine had never stooped to subterfuge; she respected that in him. So she sat down in one of the several chairs that were arrayed to one side of the window, in front of his desk.

Verlaine nodded his thanks for her cooperation and picked up a flat-form docket from his active file, backing up against the forward edge of the brilliantly polished wooden desktop until he was sitting on it, file in hand.

"Chilleau Judiciary got off on the wrong foot with Andrej Koscuisko from the very start," the First Secretary observed, mildly. "It's past time I faced up to my responsibility for what's gone wrong there, Specialist."

There were reasons Verlaine might have for taking time out of what had to be a hellishly grueling schedule of political coordination to talk about a single individual.

Koscuisko was the Ship's Surgeon assigned to the Jurisdiction Fleet Ship *Ragnarok*—Ship's Inquisitor. Several months ago Verlaine had sent her to Burkhayden to obtain Koscuisko's services for Chilleau by fiat, and Koscuisko had reacted by doing the one thing no one could have anticipated—reenlisting in Fleet, when no other offered inducement had moved him from an apparently single-minded determination to be done with the practice of Judicial torture and go home.

Koscuisko was just one man, though his public profile was higher than most due to the personal notoriety he had won at the Domitt Prison: but Koscuisko also had family, and his family was very influential within the Combine.

When the Dolgorukij Combine spoke Sant-Dasidar Judiciary and its Sixth Judge were obliged to listen, or risk expensive and awkward civil challenges. The support of the Koscuisko familial corporation could be the key to the Combine's endorsement of a chosen candidate, and the Sixth Judge had to defer to the Combine's wishes if she meant to keep the peace. That meant that the Sixth Judge's support for Chilleau's bid lay with the Dolgorukij Combine to grant or to withhold.

Nor was Koscuisko simply one among a powerful family, but the inheriting son of the Koscuisko prince, and would be master of the entire familial corporation in time. That made him the man with whom Sant-Dasidar Judiciary would expect to have to deal during much of the tenure of the new First Judge. It was in the Sixth Judge's best interest to cultivate Koscuisko's goodwill accordingly, and pay careful attention to his feelings.

"I have read your report, Specialist Ivers, and I have decided. Chilleau Judiciary has wronged Koscuisko, and it is my responsibility because it was my doing. But the timing is awkward."

Funneled special assignments in Koscuisko's direction to keep the pressure on, assigned him to the *Ragnarok* even knowing that three out of three of the *Ragnarok*'s previous Inquisitors had been unable to tolerate the work to which Fleet Captain Lowden had put them. Verlaine was right; he had wronged Koscuisko.

Clearly Verlaine meant to send her to Koscuisko now with concessions. Jils didn't see where timing could really affect Koscuisko's reception of whatever Verlaine had to say one way or the other; she knew Koscuisko's feelings about Chilleau Judiciary. And Bench Specialists didn't run personal errands with political motivations behind them. "What would you like to tell me, First Secretary?"

"It goes deeper than just Koscuisko. Though he must be admitted to be the most visible symbol of the entire system."

Of what? Of Inquisition?

Verlaine set down his flat-form docket and cast off from the desk, starting to pace. He was a very thin man, not tall, but very quick in his movements; he frequently gave Jils the impression that the energy of his mind could not be contained within his body. "The Second Judge has agreed to issue a statement of intent. Her proposed agenda."

It would be the formal announcement of her desire to step into the First Judge's position. No one had issued such a statement to date; it had only been twenty days since the death of the First Judge had been reported. It had been a surprise. People were scrambling.

"When she does she will challenge the rules of Evidence as in the best interest of the rule of Law and the Judicial order. It will be controversial. I must have Koscuisko on her side."

Jils was startled into a question. "Rules of Evidence, First Secretary? Does she really mean to question the Protocols?" Because the Second Judge was a brave woman if she did mean to do that.

The Bench had come to rely more and more on Inquisition as its instrument of state over recent years; that was why there were Ship's Inquisitors, Judicial torturers. And still civil unrest continued to increase, regardless of—or even possibly as a result of—the increasingly savage methods to which the Bench resorted to contain it.

"It costs too much," Verlaine said, simply. "In more than just money. But more than that, it's just not working, Specialist Ivers. The more the Bench leans on confession extracted under torture for validation, the less credibility the rule of Law can hope to retain. She will need all of the help in this she can get. She will need Koscuisko's support."

For a Judge to question the usefulness of her own Inquisition was a genuinely stunning development. If the Second Judge spoke out against the Protocols, she challenged the most useful weapon in her own inventory. There would seem to be little political capital to be made with such a slap in the face of the status quo; was it possible Verlaine meant exactly what he said, that torture did not help keep order in the long term, and cost too much besides?

"I know better than to accuse you of trying to deploy me on a partisan political mission." It wasn't done. "So where do I fit into all this, First Secretary?"

Pivoting in mid-pace Verlaine turned back to his desk and the flat-form docket, which he picked up and held out to her. "Except that that's just what I'd like you to do, Specialist Ivers. Complete a personal errand, in a sense." The note in Verlaine's deep voice was ambiguous; nerves—or self-deprecating humor? "I can't deny my partisan interest in the potential payoff, here. I can only ask that you believe me when I assure you that at least part of my motive is genuine and disinterested."

There was something odd in the First Secretary's demeanor; he seemed almost embarrassed. Jils opened the docket and reached out to leaf through its stacked pages; then stopped where she was, page one, paragraph one, *In the circumstance of the recently renewed engagement of service, Andrej Ulexeievitch Koscuisko, Ship's Surgeon and Inquisitor, it is the judgment of this Court . . .*

Verlaine meant to cancel Koscuisko's Writ.

Without prejudice. Having been extended under and as a result of inappropriate duress contrary to the rule of Law and the Bench's responsibility to protect its citizens from unreasonable and unlawful imposition.

There was more. There was an advance copy of the Second Judge's proposed statement of intent, and Jils could pick out the pertinent titles with ease. *Regrettable vulnerability of the system to abuse. Multiple instances of failure, not excepting Chilleau Judiciary's own shameful failure to protect the rights of displaced Nurail souls at the Domitt Prison. Immediate moratorium on imposition of the Bond and granting of any new Writs to Inquire.*

There it was, in plain text; and that meant that this was not a flat-form docket but an incendiary device capable of destroying Chilleau Judiciary at one blow in the wrong hands.

"Are you sure about this, First Secretary?" She had to ask; she had to hear it from him. If Koscuisko was minded to be vengeful he could create a very great deal of trouble for the Second Judge by leaking this to her anticipated opponents before she had a chance to make her case. The Fifth Judge at Cintaro in particular would pay a very great deal of money for the document in Jils's hands.

"It's the only way I have any hope of convincing Koscuisko that

I'm serious. I was wrong; he's suffered for it. I need his help. But I mean to try to make things right whether or not he's willing to support the Second Judge, Specialist Ivers."

Because the Bench judgment was to be executed at Koscuisko's will and pleasure. It was already fully endorsed. All it needed was his seal to make it official. All he had to do was sign, and he was clear of Fleet and Inquiry forever.

No quid-pro-quo for Chilleau Judiciary; no if then, else. Jils thought about it. As Verlaine had warned her, the errand he proposed had clear political overtones; and yet she was a Bench intelligence specialist, she was expected to make up her own mind about whether to accept or reject any given assignment. That included taking her own counsel about whether the immediate partisan impact of her mission was outweighed by the greater good of the Judicial order.

"Where is the *Ragnarok*, First Secretary?"

All right. She'd go. She'd carry this liberating document to Andrej Koscuisko, and find out whether he would even see her, after what his last interview with her had cost him. But she'd wait to see whether she would trust Koscuisko with the full power Verlaine offered to put in his hands.

"In maneuvers at the Pesadie Training Grounds, Bench specialist. But Koscuisko's due home on leave. If you're willing to perform the errand, agents of the Malcontent will see to the necessary arrangements, on Azanry."

On Azanry, where Koscuisko's family was?

Verlaine certainly had the political angles tabled out as acutely as he could. A Bench intelligence specialist taking relief of Writ to the inheriting son of the Koscuisko familial corporation in the very heart of the Dolgorukij Combine . . . where every move a man like Andrej Koscuisko made would be seen, analyzed, interpreted, then acted on by an immense and arcane machinery of tradition and ethnic solidarity. Working toward the will of the Koscuisko prince . . . or of the man who would be the Koscuisko prince, and perhaps there was not even so very much difference at this point.

"I'll take your Brief to Azanry." What was owed Koscuisko was fairly owed. She'd been there when he had been forced to gnaw off his own leg to escape the trap that Chilleau Judiciary had set for him, the trap that she herself had sprung on him. She had a right to be there when Chilleau prised open the jaws of the trap and apologized and begged him to accept a replacement leg with the sincere compliments of First Secretary Verlaine. For the rest of it—

"Thank you, Specialist Ivers." Verlaine knew that he was asking her to intervene in a more-or-less personal relationship between Chilleau and Andrej Koscuisko, but that was all right. He'd read her report. He knew what she'd had to say about his attempt to co-opt Koscuisko in the first place. "I appreciate your cooperation. We'll alert the Malcontent to your expected arrival."

For the rest of it she'd review the docket, and if its contents conformed with the rule of Law she'd do what she could to enlist Koscuisko's cooperation in turn. And while she was there, on Azanry, maybe she'd ask the Malcontent for something on her own behalf.

Garol Vogel had dropped out of sight on an exit trajectory from Port Burkhayden months ago, and had not been heard from since. Maybe the Malcontent knew what might have happened to him. No other source of information Jils had consulted had been able to offer any help.

Bench specialists were supposed to be difficult to seek, locate, identify. But not by other Bench specialists. "Very good, First Secretary. I'll keep you informed." She couldn't shake the feeling that more had gone on in Port Burkhayden between Andrej Koscuisko and Garol Vogel than she'd realized.

If the key was on Azanry somewhere, Jils meant to find it.

The little Wolnadi—one of the *Ragnarok*'s complement of four-soul fighters—careened past its target on a high oblique trajectory to plane; weaponer Smath screamed, from her post on the aft cannon, and Lek Kerenko grinned with pure delight to hear her curse. "Damn you, Lek, slow down!"

He would not slow down. It was just a training exercise; but Security 5.1 had the best kill-time on board the Jurisdiction Fleet Ship *Ragnarok*, and Lek did not mean to yield the honors to anyone.

"On target, Smish!" He didn't have to yell—he had the inter-ship. She wouldn't let the team down. She was eight for eight out of the gate, perfect record, confirmed target kill on all vectors.

"Trajectory shift on proximal target," Murat warned. Lek frowned in deep focus on the new data Murat sent through and made a quick rephase calculation in his mind.

Fleet didn't mean for 5.1 to finish this target run with a perfect score. Pesadie Training Command wanted evidence of substandard performance on the *Ragnarok*'s part, to support cancellation of the First Judge's research program; they weren't going to get it.

"Lateral eight point from directional?" Lek asked Taller on power flux, coding his approaches. Taller's post was right next to the navigation comps. The Wolnadi fighter was a small craft. Lek could see Taller shake his head, scowling.

"If we have to. If you're sure."

Yes, they'd pushed the propulsion systems hard from the moment they'd cleared the *Ragnarok*'s maintenance atmosphere. But that was what the ship's engines were there for. Motive power. Maneuverability. Lek knew his ship. The Wolnadi would do it.

"If I take a sub on target minus-two, can you pick off target minus-three on the way?" Lek asked Smish, just to let the weaponer know what he was doing. Because he already knew that she could do it. If she couldn't do it, he wouldn't be asking.

"We're already good on time, Lek, why push it? Yes."

She was frustrated with him, because he was pushing her hard, as well. It was an unusual position to be in, a bond-involuntary telling un-bonded troops what to do; but the *Ragnarok* didn't have enough bond-involuntaries assigned to make up a second full team after 5.3, so there they were.

Security 5.1, Lek's team, did have an un-bonded navigator assigned; but Eady was on fifth-week rotation this cycle. And Lek was better than Eady was. "On target. Fire through."

If she couldn't make the target minus-two kill before they hit target minus-three, they'd lose points on execution. The flight sphere was set up to maximize the challenge, and the targets were to be taken in order. The targets—the little remote decoys—were moving; Lek just had to move faster. That was all.

"Confirmed," Murat said approvingly, from his post on observation scan. Lek didn't have time to congratulate Smish on her marksmanship, though, because she had mere fractions of an eighth to refocus her considerable prey instinct on the next target.

"Minus-two on monitor. Please confirm target acquisition."

Lek shoved the linear propulsion feeds to the maximum, firing his laterals as he went to spin the ship and finesse its trajectory. The next target was well below the arena's theoretical floor axis, and fast approaching the boundary, but he could fly through the center of the arena, and that saved time. Nothing to go around.

"Target minus-one within six degrees of escape," Murat warned. Lek checked his stats. Fleet really did want them to fail the exercise. There was no way to get from one target to the other in time. Was there?

He could do a fly-through, maybe, if Taller could give him a pulse to shield their forward path, and clear the debris from the target so that he could take a direct line on the next without fear of hulling out on some piece of scrap metal—

"I confirm target minus-two. Targeting. Firing."

Smish was too busy concentrating on her own task to yell at him. Lek was just as glad. He knew what he was doing, and they knew that he knew what he was doing, but his governor would not let him take chances with the ship if he made the mistake of letting himself become nervous about his margins. So he had to avoid getting nervous; or else his governor would conclude that he had destruction of Jurisdiction property in mind, and shut him down.

The sensor screen lit up with the impact report from the target's remains. The kill was good. "Blow me a hole, Taller," Lek suggested. "We can still catch the last one."

Taller sent a plasma burst out ahead of the fighter's path, shaking his head as he did so. "Whatever you say. But we're already ahead, Lek, you don't have to prove anything."

Lek threaded the Wolnadi through the narrow passageway that the plasma bolt cleared through the debris of target minus-two. "Ahead isn't good enough. We're maximizing. Smish. Target acquisition?"

Nobody flattened the line. Nobody had hit all the targets in sequence and on time in the weeks they'd been here. He had a chance. With Smish's eye for her targets and his feel for his navs, they could do it.

The last target was on-screen. Lek could see it; they were heading straight on, and the subtle blue sheen of the flight sphere's containment field glowed dimly against the backdrop of black Space and distant star-fields. It was going to be close; their quarry was doing everything it could to escape.

"Targeting," Smish said.

Lek eased the propulsion up just a hair, one eye to his return trajectory. He needed power in reserve to return to base. "Firing. Confirm kill on three. Two. One."

The forward display screens blossomed, then blanked as ship's on-board display recalibrated itself. Explosion; good. That was it for the last of the targets, then.

Lek heeled the ship into its return arc and brought its speed up as quickly as he dared. All he had to do now was get back to the *Ragnarok* on time, and they would have beaten Pesadie for good and all. After years of being mocked by their Fleet counterparts as idle vacationers on an experimental test bed—if not worse—the crew of the *Ragnarok* had shown Fleet that they could obtain and execute with the best of them.

Pesadie Training Command had done everything it could to discredit the technical and fighting abilities of the Jurisdiction Fleet Ship *Ragnarok*, under cover of capability evaluation. But the *Ragnarok* had accomplished every task, exceeded every benchmark Pesadie had set against them; and defended its honor, to the last.

Jennet ap Rhiannon stood on the observation deck of the Engineering bridge with her arms braced stiff against the waist-high railing, looking down through the soundproof clear-wall into the well of Engineering's command and control center, where the *Ragnarok*'s last battle exercise was displayed on ship's primary screens.

It was a pleasure to watch the Wolnadi fight. None of the crews had embarrassed the ship, but this one seemed to be particularly aggressive, and Jennet sent a question back over her shoulder to Ralph Mendez while she watched. "Security 5.1, First Officer?"

The Wolnadi took its target on a high hard oblique roll, clearly planning on blasting through its own debris field on its way to the end of the set. She could see the final target start to move toward the perimeter; someone in Pesadie Training Command had noticed the Wolnadi's successful attack as well, and was taking measures to challenge their final approach—to make it as difficult as possible to get the final kill.

"That's them, Lieutenant," Mendez replied, Santone dialect still flavoring his syntax even after all of his years in Fleet. "Look at him go. Would you have thought a bond-involuntary could show so much ginger, and get away with it?"

No, she wouldn't. Bond-involuntaries were much more likely to be characterized by an aggressively—or defensively—conservative approach to life, for their own protection.

"Kerenko, I think," Lieutenant Seascape said, from the shadows behind Jennet. "I thought Koscuisko was taking his Bonds home?"

"Andrej's taking Security 5.3, Lieutenant," Mendez corrected. "Kerenko's on 5.1. He wanted to take all six of them home, but he can't take St. Clare anyway, no new governor yet. And Fleet would only authorize one Security team."

That was right. There were only six bond-involuntary troops assigned to the *Ragnarok* right now, well short of the hypothetical full complement of twenty-five. Nor were bond-involuntaries the only troops the *Ragnarok* was shorted; there were only three Command Branch officers left on board, since murder in Burkhayden had removed both Captain Lowden and Lieutenant Wyrlann from the chain of command several months ago. Acting Captain Brem, acting First Lieutenant ap Rhiannon, acting Second Lieutenant Seascape, and that was it.

"That ship sure doesn't move like a failed technology," Jennet said, though she knew there was no sense in being bitter about it. The *Ragnarok* was shorted Command Branch and bond-involuntaries alike because everybody expected the ship to be scrapped as soon as the new First Judge was seated. Such was the future that awaited the pet research projects of dead First Judges. "Whoever gets that team will get quality."

"Son of a bitch," Wheatfields growled from his post in the pit of the Engineering bridge below, his voice projected into the observation deck from the station's pickups. "Be careful with those vectors, damn it, that's an expensive piece of machinery."

The Wolnadi's weaponer hit the target solid and true, and the starburst blossom on-screen was familiar and beautiful in its way. A pulse from the Wolnadi's forward jets cored the debris field and the Wolnadi dove through close behind it, only just trailing the newly emptied space. Jennet could appreciate Wheatfields's nervousness: if the navigator misjudged his speed, he could hull the fighter. But it was all part of the age-old conflict between Engineers and pilots, after all.

"He'll be careful, Serge," Mendez assured Wheatfields. Wheatfields looked up toward them resentfully—so he was on return feed, listening as well as sending. "Or you can take it out of his hide. If there's any hide left." After Mendez himself was finished with Kerenko, should Kerenko make a mistake. Wheatfields did not seem to be impressed, turning back to watch the screens without comment.

The last target was running for the perimeter of the exercise field as fast as it could; if the target escaped from the containment field, the kill wouldn't count. Pesadie didn't expect them to perform well. Pesadie had made that perfectly clear, and it wasn't supposed to be easy—but Pesadie's aggressive tests had gone well past fair challenge.

Jennet knew that Pesadie had expected them to play along, and queer their own performance. She wanted the kill all the more badly for that. The fighter gained on the target moment by moment; there was the shot, but was the kill good?

Explosion. Dead target. Jennet tightened her grip on the railing with satisfaction, tracking the fighter's progress on-screen. Beautiful.

It had been close, though, so close that the containment field itself showed signs of reaction to the impact. The faintly glowing blue sphere that delineated the flight sphere was distorted, wavering, pulsing from dim to bright and back to dim again as it absorbed the kinetic energy from the particles of debris that the explosion had sent right up against its borders.

The containment field's boundary belled outward for a moment or two, just touching the tiny blip of an observation station hung clear of the flight sphere to track the execution of the exercise. Jennet shook her head.

"Anybody on that watch-ball's going to get vertigo." Because the containment field's energy had set the station into a perturbation wobble. In her student days it'd been a standard prank—getting as close to the containment field as she could, in order to destabilize the containment barrier and rattle any rank that was observing in the backwash.

There was another explosion. Jennet stared. The observation station? But how? The fighter was well on its way back to base, there had been no round fired . . . and if she was right—she hoped she was wrong—

Jennet turned her back on the Engineering bridge to face Ship's Intelligence Officer, who was hanging from the ceiling at the back of the dimly lit observation deck with her great leathery wings folded demurely around her. "Two?"

First Officer was staring at the screen as well. So he had the same concern. "Yes, your Excellency," Two said, her mechanically translated voice calm and cheerful, as it was programmed to be.

Jennet sank back against the railing, stunned. She wasn't an Excellency. The only Command Branch officer who rated "Excellency" was the senior officer assigned, and that was the acting Captain, Cowil Brem. So Brem had been on that observation station. And he was dead. What had gone wrong?

"They're going to want to interrogate the crew." Mendez had straightened up to his full height, folding his arms across his chest. He didn't sound happy; she didn't blame him, because he was right. Fleet would want to talk to the crew of the Wolnadi to explain their role in the explosion.

The Wolnadi's crew had no possible role in the explosion that she'd seen—they'd been heading back to the *Ragnarok* before it had happened—but they'd been closest, and it was the obvious explanation, wasn't it? Training exercise, live fire, death of the commanding officer. Worse than that, this was the third Command Branch officer assigned to the Jurisdiction Fleet Ship *Ragnarok* to die by violence within the past few months.

Someone was sure to see conspiracy at work. There were two problems that faced them, then, and the fact that no one deserved to be threatened with the penalty for killing a Command Branch officer when it had been an accident was only the first. The second problem was that once Fleet started asking questions, it almost never stopped with only three or four confessions.

"Seascape. Go and get Koscuisko. Tell him he's leaving now, right now, Captain's orders." She knew what she had to do. Fleet would want to test for Free Government plots, or maybe even mutiny. They'd start with the crew of the Wolnadi and go on from there.

Mendez was looking at her, somewhat skeptically, and Seascape hadn't moved yet, waiting for a cue. Jennet didn't blame her. But she didn't have time to stop and give a speech about how unsuited she was for Command, unexpected responsibility, the help she'd need from more experienced officers if she was to hope to avoid discrediting her Command. Brem was dead; she was the senior Command Branch officer on site, and that made her the acting Captain of the *Ragnarok*.

"First Officer, please go and get that crew to the courier as soon as they dock. I'll meet you there. I'll explain to 5.3. I want those people out of here."

Fleet couldn't ask them questions if Fleet couldn't lay hands on them. Let Koscuisko take 5.1 home with him on leave, not 5.3. By the time Koscuisko was back Fleet would have straightened everything out, so long as she could ensure that they didn't just take the path of least resistance at the expense of the crew of the *Ragnarok*.

"Vector transit is logged, Lieutenant," Wheatfields said, his voice calm and matter-of-fact over the station pickup. Turning around, Jennet gave the Engineer a crisp nod that was equal portions of acknowledgment and thanks.

"Never mind explaining to 5.3," Mendez said. "Explaining to Andrej. That'll be the test, Lieutenant. I'll be waiting to see you do that. Coming, Seascape?" He would go along with it. He agreed with her. So he knew she was right about Fleet.

"I'll talk to Pesadie once Koscuisko is on vector," Jennet said to Two, who was just hanging there, taking it all in. "Did we even know where the observers were? I know the fighter didn't." Most observation stations were unmanned. But it wasn't because they were dangerous, in any way. What had caused that explosion?

"We had no idea." Two's translator was permanently set on "chipper," no matter the seriousness of the situation. "Were it not for the deviousness of your Intelligence Officer you still would not know. Please be careful, Captain. We have had very bad luck with our Command Branch lately."

Yes, Two was brilliant; but the joke was still in poor taste. If it had been a joke. Did Desmodontae joke? Was there a concept of humor in the Desmodontae worldview? Who knew? Two was a bat. Hominids were her natural prey. A much less intellectually sophisticated hominid species, perhaps, but Jennet knew quite well that on a certain level she looked like lunch to Ship's Intelligence.

"I'll keep it in mind. Keep Fleet off if you can, please."

She had to get out to the courier bay in the maintenance atmosphere, where Security 5.3 was only waiting for their officer of assignment to leave his going-away party before departing on home leave for Azanry in Koscuisko's system of origin, the Dolgorukij Combine. They had probably been looking forward to the vacation. And she was going to deny them the treat at the last possible moment.

It was ugly, but it had to be done. She had to get that fighter crew out of the way before Fleet could start talking about Protocols.

Surveying the scene in his office with satisfaction Andrej Koscuisko—Ship's Surgeon, Chief Medical Officer, Ship's Inquisitor—drained his cup and lofted it high over the heads of three intervening revelers to where his chief of dermatology sat tending the dispenser of punch. "How does this happen?" he called, with challenge and confusion in his voice. "There is a cup, and it is empty."

And only then did it occur to him to hope that Barille would not try to toss it back to him, once refilled. There was already enough of a mess on the floor: snack wrappers escaped from the waste container, bits of paper garlands.

Barille bowed cheerfully from his post. "The situation shall be speedily amended. Sir."

Andrej Koscuisko was not exactly drunk. But he was unquestionably in such a very good mood that not even the unexpected appearance of the Ship's Second Lieutenant—Renata Seascape—could perturb his genial humor. He was on holiday. He was going home. He was taking his people with him, or at least some of his people.

"Lieutenant. A surprise." She stood in the doorway to his office, which was full of people and decorated for the occasion with colorful garlands of fish tails and fins and cheerful smiling fish-faces. Andrej had at first tried to believe that they could have no idea how rude it all was; but there was no real use trying to pretend that Infirmary had not in all this time learned that Dolgorukij men customarily thought of their genitals in piscine terms, so it was a mark of affection, really. "Come in, sit down, have a drink. Have several. There's plenty."

And it all had to be gone before the next shift came on, because one really did not party in Infirmary, not even in the Ship's Surgeon's private office. Which Mahaffie would be sharing with Colloy and Hoff during his absence, and Andrej wished them all joy of the documentation, with a full heart.

Seascape smiled and bowed. "Thank you, your Excellency, no thank you." She had to raise her voice to make herself heard; Volens had started to sing. Something about a river, Andrej thought. "Sir. Your presence very urgently requested in courier bay. Time to go, sir. Please come with me."

Time to go? Rising from his desk Andrej squinted at his timepiece. Surely not. Someone threw a fish-fin at Seascape and it stuck in her hair, but she was otherwise unmoved. Well. Perhaps it was time. Because he was tipsy, and could have mistaken the schedule.

"If you say so, Lieutenant." It was a tricky business, making his way to the door; it meant getting past Aachil, and Aachil always got a little over-affectionate when he was drunk. Not like Haber. Andrej wouldn't have minded kissing Haber, but he rather drew the line at Aachil. "Gentles. Thank you for your good wishes, good-bye, I'll be back in three months. Please do not save any documentation for me. I grant it all to you, with all my heart."

The party was in full spate. It would do very well without him. Barille was in pursuit, with a full cup of punch; Andrej couldn't very well have Barille coming out into section with uncontained liquor, could he? "Yes. Thank you." Almost to the door. Andrej drank off half the cup before handing it back. "But really, I must go. The Lieutenant says so."

She was getting impatient, too. "If you please, your Excellency, we've got to get to courier bay."

That was odd. What urgency was there, really? Everything was ready to go, his kit packed, his people cleared. But not understanding what was happening was something that a man grew to accept when he was drunk, or even when he was merely not exactly drunk. So rather than argue with her Andrej put his arm around her shoulders— for support and stabilization only, of course, he was a little unsteady on his feet. "Yes, yes, Lieutenant, coming immediately. Tell me. Have you ever to Azanry been?"

He was going home. It had been nearly nine years. He was not going home to stay, to try to rebuild a life of some sort after eight years dedicated to the practice of atrocity as a professional torturer; no, that fantasy had died months ago, when Bench intelligence specialist Jils Ivers had brought him word from Chilleau Judiciary that had forced him to re-engage with Fleet, to save himself from the administration that had been responsible for the Domitt Prison.

But he was going home.

Bench intelligence specialist Garol Vogel had shown him a Bench warrant with his name on it, in Port Burkhayden. Someone wanted him dead. If someone with the power to obtain a Bench warrant truly meant that he should die, the odds were good that he did not have long to live. So he had to take care of some personal business before he could be free to concentrate on who and why and how he was to protect himself. He had to ensure that Marana would be all right if he was killed; Marana, and his young son Anton.

"Never had the pleasure, your Excellency, though I understand it's very beautiful," Seascape said. "Here's the lift, sir. It'll be this way."

What? Oh. That was right. He'd asked her a question.

"I suppose one's home is always beautiful." The half-cup of punch he'd downed on his way out of his office had fuddled him, but the walk did him some good. His head was just clear enough for him to realize what an inane thing that had been to say. Stildyne's home had never been beautiful to Stildyne, for instance, as far as Andrej had ever heard him talk about it.

Or perhaps Stildyne's had simply never been home at all in the sense that Azanry was Andrej's. That could be. Stildyne's childhood and upbringing had apparently been as ugly as Stildyne himself was, also through no fault of Stildyne's own.

The lift doors sealed behind them; they were alone. Andrej leaned up against the back wall of the nexus lift, waiting for the fog to clear from the forefront of his mind.

"Your Excellency, there's been a change of plan," Seascape said.

Andrej stared at her, wondering what she was talking about. "How do you mean, Lieutenant?"

Seascape seemed uncomfortable, but resolute. "Necessary to make a last-minute substitution, sir, Security 5.1 for 5.3. We're to be met by the First Lieutenant. She'll explain, but you should at least be forewarned."

Substitution? What nonsense. And yet it didn't seem to be a joke; Seascape seemed quite serious. Any number of things to say occurred to Andrej, but she was the most junior officer on board—so whatever was going on was not likely to be her fault. A man had to take care how quickly he took offense, when liquor might be interfering with his perception.

The nexus lift stopped; it wasn't far to the courier bay from here. One turning, three turnings, straight on; First Officer stood in the corridor waiting for them, pointing them toward the ready-room with a gesture of the arm and hand before he followed them into the room to close the door behind them.

Through the observation window in the connecting door, Andrej could see his Security 5.3, drawn up in the muster room adjacent. What were they doing there? They were supposed to be waiting at the courier itself, not on standby.

The ship's acting First Lieutenant ap Rhiannon stood between Andrej and the door to the next room. She waited until Mendez had sealed the door, and then she spoke. That was a little forward of her; perhaps the impertinence could be excused on a formality, as her superior officer was not on board.

"Your Excellency. I regret that I must make an alteration to your travel plans, sir. It will be necessary for you to take Security 5.1 rather than your previously selected Security 5.3 home with you on leave. And it is critically important that you leave immediately."

Said who? Jennet ap Rhiannon? Andrej folded his arms across his chest and raised his eyebrows at her skeptically. She was shorter than he was. And he outranked her. Who did she think she was, to tell him what to do?

"I'm not inclined to make any such substitution, Lieutenant." He'd been through a great deal with 5.3, or rather they had been through a great deal with him. Because of him. On his behalf, for his sake. "I have clearance for 5.3. I'm taking them with me. What possible interest could you have in interfering with my holiday?"

And yet the First Officer was here, and he was not jumping down her throat for overreaching her position. First Officer rarely tolerated breaches of rank-protocol; Andrej therefore asked the question in a curious, rather than an overtly hostile, tone of voice. Oh. Perhaps a little hostile. Perhaps. He didn't like Command Branch interfering with his life. Captain Lowden had had altogether too much to do with Andrej's life, until someone had killed him at Port Burkhayden.

"In the recently completed exercise from which Security 5.1 has just returned, a target was destroyed near the containment perimeter." All right, she clearly seemed to feel that she was making an explanation. He would wait. "Shortly afterward, an observation station proximal to the final kill exploded. I don't know if 5.1 knows about the explosion. I'm quite sure they don't know where our own remote observation team was when the explosion occurred."

Andrej began to see where the argument was headed. He didn't like it. "Lieutenant, I have promised these people, and long anticipated this. Is it truly necessary?"

Even through the liquor and the partying, however, Andrej's mind could track the logic. Command Branch officer dead. Explosion proximate to fighter manned by Security 5.1. *Interrogate the crew for any potential evidence of conspiracy to commit a mutinous act. Aggressively investigate all implied or explicit disaffection among the crew.*

"Your Excellency, through the death of acting Captain Cowil Brem I have assumed command of the *Ragnarok*. In the legal capacity of your commanding officer, I direct you to take Security 5.1 and clear this ship with all expedient speed."

How dare she use such language with him? She had the technical authority, but it was just that, a mere technicality. And yet she was right. She was the senior Command Branch officer, and that made her acting Captain.

That didn't mean he had to like any of this a bit. "First Officer. What have they been told?" It was capitulation on his part, and she would recognize it as such. But he dared not leave without understanding exactly what Lek Kerenko knew, and what supposed; Lek was bond-involuntary, and vulnerable.

"I told 'em that Fleet would try to pick the team apart, to cover for the embarrassment of being blown out of the water by an experimental ship. So they were going on assignment. Captain's direct and explicit orders."

Well, it would do, and it was all he had. Very well. "I will say goodbye to my Security," Andrej said firmly, and not very respectfully either. "And then I will leave straightaway. By your leave, of course, Lieutenant."

He didn't wait for leave. He went through the intervening door into the muster room, where Security 5.3 stood in formal array, waiting for him. There was to be no chance to explain; what the Lieutenant proposed was to willfully evade normal Judicial procedure by removing persons potentially of interest from their immediate environment, and that might create trouble in the hearts and minds of bond-involuntary troops.

Bond-involuntaries had been carefully schooled in the performance of their duty. Emotional conflict was the signal for the governor that each had implanted in their brains to punish what was clearly either a transgression or intent to transgress. So he could say nothing to his people except that he was sorry, that he would miss them, that they would be sure to come with him next time.

She was overreacting. Surely. Yet he had seen too much during his term of duty to be able to believe that there was no chance of her worst fears becoming reality.

Stildyne could see Koscuisko in the next room, talking to 5.3. He wished Koscuisko would hurry up. The sooner they got clear of this the easier it was going to be to manage; and starting this exercise with Koscuisko already in a filthy mood was not what he had anticipated— but a man could only deal with what he had to work with. Not what he wished he had.

Koscuisko stepped through the door into the courier bay, and Security 5.1 came to attention smartly, lined up beneath the belly of the craft and waiting only for Koscuisko's word to be away. It was a nice courier; a Combine national, the property of the Koscuisko familial corporation in fact. One of the things that still amazed Stildyne after four years and more with Andrej Koscuisko was how inconceivably rich the man was—at least so far as disposition of material goods was concerned.

"Thank you, gentles, and we must leave very soon, but I want a moment. Stand down. Stildyne. Kits on board?"

Stildyne knew what urgency First Officer had concealed behind his calm demeanor and his careful drawl. If First Officer was worried Stildyne was near frantic; but Koscuisko would not be hurried.

"Cleared and ready for departure, your Excellency, immediately. As the officer please."

Koscuisko frowned at him a little over that. He didn't usually resort to formal language with Koscuisko; it was almost a form of bullying. It was the only way Stildyne could come up with to express the urgency he felt. First Officer wanted 5.1 clear of the *Ragnarok*. Stildyne didn't know why—exactly—but that didn't concern him. First Officer knew what he was about.

"These people have just come off exercise, Chief." There was a touch of admonition in Koscuisko's voice, a hint of reproach. "And in particular the navigator has been worked hard. Not that the entire crew has been less fully challenged, but do we demand that Lek perform a vector transit now? This moment? Lek. Should truly we be asking such effort, from you?"

All right, maybe Koscuisko was not simply being difficult because he was angry and frustrated. It was possible that Koscuisko was checking to be sure that Lek was centered, clear, and well within the tolerances imposed by his governor. "It's just a vector transit, your Excellency." Lek didn't quite shrug, but the idea was there. "Not a problem, sir. And Godsalt has already done the calculations."

There was no halt or hesitation in Lek's voice. If Lek had any apprehension, he would let them know by using more formal and submissive language—"as it please the officer." For Lek to use "your Excellency" and "sir" in direct address meant that there were no issues with his governor for Koscuisko to confront. Koscuisko nodded, and made an effort to clear the trouble from his face. "Well, then, let us be off, there is no time like the present. Chief."

Stildyne didn't need to say anything. Koscuisko went up the ramp into the courier. Stildyne nodded, and 5.1 broke out to man the stations—finalize the checks, close the ports and portals, seal the courier for launch.

Stildyne himself followed Koscuisko up the ramp, slowly. Thinking. Wondering. Why was First Officer in such an apparent hurry to get these people away from the ship? What did Koscuisko know? And what would Koscuisko tell him?

It was an unfortunate complication to the start of a man's holiday. But maybe once they'd passed this rocky bit the track would be smooth and level for the duration of Koscuisko's home leave.

CHAPTER TWO

Damage Control

Admiral Sandri Brecinn sat at her ease in her war room watching the course of the exercise on the massive screens that filled the whole half of the room: top, bottom, sides. "What do they think they're doing?" she demanded, watching, as the Wolnadi made an audacious move on its next-to-last target. "Eppie, I'm going to want a blood test on that navigator. He's got to be on something."

An appreciative chuckle ran through the room, passing from sycophant to toady to sidekick. Brecinn stretched comfortably. She was in her element, surrounded by her people, and they all knew that nothing the *Ragnarok* accomplished during this exercise would make any difference in the end. The *Ragnarok* was history. History, and a very significant addition to her asset account.

"You might have to hold the crew here for a while." Eppie, her aide, picked the line up and stretched it out ably. "Once you start looking into such things. Who knows how far it goes?"

Brecinn liked Eppie. Eppie was a reasonable person. They were all of them reasonable people, people one could deal with, people with whom one could do business. Well, almost all of them. Some of the observers were unknown quantities. The armaments man, Rukota, for one; Brecinn didn't know too much about him except that he was very solidly protected—his wife had an intimate understanding of long duration with somebody's First Secretary.

The Clerk of Court that Chilleau Judiciary had sent to take legal note of the proceedings, however, was a woman with a very interesting past about whom Brecinn's sources wished to say surprisingly little; that piqued Brecinn's interest. Noycannir was just a Clerk of Court, one who didn't seem to be very well placed. Her apparent status was inconsistent with what little Brecinn had been able to find out about her contacts. So was she a different sort of an observer? And why exactly was she here, under cover as an exercise observer?

If Noycannir was here on a secret mission she had yet to approach Brecinn about it, which showed a lack of respect on Chilleau's part. Chilleau was getting too self-confident by half. The Selection was far from certain, and—favorite or no favorite—Chilleau's victory would not be guaranteed until the last Judge had logged the consensus opinion of the last Judiciary. That was weeks away.

"No sense of propriety." Brecinn vented some of her frustration with Chilleau Judiciary at the expense of the Wolnadi crew on-screen. The *Ragnarok*'s fighter had taken its next-to-last target; it had only one left. "Anybody with a feather's-weight of sensitivity would settle for a solid showing. Instead of this—shameless display—"

That crew knew as well as anyone that the program was as good as cancelled. If they had any sense at all, they'd be doing what they could to facilitate the cancellation, and hoping for a few crumbs of the spoils to drop their way. If they were reasonable people, they'd play along. Nobody was going to be looking closely at anybody's personal kit once the ship was decommissioned, after all.

The Wolnadi closed on its last target. Brecinn frowned.

There was an observation station right there, just there, to the other side of the containment field. The *Ragnarok*'s observation party was on that station. The Wolnadi wouldn't know that, or at least they weren't supposed to know. What was she worrying about, anyway? Brecinn asked herself, and took a deep breath, willing herself to relax. The odds of the fighter missing the target, breaching the containment field, and hitting the observation station were low indeed.

Maris had sworn that the stock he had stowed there was stable. Fresh stuff. New loads. Rocket propellant didn't start to degrade until it got old, unless it had been contaminated. Maris knew better than to have sold her inferior goods. He knew she needed them to satisfy the debt she owed to reasonable people.

And the fighter didn't miss the target. Admiral Brecinn sat back in her chair, satisfied and annoyed at the same time—satisfied, that she'd been concerned over nothing; annoyed at the fighter's arrogance in pushing for a perfect run.

The fighter heeled into its trajectory, starting back toward its base ship while the debris from the target blossomed in the familiar dust-rose of a solid kill. The target had been very close to the boundary; the plasma membrane of the containment field belled out, fighting to absorb the energy of the blast, and kissed the observation station, sending it tumbling.

There was a murmur of amusement from the observers assembled, nine in all, seated in ranks arrayed before the great monitoring wall—getting a lick from energy wash was a harmless mishap, a pratfall, more amusing than anything else unless it was your bean tea that got spilt. Still Brecinn frowned, despite herself.

Armaments were intrinsically unstable to a certain degree, but it was a moderate degree, a very moderate degree, and it wasn't as though she could have redirected the *Ragnarok* party. They'd made the selection at random from the available platforms as part of the exercise protocol.

She hadn't thought about excluding that one station until it had been too late, not as though she really could have without drawing attention to herself, and not as if that was the only station she was using for storage. The storage spaces were all inerted anyway. Why should she worry? Nobody paid any attention to what might be stored out on unmanned observation stations. Nobody cared about miscellaneous stores.

There was a sudden flare on-screen, and the room fell silent. Brecinn stood up, staring.

"What was that?"

It couldn't be. It would be such disgustingly stupid luck.

"Observation station, Admiral," the technician on duty said, disbelief clear in her voice. "Seems to have exploded. No coherent structure on scan."

No trace of a lifeboat, then. They hadn't had time. They hadn't had warning. There was plenty of debris; that was all too depressingly obvious, and somewhere in that debris floated the probably fractionalized bodies of the people who had been watching the exercise from remote location. The *Ragnarok*'s acting Captain. A Command Branch officer. That meant a full-fledged accident investigation. She couldn't afford one.

Some of the debris in that cluster would bear unmistakable chemical signatures of controlled merchandise—armaments, bombs—that could be traced back to specific points of origin, failures in inventory control, even the occasional warehouse theft. It would be difficult to explain, almost impossible to overlook. Unimaginably expensive to deny.

"Poll all stations," Brecinn ordered. "Let's be sure of our facts before we send any formal notices. We'll take a short recess while we confirm whether the station was manned. Two eights, gentles, and reconvene here."

Taking a recess was risky. They were her staff, true enough, but they would be watching for the first hint of uncertainty on her part to gut her carcass and throw her to the scavengers while they hurried to harvest everything they could salvage ahead of a forensic accounting team. She had to have time to think.

One by one, her people stood and left the room. The Clerk of Court from Chilleau Judiciary excused herself; the armaments evaluator from Second Fleet put his feet up on the back of the chair in front of him, with every apparent intention of having a nap in place. Fine.

Eppie and one or two of the others would have gone directly to her office. They'd be waiting for her. *Damn the* Ragnarok *and its crew anyway*, Admiral Brecinn told herself crossly; and went to join her aides and advisors for private conference.

Strolling thoughtfully through the halls beneath the Admiral's management suite Mergau Noycannir switched on her snooper with a casual gesture that mimicked rubbing behind one ear; and was immediately rewarded.

". . . damage assessment, as soon as possible. We needed those rounds to fulfill a contract coming due. We'll have to make up the difference in cash, if this gets out."

Eppie, Mergau thought. It was a daring act of espionage to have planted a snoop on the Admiral. As it was, she could only afford one of the timed sneakers. One quarter of an eight, and then it would disintegrate into anonymous and untraceable dust. With luck, no one would even have discovered that there had been a transmission.

"That means an inventory of all the stations. Not just to discover what went up. To be sure we know what's where." Admiral Brecinn's voice, annoyed and anxious. From the way the others' voices rose and fell in volume, Mergau guessed that the Admiral was pacing.

"We'll have to cover for it somehow, Admiral. After all. Command Branch. Bad luck all around."

She'd suspected Brecinn's command of black marketeering from the moment she'd arrived. She recognized some of the names and faces from the secured files at Chilleau Judiciary. Here was evidence; but more than evidence, perhaps.

"Our counterparts are counting on us to be well placed for the new regime. We lose their confidence, we lose everything. We've got to contain this somehow." The Admiral again, and she sounded just a little—frightened. Mergau Noycannir knew what frightened people sounded like. She recognized the subtle quavering behind the fine false front.

"Admiral, it was an accident. It could have happened to anyone." Mergau knew better. Brecinn apparently did, too.

"People who conduct business with professionals don't have accidents, Eppie. No. We can't afford to let it be an accident. We need a cover, and we need it fast."

Mergau knew her time was running out; the snooper would stop transmitting at any moment. She could extrapolate well enough from what she had heard, however, and with that she could build the perfect solution to the Admiral's problem. Her problem as well.

Admiral Brecinn needed to cover the fact that the explosion that had just killed the *Ragnarok*'s acting Captain had resulted from the illegal stockpiling of stolen armaments for sale on the black market; Mergau needed all the protection she could get.

Admiral Brecinn only knew that Mergau was a Clerk of Court at Chilleau Judiciary. She didn't know how low on the First Secretary's table of assignments her placement had become. Mergau naturally had not hastened to explain how sadly reduced her position was from the days when she had brought the Writ to Inquire back from Fleet Orientation Station Medical at the First Secretary's desire; and she did have contacts, even yet.

That was how she had arranged for the forged entry of Andrej Koscuisko's name on an unauthorized Bench warrant.

Had the Bench warrant been exercised, it would not have mattered, in the end, whether it had been forged or not. Once the thing had been done, the Bench would have been forced to stand behind it, or admit to the falsification. The Bench couldn't afford to do that. They'd have had to defend the warrant as true, if anyone ever found out about it— not that there'd been any reason to fear that anybody ever would.

But the Bench specialist to whom it had fallen to execute the warrant had recorded it as written against somebody else entirely, and that raised all kinds of difficulties.

Someone had said something that Mergau hadn't quite caught, handicapped as she was by the directional nature of the snooper. Admiral Brecinn's response made the nature of the question clear, however. "Ap Rhiannon. Priggish little self-important bitch. Crèche-bred. Of all the luck."

A tiny spark of heat against the skin at the back of her ear, too brief to be painful; the snooper died, and destroyed the evidence of its existence. Where she'd tagged Brecinn, the Admiral would not even notice the snooper's disintegration.

Mergau continued in her thoughtful meditative stroll, heading for the water-garden outside the canteen. There was a great deal to think about here. Admiral Brecinn needed help. Mergau needed protection. Mergau didn't know quite how it was going to play out, not just yet. But she was confident.

Somewhere in this morning's events she was going to find the key to her salvation, and defense against the chance that some Bench specialist would turn up some day to confront her with her failed attempt to satisfy her vengeance against Andrej Koscuisko with a Judicial murder.

The observation deck cleared out. The Admiral had left the room; her staff had melted away into the figurative woodwork. The Clerk of Court that Chilleau Judiciary had sent to observe the exercise had similarly excused herself. That meant that the room was as clean as any on station just now, and General Dierryk Rukota had no particular desire to go anywhere.

The technicians were still here, of course, working the boards:

status checks, population reconciliation, traffic analysis. All to try to determine for a fact whether the *Ragnarok*'s Command had been on that observation station when it had exploded.

Someone brought him a cup of bean tea, and Rukota accepted it with a nod of grateful thanks. Good stuff, too. He had no grievance with technicians. He just didn't think he liked Fleet Admiral Brecinn, or her pack of scavengers.

Everybody knew that the *Ragnarok*'s research program was due for cancellation with the selection of a new First Judge. It was traditional. New First Judges needed all the leverage with Fleet that they could get, especially during the early formative years of their administration—leverage a new research program, with a generous provision of funding from tax revenues, could provide. That didn't mean they had to be so obvious about it.

The *Ragnarok*'s black hull technology was the culmination of twenty-four years of technical research, hundreds upon thousands upon millions of eights of markers Standard, untold hours of labor, and the product of the focused intellect of some of the finest mechanical minds under Jurisdiction.

It was bad enough that the program had to be at least suspended while the new First Judge, whoever she was, decided exactly what to do with it. Rukota wanted to see Fleet concentrating on doing what it could to harvest the lessons learned to date, rather than blowing it all off as yesterday's news. The ship had performed well in test and maneuvers. There were solid innovations there in its design.

Flying on the order of that last fighter's run spoke for esprit as well; people who didn't care about where they were and what they were doing couldn't be bothered to shave their fuses like that. So the ship had more than just its experimental technology going for it. And Fleet would throw that away, too, dispersing the crew in every which direction when the time came to decommission the hull.

It was a very great shame to put so much into a battlewagon and never let it meet the enemy. And yet the enemy—the Free Government—was not one that could be met with at all, by even the greatest of battleships. They were small and only loosely organized, poorly armed, ill provisioned.

Fighting the Free Government with great ships like the *Ragnarok* was a little like deploying a field gun against the small annoying birds that were forever mocking one from the trees downrange. They were always long gone before a round could impact. All a person ended up with was wasted ammunition, and an overabundant supply of surplus toothpicks.

Rukota sipped his bean tea and stared into the great sweep of the observation screens, brooding. Jurisdiction Fleet Ship *Ragnarok*. He knew an officer on board that ship; he'd been young ap Rhiannon's commander not too long ago, when he'd had a stubborn pocket of resurgent civil resistance to deal with and she'd been sent to command his advance scout ships. It hadn't been a pleasant experience, at least not for him.

Ap Rhiannon was crèche-bred, inflexible, intolerant, and all but unteachable. When she'd seen that elements within Fleet's own supply lines had been aiding and abetting the insurrectionaries—for a nice profit—she'd redirected her assigned ships to intercept an arms shipment, and shut the pipeline down.

There had been a very great deal of embarrassment in upper Fleet echelons. He'd been blamed for not keeping a closer rein on her, when it hadn't been any of his doing one way or the other. She hadn't even told him. That had given him deniability, and saved his career; but it had bothered him at the same time, and bothered him still.

Had she not told him in order to reserve the blame for herself, when blame came—as it was almost certain to? Or had she not been able to decide whether he was in on it?

She'd made her point about black-market traffic in armaments. And been assigned to the *Ragnarok* for her pains, a dead-end assignment on a dead-headed research vessel headed for decommission with a crew that fleet had notoriously been packing with malcontents and malingerers for years. And here he was, for his own part, pulled off-line to provide administrative support on training exercises. As close to dry-dock as an officer could get.

He knew where the *Ragnarok* was on-screen; its position was marked, and with its maintenance atmosphere fully expanded the lights were easy to pick out against the black backdrop of space. So when something disengaged from the *Ragnarok* and started moving out and away from the ship it caught Rukota's attention. Small blip. Picking up speed quickly enough to indicate a courier of some sort.

Rukota leaned his head back against the low headrest of the chair in which he sprawled, and caught a technician's eye. "What's that?" Ap Rhiannon coming to see Admiral Brecinn, perhaps, though what her purpose might be was not something Rukota felt he could easily guess.

The technician squinted at the light-track, and then consulted a log. "Oh, Ship's Surgeon, General. Home leave."

Right. The blip wasn't tracking for the station. It was angling out toward the Pesadie exit vector, leaving the system. Ship's Surgeons were ranking officers; they were also Ship's Inquisitors, and Ship's Inquisitors never, ever, ever traveled without Security.

There was a thought at the back of his mind, a vague and unformed suspicion that there could be something interesting about that courier. If he thought about it—

If he thought about it, he might discover something that he'd have to call to somebody's attention. It wasn't any of his business. Pesadie was jealous of its rights and prerogatives; they didn't need any help from him. He had as much as been told so, and by Admiral Brecinn herself.

Shifting his feet from the back of the chair in front of him to the floor, General Rukota put it all out of his mind. Pesadie Station was responsible for its own Security. Let them deal with it.

"Thanks," he called over to the technician, still hard at work on the assessment task. "Good bean tea. Best of luck with damage control."

So long as he left the area he didn't have to worry about keeping his own suspicious mind in check. A quick nap before Admiral Brecinn reconvened, and any miscellaneous thoughts he might have would be safely put to rest.

Andrej Koscuisko was very close to sober and not entirely happy about it. Standing behind the navigation console in the wheelhouse, he watched the forward scans, listening to the traffic in braid over the inter-ship channels.

Lek—their navigator—was tired. Combat evaluations were intense enough to be exhausting even with dummy ammunition, and these had been live-fire exercises. If Lek was given a chance to start to wonder about all of this . . .

"Courier ship *Magdalenja*, Dolgorukij Combine, Aznir registry. Koscuisko familial corporation ship. Requesting release of pre-cleared passage."

Lek sounded steady enough. And once they were on vector Andrej could have a quiet talk with him. There were drugs on board. He never traveled without drugs strong enough to overrule even a governor, and after what had happened to St. Clare—whose governor had gone critical at Port Burkhayden, and nearly killed him—Andrej had stocked his kit for triple redundancy. He was taking no chances with his Bonds. He was responsible for them. They trusted him to take good care of them.

The courier was approaching the perimeter of Pesadie Training Command's administrative space, ready to clear the station. From here it was only a matter of three hours' time before they reached the exit vector. The vector was patrolled, of course; exit from Fleet stations was controlled as strictly as authorized entry. But the transit plan had been precleared. There was no reason for anyone to challenge his departure; Andrej concentrated on that. No reason.

"We confirm, *Magdalenja*." Pesadie Station's port authority sounded bored. Almost casual. "For the record, confirm souls in transit, please."

Lek looked around and up, back over his shoulder, seeking guidance from Andrej. Or perhaps from his Chief, Stildyne, who stood to Andrej's left; but this was Andrej's arena. He knew what to do. Ap Rhiannon surely had not intended her ruse to go on record so soon after its initiation.

"Voice confirm," Andrej said, and if he sounded a little irritated it was because he was unhappy. "I am Andrej Ulexeievitch Koscuisko, Chief Medical Officer assigned to the Jurisdiction Fleet Ship *Ragnarok*. Traveling home on leave with my Security also duly assigned, and I have not been home in nearly nine years, so I would appreciate your cooperation in expediting clearance."

Meaning, *if you dare insult a ranking officer by insisting on a voice-count just because it is the letter of the procedure, said ranking officer is entirely capable of taking it personally, with subsequent negative consequences to your very own personal career. Which will be ending.* Andrej didn't usually resort to bullying, but if a man was going to pull rank there was no sense in being the least bit subtle about it.

It took several moments for the voice confirm to clear; to claim to be Andrej Koscuisko was not something that could be lightly ventured. He held the Writ to Inquire, and could lawfully deploy the entire fearful inventory of torture in the Bench's Protocols on his own authority. Making a false claim to the authority of a Judicial officer was a capital offense; and an abomination beneath the canopy of Heaven to take pleasure from the suffering of prisoners in chains—

But that was an old guilt. Old, if ever present, sin. No less deep and damnable now than the day Andrej had first begun to realize that he was a monster, but it had been nine years, Creation had not risen up to swallow him and take him to his punishment, and Andrej needed his wits about him to get past this procedural check and to the exit vector. He could not abate his sin by brooding on it. There would be time enough for that in Hell.

"Thank you, your Excellency." The Port Authority sounded much less casual now. "No offense intended, your Excellency. Cleared to vector. If I might presume to offer personal good wishes for a pleasant holiday, sir." *No, you insolent groom's boy, you may not.* It was presumptuous. But Andrej had already made himself unpleasant. He wanted the Port Authority to be too grateful to be out from under his displeasure to think about placing any additional administrative requirements in his path.

"You are very kind, Control, thank you. *Magdalenja* away here, I think? Yes?"

This was Lek's signal to pick up the thread, and he did so smoothly, with no hint of tension in his voice. "*Magdalenja* away here, Pesadie. Going off comm to prepare for vector transit."

Clear.

The corvettes standing by at the entry vector could still cause a fuss, but it was much less likely that they would do so now that Andrej had snarled at Pesadie, and they had been unlikely enough to interfere with him in the first place.

It was just his nerves. And his nerves weren't the nerves he should be worrying about. "Mister Stildyne, may I see you for a moment?"

There was a private lounge just off the back of the wheelhouse, and it had all the privacy screens on it that a man could wish. Stildyne followed him into the lounge and pulled the barrier to, sealing the room.

Andrej went to the drinks cabinet at the far end of the lounge and considered the available options. Wodac. Cortac brandy. The proprietary liquor of the nuns over whom his elder sister was abbess, widely renowned for its healthful botanicals. Alcoholic beverages from one end of the Combine to the other, and all Andrej really wanted was a cup of hot rhyti, and something for a headache,

"How are we to hope to manage, Chief?"

Stildyne was up to something, behind Andrej. Andrej could hear the little chime of metal against fine Berrick ceramic ware, the seething of liquid coming to a boil. *Trust Stildyne to have found rhyti*, Andrej thought, gratefully .

"Well, you're not helping, your Excellency. It's not a problem so far. But if you're paying too much attention to Lek he'll start to wonder."

Stildyne was right. Of course. Andrej smelled the rising fragrance of top-quality leaf, and smiled almost in spite of himself. He was going home. It was only for a visit, and he had a very great deal that would have to be accomplished; but he was going home. He had not been home in more than nine years. He was going to meet his son at last.

"I can explain, Chief. Lek is Sarvaw. I will have a quiet talk with him. You may not appreciate quite what it is to be a Sarvaw, and be borne deep into the heart of enemy territory." It wasn't that Stildyne hadn't heard about the peculiar relationship between Sarvaw and other Dolgorukij, over the years. Yet how could any outlander really understand?

Stildyne had come to stand behind Andrej now; holding out a cup of rhyti. Beautiful stuff. Very hot, and milky, and smelling every bit as sweet as Andrej liked it. Stildyne was good to him. "We may need to lean on that, your Excellency, but first things first. We'll clear the vector. Then you should probably go talk to people. I'll leave you to your rhyti."

And sober up. Stildyne didn't have to say it. After more than four years together they understood each other better than that. It wasn't the norm for relationships between officers of assignment and Chief Warrant Officers, no, but had it not been for Stildyne's willingness to exceed the normal parameters of his assigned duties Andrej was very sure that he would not have survived Captain Lowden.

"Very good, Mister Stildyne. Thank you."

Andrej had enough to get through at home, if he was to hope to leave Azanry prepared to seek the unknown enemy who wanted him dead—someone with the Judicial influence to have obtained a Bench warrant for his assassination, one that Garol Vogel had declined to execute almost as an afterthought, months ago, at Port Burkhayden.

He didn't know when he would find the time and strength and courage to address the thing that had gone wrong from the beginning between himself and Security Chief Stildyne.

Jennet ap Rhiannon sat in the Captain's office with Ship's Primes around her, watching the monitors.

She wasn't sitting behind the Captain's desk; the kill was not confirmed. It would be premature. This office had the access they all needed to be sure they were on top of what Pesadie might be up to, however, so there was no choice but to gather here, whether or not the issue of the captaincy was unresolved.

Wheatfields didn't fit very comfortably into the chair in the conference area. But Wheatfields was oversized. There was no way around it. The Chigan ship's engineer was a full head taller than the late, and by and large unlamented, Captain Lowden had been; and Lowden himself had been toward the upper limit of the Jurisdiction standard.

"There's no room for misinterpretation in the ship's comps. Not as though that ever stopped Fleet," Wheatfields was saying, his eyes fixed on a monitor. "We were firing training rounds, even though they were live, so the explosive payload was reduced. That last target was destroyed well in advance of the explosion on the observation station. Whatever set the remote station off, it wasn't one of our rounds."

They were tracking the courier ship on its way to the vector. Three hours had elapsed since its launch; the exit vector security had yet to go on alert. Another half an hour and the courier would be on vector, functionally out of reach for days, at minimum. Out of Pesadie's reach forever, if she had anything to say about it.

First Officer took a drink of bean tea and grimaced.

"This stuff gets nastier every day. We ought to press for resupply while we're here, now that we're going to have to wait an investigation out. What's the Admiral up to, Two?"

Jennet shared Mendez's sentiments about the bean tea. The *Ragnarok* had always had a certain degree of difficulty breaking stores away from Fleet depots—as an experimental ship it had always taken second best. Things had begun to deteriorate at a discouraging rate after Lowden's death, though. Lowden had been as corrupt as imaginable in some ways, his personal misuse of interrogation records among them. But he had at least had the political influence required to keep the *Ragnarok* well stocked.

"No official communication." Two had to stand in her chair; she didn't sit at all in any conventional sense. Since she was fully two-thirds of Jennet's own height she was unnaturally tall amongst the assembled officers as they sat, but the Captain's office had no provision for Two's preferred mode—which was hanging upside down from the ceiling. "Traffic suggests a full-scale inventory on all observation stations and several warehouses besides. We have some eights in which to decide what to do. Perhaps as much as two days."

Two's voice was mostly out of range of Jennet's hearing. The translator that Two wore gave her an oddly accented dialect, but at least it was female, like Two herself.

The translator always took longer to process than it took Two to speak. Two sat there solemnly with her black eyes seemingly fixed on Jennet's face, waiting for the translator to catch up. It was an illusion, that fixed regard. Two didn't actually see any farther than the first flange of her wings' extent—an arm's-length, more or less.

"I'm still not sure what it is, exactly, that you mean to accomplish, your Excellency."

Ship's First Officer had always been very straight with her. There was no disrespect in his tone of voice; there was no particular change in his demeanor. Jennet could understand that. These people were all senior. She was the third person to be acting Captain of the *Ragnarok* in a year. And Mendez had never paid as much attention to rank and protocol as others in his grade class: that was the only reason he hadn't been drafted into Command Branch himself, long since.

"I'm making it up as I go along." There wasn't any sense in pretending to be smarter than Ship's Primes. She needed their agreement to do anything, rank or no rank. When it came down to it rank only existed so long as everybody agreed that it was there. "The best way I could think of to keep these crew out of Fleet's hands was to get them out of the area. If Pesadie can't get started on them, they can't begin to touch the rest of the crew. They'll have to try something else. A real investigation, maybe."

"All they have to do is wait till the crew comes back." Wheatfields was calm, dispassionate—uncaring. She'd learned that about Wheatfields. There was very little that aroused his interest, and practically nothing outside of Engineering. "What does this give us? Apart from irritating Pesadie, and I don't care, it's your neck anyway, Lieutenant."

In the months she had been assigned to the *Ragnarok*, the number of times Wheatfields had spoken to her could be reckoned up on the fingers on her hands. Or even on the fingers of Wheatfields's hands, and he had only the four fingers and the thumb to her five, since he was Chigan and not Versanjer.

To Jennet's surprise it was Two who answered for her. "Pesadie must provide some suitable answers to questions from Fleet while they wait for the crew. Or even while they send for the crew. Pesadie maybe cannot wait. They'll have to start some alternate investigation. It will only show that the *Ragnarok*'s fighter could not have fired on the observer."

Well, not that that particular issue would be a problem in and of itself. There were too many copies of the record, surely. At least three copies of training records were maintained by Fleet protocols; one of these was on the *Ragnarok*, and not under Pesadie's direct control accordingly. If Pesadie wanted to tamper with that, Pesadie would have to get past Wheatfields to do it.

But the easy answer was that the round that the Wolnadi fighter was to have deployed had been exchanged for a more lethal weapon intended to destabilize the containment barrier, communicating sufficient disruptive energy to cause the station to explode—killing the *Ragnarok*'s Captain by design.

It would be easy to prove out by confession once Pesadie got their hands on the Wolnadi's crew. Not every Inquisitor with custody of a Writ to Inquire had Koscuisko's delicacy of feeling where truth and confession were concerned.

People could be made to say anything, under sufficient duress—unless they were fortunate enough to die before they could compromise themselves. Their crewmates, other Security, Engineering, the entire crew of the Jurisdiction Fleet Ship *Ragnarok*, up to and including—she realized with a start—its acting Captain, ap Rhiannon, already unpopular in some Fleet circles for having taken an uncompromising approach to black-market weapons dealing in the recent past.

Mendez was watching the monitor, drinking his bean tea absentmindedly. The on-screen track that represented Koscuisko's courier had closed on the entry vector, and was gone. "Well, that's put one of however many parts behind us," Mendez said. "Koscuisko's away. So now we'll all find out. Not that I'm arguing the abstract point, Lieutenant, your Excellency. If you can make this work, we'll all be just as happy about it. With respect."

"We'll get formal notification from Pesadie Training Command about Cowil Brem." There were things they needed to see to in the time they had left before an audit team came on board. "We'll take it from there. Wheatfields will sanitize the Wolnadi line. Let them try to figure out how we're supposed to have done it. Two will be listening to Pesadie while they think about it."

She stood up. And, somewhat surprisingly, Wheatfields and Mendez stood up as well, while Two hopped down out of her chair, bracing herself against the floor with the second joints of her great folded wings. Respect of rank. It was an encouraging sign.

She didn't really care if they gave her the formal signs of subordinate rank relationship or not, though. All that mattered was that they came together to protect the *Ragnarok* and its crew. Somebody at Pesadie had been storing something on that observer that they oughtn't have; it was the only explanation she could see for the explosion.

And it was her duty to the *Ragnarok* to ensure that nobody made a scapegoat out of its crew to cover an administrative irregularity: not with lives at stake.

"We have the Pesadie vector, your Excellency." Turning away from the station as he spoke, Lek stood up and bowed to his officer of assignment. Koscuisko could see perfectly well for himself. The publication of the fact was a mere formula, but ritual was important, especially in the lives of bond-involuntaries. "Three days, Standard, to the Dasidar exit vector, Azanry space."

Koscuisko nodded briskly in appreciation. "Thank you, Lek, ably piloted. Now. Let us all to the main cabin repair, so that I may put you on notice, the ordeal which you face when we are at home on my native world."

Koscuisko was considerably relaxed, from a few hours ago; but not

for the otherwise obvious reason, because Koscuisko didn't look or
sound as though he'd been drinking. Recovered a bit from his going-
away party, then. Lek followed his fellows, taking advantage of his
position to linger for just a moment in the wheelhouse.

It was a pretty little courier, and it spoke his language. Or at least
it spoke a language he had learned as a small child, before his trouble
with the Bench, before his Bond. He'd understood why Koscuisko
had selected Security 5.3 to take home with him on holiday, given
that Koscuisko could take only one team; Koscuisko had tried to get
as many of his Bonds in one basket as he could, and there was
nothing personal about Lek's situational exclusion from the
privileged party.

But none of the others were Combine folk. It made Lek so
homesick to be talking to Koscuisko's courier that he wished he was
back on the *Ragnarok*, rather than going with Koscuisko to Azanry. So
close to home. So far away from his own people.

Distracted for a moment by the strangely painful familiarity of the
courier's accent, Lek lingered a bit longer than he had intended.
Someone stood in the doorway between the wheelhouse and the rest
of the ship; someone big and solid and silent, patiently waiting.
Stildyne.

"Sorry, Chief." It wasn't Stildyne's fault that Lek was Sarvaw, after
all. "Daydreaming. Coming directly."

Stildyne could easily have made a point about it, but he simply
turned and left the room. Stildyne had mellowed since Koscuisko had
come on board; he'd been considerably rougher to deal with when Lek
had first met him—though he'd never been abusive. He'd taken some
of the customary advantages from time to time, true enough, but he'd
always been a reasonable man, and fair. Koscuisko was too hard on
Stildyne. Koscuisko didn't understand how much worse than Stildyne
warrant officers could be, when you put some of them in charge of
bond-involuntaries.

Glancing around quickly to make sure that everything was in order
Lek followed his Chief out of the wheelhouse and into the main cabin,
where the officer of assignment was sitting on a table at the far end of
the cabin, swinging his feet. He'd changed his dress boots for padding-
socks, Lek noticed.

The rest of the crew were seated in array in front of Koscuisko, except for Stildyne standing in the doorway. Lek found a place at Smish's left; Koscuisko nodded at Lek and began to speak.

"We have not had a chance to talk, gentles, because we were in such a hurry to be gone before someone could change their minds again, and send me away with people of Wheatfields, from whom all Saints preserve me."

That was by way of a joke. Ship's Engineer was a moody and difficult man with very particular reasons to detest Ship's Inquisitors; Koscuisko was a proud and self-assured officer who was accustomed to having his own way. The personalities had not blended well on board the *Ragnarok*. Over the years a species of truce had gradually evolved between them, but it was still a fragile sort of detente.

"We are to be on holiday, gentles, and yet the environment into which I bring you is not one in which we can all equally be comfortable." Koscuisko didn't look at Lek when he said it. Koscuisko didn't need to. They both knew who Koscuisko's thrice-great-grandfather had been. Koscuisko didn't need to know the details of Lek's family background to understand that he led Lek into the presence of his enemies.

On the other hand, though Koscuisko was the living descendant of Chuvishka Kospodar, he was not Lek's enemy. Koscuisko had earned Lek's trust over the years they'd been together on the *Ragnarok*, and in so doing had made Lek more free, even under Bond, than Lek had ever hoped to be until the Day when it expired at last—if he lived that long.

"We go first to a place that is called the Matredonat. It is my place. My mother's family made of it the present when my father cut my cheek, what would that be, when I was held up to the world as his inheriting son."

The details of Aznir blood-rites were arcane and not widely published, but Koscuisko's general meaning was clear enough. "Living at this place you will meet my friend Marana, and my son. I also will be meeting my son, for the first time, as you are. He is eight years old. His name is Anton Andreievitch, because I am Andrej his father."

Lek knew by the eager tension in Smish's body beside him how interested she was in this news. They were all interested. There had been guarded talk among them, but Robert St. Clare—who knew more about Koscuisko than anyone on board, including Stildyne—had either been unclear on the details or too reticent to gossip about them. Koscuisko's friend Marana, Koscuisko had said. It seemed an odd way to describe the mother of his son, even given that Koscuisko was Aznir and Aznir were peculiar.

"This place of mine, the Matredonat, is in the farmland, but there are hills behind. There is riding. One may swim in the river if one does not mind the fish. They are very large fish. And that brings to mind a point."

If Koscuisko's estate was in the grain-lands Koscuisko would be talking about the old ones, the huge, old, wise, green-and-gold fish with their solemn expressions and their faces that were like the private member of a man. His fish. The old ones were as long and sometimes longer than a man was tall, and the roe that the females carried was worth its weight in hallucinogenic drugs. Lek wondered if the others knew that when a man like Koscuisko spoke of his place, he meant an estate the size of a respectable city, or larger.

"Lek and I have blood in common, in a way. He will be able to explain much when I am not with you." Koscuisko's reference startled Lek out of his meditation; Koscuisko was being very frank indeed, to admit to genetic ties between Aznir and Sarvaw. "Among these things about which it may be necessary to explain are requirements of hospitality. You are to be lodged each of you apart in guest quarters, because you are my Security. The household will wish to ensure that you lack for nothing that will increase your comfort under the roof of the Matredonat."

This was going to be awkward. Stildyne did have women, from time to time, but women were not his preference. Maybe Koscuisko's people would make allowances for the fact that Stildyne was an outlander, Lek decided. Maybe they'd call for a Malcontent. If they did that, Stildyne was in for an interesting experience . . .

"The difficulty here is this, Miss Smath." Why Smish? She tensed beside Lek, when Koscuisko said her name. "There is no tradition in my house of a woman warrior. To Security is to be offered the hospitality of the house."

Suddenly Lek realized how long he had been away from home. How thoroughly he'd learned to think in Standard. He had not even thought about it. Koscuisko was right.

"It will be a little unusual. But you need not feel the least bit reluctant to decline, should your interest not tend in that direction. I assure you that you will not give offense."

Warriors were greeted with soft words and warm embraces, granted the privilege of taking comfort with the women of the household. The fact that Smish was a woman herself would be considered secondary to her role as a warrior, a Security troop. Someone was probably going to offer sexual hospitality to her and so far as Lek knew Smish had as much interest in having sex with women as Stildyne did—or even less.

"Thank you, sir." Smish sounded a little confused overall. She wasn't Dolgorukij. She wouldn't know. "I'll keep it in mind."

Koscuisko nodded. Then Koscuisko turned his attention to Lek himself, looking directly at him while speaking in general to the team. "There will be much that is strange. I can only guess, remembering how it was when first I left Azanry for the school at Mayon. I could not warn you about everything if I talked for three days, and I would rather have something to eat."

Home food, Lek thought suddenly, and smelled remembered fragrances in his imagination. Thin little cakes made with soured grain mash and cream. Thick soups of stewed root vegetables, and when times were good meat to go with cabbage and water-grass.

"Therefore I will only say this, though I repeat myself. I request you all pay particular attention to what Lek does and says while we are home. In this way you can be sure of keeping your dignity in the land of the outlander."

It was a sensible suggestion, yes. But it was much more than that, though none of the other people here might realize it. Koscuisko told them all to point on him, Lek Kerenko, Sarvaw. That would be a sign to the Dolgorukij into whose territory Koscuisko was carrying them all, and Lek was grateful to Koscuisko for having thought of such a natural way to give him face in an unfriendly environment.

"And now I mean to go and lie down. Perhaps Lek will consent to discuss with ship's computers on your behalf and find out where the liquor has been stored. There are three days from here to Azanry, and we are on holiday."

Lek didn't want liquor. He wanted root stew and cabbage-stuffed sausages; but this was an executive courier, and there was no hope of finding such homely food as that. He'd just have to make do with pearl-gray roe and cured fish wrapped in flour skins, he supposed. It was a hard task.

But someone had to do it.

CHAPTER THREE

Reasonable People

Admiral Brecinn stepped down into the observer's pit at her headquarters at Pesadie Training Command with some inventory reports in hand. It had been a day since the anomalous incident had occurred; it was time to put the *Ragnarok* on notice. The inventories had put her on notice as well. She was going to need a strong bargaining position to hold her own against the reasonable people, when they demanded their merchandise. She didn't know where she was going to find the leverage.

"Contact the *Ragnarok*, if you please," she said, nodding to the technician at the comm station. The full complement of observers were here, just for the sake of the formalities. The inventory had had to be done twice, which had complicated things. Once for the official record, and once for the other record, the real record, the one that showed her where she stood in the profit and loss registers in her dealings with undocumented trade.

All right, illegal trade, but it was only illegal because people elected a too-narrow interpretation of the laws. Reasonable people knew how to conduct business without undue administrative procedure getting in the way.

The signal cleared from the *Ragnarok*, its position in the training area highlighted by a pinpoint halo on the star map even as the interface screen opened across much of the forward display area.

Projected in this way Jennet ap Rhiannon was about twice life-size, seated at the desk in the Captain's office, her First Officer standing behind her, looking bored.

Admiral Brecinn didn't know much about the Ragnarok's junior lieutenant and she didn't really care. Reasonable people had hinted that ap Rhiannon was not the sort of intelligent and responsive officer Fleet needed, which was a shame. Fleet needed good officers, especially in the lower ranks.

As the links all fell into place along authenticated lines of communication, ap Rhiannon stood up. Not a moment too soon, Brecinn thought, with contemptuous amusement. Junior officers rose to their feet in the presence of superior officers. Ap Rhiannon was being close to insubordinate.

"Pesadie Training Command presents its heartfelt sympathies to the *Ragnarok* on the loss of its Captain." Brecinn opened the engagement on the offensive, without waiting for whatever ap Rhiannon might have wanted to say by way of ingratiating herself. From what Brecinn had seen and heard of ap Rhiannon, she didn't have the sense to know when she ought to be doing her best to curry favor . . . like now, for example. "And expresses its concerns over the cause of this distressing incident."

Brecinn chose the word carefully, and employed it for full effect. Incident, not accident. Whether or not ap Rhiannon had the political sense of the average bulkhead was none of Brecinn's concern. The word would put ap Rhiannon's people on notice that Pesadie thought there was quite possibly sabotage afoot: ap Rhiannon's people, and Brecinn's observers, as well.

"Thank you, Admiral Brecinn." On-screen, ap Rhiannon had seated herself once more. She was clearly intent on pushing the rank privileges associated with her status as acting Captain of the *Ragnarok* to their fullest. "We are also deeply distressed by the unfortunate accident that has deprived Fleet of not only one Captain, but several other valuable resources as well."

Ap Rhiannon's choice of words in turn was lost on no one in the room. Brecinn had said incident. Ap Rhiannon said accident. It was just short of calling the Admiral a fool in public.

Ap Rhiannon only dug herself deeper into her own trap as she continued. "In my capacity as the senior Command Branch officer on board of the Jurisdiction Fleet Ship *Ragnarok* I respectfully request the immediate assignment of a duly detailed Fleet Incident Investigation team to determine the exact cause of the accident."

A what?

Brecinn was all too fully aware of the attention of the observers in the room fixed on her, wondering how she would react to this. She couldn't allow it.

"You are doubtless aware that there are no such teams assigned to this Command," Brecinn noted, coldly. This was an intolerable imposition on ap Rhiannon's part. "In the absence of a duly selected First Judge Presiding, no such teams can even be chartered."

Ap Rhiannon was counting on just that, though, Brecinn realized suddenly. Ap Rhiannon was technically well within her rights as acting Captain to demand a Fleet Incident Investigation team. In fact, now that she had made her claim in official transmission—and in front of all of these witnesses—Brecinn was left with no choice but to accede.

"Understood, Admiral Brecinn." Ap Rhiannon was clearly trying hard to keep the note of gloating out of her voice. Brecinn was sure of it. The ghost of a jeer crept into her language, nonetheless. "With all due respect, I cannot insult the memory of my former commanding officer by accepting anything less than the most careful investigation of the accident that took his life."

It would take weeks, at minimum, to locate a Fleet Incident Investigation team that could be assigned. Then it would take weeks more to wait for the new First Judge to be seated so that an administrative investigation order could be issued. Fleet Incident Investigation teams were not ordinary, everyday affairs. The Bench liked to keep an eye on them.

"As you wish, ap Rhiannon. I will forward your stipulation to Chilleau Judiciary on priority transmit." She'd confused the people who were watching her. She could tell. Even that Clerk of Court from Chilleau Judiciary was staring at her, while the expressions on the faces of her staff smoothed quickly from surprise into undisguised admiration. They'd guessed her strategy. She'd just reminded them all of why she was Admiral.

"In the interim period, however, evidence must be carefully placed on record by a neutral observation party. I will send a preliminary assessment team as soon as possible to begin this important preparatory work."

She didn't have a strategy, not yet, but nobody else needed to know that. She'd think of something. Ap Rhiannon couldn't bar a properly constituted preliminary assessment team, not with her request for a Fleet Incident Investigation team going forward.

Ap Rhiannon apparently realized that she was outmaneuvered; she was churlish about it. That was all right with Admiral Brecinn. The Lieutenant shouldn't have tried to get clever with her. "As you say, Admiral Brecinn. We will await your preliminary assessment team. Will that be all, Admiral?"

Ap Rhiannon underestimated her opponent if she thought she could seal off her boundaries so easily. "We'll let you know when the team is on its way. Pesadie away, here." She terminated the communication link with a forceful nod of her head to the technician on the board, and smiled. *Take that, you pathetic amateur.*

It was half for show and half pure honest spite, and Brecinn could see by the expressions exchanged among the reasonable people on her staff that it served the purpose. They believed she had a master plan. So she would, in time.

Brecinn rose to her feet to signal that the morning's work was winding down. "Thank you, gentles; and good-greeting to you all."

She had one day before she'd have to talk to anyone about it. There was no time like the present to be started. Forcing a confident stride, carefully keeping a serene smile on her face, Brecinn fled with all deliberate speed to go to ground in her office, and make plans.

Mergau Noycannir had not been idle since the snoop she'd planted on the Admiral yesterday had shown her a possible line of approach.

Despised and discarded at Chilleau Judiciary she might be, but she had contacts that had yet to fail her, developed over the years with favors and information and the general exchange of mutually profitable courtesies that characterized the conduct of business from one end of Jurisdiction to the other. She hadn't needed more than a few quiet inquiries to get her all the information she could wish with which to build a strategy.

Following Admiral Brecinn out of the observation hall Mergau kept close enough behind her to make it clear to the others that she meant to talk to their superior officer, in order to forestall any such actions on their own part. She waited to speak until the Admiral had passed through her administrative complex and stood in front of her office door, however, because what she had to say was to be between the two of them alone. "Excuse me, Admiral. I have a concern. May I have a moment?"

Brecinn was a tall woman. Mergau could not see her face, standing as the Admiral was with her back to the administrative area, caught in mid-movement as she set her palm to the secure on her private office. Mergau could see the fabric shift across the back of the Admiral's shoulders, though, and it was as good as a scan-reading.

"Dame Noycannir. You surprised me." Yes. Mergau already knew that. She waited. "By all means, then. Come in. What can I do for you?" Her presence was not welcome, Mergau could tell that easily enough. But unless she missed her guess, she was about to make herself Admiral Brecinn's very close friend and intimate acquaintance.

The door opened. Brecinn stepped through into her private office. Mergau followed. The lights came up as the Admiral crossed the room. Mergau looked around her appreciatively. Large office. Very nicely done, lots of plants—conspicuous consumption of water; at a headquarters located on an asteroid platform that was as good a rank-signal as anything.

The Admiral had a taste for architectural forms in furniture, it seemed, very expensive stuff. The two Perand chairs in front of the desk alone were worth three or four times Mergau's annual salary on the casual market. "Please," Brecinn urged. "Sit down." She was playing it well; Mergau could appreciate that. There was little indication in her tone of voice of the impatience that she had to be feeling.

Mergau settled herself in one of those very severe, very expensive Perands. "Now that I have your attention I'm not quite sure where to start, Admiral. Can I be sure that our conversation can be privileged?"

Meaning, *Are your privacies in place*? And, by extension, *I want to talk business, and it's not precisely open-air business*. Admiral Brecinn toggled the remote, looking past Mergau as her door sealed itself shut.

"Privacy is in effect, Dame, at your request. What is this all about?"

Mergau frowned, to present the appearance of concentrating. "Well. Yesterday's unplanned and unfortunate event. Very awkward.

One anticipates a good deal of interest from Fleet—too much interest for any reasonable person to be asked to tolerate, if you ask me."

She used the phrase with deliberate intent. She herself had always been careful to minimize her exposure to reasonable people as a class: because benefit bred obligation. But everybody knew about the existence of reasonable people. And Clerks of Court had more opportunity than most to place themselves in a position to be of use, and to gain insight.

Admiral Brecinn did not react to the phrase in itself. She was clearly testing Mergau out, unsure of Mergau's position. "Well, it is very unfortunate, Dame. Yes. And it will be an annoyance to have a stream of investigators through here. But what can we do? Cowil Brem is dead."

Very deliberately, Mergau shrugged. "Accidents happen. Why should they be allowed to upset the normal course of operations? Fleet has enough upset on its hands just now. The Bench is not well served by diverting police resources to investigate miscellaneous training accidents when they're needed to keep the peace during the selection process."

Civil unrest was a fact of life. It was only to be expected that it would increase during the period of uncertainty between the death of one First Judge and the selection of the next.

"You state the obvious, Dame, but what can be done? And you'll excuse me, but I have a lot of work to do. So if . . . "

Mergau held up her hand to stop the Admiral, interrupting politely but firmly. "That is my issue exactly, Admiral Brecinn. What is to be done? I think I may be able to offer some assistance."

On the face of it, it was an impertinent thing to say. Mergau put full weight on the words, enough to give the Admiral pause, and was rewarded with Brecinn's raised eyebrow, encouragement to continue.

Mergau leaned forward. It put her at an odd angle because of the peculiar slope characteristic of the chair; hominids of Perand's class were by and large longer in the torso than the Jurisdiction standard.

"Admiral Brecinn. Let me be utterly blunt with you. There's been an accident. There will be an investigation. It will cost money, and investigations almost always get out of control. Unimportant and unrelated issues are turned up by auditors anxious to justify the expense of their investigation. It's all so unnecessary."

She had Brecinn's full attention now. The Admiral wasn't giving her many cues; Brecinn was corrupt, but not stupid. Mergau liked dealing with corrupt people. Stupid people were just boring; and frequently endangered one's own goals.

"All we need is a suitably logged confession set, Admiral, and we can close this unfortunate incident with minimal expense and exposure. I can help. If you are interested."

Picking up a decorative stone from her desk Brecinn turned the smoothly polished thing over and over in her fingers; thoughtfully. "It's my fiduciary duty to the Bench to weigh the costs and benefits of all planned approaches, Dame." Brecinn still revealed nothing—unless her use of the loaded word *fiduciary* was intended to hint at the underlying rewards that Mergau might expect to share if she came up with a good approach. "But surely it's premature to speculate about mutiny. Assassination."

Mergau shook her head. "Not at all, Admiral. I am completely confident of my information. The Second Judge does not like to publish the fact, but I hold the Writ to Inquire for Chilleau Judiciary, Admiral Brecinn. And I say that the crew of that Wolnadi will confess their Free Government connections and treasonable intent for the Record in due form, before they die. All you need to do is provide me with the crew."

It wasn't exactly true to say that she held the Writ to Inquire for Chilleau Judiciary. Her Writ had never been revoked or rescinded, to spare the First Secretary the embarrassment of putting the failure of his experiment on record. But he hadn't used her Writ for years, not since she'd failed to get results from those Langsarik prisoners that the Bench specialist had brought to Chilleau Judiciary. Not since the Domitt Prison. More than four years.

Admiral Brecinn didn't need to know that.

Mergau had failed to get the information out of Vogel's Langsarik prisoners, and Vogel had taken the surviving Langsariks and turned them over to another Inquisitor. She'd been operating under a handicap; she'd been on Record, her actions had been recorded for the purposes of Judicial review. She had not dared subvert the Protocols. This would be different. All she needed were confessions on Record. Nobody would be there to observe how she had gotten them.

"You're very sure, Dame Noycannir," Brecinn said. She didn't sound perturbed by Mergau's suggestion; nor did she sound convinced. "It could all come down to some harmless accident. How will we know?"

Mergau relaxed into the deep curve of the back of the Perand chair. "You're right, of course, Admiral. It could all be a silly misunderstanding. Nobody's fault. An accident."

Exactly as it had been, in a sense. It was just bad luck that the senseless accident had taken several lives, and would expose some awkward, off-the-record financial arrangements and material transactions.

"We should evaluate the situation up front with clear and unbiased minds, that's all. The incident will take investigation. The crew will be interrogated." At least, in Preliminaries. So long as charges had not been preferred, that was a fairly innocuous process. But charges would almost certainly be preferred sooner or later against somebody. All Brecinn had to decide was whether she was willing to risk those charges against herself and members of her staff rather than some Security crew from a test-bed ship due to be off-lined soon anyway.

What was it to be? Minimizing the damage, the exposure, the risk at the cost of a few crew from the *Ragnarok*, or letting delicacy of feeling overwhelm common sense, and the greater good of the majority?

"There will necessarily be a series of collaterals," Brecinn noted. Mergau knew by the fact that Brecinn was thinking about it that she was halfway there. "We're not just talking about four people here. And there's bound to be Judicial review. Command Branch requires it."

"The Bench has other things to worry about right now, and among them is its sacred duty to maintain public confidence in the rule of Law. If anybody wants to ask any questions when it's all over it's only going to raise unnecessary issues, and the Bench is going to have its hands full with political stabilization for the next few years."

Brecinn wasn't looking at Mergau any more. She was staring past Mergau's left shoulder at the far end of the room, her face all but expressionless. "We do need to be here for Chilleau Judiciary when the new First Judge is seated," Brecinn agreed thoughtfully. "And that means with our credibility intact. If we risked a scandal now it could cost Chilleau support she'll need. We can only provide it if we've put this behind us by the time the Selection is made."

Just so. Mergau sat quietly, content to let the Admiral do the job of convincing herself to sacrifice lives on the *Ragnarok* to political expediency. The personal benefits—escape from exposure as a black-market trafficker, negotiating leverage with reasonable people—were strictly subordinate to the greater good of the Judicial order. Of course.

Brecinn took a deep breath and focused her eyes on Mergau's face. "What's your interest in all of this, Dame?"

Almost there. Mergau smiled. "You mean apart from my keen awareness of how much the First Secretary values the support of Pesadie Training Command?"

Verlaine cared no more for Pesadie's political support than for any other such Fleet partisans. Brecinn didn't need to know that. Brecinn was more than willing to believe herself to be an important key to Verlaine's long-term strategy.

Mergau let her head sway on her shoulders, ever so slightly, in a gesture of complicity and conspiracy. "And apart from my personal interest in doing the best for the next First Judge, I'd like to do business with you, Admiral. We could consider my assistance in this little matter services on account, for the future. On deposit, if you will. I know there's interest to be had, if I can demonstrate to you that you can rely on my discretion."

As far as that went. It didn't have to go very far. The plan, in fact, didn't go any further than what Mergau had proposed just now; she was still thinking things through. But if she pulled this off, she could earn invaluable protection . . . and blackmail opportunities, if it came to that.

Admiral Brecinn leaned forward over her desk and offered Mergau her hand, in the quaint, old-fashioned manner that some people had of doing business in good faith. "I begin to see the long-term requirements of the situation," Brecinn said. "Thank you, Dame. It's never easy to believe treason of any Fleet resources, but our duty to the Judicial order clearly requires us to investigate. The more quickly we can resolve things the better it will be for everyone."

This transparent rationalization required a solemn response from her, and not a hearty chuckle. "Quite right, Admiral. I will tell the First

Secretary that I have offered my services, and extended my stay. If you could detail an aide to show me what facilities you have available. And I'll need access to the Record on site."

No time like the present to be started. The Admiral would have work for her very soon, of that Mergau could be confident. "Of course, Dame Noycannir. I'll send someone to you in quarters directly."

She would gain armor here that would protect her even from the chance that Garol Vogel would return from wherever he had gone, and uncover the forgery of the Bench warrant that should have ended Andrej Koscuisko's life. Somehow, Mergau knew that she would be coming out of this more powerful, more influential, more secure than she had ever dreamed of being.

When General Dierryk Rukota reported to Admiral Brecinn's office he was surprised to find Dame Mergau Noycannir in company, and a clearing signal on the communicator screen at the far end of the office. The signs were not good. But what was Noycannir doing here?

"You sent for me, Admiral." Rukota had been detailed here to observe as a representative from the Second Fleet; Admiral Brecinn was not in his chain of command. He didn't worry about observing all the formalities. He'd be polite, but he was an artilleryman, not an administrator.

At least he'd used to be an artilleryman before he'd attracted the wrong sort of attention from the reasonable people that seemed to fill Fleet's administration these days. His tour of duty with ap Rhiannon had been the last straw, apparently, because he'd been on one detail or another ever since, and there was no hint from anybody about a return to an active line posting yet.

"Yes, thank you, General. I'm just putting a call in to Second Fleet." Brecinn in turn barely acknowledged his rank, though she could hardly avoid acknowledging his presence. Maybe she wasn't entirely to blame for that. Second Fleet wasn't particularly on Brecinn's side, and exercise observers were frequently called into play as double agents to collect information on mismanagement to be used, if necessary, to offset any criticisms that Pesadie might level at the Fleet resources undergoing evaluation.

Noycannir hadn't stood when he'd come in; so she felt she was on an equal rank footing with him—a change since yesterday. The implications were intriguing. He'd heard gossip about Noycannir from his wife, during their infrequent rendezvous.

There were disadvantages to being married to one of the great beauties of the age; one of them was not having her all to himself. Another was having to put up with the jokes that people made about children that looked like almost anybody other than their mother's husband, but Rukota knew better than to care. They were all his children. She was his wife. He was their father, no matter who the sperm donor might have been.

Since nobody was standing on ceremony he guessed he would just seat himself and say the first thing that came into his head. Brecinn was barely paying attention to him anyway. "Why are we waiting to talk to Second Fleet, if I may ask?"

"We're going to ask Second Fleet to extend your detail, in order to accomplish a very sensitive task for us," Brecinn said. "I know it's an imposition on your time, General, but you're really the very best person we have at hand for this mission."

It was the preliminary response team. He just knew it. Admiral Brecinn had only two choices for a commander to field such a team: someone from Pesadie; and someone not. If they sent a team comprised entirely of people from Pesadie, there would be protests and accusations of partisanship from the beginning of the investigation. And of all the other people here to observe the *Ragnarok*'s training exercise—numbering two in total—he was the only person who could credibly be detailed to command an audit team, howsoever ad-hoc and informal.

Second Fleet was on the line—Brecinn's counterpart, Command General Chehdral herself, Rukota suppressed a sigh. Chehdral was not part of the network of corruption as far as Rukota knew, but she had no particular use for him—not because of any personal animus, but because she was fully staffed for officers in his grade. Chehdral would be just as glad of something that would occupy Rukota's time for a while longer. It would be the assessment team for him for certain, then.

"Admiral Brecinn. What can we do for you?" It wasn't really a question, just a polite sort of a greeting. Not much of a greeting, either, come to that.

"General Chehdral, I've been privileged to enjoy the support of one of your command in recent weeks. You sent General Rukota to participate in evaluating the training exercises we have been conducting with the JFS *Ragnarok*. We'd like to keep him on for a few months. We need the line commander's insight on some issues that have come up."

Well, it wasn't as if she was likely to come out and say "The *Ragnarok*'s Captain has been blown up and we need someone to help us control the damage." Was that what they wanted him to do? Manage the fallout? Or just pin it on the *Ragnarok* and get on with life?

"General Rukota is with you?" Chehdral asked. "Yes. General. What do you hear from your family?"

His wife was in retreat, helping the First Secretary at a Judiciary not to be named manage his not-inconsiderable stress. His children were with their mother, with his parents, or in school. Nobody particularly needed Rukota himself. His was a relatively small role in the life of his family.

"They are well, General Chehdral, thank you for asking. There is nothing at home that requires my personal attention." He couldn't pretend to be needed at home, though he appreciated the offered escape hatch. It was clearly of no particular interest one way or the other whether Rukota stayed or not, for Command General Chehdral. She shrugged.

"You are seconded at Admiral Brecinn's request, General Rukota, to serve as needed or until further notice. Orders to follow. Are we done, Brecinn? This is Command General Chehdral, Second Fleet. Away, here."

She always had been a woman of few words. That Rukota was inconvenienced by the words she had shared with him was not her issue.

It was quiet in Brecinn's office, so Rukota took the initiative. "What do you expect to accomplish with the fielding of an immediate response team, Admiral?" His question came out sounding perhaps a little more confrontational than it really needed to be. Brecinn did not seem to notice.

"Dame Noycannir has prepared a brief." A flat-form docket, which Brecinn held out for him to take. He had to stand up and lean forward to take it. He'd never liked Perand chairs; they compressed the spine and gave him muscle cramps. "Due to the extended period of time likely to elapse between now and the arrival of an accredited Fleet audit team, it's imperative to capture what physical evidence there may be. It would be too easy for vital information to be lost."

Or discarded. Or destroyed. "Physical evidence of what, Dame, exactly?" Rukota asked, looking at Noycannir. If this was about an honest attempt to protect the truth he was a Chigan's bed-boy. "It seems a little unusual to send an investigative party to the *Ragnarok* to seek evidence pertinent to something that occurred on an observation station."

Noycannir dropped her eyes, almost coyly. "You'll forgive me if I protect privileged sources." As though she had some. Perhaps she did. He had no reason to suspect that she was making it all up. Did he? "There are disquieting indications. We need to establish a baseline as soon as possible."

Either she was truly in a position to know something, or she and the Admiral meant to blame the accident on the *Ragnarok* somehow. She was a Clerk of Court at Chilleau Judiciary, true; she could be operating on a level much different than that about which Rukota's wife had told him.

Or she could be dirty, as Brecinn was dirty, as Pesadie Training Command was dirty, as increasing numbers of Fleet administrative staff appeared to be. Reasonable people. So why select him?

He'd worked with ap Rhiannon before, and lived to tell of it. Did they assume that he resented the trouble that ap Rhiannon had caused him, and would turn a blind eye to plots on the part of Pesadie—or even actively forward them? Or did they mistakenly believe that his presence on Brecinn's hunting party would put ap Rhiannon off her guard, convince her that she had a friend in him who would protect her interests?

"When do we leave, Admiral?" He would read Noycannir's brief. And he would keep his own counsel. Who knew? Perhaps by the time the accredited team ap Rhiannon had demanded arrived to take charge, he would have some interesting things to say to them. About Admiral Brecinn. And about Mergau Noycannir.

Anything was possible, in this age of wonder.

Bench intelligence specialist Jils Ivers sat beneath a canopy on a crossing-craft in the middle of a great blue lake, her eyes resting on the brilliance of the snow-covered mountains that garlanded the horizon.

The men who rowed the crossing-craft were singing. *If you row well enough the Autocrat may see/And then the Autocrat may chance to smile/And then good fortune will descend upon your house.*

There was an island of gray rock in the middle of the lake, and administrative buildings glittering in the sun. Old-fashioned architecture. The Autocrat's summer residence was in the middle of lovely Lake Belanthe, which lay in the embrace of the goddess Perunna—after whom the right-most range of mountains had been named.

Then all of your sons will have eight sons/And you will have a daughter of such beauty and ability that she will come into the house, into the Autocrat's house/And there the Autocrat may see, and then the Autocrat may chance to smile.

It was an old song, by its syntax; Jils wasn't sure she caught more than half of it. Garol might have been able to translate for her. Garol was good at languages, and had an apparently solid grasp of High Aznir by report; which was a little humorous, because Garol didn't even like Dolgorukij. Garol's nature was not at base suspicious, but he had learned to be wary, and among the things to which Garol had elected to take general all-purpose undifferentiated exception was the Dolgorukij Combine and all of its works and adjuncts.

Your daughter will have sons of noble blood to grow in power and prosper in wealth/The breeding-grounds of Geral will be yours, the seven looms of Dyraine of the weavers/You will have the holy grain to feed your house/And be welcomed as a guest in all Koscuisko's strongholds.

The crossing-craft drew near to the island and slowed.

There was a man at the docks waiting for her. Jils tried not to be glad to see him; at this distance he could well be some other Dolgorukij than the one she was looking for, and even if he was the right man he might not have any information. Or elect to share it.

People in uniform clustered around the crossing-craft as it tied up. Someone pushed a roll of fabric down the stone steps—a rug. An expensive rug, and though the waters of Lake Belanthe weren't salt using a hand-knotted rug of such elaborate pattern for a traction-mat was surely not the way to preserve a work of art. That was the whole point, Jils supposed. Conspicuous consumption. The Combine was rich.

The Combine was filthy rich, and had always had an agricultural surplus with which to support labor-intensive handicrafts, and as long as people could earn a decent living replacing rugs used as traction-mats who was she to think twice about it?

"Specialist Ivers," the waiting man said. It was the Malcontent Cousin Stanoczk, yes. "Good to see you. Did you have a pleasant crossing?"

The crew held the craft so still it was almost as though she was already on solid ground as she stepped out. The angle of the steps was a little awkward; she found herself glad of the extra purchase that the rug provided. The stairs were worn to a slope. They were old. On other worlds they might have been replaced, or the lake bridged; but Dolgorukij treasured old things as they were.

"Smooth as anyone could wish." There wasn't much of a breeze up across the lake, but thanks were owed to the crew as well. A rowing crew could make the smoothest passage rough if they were minded to. "These men are impressive, Cousin."

She didn't feel up to choosing the correct Dolgorukij form of the word; there were entirely too many ways to call someone cousin in Dolgorukij, each one with its own meaning and message about relative status, the degree of intensity with which one desired a favor, and the depth of obligation that one was willing to accept in return. Jils stuck to plain Standard. It was much safer that way.

"Indeed, Specialist. Combine-wide champions for speed as well as endurance, three years running now. Someone will take your box up to quarters. If you'd care to come with me, and have a glass of rhyti?"

If she had to. "Very kind." She didn't like rhyti. She'd learned a lot about it over the years, though. Verlaine had set her on Andrej Koscuisko to keep an eye on him, and Koscuisko drank rhyti. She'd gotten interested almost despite herself. "Thank you for meeting me, Cousin. I wonder if I could have a quick word or two with you on a personal matter."

Cousin Stanoczk reminded her of Koscuisko, if rather vaguely. The two men were related, if she remembered correctly; but Cousin Stanoczk had a very deep voice and Koscuisko was tenor, Cousin Stanoczk had dark brown eyes and Andrej Koscuisko's eyes were so pale that they almost had no color at all, Cousin Stanoczk had hair the color of wet wood and Andrej Koscuisko was blonder by several emphatic degrees.

Still, it was the same general form—not tall, deceptively slight, with shoulders whose slope belied their power and hands whose surpassing elegance belonged by right to an artist or a surgeon. What a Malcontent was doing with such hands Jils didn't know. Perhaps Stanoczk painted; it was unlikely that he practiced medicine, because medicine could be hired nearly anywhere, and Malcontents specialized in services that could not be hired or purchased at all.

Cousin Stanoczk grinned. He had very much the same surprising and open smile as Koscuisko had from time to time—one that showed a lot of small white teeth. "Be careful what you do, Specialist, the Malcontent is always at your service but will almost always find some favor to solicit in return. Sooner or later. That said, speak, I listen."

The worn stone walkway from the dock led them up a long shore of shallow steps into a green plaza where water birds were browsing in the grass like flowers on feet. Webbed feet. *How did they keep the walkways clean?* Jils wondered.

"Garol Vogel, Cousin. I don't mind telling you in confidence, as one professional to another. He's disappeared."

At the far end of the plaza there was an old wall with a high-arched gate that stood wide open. There were more lawns beyond. The guards were all in fancy dress; it was easy to overlook the fact that they were apparently also heavily armed. Once they passed through the pedestrian gate she saw yet more guards, as well as a great curving walkway paved with crushed stone, an immense stone facade with who knew what behind it, and a pretty little pavilion to one side toward which Cousin Stanoczk began to guide her.

"I've heard words spoken about it here and there, Specialist. Burkhayden, wasn't it?"

There was nothing unusual about Stanoczk already knowing. The intelligence community exploited its contacts with the Malcontent and others of its ilk, fully aware that it was being exploited right back. "Yes, that's right."

As they drew nearer Jils could see that the pavilion stood at the side of an ornamental stream, and that there were people in it. Three people not in uniform; the other three people there would be guards or servants, then. On the far side of the little stream there were musicians sitting in the shade of a large willowy tree, playing stringed instruments. The Dolgorukij plucked-lute, Jils suspected.

"Is it that you are concerned about him, Specialist? It seemed to me that Garol Aphon was more likely than even the average Bench intelligence specialist to be fully capable of taking care of himself. If I may say so to you, without giving offense."

No. She knew what he meant. Garol was professional. Some Bench specialists lost their edge over time. Garol's was one of those edges which might look dull, but if you made the mistake of presuming upon it you'd never even feel the slice as your head rolled one way and your body fell the other.

The people in the pavilion were waiting for them. One of them was seated—a young woman. The two other non-servants there were older than the young woman; that meant she had rank, whoever she was, to be sitting while her elders stood.

The Autocrat's Proxy. The Combine certainly meant to extend every courtesy to Chilleau Judiciary.

"He may have been working on something, Cousin." Jils slowed her steps, both to collect her thoughts and to finish this one. She hadn't anticipated being brought before the Autocrat's Proxy, not so soon. Did she know who those other people were? Had she seen them somewhere before? "Nobody knows."

Some Bench specialist was always supposed to know what another was doing. Not all of what the other was doing; not always the same Bench specialist. But somebody was always supposed to know. It was just common sense. And nobody knew about Garol. Or else nobody was willing to say.

"So Vogel is in more deeply to his investigation than imaginable, or is perhaps simply either dead or disappeared?"

She'd thought about that. Dead she couldn't really believe. Accidents happened to everybody. But Vogel took a lot of killing; it wasn't as though it hadn't been tried before, on more than one occasion, and sometimes with a very great deal of enthusiasm indeed. "Call me sentimental. But I think he'd find a way to let me know if he decided to disappear."

They weren't going to be able to keep the pavilion party waiting.

Stanoczk quickened his pace, but it was subtly done, not in the least
bit obvious. "Let me put it to my Patron, Specialist, may he wander in
bliss forever. Because for now it is my duty, as well as my pleasure, to
bring you into the presence of the Autocrat's Proxy, who will receive
your credentials in a while."

He had Jils worried for a moment, the quick moment between
"receive your credentials" and "in a while." Her credentials were in
her box, along with her dress uniform. The young woman who sat
waiting for her was not in court dress, however, but in a pretty if rather
plain long dress with loosely pleated sleeves and a wide skirt.

Jils climbed the few stone steps into the shade of the pavilion. There
was a charcoal warmer sunk into the floor on one side, Jils noticed;
welcome, because it was cool in the shadows. The others were a man
and a woman, similarly not in court dress, but more formally attired
than the young woman; Jils hadn't quite placed them yet.

She bowed politely, saluting the Dolgorukij Combine in the
presence of this Autocrat's Proxy. There were eight Proxies in all,
young people of the very best families who would spend twenty years
in diplomatic service. This one looked younger than most, but very
self-assured regardless.

"On behalf of the First Secretary at Chilleau Judiciary," Jils said. "I
present the greetings of the Second Judge. I am Bench intelligence
specialist Jils Ivers, Proxima. Thank you for receiving me like this."

She wasn't exactly here on behalf of the Second Judge, but it was a
signal honor to be thus presented informally. The least Jils could do
was give the gesture as much weight as possible, in return.

The young woman smiled, and waved for a chair. "Very welcome,
Specialist Ivers. We will have the ritual later to repeat, I'm afraid.
But we have been advised of your desire to make to my brother
presentations, and I wondered, have you our mutual parents met?"

Jils stared, genuinely startled. Her brother?

How could she not have realized that this was Zsuzsa Ulexeievna
Koscuisko?

She'd never met Koscuisko's parents. She'd only seen the records,
stills and clips, and those were always formal presentations. She sat
down.

"Haven't had the pleasure." Now that she'd sat down the others
did too, Koscuisko's mother and Koscuisko's father, the Koscuisko

prince himself. Cousin Stanoczk was nowhere to be seen. Malcontents were like that, Jils supposed.

"My lord father is Alexie Slijanevitch, and my lady mother is Ossipia Carvataja. We are all wondering. Andrej comes home, it is the first time in years, you have seen him in Burkhayden where all the officers were being murdered. How does he? My brother."

Nothing like his father, that was how Andrej Koscuisko was, because his father was a tall man with black eyes and a magnificent beard. Koscuisko had no beard. He appeared to take after his mother's side of the family, because she was slim though she was tall as well. Oh, there was no telling. What good did it do to look for people in their parents' faces?

"I'm not sure what to say, Proxima," Jils began cautiously. "Senior officer, well respected, popular with bond-involuntaries. That's a little unusual, by the way. What can I tell you?"

The Autocrat's Proxy gave a little impatient bounce in her chair where she sat. "Oh, but he has not in all this time come home, and now. And does he speak of his family. And has he been happy in Fleet."

"My daughter does not say one thing, because she is a devout and filial daughter," Koscuisko's mother said, before Jils could formulate a response. Koscuisko's mother had a beautiful voice, rich and deep and calming to listen to. "But my son does not often write. And with his parents quarreled, when he last left, so that we find ourselves anxious. If he will not ask to be forgiven, what shall we do? So of his state of mind and temperament we seek such information as you may be able to give to us, trusting in your discretion. Even though you are a stranger. It is not worthwhile to be too proud, when it has been this long."

Her son Andrej was not filial.

Her son Andrej had quarreled with his father bitterly, and yet had been unable to convince or to prevail; had gone to Fleet Orientation Station Medical in obedience to his father's will after all, and had learned there that he was not merely exceptional in the art of torture, but enjoyed it.

The damage had already been done before Koscuisko had left Azanry. Now his family sought a strategy for reintegrating the oldest male child into his family, not knowing what Koscuisko's own attitude was going to be.

Jils didn't think Koscuisko was going to beg to be forgiven for not having wanted to go to Fleet Orientation Station Medical. Was there a way for her to get across to these three essentially sheltered people the enormity of the burden that the Bench laid across the shoulders of a thinking, feeling creature when it issued the Writ to Inquire?

It had been her errand that had caused Koscuisko to resubmit to Fleet, when he had been planning to go home. She was under obligation, in a sense. "The Bench owes more deep a debt to your son than it can readily repay, your Excellency. Excusing your presence, Proxima, I would ask that you make allowances for how much the Bench has asked from him."

Koscuisko was unlikely to ask forgiveness for anything. Koscuisko had a stubborn streak, from all Jils had studied of him, and eight-plus years in Secured Medical had only strengthened the native autocracy of his character. "There is no harder task than that to which the Bench has put your brother and your son, and he has done his Judicial duty thoroughly and well—"

If she could sweeten Koscuisko's path back to his home, it was only what was owed the man for what she'd done to him, when she had forced him back to Captain Lowden.

The courier ship *Magdalenja* was halfway between Pesadie time and the Aznir mean standard—toward the end of the day by any measure. It was late in third shift, maybe even shading into fourth by now; and Security Chief Stildyne sat in Koscuisko's cabin, smoking one of Koscuisko's lefrols and beating his officer of assignment at cards.

Koscuisko set a "hemless" playing token down across his last remaining single-loom sheet and shook the dice. " 'She was bereft and wandered on the sere hillside with none but one last lambling to console her,' " Koscuisko quoted, but it did him no good. The dice fell Stildyne's way, two "kerchiefs" and three "napkins." It would take at least a "double apron" to match Stildyne's hand. Koscuisko was doomed. Yet again. Koscuisko slumped against the padded back of the chair and shook his head.

Now it was Stildyne's turn to quote. " 'The sun rose' . . . ah . . . 'in beauty like the maiden of the middle way as Dasidar in glory rode home to claim Dyraine.' Three goslings, your Excellency, that's the rest of the maintenance atmosphere you owe me, as well as the Engineering bridge."

Koscuisko scowled, but it wasn't serious. "I have never in fact spoken to Wheatfields about wagering either, Chief, so I suppose it's just as well. How is Lek doing?"

Reaching for the tokens, Stildyne started to tidy up the board. Three games was about his limit. He had only started to read the old saga of Dasidar and Dyraine a year or two past, in order to be able to distract Koscuisko by playing cards with him. He didn't have Koscuisko's command of the couplets.

"You might want to remind yourself that he's already thirteen." Lek's Bond was that old, that was to say; Lek had survived as a bond-involuntary for that long. Koscuisko called his troops by their first names. He had never called Stildyne anything but Chief or Mister.

Koscuisko knew his name. Stildyne was in no doubt of that, but his officer of assignment had never forgiven him for having once made a mistake, not even after all these years. Stildyne was almost through being bitter about it. "He hasn't lived this long by borrowing trouble. And he's been told that the Captain ordered the substitution to keep Fleet from trying to queer the performance scores."

"So long as Lek believes it, we have no worries. Yes. And the others will look out for him." Koscuisko sounded uncertain, worried. Koscuisko liked to fret. After what had happened to Robert St. Clare at Port Burkhayden, Stildyne couldn't blame Koscuisko for worrying; a governor gone terminal meant unimaginable torment and near-certain death for a bond-involuntary. Koscuisko still didn't know exactly what had pushed Robert's governor over the edge that night, and Stildyne had no intention of ever telling him.

"No, Andrej, Lek doesn't have to believe it. He only has to focus on the fact that he's been instructed to believe it."

There was a moment's pause as Koscuisko thought about whether he was going to take exception to Stildyne's use of his personal name.

It was true that Stildyne permitted himself that degree of intimacy only rarely. But also true that Stildyne and Koscuisko alike were sitting at the table with their collars undone, and Koscuisko in rest-dress was as casual as Koscuisko ever got when he was sober: the full dark pleated skirtlike trousers, with the stiffened half-moon of starched fabric at the small of Koscuisko's back; the very full blouse wrapped closed across Koscuisko's chest; the wrist-ties left untied; and the white padding-socks on Koscuisko's feet, with the big toe gloved separately.

When Koscuisko raised his hand to push his blond hair up off his forehead, his blouse shifted to show his collarbones: and Stildyne bit the inside of his cheek to stifle his sigh of resigned and impotent desire, concentrating on packing tokens into the box. Linen-markers. This one for a hemless garment, this one for a seamless garment, this one for a single-loomed sheet of fabric, this one for this manner of embroidery and this one for that manner of embroidery, and so on.

It was a good game to play with Koscuisko. It took concentration. While Stildyne was playing cards with Andrej Koscuisko he could almost forget all about the fact that he could never have the man.

"As you say, Chief," Koscuisko agreed, finally. 'Chief' was more intimate and friendly than "Mister." Koscuisko didn't reject Stildyne's advances; he simply declined to respond to them. "When we get home, I mean to call for a Malcontent. I'd rather not have to rely on just Lek's discipline to keep him safe."

It was what Koscuisko's Security did their best to do—keep Koscuisko safe. Safe from himself; safe from the sick fantasies of his dreaming mind. Before Koscuisko had come to the *Ragnarok* it had not been so bad for him. Robert had told Stildyne that. Koscuisko's former Captain had kept Koscuisko clear of Inquiry as much as possible—not from any misguided sense of decency that anyone would own to, but from simple practicality.

Perhaps the distaste commonly shared by military professionals for subjecting prisoners to torture had had something to do with it after all, but Captain Lowden had never had any such misgivings or reservations, and it took more than just Robert St. Clare to handle Koscuisko in the depths of a self-punitive drunk after yet another of Lowden's all-too-frequent exercises.

Four years of conspiracy between bonded and un-bonded and Chief Warrant Officer Stildyne alike, trying to keep Koscuisko from the abyss of horror. It was no wonder that Koscuisko took such good care of his people. That wasn't the reason Koscuisko did it, though. It was effect and cause more than cause and effect.

"Malcontents have Safes, your Excellency?" This was an intriguing concept, and called for increased formality. Safes fed a signal to the governor in a bond-involuntary's brain and silenced it for as long as the Safe was within range. They were very carefully controlled by Fleet and the Bench accordingly, because what would become of the deterrent power of the Bond if it could be gotten around without official sanction?

"If there is any way to obtain one, it is a Malcontent who could accomplish the task," Koscuisko said; and yawned. "Thank you for your company, Mister Stildyne, I imagine I am ready to nap, now."

Stildyne closed the board around the box of tokens, and stood up. "My pleasure, sir. We'll play for the labs next time, maybe."

Smiling, Koscuisko waved a hand in friendly dismissal.

Stildyne didn't want to go.

He wanted to stay, to help Koscuisko out of his rest-dress, to help Koscuisko into his sleep shirt, to put Koscuisko chastely to bed—all things that were permitted to him when Koscuisko was drunk enough. When the fact of Koscuisko's incapacity made the very idea of taking advantage of it intolerable. It was Koscuisko's fault. Before Koscuisko, he would not have thought twice about taking what he wanted so long as he was strong enough to get away with it.

Koscuisko had ruined him. Life had been so much less complicated before Koscuisko had come into it.

Stildyne let himself out and closed the door behind him, nodding to Murat, whose turn it was to sit the night watch. Murat knew. They all knew. " 'Night, Chief," Murat said.

In their own way they all took care of him as well as of Koscuisko, so that they made a tidy little fraternal community, Koscuisko taking care of Security who took care of Koscuisko.

Was it worth it, to trade the easy and immediate gratification of physical desire as it arose for membership in such a community, when all it cost was the pain of unexpressed and unrequited passion?

"Have a good watch, Murat."

He had alternatives, Stildyne knew. And no intention of exploring them. He went down the corridor to his berth, thinking about how soon they could expect to make planetfall on Azanry.

CHAPTER FOUR

Family Matters

Great *Ragnarok* had been built according to the plan of a cruiser killer warship—carapace hull above, docking facilities below—opening onto the maintenance atmosphere that clung to the belly of the ship, contained by a plasma field. General Rukota braced himself as his courier approached the boundaries. There was a peculiar sensory effect associated with passing the plasma containment membrane from space into atmosphere; it made his skin crawl. He had never gotten used to it.

"Eleven eights to docking, General." The navigator was one of Admiral Brecinn's people, but carried more rank on her shoulders than a navigator usually bore. All of the team were relatively senior for their roles; it increased his suspicion that these people were committed to some ulterior purpose. Rukota didn't like it. "Thank you, Navigator. Send the request and stand by."

Yes, it was gratifying to a man's ego to be giving orders to people more accustomed to giving their own than taking anybody's. Still, ego gratification only went so far with Dierryk Rukota. No man as ugly as he had been all of his life could afford to nurture too much ego. Every time he caught sight of himself in a mirror, it reminded him. But so long as his wife didn't care, it made no difference if his mouth was as thin as the edge of a dull knife and his eyes nearly as narrow, to speak of only two of the most obviously unfortunate aspects of his face.

"Clearance is logged, General. We're expected. Well. We'll just have to hope that the evidence hasn't been compromised already."

What made the navigator suppose that there was evidence to be compromised in the first place?

Did she expect him not to realize that the mission upon which he had been sent was at least as likely, if not certain, to compromise evidence—if it was not actually bent on fabricating evidence that did not exist?

Rukota couldn't decide how best to answer, and therefore decided not to. He was technically in command of this mission. He didn't have to make nice with anybody.

The courier cleared the maintenance atmosphere with the familiar and unpleasant feeling of insects tunneling through his joints. Rukota concentrated on what the screens showed, to distract himself from his discomfort.

The entire working area of the *Ragnarok*'s underbelly lay open to the maintenance atmosphere, with the plates that would hull over the ship for vector transit stacked into a solid wall fore and aft. There wasn't much activity: some tenders, one craft in free-float with its crew on EVA, their umbilicus tethers glinting in the powerful illumination from the *Ragnarok*'s docks.

Their destination was a slot in the hull of the ship, an envelope of stalloy big enough to park the Captain's shallop—her personal courier—in. As the navigator maneuvered toward the slip Rukota thought he caught sight of a familiar figure in the basket of a crane near the entrance to their docking bay.

Short person. Stocky. Hair smoothed back severely across a rounded skull typical of a class-three Auringer hominid, but if it was who he thought it was she had six digits on either hand, and that meant Versanjer instead. He'd thought it through one day a few months ago when he'd been in a particularly bad mood.

Twenty-seven years ago the Bench had put down a bloody revolt at Versanjer. The slaughter had been horrific. And the vengeance of the Bench had not stopped at the execution of most of the adult population; the Bench had taken the children as well. Put them into crèche. Raised them to serve the Bench with fanatical devotion, making of the daughters and sons of dead rebels paragons of everything against which the insurrectionaries had rebelled.

The navigator brought the ship into the bay, and the tow drones took control to complete the landing sequence. Rukota decided that he needed some air. Following the system engineer up through the topside observer's station Rukota straightened carefully, standing on top of the courier's back.

Something fell past the mouth of the docking slip, something big and black and silent.

"Oh, no," the system engineer said, as if someone had asked her a question. "I don't deal with those things. All yours, General."

She scurried back down into the body of the courier with unseemly and ungraceful haste. Rukota looked at the now-closed hatch for a moment, thinking about it; then he threw the catch with the toe of his boot, securing the hatch from the outside. Let the crew wait for the inorganic quarantine scans to cycle through before they left the ship. It would serve them right for abandoning him to a Desmodontae.

Something else was coming toward the mouth of the docking slip, but Rukota had an idea that he knew what this was. The crane. The basket came down across the mouth of the docking slip slowly, then slid carefully into the bay itself until it rested level with Rukota where he stood.

Jennet ap Rhiannon opened the security cage's gate and beckoned him in with a wave of her hand. "General Rukota. A pleasure to see you."

If she said so. He couldn't say the same for her, and if he had been in her place he would consider his mission to be about as welcome as the tax collector the morning after an unreported gambling coup. Rukota stepped into the basket without comment, and ap Rhiannon moved the crane out and away from the docking slip.

He could see the Desmodontae now. A great black web-winged creature out of a horror story, a giant bat, subsisting on plasma broths that replaced its native diet of hominid blood. The *Ragnarok*'s Intelligence Officer. One of the very few non-hominids with rank in all of the Jurisdiction's Fleet, her presence here on the Ragnarok part and parcel of Fleet's confusion over what to do with her and what to do with the ship itself.

His wife said that Two had something on somebody, but that nobody had ever been able to decide if Two realized it or not.

"To what do I owe the honor of this meeting?" Rukota asked,

watching Two carefully as she executed her aerial maneuvers. It was probably difficult for her to be confined on shipboard, rank or no rank. Rukota supposed he himself would grasp any opportunity to fly if he had been a bat.

"We'll have a formal in-briefing later on, of course," ap Rhiannon assured him. "I was surprised to hear you'd accepted the assignment, General. I'm sorry. We don't have anything for you."

Of course she didn't. What else could she be expected to claim? "Brecinn thought I'd be an impartial observer." Or a cooperative patsy. Maybe that. "Second Fleet doesn't have much work for me just now. So here I am. Don't get any ideas, Lieutenant."

There had been awkwardness, during their earlier assignment together. The gossip about Rukota's wife was widespread. Ap Rhiannon had apparently become intrigued by him, if for no other reason Rukota could guess than sheer contrariness. He had had to remind her that he was her superior officer.

Now she was the acting Captain of the *Ragnarok*, and technically outside his chain of command. Was he going to have to defend his virtue?

The Desmodontae was coming at them in full soar, gliding by very close overhead. Talking to herself, evidently, from the vibration Rukota felt in the buttons on his blouse. Maybe it was just her echolocation. Either way he wished she would stop it.

"Have you met my Intelligence Officer?" ap Rhiannon asked. Two did a spin and roll, landing on the arm of the crane and stopping abruptly. It was unnatural, that sudden absolute stop. Rukota held on to the railing. He didn't like Desmodontae. They made him nervous.

Crawling up the crane's arm to the basket Two climbed over the rim to hop down into the security cage, smiling up at Rukota cheerfully. It looked like a smile, at least; her mouth was open and the corners of her lips curled up in her face. Rukota could see her very white, very sharp teeth, set off to dazzling perfection by the black velvet of her pelt.

"Pleased," Two said. Her translator had no accent, but Rukota suddenly thought about the farce stereotype of the Briadie matron, all flamboyant hand gestures and shrill nasal tones and insatiable nosiness. "Rukota General. Seventeen thousand saved at Ichimar, and casualties held at less than one in four sixty-fours. Very impressive."

And a long time ago, but it was kind of her to mention it. "Very gracious, your Excellency. What's your take on all of this, if I may ask, ma'am?"

Ap Rhiannon seemed clearly intent on controlling the investigation from the beginning. He could appreciate that. It was her natural right as the acting Captain of this ship. If she was going to give him access to her Intelligence Officer, though, he was going to take advantage of it.

"We have nothing to give or take," Two assured him, happily. "But don't take my word on it. Take your time. Enjoy your investigation. The food is not good, by report, and accommodation cannot be said to be luxurious, but what is ours is yours."

Ap Rhiannon was not so happy as Two seemed about it all. "I'll tell you what I think, General. I think Pesadie wants to find someone here on board of the *Ragnarok* at fault for that explosion. The plain fact that it's incredible is not enough to stop some people. I won't have it."

There wasn't anything he could say in response to this, because she was right on all counts. "Then the audit will show that you're clean, Lieutenant. And we'll be out of your way in no time."

He hadn't convinced her. No surprise there. He hadn't sounded convincing to himself. "We've already done one assessment, General, ammunition, equipment calibration, electromagnetic emissions. Everything. Unexceptional on all vectors. So what? If evidence is not found, it can be created."

Yes. That was the way it was. "So Fleet will run a few tests, and ask a few questions. You could lose a troop or six. That's the way it goes, Lieutenant. There's a Command Branch officer dead, and there has to be an explanation somewhere."

"Pesadie can just find its explanations at its own expense. I have no intention of throwing a single life into Fleet's maw, Command Branch or no Command Branch. These are my crew now, General, for howsoever short a time, and I will defend them. Are we clear?"

Two shifted her wings with an embarrassed sort of a shrugging gesture as ap Rhiannon spoke, and it was all Rukota could do not to jump.

"I'm just here to take the baseline, Lieutenant." Yes, they both knew how easy it was to fake a baseline. But if she'd learned anything at all about him during their previous acquaintance, she would know that he didn't play games. "It doesn't matter to me one way or the other. If there's nothing here, that's what I'll tell Brecinn. If there's something here, you'll see it before she does. Can we just agree on that?"

So that he could get out of this crane basket, and away from the *Ragnarok*'s Intelligence Officer. He was probably sweating.

Ap Rhiannon glanced up into his face for a moment before she nodded, finally. "Very well, General. Welcome aboard."

Oh, absolutely. A hostile Captain and suspicious crew to one side of him, a team he mistrusted—and whom he suspected of having their own agenda—to the other: just his idea of a welcoming environment.

"Thank you, Lieutenant." Technically she was an Excellency, he supposed. But she'd been his subordinate Officer, once upon a time before, and he didn't know quite how to relate to her as anything else. What did it matter if he antagonized her? She wasn't happy about any of this anyway. "Pleased to be here. Well. Actually, no. But we'll do our best with what we've got."

With luck, he wouldn't have to spend too much time with the Intelligence Officer.

But, with luck, he wouldn't have been here in the first place; so Rukota sighed and resigned himself to the fact that he was going to have an opportunity to grapple with his fears, and climbed back out of the crane basket—when ap Rhiannon returned him to the docking slip—to open the hatch in the top of the courier and let his team come out.

Cousin Ferinc stood in the young master's schoolroom with Anton Andreievitch in his arms, looking out the tall window across the courtyard to the old wall and the river beyond.

"There, now, that's better," he said encouragingly, as Anton rubbed his nose and wiped his eyes. In that order, unfortunately, but there were limits about what could be expected of an eight-year-old—even one so self-possessed as Anton Andreievitch Koscuisko. "Here's Nurse, young master, time for your bath. You can tell me all about it when I get back, but be good and don't fuss, or I shan't bring you a wheat-fish from Dubrovnije."

Anton's bright blue eyes widened. "I shall be very good," he assured Ferinc, solemnly. "And shan't fuss at all. I promise."

He always kept his promises, too; at least, as well as a child with the handicap of a developing attention span to contend with could manage it. He was like his father that way.

Ferinc put the child down. "Good man. Go along, I'll just speak to the Respected Lady, and I'll see you in a few days. Don't forget. I'll bring you a wheat-fish."

He usually tried not to think about Anton's father. Over the years it had become easier than he would have imagined not to think about Anton's father. He still had dreams, but Cousin Stanoczk had reconciled him to that. Cousin Stanoczk was not Anton's father. But he did look a very great deal like the man, especially in the dark of a dimly lit cell.

Ferinc watched Anton Andreievitch out of the room, smiling gently to himself: Anton was such a little man.

Anton Andreievitch's mother spoke from behind him, and called his attention back to where he was. "And for me, Cousin." It was a word for cousin that she used only seldom, and never except when they were alone. "What will you bring me from Dubrovnije if I am very good, and do not fuss?"

There was tension in her voice, and not a little bitterness. But there was to be no help for it. Andrej Koscuisko could not find him at the Matredonat. It would ruin everything.

"Surely the Respected Lady has nothing to fear," Ferinc said with tender assurance, turning to face her. "What is it, Marana? Tell your Cousin Ferinc all."

She smiled bravely at his teasing, reaching out for him, drawing him to her by pulling at the braids that he wore to each side of his face to keep his hair out of his eyes. Malcontents alone of all Dolgorukij men wore their hair long; at least some of them did, and Ferinc had let his hair grow as part of his way of separating himself from his former self. There were drawbacks. This was one of them.

"I have not seen Andrej for more than nine years, Ferinc. Nine years. And yet he is the master of this house, lord of the Matredonat, and all that is in it."

Master of her body, at least in principle. That was the traditional understanding of her position here, at any rate.

"It will probably be a little awkward. Yes." He had his arms around her now, and the trusting warmth of her body against his was familiar and comforting. She was tall for a Dolgorukij woman. But he was taller. He was not Dolgorukij, either. "Nothing I have ever heard of thy lord would make him out to be a man to impose himself on a lady's privacy. He is probably as nervous as you are; consider, you know I'm right."

She raised her head and looked up at him sharply. It couldn't be that she had misunderstood him; they were speaking of Koscuisko in his capacity as a normal social creature. Not as Inquisitor. "But I'm not a lady, Ferinc, I'm a gentlewoman of yes-all-right-passable breeding—but poor judgment—who bespoke a child from a betrothed man before his sacred wife had been bred to his body. There are far simpler ways to say just what I am. You know them."

Willful misunderstanding was to be his tactic, Ferinc decided. "Yes. Among them beautiful. Devoted. Precious beyond price. The hearth-mistress of the Matredonat—"

No, none of those were the words she had had in mind, and she pushed him away from her with a smile. " 'In the mouth of the Malcontent, excrement is honey.' You will be gone for how long, Cousin?"

Not so quickly as that, Ferinc decided, and closed the distance between them to embrace her. "Would I dare to kiss you," he asked; and did so, carefully, gently, thoroughly, "if that were true? Be fair, Marana."

She made a face at him, her hands at the back of his head, smoothing the long hair that fell unbraided down his back. "Lefrols, then, and it is very much the same thing if you would like to know my opinion. Answer the question."

"Three weeks, maybe longer, Respected Lady. I don't know for certain. I won't know until Cousin Stanoczk tells me, and he hasn't yet." Koscuisko would be home for at least that long. Anton would be reconciled to Ferinc's temporary absence after a day or two, and then six weeks would seem no longer than three to him. Marana was not likely to be as understanding, but there was nothing that Ferinc could do about that.

He was not going to Dubrovnije. But that was nobody's business but the Malcontent's. He would have to send for a wheat-fish for Anton Andreievitch.

"Think of me while you are gone, Cousin." Marana stepped away from him and back into her status; one almost saw the power descend upon her shoulders like a shawl. "Yes. I'm nervous. It's beastly of you to leave me now. But one does not expect decency from Malcontents."

She was not actually angry at him. If she knew what duty called him away from her, she would be. She would be more than angry. She would be horrified and betrayed, and would quite possibly refuse to so much as see him again, ever again.

She was right about one thing at least, though. It was nobody's business but the Malcontent's. It could be true that Mergau Noycannir at Chilleau Judiciary had no good reason to know Andrej Koscuisko's exact whereabouts: but the Saint had accepted the bargain she'd offered, and would fulfill its side of the contract. It was one way to be sure that they knew what she was up to, after all.

"The peace of the Malcontent be with you, Respected Lady. I will think of you. Depend upon it."

She was to be Koscuisko's wife, though she didn't know it yet. Ferinc was not sure she would still be his lover when he returned. "The Holy Mother has ordained that women need not bless your divine Patron. So I will say only good-bye, Ferinc."

It was in the hands of the Holy Mother. In whom he did not believe, but it would be imprudent to remind his Patron's goddess of that. "I'll be back to see you in a few weeks, Respected Lady. You have the home advantage with your lord; he is almost a stranger here. You will manage beautifully."

Women were absolved from blessing the name of the Malcontent; Malcontents, from begging leave, as from most—if not all—of the otherwise common rites of ordinary life. Ferinc left Marana in the nursery and went down the hall to make his way out to the motor stables. There was a ground-car waiting.

Marana, in the embrace of her lord, soon to become her husband as well as her master. Marana, in Koscuisko's bed—

He had to get out to the airfield in time to find his covert. He would simply have to submit the whole problem to Cousin Stanoczk, the next chance that he got to be reconciled.

Andrej Koscuisko stood behind Lek as the courier made its final approach to Jelchick Field.

The *Magdalenja* had made atmosphere, dropped out of space into stratosphere, several hours ago; it had shed the thermal load acquired in its re-entry over long, slow, high-altitude orbit, and it was ready to make planetfall in fact.

"We have for the final approach your clearance codes, *Magdalenja*. Stand by."

The Standard was precise and uninflected, but the syntax was Dolgorukij. Andrej watched the long hills, the great broad course of the river Trijan, the black-green slopes of the spacious game preserve with its old forest scroll beneath the hull of the courier: home.

There were veserts upon veserts of fields in grain, still green and silvery in the sun; it was yet midway into the growing season, and Jan Seed-of-Life had only begun to show the long black beard that marked him for a man and ripe for slaughter. Well, for harvest, but harvest was slaughter, and tradition required it be approached with reverence and care.

"Thank you, Jelchick. Final approach. Beacon scan initiated."

In all of the years that he had known Lek Kerenko, Andrej didn't think he had even once noticed that he had an accent. The blood of his ancestors in the fields below reached out to him, cried out to him—corrupted him. Lek sounded Sarvaw to him, and Andrej shuddered to hear it. If he could think such a thing—he, who owed so much to Lek for openhearted charity—if he could think the word with scorn, how could he hope to keep Lek from shame at the Matredonat?

The courier slowed perceptibly moment by moment, falling fast. Jelchick Field took a sudden approach, but it had been the most suitable airfield—the one closest to home. Andrej was not going to Rogubarachno, the ancient house in the plains of Refour where he had been born; only later would he travel to Chelatring Side in the mountains, to attend to political business with his family.

They were for the Matredonat, an estate that belonged to him personally in his capacity as the son of the Koscuisko prince, the place where he kept Marana and his child. They were going there first. It had been negotiated. It had been agreed. So why were there riders in array at the very edge of the airfield, a hunting party, and one rider on horseback sitting apart from the rest?

"Send a security query, Chief," Andrej suggested. He would not send the question himself. Let Stildyne do it. "Find us out who those people are. The airfield is secured. I want to know." He needed all the advance warning he could get, if they were who he suspected they might be.

Stildyne stepped away from beside Andrej without comment as Lek drew the courier into its final descent. Andrej could see the emergency equipment drawn up alongside the end of the travel-path, could hear Lek talking to the traffic control center; but had eyes only for those people well out of range of the courier's engines, waiting.

If he did not take care, Andrej told himself, he would convince himself that he recognized that one tall rider. And that was clearly impossible. He had not so much as seen his father in almost nine years.

Stildyne had returned. "Says it's the landlord, your Excellency," Stildyne said. "At least that's what I think they said."

" 'Master of field and grain, river and mountain'? Is that what they said?"

Stildyne didn't so much nod, but merely lowered his head in confirmation. "So what does it mean, sir?"

Closing his eyes for one brief moment of frustrated fury Andrej swore. "All Saints in debauch. My father, Chief. Probably my mother. Doubtless at least the youngest of my brothers, but it was not what we had planned. I'm not prepared for this."

It was far too late to tell Lek to abort the landing, and break space again. Nor would it have been fair if he'd let himself be forced so far as that. He wanted to meet his son.

"His Excellency presents his compliments," Stildyne said, as if it was a question. "And regrets that an unfortunate desire to see you all in Hell prevents his meeting with you at this particular time or any in the foreseeable near future?"

As angry as Andrej was, he had to laugh. "Someone has corrupted you, Chief. You sound like a house-master in a bad mood. No. There is to be no help for it, and everybody knows that the prince my father left me with no choice when he elected to attend this event. I will have to go and kneel and beg for blessing."

The courier had come to a complete halt, the ventilators equalizing atmosphere. Andrej took a deep breath to calm himself. He almost believed that he could smell the hot dust of the grain-lands in the summer. "When we approach them, hold the team at the same remove as my father's house-master will be standing, with my father's mount."

"We brought smoke, your Excellency." Lek surprised Andrej by speaking up, and Murat beside him took up the skein, in braid.

"We wouldn't even use irritant fog. Just smoke."

"Lay down a good field," Smath added. "Run for it. Evasive action. Just to keep in practice, sir. Just say the word."

They were so good to him. Or perhaps they simply preferred not to start a vacation with their officer of assignment in a filthy temper: so one way or another he owed it to them to face up to the coming ordeal like a man, and get it over with.

"Thank you, gentles, but the word must be 'no.' I will go and speak to my father. You may watch if you like. You will not see many Dolgorukij so tall as he is."

Meeka had inherited all of their father's height, and their father's beautiful great black beard as well. Neither Lo nor Iosev nor Andrej himself stood any more near such height than the shoulder to the head. There was no telling about Nikosha, who had been a child; but even so, Nikosha seemed to take after their mother for his frame and his physique.

The ground crew had arrived. Andrej could hear Taller making the required polite conversation. A moment or two, and the passenger ramp descended, opening the side of the courier to the sight of late morning and the faint but unmistakable fragrance of sirav in bloom.

The perfume of the weeds of the country seized Andrej's brain like a drug. He could not bear to stay inside the courier breathing Standard air for one moment longer. He had to get out. Even though it meant he would have to go and confront his father, he had to get out and breathe the air, feel the pull of his own earth, the caress of the warmth of his own sun.

Nine years.

He had spent years at school on Mayon before he had gone to Fleet; he had had difficulty with Mayon's gravity as well. Off. Ever so slightly off. It had taken weeks for the uneasiness in his stomach to settle, but he had been away from home too long, and now he felt the land-sickness in his stomach all over again.

It was probably just nerves.

Out there in the near distance the hunting party was moving in bits and pieces, reacting to the appearance of the courier's passengers and crew. It would be over all the sooner, and the more quickly, he engaged; therefore Andrej waited until Murat had finished his post-flight checks and spoke.

"If you please, Mister Stildyne."

He was an officer under escort, his uniform a stark contrast to the hunting costume that his father wore. Men in their family did not wear black boots in the summertime, nor boots of hard leather of any color unless they were at court or at war. The blouse of the trousers was not creased unless one's housekeeper were clumsy, stupid, incompetent, or insolent; no man of rank would fail to wear a broad belt over his jacket, from which to hang a pouch of this or a string of that. All in all, he was quite possibly as alien to them as Andrej's father and his people were to Security 5.l.

Climbing into the waiting ground-car Andrej nodded to Taller, who had taken the driver's seat. Taller knew quite well that they were taking a detour on their way to traffic control. Once Smath had hopped on board with the last of the luggage Taller headed out for the far side of the airfield, where the hunting party was gathered just to the near side of the security fence.

When the distance had shrunk to eighty paces or so Andrej stopped Taller with a gesture, and Taller secured the vehicle's drive before joining the rest of the team on the ground.

His people formed up in the standard square around him with the efficiency of long practice and the ease of clear, if unspoken, communication. Andrej started through the long grass toward the hunting party, and three riders came down from the little rise that the hunting party had invested to meet him partway.

When they had closed one quarter of the distance Andrej's father dismounted. So of course the escort dismounted as well, one of them taking the reins of Andrej's father's horse.

One half of the distance, and the two men who had accompanied Andrej's father stopped. Andrej didn't hear any word from Stildyne, but his people stopped too, Taller and Lek each taking a step to either side to give Andrej clear passage between them.

When Andrej was close enough to see his father's face, close enough to meet an outstretched hand, he stopped and stood and waited for his father's word. Looking up into his father's worried blue eyes Andrej wondered what there was that he could say, what there was that he could do. He knew the obvious answer: he was to kneel and beg his father's blessing. But it was not as simple as that.

This man was his father, and loved him, drinking in his face with an expression of fond thirst.

And yet Andrej's knees could not be convinced that they should bend. His father, yes, but also the man who had sent him into Hell nine years ago and demanded that he abide there, the man who—once all had been said and done at the Domitt Prison—had rebuked him for unfilial behavior in having challenged Chilleau Judiciary in so public a forum. The man whose acceptance of Chilleau's persuasions had left Andrej with no other escape from a servitude more horrible than even that which he had endured under Captain Lowden's command than to submit himself to Fleet for four years more.

At the same time, this man had not truly done much of what Andrej found to blame. His father had been an officer in mere Security, and at a time when Inquiry had been informal and field expedient, bearing no discernible relation to the Protocols in their current form. His father could have no conception of what Andrej's life had been like with Captain Lowden as his commanding officer.

This was a Dolgorukij father in the presence of a wayward son, and as much as Andrej regretted the shape into which his father had forced his life, there was no sense in reproaching a man for what he had no idea that he had done.

In the end, it wasn't his father's fault at all.

He could at any point have turned his back and stepped away from duty and obedience that required he execute sin and practice atrocity. No one had forced him to his duty but his own will to be dutiful. He had not in all of this time turned his back and said no, because he had not had the courage to shame his father and distress his mother.

Was that truly adequate an excuse to cover the torture and murder of feeling creatures?

Having submitted to such crimes to keep the pride of his family from stain and reproach, was he now going to shame his father in front of so many of the household by refusing the basic duty of a child in the presence of its father?

It was the act of a coward to blame another for something that was not truly their fault but one's own.

Finally Andrej's knees began to bend. He lowered his head to show his father the white of the back of the neck above the collar. Maybe it had taken all these years for Andrej to grasp the idea that he did not have to be a filial son, but so long as he was here and had committed such horrors in the name of filial piety and the Judicial order, it would be mean-spirited of him to deny his father the respect that should naturally be between father and son.

It was not his father's fault.

His father reached out to him as Andrej started to kneel and prevented him from kneeling, drawing Andrej to him instead, to be embraced both gently and fiercely.

His father seemed to be weeping, and the notion sent Andrej into a panic that he didn't really understand. So many people he had hurt so far beyond the power of tears to express, or cries, or screaming. Why should one man's purely emotional grief distress him so?

"Please, sir."

His father relaxed his grip on Andrej the moment Andrej spoke, but he didn't let go of him. Andrej stood in his father's embrace in an agony of confusion and embarrassment; too much happening too quickly between heart and mind for Andrej to be able to make sense of it.

"Please, sir, don't distress yourself. I have been wayward and unfilial, but I am your child still." And yet he was going to go from here to the Matredonat, where he would once again defy his father and insult his mother by acting as though he were an autonomous person rather than somebody's child.

His father tightened his arms around Andrej one last time, then let him go. "And yet Cousin Stanoczk has hinted, son Andrej. You know that you cannot have my blessing for your intended actions."

What was worse, his father apparently knew what he meant to do. How had Cousin Stanoczk come by the knowledge?

Was there ever any knowing, with Malcontents?

He'd spoken to a priest on their way out of Port Burkhayden, in order to be sure of the correct and complete ritual. That was perfectly true. He just hadn't expected it to get back to his father, and for the Malcontent to have transmitted the information made Andrej wonder what the Malcontent had in mind.

"I am bound for four years more at least, sir, and my ship of assignment has only recently lost two of its officers, even though we are not actively engaged." One of whom he had himself murdered, but he wasn't going to trouble his father with that surely trivial piece of information. And he had no idea whether the death of Cowil Brem was public knowledge as yet. "I must think of my son."

"As I of mine." Well, the Koscuisko prince had more than one son, and they both knew that. But Andrej was the oldest of Alexie Slijanevitch's male children; that meant he counted for more than the rest of his brothers taken together. "And I have for too many years played Sanfijer to your Scathijin, son Andrej. I don't pretend that Scathijin did not bring the most part of his grief upon himself. But Sanfijer had no one but himself to reproach for the fact that he had not been more natural a parent."

Never, never, never had Andrej ever imagined that it could be possible for his father to say such a thing to him. The surprise betrayed him to himself, and the frustrated affection and aggrieved resentment of the years brought tears to his eyes.

"I do not ask for your forgiveness, sir, as I do not deserve it." He was become unfilial. He would remain so. His father forgave it, even before the fact. "But to have your forgiveness for my fault. It would be almost as good."

It was a fault only in the context of their culture. Andrej had just realized he was no longer fully part of it; but his family was. His son would be raised here on Azanry, and have to find a way to fit himself into the society to which Andrej had been bred and born. It seemed the traditions of his ancestors had power over him that he had not begun to suspect.

"I bless thee as my unfilial son Andrej," Alexie Slijanevitch said, very solemnly, but there was the unmistakable softness of a loving parental heart within and around the words. "That is to say, my child, who has been a man in the eyes of the greater government of this Jurisdiction for these years past. Your father's blessing on your misguided, ill-advised, self-willed, and all too clearly Koscuisko head, son Andrej, with a full heart I grant it."

Something inside Andrej's chest seemed to crack open, flooding his body with grateful warmth. He bowed over his father's hand to kiss the family seal that Alexie Slijanevitch wore on his right hand; and his father embraced him once again, and held him close for a long moment as Andrej struggled for control of his emotions.

"Now. I have already violated the terms of our agreement, son Andrej. We know you are on your way to the Matredonat." His father put Andrej away from him at arm's length and looked him in the eye, lovingly. "You will perhaps forgive us in turn for having wanted too badly just to see you. Go and kiss the hem of your mother's apron, and come to us at Chelatring Side when the Autocrat's Proxy arrives."

It was almost unfair.

He was to have his father's forgiveness and his mother's understanding after all, and it was all only now. Only now that he was under some mysterious and undefined sentence of death, only now that he had already made contract with Fleet for another four years.

If he had known that his father would have softened so much toward him as to be able to cite the story of the filial son wrongly accused—the tragedy of Scathijin the Self-Minded—he might not have done it. He might have come home and trusted his parents' change of heart to keep him safe from the threat of Chilleau Judiciary.

With a full heart Andrej hurried through the tall grass of the un-mown verge between the pavement of the airfield and the perimeter to see his mother, his head too full of wonder and amazement to have a thought to spare for anything but the moment.

They were too far away to hear what was being said, but what Stildyne could see was startling enough.

Koscuisko's father.

Stildyne had only negative associations with the concept. His own father was a man he'd hardly thought twice about since the day he'd sworn to Fleet to get off-planet and away before the local authorities started to make inquiries. The chances of anybody really caring who had killed Stildyne's father were vanishingly small, and the pitiful remains of Stildyne's young sister were no more grievous a motive in the world that he had left than other wrongs his father had done.

He'd never embraced his father that he could ever remember, and had successfully avoided other sorts of physical contact from the day when he'd been old enough to hit back. His younger sister hadn't had a chance. She'd never gotten quick and clever enough to escape. She hadn't lived long enough.

And here Koscuisko bowed to his father.

Was about to kneel, if Stildyne read Koscuisko's body language correctly, and he had studied Koscuisko's body language with care and keen attention for years now. Koscuisko was embraced by his father, and bore it; then bowed over his father's hand.

There was something wrong. There was something altered in the slope of Koscuisko's shoulders, something alien and unknown creeping into Koscuisko's body to make him a different man, one whom Stildyne did not recognize. What was it?

Koscuisko ran up the slope at a quick jog; the people between him and wherever he was going gave way to him, bowing, until he reached his goal.

Smish Smath had the best eyesight at distance, so Stildyne asked her, though he thought he knew the answer. "Who is that, Smath, can you tell?" He spoke quietly, moving his mouth as little as possible to preserve the appearance of waiting in respectful silence at attention rest.

After a moment, Smath answered. "Tallish woman compared to the women around her. Dark hair, fancy headdress. His Excellency takes her stirrup. Maybe what—kissing her knee?"

"Her apron," Lek corrected, tolerantly. Lek didn't have Smish's keen sight, but he did have the advantage of knowing what went on between Dolgorukij. "He'd be kissing the hem of her apron. His mother. The sacred wife of the Koscuisko prince. A Flesonika princess, if I remember right. Old blood, in his Excellency's family."

Family. What a concept.

Koscuisko's father mounted and turned his horse's head, and the hunting party started to move. Koscuisko himself started to walk back to where Stildyne and the others were waiting for him; even mounted, the Koscuisko familial retainers backed the horses out of Koscuisko's path rather than turn their backs on him. They all seemed so much alike, in a sense; the body types were similar and yet strange to Stildyne.

In the midst of that crowd of Dolgorukij, Koscuisko seemed strange to Stildyne, and the realization was an unpleasant one.

Andrej Koscuisko was his officer of assignment, a man whom Stildyne had trained on an almost daily basis for physical fitness and to improve on the fighting skills that Chief Samons—Koscuisko's Chief of Security prior to his assignment to the *Ragnarok*—had so ably established in him. A man Stildyne had nursed through countless drunks and alcohol-induced psychotic episodes, dreams so vivid and horrible that they could not be dismissed as simple nightmares, agonies of mind and spirit that had sensitized Stildyne to the concept of guilt and sin and spiritual pain for the first time in his life.

This Andrej Koscuisko was none of those things. Koscuisko had been transformed from the man Stildyne knew and understood into a complete stranger, somebody's son, a man with a community so alien and self-contained that Stildyne could not begin to reach out to him.

These people were Koscuisko's family. All of these people were, in a sense. And here in the midst of his family, what need did Koscuisko have of Stildyne—or anybody?

Koscuisko walked down the grassy slope to rejoin them, but he didn't look the same. His posture was different. Not even his face was truly familiar; he looked years younger than he had when they had landed, and his uniform did not seem to fit, somehow. It seemed wrong on him. It was the clothes that those other people wore that would be natural on this Koscuisko's body; Stildyne had never even seen Koscuisko in anything but a uniform, or pieces of a uniform, or in no uniform at all.

Stildyne hated this.

He had anticipated Koscuisko's re-absorption into his birth-culture; he had resigned himself to the probable fact of Koscuisko's becoming so involved in personal business that he would have little time or attention to spare for his Security. But he had not realized that Koscuisko would become an alien to him, a man he could recognize only on a superficial level.

As painful as it was to be held at an arm's length by his officer of assignment, it was worse than Stildyne had expected to realize that Koscuisko might be so far away from them in spirit once he had got home that there would be no reaching out at all to make or deny contact.

Koscuisko reached them, nodding to Stildyne to signal that they should all get back into the ground-car and get on with their business.

"Blessed or berated, your Excellency?" Lek asked. Stildyne was surprised that Lek spoke, but Koscuisko didn't seem to be, so clearly it was something to do with the culture that Lek and Koscuisko had in common.

Koscuisko tilted his chin a bit, looking up into Lek's face as Koscuisko climbed into the ground-car. "Blessed as well as I deserve, and a good bit better than that. My father says he will not Sanfijer my Scathijin. So it was much better than I had feared, even though the Malcontent has been talking."

Lek could probably explain that to them all later. "Right," Stildyne said, just to regain some illusion of control. "Let's just go clear in-processing and be out of here, your Excellency, shall we?"

What was a scathijin, and how did one sanfijer, and why was that something that Koscuisko and Lek both seemed to understand was a good thing for fathers not to do to their sons?

This Koscuisko was a stranger to Stildyne. Having Koscuisko a stranger was almost like not having him at all; and unhappiness of a sort Stildyne had never felt possessed him, as they drove off to the airfield's receiving station.

Cousin Ferinc sat in his secured observation station, watching through the heavy plate-glass window as the ground-car came across the tarmac toward the administration center where Koscuisko's people would surrender custody of the courier ship, and have their purpose and presence here cleared and documented, by the grace and favor of the Autocrat.

There was no further sign of Koscuisko's family; the hunting party was gone from view. Cousin Stanoczk—Ferinc's reconciler—said that Ferinc was to come to Chelatring Side some day, to view the Gallery. Ferinc was hungry for it, for the chance glimpse he might have there of Koscuisko's father and Koscuisko's mother and the youngest of Koscuisko's brothers, the barely twelve-year-old prince Nikolij. Nikosha. Koscuisko's favorite brother, it was said. There was no love lost between Koscuisko and his brother Iosev who was the next eldest of the Koscuisko prince's sons, and . . .

Ferinc shook his head, angry at himself, and tied his braids together at the back of his head to keep them from falling across his face. Stanoczk tolerated his obsession with Andrej Koscuisko, but only just. And without Stanoczk's charity there was no hope of reconciliation for him in the world. He dared not risk incurring Stanoczk's disappointed anger.

It was so hard.

The communications booth was fully equipped for secure transmit, but no one here would have listened in had it been open. There was no profit to be had from interesting oneself in the Malcontent's business, that was no one's business but the Saint's alone. Ferinc sent the codes that he'd been given into the relay stream with the toggling of a switch; and spoke.

"Swallow's nest, for client at Chilleau Judiciary. Transmit on schedule. As follows, confirm receipt."

He could watch. He could. It would take moments for the screen to clear, because the client at Chilleau Judiciary was suspicious and trusted no one. And was not, in fact, at Chilleau Judiciary, but Ferinc wasn't supposed to know that. Not supposed by the client to know that, at least.

The ground-car pulled up to the foot of the loading dock, almost immediately below the window. They couldn't see him. The panes were treated for thermal management. He knew they couldn't see him. They had no reason even to look.

Ferinc stared down at the party gathered on the tarmac. Security. Chief Stildyne he recognized, with pained surprise; he was a hard man to forget, and that could have been Ferinc himself in Stildyne's place, though their acquaintance dated from before Stildyne's promotion. Petty Warrant Officer Stildyne, and Ferinc. They had had some times.

Oh, he could not think of that, and most especially not—

There was Andrej Koscuisko himself, climbing out of the ground-car, pausing half in and half out to share some joke or another with one of the Security. Ferinc stared hungrily at the man who had haunted his dreams, haunted his nightmares ever since. It had been more than seven years. It felt as though it had been yesterday that Koscuisko had made his mark on Ferinc, body and soul, and left him ruined and destroyed forever.

It had been deserved. Ferinc knew that. And yet he could not shake the horror of it, and the ferocious intensity, and that slim blond officer who stood there smiling—talking with Stildyne—still owned him.

Koscuisko doubtless thought it was all over. If Koscuisko ever thought of it at all, and why should he? What had Ferinc been to Koscuisko, after all, but a man meriting punishment, out of so many that had come under Koscuisko's hand?

The transmission's chime repeated for the third, and then the fourth time. Ferinc turned away from the window.

"Confirming arrival of Andrej Koscuisko with party of Security assigned." Security 5.3 had been expected; Ferinc had made it his business to find out about them, in order to let Marana know what to expect. This wasn't Security 5.3. There was a woman there. But the client hadn't asked; she only wanted to know when Koscuisko set foot to his native soil—so it wasn't up to Ferinc to tell her.

Cousin Stanoczk said that the client was unstable, unnaturally obsessed with Andrej Koscuisko and desirous of knowing his whereabouts from moment to moment. Cousin Stanoczk was most likely to remark on the client's instability of mind when reproaching Ferinc for his own obsession.

The Malcontent made good profit from the weak-mindedness of persons unnaturally interested in specific Inquisitors, however. The client at Chilleau Judiciary paid well for her reports. In kind, and in specie. And Ferinc himself was bound to the Saint on Koscuisko's account, self-sold into slavery of his own free will out of his desperate need to be reconciled with what he had seen in the mirror of Koscuisko's eyes in that cell at Richeyne, so many years ago.

It would be a moment before the countersignal cleared, because the client had been linked on redirect. That always slowed things down. Ferinc went back to the window.

The transit-wagon had come up for Koscuisko's party now. Koscuisko—having apparently stepped through to the airfield master's office for a quiet official signature or two, while Ferinc had been transmitting his report—was coming out of the building, Security forming up around him in perfect order.

Precise to the mark, a pleasure to behold, professional, competent, completely secure in their roles and who they were and what they were called upon to do at all times—

The pain of loss in Ferinc's heart was nearly physical, looking at them. And it was Koscuisko who had ruined him, Koscuisko who had destroyed him, Koscuisko who had taken it all away from him forever and left him broken and bereft.

Just as he reached the transit-wagon Koscuisko looked up, back over his shoulder. Looking up at him. Ferinc shrank back and away from the window, shuddering in terror. Koscuisko could not know. He could not.

What would Koscuisko do if he ever learned the truth behind the role "Cousin Ferinc" had come to play at the Matredonat—Koscuisko's child, and the woman who was soon to find herself Koscuisko's wife—

The relay stream's confirmation signal was noise without meaning. Ferinc reached out his hand to shut it off, barely conscious of his own actions.

Then Ferinc sank to his knees on the floor of his secured communications station and wrapped his arms around his belly to keep his stomach from turning itself inside out, and rocked back and forth in agony, remembering when.

CHAPTER FIVE

Home is the Hunter

Marana Seronkraalya stood in formal dignity well to the front of the assembled household arrayed on the graveled ground before the great doors into Andrej's house and wished with all her heart that Cousin Ferinc could be here with her.

She hadn't seen Andrej in more than nine years.

He had sent letters, gifts, tokens, records, but she could no longer hear his voice in his letters, and when she did hear his voice—in the records that he made from time to time, the hologrammic cubes—it was not the voice of the young man she remembered. It was not the face of her Andrej.

Her son stood waiting in the forefront of the household behind her, with his nurse, wearing his best clothes. His little coat. He should have had the white and red and gold of the son of the son of the Koscuisko prince, but wore the blue-and-yellow of the son of the master of the house instead. Why should she resent the colors Anton wore? It had never been a possibility. And it had been her choice to take a child of Andrej's body before he was married. She had known that his family would resent the claim she made. She had not cared.

She had come to care. For her son's sake she was prepared to demand that the entire Combine reverse itself, and conform to her desire. She had not anticipated the effect that her child would have on her ability to accept the place of a man's second and secular wife and see another woman's son take pride of place over her beautiful Anton.

Closing her eyes against the glare of the bright sun Marana struggled for psychological balance. It wasn't Andrej's fault. It wasn't even her fault. Who had known? His letters were unfailingly kind, and sometimes all but heartbreaking. And yet his letters never really spoke to her as Andrej had once spoken to her. There was the work that Andrej never discussed; it stood between them.

This is not about me, Marana reminded herself, opening her eyes. This was about Anton Andreievitch, who had never met his father. Anton knew what his father looked like; she was careful to keep plenty of pictures. Cousin Ferinc spoke frequently and with admiration of Andrej to Andrej's son, and Andrej sent records to Anton from time to time in which it was clear to her that Andrej had no idea how to speak to a child, no idea of what Anton knew or understood at what age, no possible understanding of Anton's own personality.

She smoothed her palms against the apron that she wore, a formal apron, almost as long as her old-fashioned skirt which dropped to her ankles. There was a little breeze; it was a very pleasant day. The branches of the ranks of shield-leaf trees lining the grand *allee* leading from the side of the house at her left to the motor stables and the stables proper beyond rustled pleasingly, and sent their subtle perfume far and wide.

The house itself all but glittered in the sun, its windows washed, its pillars whitened, its black-slate roof scraped and oiled, its every odd corner and half-forgotten closet cleaned and freshened and made beautiful to receive the son of the Koscuisko prince. It was her home, after all, and he was but a guest in it—all things considered. He had lived here for only a short time out of the years during which it had been in his possession, and she had been here since before Anton was born.

There were people coming from the motor stables, a party of men emerging from the shadows of the *allee*. She knew when they'd arrived; she'd been getting the reports in series as they had left the airfield and passed onto family land and thence to the estate perimeter of the Matredonat. She had waited until the very last to call the nurse out with her young son Anton. He was a very intelligent child, but he was a child still. His attention span was limited. She didn't want him to have time in which to become frightened.

If only Cousin Ferinc were here Anton would not be frightened. Anton loved Cousin Ferinc almost as much as Anton loved his nurse, and Cousin Ferinc seemed genuinely fond of Anton. She was Anton's mother. She could tell.

Six people.

Marana watched them come. It was a long way from the end of the *allee* to the front of the house. The Matredonat was a large house, as befit the gift of the family of the mother of the son of the Koscuisko prince to that son on the occasion of his acknowledgment by his father as his father's son and heir. The cutting with the knife at the inside of the cheek, on the steps of the family's estate at Rogubarachno; the solemn declaration of blood to blood, Koscuisko to Koscuisko. Andrej had been eight years old.

Anton was eight.

Anton had had no such public trauma, nor would have. That was a privilege reserved for the first son of the Ichogatra princess, the woman who had been betrothed to Andrej since his eighth year, the woman who would be Andrej's first and sacred wife. It would be *her* son, not Anton, who would stand beneath the canopy of Heaven and submit to wounding at his father's hand, the cut, the kiss, the declaration. *Give me to drink of thee.* Andrej had not even met the Ichogatra princess more than a few times in his life, and had not thought he liked her particularly well on those occasions—at least from what he had said to her about it.

She needed to focus.

Six people. Ferinc had told her how they would be. Two in front, Security. Andrej next. Two in back, and the chief of Security last, outside of the box of secured space in which they kept their officer of assignment and one step out of alignment with his back. One step to the right, because Andrej was left-handed.

She couldn't get a very good look at Andrej, not with those Security in the way. Her messengers had said that his family had gone to meet him at the airfield; they had never come to the Matredonat. They had never asked her to them at Rogubarachno or at Chelatring Side. She had known that she was snapping her fingers in their faces when she had decided on a child before Andrej's marriage, but she had not understood how angry it would make her for them to slight her son.

She could see Andrej's figure now, at last, as the party drew nearer.

All in Fleet uniform, and Andrej wore the raven's wing. It was very odd for so young a man to wear the color of age and piety, but it was the Fleet color for a man of Andrej's rank. It had no reference to what the color signified on Azanry.

She could see his figure, but it was not familiar. Not more so than that of any man might be, familiar only in that it was Aznir Dolgorukij of the shorter run.

Something was odd. One of the Security was female.

Ferinc had not said anything about a woman in Andrej's Security; and he had said they would all be green-sleeves, all bond-involuntaries, all Security slaves except the Chief of Security who was called Stildyne. She saw only one man with the bit of green on the cuff of his sleeve and the edge of his collar. Ferinc had not known about this.

They passed in front of her at a small distance of five paces' remove, and when Andrej stepped on a magical spot that was directly in front of her they all stopped, very suddenly, without a word or gesture of command that Marana saw. It startled her. Then all at once they turned toward her, and Marana stood face-to-face with the father of her child, the loving friend of her young age, for the first time in more than nine years. Her Andrej.

The Security who stood to either side between her and her lover took a side step each, so that no one stood between them. Marana stared fearfully at Andrej for a moment, trying to see something in his face that would reveal the man that he had been and remind her that she had loved him once.

It was his figure. His shoulders, although he was filled out and hardened in some way. His hands, his booted feet, the way he carried his head, the never-quite-tidy fringe of hair across his forehead, the always-almost-smiling look to the corners of his mouth.

She could not see his heart. It was his face, but there was little she could really recognize. "You are welcome to your house, my lord."

The words were practiced; there was comfort in the ritual. She had never spoken them to him before, but she knew her lines. It was just not being able to believe that it was him that made it awkward. "Stop and take refreshment, for this house and all that are within are yours. Therefore be pleased to stay with us a while, and walk amidst these gardens green; my arms long to embrace you."

He was not looking at her. He was looking past her, to where the household stood assembled, the members of and the members in his Excellency's household. He was an Excellency in Fleet as well; Ferinc had explained it to her.

She thought that his considering gaze stopped when it fell where Anton would be standing, with his nurse. Andrej opened his mouth to answer her, but what he said was not the lines expected.

" 'How shall I come into this house when she who holds the keys is sacred to me? Not as your master, lady, but your suitor true and dedicate, to seek your blessing as that of the Holy Mother of us all.' "

She could not breathe.

There was a clattering sound that rattled in her ears, what was that noise? It was the jug of milk upon the tray that the wife of the kitchen-master held. That was it. It rattled on its tray as Geslij trembled, struggling to keep her body still.

The wrong words for a man to take possession of his house and everything that was in it, and her.

Not Powiss and Empeminij, but Dasidar and Dyraine, the end of the tale, the triumphant conclusion of the saga when the hero to whom all Dolgorukij traced their ancestry besought the beautiful and beloved Dyraine of the weavers to be his sacred wife.

The words that all Dolgorukij had used to marry ever since, but only once. No man would dream of marrying as Dasidar had been forced to promise himself to Hoyfragen, not after the offense that Hoyfragen had given Holy Mother and all Saints under Canopy, not after how nobly Dyraine had suffered to prove her merit matchless and unstained by any act in which virtue was not queen.

She knew the words to say. She just could not quite bring herself to say them, and said to him instead "What are you thinking of? You've got it all wrong. How could you have forgotten such a thing?"

The rattling of the milk jug on the tray that Geslij bore grew ever louder. In another moment, Geslij was going to drop the milk jug entirely; that would be a very bad omen.

"I wish I could have warned you, Marana," Andrej said. There was the ghost of the voice of the man that she had loved in his words; even though he still said "warned," and not "obtained your permission." "I couldn't risk the chance of interference. Please. Be my bride, and make your child my son. This must be done. I promise you."

Her child was his son. That wasn't what he meant. He meant son and heir. Legitimate; inheriting.

He meant to spurn the Ichogatra princess for good and all, and make her—gentlewoman though she was—the mother of the son of the son of the Koscuisko prince.

She was light-headed with shock and bemusement. She could get only very little meaning out of what he said, and what meaning she could grasp seemed too fantastic to be truly understood. Giddy with the unreality of it all, she folded her hands across her apron—to steady herself, as much as because that was what it was to be Dyraine—and raised her voice to say the words that she had never thought to hear coming out of her own mouth.

"'I will be mistress of your hearth and bed, my lord, gladly and with my great entire goodwill, and may the Holy Mother bless and preserve us both to serve all Saints beneath the canopy of Heaven.'"

Reaching out to one side, not daring to look, Marana steadied the milk jug on the tray that Geslij bore. And just in time. Geslij's trembling had so perturbed the jug's contents that some of the milk had slopped over the rim, and made it slippery.

"'Will you not come and drink with me? Let us be glad and take shelter in one another, so that we may have joy and comfort all our lives.'"

House-master Chuska stepped up to the other side of Geslij with the cup, antique and priceless, shining in the brilliant sunlight. Geslij poured the milk and Chuska passed the cup to Marana for her to offer to Andrej, who received it gravely in both hands, raising his voice to begin the end of the ritual, line by line in proper form.

"'Sacred are thy feet to me, lady, for the bearing of the weight of this my child. Sacred is your apron to me, lady, for the cradling of the frame of this my child. Sacred is your breast to me, for the nurture and the comforting of this my child. And sacred is thy mouth to me, lady, for the speaking of the name of this my child.'"

Each sentence had to be interspersed with sips from the greeting cup. Andrej conducted himself with grace and precision; he knew as well as she did that the eyes of the entire population of the Matredonat were fixed on him, how carefully they all listened to be sure that it was done correctly. Once the final word was spoken, there was no going back; he had made witnesses of them all.

When a man married his first and sacred wife before she bore his child, the words were formulae and could be gotten around; but there was no dispensation under the canopy of Heaven that could sunder her from Andrej now, nor Andrej from her, not with the fact of Anton in evidence.

It was the stuff of opera and romance, melodrama, but also law and feud and bloody warfare. For as long as Dolgorukij had told each other stories of Dasidar and Dyraine, a man who cried the full four Sacred-art-thous had made his choice public and irreversible. Andrej emptied the cup and held it out to Chuska, looking at Marana.

"And I hope to be forgiven, once I have but had a chance to speak to you." Because he made her position at once unassailable and more difficult than ever, and he who had done this thing would not be staying to help her bear up beneath his family's displeasure. There would be unpleasantness. She could not imagine that he had his father's blessing to publicly insult the Ichogatra princess and unilaterally revoke all of the complex business relationships that had been years developing—all based on the clear understanding that the Ichogatra princess would be Andrej Koscuisko's sacred wife, and that the benefit that Koscuisko's family enjoyed from the match would accrue to an inheriting son with an Ichogatra mother.

It was beyond possibility that the Ichogatra princess would accept anything less than the first place in Koscuisko's household—for herself or for her children. That was to have been Marana's place, the subordinate wife, the secular wife, the acknowledged but not-privileged children, the match a man made for pure affection and not by his father's devising. The Ichogatra princess would never consent to take second place to a mere gentlewoman.

"We will talk about it later." If he thought for one instant that he was to escape explaining, he was mistaken. "We have already upset your son, Andrej, by this unexpected departure. Now come with me and greet your child. He will be worried. He will not understand what is going on."

Anton Andreievitch had just made an unimaginable leap in status over the heads of the sons and the daughters of Andrej's brothers and married sisters. Over even Andrej's brothers themselves, conceptually. The enormity of it all should stagger Anton, but he was only eight years old, and fortunately would only understand that something unusual had occurred.

Andrej held out his hand; Marana took it. Turning around, she led her now-husband to where Anton Andreievitch stood bravely in his little blue-and-yellow coat, waiting to be introduced to the alien creature in black that was his father.

It had been so long since he had seen her that Andrej couldn't tell how angry Marana might be, or what might be going on in the privacy of her mind. Once they had been so close that they knew each other's joys and disappointments as though they had shared one mind between them; now she was a stranger. Nor could he afford to open up his heart and mind to his Marana, ever again, for fear of what she might see there.

Her legal position and that of their son was as firmly grounded now as he could make them. She would have power, but Andrej was afraid she would have very little support. The election was unblessed. Marana was to remain the anomaly, the gentlewoman, the woman who would continue to represent the loss of face and failure of contractual arrangements that this marriage entailed. He was leaving. He had the easy part.

She led him by the hand in the correct manner to where a little boy was standing, waiting with his nurse. Little brown shoes of soft brown leather. A tiny jacket of blue, and yellow trimmings; an absurdly formal lace cravat, and a face that wrung Andrej's heart because it was like Marana's face and like his own, together, and yet a face distinct unto itself.

He had seen pictures. Hologrammic records. Nothing had prepared him for this moment.

"Here is your son, my lord," Marana said. "And if he is not filial, may all Saints under the canopy of Heaven rise up to rebuke me. This is your child, whom I have named after his father to be Anton Andreievitch."

For a moment the absurdity of the situation, the tyranny of tradition, threatened to overwhelm Andrej. Filial. *If he is not filial may all Saints rise up to rebuke me.* Why should Andrej Ulexeievitch rejoice in a filial son, when he himself was not a filial son?

Why should any son be filial, when it had been in the name of filial piety that Andrej himself had sacrificed his honor and his decency and his ability to sleep untroubled by his dreams, and become Inquisitor?

"He has his father's name, lady, and I am very pleased to know him for my son."

The ritual just completed would not have been reviewed beforehand with this little boy, but they were safely returned to anticipated ground now. This piece of the homecoming speech was the same for almost any circumstance. The little boy looked up into Andrej's face with a look of relief and expectation.

Andrej didn't want to waste a moment longer with ritual and ceremony; this was his son. But his son was a child, and children could be frightened easily by the unexpected. Anton had lines that he would have been coached in and rehearsed to speak. There was no help for it but to go forward.

Andrej finished the required text. "If he can also claim his mother's courage and her strength, he will be blessed indeed. Anton Andreievitch. Do you know who I am?"

Anton was concentrating so hard on what he was to say that it seemed to take a moment for him to realize that this was his cue. He gave himself a little shake, then, that reminded Andrej almost irresistibly of a puppy climbing out of an unwelcome bath. "You are my father, sir, Andrej son of Alexie who is son of Slijan before him. Give me your blessing, sir, I beseech you, so that I may grow in wisdom and in learning to become worthy that I bear your name."

It seemed a very long speech for a little boy to have to learn. Full of archaic constructions and little-used words. It was the end of the speech making, though; or almost the end.

"With all my heart I bless you, my own son." Now it was over. Now Andrej could sink down slowly to crouch on his heels at Anton-height and look at him, really look at him. His son. His. "Come to me, then, Anton, let me have a kiss. I am so glad to finally meet you."

Anton did not seem inclined to do any such thing. Why should he run into a stranger's arms, and kiss him dutifully? Anton's nurse gave Anton's shoulder an encouraging pat that was at least one part gentle push. Anton stepped forward. Putting his little hands on Andrej's shoulders he kissed Andrej shyly, one cheek, the other cheek, the first cheek again.

Andrej held out his arms and Anton, if a little reluctantly, permitted himself to be picked up.

Andrej stood with his son in his arms. He hadn't thought Anton would be so light. "Your mother has told me so many good things about you." And people would tell Anton things about Andrej sooner or later that were not wonderful at all. "I'd like to introduce you to my Security, because they have heard all about you. From me."

A lie. But perhaps one that could be forgiven him. Andrej didn't like to talk about Anton; he was ashamed of never having met him, though his rationalizations for not having gone home were well rehearsed and firmly in his mind to be available whenever he might need them. And what business was it of anybody's but his own? What difference did it make to anybody whether he had a child or not?

He carried his child slowly back to where Security waited, noting with amusement that the look on Chief Stildyne's unlovely face was almost one of horror. Security did not have much to do with children as a rule. Still, Anton was a brave young soul, and looked up into Stildyne's ravaged face with grave courtesy that showed no tinge of fear or horror, putting his arms out unbidden to be held by a man of whom Andrej himself could be afraid—and yet was not, knowing in the marrow of his bones that Stildyne would never do him harm.

Did Anton know that? Was there some special insight that a child's heart enabled that gave Anton the power to look into Stildyne's very ugly face—the flattened nose, the mismatched eyebrows, the cheekbone smashed up beneath the eye, the thin pale lips, the narrow squinting eyes—and see only a man who loved his father?

"My Chief of Security," Andrej explained, as Stildyne held the child in his arms and the others gathered around him. "Like unto the house-master, and these the people of his team. His crew. How do you say it in plain Standard, though? His what?"

"His watch, sir?" Anton guessed. It was the first thing Anton had said to Andrej after the rehearsed speech of welcome, and it was very apropos. Lek Kerenko caught Andrej's eye and grinned, openly and freely, with obvious approval

"Quite so." Andrej was a little surprised, even, because it was the best word for the problem. Also because Anton had clearly been not only listening, but thinking. "Here is my good Smish Smath. Do you see many women on guard-watch here, Anton Andreievitch?"

He was going to have to cut this short in a moment. The household stood waiting; he had to let Anton lead him into the house. It would not be so very much longer, though, surely.

"No, my lord father," Anton said, with his eyes so wide that the whites showed all around. "Is she very fierce?"

And Andrej wanted his Security to know his son, because Anton Andreievitch was the best part of himself that he had left to share with people who had earned his deep regard and gratitude.

It got very late, and Marana was exhausted from the emotional strain of the day and its shocking surprises.

Andrej and his people were still on a different time, perhaps; and Andrej seemed to be genuinely besotted with his son, which more than anything endeared the stranger with the face of the friend of her childhood to her once more.

He might have become a stranger to her; he might not move or sound or even smell like Andrej as Marana had once known him. But at least he knew to cherish their son Anton. She could forgive him much for that, and save the aching outrage that she nursed with regard to his long absence for later contemplation.

She had a much more immediate situation to address. The household had to be allowed to stand down, and to sleep. The master-bedroom suite had been opened for Andrej Ulexeievitch for the first time in more than nine years. There was to be no getting around it; custom and practice and common expectation required her to wait upon her husband in his bed.

There was no escape that Marana could see. As soon as Andrej had sent word that he was coming home, she'd known that she was going to have to sleep with him, at least in the most obvious sense of the term—in the same bed. This bed was an antique, an old-fashioned Dolgorukij autocrat's bed with two tiers of steps up to the platform, its great carved headboard with the family seal of one of Koscuisko's maternal antecedents, more than twice as wide as it was long, with room for a man and his wife and the nurse and the baby.

When Ferinc came to speak privately with her he cradled her close in the dark in her own bed and slept with her in his arms, with his dark hair spread over the pillow.

Being in this bed with Andrej was almost not even being in the same room. There were two sets of curtains that marked the bed space off from the rest of the room, marked off in turn from the rest of the house by its own interior walls, like a house inside a house.

What was she to do? Engage with him? How could she?

She thought about feigning sleep. That had the burden of tradition to recommend it, a signal Andrej would understand without any potentially dangerous words exchanged. To feign sleep would only put things off, however; she would still have to face him tomorrow. And tomorrow night. And the night after that. She was expected to sleep with him for five nights running, in token of her gladness at his return—tradition. It would be awkward to feign sleep for five nights running. It would not be fair to Andrej.

Marana sat at the edge of the great bed in her dressing gown with her hands in her lap, trying to decide how she was to approach this. What she was to say. The problem wasn't Ferinc, not really; Andrej would be hurt, perhaps angry, if he ever found out, but she was well within her rights to accept reconciliation from a Malcontent in the absence of her lord. In the long absence of her lord. In the long and frequently silent absence of her lord, who scarcely spoke to her from his heart, even when he did send her some word. No.

The problem was not really so much Ferinc, and why should it even become an issue, when Ferinc was Malcontent and people minded their own business where Malcontents were concerned?

The problem was Andrej. The thought of exchanging intimacies with a man she had only just re-met made her skin crawl, and yet Andrej gave no sign of any such reservations.

Andrej was coming in through the bed curtains to his bed now, in sleeping dress as she was; which for a man meant a shirt, of course. And slippers and a robe, as well, but there was no way around it—this was a man who was naked beneath his garment, and he was coming into the bed enclosure to sit down next to her.

Looking at her he smiled with a sort of defeated hopelessness, and Marana realized with a shock of icy horror that not only was Andrej stark naked beneath his shirt but so was she. She looked at her hands, and not at him.

Seating himself at the edge of the bed at a respectable arm's length from her, Andrej spoke, almost the first time he'd spoken directly to her since he'd arrived. "This bed is the size of my room on the

Ragnarok," Andrej said. "And I'm an officer. I have twice as much space as anybody. You could put a full Security team into a room the size of this bed. I had forgotten. It is a little bit intimidating, Marana."

She didn't know what she could say. He had offered her conversation, clearly trying to solicit her reaction. She had no reaction. She was benumbed with disgust and dismay to think that she was naked in a bed with a naked man who might as well be a complete stranger.

"That's why there are curtains, my lord. To dampen the echo." She didn't want to be hurtful or cold to him, just because he was a stranger. He had a right to expect at least basic courtesy from her. He had just made her the second-most important woman in his entire family, not excepting his elder sister, not excepting Zsuzsa, the Autocrat's Proxy.

Her son would inherit the controlling interest in one of the oldest, richest, most powerful familial corporations in the entire Dolgorukij Combine. Surely that called for friendly behavior, at least, on her part.

"And the entire bed, perhaps the size of the bolster. Perhaps not quite so large as that. You have slept in decent beds these years past, Marana. Tell me, which side of the bed is it that you prefer?"

She could set that bolster between them, under pretense of desiring the support. Then it would be less like being in bed with him. "I take the near side, Andrej. When Anton was a baby, it was this side that was nearest to the nursery." Not this same bed, of course, but her own bed, in her own apartment. The bed that Ferinc shared with her from time to time, and took the far side of the mattress when he did.

Andrej nodded, but did not get up immediately to go to the other side of the bed. He was looking at the bed curtains right in front of her. Maybe he was just not looking at her, Marana thought, and the fact that there were curtains there was incidental.

"My lord father and my lady mother came to the airfield today, Marana. I suppose you heard."

Yes, she had, and she had therefore no need for him to tell her; so he meant to tell her something else.

"I do not have my father's blessing, to have insulted Lise Semyonevna. But neither was blessing withheld. I'm sorry to have put you in this position, Marana. It was only because of Anton. There are things I may not tell to even you."

A man did not take a sacred wife as Andrej had taken her today. A man sued for acceptance as a husband. She could have spurned him; he had named her sacred to him, but as masterfully as though she had been a share-owned mare. Very high-handed behavior on his part. Had it not been for what the change would mean for her son Anton she might have slapped him, instead of quoting Dyraine to his Dasidar.

At least he knew that he was in the wrong. "He doesn't seem afraid of you." She wanted to be loving. She wanted to be charitable. Maybe if she talked about their son; they had Anton in common. Only Anton. Nothing else; not any more. "I think that you have almost won him over. That gives you credit in his mother's eyes, my lord."

Andrej smiled with gratitude, but twisted his face up into a grimace of distress almost at once. "What is this 'my lord,' Marana? Must it indeed be so? I can't pretend to be the man I was. I don't know you. You don't know me. And yet we loved each other once, I believe we did. I trust we did. I'm almost certain I remember."

His cry was from the heart. "All right." It startled her to realize how close his thoughts moved to match her own. "But it's expected, Andrej, 'my lord husband.' You know that it is."

The formal language was a species of barricade that she could raise to hide behind. It was too bad that Andrej knew that as well as she did. He stood up.

"If you do I'll call you 'Holiest-unto-me,' Marana, I will. And it will be your own fault, too." The sound of his voice was mild and only humorously annoyed. "If we were to pull the pillow down the middle of the bed it need not be too embarrassing to lie together, Holiest-unto-me. So long as someone wakes before the servants come, to set the bed to rights."

Marana stood as well, and felt a strange and unexpected tremor in her belly to hear him speak. It had been her thought, too. It had been her thought almost exactly. Was there something of the Andrej she had loved still there within him somewhere after all? Kept she in any form some faded trace of who she'd been when she'd been his Marana?

"It's been a long day, Andrej." She could say it. The name had an unusual flavor in her mouth, but it was not an unpleasant one. "And you are not on home-time yet, I would guess. It would be better not to risk the scandal. Leave the pillows where they are. If we shall chance to touch by accident, it's nothing that we have not done before, once of a time."

He was untying the sash of his bed robe, and paused, resuming the task only much more slowly. "There are, after all, these years to stand between us," he agreed. "We will not need the pillows. You're quite right. They will be after me for laps tomorrow morning, Marana. You will have the room to yourself to take your breakfast."

Keeping his back to her he laid his robe aside and climbed into the bed. There was something in his body that she knew. Not in the body itself so much perhaps but in the movement of it. Something. She turned down the light.

In the dim golden glow of the votive lamp that burned within the lattice niche of the headboard before the icon that was treasured there Marana took her robe off and got into bed herself, shifting a bit toward the middle of the bed as she pulled the covers up over her bosom.

She reached out her hand, not looking, lying on her back.

After a moment she felt his hand, similarly extended at length across the expanse of the bed linen to touch her fingers—and her fingers only—with unspoken and tentative address.

Thus it was she slept.

Andrej Koscuisko awakened in the dark, not knowing what time it was, not knowing where he was for a long moment. He knew that he was safe, but it took him some thought to gather together the threads of the past day's events and decide what he was doing here in this immense bed.

He'd slept here before, but not for years.

He had made planetfall, he had done his in-processing, he had come home to the Matredonat and made his declaration beneath the canopy of Heaven, Marana to be his first and sacred wife, Anton, his son, to inherit.

This was why he had come home.

Not to astound Marana and infuriate his parents, but to set Anton firmly in place before he turned his attention to the underlying issue, the constant trouble that had dogged his waking moments since first Garol Vogel had shown him the Bench warrant at Port Burkhayden. *As regards the person of the following named soul the bearer is to exercise the solemn ruling of the Bench in support of the Judicial order.* His name.

Vogel had left the warrant with him, and Andrej had brought it. He wanted to take it to the Malcontent, but first he had had to be sure that no matter what happened Anton would be safe.

Unless he could discover who wanted him dead, he could not count on living to engender other sons; so it only made sense that he have no other wife than Marana. He had no fond hopes of convincing his parents of this. He dared not tell anyone but the Malcontent.

Garol Vogel's Bench warrant had not been for Captain Lowden. Therefore Garol Vogel had not exercised it. Then who had killed Lowden, and why had Vogel made the claim that he had, to cover it up?

If it had been Vogel, Bench warrant or no, there would have been nothing to cover up. Vogel was a Bench intelligence specialist. He had the authority to take the Law into his own hands. The existence of the Bench warrant with Andrej's name on it could only mean that someone else had killed Captain Lowden and that Garol Vogel was protecting somebody.

It would be all too easy for any intelligent person to turn their attention to Andrej Koscuisko, the man whose name was on the Bench warrant, a man much worked upon by Captain Lowden, a man whose whereabouts could not be accounted for during crucial hours at Port Burkhayden that night. A man who might conceivably have been mistaken for a Bench intelligence specialist in the dark and confusion of the service house on that fatal evening.

Andrej needed the resources of the best secret service there was. Andrej needed the Malcontent, if he was to have any hope of getting through to the truth behind the Bench warrant. But he could say nothing to anyone else about its existence, and that meant that any excuses he could offer for his behavior would be facile and unconvincing.

He was awake, now. Not just waking up—wide awake, clear headed; he even felt rested. That probably meant it was his normal rising time—early morning, on the Matredonat's schedule, time to go to exercise with Security.

Lying in the bed for one moment longer Andrej stretched himself, listening to Marana breathe. It would be less awkward for them both if he was gone when she got up. Exercise made a good excuse, one that the household could understand. He was expected to renew carnal relations, to possess himself of her body once more. And he didn't dare touch her.

Her breathing sounded deep and regular. If she was awake, she was encouraging the charade, pretending to be asleep, playing along. He had forgotten how well they had once understood each other.

Sliding carefully out from under the sheets Andrej climbed down through the double row of bed curtains into the room, leaving his robe and his slippers behind. There was little risk of waking her by disturbing the bed. It was a big bed. It had been brave of her to reach out to him in the night, but even so formal a contact as that had been almost distressing.

There was too much between them.

When he and Marana had become lovers they had been much younger, and among the very first of each other's loves. She had not been the first woman he had known, but she had been the one he most sincerely wanted, and she had desired him. Once. Long ago. Then he had gone away, to the Fleet, gone as his father had told him to learn how to torture in the name of the Law; and found out such horrors about himself that destroyed what innocence he might have had in lovemaking entirely.

He still liked women. He could engage with them in any of the conventional manners, and have satisfaction, and even give satisfaction. But there was the other thing; there was pain.

The impact it had on him was so much more than merely sexual. The pleasure possessed him body and soul, heart and mind, terrible and transcendent, and overwhelming in its sheer power. Sexual pleasure was sexual pleasure, and it was still available, but it was an almost trivial thing set against the reaction that Andrej had learned that he could have to the suffering of souls in the torments he inflicted.

There were two problems.

One of them was that the suffering that the Bench decreed was so grotesquely out of proportion to the supposed crimes it was meant to address that there was no rational purpose to it, no excuse, no justification. It was wrong, but worse than wrong, it was ineffectual, an atrocious imposition on captive bodies that had no relation to justice or any good effect.

The second was that whether or not it was wrong for the Bench to torture its criminals, it was not right for any decent man to enjoy it. Not even if the Protocols had truly been just and judicious could it be right for the officer charged with their implementation to take so much pleasure as Andrej had in the suffering of feeling creatures fallen foul of Jurisdiction.

And Andrej took pleasure in the Inquisition, a drug so intense that his first experience had been addictive almost at once. He was soiled in flesh and in heart and in spirit by the degradation his pleasure entailed. How could he hope to strip away the years of sadistic indulgence and stand before the friend of his childhood as her true lover?

It was only decent of a man to wash before he approached his lover for intimacies. No amount of washing could remove the stain of sin that was on him. He would soil her if he touched her, because he was corrupt, and his desire had been too compromised by the helpless suffering of his victims to share with an honest woman ever again.

His pleasure itself was compromised. It would be an offense to drown in her arms who had drowned on dry land in Secured Medical, overwhelmed not by the attainment of the sacred ocean within women's bodies but by the gross lust that was within him for mastery.

He hadn't quite thought it all through before now. He'd had too many other things on his mind. But now that he had come home to be her husband, it was all too clear that he could never be any such thing in the physical sense ever again. She had been honest and true to him, even before the wedding-rite had made her holy. And he was a man too corrupt with obscenity to touch her flesh without soiling it.

He needed to think. Exercise would serve.

Andrej did not really care for exercise in and of itself, but Stildyne had a right to expect Andrej to take reasonable measures to cooperate with the efforts of the Security who would be expected to die if need be to protect him from harm. And he had come to rely on Stildyne's demands to give structure and order to his daily life, even when it could have no possible meaning.

Going through the dark bedroom to his dressing room Andrej exchanged his sleep shirt for an exercise uniform and let himself out into the inner hallway, where his people would meet him.

There was only Stildyne, waiting in the corridor, standing there talking with the porter, the elderly woman whose duty it was to sit outside Andrej's bedroom during the night in case he decided he wanted something from the kitchen. Or anything at all. Stildyne alone;

Andrej looked up at him, a little confused, and as Stildyne started off down the hall with him Stildyne explained.

"You wanted to give your people a holiday, your Excellency. And they're pretty tired."

As if that meant anything. They were Security. They were expected to execute Stildyne's will and instruction, regardless of how tired they might be. This was funny. Andrej never would have thought to hear such a thing, not from Stildyne.

"So I've put them on their honor to do their own training. It's just you and me. The house-master tells me where we could go do laps, and it will be a change to be running outdoors." Rather than on an exercise track on board of the *Ragnarok*, which ran the perimeter of the ship along the carapace hull.

It was up to Stildyne to decide on the training schedule one way or the other; if Stildyne felt his people could be excused early morning exercise, could be allowed to sleep late, it was Stildyne's business. Andrej followed Stildyne out of the master's apartments, out of the house, out toward the river past the motor stables down the long *allee* of trees, distracted by the strange and the familiar alike.

Familiar, because this place was his. These grounds, these fields, this house and everything—and everybody—in it, were his own. Possession; and responsibility.

It was a beautiful morning. The sun was not yet clear of the mountains on the horizon, and the little fog from off the river set everything into soft focus. It smelled like home, a unique and indescribable combination of dirt and vegetation, air and water for which Andrej had been longing for years without even realizing his homesickness. It was good to be back home, in his own place.

He was depraved, unfilial, a sinner. But he was a depraved unfilial sinner who was at home.

Stildyne strolled thoughtfully beside him, silent in respect for Andrej's thoughts. Stildyne was long accustomed to the fact that Andrej didn't speak much before breakfast. It took him a while to turn his attention outward in the morning. But something had caught Stildyne's attention.

Andrej sensed a change in Stildyne's demeanor, and glanced up and over at him to see what it might be. Stildyne was watching someone who appeared to be watching Stildyne through the trees, someone who walked on the other side of the ranked shield-leaf trees and kept them in view.

"Something, Mister Stildyne?"

Stildyne shifted his eyes from his target to Andrej and back in the direction of their companion in the distance, pointing without seeming to point. "He's following us. He picked us up the moment we stepped out of the building. I don't know enough about the people here to be able to say, but it seems to me that there's something out of place about that man."

There was no necessary reason why Andrej's own house security should not have a post on them. To keep Andrej's outland Security from getting lost, if for no other reason. And with Andrej back after nine years' absence there was nothing insulting—perhaps the opposite—about an impulse on House-master Chuska's part to send someone with Andrej in case he forgot his way. It would only be looking out for their master, a mark of respect and delicacy of feeling.

But once Andrej had a look at the figure who was following them he knew it wasn't house security. "Men don't usually wear their hair long here. You're quite right, Chief."

Their shadow was keeping his distance, too far off for Andrej to be able to guess whether he knew that man or not. But he could see the man's figure and the more obvious details of his dress. Decent Dolgorukij men wore beards, yes, if they grew beards at all and were old enough. But no decent Dolgorukij male ever wore his hair long down his back. That was no decent Dolgorukij.

Andrej explained, because Stildyne was waiting. "That is a Malcontent, Chief. A religious professional of a particular sort. You've heard of Malcontents?"

Maybe he had and maybe he hadn't. Stildyne was a Security warrant, and had had contacts in intelligence fields, once upon a time. "Heard about them, yes, your Excellency. What do you think he's up to?"

Shaking his head, Andrej smiled. "There's no use even wondering, Chief. The Malcontent does as the Malcontent pleases, and the Malcontent's business is for the Saint alone. You needn't worry."

"Looks familiar somehow," Stildyne remarked, as if clearly aware that a Malcontent shouldn't be. Andrej had to grin.

"If you'd met a Malcontent you'd remember, Chief, trust me on this. We approach the river. Shall we run?"

He didn't know what the Malcontent might be about and he didn't care, because there was no way he would ever find out unless the Malcontent should reveal the information for the Saint's own purposes, and there was therefore no sense wasting the energy.

"Very good, sir. After you."

Just he and Stildyne, in the early morning, on a worn old track that ran alongside the river down to the nearest bridge. The Security they had brought with them were on vacation, Stildyne had said, and came alone. Stildyne had Andrej all to himself. Stildyne was on a holiday of a sort as well, Andrej mused, and this was one of the treats he had granted to himself, morning exercise alone with his officer.

Andrej could see no objection to so harmless a self-indulgence on Stildyne's part. And he did owe Stildyne laps. He always owed Stildyne laps. He would die owing Stildyne laps.

But not before he laid that Bench warrant before the Malcontent and asked the Saint's assistance in identifying who on the Jurisdiction's Bench wanted him killed, and why.

CHAPTER SIX

Disquieting Undercurrents

It was four days into his investigation, six days now since the accident. General Rukota stood on the flight-prep line in the *Ragnarok*'s maintenance atmosphere with the Ship's Engineer louring beside him, watching Pesadie's preliminary assessment team work through an operational audit on yet another Wolnadi.

"Willful obstruction of an authorized Fleet investigation," Rukota pointed out. "As has characterized the approach of this entire Command from the date of the incident. I have never encountered such a concerted effort to be unpleasant in any situation into which I have had the misfortune to be placed in over twenty years of service of the Judicial order."

Rukota himself was a tall man, unaccustomed to the company of people who could look down on him. Wheatfields was slender, but unquestionably very tall, and rolled a little twiglet of wood from one side of his mustachioed mouth to the other before condescending to favor Rukota with a response.

"Flatterer." There was no hint of any personal animosity in Wheatfields's voice. There was no hint of any emotion whatever. "I suppose you say that to all the people you're trying to screw."

Closing his eyes in a momentary spasm of frustration, Rukota reminded himself that it was nothing personal. Wheatfields just didn't like strangers getting into his Wolnadis any more than Wheatfields was likely to tolerate strangers taking more personal liberties. Rukota was right with him, on that. He didn't like the Pesadie team either. They were too obviously looking for something. They weren't finding it, but they had no business coming here with any preconceived ideas on the subject of whether there was anything to find in the first place.

"No, your Excellency, I usually take a more traditional approach: 'Hello, what's your name, did you know that artillerymen can do it on a full three-sixty transit?' You know. Why don't you just go ahead and tell us whose Security it was?"

Wheatfields glanced sideways at him for a thoughtful moment, as though he was carefully evaluating Rukota's facetious overture. Rukota felt a twinge of uncertainty: he didn't want Wheatfields. He didn't care for engineers; he'd always found their approach to intimacy to be entirely too focused on technical details to make for an enjoyable engagement. If he was going to try men at all a Chigan would be the place to start—there was no question about that—but when Wheatfields answered, Rukota realized with disgust that Wheatfields had been having him on. Making him think. Playing games with his mind.

"No, I don't like the psychology of it, Rukota. The minute we say 'Look here for a malfunction, if any,' we've introduced the concept, and there isn't any malfunction to find. The best way we have of proving that is to let your people run a really thorough test on everything here. If they can't identify the subject craft on empirical evidence alone—you have your answer."

In more ways than one. Wheatfields's reputation should have warned Rukota that Wheatfields was teasing. It had been years since the Judicial mistake that had resulted in the horrible death of Wheatfields's lover, spouse, partner, whatever it was that Chigans called each other when they mated.

Chigans didn't necessarily mate for life—the peculiar population dynamics of Chigan society encouraged a rather more fluid approach to intimate relationships—but Wheatfields himself had by report been deeply scarred by the emotional trauma. It had been an exceptionally egregious lapse of good judgment on whoever's part to have let Wheatfields look at the Record of his lover's torture.

At any rate Wheatfields had been as celibate as a woman in a Chigan enclave ever since, by all reports, and had a reputation for being unpleasant. Rukota supposed he was lucky that Wheatfields was speaking to him at all. Part of the investigation, yes, but that didn't mean that Wheatfields would have acceded to an interview if he'd been feeling difficult.

Wheatfields had been daring the Fleet to discipline him for years, and Fleet to its credit had turned its back on behavior that could easily have meant Wheatfields's dismissal in disgrace. It was his death that Wheatfields was looking for, anyway.

"At the rate we're going it'll be weeks before we're finished, your Excellency." There were twenty Wolnadi fighters in the *Ragnarok*'s inventory, twenty-three if you counted the reserves. And Wheatfields probably was. Just to make his point. "What's your investment in hanging on to a bunch of admin types from Pesadie Station for that long? I'd think you'd want us off as soon as possible."

Four days, and this was only the second Wolnadi that Pesadie's team had worked on. Operational audit took time, especially when the Ship's Engineer held so close to his principles and absolutely declined to offer assistance from the *Ragnarok*'s resources—all in the name of ensuring a true and pure result, of course.

Wheatfields smiled. Rukota noticed with astonishment that Wheatfields could actually look pleasant, when he smiled, and really very engaging when he almost laughed.

"Operant behavior," Wheatfields said. "We haven't had staff to run audit on everything. This is an opportunity, Rukota, free labor for as long as it takes. I'm sorry about the environment, though. The stores are pretty low. Nothing personal."

Wheatfields was right about the quality of life on board of this ship. Worse, there were maintenance issues that could only result from increasing starvation for replacement articles and consumables. The *Ragnarok* hadn't been at Pesadie Station above two months; there had to be a more pernicious reason for the state of its stores than just the timing of its depot visits. Somehow or other the *Ragnarok* had simply not been getting its stores in.

"You want me to believe that your people weren't out there on overtime to sanitize that exercise craft?" Rukota demanded. Because if Engineering truly hadn't done an operational audit on the craft before hazarding the findings of the assessment team, the *Ragnarok* was naively convinced that innocence was adequate protection against harm. That would be deeply troubling, because of its stupidity, but also because the *Ragnarok* could only think that if they already knew that there was a reason that would be revealed, and from outside its boundaries.

"Just enough time to satisfy ourselves on the fighter in question."

Wheatfields's candid response made Rukota feel better . . . and then made him feel worse. Wheatfields was confiding. Wheatfields was extending the handshake of truce, and inviting Rukota to become complicit in the *Ragnarok*'s cover-up. It was a risk for Wheatfields to take. Rukota was supposed to be an impartial observer. He had a duty to the Bench.

What duty?

The people that Admiral Brecinn had sent along with him were not in the least bit neutral. They almost didn't even pretend to be. So why should he hold himself to a higher standard, when everything around him was so corrupt?

"Well. You've got to grab resources where you can find them, I suppose."

Because it was his honor, that was why. He couldn't quite turn his back on Pesadie and ally himself with the *Ragnarok*. He couldn't. He had a duty. And his own integrity to consider—at least what was left of it. "No chance of a stash of good bean tea on board, is there? I mean decent stuff. The bean tea in mess is enough to drive a man to desperation. By which I mean khombu."

With clear regret, Wheatfields shook his head. "Sorry, Rukota. Don't even try it. You'll never find my supply. You'll just have to suffer."

That was right. Chigans drank bean tea. He should have remembered.

Wheatfields went off for a word with one of the Security warrants and Rukota stayed behind, watching the assessment team work on the Wolnadi and wondering if he could get a word through to his wife. *Desperate straits. Please send bean tea.*

There had been some stores with them on the courier ship when they'd arrived, the standard issue and survival rations. Meat broth, for one, which had been the only thing that had saved him thus far. When that was gone, they would have no choice but to share the *Ragnarok*'s common mess: and Rukota did not know how he was to face that prospect, and survive.

⊕ ⊕ ⊕

In all of the years that Ferinc had been here, he had never been so reluctant to approach the Malcontent's cell in the Brikarvna safe house as today.

He was usually happy to be called to open his accounts for examination, because it meant that Stanoczk would be there, and Stanoczk would not deny him reconciliation. This time it was different. Stanoczk would be angry with him. He had transgressed.

That Stanoczk would deny him was unthinkable. The all but certain fact of Stanoczk's disappointment was almost as horrible as the thought of being sent away alone, unblessed, uncomforted, un-Reconciled. Ferinc knocked.

It was an old place. It had doors made out of wood, heavy and hung on actual hinges, and when they closed behind one the report of their impact was muffled against the wood that lined the walls into a dull, thudding sound of very oppressive—or promising—finality.

"Step through," Stanoczk called from inside the cell, but Ferinc hesitated, wondering if he should not turn around and go away. He had not done as he had been supposed to do. Stanoczk would be unhappy with him.

And still he was a man, and would stand evaluation like a man. Koscuisko had ruined him, destroyed him, annihilated him, but Koscuisko had not yet made him into a coward.

Ferinc went in, closing the door behind him with quiet resignation. Stanoczk was there, sitting at the long low table, drinking a glass of rhyti. There was only one chair at the table. Ferinc bowed over Stanoczk's hand to kiss his knuckles, a formal and traditional greeting that he had learned to give with affection. Stanoczk did not take Ferinc's hand in return. Stanoczk was that angry.

Sitting down on the floor at a polite distance Ferinc folded his legs for compactness's sake, and waited. He had been in the wrong. This would not be easy. But Stanoczk was his reconciler, and would not let him suffer so long as the peace of the Malcontent was within his power to grant.

Had it not been for Stanoczk, Ferinc believed that he would have killed himself years ago. After Koscuisko.

"What news do you bring from the Matredonat, Ferinc?"

Cousin Stanoczk's deep voice was low and level. He didn't look at

Ferinc. Ferinc could be grateful for Stanoczk's candor; he would not draw the painful confrontation out.

"All seems well, Stanoczk; the child learns not to fear the stranger, the lady grows accustomed to his presence. They say that they sleep in the same bed, but not together."

He wasn't supposed to know. He was supposed to have kept clear of the Matredonat until Koscuisko was summoned to Chelatring Side.

"Tell me, Ferinc," Stanoczk suggested. "Explain. You haven't been reckless in the past. Sometimes almost I have heard praise for you. Talk to me now. Why did I have to seek here for you, when I expected you in Pirlassins?"

Resisting the temptation to solicit reassurance, Ferinc concentrated on the report Stanoczk required. To keep things from one's own reconciler was as much as to shut one's own mouth against sustenance when one was starving.

"I met the party at the airfield, Stanoczk, as I was directed. I sent the report to the person at Chilleau Judiciary. It was acknowledged."

Stanoczk had set his glass of rhyti down, and was preparing to smoke a lefrol. The simple ritual always made Ferinc shudder. Andrej Koscuisko had been smoking a lefrol. "You also had acknowledged your instructions, Ferinc."

That cell had been bigger than this one, better lit, much colder; but it had been as bleak and comfortless, and the stone floor had been as hard.

"It was an error of judgment. I looked out of the window. I knew that Chief of Security, Stanoczk, before he was a chief warrant officer. Oh, I could ruin him—I know things about Stildyne that Koscuisko would not tolerate—"

"We aren't talking about the warrant officer," Stanoczk reminded him. "Go on, Ferinc. I am hoping to be able to excuse you. Help me."

Stanoczk was angry. And Ferinc was heartily sorry for it. Sorry that he had betrayed his discipline; sorry that he had seen Koscuisko; and sorry that he had made Stanoczk angry. There was no way to make it right.

"Oh, I went to look out the window, Stanoczk, and he looked up. Him. As if he knew that I was there. Marana was so unhappy. To think of him in her arms, in her bed, I couldn't stay away. I had to see for myself that she was all right. And then I saw them by the river, Koscuisko, and Stildyne, and . . . "

He didn't want to say this.

He couldn't keep the truth from Cousin Stanoczk.

"I think he may have recognized me. Stildyne. Koscuisko wouldn't. I don't think that he would, not from a distance, not like this. Surely he didn't know—he couldn't have guessed—"

"You let yourself become distracted, Ferinc, and I do not tolerate being disregarded." Stanoczk's warning called him back from the edge of the abyss—as Stanoczk had so many times before. Stanoczk's voice. And Stanoczk's touch.

And the skillful, loving passion of Stanoczk's caress, which had the power to turn the self-punitive fury harmlessly into the emptiness of the past, the power to turn him back from the edge of madness toward a species of fury of a more benign sort, raging in his mind and his desire; quieted to Stanoczk's word in the embrace of the Malcontent.

"I'm sorry, Stanoczk." At least Stanoczk would know he was sincere. "I should have fled to this place and cried for mercy. And instead I went back to the Matredonat. Are you very angry with me?"

Rising to his feet Cousin Stanoczk began to pace, smoking his lefrol, his head bent to regard the floor very thoughtfully.

"After all these years, Ferinc, and to be put back into that place in your mind so suddenly and so completely. It is as though we have not helped you find any healing, at all. If I can't reconcile you to your past they will excuse me from the exercise and try to fit you to another man, one who can better share the true peace of the Malcontent with thee. I don't want that."

Ferinc heard Stanoczk's language drop into the familiar, intimate mode of address, and felt fear gripping his heart. He hadn't stopped to think about that. He hadn't stopped to consider the effect his selfish action might have on Stanoczk at all.

"I don't want another reconciler." He had come much closer to the mystical understanding of the Malcontent with Stanoczk as his tutor than he had ever hoped. "How shall I beg to be forgiven? Do not deny me reconciliation, Stanoczk. I couldn't bear it."

Stanoczk turned so sharply on his heel that for a moment Ferinc saw Stanoczk's cousin, and not Stanoczk himself. Koscuisko had had a quickness about him. It had been very unnerving.

"You do not ask forgiveness of any Malcontent, Ferinc, surely you know so basic a thing as that by now. Nor may I deny you reconciliation, even if I wanted to. It is as much as my soul is worth. But neither your wishes nor mine will change the fact that you are not of the Blood. The Malcontent has taken you on trust and out of compassion for your suffering because of the man who is responsible for it, and should I fail to help you to find peace, I fail our divine Patron. May he wander in bliss."

In bliss and in intoxication. The Malcontent had been a very famous lover of liquor, in his life: liquor, lovemaking, and laughter.

"What happens now?" Ferinc asked, looking at his feet folded beneath him, on the floor. "I want to go back and see him again. I want to be sure Marana is all right. I love Koscuisko's child, Stanoczk. What am I to do?"

He watched the ash fall from Stanoczk's lefrol to the floor, and shuddered. Stanoczk turned back toward the table, and sat down.

"I will bring the Bench specialist to the Matredonat, Ferinc, she will an interview with Koscuisko conduct. You may during that time speak to the lady. The Second Judge still believes that she needs this Judiciary to win her bid, and has offered concessions that we want. We particularly need to secure them before Chilleau Judiciary comes to understand that it need not sue to the Combine for victory."

Was Stanoczk speaking of neutral issues to calm his nerves, to avoid an unpleasant necessity?

"If she has so much support, it bodes well for the transition, doesn't it?" Clearly the more people that supported Chilleau Judiciary, the fewer who would be rioting when the Selection was announced.

Stanoczk shook his head, however. "The transition may run well, Ferinc, you will be glad that you are sequestered and here before too much longer, though, I think. Will you speak to Koscuisko, and seek peace?"

Yes.

No.

He'd had fantasies. But after what had happened to him at the airfield, Ferinc had to admit to himself that he did not have the nerve. "If you think I ought, Stanoczk. What shall I say?"

Stanoczk shook his head. His expression had grown less serious, less stern, and he was leaning back in the chair with his knees splayed at a very informal angle, a very much more relaxed picture indeed. "It was a question, not a challenge, Ferinc. I see it all so clearly. 'Hello, you may not remember me, but you had cause to discipline me once, and since then I have been providing comfort to your wife and a role model for your son. I only thought that you should know because I have no hard feelings.' Yes. I can imagine."

When Stanoczk put it that way, it did sound funny. Not a threat at all. Encouraged, Ferinc put what he could only hope was an expression suitably mild and innocent on his face, and shifted on the floor so that his knees were underneath him, and he was that much closer to Stanoczk. He was taller than Stanoczk. He was almost eye to eye with him, and could set his elbow to the table to look up into Stanoczk's skeptical face confidingly.

"Shall I just go and get started on a suitable speech, then?"

It was a very cheeky thing to say to one's religious teacher, the official representative of the religious order that had taken him in those years gone by and made the Fleet forgive the charges brought against him for desertion. Ferinc was counting on that.

And Stanoczk laughed. "You'd be better advised to give some serious consideration where you are here and now, if you hope to avoid falling into error. It is my opinion that you have gone too long without adequate reconciliation, it will take days to sort you out, and that will have to wait. Still. We have some hours. And so you may be confident that I mean to examine you with the strictest diligence, within the limits of the time that we have here and now."

Oh, he could write his speech for Koscuisko tomorrow, then. Because when Stanoczk was minded to be thorough the process of reconciliation could go on and on. Rigorous though it was there was no substitute for the deep and profound peace, the inner security, the sense of calm and well-being that resulted from the reconciliation of the Malcontent.

There was water and a warmer, rhyti and food. The cell was small, but it was a secure safe place, and there was a thick pile of bearskins in the corner to guard against the chill as the hours wore on. He was alone with Stanoczk, whom the Malcontent in his mercy had granted to Ferinc to reconcile his pain with the mysteries of the Holy Mother's

Creation. There was nothing he could say to Stanoczk that would surprise, shock, or offend him; he was safe to open the dark agonies of his soul, and know that Stanoczk would handle him gently.

For these few hours he could be as happy as if he'd never even met Andrej Koscuisko.

Another day, General Rukota told himself, swallowing back his sigh of resignation. Another hostile and combative communiqué from Pesadie Training Command.

"Acting Captain ap Rhiannon." The voice of the recorded image of Admiral Brecinn on view in the Captain's office gave every ounce of the venom doubtless intended to the word *acting*, to emphasize ap Rhiannon's tenuous claim to any rank at all. "We all approve of thoroughness. In theory. But it has been eight days."

"I fully endorse Pesadie Training Command's desire for a careful and complete investigation." Ap Rhiannon's own voice on record was smooth and validating in turn, for all the world as if she had believed that to be what the Admiral was saying. Rather than exactly the opposite. Rukota looked to ap Rhiannon, who was sitting alone in the briefing pit. She was drawing circles in spilt shirmac tea on the table in front of her, not meeting his eyes.

Rukota could appreciate that. It was one thing to say the words once; quite another to maintain that brazen composure the second time through, listening to herself. Knowing how confrontational the words had been. "It is for this reason that we so much appreciate the continued support of Pesadie Training Command, Admiral Brecinn. The investigation is well under weigh. We hope for completion within seventy days."

The Admiral, to her credit, had not actually sputtered. "See if you can't find some way to hurry things along. I have no intention of allowing the monopolization of my valuable personnel resources. That will be all, Lieutenant."

Rukota couldn't really blame Brecinn for "Lieutenant." Ap Rhiannon had provoked her. And yet ap Rhiannon hadn't done it to be provoking; she appeared to have a genuine motive that Rukota had not yet been able to decide if he could credit.

The record stopped. Ap Rhiannon looked up from her artwork with an expression of anxious tension on her face. "I don't like her," ap Rhiannon said, as though there had been any doubt. "I don't suppose that you could shut her up for me."

Rukota shook his head, walking slowly to the briefing pit to sit down. "You know better than that, your Excellency." He didn't mind giving her the rank. She had to deal with Brecinn, after all. "And in every conflict, there is usually a point on either side. With respect. But your Engineer is a very difficult man. And it's catching."

Don't shoot me, I'm an artilleryman. I only fire the cannon. I don't even know what's on the other end of the round. It was an old joke. Rukota wondered if he dared make it.

Ap Rhiannon frowned. "Difficult, how do you mean 'difficult'? You know what he's been given to work with. If he hadn't had an attitude problem to rub off on Engineering, Engineering's attitude would have rubbed off on him. And I don't blame them either. You can see the environment Fleet expects this crew to deal with."

Rukota stretched his legs out in front of him and studied the toes of his boots. What was on ap Rhiannon's mind? She was crèche-bred. Troops were disposable, for crèche-bred. Duty to the rule of Law was everything. "That's no excuse for failure to cooperate, your Excellency. We all have our own challenges."

The look she gave him was equal parts confusion, anger, and disappointment. "Some of us more than most, General, and none of which include volunteering for martyrdom. Brecinn is not going to turn this into a training accident. The training accident was strictly coincidental."

That was stating things a little strongly. He knew what she meant, though. But how far was she willing to take it? This was a side of ap Rhiannon he hadn't seen before. She appeared to have personal feelings about the matter. He hadn't thought crèche-bred were issued any personal feelings.

"It's a reasonable suspicion, your Excellency, be fair. I'm not Fleet's most particular officer. You know that." He was in fact not very keen on rank and protocol unless he needed them to get the job done. Ap Rhiannon did not insult him by pretending to protest anything to the contrary, so he continued without any such hypocritical interruptions.

"But I've seen things on board of this ship that could make even me wonder. Another officer might easily decide to call the complaints seditious. And Brem was the third of the *Ragnarok*'s officers to go. It's only been a few months, hasn't it?"

She stood up suddenly, with a gesture whose angry violence startled him. "No, General. Any such expressions of discontent are more than understandable. You should have a look at the *Ragnarok*'s transfer history sometime; it's fascinating. Fleet has been packing us with problems for years. I don't like feeling like a target, General, but if this ship hasn't been set up as a fire-ship, I've never seen a fire-ship in my life."

Fire-ship. It took him a moment, then he understood. She meant that Fleet was using this ship to warehouse its undesirables until such time as Fleet could wipe them all out in one swift conflagration.

"I'll grant you that the mess has fallen to near-punitive levels." There was no point in mentioning that ap Rhiannon herself fell into that category, because ap Rhiannon was thickheaded and stubborn and difficult but she wasn't stupid. "But that doesn't mean Fleet's willing to throw lives away, your Excellency. Your concern gets the better of you."

As soon as Rukota said it he wished he hadn't, because that was clearly exactly what Brecinn had in mind, and what ap Rhiannon was resisting with every weapon at her disposal. Ap Rhiannon had few weapons compared to the commanding officer of Pesadie Training Command, so perhaps it was inevitable that her deployment lacked finesse.

How had the Bench failed Jennet ap Rhiannon?

She was crèche-bred. She had been raised to show no tolerance for disloyal behavior or qualified opinions on anybody's part. Anybody— peers, subordinates, superiors. But the crew of the *Ragnarok* sounded like a crew with serious problems of disaffection, and ap Rhiannon was defending them. Not calling in a Fleet Interrogations Group to conduct a purge.

She smiled at the wall where the image of the Admiral had been. "You're very right, General. Nobody's throwing any lives away. These are my lives. I'm responsible to the Bench for them. And I'm not letting a single soul on board of this ship pass into Fleet's hands without a fight."

There were in some ways some aspects of ap Rhiannon's own behavior that could possibly be potentially interpreted as giving the appearance of mutinous intent.

Rukota stood up slowly, but with determination. He had to get out of here. Something in the atmosphere was clearly affecting his brain. The atmosphere scrubbers were failing. Yes. That had to be the explanation.

"By your leave, your Excellency. I'll be getting back to trying to ignore my preliminary assessment team."

If one of Fleet's own prized paragons of devotion to the rule of Law could sound like a battery with its primer gone bad, there was no longer any sense nor reason in the world.

The plasma-sheath generators near the leading edge of the *Ragnarok*'s upper hull spooled their atoms-thin gauze in a ceaseless churning. Filament-tissue, invisible to the average hominid under Jurisdiction, fabric flowing like water up over the carapace hull and down along the maintenance atmosphere in constant motion, the sheath both protected *Ragnarok* and fed its great fusion converters, pulling the trapped dust and debris of both planetary and interstellar space into the ship's engines.

Passing through the energy inferno, the sheath was constantly cleansed of matter and cycled back to the outer hull once more. Self-healing, tolerant of whole shuttlecraft passing through, and yet capable of absorbing the constant bombardment of subatomic matter, the plasma sheath fed the *Ragnarok* on whatever space had to offer, guarding the hull jealously—guarding the lives within.

Feeding the ship, and cleaning it, the sheath carried the industrial waste of the furnace process itself the entire circuit of its rounds to pass the dross back through the fusion converters and abandon it to nuclear disassociation.

The entire process was below the level of the *Ragnarok*'s consciousness, like breathing. Engineering was aware of it, in the background, and kept a close watch on the rate of spool and the yield from the outside, but for the most part, plasma-sheath generation was entrusted to ship's computers.

Like the normal breathing of the average animal, occasionally something irritated one of the generators, and it coughed.

There was a little remote traveling in the plasma stream, as if dropped there through the cyclers at some point after that portion of the fabric of the sheath had left the furnace. Just a little smaller than one of the spooling-ports, perfectly round and smooth—catching on nothing—it fell from the ship embedded in the plasma, like a piece of grit surrounded by a protective layer of mucoid tissue.

Once it had left the ship, however, the little remote took surprising action, kicking itself away from the *Ragnarok*'s hull, tearing itself free with a sudden convulsive gesture.

Away from the ship, it dropped, inert and silent, traveling on the inertia of its escape until its sensors told it that it was clear of the ship's communications intercept net.

And then it began to transmit.

It was too small, too primitive, to do anything but send its tiny packet of information. It was preset for one exact target receiver, burning its limited power supply with reckless profligacy in its urgent need to make its message heard.

It had things to say, to the right people. It knew who had been on board of the ship nearest to the observation station when the station had exploded. It knew which team it had been, and which Wolnadi. The names were required; the Warrant could not be written without the names, and without a Warrant, there could be no serious challenge to the *Ragnarok*'s custody of the individuals in question.

It sent the names on transmit, and fell silent.

Ap Rhiannon had asked Dierryk Rukota to join her in the Captain's office. He wasn't much occupied this forenoon, tired of watching the assessment team go through one Wolnadi after another and sensibly resigned to the futility of trying to talk to the Ship's Engineer; so he'd come directly.

He beat her to it, finding himself when he got there with nobody but the First Officer for company. The First Officer, however, was apparently too absorbed in some documentation to more than acknowledge his presence with a polite, if uninterested, nod.

Rukota looked around. This had been Captain Brem's office. It looked unoccupied—as though Brem had only begun to move in before his unexpected death. None of the decor looked particularly like ap Rhiannon to Rukota; had she moved in at all? Or was she still operating out of a Lieutenant's office, being punctilious about her rating? It'd be like her.

"Well, if the Captain isn't going to use this space, I wish she'd loan it to me," Rukota said to the room. The Captain's office was one of the larger administrative spaces on board of the *Ragnarok*, and it was quite emphatically roomier than the squad bay that Mendez had allotted to the Pesadie team. "I could fit my whole crew in here. With some space left over for a bean tea service," he added, a little unfairly, eyeing the quite obviously unused service set to one side of the room. If there was any hope at all for good bean tea it was nowhere on board but here, since Wheatfields had declined to share his.

Mendez set his flat-form docket aside as the admit warning sounded. "Haven't had it fumigated yet, General. And my Captain needs the space to talk to your Admiral."

Rukota was minded to object to Mendez's assumption that Brecinn was "his" Admiral, but found the First Officer's unselfconscious reference to ap Rhiannon as his Captain too interesting to interfere with. And ap Rhiannon was here, now, after all. No bickering amongst the troops in the presence of Command Branch, Rukota reminded himself.

"General Rukota."

She came into the room with a precision of Security whose posting of themselves at the door was beautiful to watch. Rukota had noticed that, about the *Ragnarok*; all of the normal morale indicators were absolutely topnotch as far as crew demeanor went. He'd been trying to convince himself that they were all simply on their best behavior with outsiders present; but the ability of a pair of troops to post in perfect synchronicity was not something that could be turned on and off for company. It was either a consistent habit of living, or impossible.

Bowing his salute in response, Rukota felt it better not to speak until spoken to. She clearly didn't have a great deal to say to him. Seating herself at the Captain's desk, she gestured for him to come and stand behind her. Mendez took a position beside him, at her right shoulder, and petrified without a moment's notice into an archetypal image of a First Officer present for a Captain's transmission.

Rukota didn't think he could match the pose. Moreover, he could not help but feel that he would only look pathetic if he tried. At least he understood why he was here, now; ap Rhiannon had some sort of an official communication to make.

"This is Acting Captain Jennet ap Rhiannon, Jurisdiction Fleet

Ship *Ragnarok*, for Admiral Sandri Brecinn. Pesadie Training Command."

The usual preliminaries, and then Admiral Brecinn appeared in holographic projection at one-and-four-eighths' life-size in the room in front of them. It was a good deal closer than Rukota had ever gotten to her, and the experience was not an entirely pleasant one. She looked rather older, and very tired.

She also did not look to be in a very good temper. "You have results to report, ap Rhiannon?" Granted, Brecinn had no motivation for observing the niceties of Fleet protocol; she seemed to be alone in her office, and ap Rhiannon was only acting in the capacity of Captain. Rukota thought her choice of words unnecessarily short, all the same.

"Preliminary results, Admiral. I am calling to report that the Wolnadi fighter that was nearest to the scene of the accident when it occurred has been identified by the preliminary assessment team. My Engineer has transmitted the information to me. I will be asking General Rukota to prepare an in-depth analysis."

Rukota heard her, but he didn't believe it. He kept his face clear and his expression serene by main force of will. It was times like these that being ugly was useful; people generally spent as little time as possible, looking at him, and were less likely to notice a continuity glitch accordingly.

If the Wolnadi had been identified, it was news to him.

"And not before time, Lieutenant." Brecinn sounded gratified, almost gloating. But not surprised. Suddenly Rukota had a very unhappy feeling that something even uglier than anticipated had occurred. Had one of the team come by information by stealth, and transmitted it?

It was hard to imagine. There was a genuine coherence to the crew of the *Ragnarok* that Rukota found intriguing, and that would be hard to reconcile with treachery on the part of any of the souls assigned.

Admiral Brecinn addressed him directly, calling his attention back to his immediate environment. "I was beginning to wonder what you were taking so long at, General. When may I expect my report?"

He could answer this one honestly, which always helped. "I'm unsure as yet, Admiral. The information is just in. I haven't had a chance to consult with the team."

And yes, he would play along with whatever it was that ap

Rhiannon had in mind. It was poor policy to contradict Command Branch in front of other officers. He could afford to wait until he knew what she was up to before he decided what his considered response would be. He didn't owe Brecinn anything in particular, one way or the other.

"Well. Fair enough, I suppose. Don't keep me waiting. Anything else to report, Lieutenant?"

Brecinn's insistence on ap Rhiannon's junior status was beginning to grate on Rukota's nerves. The crew of the *Ragnarok* didn't seem to mind "Captain" ap Rhiannon; they corrected themselves easily enough when they said Lieutenant, or at least they had in Rukota's limited experience. If the crew of the *Ragnarok* didn't mind, why should Admiral Brecinn?

Whether or not ap Rhiannon experienced a like sense of aggravation, there was more than a touch of asperity in her voice as she replied. "Yes, Admiral, in fact. I have shortages to report, and it's impacting health and welfare. We were to have been at the resupply station days ago, Admiral. I have got to go and get some of these requisitions filled."

Brecinn had not been expecting anything of the sort out of ap Rhiannon, either in subject or in delivery. It was all too clear from the momentary wobbling of her stream-snapper's beak of a mouth. "You've already been told three times that there simply are no replacement converters available for that secondary fusion. I've told you, there's a shortage on, or don't you believe your own supply reports?"

What shortage? Rukota wondered, hoping his face was appropriately blank. Shortage of converters for fusion furnaces? That was ridiculous. Why would Fleet tolerate a shortage in such a critical area? Motivation and weapons systems had the very highest priorities. He must not have caught something, somewhere.

"Understood, Admiral Brecinn. But I have other requisitions against existing inventory for nutritures. Meds. On-board recycles. Some of these have been outstanding from the beginning of the recent exercise."

Oh, really? That could explain why the bean tea was as bad as it was. If he'd known ahead of time, he could have packed an extra store for his personal use; although that might not have been interpreted as a friendly sharing gesture.

"General Rukota? What do you have to say about all this?"

Brecinn's abrupt, direct address startled him beyond his ability to cover it up. Was she calling ap Rhiannon a liar? Or simply a poor judge of logistical requirements? Did it matter? Brecinn clearly did not care how she spoke to ap Rhiannon, Command Branch or no Command Branch. It made a man feel very uncomfortable: apart from the gratuitous rudeness of the gesture, what made Brecinn think that she could get away with it?

"The scope of the assessment team's brief does not extend to the *Ragnarok*'s requisitions-in-holding." He could hear his own stiff outrage in his voice. And he was trying to be polite; because he believed that discipline and courtesy were supposed to move up, as well as down, the command chain. "As far as anecdotal evidence is to be trusted I can personally vouch for the generally depressing lack of required sensory characteristics in Ship's Mess."

But Brecinn was already pulling her head back beneath the bony shell of her figurative carapace. "Well, as long as it doesn't interfere with the investigation, I suppose you may as well go resupply," Brecinn said, with a dismissive frown. "Rukota, I'll be waiting for your report."

Ap Rhiannon had given her what she wanted, the promise of a report. Brecinn clearly felt she could afford to play from her rank. "But I don't mind telling you, Lieutenant, that to my mind identifying the saboteurs responsible for the murder of Captain Brem should be somewhat more important than stocking up on sweetener for your fast-meal mush."

"Thank you, Admiral Brecinn." Ap Rhiannon for her part sounded absolutely unmoved, as if she had not even noticed Brecinn's rudeness. "For my part, I was raised to believe that the health and welfare of the souls entrusted to my Command under the rule of Law was much more important than playing pointless political games with anyone. I state once again for the Record that the evidence will show that the *Ragnarok* had no part in the death of Cowil Brem. Departing for resupply, by your leave, Admiral."

Admiral Brecinn waved ap Rhiannon off with a cavalier gesture of her hand. "Do what you must, Lieutenant. I need by-name identification of the crew of that Wolnadi, General, so that the documentation can be prepared for a formal Inquiry. The sooner we can complete the necessary reports, the better off we will all be in the long run. I trust you take my meaning. All of you. Pesadie Training Command, away, here."

It was a mistake on the Admiral's part, an error. Rukota knew it in his bones, even though he did not yet know exactly why it was an error.

Cutting the signal with a decisive gesture ap Rhiannon stood up; and remained for a brief moment with her back to them, leaning on the table's surface as though she was tired. Rukota supposed that it was abstractly possible that she was, but there would be no getting such an admission out of her.

Then she straightened up, and looked back, over her shoulder at them. "Let's get out of here," she suggested. "Before we run into any interference. You know what to do, First Officer. General Rukota, thank you for coming. I felt you would wish to be present."

"Tell me about this information your Excellency has just provided," Rukota suggested, unwilling to go away quietly. "Does the preliminary assessment team know about this?"

Ap Rhiannon smiled. Mendez didn't. They were in this together, Rukota realized; and he was complicit as well, at least by implication. "It's possible," ap Rhiannon said. "We think we've had a leak. But as long as she thinks she's got the names coming, we can win a little time to maneuver."

Well, to the resupply depot at Laynock, for instance. Except that the Laynock depot wasn't the only depot that was accessible from the Pesadie exit vector. And he wasn't going to think about it. It was none of his business. "If she's got the names already, it's all academic, your Excellency."

Ap Rhiannon shook her head. "It's not official. She can't admit to having the names until your report transmits them. And once she has the names, she'll want the troops. I don't know how we're going to protect them, exactly. But we've got to think of something."

A vision from the recent past rose up on the mind's eye of General Dierryk Rukota. A shuttle. A courier. Clearing for Azanry, if he remembered correctly. Hadn't the technician said it was the *Ragnarok*'s Chief Medical Officer, going home? One of the Ship's Primes. Traveling with Security.

Ap Rhiannon was playing more dangerous a game than Rukota

would have imagined, if she had done what he suspected. Her career was at risk, at the very least; and for what? Reluctance to surrender four souls to Inquiry, to torture?

Or educated expectation of how the scope of Inquiry would widen with its own inexorable logic from four to sixteen to two hundred and fifty-six?

"What's my place in this mess, then, your Excellency?"

Ap Rhiannon almost smiled. Almost. "Let that assessment team do what they came for, General. Ask them when they'll have information for you to prepare your report. It's their job, after all. With respect. General." *Stay out of it. You aren't part of it anyway. Keep clear.*

Rukota was disgusted enough to do just that. He bowed in salute. "Very good, your Excellency. Returning to assigned offices as instructed."

She hadn't a prayer of making it work, whatever it was. But he understood her motives and her rationale. And he liked them better than he liked Pesadie, with its corrupt Admiral and its opportunistic staff of reasonable people.

If Brecinn was going to enforce her will against the Jurisdiction Fleet Ship *Ragnarok*, it would be without aid and comfort from General Dierryk Rukota.

Well satisfied, Admiral Brecinn toggled into her on-station braid for Dame Noycannir to share the news. Not just the news she had just gotten from that tiresome little petty officer on the *Ragnarok*, but the other news as well, the news that had made ap Rhiannon's call welcome but not exactly a surprise.

Names. Names and identifications, received just this morning from remote. "Mergau. Yes. If you would come and pay me a visit, please. A note from a mutual friend with news that may be of interest."

They'd had two weeks to prepare. Noycannir had everything she needed to conduct a valid, legal Inquiry; with the names, she would be able to start to set up her strategy. Her interrogatories. Her in-depth personal file analysis, looking for the evidence of disaffection and corruption that would explain what they had done—and support the confessions that Noycannir had promised.

Sacrificing four lives to the rule of Law was not something to be done lightly. And yet Chilleau Judiciary would need Pesadie's support, in the coming weeks. The Second Judge would surely make her declaration soon. Pesadie had to be ready to defend the Second Judge's claim against any challenges, had to be in position to move against civil unrest; for the greater good.

She couldn't do that if Pesadie was compromised by an unfortunate, ill-timed accident. She could not afford the compromise. She had to be ready to deploy all of her resources, to stabilize the sector should the Selection be contested, to achieve the privileged position in the new administration that the reasonable people with whom she did business expected her to gain and maintain for the mutual benefit of all parties.

It was only four lives.

Noycannir would find a way to hold it to four. Surely. Noycannir was a reasonable woman herself. And four lives were as nothing, compared to the greater good, compared to the lives Pesadie would save by being there and being ready to act to restore order.

Forty lives were not too much to pay for that. So four were not worth mourning. It was to be their glory to give up their lives to ensure a safe and stable transition when the Selection was announced. Theirs would be a sacrifice no less noble for being hidden for all time. Yes.

It was only six days to Laynock and back. It would be at least three before ap Rhiannon would force herself to release the official report with the names. By the time the Warrant had been endorsed at Chilleau Judiciary and returned, the *Ragnarok* would be back at Pesadie Training Command.

Noycannir had enough to worry her. There was no sense in cluttering her mind with unnecessary details. Brecinn had the names; that would be more than enough information for Noycannir to start to work.

CHAPTER SEVEN

Thresholds

Mergau Noycannir looked over the list of names that Admiral Brecinn had handwritten out for her, realizing with joy in her heart that this was even more perfect than she could have hoped.

"These are to be the prisoners, then?" she asked, hoping the note of admiration in her voice was suitably transparent. Brecinn was vain; it was not difficult to handle her. "Your team is to be congratulated. When must I be ready to begin processing?"

She'd presented Brecinn with a conflict of sorts, between Brecinn's desire to bask in her acclaim and the fact that she didn't have a good answer for the question. "I don't mind telling you that the *Ragnarok* is not being reasonable at all, Dame Noycannir. Why am I not surprised? I'll be able to get a Warrant as soon as the official report is released, and we'll have the prisoners very shortly after that. Four days?"

Impossibly optimistic, Mergau was sure. But that suited her purpose just as well. She didn't need the prisoners. She just needed to know who they were going to be to mount a coup that was so daring it would win her power and influence beyond her fondest hopes.

"Very good, Admiral. I've got some preliminary data pulled on the *Ragnarok*'s Security. I can start to bring it all together. Shall I get started?" Mergau stood up as she spoke, to indicate her eagerness to be on about her part of this important task. To tell Brecinn that she was leaving, now, but doing it politely.

"You have everything you need, Dame?" Brecinn asked. "Good.

Yes, thank you, we can't be on top of this unfortunate situation too quickly. It's gone on for far too long already. Ap Rhiannon will be sorry. I promise you that."

Mergau didn't care about ap Rhiannon. She had her own agenda to put forward.

The fact that the named Security were all people assigned to Andrej Koscuisko only made her task more poignantly appropriate.

"No matter how clever these little officers think they may be, sooner or later they all pay, eh, Admiral?" Mergau agreed, and bowed. Leaving the room on a graceful note of conspiracy. Not bothering to point out that Admiral Brecinn herself might well be one of those "little officers" who would eventually pay.

Not before Koscuisko paid. And Koscuisko had so much to pay for. Everything that had gone wrong with her life went back to him; but she would have revenge—all the more sweet because his own people, his own precious and famously cherished Security, would be the instrument of her ultimate victory.

Hurrying through the halls, Mergau made her way to the out-of-the-way stores-room that had been configured for an interrogation arena, a theater of inquiry.

Had she everything she needed, Brecinn had asked. The instruments of torture were here, the drugs from the Controlled List, restraints and implements, shackles and chains; all secondary, though Brecinn did not know it.

What was truly crucial to her purpose was the Record: and the equipment Mergau needed to effect her plan. She'd told the Admiral that she would gain confessions to whatever Brecinn decided the story should be; she hadn't lied. She'd only stretched the truth a little.

She had realized what she could really do with this opportunity only gradually. Pesadie Training Command was a testing facility; its judicial records were naturally weighted in just the direction she needed to go—insubordination, sabotage of training exercise, failure to comply with instructions received from exercise commanders, mutinous intent.

She could hardly have hoped for so generous a field from which to choose had she been free to survey all of Chilleau Judiciary's records. Koscuisko's people. She would send a message to her spies on Azanry. She would know exactly where to find him.

Koscuisko was no match for her in cunning or in strategy; it was only the unfair advantage of his medical training—the product of the privileges of wealth and rank—that had made her look bad in front of her Patron, that had persuaded the First Secretary to devalue her worth and her abilities.

Mergau checked her secures and engaged the privacy barrier. "Smish Smath," Mergau said to her voice-trans. Secure. No one could forge her voice. She had to be very careful. Nobody had done what she planned to do in all the history of Jurisdiction. "Murat Spodinne. Taller Archops, Lek Kerenko."

More luck, on top of luck. Kerenko would be easy. He was one of Koscuisko's Security slaves, a bond-involuntary troop. There was no need to create a confession for Lek Kerenko; all she needed there was a simple "expiration of a Bond during the process of Inquiry, without prejudice."

The others would have misled him all along, of course; by definition, a bond-involuntary could not plot mutiny. The governor would not allow it. Once she began to probe and test for what knowledge he might have, his governor—the story would go—would so work on him, in combination with her keen interrogation into matters that he should have seen and noted and reported to his First Officer, that he would die of self-inflicted punishment.

She would be sure to specify that he had not been at fault in any way. That way, his family would not have to repay the Bench for the costs of his training and his keep, Andrej would be grateful to her for that. She would see to it.

Three confessions. Only three. Smath would be the most challenging. There were relatively fewer women in Security; they tended to be absorbed in Engineering instead because of their superior skills in operating under pressure. They were disproportionately underrepresented in Brecinn's records accordingly. Women were more logical, better at covering their tracks, harder to catch up doing something stupid.

She'd make do. She had the Record here.

"Index on class of hominid. Sex. Physical characteristics." She'd preselected the data files on the cases that would match any of the *Ragnarok*'s Security; this would be a much swifter search. "Execute."

Andrej Koscuisko had been there at Fleet Orientation Station

Medical when Verlaine had sent her to take the Writ to Inquire, and come home as Inquisitor to Chilleau Judiciary. She had done the best she could. It had been hard. And Koscuisko had done better.

In an evil hour she had commended Koscuisko to her Patron while she was still at Fleet Orientation Station Medical, to spite the station's administrator and her Tutor, to put them all on notice that she was a force to be reckoned with and had the immediate ear of the First Secretary. That they had good cause to be careful how they misused her, because she had more power than they seemed to realize. It had been a mistake.

Verlaine had compared her to Koscuisko and found her wanting. No matter how hard she tried when she returned to Chilleau Judiciary, Verlaine had Koscuisko always in the back of his mind, pointing out her every small miscalculation, jeering at her every failure. Every defeat.

Koscuisko was a rich man from a powerful family; he had education and a certain degree of personal charm. People were so easily impressed by superficialities. They ascribed talent to Koscuisko that no one could hope to match, and built him up into a sort of legend against whom a mere mortal was powerless to compete. But just because she did not have Koscuisko's medical education did not mean that she lacked for knowledge of the Record . . . and how it could be used.

She had technical knowledge of Bench Record devices that few other people could hope to touch. Her access codes had never been revoked—Verlaine had thought he could yet find a use for her access, she supposed, as legal cover for some desperate act.

Now she would make use of her Writ against them all. She would use her knowledge of the Record to create a false history of interrogation and confession for three of the four Security troops who were on that Wolnadi fighter.

It would be a daring piece of work. The technical integrity of the Record was the cornerstone of the rule of Law and the Judicial order. No one had ever forged a Record. No one would ever dare reveal that she had done it. If the Record lost credibility, the Bench lost credibility. For the good of the Judicial order, Chilleau Judiciary would be forced to formally accept her forgeries as the truth.

She would take the Record to Azanry to confront Andrej

Koscuisko. He was the Ship's Inquisitor on board the Jurisdiction Fleet Ship *Ragnarok*. It would be his duty to accompany her to Chilleau Judiciary to conduct the investigation. He would have no choice. And once she but had him in her hands, he would have no choice about anything, anything at all, ever again.

She would bring Koscuisko to Verlaine, a very special gift, captive, revealed as a co-conspirator in the death of Cowil Brem—and who was to say that he had not been involved in that of the *Ragnarok*'s other recently dead officers as well? Was there to be no limits to the depth of Koscuisko's guilt? Verlaine would be gratified.

If he were not grateful, he would have to seem to be. He would be unable to reject her gift, not unless he was willing to risk not only his career, but that of his Judge as well. Verlaine would be forced to keep Koscuisko secured, concealed, hidden away, her prisoner; or be destroyed. And she would be secure.

She would have knowledge that could destroy the new First Judge and destabilize all of Jurisdiction space: knowledge that the Record could be forged, knowledge that Chilleau Judiciary could be blackmailed into compliant silence. She would be First Judge, because Verlaine would not dare deny her anything.

Pesadie Training Command would get its just reward.

And Mergau Noycannir would be revenged at last on Andrej Koscuisko for all of the humiliations she had suffered in the past because of his wealth, his education, his position, the unfair advantage he enjoyed as an Inquisitor, putting her to shame in the eyes of her Patron.

Andrej Koscuisko walked hand in hand with his son in the garden, feeling the warmth of the afternoon sun like a blessing on his face. His home sun. His body knew this air, this gravity, this light. It was almost physically painful to be here in his own place, the world that had bred him, the sun that ruled the chemistry of his blood. Home ground.

Anton looked up at him from time to time, strolling with him, but said little. Andrej didn't mind. What did he have to say to this young boy?

"Do you like the summer, Anton?" Andrej asked.

He knew there were other things that fathers were supposed to say. Studies. Saints. Obedience. Hunting. Things a young lord had to learn and know. Andrej didn't care. And he didn't have time. He would be leaving soon. If he was lucky, he'd be coming back; but if he wasn't, he would at least know something of the person his child was. Someone else would teach Anton who he was supposed to be.

"Summer is empty, sir," Anton replied, after a moment's apparent thought. "I like harvest. Harvest-time is full. I see people I only sometimes see in summer. I like harvest."

What was he to make of such a claim? Andrej wondered.

It was true, wasn't it?

In the summer the house was empty. Everyone was dispersed out into the fields, all across the estate. There was so much to do, and so much day in which to do it. Wasn't part of what made harvest glad the knowledge that the heavy work was done until the spring?

"Harvest is good," Andrej agreed. "I also like snow. Not wind. But snow. I never liked the wind, Anton."

Now Anton smiled up at him with an open, candid expression that wracked Andrej's heart, for reasons that he wasn't sure he understood. "Ferinc says it's words in the wind, sir."

Yes, that was what Andrej had been taught. Words in the wind, messages gone astray, and if you could catch the whole of the message the soul who'd breathed it would be free at last. "Who's Ferinc, son Anton?"

"Cousin Ferinc, sir; I love him very much. If he hadn't gone to Dubrovnije I would show you to him." Malcontent, then. Anton would show his father to his friend?

Andrej frowned up at the clear blue sky, surprised to feel the pain in his own heart. He shouldn't feel pain; he should be grateful. Anton had a special friend that he loved. It wasn't as though that would have been different had Andrej lived at home all of this time; Dolgorukij fathers and their sons were never friends. There was too much to stand between them. Anton called him "sir" with grave and unfailing respect. What might it be like to be called "Papa"?

The sun caught on the glass panes of one of the garden gates in the distance. Someone had come in from the other side of the garden, the side that faced the motor stables. Andrej sighed. "Yes, I would like to meet him, Anton. Since you love him, I must love him also. Now you must go with Lek. He'll take you back to the house. I have company come."

Anton stood waiting on the garden path, and after a moment, Andrej realized that Anton was waiting to be kissed.

Crouching down on his heels, Andrej kissed Anton on the cheek, and Anton put his arms around Andrej's neck to hug him. It was peculiar behavior for a Dolgorukij son, to hug his father. Whoever Cousin Ferinc was, he had taught Anton to be a loving child.

Suddenly Andrej felt overwhelmed with gratitude that Anton felt free to offer him affection. Of all things. Had he ever, ever hugged his father? Or had they been too formal with each other from the start?

Anton went away hand in hand with Lek, whom Andrej particularly wanted to show to his household as someone to be trusted with the most precious thing he had. His child. And corning down the garden path was his cousin, Stanoczk, and the Bench intelligence specialist, Jils Ivers.

"The peace of the Malcontent is with you," Cousin Stanoczk said, formally. "You know the Bench intelligence specialist, your Excellency?"

Of course he did. He had spent some very unpleasant moments with Ivers in his office on the *Ragnarok*; but it was not a question of personal fault. He had seen her within the past year. He hadn't seen his cousin Stanoczk for far longer than that. "Bench specialist," Andrej nodded. "But, Stoshik, how long?"

Now Stanoczk grinned at him and relaxed. "Some time, Derush. Do you embrace the Malcontent, or have you too much dignity?"

There were two kinds of joke there, whether or not Stanoczk meant both rather than just the one. The first was that Andrej would embrace a Malcontent who was his blood relation, but he had not yet "embraced the Malcontent," which was quite a different proposition.

The second was that he himself, Andrej Koscuisko, might pretend to disdain the Malcontent, whose moral turpitude was strictly relative to Combine mores—when his own sin was atrocity under the laws of almost any well-developed moral community.

Andrej held out his arms for his cousin, and embraced Stanoczk with a full heart. He and Stoshik had been playmates when they had been children, never minding the gulf of rank that stood between them. Before Stoshik had elected the Malcontent. It was a very comforting embrace; but that was Stanoczk's business, after all—comfort, and reconciliation.

Finally Stanoczk pulled away, and laughed, holding his hand to his eyes for a moment. Stanoczk had brown eyes, brown hair, a deep voice; but otherwise he and Andrej alike were the very types of the blood of the family of their mutual maternal grandmother. The Kospodar line. Chuvishka Kospodar, in fact, from whom the Sarvaw nations had yet to recover.

"It's good to see you, Derush." Stanoczk used the childish diminutive rather than the more formal adult pet name. It had been a long time. "I need to speak to you on the Malcontent's business. Later. Is the Bench specialist to stay? Because I could to Beraltz go and speak."

House-master Beraltz, Stoshik meant. Andrej turned to Ivers, who had watched him greet Stanoczk with reserved good will. "If you have no other business, Specialist, you are welcome to a place at my hearth."

Perhaps "welcome" wasn't quite the word for it, and it was only his hearth in principle. It was much more Marana's hearth, Beraltz's hearth, the hearth of the people who had lived here and seen to the estate these nine years past; but still, in point of protocol, it was "his" hearth.

"Cousin Stanoczk says we're expected at Chelatring Side in eight days' time," Ivers said. "An expedition in force, I've been told. Thank you, your Excellency, you're very kind."

That was right. He had to go into the mountains. The Autocrat's Proxy would come to take the pulse of the Koscuisko familial corporation, and though Zsuzsa would doubtless know their father's prejudice already, it was all part of the play of the Selection for the grand rounds to be made.

The Autocrat called her people to herself when she wanted to issue a decision, to let them know her will. The Autocrat came to her people one by one when she sought their advice and their opinion: and so it had been since the days of the Malcontent's life beneath the canopy of Heaven.

"Go and tell my Chief of Security," Andrej suggested to his cousin. Stoshik took himself away on Andrej's not very subtle suggestion, and Andrej turned to Ivers. "Stildyne says he has worked with you before, Specialist. But since you go to Chelatring Side to hear my father's will, what use do you have for one mere Andrej? Walk, and talk to me."

It was a beautiful day. It would be midsummer soon. The breeze from the river smelled of growing things, the bosom of the Holy Mother, the skin of the great green-gold fish of the Matredonat. Someone would bring refreshment. A man could not walk five paces in his own garden without someone turning up with a laden table.

"First I have to tell you that the First Secretary at Chilleau Judiciary sent me in full knowledge of the fact that you might feel that he's attempting to bribe you."

She didn't look at him, but at the great hedge at the far end of the garden, well beyond the maze. She took a very formal tone with him, one that made the word *bribe* all the more unusual in context. "Chilleau Judiciary can't do anything just now without a political interpretation being cast on it, after all, your Excellency. So it's important that you understand that what I've been sent to tell you is independent of your family's advice to the Autocrat. And of the final decision at Selection."

The gravel on the path was crushed pink rock quarried in the hills around the Serah. It had been so long since he had felt it crunch beneath his feet. "Yes?" He didn't know what she was talking about.

She seemed to realize this with a sigh. "When I saw you last, your Excellency, it was to bring you an offer from First Secretary Sindha Verlaine. You took an unexpected action to assert your independence, your Excellency. The First Secretary regrets his ill-considered action. I have with me fully executed Bench documents for relief of Writ, sir."

Relief of Writ?

Andrej stopped in the middle of the garden path with the late morning sun warm on his shoulders, squinting toward the river. "I don't understand what you're trying to tell me, Specialist." He was afraid to believe what he thought she was saying.

"Your re-engagement with Fleet was essentially coerced. It can be put aside. I have the legal instrument. Stay home, your Excellency. The Bench regrets its lapse in judgment. Sir."

The words made no sense. She spoke Standard, not Aznir, but he had been tutored in Standard from a young age, he knew the language. It wasn't that.

Andrej shook his head with violence. It was as though he had gotten water in his ear sinking too deeply into the bath, and couldn't find his balance. "Your humor is ill chosen, Specialist Ivers." He wanted to believe that it was possible, and it couldn't be, because he wanted it far too much. "Why have you come?"

"I've brought the documentation with me, your Excellency," she insisted firmly, but as if she was fully sensitive to the confusion it created in his mind. "Since you have been so generous as to offer me your hospitality, sir, perhaps I could meet with you later today or tomorrow, and display my proofs. I know it must be difficult to credit. But I'm telling you the truth. The First Secretary is not playing games."

She almost said "*Any more games.*" He knew she had. Could it be true?

"Why?" Andrej asked, wonderingly. "Why, after all these years, would Verlaine have come to such a conclusion? Does my old schoolmate Noycannir no longer have his ear?"

Ivers looked confused. But Ivers knew Noycannir; Ivers had brought her to Port Rudistal, years and years and years ago. Noycannir had thought that she was to assume control, but the Domitt Prison had already been taken off-line, and under Andrej's personal command.

"There are political implications." Ivers's tone was grave and reserved. Of course there were. They could not escape them, not under the current unsettled circumstances. "But I've spoken to the First Secretary, your Excellency. I believe his motivation to be genuine. If opportune."

The house-master's catering party had come into the garden from the gate nearest the kitchens, and he could not discuss this matter in front of the house staff. They were discreet; they would keep it in the family—but the family in which they would keep this news comprised every soul at the Matredonat.

"Freedom?" he asked, watching the house-master's party nearing with tables, hampers, linen.

"It is the judgment of the Court that your extension was only solicited as a result of improper pressure. 'Unreasonable duress,' I think it says. There is more."

Could it be true? Did she in reality offer him the escape he had believed denied him? Was he to stay here on Azanry, in his home, with his child, and never be the instrument of atrocity again?

"Too much, Specialist Ivers," Andrej said finally, putting one hand to her shoulder to communicate the depths of his emotional confusion. "I cannot grapple with this suggestion here and now. We will take rhyti. There is to be no help for it. Tomorrow in the morning, after breakfast, come to me in the library, and show me the documents you have."

She wasn't playing games with him. Bench intelligence specialists didn't play games. She knew what she was saying, as she had not more than one year ago when Captain Lowden had sent her to speak to him on board of the *Ragnarok*.

A full banqueting-hall of local gentry was coming to the Matredonat for dinner; there was to be dancing in the gardens after dark. Her offer needed more concentration than he would have to spare until tomorrow. He needed time to think about what she had said, and make up his mind about whether he had interpreted her correctly or not.

"At your Excellency's disposal, sir, entirely." She knew that what she brought was world-shaking for him. If she believed that he was to be free, how could he doubt?

He would be free. He could stay home. He would learn to be a husband to Marana, if she would permit it. He could become a father to his son, in place of some unknown Malcontent. And he could engage with the Malcontent to see if there was anything a man could do to atone for such sins as he had committed. He could be reconciled to his family, his father and his mother.

All he would have to do then was discover who it was that had wanted him dead; and if Chilleau Judiciary offered him freedom, did that mean that the threat had not come from Chilleau Judiciary, or was being withdrawn?

He would never see his Bonds again, not until the Day dawned for them and they came to him. If the Day ever dawned. If they ever came to him after that. Yet when last year he had believed that he was going home at the expiration of his tour of duty, he'd known that he could not take his Bonds with him.

The fate that had faced them then had been far worse than it was now. Captain Lowden had been in command of the *Ragnarok*. Andrej had shuddered to think of people for whom he was responsible, of whom he was fond, suffering Lowden's whims and jests without him to protect them. But now Lowden was dead.

Andrej didn't know much about Jennet ap Rhiannon, but she was nothing like Griers Verigson Lowden. The bond-involuntaries assigned to the *Ragnarok* were as close to safe as they could be. First Officer would look out for them. Stildyne would be there.

And they would want him to be free, even at cost to themselves— as he would wish for them. He couldn't let that become an issue in his mind: or not an insurmountable barrier. Once he had seen Ivers's documentation with his own eyes, he would know whether he was to send Stildyne back to the *Ragnarok* an orphan.

Dierryk Rukota was lying on his back on the bench in the squad-bay that First Officer had assigned to the preliminary assessment team, chewing on his thoughts and trying to digest his mid-meal, when the admit at the door sounded with unexpected urgency, and the *Ragnarok*'s Intelligence Officer came storming through in a great rustling of wings, with four or five Ship's Security behind her.

"I have no intention of tolerating, no, it is not prudent!" she shrieked at him, her momentum carrying her clear to the far wall of the squad-bay where she scrambled up onto the surface of the desk-ledge and glared at him horribly. "At the very least a formal protest, and you will be very lucky if the Engineer does not have you simply locked off. I would not regret seeing it."

He couldn't speak for the shock of the surprise, the clear sense of assault and the fear he had of predators with such sharp glittering teeth. Half-stupefied, he could only freeze—still lying on his back— and wonder, for the crucial moment that it took her to find a foothold at the top of the empty equipment locker. Clambering up, she inverted herself, wrapping her wings around her in a thunderous gesture of high dudgeon and rocking sullenly back and forth in expectant silence.

For a moment he considered whether the particularly nasty bowl of soup he'd gotten for his mid-meal had poisoned his brain somehow. It could be a bad dream, couldn't it? Delusions. Why would the Ship's Intelligence Officer, one of the Ship's Primes, have come down to the dismal space that Mendez had assigned to them, in person? And—in the unlikely event that she had decided to indulge a taste for fresh raw Rukota—what conceivable reason could she have for bringing witnesses?

He sat up carefully, taking stock of the situation. He was trapped in here, alone, with her. Security was at the door, but by the looks of them they were not inclined to intervene should Two take it into her head to tear his throat open for a snack.

"Your Excellency. A very great pleasure, ma'am. To what do I owe the honor?"

Her great black leathery wings filled the room like an explosion as she gestured. "I am not mollified; you are not in order. I am keeping all of them. Confined to courier. You will have to sleep in some room else."

All right, it was Pesadie's team. They'd done something; or something that they'd done had been traced back—the information ap Rhiannon had announced to Admiral Brecinn, perhaps? "If her Excellency would be graciously pleased to explain, ma'am."

Two was still muttering, and how she managed that with a translator Rukota could not fathom for the life of him. Not that he wanted to dwell on that particular phrase—*the life of him*—with an obviously angry Desmodontae in the same small room as he was.

"As if you think that I am stupid. Lax. Remiss in procedure," she accused, shifting her wings with an angry sort of irritated restlessness. "As if you think we are to be simply walked in on and queried by any uncleared parties. As if you have no knowledge of plain Standard or good discipline. It is intolerable, I remind you!" she shouted yet again, her wings an agitated scrim against the back wall.

"Yes; ma'am, but if you'd just give me the worst of it. I am responsible for the conduct of the team, after all." Technically, at least. In fact, they'd made it all too clear that he was only there for show: but at least the Captain and crew of the *Ragnarok* seemed to understand that as well.

Two dropped from her perch; Rukota shut up. Scuttling forward on her strong little feet, using the primary joint of her wingtips to hurry her along, she paused before Rukota on her way out of the room, lifting her sharp black face toward Rukota's with an expression of immense dignity, only somewhat weakened by the fact that she surely could not see him.

"Members of your party have been found using guest-code to access ship's computers."

Rukota closed his eyes with involuntary pain. Violating Security protocols was a willful endangerment of Fleet resources, not to speak of lives.

"And once members of your party had accessed ship's computers, they tried to command-prime to the First Officer's administrative log. It is just as well that our Captain did not notice. For myself I do not care, but there is a default penalty, yes?"

Indeed there was. The default penalty for compromising administrative security was six-and-sixty, and dismissal from service without benefits. Jennet ap Rhiannon was entirely capable of invoking it; she would probably not make dismissal stick, but nobody on board would stand between those people and the whip. Rukota set his teeth against a grimace of disgust.

"Thank you, your Excellency." They had put him in an absolutely unacceptable position, that of being responsible for an act that he had not authorized and of which he deeply disapproved. "I'll see to it that it's so noted in the official report. Confined to courier, you said, your Excellency?"

She glared up at him for a few breaths longer before apparently making up her mind. "We will not speak of it again. First Officer has found a place for you, we are short a Ship's Third Lieutenant. It is at least a clean berth."

It occurred to Rukota that for the second time Two had rather pointedly excluded him from the well-deserved quarantine of the preliminary assessment team. He was grateful, if surprised. He didn't like those people.

"I'm very much obliged, your Excellency. I'll take them off your hands as soon as we return to Pesadie. From Laynock, am I right?"

She was between him and the door, with her back to the Security troops she'd brought with her. Looking up into his face, Two laughed.

It was unmistakable. She opened her sharp-muzzled mouth wide, affording all too clear a view of her very beautiful, very sharp white teeth; curled the corners of her black lips back happily, and panted, the tip of her cunning tongue quivering with genial hilarity. He couldn't hear a thing but he knew that she was laughing. This was something she had learned to do, apparently, to communicate with hominids, and it communicated very well.

"Impertinent," Two said, and with a sudden movement of one wing sent Rukota staggering back against the wall to collapse onto the ledge where he'd been sleeping. "My Captain will have a word to say to you, Rukota. Someone will come to show you to quarters. Good-bye."

Tucking her head down to her chest abruptly, Two scuttled rapidly from the room, and all of the Security went with her. The *Ragnarok* was not going to Laynock at all. They didn't care if he knew it. What was a man to make of all of this?

Third Lieutenant's billet. So ap Rhiannon had not vacated the First Lieutenant's quarters, and Seascape was logically in the Second Lieutenant's berth. Was that where he fit into all of this? Impossible.

Impossible that they should think to add him to the crew of the *Ragnarok*. Impossible to think that they could use an artilleryman. Impossible to imagine any set of circumstances within the realm of possibility that would enable such a situation. Warships did not select their own officers. Officers did not select their own assignments.

Ships released to resupply went to resupply and returned to their Command of assignment. Or they were in violation of standard operating procedure. In the jaundiced view of Pesadie Training Command, violation of standard operating procedure could all too easily be interpreted as—

He wasn't going to think about it; he was going to wait and see.

My Captain, Two had said. Not "acting." Captain ap Rhiannon.

He'd wait to see what ap Rhiannon would tell him: and then he could decide how soon he should get seriously worried about what was going on, on board the Jurisdiction Fleet Ship *Ragnarok*.

Morning at the Matredonat.

As accustomed as Jils Ivers was to moving in circles at all levels of society, the luxury of Koscuisko's house rather stunned her. It was not so much a richness of food and drink and bed linen and appointments, though those would not shame a First Secretary—or even a Judge herself. This was a more profound wealth than material: all of these people with nothing whatever to do but wait upon her hand and foot, figuratively speaking, and Jils had no doubt that it would be literally speaking had she been inclined to accept a more extreme degree of body-service. All of these people.

Things that could be done by machine, by automated process, were done by hand here at the Matredonat, because Koscuisko had the money to afford to support human souls to do work that machines could do at less cost and in much less time. It was a species of conspicuous consumption that she had only very rarely encountered elsewhere in her travels on behalf of the Bench, and then only in much more primitive societies.

Koscuisko's private library was on the ground floor of the master's private house-within-a-house, a great, cool room with an immense hand-loomed carpet of considerable antiquity and value beyond price, tall massy shelves stacked deep with old-format printed texts bound in the tanned hides of animals, and an immense long study table in the middle of the room the approximate size of a one-soul courier. Jils looked at the shelves of books and scanned the titles, some of them unreadable from a distance, the gilt rubbed black with handling and age.

Garol should be here. He could probably read some of that.

Koscuisko closed the flat-form docket and pushed it away from him a little space, turning toward her in his chair and taking up his flask of rhyti. He'd asked her to sit just at the end of the long side of the table, so that she was on his right, and there was not the great span of the table between them. It was almost intimate.

"This represents an unimaginable reversal on the First Secretary's part, Bench specialist. Does it not?"

The rhyti server was near at hand; she had her flask as well. She preferred almost anything to rhyti, but she hadn't let on, yet. She was waiting to see how long it would take for the house staff to come up with that particular piece of intelligence from other sources. It was an experiment. "It may seem so, your Excellency. But from my point of view it's a consistent stage in the development of Verlaine's thinking. That's one of the things that convinces me that he's telling us the truth with this offer."

Not the Bench order for relief of Writ. There was no controversy there; Koscuisko would execute it. There was no hesitation on Koscuisko's part over the Judicial order that would make him a free man. It was what else the First Secretary had sent that gave Koscuisko pause, and rightly so, because the implications were staggering.

"Speak to me, Dame Ivers. Permit me to share the benefit of your insight, because I do not trust this damned soul further than a starving wolf in the dairy, and yet I cannot but respect your professional opinion."

The Domitt Prison. Verlaine had not been to blame for that atrocity, perhaps, not directly; but he was responsible. Jils had never heard him try to pretend otherwise. It was one of the things that most annoyed Verlaine about Koscuisko. Verlaine had been in the wrong and Koscuisko had told the world. Regardless of what the formal decision of the special Court had been, Verlaine knew his honor to be justly tainted forever by what had happened to Nurail prisoners at Port Rudistal in a prison to which he should have paid more careful attention.

"His Excellency will recall from his orientation that the First Secretary had sent a Clerk of Court to qualify for the Writ."

Mergau Noycannir, whom Verlaine had pulled out of a gutter somewhere and nurtured as his protégée. Ruthless. Determined. And willing to do anything for the First Secretary's approval; a potentially very useful person to have on leash if only she could be kept on leash, because such people had no sense of proportion.

"You came to Rudistal with her, as I recall, Specialist. Yes."

Noycannir had no formal medical background, and proved ultimately incapable of mastering the intricacies of the Bench's Protocols. There had been no way to tell before they'd tried, and the sacrifice asked of Noycannir had been extreme. "The First Secretary's choice of representative was not perhaps fortunate." Verlaine had had no one else from whom he could have demanded so stern a proof of dedication as to go to Fleet Orientation Station Medical and become a torturer.

"If you will however consider the motives behind the attempt. He wanted an Inquisitor not under Fleet controls, to break the monopoly Fleet had over Inquiry and reclaim the Judicial function for the Bench. This was his motive. The First Secretary became interested in you because of your ability. I respectfully suggest you consider two aspects of that instinct on his part."

Koscuisko stood up and began to pace, but he was listening. Perhaps he was remembering things. Jils knew what sort of pressure Verlaine had put on Koscuisko, in his attempts to force Koscuisko's cooperation.

As many special field assignments as Fleet would tolerate, making Koscuisko's life as difficult as possible while he was assigned to Scylla—to make the point about Verlaine's influence, and how much easier Koscuisko's life would be with Verlaine as his friend.

Assignment to the *Ragnarok* under the command of Fleet Captain

Lowden after Koscuisko had cried failure of Writ at the Domitt Prison, knowing what Lowden's record with Inquisitors was like— perhaps the single most ignoble, pettiest, and least worthy action to which Jils had ever known Verlaine to stoop.

Verlaine had hoped month by month that Koscuisko would yield to the strain of serving Lowden's corrupt interests, and petition to be called to Chilleau Judiciary. Koscuisko had not. Whether it was sheer stubbornness on his part, or whether Verlaine had underestimated Koscuisko's sensitivity to the plight of the bond-involuntaries under Lowden's command, Koscuisko had lasted out his full tour of duty; at what cost to himself Jils could hardly even guess. His determined resistance had frustrated and angered Verlaine—emotions tempered by the special heat that came from Verlaine's knowledge that he was in the wrong.

Finally Verlaine had backed Koscuisko into a corner with a threat to annex his Writ, and Koscuisko had kicked the bottom out of the box in which Verlaine had thought to trap him, and put the entire Jurisdiction Fleet between them. Again.

Now Verlaine had finally decided to admit that his behavior had been inappropriately motivated, and worse, it had been—there was no other word for it—unjust. Cruel and unjust.

Jils kept talking, because Koscuisko was clearly still listening and thinking while he paced. "Your reputation, your Excellency, maximum results with only the minimum amount of force required, no more. Even your Tenth Levels, sir, shockingly effective demonstrations, maximum invocation of deterrent terror where the verdict of the Bench called for the extreme penalty. Surely you can see that you are the man that Verlaine would want if he had begun to have reservations about the entire concept of forced confession. You do it so well."

Verlaine was conservative; he hated waste, of any sort. Koscuisko was the single most efficient Inquisitor in the entire inventory. Koscuisko didn't waste pain or blood, lives or limbs, not when he was given his own head. And in those instances in which Koscuisko had been handed a life out of which to make a public example, he hadn't wasted that, either. He'd exploited the resource to its absolute fullest, so that it was Koscuisko's work that people remembered when they called to mind the extreme penalty under Law for treason.

"I won't be pushed, Bench specialist," Koscuisko said. "I have been sufficiently imposed upon, to my mind. And behind the First Secretary's crude bullying I cannot but suspect I catch a whiff of a bitter old acquaintance."

It was true that Noycannir had carefully presented Koscuisko in the most annoying light possible before Verlaine. But Noycannir's influence had waned over time.

"He is not accustomed to being defied or resisted, your Excellency. You brought out the worst in him, and there's no excuse for it. But you win. There is nothing more that he can do to make you his for the use of the Second Judge. His realization sheds too strong a light on the deficiencies in his own behavior. He perceives his clear duty to make what amends he may. And he is truly of a mind that Inquiry is a waste of lives, and no longer in the best interest of the Judicial order."

"Do you believe this to be a genuine statement of policy, Specialist Ivers?" Koscuisko asked, standing at the table behind his chair, nodding at the flat-form docket. "Because if it is genuine, I must endorse it. The personal history that I have with Chilleau Judiciary and its people would not deter me for an instant. If I but knew."

"He's convinced me of his sincerity, sir. And an enriched sense of cynicism is part of our initial issue when we sign on." It wasn't as though Verlaine was the only person within the Judicial structure who had come to believe that the system no longer served a useful purpose, if it ever had. Inquiry had been an experiment that had taken on a life of its own; the initial result of institutionalizing torture as an instrument of State had been very positive, but those results had been short-term. Terror could stabilize a population for a few years, but then it began to create a complex of destabilization all its own.

Koscuisko sat down. "I will faithfully consider it, Bench specialist." He had clearly already made up most of his mind. It was only the possibility of duplicity on the First Secretary's part that troubled him. "For the rest of it. I will of course accept the offered relief. But how are my people to be managed, if I have become a private citizen?"

Koscuisko felt somewhat less strongly about his un-bonded troops, perhaps, if only because they did not need as much protection. But it was still obviously an issue in his mind.

"Once you have countersigned the document, sir, I will transmit it to Sant-Dasidar from the nearest Bench offices. It will take two to three weeks after that for all your voice-clearances to be purged. Until such time as you can no longer invoke the Record you remain a Judicial officer, your Excellency. Although with these documents on record your status will clearly be in the process of changing."

If Verlaine had been able to break Koscuisko's bond-involuntaries free from Fleet and bring them to Chilleau Judiciary years ago Koscuisko would have come with them, almost certainly. Jils kept talking. "Until then the Bench will wish to continue to protect its officer. Your people can return to the *Ragnarok* once your clearances have all been purged, your Excellency, and at your instruction I will leave immediately for Bench offices, if you should wish it."

Because otherwise she was scheduled to travel to Chelatring Side with Koscuisko seven days from now, to be present when the Autocrat's Proxy took her formal poll of the Koscuisko familial corporation. She had intended to leave for Bench offices afterward; that was what Cousin Stanoczk had arranged. But if Koscuisko was impatient she would not be surprised, nor was she unwilling to change plans. Koscuisko thought about it.

"It is only a few more days, Bench specialist, and I am at home already. If I am to trust the First Secretary, I will trust that this is a done deed. No, do not change your plans on my account. It would only call attention. I need to think and plan how to reveal this to my family. Give me the document. I will make my mark."

Koscuisko's signature, holograph endorsement, and his seal. The thing was done. All that was left was for it to be recorded, and that was the merest technicality.

"Thank you, your Excellency. As you wish, sir."

Koscuisko was pale. And yet looked so much younger. "Thank you as well, Bench specialist, and now excuse me if you will. My heart is full. I need to be alone here for a while."

To offer a salute by way of courtesy was not appropriate; he was no longer an officer, except for the formality. Something Jils had heard came to her mind, instead.

"According to his Excellency's good pleasure," Jils agreed. A Dolgorukij formula, for a Dolgorukij autocrat. Her mission was accomplished. Andrej Koscuisko had come home at last; and now would stay.

CHAPTER EIGHT

The Malcontent

On the morning of the ninth day since Andrej Ulexeievitch had returned to Azanry, Marana pulled open the great curtains that draped the windows of the master's bedroom and looked down into the gardens below. It was well past breakfast; she had lain sleepless for long hours in the night, struggling with her sense of fairness and duty, and consequently slept later. The light in Andrej's bedroom was different than in her own and provided few clues as to the time.

As Marana looked out over the garden in the midmorning sun, Andrej Ulexeievitch himself came out of the house below her, rushing into the garden like a man in pursuit of some elusive goal. She frowned.

He had had an appointment with his guest, the Bench specialist, in the morning. He had seen Specialist Ivers for a few words in the garden yesterday as well. He hadn't said anything to her about the meat and matter of the conversation; he hadn't seemed disturbed or unhappy—yet who was she to say?

His outland Security were there, spreading themselves well out along the perimeter of the garden. But Andrej was headed for the maze. Security would not be able to track him there, unless he wore a blip; it was an old maze, and very cunning. Nor would she be able to see where he was, because the latticework of living centuries of shrubs had roofed the maze over solidly. In the winter, yes, she was able to see her son Anton running through the maze with his pet mas-hound, if there wasn't any snow and he wore something brightly colored.

She wanted to know what was on Andrej's mind. Shrugging into her robe—glad that her woman wasn't there to insist she dress—Marana hurried down the private stairs and out of the house, into the garden. Nodding at Andrej's master of Security, Marana went straight for the maze, and in. She knew the maze. She didn't know which way Andrej had gone, but she could guess. They had once had a favorite place to go and be lost in—

Turning a corner, Marana caught sight of him as he went around the crisply trimmed edge of the shrubbery hedge, trailing his left hand across the green leaves as he went.

"Andrej!"

He had found the bench in the arbor that had been their trysting-place of old, and sat there with his face in his hands, rubbing his eyes. Something was wrong. She flew to his side and took his right hand in her own, and he let her carry his hand away from his face without protest. He would talk to her, then.

"Andrej, what's the matter?"

His hand worked in her anxious clasp, his fingers fluttering with emotion. "It's not wrong at all, Marana, but it's so far from right. I don't know what to do."

She waited.

After a moment, Andrej turned to her and took her hands between his. "Marana. When I came home, and so far abused your goodwill as to marry you. It was not because I thought you might still love me, or had pined for me in solitude for years. But to protect our son."

Someone must have told him about Ferinc. Marana felt a chill in the pit of her stomach: she had thought she could explain—but she had yet to broach the delicate subject, and now it was too late.

Andrej spoke on, without asking or apparently expecting a defense from her. She was under no obligation to defend herself. She knew her rights, and Ferinc was one of them.

"And only then because I have had warnings, Marana, of a powerful enemy who wants me dead and has the means to accomplish this. I was almost assassinated at Port Burkhayden, Marana, and I place my life in your hands to tell you even so much as that."

He didn't want to go into details. She could sense it. She agreed.

She didn't want him to go into any details either: she didn't want any knowledge that could be used against him. "Tell me, Andrej," she encouraged. "Has something changed?"

"Everything is changed except that." Releasing her hands with a gesture of hopelessness he pleaded with her, palms up, as if gloomily convinced even before the fact that he could not express the enormity of it. "Chilleau Judiciary offers me freedom. And more than that, in return for my voice in my father's ear, but freedom without qualification. Marana. I would never have dared bind you to me in such a way if I had thought that it would mean imprisonment for you."

She was safe to ignore the latter half of his speech; she thought she understood the former. He was being yes-or-no again. It was so very Andrej of him that she felt her heart soften with remembered love. "Relieved of your duties, you come home to be a husband to your wife and a father to your son. How can that not be right, Andrej? Speaking of the portion that regards our son in particular."

Andrej resettled himself on the cool stone bench, at a little farther remove than that at which Marana herself had sat down to speak to him. "Had I only known that I had time. I might have won your permission beforehand. I might not have flouted my father's will, again."

Marana hid her smile of recognition. Yes, he had behaved in a very high-handed manner. Yes, he had been arrogant and self-willed, and focused completely on his own agenda to the absolute exclusion of anything else. That was what an autocrat was expected to do. And Andrej's aim was the protection of his son; surely he could understand that that fact won him some consideration from his son's mother.

"Surely to have you home is a good thing," Marana encouraged him, gently. "You have a child. He will grow to love you. You so often wondered whether you were doomed to inspire only fear and filial duty." That there were issues between Andrej and his father was a fact of life unchanged in the years Andrej had been way from home. "You will have work to do. To repair relationships with the business interests of the Ichogatra."

He looked at her almost reluctantly with his head lowered, grasping the edge of the seat of the stone bench in either hand. "But do we have a future to make between us, Marana? If I am to be home.

I would like to know if we might try to see if we can remember what it had once been to have loved one another."

Her heart went out to him, trying so hard to do the thing that was right, trying so hard to determine what that might be. She slid across the bench closer to him, and this time he did not stir. "When Pellarus came back to Osmander, he was changed," Marana pointed out tenderly, not minding if her own uncertainty sounded in her voice. "And it was time before she knew him for her lord. But she did come to know him."

Andrej nodded in apparent acceptance of the offer, or at least of the spirit that had inspired it. "Pellarus was changed by ordeal and honorable battle," Andrej objected regardless, stubborn for all his clear understanding of what she meant to offer to him. "Osmander had not made a life for herself. As another woman very properly might."

Marana had made up her mind now, and was determined. "I am your wife, Andrej; you my husband. It's not for you to say whether Ferinc should be an obstacle. I say we should approach it as Pellarus to Osmander, and see if there is truth for us in the story. Else, we will negotiate. But I would like to try, because sometimes when I am not paying attention it seems that I remember loving you."

Turning to her Andrej raised his hands to take her by the shoulder and caress her face with trembling fingers. "It is so much to think about," Andrej said, in a voice that was heavy with tears and wonder. "And all at once. It's been so hard to meet Anton, knowing I was going away, that to think I need not go away is almost too much happiness. I cannot deserve this, Marana."

What could he mean? " 'If happiness were deserved how few would ever be.' " It was an old adage, no less true for its antiquity. "Strive only to be worthy of it. Not to deserve it."

She leaned her forehead against his, and in a breath remembered with so forceful a rush of shared delight that it nearly overwhelmed her. His face had changed, his manner subtly altered, his language edged with harsh experience, his eyes grown weary from looking upon alien visions. But his smell was Andrej.

It was Andrej with some overlay of age and maturity; his personal linen did not take the scent that she remembered, he dressed his hair with different toiletries than those he had once been accustomed to use.

It was still him. Beneath the influence of soap and cloth, the underlying truth of his body was the one that she remembered. It was so easy to put her mouth to his and taste his kiss, drunk in the moment with the certainty of her senses.

There was an alien flavor to his mouth. He was an older man than he had been, his kiss was not as sweet as when they had been children. But she could recognize enough. His smell, the taste of his mouth, the remembered shifting of his body against hers—Andrej.

He would come home, and stay. Anton would learn to love him. With Andrej at her side, there would be nothing to fear from the spite of his family.

With Andrej home it would be different, now.

There was someone on the grounds of Koscuisko's manor house that Chief Stildyne thought he recognized, and Lek was not the man to argue with his Chief. Their officer had gone into the maze in his garden; his lady had gone in after him, and so far as Lek was concerned anything he could find to focus his attention away from what was likely to be happening in the maze was all to the good.

Smish Smath chirruped, her little trill a very creditable imitation of a local warbler. Lek recognized her accent all the same. Leaning away from his post just enough to catch her hand signal, Lek read the signs. *Quarry bearing Taller to Murat. Intercept at twenty-four eighths. On one. Two. Three. Four.*

Taller to Murat told Lek what direction to seek; *twenty-four eighths* gave him the distance. It would be a stretch at the sprint, but he could do it. There was a relatively clear field between the maze and the outermost perimeter, but once past the gravel track of the promenade there were trees and plantings to muddle the pursuit.

If the quarry gained the garden wall, they would lose it. There were too many directions in which a man could run to hide, and no way to alert the house security in time. Perhaps that was best. Perhaps Stildyne was crying the alert. It was in their best interest as Stildyne's team on site to ensure that Stildyne not find himself in need of outside help.

Lek ran for the goal as though the Aznir were on his heels with the dogs, and the Devil after. Taller had flushed the game. Lek could hear someone running, and altered his course to intercept, pushing for each extra bit of speed that he could muster. This was for Stildyne's face. He couldn't let Stildyne down in front of all of these Aznir. He would not.

Lek could hear the quarry, but still could not quite see it. Whoever it was ran very well and very quickly, but Lek had had the advantage of direction. Lek knew where he was to look for his prey; the quarry didn't know where to expect Lek. Seeing his chance, Lek, shifted his pursuit track in a wide arc to cut across the fleeing man's path and terminate his flight.

The target saw his danger and veered off toward a break between two trees, but the shift in direction cost him time. Lek launched himself for the quarry and landed him, crashing to the ground against the base of a tree trunk, with his arms wrapped around the waist of Stildyne's prey.

The others were with him, now—Smish and Murat and Taller—wrestling with the man Lek had brought down, subduing him by degrees as he struggled. Once he felt sure that the others had a good grip on the man, Lek pushed himself away from the prone body to stand up.

What he saw froze his blood. The man was Malcontent.

He wore his hair long down his back, but worse than that, as Taller and Smish pinned his shoulders to the ground Lek could see the crimson halter around the prone man's throat, exposed, revealed by the struggle that disarranged his clothing and pulled his collar wide.

Lek leaned into his shoulder and struck Taller as hard as he could to shake him free, pushing at Smish at the same time. He'd startled them. They went down.

Lek reached down to embrace the Malcontent, to help him up, to beg forgiveness for the error they had made and explain that his off-world companions had not known that they were making such a terrible mistake. Murat landed on his back, flattening Lek across the Malcontent's body.

Lek started to become confused. This was a Malcontent. The person of the Malcontent was sacred. He couldn't let these off-worlders abuse a Malcontent. He was one of these outlanders, though. He was supposed to do as his Chief ordered, and his Chief wanted this man stopped and secured. But this man was Malcontent. He couldn't let them impose violence on the person of the Malcontent; it was a sin, and yet—

"That'll do," the Malcontent said firmly, but it wasn't a Malcontent's voice. It was some warrant officer or another, speaking plain Standard. Maybe not a warrant officer. But it was Standard. And it certainly sounded like a warrant officer to Lek. "Disengage, and terminate your exercise. Very well done indeed, and me with the advantage of knowledge of the terrain. Where is your Chief?"

Lek helped the Malcontent to rise, while Smish and Taller came up on either side, predictably confused. Lek didn't blame them. He was confused himself.

"He's Malcontent," Lek explained, as Chief Stildyne joined them. "No man may touch the sacred person of the Malcontent. Well, not without leave and permission. We almost made a horrible mistake, Chief."

He was confused and uncertain, and beginning to be afraid. He knew that the person of the Malcontent was not to be approached with violence. But did Stildyne? And more to the point—did his governor know that?

Stildyne shook his head. "He's not Malcontent, Lek," Stildyne said, with absolute assurance. "He's not even Dolgorukij. I know this man, or at least I used to know him. He's a deserter from Gotrane. Not Malcontent at all."

"That was then," the Malcontent said. "This is now. You, troop, Lek? Don't worry. It's all right. Do as your Chief tells you. And the peace of the Malcontent be with you. It's all right."

The Malcontent wasn't moving, wasn't giving anyone any reason to have to hit him. That helped. What the Malcontent said was confusing, but Lek thought he could make sense of it if he tried. Stildyne thought he knew the man. Maybe Stildyne had. An outlander, electing the Malcontent? Because he didn't look like any kind of Dolgorukij to Lek, let alone Aznir. Stildyne was right about that.

Stildyne came forward, keeping a wary eye on the Malcontent. "We're sorry, Lek, we didn't realize. But I do know him. And I do need to know what he's doing here. Is this going to be all right for you?"

There was no time like the present for the Malcontent to escape, because Lek's team was paying attention to him to the exclusion of anything else. But the Malcontent wasn't fleeing. The Malcontent

NlQdXRXpKzWClu

simply stood with his back to the trunk of the tree, waiting calmly. Lek shook his head vigorously, to shake out the confusing thoughts that warred within him.

"You can't push him, Chief, you can't. He's Malcontent. He's a sacred person. Please."

"There'll be no pushing, Lek, put your mind at ease," the Malcontent said kindly. He had a soothing tone of voice whose combined accents—warrant officer, Malcontent—were very comforting. "Your Chief has questions, fine, we'll talk. That's all. He's telling you the truth. Come on, then, let's go to the house, but I don't want your officer to see me."

Taller and Smish were at Lek's sides, watching him. Murat stood behind him, and put his hand out to Lek's shoulder. Lek stood for a moment, letting things settle out. Yes. He was going to be all right. It was not going to be a problem. It could have been. It had almost been. But it was all right now.

"Ready, Chief," Lek said. Now he was curious himself: an outlander, bound to the Malcontent? He wouldn't have believed it possible.

Whatever Stildyne might have to say, Lek hoped he'd get to listen in.

Marana took her leave with a tender kiss, and Andrej leaned back against the hedge that surrounded the bench and watched her go. It had been their bench. Perhaps it would be their bench again, someday.

He waited several moments to give Marana time to gain the house, to go up to their room and finish dressing. It was mid-morning; soon there would be mid-meal. He would see Anton during the break from daily studies.

He was going to have to talk to Chief Stildyne.

A year ago, when he had first thought he was going home—before Jils Ivers's embassage from Chilleau Judiciary had turned his life in such an unexpected direction—the single thing he had found to regret in the prospect of freedom was that he could not take his troops with him. Bond-involuntaries belonged to the Bench. Un-bonded troops could make their own decision to stay with Fleet or follow him into private service in his House, but the bond-involuntaries had no such flexibility.

He was going to have to tell them that he was leaving; it was not going to be easy. Standing up at length—stretching himself, a little stiff from long sitting—Andrej started for the entrance to the maze. He would find Stildyne nearby, or someone who knew where Stildyne was.

Right now there were only four people at the Matredonat who knew what Ivers had brought: himself, and Jils Ivers, Marana, and almost certainly his cousin Stanoczk. But Stoshik hadn't been at dinner last night, though he'd said that he and Andrej needed to meet. Andrej wasn't sure Stoshik was on the grounds at all; Malcontents were like that. They came and went on their own schedule, taking and asking leave of nobody.

One of the house-master's people was waiting, well clear of the mouth of the maze itself. Not one of Andrej's own Security. That was odd.

"Prosper all Saints," Andrej said, giving the man leave to speak to him.

"To his Excellency's purpose and the profit of his House. Your outland Security are anxious to speak with you, your Excellency, in the library in the master's quarters."

"Is something wrong?" Andrej had intended to look in on the schoolroom, but that was in another part of the house altogether.

"It's not for me to say, your Excellency. It's the Malcontent's business."

Andrej frowned. Was Stoshik returned? What would Stoshik be doing with Stildyne in the library? Well, there was the obvious, of course, since Stildyne and he held a sexual preference in common, and Stoshi's sacred duty was to offer reconciliation to unhappy souls. But if it were so simple as that it was unlikely that Stildyne would welcome company. Stildyne might not know about Malcontents, who could be much more aggressive on their home ground than outside of Combine territory; there was only so much Lek was likely to have explained.

Taller and Murat were at the door to the library, which meant that Lek and Smish were within. Nodding at them to keep to their post Andrej went through into the master's library, closing the doors behind him. What was going on?

Stildyne had a man seated in front of Andrej's great desk that fronted the tall windows overlooking the garden. Smish and Lek were there.

The Malcontent was not Stanoczk.

The Malcontent was some tall, slender creature with green-tinted eyes and dark hair, whose long-fingered hands lay still and calm on the arms of the chair in which he sat, but whose fingertips were white with tension. Andrej spared only a quick look at the Malcontent on his way past to confront Stildyne, who stood beside the desk. "There is a problem, Chief?"

The Malcontent had given a start when Andrej entered the room. Was it the man Stildyne had called to his attention at exercise several days ago, on the morning after his arrival at the Matredonat?

"I'm not sure if it's a problem, your Excellency." Stildyne sounded more uncertain than he usually did. Andrej wasn't sure he liked the implications. "This man has been keeping an eye on you ever since we got here, and we caught him trying to observe you in the maze. Lek says he's Malcontent. I say he's a deserter from Chambers at Gotrane. I used to know this man. There's a discrepancy here that concerns me."

Lek was in the room, but he didn't look distressed to Andrej. He looked a little dusty, yes. Andrej beckoned Lek to him; Stildyne stepped away. "You say Malcontent?" Andrej asked. Lek nodded, very confidently.

"He wears the braid, your Excellency. And gave me peace."

Both convincing from the worldview of a Dolgorukij who had never been off-world; but not conclusive proof, particularly where Security warrants were concerned. Stildyne was a suspicious man. It was his job. "What is his name?"

"He says Ferinc, your Excellency, Cousin Ferinc. Chief says differently."

Lek and Andrej both knew that what a man's name had been before he elected the Malcontent had no particular relation to what he would answer to once he came to be called "Cousin." But if this was Cousin Ferinc, of whom Anton spoke . . .

"Really," Andrej said with interest, pitching his voice to carry to where the Malcontent sat under Smish's observing eye. " 'Cousin Ferinc'? The man my child loves. You were to be at—where was it?"

The Malcontent didn't want to speak, it seemed. Andrej could be patient. There was something odd going on here; he would call for Stanoczk if he had to. This was his house. He had a right to know what Malcontents were coming and going, and for what reason, at least approximately. "You can tell me, Cousin, or I will ask my Cousin Stanoczk. It is all the same to me. You have distressed my Chief of Security."

The Malcontent raised his face, so that the light caught his profile. Rather fine features, but not particularly Dolgorukij. Very strange. Some outlander's bastard, hounded into the Malcontent by his exotic looks?

"Dubrovnije," the Malcontent said. "I promised to bring him a wheat-fish. Your Excellency."

Dubrovnije was the right answer; Andrej started to turn back to Stildyne and the next question, before his mind quite caught up with his senses. "A man may desert and throw himself upon the Malcontent for protection, Chief. It is the right of every child—"

Under Canopy. Stildyne knew that. Stildyne had been newly assigned, he to Andrej, Andrej to the *Ragnarok*, when some Sarvaw mercantile pilot had elected the Malcontent to evade prosecution for piracy. Years ago. But suddenly Andrej was convinced that he recognized Cousin Ferinc's voice, and it had been even longer ago than the incident with the Sarvaw mercantile pilot.

"He's not Dolgorukij, your Excellency," Stildyne said, watching Andrej's face. Stildyne would know that Andrej had realized there was a problem. "I think he may have been Amorilic. Maybe. Petty warrant officer."

"Girag," Andrej confirmed. Stildyne's eyes widened marginally in surprise; Stildyne hadn't expected Andrej to recognize him. And yet Andrej knew who he was, now. "Petty Warrant Officer, Haster Girag, wasn't it? Cousin?"

That was the man. The Malcontent shifted uneasily in his chair, as if to hide himself from Andrej, turning his face away.

"You know this person, sir?" Stildyne asked. Carefully. There was a layer of inquiry in Stildyne's voice that Andrej could not quite interpret, but it would keep.

"Haster Girag," Andrej repeated, and closed the distance between him and the Malcontent to stare down into the man's pale face implacably. "You. A deserter. And you come into my house? You endear yourself to my child? Why should I tolerate this obscenity, 'Cousin'?"

He knew who it was. He remembered. Girag had taken liberties with prisoners in his custody, liberties outside the Protocols, unsanctioned and unlawful. Andrej had punished him. It had been at least seven years. Possibly longer.

Cousin Ferinc stood up, finally, but it was only by way of putting some distance between Andrej and himself. "It wasn't meant to go that way, your Excellency." He made Cousin Ferinc nervous, Andrej noted, and followed Cousin Ferinc step for step across the room, stalking his prey without mercy. "And I don't blame you for having questions. But I don't have to explain myself to you. I'm under direction from my reconciler. And if you don't mind I'll be going. I've promised to bring Anton Andreievitch a wheat-fish. From Dubrovnije."

This was intolerable cheek. Haster Girag had been a bully. An abuser of prisoners. A sexual deviant, or if not a sexual deviant, then at least a man who found amusement in sexual perversion. It was beyond imagining that the Malcontent knew this man's history and still tolerated his cultivation of a friendship with a child, any child. No. Not any child. His child. Anton Andreievitch Koscuisko.

"You will not give any such thing to my child, Cousin Ferinc—not until I have had a chance to be sure that your reconciler knows just what you are. Who is it to whom I must appeal? Name this man, Ferinc, if you please."

Cousin Ferinc had his back up against the library bookshelves and stood there trembling, with the stink of the fear-sweat upon him. There wasn't any place farther for him to go. He was afraid of Andrej; Andrej could tell. He had good reason to be afraid of Andrej. It was prudent and proper, just and judicious that it should be so.

But Andrej was not going to threaten Cousin Ferinc.

Cousin Ferinc wore the halter of the Malcontent, and Andrej knew as well as Lek how much genuine immunity hung by that red ribbon around the neck of the slaves of the Saint. "It is his Excellency's cousin Stanoczk," Cousin Ferinc replied, in a voice that spoke volumes of shame and of humility.

Andrej saw it all in a sudden flash of insight, and closed his eyes. Of course. He had turned Girag's perversion back on the man, as suitable punishment for Girag's misuse of prisoners. Now Girag enjoyed reconciliation in like form from Cousin Stanoczk. Andrej's own cousin Stoshik. The obscenity of it was almost too much to be borne.

"I understand." He wished he didn't. "Give my good Lek peace, Cousin Ferinc, and go. Do not let me see your face again. And have no contact with my child until I have had a chance to explain to Stoshik why your hands should be taken off at the wrists before you should be allowed to so much as touch such innocence."

Girag's offense had not been against children, no. Not against women either. It had been the constraint of people otherwise his match or more that had seduced Girag. Grown men. But it was bad enough at that.

Ferinc bowed his head. "By your command, your Excellency, under your roof." He seemed to master himself moment by moment as he spoke, and gave Lek peace very prettily. "The peace of the Malcontent is with you, Lek, be easy."

There was finger-code passing between Stildyne and Ferinc, but Andrej ignored it. It wasn't any of his business. He didn't even want to know. When Ferinc had left, Andrej turned back to the room from staring at the backs of the books on the shelves of the library. "Chief. I need to talk to you. Gentles, if you would leave us, for a moment."

Lek was apparently secure, though quite possibly confused by the crosscurrents raised within this room by a Malcontent who was not Malcontent at all. Or who was not Dolgorukij. It was all right for Lek to be confused, so long as he was not in conflict within himself. It was with internal conflict that Lek became vulnerable to his governor.

Stildyne seemed confused as well, but determined on something. Once the doors had closed behind Lek and Smish, Stildyne spoke, to have the initiative. "You also knew this man, your Excellency?"

That was right. He was someone Stildyne had recognized. Girag and Stildyne had had history together of some sort.

No, Andrej thought suddenly, with a spasm of apprehensive fear. *Not that sort of a history. Surely not.*

Yet why not? Was it impossible that Girag and Stildyne had been lovers? It was still a far cry from abuse of prisoners outside of Protocol—"He was senior man on a detachment at a holding facility in Richeyne." He would simply have to lay the whole thing out, and let

Stildyne say what he would about it. What did it matter? He meant to break the bond that was between them; he would leave Fleet.

No.

He would leave Fleet, but that would not break the bond between them. He owed Stildyne honesty. "My Captain had been forced to second me to some Judicial investigation there. That man liked to play with prisoners, Stildyne. It was his practice to demand sexual favors in exchange for food and water. It is abuse of prisoners outside of Protocol."

Any Inquisitor could demand sexual favors, on pain of torment. It was recognized, if not codified, as useful in eroding the self-respect, and contributing to a good outcome accordingly. That wasn't the point. The point was that even an Inquisitor was expected to observe the Protocols. Rape wasn't part of accepted protocol until the sixth level of Inquiry; and any demand for sexual services was a species of rape, so far as Andrej was concerned, regardless of whether or not an assault went with it.

What Girag had done was perhaps not so unusual a thing for a man with power over prisoners to demand. Andrej had not been naive then; he was not naive now. But whenever Andrej stepped into a prison, he expected to have absolute control over what abuse his prisoners were to be required to endure, and Girag had violated the sole right of an Inquisitor to inflict atrocity under cover of Law.

"I very much wanted to deliver him to those same prisoners, Mister Stildyne, but it would have been inappropriate. I found willing recruits among station Security instead. I am ashamed to explain what I did to him, Chief, but I don't think I'm ashamed of having done it."

Certainly compared to other things that he had done, his afternoon's sport with Haster Girag paled into all but absolute insignificance. Except for Haster Girag, perhaps. Perhaps he *was* ashamed.

Perhaps the imposition had been excessive. Something had clearly shattered Girag's life; perhaps confronting his own hunger and being forced to admit it for what it was had been too much for him. It had been too much for Andrej, after all, if the specific nature of the thirst was not the same. He had never recovered from the realization that he was a monster.

After a moment's thoughtful silence Stildyne spoke.

"Well. You should know, though." There was an unusually grave note of deliberation in Stildyne's voice, as though he faced the Court. "My previous acquaintance. We used to have parties. We used bond-involuntaries for entertainment. You would not have approved of my own conduct. Sir."

Andrej stared up into Chief Stildyne's ruined face with shock and horror. He knew perfectly well that prior to his arrival on the *Ragnarok* Stildyne had been in the occasional habit of exploiting his access to bond-involuntary troops for sexual purposes. He couldn't change any of what Stildyne had done; only what Stildyne did ever after, as long as he was responsible to Andrej for the welfare of those troops. It was unthinkable that Stildyne would revert to previous abusive behavior once Andrej was gone. So why was Stildyne telling him this?

"To you I would trust my child in a heartbeat, Chief." He knew perfectly well why Stildyne was telling him such things. And he had no cause to scorn Girag as diseased. His own hands were far more deeply soiled than Girag's had been, though his sin was sanctioned by the Bench in support of the Judicial order. What were the games of pain and sexual dominance that Girag had played, compared to gross and unjustifiable murder? "But Girag has cause to bear a grudge. I cannot risk him next to my child."

Stildyne looked skeptical. "I see. Thank you, your Excellency. But if you did. Trust me with your son, I mean. What would he call me? Chief? Or Mister?"

The question made no sense. Too much had happened today, and it was still short of mid-meal. Andrej needed to go into a dark quiet room, and think. It was the wrong time to tell Stildyne that Andrej was not going back to the *Ragnarok*.

"He might very well mistake your worth, and call you Brachi," Andrej admitted. "Being a child. And not understanding the respect due to a man in your position."

There was a flicker of surprise in Stildyne's eyes, but it went very quickly. Stildyne bowed. "I'll see about Lek, your Excellency. And ask the house-master to send your cousin Stanoczk, when he can be found."

Yes, that would be good. Andrej sat down at the great desk in the library and buried his face between his hands. This had been unexpected. Unnecessary. And he had not told his people. He would have to tell them. Soon. Not now. It would raise too many issues of judgment and abandonment if he told Stildyne now, in the face of Stildyne's painful revelation about his past.

"Thank you, Mister Stildyne. I will sort myself out between now and mid-meal." It was going to take him much longer than that; so there was no time like the present to be started.

What could have possessed Haster Girag to elect the Malcontent? What could have possessed the Malcontent to accept him? Who had made the decision to permit Haster Girag to come to the Matredonat and cultivate Anton Andreievitch, and who was Andrej Ulexeievitch to judge?

But Anton was his child. And the thought that Anton should admire such a man as Andrej knew Girag to be was more than he could rationalize, even him.

Ferinc bent his head and made for the escape of the library doors with all deliberate speed, struggling to maintain control of himself. Koscuisko was furious with him; Koscuisko had a right to be.

But Ferinc was Malcontent. He could not be threatened; the degradation of his status as a slave of the Saint gave him immunity. No casual punishment assessed by any layman could compare to the humiliation of the red halter.

He was not even legally a person, but an object. Slavery was illegal under Jurisdiction, but there were exceptions for religious observance, and the Malcontent was one of them. Koscuisko could not touch him. He was an object belonging to the Saint.

And yet it was his doom—as Stanoczk had regretfully suggested— to remain outland and fundamentally un-Reconciled in his heart of hearts, because one black day years and years ago Andrej Koscuisko had mastered him, and he had been a slave ever since. Not to the Malcontent.

I can explain, Ferinc signaled to Stildyne, as he forced himself to walk across the room rather than running. He had not used the finger-code for years, but he was confident that Stildyne could still understand his accent. *No threat to the officer. Truth, Stildyne.*

Stildyne need not be angry at him for being here—he was no threat to Koscuisko or to anything that was Koscuisko's, and among the things that were Koscuisko's were the woman and the child that he had grown to love for their own sakes, and no taint of Koscuisko about them. Koscuisko himself had disappeared from Ferinc's mind here, years ago. He had been almost at peace, and now he was damned.

Cousin Stanoczk would be disgraced in Chapter. Ferinc had been disobedient, undisciplined, but worse than that had revealed by his behavior that despite the most concerted efforts Stanoczk had made on his behalf he was still fundamentally un-Reconciled. What would become of him?

He cleared the threshold and gained the outer hallway, but Koscuisko's Security were not stepping away. The bond-involuntary Lek Kerenko had one hand to his elbow, but very gently, as if to give support; the woman cocked her head at him, gesturing down the hall.

"Chief's room down this way, Cousin," she said, and she used a Standard word for *cousin* that sounded oddly in Ferinc's ears. "Come on. You can have a drink. You look as though you might not mind one, if I can say so without giving offense."

Of course. They read finger-code as well. It had been bond-involuntaries who had invented it, after all, as a means of communicating between themselves without compromising their discipline. Ferinc had bullied the knowledge out of bond-involuntaries, knowing how to exploit their vulnerability to their governors; that was how he'd learned it. Lek's fellows clearly had the knowledge, as well, but Koscuisko would not have permitted his Bonds to be coerced into teaching it.

It was a telling detail that spoke of the exceptional trust Koscuisko had earned from his Bonds, more evidence to Ferinc of what he'd lost. He couldn't speak. He let them escort him down the hall to a room near the end of the corridor, where the house-master had placed Koscuisko's chief of Security. He knew these rooms. There was more familiar here than not.

Lek poured out a drink for him, fully half a glass of cortac brandy; Ferinc took it with a nod of thanks and had drunk half of it down before he realized that the house-master had given Stildyne the good stuff. The really good stuff.

The liquor calmed his nerves. He took the balance of it with more respect and consideration, listening to the voices in his mind drop off one by one into a drugged stupor. After a while, Stildyne came into the room, and the Security left.

Stildyne sat down. Ferinc looked up at him a little stupidly, feeling the liquor. He didn't usually drink. "What did you tell him?"

Stildyne looked thoughtful, and much older than Ferinc remembered him. "You and me. Parties. Bond-involuntaries. He would have tortured himself, trying to guess and never just corning out and asking."

Ferinc shook his head, regretfully. "You needn't have, Stildyne. You owe him no explanations. Surely." Even as he said it, he knew better. He knew things about Stildyne that he had not guessed before Andrej Koscuisko had come into the library. It was only more evidence of the fact that Koscuisko was a terrible and corrosive sort of metamorphic agency. Stildyne. Of all people.

"You're right, of course." Stildyne's agreement was amused—on multiple levels. "But it doesn't make any difference. You'd better leave. He doesn't want to see you."

Ever again. "Let me have a word with his lady, Chief," Ferinc asked humbly. "Just so she knows. In case there's gossip. I had leave from Cousin Stanoczk to make sure she was all right, not to spy on Koscuisko. I wasn't to have been caught skulking in the garden."

Stildyne nodded. "If you do it now, you should be all right. Himself is in a state; he'll not be stirring. But I don't understand, man. Why are you here?"

"I truly mean no harm, Stildyne. I came looking to make up a lack, years ago. I thought that I was doing well, really. Stanoczk says that he has failed me, but it's not his fault."

Nor was it Koscuisko's.

What Koscuisko had done to him had not made him the moral cripple that he was. He had always been a moral cripple. Koscuisko had only put the fact in front of him, where he could not avoid recognizing the truth of it. That was all. For that, Koscuisko deserved his thanks; and yet Ferinc could not imagine trying to explain any such thing to him.

Maybe to Stanoczk. Maybe. If Stanoczk would speak to him. If the Malcontent did not send him away from Cousin Stanoczk forever, and try some different approach to the reconciliation that was his right—even though he was a slave.

"Some lacks are never going to be made up," Stildyne said, in a voice that was almost sad. Almost. But this was Stildyne. On the other hand, Koscuisko had Stildyne, too. "The dogs in this house are cherished more tenderly than I ever was, Haster. Ferinc. Sorry."

As if Stildyne was thinking about his past, and not his present.

"I'll be away." Ferinc needed to see Marana, and then he needed to run. He would go to the chapter-house at Brikarvna. Stanoczk would know where to find him there. "I'm sorry for the trouble I've caused you, Brachi. I should have known better than to try to steal a glimpse."

It was an echo from a long time ago. Warrant to warrant. Stildyne smiled. "Yes," he agreed. "You should have. But it's lucky for the troops that they caught you, all the same, or I'd have had them on remedials for months."

And he could have been in Stildyne's place. He could have been Stildyne. Chief Warrant Officer. Trusted and valued, and rejoicing in the care and tutelage of professional Security troops, only one step short of the Ship's First Officer.

To be Stildyne, he would have had to have been Stildyne all along, though. Stildyne hadn't ever minded taking advantage of opportunities. But he'd taken much less advantage than Ferinc. Stildyne had always been a practical man. Ferinc had been a bully—he knew that—and bullies were trying to conceal the fear within themselves, and Koscuisko had opened him up and laid it bare in front of the entire world.

So he could not have been Stildyne. There was comfort in that realization that Ferinc took with him to go to see Marana, and say good-bye to her.

Someone came quietly into the room, closing the great double doors behind them. That was odd. Andrej hadn't heard anybody ask for permission. Maybe he'd been too caught up in his own misery to have noticed.

"For one day merely I leave you to your own devices," someone said, in a deep voice that was both distressed and bantering at once. "And what do I return to find? You have ruined my poor Ferinc, Derush, and I particularly wanted to beg you to forgive him, and grant him peace."

Cousin Stanoczk.

Andrej raised his head from his palms and blinked, trying to focus. What time was it?

"Have you called for rhyti, Stoshik?" Andrej was thirsty. It was probably past mid-meal. "Sit. Talk to me. I need to speak to you. But what is this of so-called Cousin Ferinc, first of all."

He couldn't keep the disgust out of his voice. The shock had been too great. Stanoczk went back to the doors and let the servants in to lay the table; Andrej watched the process dully.

Stanoczk poured a flask of rhyti and sweetened it with a liberal hand. The servants left. He brought the flask of rhyti over to where Andrej sat behind the desk and set it down at Andrej's hand; seating himself on the desk's surface beside it.

"He is a deserter, Derush. He came five years ago, no, six years ago, about a year after you had taken his discipline on yourself, and spared him legal sanctions. We intercepted him on his way into Azanry as a tourist. Fleet said that we might keep him or send him back. And we had learned the story from him, or as much as he was capable of telling us."

It was good rhyti. Andrej took another drink, and his mind began to sharpen. "Why deserter?"

Stanoczk shrugged. "His life had become intolerable to him, Andrej. You proved him to himself all too effectively. We considered that it was your intervention that had sent him to us, and made the offer, and were accepted."

An outlander, taken into the embrace of the Malcontent. It was unheard of. "Nothing that was done to him was worse than he had done, Stoshik. The Saint owes him nothing. He is a corrupt man."

Cousin Stanoczk shrugged again. "Yes, but it was you, Derush, and you are so much better at it than he ever was. Your impact was all the more shattering. And the Saint's proper business is with damaged goods. It is our holy charge, you know that; those who are pure and uncompromised have their choice of Saints, but for Ferinc there is only the Malcontent or to be damned."

Andrej couldn't argue with him on that. Cousin Stanoczk was the expert, after all. So instead Andrej said the thing that troubled him most deeply about finding Girag here at the Matredonat.

"Knowing what he was, though, Stanoczk, you let him come here, to this house, and endear himself to my son. To my son, Stoshik. How could you put my child at such a risk? Girag should hate me. The Holy Mother only knows what such a man might do to be revenged."

Marana had said something about Ferinc earlier, when they had spoken together in the garden. What had it been?

"You would be happier if he did hate you, I think, Derush," Cousin Stanoczk said gently. "He does not. You terrify him still. He knows that he has been a sinner. He has learned to do the Malcontent's work here honestly and honorably. He teaches Anton to love you every day, Derush, you will not deny his worth once you have come to know him better."

Andrej didn't like the way this conversation was trending. He stood up to distance himself from what Stanoczk would say, taking the flask of rhyti with him. "Well, I am home, Stoshik," he said. "And mean to remain here. I have told no one but Marana. So there is to be no need of Malcontents to teach my son to love his father. You can have him back. Take him away. I don't want to see him here. Ever again."

Stanoczk stayed where he was, sitting on the desk with his back to the room. "Perhaps it is so," Stanoczk said. "But for the goodwill he has nurtured in your child there are thanks owing, Andrej, and the Malcontent has a word to say to you about your household. Will you hear me?"

Andrej wasn't interested. Still, Stoshik was a Malcontent, a religious professional of a particularly dangerous sort. Starting his life once more at home here on Azanry by setting himself at odds with the Saint was not good precedent. A man could have all Saints against him and prosper under the protection of the Malcontent; and if a man outraged the Malcontent, all Saints could not protect him from ruin.

"To you, Stoshik, I listen," Andrej agreed. "And also to Cousin Stanoczk. Out of my respect for your divine Patron, may he wander in bliss." Stanoczk was his cousin, and Andrej loved him, Malcontent or no. Stoshi nodded solemnly, as if accepting the terms Andrej laid down—such as they were.

"You will stay here at home, you said, Andrej?" Stanoczk asked, as if he didn't know. Perhaps he didn't. It was always safest to assume that the Malcontent knew everything, except what one was going to do next. "We seek an understanding with you, Derush, you are your father's son. For the sake of your soul you should forgive Ferinc, and thank him for the good service he has done here these years past."

There was no man free from the Malcontent, no soul without some hidden shame in the past that the Malcontent could use against it. Or was there? Was any of his own shame hidden, shameful as it was? He had never sought to deny the horror of his crimes to himself or to anyone.

Yet he did not want to contemplate the day when his son should start to understand just what he was. Perhaps that was what the Saint held over his head. "You go too far, Stoshik." It was worth consideration—how a man without shame might be invisible to the Malcontent. "Thank him?"

"For the good service he has done you, Andrej, in making you a hero to your son. And strengthening the spirit of the lady your wife, to face her daily trials."

The flask of rhyti Andrej held dropped to the carpeted floor and bounced, splashing hot sweet liquid all over the rug.

Marana.

That was what she had meant when she had said it. *It is not for you to say whether Ferinc should be an obstacle.* He hadn't understood. He had been thinking about other things. Not only Anton, but Marana, was there no end to this nightmare?

But Stanoczk was just telling him. So that he would know. So that he would not be surprised. So that he could rule his household wisely and with benevolence and charity. No man might raise his hand against the Malcontent. Stanoczk was only warning him, for his own good.

"If a man is to thank the enemy that comes into his home and woos his child and corrupts his wife, then a man is not the master of his household." This was beyond all imagination. Stanoczk could not be serious. "Suppose instead I hunt this person down and scourge him naked from my boundaries, Stoshik, what penance must I pay for such a crime as that?"

Stanoczk stirred himself from the desk to come and take a napkin from the table that the servants had laid, crouching down at Andrej's feet to blot the spilt rhyti up from the rug. "You will do nothing of the sort, Derush," Stanoczk scolded, but very gently. "If you spoke again to Ferinc, you would know it is not revenge on his part. It has been the ordeal we set him to in order to test the quality of his obedience, to send him here. It is our fault if he loves your child. Promise to consider that you might forgive him, Derush; it is deserved, I attest it to you in the name of the Saint himself."

To consider the possibility of forgiving Girag for coming here was distasteful, but at least Andrej could agree to do so much and still be honest. "I have said he is not to show himself to me again, Stoshik. But I will talk to Anton. Perhaps Marana also. And I will consider my debt accordingly. Yes. I promise."

Stanoczk was done mopping up rhyti, and fixed himself a flask. "Good, it is well. Thank you. Now also your Stildyne. You have no cause to hold him so far from you, Andrej. You owe so great a debt that you cannot repay."

Outrageous. "When was it that I invited you into my bed, Stoshik? You exceed all bounds of propriety."

Stanoczk turned to face Andrej, very serious. "Well. We were told that there was an issue, Derush, that required the intervention of my Patron. And it is my only pleasure in life, to meddle in the private lives of other people, having none myself. You cannot blame me."

Stanoczk had hardly ever been serious a moment in his entire life. It was how Stanoczk managed the pain that had propelled him into the embrace of the Malcontent. Had Stanoczk not been Dolgorukij, it could have been much simpler; he need not have suffered for desiring men if he had been born to a more liberal culture. Stoshi could have been born Chigan, and been happy.

"True enough." Stanoczk looked at him; Andrej could only admit to the plain fact. "Have you been told also what it is, this issue? Or does the ritual require that I lay it at your feet in plain language?"

"That would be telling," Stanoczk said. "Speak to me, Andrej, in what way can my divine Patron reconcile you to the life that the Holy Mother has decreed for you beneath the Canopy?"

Maybe it was just as well to do it now. He was already benumbed by shock and distress. What better time to talk about his own death?

"You brought to me Specialist Ivers yesterday, Stoshik." The document was in a secure drawer in the library desk, along with the other things he had for his cousin. He had put them there this morning, when he had come down for his interview with Jils Ivers. "Did you ever know another Bench specialist who worked with her? Garol Vogel."

"Garol Aphon Vogel." Stanoczk nodded. "Yes. A sour and

suspicious man, Andrej. I like him." *Like,* not *liked.* That was potentially interesting. Ivers had said that Vogel had not been heard from.

"I saw him last at Burkhayden, it has been some months. The last time I spoke to him he gave me this, and suggested that I seek the advice of the Malcontent."

The Bench warrant. Andrej drew it out of its secure place and passed it to his cousin, whose dark eyes widened at the sight of it. Yes. Stanoczk knew what a Bench warrant looked like.

"In the shortest possible statement, Stanoczk, someone wants me dead, and has the means to get the Bench endorsement. I must know how to protect myself, if I can. If I cannot, there is no sense in asking me to forgive Haster Girag, as I will not be available to do any such thing. Help me, Stoshik."

In silence Stanoczk took the Bench warrant and opened it out in careful hands, looking thoughtfully at what elements Andrej could not guess.

Andrej could wait for Stanoczk to meditate on the document, and its meaning. He had something else in his desk. While Stanoczk turned the Bench warrant over in his hands and held it up against the light, Andrej took the notebooks out of the secured drawer, stacking them in chronological order.

He had almost forgotten all about them. But in Burkhayden he had had a dream that had reminded him of what a treasure he possessed, and how little he deserved it, and what his responsibility to posterity was with regard to it.

Finally Stanoczk sighed, and put the Bench warrant away in his blouse. "We cannot allow it, Derush, we rely on you for the future. I will submit the problem. What else?"

"I might ask you, Stoshik," Andrej, countered. "A man does not seek aid from the Malcontent without paying the price."

Cousin Stanoczk shook his head. "My Patron does you no favors, Derush. This is a question of Combine politics. You have the natural right to demand the Saint's protection, without prejudice. I can't pretend to extort concessions. Unless you would be kind to my Ferinc. I've become fond of him, Derush."

Andrej could only shake his head in wearied wonder.

"You are all surprises today, Stanoczk. I have these documents. I need them to be safe and secured, if I am dead. They will be worth much more than money, in a generation's time."

And the Malcontent would know best how to conserve the information for the Nurail, still forbidden access to their own cultural heritage by the bitter and unreasoning enmity of the Bench. What Andrej had belonged to them, and had to be cherished carefully till it could safely be returned.

"This is then what, Derush?" Stanoczk asked, curious, picking up one of the notebooks to leaf through it. "Your penmanship has not improved with time, I must say."

Andrej had to smile at that. "The circumstances were challenging. It was at the Domitt Prison, Stoshik. The Nurail there had no chance to pass their weaves except to me who was their torturer, but were willing to use even their own murderer as the tool to see the weaves remembered. Written down."

Stanoczk let the leaves of the notebook riffle through his fingers. "It explains the hurried hand, I suppose. Does anybody know? They are proscribed under Jurisdiction, Derush, on pain of offense against the Bench itself."

Yes and no. "Nurail may not sing their weaves, Stoshik, but there is no law that says a Dolgorukij may not write them down if it suits his fancy. Also I hold the Writ to Inquire, and may do many things with impunity forbidden other men."

"Such as to my Ferinc," Stanoczk agreed, but as if it was by the way. "I should not grudge you that. You did not ruin him. Had you not destroyed him he might never have reclaimed his sweet humility, which I love. Only you are not to tell him that, because I have little enough influence with him as it is, and should he realize that I am fond, he will take advantage, and be misery to deal with. More misery, rather."

Andrej didn't want to talk about Ferinc. He didn't want to think about him. "Will you take these? There will come a time when the Nurail will have leave to come and find them, and they must be safe till then."

Stanoczk nodded. "I will go to Chapter, Derush, and put these in trust for the future, and ask about the warrant. When I return to go with you to Chelatring Side, I will tell you what the Saint may have found out."

There was nothing more that Andrej could do about it until Stanoczk came back, then. And he needed to speak to his Security before the sun set on the day. The news would come out. He had a clear duty to his people that they should hear of it from him.

"And I in turn will sound out my child and his mother, and give careful thought to if I should tolerate that your Ferinc breathes the same air as I do. It is my pledge to you, Cousin."

Stanoczk came to embrace him, but informally, as his kinsman rather than as a Malcontent. "It really is so good to see you, Derush," Stanoczk said. "You have been away for so long. Your family has missed you. I have missed you. Save a place at supper for me, in six days' time."

Andrej nodded, unwilling to speak, feeling overwhelmed by a species of nostalgia for the place where he was, the place where he could stay, the place that was his place. Stanoczk let himself out, with the notebooks—and the Bench warrant—secure in his custody.

An hour. He would take an hour to compose himself. Then he would have to tell Stildyne that he was not going to go back with him to the *Ragnarok*.

CHAPTER NINE

The Appropriate Channels

Marana had gotten a late start to the day, late in rising, much later in dressing, and only now was sitting down in the nursery office to review the status of Anton's lessons with the house's master of children's education.

"The lesson plans have fallen a little behind, Respected Lady, but it is only to be expected," Housemaster Janich said, but comfortingly. "Under the circumstances. Our young lord's father does not come home every day."

Marana closed the schedule log carefully. Nor would their young lord's father be coming home ever again; he was here to stay. But it was for Andrej to make the announcement.

"Still, this is a lag of three days." The single most pernicious fault that Aznir culture found with the members of its hereditary aristocracy was in the tendency of many to substitute privilege for perception. "How are we to recover?"

Anton Andreievitch had needed the very best education because he had been fated for a life as a bastard child, who could reasonably expect a good position within the Koscuisko familial corporation, but whose performance would be under constant scrutiny by the partisans of legitimate children jealous to ensure that no undue special favor was shown him. Now she didn't have to worry about that any longer.

Now Anton needed an even better education, because he was to inherit the controlling interest in the familial corporation one day. Then history would judge her worth as a mother, and the value of her love for Andrej Ulexeievitch, by the prosperity that Koscuisko should enjoy during Anton Andreievitch's tenure as its master.

Therefore she would have to pay twice as much attention to Anton's lesson plans. The family would do its best to intervene, to take control of so important a task away from her. She would be ready to defend her primacy; she would accept help, but she would not yield control. Anton was her son.

Janich frowned. "The young lord does well with his languages, Respected Lady. Perhaps some time could be found in the schedule for Standard grammar and syntax. I will create a recovery plan, if this suggestion meets with your approval."

And above all else Anton had to be allowed to be a child. It was lucky that he was intelligent and biddable; he did his lessons with as much diligence as one could ask any child his age, and learned them well. Ferinc helped Anton with his language. How was that going to work, with Andrej home?

"Thank you, house-master. We might find a way to do a science lesson outside of the classroom as well. If it can be worked into Anton's play."

Ferinc was here, standing in the open doorway to the nursery office, looking very pale. Janich had noticed Ferinc as well. "Very good, Respected Lady, until next time. With your permission."

Janich had gotten more formal with her. Before Andrej had come home, she had been "Respected Lady," but no one had taken leave of her "with her permission."

Ferinc stood aside, smiling in wordless response to Janich's greeting as the house-master left the room. Marana stood up and waited for Ferinc, who closed the door.

"What is it that they say about Malcontents, Respected Lady? That there is no trust or honesty in them?"

Something had happened. Ferinc was much worked upon by some emotion or another. Andrej knew about Ferinc; he had told her so in words that implied without accusing, earlier today, in the maze in the garden. Had there been some terrible sort of confrontation?"

"They say such things about all Malcontents." Not Ferinc. Ferinc was her very great comfort. Almost her friend. "What is it, Ferinc?"

Ferinc reached into his blouse for a case of some sort, as long and as broad as her hand. No, as his hand, and Ferinc had long hands. Wincing slightly. "I'm lucky these boxes are as crushproof as they are, Marana, or else it would have been all over. Has the fish survived?"

Marana opened the case. A wheat-fish, secure in a padded container, carefully wrapped to avoid breaking off any fragment of the long whiskers in the beards of the heads of grain that had been used to plait the ancient good-luck charm. "How is that have you been scuffling? Ferinc."

He was looking at the wheat-fish, not at her. "I'm glad. You must give it to Anton for me, Marana, and tell him that I love him, but I have to go away on the Malcontent's business. The thing I never told you was that I had known your husband, once, under different circumstances. He has forbidden me to see his son."

In all this time, Ferinc had given no hint—"He has good reason, Marana," Ferinc added hastily. "The Malcontent knew, of course, but there are personal feelings. And. To be honest. I never meant to love either of you."

It was worse than just that Andrej had discovered Ferinc to be her lover, before she had been able to come up with a good strategy for telling him. She had been the lover of a man whom Andrej had known, and did not like.

There were so many questions that she wanted to ask. *Were you a criminal? Why doesn't he want you to see Anton? Is he jealous? What is it? Doesn't he realize that Anton loves you? Not that I—*

Ferinc was Malcontent, and any such questions were not to be asked. Marana swallowed hard, instead. "You deserve better for your care of Anton." He had been as tender a parent as any woman could wish, and Anton was not even his son. "Is this to be forever, Ferinc?"

Too much was changing too fast. She had not thought far enough ahead, perhaps. There had been too much to do to cope with the immediate changes resulting from Andrej's declaration of the Sacred-art-thous to leave her any room to think on more than the issues that lay directly before her.

Ferinc stood very close, and touched the hair beside her face. But not her face. "It's his concern that makes him stern. So if Cousin

Stanoczk can speak for me perhaps I'll be allowed to see Anton. But you, Respected Lady, you owe your husband duty and honor, and a chance to be your husband. You know it's true."

Yes. She knew. It didn't make it any easier, though.

"What becomes of us, if Andrej and I marry?" In the true sense, rather than the formal sense. "Ferinc. All of this time." He had been so great a comfort to her. She was torn between the duty that she owed Andrej, both as a man and as her husband, her duty to be honest and true; and reluctance, inability, to discard five years and more of Ferinc's quiet support.

"I will think about you on cold lonely nights, and wonder if you miss me," Ferinc said. But wickedly. There was a streak of play running throughout his personality that took much of the sting out of even so melancholy a thing to say as that. "And tire my lover with I-remember-when until she kicks me out of bed, and bids me go hang myself. And then it will truly be a cold and lonely night."

She'd known that it was going to come to this. Part of her had known that, anyway. She took him by the braids on either side of his face and kissed him, very carefully. *Good-bye.*

They didn't embrace. The kiss was enough. He looked at her for a long moment, as if he was committing her face to memory and smiled, fondly, without much pain.

Then he kissed her nose. "Give Anton his fish," Ferinc reminded her. "And my excuses. I've got to go. Thy lord has sent me away, and we don't like to provoke the inheriting prince, because we have to apologize and it's the wrong direction for the Malcontent's preferred mode of operation, isn't it?"

It was the end for them, one way or another. Andrej was to stay. If they were lovers ever again, it would be different. That was unavoidable. " 'Till later, Ferinc."

Nodding, Ferinc left, and closed the door again behind him. She was alone. She owed Andrej a chance to be her husband in a modern, Standard way, as well as the traditional manner. She'd see what he had to say to her about Ferinc, and then decide.

But now she would carry a wheat-fish to Anton at his lessons, and interrupt his day just to tell him that Cousin Ferinc had loved him.

Stildyne set a watch on Lek to be sure he remained at peace with his governor, and went back to his room to see whether the bottle of liquor that was there was alcoholic throughout.

In time he began to sense a particular fragrance in the corridor through his open doorway, and knew that Koscuisko was on his way. Lefrols. Koscuisko's smokes. A peculiar weed, and foully odiferous, but it meant Koscuisko to Stildyne, and that was usually a good thing. Even when it was a bad thing.

Koscuisko hadn't changed since the morning, and it was late afternoon. He looked as though he had been sleeping on the desk, with his head buried in a pile of bound text—his face was creased, his eyelids falling half shut.

Coming into the room Koscuisko closed the door, and sat down, and reached for Stildyne's glass. There was only one glass on the table. That would explain it. For a moment Stildyne was alarmed, because Koscuisko could drink him under the table and tended to run through bottles of liquor at a phenomenal rate when he was minded to self-medicate; then he relaxed. This was Koscuisko's home ground. He probably had barrels of the stuff.

"What is it," Koscuisko asked, holding out the emptied tumbler for a refill. "About what name you should be called. Talk to me about this, Mister Stildyne."

Why not? Haster Girag had raised hard truths about Stildyne's past that he'd never shared with Koscuisko; and he had been drinking. Koscuisko was doubtless already skeptically disposed toward him after the morning's revelations; if he was going to quarrel with Koscuisko, he might as well do it when he didn't have to compromise a period of amity and good communication to say what was on his mind.

" 'Chief,' " Stildyne said. "And 'Mister.' Never Stildyne, I suppose I could understand that, not without a 'Chief' or a 'Mister.' Robert you love. Him you call Robert. Lek maybe you don't love so much as Robert, but you call him Lek anyway."

Koscuisko watched his face, as though waiting for him to make his point. "Mister Stildyne. I call my orderlies also Heron and Diris and Lupally. A man should not call responsible people by their first names. It is not of due respect showing."

Koscuisko's dialect was deteriorating. They'd been here for some days now. The house staff spoke Standard, by and large, when they were talking in front of Koscuisko's Security, but Stildyne strongly suspected that they all spoke their own language when they were alone. Or speaking to Koscuisko.

"Well, where I come from, you call a man by his last name when you have no relationship. But people that you know you call by first name."

That wasn't exactly true. He didn't come from anywhere in particular. It was just a conflict between styles—his style, Koscuisko's style—and Koscuisko had the rank, so it was not unreasonable for Koscuisko to assume that his style should define the terms of the relationship. It was all just the issue of whether there was a relationship. Of course there was a relationship. Stildyne was a Chief Warrant Officer, Koscuisko was his officer of assignment. That was a relationship.

"Were you with Girag then on the basis of Brachi and Haster?" Koscuisko asked, thoughtfully. It was not a challenge or a taunt; it was just a question. It was very, very good cortac brandy; it seemed to slip down almost by itself.

To everlasting confusion with it all. Stildyne poured the glass Koscuisko sought and kept it for himself, passing the bottle back. Less effort that way. The bottle needed refilling less often than the glass. "I'm not sure I remember. There was a crew of us at a Fleet base at Gotrane. We probably didn't know each other all that well."

Koscuisko took the bottle but didn't drink from it, looking around him absentmindedly—for the glass. Stildyne knew that was what Koscuisko was looking for. "One is on intimate terms with one's house-masters, but one does not call them by their private names, Brachi. Unless it is in private. And I dared not ever use Chief Samons's name but once in my life that I can remember, because it was so important to try to avoid noticing what a spectacular beauty she was."

Brachi. Koscuisko had said it. Koscuisko was not drunk—or nothing like as drunk as he had to be before he started to get sentimental. He was not teetering on the brink of total psychological collapse. No one held fire to the soles of his naked feet, and that was just as well, because Stildyne would have had to kill them had anyone tried. Stildyne himself was more drunk than Koscuisko, and on only a little more liquor.

"Nor wished ever to use mine. For fear of being misinterpreted," Stildyne said sourly, being drunk. Rising to his feet, he went to the drinks cabinet and took out a clean glass for Koscuisko. And another bottle of something. Just now he didn't care what it was, exactly, so long as it had alcohol in it. "Now you are three times as determined. Now that you've heard about my past."

Koscuisko looked at the empty glass Stildyne set down before him for a long moment. Sighing, Stildyne plucked up the bottle from Koscuisko's hand and poured; then at last Koscuisko seemed to realize that it was meant for him.

"Your past distresses me, Brachi, but it is past. And means you are more greatly to be honored for that you have changed your manner."

No, it didn't. He hadn't left off taking the occasional bite out of a bond-involuntary because he had developed any moral scruples. He had learned not to take advantage of them because Koscuisko disapproved. And that was all.

If there was more to it, Stildyne didn't even want to know. He'd heard about morality. It seemed an unnecessary complication to life in an unjust and uncertain world. Koscuisko had opened his mouth as if to say something, and then closed it again. Stildyne waited.

"And I have struggled this day with how to say this to you, Brachi. But I also have a chance to step away from abuse of those within my power. It is the message that Ivers has brought."

What was Koscuisko saying? Koscuisko had never abused his Security, nor any member of his staff—except the orderly who'd been caught stealing drugs. Koscuisko had beaten her very thoroughly for that, and then forgotten to report the crime to the Captain or the First Officer, to keep the woman from prison. So far as Stildyne knew, there had never been any further problem with the orderly in question.

"You meant to come home last year, sir." So there was only one other thing else that Koscuisko could possibly be talking about. And only one thing it could mean. "Has there been some movement on the part of Chilleau Judiciary?"

Chilleau was expected to put a bid in for First Judge, and it would be a solid bid. As far as Stildyne's limited interest in politics went, he understood it to be a very real candidacy. Koscuisko was Stildyne's officer, but—though it had been easy to overlook on board the *Ragnarok*—Koscuisko was in fact a great deal more. Chilleau Judiciary would want Koscuisko's voice on their side. Stilled, if not raised in active support.

"I have executed documentation. It was this morning. I only heard last night. And I so much regret leaving the people behind, Brachi, but I am to be relieved of Writ and sin no more against the natural laws of decency."

I so much regret leaving you behind, Stildyne thought to himself. A fantasy; but an appealing one. When what Koscuisko meant was Lek, and Smish, and Pyotr, and Taller, and Murat. Godsalt. Robert St. Clare.

Stildyne knew what Koscuisko's people would feel when they found out. It was pure selfishness of him to wish Koscuisko bound to his Writ, in order to have him back on the *Ragnarok*.

"Revocation of Bond, then, in a sense." Freedom unimagined and wonderful. "We'll all be very happy for you, sir. I'll write to you. If you would like to hear."

Lowden was dead, and unlamented. Stildyne didn't know anything much about ap Rhiannon, but he knew that First Officer had been taking careful notes, over the years, of the ways in which Koscuisko had protected his people. First Officer was a very intelligent man, for an officer. It wasn't going to be the same with Koscuisko gone, but it was never going back to Lowden days. Stildyne was sure of that.

Koscuisko nodded, in apparent appreciation of Stildyne's calm acceptance. Calm on the surface, at least. He had believed Koscuisko to be going home less than a year ago; he had had practice in imagining his life without Koscuisko in it.

Whomever they assigned as Chief Medical Officer could hardly be one-eighth the trouble that Koscuisko had been. If they assigned a new Chief Medical Officer at all, with senior officers in such demand these days.

"I should speak to the gentles," Koscuisko said. "Do you tell them first? Or do I?"

"I'll do the dirty deed, sir. Let it alone. You can make a speech when we say good-bye. When do we leave?"

If Koscuisko had accepted relief of Writ, Stildyne's people didn't have an officer of assignment any more. Technically speaking, they probably should be on the next courier out to rejoin the *Ragnarok*, bringing the news with them.

"You shall not, before time," Koscuisko said, decidedly. "The Bench specialist says that there will be some days before the documentation is complete. And that until my codes have been revoked, I am still entitled to the Bench's protection as a Bench officer rather than a private person. And it was to have been a holiday."

A good story. It would probably work, too, especially with the backing of the Bench specialist. If Chilleau Judiciary wanted Koscuisko's goodwill this badly, they were unlikely to risk tainting the enthusiasm of his endorsement by petty insistence on the proper allocation of Fleet security resources.

"I'll tell them," Stildyne repeated. "It's my job. You'd better go and dress, your Excellency—it will be dinner soon."

Koscuisko nodded, accepting both direction and the reasoning behind it. The simple gesture went to Stildyne's heart; would he ever again have an officer who listened so well to him? Rising to his feet Koscuisko went to open the door, to leave the room; but paused with his hand on the latch-lever.

"Will you come to me, when you retire?" Koscuisko asked. "I would welcome you to join my household. Though you would almost never hear yourself called Brachi, even then."

There was no point Stildyne could see to it. But no sense in giving gratuitous offense. Koscuisko doubtless meant well, even if it was plainly guilt that had inspired the offer.

"Thank you, your Excellency. I'd be honored." He was years short of being able to retire, if he lived that long. Koscuisko would have forgotten all about it, when the time came. Or if Koscuisko hadn't, Stildyne would have come up with some good excuse, by then.

Still, why not? Since he had nowhere else under Jurisdiction to be, why not find a comfortable berth among the many members of his Excellency's household in which to spend his declining years?

Because he wouldn't take favors from Koscuisko. He'd die sooner than turn into Cousin Ferinc, never recovered from Koscuisko's mark on him, obsessed and distracted to this day.

Koscuisko bent his head and left the room. Stildyne sighed, and put the bottle away from him, and left the room himself to go to find some rhyti in the kitchen. To give himself time to think, and sober up, and make up his mind on how he was to tell Koscuisko's people that they were going home to the *Ragnarok* without Koscuisko, who had taken such good care of them over the years.

⊕ ⊕ ⊕

In the summertime the light lasted beyond the hour at which a young lord should properly retire to his bed, making the young master of the house fractious with reluctance to go to sleep.

Marana sat in the master's parlor after dinner stitching a piece of fancywork, waiting, listening. Andrej sat at the desk next to the double-harp and read over accounts. She knew that it was not because he was concerned, but because he was expected to review the journals when he came back to his house, and assure himself that the books had been honestly and honorably maintained in his absence. He would have to call an assembly within a day or two and thank the house-masters in each department for their good husbandry of his resources, and distribute tokens of his appreciation and approval. Tradition.

Not all of the traditions of family life were in church records or the acts of saints, however. Andrej had been away for years. She owed him her decision, and she owed it to the love that they had once borne for each other to make it soon.

There was a pounding of young feet down the carpeted corridor outside the room, a gleeful shriek of slightly manic excitement; it was Anton, pursued by his devoted but distraught nurse, coming flying into the room with something in his hand.

When Anton saw his father in the room he stopped, visibly taken aback, unsure of how he was to proceed without error. Anton's delight in his treasure was too much for his dignity, though, even in the presence of his awesome and alien father; smiling, Anton advanced upon Andrej, holding out his prize.

"Look what I have here, lord father, Cousin Ferinc has brought me a wheat-fish. From Dubrovnije."

Andrej had half turned from the desk to face his child, holding a stylus in his left hand, arrested in mid-notation by Anton's unexpected appearance. She could not read his face. Ferinc had told her that there'd been history between them; but Anton loved Ferinc. Now, which would rule? The personal disgust that Andrej had for Ferinc, or a true father's willingness to be tender of his child's passions, and handle them with care and with respect?

"Indeed?" Andrej asked Anton, his voice soft and affectionate. "May I see?"

Anton stood at his father's side as Andrej admired the wheat-fish, with its fine black beard and its gleaming body of woven golden straw. Two blond heads bent over a wheat-fish, Anton gazing up at his father's face with transparent adoration, Andrej's own face shadowed by the tilt of his head but concentrated clearly on his son. She had never seen Andrej so strongly in Anton, ever before. The visceral reminder of who Anton was and why it was that he should be so like Andrej caught her by surprise, a movement in her belly as though Andrej's hand lay across her womb where Anton had been cradled as he grew.

"I was having my lesson. He gave it to my lady mother. I must write him a note . . . " No, Ferinc had brought it to her and fled, because Andrej had told him that he wasn't to see Anton ever again. But he had kept his promise to Anton. "Isn't it fine? I have never seen so nice a wheat-fish in my life."

Marana smiled, but she was still waiting to know what Andrej would do.

"This is very special, I think," Andrej said, playing his fingers delicately along the long beard of the grain heads. "No common wheat-fish has so black a beard. I am impressed. Ferinc must have picked it out for you very carefully. I'd better give it back to you, though, and you must take very good care of it, and tell him your thanks for his kindness."

Black-bearded grain was the most holy. Andrej was right; it was a special fish. Andrej would have been within his rights as a Dolgorukij parent to have taken it away and destroyed it; Anton had not asked Andrej's permission to accept gifts from a man who was not related to him. Andrej did not. Andrej praised the wheat-fish and its donor and Anton's keeping of it instead. It was his pledge. There were to be no recriminations.

"Ferinc is very good to me, sir. I wish I could have taken him to meet you. But I didn't have the chance."

"Perhaps next time, son Anton. I am sure he must be a very good friend to you to have brought you this fine gift. Go and show your lady mother. And then you must go with your nurse."

Anton took his wheat-fish and kissed his father's cheek with spontaneous affection, pure and true. Andrej had passed. Andrej had declined to slander Ferinc to Anton who loved him, though Andrej himself, by Ferinc's report, despised the Malcontent. He had earned the right to try with her, to see if they could be wedded again as fiercely as they had once been, before they were married.

Marana praised Anton's treasure, kissed him, sent him away; and stood up. Andrej had turned away from the desk to look after Anton and watched her now, his attention apparently arrested. Setting her needlework aside, Marana closed on Andrej across the floor of the parlor.

When she was less than an arm's length from him she put her hand up to her hair, slowly, keeping her eyes fixed upon his face all the while; and pulled one of the long bone pins that kept her headdress secure, loosing a thick braided strand of her heavy, wheat-colored hair. His pale eyes were darker by the moment as the pupils widened; an encouraging sign. Holding out the pin, she waited for Andrej to raise his hand to receive it, dropping it into his open palm.

One moment longer she stood, looking at him. He'd said nothing to her about Ferinc. If he said nothing now, he never would. She turned around. Slowly, she walked out of the room, doing her best not to strain her ears to hear if Andrej had got up to follow her. She was willing to try to reach out to him. Was he willing to meet her midway?

He was behind her.

He followed her down the hall to the bedroom. Marana plucked the pins out of her hair one by one as she went, Andrej following after to gather them up as they fell, and her hair draped ever more loosely around her shoulders with every discarded pin.

The bedroom door stood open; the servants had been here. The curtains were drawn back from the great bed, the lamps turned to a welcoming yellow glow, the windows open to the deepening twilight to let the cool air come into the room. Andrej shut the door.

She was too shy of him to turn around, and that was humorous, because she was the one who had laid claim. Andrej was close behind her, at her back; he put the thick hair away from the back of her neck with a careful hand and kissed her there, thoughtfully. It made her shiver.

Andrej seemed to find that an encouragement. Lacing his fingers through her hair he kissed her neck, her throat, at the back and the side of it, with contemplative moderation. Pressing his lips against her skin; tasting the salt of her body with a considering tongue, slowly.

She turned around, with her long hair trailing slowly through the open fingers of Andrej's right hand. He wore country-dress, very informal. She had not seen his body in all this time, and yet his body was her property, in a sense. She had a right to assess its condition.

She opened the front plaquet of his simple smock, the embroidered band that ran down the front of the garment from shoulder to hem, offset from the collar by the traditional hand's span. Since it was summer, the garment that he wore beneath was as thin as gauze; the heat of his skin beneath her fingertips, even through his undergarment, brought the blood to her cheek, as though she stood too near the fireplace.

Smoothing the open smock back along his shoulders, she put her palms flat to his undershirt and felt the flesh beneath. Andrej. There was something still familiar about the fall of his ribs as they belled toward his diaphragm, the contours of his skin stretched over them; her hands remembered.

She needed the heat of him. She was cold. She put her hand to the back of his neck to draw his mouth down to hers for a kiss, but there was something at the back of his neck that startled her, and she drew away from him with her mouth still half open as it had been to seek his mouth. There was a line, there, across the back of his neck, beneath his skin, between the back of his ears and his hairline at the nape of his neck.

A scar. She touched it with her fingers, and Andrej stood with his hands at her waist and waited for her to be satisfied. Scars. Why was he scarred there? Where else was he scarred, that he had never mentioned to her in his letters?

Sliding his hands up from her waist Andrej gathered her to him and kissed her mouth. She could feel the tension gather in his body. There were his fingers at the back of her shoulders pulling the knot of her kerchief free, pulling the kerchief itself away from her shoulders; uncovering her bosom. It was summertime; her dress had no sleeves. There was no obstacle to interfere with Andrej's unbuttoning her bodice and peeling the fabric open, down her arms, to the floor.

He held her with an arm around her waist and slipped his fingers beneath the garment's neckline to touch the naked skin of her softly rounded shoulders. The sensation made her catch her breath. Andrej's breath seemed to come a little shakily on his own part; he turned the neckline of her undergarment back to bare her shoulder and kissed her where her neck met her body, and shuddered with desire.

Skin. She wanted skin. He was distracted; he was not paying attention. Taking a fistful of linen in each hand Marana tugged up and away to free his undergarment from the waistband of his full trousers. The undergarment had no fastening; it wrapped across the front of Andrej's body, and in the winter it would close with ties—but for now, once she had the hem free, it was easy to pull open and away.

Marana backed away, toward the bed; Andrej watched her go. She looked into his face, wondering if he had second thoughts. She felt so naked, with Andrej watching her. It was intolerable that she should be timid in front of him.

Marana shook her head, and her hair settled like a fine spun shawl across her shoulders. Andrej closed his eyes and bit his lip, the fish that had carried his half of their child into her ocean stiffening visibly beneath his wrap even at several paces remove. Yes. That was better.

She climbed onto the bed, unfastening her hip-wrap as she went. Andrej followed her, his mind apparently focused on her shoulders. Rolling beneath him on the bed's surface, Marana tucked her thumbs beneath the band of his hip-wrap, and then that was gone, too.

Here was the fish in which they had both once delighted. Marana embraced it between her palms and stroked it with affectionate greed; she had not had Andrej's fish since the night before Andrej had left the Matredonat, more than nine years ago. It had been a brisk fish, then.

Andrej knelt on the bed and trembled while Marana beguiled herself by caressing him; then he caught her hand away and carried it to his lips to kiss her palm. Taking control of the encounter, prisoning her hands in his to protect himself from the distraction of her touch while he tested the curve of her flesh with kisses, tasting her, drinking her fragrance, relearning the feel of her body against his cheek.

He touched her as carefully as though they had never known each other. In all the years that he had been with Fleet, Andrej had been unlikely to have been celibate; what did his hands remember? Was it one woman? Any five women? Or simply the knowledge of alien woman-flesh?

She had known no other lover but Ferinc while Andrej had been gone. But Andrej had been her first love and her first true lover. Even after all of these years, her body remembered that, and craved the caresses that she and Andrej had practiced together to increase their pleasure in one another.

"Andrej," Marana whispered, hoarsely. "Come to me. I want your fish, Andrej. Let me feel him wriggle to his place."

He raised his head, he shifted his body, he half lay over her with his arms straight to the bed on either side so that she felt the heat of his bare flesh, but had no contact with it. His face was flushed, his mouth gone ruddy, his eyes glittering with erotic intoxication beneath their half-closed lids.

"Come to me," Marana urged him. Using small words, speaking to his fish. Her own minnow, the fishlet between her thighs, surged for the pressure of his body; she was not thinking very clearly herself. "Now."

He settled himself against her. In small and careful steps his fish tested the straits of passage, venturing ever more deeply within her with each trial. He had forgotten what it was to lay with a woman of his own race, perhaps.

She ran her fingers down his back with fierce hunger, pressing as deep into the long muscles on either side of his spine as she had strength. The bending of his back in reflex beneath her hands caught at his hips like pulling at the string of a longbow to bend its tip, and Andrej's fish was at home within her. Hers.

Every thrust of Andrej's fish maddened her minnow even more; the passion that consumed her was beyond naming. It was hot in the room; her skin was on fire, she could feel the sweat on Andrej's belly against hers as his fish strove within her, and the salt scratch of his fish's beard against her body worked upon her flesh like the judgment of Heaven.

He destroyed her.

He was her lover and her husband and the friend of her childhood, and even so he destroyed her without mercy, utterly and entirely, and completely. She screamed in terror and in ecstasy as her entire body caught fire and was consumed from the inside out with living flame.

The bed would burn. The room would catch the blaze, the house would be destroyed. The roof would come down through the blackened structure; they would be buried alive in fire and smoke—

Slowly, very slowly, Andrej collapsed in her arms, and fell over onto the surface of the bed to one side of her. Drowned. The fires cooled as the tides retreated, the bed's cover damp with sweat and exercise. The house would not burn. She carried the ocean within her; they were safe.

Andrej reached out a hand behind him and pulled the bedcovers up from the far side of the bed, pulling her limp body to him away from the rumpled portion of the bed to cover them both with the draped coverlet and rest in the middle of the bed now, together, and for the first time since Andrej had come home. Nestling his face against the back of her shoulder, Andrej slept almost at once.

She rested with him for a little while, her body still shaking within itself in the echoing reverberation of the pleasure he had given her. It was different than when Ferinc loved her. But it had worked. She could still be Andrej's lover; she could be his wife. She could adjust, adapt. There was strangeness to his body—exciting as well as intimidating—and he was not the man that she had known. But neither was she the woman that he might have remembered. It was not impossible that they should begin again, and perhaps be happy.

His sleeping smell had something in it still of the Andrej who had once been hers. Marana set her mind on hope for the future, and slept.

CHAPTER TEN

Alternate Means of Procurement

Cousin Ferinc sat at the receiving station, watching the traffic analysis reports; he didn't pay much attention to the fact that someone had come into the intelligence station until a hand came down on his shoulder. By then it was too late.

"What interests you, Ferinc?"

It was Stanoczk. And Ferinc was to have met with Stanoczk, almost an hour ago. He had let himself become distracted. How could he do that? Stanoczk was his reconciler. And his reconciler was the single most important person in the world to him . . . after Anton Andreievitch, and Marana, and perhaps Andrej Koscuisko.

Turning in his chair Ferinc stood up quickly, taking Stanoczk's hand away from his shoulder to kiss Stanoczk's knuckles in greeting. "Stanoczk. I'm sorry. You startled me."

"You should not have been startled," Stanoczk pointed out. "You should have been waiting for me. Elsewhere. I despair of you, Ferinc. What have you found?"

Sometimes his gratitude for Stanoczk almost overwhelmed him: Stanoczk's patience and forbearance, equable temper and genial goodwill. The hand of the Malcontent rested lightly on Ferinc, because it was Stanoczk's.

"If it's Noycannir, she could have done it." No, wait, that didn't make much sense. "I've found something interesting. It's proximity, but it's suggestive."

Ferinc nodded at his analysis screen, wanting Stanoczk to see, hoping Stanoczk would find the information interesting. Maybe interesting enough to overlook Ferinc's lapse in leaving his own reconciler to wait, and wait, and finally come find him. Malcontents were beaten for lesser faults; more or less frequently, as the need and inclination required.

Stanoczk scanned the screen and raised an eyebrow.

"What does this mean to me, Ferinc?"

Stanoczk had to see it. It was that obvious. "Just look how depressing a person she must be. Over the last three years. Five suicides. Five."

A Clerk of Court on the Second Circuit; an evidence disposition manager at a sub-court headquarters; a Security troop on detached assignment for debriefing of troops at a Fleet station under the Second Judge's aegis. A third-level communications specialist at Chilleau Judiciary.

And his favorite: a documents release controller at Fontailloe Judiciary itself, where the First Judge presided. That one had been carefully investigated at the time, because of the sensitive nature of the dead woman's job. Everything had cleared. Ferinc didn't think they'd looked hard or long enough.

"Ferinc, despair is more bitter a pain than many can bear. Surely you know this." But Stanoczk was still looking at the screen; the cross-tracking, the time elapsed between a personal contact with Mergau Noycannir and the unfortunate death of an officer of the Court by her own hand. "None of them murdered?"

That was the question, of course. In one instance at least, the cause of death had been recorded as due to an overdose of a recreational drug; there had been a record left. The drug had been of such exceptional purity that a pharmacy audit of the Court's administratively attached medical personnel had been conducted. There had been no findings, and the investigators had left it at that.

There was no recorded curiosity about the chemical signature of whatever batch the drug had come from, and Ferinc thought that was a shame, because he was almost ready to convince himself that such a trace would have led far away from the actual site of the incident and back to Chilleau Judiciary.

Maybe the trace *had* been done. Maybe it had led back to Chilleau

Judiciary. Maybe the investigators had assumed a political assassination, and elected for prudence over justice.

"The pattern intrigues, Ferinc," Stanoczk admitted. Ferinc had been confident that it would.

What would one have to do if one set out to accomplish the unthinkable, and subvert the justice of the Bench? Bench warrants did not come out of nowhere. They had to be validated and cross-validated at every step of the process of issue; at any given time, somebody knew where it had come from and where it would be going.

And the further along the process of issue moved, the fewer obvious questions were likely to be asked about the integrity of the validations that the warrant had collected.

When a man came before the Court to argue in the face of the grieving widower's tears that he was guilty of manslaughter, but not murder, for the death of the security guard during an attempted robbery by cause of temporary intoxication depriving him of the use of his reason, it rarely occurred to anyone to ask whether the security guard was dead.

"There is a flaw in the argument, of course," Ferinc pointed out, as Stanoczk frowned over the data. "I am starting from a supposition. So I may be entirely mistaken. But why is it worth so much to her to know exactly where Koscuisko is?"

Stanoczk nodded, but Ferinc hadn't asked a question in a form that Stanoczk could answer with a nod. "I think we need to prefer the question, Ferinc. And also. I have sent the Malcontent's thula to Chelatring Side."

The two halves of that did not quite connect, but they came close enough together that Ferinc could draw the bridge between them. Andrej Koscuisko would arrive at Chelatring Side within five days' time to be present as his father gave the Autocrat's Proxy the wishes of the Koscuisko familial corporation as regarding the Selection of a new First Judge.

The Second Judge was scheduled to announce her candidacy within the next ten days. Now that Verlaine had bought Koscuisko off, there was little doubt that Koscuisko would support the Second Judge.

It was the Malcontent's mission to maximize the concessions that the Combine could demand in return for its support, before Chilleau

Judiciary realized that it would win its bid—and no longer needed to purchase the support of member worlds.

"I could tell Noycannir that Koscuisko stays at home," Ferinc suggested. "There's no telling but that I might be marked for a convenient suicide myself, in the near future. I can feel no particular sense of obligation, with that in mind."

Grinning, Stanoczk shook his head. "There is no such word as suicide in the Malcontent's vocabulary, Ferinc. No. We will fulfill our contract. We do not yet know that her motive is sinister. And . . . "

Ferinc waited. Stanoczk seemed to reconsider what he was about to say. Shaking his head as if to clear it, he continued.

"And she is at Pesadie Training Command, and expected to remain there. Those deaths, they have all occurred after she had been physically present. But you will see to it that the thula is ready should we need to bring news with speed. And open up the Gallery for me, Ferinc. I want to take your Stildyne on a tour."

Ferinc paled. He couldn't help himself. "What business does Stildyne have with the Malcontent?" Even as he asked it he knew the answers, both of them. He knew. And it wasn't his to ask. Stanoczk put a hand to Ferinc's shoulder kindly, but didn't answer; Stanoczk changed the subject, instead.

"You have spoken to the lady?" Yes, several days ago. He hadn't seen Stanoczk since. He hadn't wanted to. He'd had permission to see Marana, but not to create a disturbance in the garden and arouse the wrath of Andrej Koscuisko himself.

"She knows where her duty lies. And accepts it." Willingly, he could have added, except that he wasn't sure how willing that acceptance was. Or how willing he might be that Marana could turn her back on him, and seek the embrace of her lord. "I'm going to miss Anton. Worse than poison."

Not the best choice of phrases, considering the several drug-accomplished deaths—murders, or suicides—that he had just been reviewing. But the point was made. Why did Stanoczk shake his head, as if in wonder?

"What has happened to you, Ferinc?" Stanoczk asked. "You speak as a man with no feeling about the other man, in your life."

What did that mean? Koscuisko? "Did you talk to Koscuisko about me?"

Now Stanoczk snorted in apparent disgust. "Egoist. Have I nothing better to discuss with my own cousin? As though he could be bothered about you, with other issues on his mind."

That was true. Koscuisko had given Stanoczk the Bench warrant on the same day that Ferinc had given Anton's wheat-fish to Marana and fled. Perhaps Koscuisko had been distracted when he'd seen Stanoczk.

"I only wondered. I am forbidden to see Anton until he's had a chance to consult with you and ensure that you know what sort of a depraved creature I am. The sooner you and he have that discussion, the sooner I may seek for visitation rights."

Stanoczk gave him a shove that sent him staggering, but it was pure affection on Stanoczk's part. Ferinc could smell it. "Visitation? And rights! You are Malcontent, Ferinc, or at least we have pretended that you may someday be a Malcontent in fact, and you can speak such a word? You are impossible, Shut up. Get out. Go to Chelatring Side."

He'd forgotten.

"Visitation privileges?" he asked meekly, with a grin he could not quite repress and a sharp eye out for Stanoczk's boot. Stanoczk was quick with his feet, when he was provoked. "Opportunities, options, avenues, potential approaches—"

"Shut up, shut up, shut up!" Stanoczk cried, almost helpless with laughter. "May all Saints witness what I have to do, to treat with such a donkey. Out. Get out. Go. And I will meet you."

Stanoczk was right. Something was changed. He had seen Andrej Koscuisko, and lived. Open up the Gallery, for Stildyne's benefit?

He had a lot of work to do. He needed to get his reply through to Noycannir at Pesadie, still pretending that she was at Chilleau. And then he needed to bestir himself and get into the mountains, to the Koscuisko's stronghold at Chelatring Side on the breast of mighty Dasidar himself, to see to it that the thula—a Kospodar thula, one of only twenty-seven ever made, the fastest ship of its size or any larger under Jurisdiction—was ready to serve the Malcontent's purpose. Whatever that would turn out to be.

He had faced Andrej Koscuisko, and Koscuisko had been angry at him, and he had not fallen to his knees and begged for mercy. The peace of the Malcontent was his at last.

He could even share his reconciler, without too much distress; and hope that Stildyne might find a share of that peace, in the Gallery.

⊕ ⊕ ⊕

There was no signal at the door, and yet it opened.

Admiral Brecinn looked up from her desk with surprised displeasure: who dared enter her office without signaling?

More to the point, who could? The door had been secured—

Mergau Noycannir. Standing there in the now-open doorway with a flat-file docket under one arm. Brecinn could not read Noycannir's expression; the office was dim by choice and the light coming through from the corridor beyond put Noycannir's face into shadow.

"I beg your pardon, Admiral," Noycannir said. She certainly sounded confused and apologetic. "They told me you weren't in. I meant to leave a message."

An important message, no doubt, or else she wouldn't have forced the door's secures to leave it on Brecinn's desk. Brecinn smoothed her involuntary grimace of irritation away with an effort. "Come in, Dame. Close the door."

Yes, she'd had her people say that she was unavailable—especially to Noycannir. Noycannir might ask questions that Brecinn wasn't interested in having to avoid just at the moment. It had been five days since the *Ragnarok* had left for resupply at Laynock. Brecinn had told Laynock to expect the *Ragnarok*, and ensure that its resupply contained every surplussed ration and expired supply set they could get rid of.

It was an opportunity to take the garbage away and shut ap Rhiannon up at the same time. The redirected stores might not be very exciting in terms of market value, but what was the sense in wasting an opportunity? She hadn't heard back from Laynock. The *Ragnarok* was evidently dawdling.

Noycannir approached the desk, but didn't sit. Just as well—Brecinn hadn't invited her. "I wanted to let you know," Noycannir said. "I feel I should make a short visit to Chilleau Judiciary to see what's become of that warrant. It must be caught up in processing somewhere. We haven't received it, have we?"

It was not surprising that the Bench warrant for those troops had not come back from Chilleau. She hadn't requested one yet. She needed the official report from the preliminary assessment team; she hadn't gotten it. The *Ragnarok* was not merely dawdling, but dragging its feet, and there hadn't been a sound out of the assessment team for days. That was the only thing that stopped her from sending a corvette after them: if something was wrong, she would have heard something.

Could ap Rhiannon have detected the leak, and plugged it?

Possible, if improbable. For that to happen, ap Rhiannon would need the cooperation of Ship's Primes, and Ship's Primes were very unlikely to cooperate with any one mere junior officer, especially one as abrasive as ap Rhiannon. Besides which, even with the cooperation of Ship's Primes, ap Rhiannon could not plug every leak.

"No, we haven't gotten our warrant approved. Thank you, Dame Noycannir." The *Ragnarok* would be back soon; there was a natural limit to how long they could make a simple supply run last. She'd see to it that the report was suitably back-dated, and make a stink about Chilleau Judiciary's loss of an important Fleet disciplinary document.

It would remind Chilleau of Pesadie's importance to the successful transition of the Bench to its new First Judge . . . because Chilleau could not afford to treat the investigation into the death of Cowil Brem, a Command Branch officer, with anything less than the utmost discretion.

So it wouldn't matter, in the end, that ap Rhiannon was dragging her feet on her report. Brecinn would have names and a warrant. Ap Rhiannon would have only the extra demerit marked against her name in the intangible register of Fleet and reasonable people everywhere. "I appreciate your assistance in this matter. When will you return?"

Noycannir frowned slightly, as if in thought. "Well, that naturally depends on what the problem with the warrant might be, Admiral. It could take days. Shall we say—back in nine days, to get to work?"

Brecinn stood up. "Well, good travel," she said, extending her hand. "And good hunting. I hope I don't need to tell you how important your effort is to our readiness as we stand by to support the Judge at Chilleau." She wouldn't say "Second Judge," and it was too soon to say "First Judge." Noycannir would take her point. "Nor how deeply we all appreciate your energetic pursuit of mutually productive goals."

Noycannir's smile was a little cynical, but Brecinn didn't mind. "Just as you say, Admiral. I'll see you in nine days' time or less, then."

Well, it would probably be longer than that, but Noycannir didn't yet know that she would be staying to see the new request for a Bench warrant through channels. That was all right, too. Noycannir would be expecting to profit for her intervention. Let her work for her profit.

And ap Rhiannon just dug herself deeper into her own oubliette day by day by day. There would be a reckoning. Admiral Brecinn was not a vengeful woman, but ap Rhiannon's intransigence was an insult to Fleet itself. Fleet would settle with Jennet ap Rhiannon.

And the *Ragnarok* would be transferred from a draw on resources to a source of tremendous profit, once the new First Judge cancelled the program and forgot all about the ship's existence.

"With Security as well, Dame?" courier ship captain Gonkalen asked, reading the documentation that Mergau had presented. "With respect, it seems a little odd to take Security to Chilleau Judiciary."

Gonkalen looked a little uncertain, but Mergau was sure of her documentation. She hadn't spent all of the past several days creating her forged Record. She'd found time to ensure that she'd be able to get what she wanted when she was ready to make her move.

"Can't be too careful in uncertain times, Gonkalen, and Chilleau Judiciary's own resources are probably fully deployed just at present. It's a mark of thoughtfulness on the Admiral's part, really. Is there a problem?"

No. There was no problem, not unless this Gonkalen meant to argue with Fleet Admiral Sandri Brecinn about her disposition of her own resources. He passed the dispatch order back to her, and bowed. "Of course not, Dame. When do you wish to leave?"

"How soon can we leave?" She knew the correct answer to that question; she had chosen this ship with care. A fast courier, with transport for a Security team, and a storage area that could be secured. That was for Koscuisko. He would board the courier as a Bench officer on detached assignment; he would arrive at Chilleau Judiciary her prisoner, her slave.

Gonkalen shrugged. "At your convenience, Dame. There is a Security team on standby at all times."

That was the right answer, fortunately for Gonkalen. Mergau nodded. "Here are my effects, Ship Captain. I'd like to leave immediately, if you please."

Once they'd cleared Pesadie, they would start to spin for vector transit—but not for Chilleau. Gonkalen would be surprised, but she'd be his superior officer by virtue of Admiral Brecinn's delegated authority. It would be a secret mission. There would be no questions asked; or at least none answered.

Azanry, in the Dolgorukij Combine, and Koscuisko would be at the old fortress known to the locals as Chelatring Side. She had the flight plan. She had the administrative clearance codes, for use when the time came. Her appearance would be sudden, unannounced, surprising. He didn't have a chance.

"As you direct, Dame Noycannir. Within the hour."

By the time it occurred to Brecinn to wonder where she was, she would be on her way to Chilleau Judiciary with a prize under lock and key that would render her position unassailable for the rest of her life.

Silboomie Station experienced a fair level of activity during a given shift, but a visit from one of the big battlewagons in the cruiser-killer class was unusual enough to be an event. They'd had a day or two to anticipate it, as well; once the loading drills had started to pool into the supply set to be ready for the gaining ship's barge, it had been clear that the size of the ship was to be extraordinary.

That the ship was not only a cruiser-killer class warship, but an experimental model—a test bed for the still developmental and controversial black-hull technology—had only added excitement upon interest. Half the station was out upon the dispatch apron, high above the loading area, to watch the slow descent of the ship's barge down to the loading level.

The clear-space of the station was clearly marked with illumination globes for the entire hemisphere, so that there would be a constant source of light, even when the station's orbit carried it through the night shadow of the cold dead world that anchored it in Silboomie system. The ship's marks were clearly visible, once in range; great *Ragnarok* itself, whispered and gossiped about as much because of the people on board as the innovative promise of the black hull.

Scanner Habsee, the Supply Officer on shift, counted the people who were watching the spectacle, and shook her head. Nineteen heads, and only thirty-six on Station. It was just as well that theirs was an oversight function, restricted to maintaining the automatics and administering the appropriate releases and secures. Because if the work relied upon the living, rather than the mechanical, it would have come to a standstill just now, to watch the *Ragnarok*'s barge come in.

From Habsee's post in the control pillar, she could see the pilot platform on the barge as it sank past her line of sight. There were three people on it, and one of them had to be the Engineer, since he was required to attest to the receipt and valid need for supplies transferred.

One of the people on the pilot platform was tall enough to be the Chigan engineer Serge of Wheatfields, notorious throughout Fleet not so much for his own accomplishments—which were respectable—as for what Fleet had accomplished against him. There was a question to be raised though, over whether the adjective notorious could be applied to any of the *Ragnarok*'s officers in comparison to its Ship's Surgeon, whose reputation outshone that even of the late, unlamented Fleet Captain Lowden for dreadfulness and horror. Supply Officer Habsee wondered if the Engineer was ever jealous of Andrej Koscuisko.

With the Engineer at the wheel on the pilot platform the barge slid into its preprogrammed docking slot without a single jolt or jar, not so much as a flash of proximity warning lights. Locked off, ready to commence loading, the barge engaged its interface protocols with the Station's cranes, and the transfer process began.

Descending the ladder set into the side of the barge, the three people who had ridden it down began to make their way across the tarmac to the lifts. And suddenly something fell out of the upper atmosphere, something huge and black, erratic in its movements, swift and sudden in its turns.

Habsee could hear the exclamations of the onlookers over the monitors: fear, confusion, wonder. Recognition. It wasn't a huge black awful thing falling from the underbelly of the *Ragnarok*. It was only the *Ragnarok*'s Intelligence Officer, taking advantage of the joined atmospheres to fly the extra distance rather than ride on the barge.

The Desmodontae came in swift and low, heading straight for the control pillar; to climb up the outer wall, Habsee supposed. It disappeared from sight below the lip of the tower's balcony, only to reappear—climbing up over the outer railing—even as the lift doors opened to discharge the other members of the *Ragnarok*'s supply party.

Habsee went to her post, to greet them formally from behind the transfer-desk. There on the desk's surface was the supply manifest, complete and cross-checked, ready for receipt signatures and release of responsibility.

It was rather a full manifest, she'd noticed. Maybe the ship had been out beyond range of resupply for the months since the death of Captain Lowden. Some of the staff thought that the *Ragnarok* had been on training maneuvers at Pesadie Training Command, though, and not out in the Fringe at all.

It wasn't any of their business, really. They were reasonable people. The ship requested the support; Silboomie Station supplied it. That was their job. Their mission. Asking questions about clients' recent active postings was not included in the mission statement.

"Welcome to Silboomie Station, gentles," she said. She could hear a scrabbling sound behind her, to her left, as the Desmodontae let itself in from the outer balcony. "Your manifest has been prepared. I think you'll find everything in good order. I'm Scanner Habsee, the shift Supply Officer."

The Desmodontae had scuttled past the desk to take its place with the other crew from the *Ragnarok*. "Ship's Engineer," the tall Chigan said, confirming her previous guess. "Serge of Wheatfields. Logistics Control, Pinapin Rydel. Stores-and-Replenishments, He Talks. The Intelligence Officer, Two."

Logistics and Stores-and-Replenishments nodded politely in turn, but the Desmodontae only stared. What was it doing here? Logistics and Stores-and-Replenishments one expected, but what did an Intelligence Officer have to do with a routine resupply? Had there been an undiscovered shortage of the nutrient broth that Desmodontae used for food? What?

"As you'll see from the manifest, we're ready to validate," Habsee replied, a little nervously. "Will you be wanting to spot audit prior to acceptance, your Excellency?"

Many Engineers did, as part of good prudence, and to ensure that they were receiving what they had requested. It was different for commercial transfers, of course. Smaller orders could be more easily verified, and commercial transfers involved money. If the *Ragnarok* didn't get what it expected, they'd just reorder. Silboomie Station was a chartered Fleet support activity; they took what Fleet paid, and were grateful for that much. They had their own ways of making sure that the margins were acceptable.

"Won't be necessary this trip. We're all reasonable people, after all, aren't we? And Two has validated the audit trail." The Engineer's response was a little confusing, but he kept talking, as if what he'd just said had been easily understandable. "There are some additional stores we're particularly anxious to pick up, now that we're here. They weren't on the pre-trans manifest, we'd like to do an ad-hoc add-on."

Happened all the time, especially where reasonable people were concerned. As long as there weren't too many last-minute requests, they could usually locate and load the desired commodity before the barge had finished clearing its original manifest.

"Of course, sir. Material class code?"

The Engineer glanced down at the silent staring Desmodontae at his side, and the Intelligence Officer turned its black-velvet muzzle up in the Chigan's direction and spoke.

"Standard deck-wipes, by the octave, each," the Intelligence Officer said—and its voice was female. Female, and oddly cheerful, somehow. "But a particular lot, if you please. It should be located at encrypt serio trevi-spikal-conjut-seven. Sector four. Line two. Crane access seventeen."

Deck-wipes weren't an acquisition item, under normal circumstances. They were as easy to come by as they were easy to dispose of, by the octave, each. Scanner Habsee didn't wonder; she knew how to mind her own business, and she had to scramble to get the matrix coordinates loaded, because by the time she had grasped what she was being told, "Two" was already halfway through the location sequence.

"I confirm encrypt serio trevi-spikal-conjut-seven . . . " The information came up slowly, the cross-reference seeming to require longer than usual to complete its search. "With respect, ma'am, according to the register it's a shipment of tallifers, special hold for experimental—"

Two raised one clawlike hand in a swift gesture of warning, and most of one wing came with it. Habsee shut up, startled into silence.

"There is a very good reason for such an entry," Two said, solemnly. "We, however, have strict instructions to receive deck-wipes from that coordinate. We are not to leave without them. It would, of course, help immeasurably if you could slip the package into mid-manifest, and excite as little notice as possible."

As long as there were no inadvertent misunderstandings. Habsee invoked standard handling on emergency override, to get the package moved without the flag-action of a special transfer. Fortunately, the index location was only one or two processes deep; it had been placed quite close to the loading apron—doubtless deliberately.

Two was the Intelligence Officer, after all. If there were Intelligence issues involved, Habsee rather wanted to get rid of it as soon as she could.

"It will be one moment." Habsee frowned in concentration, working the problem on-line. Pull a heavy lift off a mid-process, get it to the closest entry site. Find the package—there; load the package. It was remarkably heavy, for its size.

Habsee adjusted the counterbalance resists. The load stabilized; she keyed the global-domain. "Attention on observer. Maximum load limit on dispatch apron has been exceeded, return to post." She was expected to run the idlers off from time to time; and they had already had the better part of the treat—the *Ragnarok*'s barge docking, with the dramatic appearance of the Intelligence Officer as an unexpected thrill. "Repeat, maximum load limit exceeded, return to post."

Clear the area. By the time the lift with the special consignment cleared the front end of the massive stacks to make its slow ascent from two levels down, the dispatch apron was effectively deserted. Not that the movement of the special requisition was really hidden or concealed in any sense, no. It was just as not-obvious as it could be, given the restrictions under which she had to operate.

Then it was done. The special consignment was placed forward, and the loading barge took it up as if it had been waiting for just that. The next four packages in their dull gray, featureless containers slid onto the barge immediately afterward, hiding the special package from sight. The Engineer stepped forward and set his mark against the manifest, bending his head to the ident-scan with solemn, bored gravity.

"And that's that," Habsee said, as the ident came back true blue and the manifest ticket faded into SHIPPED from STORES. "Pleasure to be of service to you, gentles. And good-shift."

Special packages and cruiser-killer-class warships aside, it was just the same thing that she did shift in, shift out, for shift after shift after shift. It was all either "Shipped" or "Stores" to her, and once shipped, it was no longer of any interest to Scanner Habsee whatsoever. She sent a standard notification to Pesadie Training Command to confirm disposition of the special consignment, and went back to her daily tasks without a second thought.

Jennet ap Rhiannon stood on a loading apron in the maintenance atmosphere, watching as the maintenance crew unshipped the case of deck-wipes that Wheatfields had brought up from Silboomie Station. Two had traced its provenance through avenues known only to her; Two said it would be evidence. If it was a shipment of tallifers, it would mean one less hope for making their case against Pesadie Training Command.

"What good does it do us, your Excellency?" Mendez asked, from beside her. Mendez to the right of her, Two hanging from a support beam to the left of her, and Wheatfields standing—as was his habit— apart, watching the crew, chewing on a twig of something or another: Command and General Staff, Jurisdiction Fleet Ship *Ragnarok*.

Only Lieutenant Seascape was missing; she was up in a crane where she could watch the crew work from above. It was a big case of deck-wipes. Twice Wheatfields's height. Three or four times as long as Wheatfields was tall. One Wheatfields deep.

"I'm hoping it will be ammunition, First Officer." She appreciated the fact that he called her "Excellency," even though she knew he knew it was merely a courtesy title. She could not bring herself to call him "Ralph." "It should prove that Pesadie is corrupt, and trading in armaments. Therefore there is also a strong possibility that the explosion that killed Cowil Brem was related to black market munitions."

"Wait," the Ship's Engineer said suddenly, then lapsed back into his customary sullen silence. Jennet waited. On the crane overlooking the platform, Lieutenant Seascape leaned over the top of the crate as the crew winched its top cover clear.

For a moment Seascape remained just as she was. When Seascape raised her head to look across to where Jennet stood with the other officers, it seemed that her expression was a mixture of horror and delight. Then Seascape urged the crew to hurry as they took down the great side panel that concealed the contents of the crate from Jennet's view.

Bending over the crane's basket, Lieutenant Seascape hooked the cable onto one of the lift points on the crane. Jennet hoped she was tethered into the basket; it was a long reach.

The winch started to work, the great side panel lifted, the maintenance crew guided it carefully across the platform to where it could be laid flat. The outline was clear, but the blanket was still in place, and a person could still tell herself that they were mistaken.

The blanket lifted clear. There could be no mistake. It wasn't a case of deck-wipes; so much had been obvious from the first glimpse they had gotten of the contents of the crate.

"Sanford in Hell," First Officer swore, but reverently.

It was the main battle cannon for the forward emplacement of a cruiser-killer-class warship, beautiful, deadly, and efficient beyond measure.

Jennet waved at Seascape, calling out to her. "Thank you, Lieutenant." She needed to know exactly what else was in that container, now that the basic fact was confirmed and undeniable. "Carry on."

"Somebody will get the Tenth Level for this," Mendez observed. "Selling off Fleet armament. What's next?"

Jennet looked up to where Two hung from the crossbeams, scratching her neck with her wing. Mendez knew. Mendez had to know. "At least it gives us some leverage," Jennet said. "But it means going to Taisheki."

That was where Fleet Audit Appeals Authority had its base. And so far she had left Pesadie Training Command on false pretenses, though the action could be excused as a misunderstanding if Fleet was generous and willing to overlook it; but once they left Silboomie Station for Taisheki, they were at war with Pesadie. There was no other way around it.

"What exactly do you mean to appeal to Fleet, your Excellency?" Mendez asked, but calmly, without challenge. Playing the Devil's advocate. "What has Pesadie done? Except for demanding some troops and, oh, been implicated in black-market profiteering with Fleet's battle cannon, just a little."

"Demanded surrender of Fleet resources to face the Protocols based on illegally obtained information, demonstrating a clear preconception prejudicial to the rule of Law. Two's found Brecinn's marks all over this case of deck-wipes, which proves she's corrupt. The last person who should be investigating the death of Cowil Brem is an officer who has something to hide. What was she storing on that station, anyway? Why did it explode?"

Wheatfields raised a hand and took the twiglet out of his mouth. "Taisheki," Wheatfields said. "Three days, your Excellency, maybe five, First Officer."

Mendez hadn't asked, but Wheatfields was answering anyway. Jennet felt something in her gut relax. It was only an implicit agreement to go to Taisheki, but it was enough, and it heartened her more than she could say. They'd challenged her decisions, but they'd accepted them; this was the closest they'd come to an endorsement yet—and she needed their support, if she was to have any hope of making this work.

"What about the Bonds, First Officer?" Six bond-involuntary troops were on board, assigned to support Koscuisko at torture work in Secured Medical, governed to obedience. And Koscuisko wasn't here to keep them comfortable with the situation, to assure them that they were not to blame for the fact that the ship was operating well outside its normal range of procedures. There could be trouble with their governors.

If Wheatfields had agreed and Mendez was not objecting, they believed that the crew would accept the decision. It wasn't value neutral. Making an appeal to the Fleet Audit Appeals Authority had consequences. If their appeal was not sustained, there could be disciplinary action, loss of rank and pay; disciplinary action that should properly be restricted to the ship's officers—but the odium attached to having made an appeal that was not sustained would attach itself to the entire crew. Transfer out would be difficult, if not impossible. Nobody wanted troublemakers within their Command.

And there was more. If an appeal was not sustained, it opened the possibility that Fleet would elect to investigate the *Ragnarok* for mutinous intent. There was only one reason why so desperate a course of action as an appeal could be contemplated: the fact that Brecinn had made it clear that "mutinous intent" was exactly where she was going anyway.

Mendez did not quite shrug. "So far, so good, your Excellency," Mendez said. "And making an appeal is within your authority. Medical will keep an eye out. And there's Koscuisko's influence to consider; he's corrupted them to a significant extent."

This was an intriguing claim. "How do you mean, corrupted?" Jennet asked.

"Gained their trust, your Excellency. Convinced them that nobody's going to get unreasonable on 'em without going through him first. Ruins the whole effect, but there you are."

She'd heard gossip about Koscuisko's relationship with his Bonds; she hadn't thought it through, but Mendez was right. The whole idea was for bond-involuntaries to be incapable of transgression, because punishment was so horrible and so immediate. But the governor reacted to internal stress states to make its determination of whether punishment was in order; without those cues, the governor did—nothing.

"Will you go on all-ship, First Officer?"

Mendez nodded. "I'll make the announcement, your Excellency. Serge. How long to vector transit?"

Wheatfields did something peculiar, even for him.

Raising one arm high overhead, he drew a great looping circle in the air, three times, five times, before he dropped his hand to tuck his twiglet back between his teeth. "Twelve hours," Wheatfields said.

She could see movement at the far end of the maintenance atmosphere. Engineering was already moving to hull the maintenance atmosphere for vector transit.

"I'd better get, then, your Excellency. With permission."

Jennet returned Mendez's bow with grave precision. Wheatfields nodded and excused himself, and she couldn't tell whether he had actually saluted her or just been momentarily distracted by something underfoot.

Two hopped down from her perch and scurried off after Wheatfields, her bow over and done by the time her translator got to the end of "By your leave, Captain." Jennet ap Rhiannon stood alone on the apron, watching Seascape strip the coverings off that beautiful cannon.

Maybe once they were on vector she could send Rukota to Engineering, to help install the battle cannon in its place. She wanted the cannon in place. She thought that they might need it. The

Ragnarok's own armament was on the light side, always had been. It was an experimental hull. It had never been equipped to defend itself. Until now it had never faced an environment in which it might be required to.

Defend themselves—against even Fleet? If it came to that. She was not going to throw anybody's life away without a fight. The rule of Law would be upheld. It would. She looked at the battle cannon, and shuddered.

But she had work to do, if she was to be prepared to transmit an appeal to the Fleet Audit Appeals Authority at Taisheki Station. She would need to have her Brief in order. And request Safes, for the bond-involuntaries.

She left Seascape to supervise the birth of the battle cannon and exited the maintenance atmosphere for her office, to get to work.

General Rukota hadn't seen much of the officers of the *Ragnarok* since the preliminary assessment team had been confined to quarters. He looked in on Pesadie's people once a day because it was his duty, but he wasn't any more interested in talking to them than they to him, and the visits were short accordingly.

Something was clearly in the air; he'd known that since Two had not-told him that they were not going to Laynock for resupply. But the crew of the *Ragnarok* had discipline: whatever it was, he wasn't hearing gossip. He spent his day in the Lieutenant's quarters they had set aside for him, writing letters to his wife and children for some future and possibly never-to-come date when he would be able to transmit them.

He worked on his official report, the one that Admiral Brecinn was expecting, the one with the by-name identification of the troops who had been on the Wolnadi at the time of the explosion of the observation station. But he didn't spend too much time on it. He saw no particular point; ap Rhiannon was not about to surrender those troops, so taking his time was doing her a favor, really.

The longer it took him to prepare the official report, the longer it would be before ap Rhiannon would have to stop defying Admiral Brecinn and start defying a Bench warrant with the full weight of Chilleau Judiciary behind it, which was going to be much trickier than merely refusing to cooperate with Pesadie Training Command.

He worked on his memoirs instead. Some of the officers he had known in his career deserved commemoration, some of the battles he had fought had been worthy of preservation for the lessons they could teach, and he had his theory of armament to propose and develop. Plenty to do.

Twice a day he went to exercise. Individual training in the morning; group combat drill in the evening, when he could find someone in the arenas to spar with him. He could almost always get a bout with one particular team of Security that was apparently on its fifth-week duty, in Medical.

Individual members of any Security team—the Captain's Security 1-point, Intelligence's 2-point, First Officer's 3-point, the Engineer's 4-point—could be and were posted to Medical to maintain their basic field medical skills; but the only time an entire team did fifth-week duty in Medical was when they were bond-involuntary, and the only place bond-involuntaries could be assigned was to the Chief Medical Officer, because he was Ship's Inquisitor. Security 5-point.

But Rukota had seen the Security manifests. There were only six bond-involuntary troops in all on board of the *Ragnarok*, and four of them were to have gone home with Koscuisko on leave. Therefore Jennet ap Rhiannon had switched Security teams. So she couldn't surrender the troops that Brecinn was demanding, because they weren't even on the *Ragnarok*.

That was ap Rhiannon's business, though, not his; and was certainly nothing to do with the troops themselves. They gave him a good workout. They pressed him hard enough, but not too hard. They worked so well together. Good people. It would be a shame to let Pesadie Training Command torture them to death.

He was just getting cleaned up after his evening's exercise, toweling off his thinning hair, getting dressed, when Security came for him. "General Rukota?"

One of the senior Warrants, Miss Myrahu; he'd interviewed her about the audit problem. She was standing in the doorway of the dressing room, but it was nothing personal; there was no segregation of the sexes in Security arenas and he was more clothed than not anyway, by now.

"Speaking. Excuse my state of undress. What do you want?"

Maybe Brecinn's people had tried a breakout and been shot down.

A man could fantasize. If they had, though, wouldn't that cause damage to the courier? And it was a nice courier. It deserved better. When this was all over he would have it fumigated. Exorcised. Apologized to, at the very least; as far as he could tell it was an honest ship.

"If you'll come with us, sir. Captain has requested an interview."

Had she, indeed? Well, why not. It wasn't as though he had any urgent business of his own; he was curious, too, to see what ap Rhiannon might tell him—if anything—about what was going on.

"Very well. At your disposal, Miss Myrahu, lead on."

His escort took him down to the engineering bridge in the very core of the ship, the single second-best shielded area on the *Ragnarok*. Was it his imagination, or was the atmosphere in the corridors a little more tense than it had been earlier today?

They stopped him at the entrance to the observation deck, signaling for admittance; when the door opened, Security turned around and went away, leaving Rukota alone—or as alone as a man could get, on board a cruiser-killer—to step across the threshold on his own.

The observation deck over the engineering bridge was a gentle curve of clear-wall, railed off, but otherwise with a full range of sight—and sound. Ordinarily they would be able to hear everything that was going on, but the feed seemed to have been turned off temporarily.

Either way, the people working below in the engineering bridge couldn't hear them. It was better not to distract ship's engineers while they were concentrating. A momentary distraction could have serious consequences during a vector spin, and what might earn an inattentive Security troop an especially pointed thump on the head on the exercise floor could cost the entire ship its very existence, if it came at the wrong time.

Pausing on the threshold, Rukota took it all in. It was dark on the observation deck, to cut down on distractions. But the command structure of the entire Ship was here, the Captain—acting Captain—ap Rhiannon, the Ship's First Officer, the Intelligence Officer, even the one other Lieutenant who had been unfortunate enough to be assigned here. Command and General Staff, Fleet Jurisdiction Ship *Ragnarok*, with sauced-flats and—so help him—bappir. Bappir, on the observation deck of the engineering bridge.

He was dead, and gone to his reward. Or he was dead, and for his next task—a few octaves with Jennet ap Rhiannon, trying to teach the mulish young officer about self-preservation and protocol.

"General Rukota." Ap Rhiannon beckoned him in, waving him to a place at the rail where he, too, could look down over Serge of Wheatfields's dark close-cropped head to the great visual field that occupied one wall of the engineering bridge. "Come in, sit down. Have a flask of bappir. Have two, you may as well."

He couldn't see well enough to be able to read the mechanicals' displays from their removed vantage point. It didn't help if he squinted. The First Officer handed him a slice of sauced-flat, adding an extra handful of ponales across the top in a gesture that was apparently intended to be friendly.

Santone could eat ponales; their mouths had all been cauterized from the inside out by a steady diet of the acerbic fruit from childhood. If First Officer expected him to eat ponales, however, he was going to need more than two glasses of bappir.

"What's this all about?" *Your Excellency*. He'd forgotten the "your Excellency." He remembered in the middle of a mouthful of sauced-flat, and by then it was too late.

"Well, in the simplest possible terms, it's this." Ap Rhiannon hadn't seemed to notice. She was leaning on the railing with a flask of bappir in one hand, tracking a scan somewhere down in the pit of the engineering bridge as if it meant something to her.

"We're being set up to take the blame for something we didn't do, and there are lives at stake. That preliminary assessment team had cleared the craft implicated well before anyone broke into Security. And Brecinn's been telling us we can't get resupply on critical goods, but once you leave Pesadie Training Command's sphere of influence, the shortages don't seem to exist."

Once you leave Pesadie Training Command? Of course. Why not? It was major resource deployment contrary to standing orders, that was all, unless anyone really believed that Brecinn had had some place other than Laynock in mind when she'd released the *Ragnarok* to go to resupply. A little spot of failure to obey lawful and received instruction. Oh, maybe a little mutiny. Just a little one.

"I'm not about to give away four crew. As nearly as we can tell"— glancing at First Officer for confirmation—"most of the rest of the crew doesn't like the idea either. Either that, or they realize that four is never enough for Fleet. We feel the only real option is an appeal."

Much good that would do her. An appeal could be accepted or rejected at the Pesadie level, and that would be that. What was she talking about? The only "appeal" worth making would be to the Fleet Audit Appeals Authority. And that was clearly out of the question.

"I've never seen the *Ragnarok* do a vector spin," ap Rhiannon concluded, straightening up, standing away from the rail. "And we know we haven't been providing you with much by way of entertainment. Are there any ponales left?"

The Intelligence Officer was keeping to herself, eating a custard. Two wouldn't be able to get much out of watching, not glassed-in as they were. Perhaps she was hearing transmissions. Or perhaps she was simply enjoying the custard, in the company of the *Ragnarok*'s other officers. The *Ragnarok*'s soon-to-be-cashiered officers. The *Ragnarok*'s lucky-if-they-weren't-all-summarily-shot officers.

"You're going to Taisheki." He might have known, the moment she'd started talking about vector spins. She would hardly be making so much fuss out of simply returning to Pesadie Training Command. "You are out of your mind. Individually and collectively. With respect. More bappir in that jug, is there? Lieutenant Seascape?"

Grinning, the Lieutenant pushed a full jug of bappir across the curved rail-table toward him. Ap Rhiannon laughed, but it didn't sound as though she had much pleasure in it.

"General, either I go to Taisheki, or Pesadie helps itself to the *Ragnarok*'s crew as it sees fit. And for no purpose, no valid purpose that supports the rule of Law."

Maybe ponales on sauced-flats weren't quite so bad. Maybe it was strong bappir. They all looked as though they hadn't had much rest over the past few days; even Two's pelt betrayed a suspicion of dust, around the feet. The hands. Whatever. He had done nothing but rest. The bappir went past them, and right to his head.

"Well, it's your career. And your career. And his, and quite possible yours as well," he noted, glancing around him at ap Rhiannon, the First Officer, and Wheatfields, in the pit of the engineering bridge below them, and the solitary Lieutenant left on board. "Can it really be worth hauling the entire ship to Taisheki? For what? All right, four lives. All right, four innocent lives." The enormity of the undertaking rather stunned him, bappir or no bappir. "Seven hundred people on board this ship, Captain."

And each of them willing to accept the blame and the burden, the permanent brand of a troublemaker and a dissident, to go crying to the Fleet Audit Appeals Authority at Taisheki over a mere four lives? Howsoever dirty the plot, howsoever innocent the lives, there were just four of them, and there were more than seven hundred people on board the *Ragnarok*.

"None of them with a great deal to gain," ap Rhiannon countered, somberly. "And all of us with entirely too much to lose." Yes, advancement, promotion, hope for the future in Fleet. A career. No, that wasn't what ap Rhiannon had been getting at, at all. "If we don't fight it, we may as well have colluded from the beginning, as though we're the kind of crew that really would sell ourselves just to stay out of trouble—"

"Attention to the Engineer, with respect, Captain," Mendez interrupted, gesturing toward the pit of the engineering bridge with his flask of bappir. "Might want the sound up. Lieutenant?"

Ap Rhiannon looked confused for a moment, but Mendez wasn't talking in her direction. It was Lieutenant Seascape who made the necessary arrangements, plaiting them into the braid.

" —increase spool rate on plasma sheath," Wheatfields was saying. The plasma sheath was the ship's respiration, and the faster the ship was to move, the more quickly it had to breathe. "Cassie, reduce your rate of acceleration. We're going to come up on it smoothly. I said reduce your rate, Cassie—"

There was urgency, but little sharpness, in the Engineer's voice. "Thank you, Cassie, sorry about that. Sela. We should be starting to cook in tertiary furnace."

And the plasma sheath had to thicken to catch the increased rate of particle bombardment, as well. Which of course implied that the ship's engines would start to run hotter than the usual tolerances. The only thing that could draw the extra energy off the furnace before the activity level began to reach critical parameters was to thin the sheath and slow the ship down—or take the energy and turn it into speed, enough speed to take a mass of the *Ragnarok*'s dimensions and shoot it like a projectile into the vortex of the vector, where even the *Ragnarok* could experience something akin to faster-than flight.

"Tersh and quat both coming along nicely, sir. Preparing overflow energy dump to the pintle batteries."

Space was mostly empty, and the vectors were the fastest way through it. The vectors were characterized by the absence of large objects in their vicinity; some speculated that they were pinholes in the fabric of space of some sort, formed long ago by the passage of a mass so dense that it had left a relatively stable deformation in the universal fields behind, clearing out most of the existing matter from the area as it went. They had to be old, if so, because enough minute particulate matter had accumulated in the area over time to feed the *Ragnarok*'s engines.

"All right. Watch it, Cassie. Ilex. Start the spin. Don't forget that we've selected left-helical twist, and get ready to set your mark."

The vector was clearest—fastest—in its center, the vortex, but getting there and staying there could be a bit complex. They needed the correct trajectory to counter the characteristics peculiar to the vector itself. The *Ragnarok* had to line up on the vector and gauge its approach just right to ensure that they would hit the vortex and go straight through to Taisheki.

"Begin your offside roll, mark. Four. Five. Six. Seven. Mark."

They didn't feel a thing, of course. They wouldn't. If they were out in the maintenance atmosphere standing on the hull, perhaps they would feel some vibration, but no more than that. But the blank star field on the massive display at the far end of the engineering bridge cleared, and re-imaged on a vector dynamic that made the speed and character of the ship's maneuvers graphically accessible, even to a mere Fleet Ground Landing Forces officer like himself.

"We hit that one just a shade too hot. Cassie, you're going to have to back down just a slice. Pumet, give me a fractional retard and second and third."

There were machines here to do to work of setting the ship on vector spin. It could be done without the help of mechanicals, but only theoretically, and only with smaller craft—with correspondingly less complex characteristics.

The fact remained that even the expert systems on this experimental model failed when confronted with the combined effects of seemingly unrelated factors. The mechanicals, the expert systems, the professional machines—*Ragnarok* relied upon them to maintain life support, motivation, respiration. It was more of a job than a mere seven-hundred-plus organics could manage between them. But only organics could manage the chaotic interplay of multiple events at the extreme limits of the on-board systems' tolerance.

"Stay on acceleration. Perfect. Coming up on second mark. Are we pulling any extra drag on that hull-flap section we had to seal manually?"

All of which taken together meant that although the Engineer might not be able to get the *Ragnarok* on vector without the mechanicals, the mechanicals alone could not get the *Ragnarok* on vector as well as they could with the Engineer to make adjustments.

The mechanicals only knew whether or not there was extra drag on hull-flap section whatever. They had no way of knowing why it might be so, or what kind of other effects the manual seal was liable to have.

The ship's spiral hit the second glowing graph point on the screen's display. Serge of Wheatfields was tapping the rail on his console, clearly deep in concentration. "That's good. Pumet, left retard. Sela, check the spool to speed, how are we doing?"

The third mark was coming up on-screen, and Rukota almost thought he could see the fourth—still faint and dim. "That's as it should be. Cassie, we're feeling a little sluggish—do you agree? Pumet, let it warm up a couple of layers."

They hit the third mark, and the spiral path on the display screen was beginning to make Rukota dizzy. The fourth mark was up within a scant eighth of the third, and the marks came ever more quickly as the *Ragnarok* gained momentum and the spin it needed to hit its mark on vector.

"Lift those retards, Pumet, keep it as smooth as you can." Wheatfields had less to say, and was speaking softly and quietly— careful not to disturb concentration. "All right, now, gentles. Seven eighths to vector spin. Go for it."

The cruise-marks on the display screen blurred into a single point of light that circled around the screen's perimeter, spiraling ever inward. Rukota took hold of the railing to keep his equilibrium. Watching the target blips as the ship's course proceeded was like watching a sleep-spinner. He didn't want to embarrass himself by falling over.

"This—is going to be—the smoothest—sweetest—vector spin, in the history of the Jurisdiction Fleet—"

And the single point of light that was all Rukota could see of the ship's course markers circled closer and closer to the center of the screen, each rotation tighter, each period shorter and shorter and shorter.

"Two eighths to vector spin," Wheatfields said.

The light point was a throbbing pool in the center of the screen, the target blips too close to one another to distinguish them individually. Then—as Rukota stared in fascinated wonder—the light point shuddered and condensed into a single solid point dead center in the screen that fixed and held and shrank into oblivion.

The Engineer turned at his post and looked up at the observation deck, to where ap Rhiannon leaned over the rail intense concentration.

"Captain, we have the Recife vector."

Unclenching her hands from the railing, ap Rhiannon took a few deep breaths—as if she had been holding her breath, and hadn't realized it. There were subdued gestures of triumph and relief from the crew down in the engineering bridge pit; ap Rhiannon keyed the cross-transmit.

"Thank you, Engineer. The First Officer and I have taken the liberty of asking your relief shift to come on early. I hope that you may all join us in Mess area next forward for bappir and sauced-flats. It isn't much, but it comes with our sincere thanks."

Nodding, Wheatfields turned back to the pit. "Thank you, Captain. Well done, all. Let's just braid our loose ends, and let the next shift on, shall we?"

Mendez turned off the cross-transmit, and the Lieutenant shut down the transparency factor so that the observation deck no longer offered the view of the engineering bridge that they had recently enjoyed.

Ap Rhiannon drained a flask of bappir, staggering just a bit; the Intelligence Officer, behind her, steadied her unobtrusively, without seeming to have noticed anything. Ap Rhiannon wasn't drunk; Rukota knew better than that. Ap Rhiannon was probably just exhausted. For all he knew she'd been sitting up shifts, fretting about her people, trying to convince herself that going to Taisheki was the right—or not merely the right, but the best and only—thing to do.

"I've got a favor to ask you, General Rukota." There was no uncertainty in ap Rhiannon's voice, however. The *Ragnarok* was on vector for Taisheki; there was no changing that now. And therefore no reason to waste any more energy on worrying the issue. Obviously. "We found a beautiful piece of armament at Silboomie Station, hiding out in a case of deck-wipes. Main battle cannon. Would you advise the Ship's Engineer on installation, once he's had a bit of recovery time?"

She'd taken the *Ragnarok* and left Pesadie without explicit clearance; she'd taken resupply—so that she could run without access to Fleet stores for a while—and she had taken the Recife vector for the Fleet Audit Appeals Authority at Taisheki Station. And she had convinced the Ship's First Officer, and the Ship's Intelligence Officer, and of course most importantly the Ship's Engineer, to do as she said, and go.

It was a fearfully desperate thing to do, for a mere four lives. A crew that would consent to hazard careers and pensions for such a slight piece of principle—had no place in the Jurisdiction Fleet of Admiral Sandri Brecinn.

A crew that would agree to defy authority and jump the chain of command to appeal for the lives of four Security was either a working unit with clear common goals and an awesome sense of self-respect, or it was actually, honestly, two steps short of the kind of mutiny that even he would have to acknowledge. Perhaps the *Ragnarok* was both things, at once.

"Battle cannon, you say." Contraband, clearly. Ap Rhiannon didn't like black marketeers. "Of course. At your Excellency's disposal entirely." He didn't like black marketeers, either.

She was looking up at him directly, with a curiously forlorn expression buried deep, deep, deep in her professionally unreadable black eyes. "Maybe we can talk again," she suggested; there seemed to be something more that she wanted to say, but had thought better of. She was right to suppose that she had some explaining to do, but he could wait. "But for now you'll have to excuse us, General."

"Wanted in Mess area next forward. Of course." He bowed in salute, carefully, rather more respectful of "Captain" ap Rhiannon than he had been inclined to feel before.

She in turn nodded, her own gesture somewhat less of an

acknowledgment of courtesy offered a temporary position and more an acceptance of acknowledgment of rank. She wasn't thinking about it, no; she seemed too tired to be thinking on so deep a level—or so trivial a one—as that. She was getting comfortable with "Captain." Maybe she was earning it.

"Later, then. Security, return General Rukota to quarters— Wheatfields will want to know where he can find him. First Officer, Two, if you would please come with me."

He would much rather have gone with the *Ragnarok*'s senior staff to Mess area next forward.

And beyond?

CHAPTER ELEVEN

The Procession of the Sirdar

And when the last piece of sauced-flat had been eaten to its crust, and the last half-a-flask of bappir had been swallowed, Jennet ap Rhiannon left the last of the mess areas she had been visiting since they'd made the Recife vector and returned to quarters. She was so tired that only the wake-keeping drugs she'd gotten from Medical were keeping her going, so tired that she nearly lost her way twice, so tired that she kept forgetting that the people behind her were her own Security escort— or the acting Captain's Security escort, at any rate. She felt no sense of ownership or identification with them.

She felt very little.

When she got to her quarters it was a moment before she realized that they were her quarters, and not someone else's, because there was a Security post outside the door, and the only time Security was posted outside an officer's quarters was when it was the Captain's quarters.

She was so tired that the door was coming open and she was already moving into the room before she realized that the Security post was 3.4, not l.-anything, and what that implied about who was within the room and what he was doing there.

And then quite suddenly she was wide awake. Security 3.4 was the First Officer's. Ralph Mendez was sitting in the room, at the worktable, leaning his forearms against its edge and pushing an empty cup of what had probably been khombu from side to side between his hands.

Mendez was responsible for Security, as well as for Operations. If an officer offered an act of sedition or mutiny, it was Mendez's job to take the officer into custody until such time as the question of guilt or innocence—error or intent—could be placed in the hands of a Ship's Inquisitor for discovery and investigation at the Advanced Levels of the Question.

The door slid closed behind her, and they were alone. She could take him, from this distance; she wore knives, and she knew how to use them. But she could not take the First Officer, and the Security at the door, and the rest of the Security on board. And it was better not to jump to conclusions, no matter how obvious it all seemed.

"First Officer. A surprise. Have you been to bed at all, your Excellency?" She'd approached the Engineer first; there had been no other option. The Engineer was the person who was ultimately responsible for where the ship actually went, and how it actually got there. And she'd seen the Intelligence Officer next, because once she could feel confident that Wheatfields would at least listen to her, she had needed to be sure that no one was paying any particular attention to the *Ragnarok*'s movements.

By the time she'd got past the two of them, the *Ragnarok* had already reached Silboomie Station, and Mendez had seemed comfortable enough with developments—if not exactly enthusiastically supportive. Enthusiasm was not to be expected. Nobody wanted to do this.

Well, she'd known it had been a gamble, from the start. They couldn't all be successful. An unsuccessful gamble had only one possible outcome for crèche-bred, and that was death.

Stretching in his seat, Mendez yawned and set his empty cup upside down on the tabletop. "With respect. You should ask, your Excellency. I have an authorization from Dr. Mahaffie, here—"

He didn't need an authorization. He could arrest her on his own authority. That he would arrest her was obvious; they had already cleared out all of her personal effects—they were that sure of her. Her quarters were as featureless as though she had never slept here.

" —and Dr. Mahaffie says that if you don't shut yourself up in quarters, your Excellency, and get at least a shift-and-a-half's rest, he will issue a dose. Enough sleeper to stop even Jennet ap Rhiannon in her very determined tracks. And I've got the handgun here to make the delivery, too. I'll shoot you down in the corridor, that's a promise."

Dr. Mahaffie did not hold the Writ. Andrej Koscuisko did. She had no illusions about what awaited her. She knew what the punishment was, what it looked like. Her entire class had watched, day by day, hour by hour, for the two and a half days it had taken the assigned Inquisitor to execute Yordie for failing in his field test.

Koscuisko was better than any borrowed Inquisitor. It was widely acknowledged that Koscuisko was the best there was. But Koscuisko wasn't here, and Mahaffie didn't hold the Writ, so what was First Officer talking about?

"What do you think the feeling is amongst the crew, First Officer?" She'd pretend that she had no idea why he was here. She'd pretend that she had no idea that he was not in with the rest of them, all the way. She could kill him, rather than let him net her for Andrej Koscuisko.

There was no point in killing him.

He had dealt honestly with her; he had not said anything, one way or another, that would be inconsistent with arresting her. And she could not escape from the *Ragnarok* with just a knife or two. Or rather, although she could, she would only escape at the cost of one or more of the lives that it was her business and her sacred duty to preserve, not to destroy.

She hadn't thought about Yordie for years, except for nightmares. The last Tenth Level Command Termination that Andrej Koscuisko had performed had taken nearly seven days . . .

"You've got to understand, Captain. Nobody on board this ship wants trouble with Fleet. On the other hand most of us on board are already in trouble with Fleet. I believe Serge mentioned something like that to you before."

She didn't know what he was talking about. She leaned her back against the closed door and waited for him to start making sense.

"And most of us have been kicked in the face before, and we're tired of it. Most of our people are with you. And the ones that aren't with you, aren't against you. There is only one little thing."

What little thing was that? It had lasted forever, Yordie's dying. It had gone on for so long that it had ceased to be horrible, and become boring, tiresome, tedious. She could remember hoping that each scream would be his last, and no longer because she had been his crèche-mate, but because she was sick and tired and disgusted at him for screaming. For his weakness. And that had only been two and a half days.

Koscuisko could make her scream like that; she had no doubt of it. Somehow the humiliation of ending her life so meanly, her pathetic puling recorded for all time in the Record, was even more horrible than her appreciation of the kind of pain that it had taken to make Yordie so shamelessly frantic with sharp unbearable agony that he had not been able to preserve a single shred of the dignity that had been his birthright.

As long as there was no active resistance, there need be no loss of life; except for her own, and that would not matter. Within the space of a very short time her life would mean nothing at all, and her death would be merely inconsequential. "What 'little thing' is that, First Officer?" She would play along. She would not make things needlessly difficult. It had been a good effort. It had almost worked.

"You have insisted on your prerogatives as a Second Lieutenant, your Excellency. It was one thing when you were acting First Lieutenant, and even understandable when you became acting Captain. But the Recife vector has changed all that."

As a prisoner she had no privileges. She knew that as well as he did, if not better. What was the point of all this?

"If you're going to ask people to follow you to Taisheki, you've got to acknowledge their agreement. You've got to live up to your end of the contract. These people aren't going to Taisheki with any Fleet Second Lieutenant, not even a crèche-bred one. They're going to Taisheki with Captain Jennet ap Rhiannon. I want you to lose the 'acting' bit."

She'd already lost her Captaincy, her First Lieutenancy, her basic rank of Second Lieutenant. "Very well, First Officer." She was tired of waiting for him to say the words, to come to the point. She just wanted to go to sleep.

"You will occupy the Captain's quarters, and you will use the Captain's office. We've moved your personal possessions. If you will follow me."

Captain's quarters? That was an unusual way to characterize a prisoner holding cell. Unless it was a phrase left over from the days of Captain Lowden, since Lowden had tended to handle prisoners as though they—and Andrej Koscuisko—had been personal possessions, rather than Bench resources.

Something was just not adding up.

Rising to his feet, Mendez gave the signal, and the door slid open again behind her. She waited for the Security to seize and secure, but nothing happened. Mendez merely came forward, and gestured toward the door.

The Security she'd brought with her were still posted outside, and saluted as she stepped across the threshold. Security fell into formation behind her, and Mendez himself took the subordinate-escort position at her left elbow.

She started walking, because it was habit, because they were not to initiate movement on their own; unless she was a prisoner, of course, in which case they would carry her at their own will in their choice of direction. She'd forgotten. She let First Officer direct them, remembering that she was a prisoner. But they weren't going toward the holding cell out in Secured Medical, forward. They were heading back down into the shielded heart of the ship, instead. The Captain's quarters.

Ship's Primes had sleeping space within the shielded core, rather than toward the upper hull where more disposable Lieutenants were assigned to sleep. Ship's Primes had two entire rooms at their personal disposal, outer and inner, and the things in the outer room of the Captain's quarters were her things.

Her personal shrine to the rule of Law, the religion of her childhood. The trophies she had taken—the weapon that had wounded her at Atrium, the ship's pennant from her first Vorket command, her personal commendations.

There was no way they meant to secure her in these quarters, rather than in a cell. So they didn't mean to secure her at all. They only meant for her to be their Captain.

She lost control over the terror and the tension, the relief, and the fearful weariness within her. She staggered toward the table, and First Officer was right with her, making sure that she sat—rather than falling—down.

"Thank you, First Officer." And the entire ship, by proxy. She could not refuse the honor, not if she meant to have their continued cooperation. "You don't know what this means to me."

It meant that she was not going to die. Or not just yet. The greater meaning was beyond her, at the moment. She was very tired. And the wake-keepers were wearing off, and all at once.

"Only what you've earned, Captain. Now get some rest."

She put her head down on her crooked forearm resting on the table's cool polished surface, and went to sleep.

The message had been laid casually atop the day's stack of administrative notices, by design. It wasn't the sort of thing to draw attention to itself, but her aides knew what it meant and that it meant a problem.

Pesadie Training Command modular packet released from storage to Jurisdiction Fleet Ship Ragnarok *on direction, receipt executed by Ship's Engineer, Serge of Wheatfields, countersigned. Dated, validated, two days old.*

While she had been talking to Noycannir, while she had been calculating turnaround and reissue time, the *Ragnarok* had gone to Silboomie Station—not Laynock Station at all—and they had absconded with the single most valuable item in her private inventory.

It wasn't her item. She held it in trust for reasonable people, because she had the means to arrange secure storage and document an audit trail that would cover disposition when the highest bidder had been selected, payment received.

It was immeasurably worse than when she had lost all of those munitions when the observation station had blown up with the *Ragnarok*'s Captain on it. How had the *Ragnarok* known?

Wasn't it obvious?

She had underestimated the *Ragnarok*. Somebody—maybe Jennet ap Rhiannon, unlikely though that seemed—had turned out to be reasonable after all. Someone had been found to surrender the information, because reasonable people could be relied upon to know what was reasonable to do. Ap Rhiannon wanted that module for herself.

Was she going to sell it? Hold it for ransom to force Brecinn to cancel her planned recovery from the training accident? Use it as a bribe to acquire position within the informal hierarchy of responsible people?

If there had been a sellout in the works, Brecinn would have heard about it by now. Surely. Wouldn't she have?

Or had someone on her staff already sold her out?

Had that been how ap Rhiannon had known to go to Silboomie

for the special module? Were reasonable people already making arrangements to abandon Brecinn as last year's hero, and do business with ap Rhiannon instead? She'd been an idiot not to see it. Who was better placed to part out the *Ragnarok*, to sell off its assets, to skim its stores than ap Rhiannon herself?

This called for an immediate reconsideration of plans. She needed to see where Noycannir was in her process. What was ap Rhiannon going to do? Silboomie Station. Not Laynock. Where could you get to, from Silboomie Station?

Fleet Audit Appeals Authority. Taisheki space. Maybe that was all right. She had contacts at Taisheki.

Signaling for attention on her voice box, Brecinn called up the central communications deck. "Send a message to Chilleau Judiciary. Priority transmit. Dame Mergau Noycannir, sole recipient." She'd see what Noycannir had to say to her, and then she'd decide what to do.

Who could have guessed that a minor training exercise could explode into a fight for her very survival?

Lek Kerenko stood at attention-rest with his team alongside the transport craft, listening to the voice of his ancestors. shouting for attention in his brain.

Chelatring Side. The Autocrat's Proxy. Chuvishka Kospodar, the rape of Prishklo, the slaughter of the Sivarian innocents, the walls of Erchlo, the dead lake at Immer. The blasted remains of Chatlerin, on the coast.

Koscuisko was the enemy, had carried him here into the heart of the enemy's territory, was carrying him farther still to Chelatring Side to see the Autocrat's Proxy and to meet the great-great-granddaughter of Chuvishka Kospodar himself.

Koscuisko was the three-times-great-grandson of Chuvishka Kospodar, the doom of the Sarvaw, the man who had unleashed the Angel of Destruction against an unarmed and defenseless population, a defiler of women, a murderer of children—

Koscuisko was the enemy, but Koscuisko was his officer of assignment. And Koscuisko himself was not Lek's enemy, but had been a good officer to him, the best man Lek had seen assigned as Ship's Inquisitor in thirteen years of bond-involuntary service.

Koscuisko was coming, walking slowly down the track to the

motor stables with his lady at one side and his son at the other, talking to the Bench specialist while the Malcontent Cousin Stanoczk brought up the rear. Andrej Koscuisko, hand in hand with Anton Andreievitch. The four-times-great-grandson of Chuvishka Kospodar, who broke away from his father when he saw Lek standing there waiting and came running over the graveled apron with his arms outspread to embrace him.

Don't run, little lord, you'll fall, and scrape your hands.

Crouching down on his heels, Lek watched Anton Andreievitch come. He could not frown at the child, anxious though he was. This child was the enemy of his blood. This child's ancestor had drowned children as beautiful and beloved as he was for the crime of being Sarvaw, born of a Sarvaw mother and a Sarvaw father—vermin by definition; nor had those children been any the less dear to their parents than was Anton to his Excellency.

Was it Anton's fault that his blood was tainted?

Anton Andreievitch put his arms around Lek's neck and kissed him. Lek held the child in his arms, and the voices in his blood murmured in confusion as Lek spoke.

"There, now, little lord, you do me great honor, but we're only going to Chelatring Side after all. You've heard of Chelatring Side, I know you have, and you're to come next time, you told me so yourself."

In all of Anton Andreievitch's life, he had never met his own grandparents—not his father's parents. Things were changed now. The Koscuisko familial corporation would receive Anton Andreievitch as the inheriting son of its inheriting son; Koscuisko had seen to that.

Chelatring Side was not ready to receive its new master-to-be, not ready to receive its new princess. There would be rank conferred on Koscuisko's Respected Lady before that happened; it was too awkward that the mother of the Koscuisko prince should be a mere gentlewoman. All very complicated, but the only thing that mattered right now was that Andrej Koscuisko was going to Chelatring Side and his child was bereft.

"Be well," Anton Andreievitch said with careful precision, kissing Lek one last time before he stood away. "Have care for yourself, Lek, until such time. As . . . "

It was a formula. Anton Andreievitch had to learn an entire catalog of new formulae, now that he was no longer merely an acknowledged son, but the inheriting son. Lek kept his face as carefully clear as possible, willing the words into Anton Andreievitch's mind. *Until such time as we shall see each other. Until such time . . .*

". . . um, until such time as we shall see each other once again, and all Saints keep you in the heart of the Holy Mother."

The Holy Mother was an Aznir whore. But that was beside the point. Surely. "Thank you, my lord, and all Saints under Canopy prosper thy purpose till we meet again."

He knew some formulae as well. He'd just never imagined that he might ever say such a thing with affection. Shifting his weight, Lek put one knee to the ground so that he could bend his neck in solemn and traditional salute; the grave bow that Anton returned to him in response almost broke Lek's heart. Anton would learn. Someone would teach him. Anton gave him face as a respected family retainer, and he wasn't; he was a mere Sarvaw, which was to say a brute animal.

"Load courier," Chief Stildyne said, with a note of amusement and tolerance buried so deeply underneath the layers of rubble and broken glass in his ruined voice that it was almost imperceptible. Koscuisko had taken leave of his Respected Lady; she came forward to take custody of her son.

Lek loaded courier with the rest of his team. This time he was not flying; the courier had its own crew. Chelatring Side was deep in the mountains of the Chetalra range, named after the goddess who had been sovereign here before the Aznir had come and their Holy Mother with them. Dasidar the Great—from whom all of the oldest, noblest families of Aznir Dolgorukij claimed descent—had set his name on the mightiest peak among the Chetalra, Mount Dasidar himself. Navigation at altitude through such a mountain range was difficult enough for a practiced crew. Lek was just as glad he didn't have to drive.

Koscuisko boarded next to last with the Bench specialist before him, as befit his senior rank; and laid his hand on Lek's shoulder as he went forward to take his place at the great windows that lined the courier's skin. "You are very kind to my son," Koscuisko said. "He is very fond of you. His mother asks that I praise you particularly for your care, and I thank you for it also."

It sounded a great deal more formal in Koscuisko's Aznir dialect than it was meant, Lek was sure. The Dolgorukij dialects in general did take on a formal sort of tone when translated into Standard, and Koscuisko with his Security spoke Standard without fail, even here. Even at home.

Lek smiled and nodded in appreciation of the compliment, while the voices of his ancestors raged in his blood. *Can you be bought as cheaply as that, Lek, and this the man who is Kospodar's child.*

Maybe there was something that his ancestors didn't understand, Lek mused, watching out the windows as the courier traveled forward slowly down the graveled drive toward the launch field.

He was only Sarvaw in an Aznir context. Outside of the Dolgorukij Combine he was Dolgorukij, and a bond-involuntary. Koscuisko did not honor him by treating him, a Sarvaw, as though he were actually a human being. Koscuisko treated bond-involuntaries as though they were human beings, when what they were was instruments of torture for Koscuisko's use. That was how Koscuisko had purchased him. Not with praise as Aznir to Sarvaw; but with respect as man to man, in context of the Fleet.

At the launch field the courier idled for several moments as the flight engines were engaged, the fuel adjusted, the change from ground to air travel modes completed.

Then it took a short run down the launch corridor and leaped into the sky on a sharp angle of ascent that was so unexpected and extreme that Lek grinned almost despite himself, as though he was on a carnival ride and headed straight for the cold hard ground.

It was not very long by airborne courier between the estate of the Matredonat in the grain belt of Azanry's largest continent and the mountains where Koscuisko's family had first established itself in the days of the warring states long, long ago. A few hours, and the courier had covered the grain-growing regions of the continent; another short period of time, and the landscape began to rise to meet them.

Steep slopes. Barren crags. Long lawns of green at impossible angles, and grazing animals navigating all but the most extreme slopes; old-fashioned buildings, low and gray and thick walled with black slate roofs pitched at an angle to shed the accumulation of snow during the winter. There were dire wolves still in these mountains, Lek knew. They could no longer be hunted except by the permission of the Autocrat and by a member of the ancient blood, because they were a last remnant of what had once been an enemy as savage as the Dolgorukij themselves.

The courier flew steady and straight, but the mountains did not level off. The mountains continued to rise beneath them.

The pilot switched the propulsion mode of the courier from thrust to float, so that they could continue the approach at a much reduced rate of speed. Lek was just as glad. The rock grew closer by the moment—great jagged peaks that looked hungry to him. They made him nervous. He didn't want to knock into any mountainsides.

It was quiet in the courier.

Nobody was particularly enjoying this but Koscuisko. Lek could hear Koscuisko making conversation with Cousin Stanoczk and the Bench specialist, noting the points of interest, naming the landmarks. Arguing with Cousin Stanoczk whether the battle of Mingche had been fought at the ford at Vsalja or on the bridge of Girnos, because *the song said stone but the bridges over the river had been wooden till well after the event but they were stone by the time the song was written down and the poet had realized that calling them "wooden" would just confuse people but people knew that they had been wooden and people weren't stupid but the song also said the banks with the high-water so it had to have been the ford, and you just stay out of this, Stildyne, whose side are you on, anyway?*

Lek couldn't imagine the Bench specialist being unnerved by the nearness of the mountains. But he was. He wasn't accustomed to land-based flights. His training had all been for engagements in deep space. That was his job, to defend the *Ragnarok*, and he couldn't have defended the *Ragnarok* here, because there hardly seemed to be enough room to maneuver for a single Wolnadi, let alone a battlewagon.

They were flying between mountains, now, following the course of a river back toward its birthplace. And the terrain was rising fast, or they were sinking fast, skimming over a ferocious and forbidding landscape of sharp black peaks whose wind-scoured flanks were like obsidian-edged knives; heading straight for the great shield-wall of the Chetalra Mountains, whose steep peaks pierced the clouds.

The black peaks rose up into the visiports of the transport, as if eager to examine its contents for a meal as the courier worked its way into the body of the goddess Chetalra. From what Lek could hear, Koscuisko was saying they had had reached the flanks of awesome Dasidar, towering above them and before them steep and frightening. The valleys were all filled and hidden with mist; there was no seeing how deep those valleys were. As they flew steadily onward toward the mountain, they ran through alternate stretches of ice and snow that shut their visibility down to nothing with brutal suddenness.

But the variant text says glassy slope. Glassy slope. Not grassy slope. So it was higher up than the bridge, there would have been grassy slopes, so it had to be the fort. Stildyne, name of all Saints, you haven't been reading the revisionists, have you? Holy Mother. Just when you think you know a man.

They were going to run into the wall.

The mountain filled their vision on three sides, with an unfathomable chasm on the fourth; the walls of Dasidar's fortress rose into the very heavens, and they were continuing to make straight for them, rising as they went. The side of the mountain was as smooth as stalloy here, polished over the ages by wind and snow and cold, and the sheer size of the rock—the closer one came to it—was terrifying, in its way.

Lek braced himself, biting his lip to stifle his cry of fear. They were going to crash. Why hadn't the officer noticed? Because the officer knew where he was going. The courier made straight for the wall, closer and closer, and Lek slowly began to realize that they were not as near to the wall as he had thought. The scale of that great wall was almost unimaginable.

Rocks he had taken for boulders were great towering crags, bits of green that he had taken for moss or lichen were clumps of trees as large as small forests, and the courier just kept heading on steadily toward the wall. But continued to climb. The wall fell away beneath them, but it did not end. There was more and more and more of it; and then the courier topped one final rise, and Lek gasped in involuntary shock.

Chelatring Side.

The ancestral seat of the Koscuisko familial corporation, set into the side of the mountain like a babe against its father's bosom, curved close into the embrace of Dasidar himself where he sat in majestic glory looking out over his conquered world, a stronghold huge and invincible, dwarfed by the rock around it for all its size.

Chelatring Side.

The walls went on forever, and the towers could not be counted. Its fortress walls were monumental, and its ranks of solar panels glittered forever-long in the bright sunlight. There was nothing beneath them now but clouds, and of the peaks that stood sufficient tall to stand in array with Dasidar the nearest was veserts upon veserts away, even by direct flight.

This was not a fortress, this was a city. This was a large city, and that such a piece of work should be the personal possession of anyone man or even group of men was almost obscene. No. It *was* obscene. There was no "almost" about it.

The courier cleared the first banked wall, and there were walls behind walls behind walls, each rising higher and higher into the sky with the weathered gray of the stone of the fortress almost the same shade as the mountainside itself. Wall upon wall, and tower upon tower, and Andrej Koscuisko sighed happily where he sat. "Home," Koscuisko said. "What do you think, Specialist Ivers, do you like it?"

The Bench specialist was staring out the window, as transfixed as any of them. "I don't know what to say, your Excellency. Description fails to capture the actual impact of the place."

"I suppose when one grows up in such surroundings, it seems more homely. Also one was accustomed to approaching it in stages, when one was a boy, before the entire installation was sealed for supplemental air. And still my brother Iosev got the nosebleed. Every year. Finally they let him stay at Rogubarachno, but he was the only one left there of my brothers; he learned bad habits."

Supplemental air? Well. Yes. Altitude. How high were they? Lek didn't want to know. Was it his imagination that he could see the curvature of the planet itself, on the horizon?

The courier cleared the second set of walls and settled to a halt in a motor court. They were well to one side of the fortress itself, but there were fortified corridors, and transport waiting. Fortified? Lek wondered. Or were those obviously thick walls, the steeply pitched roofs, the half-buried foundations simply accommodations for the winter? There was no snow on the ground within the compound, but outside the walls it lay undisturbed. How much of it was there?

"Your Excellency. That," the Bench specialist said, and pointed. "That. What is that. Is that what I think it is?"

What was she looking at? There. Not alongside the courier, but at a near remove, its glittering lines elegant and evil in the bright thin azure light.

The Malcontent Cousin Stanoczk coughed. "Yes, Bench specialist," he said. "She is. Kospodar thula."

Kospodar. There was no escaping the beast, in all of the Combine.

"Cousin Stanoczk, I thought the Arakcheyek Yards only built twenty-seven of them. What is this one—" She almost asked *What is this one doing here*? She almost did. Lek could hear the unspoken words clearly in the quiet cabin, though she had stopped herself in time.

"And this is one of the twenty-seven, Bench specialist. You would like a tour? Andrej. Permit me. Let me show off this pretty little animal. You can stand and talk to Ferinc if you do not care to see her for yourself."

The courier had been secured. Lek could hear the opening of the cargo bays. Someone was working the secures to the passenger landing ramp, and let a blast of air come in. Hot air. Lek was surprised that it was not cold, but they did lie in full sunlight.

"I have nothing to say to thy Ferinc," Koscuisko said, sourly. "Except for, 'be damned.' Here is supplemental, gentles, you must each wear one until you are indoors. You will want one to tour the thula. Go with Stoshik."

Supplemental atmosphere generator, a little soft packet that sat on the shoulder, a supple tube that lay along the cheek below the nostril and clung there of its own accord. Lek took one; the courier's navigator helped him to adjust it. His headache went away. He hadn't realized he'd had a headache.

The Malcontent broke from his place and down the ramp as soon as it was cleared, and the Bench specialist after him. Stildyne nodded; Lek followed eagerly. A Kospodar thula. He had only ever heard of them. He had never hoped to see one.

It would be something to tell the crew when they returned to the *Ragnarok*. Without their officer . . .

Lek put that unhappy thought aside. It was to be.

There was no help for it. And he needed all of his attention to spend on the thula.

⊕ ⊕ ⊕

Talk to Ferinc, Stanoczk had said. Insufferable cheek, Andrej decided. Nobody had said anything to him that would change the fact of who Ferinc had been, nor had anybody a satisfactory explanation for why Ferinc should be tolerated at the Matredonat. He was home now. He was to stay. Ferinc had no place left in his house.

That Marana had taken comfort from Ferinc in Andrej's absence he could understand, so long as he declined to think about it.

Yet Anton loved his Ferinc, and Andrej didn't know what he was going to do about that. The Ferinc that Anton loved was very little to do with the man Andrej had disciplined so many years ago; it did no good to tell himself that it was for Anton's sake that Ferinc should be denied him. Anton was a loving and trusting child. Children learned what they were shown, rather than what they were taught. To be fair, Andrej could not deny Ferinc credit for the beautiful spirit of his son, the openhearted affection that he had found so surprising and so endearing. How could those two Ferincs be the same man?

He was not particularly interested in Cousin Stanoczk's thula. Unless he missed his guess, Specialist Ivers would imagine that this was the only one that the Malcontent owned; and she was impressed enough at that, because the Bench itself could not afford any more of them. That had been why the program had been cancelled. Andrej suspected that the Malcontent had more than one thula at his saintly disposal; not because he knew, but because he—unlike the Bench specialist—had the native child's grasp of the money that the Malcontent held in safekeeping for the Saint's purposes.

He stood outside the craft at the side of the loading ramp and looked at the sky, instead. They were so high into atmosphere at Chelatring Side that everything looked crisper, brighter, sharper in the thin air. Sometimes he thought about the old times when Koscuisko had lived at Chelatring Side and only gone down to the grain fields to raid or to marry, and wondered whether his ancestors would hold him in contempt for that he had to use a supplemental atmosphere generator when he came to his own home.

He knew that he'd looked down on Iosev for chronic bleeding of the nose, as if it were a moral weakness. There were many more reasons than just that to find his brother wanting, that was so.

Someone came around from the nose of the thula toward him, and stopped dead in his tracks when he caught sight of Andrej. Andrej sighed. "Come to me, Cousin," he suggested, knowing that it was not a suggestion. "Stanoczk says that I am to have a word with you."

Ferinc looked a different man, in this thin light, than he had in the library at the Matredonat, which had been comparatively dim. There was more gray in his long fore-braids than Andrej had noticed, but his gaze was clear and level. When Ferinc dropped his eyes to bow it was with professional self-effacement, not the fear that had possessed him before. "If Cousin Stanoczk says, your Excellency, I am bound to obey."

Oh, be that way, Andrej thought to himself with irritation. *And your soul to perdition on top of it.* "My child loves you very much, and speaks of you often. Someone has taught him to be so openhearted as to gladden the heart of a long-absent father. How are we to manage this between us?"

"We" was owed Ferinc, regardless of how Andrej felt about the man personally. Marana had not approached him to moderate his ban on Ferinc, but every time Andrej heard Anton mention the name it reminded him that there was an issue to resolve.

"Permission to speak freely, your Excellency," Cousin Ferinc said, but it wasn't a Malcontent talking, it was the petty warrant officer that Ferinc had once been. Andrej didn't care to be reminded of who Ferinc had been, but that was the problem whole and entire right there, wasn't it?

And who was he, of all men, to disdain Haster Girag for what Girag had done, when he himself was so much the more depraved a beast? "Granted."

It took Ferinc a moment to collect his thoughts, but then he licked his lips as though they were dry and spoke. "I was sent for duty, your Excellency. I didn't mean to grow close to the child. I didn't see it happening. I am the slave of the Malcontent. His Excellency knows how little I have to say about where I am next to go. But, your Excellency, if I could be permitted, even if only to write from time to time."

Andrej knew that he was Anton's biological parent, his genetic sire. Ferinc was the man who had been Anton's father—the realization was liberating and agonizing, at once.

"Stanoczk is right." Andrej said it out loud, and heard the somewhat confused wonder in his voice. "A duty is owed to you, Ferinc. I don't want to see you. Deal with Marana. I withdraw my prohibition. Anton loves you. How could I love him, if I kept you from him?"

Liberating: because what he had done to Ferinc when he had punished Haster Girag—rather than reporting his criminal behavior for Fleet to punish—had not destroyed Ferinc's capacity for happiness, Malcontent or no. Ferinc could still feel and share a parent's love for a child, love that was untainted by the corruption of the torture cell.

Agonizing: because Andrej despaired of ever taking Ferinc's place in the heart of his own son. He did not deserve it; he could not truly begrudge it to Ferinc; and yet, and yet, and yet. Ferinc reached out and took him by the sleeve, as if overcome. Loosened his grip, then straightened up. "Thank you," Ferinc said. "I won't give you cause to regret it. I promise. Thank you."

And yet he had only done the right thing, because the pure parental affection in Ferinc's voice was unmistakable. Undeniable. How cruel would it have been to deny Ferinc to Anton? To deny Anton to Ferinc?

It was the Malcontent's business; so Andrej did not have to think long or hard on it, nor could he bear to. He merely nodded, and Stildyne came down out of the thula to rescue him from awkwardness, pausing in apparent confusion to see him and Ferinc together. "Your Excellency," Stildyne said. "Your assistance, sir. Lek's bonding. We may not be able to pry him loose. We need your help."

No, Stildyne had only wondered where he was, but Andrej was glad to take the offered escape route. Andrej nodded yet again; and went up the ramp into the courier to see what had gotten into his good Lek, hoping he'd done the right thing for his son.

Admiral Brecinn stared at the little ticket in front of her on her desk, her hands flat to the desk's surface as though she could stop the room from spinning by main force of will.

The treachery was unspeakable.

Dame Mergau Noycannir was not at Chilleau. She hadn't been there, she wasn't expected, and so far as Chilleau knew she was at Pesadie. Mergau Noycannir had taken the finest, fleetest courier at Pesadie and left days ago, but she hadn't gone to Chilleau at all. It all made too much sense, all of a sudden.

Noycannir had come from Chilleau to observe the exercise. When the accident had happened, she had offered her services to Brecinn as though motivated by nothing more than an eye toward her own advantage and a desire to ingratiate herself with the network of reasonable people. She had counseled patience, subtlety, tact, but it had all been a trick.

The *Ragnarok* had stolen the cannon from Silboomie Station and left for Fleet Audit Appeals Authority at Taisheki. Mergau Noycannir had disappeared.

It was a conspiracy; Brecinn couldn't quite puzzle the exact framework of it out, but she knew a conspiracy when she smelled one. There was no time to sit and beat herself for her stupidity, her trusting nature, her gullibility.

This had gone beyond a simple issue of lost profit. The loss of the battle cannon was a serious compromise. Reasonable people did not tolerate being compromised. She needed a good story and she needed it fast, and she needed to get it to Taisheki Station before the *Ragnarok* had a chance to log an appeal. She had to get her word in first.

There were reasonable people at the Fleet Audit Appeals Authority. And the cannon was worth a very great deal of money.

The *Ragnarok* was clearly trafficking; they'd killed poor inoffensive Brem because he'd discovered something inconvenient, perhaps because he'd been reluctant to participate. They'd used their stay at Pesadie Training Command to forge documentation for stolen munitions, using her own validation codes. Now they intended to present the gun to Fleet to incriminate Pesadie and divert Fleet's attention away from their own corrupt dealings.

It was not the most convincing story in the world. But it was all she had. And if it cost her everything she had left to buy credibility at Fleet Audit Appeals Authority—poverty was better than death. Poverty she could hope to recover from. Assassination was much more permanent a handicap for an officer's career.

She would see to it that ap Rhiannon, not Sandri Brecinn, paid the price for this treachery, if it took the last resources she had at her command. She would be revenged. She could no longer hope to profit from the *Ragnarok*'s decommissioning, but she would see to it that ap Rhiannon died for her duplicity.

⊕ ⊕ ⊕

There were only fifty people at dinner, sixty at most, but Stildyne couldn't get a decent count for the glittering of jewels in the bright lights. They hurt his eyes. And he was drunk already: not on any alcohol, but on the luxury that clothed his body and beguiled him with unimaginable sensuality.

They hadn't brought dress uniform with them.

Koscuisko's people hadn't said word one, but Koscuisko's people had been busy at it since the day that they'd arrived here on Azanry. Stildyne could only guess that garments had been borrowed, checked for size, when he'd thought they were merely being laundered. Because on gaining crew-quarters here at Chelatring Side earlier today, they had found dress uniform ready for all of them.

The fit was exact and the detail was precise, from the formal version of the service marks that Taller wore on his collar—from the Abermarle campaign—to the exact shade of green that marked Lek for a bond-involuntary. Of course, the shade of green had to be precise; not all hominids under Jurisdiction had the same sort of color vision, after all, so tone and saturation were as important as hue.

Perfect. But so much more than perfect. The boots had been shaped to the wear of the foot, but they were lined with glove leather so soft that it was almost like sex to set foot inside them. Koscuisko's personal linen had always been that, linen, and Security had handled it often enough over the years while managing drunken officers; Stildyne had never imagined the luxury of wearing a linen hip-wrap on his own part.

And the boot stockings were silk. And the uniform blouse was a wool spun so fine that it made a man afraid to put it on, but it lay so lightly across his shoulders that he almost felt naked. It was unnerving. His under-blouse alone was worth three weeks' pay, and the kit was complete. It was astonishing. And it made him angry, in a subtle sense; how dare Koscuisko's people treat them with so much contempt as to casually clothe them with a year's wages, and not even bother to mention it?

Stildyne stood by the side doors into the great dining room, brooding about it, watching his people. House security had posted Security 5.1 in visible positions around the officer, a guard of honor. Koscuisko's people were particularly fascinated by Smath and

Kerenko, to judge from their placement, because they were to either side of Koscuisko himself, with a clear corridor between down which the servers might pass.

Koscuisko would never wear his uniform again. He wasn't wearing his uniform now, sitting at the table, talking with Specialist Ivers to one side of him and a boy-child on the other. Not that much older than Anton Andreievitch, Stildyne thought, and nudged Cousin Stanoczk in the ribs with his elbow.

"Who is that?" The boy-child looked like Anton Andreievitch, come to that. Or like Koscuisko. That meant nothing. Chelatring Side was filthy with people who looked like Koscuisko. He had thought that Cousin Stanoczk looked like Koscuisko at the Matredonat. There were closer matches here everywhere he turned.

Cousin Stanoczk frowned, apparently confused; but his face cleared quickly. "Young prince. The youngest of the family, Nikolij Ulexeievitch. Your officer's youngest brother. Who else?"

The servers were carrying a meat course down the line behind the seated guests. Stildyne caught a glimpse of the Bench specialist's profile as she turned her head to consider the offer; she looked a little panicked, Stildyne thought. Yes. It had already been several courses.

"Father. Mother. Autocrat's Proxy." Stildyne named them off as he knew them, and Cousin Stanoczk filled in the rest.

"Thy officer's sister, actually, did you know that? Fourth born and second eldest of daughters. Younger than Iosev and Meeka, but older than Lo. There's another sister. And the oldest sister is not here tonight, because it is too awkward in today's environment, after all."

Whatever that meant. Stildyne counted them all up in his mind; Koscuisko had four brothers, then, and three sisters as it seemed. More family than Stildyne had ever had. In Dolgorukij terms, Stildyne had never had family at all, he supposed. "Why do they keep staring?"

That the guests were intrigued by Smish in uniform Stildyne could understand. Koscuisko had warned them to expect that, and the experience of their stay at the Matredonat had only confirmed the exotic appeal Smish had on Azanry. He wasn't sure he understood what was so interesting about Lek. Lek was tolerably well put together, yes, and Security were expected to maintain an appropriately lean and menacing physique. But so were Taller and Murat, and Murat was quite possibly abstractly the more attractive of the three. Being younger, for one.

Now Cousin Stanoczk shoved him, as, Stildyne had elbowed Cousin Stanoczk earlier. "What do you think?" Well, if he'd known what to think, Stildyne thought a bit resentfully, he wouldn't have asked. "And do you mean to watch all through the dinner, Chief?"

"No, Cousin, I think he's safe enough with his own people. These troops look like they mean business to me." The house security who staffed the room were as fine troops as Stildyne had ever seen; he could smell their edge. It was subtle. They more than just looked impressive. They had the juice.

"Then come with me. I've got something to show you."

Cousin Stanoczk drew him away from the room, walking backward, sidling through a panel door in the wall that Stildyne hadn't noticed being there. "He's Sarvaw, Chief," Cousin Stanoczk said, and after a moment Stildyne remembered having asked the question about Lek. "Imagine that. A Sarvaw security troop. Assigned to the son of the Koscuisko prince. The mind, it absolutely boggles."

Stildyne couldn't see what was so particularly boggling about that. "It's all Combine one way or the other, Cousin, isn't it so?" All right, so he'd heard that there was bad blood in the history. History was history. And if it wasn't history, it ought to be, once it was history. "How can they tell, anyway? You all look alike to me."

Cousin Stanoczk snorted, apparently taken by genuine surprise. "Say such a thing to either Aznir or Sarvaw and insult them equally, friend Stildyne. You will perhaps consent to trust me on this. We can tell."

The corridors through which Cousin Stanoczk led him were emptier by the moment; the area into which they were descending seemed almost deserted. There were locked doors. Cousin Stanoczk had the keys.

"But *how* can they tell?"

And where were they going? "If you had the history of this family, you might have cause to understand, Chief. I would almost say that Sarvaw children know Aznir for their enemy in their mothers' wombs. And my cousin and his Lek, they get on together?" The corridors were narrowing, and they kept climbing down stairs. Cousin Stanoczk stopped in front of one particularly large wooden door to work the secures.

Lek was a bond-involuntary. He had no choice. That wasn't what Cousin Stanoczk was asking. "His Excellency respects and values Lek equally as his other Security. Maybe there's even a community feeling between them, both Combine—what?"

Stanoczk had rolled his eyes in exaggerated exasperation, leaning into the door to open it. "If you only knew what nonsense you were talking, Chief. But, at any rate, that is why they are staring. Andrej has been playing his Lek up from the moment he arrived, to give him face. I'm not surprised that the family are fascinated."

That was all to the good. Stildyne found Cousin Stanoczk a little fascinating for his own part. Stanoczk was very like Andrej Koscuisko in some ways that had nothing to do with his physical appearance; and so completely unlike Koscuisko in others. Cousin Stanoczk flirted with him. Andrej Koscuisko had never kissed a man with amorous intent in his entire life, not in any context that counted.

"Where are we going, Cousin?" He didn't mind taking a stroll with Cousin Stanoczk. But he was beginning to wonder what was going on.

"Going, we go nowhere, we are arrived," Cousin Stanoczk said, somewhat confusingly. "You and my Ferinc had history, I understand. I thought that you might be intrigued by some of what it can mean, to be Malcontent."

Cousin Stanoczk turned and closed the door behind him, and secured it. Stildyne stood and stared.

It was just a corridor, but it seemed to be a long corridor, and there were pictures on the walls the likes of which would have been startling enough in almost any other context but which were truly amazing in a Dolgorukij one.

"What's this?"

Cousin Stanoczk took Stildyne's arm encouragingly, and started down the corridor. "It is the Gallery—technically, the Great Gallery at Chelatring Side. Or more technically, it does not even exist. This part of the house belongs to my holy Patron, Chief. Some mysteries cannot be written, but they can be shown."

Visual documentation. Pictures. Ways in which a man might discover that he was Malcontent. "Reconciliation," Stildyne guessed, trying hard to look without seeing. It was hard. They were persuasive pictures.

"In one form or another." Cousin Stanoczk's voice was cheerful in agreement, seeming unmoved by the explicit and arousing images on the walls. *Why not?* Stildyne asked himself, in despair of ruling his own flesh. Cousin Stanoczk probably saw them all the time.

"I'm not Dolgorukij, Cousin." And nobody would know that better than an Aznir Dolgorukij, because that was as Dolgorukij as they got. "Why have you brought me here?"

"I wish to take advantage," Cousin Stanoczk said, enthusiastically. "In an attempt to seduce you. Say that I may succeed, and I will be a happy man. One of these in particular I think you will especially like, Stildyne, if you would put your eyes back in your head and follow me."

This was not a dialect of Dolgorukij that Stildyne could grasp. Cousin Stanoczk was speaking plain Standard. But Dolgorukij— *didn't.* That was why they were so expensive in service houses, after all. Dolgorukij didn't, not with other men. Were those expensive Dolgorukij all Malcontents?

He couldn't think. The lovingly detailed sexual images in the paintings that lined the walls had stacked themselves firmly between his cerebrum and his brain stem, so that the only processing that was going on in his brain any longer was direct and visceral. Eye to brain to spine, and down.

His entire body was following Cousin Stanoczk with avid interest, eagerly curious about wherever it was that Stanoczk was going and whatever it was that Stanoczk might have in mind. His entire body, less his brain, which was still only slowly processing the things that he was seeing on the walls.

He had to hurry to catch up. When he did, he put his hand to Stanoczk's shoulder, and left it there; turning his head Cousin Stanoczk grinned back at Stildyne over his shoulder, and led him deeper into the Gallery.

CHAPTER TWELVE

The Great Gate

Jils Ivers had known torture, hardship, and privation in her life, and no ordeal that she could think of at this moment could be compared to a Dolgorukij formal banquet. Not because she wasn't comfortably seated; she was. Not because there were after-dinner speakers; there weren't, though the toasts had been difficult to get through on account of the amount of drinking that they involved.

There was simply too much food. And she hated to not eat every bite of it, because she never knew for sure when exactly she'd have a chance to eat again. It was torture. It was all so good. Agony.

And when the Koscuisko princess—Andrej Koscuisko's mother— rose from the table at last, with everybody else in turn rising in order of precedence to progress out into the great hall of Chelatring Side, Jils Ivers heard an orchestra tuning, and groaned inwardly. It was too much. She had to go lie down. Nobody took exercise after such a meal as this.

But Dolgorukij went dancing, and she was on the arm of the son of the Koscuisko prince, Andrej Koscuisko himself. He looked so different in civilian dress. Dolgorukij aristocrats wore fancy clothing, brightly colored, frothing at the cuffs with lace. Exotic animals, as unlike a man in the black of a Ship's Chief Medical Officer as could be imagined.

"It is only a darshan to start," Koscuisko explained, encouragingly, clearly sensitive to her distress. "My brother is shy. But would very much like the honor. If you would permit, Bench specialist."

Figures of eight, many of them already in motion. Koscuisko's youngest sister was waiting for them, with a young man; the boy Nikolij Ulexeievitch bowed to her very prettily, with almost no trace of anxiety on his face, and Jils had to smile and give in.

She had never thought of Koscuisko as a man with brothers and sisters. As odd as it had been to see him at his ease at the Matredonat with his wife and his young son, it was stranger still to see him here in a darshan-eight, dancing with his young sister, and his youngest brother serving as her squire.

Inquisitors were without family; they existed only in the thoroughly adult context of the Law, the prison, and the torture room. Andrej Koscuisko was the single most notorious pain-master in the entire inventory, and here he was the older brother in the middle of his cousins and his brothers and his sisters and his parents as well.

By the end of the figure she was beginning to feel much less uncomfortably full, but she was still grateful to be ushered to a chair behind that of the Koscuisko princess to sit down. Nikolij was an attentive host, bringing her a glass of punch and a fan with which to cool herself. He yielded up his duties to his brother with good grace when Andrej Koscuisko appeared from out of the press of people to sit down beside her.

Koscuisko's mother looked back at her son over her shoulder and raised an eyebrow. Koscuisko rose swiftly to bow over his mother's hand, but sat back down almost as quickly, smiling.

In the lull in the music between the conclusion of the darshan and the beginning of whatever other dance it would be next an elderly woman came through the mingling guests, and the crowd made way before her. Very straight she stood, very short, almost as small as young Nikolij, who was still growing; her hair was thin and yellow, but her face was youthful in its appearance for all the wrinkles at her eyes and forehead.

When she was five paces or so in front of where Koscuisko's parents sat, she stopped and planted her walking stick firmly on the ground in front of her, and waited. The room got quiet.

"The son of the Koscuisko prince has returned home," she said, her voice clearly meant to carry. "It grieves me to be the one to say, my prince. But he brings neither plunder nor slaves. And therefore, according to the ancient rules of your House, must pay a forfeit."

"Saints," Koscuisko swore under his breath, beside Jils. But he seemed to be smiling. It was some form of hazing, perhaps?

"True enough," Koscuisko's father agreed, with a rumbling undertone of amusement in his voice. "Be merciful, I beg you. He is my son. What shall his forfeit be?"

The elderly woman took another step forward. The great hall was so quiet that Jils could hear the scrape of a chair across the wooden stage as one of the musicians adjusted his place. "Family jeweler," Koscuisko whispered to her, not moving his lips. "Savage woman. I am terrified."

"He brings neither plunder nor pelf," the elderly woman repeated. "And yet has at least one thing to show for his long absence, my prince, something above price. As forfeit we think that we should be allowed to examine his items of adornment. Perhaps to contest with him at target."

"It is worse than I had thought," Koscuisko said quietly. "Do they know that Lek is my knife teacher? I am sure of it."

Lek? What was it about—then she remembered. Yes. That was right. Koscuisko's Sarvaw bond-involuntary. People had been whispering about him all night, and as far as Jils could tell he was enjoying his notoriety thoroughly. It made Jils a little uncomfortable, but she supposed that if it amused the man himself she was not the one to find fault with it.

Koscuisko stood up, moving around to stand in front of his mother and bow to his father. "In truth I am improvident and thriftless," Koscuisko said. "And yet possess treasure. If my father's jeweler will name her time and her champion, I will maintain my honor; or call her 'Younger Sister' for a year."

People seemed to be having a hard time keeping their faces straight. It was a hint to Jils that none of this challenge and rebuke was serious.

"Tomorrow, after breakfast. At such time as your head will have had a chance to clear from your night's debauch, young master."

Now people had started to laugh. The jeweler continued. "We will meet you here, upon the field of honor. And your father and your mother will bear witness, young master. May we hope to see all five?"

A different note, suddenly, some kind of hunger—genuine, and sincere. Five-knives. Koscuisko's Emandisan steel. That elderly woman wasn't the family's jeweler; she was the house armorer. Maybe for Dolgorukij it was the same thing. *Items of adornment*, the old woman had said, and she was talking about Koscuisko's knives.

"Dame Isola, you have rebuked my poverty before my mother and my father, and I will be avenged. You will have to fight to see all five. I put you on your guard."

Now everybody in the entire fortress who did not have to be somewhere else would come and watch, and cheer for one side or the other. This was a family, a familial corporation, not a military installation. But in some ways, its gestalt was not unlike that of an elite ground-combat troop unit.

The music had started to pick up again; the show was apparently over for now. Koscuisko came back for her, holding out his hand with transparent expectation that she would want to dance. "Bench specialist. This is the procession-step, very sedate. Perhaps you would consent to honor me."

Procession step. That sounded safe enough. Giving him her hand Jils rose and went with him to dance, making a note to be sure to come to the great hall in the morning and watch Koscuisko contend with his house troops for face and credibility.

The knife flew clean and true to target, and the crowd cheered. Andrej turned to face them—his parents and his sister Zsuzsa, seated at her father's right in token of her proxy rank—and bowed, smiling. Yes. He was a good shot. Joslire had always praised his natural eye, and said that the blood of the hunter was in his veins. Joslire.

"I think my son shows his worth, Dame Isola," Andrej's father called. The chairs had been moved back to a safe distance, along with the carpet that defined the privileged space. "Do you dispute it?"

Dame Isola, for her part, had stood to one side to watch the progress of the contest. Now she bowed her head. "The son of the Koscuisko prince does his blood honor. I admit it." She seemed to take it in good part, even though she had to know that the coach with whom Andrej trained—now that Joslire was dead—was Sarvaw. "The challenge is well met, my prince. And still."

Lek stood well apart, with Andrej's other Security; they were in uniform, as he was not—they still belonged to Fleet. They had been kept late, last night, and no one had come to take him to train this morning, which was just as well. Supplemental atmosphere or no, the altitude was debilitating; they all felt it, Andrej was sure. Even Stildyne. Andrej had almost never seen Stildyne walk with such hesitation, except when he had been injured in one leg on an assignment—to Ropimel, Andrej thought it was.

"Still?" Andrej's father prompted. "You have further tests to propose? Take care, Dame, this is the man who is to be your master. Do not press him over-hard."

It was an affectionate and insincere rebuke. Dame Isola bowed. "Yes, my prince, and still. The son of the Koscuisko prince has demonstrated his ability." She turned to Andrej, and her bow was respectful, but not nearly so deep as that she had made his father. "It is Emandisan steel, your Excellency, and I would very much like permission to handle it."

Of course. It hadn't been just to see whether Lek was to be granted their respect, and him Sarvaw. It was the knives they wanted. This whole thing had been a setup. She wanted to get her hands on Joslire's soul.

She was the family jeweler; she had maintained steel and adjusted side-arms for Koscuiskos for an octave, almost, almost eighty years. She had served his father and his father's father before that. Joslire might have recognized such a soul; Andrej was curious to see what she might make of Joslire's knives.

"For that you must sue to my son Andrej," Andrej's father said. Andrej could hear the possessive affection in his father's voice as he had never before in his life. *My son Andrej.* Had it been there all along? Did he only recognize it now because he had learned what it was to say *my son Anton*? "He shall decide. Thank you, my son, you vindicate your honor, and you make us proud."

Andrej bowed to his parents with his heart full of gratitude and love.

There would be discussions still when it came time to start to adjust the business considerations consequent to his having forced his father's hand and married Marana. He could never explain about the Bench warrant, not to his parents, because of the relation between it and the question of who had killed Captain Lowden if it had not been Specialist Vogel.

But he had not been more than moderately rebuked for it. He had been afraid that he would be decisively rejected, having only then won forgiveness of a sort for past misdeeds; instead, it seemed that his father understood better than Andrej had imagined that he might.

Maybe Cousin Stanoczk had told him something about the Bench warrant, Andrej decided, waiting for the houseman to carry the tray back to him with his knife. He hadn't seen Cousin Stanoczk since last night.

The houseman brought the knife he'd just thrown back to him on a fabric-lined tray; Andrej loosed its mate from the forearm sheath on his right arm and laid it beside its twin to be shared out, passed around, admired.

Dame Isola was watching him, waiting, and the look on her face was an almost hungry one. He knew what she wanted.

Reaching up over his shoulder, Andrej pulled the mother-knife from its sheath at his back, and passed it to her direct. She held it up to the bright morning light that streamed through the windows at the far wall, fingers delicate to the blade to avoid smudging, her wrist flexing subtly as she tested its weight and its balance.

"He was taller than you are," she said. "And very quick in his movements. But less restless. And also his shoulders, they were more square than yours." Joslire, whom Andrej had known as Curran. Joslire's people had come for the knives when Andrej had gone back to Rudistal to execute the sentence of the Bench against Administrator Geltoi, who had been found to blame for the Domitt Prison.

Andrej had refused to give them up. They were his knives. Joslire had said so. Dame Isola frowned. "But the balance is wrong for such a man," she said. "There is no inner core to these other knives, young master, what is it?"

Thy knives, Joslire had said, pushing the knife that Dame Isola held through the back of Andrej's hand and his own hand to sew their lives together. *Thy knives and my knives, from the first that I came to understand your nature. To the end with thee, my master. And beyond.*

Andrej held out his hand; Dame Isola passed the knife back with evident reluctance. "It was not always so." The knife slid back into its place between Andrej's shoulder-blades as easily as ever it did, and it always gave him anchor there. Security. A feeling of protection.

Chief Samons had had to pull the knife from Andrej's hand.

Because he'd needed it. Joslire had claimed the Day. It had been Joslire's right to die. If anyone could understand, it should be a jeweler, a woman whose whole life had been in steel. "It became heavier. After Joslire died."

The soul of a man was an intangible. It had no weight. Andrej could not explain it; he had no theological grounds for making any such claim. But he knew. The knife was heavier now. There was some part of Joslire in the knife that had never gone away from him, nor ever would.

Dame Isola waited in respectful silence as Andrej set the knife back in its place. Then she leaned forward, just a bit, with an inquiring and beguiling expression on her face. "And the other two, young master?"

Andrej smiled. It was, to an extent, a trick question. Because there were two more knives that he wore. One of them he usually wore in his boot. But the fifth of five knives was a secret, one to which Andrej himself was not privy. He could not show all five knives. He didn't know which one was the sacred one. Joslire had never told him.

Joslire hadn't told him till Joslire had been at the point of death that Andrej was wearing Emandisan steel, and had been all along. Andrej suspected that the sacred blade was the mother-knife, because that one was the one that held Joslire's soul; it was the holiest of Joslire's knives to Andrej. But he didn't know. And he had no one to ask.

So it had been his practice to show off four knives when the occasion called for it, but never all five at once. Not always the same four. Just never all five at one time. That way at least he could respect the spirit of the Emandisan steel, because his undoubted violation of its sanctity was due to ignorance on his part.

And he had loved Joslire, loved him still, honored Joslire in his heart and took comfort in Joslire's knives. "The other two were not required for target practice, with respect, Dame Isola. I trust you will forgive me."

Dame Isola looked for a moment as though she would make another remark; exposing his secret, perhaps. There was a definite light that spoke of arcane knowledge received in her clear eyes. But as she seemed on the verge of opening her mouth to make some roguish comment, the great doors at the far end of the hall opened with unexpected suddenness, and a squad of house security came through.

House-master Jepson was in the lead—the senior security man here at Chelatring Side. Andrej's father stood up, turning to face Jepson; who bowed.

"Special envoy from Chilleau Judiciary," Jepson said. "She demands an interview with the Koscuisko prince, on behalf of the Second Judge and the rule of Law."

There was someone with the security squad that Andrej thought he recognized. A woman. Who was that? Glancing over to catch Jils Ivers's eye, Andrej found her frowning at the woman, with an expression of open skepticism.

There were Fleet security troops behind the house troops. "I'm not expecting any such honor," Andrej's father said. "Who is this person?"

Some of the house-master's men had materialized to either side of Andrej's sister Zsuzsa, the Autocrat's Proxy, and vanished into the background with her. There had been a bit of a crowd assembled to see whether Andrej would acquit himself well in response to Dame Isola's challenge or suffer defeat; there was plenty of background into which to disappear.

The woman under escort stepped forward smartly, but she did not salute. She nodded her head, but that was all. "I am Clerk of Court at Chilleau Judiciary," she said. "Dame Mergau Noycannir. And I hold the Writ in whose support the Writ of the Koscuisko prince is to be annexed, on direction."

It made no sense. But Andrej recognized her now. What could possibly have brought Mergau Noycannir, of all people, to Chelatring Side?

Mergau Noycannir strode proudly into the great hall of the fortress place that Koscuisko's people kept in the mountains, her sharp eye missing nothing of the power and the wealth that this place displayed with such offensive opulence.

There had been a Kospodar thula in the shipyards where she had landed. The Arakcheyek shipyards had built them on Bench contract. How could there be Kospodar thulas in private hands? In Koscuisko's hands? Such wealth could not have been gained legally. She would have to call for an investigation. Later. Once she had become Queen of the Bench.

The great hall was the size of a maintenance hangar in stone, whose floors were carpeted with knotted wool, lighted by great windows and large fixtures in the ceiling; and it was full of people—a small crowd at the far end, people in chairs, more people standing. One person stood up as her escort neared.

The head Security man bowed. "Special envoy from Chilleau Judiciary," the man said. He didn't sound very respectful, to Mergau; he sounded in fact as though he didn't exactly believe her. He should know better, Mergau told herself. He would in time. She would see to it, but for now she was so close to her prize that she could almost taste the fear and despair that she would have from Koscuisko. Soon. Very soon.

The man who had risen to his feet was looking at her with an amused expression on his face. The chair beside him had emptied. "I'm not expecting any such honor," he said. "Who is this person?"

It was time to take control of this. Mergau stepped forward. "I am Clerk of Court at Chilleau Judiciary." Who was he to ask? "I hold the Writ in whose support the Writ of the Koscuisko prince is to be annexed, on direction."

The tall man shook his head. "I am the Koscuisko prince," he said; there was a note of mild amusement in his voice that Mergau found hateful. "I hold no such Writ. You seek my son, Dame Noycannir." Gesturing with his hand, he waited; and Andrej Koscuisko stepped forward from behind him.

Andrej Koscuisko. In his shirtsleeves, and looking at her with wary confusion. How she hated him. How she had waited for this moment.

"This man." She pointed. "You. Andrej Koscuisko. You are required to come to Chilleau Judiciary to pursue the investigation into the death of your Captain and the subsequent discovery of mutinous conspiracy, on board of the Jurisdiction Fleet Ship *Ragnarok*. Under the provisions of Bench disciplinary codes, your Writ is annexed for the duration of the investigation. I should like to leave immediately, if you please. There is not a moment to waste."

Koscuisko looked confused. But he was alone; he had no choice. "I don't know that the Captain is dead," he said, but it was a weak attempt. He might think that he was challenging her, standing there in the middle of a target range with his arms folded. But he could not deny her evidence. "Still less that there is any such mutiny, Dame. If

Chilleau Judiciary truly means to annex my Writ, I am very much surprised."

Whether he were surprised or not was not material. He would learn soon enough not to take such a tone with her if he did not wish to suffer the consequences.

Mergau advanced on Koscuisko where he stood, past Koscuisko's father, to confront him face-to-face. There were security troops at this house, but she had brought Fleet resources with her, and Koscuisko would have no choice but to go with her once she had made her case.

Where were Koscuisko's own Security, the Security he would have brought with him from the *Ragnarok*, his Security slaves? She wanted those people. She wanted to make Koscuisko kill them one by one, in fearful agony; and that would be the start of Koscuisko's punishment. But just the start. They were bond-involuntary; they could not disobey a direct legal order. Koscuisko would be forced to give the order. They would even subdue Koscuisko himself if she said the word.

"You force me to a disagreeable display." She meant there to be no chance of misunderstanding. They would all see. Koscuisko would be left entirely without recourse. "Since you insist. Here is the Record. You of all people understand the implications of this evidence."

Putting the Record down on the empty seat of the chair that Koscuisko's father had vacated, she set the Record to scroll through her evidence. The space between the chair and the far wall had been cleared; Koscuisko had apparently been showing off his combat skills of one sort or another. The images that the Record projected were clear and sharply focused in the air.

Murat Spodinne. Taller Archops, Lek Kerenko.

Smish Smath. Current assignment Jurisdiction Fleet Ship Ragnarok, *skill class code mission engineer Wolnadi prime. Suspicion of conspiracy to commit illegal and insurrectionary acts. Confession as accused and execution in due form.*

The Record broadcast the official language of confession and condemnation, but Koscuisko was not listening. "Explain to me, Noycannir," Koscuisko said. "How can Verlaine have sent you to bring me back to Chilleau Judiciary for whatever purpose. Having previously sent Specialist Ivers to me with fully executed documents for relief of Writ?"

Taller Archops. Skill class code weaponer Wolnadi four, current assignment Jurisdiction Fleet Ship Ragnarok, *suspicion of conspiracy to commit murder of senior Command Branch officer, insurrectionary assassination in the first tier. Confession as accused and execution in due form.*

Noycannir stared. What was Koscuisko talking about? Relief of Writ? Verlaine would never do that. Verlaine hated Koscuisko as much as she did; Koscuisko had disdained and humiliated Verlaine personally and professionally before Fleet and the public alike, at Port Burkhayden. And if anyone had heard hints of a relief of Writ, someone would have told her about it. There would have been gossip.

"You confuse me, Koscuisko, and I suspect you seek to evade your sworn duty. No matter. We will clear it up soon enough once we arrive at Chilleau Judiciary. I trust your kit is packed. Be so good as to summon your Security and we can be on our way."

Murat Spodinne. Confession denied at the Eighth Level, obtained at the Ninth Level under the provisions of emergency legal code subsection suspicion of mutiny. Conspiracy to commit murder and mutinous intent. Conspiracy to undermine the Judicial order. Confession as accused and execution in due form.

The pre-interrogation pictures, the identity validation shots, were focused a few eighth's distance from the chair, displayed in a format large enough for the assembled crowd to see them. Mergau was taking no chances.

But Koscuisko was not moving.

"Tell her that," Koscuisko said, and pointed. Mergau's vision blurred with fury: Bench specialist Jils Ivers. That bitch. Ivers had never liked her; she would say anything Koscuisko wanted her to, just to discountenance Mergau. "Tell her that the documents she carries are illusory. I'm waiting."

"No, I'm waiting, Koscuisko." She didn't care what any eight Bench specialists said. Bench specialists supported the Bench. They would have to defer to her, now, because she had the power to shake the entire Jurisdiction to its foundation, and she would. "Aren't you listening? You know these people, How can you pretend to deny the evidence of your own senses?"

Mergau could destroy it all with a single word: forgery. Bench specialists weren't stupid. If they wanted to save their skins and protect their privileges, they would learn quickly enough to take their orders from her.

Lek Kerenko. Skill class code primary helm navigator Wolnadi three, current assignment Jurisdiction Fleet Ship Ragnarok, suspicion of conspiracy to commit murder and mutiny by indirection, failure to refer incriminating evidence to proper authorities. Expiration without confession of a Bond.

Koscuisko started to speak, but he was forestalled.

"I know *that* person." It was a young woman's voice. Mergau turned her head, startled, shocked; there was a young woman standing beside Koscuisko's father, and she was pointing. "We saw him at dinner last night, very handsome. He's Sarvaw."

"The Serene Proximity is right," Koscuisko said, pointing at the image displayed large behind him, holding out one hand with an expansive and contemptuous gesture. "Lek isn't dead. And hasn't confessed any such thing, because it isn't true. Nor are Smish or Murat or Taller. Noycannir. What have you done?"

How could he ask such a thing?

Was he so stupid that he could not understand that she, and she alone, had dared to forge the Record?

Then a Security troop stepped out of the crowd that was gathered there watching, and bowed; and the impact of what Koscuisko had said hit home. The Malcontent had lied to her. Koscuisko had switched Security teams.

She'd forged the Record for nothing: these people were alive. They were worse than alive. They were here. They were visibly present for everybody to see, so everybody knew. After everything that she had done. Everybody knew that this was not a true Record. Andrej Koscuisko would not come with her to Chilleau Judiciary.

"Mister Stildyne," Koscuisko said. "Secure this supposed Record, if you please. House-master Jepson. If you would assist my people in taking Dame Noycannir into custody—"

With a scream of frustrated rage that had been building for nine years Mergau drew her glasknife and sprang at him, hearing his cry of startled agony as the knife went home and shattered in his body. Flooding the wound with neurotoxin. Incapacitating him—if not killing him outright—and she had another glasknife.

She was a dead woman here and now.

Yet if she could not have the vengeance that she sought she could still take Koscuisko down to death with her, and die happy at last.

Listening in horror to the insane claims that Noycannir made, Andrej Koscuisko clutched at whispered voices in the wind to find an anchor and hold fast. If he was swept away he would be lost.

Evidence of mutiny on board of the *Ragnarok*, and he had seen no such evidence, but it was all too likely to be true. The ship had been treated shabbily by Fleet all along, but it had gotten worse with Lowden gone. There could be mutiny, and it was his duty to root it out and punish it.

These were his people. He couldn't quite grasp what it was that was wrong with the evidence that he was hearing, but he knew that those were his people, and it was up to him to execute the vengeance of the Bench. Tenth Level Command Termination. His own people.

People to whom he owed his life, if not his soul. He couldn't think. He took hold of the first thing that occurred to him and threw it at Noycannir as hard as he could manage to push her away and shut her up.

"How can Verlaine have sent you to bring me back to Chilleau Judiciary, having previously sent fully executed documents for relief of Writ?"

He could no longer be made to punish people, any people, let alone the *Ragnarok*'s crew. He was separated from the crew of the *Ragnarok* by Judicial decree. Jils Ivers had the documents. They had not been transmitted, no, but she had them and they were fully executed. But did that still mean that his people were to be tortured, even if he was not to be the person who did it?

How could he bear to let any ordinary butcher mutilate the bodies of people to whom he owed so much in love and duty and good lordship?

Noycannir simply sneered. "We will clear it up soon enough once we arrive at Chilleau Judiciary. Be so kind as to summon your Security and we can be on our way."

Andrej's panic deepened. Could it have been some kind of a joke on Verlaine's part, after all? No. It could not have been a joke. Verlaine had sent Jils Ivers. Not even the First Secretary would dare deploy a Bench specialist on a mission of petty vengeance, just to make a spiteful joke. Raising his hand to point at Ivers in the crowd, Andrej struggled to keep his voice level; if he should show Noycannir the slightest trace of weakness he was lost, he was certain of it.

"Tell her that." He could hardly choke out the words; because it could be true, it could be a plot for revenge. It was even possible that Ivers was in on the scheme. "Tell her that the documents she carries are illusory. I'm waiting."

No. It could not be possible. Not a Bench specialist. If a Bench specialist was in on a plot on Verlaine's part to hold out false hope of escape and freedom—only to take it all away at the last minute—then there was truly no justice left under Jurisdiction; and the entire galaxy was damned.

"No, *I'm* waiting. How can you deny the evidence of your own senses?" And yet Ivers did not speak. Was she as stunned by the enormity of Verlaine's betrayal as he was? Or—was it possible—

"I know *that* person," Zsuzsa said, and her clear voice cut through a fog in Andrej's mind. "He's Sarvaw."

What?

Noycannir's evidence. It was the crew of the Wolnadi that had been involved in the training accident, yes. Jennet ap Rhiannon had sent these people home with him to keep them from the Bench. The crew on Record were here, alive and well.

"The Serene Proximity is right." There was more wrong here than any possible joke on Verlaine's part. "Lek isn't dead. Nor are Smish or Murat or Taller. Noycannir. What have you done?"

She had brought a Record with her, or at least it looked like a Record to Andrej, and he should know. It carried the counterseals, it showed the codes, it seemed genuine. But if the Record were genuine—then Noycannir had forged evidence.

The rule of Law depended upon the sanctity of evidence.

Oh, this was astounding treachery, and if Chilleau Judiciary were behind it, Chilleau Judiciary had to be destroyed. But if it was just one mad woman, it had to be exposed without mercy and without delay.

Andrej decided. "Mister Stildyne." This was far beyond any personal considerations; he had to take this Record into custody, and place it in evidence. "Secure the Record, if you please. House-master Jepson. If you would assist my people—"

He never finished his thought.

He had not been looking at Noycannir; it was a mistake. She was on him like the weight of blind remorse, she stabbed him with a knife that seemed to explode within his flesh into a fireball of anguish. Below his right shoulder, toward his side, missing the upper lobe of his lung if he was lucky, why did it hurt so much?

He was going to die. The sharp blow that his head took when he hit the ground settled his wits back into his consciousness, somehow, and Andrej knew that he had moments at best.

Her attack had taken them all by surprise. The room was full of people. Stildyne had been at the back of the crowd with Security, and prudently so; Stildyne would have moved Andrej's Security to the back of the room the moment he had realized that Noycannir had brought Fleet Security resources, just in case those troops had come to arrest Andrej's team. House security was on the other side of his father and his sister Zsuzsa. It would take seconds for any of them to intervene. He did not have seconds to spare.

Neurotoxin. The knife had carried veniwerk poison. The tissue of his body would start to dissolve within moments. Andrej rolled away from Noycannir, onto his left side, avoiding the pressure on his wounded side by instinct—but the move crippled him, because he had only the one good arm with which to defend himself, and now he was lying on top of it.

She swung at him savagely with another knife in her hand, and as Andrej ducked away from the threat he wondered how she had got them past the weapons scan. Glass knife. They would want to revise their search protocols. He rolled away from her and she rolled after him.

Andrej pulled away across the floor as best he could with one half of his body searing with agonizing pain, digging his left elbow against the floor for traction, straining with his neck bent and his head down. Trying to get away. Hoping against hope to win enough time to let his people react, and save him, but it all happened so quickly, and he knew it was only the adrenaline surge of pain and terror that made it seem as long to him.

He heard a sound. Noycannir crouched over him with her weapon raised to strike. The sound had been steel hitting stone. Emandisan steel, he knew it by the ringing of it, the stone of the floor. The mother-knife had slipped its catch and loosed itself and fallen. How could that have happened? He had no time to wonder about it.

The knife had fallen from the gaping neck of his blouse and followed the line of his arm down onto the floor at his elbow. He swept it into his hand with an awkward scraping grab of desperation and sank it into Noycannir's chest as deeply as he could manage, twisting away from her glasknife—which shattered against the stone floor and spread its poison. Rolling over and on top of Noycannir's body, using his own weight to press the blade home because he had no strength left with which to stab.

The hilt of the knife was hot now in his hand, and slippery. It seemed to resonate. Was it the sound of his own screaming? Was he maybe dead?

Not dead enough.

The rest of the world had caught up with him at last, but it was too late. They took him by the shoulders to move him from where he lay, and Andrej shrieked in agony, and passed out.

Coming to himself again after some unknown while Andrej opened his eyes, which declined to focus. He couldn't raise his head to shield his eyes from the bright lights that surrounded him; someone held a big broken gnarl-knuckled hand up carefully between him and the direct glare of the floodlights, and Andrej recognized Stildyne.

After a moment Andrej raised his left hand—inefficiently, but a man could only do as much as he could do—and gestured for Stildyne to come down to him. He wasn't quite sure where he was, on a gurney or on the floor, but he knew by the dazed fog in his mind that he was doped to the lips before and the dorsal fins behind, and he could guess that they were flushing the wound in which Noycannir's glasknife had shattered for all they were worth.

"Record," Andrej croaked. It didn't come out very promisingly, but this was Stildyne. Stildyne was accustomed to making sense out of the muttered and incoherent ravings of drunken Dolgorukij—how different could this be?

Stildyne dripped a little stream of fluid into Andrej's mouth and waited. Andrej tried again. "Record."

This time it came out almost normally. Stildyne nodded solemnly, with what looked like a smile of grim amusement on his face—though it was a little difficult to tell, against the brilliant halo of the emergency lights behind Stildyne's head.

"Secured," Stildyne said. "On lawful authority directly received. Not a problem, sir. Next."

Good. Stildyne apparently grasped the importance of keeping the Record out of Specialist Ivers's hands. Not because Ivers was in on any double-dealing; but because Ivers's duty to the Bench could well be in conflict with what Andrej knew he had to do to see justice done—or more precisely, to avoid an injustice. "Noycannir?"

It took him longer to get the longer word out, and Stildyne wasn't so familiar with this one. But Stildyne caught it and shook his head this time, rather than nodding. "Dead as dead, your Excellency. I've never seen that catch to slip on you. But it's a good thing that it did."

These things always happened so fast. They were still happening too fast for Andrej; the drugs were clouding over in his mind, moment by moment. He had to concentrate.

"Thula." He needed to get back to the *Ragnarok* as quickly as possible. There might be other elements to Noycannir's plot of which he was still unaware, elements that could continue to work themselves out on their own momentum even after Noycannir herself was dead.

That was the way of it with poisonous reptiles, or so Andrej had heard. Had Noycannir been behind the Bench warrant for his death? "Stoshik. Cousin. Stanoczk."

Stildyne moved his head to look around him, and Andrej winced at the sudden assault of the light. He needed Stildyne back to block the glare.

"Ferinc's gone for him." It was odd to hear Stildyne call Girag by that name; but perhaps it was only fair, after all. Regardless of who the man had been, he was Cousin Ferinc now. And Andrej was going to have to count on him to comfort his son for a little while, until Andrej could get home again.

There was just one more thing, then, and Stildyne would make the connection, Stildyne wouldn't need to hear it all spelled out for him. Stildyne would know.

"Uniform." He had to get the Record back to the *Ragnarok*. So he had to travel in uniform; very few people under Jurisdiction were legally permitted to transfer a Record. But once Ivers logged her documentation and his codes were revoked, he would no longer be technically entitled to wear the uniform of a Ship's Prime officer on board of the Jurisdiction Fleet Ship *Ragnarok*, let alone that of a Ship's Inquisitor.

Therefore Ivers could not be permitted to transmit the documentation that Andrej had endorsed until he had brought Noycannir's forged Record safely to the *Ragnarok* and placed it into evidence in due form, legally, lawfully, uncontrovertibly.

Maybe they should offer Ivers a ride back to Pesadie Training Command, Andrej thought; and closed his eyes. It was a mistake. He had only enough time to realize the error before he was unconscious once again.

Andrej lay with his mind adrift for what seemed to be a long time, half-conscious of what was happening around him, thinking.

Mergau Noycannir had forged the Record. That was shocking enough on its own, but there was more. She had registered confessed guilt on the part of three of his Security, three people who were not dead and had not confessed. The Record had no tolerance that Andrej knew of for reversing receipt of a confession. Once the identity codes were cross-validated, the confession had legal status; it became its own object in law.

It would be all too easy for Chilleau Judiciary to turn its back on the forgery of the Record. The woman who was responsible for the crime was dead. It would be simple prudence on the part of the Bench not to introduce the shocking fact that evidence and confession could be so egregiously forged; the Bench had stability concerns enough already.

And yet Ivers had said that Verlaine questioned the usefulness of torture in upholding the rule of Law. Couldn't he use this instance as a shocking example of the fact that the Inquisitorial system was no longer entirely in the Bench's best interest?

If Andrej did not challenge the legitimacy of the forged Record, he could not reject the confessions it recorded. Smish, Murat, Taller, Lek, they were legally dead in that forged Record; how long would it take for someone to make them really and truly dead, out of the way, silenced, no longer a potential embarrassment and reproach to Jurisdiction?

People held his body, moved his body, and Andrej paid almost no attention to what they were doing. They'd flushed the wound. Yes.

And were restoring fluid, swiftly, to minimize the strain on his circulatory system. Andrej could hear them talking, but the words made no sense, and he had issues of his own to ponder.

In order to protect his Security he had to get the forged Record into evidence as a forgery, and have its so-called evidence purged. He had no way of telling whether the information had been transmitted to any other Record, as for instance at some local Court.

He had been hearing the familiar sound of the pumps, but they shut down now. The flush was complete. How much damage had he sustained? How much of it was permanent? Had the neurotoxin destroyed lung tissue or merely muscle? He could open his eyes and find out, but for that he would have to open his eyes, and he wasn't done thinking.

He had to get the Record back to the *Ragnarok*, and that meant as an officer, a Ship's Inquisitor with possession of a Writ to Inquire. He had to ensure that his people would be safe. And if anyone should somehow force the issue and refer one of them to torture—

He would not. So long as he was the Ship's Inquisitor, he was the officer who would perform the interrogation of any assigned resources. And he would not. Drug assist, speak-sera, that he might consent to; but no more, Writ or no Writ.

The Bench could remove him only by accusing him of treason. Failure to obey lawful and received instruction was mutiny. That would compromise the son of the Koscuisko prince in an environment in which the political stability of the Dolgorukij Combine was needed to stand as a balance against civil unrest during the coming transition of power; maybe that would work in his favor, if it came to that.

But it didn't matter any more. They couldn't make him. He was the only one who could do that. Jils Ivers had offered him freedom, relief of Writ. A chance to come home and be father and husband, to enjoy the power that entailed to the inheriting son of the Koscuisko prince. He had so wanted to come home and meet his son. The offer of escape from Inquiry had been a huge and staggering opportunity, but he could not trade the lives of his people away for wealth and power.

And it didn't take relief of Writ to free him from the horrors of Inquiry. It only took a decision on his part. That was all. He had for so long told himself that he had no choice. He had for so long bathed in blood and torture, and done atrocious and obscene violence to helpless souls to rob them even of their last secrets before they died. He had believed that he had had no choice. He had been wrong about that. All of this time he had been wrong. Of course he had a choice.

It was so simple. He could do as he was bidden, or he could die. Yes, it was rational to be afraid of that death; he knew better than any man alive under Jurisdiction what a Tenth Level Command Termination could mean. But by the same token, he knew what it was not; nobody could do what he could do with pain at such a level. He knew that. It was not vanity. It was only fact.

Not very long ago he had faced in himself the fact that he had played Captain Lowden's game and tortured souls in Inquiry beyond the limits of their crime to placate his commanding officer, so that Lowden would leave the bond-involuntaries alone. Not beyond the limits of their guilt—all of Inquiry was beyond the limits of any guilt— that had been part of the problem from the beginning. But beyond even the limits of the Bench's ferocious list of torments to be invoked per the seriousness of the crime suspected.

He had done it to protect his people, but he had been wrong to do that. He had no right to beat a prisoner to save a bond-involuntary a beating, he had no right to make such decisions, he had been wrong. And had killed Captain Lowden, not because he had been wrong— there was no help for what crimes he had done, they were done, he could not call them back—but in order to protect his Bonds from imposition.

All this time he had been guilty of so far greater a confusion of the mind. He had always known that Inquiry was evil, and that he was committing sin each time he implemented the Protocols. He had known that from the beginning. He had believed that he had no choice. Now he could see it. All of this time he had traded torture for his own security, his own pride, his own parochial and misguided set of values.

How could filial piety require that he sin? Why had he ever thought that his father and his mother would be more honored in a son who committed gross atrocity than in one who refused the obscene torture of sentient souls? In what way could his duty to the Holy Mother require that he mutilate the flesh and bone of souls that were of Her own creation?

There was the old theological question, of course, of whether hominids who were not Dolgorukij had souls. It didn't matter. He knew well enough that souls who were not Dolgorukij suffered as horribly as Dolgorukij did when they were tortured. The Holy Mother Herself would cry out in anguish to witness such suffering; and if She did not, how could She be holy?

If he returned to the *Ragnarok* he could lose everything, and he had so recently been given everything: his parents' forgiveness, if not their understanding; the chance to be truly married with Marana; and a beautiful and loving child who was his son. The power of the Koscuisko familial corporation. Freedom from Secured Medical's horrible requirements, forever after. Everything.

He could not turn his back on his people. There was nothing that he owned or had enjoyed that was worth the lives of his Security: and it would only begin with the lives of his Security. He knew how Fleet inquiry was executed, after all. He better than most.

Lek Kerenko was a bond-involuntary. Lek had nothing that was his; even his body belonged to the Fleet, and the Fleet could do whatever it wanted with him, its absolute power moderated only by rational considerations of efficiency and replacement costs.

Lek had given him the only thing that Lek had left to call his own— his trust, and perhaps even a portion of affection. How could he reject so great a gift as everything from a man who had nothing for the sake of mere fields and houses, money, wealth, and the domestic comforts of a hearth to which he was still yet a stranger?

Brachi Stildyne had had nothing all his life. Stildyne had no cause to return anything to the world that had given him so little; and yet, Stildyne, who had grown up comfortless, uncomforted, tried to give comfort to a man from so different a background that he might as well have been an alien species.

Stildyne, to whom nobody had ever extended charitable kindness or sought to understand, had saved Andrej's life and helped preserve his sanity by exercising charitable kindness, trying to understand, efforts all the more remarkable coming from a man who'd never had the luxury of caring for another soul in his life.

And when Stildyne had found someone to care for, how had Andrej honored that regard—except by declining to reject it outright? How great a sinner would he be if the best thanks he had for Stildyne's strength over the years was to turn his back on his own crew and let them fall to torture, one by one?

The people here on Azanry were his by birth and blood and familial affection. But his people on the *Ragnarok* were his because they consented to enter into the relationship, and not with the son of the Koscuisko prince, not with their sibling or son or father, but with a mere man, and a more than ordinarily flawed one. He had to go back.

He'd live if he could but he'd die if he had to, and if he had to, he'd do it defending the people to whom he owed his life and his sanity. Andrej opened his eyes and started to sit up. It didn't work.

Stildyne held him as he fell back the few fractions he'd been able to raise himself off the surface of the diagnostic bed, and Andrej's body knew better than to try to argue with Stildyne. Someone adjusted the shades on the nearest light and raised the level of the bed; Andrej cleared his throat.

Stildyne was there with a flask of rhyti. The room came back into focus. Medical personnel, looking pale and very severe. Stildyne, more sensed than seen, at his side. Stoshik. Bench specialist Jils Ivers, and his father, leaning up against the wall with his arms folded and reminding Andrej suddenly and incongruously of the First Officer.

"Can Lek fly the thula?" Andrej asked, looking at Cousin Stanoczk. Cousin Stanoczk looked rather pale himself. Andrej wondered what Stanoczk might know about Noycannir's scheme that he could not reveal; or could it be that the Malcontent had not anticipated her attempt? That would truly be unnerving.

"He will have to," Stanoczk nodded, with grim amusement. "If you are to reach the *Ragnarok* at Taisheki Station."

What?

Fleet Audit Appeals Authority was at Taisheki Station. Had ap Rhiannon been unable to defend herself against Pesadie on her own? Why else would the *Ragnarok* go to Taisheki, except to file an appeal? It was a worrying indication. The only people Fleet could lay a claim to this early, without evidence, were here; but Noycannir had produced false evidence. Had ap Rhiannon been forced to surrender collateral witnesses?

He needed to review the Record; he needed to know exactly what Noycannir had placed into evidence. And then he needed to know if she'd transmitted that so-called evidence anywhere, anywhere at all. He could review the Record once they were in transit.

"When do we leave?" Andrej asked, to find out what the parameters were. Cousin Stanoczk bowed.

"At his Excellency's convenience entirely," Stanoczk said. "But you have to take my navigator." And why did Andrej think he knew exactly who that was? Later. Andrej nodded thanks and acceptance at once.

"Stildyne, I need to get dressed. Meet me at the thula as soon as you can. Specialist Ivers, would you care to accompany me?"

She was in an interesting position. It all came down to the documents, didn't it? Ivers nodded, a gesture that was almost a bow. "Delighted, your Excellency." With rank. So they understood each other. "I may never have a chance to travel on a thula again. They cost money, after all."

A note of warning, there. The Bench had evidence in hand of how much money the Malcontent commanded. There would unquestionably be an inquiry, over the coming years, into how deeply the fingers of the Malcontent truly reached. That was the Malcontent's lookout, though, and the Malcontent was more than adequately qualified to protect its interest. Andrej looked past Ivers for the medical people.

"Prognosis, Doctor. Status, please." He himself was a surgeon, not a soft-tissue specialist, and his experience of traumatic wound management was almost completely limited to the care-giving side of the equation. The house physician stepped forward and bowed.

"Gross physical trauma to the upper right-hand portion of your chest, sir, the muscle beneath the front part of your shoulder. Some of the lymph is damaged, potentially some of the lung. It's too early to tell. We got the flush-and-neutralize started in good time, but there is danger."

Of course there was danger. Every muscle in his back and side and belly on the right side of his body hurt, and a good representative sample of the corresponding elements on the left were protesting in sympathy. There was a huge empty space in his body where the upper portion of his chest was supposed to be—local anesthesia, Andrej presumed—and his mind seemed to be floating at some few measures' remove from his body in a comforting narcotic haze.

"Stabilize for transport, please, Doctor. I've got to get out of here. My duty absolutely requires that I return to my ship immediately." He recognized the expression of condescending superiority on the doctor's face; it was one of his own favorites.

"I'm sorry, sir, it's out of the question. I cannot permit it. Your wound absolutely requires immobilization while the neutralysis completes, and a single wrong move could set muscle-regeneration back days. Weeks. No."

As a matter of principle Andrej always unfailingly deferred to his general practitioners when he was the patient, whether or not he agreed with them. It was simply good protocol. Just as well that he was at Chelatring Side, and not on board of the *Ragnarok*, because he would never have dared pull rank on one of his subordinate physicians. So arrogant a misstep could undo years of careful building of relationships.

"I hear and comprehend, Doctor, but I insist. It is absolutely necessary that you stabilize for transport immediately. The alternative is not cancellation of transport but transport without stabilization, and we both know that to be a much more dangerous proposition. You are master in your own infirmary, Doctor, but I have a duty to the Bench which must override even your authority."

He knew his argument was persuasive, as far as it went, and that it was unlikely to be acceptable. Andrej would have respected the house physician less if he didn't object strenuously to any such suggestion. The doctor looked across the room to Andrej's father, scowling.

"Your Excellency," the doctor said. "This is an imprudent suggestion. I will not answer for the consequences. Your son faces serious and permanent injury, your Excellency, and possibly a fatal outcome. Relieve me of this requirement."

Andrej's father straightened up, crossing the room to come to Andrej's side. "He is my son," Andrej's father agreed. "I know this man, in a manner of speaking. So I believe what he has said, that his duty requires that he travel. As dangerous as it may be for him to travel with such a wound, it will be much worse if you will not consent to do what can be done."

The point exactly. Andrej could have smiled, but he had already annoyed the doctor, and who knew better than he that a physician was not to be challenged in his own infirmary?

"I therefore lay the blame on his head," Andrej's father said kindly, but implacably. The expression on the doctor's face reflected his clear realization that he had no choice; he would have to comply. "You are to accept no portion of the blame, Doctor. It is my son's decision. Stabilize for transport, if you please."

It was an order even a physician had to obey. The doctor bowed. "Going for transport kit directly," he said. "According to his Excellency's good pleasure."

He left the room. That left Ivers, Cousin Stanoczk, and Andrej's father, if one disregarded the technicians for the moment.

"It is necessary?" his father asked. Andrej nodded.

"It is crucial." That didn't make it easier; just explained why it had to be done. "To save the lives of my Security, and possibly many more beside. I am I regret still your unfilial son. And will challenge the Bench if I must."

It was a reference to the letter that his father had sent him after the trials at the Domitt Prison. His father did not rebuke him for the reproach, however; it was almost as good as an apology. "Come back soon, then, son Andrej," his father said. "I want you home. And you have explaining to do to the Ichogatra."

Yes. He did. And if his punishment for marrying Marana was to be the negotiation of reparations and new contracts in light of the prejudicial cancellation of the planned contract of marriage—he was still ahead of the game.

Andrej held out his left arm—with some difficulty, because his muscles ached. His son had embraced him. He could not embrace his father, not under these circumstances. But he could indicate his desire to. "I will come home when I can, sir," he said. Promised. "Depend upon it."

A long handclasp, a paternal kiss, and Andrej's father turned around and went away. There was nothing more to say. Maybe his father couldn't say anything more anyway.

He'd have to say good-bye to his mother, if he had time, but now there was only Stoshik to get through and he could leave. "Who is to beg forgiveness from Marana?" Andrej asked. "As I am taking Ferinc with me, Stoshik. Somebody must go and explain. This is the last thing anyone could have expected."

Stoshik was very pale. "It shouldn't have happened," he said. "I blame myself. Derush, we are supposed to have better care for you than to allow you to be assaulted by madwomen. Specialist Ivers, what do you know of this?"

Stanoczk had to know that Ivers knew nothing. He was just playing the scenario out; Ivers was an envoy from Chilleau Judiciary, after all. Noycannir had belonged to Chilleau. It could be made to look ugly. The Combine would make Chilleau pay dearly for the potential of the appearance of a conspiracy to assassinate the son of the Koscuisko prince.

"I probably know even less than you do." Ivers seemed to have no stomach for the play; or else her blunt frankness was her role. Perhaps that. "I will report to the First Secretary as soon as is prudently possible. But I feel completely confident in this much: Noycannir was on her own. Chilleau Judiciary has no hand in this."

Maybe Chilleau Judiciary was going to have to leave the issue of the thula alone, after all. Andrej didn't feel that he had much time; the drugs were fast overtaking his consciousness. "Stoshik, I'll come back as soon as I can. If I can. Speak to Marana for me, I beg you. This is grotesque injustice to her. But I can see no option worth considering."

"Taisheki space," Stanoczk said, his reply indirect but obvious enough. "Ferinc will have the briefing. Good travel, Andrej, Bench specialist. We can speak again when you've come home, Derush."

Stanoczk wouldn't tell him anything about the Bench warrant, not in Ivers's presence. Had he got everything? The doctor was back with a medical team, and they had brought a stasis-mover with them, an inclined sort of a mechanized bed—they meant him to be as thoroughly stabilized as possible.

How many days to Taisheki, even in a thula, and confined within a stasis-mover? Andrej closed his eyes wearily, overcome with dread at the prospect. Once he closed his eyes, they stayed closed. The drugs pulled him down into the darkness, and he was lost.

CHAPTER THIRTEEN

Order of Battle

The thula was compact and very efficient, but it had clearly been built for speed rather than comfort. Jils wasn't quite happy with the prospect of spending two or three days alone on this thula with Andrej Koscuisko alone as far as medical resources went—but neither had Koscuisko's own family physicians been; they had trammeled him up so thoroughly that the odds of his doing injury to himself were minimized. The odds of him doing anything at all were minimized.

There were Security in the wheelhouse with the Malcontent Cousin Ferinc, learning the thula; more Security in the narrow corridors outside the low-ceilinged cabin in which Koscuisko rested. She'd heard Cousin Stanoczk say that the Malcontent would have a briefing for Koscuisko. But for that, Koscuisko had to be awake.

Andrej Koscuisko hadn't awakened in the day since the thula had taken the vector for Taisheki. The house physicians would have put his medications on time-release. It was what she would have done with Koscuisko under the circumstances, but was she to sit and watch an unconscious invalid all the way to Fleet Audit Appeals Authority? She needed to talk to him.

She sat in the little cabin and waited, sharing the time with the others on board. Rank was no respecter of duty rosters, and they all needed Security to fly the thula, which meant that every waking moment she could spend on watch freed one of the Security to learn the operational characteristics of this elegant and fearful machine. Familiarity with fast spacecraft was a good thing. It decreased the chances that someone would make a wrong move and kill them all.

Toward the end of the shift Chief Stildyne came into the cabin with two flasks of something steaming and hot and offered her one. "Rhyti," Chief Stildyne said, as though he was apologizing. "Nothing much else by way of stimulants. Dolgorukij, you know. How's the officer?"

"About the same." Exactly the same. The wound was well dressed, but it still smelled like raw flesh, and Koscuisko did not move. Koscuisko couldn't move. That stasis-mover was a piece of work. "Either it's much worse than they let on, or he really annoyed them."

The latter, she thought, and Chief Stildyne by his smile seemed to agree. She wished he wouldn't smile. His lips were thin to begin with, and when he smiled they disappeared entirely, so that his face looked even more like a fleshless skull than it normally did. It was nothing personal. She liked Stildyne, he was among the best Warrants she'd ever worked with. But he was ugly.

Stildyne stood looking at Koscuisko in the stasis-mover; Koscuisko opened his eyes, frowning. Just like that. How long had he been awake? "Brachi," Koscuisko said. "Where am I?"

Stildyne made a peculiar face that Jils couldn't exactly interpret. He fit his flask of rhyti into Koscuisko's good hand before he spoke, guiding it with care. It wasn't easy for Koscuisko to drink. Stildyne adjusted the stasis-mover's indices more toward the vertical; Koscuisko drank again. "On vector for Taisheki Station, sir. Two days out. Cousin Ferinc wants to talk to you, now or later."

Koscuisko's eyes wandered, but he focused on Stildyne's face with an apparent effort. "In one day and sixteen hours, Chief, you are going to find whatever drug delivery system they have me plugged into, and you are going to pull it. I'll want to be awake. Ferinc is where?"

Stildyne took the flask away. "I'll be right back. Don't go anywhere." It was a joke. Koscuisko seemed too deep in medicated drowsiness to notice.

This couldn't be a good time, but the question needed asking. "What do you want me to do with the documents, sir?"

Koscuisko frowned again, lifting his head away from the padded headboard of the stasis-mover. "Oh. Bench specialist. Documents? Yes. Those."

He seemed to be lucid, just easily distracted. Jils repeated the question. "What am I do to with the documents, your Excellency?"

"I may need to remain at my post for some days, Specialist Ivers." He spoke slowly, but she could catch no sense that his mind wandered. Either it was an effort for him to speak, or else he wanted to be very sure of what he was saying. "I don't yet know. I think it may be best if you gave them to me. I will call for you, when I am ready."

Yes, but that meant that his relief of Writ would go unrecorded until then. "With your permission, sir." She wanted to satisfy herself that he knew what it was that he was doing. "You have for so long sought to set your Writ aside or, rather, regretted its exercise."

He nodded, with a considering expression on his face that she could not quite interpret. She pressed on, to try to see if he was truly listening. "Are you sure of what you do, sir? We don't know what may be happening. Without these documents, you remain subject to Fleet discipline. You know that."

Koscuisko's eyes tracked across the room from object to object; was he trying to focus? When he spoke, it was with perfect clarity, lucid and precise. She could not imagine that he was drugged and raving. There was too much implacable logic in what he was saying.

"Thank you for your care, Specialist Ivers. But here is the truth of it. It is not relief of Writ that frees me from the further commission of crimes in the name of the Judicial order. It is only my own determination which suffices for that. The Fleet and the Bench may do as they like with me, but I will be guided by my own heart. I cannot say decency. I'm unsure whether I have any left."

Stildyne was back with the Malcontent, Cousin Ferinc, and more rhyti. Stildyne gave her a sharp look, as though accusing her of tiring Koscuisko in his absence; but there was no help for it. She had needed to know. Koscuisko had shaken himself free of the last of his cultural conditioning: he was a free man. That made him more dangerous than he had ever been.

"News for you, sir," Cousin Ferinc said, carefully, not raising his voice but fixing his attention very closely on Koscuisko's face. "From Cousin Stanoczk. About the *Ragnarok* en route to Taisheki Station. Are you awake, your Excellency?"

Koscuisko's eyes seemed about ready to roll back in his head. Frowning, Koscuisko focused with apparent effort. "Almost, Ferinc. Speak quickly. You may have to tell me again later."

Ferinc nodded. "Appeal to the Fleet Audit Appeals Authority on improper acquisition of evidence improperly read. There is no Bench warrant for these crew, sir, but there are hints that Taisheki is not in a receptive mood, nonetheless."

"Get the documents," Koscuisko said, to Chief Stildyne. Had he lost the braid? Or was it the last thing he wanted to say before he went down once more, as he clearly seemed about to do? "And remember. Four hours before. Pull the meds. I can't stand this."

Did that mean she had to wait till then to hear what Ferinc knew of what might be happening at Taisheki Station?

She had not been offered the use of the thula's communications. She didn't think she wanted it. The First Secretary needed to know about Noycannir, but the Combine could pass on that information. If she spoke to Verlaine he might give her instructions, and she might feel obliged to implement them. To seize the Record, by force if necessary, though all she could reasonably hope for on this trip would be to destroy it.

Koscuisko needed that Record. The *Ragnarok* itself might need that Record. It was better if she avoided the mischance that Verlaine might look to his own interest and direct her to actions which would support the rule of Law but suborn justice.

Garol Vogel had been there, years ago, at Port Charid. With his Langsariks. He had found a way to avoid an injustice, but it had cost him his lifelong submission to the rule of Law. He'd never been the same after Port Charid, and that was almost five years ago. Now it was her turn.

"I'll sit for a while," Chief Stildyne said, which she knew perfectly well meant "Go away and leave me alone" in Stildyne. She was perfectly willing to. She needed to think.

There was more to this problem than Mergau Noycannir and a forged Record, and she had very little time for analysis left before the thula reached Taisheki Station and she would have to decide what to do.

From the Jurisdiction Fleet Ship Ragnarok *to Fleet Audit Appeals*

Authority, Taisheki Station, greeting. On behalf of the crew and Command of this ship the following appeal is transmitted.

Jennet ap Rhiannon sat alone behind the desk in the Captain's office brooding over the printed text, analyzing it for the eighth or sixteenth time, wondering if she had said everything she'd wanted to. Wondering if her plea had been as convincing at Taisheki Station as she felt it to be from on board the *Ragnarok*.

A recent accident at Pesadie Training Command took the life of Acting Captain Cowil Brem. Although no Ragnarok *resources were active in the area at the time of the accident, Pesadie Training Command's investigative focus has been on finding fault with the crew and craft that had just quit the area when the accident occurred.*

It just didn't come out right. The words could not express her outrage; they didn't communicate her determination.

The preliminary assessment team posted by Pesadie Training Command took covert action to subvert ship's security and obtain information illegally and inappropriately. Fleet Admiral Sandri Brecinn's direct collusion in this cover-up was made evident by her resort to improperly obtained information as a basis to demand release of troops to stand the Question.

Nowhere in these legal terms and careful phrases could she hear the words that were in her heart: *I am responsible for these troops, these troops are blameless and not at fault. Once you start on troops it never ever stops at just the four or six or eight or twelve, and I will ram Pesadie Training Command with an explosive detonation charge before I will surrender one single soul to be used to cover up for her black marketing.* It wasn't there.

She couldn't say it, not in so many words; if her appeal was to succeed there had to be an out there, somewhere. She was in no position to back Taisheki into a corner and demand concessions. If the Appeals Authority would not listen to her appeal she didn't know what she was going to do.

Further evidence indicates the potential existence of systemic irregularities within the Pesadie Training Command injurious to the maintenance of the Judicial order.

The talk-alert's warning tone interrupted Jennet's brooding. Swallowing back a sigh of resignation, she toggled into braid. "Ap Rhiannon. Yes."

"Engineering bridge, your Excellency. Requesting the pleasure of your company. I've never seen anything like this."

Wheatfields. It was unusual enough for anyone to actually hear from Wheatfields; but this was even more unusual, because he sounded excited. She thought that was what he sounded. She wasn't sure she would be able to tell, not with Wheatfields.

One way or the other she needed to go see what he was calling about. He was off-braid already, but she didn't think it was a failure of military courtesy on his part. That would have been rude. When Wheatfields wanted to be rude he generally left one in no doubt at all about it.

She hurried down from her office to the Engineering bridge with all deliberate speed, paying attention to the expressions and the deportment of the people in the hallways, showing the rank. She was their Captain. She had gotten them all into a very great deal of trouble and they had gone with her willingly. She owed them all acknowledgment of that; and a successful outcome, of course. Unless they all elected to dive into Pesadie Training Command with her.

Ship's First Officer was standing in the doorway of the observation deck when Jennet got there, waiting for her, his forehead creased in a worried frown but his face alive with what appeared to be good-humored excitement.

"Hurry on in, your Excellency," Mendez said. "You don't want to miss this. Any of it. Someone's tracking for intercept on vector. You'll never guess."

This was nonsensical. Nobody tracked for intercept on vector. There was too much vector, for one. And the speed differentials required to make any difference during vector transit were extreme, for another. Hurrying through the doorway as Mendez had encouraged her Jennet made for the railing and looked down into the engineering bridge, to see what the aft scanners were saying.

Mendez was right. There was an intercept blip. And it was moving faster than anything she had ever seen in her life. "Engineer," Jennet said. "What is that ship?"

Wheatfields looked up and over his shoulder at her from his post on the Engineering bridge below. "Do you like it?" Wheatfields asked, with a curious note of wistful lustfulness in his voice. "It's a Kospodar thula. Koscuisko's on board. Just say the word and I'll blow it up for you."

"Start at the starting place, please." To say "Wheatfields" would be rude, and "Serge" was out of the question. "Tell me what this is all about."

Wheatfields shook his head, as if in wonder. "Look at the spin vectors on that machine. I don't know what to tell you, your Excellency. We only noticed it coming at us an eight or two ago. It's not saying much. All it will tell us is that Koscuisko requests permission to come on board, and has two non-crew passengers."

"Strange," Jennet said. This was not good news: if it was Koscuisko, he logically had Security with him, and she had wanted those Security kept out of the way. "He wasn't due off leave for another two weeks at least, was he?"

Something chimed on the Engineering bridge, a transmission alert. Wheatfields nodded at one of his people, and the transmission came up on shared audio.

"Private courier ship, Aznir registry, Chief Medical Officer Andrej Ulexeievitch Koscuisko and party, two others. His Excellency wishes to rejoin his Command, and requires medical attention. Permission to come on board."

That "requires medical attention" sounded ominous. The *Ragnarok*'s maintenance atmosphere had been hulled over for vector transit; trying to pull a courier in was going to be tricky. "Engineer?" Jennet asked. "Can we rendezvous at all?"

The authentication codes were scrolling across the base of a status-screen to one side of the Engineering bridge. Voice-identity confirmed: Lek Kerenko, Security 5.1, Jurisdiction Fleet Ship *Ragnarok*.

Wheatfields shot her a look that was half serious and half mock outrage. "Do I have to, your Excellency? I want the ship. Not Koscuisko. Thula, this is Ship's Engineer, can you sustain position for entry with limited clearances?"

The containment field that held the *Ragnarok*'s atmosphere when the ship's underbelly was not hulled over could not sustain the speed at which the *Ragnarok* was traveling without potential damage. That was why they hulled the maintenance atmosphere over for vector transit in the first place. Wheatfields would want to minimize his exposure.

"With respect, your Excellency." Now that Jennet knew who was talking, she almost thought she recognized the voice. "This beast can do anything. Just try her."

Mendez stood at Jennet's side with his arms folded across his chest, frowning now in what appeared to be genuine concern. "Medical attention, Kerenko?" Mendez asked. There was a brief silence; then Security Chief Stildyne came into braid.

"Assassination attempt, sir. Neurotoxin, but he's got something he needs to read into the Record, and he was in too much of a hurry to listen to the doctors."

Koscuisko was accustomed to having his own way. Jennet felt a brief pang of concern in her belly: she hadn't precisely gotten along with Koscuisko before the accident; how were they to get along now? Because she could not afford to let him doubt that she was the captain of the *Ragnarok*.

"How bad is it, Chief?"

Content to let Mendez do the talking, Jennet watched the track of the thula as it gained on them, and listened. "He's pretty much drugged senseless, your Excellency. We'll want Infirmary to be standing by. They didn't want him traveling at all. He insisted."

"Good hostage," Wheatfields said suddenly, not looking up. "Koscuisko's an important man in his home system. We may need the leverage. I'll bring him on board, your Excellency."

She hadn't thought that far. But Wheatfields was right. She didn't have to worry about how she was to manage Koscuisko's adjustment to the changes that had occurred on the *Ragnarok* during his absence. He hadn't been here. He was not implicated or involved. He was a neutral third party—an innocent bystander. A bargaining chip.

"Very well." Let Koscuisko on board, even with the Security she had wanted him to shelter. Better Koscuisko should bring the Security back on board where she could keep a good hold of them than follow the *Ragnarok* to Taisheki Station and surrender his Security before he knew what a mistake he would be making. "Grant permission, Engineer. We'll alert Medical. Once we know what Koscuisko's condition is, we can talk."

Technically speaking it was the First Officer, not the Captain, who got to decide who was and who was not allowed to come on board. Wheatfields nodded. "As you wish, Captain. Thula. What's your name, anyway? Never mind. Sela, calculate a docking protocol. Kerenko. If it was anybody else driving, I wouldn't be doing this."

But they'd seen Kerenko's flying. They all knew that he was good.

"Standing by for docking protocol, your Excellency, and thank you, sir." Still, not even Kerenko could have that much experience piloting so exotic a ship—

It was the Engineer's lookout, Jennet reminded herself, firmly. "I'm going down to the maintenance atmosphere, First Officer." To be there when the ship docked. "Would you call Infirmary for us, please?"

An assassination attempt. By whom, and why, and what had they hoped to accomplish by murdering Koscuisko, or had it just been revenge? First things first. Let them get the thula into the maintenance atmosphere, and Koscuisko offloaded to Medical.

Time enough to press for all the details later.

When Andrej Koscuisko awoke he was in Infirmary on board of the Jurisdiction Fleet Ship *Ragnarok*, a circumstance both startling and disturbing. Startling because he had no memory of arriving; disturbing because he did not know where the *Ragnarok* was. "Mister Stildyne. What has happened?"

The drugs were clearing from his system; he felt clearheaded, if weak. He had never known a doctor for soft-tissue injury management like Narion. She knew what she was doing.

"Where to start, your Excellency?" Stildyne's response was reflective. "We caught up with the *Ragnarok* on vector. We've come off vector. The Second Judge has announced her platform. There's no encouragement from Taisheki Station on the *Ragnarok*'s appeal. You're going to live. I think that's the lot."

Whether he was going to live had not been at issue, so Stildyne was just padding his narrative. Or making sure that he had it all. "I need to place the Record into evidence, Chief, I've got to get up."

But Stildyne shook his head. "His Excellency may wish to reconsider. Fleet is not happy with Chilleau Judiciary. Specialist Ivers suggests we wait."

"She doesn't have the Record, does she? Chief? Brachi?"

"No, your Excellency." The smile on Stildyne's face to hear his first name was almost frightening. Because so much about Stildyne was. "Secured by order of the First Officer. Let me call First Officer, sir. He wants to talk to you."

Andrej didn't need to answer that. He closed his eyes; and when he opened them again, the room was full of people. Narion's soft-tissue specialty team, and him half naked on the inclined stasis-mover. First Officer. Stildyne. Specialist Ivers. Lieutenant ap Rhiannon, who'd started the entire mess by sending the wrong Security home with him.

Perhaps that was unfair, Andrej decided. Ap Rhiannon hadn't had anything to do with Mergau Noycannir. And if ap Rhiannon hadn't sent the wrong Security, they wouldn't have been present at Chelatring Side to save Andrej from Noycannir's plot by demonstrating that the Record had been forged. So he owed her an apology. And it would have to wait.

"Well, that's the excuse," First Officer was saying. "Unsettled environment, you come to us if you want Safes for those bond-involuntary troops. But I don't like it, Specialist Ivers. No. We aren't going anywhere fast."

Blinking, Andrej waited patiently for his eyes to focus. So they'd come off vector, but Taisheki had declined to meet them with Safes, as would have been standard operating procedure—an appeal was a Command action. Bond-involuntaries weren't held accountable for it, but the stresses of the situation could destroy them unless they had the protection of the Safes.

"That statement of the Second Judge's does rather threaten Fleet's power base, First Officer," Andrej pointed out, very reasonably he thought. "I wouldn't have thought Taisheki Station to be affected—"

Everybody turned to stare at him. What? Was he not speaking Standard? What was the matter with everybody?

"Andrej," Mendez said. "Good to hear from you. "How's the shoulder? Better?"

No, it felt much worse. That was the "better" part, though, because it meant that Narion was pulling back on the drugs. "I will get a report, First Officer, and let you know. Specialist Ivers. Stildyne says you want to hold the forged Record out of evidence. How can this be?"

Ivers looked down and to one side, carefully, as if collecting her thoughts. "If you mean to endorse the Second Judge's declaration. Consider. The forged Record is intimately connected with Mergau Noycannir, and thus could discredit Chilleau Judiciary. With respect, sir, now is exactly the wrong time to give Fleet any weapons against the candidacy of the Second Judge, if you agree with her declaration."

All right. Andrej supposed he could understand her reasoning. He turned his attention to the bandaging that the soft-tissue injury management team was doing; he'd never seen so much of his own flesh laid raw in his life.

Ivers spoke on, but was no longer speaking to him. "I don't understand why Taisheki Station would withhold Safes on these grounds, your Excellency. The Safes are there. They have only to send a courier. With your permission, I'd like to get to Taisheki Station and see if I can find out what's going on."

Who was she talking to? She didn't seem to be looking at Mendez. And Andrej himself was the only other Excellency in the room.

"Take the Captain's shallop. And those leftovers of Brecinn's, with you," ap Rhiannon said. "We keep the thula. Because Kerenko is driving it. And if Taisheki Station gets its hands on either, I'm not likely to get them back. But . . . "

Oh, all right. Yes. Ap Rhiannon was an Excellency by default. Acting Captain, and so forth. Andrej leaned his head back against the padded headboard of the stasis-mover and frowned, concentrating.

"Yes, your Excellency?" Ivers prompted.

"If I don't get satisfaction from Taisheki Station, Bench specialist, I can remove the *Ragnarok* to neutral territory and appeal to the Bench direct. And I will. I've come too far to let it all be for nothing."

What nonsense. The *Ragnarok* was a Fleet resource. There was no neutral territory for the *Ragnarok* in all of Jurisdiction space, if Taisheki Station should refuse the appeal. Ivers didn't bother to point this out, as though she was as aware of the patent absurdity of this claim as he was. "Yes, Captain, and we'll hope it doesn't come to that. Your Excellency."

Too many Excellencies, Andrej decided. It was making him dizzy. The only way he could tell that he was the "Excellency" she meant this time was the fact that she had turned her body back to face him. "Bench specialist."

"I need to report about Noycannir to Chilleau Judiciary, sir. The Malcontent will already have transmitted some information, but Verlaine will be waiting to hear from me. I must respectfully request that you refrain from putting the forged Record into evidence until we have time to strategize. To decide if here and now is when it should be done."

She was making sense. He was tired. Narion was probably not going to let him out of Infirmary very soon, and he dared not pull rank on his own staff without truly crucial overriding considerations. Mendez had secured the Record. What harm could there be?

"Leave also the documents that I for you countersigned, Specialist Ivers." If he didn't enter the forged Record into evidence before she logged relief of Writ, he could find himself barred from the Record, and unable to make the required statements. He couldn't afford the risk.

After a moment Ivers nodded. "Very well, your Excellency. Captain, I will go and find out what I can, and take those unwanted crew with me. General Rukota isn't returning, ma'am?"

Who was that? Rukota? General Rukota? He didn't know any Generals Rukota. What had been going on here while he'd been away?

"Nor do I blame him, Bench specialist. He's got damage-control issues of his own. Doctor Koscuisko. Welcome back. We'll get you a briefing once you've had a chance to recover a bit. You may wish to leave yourself, but we can discuss it later."

What did ap Rhiannon know? This was his ship. His crew. He wasn't going anywhere. He'd just gone to a very great deal of trouble to get back here.

"You can be ambulatory inside of two days, your Excellency," Narion assured him, gravely. "Whoever parked you on the other side did a superlative job. But you still have strong painkillers in your system. Go ahead and sleep them out, sir. Everything's under control on this end and nothing's happening fast."

Now, that was a sensible suggestion. And with Ivers's agreement to hold processing of the documents that would cancel his clearance codes, he didn't have so much concern about the forged Record going missing before it could be logged.

This would all make sense when he woke up again, he was almost sure of it. "Make sure of the Record, First Officer," Andrej said, and resigned himself to sleep once more.

"And I say that ap Rhiannon has conspired with a Clerk of Court from Chilleau Judiciary to trade in contraband munitions," Admiral Brecinn insisted. Jils kept her face clear of irritation; no one would believe that any emotion she displayed was genuine anyway. In the privacy of her own thoughts, she didn't know whether to rage or to laugh. She'd never met Sandri Brecinn; she certainly hadn't expected to find Brecinn here at Taisheki Station, rather than at Pesadie Training Command.

"The Fleet Admiral is who she is," Auditor Ormbach said, in a reasonable tone of voice. "We cannot simply discount her very serious accusations, no matter how extravagant they might seem. Work with us here, Bench specialist, please."

Brecinn was apparently feeling very sure of herself, basking in the deference being shown her by the Fleet's auditors. Jils knew that was likely to be an error of judgment on Brecinn's part. Fleet's auditors were in general not so quick to swallow a story—at least Jils hoped not.

"You've just come from the *Ragnarok*, Specialist Ivers," Brecinn pointed out, her tone at once unctuous and ingratiating. "What can you tell us that will shed light on the ship's truly inexplicable behavior?"

Brecinn's question was a challenge in good form. Jils thought about it. Brecinn had the advantage of prior persuasion on her side, having arrived here at Taisheki Station more than three days ago to make her case.

Her arrival in and of itself was suspect to Jils. Brecinn claimed that it was the critical nature of the *Ragnarok*'s crimes that had motivated her to leave her Command, but Jils suspected that upper Fleet echelons might well ask why she hadn't simply sent a courier. Or a priority transmit.

"I can tell the Bench specialist plenty," one of Brecinn's crew—a member of the preliminary assessment team that Jils had liberated from the *Ragnarok*—said. Her voice was venomous. "We've kept notes. I'm sorry about Rukota, Admiral, but he went over from the beginning. Noycannir and he must have been in collusion from the very start."

Noycannir. Yes. That was right. The Clerk of Court with whom ap Rhiannon was supposed to be conspiring was Dame Mergau Noycannir, from Chilleau Judiciary. So Brecinn hadn't heard. Verlaine had almost unquestionably been told by now. The Malcontent surely would have seen to that.

But since Brecinn didn't know, it wasn't public knowledge yet, or even leaked out into the informal communications channels that existed side by side with official Fleet lines of transmissions. Not deeply enough for Brecinn to have heard, and if Jils had been Brecinn, she would have been listening very carefully to every tidbit of gossip that she'd been able to dig up on her way from Pesadie to Taisheki Station.

"Auditor, excuse the Pesadie team," Jils suggested. The fact that the news was clearly not out gave her all she needed to determine a strategy—only a temporary strategy—but it would serve to stabilize the situation here at the Fleet Audit Appeals Authority. "I have privileged information to impart."

She waited. Station Security validated the privacy fields; she spoke again, choosing her words carefully, trying not to enjoy herself more than she properly ought. "Dame Mergau Noycannir is the Clerk of Court you suspect of conspiracy with the *Ragnarok*, Admiral Brecinn?"

Brecinn was suspicious of the question, but she was trapped. There was no choice but to brazen this out now. "I do emphatically, Bench specialist." Oh. So polite. "And I can't help but suspect that she was involved in some plot or another with General Rukota. His presence at Pesadie Training Command might be taken as a little difficult to understand. A man with his connections can write his own posting-orders, after all."

Jils nodded. "Since this suggestion has been made, there is some information I need to share with you all. Noycannir has emphatically been implicated in a plot." Had unquestionably been plotting with somebody, and where had she got the Record to use for her forged evidence, if not from Pesadie Training Command? Jils didn't know. Stildyne hadn't let her examine the forged Record, and she hadn't pressed the issue. It would all come out sooner or later: or not at all.

Brecinn seemed to know better than to let herself relax, even with this apparently encouraging information. She waited silently for Jils to continue; and the auditors—three of them—waited, too. It would be disobliging not to do so.

"But is unlikely to have been plotting with the *Ragnarok*. Because she has in fact attempted to assassinate its Chief Medical Officer. This behavior seems too contradictory for someone in collusion with the *Ragnarok*'s Command; Koscuisko was at home, out of the way. It just draws attention to Noycannir. Some other explanation must be sought." There was no need to mention the fact that Noycannir was dead.

Brecinn was not stupid enough to blurt out any self-incriminating denial of whatever Noycannir might have had to say about her; not yet. There would be time. And there would be the Protocols, when the time came, though Koscuisko was unlikely to be the man who would implement them. Ever again.

"So I don't need to tell you how delicate the situation is, Auditors. Dame Noycannir is clearly associated with Chilleau Judiciary. The Second Judge's platform attacks the entire system of Inquiry, and a Clerk of Court from Chilleau has tried to kill Andrej Koscuisko. I have to take immediate action."

Not the action that Brecinn might expect her to undertake. She needed to get to Chilleau, consult with Verlaine about the forged Record. Noycannir's crime could destroy the Second Judge's chances to be First Judge once and for all. And Verlaine had convinced her that he was sincere, which meant that Chilleau's bid for control of the Bench was the best hope for reform of the Judicial system she was likely to see in her lifetime—however much was left to her of that.

"What action, Bench specialist, if we may ask?" Senior Auditor Ormbach's voice was calm and politely curious, but Jils thought she could hear an undercurrent of amusement. Well. Brecinn had clearly felt confident of a sympathetic ear at Taisheki Station, and to a certain extent she had gotten it. But the Auditor was not turning off her own skeptical chaff detector, not even for Admiral Sandri Brecinn.

That heartened Jils. It meant that Taisheki Station might not be corrupt, though Brecinn seemed to be relying upon it to be. Jils didn't care for players in principle. Wasn't that ap Rhiannon's stance as well?

"I need to quarantine Admiral Brecinn and her team. This information is too potentially divisive to be leaked by mischance." Let alone on purpose, through a network of people who would take action to maximize their security and profit. "I will travel with the *Ragnarok* to Chilleau Judiciary to consult with Noycannir's superiors and determine what should be done. I'll want Safes. Bond-involuntary troops are Fleet resources, after all. It's our duty to safeguard them."

She didn't know how the *Ragnarok*'s Bonds were taking things. That was only part of the point. The larger part of the point was that a ship traveling under appeal put any assigned Bonds on Safe. Therefore she would put the *Ragnarok*'s Bonds on Safe: to confirm that the *Ragnarok* was traveling as a ship under appeal. A ship with a protected legal status. A very visible ship, one which could not be quietly shunted off to one side and consumed piece by piece, ship and crew.

"I understand," Admiral Brecinn said. Nobody had asked her. She did understand, Jils was sure of it; and was doing what she could to change her future. "You may rely on my discretion with absolute confidence, Bench specialist."

That wasn't going to be necessary.

"I agree to sanitary quarantine for Admiral Brecinn and her people," Auditor Ormbach said. "And to release the Safes, though I meant the *Ragnarok* to come here for them. But in light of your evidence, it is crucial that the ship not be permitted to remain in possession of a battle cannon. If their motivations are unworrisome, they should have no objection to surrendering the contraband item to be placed into Evidence."

This was unpleasantly unexpected, but not in the least remarkable. Unfortunately. "I have no personal knowledge of the existence of such a piece of contraband," Jils said, carefully. She had been told that the evidence against Pesadie Training Command included a black-market, main battle cannon, and its munitions load on top of it. She had not actually seen the cannon, however. "Consider your request, please, Auditor."

If the contraband that the Auditor demanded existed only in Brecinn's imagination, the *Ragnarok* could only prove that by submitting to an intrusive and time-consuming search by Taisheki Station resources. Jils couldn't wait. Nor could she afford to leave the *Ragnarok* vulnerable here, lest Koscuisko play his trump to protect his ship.

And if the *Ragnarok* surrendered a contraband cannon, by the time it all came to explanations who knew what the audit trail would look like?

"Questions have been raised as to the motivation and loyalty of the *Ragnarok*'s chain of command, Specialist Ivers, and an officer of the Court at Chilleau Judiciary has by your report attempted to kill one of the *Ragnarok*'s officers. If the ship is armed, I cannot let it leave here. I'm sorry. I see no alternative that would not be grossly irresponsible."

Well, Auditor Ormbach was right. As long as there was a main battle cannon unaccounted for, it would be criminal negligence on

Auditor Ormbach's part to permit a potentially compromised warship with an understandably aggrieved senior officer to leave the system.

Unless.

"Safes, Senior Auditor. I will take them with me as a token of goodwill on your part, and convey your instructions to the *Ragnarok*'s Command and General Staff." She'd get the Safes. She'd have Brecinn and Brecinn's team sequestered under strict quarantine, not an uncomfortable imprisonment by any means, but bound to be boring.

She had to get to Chilleau Judiciary, and the *Ragnarok* with her, so that she could get space between Fleet and Jennet ap Rhiannon, so that the First Secretary could offer Koscuisko his personal assurances and discuss mutual concerns. "As you say, Bench specialist," Auditor Ormbach agreed. "And we will in the mean time initiate appropriate precautions."

And she had to hold the secret of the forged Record, if she could, until after the Selection. It was not a very closely kept secret. Everyone who had been there in the great hall of Chelatring Side was in a position to know, but the Malcontent could do the damage control there. She had to trust the Malcontent for that. Bench specialists didn't like having to trust anything or anybody, but there was no help for that now.

After the Selection they could expose the fraudulent Record under Bench seal, and cancel any charges outstanding against those troops for whose sake Jennet ap Rhiannon had dared so much. She would log Koscuisko's documents then. He would be relieved of Writ. She would find a way to make it all come out right—once the Selection had been safely completed.

Stildyne helped Andrej up onto the upper tier in the little room, letting him down gently onto the slatted bench as Andrej grunted in reluctant discomfort. Andrej didn't think it was the wound in his shoulder. That was healing nicely now, from the inside out as desired; and the tissue itself was carefully protected by a therapeutic breathable membrane—one that would have to be exchanged soon, which was the only reason that Narion had allowed him into the sauna at all. And then only with strict conditions about heat and humidity.

"All right, sir?" Stildyne asked, with his hand at the back of Andrej's neck to keep his head from knocking up against the wall before Stildyne had had a chance to pad the point of contact with a folded towel. It was perhaps not absolutely necessary for Stildyne to be handling him so carefully, but Andrej couldn't begrudge it.

Stoshik had been right. He had wronged Stildyne. He was not going to make it right, either, because he couldn't imagine such a thing as that; but he could try to accept care more gracefully than he had in the past, with more self-awareness in his acceptance of courtesies that he had become dangerously close to taking for granted.

"Thank you, Brachi, it is fine." It wasn't the wound. It was his entire body. Strapped into a stasis-mover and scarcely conscious for all of that time, his arms ached and his back hurt, his neck was stiff, the muscles in his belly sore, his legs uncomfortable. They had done him good service at Chelatring Side. But he had unquestionably annoyed them. "I am more travel-sore than convalescent. It is why I so particularly wanted a sauna."

Turning away without replying Stildyne crossed to the other side of the room to settle himself on the lower bench. It wasn't far across the room, since it was a sauna. Stildyne's choice of the lower bench was the only way Andrej could look Stildyne in the eye at that small distance, what with the difference of height between them.

At eye level, the impact of the rest of Stildyne's all but naked body was manageable. Andrej had been taking saunas with Stildyne for years; he was accustomed to the experience, but it was still a sometimes stressful one. Stildyne's body was scarred as well as Stildyne's face, and if the scars were not as disfiguring, they were spread over a much larger canvas. Who was to say whether the cumulative impact was more or less awful accordingly?

"You'll have noticed that things are a little different on board since we got back," Stildyne suggested. Andrej closed his eyes and let his body drink in the grateful heat of the sauna. He could feel his muscles relax. He had not lied to Narion; it was simple therapy. The fact that he liked sauna was a side benefit only, and the fact that sauna was one of the few places on board the *Ragnarok* where a man could be almost alone was also beside the point.

"Our Command Branch officers are out of their minds. Yes. I had noticed." Lieutenant ap Rhiannon was a piece of work if he'd ever seen one, and it was hard for him to take her solemn assumption of her duties with a straight face. Except that the other officers seemed to have no such difficulty. Andrej hadn't decided yet whether they were perhaps playing an elaborate practical joke on him. "I think I like Command Branch better that way."

"Problem, though, Andrej." Stildyne's voice was grave and considered, and Andrej thought his name sounded very odd in Stildyne's mouth. Because it sounded just like "Excellency" sounded, when Stildyne said it to him rather than First Officer. "I've been talking to people. If ap Rhiannon doesn't like what she hears when Specialist Ivers gets back from Taisheki Station, she's leaving."

Andrej thought about this. Stildyne was right to be concerned, of course. Based on her actions since he had left, there seemed little doubt that the woman had become desperate. Did he not know what madwomen were capable of? Had he not the hole in his shoulder to prove it?

"I'm not sure what she might think she could accomplish by defying the entire Jurisdiction, Fleet and Bench alike." Wait, he couldn't say that. That was precisely what he meant to do. "I'm not about to leave my Infirmary at the mercy of a maniac. We have had quite enough of that already. Where the ship goes, I will go also."

He was in for the duration, now. He could not in honor leave until the issue of the forged Record had been resolved to his satisfaction, if only by placing it into Evidence. As long as it was an undisclosed forgery, it threatened his people.

And yet Specialist Ivers had been right: if he valued the Second Judge's plans for a change in the system of Inquiry, he could not afford to place so destructive a weapon as the forged Record in the hands of Chilleau Judiciary's political enemies. So long as the Record lay undisclosed, he had to keep with it; and for so long as that, he could not have the relief of Writ completed.

"I'm glad to hear that. Sir. So will your people be."

The outer door into the changing room had opened. Andrej saw movement through the window in the door. Stildyne fell silent. Stildyne was up to something. After a moment, the inner door came open; and the First Officer came into the sauna. Andrej stared. He had never seen First Officer in a sauna.

He had never seen First Officer out of uniform that he could remember, and there was no rank on the towel that Mendez held in one hand. Stepping carefully past Stildyne's scarred knees Mendez took a position beside Stildyne, close to the back wall, and laid his towel across his lap.

"Good-greeting," Mendez said. "Warm enough for you? I don't know how you breathe in here, Andrej."

Andrej didn't know what to say. He was too surprised. He had grasped that Stildyne had a plot in motion; but he had to process the apparition of Ralph Mendez, third of three so named, in a sauna before he could begin to parse the meaning of it out.

"Just getting to the good part, First Officer," Stildyne said.

Mendez nodded. "What's he say, then, Brachi?"

"Means to stick it out. At least at first mention. But I haven't explained the problem to him yet."

Andrej caught his breath. "Speak to me," he said. "Explain. What problem? I do not tolerate to be ambushed, Brachi. Confess yourself at once, and with completeness."

Stildyne looked startled; Andrej considered that he had perhaps not yet quite readjusted to the Standard-speaking world. It was true that such language could be taken as referring to formal Inquiry, here—rather than a simple demand for an explanation.

"Easy as this, Andrej," Mendez said, but considerately, as if aware of how strange what he had to say would sound. "Unprecedented circumstances make new rules. And we're glad to have you back, we're used to you, your Infirmary missed you. But. There's two parts to it. Only half is that you want to stay. The other half is if we're going to let you."

What was this *we*? "I don't understand."

"Captain knows you haven't had much time to think things through. You've come on board wounded, for one. And of all the people here on *Ragnarok* you've got the most to lose. She isn't sure she means to let you."

Staggering. Andrej sat and concentrated on taking a deep breath, calming himself, thinking this thing through.

"I could tell you a thing that would convince you, Ralph." He could. He could explain that it had not been Garol Vogel who had murdered Captain Lowden in Burkhayden, and Mendez would realize that Andrej had nothing to lose by staying with the *Ragnarok*, that Andrej was in danger—real, if of unquantifiable likelihood—of being called to give accounting for that crime. "If I have to, I will. I came back to this ship because I am more indebted to its crew than my blood kin. To suggest I go away to secure my privileges insults me."

Someone else. The door was opening again. Wheatfields, in the name of all Saints, and if there was a very great deal of Stildyne when he took off his clothing there was altogether too much of Wheatfields to be tolerated.

"I appreciate that, Andrej." First Officer took no special notice of Wheatfields, who sat down next to Andrej himself on the bench—well toward the wall, to minimize proximity. The lower bench, and he was still taller than Andrej was. It was a setup. He would have a word to say to Stildyne when this was all over. "But we need more of a commitment from you than that. We need your support. You have to believe that ap Rhiannon is your Captain, Andrej, or it isn't going to work. Serge. Explain."

Wheatfields had closed his eyes, his head tilted back to the ceiling. He made Andrej nervous, sitting so close. "It's still a dirty secret," Wheatfields said. There was something in his voice that Andrej could not understand—humor? "Or at least no one has taken official notice, yet. But it's true, that rumor of Admiral Brecinn's. We are mutinous. You'd better be sure of what you decide, Koscuisko, because once you commit to this there's no going back."

Didn't they think he knew?

"For this reason you should agree that I must be here," Andrej said. Considering whether he should perhaps be furious. "Because so long as I am here, it will be that much more difficult to notice. Have I come from my home for those days in a stasis-mover to have my motivation questioned? What do you wish for me to do?"

All right, he was furious. Yes. During the time that Andrej had been assigned to this ship, Wheatfields had told him many things about himself—his character, his sexuality, a wide range of issues relevant to his personal value and right to breathe the same air as decent souls.

But never had it been suggested that he'd run from threat and leave his people to face hazard alone. Not until now. In all of this time, not even Wheatfields had called him a coward. It was possibly the only thing that Wheatfields had not called him, once "noble and beneficent" was ruled off the list.

"You've got people at home as well, Andrej," First Officer pointed out. "You've got that boy. Your Cousin Ferinc says he's a beautiful little man, and that your wife is waiting for you to come back and warm her sheets; I've talked to him. Bonds are Bonds, Andrej. That child is your son. Are you suggesting you care more about troops than your own child?"

It was a dirty question. Had it been Wheatfields who had asked it, Andrej would have struck him. But First Officer was out of reach.

"He is a beautiful child. Much more than I deserve. And I would deserve such a wife and such a child even less if I could turn my back on the *Ragnarok*, just when I might be able to help save the ship simply by staying here. It has not been Marana who has kept me from the abyss all these years, First Officer. It has been Robert. Lek. Pyotr. Stildyne. All Saints forbid I should say Wheatfields, even."

Again with the movement in the anteroom. Again with the opening of the door. Andrej closed his eyes tightly in horror. There were only two other officers with rank to match or to exceed his own on board the *Ragnarok*. And Two scuttled when she walked. What would Two even look like, in a towel?

Jennet ap Rhiannon stepped up to the upper tier opposite Wheatfields, and met Andrej's horrified gaze with a level stare. She was not Dolgorukij; and her towel was in her lap. She could not know what it was to show her shoulders. And yet she was to be his commanding officer—

"Yes?" ap Rhiannon asked. She was crèche-bred, there was that. The habit of command was easier for her than it might have been for Seascape, for instance. If Andrej concentrated on being angry, on how sore his muscles were, he might be able to ignore her shoulders. Her bare shoulders. Holy Mother. This was beyond reason.

"I think he means it, your Excellency," First Officer replied. "Respectfully suggest you let him tell you."

Captain. Captain ap Rhiannon. Shoulders or no shoulders. Yes. That was the way to do it. "Your Excellency," Andrej said. "I had not realized that there might be a question. This is my ship, and I am under so much obligation to its crew that I cannot explain. It's true that I have better to look forward to once out of Service than the most of us, but that makes me more difficult to kill, either by accident or by Judicial mandate. I am the chief medical officer on the *Ragnarok*. Respectfully request I be permitted to perform as such."

Petitioning, and petitioning this little Lieutenant, of all people. This little Lieutenant had gotten Mendez and Wheatfields to accept her, though, and the rest of the officers and crew as well. If he respected his own medical staff, he could not disregard that judgment.

"Wheatfields wants Secured Medical for storage," ap Rhiannon said. "Any problems?"

No. None whatever. Why, did she think he'd come back to the *Ragnarok* for that? "I have no difficulty in surrendering Secured Medical for any purpose, your Excellency. To the contrary, rather." They'd have to find some place to keep the Record. Or maybe they would just leave it there. It would still be a properly secured place, after all, whether used for storage or for torture.

"Very well. If First Officer agrees. Resume your duties, Doctor Koscuisko. It's good to have you back. And I'm leaving now. It's too hot in here. No, don't get up."

He hadn't thought about it, but the others had. He could tell that he had some adjusting to do. There was silence in the sauna for some moments as the Lieutenant—as the Captain dressed. When the outer door of the changing room opened and closed again, Wheatfields stood up.

"Later," Wheatfields said, to the First Officer. "And no, I don't think we should do staff here. Don't get any ideas, Koscuisko. Nothing is changed, but a ship needs its Chief Medical."

That was a welcome home, Andrej supposed. Wheatfields let another gust of cooler air into the sauna on his way out; all of this traffic was annoying, not relaxing. Mendez yawned, and leaned back against the wall.

"Well, I don't know, it wouldn't be so bad. If it were dry heat. You're not off the hook for information, Andrej. If we need it, we still need it, and you'll still be our best man for the job."

If this hadn't been so serious it would be utterly surreal. "And you'll have it if you need it, First Officer, but it'll come out of Infirmary. Or maybe your office. With the right drugs. And none of the other—complications."

Mendez was right. If it came to getting information he could not refuse. Would not refuse, because no one else on board knew as much as he did about the Controlled List and how to use it, and letting anybody else try would be inefficient. As well as unnecessarily unpleasant. And illegal.

"You'd better start showing up for staff, then. But get dressed first, Andrej. You can't go wandering around the corridors in a towel. What a notion."

On that note Mendez left; there was peace in the sauna at last, and the friendly ticking of the thermostat as the heat increased once more to proper levels. Andrej sighed.

"I had not anticipated a challenge, Chief," he said.

Stildyne seemed to consider this as Andrej relaxed with his eyes closed, drinking in the soothing heat of the sauna. "It's not a rational choice, Andrej. You can't blame them. If they'd seen your house at the Matredonat you might never have been able to convince them."

He had a child, Mendez had said, a wife as well. Both of them waiting. But so had others here, no less dear than his, perhaps more so for having better contact. When would he return? Or would he ever?

"To say that trust and affection are worth more than property and privilege would be too much of a cliché. Even the Valcovniye saga avoided such, and you will remember that there is every other cliché in the canon in the Valcovniye, Brachi. And I therefore will avoid it also."

But they both knew it was true. Stildyne did not challenge the sentiment of this observation, apparently content to let Andrej have the last word—as had indeed been Stildyne's habit, all these years.

Andrej let the tension in his body dissolve into the steam of the sauna, and set his mind at rest.

CHAPTER FOURTEEN

Mutiny in Form

Cousin Ferinc woke up when the threshold alert sounded; someone had crossed the security line at the entrance to the thula's loading ramp. He sat up in his bed, swinging his legs over the edge to put feet to floor. It was his sleep shift, but a cruiser-killer-class warship ran four shifts a day.

It was Security. No, it was Lek Kerenko, who was coming down the corridor and talking as he came. "Really very sorry, Cousin. Permission to come on board. Captain very especially requesting. Are you awake? Anywhere?"

Speaking Standard. This was in Jurisdiction space. Ferinc shrugged his shoulders hastily into his sturdy waffle-weave shirt and tied himself decently covered across the front. "In here, Lek, coming directly. There is something the matter?"

"Captain," Lek repeated, with a turn of his head and a lift of his chin back over his shoulder. "To be seeing you. With your permission, she doesn't understand, but the officer is there."

Something wasn't adding up. Ferinc followed Lek out and down the thula's ramp to the docking apron. Lek's Captain was there, and Chief Stildyne. The Captain of the *Ragnarok*. Officers assigned, by the shade of black they wore; Koscuisko himself. Security behind him.

The sight made Ferinc blanch, but he was Malcontent, he was not who he had been. Koscuisko made no sign of intending any threat. Koscuisko looked pale, and Stildyne stood very close behind him; it had not been very long since Koscuisko had been cleared to resume his uniform. Hours at most, if Ferinc remembered the gossip correctly. He bowed with careful precision, and as a Malcontent, not a warrant officer. "Your Excellency."

She would initiate the conversation. She had the rank, even if the rank was all she had. The other officers were older, taller, more experienced; but it was all she needed, in this instance.

"They've started to mine the exit vector," the Captain said. "Specialist Ivers is en route back to the ship, but it's clear that Taisheki Station doesn't mean for us to leave. Therefore likely that it's not in our best interest to stay."

All very interesting. "Yes, your Excellency?" Mining the exit vector. That was extreme. It was also defensive; an interesting sort of a signal to send. "And what service may my holy Patron extend to your command under this circumstance?"

"I want the thula," ap Rhiannon said, and pointed. In case there could be any question here about which thula exactly, Ferinc supposed. "I need it to clear the mine field. I'll want to mount the battle cannon. And therefore."

Security stepped up, as if on cue. They were all around him. They were far enough away to present no immediate threat, but he was surrounded. "Therefore, I must regretfully take your ship, with my sincere apologies, but I must have it. Cousin. You will surrender your navigation keys."

The Devil he would.

Koscuisko put out his hand, shaking his head; they hadn't told Koscuisko. Well. Several of the officers here looked a little less than completely put together. It had been someone else's sleep shift, too; ap Rhiannon had probably come as soon as she'd been told that Taisheki Station had started to mine the vector. As soon as the Intelligence Officer had woken her up to tell her that.

"Captain," Koscuisko said. "Your Excellency. With respect. It's not his ship, it's the Saint's. He can't surrender it. There must be a way around this. Because if I allow the Malcontent to be separated from his ship by force, I'm in much worse trouble with the Saint than any seven Benches could ever cause me."

Ap Rhiannon didn't know about Malcontents and it was obvious that she didn't care. "I'm sorry, your Excellency, but you also have no

choice. I must have the speed and the carrying capacity. Serge thinks
we can clear the mine field with the thula. Otherwise it's engaging arti-
plats with Wolnadis, and we'll lose them all. I'm not asking for your
cooperation, Cousin Ferinc, I arrest you fairly and openly. You should
suffer no adverse consequences from your superiors."

Koscuisko moved to grasp the Captain's arm and remonstrate with
her. Stildyne put his hand to Koscuisko's shoulder; Koscuisko started
back with such a look of surprise on his face that Ferinc could have
laughed. Stildyne's expression had not changed.

This was fun. But it could not be allowed to drag on; Lek was
starting to become uncomfortable, among other things. It would be
self-indulgent of him to let misunderstandings multiply. Cousin
Stanoczk expected better of him.

"I cannot surrender the ship, your Excellency, or transfer
navigation keys. I have a sacred duty to my Patron. To fail in that
would grieve my divine Patron, to whose affection I am more deeply
indebted than I can explain." The Security around him shifted, just so
he would remember that they were there. It would do them no good.
He had his orders.

He explained. "I must faithfully carry out my orders to accompany
the son of the Koscuisko prince to his ship of assignment, there to
perform what tasks it should please him to nominate to me until such
time as he should send us both back to Azanry—the ship and I—and
forgive us for our errors." The Malcontent should have seen
Noycannir coming. They should have known what she'd had in mind.
It was the genuinely mad that were as dangerous as that, because their
next moves could never be predicted with certainty.

Lek seemed to relax.

"The 'son of the Koscuisko prince'?" The tallest officer would be the
Chigan Ship's Engineer, by repute. So the officer who was talking was
the Ship's First. He might have been Ship's First someday, Ferinc
thought; Stildyne would have been a Ship's First right now, if it hadn't
been for Andrej Koscuisko. No. He never would have been Ship's First.
He hadn't had the moral fiber for it. "That's you, Andrej. Isn't it?"

"At least for now," Koscuisko agreed a little sourly, his eyes fixed
on Ferinc's face. He knew. But Ferinc had just been having a little bit
of fun, that had been all. No harm to it, surely. "Ferinc, has my cousin
Stanoczk truly granted me the use of this fine beast?"

"And me with it," Ferinc confirmed. Then he wished he hadn't expressed himself in quite that way, but Koscuisko didn't seem to notice. Koscuisko turned to his Captain, and bowed.

"I withdraw my objection, your Excellency. We may in fact fully exploit this thula. Cousin Ferinc will extend every possible assistance to ensure a successful mission, is that not so, Ferinc?"

"Yes, your Excellency," Ferinc answered, obediently, but hearing Marana's tone in Koscuisko's voice. Being very stern with her child Anton. It was a shame Koscuisko had not stayed at home, but Ferinc would not be sorry for a chance to see Marana perhaps again.

Ap Rhiannon looked from Ferinc to Koscuisko and back again; then shrugged her shoulders, as if dismissing the whole interchange as parochial in nature. "Very well, Doctor, Cousin Ferinc. Thank you. I have asked General Rukota to evaluate whether and how the main battle cannon can be installed in the thula's forward emplacement. If you will work with him, Cousin Ferinc. Will the ship support it?"

It had been built as a courier. But Fleet's couriers had been armed. "Specifications support main battle cannon and subsidiary stations. I will translate ship's comps for the General, your Excellency." Whoever he was. What was a General doing on a battleship? Generals were ground forces.

"Coordinate also then with my First Officer, Cousin Ferinc, on the ship's performance characteristics. We'll need to select a crew very carefully. The mine field will be almost fully deployed by the time we can get there, and we'll need the pathway clear before we can safely start a vector spin."

Or complete one successfully, to be more precise, but he took the point. "According to her Excellency's good pleasure," Ferinc said, bowing.

Koscuisko looked genuinely startled. Ferinc was a little startled to hear it from his own mouth under these circumstances himself. "Carry on," ap Rhiannon said. "With all deliberate speed. We don't have much time."

Turning, she walked away; Security went with her.

Koscuisko gave Ferinc a fish-eyed stare. "It is true, this dish you have invited to taste my Captain?" Koscuisko demanded. "Or another filthy Malcontent trick of some sort?"

"Blood-guilt, your Excellency, with regards to the incident at Chelatring Side. Truly. I wouldn't dare lie to you, sir."

Koscuisko was not convinced. "You should know better, Ferinc, but you are Malcontent and have no shame accordingly. And no sense of proportion. If you do not need me, First Officer, I go back to bed."

The officer Koscuisko had addressed nodded. "Leave us Kerenko, Andrej. We may want to talk to him. All right, Lek?"

Lek was under Bond. And yet Lek seemed to be dealing with this outrageously anomalous situation without much difficulty. Was it true what he had heard, that Koscuisko had liberated his bond-involuntaries through the shocking expedient of treating them like feeling souls?

"Very good, First Officer," Lek said, with a crisp salute. If Lek could fly the ship on a mine-clearing mission, it would help. Because Lek could really, really fly the thula. Ferinc could never have managed to locate the *Ragnarok* on vector transit on his own. Lek was good at this.

"Over to you, General," First Officer said; to the only other man left on the docking apron who had yet to speak. "General Dierryk Rukota, Koscuisko's Cousin Ferinc. Cousin Ferinc, General Dierryk Rukota. Gentlemen. Good-greeting, then. Andrej. Let's go get our naps in."

Stildyne would stay as well. Good, Ferinc could use Stildyne. And all of the rest of the rank could just clear the docking apron and let them get to work.

"Kospodar thula," General Rukota said. He was a big man as Stildyne was big, but ugly in his own special way. Thin lips. Narrow eyes. Strong nose. "Take me through her, if you will, Cousin Ferinc. We've got to get her armed and deployed as soon as possible, if we've got a hope of breaking out."

Which did rather raise the issue of whether it was worth the effort to try. But it was their business. Not his. He just flew the ship—or navigated, with Lek on board—and followed his reconciler's orders. Or what his reconciler would have told him to do, if he'd been here.

"Starting at the forward emplacement, then, General Rukota." This would be fun. He'd never seen a mutiny in progress; wait till he got home, and told Stanoczk.

Jils Ivers stood before the Captain's Bar in the mess area where the *Ragnarok*'s officers held their staff meetings. There was a place for her at the table between the Captain and the First Officer, but she didn't feel like sitting down.

"Yes. They are mining the vector." There was no question about it; certainly no attempted subterfuge was any use. "I can't really dispute with Auditor Ormbach's point. I've convinced her that the *Ragnarok* has good reason to be antipathetic to Chilleau Judiciary. And if Brecinn's claims are correct the *Ragnarok* itself, as well as its Wolnadi fighters, is armed. Which makes the *Ragnarok* dangerous."

She didn't say "makes you dangerous." She didn't say "loose cannon." She didn't need to waste her breath. The *Ragnarok* had decided that it was in its best interest to leave the moment Taisheki Station had moved to ensure that it stayed. It was classic.

It was a disaster.

How could this ship have frozen so concretely in support of one acting crèche-bred Command Branch officer? It couldn't have. Ap Rhiannon had a lot going for her in the moral outrage department, that was clear, but for the *Ragnarok* to be functioning as well as it had been was a clear indication of genuine mutuality of goals. Ap Rhiannon spoke for the *Ragnarok*, but she seemed perfectly aware that it was the crew who were in command of the ship.

"Engineer?" ap Rhiannon asked. "Your status, please."

Wheatfields straightened up in his chair, which brought his head that much closer to the ceiling. "Escape vector for Amberlin across Taisheki vector has been registered and read in, your Excellency. By your command."

Amberlin was uncontrolled space, well forward of the rule of Law. It was a notorious nest of vagabonds, derelicts, refugees, and rabble-rousers, with a thriving black market; Jils could understand the choice. If need should be the *Ragnarok* could survive there for an indeterminate period of time, taking what they needed as they found it—or would they prey on the stores of reasonable people for supplies, as they had done when they'd acquired the battle cannon?

Since activity in Amberlin was illegal by definition, they would have no necessary concerns about abusing the innocent. Staying out of the way of the powerful criminal fleets, now—that would be an interesting problem.

"We can be assured that Fleet will not pursue us to Amberlin." Ap Rhiannon could make that statement with such absolute conviction because so far Fleet itself had been unable to make an impression on the extralegal, ad-hoc governments that fielded their fleets in Amberlin space. "And we may have the opportunity to demonstrate our loyalty on a small scale where we can, while we pursue our appeal. First Officer. What if Taisheki Station should engage?"

The *Ragnarok* clearly meant to make no secret of its intentions; the speed with which the *Ragnarok* would be traveling would be enough of a signal. Taisheki might well field its small force of corvettes. How successfully could they resist? These were all their own people. Fleet.

Mendez glanced at the Engineer's blank, impassive face before responding. "The thula will be clearing the mine field, your Excellency. It can run interference for us. Fleet won't want to have to pay the Malcontent for the machine. They're expensive. It'll be tight, maneuvering the ship back up into the maintenance atmosphere on our way out, but using it will effectively control our exposure."

The Kospodar thula was as nimble as a Wolnadi, significantly superior for speed. With a main battle cannon for ginger, it could potentially hold off any Fleet pursuit short of a cruiser-killer-class warship like the *Ragnarok* itself.

"Very well, First Officer," ap Rhiannon said. "Do you have a crew on line?"

Interesting question, Jils thought. There was only one crew here on the *Ragnarok* that had any experience at all flying the thula: and one of them was under Bond. Under Safe, now, as First Officer had distributed those she had brought with her from Taisheki Station; but there were limits. The Safe only silenced the governor itself. It was fear of the governor that ruled a bond-involuntary; at least that was the theory.

This time Mendez's thoughtful gaze rested upon Chief Medical's aristocratic Aznir face for just that one moment before he spoke. Looked pale, Koscuisko did. Of course Koscuisko always looked pale, to her. "Elements of Security 5.1 for dedicated flight, your Excellency—and Lek Kerenko won't hear of being excluded. He flew her for three days, he says, he can fly her now."

"Safe or no Safe, First Officer," Jils said, just to remind them that she was here. "There's conditioning. It's not fair to the troop. Even if he is the best man on board for the job."

Ap Rhiannon frowned, tearing bits of rewrap off the lip of her bean—tea flask absentmindedly; Koscuisko spoke.

"It is true that he desires the thula, carnally." Koscuisko was clearly unwilling to hazard his people—but sensibly aware, not only that they were not his people to hazard, but also that the entire ship was equally at risk. "Also that they speak something close to the same language. If his officer of assignment were to be present, is it not possible that he could be clear to perform?"

His officer of assignment? Andrej Koscuisko? A medical officer, commanding a combat action?

The Engineer was shaking his head, apparently unimpressed. "You'd have to be there, Andrej, not just on the com, since they could jam the com. He's got to be completely convinced that he's in the clear with you, even on Safe. And what happens if he buckles in midflight?"

"But I mean to be there, if that is what it takes." Koscuisko challenged Wheatfields flatly, without the polite fiction of deferring to Command to soften his attack. "Lek and I have much more history together than just to be assigned each to the other on board of the *Ragnarok*. He and I also speak something close to the same language."

First Officer had put his head down into his hands, rubbing his forehead with a slow repetitive contemplative gesture. Wheatfields looked to ap Rhiannon, now; and after a moment—as if realizing his error, reminding himself that he was not in fact master in this room— Koscuisko did the same.

The personality interplay was fascinating.

Mere days on board, and Koscuisko was fitting himself in as though he'd never left. With occasional disconnects, yes, which would doubtless always be arising.

"If First Officer accepts your reasoning, Doctor, it shall be so," ap Rhiannon said. She could safely rely on Koscuisko's judgment; Jils knew that. Koscuisko would never have been as good as he was at what he did if he couldn't judge how far a person could be pushed, and with what stimulus, and under what kinds and degrees of pressure.

If Koscuisko said that Lek Kerenko could pilot the thula against the Fleet in overt action against the Bench authority, then Kerenko could do it. Ap Rhiannon's reservations appeared to have a slightly different focus. "If Fleet finds out you're on the ship, though, your Excellency, they're going to want to force you into Taisheki Station."

Which attempt would logically require the diversion of at least some of the corvettes Taisheki might send after them, leaving the

Ragnarok with a clear run at the vector. But what if they were to lose their Ship's Surgeon?

"All the more motivation, your Excellency." Koscuisko's determination could not be shaken. "They would kill my Kerenko. They would take me hostage against my family and the Selection. She is a Kospodar thula, she belongs to the Malcontent. She will not betray us to Fleet."

Running his fingers up through his black-and-silver hair, Mendez blinked at ap Rhiannon with owlish eyes, green and genial. "Never argue with the medic, or the paymaster, or stores-and-receipts, your Excellency. So. Lek on the hot seat. Ferinc will have to stay here, of course, he hasn't declared war on Taisheki Station. Security 5.1 will take the rest of the flight tasks. They've had practice."

So they had. Practice under pressure, running hard from Azanry to Taisheki Station, intercepting the *Ragnarok* en route. Impressive flying.

"That weaponer has never fired a main battle cannon, First Officer," ap Rhiannon reminded him. Or at least seemed to remind him. Mendez nodded, lifting one finger of his knuckly right hand to mark his point.

"Avenham has, though, your Excellency. A few others, but she's got the most experience. Wheatfields and I have picked out a few more to man the guns we've borrowed from the Wolnadis. Close your ears, Bench specialist."

Too late. Jils sighed. "I'll be in my quarters," she decided, aloud. There was a Lieutenant's berth empty that she was using; they were keeping Rukota in another, and so far as Jils could tell he was feeling right at home. "Not noticing."

Ap Rhiannon nodded at her, so that she could take her leave and go without being rude. "I'll send for you when we're on vector, Bench specialist. You can contact Chilleau Judiciary at that time, if you wish."

Not before. That went without saying. Bowing, Jils turned and walked away, out of the room, and left the Captain and the crew of the Jurisdiction Fleet Ship *Ragnarok* to plot their mutiny in peace.

And now great *Ragnarok* stood steady—but too strong—for the Taisheki entry vector, and no one who had had any last-minute doubts could question her intentions any longer.

The mine field, the network of linked artillery stations that was to have denied the warship access to the vector, had yet to be completely fielded. Forward sensors clearly revealed the emplacement crews struggling with all of their might to throw the net at its full three-sixty orb around the near approach to the entry vector: but it would only take twelve, not more than sixteen, well-aimed shots to blow a hole in the unmanned portion of the fire wall and clear the *Ragnarok*'s route for the Taisheki vector, and Amberlin space.

Andrej Koscuisko stood in the thula's wheelhouse, listening to the confused babble of common-feeds coming in from four and five plaits at once. Emplacement crews, working at fever pitch. Two's comps talking to Engineering about the state of space ahead.

The gantry officer, talking Lek and Taller through their careful passage down past the lateral gap that had been left unhulled until the last so that the thula could go—and, of course, get back—before the final seal would be required preparatory to gaining the vector.

And, of course, the communication he was most interested in, the loudest strongest feed, Jennet ap Rhiannon versus Taisheki Station. "Fleet Receiving, Taisheki Station. This is acting Captain Jennet ap Rhiannon, Jurisdiction Fleet Ship *Ragnarok*, commanding."

The formal—lesser—rank sounded a little odd, to Andrej. It had been easier than he had expected to fall into the same habit that the other Ship's Primes had apparently developed, and take her for his Captain in deed as well as in word.

Stand by the thula, he heard the gantry officer say, *go for terce-tumble on mark. Two. Three. Four.*

"*Ragnarok*, this is Taisheki Station Receiving. Welcome to Taisheki Station, your Excellency. Please direct your craft through to docking facilities on transmit, estimated transit time three hours Standard."

There was a schematic displayed forward, beneath the primary spatial. Andrej could watch the thula make its move, sinking gently through the narrow gap remaining between the massive stalloy staves of the maintenance atmosphere's hull. It was a delicate business; he knew it from Taller's tension, Lek's concentration, and the calm steady voice of the gantry officer as she spoke. *Hold at five for now, we need to adjust. Good. Thula, make your drop.*

The thula cleared the *Ragnarok*'s maintenance hull and pivoted to align to the ship's axis. The gantry communication line went mute, to give the airspace over to the Engineer. On the public braid their Captain was not cooperating.

"Respectfully decline to enter Taisheki Station, Receiving Officer. We cannot comply with your request to submit to board and search, still less to surrender any troops assigned without presentation of a fully executed Bench warrant."

Detachment of heavy Security is on alert, Two's feed broke in. *Due to clear ready-state in two eighths, Standard. Estimated transit time to maneuver field, five eighths. These indications are on balance positive. So far.*

"Captain. Administrative procedures at Taisheki Station are at the discretion of the Fleet Audit Appeals Authority. Respectfully remind the *Ragnarok* that it has been administratively reassigned and directed to report."

Thula, take your targets, you know the grid. Field on command. The Engineer's voice was as calm as if he'd been discussing clearing a passage through a rock-cloud, rather than selectively attacking an orb of mechanized artillery platforms. At least Andrej hoped—knew they all hoped—that the platforms they were going to hit were mechanized. Because they were going to have to hit them one way or the other.

"Receiving Officer, an Appeal having been made in good form and formally accepted, the *Ragnarok* has been directed to Taisheki Station pending the initiation of an investigation. Recurrence of requirements previously protested indicates an investigation targeted against the *Ragnarok*, rather than of this ship's duly logged and registered Appeal."

The remote forward was beginning to pick up an onscreen trace. A set of eight blips, from the lower middle right octant, beginning to pulse and brighten on the screen. Those heavy Security, Andrej supposed. And the thula was to engage them as well, if it came to that; or at least stand between them and the *Ragnarok*, if they could not clear in time.

"Willing to stand by to negotiate entry into Taisheki Station after dismantling of mine field currently emplaced," ap Rhiannon suggested helpfully.

If it came to engaging heavy Security, they would find out how intent Fleet was on preserving the thula—on preserving him—from destruction. Andrej was not unafraid: but all the same, Andrej knew for a fact that it was better to be here, in the thula, with his people, even if he had to die. Better than to be alive with Fleet, if *Ragnarok* should be destroyed, whether quickly in battle or more slowly through the deliberate predations of a Fleet Interrogations Group.

"*Ragnarok.*" The voice of the Receiving Officer was beginning to show some signs of wear around the edges. "You are directed to proceed to docking facilities. Failure to comply with a direct lawful order is a violation of Fleet protocols and severely handicaps the investigation of your Appeal."

Security 5.1 was here, with Chief Stildyne on one of the weapons ports. Another weaponer had been borrowed from one of Wheatfields's teams; Wheatfields himself—Andrej noted, with a certain degree of detached amusement—seemed to be getting anxious about things, from the tone of his voice over braid.

Captain. Request vector initiate. With respect, we should start thinking about getting out of here.

But ap Rhiannon was cooperating with Wheatfields to approximately the same degree as she was with Taisheki Station— hardly at all. She didn't answer Wheatfields, not directly. She didn't need to. "Any order to place my Command at the mercy of arbitrary and unjustified Inquiries is not lawful. It will not be possible for us to comply with an illegitimate instruction. Please advise."

Target acquisition complete on fire-funnel, Taller was telling Engineering, over his board-plait. *Require clearances for sweep, at your command, confirm.*

Although the stress in the air was almost palpable Lek did not seem to be feeling any special pressure from his governor, at least not yet. Ap Rhiannon was being very clear: Taisheki Station's insistence that they enter was not lawful. The harder part for Lek would come later, when they had to defend themselves by taking offensive action.

And if he had been wrong about Lek's Safe and his personal authority, they were all as good as dead already, and the *Ragnarok* with them. At least in theory. Andrej was as certain as he had to be that they could do it, even with such a penalty for miscalculation staring him in the face from the grim shadows of the forward screens.

Taisheki Station had clearly reached the end of its patience. "As you wish, *Ragnarok.* Be advised that failure to comply with instructions will be interpreted as mutinous in intent and execution, and will be prosecuted to the fullest extent of the Law. You are directed—for the last time—to break speed and alter course for docking facilities, there to be boarded and secured pending a full Fleet inquiry."

That had cut it. Andrej scanned the back of Lek's shoulders, the tilt of his head, for any sign of conflict or of hesitation; and found none.

"Taisheki Station. You are out of order, Receiving Officer. We are unable in justice to comply with your demands. You leave us with no choice but to protect the integrity of this Command pending a full and fair investigation of our Appeal. Engineering. Your action."

Well, they were down to it, then, weren't they?

"Thank you, your Excellency." Now that ap Rhiannon had cut the braid to Taisheki Station, Wheatfields was coming over their line. "Thula, we need those artillery platforms taken out. We'll do what we can to hold the heavy Security off your tail, if need should be. Go for it."

"Confirm and comply," Lek answered, as cheerfully as if it were a leave-detail he was to move forward, and not a warship. "Thula away. Weaponers. Confirm assignment targets. Excellency, if you would strap in, sir."

It was almost the first indication that Lek even remembered that he was there. Andrej didn't want to take the single step back to his observer's station and strap in; he wanted to be as close to Lek as he could be, in case there should begin to be a problem. But he had no intention of arguing with Lek. He was far from his primary competencies—in command for legal purposes, but by no means in charge.

The thula leaped away from the underbelly of the *Ragnarok*, its transit showing on the forward screens as a sudden shift in orders of magnitude as it made for the artillery net. A good thing he was webbed in after all, Andrej told himself. There was no motion to be sensed on board the ship, no; but the rate of change on the forward display was enough to make him dizzy.

Five eighths to come to speed, six eighths after that to enter the artillery net's kill-zone. It would take *Ragnarok* nearly six times as long to follow, what with size and rates of acceleration taken into account.

That meant nearly four eights, once all the eighths were totaled, for the *Ragnarok* to transit the fields of fire, unless they cleared a hole in the net.

Four eights . . . the sixteenth part of a shift, the sixty-fourth part of a day. Too long, any way one looked at it. Even with the thula's advantage of speed it seemed too long to Andrej, because there were detail screens up along the perimeter of the ship's main forwards, and he could see the battery guns start to turn—taking aim at them.

Wasn't it about time they shot at something?

A tone on Taller's board from the chief weaponer, sounding clearly in the quiet of the wheelhouse. Taller turned in his seat and looked back over his shoulder, nodding in response to Andrej's questioning look. Oh. Good. Time for his contribution, then.

Clearing his throat, Andrej toggled his braid to transmit. He'd rehearsed this, because it was critical that he got it right, and they would have only this one chance. The thula was gaining on an artillery platform at an astounding rate: but there were so many of them out there, and all turning slowly but surely to target the Ragnarok as she came—

"This is Andrej Ulexeievitch. Koscuisko." He was thinking in Aznir, under pressure. There was no particular reason for Fleet to know who Andrej Ulexeievitch was, let alone why he might bear listening to.

"I am in receipt of direct orders from my superior commanding officer to clear the transit lane for my parent ship. I have therefore issued orders in turn that the artillery platforms capable of impacting the transit lane be removed from operation. If there are any crew on any platforms—"

One of the side-screens went white as phosphorus; they had been fired upon, though not hit. It was nothing personal. The artillery platforms that comprised the mine field would have been given pre-coded instructions to fire automatically on whomever came within range without prior clearances. Andrej finished his assigned speech as smoothly as he could, surprised at his emotional reaction—anger. They were shooting at him. Were they, indeed?

"—within the defined transit lane you are cautioned to identify and evacuate. Firing will commence in three eighths. You have three eighths to identify and initiate evacuation. Koscuisko away, the thula."

The Malcontent's ship moved more quickly than the artillery batteries could efficiently track; the arti-plats were designed to stop larger ships—and few ships as small as a Kospodar thula carried sufficient firepower to seriously endanger one of them. Would Fleet be expecting a threat from the thula? Taisheki Station surely knew from Admiral Brecinn that the *Ragnarok* had acquired a main battle cannon from Silboomie Station.

"Coming up on t-minus one, mark. Shani, Alpert. Go."

The intership braid had cleared to all-ship access, now; Andrej could hear the weaponers exchange information. They needed to hear what was happening: because Taller and Lek were responsible for getting the thula to precisely where the weaponers needed it to be, and they could only spare the three weaponers to watch for rounds directed at the ship itself.

There was a flare, off to the side of the main screen. A voice Andrej didn't think he recognized. "Successful intercept, Chief. Confirm."

They were still within target overlap, the kill-zone. Surely almost clear by now, past the barrier that the overlapping fields of fire represented, through to the other side of the mine field, where only the closest arti-plat would threaten the thula—because the ranges between them had been calculated carefully, each platform just less than twice the linear range of anyone of them. Unfortunately the thula had to close, to kill. "Successful intercept, Alport, confirmed. Stildyne, mark on target."

One eighth left to the first platform, then. The first of sixteen. They had to take out sixteen of them to clear a space through the mine field that was big enough for a ship the size of the *Ragnarok* to traverse, and still be sufficiently removed from the remaining platforms that any residual rounds could be absorbed by the plasma sheath without damage to the hull.

"Mark on target, Chief, confirmed." Stildyne's voice, yes. It was a little odd, to Andrej, to hear Stildyne addressed without rank, and hear him return his own rank in address to the speaker. The chief weaponer for this mission was a junior weapons systems analyst from Engineering; but on a mission flight like this, ability took absolute precedence. Avenham was the best chief weaponer on board of the *Ragnarok*.

It was the same in his own area, Andrej reminded himself—he

might have rank, and he unquestionably had the best qualifications for some surgeries, but that did not mean that he had any business controverting with Infectious Disease or Psychiatric. Quite the contrary.

Suddenly the braid from their parent plaited in again, an urgent message for Taller and Lek alike. "Thula, this is *Ragnarok*. We have an evacuation party on target six. Can you adjust?"

Target six. They had a preprogrammed kill-sequence laid in, and a set of alternates ready to load; all designed to prevent the intelligence that controlled the arti-plats from predicting where the ship would strike next, and moving to target them accordingly. Andrej had no idea where "target six" actually came in their list of targets. Lek took a moment to find out; but when he answered, it was a relief.

"Convert to sequence nine. Weaponer Avenham. Re-sequence after target four, advise preferred response."

Advise him of what Avenham's preferred response was to be, Lek meant—whether he was going to want a different approach. These people understood the language they were speaking. It was only confusing to him because he had no place within the tight group dynamic of this crew, and couldn't share the most part of their communications.

"Lek, switch your flyby on proximate hit when we get to it. Shani, your kill, confirm. Preparing to discharge round."

The artillery platform grew gray and ominous on the forward screens. They were going to run dead into it at any moment—but the ship spun to one side, rather than colliding, and at the nearest possible approach, just before the thula broke its head-on course Andrej felt—rather than saw—the huge flare from the thula's forward gun, as Avenham fired.

Blooming like an astraffler in the side-panel screen the artillery platform blew up, sending bits of stalloy and debris in all directions.

"Piece of work, this cannon." Avenham's voice was appropriately respectful. "Next up on four, Lek? Stildyne. Pin it in the second laterals."

Now that they were through, now that they could run behind the mine field, it would be one round after another till the gap was cleared. Great *Ragnarok* labored to gain speed behind them, and they had less than the eighth part of a shift to clear the field before their ship would enter the kill-zone. The thula threw herself upon her target as if shot from a howitzer-piece; and Stildyne—on ship's-left laterals—hit the sequence perfectly. That was two, then.

Lek ran the ship at extreme tolerance, the consumption monitors cycling at an alarming rate. Silent and tense, Andrej watched the remote sensors, fixed as they were on *Ragnarok* well behind them—*Ragnarok*, standing for the vector, and the eager convoy of heavy Security from Taisheki Station straining after her.

Three and four; five, and the arti-plat had the thula targeted a shade too narrowly for comfort, so that the energy wash blinded the screens for a long instant before the ship's auto-recovers picked up feed again.

Six and seven; eight, nine, and Lek played the thula's navigation like a man in a dream, his every gesture slow and deliberate—only at so fast a pace that he didn't seem to stop moving for an instant. He was working hard, and Taller beside him struggled to keep pace. Lek knew what he was doing; he didn't hesitate. And still the odds against which Lek had to fight to do his work were staggering, Safe or no Safe.

Ten platforms down. Only six to go. There was a voice in the forward cabinet, and it was neither Avenham's voice nor Lek's voice, Stildyne's, Lorbe's, anybody's. Andrej was confused, so focused on the target grid above the primary display that it took him a moment to realize who was talking.

"Thula. Evacuation party is reporting to host, damage to craft—translation injury. They're losing heat."

First Officer, that's who it was. The eleventh platform came up on the forward scan; Lek circled around it so that Alport could fire from the backside of his arc even as he was changing vectors for the next target. Was anybody paying attention to First Officer?

Or was Mendez talking to him? Plaiting into braid, Andrej reached for more information. "The evacuation party's craft suffering damage, First Officer. Losing heat. How bad is it?"

"The harriers are still four eighths behind us, Andrej, and we're not going to be able to afford to slow for tractor. If you can pull them on board. If not, well."

But they were running short of time, and Andrej didn't know for certain whether Mendez's braid had even fed into any plait but his. He was the last person on board of the thula who could hope to judge whether they were going to be able to pick up a damaged evacuation craft or not. "Thank you, First Officer. Thula away."

Twelve. It was a temptation to call the run off, and go for the evacuation party, and let the *Ragnarok* hazard the remaining guns. But it was unthinkable to try to stop now, unthinkable to hazard seven hundred lives to try for eight. No.

The evacuation craft had been damaged by debris; they had not fired on the evacuation craft—they were not responsible. The cold was not so bad a way to die. And the people in the evacuation party, they had all been willing that the *Ragnarok* should be forced into Taisheki Station, with a Fleet Interrogations Group all too probably in the wings. He had to keep his peace. To speak now would be to betray Lek. And not only Lek—but every soul on board of the *Ragnarok*.

Thirteen, and Lek shook the thula fiercely from side to side, running down the platform's line of fire as the guns tried to fix on them for long enough to get a target registration and shoot. One of the weaponers stopped a round midway between the platform and the ship, but the impact was too close—the thula lost her course for one terrible moment, and rolled against the shock like sea-wrack at flood.

Lek set the board to rights and closed on target. Stildyne fired the left-lateral battery and blew the platform into utter ruin. Only three to go. Those people on the artillery platform had surely expected to be well clear before the mine field was called into active play. For all Andrej knew, they weren't even Fleet resources but civilian contractors.

Fourteen. The thula heeled back on her own impulse-train and ran for the next target, eager for the kill, and the chief weaponer gave the word. "Go for it, Smath. Your hit. Good shot." It was fractions of an eighth left before the *Ragnarok* would come into range, and only one arti-plat still threatened her. One last platform and *Ragnarok* was clear to breach the mine field; the ship already had the advantage of speed in the chase, because the pursuit ships were either too small to do the *Ragnarok*'s great black massy hull much harm or too big to gain sufficient speed to close.

One final platform, only one more, and it turned its primary guns toward them, blossoming into a cloud of dust and scrap and useless chunks of trash as the thula fixed and fired and killed. The *Ragnarok* was clear.

Steady, almost stately, the *Ragnarok* made full transit into what had been the kill-zone as the remaining stations fired on the ship in a vain attempt to reach beyond the range of their emplaced guns and put a stop to its deliberate progress.

"Nicely done, thula." First Officer, again, and Andrej unstrapped himself from the webbing in his secure-shell to go see that Lek was all right. "Well flown, Lek. Very nicely shot, weaponers all. Come on home, we've got a vector to catch, and the sooner we hull over the happier Wheatfields is going to be with all of us."

Andrej didn't like the confused sideways glance Taller was giving Lek, nor did he quite understand the fearful intensity of Lek's focus on his boards. The thula did not seem to be reorienting toward the *Ragnarok*, nor to face pursuit, scant eighths behind the ship.

"Mister Kerenko?"

The expression on Lek's face was one of utter concentration, not the anguished conflict of a governor going wrong. No conflict at all. Determination, rather, and—meeting Lek's dark sharp Sarvaw eyes—Andrej knew as surely as if he had been told exactly what was going on in Lek's mind.

"We can make it work, sir. Their only chance."

Yes. Plaiting into braid, Andrej keyed into the standard emergency strand. "This is Andrej Ulexeievitch Koscuisko. We have been given to understand that an evacuation craft is damaged. It is our intent to take this craft into cargo." Switching onto ship-strand, he continued. "Weaponer, if you would direct the tractor."

Three of the pursuit ships had veered off from their primary course, moving to intercept. That was their right, perhaps. The point that First Officer had made was that the pursuit ships could not reach the damaged evac craft in time: the thula could—so there was a chance.

Why should they risk their lives—and a death about whose full horror they suffered no illusions—for the lives of an artillery emplacement crew, just recently engaged in doing all they could to set the traps that would ensnare great *Ragnarok* and every soul on board?

"Yes, sir." Avenham's voice was clear, calm, neutral. Unquestioning. "Stildyne, Lorbe, on lateral forwards, mark. Alport, you and Shani and I, off-station, onto tractor."

Because they wouldn't have gotten into this desperate situation in the first place if they had been willing, as individuals, as a ship, to sacrifice anyone's life to their own survival, if they thought that there was any way around it.

It seemed to take forever to close on the evac craft, its external signals already warning of extreme stress tolerance, losing heat. Taller toggled into braid from his station, signaling urgently for a response, trying to see whether they were already too late. "Thula to evac craft. Prepare to tractor. Evac, are you there? Please. Respond."

No, only the mechanical code, in reply. The damaged ship no longer had enough power to maintain heat and transmit voice at the same time. Only the mechanical code, but that was hopeful, because someone had to be able to move, to initiate the transmit—*Extreme emergency situation exists. Failure of integrity imminent. Please expedite rescue effort. Eight souls in custody.*

"Evac craft on scan," Avenham said.

Lek did something to his console, and the thula shuddered like a wild animal cornered in a field trap, coming around. Three pursuit craft, on the second lateral, and it seemed to Andrej that they were making entirely too good a rate of acceleration for anybody's peace of mind.

"Tractor initiate. Very low reading off evac craft, your Excellency." Avenham's warning was predictable, but worrisome. It would be frustrating if they were to lose their lives—and still come too late for the evac craft. "Give us a little drop, Lek—good. Tractor is firm, gaining cargo bay now."

The tractor could not be rushed. If they damaged the thula's cargo bay, they wouldn't be able to pressurize, and then it wouldn't matter whether they had the evac craft or not. Did he imagine it—Andrej wondered—or could he hear the subtle sound of the closing of the cargo bay doors beneath the white noise in the wheelhouse?

"Chief." It was Stildyne, talking to Avenham. "Respectfully suggest we move this thula at the first possible opportunity—"

"Go for it."

Avenham's response was all the word Lek apparently needed. The thula shuddered and it seemed to groan, but the pursuit ships that Andrej could see on the second lateral screen disappeared, and when they reappeared on the tertiary dorsal scans they were appreciably smaller than they had been before.

They were going to need him down in the cargo bay. They all knew how to use emergency stasis suits to treat cold injury and blood-gas imbalance—it was one of the first and most important things anyone learned about exo-atmospheric travel. But he was the one who knew best how to set the respiration, whether circulation should be induced, and whether neural activity should be artificially suspended until they got their casualties to Infirmary on *Ragnarok*.

He needed to be there to stabilize, in case Wheatfields could not bring himself to release the thula from full implosion field without a thorough scan, especially in the middle of preparation for a vector transit. The chance that the evac craft's distress call had been just part of an elaborate trap was perhaps not very great, but it was there.

All of which meant that he had to leave Lek here alone, more or less alone, prey to the fury of his own governor. If the Safe should fail, and him not here to rescue his Lek—

Lek was steady, solid, almost relaxed. There was no conflict that Andrej could detect in his face, in his voice, in his manner as he made his moves and sent the thula straight and clean for *Ragnarok*. Andrej took him by the shoulders from behind as he sat, smiling at Lek's questioning look, at the basic blissful confidence that underlay his evident concentration.

There was no guarantee that they'd reach the *Ragnarok* in time to come on board for the vector transit. There were no guarantees that the people in the evac craft were still alive. Yet Andrej knew that Lek's choice had been the only honorable choice, and was glad to praise him for it.

"Thank you, Lek. Very well done, indeed. You will not need me?" Lek nodded almost absent-mindedly and turned back to his boards, completely focused on his pilot's task. Taller gave Andrej a reassuring smile on Lek's behalf, and—satisfied—Andrej left the wheelhouse to get down to the cargo bay, and see what could be done for the people in the evac craft.

The officer's praise was only part and parcel of the joy Lek had in this fine thula; Koscuisko always praised their good performances, and Lek already knew that he'd done well. The officer's absence was not going to be a problem. There were reasons why Koscuisko had to leave the wheelhouse, and reasons why Lek had to concentrate all of his remaining energies on making their rendezvous with *Ragnarok*, because it would all be for nothing if he didn't get back to the *Ragnarok* in time.

"Let's see how much speed she has left in her," he suggested to Taller, easing the retards out to full liberty now that they were clear to run for home. "It'll be a little tight, maybe, but we can make it work. Pull off on reserve. Weaponer. Close ports."

The enemy still pursued, but they could not touch the thula's speed. "Closed, all ports, Lek." No weaponer was ever happy to have to put the guns away, but there was no argument. It was up to speed to save them, and not firepower. Borrowed firepower had blown a hole in the mine field and cleared a way for the *Ragnarok*; now speed was all they had to bring the ship, the crew, the officer back safely to their proper berths.

"We're starting to fling caramids," Taller warned; and the analysis of the drives was showing signs of stress—but there wasn't any help for it.

"We can afford it. Increase yield on quats. We only need another three eighths. Five eighths, max." Once they came level with the *Ragnarok* they could surrender motive power to the parent tractors, and divert all remaining power to turn the craft. It would be enough.

The massive black belly of great *Ragnarok* began to crown on ship's forward horizon. Checking his signatures, Lek frowned, but he wasn't worried yet. She had plenty of tolerance. Why shouldn't she? She was a Malcontent, after all, and a Malcontent stood in need of as much tolerance as a Sarvaw did, for mere survival. This ship and he had more in common than anyone could know—

They gained on *Ragnarok* in a great steady wave that swept them ever forward. Well beneath the maintenance hull now, and the thula yielded gratefully to his instruction to ease up, stilling herself with perfect manners to find her place beneath the still-open slot and hold there motionless, precisely matched to *Ragnarok*'s exact speed and rate of acceleration.

Lek opened braid, watching the pursuit ships behind them, but not far enough behind. . . . "*Ragnarok*, the Malcontent's thula. We request transfer to ship-comp on primary drives."

Well, she wasn't the *Ragnarok*'s thula; Fleet couldn't afford her. And the Malcontent was going to want her back, Lek reminded himself sternly; but that inevitability had no power to grieve him, not just now. Not on the crest of the rush he was riding, the flying they'd done, the way she could move.

"Thula. This is *Ragnarok*." It was Ship's Engineer who came back in the braid; Lek couldn't quite decide what note it might be that he thought he heard in Wheatfields's voice. "Ready to acquire. On your mark."

Because the *Ragnarok* needed to take responsibility for holding the ship at speed, while the thula concentrated on the more delicate process of moving herself up into the host's waiting maintenance atmosphere. "We surrender primary, at mark four. Two. Three. Four."

Yes. Smooth as the cream from an Aznir dairy cow.

There were internal communications going back and forth around him, weaponers' status reports, Stildyne talking to Ship's First, Koscuisko calling for transport on emergency stasis. The crew of the evac craft were still alive, then. It was not outside the realm of possibility—in Koscuisko's characteristically cautious phrase—that they would be all right. That was good news, but nothing that he could afford to waste any attention on.

"Commence sequence, Taller," Lek warned; not that there was much Taller could do. He fired his laterals one by one, bringing the line up carefully to put a spin on the thula—east of forward heading, dead on meridian.

It was slow, and the pursuit ships were out there, but he couldn't afford to notice them any more than he could afford to listen to Koscuisko's voice over intra-ship braid. Too much nose, and the thula spun too far east, slipping away from the meridian line. He had to hold the meridian line. And he had to hold it now.

A touch at offside tailings, and she came true. "Request check for entry window, *Ragnarok*." She didn't stay perfectly aligned; she continued to slide ever so gently to one side or the other—the basic problem inherent in any reaction-correction process. He was tightening her orb moment by moment. He needed to be able to move the instant she was solid true and stayed there.

"Move that thula, Mister Lek. You're well within tolerance. Now, if you please."

Well within tolerance, his ass. He was dead solid perfect. And the *Ragnarok* knew it.

Lek hit his basal lifts, and the thula began to rise gentle and straight into the maintenance atmosphere of the *Ragnarok*. They had to bring it into the maintenance atmosphere if they were to hope to make a vector transit before the pursuit ships could reach them; but if the hull was damaged as they tried to berth, they wouldn't be making any vector transits at all.

Taller cut the ship's screens to real actual, and Lek watched the solid thickness of the maintenance hull seeming to sink as the thula rose, so close it was tempting to reach out from his chair and try to touch it as they passed. There wasn't much clearance—but they'd known that there wouldn't be.

They were clear of the hull, and rising toward the loading aprons overhead. Made it. He cut the thula's lifts; the ship rode on tractor, safe within the maintenance atmosphere.

On the ship's screens Lek could see a crew from Engineering—in full environmentals, and tethered, just in case—moving the final sections of the hull into place with disciplined urgency. The Ship's Engineer would be for vector transit, now. They couldn't have much time, so Lek was surprised to hear him coming over braid as the chief weaponer and Stildyne came forward into the thula's wheelhouse.

"Nicely done, Mister. Very pretty handling."

Of course. Hadn't he told them that he could do it? Still, it had been tight, and there had been that evac craft. Why it should have mattered that they pick up that crew, when it was the survival of the thula that had been at stake—or its freedom, which amounted to the same thing—Lek wasn't quite certain; but it had mattered.

That was all he could really keep in his mind, just now, because he was tired, and it was comfortable and familiar to have Chief Stildyne behind him, reminding him about things he had to do.

"Shut down and leave it for later, Lek. You've done all you could for now. And everything we asked you, too. Let's go, Mister."

Thula locked in traction, mover engaged to transit to maintenance apron. Medical was already offloading emergency stasis modules, eight of them. Eight. Were there supposed to be eight? The officer had told *Ragnarok* that they'd been on time. So eight was clearly the right number.

The officer was not following the stasis modules to Infirmary, though; he'd stopped on the receiving apron to have a word with the Captain, by the looks of it. It began to occur to Lek that there were a lot of people out on the receiving apron.

There was no arguing with the Chief; Lek rose stiffly from out of his place and went meekly before Stildyne out of the wheelhouse, through the ship, out to the mover, across to the landing apron. Tired out. Well, he'd been concentrating. It was a little unusual still, how tired he felt. First Officer was out there, too, now.

"Attention to pilot," First Officer called, loudly, in his direction. Lek was confused; he'd been the pilot, how was he to come to attention? Oh. It was the other people who were supposed to come to attention.

It wasn't "a lot of people" on the apron: it was a formation on the apron, and he was in front of it. He and Chief Stildyne, but Stildyne was behind him, and as Lek tried to figure out what was happening, Captain ap Rhiannon marched briskly front and center of the assembly with First Officer and Chief Medical, halting her officer-detachment right in front of his nose.

"Mister Kerenko."

She sounded very stern. Very serious. He hoped he wasn't in trouble. He was just a little confused. Bowing sharply, he acknowledged her address, in the best form he knew how.

"As it please the officer. Yes, your Excellency."

She wasn't his officer. The officer was his officer—but Chief Medical was subordinate to the Captain. Chief Medical was here, though, so it was bound to be all right.

"Based upon your expressed willingness and with the concurrence of Chief Medical, Ship's Engineer, and Ship's First Officer, you were entrusted with piloting this thula on a mission critical to the safe escape and possible survival of this ship. You accomplished your mission with exceptional skill, Mister Kerenko."

But he shouldn't have peeled off for the evacuation craft. He'd had no permission to deviate from assigned task. He hadn't even asked for a deviation.

"Yes, your Excellency." What else could he say? He knew he shouldn't have done it. He'd known at the time that he shouldn't be doing it. And he knew that under the same set of conditions he'd do it again, instructions or no instructions. What if the officer had told him to let the evacuation craft's crew die, and return to *Ragnarok*? What would he have done then?

"In addition to this essential mission, however, your ability to pilot your craft permitted the safe recovery of eight Fleet resources, living souls. This recovery was effected under extreme pressure, Mister Kerenko, and at considerable risk to the thula and everyone on it."

No one of which, Lek realized, had raised their voice in protest. No message from the *Ragnarok* had come, to bring him back into line. It was all right?

"For your demonstrated flight mastery in piloting the thula, and for your principle contribution to saving the lives of eight Fleet crew, you are to be commended in the second degree of performance. On behalf of Fleet, the Bench, and the *Ragnarok*, I thank you, Mister Kerenko."

He'd never earned a flight commendation in all his years under Bond. Such honors weren't usually issued to bond-involuntaries, no matter what their accomplishments; still less in public, in front of what looked like every Security troop assigned to *Ragnarok*—and some of Engineering, as well.

"The appropriate entries are to be made in your personnel records. That will be all."

He was supposed to salute again, now. The bow helped him wrestle with his startled pleasure, gave him time to get his face back into order. He wasn't expected to say anything. It was just as well. He was speechless.

"First Officer, dismiss."

Ship's First and Chief Medical bowed in unison, and ap Rhiannon left the maintenance apron. His officer came forward to embrace him, with evident emotion. "It was beautifully done," Koscuisko repeated. Koscuisko had been there. It must have been so, then. "Superlative performance, Lek. Stildyne. I have to go to duty, but it was well shot as well as well piloted. I am very proud of you all."

First Officer was about to say something; but the Engineer's voice came over all-ship, and overrode him. "All stations stand by for vector transit. Beginning spins in five eighths, mark. All stations stand by for vector transit."

Or, in other words, get off the apron, out of the maintenance atmosphere and to wherever you were supposed to be, right now.

Lek's moment of glory was over—or at the least, postponed. He was just as glad of the distraction. He'd never had a moment of glory. He found he didn't have the first idea what to do with it.

Stildyne tapped him on the shoulder to get him moving, and Lek jogged after the rest of the crew to get to his post and await the vector transit.

CHAPTER FIFTEEN

The Devil and Deep Space

The thula outdistanced its hunters by a slim but adequate margin and gained the sanctuary shadow of the *Ragnarok*'s black hull. The main pursuit party was still vainly trying to come up to speed to catch the *Ragnarok*, but now that the thula had rejoined its foster parent— would the ship come about?

Admiral Brecinn blinked, and the thula was gone.

Staring at the great display station, frowning, feeling stupid, Brecinn tried to figure out what had happened. The thula had disappeared. The display was tracking *Ragnarok*, but the pursuit ships were on display as well, and there was no trail of debris and mangled metal that Brecinn could see in *Ragnarok*'s wake, no evidence of destruction. What had happened?

Senior Auditor Ormbach tapped the prediction module reporter at the front of the observer station with one well-groomed fingernail, and shook her head. "The Taisheki vector. As you predicted, Fleet Admiral. The corvettes are going to have to fall back. There isn't any sense trying to follow them from here."

Ragnarok had taken the thula on, that was what had happened. That explained the queer maneuver that the thula had performed, just prior to its disappearance—turning sidewise to the parent ship's heading, from what Brecinn had been able to gather from the target-detail screen. *Ragnarok* had taken the thula to itself. Now that thula was back on board, the *Ragnarok* would make for the vector.

Brecinn felt a pang of loss and longing. That thula was worth money. If only she could have found a way to possess herself of it. "Bloodless engagement," another of the auditors noted aloud, apparently just to make conversation. "That much to the good, at least. No lives lost."

"That we know of," Brecinn reminded them all, a bit sharply. "We don't know about that evacuation craft."

"Still, it's a Brief in the third order of magnitude at most." Auditor Ormbach did not seem to be suffering from any particular irritation at the *Ragnarok*'s escape. "The most cause against the *Ragnarok* for that would be destruction of Fleet resources with concomitant loss of life, a disciplinary offense, but hardly a Judicial one. And the crew may not be dead."

"They certainly would be if the thula hadn't gone back for them—" one of the auditors started to point out. The priority signal warning interrupted her before she could finish her point, however.

Chilleau Judiciary, Second Judge Sem Por Harr Presiding. For Taisheki Station. What could Chilleau Judiciary want at Fleet Audit Appeals Authority?

Jils Ivers. She must have talked to Verlaine about Noycannir. "Chilleau Judiciary, this is Taisheki Station, Senior Auditor Ormbach. In the war and maneuvers room, Fleet Admiral Sandri Brecinn accompanying as an observer."

The signal stepped down from global transmit to the observer station restrict, and Brecinn knew by the subtle tingling at the nape of her neck that the privacy mutes had been engaged. Verlaine didn't mind talking to Taisheki in her presence, then. That was encouraging. Maybe she could salvage something from this after all.

"What is this news of the *Ragnarok*, Auditor?" First Secretary Verlaine. Deep voice. Calm. Contemplative. Concerned about something. Noycannir's treachery? Or sensibly aware that he looked a great deal like an antagonist to Fleet, now that the Second Judge had issued her program?

Auditor Ormbach watched the projections tile across the alert-border of the far remote screens, apparently putting her thoughts together. The First Secretary was still the First Secretary. The Second Judge was still only the Second Judge, but she was the Second Judge all the same.

"*Ragnarok* has declined to enter Taisheki Station, citing as unacceptable requirements to submit to search; to surrender evidence; and to surrender crew, taken together as evidence of failure of intent to investigate its Appeal."

The pursuit ships had fallen too far away from the *Ragnarok* to do any good. As Brecinn watched the projections, the detail-insert came up with a plot projection, a vector transit line—tight, but they would be in a hurry. Either that, or the Engineer was showing off, since he could be certain that this particular vector transit was to be observed with keen interest.

"What is your current status?"

"The *Ragnarok* has started vector transit preparations for the Taisheki vector, having stated its determination to protect the integrity of ship and crew at some neutral location pending resolution of its Appeal. Possible destination, Amberlin."

"Auditor Ormbach." The First Secretary's voice paused, as though he was thinking carefully about what he was going to say next. "Andrej Koscuisko is in possession of very sensitive evidence that reflects negatively on this Judiciary. It is therefore of critical importance to the Second Judge that no punitive action be taken against the *Ragnarok* while its Appeal is pending. To do otherwise would present the appearance of reprisals contrary to the upholding of the rule of Law."

What was he talking about? What evidence?

Then Brecinn realized. He had to cover up Noycannir's crimes. He was soliciting the cooperation of the Fleet Audit Appeals Authority to help him, in return for implied benefit in the future; and Auditor Ormbach might decide to listen to him.

She wasn't about to let it go so easily. "First Secretary," Brecinn said suddenly. "Fleet Admiral Sandri Brecinn speaking. If I may, sir." And why shouldn't she? She had the rank. Not to speak of the influence.

"Fleet Admiral," Verlaine said, agreeably enough—Ivers clearly hadn't made the connection between Noycannir and Pesadie, at least not for Verlaine. "Please."

"Sir, while assigned to the Pesadie Training Command's administrative oversight, the *Ragnarok* left its area of assignment without leave, first for Silboomie Station and then for Taisheki. It has since explicitly rejected lawful and received instruction to surrender itself. There are strong indications of mutinous intent on the part of the acting Captain and an unknown number of her crew."

The majority of the *Ragnarok*'s crew actually, but there was no need to whistle against that reed. Verlaine might ask her how she knew, and she had no easy and appropriate reply.

Verlaine did not seem to understand the hints she was giving him, however. "The acting Captain is young and inexperienced with Command of equivalent complexity, Fleet Admiral. It would be a potentially tragic error on our part if we mistook a miscalculation under pressure for intent to commit so grievous a crime. I understand the officer is crèche-bred."

He couldn't mean to suggest that they interpret ap Rhiannon's insolence as a mere miscalculation under pressure, surely. Ormbach glanced at Brecinn with an amused expression on her face, but Brecinn kept her own countenance utterly expressionless. Ap Rhiannon knew exactly what she was doing; they all knew it. But when all was written and read in, it was to be the Audit Authority's careful and politically sensitive finding on the matter that was to become truth.

If Ormbach agreed that ap Rhiannon was just young and inexperienced, then Brecinn was going to have no choice but to play along—and look for a worthier and more responsive patron to support in the upcoming Selection. "We must of course take all such circumstances carefully under advisement," Brecinn said icily.

Ormbach continued, without acknowledging Brecinn's points; testing the limits of Verlaine's nerve, perhaps. "And still the *Ragnarok* has refused to enter Taisheki Station. Has blown a clearance through mine field, and is even now commencing its vector spin with a privately owned thula and an evacuation craft on board, as it happens. If the First Secretary would care to advise the next appropriate measure?"

Perfectly reasonable. Perfectly responsive to the existence of political pressures unrelated to the strict confines of the Audit Authority. She'd known that there were reasonable people at Taisheki Station, but she hadn't expected Ormbach to be quite so blatantly opportunistic, even so.

The *Ragnarok* was well into its vector spin. And it was clear that the First Secretary had made up his mind about something.

"Fleet does not have resources to spare chasing off to Amberlin after the *Ragnarok*. Senior Auditor, the Second Judge anticipates that Fleet Audit Appeals Authority will investigate the *Ragnarok*'s appeal in as full and fair a manner as may be possible, absent the ship and crew."

The on-screen tracks went blank, the scroll frozen at the last point of verified transmission. The *Ragnarok* had made the vector. There was no calling the ship back now; Verlaine was still talking, persuasively, calmly, cajolingly.

"I suggest a preliminary finding of mutiny in form. I believe we can all agree on the importance of preventing it from becoming mutiny in fact. If the *Ragnarok* will stay out of harm's reach until the Appeal has been completed, there is still good hope of proposing acceptable administrative disciplinary measures. We must not allow an error of such proportions to unbalance the Bench at the beginning of a Presidence, regardless of the outcome of the Selection."

Meaning that with so much work to do once the Selection was decided, they'd have no choice but to make an example of the *Ragnarok* if the ship continued to push its luck. Verlaine clearly didn't want it to come to that; but did he realize how angry Fleet was at the Second Judge?

"Mutiny in form." The mildest interpretation that could be put on it, and Ormbach rolled the words in her mouth with mild scorn. "As you direct, First Secretary, subject of course to Fleet endorsement." Because Taisheki answered to the Fleet, not to the Bench. It was not a bad idea, perhaps, to remind Verlaine of that.

"And in form only, Auditor, I assure you of that. There are elements at play which cannot be revealed prematurely. I ask you to excuse my silence. Fleet Admiral."

Brecinn was surprised to be called out; Verlaine had seemed to forget that she was there. "First Secretary," she replied, careful to give him no note of undue deference. Taisheki Station had just put Verlaine on notice. He was going to have to solicit their cooperation.

"Go back to Pesadie, Fleet Admiral. You have no business at Taisheki Station. Unless you have an Appeal of your own? I am in possession of some interesting information from one of my Clerks of Court, Dame Noycannir. Perhaps you would care to take advantage of the coming break in training schedules to set your house in order. For your replacement."

Ormbach looked at her, and almost sneered. Brecinn felt her face go white with fury. "Thank you, First Secretary," she said, as calmly as she could. "You'll know exactly how much of what Noycannir says to believe soon enough. I only hope it doesn't cause the Second Judge any embarrassment. But I appreciate the friendly advice, and will leave immediately."

Go back to Pesadie, yes. Where she had lost the main battle cannon with which she had been entrusted by reasonable people. Where she owed replacement in kind, good munitions for bad, for inventory lost in an accident that had been caused by the *Ragnarok*, a direct result of the selfish arrogance of its Captain and crew.

Where she had in an unfortunate moment been gulled into listening to—trusting!—a double agent for Chilleau Judiciary, who had ingratiated herself only in order to betray her to the First Secretary. Her mission to Taisheki Station had failed.

She *would* leave immediately. But she would be very careful to avoid ever arriving, because the only things that awaited her now at Pesadie were disgrace and humiliation and death.

Andrej Koscuisko stood on the docking apron of the *Ragnarok*'s maintenance atmosphere looking up into the passenger bay of the Malcontent's thula, waiting for the time when it would be ready to close.

Technically speaking launch clearance was the Engineer's function, but First Officer had asked him to perform the formalities in this case on pretext of it being an Aznir ship. Andrej had his suspicions about that, though. He thought they—the Captain, Wheatfields, First Officer—were still waiting for him to change his mind and leave. He supposed he appreciated their attempts to make it as easy as possible for him to do so.

"I will keep the documents, yes, Bench specialist," he said. Jils Ivers stood beside him. The crew that they'd rescued from the evac craft were going aboard. One or two of them would help Cousin Ferinc pilot the thula from the interim Kazar vector back to Chilleau Judiciary, where Ivers had things to say to the First Secretary. "It is nothing personal."

She could hardly argue with him on that. They both knew that he couldn't surrender his Writ so long as the status of the *Ragnarok*'s appeal was in process. Surrendering his Writ while remaining on board would make him unauthorized personnel, and generate an additional charge against the ship—that of allowing an unauthorized person to exercise command and control of his Infirmary, and failure to discharge persons no longer under orders.

"We can work it out, your Excellency. I'm sure of it." She was stubborn. He knew she hated leaving him here. "And when we do, Chilleau Judiciary is going to need your influence, sir, more I think than the First Secretary anticipated."

Because Fleet was much more angry about Verlaine's proposal than Verlaine had anticipated. Verlaine had concentrated his attention on the humanitarian aspects, the legal aspects, the civil aspects of challenging the whole system of Inquiry. He had underestimated the degree to which Fleet would feel that its prerogatives were being taken away from it.

"All the more reason for a swift resolution to this entire problem. A swift and bloodless resolution, Specialist Ivers. And he shall have my whole-hearted support, as expert witness."

Fleet was not particularly committed to the system of Inquiry in and of itself. As an institution that was at base military, Fleet cared little for the concept of dishonoring itself by torturing civilians. Information required for military purposes could be gotten very simply with the right drugs.

It was power, no more. What Verlaine proposed would significantly reduce the influence Fleet possessed in negotiation with the Bench for privileges, material, resources. Autonomy. It could be seen as a move to begin to draw Fleet more firmly under Bench control: and that was certainly how the Fleet appeared to be reacting to the concept.

"You can come with me, your Excellency."

They had been over this before. "Thank you for all of your efforts on my behalf, Specialist Ivers, to the furtherance of the rule of Law. I am staying."

She held his eye for a long moment before she acknowledged her final defeat. "As you will, your Excellency. By your leave. And with my very sincere hope for a quick resolution."

And bloodless, Andrej added in his mind. But he didn't need to repeat it, not again. She knew.

Returning her salute with a respectful bow of his own—she was a Bench specialist, she wasn't required to salute to anybody—Andrej watched her go up the ramp into the thula, with a moderate feeling of affectionate warmth in his heart for her. She had tried very hard. He liked her well enough. But she was a Bench specialist. Such people were dangerous to like, even on a professional level.

Now it only remained that he take leave of Ferinc, and probe to see what damages the Saint would assess for the use Andrej had made of his thula. It was all very well for Stoshik to claim that the Malcontent's efforts on Andrej's behalf were owed by its duty to the Autocrat, and that its loan of the thula was its apology for its failure to anticipate Noycannir's assassination attempt. That would be too easy all around. Things were never so straight-forward where the Malcontent was concerned.

Andrej waited.

Cousin Ferinc had been waiting as well, watching, and came forward once Ivers was into the thula and out of sight. Ferinc had tied his braids together at the back of his neck, using the plaits to gather his long hair into a single fall; he looked more like Haster Girag with his hair back from his face, but Andrej had made up his mind to forgive Ferinc for having been that person. There was no sense in holding any grudges. And more for Ferinc to forgive Andrej than otherwise, really.

"You take the Bench specialist to Chilleau, then home?" Andrej asked, just to open the dialogue. "I hope that Anton will not be too much distressed that I do not come back. And yet it may be that he will not notice. If the Malcontent in mercy allows that you should remain his friend."

Ferinc shook his head. "Not so easy as that, your Excellency. He worships you like a saint under Canopy; it will cause him suffering. I'm sorry. But there's no way around it. I'll do what I can."

Ferinc was right. It would be too easy to pretend that having met his son and made re-contract with Marana, he could absent himself without explanation and for an unknown period of time to pursue his personal goals. There was no use in lying to himself. He was being cruel to his son, his own son, his beautiful child, a child who loved him.

"Be his friend still, Ferinc." He was an unnatural father, perhaps, to be unable to set his son's suffering above the lives of the crew of the *Ragnarok*. And if he was, Marana would tell him. There would be no use in hoping for a life with her, not if he betrayed her son to suffer for such a small thing as four or eight or seven hundred souls; or was he being unfair?

Marana. "And be a friend to my wife as well, if she will take solace. She will have much fault to find with my behavior, and rightly so, but I fear for her contest against my family. She will need powerful defenders. Will the Malcontent protect my wife, and my son Anton?"

"He is no longer your son, your Excellency," Ferinc pointed out, reasonably. "He is the inheriting son of the Koscuisko familial corporation. It is the Saint's natural business to look after his best interest. But since you ask. I will relay the request, your Excellency, to my ecclesiastical superior. Knowing that you know better than I do what it means to ask a favor from the Malcontent."

There was no help for it. The future was too much in question. He had made his son safe in the event of his own sudden death; and in so doing, had put Anton in need of a different sort of protection.

"Aside from that, Ferinc." Andrej paused for a moment to master his own irritation; it was no use losing one's patience with Malcontents. "And the Saint aside. You were only a man at one time. It may be that I wronged you once."

Cousin Ferinc shuddered and stepped back, apparently taken by surprise. It was another moment before he replied. "On balance," Ferinc said, "no, your Excellency. It was no more than Fleet itself would have done, had the crime been reported. Much less, perhaps. Fleet would not have so reduced me in spirit, I can admit that much, yes, sir."

If Andrej had reported the crime Ferinc would have lost rank and privilege, and gone to prison for some years. Andrej had spared him that, but not because he had meant to be pitiful. No. He had broken Haster Girag because he had believed Girag deserved to be broken into the dust, and because he knew that he was going to enjoy it. And so he had.

"My motives were vengeful." And he had been drunk, in those days, on the absolute power at his command, his absolute privilege to execute it, the absolute atrocity that Fleet and the rule of Law permitted him. Required of him. "All else apart, that was a sin. I have savaged you. To elect the Malcontent is a desperate thing, Ferinc. I am to blame for it. If I were to ask you for the peace of the Saint, could you from your heart grant it, and forgive me?"

"For my own part?" Ferinc asked, as if in wonder. Yes, it was an extreme sort of a thing to ask. Andrej could recognize the selfish unreason of his demand. "And not what my reconciler has demanded? If you could not have let me see Anton. But you did. And therefore."

Coming closer to him, standing between Andrej and the ramp into the thula, Ferinc put his hand to the back of Andrej's neck; a very precise signal, for Dolgorukij, and one that Ferinc had obviously learned. "The peace of the Malcontent I give you," Cousin Ferinc said, and kissed him. Very seriously.

Breaking off suddenly, though, to straighten up, leaving Andrej to wonder—

"But not where Chief Stildyne can see me," Cousin Ferinc explained. "Might cause all sorts of misunderstandings. With all my heart, your Excellency, peace between us, and I'm out of here."

There was the sound of Stildyne feet behind Andrej on the docking apron as Cousin Ferinc ducked his head and disappeared into the thula.

The loading ramp began to close.

"You'll want to wash your neck, sir," Stildyne said, and his voice was deeply disapproving. "Maybe rinse your mouth. Malcontents. Filthy people. Or so at least they tell me."

Watching the thula prepare to take flight, listening to Stildyne, Andrej's mind went back to the night he'd had dinner with, his family at Chelatring Side, before Mergau Noycannir had arrived to attack him. Stildyne had disappeared. Stoshik also. The Gallery; and on the following day—

"One never knows what such depraved souls will get up to. No. You are quite right. Let us by all means go, Brachi."

Anton would be loved and cared for until his father could come home again. Marana perhaps also, and though there was less comfort in that idea than the first it was still good to know that he had not abandoned her entirely without resources.

And when the *Ragnarok* and its crew were safe he could go home and bow down at her feet and beg for her forgiveness, as well. When the ship was safe.

Until then he could not abandon the people to whom he owed so great a debt, on board the *Ragnarok*.

EPILOGUE

Jils Ivers came direct from the common transport docks at Chilleau Judiciary up through the maintenance corridors, past the Security checkpoints, and onto the grounds that held the Chambers offices. It was early in the morning. Verlaine would be in his office already, she was sure of it. She didn't bother to signal ahead. Security would let Verlaine know when she crossed the checkpoint. He would know that she was coming.

It was much busier in Chambers than it had been the last time she'd come through these gates, across the park, into the administration building. More than forty days from span to span, but the Second Judge had announced her program and her intentions now. The bid was active; the stakes much higher.

Verlaine was probably living in his office. She knew he had a foldaway in a closet, and kept a supply of clean linen there. The morning shift had yet to come into the offices; there were just Security there, and the janitors finishing their nightly cleaning tasks.

It was quiet. Jils relished the peace, knowing how short a period it would last. She could catch Verlaine at the start of the day. If she was lucky she would not find him at the end of a long sleepless night, still less the end of several sleepless nights run together. If she was lucky.

The door into the First Secretary's central office complex was propped open, for the cleaners. There were no lights on except for the dim lamps in Verlaine's office itself, diffusing out into the quiet office area through a gap in the not-quite- completely closed door.

She didn't hear anything. Had Verlaine fallen asleep?

Gone out to the canteen, perhaps, to ask for breakfast, taking an excuse to get away from his office while it was still early enough in the day that he could?

She knocked at the door to announce herself. "Specialist Ivers, First Secretary, may I come in?" But there was no response. So he was out. She pushed the door open and stepped into the room, meaning to sit and marshal her thoughts as she waited for him to return to his desk.

She hadn't taken four steps into the room before she realized that it wasn't going to be necessary to wait, after all. Verlaine was there. He was seated behind his desk, his head laid down across the documents that he had been reviewing. One arm had slid forward across the desk's surface, as though he had been turning a page when he had slumped forward. Blood all over. On the desk. Pooled on the floor. Dead.

She stopped and stilled herself and listened, sniffing the air. Blood had ceased to drip. And the room was cold. There were no signs that she could see of violence or forced entry. How had this happened?

She didn't think she needed to ask why he had been killed.

"Security alert," she said, to catch the attention of the room's monitors. "Complete quarantine in effect, all transport, immediately. Forensics team to the First Secretary's office. No transmission secured or unsecured. Confirm."

It took a moment, as the communications protocols alerted attendants, attendants the officers, officers the Security forces. Interpreting the orders and the physical location, cross-referencing with Jils Ivers's voice-ident, realizing what the problem was.

"Confirmed."

She waited. It would take some time for the quarantine to be properly implemented from the outside in. She could expect to see forensics within moments; that gave her moments alone still to think.

Verlaine who had been Noycannir's patron, who had obtained relief of Writ for Andrej Koscuisko, Verlaine whose administration was potentially compromised by a forged Record, whose announced program challenged the entrenched power of the whole system of Inquiry—Sindha Verlaine was dead.

She had no hope of enlisting his support in constructing a solution to the problem of the Jurisdiction Fleet Ship *Ragnarok*. The *Ragnarok* would have to be left to its own devices, now, until the death of the First Secretary could be investigated, until the Selection could be carried out and confirmed.

The Second Judge had had a strong position for First Judge. But now Verlaine was dead, and with him the strength of the Second Judge's administration as well as the suspected source of her radical plans. Now everything was cast into confusion.

The political stability of the Bench was all that stood between the rule of Law and chaos, failure of infrastructure, anarchy and barbarism. One misstep now and all of Jurisdiction could fall into dissention and disorder and the unimaginable horror of civil war.

The *Ragnarok*'s Appeal would have to wait.

For supplementary text and miscellaneous vignettes please see "Scenes from the Cutting Room Floor" at .

For news & discussion of Jurisdiction topics go to the Facebook public list "Jurisdiction Novels" (need not "friend" me to join; need not join to view).

For news & discussions away from Facebook go to the Yahoo group HisExcellency.

WARRING
STATES
A Novel Under Jurisdiction

Chilleau Judiciary's senior administrative officer has been murdered in the very heart of Chambers. Bench Intelligence Specialist Jils Ivers has been unable to ferret out the perpetrator, and that means she's the Bench's prime candidate for execution—so that justice may be seen to have been done, whether or not she is guilty.

Andrej Koscuisko means to take this opportunity to execute a daring theft—stealing six bond-involuntary Security slaves to send them away beyond the Bench's reach to Gonebeyond Space.

But the corruption of the Bench extends even further than its use of institutionalized torture as an instrument of State. Before Jils Ivers realizes who killed the First Secretary and why, the rule of Law will be rocked to its very core, and the fundamental nature of the Bench will be changed forever.

Dedication

This book is dedicated to the memory of Jeff A. Elf. He was a charitable soul who truly left the world a better place than he found it, and we'll always be lucky to have known him.

We miss you Jeff!

PROLOGUE

When the sun came up in port Ghan the city started to stir, the hem-fringes of the docks first, where the poorest people lived. The warehouses were secure. But the loading equipment and the stacked pallets were not always watched as carefully, and there were almost always bargains to be had where produce was off-loaded—fruit and vegetables that would not survive the handling between the docks and the markets in the outreaches of the port, the green and gracious suburbs where the wealthier people lived beyond the towering sound-walls that shut away most of the noise and stink of an active launch-field. Ghan was in a desert; that was why the launch-fields were there, built first and foremost in the early days where the ground was already flat and hard and packed down solid by the years of sun and heat so that the job of thermal hardening had been half-done already.

Out in ever-widening circles from the launch-fields the residence areas and the business districts went, more expensive in relation to how far they were from the launch-field. There were good livings to be had in Ghan, though, even near the docks—the inverse relationship between proximity and price could work in a family's favor, and the important thing was to save enough money to be able to send the children into the mountains in the summer where they could play in the green woods and the clear water.

Little things like siphoning off excess fuel-vapors that might otherwise be wasted helped to save money and the green woods at one

593

and the same time, because excess fuel vapors were no better for the health of lakes and streams in the far hills than they were for the people who serviced the transport craft deep in the heart of the city.

It was not time to send the children into the mountains. It was still early in the spring, and it was cold at night. People turned on their heating when they got up to warm their houses while they roused the children and made mid-meals to be carried to the workplace to save the cost of buying expensive tidbits from the street-carts. The municipal utilities were no less ready to take advantage of a savings than the people that they served, and there were places where fuel-scrubbers had been tucked away ready and waiting to take in heavier-than-air vapors from the launch-fields that could be denatured and rendered harmless for heating. Everybody knew that. Nobody cared. But everybody knew.

There was no way in which the introduction of the poison into the fuel-mains could have been accidental.

When the sun came up in port Ghan that morning people rose and went to wash and cook their meals, turning on the fuel-vents, opening up the feeder-lines into their furnaces, starting up their stoves. Port Ghan ran on liligas because it was cheap and plentiful, environmentally friendly, easy to use and safe. The chemical marker that had been added to the fuel so that people would be able to smell a leak before it could get dangerous was more than enough to cover the subtle perfume of the poison in the lines.

It had been carefully planned, carefully done, and still luck played a part. It had been colder than usual; almost everybody turned on their heat, when they got up. And it was a rest-day, so the city's custodians weren't expecting a morning rush, and were inclined at first to chalk up the failure of the morning shift to come to duty as a worse-than-usual instance of excess celebrations the night before.

When supervisors tried to contact their crews, no-one answered at their homes. When people went to look for their reliefs they didn't return, but they didn't call in, either, so there was at first no panic—no understanding that an atrocity was in progress.

The civic shelters were warmed at night and in the morning as though they had been someone's home, and the floating indigent population of the city could be counted on to come out into the streets even on holidays to make their ways to the day-labor shops and the places where they could find a free meal. But the only people who were on the street that morning as the sun rose had been on the street all night.

Nobody came away from the municipal shelters. Nobody came away at all. Only the people who had already accepted that they were going to be cold, that they were not going to be able to warm themselves in any way, only those people survived the morning.

By the time enough of the poison had escaped to set off the alarms in the streets there were more than three thousand dead, women, children, men, and two thousand more who died in the horrible two days that followed, between the poison and the panic and the rioting.

No final tally was ever agreed upon. The rioting spread across the planet, and then across the system. Fleet did not have the resources to contain the panic because Fleet was already trying to contain civil unrest in too many other areas, and there was only so much the Jurisdiction Fleet could do, in the absence of a strong central authority. The First Judge was dead. It had been a year, and there was no new First Judge. The Bench was rudderless.

Port Ghan, however, was at peace. It was the peace of the dead, but it was unquestionably the quietest place on the entire world, an open tomb; it was its own memorial. No single culprit was ever identified, and after so many dead it ceased to really matter. Whoever had done it gained no advantage from the crime, because the killing that erupted in reaction to the massacre harvested across all of Ghan's populations equally.

The true horror of what had happened at Port Ghan was not the thousands dead, and the hundreds or thousands more who died in the months that followed.

The horror of Port Ghan was that it was just another incident, just another symptom of the uncertainty that plagued all of Jurisdiction Space in the absence of a First Judge to lay down the rule of Law and to enforce it.

CHAPTER ONE

Field Expedients

Andrej Koscuisko, chief medical officer on board of the Jurisdiction Fleet Ship *Ragnarok*, sat at his desk in his office doing his best to concentrate on the controversy over whether an increased incidence of a peculiar skin rash meant that there was a mutant fungus on board, or simply that they were brewing with mother-of-grain in Engineering, or both.

When the talk-alert sounded he did not answer right away. He wasn't sure how to face what it might bring; and yet he had brought it on himself. Staff would expect him to answer promptly, however, unless he were in the washroom or possibly passed out drunk, which had not happened on duty for simply months now.

"Koscuisko, here." Therefore in order to cover his tracks as completely as possible it was necessary to respond. There were four procedures yet to accomplish, somehow. Would he be detected? If only he could ward off accusation for long enough it would not matter.

"Robert says Lek's up, sir." That was one of his surgical crew leaders. She didn't sound as though she were suspicious; Andrej took a deep breath, careful to exhale as quietly as possible. "'Respectfully requests an audience with the officer at his convenience,' I think it was. Are you available, your Excellency?"

Senior officers didn't usually come when they were called, especially not when called by bond-involuntaries, who had no rank to speak of. No status, either. Well, they had status, but it was as property.

"I am coming directly. Thank you, Jahan." At the same time he had performed the procedure himself, and people were accustomed to the display of a possessive instinct on his part where Security were concerned. The Bench had created them to serve a Ship's Inquisitor, after all. What was more reasonable than that he should think of them as his?

He tried not to hurry as he left his office for sterile quarantine, where patients were sent to recover from procedures that tapped a spine or crossed the blood-brain barrier. Telbut brain-slug was something that could happen to anybody, and among persons inhabiting worlds within the trading entity known as the Dolgorukij Combine it was more rather than less likely to turn up in Sarvaw because of the poverty of the world and their general suspicion of authority, doctors, teachers, law enforcement officers. It kept them from seeking periodic care as freely as they should.

He could see Fantin coming from the other direction with her tray of doses in her hand, and he quickened his pace a bit as he approached the enclosed bay in which his patient lay waiting. He dared not risk so much on Lek's self-control, not so soon.

"What is this?" he asked Fantin, cordially standing in front of the door. "Oh, good. I am just going in, will you trust me to see the doses put through?"

She looked up at him a little startled, apparently, and for one moment Andrej wondered whether he had gone too far. The moment passed, however; she smiled and surrendered the doses with a clear eye and a serene countenance. "Of course, sir," she said, in that familiar "we-know-how-you-worry" tone of voice. "If you'd just post to the log, though, so we know how he's doing. Ugh."

"You are very kind," he assured her, with genuine gratitude. "I will unfailingly perform this duty." Yes, brain-slugs were moderately disgusting, in theory. That didn't matter. All that mattered was that in order to extract the sexually mature symbiot before it multiplied, a man had to lie on his belly and let the surgeon send a probe up through the place in his skull where his spine descended, and lure the greedy thing out of the brain in pursuit of a supposed mate.

Fantin went away about her business without any apparent second thoughts. Andrej collected himself; then turned, and opened up the door. Robert was there. Robert did not look happy. Had something gone wrong? They would have called him. They couldn't not have called him. They weren't supposed to know what he had drawn out of Lek Kerenko's skull, instead of a non-existent brain-slug.

Lek pushed away from the cradle-chair in which he had been laid to rest six hours ago, after the procedure; pushed himself up and away with such violence that Robert was hard pressed to restrain him, even though Robert had the advantage of leverage, since Robert was already standing.

For a moment Andrej was afraid that Lek would say something incautious. "This troop respectfully wishes the officer good-greeting," Lek said; *he should have known better*, Andrej told himself, *than to fear that Lek would abandon his self-discipline*. On the one hand, whether or not Lek knew what Andrej had done to him, he was still the product of careful training and years of experience in living with a governor in his brain to see to it that he followed orders.

On the other hand, Lek also knew that to speak to his officer of assignment—which was to say, Andrej himself—with such elaborate formality carried an unspoken message that did not need to be translated. *With respect, your Excellency, I could perhaps be more angry at you than I am right now, but I'm not sure how.*

"Do not be annoyed with me, Lek." Andrej set a humorous and affectionate tone to his voice, so that nobody who chanced to overhear would wonder if something were genuinely wrong. "I think no less of you for having one. Many decent people in this life have found themselves infected, and through no fault of their own."

It was too soon to be talking to Lek; he was overwhelmed by his realization, and still somewhat befuddled by the meds Andrej had used. "But it's been part of my life for so long." Lek was doing his best to keep his own tone of voice light, but Andrej could read his tension from a fair distance and more clearly as he came nearer. "How am I ever going to learn to live without it? Always there. And it'll come back, sooner or later, I know it will."

Andrej had been unable to discuss any of this with Lek beforehand, and he dared not risk any very frank language now. There was a good chance he could get away with Lek, at least for now. How he was going to take care of Godsalt, Pyotr, Garrity, and Hirsel he did not know.

"Well, that's up to you," Andrej said sternly. "Stay out of insalubrious environments. Clean living, friend Lek. If you don't want to have a brain slug pulled out of your head again all you really have to do is stay away from places where there are such things, and that can't be too difficult, can it?"

There were governors to be had in major administrative centers throughout Jurisdiction space. How was Lek to avoid them? By getting out of Jurisdiction space, of course. Simple.

Of course it wasn't all so easy as that. Lek knew it; Andrej could tell. He desperately needed to be able to talk to Lek some place where there would be no danger of being overheard; but there was only one such place on board the *Ragnarok*, and he was not about to take Lek to Secured Medical.

For one, he meant to never enter the torturer's chamber in which he had exercised his Writ to Inquire ever again. For another, the Captain could over-ride even there, and people would be curious. The temptation to see what could bring Andrej Koscuisko to Secured Medical, especially with one of his bond-involuntaries, would be too much to expect anyone to withstand.

"Now. Robert will sit with you, and keep you company. It is a minor procedure, but there is no taking chances with brains, and I mean you to stay quiet and rest. My cousin Stanoczk will be joining the ship at any hour, and you must conserve your energies for the inevitable excitement."

Lek Kerenko was Sarvaw. He knew that Andrej's cousin was a Malcontent—an agent of the secret service of the Dolgorukij church, a slave of the Saint and typically up to all sorts of mischief. Andrej had some very particular mischief in mind, and Stoshi was coming to tell him whether the freighter would be waiting at Emandis Station to take Lek and Robert and the others far, far away from places where people could be placed under governor for crimes against the Judicial order.

What if Stoshi should fail him?

Stoshi would not fail. Andrej was the inheriting son of his father, the Koscuisko prince, the single man who could direct the resources of the entire Koscuisko familial corporation. More than that, Andrej was the father of an acknowledged inheriting son of his own, and while a line of inheritance could be directed away from a man with no sons it had almost never failed to accord with tradition in cases where there was already an heir's heir in training.

If he had been killed before he had made Marana his wife, and their son his heir, the position of inheriting son might have devolved upon Iosev—the next oldest of their father's sons. Andrej wondered what Iosev's son felt about that.

He was brooding, and he had no business doing so. With a cordial nod to Lek—who sat there watching as though to read his mind by main force of will—Andrej shifted his weight, ready to turn and go. The gesture seemed to provoke Lek beyond all hope of self-discipline; Lek was on his feet and face-to-face with Andrej before Andrej had had time to realize that the sound of falling objects that he heard was Robert, knocked backwards by the impact of Lek's swift lunge.

Lek didn't speak. Instead he reached for Andrej's hand and grasped it in his two hands, trembling. "No, don't leave me here with Robert," Lek said, with a tremor in his voice that matched the shaking of his shoulders. "Please. Sir. He'll want to sing. I've done nothing to deserve it."

It was very forward of Lek to touch him, let alone restrain him in any manner. Lek's fingers moved against the backs of Andrej's own, but not because Lek was overcome with emotion. Finger-code. Andrej did not read finger-code very well, but Lek used small words, easy to understand. *All of us*?

"And yet that is my firm determination, Lek, and you may as well resign yourself to it." He meant to steal all of them. "Perhaps you will be the first to hear the saga with which he has so often threatened us. What is it, Robert? That of the exceptionally wayward flock, and the male animal of unusual endowment?"

But you're the first one. Andrej hoped Lek could find the meaning in his words, because he himself was not much good at finger-code.

"I'm insulted," Robert grumbled, picking himself up off the floor. "My tender feelings are cruelly bruised, your Excellency. Just for that I'm going to wait. Some day. When we're all together. Then I'll have a tale to tell."

"Later, then, Robert," Andrej agreed.

This is too much, Lek said, finger to flesh, Andrej's hand held in his own. *Can't believe it. Why*?

"Perhaps once we have reached Emandis Station, and you are all to come with me to visit Joslire's grave-place." Where they would be, temporarily, not under threat of random surveillance, in a burial yard. A funeral orchard. Whatever. "Then we will all have cause to mourn together, and his spirit will be appeased."

Joslire had preferred to die and be free of his governor than live as a Security slave. Even when Andrej had told him that there was an official petition to free him and the others whose quick action had saved the *Scylla* from sabotage, even then Joslire had been fixed in his mind on freedom and had embraced his own death with joy.

Whether Joslire would have approved of what Andrej was doing Andrej was not sure; it was theft, after all, in a way. But Joslire had been dead for more than six years, and was therefore unlikely to interfere in any material fashion.

Lek nodded. *We'll talk about it when we can. Very well, sir.* The fury had gone out of him; face to face with the enormity of what Andrej had done to him Lek staggered, and fell back against Robert who stood ready there to steady him. "Holy Mother," Lek said, in a voice whose sincerity resounded clear and pure and true. "Begging the officer's pardon, your Excellency. My head. Herds of—herds— trampling—"

It was not the surgery itself that was giving Lek a headache. It was the realization that the grim enforcer with which he had lived in intimate contact for years was gone. Robert passed him a dose over Lek's shoulder, and Andrej put it through.

"Rest and be still," Andrej ordered Lek. "I will be by to check on you again later."

Lek nodded, clearly beginning to feel the action of the drug. Robert took charge, herding Lek over to the cradle-chair to lie down as he had been ordered. Andrej left Lek in Robert's capable hands—hoping with great fervency that Robert would not attempt to sing—and let himself out of the room to go and see whether the *Ragnarok* had dropped vector at Connaught, where Stoshi was to meet them with letters from home and word on the progress of a plan to steal the Bench's property.

The room was dark, the air warm and still. When her talk-alert went off Vaal woke with a start that shook her whole body, and she slapped at the respond with vehement force.

"What do you want?"

Her lights came up in response to her activity. Yes. Same room. Nothing had changed. She was still at the Connaught Vector Authority. None of the problems with which she had been wrestling had gone away, and the only thing that an emergency call during her sleep-shift could possibly mean were more problems, even juicier ones than she had already. A five-ship civil mercantile fleet outbound for Emandisan space, but Fleet wanted everybody stopped and searched and interrogated over any irregularities, and something horrible had happened in Port Ghan. She didn't have facilities for interrogation. She was going to have to call on Fleet.

Jalmers was on the duty boards; he sounded nervous, very nervous. "Sorry to intrude, ma'am. Ship off vector not responding to hail."

Ridiculous. "So web it out and wait, or what aren't you telling me?" Standard procedure. Ships came off vector without responding to hail, you locked their navs with a seizer. Few ships were willing to hit a vector with their navs off-line, especially the Connaught vector, which was a little less tolerant than most.

"Um. Shielded navs, ma'am. Respectfully suggest the situation requires your presence."

Shielded navs? Well, there were other ways to stop a ship. Technically speaking shielded navs were slightly illegal, though nobody worried too much about little things like that with all of Jurisdiction in an uproar over the still-undecided issue of who was to be the next First Judge. If she'd been a terrorist, though, fleeing from an attack on the great granaries in the Narim asteroid belt or the water treatment facilities at Lucis, she would certainly be tempted to shield her navs so that tracing her to the scene of the crime would be more difficult. That commercial fleet they'd stopped earlier today had had respectfully naked navs, but it would do them no good when the Fleet sent an Inquisitor to find out the truth about who they were and where they were going. Vaal sighed.

"Takame eight. Away, here." By the marks on the chrono she'd just barely gotten to sleep, too. She was having a bad day. A bad year. All of Jurisdiction was having a bad year. But she was the one who was going to have to place those people in the hands of professional torturers.

She pulled her boots back on—cold and clammy from the shift's sweat—and went out of her small room in quarters into the narrow hallways of the station. Vector Control was an administrative station, small, out of the way, of little interest to anybody. Vaal had enough armed escort craft to control five more ships, but that was about the limit of her power. Fleet had planned to expand the Connaught Vector Authority—there was a station under development near the vector, residential facilities, recreation, schools, a clinic—but plans for the future of the station were on hold. There was no First Judge. There was no unified central authority. People still paid their taxes and Fleet still regulated trade, but it was not the time to call for any special levies that might not be supported. That was just asking for trouble.

When she reached her command station she found her crew tense, white-faced, and unhappy; and as she moved toward her seat— looking to the main screens at a visual of the problem—she could understand why. "Give me hailing," she said, hoping that the hails were not already open because it was so embarrassing when that happened. "Unidentified ship. I can see that you're a cruiser-killer. Please respond."

It was huge, onscreen. It was huge in actual fact, Vaal knew that. She'd toured a cruiser-killer class battlewagon as a part of her orientation, only three years ago. Battlewagons were serious business. She hated the idea of getting in one's way, and yet she had no choice. If her duty required her to stop that mercantile fleet outbound for Emandis space, it certainly required her to confront any resource of this size trying to use the vector for which she was responsible without so much as logging its idents.

"Look—" somebody whispered, loudly enough for Vaal to overhear. The belly of the ship on screen was still hulled over from its vector transit. The panels that covered the maintenance atmosphere— the great glossy expanse of the carapace above —weren't really black, technically speaking, but it was black hull technology.

It had been all over the research braids, when she'd been a child. Black hull technology, the enlightened investment of the First Judge at Fontailloe, the enormous outlay required to integrate a new propulsion and navigation and communication paradigm onto the only test bed that could truly test its promise, a Jurisdiction Fleet Ship of the top class deployed but never commissioned. Jurisdiction Fleet Ship *Ragnarok*.

There was a clear-tone, and an answering feed came through. It was not reassuring. "You're mistaken," the comm said. It was a man's voice, calm, even soothing. "You don't see anything of the sort. Why? Because we're invisible, that's why. And everybody will be much better off if it's left that way."

The on-screen cleared. Vaal knew that the man was an Engineer, because he was on the Engineering bridge—which she recognized from her orientation. She knew he was Chigan by his height and the calm serenity of his expression. And she knew he was Serge of Wheatfields because that was the name of the *Ragnarok*'s Ship's Engineer. Vaal fought the temptation to close her eyes in pain. She didn't want to be here. She didn't want to do this. She didn't want to try to tell a senior Fleet officer that he was blowing smoke, and especially she didn't want to have anything to do with the *Ragnarok*, because where the *Ragnarok* went, trouble followed.

"I have an assigned duty to see you." The on-screen Engineer relaxed back in his seat with an expression of amused pity on his face. She had to go on, regardless. "And to survey your whereabouts over the past eighty shifts, by executive order. You will unshield your navs, please, your Excellency."

Now her people were staring at her as though she had taken leave of her senses. It was a Fleet ship. She could see that it was a Fleet ship. She would never dare challenge a Fleet ship, but without verification and validation orders, did she know it was really what it appeared to be?

"Not likely," the *Ragnarok*'s engineer said. "I'd suggest you take our word for it. Or not. Since we're invisible. We'll be a few days to make a rendezvous at Connaught Yards and then we'll be out of your way. Nobody wants any trouble, needless to say."

She was supposed to stop ships that would not verify. She was supposed to close the vector and send an emergency call to Fleet. How could she send an emergency call to Fleet over a Fleet ship? She could close the vector by activating its defensive fortifications. Jurisdiction Fleet Audit Appeals Authority had tried to stop the *Ragnarok* with a mine field at Taisheki Station, a year ago. It hadn't worked. Taisheki had only lost its mine field, and those things were expensive.

"Reluctantly unable to authorize docking and use of facilities." What she could do? The *Ragnarok* could still get what it wanted at

Connaught, though—whatever it wanted. If it couldn't dock it could board. There was a Security force at Connaught Yards but it was not a big one.

If she went into lock-down, the *Ragnarok* would have to blow the yards to pieces to get at supply, and who was to say that the *Ragnarok* wouldn't do just that? Rumor had it that the *Ragnarok* had mutinied. Or not. Rumor failed to agree, and there was no official Bench position on the issue because without a First Judge the Bench was not in order.

The engineer on screen sighed, and shook his head. "I hoped it wouldn't come to this," he said. "But I'm going to have to tell my Captain on you. How long have you been at Connaught Station? Not counting tomorrow?"

There wasn't room for the *Ragnarok* at Connaught Station. She didn't have facilities. She had five merchant ships on impound, there, harmless traders by every indication, waiting for Fleet to send an Inquisitor to find out who they were and where they were going. They said they'd come from Wahken, but that had to be by way of Ghan, and there had been murder done there, and atrocity. She could not release those ships without legal verification of their route and identities. She had an idea. "With respect, your Excellency."

He had been about to cut his transmission and stand up, by the looks of things; he let his weight back down with an expression of mild surprise on his face that he kept politely clear of any petty gratification. No. She couldn't let him go to his Captain. She didn't know what she would do if she was faced with the acting Captain of a possibly mutinous ship attempting to give her a legal order. She would have to call for Fleet convoy. That was expensive and would probably not arrive until after the *Ragnarok* had gone wherever it was going and would only annoy everybody.

"Let me explain."

The *Ragnarok* had more notoriety than just that gained by the rash actions of a brevet Captain. Before Jennet ap Rhiannon the *Ragnarok* had been commanded by Griers Verigson Lowden, a thoroughly unpleasant man with thoroughly unpleasant manners. Lowden had in turn commanded the *Ragnarok*'s Inquisitor, and the *Ragnarok*'s Inquisitor was just the man she wanted for the job—if his services could be had.

"I'm holding ships in quarantine. I can't release them without official clearance. There's someone on board of your ship who could help."

Andrej Koscuisko, the *Ragnarok*'s Chief Medical Officer—ship's surgeon, Ship's Inquisitor. There was not a more fearful name in the entire inventory, but there was something about Koscuisko, about his reputation. One of those ships had come from Rudistal. Koscuisko had history there. It could work.

Maybe she was going to be able to get those people away from here before Fleet sent Inquisitors, after all.

Dierryk Rukota was an artilleryman, on board the *Ragnarok* by accident—more or less—but remaining of his own free will. They'd tried to get rid of him; they'd tried to get rid of Koscuisko, come to that, once Koscuisko had returned to his ship from home leave in a hurry with an explosive piece of evidence in his possession.

Koscuisko had stubbornly declined to go, even when the ship's status had trended slowly and almost irreversibly from unhappy to mutinous. He had more to lose than anyone on board, at least in material terms. As for Rukota he had nothing to fear for his family, and little to lose that he had not already given away for the sake of his duty and his honor.

The First Secretary with whom his spectacularly beautiful wife had so intimate an understanding had not been Sindha Verlaine and was consequently not dead, but still fully capable of protecting both dear friend and her children.

Rukota's career had been all but over when he'd arrived here, the victim of one too many self-inflicted wounds. What future he might have been able to salvage in Fleet had disappeared the moment he had decided not to accompany the rest of Admiral Sandri Brecinn's corrupt audit team back to Taisheki Station.

There was therefore no reason why he should not remain on the *Ragnarok*, unlike Koscuisko who had property and position and who was worried about his new-made wife and his son. The truth of the matter, however, the real reason Rukota stayed, was simpler even than that; he was having fun. He was having more fun than he could remember having for a long, long time.

This ship had a humorless crèche-bred maniac for a captain, a First Officer with no sense of political expediency, a chief medical officer widely understood to be a flaming psychotic, and an Engineer with a disconcerting but honestly-earned reputation for making pretzels out of Fleet bureaucrats who looked cross-wise at him; the Intelligence officer was a bat. A girl bat.

An old bat, he had been given to understand, but one whose personality was so cheerfully idiosyncratic that after these few months on board Rukota was beginning to forget that he had always been uncomfortable around Desmodontae. It was nothing personal. Something to do with the gleaming canine teeth in the smiling black muzzle and the fact that Desmodontae in their native system farmed hominids for cattle.

He had no business being here. This was a Jurisdiction battle-wagon, a cruiser-killer class warship; he was an artilleryman. His expertise was in artillery platforms and mine fields and even old-fashioned terrestrial field pieces, because sometimes there was just no substitute for a good old-fashioned siege piece. Or two. Or three. But the *Ragnarok* was short of Command Branch officers, and he was one; the ship had never been armed, it was an experimental test bed, so they needed him to talk about cannon. The main battle cannon. Was a ship of war all of that different from an artiplat? It moved a great deal more than an artiplat in geosync was supposed to do, but Rukota wasn't sure that really made much difference, for his purposes.

He'd been ap Rhiannon's commanding officer once upon a time, and had been marked for life, not to say traumatized, accordingly. Now she was the brevet captain of the *Ragnarok* by default—the most senior of the total of two Command Branch officers left assigned—and that made her the boss. That didn't bother Rukota. He could still pull rank if he had to, within the context of military courtesy of course, but so long as she didn't try to take him to bed he foresaw no problem.

He spent most of his time with Engineering and Security working on the ship's manifest. Infirmary—the generic term covered all of the *Ragnarok*'s medical facilities—was less familiar to him; but he knew how to interpret the quickly smoothed-over frowns, the quick glimpses of boots and smocks' tails disappearing around corners. The staff was unhappy. They knew why he was coming—and they meant to be sure that Koscuisko was forewarned, or he missed his guess.

It cheered Rukota enormously to be conspired against, in this manner. In the increasingly ugly, competitive, each-for-his-own world of Fleet, a unit that remembered how to come together was as good as a cold drink on a hot day: refreshing.

Turning a corner—he'd made sure to get a schematic from Intelligence, he knew where he was going—Rukota heard footsteps behind him, but declined to rise to the bait and turn around. Someone had been detailed to slow him down and divert him, so much was clear. Now, who would it be, and what kind of story would they try to sell him?

Whoever it was behind him broke into a sort of a jog-trot to close the distance. Rukota knew that signal: Security. That was a Security pace, suitable for situations where one wished to move quickly but not so quickly that anyone got left behind an obstacle. His first real acquaintance on board the *Ragnarok*, if it could be so described, had been made with Koscuisko's bond-involuntary Security, the ones Koscuisko had meant to take home with him on leave and been obliged to leave behind at the last minute. That substitution had turned out to be fortunate, and the saving of several lives at least.

"Good-greeting, General Rukota," the Security troop said, slowing to a respectfully matched pace half-a-step behind Rukota and to his left. He was right-hand dominant; most hominids were. Koscuisko was left-handed, and it was only one of the many perverse things about the man, but that was not the troop's fault. Robert St. Clare. Nurail. There'd been a problem with St. Clare's governor at Port Burkhayden, Rukota understood; his governor had died on him, and St. Clare had been lucky that he hadn't died with it.

"And you, Robert. Are you here on fifthweek?"

Everybody on the *Ragnarok* did fifthweek, a periodic rotation from their normal assigned duty station to somewhere different. Bond-involuntaries could only do their fifthweek in Infirmary, though, because they needed specific medical skills to support their officer—and to keep them close to their officer, as well, for their mutual protection.

St. Clare was not wearing Infirmary whites, however, but his Security colors. St. Clare didn't blush, no, he answered Rukota candid and open-faced as any man, and Rukota's sense of respect—and amusement—only grew.

"Sent to fetch his Excellency for laps, if the General please." It was an inside joke, Rukota had gathered, Security Chief Stildyne, and

Koscuisko, and laps. "The officer saw Ship's Engineer on the tracks the other day and has refused to return. This troop is to tell the officer that a Security detachment will be standing by to prevent any accidental mechanical, ah, accidents."

There was no real need for St. Clare to choose his words carefully so as to avoid falling into error; there was no governor there to punish him, but bond-involuntaries were carefully trained, thoroughly conditioned. Maybe it didn't really even matter that the governor was gone. It took months of adjustment to prepare the occasional man who survived his sentence to be returned to normal life, after all.

Rukota stopped, and held up his hand. "Let's just pause for a moment," he suggested. "And I'll predict the future. We'll get around the corner, but at some point between the next turning and the one after that you'll lose your footing and knock into me. It'll be an accident, of course, and you'll be horrified, and I'll quite naturally take appropriate pains to assure you that there has been no violation."

Operant conditioning didn't require unfailing negative reinforcement. So long as the negative reinforcement was negative enough it didn't really matter whether it was there every time. The strength and persistence of the conditioned behavior depended on the intensity of the stimulus that either rewarded or punished it, and if there was anything that could do a better job of negative reinforcement than an artificial intelligence with direct linkages into pain receptors in a man's brain, Rukota didn't know what it was.

"If I don't take long enough to do that, you'll suddenly realize that you've wrenched your ankle, but very oddly there won't be a soul in corridors, not even though we're between Pharmacy Restock and Issues, which by the breadth of these corridors is generally well-traveled. And it's all so unnecessary. I don't want to ambush your officer. I do have to pass on a message to him."

If he was wrong he might have just done an unkind thing, the sort of thing he himself had never tolerated—bullying a bond-involuntary troop, pressuring them until the stress convinced the governor that something was wrong and punishment was in order. He waited; then he turned his head. St. Clare was looking straight ahead, and the only part of his face that was smiling was such a minute number of muscles in his eyelids that he couldn't be accused of smiling at all by any reasonable soul. But he was smiling. For a bond-involuntary it was as good as a broad grin.

"With respect, General. This troop regrets having no idea what the officer means to imply, due to this troop's limited understanding and inability to grasp advanced concepts of cause and effect. Had considered attempting to lock the officer in a stores-room, but not the officer's suggestion. Request permission to offer thanks. This troop appreciates the opportunity to benefit from superior wisdom and understanding of tactics and strategy. Sir."

Oh, very good. "What's the plan, then? Do I hunt him through Infirmary, or lay in wait outside of quarters?" Rukota started moving again, confident that he and St. Clare understood each other. He might still get knocked to the floor or locked in a stores-room, but at least he and St. Clare were clear on whether or not it would be an accident. It was a pity, in a sense. It might have been worth being locked in stores to hear what story St. Clare could possibly have come up with to cover.

"His Excellency is usually in his office at this point in shift, if the officer please," St. Clare said blandly, as coolly as could be imagined. "Which is why this troop was sent to fetch him from there for laps. If the officer will follow me."

It was with a sinking feeling in his gut of having been played for a fool, and richly deserving it, that Rukota followed St. Clare the rest of the way through Infirmary to Koscuisko's office. In which Koscuisko sat, as calmly as could be imagined, apparently hard at work on clinic reports—but in Infirmary whites, rather than his duty blacks. Medical officers didn't wear Infirmary whites unless they were actually in Infirmary. For a moment Rukota thought he remembered a whisper of a recent rumor about Koscuisko and bond-involuntaries, but it was gone before he could grasp it.

One way or another, he'd been out-maneuvered, for whatever reason. There was no shame in that. It was just too bad that such successful strategic misdirection could be done by bond-involuntary troops and not fifteen out of sixteen of the junior officers that Rukota had been privileged to know—though perhaps ap Rhiannon herself might be admitted as belonging to the one out of sixteen category.

"Your Excellency," Rukota said. He was senior in rank on the face of it, but he was not the senior Command Branch officer on board.

That was ap Rhiannon, by default. And therefore, in the hierarchy of military courtesy, he was to address Koscuisko respectfully by title, whereas Koscuisko was free to address him by rank. Which was respectful enough. "The Captain expects you on the courier launch apron in order to brief you prior to your immediate departure for Connaught Station. There is a call on your professional services."

Of which fact Koscuisko had clearly already been apprised, even if the Captain wished to respect his dignity—and ensure that her instructions were perfectly clear—by sending Rukota to communicate the information to him personally, face-to-face. Koscuisko stood up. "Has Stildyne been told?" Koscuisko asked, but Rukota was certain that it was just for form's sake. "I shall need my kit."

Koscuisko knew that someone wanted information, but Koscuisko was annoyed, not worried. Ap Rhiannon had been very clear on what she expected from him as far as Inquiry was concerned, and Secured Medical had been converted into storage space for some time.

"I've no doubt that Chief Stildyne will be meeting you on the docks, your Excellency. Perhaps you should take Robert with you, as well." Because an Inquisitor was accompanied by bond-involuntaries any time he left the ship—both for his own protection and because the only reason an Inquisitor left his ship unless he was on leave was in order to execute the Protocols against an accused, and the Bench had made bond-involuntaries specifically to give Inquisitors captive hands with which to do the dirty work.

Rukota wondered suddenly whether Koscuisko's man Pyotr would be allowed to travel; he remembered the whisper, now. There *had* been a rumor about bond-involuntaries. One of them had been suddenly diagnosed with a brain-slug, and another almost as suddenly came down with a moderately rare case of crystallization of matter in the limbic system or something of the sort. It was none of his business, however.

"We'd best not keep the Captain waiting, Robert," Koscuisko said, sorting his documents-cubes into a tidy array and standing up. "Let us be going directly. Thank you, General."

Speculation and rumor were just that. Where there was a dust cloud, there was a dust cloud; no more, no less. Surrendering any residual curiosity to the basic good sense of minding his own business Rukota went whistling down the narrow corridors of the *Ragnarok* to go see the Ship's Engineer and review the requirements for the *Ragnarok*'s battle cannon.

"This then is the officer in charge at the Connaught vector control," Andrej Koscuisko said, with his arms folded across his chest and one hand wrapped around his elbow to keep a firm grip on his upper arm. To prevent himself from hitting her absent-mindedly, Vaal thought; but did her best to keep her military bearing. Of course she was afraid of him. That was Andrej Koscuisko, and everybody knew that he was either completely out of his mind or ought to be. "Tell to me again what service you mean me to perform for you."

Her people had gotten her up altogether too early into her rest-period, and after that things had gone very quickly. She was supposed to be asleep, not standing in her office face-to-face with a notorious painmaster. A professional torturer. The opportunity that Koscuisko's presence suggested could not be wasted, no matter how much it upset her to be talking to a man with his history.

"Thank you for coming, your Excellency." It hadn't been *his* sleep-shift. No, he looked fresh and rested, and the beautifully tailored curve of the black fabric of his over-blouse seemed to breathe a clean bright fragrance of citrus and snow. That was nonsense, it had to be. Snow didn't have any fragrance. It was just fluffy ice. "We have orders pertinent to the terrorist attack at Ghan that require us to stop any specified traffic through the vector that doesn't have a valid audit stamp."

Ghan was different from other recent mass casualties. Someone had gone to great lengths to maximize murder, and there seemed to be no sense to it, but was there ever any sense to terrorist activity? The fuel pipes could have been poisoned at any time over a period of days, with the right time-release, and up until the morning on which the port had died traffic had been leaving Ghan on the usual closely timed schedule of a busy mercantile port. There had been a lot of traffic, and the records were for the most part unrecoverable, destroyed in the fires that panicked rioters had set.

"And you have to feed them until Fleet can spare an Inquisitor," Koscuisko added. His tone was not very cordial. Officers at his level of rank didn't have to be cordial, unless it was to their own senior officers. Few people under Jurisdiction outranked a Ship's Inquisitor.

Andrej Koscuisko was more than just a Ship's Inquisitor. Andrej Koscuisko was widely reputed to have the truth-sense on him. Whether there were such a thing as truth-sense or not Vaal neither knew nor cared. He was a professional uncoverer of secrets. He would know if she was keeping any.

"When you're a maintenance technician everything looks like a salvage job, your Excellency." When you were an officer who dealt with sabotage and treason, everything looked like the one thing or the other. Inquisitors saw everybody as guilty, in part because once an Inquisitor was called in everybody either confessed or died. Usually one, and then the other. By a quick flash in Koscuisko's very pale eyes Vaal deduced that he had taken her meaning; she hurried on while she still had the nerve.

"Five of the ships we're holding are from Port Rudistal outbound for Emandis space, your Excellency. The story is that they are to establish a mining colony on one of the slow-moons in system." The truth was that they meant to take the vector through Emandis to Gonebeyond space, and escape from Jurisdiction entirely. That had been her conclusion, at any rate. "If you could just verify their story, sir. We could let them go on about their business."

She had to feed them, yes. That was so. She had a legitimate reason for wanting them out of here as soon as possible. Technically speaking Nurail were classed as displaced persons confined to a limited number of systems where labor was in short supply.

The Domitt Prison was closed—Andrej Koscuisko had closed it, years ago, and exposed a catalog of horrors that remained one of the blackest blights on Jurisdiction in recent history. Hadn't the Nurail earned the right to flee the Bench for Gonebeyond if they could? The Domitt Prison was drenched in the blood of Nurail men and women who had, in the end, been guilty of no crime but that of wanting to be free.

"Take me to your facilities, then," Koscuisko said, unfolding his arms. His voice was no longer quite so glacially superior. "Have you a manifest of the cargo?"

She had. "There are one or two anomalies," she admitted. "Some of the equipment appears to be make-shift. Ore-crushers are expensive. I expect a good mechanic could make do with a lighter, more portable vehicle." Agricultural equipment ran significantly smaller and lighter than mining equipment. Nurail had limited funds. It only made sense that they'd had to pool their resources and buy what they could, knowing they'd have to retool when they got to the mines. And if they never got to the mines, but ended up somewhere else—oh, well. There were no economic enterprises without risk.

"No matter," Koscuisko said, and waited while his silent standing Security opened the door to Vaal's office to let them all out. "I will take the manifests as audited. Send to me your persons of interest. Have you holding facilities?"

It was with difficulty that Vaal mastered the warm rush of gratitude that she felt. It would not do to show any unexpected emotion. People might think. Koscuisko was going to play along, he'd said so. Well, he'd said *send to me your persons of interest*, but it amounted to the same thing.

"No cells at the hospital, your Excellency, but we can hold people in a clinic wing. Since there's nothing there. You will wish to use—ah—"

There was no Secured Medical, no dedicated torture room. Not in a small hospital at an administrative station. Koscuisko smiled—yes, actually smiled—and preceded her out of the room, according to the protocols of military rank-courtesy.

"I will want bedding enough to keep my people," Koscuisko said. "Also open for me a field kitchen so that people may eat. I do not need Secured Medical, Vaalkarinnen. I am accustomed to working with minimal infrastructural support. That is why the Bench has granted to me Security."

Bond-involuntary security, yes, of course. Green-sleeves, marked as Security slaves by the thin edge of poison-green piping that trimmed the cuffs and collars of their uniforms. She wished he hadn't said that, about infrastructure; some of the most famous horror stories about Andrej Koscuisko had to do with his genius for improvisation.

"As you say, your Excellency." It was too late now, one way or the other. She had called for Andrej Koscuisko. She would simply have to trust that nothing would go awry. If it did, it would be her fault.

If it all worked out, though, she need have nothing in her memory to accuse her. She would put her trust in Koscuisko's reputation for anarchy—and for having a weak spot for Nurail after so many of them had been cruelly murdered, a significant number by Koscuisko himself, at the Domitt Prison in Port Rudistal, so many years ago.

CHAPTER TWO

Reminiscences

How often had he found himself here? Andrej Koscuisko asked himself, with an emotion that he could not quite identify or bear to examine too closely. Some makeshift torture-cell in some station with a problem and no solution in view. Prisoners. Security. Drugs. All of his favorite whips.

"Just like old times," he said to Stildyne, who was hovering—just a bit. He was wrong about the whips. He hadn't brought them. There was no sense in testing one's resolution; and a whip was traditional, but unnecessary. Andrej was Dolgorukij born and bred. Dolgorukij had respect for tradition, and his family was among the more traditional of the great Houses of the Dolgorukij Combine in these latter days. If he'd brought a whip he would have had all that much more difficulty refraining from using it.

"Don't get started in on that," Stildyne replied, setting an array of doses down on the shining surface of the sterile table in front of them. "You'll only work yourself into a mood. And you've been in a mood ever since you got here."

Just now? Or five—nearly six—years ago, when he had joined the crew of the *Ragnarok*, and met his new Chief of Security? It was perhaps better not to ask, Andrej decided. Brachi Stildyne had taken good care of him and good care of his people as well. There was nothing to be done about the fact that Andrej could return Stildyne's awkwardly expressed if deeply felt regard with gratitude and respect, and nothing more.

The best way he could communicate the gratitude that he owed was to do as he was told and not argue. Yes, he was the superior officer. Yes, technically speaking it was Stildyne who had to shut up and get on with his work. It was also true that Stildyne had spent more time holding Andrej's head over the basin of the toilet than could reasonably be expected of anybody save a wife or a servant, and Stildyne was neither.

There was a subtle sound behind Andrej's back; Stildyne looked over his shoulder, and called "Step through."

Robert St. Clare, with lab results in cube. "The officer's documentation," Robert said, passing the cube to Stildyne. "And the officer's rhyti coming directly."

Rhyti now; liquor later, perhaps. It wasn't that Andrej didn't know how to be humiliated at being so drunk that he had to be washed and changed like an infant, wrestled into bed, forcibly restrained from taking unsafe actions with sharp objects. He knew perfectly well how contemptible a drunk he was. The humiliation of his drunkenness was a species of punishment that kept him returning to drink when he could no longer bear the fear of his own dreams.

Had it not been for Stildyne's nursing and the support of his people, his own medical staff would have had to confine him on ward as self-destructive, and then he would have been publicly humiliated every time. For all he knew his medical staff would have liked to do just that, though not out of any particular desire to humiliate him. Captain Lowden had seen to it that they left him alone—and placed the entire burden of his care in the hands of bond-involuntaries, like Robert.

Now Captain Lowden was dead, but Andrej's medical staff was apparently willing to trust Security with the care of drunken officers. If he'd known that his staff was going to take that approach, Andrej told himself, he might have murdered Lowden much sooner than he had.

And it was better not to think of it, because although Bench Intelligence Specialist Karol Vogel had claimed responsibility for the assassination—Lowden had needed killing, and Vogel had the authority—it would still be Tenth Level command termination for Andrej if the truth ever came out. He was living on borrowed time.

"Clean scans." He would keep his mind on his own business; that was the best bet for staying out of trouble—and keeping his people clear of trouble, besides. "Ask for navigator Dawson, Robert, please." The reports told him the blood-lines and blood-chemistry, and that information in turn told him what he could use on whom to what effect. Dawson was Nurail without detectible admixture. The Bench had dispersed the Nurail in order to destroy their identity as a people; it was not likely that Dawson's children would be pure-bred.

But it was likely that they would be handsome, Andrej decided, watching as Godsalt and Kerenko brought Dawson in. Dawson was a tall young man with a figure rather like Robert's own, but something had gone wrong with the side of Dawson's face so that it was pulled to the left around the mouth ever so slightly; and the color of Dawson's eyes—Andrej noted, as his security sat Dawson down—was unusual.

"Dawson, that's your name?" Andrej asked. "My name is Andrej Koscuisko, and I hold the Writ to which you must answer. I have some questions for you."

There was nothing on the table between them but doses. The table itself was in the pharmacy prep room; spacious, airy, well-stocked with everything a man might want for healing—but there was no staff to make that healing happen. Depressing.

"I'm called Chonnie Dawson, yes," Dawson replied. "—your Excellency." The rank address came at the last minute, almost as an afterthought. There was no disrespect in Dawson's tone, but no particular fear, either. Wariness. Anxiety. No terror. Andrej was glad that Dawson wasn't afraid of him. It was going to make talking to him much easier.

"Have we met?" At the same time there was no sense in letting familiarity pass unnoted; too comfortable a relationship created its own difficulties.

Dawson raised his eyebrows. "Twice, as his Excellency please." He put out his hand to the tray of doses as he spoke, moving slowly and carefully, leaving plenty of time for Andrej to tell him to keep his hands to himself. "You murdered my father."

This convoy claimed to be from Rudistal, so that would logically have been in the Domitt Prison. What was Dawson's point, reaching for the doses?

"Hardly a distinguishing characteristic." Andrej watched Dawson's hand. Dawson was doing his best to make a deliberate gesture. There was something Andrej was supposed to see. "You're curious about these doses, I see?"

"You're right, I'm sure, your Excellency. About distinguishing characteristics, I mean. It's only the fact of it being my father makes the connection personally significant to me." Dawson had reached for one of the doses, apparently at random, and picked it up. "Which of these did you use on him?"

Distinguishing characteristics, Dawson had repeated. As Dawson raised the dose to eye-level, the oily frayed cuff of Dawson's sleeve-jacket fell away from his wrist, the fabric pulling against the flexed elbow. Dawson had worn manacles for long enough to scar him. They were old scars, though. He must have been quite young when he had got them, Andrej realized.

For no particular reason Andrej caught the joke, now. He remembered a boy in transit, on their way to Port Rudistal—a young man, fifteen years Standard, perhaps. That young man had had green-gold eyes with a ring of yellow like a sunburst around the aperture of the pupil. It wasn't a common eye-color for Nurail, who ran to the black in that area.

"Well, you must understand that in those days my sense of humor was imperfectly formed."

He ignored the ghost of a snort from Stildyne, who had posted himself behind Andrej's chair. There were men on either side of Dawson already, and Stildyne knew that they were good because Stildyne had trained them. On one memorable occasion more than a year ago Andrej had been forced to defend himself in a knife-fight; Stildyne hadn't recovered. Andrej had—from his wounds—but Stildyne brooded bitterly over how easily it could all have ended badly.

"Somebody had said that your father was an important man. I wanted to see what there was to him."

Not just an important man. The war-leader of Darmon. Had Andrej realized at the time that he had accidentally abetted the successful escape of the last remaining member of that family at large? How could he have known? He hadn't met the war-leader until weeks after he'd arrived at the prison. By that time a young man whose wounds Andrej had treated, whose manacles Andrej had absent-mindedly removed and set aside, would surely have been long gone.

"Different from here and now in what way?" Dawson asked, politely. Dawson wasn't Dawson. Dawson was Chonnie, the son of the war-leader of Darmon. Chonniskot Sillerbanes—Chonnie's got silver bones—he was that precious to his people, at least as an idea.

Andrej's sense of humor was different now in a number of interesting ways. "For one, this person at my shoulder was a woman of striking physical beauty. For another, we had a great many questions to ask, while here and now there are only two or three questions that interest me at all."

Twice, Dawson had said. Dawson was eyeing Stildyne with an expression of awed horror on his face, but Dawson had companions as beautiful. Didn't he? There'd been a man with a great long livid gash across his face. Andrej had seen the two of them, Dawson and Beauty, in a dream in Port Burkhayden on the night that he'd killed Captain Lowden. Maybe it hadn't been a dream.

"Questions," Stildyne snarled at Dawson, who fell back, dropping the dose to the tray with a clatter. "Pay attention."

Andrej stood up. It was going to be harder than he had realized, this sitting and asking questions. Of course it almost always started with asking questions. But then it had almost always gotten a little bit extreme from there, and there was a blood-eyed beast in him that wanted to hear this perfectly harmless—or relatively innocent, anyway—young man speak to him in tones of anguished fear.

"Window," he said, gesturing to explain himself, yes, in case anybody was wondering. "Wouldn't normally have one for this business. People don't like to have to see. Unless they're the kind who likes to watch, of course."

Captain Lowden had liked to watch. Lowden had done more; he'd violated the trust and confidence of Fleet by trading on markets that Andrej didn't even want to think about, using illegal copies of interrogation records—torture—as currency. And the Malcontent, the secret service of the Dolgorukij church, had told him that the market was too vigorous to be shut down; Andrej would not put it past the Malcontent to be actually trafficking in the name of the Saint himself.

What would happen when the time came that his son should chance on such a record, and see with his own eyes the things of which Andrej was capable?

"Questions, your Excellency?" The tone in which the young man asked was interesting. It was cautious and wary; but there was the smallest hint of forbearance—even encouragement. *You can do this.* Of course it was in Dawson's best interest to get questions out and over with. Dawson would be eager to be getting away.

"It has not been eleven days since horror was visited upon Port Ghan and those who live there by some enemy of order and civil law. The Connaught vector is only two or three days off from Ghan. And your party cleared the entry vector from Port Ghan to Connaught nine days ago."

It was quiet in the room behind him. He could almost hear people breathing. The Security troops he had with him were bond-involuntaries; they knew how to be as silent as the dead, or more so, since the dead were frequently surprisingly loud in the first few hours at any rate.

"We heard," Dawson said. There was an echo in his voice of a man much older, and accustomed to duty. A war-leader. The son of his father. "And we were there. But we were on vector before the news started to come out."

Which meant nothing, of course, since any reasonable maniac would take care to arrange things just so as to be well clear before the city started to die. "Come here to me," Andrej said. He had to know, and he didn't want to sit down. He knew how to get answers. He knew all too well. "And tell me that you had no hand in vengeance upon Pyana."

Most, if by no means all, of the dead had been from that genetic group, the ancestral enemy of Nurail everywhere and the party that had convinced Chilleau Judiciary that the Nurail were dangerous and had to be put down. It might have been a coincidence, all the same.

There was the sound of the chair's brace sliding over the floor, and Dawson came up behind him. "All right, we'd nothing to do with it. There. I'll be going now, it's been very interesting, but there are people waiting for supplies at Bell."

"You're not going to Bell," Andrej said, firmly. "Or at least you're not stopping there." No, a small commercial fleet of Nurail headed into Emandis space was more likely to be seeking the vector for Gonebeyond. What was it? Dar-Nevan? "Mister Kerenko. If I might have those doses, please."

He was going to have to step away from the window, and that was too bad. But whether or not something horrible was going to befall to Dawson, anybody outside the window who saw anybody at the window would be likely to conclude that something very unfortunate was happening to somebody, and Andrej didn't wish that experience on anyone.

"Your scans indicate a subcategory six hominid of very strong definition." Nurail, and Pyana. When it came down to it Nurail were Pyana, and vice versa, but there was no sense in being insulting. "Here are three doses for Nurail, designed to disable your internal editors and deprive you of your natural ability to dissemble."

He knew these drugs. He'd purchased the life of Robert St. Clare from the Bench with one of them, years and years ago. "Naturally there are ways to beat it, but it doesn't have to overwhelm you to be effective. It only needs to make it difficult enough for you to dissemble that I will know. You will sit down."

Dawson was a brave young man, but not stupid. Only a stupid man would feel no fear in the presence of a torturer with drugs. There were drugs that did much more than loosen tongues—Dawson sat, but could not quite keep still. His eyes when he met Andrej's gaze were defiant and still hopeful, as though he were doing his best to believe that nothing was going to happen to him. When Andrej approached him with the doses in hand Dawson struggled, but not for long; as soon as the first dose went through Dawson froze, and suddenly started to grin, going rather limp and boneless against the restraining hands of Security as he did so.

"Damn," Dawson said. "This is good stuff, Uncle. Mixmox, isn't it? I had some once. Only once. Can't afford it. There was a woman—"

Uncle. A Nurail authority figure; Andrej had been called that by Nurail before. Standing at the table in front of the seated and now-intoxicated man Andrej put his head back, staring at the ceiling, taking deep and calming breaths. He was not going to hurt Dawson. He didn't have to, and nobody could make him. He wanted to hurt Dawson. He wanted very much to make Dawson suffer, but he was not going to. And Stildyne, standing at his back, Stildyne would not let him hurt Dawson, either.

"I'm happy for you," Andrej said at last, and sat down with the chair pulled away from the table. "What were you doing in Port Ghan? Tell me."

"Port Ghan," Dawson said, and seemed to stop and think.

Although he all but crossed his eyes in concentration Andrej could sense no cues that would tell him that there were hidden secrets here; he had already told Dawson that he knew Dawson was not taking a convoy to Bell, not exactly, so it was not as though that could be said to be a secret.

"Solar cells. It took months to collect the load, couldn't buy too many at once, people might remember you and get suspicious."

One set of cells might be needed by any prudent person as a back-up, but not twenty. Unless a person had twenty buildings to power, or a person was taking them out beyond the reach of Jurisdiction into an environment in which there were no solar cells to be had unless one had brought one's own.

"Did you get them?"

Dawson was very drunk on the drug now, and snorted with unfeigned derision. "Did we? Who do you think you're talking to? We got them. And then we left."

No, not entirely unfeigned. There was the very small shade of a wrong note in Dawson's voice. Dawson would like him to believe that Dawson was more drunk than he actually was. He could increase the dose; but why? It was just as effective for him if Dawson thought he didn't know.

"It would be difficult to blame a man for seeking to be revenged on an enemy who had served his entire people so villainously," Andrej said, to be saying something. "Especially if a man felt more responsible, perhaps, because of a traditional family position, for instance."

Dawson had started to shake his head before Andrej had finished speaking, but was yet polite enough to wait to raise his voice. When he did it was a denial as emphatic as that which Andrej had expected, but the direction in which Dawson took the denial was surprising.

"Yes, and then their people must take revenge for their hurt, and your people for the hurt that their people will do if they can in response to the hurt that you have done them for the hurt that they did you. Let me tell you a thing or two about the law, Uncle."

Very strange. Andrej could sense the amusement and confusion with which his Security heard this outburst, but only because of long acquaintance. The self-discipline of a bond-involuntary was terrible to contemplate. Andrej was counting on that self-discipline to see them all safely through, but he couldn't afford to think about it, because Stildyne might hear him and he hadn't had a chance to talk to Stildyne about what he had planned, not yet.

"Tell me," he agreed, encouragingly. "I would have thought that you would have no interest in speaking of the rule of law."

Dawson hadn't said "the rule of law." He apparently decided that no correction was needed, however. "It's there to stand between us and our own annihilation. Not here, maybe, no." "Here," under Jurisdiction, the law had been used by Pyana against the Nurail to obtain the annihilation of Dawson's folk. So Dawson wasn't speaking of the rule of law under Jurisdiction.

"There has to be an agreement," Dawson said, "Or there's no community. There must be an end to vengeance once and for all. We got together and talked about it, and we decided. Unless we share our hearths we'll all die, and the weaves with us."

At this particular moment Dawson did not sound drunk at all. Andrej frowned. "Brachi," he said; then he remembered that he did not call Stildyne by his name in public, but could not call it back. "Remind me to check the pull dates on these doses. Something is not right. A Nurail speaks to me of abandoning feud."

And yet he knew one particular Nurail whose capacity to return resignation for great wrong permitted him to live a happy life, if any bond-involuntary could be said to have a happy life. Robert was considerably happier than Andrej himself in some respects; but Andrej felt it was almost insulting to Robert to even think such a thing in light of what Robert had suffered, and put the thought away.

It was just that Robert had no particular rank, that was all—bond-involuntaries could lead even the smallest work-units only when the group was entirely comprised of other bond-involuntaries, under most circumstances. It meant that there were many more women on board the *Ragnarok* with whom Robert could hide in a store-room for a few moments than were available to senior officers. Yes. That was the way to approach it. Robert had lost his family and his freedom, but at least Robert could go fishing, every day if he liked.

"Is it only fear of consequence that has kept your life so long, Uncle?" Dawson asked. "Do you believe that? I held your life in my hand not two years gone, in Burkhayden."

It was not something Andrej had ever felt comfortable thinking about. No, there had been few assassination attempts against him; yes, he was visible and notorious. Stildyne was growling in a sort of sub-vocal way, however, so Andrej moved to forestall loss of control over the situation.

"You mustn't ask such questions in front of Security," he said, so that Stildyne would know that he had noticed. "I always thought it only reasonable that you should hate me, though. All of you. There are so many of you." In the general sense, at least.

"We may hate you yet." From the tone of Dawson's voice his personal feelings were far from dispassionate. "Don't mean to kill you for it, that's all. Because if Nurail continue to kill other Nurail they have good reason to hate, there won't be any Nurail left for our children to hate. No children."

Andrej had to stand up again. Something was profoundly disturbing him here, and he could not afford to stop and think it through. He nodded to Security to have Dawson stand up; Dawson kept his balance very well, for a man on drugs. Maybe there *was* something wrong with the dose-lot.

"Now you are making me nervous," he said. It was only the truth, however mocking it might sound. "But I almost believe you, now. About Port Ghan, if nothing else. Give me your hand and swear to me on your father's death and the manner of his dying that you and your people are not to blame for it, and I will be satisfied."

Dawson had gone white in the face; was the drug catching up with him? He seemed to be feeling some sharp discomfort beneath his skin. As Andrej watched, Dawson's face cleared of hatred and contempt, and the ferocious anger in his eyes was replaced with something much more disturbing. Hope. Hope, and distance, of a sort.

"I so swear," Dawson said, and put out his hand. Left-hand dominant, Andrej noted. That was almost funny. He was left-hand dominant as well, but if Dawson's father had been left-handed Andrej did not remember even noticing. "On my father's death, and the burning of his corpse in the furnaces. And on the manner in which you killed him, torturer. There is no one among these people who has had any part in horror at Port Ghan. Not even if they *were* Pyana, there."

Curious to see how far Dawson would go Andrej put out his own hand in turn. Dawson took it. There was no sudden shock of antipathy so strong that it repelled the threat of physical contact with a father's murderer. Dawson frightened Andrej, now. How could such strength be natural?

Dropping Dawson's hand Andrej stepped back half-a-pace. "Very well." Dawson was watching him with what seemed to Andrej to be almost equal parts uneasiness and fear—that he would go back on the promise he had made, perhaps? "I will have to interview each ship's commander, and perhaps three or five others. In order that the record be complete, and no question remain. You may have your representative at the interviews. It may be reassuring to them."

"And I've got just the man for the job," Dawson replied. "Thank you, your Excellency, and I don't suppose there's an extra one of those doses about that wouldn't be missed? No? Oh, well."

It was perfectly true that Andrej needed to talk to enough people to reassure the vector control officer that Dawson's party could be released. But it was also true that this unexpected assignment offered opportunity, as well as challenge. There was a surgery here.

The operation was actually a rather simple one; only the fact that the slightest perturbation in the process would mean an agonizing death complicated matters. That and the fact that it was illegal, but he had not been notified that his Writ to Inquire had been rescinded, and until it was he remained immune from prosecution for any crime he might wish to commit short of mutiny, as represented for instance by the wanton murder of a superior commanding officer. What was a little misappropriation here and there in the face of such immunity?

"Send that person to me this evening." It was mid-afternoon already. "By which I mean, halfway through third-shift. I will have a list."

Between now and then he would go and check the surgery, and undoubtedly discover that the surgical machines were in need of calibration. It would be several days before he could be finished with his investigation, and leave; and the *Ragnarok* was still several days away from finalizing its supply manifest with Emandis Station. Andrej was expecting to rendezvous with his cousin Stanoczk, whose aid he had enlisted in his purpose. Several days, six bond-involuntaries, three of whom required no surgery; he did not have very much time.

Security took Dawson away. Andrej was alone in the room with

Stildyne. After a moment Andrej spoke. "Send someone to inventory stores," Andrej said. "Physical inventory. Controlled List. I'm concerned about the quality of stores."

No, he was not. He simply wanted a decent excuse for pulling excess medication for the *Ragnarok*'s ship's stores without being too obvious about it. Would the ruse fool anybody?

It didn't matter. "I'll set Robert right on it," Stildyne said, and left Andrej alone, to brood about justice and retribution and mortality.

The angry grief that the Second Judge held so fiercely within her heart seemed almost to shimmer visibly in the brutal heat radiating off the baked flat clay walls of what had been the Chively Dam. Jils Ivers waited, silently, at a respectful distance; she'd seen the horrific aftermath of natural disasters before. This one had not been natural.

The Second Judge Presiding at Chilleau Judiciary was a tall hawk-boned woman with pale hair and brown eyes who picked her way through the rubble at the base of the breach in the dam with grace and assurance. As she turned her head down to mind the shifting of the wall's wreckage, she happened to glance behind her, and caught Jils' eye. Jils knew how to read the subtle gesture of that minute nod and came forward to accompany the judge on the way across the broken threshold of the dam.

Chively had been holding the spring run-off from the Ato watershed for generations. The city had grown up on either side of the spillway's watercourse to nestle in the shadows of the beneficent protector of them all; there might never be a true tally of the lives that had been lost when somebody had blown the base wall and loosed the accumulated weight of Chively Lake, as old and venerable as an inland sea, over the roofs and highways all from the way from Chively to the ocean.

"Only a year," the Second Judge said. "In the name of the Law, Ivers, if you had told me that people could do such a thing to one another. Under my own presidence."

It wasn't the sort of thing that really called for an answer, or to which there was an answer. Only a year. Jils stood with the judge on the sloping slab of a piece of dam-wall, sheared away from the breach with explosive force under the pressure of an almost unimaginable weight of rushing water. The broad scar of the water-course was as smooth as the back of her hand. It was an effort to look down and away toward the remains of the city and realize that the bits and fragments of rubble and rock were each of them the size of a small school, in which all of the children had been killed.

"There's no underestimating the corrosion of anarchy." She was sorry that she hadn't found Verlaine's killer. She was almost sorry she wasn't Verlaine's killer. It would have been so easy to lay the blame on the person who had discovered the body in Chambers that the only reason the Second Judge hadn't—so far as Jils could guess—was that it wouldn't have done the slightest good. The problem wasn't so much that Verlaine's murderer was as yet unidentified, unfound. The larger problem lay in the fact that nothing could bring him back.

"Go to Brisinje for me, Ivers." The courier ship was waiting for her, there, a short distance removed, resting on the scoured surface of the flood-bed. It was dry, now. It would be months before the water level in the holding-basin behind the ruined dam wall was high enough to wet the base of the rocks there. "Tell them it was all a subtle ruse. Tell them that Sindha isn't dead, and that his dying wish was to see his life's work come to fruition. Maybe not at the same time, no, but tell them. And then get back here. When you have a suspect I want you to fetch Koscuisko for me."

A *viable* suspect, of course. That was what the judge meant. There were no lack of suspects—political enemies, agents of other Judiciaries angling for advantage, Free Government terrorists aiming to destabilize the Bench by throwing it into disarray, even Fleet assassins bent on countering a challenge to Fleet's autonomy and privileges. Plenty of suspects.

Plenty of dead ones, particularly, but the Second Judge had passed the point of being angry enough to authorize extreme measures on speculative grounds. Plenty of suspects, plenty of confessions, a useful opportunity to purge the body politic of undesirable elements, and yet they were no closer to a lead than they had been a year ago.

It went without saying that the Second Judge would much rather have sent Karol Vogel to Brisinje to represent Chilleau Judiciary. But Karol Vogel was not here. Nobody that Jils had spoken to or contacted seemed to know where he was or what he was doing, unless there had been information in the odd little quirk that the Malcontent "Cousin" Stanoczk had gotten to the corner of his mouth when Jils had raised the question with him. And there was never any telling, with Malcontents.

"As you say, your Honor." The Second Judge didn't want Koscuisko to solve the mystery for her—it was Jils' job to discover who was responsible for the killing. That hadn't been her point. No. The Second Judge wanted Andrej Koscuisko to execute her vengeance with the demonic flair characteristic of his notorious genius. "Your front office said there was to be material for me to take with me." Andrej Koscuisko would execute no Tenth Level ever again, not even if his life depended on it. He had successfully convinced her of that.

All of Jurisdiction space needed the Selection to be resolved, and a new First Judge to be named to be the supreme authority so that peace and order could be restored. Needing the Selection to be resolved so Andrej Koscuisko could surrender his Writ to Inquire and go home was a very small part of the greater problem; but it *was* a part.

The judge turned to look back over her shoulder; there were several clerks of Court in her party, as well as Security. "These are the completed traffic assessments," the judge said, nodding for one of the clerks to pick her way awkwardly through the debris. "Thirty-two days before and after, all vectors. The last pieces just came back from analysis yesterday."

There was something wrong with what the judge was saying, but Jils couldn't afford time to think about it now. Holding out her left hand to the clerk the judge passed a flat-panel data display to Jils, who accepted the flat-panel with a respectful bow. Data could contain evidence, and evidence could cost lives. It was worthy of the respect due any potentially dangerous weapon.

"Very good, your Honor." Jils could see from the activity of the ground-crew down range of the courier that it was ready to launch. "I'll give you regular reports, and hope to return to my primary task as soon as possible."

The murder investigation was her primary task. She remained the single strongest default suspect; she knew that to be true. She couldn't afford to let it interfere with her reason or her judgment. She knew perfectly well that she had not stabbed Sindha Verlaine, even if she still had very little idea who actually might have done.

Would the judge give Jils over to Koscuisko, to try to settle her own mind once and for all? She'd think about it later.

The courier was waiting for her, the roaring of its jet propulsion escape engines sounding curiously hushed within the great bowl of the destroyed dam. It was a tidy little beast with modestly raked canards, a standard model of vector courier wearing the marks of the Emandisan Home Defense Fleet. Boarding, Jils secured her kit before joining the pilot in the wheel-house.

Through the courier's forward viewports she could see the judge walking away back into the wrecked breach in the dam-wall as the flight techs deployed the field blast-barriers so that the courier could lift. She wondered, suddenly, whether the judge had wanted to be personally assured that Jils was safely loaded, and would not take advantage of an opportunity to disappear.

It was an unsettling thought, but the joke was on the judge. If she had murdered Verlaine—if she'd had the skills to bypass all of the security that surrounded the office and the person of the second most important soul, the most important man, in all of Chilleau Judiciary— a few of the judge's Security would not stop her from disappearing.

The pilot was a man of moderate height whose amber skin and black eyes were as Emandisan as the fleet-marks on the courier. He greeted her with a polite nod, neither smiling nor frowning. Emandisan characteristically presented a stoic and serene front to the world and to each other.

"Let's get out of here," Jils suggested. Had an Emandisan killed Verlaine? Emandis exported security operatives, sharp-shooters, military snipers. There had been a political upheaval in the government at Emandis perhaps five years ago. Chilleau Judiciary had been identified with the ousted government's disgraced officials. Were the Emandisan holding a grudge?

"Very good, Bench specialist," the pilot said, locking into the comm braid. "Courier Gamesil, prepare to launch, secure for lift. Launch control. Request permission to escape atmosphere outbound for Brisinje Judiciary via Anglerhaz."

Traffic at Chively was very heavy these days as the local government struggled to get disaster aid to the area and to the people who, having survived the terrorists' breach of the dam, had been displaced by the horrific if inevitable result of emptying the great lake of Chively in so astonishing a fraction of the time that it had taken to grow the lake to its former extent. Jils, however, was traveling for the

Second Judge, and the Second Judge was anxious for Jils to be off and away to represent her interest in the convocation of Bench specialists at Brisinje, where the Ninth Judge presided.

"Launch control here," the control station said. "Cleared to exit, courier. Going home, I take it, good space to you."

"And to all those who have to travel through the dark." The pilot returned polite phrase for polite phrase, but Jils thought that he sounded a little distracted by more than just his pre-flights.

She waited until the courier was on trajectory and headed out of atmosphere before she asked her question. "Have you been traveling long?"

The look he gave her was surprised but only mildly: perhaps he was too absorbed in his task to notice being surprised, and of course it didn't take a Bench Intelligence Specialist to put "going home" together with a tired pilot and derive a long mission.

"Seems like much longer than just four months, Dame Ivers. Yes, ma'am. —Anglerhaz vector in twenty-four, and expected drop in Brisinje by four days."

"Thank you, pilot." She'd just be getting aft to brood, then, or maybe get started on the data that the judge had given her as she left. Unlike Karol Vogel, this pilot was apparently perfectly confident of his vector spin calculations. No cross-check would be solicited or required.

Karol Vogel and Jils had partnered at Chilleau Judiciary for years, and partnered well, too. The sexual tension that had been between them had been the comfortable background pulse of a heartbeat, something that made it pleasant to be in each others' company— bearable to be sequestered together, sometimes in impossibly small places, without losing perspective.

He'd been moody and broody the last time she'd seen him. She'd thought she understood—he'd been carrying a Warrant, an execution or assassination order, and Karol had always found killing mildly distasteful—but it had run deeper than that. Because Karol had dropped out of sight on his way out of Burkhayden and had not been seen since.

It hadn't made sense, though. Captain Lowden, the *Ragnarok*'s notoriously corrupt commanding officer, had been dead before the fire had started in the service house that night; forensics had said so.

It wasn't like Karol to set buildings on fire; he had always been careful in the past about endangering uninvolved bystanders, and a fire in a service house was a recipe for disaster. All of those patrons in all of those rooms, and the power had been off in Burkhayden that night. It was only a lucky accident that there had been so few injuries—and no fatalities—in the evacuation.

In the secure privacy of her small passenger bed-cabin, Jils laid the flat-panel down on the table and addressed its secures, verifying her identity with the chop she wore around her neck. It was a very full collection; she could tell that as the initiating diagnostics ran. She'd been waiting for the traffic reports from the very start—from the moment at which it had been reported that something had gone wrong at Upos and destroyed the gate records, covering eight days' worth of data from the stores. From the backup. From the virtuals. From the disasters. Physically destroyed.

The records hadn't been physically destroyed at Wellocks, no, only part of the damage had been fire and corrosion there; but what they had recovered had been irretrievably over-written by a very sophisticated blanking protocol that Jils wanted for her own. And Burig as well, not only the two vectors out of Chilleau itself but two of the vectors from which one could gain access to the Wellocks vector and thus to Chilleau—oh, it had been thoroughly done.

Panthis and Ygau had been unharmed, undamaged, un-attacked except for some minor damage all too clearly designed to dilute the focus of an investigation by widening the field of avenues that had to be investigated. There wasn't much doubt in Jils' mind about that. The key to the problem was to be sought first where the unknown quarry had tried to hide it most completely. There'd been Fleet at Burig, Fleet at Ktank, Fleet at Upos and Wellocks and Panthis as well; so if it was a Fleet initiative Fleet had certainly had the resources in place to cover its tracks. Yes, if it had been Fleet.

Months to restore the traffic reports by tracking every ship that had arrived at any vector it could have reached from any of the vandalized vectors. Months to collect and rationalize and sort the data, to try to make information out of it. It was up to her, now. There were still connections and clues that could not be elicited from any of the non-sentient analysis tools at the Bench's disposal.

Report of traffic, Bury Vector, inbound and outbound, minus sixteen to plus eight. Analysis record. Do you wish to proceed? And yet something made Jils pause, and secure the log, and stare down at the flat-panel on the table for a long moment, thinking.

It was an analysis record, and an analysis record by definition was an extract. The judge had publicly entrusted her with sensitive documentation; but the sensitive documentation with which the judge had entrusted her was derivative. Second-hand. Nothing that couldn't be easily replaced, re-run, and—perhaps crucially—compared against a master record to check for errors and omissions.

The Second Judge probably had her own people working on it already. It was just a piece of window-dressing, even if it was also something Jils had been waiting for. And any of the other Bench specialists she was traveling to meet at Brisinje would reach the same conclusion as Jils had, as quickly or more: if something compromised this data, there was no harm done. The judge didn't expect Jils to get anything out of it anyway.

This was not encouraging. It didn't always take a warrant to authorize a Bench specialist to carry out an execution or Judicial assassination. Warrants were required to communicate the Court's decision that someone had to die for the good of the Judicial order; Bench specialists were empowered to make their own decisions, about whether someone needed termination.

Jils was going to Convocation, to represent the Second Judge's interest. There would be a Bench specialist from each of the eight other Judiciaries, even Fontailloe, which by long-standing custom could not compete for the position vacated by the death of the previous incumbent. Eight Bench specialists, each of whom had the legal right to kill when it seemed necessary, so long as they felt they could justify their decision before a panel of their peers after the fact.

A target didn't even have to be guilty to need killing. Sometimes it was enough if a public perception of guilt existed, if failure to demonstrate some sort of sanctions would encourage defiance of the Bench, if it was taking too long to find the guilty parties and the public had begun to wonder, if the greater good of the Judicial order demanded a quick close to a problem so that that everybody could just move on. Any one of those people could take her life if they decided she was or might as well be guilty. She would do the same.

They'd have to take her by surprise if they took her at all. Had the judge's choice of data been a subtle warning, then, a reminder that a dead Bench specialist could not speak for the rights of Chilleau Judiciary?

It was four days Standard between here and Brisinje, even by elite courier. Computer analysis and statistics could only go so far. It could take months for even the most sophisticated computer analysis protocol to surface a connection that a human with the right background could make in a single flash of insight. Whether or not somebody else was already working on this information, it was her business to see how far she could get with it.

Whether nor not somebody was going to try to kill her at Brisinje, Jils had no intention of losing sight of her goal: to discover who had caused the turmoil that was costing lives and resources from one end of Jurisdiction Space to the other, who had thrown Chilleau Judiciary into such disarray, who had cast Jils Ivers herself under suspicion of murder. And kill them.

Out of monographs. Sick of the Keldar mysteries. Out of patience with even Dasidar and Dyraine, and he had never been a man capable of gaining a meditative trance through prayer. Four days of questioning had left Andrej bored to a perceptible degree, but at least it was almost over. Just one or two more interviews. That was all he needed. He had finished in the surgery; now all five of his bond-involuntaries had headaches and wore their Safes for show and necessary camouflage. He had six bond-involuntaries, but Robert's governor had been legally and lawfully pulled, in Port Burkhayden. The thing was done. Stildyne was suspicious. Andrej hadn't decided how much he dared tell Stildyne, but he was going to have to tell Stildyne something.

It was the middle of the morning, but his interviewee was only just now arriving, and that was annoying. Andrej couldn't blame the wench for being nervous, not really, but he was bored and irritable accordingly. "Your Excellency—"

He turned from brooding out of the window with a touch too much anticipatory greed so that his interviewee, the ship's stores inventory officer, shrank back visibly, backing into her escort. If he were to get as drunk as he thought he might like to be, it would be a week before he could promise the vector control officer that she could release her detainees, and if that happened Fleet's interrogation group might catch up with them and decide to do just a little spot-checking in light of Andrej's status as a might-be mutineer. That wouldn't do.

The stores inventory officer was a redhead who reminded him vaguely of somebody. Maybe she was one of those women who flirted when she was terrified? He could hope. But not much.

"Come on, Hatt," her escort said. "You know we've got to get it over with. Have any of the others been so much as touched? Come on."

Birrin Banch was the mess officer, the man Dawson had sent to represent the interests of the detainees and observe the proceedings to be sure that Andrej did not lapse into any old, bad habits. Dawson need not have worried, Andrej told himself bitterly. Stildyne was not about to let him lapse into any old bad habits either, and it was very tedious of Stildyne to be that way, too. They were none of them any fun at all.

Did they have the first idea of how much it tormented him to be here in this place, to be constantly in the company of people who were frightened of him—with good reason—but who could not be touched, not in any interesting manner?

The woman, Hatt, seemed to collect herself. She squared her shoulders and marched in through the door from the corridor to step right up to the table in the middle of the room, seating herself with a species of nervous bravado that Andrej could recognize and empathize with. Yes, she was frightened—and disgusted by him. There was to be no flirting, clearly. That was too bad. He liked red-heads. Women, for that matter.

"Has Birrin here told you of what will happen?" Andrej asked politely, keeping his distance. "There are doses there, on the table, whose effect is to relax you and make it easier for me to tell that you are truthful. Or not."

Not all of the people to whom he had spoken since he'd started here had told him the truth, but it hadn't mattered. It was only one sort of truth he needed, that which pertained to complicity in the disaster at Port Ghan. The confidence that came from believing that one had put one over on Andrej Koscuisko was as effective as any drug in the Controlled List, and considerably cheaper. Not that the cost concerned Andrej personally, no, but this station had not been re-supplied for some time, and there was no telling when they would be able to refresh their stores of high-grade pharmaceuticals.

"I've nothing to lie to you about." She had a thin tight voice full of resentment. She was angry because she was afraid. "Dose or no dose. Ask."

Fair enough. "I ask you to accept these doses, then. I will not force them on you." He hadn't asked Dawson. But the deeper he got into this the more clear it was to him that things were clean, and people had a right to be elect to be terrified and overstressed if they liked. It was all the same to him.

If it had been the way it used to be Security would have held the prisoner for the dose, and then he would have done anything he liked to, anything at all. Captain Lowden had been good to him. Captain Lowden had seen to it that he had as much recreation as he could stand, and then some.

Hatt turned her head to look at Birrin, who nodded reassuringly. *Go ahead. It's all right.* Taking a visibly deep breath Hatt nodded and turned back to Andrej. "Do as you like."

How could she know? It wasn't what he liked that troubled him. It was the fact of liking it. He had had such freedom, and been its prisoner. Now he was free of the freedom to commit atrocity, prisoner of his own determination and subject to the penalty of death by his own free will.

He put the dose through at the back of her shoulder through her garment, then sat down. It would be a moment before the dose began to take effect. Andrej looked around for whomever was handy, catching Godsalt's eye. A flask of rhyti. By the time Godsalt had brought the beverage Hatt was very relaxed indeed. Taking a deep breath and closing her eyes she smiled with evident appreciation.

"Do you take rhyti, Miss Hatt?" Andrej asked, surprised. Dawson's observer shifted where he sat, just a bit, but Andrej already knew that Birrin didn't take rhyti.

"Yes, please, if there's to be had." The eagerness of her response was unfeigned. "Beautiful stuff, that. At least by the perfume of it."

Godsalt hadn't needed Andrej's implied instruction to bring a second flask, one as milky as the first. Less sweet, Andrej hoped. Dolgorukij liked sweet things to be sweeter than the general taste of many other sorts of hominids. It was because the Dolgorukij base metabolism ran high to the Jurisdiction standard.

"One is a little puzzled," Andrej said politely, watching her take a clearly appreciative sip of the hot infusion. "One has rarely met persons not from Combine worlds who care for rhyti."

There was a limited luxury market for good-quality rhyti, true enough, and naturally it was a staple of ethnic restaurants. There was not much demand for Dolgorukij cuisine outside markets with displaced Dolgorukij populations, though. Where would Hatt have had occasion to acquire a taste for it?

"In Port Rudistal I had an information service," Hatt said. She was sensitive to his confusion, Andrej guessed. "One of my clients was a guest of a religious establishment. They always offered rhyti. Cakes. Pastries. You didn't dare eat for a day you went to see the cousins at the sister's house."

No, wait. A feeling of unrest had started to build in Andrej's mind as Hatt explained, and it got worse as she got further. A religious establishment in Port Rudistal, and they served rhyti, so it was a Dolgorukij religious establishment. There was only one Dolgorukij religious establishment in Port Rudistal that Andrej knew anything about—the one that he had himself had established so that the Nurail service bond-involuntary who had shared his bed while he was at the Domitt Prison need not go back to enforced prostitution once he was gone. It couldn't be Ailynn that Hatt was talking about. Cousins, she'd said cousins, well, that could be anybody, but cousins at the sister's house—Ailynn.

"I think I know of that establishment," Andrej said. He didn't have any brief to talk about it; he was here to ask about Ghan, and for no other reason. He had to finish his inquiries and let these people go so that he could have a word with Stildyne about bond-involuntaries. "If I do, it is a woman named Ailynn."

Hatt nodded. "It's well his Excellency should know, it's your own house, after all. That man of yours. The one who died there." Joslire, she meant, Joslire dead in the street. "I met Birrin there, did you know?"

Was that why Birrin had seemed so uncomfortable? He'd been steady enough over the past days, acting his role of advocate-observer with quiet competence. But now he gave unmistakable evidence of nerves. Andrej could smell it in his sweat.

"That's none of my business, Miss Hatt." He wanted to ask how things were. The Bench had called him back to Rudistal to execute judgment against Administrator Geltoi, tenth-level command termination. He'd made a good demonstration of it. It had been a public execution, it had been important that it be as horrifically impressive as possible. Kaydence had been there with Ailynn at that time. And a party had come from Emandis space demanding the return of Joslire's knives, but they were his knives now. Joslire had given them to him.

He was letting himself become distracted. Emandis and Joslire's knives were very much on his mind; he'd asked Two for research on any family Joslire might have left, and hoped to visit the place where Joslire's ashes had been buried. They did it in orchards on Emandis, he understood. "I've no interest in extraneous matters. I only need to know about Port Ghan."

She shuddered and put her hand to her mouth as if her stomach hurt her suddenly and very badly indeed. "Horrible," she said. "Children. Animals. I thought the furnaces at the Domitt were the worst thing I could ever see, your Excellency. I was wrong."

Andrej thought he knew what she was saying, but he had a duty to be sure. "You saw the children dead at Port Ghan?" he asked, carefully; just because he wanted her to be innocent so that he could let them all go did not mean he could take any short cuts. Because it was horrible, at Port Ghan. Children. Yes. And their parents and teachers and friends, every living thing within the entire zone serviced from that one fuel distribution station, all dead.

"No," Hatt said, too clear and honest and mildly confused for there to be any ambiguity in her meaning. "I saw the furnaces. And the pit. But I've seen pictures from Port Ghan. Horrible."

Birrin was more uncomfortable moment by moment. It piqued Andrej's curiosity; nothing to do with Ghan, surely, but something to do with the Domitt Prison. "Tell me, Miss Hatt," Andrej said. "Do you know anything about who was responsible for that? Anything at all?"

What she said next caught him by surprise, again. This interview was full of perplexities—"He was a guard, that's true. But the days of blood for blood are over. Birrin's a good man. It doesn't matter what he might have done, before, and it's yourself that shares the shame of what happened there, but do we count it against you? No. We're mindful of your word that stopped the burning. It more than counts. With both of you."

Andrej understood. "And we are both rightfully humbled," he assured her, not looking at Dawson's observer. "But as to what has happened at Port Ghan. I ask if you have any knowledge of who is responsible for that. You were there. Did any among you put the plot forward, in any way?"

Opening her mouth to answer him with strong words she seemed to collect herself, to remind herself that after all the whole point of the thing lay in that question. She shut her mouth and swallowed once, and then spoke.

"I had no knowledge of it," she said. "And have gained no knowledge since. No, your Excellency. We took on goods at Port Ghan, but brought none, nor did anybody but a few even go out of ship. For fear of arousing suspicions. You can guess."

True enough—they would have minimized their contacts in the port, and he could indeed guess why. "Thank you, Miss Hatt. Gentlemen, if you would see Miss Hatt safely back to her place, please." He did not offer to excuse Birrin. Birrin did not attempt to leave.

When the security were gone and Hatt with them, Andrej leaned back in his chair and looked at Birrin, curious. "You're Pyana. Not Nurail at all."

"You pretend you can't tell?" Birrin demanded, but it was in a tone of voice that was defeated, almost helpless. "Yes. I was a guard at the Domitt Prison. His Excellency would not remember ever seeing me."

Well, Birrin hadn't been a work crew boss or among the unauthorized and unofficial torturers from that one long ugly barrack, or he would not be here. It didn't mean he hadn't committed abuses. It was merely that so many crimes had been committed there that bringing the worst of the criminals to account had exhausted the resources of the Judicial system. After a point there was no point in criminalizing bullying, distasteful as it was.

"But you saw me? We were there together?"

Birrin nodded, his face full of shame. "I was in the guard mount on the morning that you turned off the furnaces. There was something that was beyond natural about the fog, that morning, and I was afraid."

Andrej wasn't sure he quite followed Birrin's line of thought, but he wasn't trying very hard. If he wanted to remember he'd have to think about it. He didn't want to think about it. He relived it all frequently enough, in his dreams—

"We are both well quit of it. That's all that matters." And yes, he understood very well why a Pyana with blood-guilt to atone for might be here among these Nurail. "It can never be made right, but we have finished with it, you and I."

There was no making amends—at least not for him. His crimes had been too great. For Birrin, Andrej had no doubt that his atonement overbalanced whatever fault he had committed, but the important thing was only—first—to stop. To quit. It didn't matter in the least how sorry you were about what you had done if you were at the same time still doing it.

"Done," Birrin agreed with a nod. There was a peculiar catch in his voice; what was on his mind? "I've watched you, and I can't tell. Am I the only one who—sometimes—who is sorry that it's over?"

For all the hesitation in Birrin's voice there was no mistaking his meaning. Andrej stared, and Birrin stumbled on, clearly feeling more miserable by the moment.

"And it's not that I would ever do it again. I think about the things I did, I can't believe it was me, I know I did them, I can't imagine doing anything like that. But I can't stop wishing. I remember things when I'm not thinking about it. It was so easy. It felt so good, to have so much power."

Certainly Andrej knew what Birrin meant. "You can't help it." Neither could Andrej himself. "Of course you remember. It's your mind trying to make sense of it all. 'How could I have abused those people,' you ask yourself."

"What do you do?"

Birrin had been a prison guard. His crimes, whatever they had been, could hardly be comparable to those that Andrej had committed in the name of the Judicial order. But Birrin was in pain, and this was no time for perverse pride. "I stay out of situations that remind me, as much as I can," Andrej said. "And if the truth be told I drink a great deal, friend Birrin, though I cannot recommend that as a strategy."

"You miss it also?"

Andrej could hardly bear to answer, for a moment. Yes. He missed it. He wanted—"Fiercely, but it is only right, that I should be in pain." He didn't want to talk about it. Had Birrin heard what he needed to hear, to know that there was nothing uniquely monstrous about longing for days of power and lordship that were over, when they had been enjoyed at the expense of other feeling creatures? "Let us go to the vector officer. I have all the information that I need to release the convoy with full confidence."

All of this time, Birrin had stood at his post, leaning against the wall just to one side of the doorway. He turned without another word, and waited; Andrej stood up and followed him, resigned, depressed, but glad at least that he could help Dawson's convoy on its way.

CHAPTER THREE

Manifest Irregularities

Jils Ivers stood up from the small table of the passenger cabin and stretched with her hands at the back of her waist, her fingers not quite touching the track of her spine. She was getting nowhere.

Her mind kept wandering; she couldn't concentrate. She found herself scanning the scrolled sections on her viewer, awakening to the fact that she couldn't remember a thing about the last sub-segment or the section prior to the one on which she'd just stopped, going back to find the last place she could remember and discovering that she didn't recognize a single data-point between where she'd left off last and where she was now.

She could almost have believed that someone had laid down a hypnotic subliminal in the text except that she didn't believe in subliminals. She'd never validated a single instance where they'd worked with any degree of consistency at all. She'd known that she was stressed. She hadn't realized that it was as bad as it was. She knew what to do about stress, though.

Closing up the data reader, Jils tucked it away in the secured locker with her kit and then started to clear the room. The hollow globe was really the best solution. She had stowed the table and was latching the bed into its wall-mount when the talk-alert sounded; it was the courier's pilot.

"Twenty hours clear of Chilleau, Dame," he said. "There's news from Brisinje, we won't be coming in to the launch-fields near the city. They're burning. Trade protests of some sort, they say."

The Bench was all about regulation of trade, at its heart. Yes, its form was that of a Jurisdiction—nine judges on the Bench, each responsible for lower courts and circuits and the entire range of governance; but when it came down to it all the Bench was really interested in was protecting and perpetuating itself for the greater good of the Judicial order and the maintenance and regulation of trade.

Jils sighed in frustrated resignation. "All right. Has anybody put their name to it?" Twenty hours clear already? She hadn't really noticed the passage of time. She was sure she'd learned the first few sections of that data by heart, but that was a poor return on a Bench specialist's time.

"There's a preliminary report on it, Dame, but nothing official. I'll let you know if anything comes in."

Right. "Thanks, pilot, Ivers away here." She'd spoken to him four or five times on her way to or from the galley; personable sort with an unusual name. Weren't they all unusual names? The pilot was Emandisan. She'd track down her nagging sense of recognition later, when she had time. Jils reached for the pull-strap above the lintel of the door that separated cabin from corridor and pulled.

The ceiling-panels moved apart to either side of the cabin; there was the exercise apparatus stowed and waiting. Its own pull-strap fell free of the ceiling panels and Jils put her weight to it to deploy the device, an exercise globe, flattened for storage but unfolding into the metal skeleton of a sphere as it descended.

Each of the cabins contained a piece of stowed equipment in its ceiling compartment. She had made sure that she got the cabin with the globe. There were times when the only thing to do was to step into the cage and strap in and work it into a freely-spinning inertial resistance training machine.

The straps of the man-mount in the middle unfolded and fell straight from their anchors as the globe completed its descent, and something fell to the floor. A piece of paper. Caught up in the apparatus from the last time it had been deployed, perhaps?

She didn't care. This was a well-maintained little courier, but things could be overlooked, and a stray bit of paper in an overhead storage bin was no big deal. Opening the door of the spherical cage Jils stepped inside and started to strap herself in, thinking. How far had she gotten in the data?

She'd gotten through most of the Terek vector's records, only partially distracted by its casualty list. Terek was powerful—giving access to more than five exit vectors—but loose; it was easy to end up where you didn't expect to be, if you didn't pay attention.

Some of the Terek's multiple exit vectors were in undeveloped territory. There were supposed to be emergency depots at even those, in theory; but with Fleet stretched thin and complaining about resource starvation, if the resupply and maintenance crews hadn't been by and the last ship had taken atmosphere, you could find yourself without enough good air to last until next planetfall if you had to turn around and take the vector right away. Setting the wheel in motion was a gradual process, and she had to exert herself to get the wheel started. That was the whole point, after all. There'd been a lot of traffic through Terek lately, at least during the audit period. Never any shortage of people willing to risk their lives to save time and resources. A really good pilot had nothing to fear from the Terek vector, true enough.

The wheel was beginning to warm up and start spinning, slowly. The piece of paper in the floor was like a visual brake that interrupted Jils' train of thought every time the rotation of the wheel carried her past. That wasn't just an ordinary piece of maintenance log-sheet. There was something disturbing about the way in which it was folded.

Terek vector, Jils told herself, firmly. Ships could occasionally slip through Terek during a solar disturbance that reduced the capacity of the vector control's recording devices. Might a ship have come in the wrong direction—from Gonebeyond—carrying an assassin?

Why wasn't that piece of paper resting on the floor moving in the air-currents that the movement of the exercise sphere created as it spun faster and faster? Just how heavy was it? She'd seen heavier paper and thinner paper, and even metal foils could be used for hand-writes from time to time. Metal foils could be quite heavy. But if it was a metal foil would it have fallen the way it had?

She braked the machine with the weight of her body, going limp, leaning back against the harness. This was no good. She wasn't getting anywhere. The wheel spun to a stop; Jils unstrapped herself. Reaching through the metal frame of the sphere Jils picked the damned thing up and unfolded it. Heavy paper—sketch paper—and a simple cartoon in which Jils recognized a message.

It was a hanged man. A stick figure on an old-fashioned tee-frame, the noose—a specific noose, a technically correct detail—clearly indicated. And across the stick figure a scrawled strike-out heavy and black as if the person who had done the cartoon had wished to call the image back. Jils knew better than to imagine that to have been the case, however, because she recognized the style.

She always sought the cabin with the globe. She frequently diverted herself with exercise when she was thinking hard about something, and she had been thinking hard ever since she'd found Verlaine's body.

The doodle would mean nothing to anybody else; it had been left there for her, only her, in the hopes that chance would bring her to this cabin. The news of a Convocation had been leaked months ago; that it was to happen at Brisinje was common diplomatic knowledge. Chilleau Judiciary had no Bench specialist to send but her. The odds of Jils traveling to Brisinje on this one courier were by no means as long as they might at first though seem; and who knew how many doodles had been planted in how many cabins, and by whom?

Karol Vogel wanted her to know that Simms "the Hangman" Balkney had not done the murder of First Secretary Verlaine.

Ever since she had realized that Karol had gone missing she had sought for news, clues to his whereabouts, some sort of a hint about what he was doing—any scrap of information that might explain why he had disappeared so disgustingly completely on his way out of Burkhayden space, nearly a year ago, now. She had found nothing. She knew what the doodle meant in the immediate sense, at least on the surface; but what its meaning might carry as a deeper message—and how long it had been here, waiting for her—she could not afford to stop and brood about.

Would Karol be in Convocation? Surely not. But Balkney might well be. At least Karol wasn't dead, or hadn't been, recently enough to have left her a message.

She left her cabin as it was and took the piece of paper to the wheelhouse where the pilot sat at his station. He looked over his shoulder as she came in and started to rise, but she waved off the courteous gesture and sat down in the second seat at the pilot's right. What was she going to ask him? What was she going to ask first?

"Feed from Brisinje space," the pilot said, and cued a visual. "It's shameful."

She could see the pearl-gray globe of Brisinje, its great oceans, the brilliant white sands of its countless beaches outlining the landmasses clearly even hours and hours away; she could see the dark smudge in the atmosphere at Brisinje's equator feathering like a plume from Brisinje Judiciary's seat on the famous Reggidout River. It was the gem of the Judiciary, so pure and clear a river that it was celebrated throughout the Judiciary and even beyond; and the black smoke lay across that beautiful blue thread for what had to be octaves and octaves.

She didn't have to wait for the reports to be written to know the cost in human suffering. The river had no defense against the outrage that was done to it, and on behalf of the white sand beaches and the clear blue river Reggidout Jils knew a special kind of anger in her heart.

"We're scheduled in at Imennou," the pilot said. "Priority override, we're the last party to arrive. You'll be met."

She'd just bet. Met by a guard of honor, yes, but one that was a guard detail beneath it all. They needed her for Convocation, though; Karol wasn't here to speak for Chilleau and there was nobody else who'd been associated with Chilleau at any recent time who wasn't already absorbed in the affairs of other Judiciaries. That gave her a reprieve of sorts. Perhaps.

She opened her mouth to ask a question but closed it again when she realized how little good it would do her. She could ask the courier's pilot where he'd been, and he would tell her; she could check its records, for that matter.

She could ask the pilot if he knew where Karol Vogel was, but Bench specialists could travel unregistered; it was part of their privilege package. They were not obliged to tell anyone where they'd been or were going. If Karol had been here the pilot might well have been instructed not to mention it, and pilots were by definition conscientious and careful people, as a rule. If Karol had not identified himself, he was traveling as someone else, in which case a passenger list in and of itself would do her little good.

What did it matter? Karol had been here, and left her a message. "Imennou." She wasn't sure she even knew where that was. "How long to Brisinje from there?"

"Six hours by ground-car, they tell me, Dame. I've never ridden in a top-of-the-line ground-car. Is it true that they stock the refreshments bar with all of your favorite snacks?"

"Bench specialists don't have favorite snacks." It was the response he would expect; she'd play along. "And we live on plain water and survival rations. It's to avoid establishing a pattern that could be used to locate and identify us when we're under cover. And when you've been living on survival rations almost anything else counts as a favorite snack, believe me."

The pilot grinned. "I'll send ahead, Dame," he promised. "Refreshments bar to be stocked with plain water and survival rations. Supplement tabs."

She almost had to laugh, and missed laughing so much that she did. "Very good," she said, with an assumed frostiness of dignity. "Carry on. I'll just be going back to quarters."

She didn't want to watch the world come closer. She didn't need a clearer hint of how Brisinje was suffering from fire and sabotage. The fuel tanks on the launch-field had been breached. The toxins in the atmosphere would be damaging the river's flora and fauna for years. It was criminal. But that was stating the obvious.

If she survived the Convocation she would ask to be allowed to stay on at Brisinje, and see the villains punished herself, if possible. If she didn't get through to the truth about Verlaine's death her own execution was all but inevitable.

"True enough," Koscuisko said to the convoy commander Dawson, standing on the platform before the last of the mercantile ships to be unshackled. The unchaining was figurative, of course; it seemed to Stildyne that what Koscuisko had just offered to tell Dawson about Dawson's father was likely to be distressingly concrete. "He might have liked you to know, all the same. Shall I tell you?"

Dawson looked at the vector officer, who seemed to shrug her shoulders as well as anybody could while she was standing on her dignity. She was operating at a significant handicap in the dignity department because she was on Koscuisko's right, and Koscuisko could project ferocious self-possession in his bare feet and a soiled nightshirt. Stildyne had seen him do it.

Looking back over his shoulder, checking the progress of the preparations for departure, Dawson took a deep breath and thinned his lips with an expression of resignation. "I repeat that I can't imagine what a man might want to hear about his father's death by torture," Dawson said. If there was hatred in his voice Stildyne couldn't place it. "Speak as you like, Uncle."

The familiar tone that Dawson took had surprised the vector officer, so much was obvious. She knew how to take her cue from Koscuisko, though; that was obvious as well. And Koscuisko didn't seem to be bothered by the imputation of kinship.

"I paid little attention to it at the time," Koscuisko said. "And only now realize what it meant. Your father knew that you were not taken. I showed him the list of friends and family known to be dead and in custody, you were not on it."

A strange light leapt into Dawson's coppery eyes as Koscuisko spoke, but it seemed to die away as quickly as it had kindled. "It's a small matter," Dawson said. "Thank you, but I—"

Koscuisko shook his head emphatically. "Excuse me that I insist, Dawson. It is no small thing. I meant to dishearten him by showing him that all was lost, and he knew by my showing that hope remained. Had that changed during the course of our acquaintance I would have told him, he would have known to be sure of that, and it had been some weeks. Months. That you had not been taken or identified among existing prisoners meant good hope. I left him little enough to take with him as he died."

The whole Domitt Prison thing had been before Stildyne's time, though it had been at Rudistal that he had first met Andrej Koscuisko. Fleet had elected to effect Koscuisko's formal transfer from *Scylla* to the *Ragnarok* while Koscuisko was back in Port Rudistal to execute the sentence of the Court against the Domitt Prison's administration. He'd met Koscuisko's former chief of Security, and made some assumptions about their relationship that had created problems for him later. He was glad he hadn't been there the night Koscuisko had taken Joslire Curran's life, though.

"And he left you with the weave." Dawson had gone pale. "I never learned my mother's weave, Uncle, nor my father's either. And you. You wrote them down. You said so."

Had Koscuisko had conversation with Dawson that Stildyne hadn't known about? It was possible, if difficult to imagine. Stildyne liked to know where Koscuisko was, and with whom. It was his job. Koscuisko only nodded, though, so it had clearly happened, somehow.

"Eight and eighty of them," Koscuisko agreed. "And have given the text to the Church to be protected, since there is no security on board of the *Ragnarok* for any of her crew. No personal criticism is meant by this, Brachi."

Of course not. It was the security of the *Ragnarok* as an entity that Koscuisko meant, not the quality of protection provide by any of its Security teams.

"Does the Dolgorukij church speak scream?" Dawson asked, with an almost completely suppressed tremor in his voice. Koscuisko shook his head.

"Not so much in these latter days, but my cousin Stoshi can read my handscript better than most. We have a similar handscript, or at least we have had in the past."

That was true. There was a family resemblance. Stildyne was in a position to know, having seen one or two examples of the writing of Koscuisko's cousin Stanoczk. It had been a shame that he hadn't been able to keep them, but the matter of the notes that Stanoczk sent to Stildyne was not such that Stildyne could take the risk of accidental disclosure.

"What must we do to get the weaves back, then?" Dawson demanded. The maintenance crew was coming off the last of the convoy ships, and the members of Dawson's crew who had been detailed to accompany them looked satisfied and eager. They would be leaving soon.

"It is your property, or rather the property in common of any Nurail. The Saint holds the manuscript in trust, and will transcribe it. I meant in this way to be sure the books were safe." It was technically illegal to transcribe Nurail weaves, and had been for years; part of the Bench sanctions. Of course Koscuisko could do so with impunity. The Law did not apply to Inquisitors, or applied only in a limited sense.

The vector officer's maintenance chief had waited politely for Koscuisko to stop talking. Koscuisko could see her waiting as clearly as Stildyne could, of course, and raised his eyebrows at the woman, inviting her to speak.

Which she did, to her vector officer, as was appropriate. "Cleared and registered, vector officer," the maintenance chief said. "Buy-off on all stats. Ready for immediate departure."

Vector Officer Vaalkarinnen nodded. "Get out of here, Dawson," she said. "I wouldn't waste any time. Go. Move. Shift."

"And take your surgical kit with you," Koscuisko added. The vector officer looked up sharply at Koscuisko as he spoke, but Garrity and Hirsel, taking their cue, were already moving the two solid crates forward at as brisk a pace as the assists would tolerate.

Dawson offered the vector officer his hand; she seemed to think about whether she would protest, but apparently made up her mind to let it go. She shook Dawson's hand, and Dawson turned away to hurry into the open passenger loading ramp of the nearest ship with Garrity and Hirsel following close after.

"I looked at their manifest," Vaalkarinnen said to Koscuisko. "They're not carrying surgical kit. Just standard medical maintenance and emergency."

"And I have done an inventory of your medical facility, Vaalkarinnen. Do you know how outdated a significant portion of your stores have become? I have been forced to destroy *materia medica* that might otherwise fall into the wrong hands. You will have to make do with a single inventory-set until your replacement stock arrives from Emandis Station. It may be ten days but I have placed the requisition on urgent status."

Was that what Koscuisko had been spending all that time in the station's surgery doing? Building a colonization medical kit for Dawson's fleet? Stildyne wouldn't put it past him. And it would explain. When Koscuisko got off on a medical tangent Stildyne tried to stay out of his way. Koscuisko had threatened him with reconstructive surgery more than once, and Stildyne was not taking any chances.

"Thank you, your Excellency." Koscuisko had left Vaalkarinnen with nothing else to say. She sounded sincere enough all the same. Stildyne could empathize with the dilemma that she'd been in, and with Koscuisko here she had been able to release the entire convoy without so much as a bruise or a yelp or a drop of blood. "I understand that I am responsible for imposing on you. I'm very grateful to you for your assistance."

Well, it wasn't as though it had been Koscuisko's idea, precisely. Koscuisko said as much. "Your sense of conservation is to be heartily applauded, Vaalkarinnen." The sincerity in Koscuisko's startled a blush out of her. Stildyne wondered if she minded. Blushing was a much under-rated ability, so far as Stildyne was concerned. He didn't think he'd ever been able to do it. "I applaud your dutiful care of souls under Jurisdiction. I have said as much when I made my report."

"His Excellency is very kind." Her blush had deepened, but she gave no sign of being aware of it. "If you'll excuse me, sir, I'll return to my duties, now. Please clear the docks for release of convoy."

Koscuisko returned her salute with a cheerful, almost casual nod. He watched her back in silence for a moment before he looked around him, carefully, and spoke again. "I wish to speak to you about a matter of some delicacy, Brachi."

That could mean almost anything. Anything which might be interpreted from Koscuisko's parochial Dolgorukij point of view as potentially representing a remark about deficiencies in a person's performance of their duty was a matter of the utmost delicacy, and the Dolgorukij interpretation of "duty" extended all the way from what a man had for fast-meal to the manner in which he shat the following morning.

It was with somewhat mixed feelings that Stildyne, taking a survey himself before responding, saw someone who was probably Dierryk Rukota by his size and shape and the color of his uniform pausing at several marks' remove to receive the salute of the vector officer and exchange a few words with her.

"Have to wait," Stildyne said. "Artillery officer abaft the labbord beam."

He had no idea what it meant to be abaft the labbord beam, except in the general sense of approaching. The phrase came out of his mouth from the antiquated retrieval systems of his childhood memories, which was a surprise in itself as he hadn't remembered ever having had a childhood.

"The bonds," Koscuisko said. "I have stolen them. I need to talk to you about what happens next."

Stildyne had in fact suspected as much, but Koscuisko had handled things carefully and the fact that he had had serendipitous access to a surgery where nobody was watching him come and go down here on Connaught Station meant that nobody else would have thought twice. General Rukota was moving toward them again, however, so Stildyne had to put away his feelings about Koscuisko's confession and his apparent desire to make Stildyne his co-conspirator for later examination.

"I'll look out for them," Stildyne said. "We can talk later. When we get to Emandis, or is there something I need to know sooner?"

Koscuisko had turned around to watch Rukota's approach. "I would want you to know before I tell them," Koscuisko said unhappily. "Out of respect, if nothing else." What did that mean, when "respect" was all he was ever going to get from Andrej Koscuisko? "But you are right. It will be safest."

Koscuisko had a privacy field available to him in his office, where it was understood that sensitive formal discussions on medical issues might take place. Koscuisko couldn't have him in to the office for a private tête-à-tête without somebody in communications getting too curious about it, though, not unless Stildyne was under medical care for one reason or another.

The temptation for someone to do a periodic maintenance override when the standard "privacy field invoked" notification came up in the communications center might be too much to expect a bored technician to resist, and the Ship's Intelligence Officer herself was one of the most bored people on board the JFS *Ragnarok*, from what Stildyne knew of her history. Either bored, or unnaturally curious— the effect was the same, and he had been grateful enough for Two's prying in the past when he had needed to know where Koscuisko was. One way or another Koscuisko's feeling that he didn't want to talk about next steps on board of the *Ragnarok* made perfect sense to Stildyne.

"Later, then, your Excellency, and I'll look out for it." Stildyne didn't know how good Rukota's hearing was, and did not want to risk calling Koscuisko "Andrej." Stildyne wasn't sure he'd ever heard anybody use Koscuisko's name in all of the years that Koscuisko had been assigned. Except for Captain Lowden, come to think of it— Lowden had enjoyed flaunting his superior rank—but Lowden was dead, and Rukota hadn't been with the *Ragnarok* then anyway. "General Rukota, sir."

Rukota didn't need to tell Stildyne to stand at ease; Koscuisko was the superior officer, so it went without saying that Stildyne was doing as Koscuisko had instructed him. Rukota gave Koscuisko his salute accordingly. "Thanks, Chief. Your Excellency. Captain sends me to retrieve you as soon as possible. Wants your report on our current virus situation, sir."

Garrity and Hirsel had come back out of the ship and were waiting at a polite distance. Koscuisko nodded. "Very well, General, let us go to the transport ship. Mister Stildyne. Have the gentlemen pack."

Not as if there was much to pack, although Koscuisko would be anxious about the rhyti-brewer. He was running low. His cousin Stanoczk would be bringing a fresh supply of leaf, Stildyne guessed. "Very good, your Excellency. Right away."

And he'd find out all about whatever else was going on when Koscuisko got to Emandis proper. The sooner they got there, then, the sooner Stildyne would know; so there was no time to be wasted, and he went off to quarters with Hirsel and Garrity in tow to get packed and report to transport for return to the *Ragnarok*.

The approach to Imennou launch-field was grimmer and more depressing moment by moment as the courier flew through great greasy clots of black soot even in the upper atmosphere. It was more similar to flying through the ash-cloud days after a volcano had blown out its side than anything Jils could think of, except of course that volcanic ash would settle and work its way back into the soil and improve the drainage of the fields and generally display its positive side in time.

There was no excuse for the roiling gouts of ash from Brisinje's launch-field. It would take a much longer time for each particle to settle out of atmosphere, longer still to sink into the background and degenerate and yield what nutrients or supplements the Brisinje florae and faunae could take for their use from burned fuel and vaporized metal.

By the time the courier touched down at Imennou launch-field, Jils was even more depressed about the whole thing than she'd already been from her first glimpse of the cloud over the Reggidout River; it was out of proportion, she knew that, but all of the tension she had been unable to banish or sublimate over the months of the murder investigation seemed to have surfaced strictly in order to attach itself to the first good external cause she could find.

Imennou was a pretty launch-field, with white walls for blast containment and cheerful green vines of crimson-and-gold trumpet-shaped flowers draped over almost every vertical surface. The architecture ran to flat roofs and low buildings, nothing more than four levels above ground; so that as the courier ran its excess momentum out on the launch-field one saw nothing more than the flower-covered vines, the brilliant white of the blast walls, and the deep blue sky beyond.

It was a restful sight, presenting the illusion that one was almost alone. Illusion: and almost, because there were of course people waiting for them behind the window of a thermal barrier—Security by the color of the uniform—and a ground-car on the track at the back wall by the sliding gate.

The courier slowed as it neared the waiting party. She could count the Security from her place in the wheelhouse; Security she understood, but there was someone there who was not Security, and something inside her chest-wall somewhere believed she recognized him.

"Flown into Imennou before?" she asked the pilot, whose handling of the landing had been expert. It didn't have to mean that the approach had been as smooth as it had been because the pilot was already familiar with the air-currents and the prevailing weather conditions, but the skill displayed in the landing had been a potential hint, and if the pilot was familiar with the area maybe he'd know who those people were.

"Not really, Dame. Through Brisinje, mostly. Ferried your counterpart, there, from time to time, if it's not a breach of confidence to say so."

No, of course it wasn't. Not unless the pilot had been instructed to say nothing, and if he'd been told to keep shut he'd never have mentioned it. "If I didn't know better I'd be tempted to guess that I know him," Jils said carefully, soliciting the name without coming right out and asking for it. The closer the courier got, the more familiar that one man looked. Above average height for a Jetorix hominid, his arms crossed over his broad chest with his hands wrapped around his elbows in a very familiar fashion, an easy smile, hair that curled and waved around his temples and fell to his strong shoulders like the decoration of a ritual mask—

"Specialist Delleroy," the pilot said, as if he hadn't noticed being pumped for information. "I don't have much experience with people at your level, Dame, if you don't mind my saying so. He's got the common touch, though, doesn't he?"

And surely there was not another Bench specialist in known Space who stood quite so confidently and self-contained as that, perfectly calm, perfectly ready for any event, perfectly in command of the very ground on which he stood. Delleroy. Padrake Delleroy.

She wasn't going to think about his common touch, or his uncommon touch, or any of the different sorts of touches at which Padrake excelled. It hadn't been five years; she'd thought it was hard enough five years ago, but seeing him there, now, as if he was waiting for her, was almost more than she could bear.

There was refuge and sanctuary to be had in Padrake's embrace. No one had ever made her feel so cherished, so vulnerable, so taken care of—all things to be avoided like a death sentence, by a Bench specialist, because any sort of loss of objectivity could be just that, and when a Bench specialist failed and died there was too good a chance that innocent civilians would suffer for the error as well. It was just the nature of the profession.

Padrake had understood that as well as she had; they had parted by mutual agreement, severing their swiftly-becoming-too-close relationship while it could still be done without hurt and recrimination. She hadn't seen him since because she couldn't help remembering how good it had been with him, how it had just kept on getting better, how she could have given up her career and her duty and her mission and lived happily as Padrake's partner if only she had not been Bench specialist Jils Tarocca Ivers. If only.

That wasn't the point, she admonished herself. The point was that it hadn't been feelings of hostility that had kept them apart, but rather too strong an echo of the reasons why the connection had had to be severed in the first place.

"I do know him, then." She'd been silent for almost too long; the pilot would be wondering. "I hadn't realized he was at Brisinje, though. I hope he's not driving. He's a demon, in a land transport."

"Been here about five years that I know of, Dame." The courier was stopped; the pre-disembarking checks were running with the efficiency that characterized everything on this ship, including its pilot and crew. "There's the all-clear. Free to disembark, Bench specialist, and it's been the honor of the Emandis Home Defense Fleet to have provided you with transport, on behalf of the rule of Law and the Judicial order."

Formal and polite, as well as efficient; but there was nothing obsequious about the reading the pilot gave the standard formula. "Thank you, pilot, it's been a very enjoyable trip." Maybe that was the wrong word. But it was said. All she could do was move on.

Her kit was already packed and waiting; Karol's note was tucked into her blouse. Down the ramp and out into the all-but-painfully clear sunlight; suddenly the white of the blast walls was almost glaring, too intense to be looked at directly. Was that the reason why so much of the surface was covered with flowering vines? To cut down on the dazzlement?

Padrake had started toward her as she cleared the ramp from the courier's loader. Now he broke into a lazy sort of a jog, something she remembered as hellishly ground-eating even while it looked almost effortless. For a big man he was very light on his feet, as befit a specialist renowned for his subterfuges and stratagems.

"Jils Ivers! Really you!" he crowed, and took her into his arms for a warm embrace. Which he loosed before she had a chance to decide exactly how she felt about it but not before she noted that he was using the same scent in his toiletries as he had before, something with crisp notes and elements reminiscent of roots and fragrant bark and sharp spices all at one and the same time.

"So good to see you, Jils. I hoped it would be you, how many Bench specialists named Jils Ivers could there be? But still it could have been a ruse on the part of the Second Judge to keep you for herself, at work on a criminal case when the fate of the Jurisdiction is to be determined. Glad it wasn't a ruse. How are you, how have you been?"

How did he think she'd been, living under suspicion and the constant possibility of being assassinated lurking just out of sight behind her chair every waking hour? "Well, all the better for the seeing of you," she mocked him, gently, with one of his own catch-phrases. "Padrake. How have you been keeping yourself?"

"Busy." Of course. He seemed to remember himself only barely in time to refrain from attempting to carry her kit bag, something a man with Padrake's background did almost by reflex in the company of women but which she had suffered only as a special favor during the days of their intimacy. One did not presume to fetch and carry for Bench specialists; not even, or especially, if one *was* a Bench specialist. "This way."

The ground-car that was waiting for them could well be the First Secretary's official vehicle; it almost had to be, unless Brisinje was in the habit of provoking its subordinate Courts by flaunting its wealth. Not a good idea, in Jils' estimation, but some administrations did take the stance that a convincing enough display of power and luxury could contribute to the public weal and welfare—so long as it was perceived to be attainable. So long as people believed that anybody could grow up to be First Judge; or at least First Secretary, if they were men.

"Nice transport, Padrake, have you been prospecting in ice-fields in your spare time?"

He snorted. "You know better than that." Yes. Bench specialists didn't have any spare time. "It's a long ride overland to Brisinje, six hours, maybe longer. No-fly zone in effect because of the unpredictable thermals and the smoke, and nobody was using this, so why not? Hop in."

The driver would be in the front compartment of the ground-car, shielded, isolated in the cabin. The ground-car opened its doors politely as she approached, the near recliner offering itself to her; as she sat down and let the recliner carry her into the interior of the car she felt the padding adjust itself around her body, a little more support here, a little lower for the neck-roll there. It was a very nice ground-car indeed.

She lay back and gazed up into the star-field displayed against the inside of the roof while Padrake's recliner moved around into its position in turn. The doors closed themselves, the security bands crept slowly and meekly across her belly, across her thighs, to meet and mesh and welcome her in so that she would be protected from translation injury in the unlikely event of an accident. Or at least prevented from becoming a translation injury herself. Security webbing could do little to stop objects from coming toward her at a high rate of speed; the ground-car had other defenses, for that.

Suddenly she wished that Padrake had taken a much less comfortable car. She was so tired. She could hear the subtle crackling sounds in her spine and in her neck as long-tense muscles relaxed; if she wasn't careful she was going to fall asleep, she knew it. Maybe there were stimulants on board?

Reaching for the slider that secured the refreshments bar Jils opened it to have a look at what was available to her. Luxury goods. Expensive sweets; premium savories; small containers with some of the most intriguing names in mood-altering potables in known Space. All strictly legal, of course, that went without saying; conspicuous consumption. Jils frowned. She wasn't sure she felt quite comfortable indulging herself in Neris extract or banner-honey or nectar of obaya while Brisinje's launch-fields were burning.

"Something the matter?" Padrake asked. "There's kilpers, if you want some. Jade-pressed and shell-filtered, the best stuff, or so people who drink kilpers have told me."

Shaking her head Jils reached for a retort-flask of rhyti. It was the least expensive drink in the cabinet, and it was expensive enough from the label—she'd learned a bit about rhyti and where it grew and what made its grades, keeping up on Koscuisko at Verlaine's instruction.

Most commercial rhyti was a soft sweet mild pale beverage, but what Koscuisko drank was brewed from the leaf from one series of hill-stations that caught the rain and the wind in the right way or had a unique blend of minerals in its soil or some such combination of factors that yielded an herb that steeped as red as fury and as sharp as iron. It was no wonder he put all that milk and sugar in it. Koscuisko's favorite would take a person's stomach lining right up, surely, if drunk incautiously.

"I was expecting survival rations and water," she lied, to cover her discomfort. "My pilot promised me."

Padrake seemed to consider this claim for a moment, his head half-inclined toward her in the soft soothing yellow cabin light. The ground-car had started moving; she could see its route-reports update, alongside the front console. She scarcely felt it. "I think I've seen that make of courier before. Only one in active service, if I'm not mistaken—Fleet size restrictions, of course. If it's the ship I think it is I might have met the pilot, interesting fellow, who'd you have?"

There was something about the rhyti that was peculiarly delicious.

What was it? Surely she was not to be doomed to develop a taste for expensive leaf? Had her issue with rhyti been the result of foolishly restricting herself to what a reasonable person could afford?

"I didn't spend more than a few hours in the wheelhouse. I had work." Which she hadn't done, looking for clues about Karol's note; but Padrake didn't need to know that. "Seemed a competent sort. Emandisan. Ees-ihlet, I think he said."

"Ise-I'let." Padrake's accent made sense of something Jils' ear had almost, but not quite, grasped. She'd heard the name before. She'd thought so at the time, and not wanted to make an issue of it; now— unwilling to open herself up to teasing from Padrake about losing her powers of recall—Jils shrugged, and put the information aside.

"Yes, something like that. He and I were talking about ground-cars."

"Well, if anyone could have gotten you in to Brisinje under these conditions, it would've been him. —Work, you said. The murder? My money's on a jealous subordinate, if you ask me."

Of course. "I can tell you," Jils said confidentially. "For your ears only, needless to say. Not to breathe a hint to another living soul, and so forth. The clerk of Court did it."

The Clerk of Court had always done it. It was rule number one of popular entertainment. Sometimes she was a Free Government agent in deep cover trying to destabilize a struggling community by cruelly murdering a popular and hard-working Judge and blaming it on the devoted and dedicated First Secretary. Sometimes she had been misled by the First Secretary in his youth, and her child was dead, probably through the long-term effects of something the First Secretary had done to worm his way into the Judge's trust and confidence by making things other than they actually were.

Sometimes she had actually aimed for the position of First Secretary herself, which was widely understood to be a bit unfair since after all the most gifted legal scholar under Jurisdiction couldn't hope to be First Judge, not ever, if he was the wrong sex. Administrative posts were a masculine reserve by and large almost by way of a consolation prize.

People had been arguing the issue of men and the Law for as long as there had been a Bench. The one thing that could always be relied upon was that in the ultimate analysis nobody could bring themselves to entrust the highest posts to creatures as ruled by passion and the short-term imperatives of a male's biological role in reproduction as men were. And it was always the clerk of Court who had done murder in Chambers.

It was perfectly true that Undersecretary Tallies—one of Verlaine's protégées—would have had to wait for years and years to be First Secretary himself under any usual circumstances. And there were unquestionably plenty of places where the sudden vacancy at the top had resulted in windfall promotions for numerous intelligent and ambitious people.

None of whom, unfortunately, had enough of a motive to murder the man who had made their places for them, and all of whom had either good record of where they'd been or other valid and convincing evidence to disqualify them from the list of possible assassins.

There *was* a clerk of Court who would have been first on Jils' personal suspect list: psychologically unbalanced, a woman of great cunning but little long-term planning ability, someone who had undergone a fearful ordeal at Verlaine's direction to further Verlaine's agenda and had seen it come to nothing. Who had found herself ignored, back-officed, deprived of Verlaine's confidence and access and finally even any particular regard—it was just too bad that Mergau Noycannir had been dead well before Verlaine was killed.

Jils hadn't been able to puzzle out how Noycannir might have gotten around Verlaine's security, but it was an attractive fantasy to entertain because it was satisfying, comprehensible, made a great deal of intuitive sense, and was also strictly hypothetical, so that a woman could dream all she liked about how Noycannir could have done it.

How could Noycannir have done it?

The ground-car traveled; the cabin was pleasantly cool and quiet and dim. She'd had a flask of rhyti, but rhyti contained a range of chemical compounds that could relax the stressed as easily as they could raise the alertness level of the relaxed or fatigued; there were hours between here and Brisinje, and she was so tired. She closed her eyes.

Forensics was still trying to work out exactly how it had been done, how someone had gotten the monitors to watch their own records and take them for live action. Passive sensors, active surveillance, motion detectors, samplers and scanners and sniffers—and all of the resources compromised, gotten around, fooled into looking the other way while convinced that they were keeping an active guard. Someone had known a great deal about the most sophisticated security the Bench had available: it limited the pool of available players. But not enough.

The recliner adjusted itself to the progressive relaxation of her body, offering warmth where its pinpoint sensors detected muscle stress, firm cushiony support beneath her knees and thighs and angles that had started to just lie there. She stretched, sighing, and turned her head away, finding just the right angle for her head against the high back of the recliner. It was a good angle. She decided to stay there for a while.

There were private enterprises whose security systems were as complex—or more—so there were people in private enterprise who knew how to get around them. And the issue of who, exactly, was only part of the interest of the question. Why had Verlaine been murdered? If they knew that, they would know where to look for the who, and until they could determine the answer to that question it was a long slow search for evidence and the identity of the perpetuators.

Something shifted, near her side; she heard Padrake move—to catch something, she thought—and opened her eyes, blinking at the schematic that displayed their route, trying to focus. Had she fallen asleep?

Something had slid over to one side on the luggage-stow overhead, that was what it was. Padrake was just setting things to rights. Her kit. His reader-panel. Whatever else was up there. He could be a bit compulsive about neatness, but there were circumstances in which his personal dedication to symmetry and balance and not leaving things undone or worse half-done could yield very enjoyable results, which she was not going to contemplate because she didn't need the distraction.

Once upon a time she and Padrake had known how to take advantage of a ground-car and a few stray hours. That was over; but it was a useful reminder—she still knew how to take appropriate advantage of opportunities such as this when they were offered. Why shouldn't she? This was Padrake. She knew him. She was as safe with Padrake as she would have been alone.

Stretching and settling herself with a clear intent she closed her eyes again. "Wake me when we get there," she suggested, and quieted her mind to sleep.

CHAPTER FOUR

News from Far Places

Security Chief Stildyne signaled at Koscuisko's office door with a fair degree of intrigued anticipation in his heart. It was a very unusual feeling, because for years he'd forgotten what it was like to have any feeling in his heart at all. "Due on dock in sixteen, your Excellency. Shall we go?"

The door slid open without a return signal and Stildyne stepped through with a small and secret grin. Koscuisko had mixed feelings about the Malcontent "Cousin" Stanoczk, a man who in this instance was actually Koscuisko's blood relation as well as "Cousin" by religious title.

Stildyne had some feelings about Cousin Stanoczk as well, mostly having to do with the fact that he was very like Andrej Koscuisko in some ways and completely unlike Koscuisko in other rather interesting ways. Cousin Stanoczk was coming aboard just before the *Ragnarok* started the preliminary approach to its vector spin; so he'd be staying for several days, until the *Ragnarok* came off vector in Emandis space. Stildyne had an issue or two to present to Cousin Stanoczk for reconciliation.

"I am directly going," Koscuisko said, standing up from behind his work-table. "For a moment I was concerned, Brachi, that you meant to scold me for laps."

Oh, better and better. "Yes, if you're going to bring it up. But we can discuss that later."

Giving Stildyne a disgusted look Koscuisko set the jumble of data-cubes on his desk-surface into array. "Of bullying you will please restrict yourself to a single item at a time. And if I hear any words from Stoshi I will know that you have been telling tales, so comport yourself accordingly."

So much unsaid, and that was better than an hour-long monologue. Stildyne's smile broadened almost despite himself; Koscuisko shuddered theatrically, and left the room, shielding his eyes with one hand as he passed the clearly horrifying sight. Stildyne didn't mind.

He knew perfectly well that he was ugly. He'd been born ugly, raised ugly by ugly in the middle of ugly's eldest brother, and improved on ugly by acquiring appropriate decorations over time— a by-now-permanently deformed nose, the scar tissue that had made it possible for him to raise a single eyebrow because the other wasn't working any more, and similar beauty marks too numerous to mention.

Until Dierryk Rukota had come on board he'd been the ugliest man assigned to the Jurisdiction Fleet Ship *Ragnarok*, and even now the question was undecided. They met for regular competitions on the killshot court. Stildyne was confident that in time his native ugly and accumulated enhancements would prove more than even "Sharksmile" Rukota's charms could match, superior rank or no.

By the time Stildyne and his officer reached the docks in the *Ragnarok*'s maintenance atmosphere, the courier was already clearing the hull, which had been opened only so far as necessary to let a ship pass into atmosphere. It wasn't prudent to make a vector transit with an unprotected atmosphere. Even if you could replace it, there was drag on the hull to be considered, and the risk of a rogue particle— even on vector, the emptiest space in known Space.

"He has brought the thula," Koscuisko said. "I hope this does not mean also his pilot." There was an unusual tone in Koscuisko's voice, one of hunger and resentment. Stildyne knew that Koscuisko was still struggling with things he had learned—and people he had found— when he'd gone home to marry his wife and make an heir of his son; he didn't think that Koscuisko had anything to worry about. The Malcontent Cousin Ferinc was unlikely to have come.

Regardless of what Koscuisko felt about it, Ferinc had impressed

Stildyne as being genuinely—and passionately—invested in the welfare of Koscuisko's child. Also Koscuisko's wife, but Cousin Stanoczk had explained that men were expected to turn a blind eye to Malcontents in their households, or suffer the displeasure of the Saint.

"Surely not, sir," Stildyne said soothingly. "Ferinc's probably too busy." Or perhaps that wasn't so very helpful, after all. Fortunately the courier had docked and the ramp had descended, so Koscuisko didn't have time to consider how deeply he would elect to be offended at the reminder.

"You are as helpful and supportive as ever," Koscuisko noted sourly. "I should complain to Stoshi about you." Rather than the other way around, that was to say, clearly enough. "See if I do not. It is not to be enough that a man is to be hounded for his laps. There is no justice in the world, no charitable forbearance, no—"

Koscuisko's Cousin Stanoczk came down the ramp, and Koscuisko shut up. There were ways in which Koscuisko might be said to be afraid of his Malcontent cousin; Stildyne had often considered attempting to discover what the trick was, but there were more interesting questions to be asked.

Behind Cousin Stanoczk followed not another Malcontent—certainly not the Cousin Ferinc about whom Koscuisko was so exercised in spirit—but someone Stildyne recognized as being potentially even more controversial.

"Derush!" Cousin Stanoczk called happily, and quickened his pace down the ramp to trot up to Koscuisko where he stood and embrace him with an enthusiasm that was not notably reciprocated. "It is good to see you. And Chief Brachi Stildyne, yes, you are looking well." Cousin Stanoczk didn't offer to kiss him, at least not in public. Probably just as well. "You remember the Bench specialist, I expect?"

Following Cousin Stanoczk down the ramp and toward Koscuisko at a much more moderate pace, keeping his distance. A man of middling height—taller than Koscuisko, but that wasn't difficult—with an iron-gray moustache and clear blue eyes whose weariness was general to all life: Bench intelligence specialist Karol Aphon Vogel. Stildyne recognized him if Koscuisko did not, but Koscuisko apparently did.

"Specialist Vogel, yes." Koscuisko seemed at least as wary as he was surprised. "To what do we owe the honor? There are people who have been looking for you."

Vogel nodded very politely, all but bowed. Bench specialists were under no obligation to salute anybody, let alone mere Ship's Inquisitors. Vogel was a thoughtful man, however, polite, and the less he reminded people that he was a Bench specialist the more likely they might be to forget that he was uniquely dangerous, Stildyne supposed.

"You're holding evidence that I'd like to have a look at, your Excellency. Cousin Stanoczk was kind enough to offer me a lift."

Now Cousin Stanoczk took Koscuisko by the arm and turned him toward the airlock that gave access to the interior of the ship. The multi-chambered airlock was open, of course; it was only ever closed when the maintenance atmosphere had to be purged for periodic refresh. Cousin Stanoczk seemed very sure of where he was going, but why not? He was a Malcontent.

In light of the Malcontent's access to things Stildyne wouldn't be surprised, he reminded himself, if it turned out that the Saint had a cruiser-killer class warship just like the *Ragnarok* of his very own. People who could afford a Kospodar thula—so expensive a piece of machinery that even the Bench had been unable or unwilling to afford more than a few of them—were clearly capable of presenting all sorts of similar surprises.

"You would do well to secure your craft before you leave the area," Koscuisko grumbled. "I will not be held responsible. Wheatfields desires the thula. I hope you have brought war-hounds."

"Only the crew," Cousin Stanoczk assured Koscuisko in reply. "Nobody you know. Trust me on this."

He was lying. Stildyne was sure of it, lying, why didn't Koscuisko detect the smell of it immediately? Maybe Koscuisko just declined to notice, because Stanoczk was Malcontent and Koscuisko's socialization would not allow him to challenge the Malcontent on much of anything. Or maybe, just maybe, possibly, Koscuisko didn't see that. Hard to believe. But Koscuisko hadn't spent as much time watching people who looked a great deal like Cousin Stanoczk in terms of their size and build and habit of speech as Stildyne had, over the years since Koscuisko had been assigned to the *Ragnarok*.

He'd have to ask Cousin Stanoczk about it. Unlike Koscuisko, he had no problem challenging Malcontents on things. There were ways in which challenging specific Malcontents could be a lot of fun, in fact, though Stildyne didn't really think he should be thinking about that with Koscuisko and Cousin Stanoczk alike right in front of him. He waited respectfully until Vogel had followed the two of them before falling into place behind Vogel, instead.

There was only one piece of evidence in Koscuisko's custody that a Bench specialist was likely to be interested in. There was only one piece of evidence in Koscuisko's custody at all, just at present, if it came to that. A clerk of Court from Chilleau Judiciary had come to Chelatring Side, the ancestral fortress of Koscuisko's family, to draw Koscuisko into some sort of a trap; and had used a forged record as bait.

The clerk was dead.

Koscuisko had returned to the *Ragnarok*—after putting the longed-for freedom that First Secretary Verlaine had offered him on hold—because so long as the forged record existed the false evidence it contained had to be handled carefully, and the lawful custodian of any given record was an officer in possession of a Writ to Inquire.

Cousin Stanoczk would have been interested in how the forgery had been done as a matter of abstract principle. Bench specialist Ivers, who had been present at the exposure of the record's evidence as false, had been too deeply shocked at the implications of its very existence to have expressed much interest in the mechanics, at the time.

Vogel had gone missing out of Burkhayden months before all of that had happened, however. So what Vogel had to do with the evidence in Secured Medical was beyond Stildyne.

"For that you must to the captain speak," Koscuisko said over his shoulder to Vogel, as Cousin Stanoczk drew Koscuisko on.

When Vogel began to produce the appropriate rote response— something along the lines of "naturally nothing will be done without Brevet Captain ap Rhiannon's knowledge and consent," Stildyne expected—Koscuisko shook his head and cut him off.

"No, I mean that you must speak to her. The Engineer has crates of disposable vent-solvents stacked five tiers deep in Secured Medical, and I do not have the authority to order them moved."

True enough. When Koscuisko had returned to the *Ragnarok* his presence had been accepted only upon understanding of some rules and guidelines—some Koscuisko's, some ap Rhiannon's. Among those rules and guidelines had been Koscuisko's warning that he would execute the Protocols only on a strictly limited footing; and ap Rhiannon's answering requirement that Koscuisko would do nothing whatever in Secured Medical, which would be made over to the Ship's Engineer for a closet. There were things in Secured Medical to which Koscuisko alone had access, that went without saying. But to gain access to them he had to get past Wheatfields' crates.

"We are going to staff meeting, even now," Cousin Stanoczk assured Vogel. "My cousin would know, but he is not good about staff meetings. No doubt his captain will be speaking to him on a not very distant occasion about that fact—" perfectly fair, Stildyne knew, Koscuisko was a very unsatisfactory attender of staff meetings, but always had been, it was nothing specific to Jennet ap Rhiannon—"—but for now he evades censure because he is prompt to the mark, and with company. He is grateful to me for this. Is he not? Look you, Chief Stildyne, have you seen such a sincerely grateful scowl in all of your years?"

He wasn't seeing any such scowl right now, because Koscuisko had turned around. "Never," he admitted truthfully, wondering if it had been strictly necessary for Cousin Stanoczk to remark on "all" his years.

Cousin Stanoczk shook Koscuisko by the shoulder enthusiastically. "See? See? We are all in agreement, Derush. No, don't thank me." A request more likely to be honored than many of Cousin Stanoczk's, Stildyne expected. "Chief. I will come and see you later, if I may. I will tell you about staff meetings, and many other interesting things."

Yes, he'd just bet Cousin Stanoczk would. He'd been hoping for it. "I'll be waiting," he promised. "Your cousin owes me laps, though."

"Then I shall see to it that he is safely out of the way, and will not interrupt. I have letters for you, Derush. Also for your good Kerenko."

They were at the lift-nexus that would carry Koscuisko and his cousin and Vogel deep into the heart of the *Ragnarok*, to the officer's mess. To staff meeting.

The frown Koscuisko gave Stildyne as he turned around in the lift to face front was worth three month's pay for its combination of betrayal, resentment, and underlying amusement. Stildyne bowed to that frown, feeling very cheerful, and went away to his office to wait for Cousin Stanoczk to come and fill him in on all the gossip from Chelatring Side.

⊕ ⊕ ⊕

The officer's mess on the *Ragnarok* was actually a common-room of sorts. The chief warrant officers and shift supervisors took their meals here, and Ship's Primes and Command Branch; Andrej's department chiefs ate here as well—but below the Bar, which had always seemed unreasonable to Andrej. They were older than he was—or had been, in the earlier years of his Fleet duty—considerably more fully qualified for leadership by virtue of actual experience, and everybody knew that the only reason an edge-new surgeon from Mayon's colleges took pride of place was because Fleet granted special privileges to Inquisitors, one of which was rank.

Ship's Inquisitors with a decent sense of their own shortcomings sat quietly back and let senior officers run the section. Most of the people who elected to enter Fleet Orientation Station Medical to qualify for a Writ to Inquire were decidedly under-qualified, after all; medical students who could find anything else to do with their certifications, anything else at all, generally took other routes in preference to accepting rank in Fleet when rank came with particular responsibilities.

Andrej knew that as an honor graduate, a man with the generously bestowed praise of his teachers and the administration of the Mayon Medical Center, he was an exception to the rule of mediocrity in ship's surgeons. The fact had never afforded him much satisfaction. A patient had nothing less than an absolute right to expect the very best a surgeon could possibly manage to provide; no healing he was fortunate enough to effect through skill and education and the grace of the Holy Mother of all Aznir could balance out a single blow struck in cruelty, to punish or deter, in Secured Medical.

"No, we ask for all nine battle cannon," the artilleryman, Dierryk Rukota, was insisting, as Andrej reached the open doorway to the officer's mess. "All right, so we already have one in reserve. If we only ask for eight we only remind people that we've got one. That gun is contraband. We shouldn't be counting it."

One wall of the officer's mess could be covered with a plot-scan for schematics or strategic planning. Rukota stood there now, one hand to the wall, arguing with the captain; brevet or acting captain ap Rhiannon, a short woman with her hair done up with the pins that bore the rank-markers peculiar to crèche-bred, her shoulders squared, her arms akimbo, all points skeptical in her body language and her expression alike.

"Two says Emandis Station only has nine battle cannon. One full issue, so they can respond to replacement requests. If we ask for all nine they can decline to issue any. It would leave them without a cannon in reserve until they can get a new issue from Central Stores, and that could take months in this environment."

"Which is Emandis' problem and not yours, your Excellency, you are looking for your base load, any depot rated for full replenishment has a charter to be able to respond at any time, and if they only give us eight—if we asked for eight we'd get seven. Maximum. We put in for nine battle cannon, your Excellency."

Rukota had the rank-tags right in his speech, but there was not much to doubt in Andrej's mind that Rukota actually saw a junior officer in front of him. He had that issue himself, to a lesser extent. She had warned him—Stildyne as well: if he wanted back on board the *Ragnarok* on anything like a permanent basis he was going to have to accept her as his captain, not because she had earned it, but because that was the way it was. He was rather proud of the progress he'd made, but it was also true that she was not over-punctilious about her perquisites—sensitive to the limitations inherent in the situation.

Had it been as difficult for his clinic chiefs to call him "sir"? It could only have been more distasteful yet; ap Rhiannon was very young, but she was not a professional torturer.

Neither was he, any longer. He and ap Rhiannon had agreed. He would use a speak-serum if information was truly required; she would not direct him to return to Secured Medical, not ever. How was she going to react to this?

Stoshi coughed politely, apparently unhappy with the rate at which Andrej was proceeding to the introductions. The captain glanced over to where Andrej stood in the doorway, looked away again to the schematic on the wall—the *Ragnarok*'s armaments plan, how many of how heavy of what to be put where. She had no more turned back to the schematic than her head jerked back to stare at Andrej again, however. Andrej dared not smile.

"Please excuse my tardiness, your Excellency," Andrej said, and bowed to his superior officer. "I was meeting this disgusting person on the docks. He is called Cousin Stanoczk, a religious professional, a Malcontent. And yes. We are also in fact related in the same degree."

When they'd been children it had been a joke to play on people who didn't know them very well; from a suitable distance the fact that Stoshi's eyes were dark and Andrej's pale did not distinguish them immediately. There had been pranks. But Stoshi's voice had gotten deep and resonant, and Andrej was still tenor. There were other differences between them—but Andrej was not going to speculate on how well his good Chief of Security might have studied on what they were.

"Doctor." She sounded surprised; yes, he almost always found a good reason why he was not needed at staff meetings. "Cousin Stanoczk, Two warned us that you were coming. We're pleased to grant you the freedom of the ship. We're indebted to you for the previous use of your thula."

"Yours" in the general sense, of course; it wasn't Stoshi's thula, it was the Malcontent's thula. "You are very kind, your Excellency. The Saint is pleased to have been of service. I impose upon you now for a different purpose, however; to request a favor, which Specialist Vogel will explain."

Whether Vogel would remember ap Rhiannon was not something Andrej felt inclined to guess at. It seemed clear that ap Rhiannon remembered Vogel.

"This person was not on your passenger manifest," Two said accusingly, rustling her wings. She was standing in a chair at the table above the Captain's Bar, on the raised platform where only Ship's Primes and Command Branch were supposed to sit; bored, surely, Andrej imagined, because she couldn't see the schematic that the captain and Rukota were arguing over. Perhaps there was a tone-map of some sort there for the benefit of bats.

Andrej stepped into the room and to one side, to make way for Vogel. Vogel stopped on the threshold and bowed, very properly indeed, first to the captain and then to the other officers—Ship's First, the Engineer, Ship's Intelligence—gathered around the table on the platform. First Officer had stood up, Andrej noted.

"I'm very gratified to hear it, your Excellency," Vogel said to Two. "A person's got to have some secrets, after all." And Bench specialists didn't necessarily show up on anybody's manifest. "Captain ap

Rhiannon. I've come to request access to a piece of evidence that your Ship's Inquisitor is holding in Secured Medical. In order to pursue an investigation I'd like to examine the forged record that Koscuisko brought back here from Azanry when he returned from leave."

When he'd cut his home leave short and come back to the *Ragnarok*, Vogel meant. Or maybe not. Maybe Vogel didn't know the details. Why would Vogel care that Andrej had left his wife and child without even a good-bye, in order to bring evidence back to a ship which had somehow transformed itself into a dangerous mutineer in his absence?

Ap Rhiannon sat down at one of the tables that had been pushed back toward the front wall of the room to clear a space for close-up study of the schematic on the wall. "Interesting," she said. "Who says we have any such item on board? A forged record, you say. I'd expect a Bench specialist to be much more careful with his language."

Specialist Ivers had been anxious to keep its very existence as quiet as possible. It had been Mergau Noycannir, an old enemy and quite mad, who had brought it to Azanry—to Chelatring Side; Mergau Noycannir had been a clerk of Court at Chilleau Judiciary. The incident could have been used to discredit the Second Judge just when the Selection was due to be made. It was still a potential weapon, Andrej supposed, but more than that it was their best evidence that the alleged conspiracy to murder to previous captain of the *Ragnarok* was a frame of particularly shocking illegality.

The Record in concept was still the cornerstone of the Law, the impartial keeper of legally admissible, lawfully obtained evidence. If evidence that was not legally admissible or lawfully obtained could be put on record then the entire system that relied on evidence would lose its credibility.

"I understand your concern, your Excellency, and speak as bluntly as I do only because I believe myself to be in the company of people who are perfectly well aware that a Record has been compromised. Now I will share another piece of dangerous information with you, so that you'll understand why I'm here. I have evidence that the forged record that your chief medical officer brought here from Azanry is not the first such forged Judicial instrument. I believe in fact that at least one judicial warrant has been similarly improperly released."

A warrant? Or could it be *the* warrant, the one Vogel had given to him at Burkhayden before he'd left, the one with his name on it—an execution order that Vogel had claimed to have exercised against Fleet Captain Lowden of unlamented memory?

Not possible. Vogel couldn't be talking about that warrant. If he'd believed that warrant to have been forged he wouldn't have exercised it. If he hadn't exercised it, then Lowden had not been executed by Judicial decree. If Vogel hadn't killed Lowden someone else had. If Vogel hadn't been the person that the harried house-master at the service house had shown up to the suite that Lowden was occupying shortly before the murder had taken place, then it might even have been Andrej himself after all.

And he'd given that warrant to Stoshi, besides. But he'd asked Stoshi to investigate, and what would be more natural than for Stoshi to have called in a Bench specialist? Stoshi wouldn't have known the background. Andrej hadn't told him. How could he have told the Malcontent—"Stoshik, I have murdered my commanding officer because he tried to send an innocent man to torture. He did send an innocent man to torture. Vogel had come to Burkhayden to kill me, but he pretended it had been Lowden all along, because Vogel didn't like Lowden even more than Vogel doesn't care for me." No, impossible, clearly impossible.

Ap Rhiannon had no such insight to paralyze her. "If you say so, Specialist Vogel. What do you hope to gain by examination of the record?"

"It's taken time to analyze the warrant, your Excellency, but I believe I've isolated the forgery's fingerprints. There's a genuine authorization imbedded there, but in such a way that there had to have been collusion. I suspect that there's genuine evidence similarly imbedded in the forged record, and you may recall that all such authorization codes are specific to an individual or judicial center."

That was true. A Record was legal evidence in part because its contents were placed on record by a legal officer. Ship's Inquisitors served a dual function for that purpose.

Ap Rhiannon frowned. "Locate the code, find the origin? If I was forging a record I'd see to it that you couldn't track me, Bench specialist."

"Indications are that the forgery might not have been that carefully done, your Excellency. There are signs of an unskilled user. The Bench warrant would never have been examined after its exercise, had it not been for specific, suspicious circumstances. The record might have been built to accomplish only a specific, time-limited purpose, to be safely destroyed as soon as possible by the woman in whose possession it was at the time that the forgery was discovered. There's a risk. You'd like to know, though, as much as anybody, I'm certain of it."

The captain shook her head. "Not really. Koscuisko says the record is forged and I believe him, but that doesn't mean I want anything to do with it. Serge, can you get a path cleared through to Koscuisko's evidence locker?"

"I'll have to send my crew through decontamination afterward," Wheatfields said. "Give me three eights, your Excellency."

Ap Rhiannon nodded. "Done. General Rukota, please accompany the Bench specialist to Secured Medical to represent the interests of this Command. Doctor, every professional courtesy, and so on." She was speaking to him, now, so Andrej had to do his imitation of a man who had been paying close attention. "Specialist Vogel, it will be a few eights, and I don't care to have Bench specialists wandering around my ship without more of an idea about why they're here and what they're looking for. How does a ready-room in Security sound to you?"

Well, that was moderately rude; Vogel had told her why he was here and what he was looking for—but Andrej couldn't fault her for not being too ready to take Vogel's statements at face value.

Vogel bowed his head. "I'll be very comfortable, I'm sure, your Excellency. I'm told that the bean tea is much improved lately since the *Ragnarok* got restock at Silboomie Station. Thank you."

"Right. Very well, then." Ap Rhiannon shifted her gaze back to Dierryk Rukota, who had been standing there quietly with his back to the schematic on the wall, his arms folded. Perhaps coincidentally directly in front of some details on the *Ragnarok*'s combat readiness assessment, Andrej noticed. "We'll continue this later. First Officer. Let's review the munitions stores, shall we?"

Rukota bowed to ap Rhiannon and came forward for Vogel, not quite putting an arm around Vogel's shoulders but something close to it. "Ready room it is," Rukota said cheerfully. "Do you play cards?"

Stoshi tapped Andrej on the shoulder and jerked his head toward the corridor behind them. Oh, Andrej supposed Stoshi was right; they were dismissed. Wheatfields would be looking for him at his duty station. It was mid-shift. He had documentation to review, always documentation to review, and he wanted to make an appointment to consult with his Chief of Psychiatric, Doctor Farilk, on a personal issue.

Andrej made his salute to his captain, who nodded crisply in return. Stoshi had him by the arm; Wheatfields was staring. No. He was not even going to begin to travel in *that* field.

Still and all, and quite apart from the aggravation that Stoshi could represent, they were related and had been much together as children and he was fond of his cousin. When they reached his office—Andrej willfully ignoring the stares they got as they went past, what, had these people never seen a Malcontent before?—Andrej and went to the rhyti-brewer, to draw the both of them a flask.

"You travel with Bench specialists in these days?" he asked, just to open the conversation. "The Saint keeps strange bedfellows."

Stoshi accepted the flask that Andrej offered him with a cheerful grin. "Else would not be the Saint, Derush, may he wander in bliss. The first thing that a person discovers in search of the truth behind an article was that there was an unhappy man who had left himself in Gonebeyond to research a similar problem. It is always good to use someone else's resources, Drushik. The Saint approves. It leaves much more money to buy drink."

It did make sense. Vogel had been unhappy about the Warrant; that was why Vogel had not exercised it against its named intended, Andrej Ulexeievitch Koscuisko. If he thought about it he wouldn't expect a Bench specialist to simply let such a question drop; and it had been Vogel, after all, who had suggested that Andrej enlist the assistance of the Malcontent.

The record had come from Mergau Noycannir, Chilleau Judiciary. Vogel wouldn't have known exactly where the Warrant had come from—that was held in confidence to minimize reprisals after the fact—but the obvious truth was that the simplest explanation for its existence led back to Noycannir. How had she obtained it? How had she forged the record? Andrej had not attempted to examine the record himself; he was not a forensic specialist.

"How are things at home, then, if you have brought me news?"

He didn't want to go to his desk. There was documentation there.

Work that he had to do, and meant to be neglecting, in the next several days—once they arrived at Emandis Station. He led the way to the two-chair conference area at the back of his office, instead, invoking the privacy field on his way. No one would think twice about it, and they were more than welcome to sneak by his open door and stare; a man couldn't conspire with his door open, could he? They didn't see many Dolgorukij in Fleet. At least not on the *Ragnarok*, whose population had been more stable in recent years than was the Fleet norm because of the fact that people posted to the *Ragnarok* very frequently had absolutely nowhere else to go.

"I have brought letters, Derush," Stoshi said. In his courier-pouch, in fact, that he was wearing over his shoulder, and which he unlimbered as he spoke before he sat down. "And words about the melon-harvest, but that will wait. You are to be stuck with me for several days now, after all. What does one do on board of a warship for a party?"

"One assigns oneself extra laps, Stoshik, and takes a cold shower." Parties. On the *Ragnarok*. The very idea. Yes, he'd had a going-away party as he was leaving for his visit home—ultimately cut short; the visit, not the party, which had been going strong when he'd left it. "We are all sober and hard-working and abstemious here and have no recreation to offer Malcontents."

Oh, as soon as Andrej said it he wished that he had not. Hastening to continue before Stoshi could make an impertinent remark about one's Chief of Security, Andrej grasped at the thought uppermost in his mind and voiced it with a sort of desperation. "What is it that you have been doing, to find the Bench specialist? Dame Ivers would very much like news of her companion."

Stoshi shook his head. "I am prevented by my promise to Karol Aphon, Derush, who feels that it is up to him decide when he is ready to return from Gonebeyond space. Where he's been courting the Flag Captain, the Walton Agenis, and I'm fond of the man who has been married to her niece even if he is a Sarvaw born and bred. No. I've been to Rudistal, and borrowed some resources from the Church there that you might remember if I asked you for a pocket-handkerchief that had no hole in it."

As references went this was one of Stoshi's more obscure, but whether by premeditation or accident it hit on things that had been very much on Andrej's mind recently since his work with Dawson's people down on Connaught Station. Handkerchief. Kaydence, one of the bond-involuntaries who had been with Andrej at Rudistal, a man granted revocation of Bond for his role in saving the *Scylla* during the battle over Eild. The nun at Rudistal that Andrej had hired out of the service house and installed to pray for Joslire's spirit; Kaydence had taken up with her, with Ailynn, Kaydence who had so frequently been on Chief Warrant Officer Caleigh Samon's disgraced list for a worn spot in his boot-stocking or failure to produce a clean, mended white-square. So that was it.

"Dangerous avenue for investigation, surely." Kaydence had been Bonded for incautious play in security systems; it was something he apparently found very difficult to control, his passion for getting into computing systems that were none of his business just to see what might be there. Andrej had invoked those skills at the Domitt Prison to discover the horrifying truth about how Administrator Geltoi had been stoking his furnaces all of that time to save on fuel.

Now Kaydence was a man reborn, a privileged citizen of the Bench exempted by the Bench instruction from most taxes and legally immune to many forms of punishment for petty civil transgressions; but warrants were Bench instruments, and if Kaydence was investigating that meant that he would necessarily be at play in Bench judicial systems, and how could he risk it? How could Stoshi permit such reckless behavior?

"I have my own resources dedicated to special areas of the hunt, Derush, do not become concerned. We would not endanger either the person at Rudistal or the one with whom he consorts. No, we rely on that person for advice and strategy. Technique. In order to ensure that the Saint may not be associated with the smuggling of Nurail, which is none of the Saint's business."

Andrej closed his eyes with a grimace of pain. Oh, Kaydence. A grown man, and one who had survived horrors that Andrej could not even imagine—though he had been responsible for several—and involved with the smuggling of persons out of Bench control? Nurail refugees, escaping to Gonebeyond.

Joslire would be proud to have his name associated with such an enterprise. And that of course led Andrej back very naturally to his concern, in seeing Stoshi, the reason Stoshi had come, the thing that

Andrej needed Stoshi for. "That cannot be condoned. To attempt to cheat the Bench of the lawfully adjudicated punishment that a man has earned by his own crimes? It cannot be tolerated."

Stoshi nodded enthusiastically. "Indeed not, Drushik." *But it can be arranged.* Andrej was counting on Stoshi to have done just that. "And desperate men are no respecters of property, either, not chattel or goods or transport, whether in Chambers or the city or in Church." Or somewhere close to the memorial barrow where Joslire's ashes had been laid to rest, where his tablet was to be found. Andrej meant to visit Joslire's tablet, if there was one.

"You know how it is sometimes, Derush," Stoshi continued. "A man knows that he should not say thus and such a word, because it will inspire an idea that might not have occurred otherwise to a person of weak character. It would be best if you held this carefully in mind, because it may be that there is a Khabardi small-freighter that must stop over near the city of Jeltaria, and you would not be the man to introduce the concept of wrong-doing to one who is only his assigned duty currently performing."

So Stoshi had done as Andrej had asked him. There would be a ship, loaded, fueled, waiting, with a pre-approved exit trajectory through the dar-Nevan vector for a perfectly innocuous destination that it would never reach. All that was left now for Andrej to do was to explain to his gentlemen and wave good-bye as they left, because it was not to be imagined that a man once freed of his governor would wait meekly for the day when he would be enslaved again in so horrible a fashion.

"You have not answered my question." He couldn't keep the gratitude out of his voice; but he would wait, to weep, until his gentles were gone from him. "At home. My son. Marana. Tell me how it goes."

Leaning forward Stoshi reached for his courier-pack and opened it. "Letters, Derush. Your parents. House-masters' reports. Here is the one that you want, though, I think."

Yes. A heavy square of thick white paper folded very carefully by a young person, its face inscribed with a deliberate hand whose hesitation of line, and the thickness of it, spoke of a young lord with a large stylus being as careful as he could manage with the dangerously wet ink. *To my lord father, Andrej Ulexeievitch Koscuisko, of our family prince and heir.*

He'd had letters from Anton from time to time in the past, but seeing this one had quite a different impact on Andrej than they had before. It was so formal. And now that he had met the child his longing to have him in his arms right here, right now, was almost too heart-piercing to be borne.

"Also, these." Stoshi had not ceased to draw letters out of his bag. "The lady sends to you, Derush. I do not know if she speaks here of Ferinc, but he has never in all of the years that I have known him been so close to happy. I am grateful to you for this, because I have become very fond of him, though he is not of the Blood."

No, Cousin Ferinc was not of the Blood. Cousin Ferinc was Stoshi's pet animal, and pets were not evaluated according to their pedigree. The issue was a sore one with Andrej; he had known Cousin Ferinc by another name before the man had fled to the protection of the Malcontent, the only off-worlder—in Andrej's knowledge—to have been granted the protection of the Saint. It was because of his own fault, his crime against the man. And yet to return home and find a criminal—one whose crimes were so sordid, whose punishment had been more sordid still—so closely associated with his own now-wife Marana, and loved so tenderly by his own son . . .

"In all of that time believing that I had duty, Stoshik," Andrej said. "I was losing something that I did not even understand. Day by day. It is not only my honor and my sleep that Fleet has cost me. My son's life, Stoshik, my son, and thy Ferinc has been a better father to him than I will ever be, forever after."

"And yet what do you imagine would have been different if you had been at home, Derush? Thick-headed. Your father would have married you to that Ichogatra princess, and the respected lady Marana would have been separate from you until you'd bred a boy to your princess wife regardless. And also there would not have been Ferinc, for whom you have finally done what I have sought to do and failed all of these years, Andrej, and freed him from himself at last."

Tapping Anton's letter against the fingertips of his right hand with an abstracted sort of confusion Andrej tested Stoshi's claim against his own knowledge of his birth-culture for some flaw, and was unable to find one. The failure gave him no comfort. He looked down at Anton's letter, seeking understanding, but just looking at it made Andrej want to weep for all the time he could have had, had he but realized much sooner that he had no one to blame for the stubbornness that had kept him at his post except himself. Oh, and perhaps the fact that it was treason in the first degree for a man who held the Writ to Inquire to quit his post—but even that perhaps could have been gotten 'round.

"'Yes, good, thank you, Andrej, my special charge in the name of the Saint is now much happier keeping warm the bed of your wife, and loving your son.'" Andrej couldn't keep a species of savagery out of his voice, though he could see the humor. And Stanoczk, shameless and heartless alike, actually laughed, and leaned back in his chair to sup his rhyti.

"Yes, and shows that there is a wolf I had not suspected after all who bares his teeth at your family and sets them all at bay. It is impressive. He could not fight for Marana and your child any more ferociously if they *were* his, Drushik, and not on loan."

Oh, this was intolerable. "And this is comforting to me?" Andrej demanded. "What sort of new challenge do I face when I can go home, Stanoczk, a duel for the affections of my own Marana? There is strange comfort in this missionary work."

Closing one eye to obtain a better focus Stoshi peered into the depths of his rhyti-flask, and clearly found it wanting in its emptiness. But Stoshi was clever, and accustomed to doing for himself; rose to his feet and started across the room toward the rhyti-brewer.

"I can't speak for your lady-wife, Derush," he said with his back turned to Andrej, drawing a fresh flask. "But you need have no fear for the place you have in Anton's heart. He adores you like a saint under Canopy. Surely it is just as well, if you can't say when you will go home. You know that your family has much of an adjustment to accomplish. Marana needs a wolf."

He didn't want the place of a saint under Canopy in Anton's heart. He wanted Ferinc's place. It should be his, to be the wolf to protect his wife and child. How could he call himself a man, and let another do it?

"What else have you for me?" Andrej asked, putting away his morose self-pity for the time being. Malcontents had no patience with self-pity. If there was anybody in this room with genuine cause to feel sorry for himself surely it was his cousin Stanoczk, condemned to choose between a life of fear and lies on the one hand and the total loss of family, property, rights as a citizen, even title to his own person on the other, and all because he had been born both Dolgorukij and a man who desired the caresses of other men.

For that Stoshi had elected the Malcontent and a life as a slave, albeit a peculiarly privileged one, rather than attempt to deny his own nature which the Holy Mother herself had decreed for him at the moment of his soul's rebirth; and there were so many other places where he could have been born instead, in which a man's choice of a partner to love and cherish was not restricted to the opposite sex.

"Oh, this? This is for your Kerenko, Derush, Anton has written to him about the sparrows. Something about the sparrows in the gutter outside of his bed-room. I will go and find him and deliver it myself, I have promised very solemnly."

A much thinner letter, to be sure, and the same thick childish hand—but with much more assurance in the lettering. *Right trusty and well beloved*. It was a formula that had been ancient when the Blood had come to Azanry from wherever it was that they had come from. Andrej didn't know which of the theories about that he preferred, but he didn't mean to be distracted from the point that this raised.

"He is a dutiful child." The highest praise a parent could bestow: dutiful. Filial. But Anton was so much more, and duty was so trivial a thing beside loyalty and love. "Also very charitable, to remember Lek. It gives me hope for the day when he comes to understand exactly what I am. My family—they mustn't be allowed to spoil that."

It hadn't mattered to him so much before he'd met his child. So long as his son was an abstraction in his mind, a stranger with a limited vocabulary and no learning to speak of, the knowledge that some day his child would understand the shameful truth behind the spectacular acts of cruelty attributed to Andrej's name had been one that had troubled him only on an abstract level.

He had lost perspective. He had met Anton. If he was a lucky man he would be dead before he had to face the horror in his child's face, and try to condense an answer to the inevitable "How?" out of the fog of blood that filled his brain.

"You will go home, Andrej, and protect him yourself. What does it matter, in the end, who is to be First Judge? There will be famine in Supicor if we cannot reach them with grain, but they are not

Dolgorukij in Supicor, so do we honestly so much care?" Yes, he did, but Andrej knew what point Stanoczk was making. "What may happen on Sarvaw should the selection pend for very much longer, though, I cannot say. And that reminds me."

Stoshi bowed over the table to pass the flask of rhyti to Andrej, as if it was the most gracious gesture under Canopy to give a man a flask of his own rhyti—in a glass to which some forward Malcontent had already pressed his notoriously filthy mouth, and where *that* had been recently, Andrej did not wish to so much as speculate—when he had not finished the entirely adequate flask he had himself started out with.

"I will carry this away to your Kerenko, and see how you have exercised your good lordship since you have returned. And then I shall have a word to say to thy Stildyne. You will find me on the thula when you want me, Derush, so long as you do not finish your letters within the next six to eight hours."

Your Kerenko, but *thy* Stildyne. The variance in intimacy was all too telling. "I wish you good hunting," Andrej said, a little sourly. Surely it was in poor taste for Stoshi to flaunt his religious duty in Andrej's face in this manner. But that was part of the privilege of the Malcontent, after all, no one expected any good of such depraved souls—which only made Anton's fondness for Ferinc all the more galling. Andrej knew how depraved a soul Ferinc had been, once upon a time. And for any crime Ferinc had done there were worse crimes to be laid against Andrej's own account, and so many of them.

"Stoshik, I—"

He didn't want to go back out to Secured Medical. They would expect him to wish to avoid it; all except Wheatfields, perhaps. Of all the people on board it was the Ship's Engineer who was most likely to guess at Andrej's secret. It would not surprise Wheatfields if he guessed. It would not surprise Andrej either.

"It is only Stanoczk, Derush, not Stoshik-eye." But Stoshi had stopped, halfway across the room, and very conveniently still within the privacy barrier, too. A Malcontent was shameless, but discreet. "What is it that you say to me? Bearing in mind that you and I can talk, but later, because I have my rounds to do."

Andrej would not go to Secured Medical alone. He was not even permitted to do that; so he was proof against the trouble of his own spirit. If he attempted to creep back into that place at some odd moment, he would be discovered. And then he would be expected to explain.

"It does not import. Go on about your disgusting Saint's disgusting business, Stoshi." He tried to lighten his tone. Stoshi would not be fooled; but Stoshi would respect Andrej's desire to talk about it later. Stoshi waved and was gone, trotting briskly out into the corridor with the letter Anton had written to Kerenko in his hand. One of the Security that had accompanied them from the docking bay to the staff meeting and thence back to this office would be jogging after Stoshi, trying to keep up. Should he check in with Engineering, and see how things went? Should he perhaps seek out Brachi Stildyne?

No. Stildyne would have other things on his mind. And perhaps he didn't even really want someone who knew him as well as Stildyne did to be there when he went back to Secured Medical for the first time since he'd placed that record into evidence.

The first time while he was awake, at any rate. He had been to Secured Medical in his dreams, and that was no particular innovation; it was the emotion that accompanied the visits that had changed. Regret, but not for what he had done; for the fact that it was over. He missed it. He knew exactly what had been on that man Birrin's mind. He missed the overwhelming passion and the savage joy, transcendent pleasure that was so much more than merely sexual.

It was humorous. It was a good joke. He had taken secondary honors in psychopharmacology. He was supposed to understand the mechanics of addiction, physical and psychological. Why hadn't he, of all people, realized that a man could not take in so powerful a drug as mastery for all those years, and not feel its lack keenly when it was no longer available to him?

There would be good to come of this, surely. Some year perhaps Farilk or some other qualified psychiatric doctor would write about the combination of hormones or the brain chemistry that made torture so irresistible a drug for flawed souls like his. It would assist in the diagnosis and treatment of sociopathology and the criminally insane, perhaps.

Only just for now and even in the midst of so many so much more important things Andrej was suffering withdrawal from the habit of the past eight years, and did not know how he was to live through it without bringing shame on himself and everyone around him.

CHAPTER FIVE

Brisinje

The ground-car and its escort had loaded, left. Shona Ise-I'let sat at his station in the wheelhouse of his courier, waiting; where was his refuel, where was his atmosphere refresh, his ground crew?

The landing management people had completed their checklist and gone. Yes, the courier had landed. Yes, the engines were safe to hot-fire. Yes, he had sustained no thermal damage, at least none that mattered to any of the standard diagnostics. He'd be happy when he got home and had Emandis diagnostics; they were much more thorough. Fleet said unnecessarily so, but it wasn't Fleet's courier. Fleet just borrowed it from time to time. He'd been at Chilleau. He'd wanted to get back to his home Judiciary anyway. It didn't bother him to ferry a Bench specialist on his way. He'd ferried Bench specialists before. Interesting people.

The ship grew quiet, though he knew that the three other crew the courier carried were busy at their own preflight tasks. He couldn't start his pre-flights until the additions-and-amendments had been run. He could make it to Emandis Station with the atmosphere he was carrying, he'd taken on atmosphere fresh at Chilleau and he had oxygen generators on board; but it was imprudent to make a practice of it, and the port authority wouldn't clear him for departure until he could certify that life support had been independently audited and passed—since he was using a civilian launch-field. It was a very pretty little launch-field. There were red flowers. He wanted out.

He toggled into braid and waited for the port authority to notice that they had a courier to clear for immediate departure. "Launch control, may I have a ground crew, please? Need to be getting on."

"Be right with you, courier, on pending."

Leaning back in his clamshell Shona stretched his legs and looked up through the wheelhouse's view-ports at the sky. Beautiful evening. All of the smoke and haze in the upper atmosphere caught and refracted the sunlight.

Shadows lengthened. Sighing, Shona keyed his transmit. "Need a ground crew, please, launch control. Required to return to my station upon completion of courier duty."

Things had quieted down in launch control, to judge by the swiftness with which the response came. "Sorry, courier, didn't mean to make you wait. Just finding the overnights. We've got you nice billets, though, to make up for the delay."

Worried, Shona took a moment to phrase his next words carefully. "Not a problem, launch control, but we're not billeting. If I could just get a ground crew, please. I'm due at Emandis Station in two days."

It was two days between Brisinje proper and Emandis Station. The *Ragnarok* was there. The last he'd heard from friends in Stores and Issues had been that the resupply was being pulled for 7.7.1 by the Standard calendar, and that was today. Load out would take seven days at the absolute most; the *Ragnarok* would be leaving Emandis Station in seven days. He had to be there before that happened. He had promised himself. He had promised his brother, on the hillside.

"I'm sorry, courier. Unable to oblige at this time. We're down to three ground crews and they're all working priority. Is there someone at Home Defense that we need to clear you with?"

No. His superiors knew that a courier's schedule was irregular, that Shona couldn't always say exactly where they'd been or how long they'd been there or what they'd been doing. The Bench specialist at Brisinje preferred to use home defense fleet couriers for exactly that reason, because they were more independent—had more autonomy, offered more flexibility, than the Jurisdiction Fleet. His need to get back to Emandis Station was strictly personal. The crew was overdue for stand-down, yes, but they could do that here just as well as anywhere else.

The one thing they could not do at Imennou or Brisinje was watch the great curved hull of the *Ragnarok* maneuver into close orbit and hold for resupply, and watch its personnel come off for personal time, and wait and wait and wait until they saw the one man Shona had to see. Koscuisko. Andrej Koscuisko. Ship's surgeon, Ship's Inquisitor, the man who had taken Joslire's life. To do that Shona had to be at Emandis Station.

"Thank you, launch control, not necessary." If there were only three ground crews available, and they were on priority already . . . "Do you have a projected for us? Really very anxious to get back."

"Sorry again, courier, could be a week. There are cargoes pending with pharmaceuticals and no place big enough to handle the booster but one at a time unless you haul all the way to Pilos. Which we're doing."

A week. Two days from here to Emandis Station; if he didn't get away from here inside of four days he might never see the *Ragnarok* again, and what would his brother's spirit have to say to him then— to have had the chance to put out his hand to Joslire's killer, and failed to meet Koscuisko face to face?

"Understood, launch control." None of it mattered to anybody else, except perhaps his crew. And they could no more create a ground crew out of dust and twigs than he could. Joslire had been his brother and Koscuisko carried five-knives, but pharmaceutical shipments had to be given the priority, because honor and obligation could only ever be placed ahead of one's own life, not that of uninvolved and unknowing parties. "Will go on whatever you can get us. Thanks for your help. Maybe we can lend a hand with scheduling."

They'd cross-trained in dispatch and maintenance, of course—it was the logical extension of the tradition of their cultural heritage. No one was privileged to enjoy glamour and glory who did not also put in his time on supply and transport. There were no elites among Emandisan: except for knife-fighters, and they were different.

"We could really use some extra bodies if you can manage. Thanks. We'll get you off as quickly as we can."

Keeping busy might not get them off any more quickly, but at least they'd be doing something positive to contribute to recovery from the problems created by whomever had vandalized the launch-fields at Brisinje proper. Shona didn't know who, if anyone, had taken credit, and he didn't care; he didn't know anybody who did. Vandalism never made a point, unless it was about the cowardice and stupidity of the sort of people who engaged in it.

"We'll report soonest, launch control. Courier out."

All right. He was stuck here. As was the rest of his crew, but none of them had a dead brother on the hillside with things to say to the man who was carrying his knives. He'd keep busy, he wouldn't brood about it, and he'd just have to trust in his luck and his brother's honor to see him through to the day when he could stand face to face with the man who had killed his brother, and restored honor to his family.

By the time Jils shook herself awake the ground car was tracking through the traffic of an obviously prosperous business district. The deep public walkways with their generous plantings and welcoming benches were only sparsely populated, however, and there seemed to be more rubbish in the street than could be indicative of a well-ordered city in control of its own destiny. A subtle black smut hung over it all, the soot collecting from the air to smear the sides of the white buildings like a sort of a nightmare-ivy.

"Arik hates to come through the city any more," Padrake said, looking past her through the window on her side of the car. "He's taking it personally. I have to admit I hate to see it myself."

He couldn't be talking only about the burning launch-fields, clearly. But Jils had seen similar signs of civil unrest at Chilleau Judiciary: people not quite comfortable in public; evidence of increasing carelessness, apathy, on the part of a city's custodians.

"Who's Arik?" she asked, curious, because the sound in Padrake's warm clear voice was one of confidence and sympathy. A friend? A lover?

Padrake smiled a little and settled his shoulders against the padded back of his shell, staring straight ahead now at the schematic display that told them where the ground car was relative to his goal. "Oh. Tirom. Arik Tirom, Jils, the First Secretary. A man of intense conviction. You'll meet him soon."

And Padrake was on a first-name basis with him? Interesting. "How long have you been at Brisinje, then, Padrake?"

Tilting his head to one side Padrake half-turned to face her again with a quirky expression on his face that sank straight into her stomach, and warmed her there. "Oh, don't worry, Jils. You'll meet him." This was repetitive, but Padrake seemed convinced that it answered all questions. "No harm to it, he's just a personable sort. And there's no reason to be rude. Two years."

Two years what? Oh. Two years at Brisinje. She wondered what he'd been doing before then, but it wasn't the sort of question Bench specialists asked each other—or answered.

The car turned away from the business area of the city, through long empty stretches of ground transport lanes toward a cluster of buildings whose white brilliance—besmirched with soot and ash—made them look unutterably tawdry in the setting sun. The smoke of the Brisinje launch-fields was behind them; so the river was on the other side. Chambers, Jils supposed. The car cleared security and slowed to trundle through the beautiful well-kept grounds of Brisinje's administrative center; here was no sign of unrest or violence, but Jils knew that it took security to keep it that way.

She walked side by side with Padrake from the motor stables up through floors of office space into the upper levels of the administrative center. Padrake had changed; he was different, and Jils couldn't quite put her finger on it. Yes, it had been years since she'd seen him; but there was something odd in his manner itself: he was cheerful, pleasant, engaging, pointing out things and people, beguiling her with conversation.

As they neared what had to be the First Secretary's office complex Jils finally realized what was wrong with Padrake. He seemed to be at peace with himself and the world; that wasn't like Padrake. What had happened to him?

She'd seen enough of Chambers to be able to tell what was what; they were in the heart of the administration. People knew Padrake, and looked at her with calm polite interest; what had Padrake told them about her? Nobody seemed to have a question of murder at the back of their mind, and after weeks of living with the unexpressed suspicion at Chilleau the relief was as significant as it was unexpected.

"Here we are," Padrake said, and leaned into a door to push it to one side. Padrake's office, and in the middle of Brisinje's administrative complex, in the heart of Chambers. This was interesting. Emphatically unusual. Was he so comfortable here that he no longer cared what it looked like to be so close to the judicial offices, to occupy space like a member of the administration?

It was a nice office. Jils set her kit bag down beside a gracefully curved and elegantly padded Kartmanns chair, looking around. A large window with a restful view of an apparently extensive botanical gardens; a beautiful desk, clear, glossy, all but entirely innocent of anything that looked like it might represent actual work. Still Padrake had said that they were to go into isolation together; that might explain it, he'd cleared off his desk, and what he hadn't cleared off he'd secured appropriately. Padrake had always been a meticulous man, careful, precise. Tidy.

She sat down. "You have a briefing for me?"

He'd said so. Circling around to behind his desk he drew a flat-file docket out of one of its slots and held it out to her, keying a toggle-switch at the same time.

"Delleroy here, Specialist Ivers just arrived. Can I get in?" The transmit was on directional, so much was obvious; Jils didn't hear the response, but Padrake nodded. "Thanks, we'll be right there. Jils. Let's go meet the First Secretary. He's been anxious for your arrival, as have I."

All right. Jils closed the docket with a shrug; Padrake clearly had things on his mind, and he could be difficult to stop or stay when he had his Jetorix up. A man of immense and persuasive determination, Padrake Delleroy, and the years that had silvered those several strands in amongst his beautiful mane of black hair had not apparently made any appreciable dent in his momentum.

Just five doors down to the inner office. Padrake was expected, the doors stood open for them, the Security post bowing them through past the clerks' stations into the First Secretary's office. It was bigger than Padrake's, and the view was of the river; Jils saw the First Secretary at Brisinje Judiciary—Arik Tirom—look up from the view-screen on his desk as Padrake opened the door into the office and invited Jils to precede him into the room with a sweeping shooing gesture of his free hand.

The First Secretary was a man of medium height but significant shoulder, whose broad high forehead and long heavy braid of stunningly black hair indicated that the brown-ivory color of his skin was that of a Manicha hominid, class one. Meeting Jils' eyes, Tirom stood up quickly and nodded his head in a polite greeting; "Specialist Ivers," Tirom said. "I've heard so much about you."

And that could go in several different directions, too, Jils thought. She stopped when she was two paces shy of the front of Tirom's beautifully polished sand-grass veneer desk, and bowed. "I'll admit to any good things, but for most of what you'll have heard I'll plead duty to the rule of Law, First Secretary. Pleased to make your acquaintance."

Padrake had closed the door behind them, and now he came to join Jils at the desk. Tirom had not sat back down. "Specialist Ivers is just now in, First Secretary, redirected through Imennou. I've taken the liberty of having a beverage service sent up."

She hadn't planned on sitting down and having a talk just this minute. She'd had a long transit; she'd gotten an unexpected and ambiguous message from Karol Vogel, and the First Secretary was saying something so she had better pay attention.

"Thanks, Padrake, I could use a break. If you'd care to sit down, Specialist Ivers?"

It was her practice to be polite to senior administrative officials, unless they had given her specific reason not to be. It only surprised them more when one had to pull rank on them—rank that technically did not exist, but rank that was hers as a representative of the entire Bench and which therefore over-ruled that of any one single Jurisdiction's administration. The moment of surprise between realization that someone had just said "no" and the reaction was frequently the moment at which the entire carriage of an investigation depended, and Jils had been glad of it on more than one occasion.

"Very kind, First Secretary. Thank you." Right now she was the one who was a little stupefied with a combination of stress and fatigue. The arrival of the beverage service saved her from the immediate embarrassment of having to say anything intelligent right then, so that by the time kilpers had been handed all around and the trays of crisp snack cakes and fruit had been passed, and everybody had settled back in the cushiony embrace of the very comfortable chairs in Tirom's conversation area, she was ready to engage.

"Padrake hasn't briefed me yet on the status of the convocation," Jils noted, politely. That was a little unfair, perhaps—she'd been asleep, after all—but true. "Am I the last to arrive, First Secretary?"

Tirom nodded with an air of understanding more than had been said. "Old friends with a lot of catching up to do," he said, and finished off a slice of fragrant golden-fleshed melon with evident relish. "I quite understand. And you'll have plenty of time to get your feet under you, Specialist Ivers, you're not in one of the chairs until the preliminaries have been completed."

Preliminaries. Bench against Bench against Bench, one-on-one, and then winner against winner, Supicor against Dasidar and Dasidar against Haspirzak and Supicor against Haspirzak and so forth—and at the end of it all, only then, Chilleau against Fontailloe against the strongest other candidate on the Bench, for one final contest to decide the Selection based on the finest macro-analyses the Bench could offer.

"I've been following a little of the developments. But not very clearly." Much of what was going on was behind the scenes and not accessible even at Bench offices to people without a specific need to know. There was probably more that the Second Judge had simply not bothered to share with her. Jils knew that the Judge had been hoping that Karol Vogel would turn up and spare her the necessity of sending Jils to Convocation. And Karol should have turned up. It was hard for Jils to understand what could have been important enough to keep Karol away from Chilleau at this crisis point in the Bench's history.

Unless it was Karol who had assassinated the First Secretary, that was, of course. If he had it was not with the Second Judge's knowledge or consent—that went without saying. And her mind was wandering again. This was not good. She needed some time to stand down, to clear her mind and concentrate on what she was going to do. She had to forget all about Verlaine's murder just for now. She would have enough on her task list without worrying at old problems, except to rest her mind from Convocation issues.

"You're to become more familiar than you'd really care to be with the arguments, I'm afraid, Specialist Ivers."

She was glad that he didn't try to call her Jils. "Yes, First Secretary, quite so. Do you have a personal opinion you would care to share, though?"

Padrake set his flask down on the table with a decided gesture, pinching his upper lip with his thumb and forefinger as though to clean some moisture from his mouth. "*I* certainly do," he said. "My personal opinion is that Brisinje should take it."

Tirom just grinned at her, rolling his eyes at Jils as if to say that this was an old quarrel that she was not to take seriously. Of course

Padrake would speak for Brisinje. That would be his role exactly: to speak for Brisinje, but Padrake had to know that Brisinje was not in serious contention, though it would be as carefully represented as any of the others. Brisinje was the newest Judiciary, with the least powerful and influential set of historically-developed alliances and relationships with other Benches.

That was precisely why Brisinje had been selected as the best place to hold the convocation: it was as close to neutral territory as any place under Jurisdiction. For a more unaligned location they would have to go out into Gonebeyond space, which was clearly impossible.

Tirom opened his mouth to joke back at Padrake, but before he could speak there was a sound at the alert on his desk.

"Fleet Captain Irshah Parmin, Jurisdiction Fleet Ship *Scylla*. Ready to proceed with detachment to Emandis Station for resupply, First Secretary."

It was a woman's voice, and Jils knew that Irshah Parmin wasn't a woman, though she'd never met the man in person. But it wouldn't actually be the Fleet Captain calling, but his First Officer on his behalf. *Scylla* did in fact have a female First Officer—Saligrep Linelly, a woman due for her first command, but who had made no move to demand one, apparently comfortable where she was and willing to lay low until the environment had become more settled once again.

There were plenty of excellent First Officers in Fleet who didn't want to transition to Command. They tended to be the best, as a matter of fact—people who knew that they would never do another job better than the one they were doing right now, or people whose political intransigence, whose personal integrity, had marked them as people who would decline to execute orders to which they took exception.

There were captains like that, too, and the Bench had sought to address the problem of Command Branch officers who insisted on thinking for themselves by raising up its own. Crèche-bred Command Branch, children culled from the ranks of orphans to be brought up with the most thorough indoctrination the Bench could design to do as they were told to preserve the rule of Law and the Judicial order.

It was a good theory. But in practice it had been too successful, producing either mindless martinets or signal failures like Jennet ap Rhiannon, the brevet—acting—captain of the Jurisdiction Fleet Ship *Ragnarok*.

Tirom frowned, as if he was trying to remember something; started to shift to stand up and go to the desk—to look for a reference, perhaps—but apparently thought better of it, and relaxed back into his chair again.

"Thank you, *Scylla*," Tirom said. "Have a good transit. See you when you get back, Tirom away, here."

That was the communication center's cue to cut the transmission and return the First Secretary's office to private status, off monitor. "*Scylla* away," the *Scylla*'s First Officer said, and the clear-tone clicked through. Still Tirom frowned.

"There was something about that," he said, mostly to Padrake. "I can't bring it to mind right now. Can't have been very important. I hope."

"Not as if you've got any worries about those people," Padrake agreed. "Not like the other places."

Tirom nodded, and spoke to Jils. "They've been our Fleet assigned resources for three years, now, Specialist Ivers. Sixth Fleet detached at Brisinje. Very formal relationship, but no inappropriate pressure. Not like what's going on at some of the other Judiciaries right now."

"You'd like a little more cooperation on access to their Inquisitor, of course," Padrake said, as if reminding Tirom of the fact. "The man himself is willing to do his duty, from what I understand. But Captain Irshah Parmin balks."

Tirom nodded. "Well, that's a chronic issue, isn't it? I don't like to think what we'd have had to put up with if Verlaine's reforms had gone through. No offense, Specialist Ivers."

Tirom apparently made the assumption that Jils had been personally—as well as professionally—committed to Verlaine's announced agenda: an immediate halt on the issue of any new Writs to Inquire, no new orientation classes once the current cycle had been completed, an in-depth examination of the cost and benefit of the entire system of Inquiry and the Protocols.

Its monopoly on the exercise of legal, Judicial torture was one of Fleet's most jealously cherished prerogatives. Jils wondered if Tirom was one of those who believed that Fleet had been behind Verlaine's assassination.

"That's right," Padrake said suddenly. "The *Ragnarok*'s going to Emandis station. You wanted to speak to *Scylla* about that. Warn them, no untoward incidents, delicate situation with Convocation, and so forth."

The two ideas—Verlaine's reforms, and the *Ragnarok*—connected through Inquisition, clearly enough. Whether or not Padrake and Tirom were aware of the fact that *Scylla* had been Andrej Koscuisko's first ship of assignment, Andrej Koscuisko was the first person anyone would think of when the general idea of Inquisitors came up, and right now the entire Bench was acutely aware that Koscuisko was on board the *Ragnarok*.

What it meant, she was sure nobody could figure out. Dolgorukij were in general ferociously conservative people, what the *Ragnarok* was doing was reactionary at best, and yet Koscuisko had returned to the ship voluntarily and was apparently intent on staying there, thus reducing the range of punitive actions that the Bench could take against the *Ragnarok* without offending the powerful Dolgorukij Combine to a very narrow range of highly unsatisfactory and mostly symbolic gestures of disdain.

Jils, however, knew precisely why Andrej Koscuisko had returned to his ship. Further than that, she knew that Koscuisko had asked her to put the recording of the relief of Writ that Verlaine had offered him on hold until the *Ragnarok*'s appeal had been decided: an act of significant personal courage on his part, in her estimation.

Both she and Koscuisko knew that pending his relief of Writ he could be called to duty at any time as a professional torturer as well as the *Ragnarok*'s chief medical officer and ship's surgeon. Both she and Koscuisko knew that he would refuse to execute the Protocols unless he could do it according to a strict standard of his own, and that nothing above the third level would fit that definition. Also that refusal to implement the Protocols at an adjudged and authorized level was an act of mutiny, one of the very few crimes for which even an Inquisitor could and would be prosecuted at the Tenth Level.

Tirom was rolling a cookie on edge on his snack-plate as though the gradual erosion of the crumb held a message for him. "Yes," he said. "Quite right. I wanted to discourage *Scylla* from having any contact with that outfit. I particularly wanted to ensure that any ship-to-ship communications were on record and between officers only."

Tirom was afraid that something on the *Ragnarok* was catching, or could spread from crew to crew like an infection. The real problem with the *Ragnarok* wasn't its crew. Jils had been there; she knew. The problem with the *Ragnarok* was that its officers were non-compliant, and its commander Jennet ap Rhiannon had been so thoroughly indoctrinated by her Bench crèche teachers that she did not doubt for one instant that her duty to protect her crew from illegal imposition was self-evident to any right-thinking person.

"But you know Irshah Parmin. You can be confident of his discretion." Padrake spoke as if of a predecided solution, reaching for a fresh flask of kilpers. "None of the pressure Fleet's putting on Haspirzak, for instance."

Jils stirred her now-lukewarm kilpers and listened. She hadn't kept up on everything that was going on.

Tirom made a face, and shook his head. "I'd like to see anybody attempt to suggest that the Emandisan home defense fleet wasn't up to any incidental increase in civil unrest. Fleet has no basis for trying to squeeze more tax revenues out of Brisinje for more ships and crew. You don't see them kicking up at Sant-Dasidar either."

The Emandisan home defense fleet, the Dolgorukij Combine's home defense fleet. The Bench had been quietly waiving one restriction on the Combine fleet after another, over the years. What harm did it do to let the Combine maintain more ships, heavier armament, more crew than the original accords had permitted? There was only one Combine, and nine Judiciaries. The more money the Combine wanted to put into its home defense fleet the more available resources there were for Fleet to borrow for one reason or another when they wanted a little extra muscle that they didn't have to pay for.

"That's right," Padrake agreed cheerfully. "So long as they don't go Langsarik on us. I'll show Specialist Ivers to her quarters, Arik, see you tomorrow?"

As a subtle way of taking control of the conversation and ending it, this was nothing of the sort. Jils covered her surprise. It was difficult not to pass judgment on both of them, but she clearly didn't understand the nature of their relationship so it was best to avoid disapproving of it until she had better information.

"Opening ceremonies," Tirom confirmed with a sigh. "Make sure that Padrake gives you a good dinner, Dame, because you're going to be eating pre-packs for the rest of the convocation."

Lovely. But reasonable. Convocation would be conducted under quarantine, Bench specialists weren't generally known for their culinary skills and it wouldn't be appropriate to ask them to cook for one another if they were, what with all of their energies needed for the work of the convocation itself. Pre-packs were the obvious, if unpalatable, solution.

"I'll do so without fail, First Secretary," Padrake answered for Jils, with a polite bow. "Jils. Shall we?"

There were worse offers. She was tired; she'd had enough of duty, responsibility, the rule of Law and the Judicial order—at least for one night.

Just for tonight she was simply going to go along with Padrake, have a good dinner, find out what had been going on in Padrake's life. And let the rest of it go until tomorrow.

The archived image on the screen was identified by its margin-codings having been generated off parallax from Taisheki Station on the occasion—nearly a year gone by, now—of the *Ragnarok*'s declining to stop in and stay for a while.

Information and data received from the ships and monitoring stations in the immediate area had been used to build a picture that could be viewed from any angle; to Caleigh, it seemed as though she were in a neutral observer station standing well off of Taisheki watching the *Ragnarok* heading for the entry vector and the artillery platforms that were there waiting for it.

But there was more than that—there was a thula. A Kospodar thula, weaving its way in amongst the artillery platforms, blowing them up, one by one by one, and even with the data-refs that the footing line was displaying on the screen it was hard to believe that the picture had not been doctored to increase the relative speed of the little ship.

"I want it," Ship's Engineer said. "It's my natal day, Captain. Have I ever asked you for anything? I want that thula. I've never seen anything move like that in my life."

Chief Warrant Officer Caleigh Samons had been assigned to the Jurisdiction Fleet Ship *Scylla* for eleven years, most of which had been about as good as anybody would expect. She'd handled Security teams for the chief medical officer, which meant of course that she also managed bond-involuntaries for the CMO's use in his or her role as Inquisitor.

Up until the time Koscuisko had been assigned she had touched those teams as lightly as possible, not wanting to know what use their officer of assignment made of them, perfectly content to restrict herself to training and physical conditioning. They were condemned criminals, after all, but they were there because they could be forced to do things that few people would do of their own free will, and nobody liked to think about that.

After Koscuisko it had been different. Koscuisko had been young, naïve, inexperienced, at ease in surgery and nowhere else, conscious of his general lack of experience in every aspect of Infirmary that mattered; but Koscuisko had insisted on engaging with his personal discomfort, pressing forward to learn and gain in understanding even at the cost of being made to look foolish, and Koscuisko had not been content to turn his back on bond-involuntaries. They were not objects. They were not beyond help or hope. All Koscuisko had done was to look into their faces in the same way he would look at any soul, and it had changed things forever.

The captain had seen enough of Koscuisko's relationships with his Security to respect his junior officer more deeply than he'd ever cared to admit to Koscuisko. A man like Irshah Parmin was accustomed to taking an officer's measure by the way he treated his subordinates when nobody was there to see, and it had become clear that whatever Koscuisko was doing with his people it was powerful enough to transform them from men who lived in fear, condemned never to act but always only react, into people who had realized that there was a way after all for them to reclaim a portion of their freedom in their own minds, in their lives.

It was only because of Koscuisko's relationship with his Security in general and the bond-involuntaries in particular that Fleet Captain Irshah Parmin had not enforced the letter of the laws of military courtesy and discipline against Koscuisko on a daily basis.

And ever since Koscuisko had cried failure of Writ at the Domitt Prison, the captain had blamed himself for failing to put the fear of Hell into his young officer, convinced that if Koscuisko would not learn that discretion was the better part of valor he would never survive his time in Fleet. She knew.

The captain had discussed the issue with her on more than one occasion, using her as a sounding-board to work out the itch of his personal aggravation so that he could evaluate and judge some stunt that Koscuisko had pulled on its own merits rather than its potentially implied disrespect of, and consequent insult to, Koscuisko's chain of command.

She hadn't heard too much about it in the five or six years since Koscuisko had been transferred away to the *Ragnarok*, except when the captain chanced to express his frustration with his CMO's performance by comparing it to the ship's surgeon he'd had in Andrej Koscuisko. At such times it was clearly not helpful to remind the captain that while Koscuisko's technical competence in surgery could not be faulted, Irshah Parmin had found fault with almost everything else about the man.

The captain pushed the toggle-feed on the bar in front of his chair to its neutral position, and the image on the far wall of the officer's mess froze on a slice of the archival record. She'd heard about it; but this was the first chance she'd had to see it—that was why the captain had sent for her especially. Shared experience of aggravation.

"So long as I'm not needed here, your Excellency, I'd be more than happy to take a temporary posting to help handle the processing, when they run the *Ragnarok* to ground. Imagine. Interrogating Andrej Koscuisko. What a privilege that would be."

That was Doctor Weasel-Boy. Doctor Lazarbee, but it was almost impossible to think of him by that name. Sooner or later she was going to slip and call him Weasel-Boy, she knew it. It was just as well that she had bond-involuntaries to learn from: there would be less danger of making a slip if she took care to address him as "your Excellency."

Captain Irshah Parmin didn't seem to have heard Weasel-Boy speak. "Look at that son of a bitch," he said. "I heard that he was on that monster. Him. A surgeon. I knew he was a problem, but I never dreamed it was catching."

From Koscuisko to the entire ship's crew of the *Ragnarok*, he meant—Caleigh thought. "That's not fair," First Officer said. "He never bit anybody the entire time he was here. And that lieutenant ap Rhiannon had a reputation of her own, don't forget, capable of anything."

Irshah Parmin smiled, but shook his head. "It's him, I tell you. Four years under Lowden would make a rabid dog out of anybody."

There'd been betting, though Caleigh wasn't supposed to have known about it. It was nothing personal. They'd all heard about the *Ragnarok*; four Ship's Inquisitors in five years. An accident in a service house, an accidental overdose, something very regrettable in Secured Medical that not even the gossips would talk about; what had happened to the other one?

"He seems to have done almost everything except his plain duty." That was Weasel-Boy again. For a disagreeable man he had an unusually sonorous voice; she was still getting used to it. Cognitive dissonance, she thought it was called. "Did this joker ever actually do any work? Any work at all?"

The question was in poor taste on more than one level, one of which was the fact that it implied criticism of Irshah Parmin, Koscuisko's former commander. And everybody on the captain's staff in this room, with the possible exception of Weasel-Boy himself, had seen evidence of Koscuisko's surgical skills for themselves, never mind his other duties.

Sighing, the captain keyed the toggle back a few instants and then forward again. The Kospodar thula moved like a much smaller ship, lithe and agile; even at extreme magnification the speed with which it moved was remarkable to see.

"One of his Bonds flying that thing," Caleigh said, proudly. "That's the rumor I heard, anyway, Captain."

"Well, of course the man was on Safe at the time—" Weasel-Boy started to protest.

The captain raised a hand. "Let's just avoid spreading any wild irresponsible rumors," he said. "It clearly couldn't have been a bond-involuntary, that would have violated restrictions and requirements. So the question of Safes is immaterial, and I don't want to hear anything more about it."

Caleigh bowed, solemnly, well and truly reprimanded. Or something. Irshah Parmin winked—but so quickly she couldn't be sure she'd seen it—and continued.

"The point, gentles, is that the *Ragnarok* is clearly capable of anything." Shooting its way out of Taisheki Station to avoid being forced to surrender any crew to Inquiry, knowing full well that a Fleet Interrogations Group had been seconded. Well, shooting out an artillery net that was being fielded to prevent the *Ragnarok*'s access to the exit vector, at least—with a battle cannon on a private courier, and where had the *Ragnarok* come up with one of those, unless it was true about the case of deck wipes and Admiral Brecinn's arrangements with reasonable people?

"And as we are en route to Emandis Station we may be unfortunate enough to encounter this dangerous renegade. Emandis Station is administratively assigned to the Emandisan home defense fleet, which has jurisdiction, and it would be prudent of us all to remember that everybody is very sensitive about their prerogatives these days. No trouble."

Doctor Weasel-Boy snorted contemptuously. A relative newcomer, he hadn't encountered the rough side of the captain's temper yet. It'd only been a few months since he'd been transferred from the *Galven* at Ygau. Koscuisko's successor hadn't been half the surgeon Koscuisko had been but she hadn't needed a fraction of the management, either, and the ship had gotten along very well with her.

If she used bond-involuntaries to execute the Protocols that was what bond-involuntaries were for, and Parmin had never liked sharing his medical officer with the Bench and did so as sparingly as possible. It had been a good few years. What Doctor Weasel-Boy's regime would be like was anybody's guess, but he hadn't made a promising start by going through channels suspected of being reasonable in order to arrange a mid-assignment transfer. They'd been sorry to see Doctor Aldrai go.

"No down-leave?" First Officer asked.

The captain shook his head. "I see no reason why my crew should suffer because there are questionable influences at large. Downtime will be duly authorized, just exercise your discretion, that's all. As a matter of fact I'd like to have a word with you and Chief Samons, First Officer. Has anybody got anything else? Thank you, next time."

The Ship's Engineer and the Intelligence officer had both been with *Scylla* for as long or longer than Captain Irshah Parmin himself. They knew they'd been asked to clear the room, if Doctor Weasel-Boy didn't. The officer's mess was emptied within moments, despite the doctor's evident desire to stay behind and keep up on the events, whether or not they were any of his business. Especially if they were none of his business.

Once the door had closed behind the Intelligence officer and the clear-signal had sounded, Irshah Parmin stood up. "Will there be trouble, Salli? Strong feelings on board, I gather."

First Officer thought for a moment, and shook her head; her expression was one of grudging satisfaction—as though she had decided what was going to happen, and had determined that it was what she would have done in the same place, but couldn't bring herself to go so far as to admit it, possibly even to herself. "We don't know what ap Rhiannon is going to do. But if I were her I'd be making liberty as available as possible."

Irshah Parmin frowned. "She'll lose half the crew. And be unable to shift hull."

First Officer nodded. "Exactly so. People have had several months to think about what happened at Taisheki Station. What options did the crew have there? But at Emandis Station they can quietly turn themselves back over to Fleet and plead clear and present danger to life and limb."

"And she'll let them." Irshah Parmin made a face Caleigh recognized, something with a thrust-forward under-jaw and a pursed mouth. "It's the only way to be sure of their support. And no one who has the chance and doesn't take it will have much credibility if they try to convince the authorities that they'd been prevented, later."

He sat back down again and put his head into his hands, in a rare gesture of perplexity. "I can think of one hopeless case who won't be leaving. I failed that young officer, Salli. I never got through to him."

There was more to it than that. Caleigh knew it. Whatever residual sense of personal responsibility the captain might elect to cherish for his once-officer, there were reasons to be concerned about Koscuisko's fate if the *Ragnarok* were left undefended by mass defection; and even more reason for concern should the *Ragnarok*'s crew *not* take their first opportunity to extricate themselves from a very awkward situation that could turn lethal at any moment.

Koscuisko had enemies in Fleet. It went far beyond inter-system rivalry; he had made more enemies than he had inherited, earned them fairly through his own effort and by his own volition. The Intelligence officer had heard a rumor about a Bench warrant out on Koscuisko's life, but nothing seemed to have come of it. Caleigh would have been surprised if it had, with a Selection pending.

"You want to talk to him," Caleigh said, slowly, forgetting in her awe to add "your Excellency" or "Captain" or even "sir." "All of these years and you haven't had enough."

Koscuisko was ap Rhiannon's problem. But Irshah Parmin didn't trust Koscuisko's captain to be sensitive to some of the specific threats that had accumulated around Koscuisko like the scent of blood and steel and the cold pavement of an alleyway where a man lay dying under a mercilessly clear night sky. Koscuisko had a perfectly good captain of his own, but Irshah Parmin was Caleigh's captain and First Officer's as well.

"Ap Rhiannon will send him down," he said, straightening up. "She's sure to. She can't take the risk of keeping a man like that on board unless she's sure of him. At least I wouldn't risk it, and has anybody ever been sure of Koscuisko?"

Yes, Caleigh thought. Koscuisko's bond-involuntaries had been sure of him. There was a limit to how well Koscuisko's bond-involuntaries could protect him, however; against one man in particular even their powers had been limited. That one man had been Andrej Koscuisko, of course, and Caleigh didn't think anybody could have done a better job of protecting Koscuisko from himself, howsoever incompletely.

"So when we get to Emandis Station find out where he is, that's all. I just want to talk to him."

He didn't sound convincing. He didn't sound convinced. When Verlaine had gotten Koscuisko assigned to the *Ragnarok*—in a move that had been widely perceived as an act of petty vengeance on his part for Koscuisko's role in embarrassing the Second Judge and Chilleau Judiciary over the Domitt Prison—Irshah Parmin had taken it almost personally. *If I'd only taught him better he might have handled it differently.*

"Are we arresting him?" First Officer asked quietly.

Irshah Parmin grimaced, as if in pain, and shook his head. "No. No. Protective custody, maybe. Maybe he doesn't understand the trouble he's gotten himself in to this time. Just talk. You'll have to collect whoever he's got with him, though, so plan accordingly. All right?"

From the look the First Officer gave Caleigh it was clear that they both agreed on how uncomfortable Irshah Parmin was with this entire conversation. "Very good, sir," First Officer said. Maybe Koscuisko wouldn't mind, Caleigh decided; maybe he'd be pleased to come and visit with a former commander, and his Security with him. Maybe it wouldn't even have to be at gunpoint.

What lawful pretext Irshah Parmin imagined he could possibly find for poaching on another ship captain's senior officers Caleigh couldn't guess, and believed that she knew better than to expect that there was one. "Quiet and discreet. Wouldn't do to insult the Emandisan home defense fleet, of course, your Excellency."

"It's an internal Fleet matter." Irshah Parmin sounded genuinely surprised, as though the potential for conflicts in jurisdiction had not occurred to him. "No concern for Emandis either way, surely, Salli. I've asked Bassin to run a whisper on it so we'll know if Koscuisko comes down and where he goes if he does. Thanks, both."

Bassin Emer was the ship's Intelligence officer. So the captain had had this on his mind for some time now. Jurisdiction space was vast; Fleet small by comparison. It was by no means astonishing to contemplate encountering a former officer of assignment at one point or another so long as she, and they, remained in Fleet.

But she had never imagined herself in a position to detain Andrej Koscuisko. She wasn't sure how she was going to do it. She could only hope that Ship's Intelligence would have good information—or, failing that, no information at all.

CHAPTER SIX

Convocation

Chilleau Judiciary had had no shortage of potable water, but Chilleau had been on an ancient delta through which a river had not flowed for octaves, the Sannandor having long since disappeared into a desert that had once been a vast inland lake. People didn't sit in tubs of water, at Chilleau Judiciary; they showered, or they bathed in public wash-houses and never minded the amount of filtration and purification required to make it cost-effective to run such an enterprise.

It was an interesting change to be at Brisinje on the river in a world that had been colonized for a mere sixty generations. Jurisdiction had come late to Brisinje and brought wisdom, knowledge, prudence with it. There was no danger that the Reggidout River would suffer the fate of the Sannandor—at least not through the intervention of demands for irrigation or generation of hydroelectric power.

It was good, yes, but it made Jils a little bit uncomfortable. Padrake had shown her to this luxury suite on an upper floor of one of the beautiful buildings in Brisinje's judicial center, and left her to rest and change; she'd been somewhat taken aback by the palatial dimensions of the place—a library, a lounge area, a dining room, a bedroom, a washroom the size of her whole apartment at Chilleau, and all with a panoramic view of the river and the mountains beyond. Except for the washroom, of course, where a person could feel a bit exposed no matter how familiar she was with unidirectional polarization of view-pane materials.

There wasn't much by way of a view just now, that was true; the smoke from the launch-fields filled the atmosphere and soiled the beaches, though no hint of any unpleasant odors made it past the filters into her suite. This was an apartment fit for a Secretary, for a First Secretary, for a District Judge; and not for one hard-working supposed-to-be-functionally-anonymous Bench specialist. She'd have to ask Padrake about it.

After her bath.

The tub was something to see, round, with benches and steps up, and its water temperature was zone-controlled, and its pulse-jets felt almost as good against her tired muscles as the touch of a professional masseur might have. The fragrance of the water-lotion she'd selected was clean and crisp and very relaxing, and there was a stack of warmed toweling waiting for her when she got out.

She lay her head back against one of the contoured scallops in the tub's lip and let her body float on the powerful current of the water-jets, counting the stars that twinkled in the ceiling—cleverly painted so as to appear domed—and traveled across the ceiling in a slow progression possibly designed to follow that of the actual night sky above Brisinje, since she didn't recognize anything obviously familiar about it. The white noise generator with its transmit in the walls surrounded her with a soothing sound of surf against a shore.

She could easily fall asleep again, cradled in this huge tub of hot water. But Padrake had said that he'd come back to take her to dinner. She couldn't risk being caught naked in the tub; she might not get her dinner until breakfast-time, if that happened.

Reluctantly Jils pulled herself out of the bath, dried herself on warmed towels as soft as a midsummer breeze, wrapped herself in a cool silk robe with full sleeves and long skirts and went out into the bedroom with its plush white carpet and its very large bed to see about getting dressed.

The bed was the only thing with reduced power to impress her. She had been Andrej Koscuisko's guest at the Matredonat, she had been the guest of the Autocrat's Court, she had been welcomed at Chelatring Side in the Chetalra Mountains where the Koscuisko familial corporation had its ancestral seat; she had slept in beds large enough for an entire family.

The traditional master's bed in an aristocrat's household was big enough for the master, his sacred wife, the nurse, and an infant child. The guest bed she'd been provided had been large enough to require a map to get in to and out of. She couldn't think about the linen bills without shuddering. It was no wonder Dolgorukij households were so large. Keeping up with the sheets would be a full-time job for a crew of six, and she didn't even want to contemplate how much power it required to dry all of that linen in the wintertime when it could not be hung out to take advantage of the sun.

She hoped Padrake wasn't hoping she'd need company to keep her from getting disoriented and lost here. As lovers they had been rather spectacularly successful, that was true; and she still thought of his embrace from time to time, dozing, when she had nothing better to do. But intimacy couldn't be just picked up where it had been set down, not after the passage of years. Could it? Would she mind very much if he tried? What harm could it do to put everything aside for a few hours and live in the moment, when that moment could have Padrake's caress in it?

There was no guessing whether Padrake's interest remained, she reminded herself, pinning up her hair in front of the huge mirror. She didn't see much change in the image that was reflected there—she was still short, still square-shouldered; her eyes were still blacker even than her hair, which was still thick and glossy and needed a trim because it was getting to be too heavy to wear comfortably in a tuckaway.

She'd never had much of a figure; keeping in combat trim tended to harden and re-align any curves. But she had the appropriate feminine secondary sex characteristics in the appropriate locations. So did any other woman in known Space, too—well, by and large. No reason to believe there was anything of peculiar interest to anybody about *her* body.

Thinking to invoke the latest news on the reader in the library she went out into the lounge area to get to the other side. Padrake was sitting in one of the great cushioned chairs, watching the colors change as the sun went down and its declining rays caught the ash-particles in the smoke of the launch-fields in new and ever-shifting patterns. Confused—she hadn't expected to see him there, and she felt at a bit of a disadvantage, being only half-dressed—she stopped, abruptly. Padrake heard something, or perhaps sensed something, and turned his head to look at her over his shoulder.

"Ready for dinner?" he asked, cheerfully. "I thought you might be tired, so I had something sent up. That way you don't have to face your footgear."

Boots were regulation, but a person got tired of them after five or six days. It was a thoughtful gesture on his part. And why should it bother her to think that she had nothing on under her robe? Padrake didn't seem to think it was the least bit out of the ordinary.

"All right." It would give them a chance to talk. And Padrake hadn't changed his clothing, so it wasn't as though he was likely to have courting on his mind. "What's on the menu?"

"Cold supper, merely." He waved her ahead of him into the dining room. "But a very nice view. A little obscured tonight, but it's an interesting effect when the moon comes up."

Fruit. Several beautifully tall flagons of iced beverages, lightly sweetened red citrus, black thick Gremner berry juice, rhyti from fragrant green leaf, more. An immense tray of varietal cheeses, dishes of seven different kinds of pre-cracked but unshelled nuts, several platters of cold sliced meat of one sort or another. A cold cream-cake with ruby-red berry syrup dripping almost obscenely down its snowy flanks.

Padrake pulled a chair away from the table, politely, and pushed it back in once she'd seated herself. "No waiters," he said. "I thought you'd rather do without. And I don't dare risk anyone here hearing one of your better stories, Jils, I'd never live it down. Crackers?"

Yes, he was. Utterly crackers, but in another sense perhaps than he had meant. "I could get used to this rich living," she warned, reaching for a bowl of grapes. Huge, purple, seedless, and chilled. Heaven. There was wafer-melon there besides, its layers of succulent orange flesh lifting in tiers from its core as it reacted with the air. "A few days of this and I'll never go back to Chilleau."

"Promise?" he asked eagerly; but then slapped his thigh with one hand in a manner that told her he meant her to take it for a joke. "Well, bring on the milk-baths, then. Why would you want to go back to Chilleau anyway? From what I hear they haven't been treating you very well. As if anybody seriously thought."

Yes, as if anybody seriously thought. But it was kind of him to let her know that he, at least, didn't believe that she had done it. She wondered if Balkney thought she had. Then she wondered whether

Widowmaker was at Convocation as well, because she and the Hangman had married, and the Widowmaker had retired her uniform to bear children—three, maybe four by now. Bloodthirsty babies, if they were anything like either parent, but she'd better not think of babies and baby-making just at this moment with Padrake in the room. His physical presence was so very there. It was distracting.

"Seriously," she said, trying to discipline her thoughts. "Is this how Bench specialists live at Brisinje? Not that I'm complaining, and I know I'll be paying for it. Still. This is the sort of treatment I'd expect out of, say, Aznir Dolgorukij." Just to pick a benchmark of flamboyant and conspicuous consumption. "What would people say?"

"Nothing at all, if they have a decent amount of respect for the Law." Padrake crushed a cracked nut-shell between the heels of his palms and let the fragments drop to the table's gleaming surface as though he were a shaman, casting bones. "Think of what the life of a Bench specialist is, Jils. We spend years in the worst possible environments, we're barred by the nature of our duty from having friends or families, at least for the most part. All we have is each other, and we're not very good company as a rule, are we? We might as well be Dolgorukij Malcontents, but they live better. We deserve a little taste of the good life for ourselves."

He popped the nut-meat into his mouth as if to illustrate his point. "We're the people who make the good life possible. You can't hire people like us, we're not for sale, we do our duty because it's our duty. And for what? So some Judge who wouldn't last six eighths on the streets of her own capital can suspect us of murder the moment things go wrong with her plans?"

Padrake had a persuasive rant to him; he was one of those men who didn't mind in the least listening to himself talk, and it was all right because nobody else minded either. There was a sort of music to his cadence, when Padrake was on a rant. The closest thing she'd ever heard to approach it was one altogether too-late evening when she'd been in deep cover in some desperately poor hovel of a public-house and a skinny, unwashed Nurail in the corner had started to sing.

He hadn't had a good voice. It hadn't been a pretty tune. It had raised the hair at the back of her neck straight up into the air and sent an electric jolt down her spine to her toes and back up to tingle in the crown of her head, and she'd realized—with the one small portion of her mind that didn't belong to that dirty, smelly, unkempt Nurail completely and entirely, at that moment—that she was sitting in the presence of a weaver.

Padrake had a touch of that power in him. She'd wondered, from time to time, whether he was hiding any Nurail at the back of the closet of his genetic profile. "If any of us wanted wealth and power, we'd not have passed the basic psychologicals," she reminded him. "And you used to be savage enough about Fleet personnel who enjoyed their perks a little too well. Changed your mind?"

"Now you're trying to talk sense." He threw a bit of nut-meat at her. She rolled it up in a slice of filleted cold roast, dipped the roll in mustard-and-vinegar relish, and took an emphatic bite by way of showing how little threatened she was by his behavior. "Stop it. I just don't see why we shouldn't enjoy some of the respect that we've earned. And we're going into isolation, don't forget. Pre-packs. Ugh."

There were arguments to be made on both sides of that issue—the enjoyment of luxuries issue, not the pre-packs one. She'd argued it with Karol often enough, but on the Padrake side of the question. She wasn't going to indulge that line of thought. "Tell me about the isolation. Who's come? You're speaking for Brisinje, I know that, but who's at Supicor these days?"

A man with a persuasive rant, and a terrible gossip. It was one of the most enjoyable things about him, he always knew things, and he would tell you what was being said about you behind your back as well; so it wasn't as though he was deceitful in any sense. Not really. And a wonderful lover, but that was history.

"Nion is here for the Seventh Judge at Supicor. New kid. I don't know too much about her, except that she came out of Core. Tough. She'll be good if she lives long enough. The really interesting thing, though, is the Bench specialist out of the Sixth Judiciary. Guess."

The Sixth Judge sat at Sant-Dasidar, and that Judiciary included all of the Dolgorukij Combine. "Don't tell me. Not Sarvaw."

"Better than Sarvaw. Female. A female Bench specialist from the Dolgorukij Combine, she's Kizakh, I believe. There are rumors about her, Jils, indicating that the string she wears her chop on isn't just any old bit of red cord. If you get my meaning."

Malcontent. That was what Padrake was implying; that the Bench specialist at Sant-Dasidar was a Malcontent, and wore the Saint's halter, the symbol of her slavery.

Stubbing her rolled-up slice of meat in the relish-dish in much the same way as she had seen people stub out the lefrols they'd been smoking, Jils considered the implications.

"Well. It'd make sense, I suppose, but I didn't think the Bench ever commissioned talent out of system government." That wasn't exactly true, but close enough. "I guess it would fit, in a perverse way. It'd take a really unusual personality to make a Bench specialist out of a female Dolgorukij, what with the cultural biases. So she might as well be Malcontent. She's not likely to have had any chance of fitting in on her own. Who is this woman?"

"Name of Rafenkel. Blonde hair, brown eyes, soft voice, impressive vocabulary. Oh. Capercoy's here for Cintaro."

She hadn't seen Capercoy for years, either. Under the influence of her hot bath and the delicacies on the table Jils decided to risk a blunt question. "Any of them likely to be carrying a Bench warrant with my name on it?"

No, she hadn't surprised him. She would have been surprised if she had. He just took a moment to think, pouring her a glass from one of the flagons. Thick peary juice, by the perfume of it. Peary juice with a slice of citrus to keep the sweet sharp and focused on the edge of the senses.

"I don't think so, Jils. Despite what any given Judge might think, people who actually know are not going to take the idea that you killed him and then tried to discover the body seriously. Too many problems. And there's the other thing."

What other thing was that? It certainly was good juice. She held out her flask for a refill, listening.

"You're here from Chilleau, to observe and then defend. We need to get this done. We all know that. You're as safe as any of us until the Selection is decided, Jils, you can have my life on it."

Oddly enough that was comforting. It wasn't the same as claiming that nobody with the lawful authority to murder her for cause believed that cause existed. Pointing out that it would not be expedient to murder her until an answer had been agreed to in the matter of the Selection was much more limited an assurance, but much more solid regardless.

"Well, it's my life, not yours." But she appreciated his candor. "I'll have that tray of the semi-soft, please."

She couldn't quite eat, drink, and be merry. She'd always preferred moderation in most things anyway. But she'd been warned: pre-packs for the next while; and, whether or not she was comfortable with what seemed to be an assumption of earned privilege, there was no sense in letting this feast go to waste.

The light-access ports in the cave-roof high above shone against the darkness like stars from the surface of a low-atmosphere moon, brilliant, steady, dangerous to gaze upon too directly for too long. Even though the ventilation-shafts were sunk through level upon level of igneous rock to provide air to the cavern complex, the solar reflectors and refractors that carried what there was here of ambient light down through the earth were efficient enough to transmit intensities of light that were not safe to be long gazed upon with an unshielded eye.

Erenja Rafenkel sighed, and dropped her head to focus once more on her target. She liked deep places as well as she liked high places, which was not particularly. Yes, she was actually Kizakh Dolgorukij by birth, but her people had been city people. Tradesmen and mercantile women. Skilled piecework in fabric, wood, and ceramics, born and bred to an urban environment for generations and as attached to the famous high aeries of the Chetalra Mountains of Azanry as she was to any other abstract and otherwise meaningless concept.

Rivers she understood; rivers had featured in some of the happiest memories of her childhood—walking in a public park on her saint's-day, hand in hand with her mother or her father or an aunt or uncle down a gentle path along the riverside. Feeding the ducks on bread-crusts.

There was a perfectly beautiful river in Brisinje, but it might as well have been in Tuberchiss for all the pleasure she could take in it. It was well north of the ancient and blind shore on which she stood. Some octave it would wear its way finally down past its bed into this cavern, perhaps, and then there would be a cataract of spectacular beauty to enjoy but nobody to enjoy it with the cavern flooded out.

She was being watched. The skin at the place where the fur over her shoulder would lie if she was dire-wolf instead of Dolgorukij was prickling as though it remembered what it had been like to raise its hackles. She welcomed the knowledge; there was always the danger, in throwing a knife, that concentration would blinker the senses and shut away peripheral information that could be crucial. It made her aim much less reliable. But keeping her senses open to all the input around her would keep her alive, in the long term, much longer than simply superlative aim with a throwing-knife.

The range was a stretch of the midnight beach that ran between the cavern walls and the black lake, almost unimaginably old, lit with all-spectrums to supplement the channeled light of Brisinje's sun and moons. There was no sense in speaking to Bench specialists about "alien environments;" few environments were totally alien to a Bench specialist with anything more than a handful of missions in memory, and yet this one was as fantastic as any Rafenkel had seen yet.

This facility had been a research station, a place to study rock formations and analyze the chemical composition of the cold but living water and catalog the life that had adapted to this bleak and nearly eventless ecological niche. Once its presence had contaminated the environment past hope of remediation, the station had been abandoned; functionally forgotten, it made a good site for a convocation the likes of which the Bench had never seen—a gathering of Bench specialists to decide the fate of the Jurisdiction.

Steadying her arm, she took aim. The air was pleasantly cool, and the flavor of the moisture in the air was sharp and clean like that of an autumn wind. Whoever was watching had stilled their breath, but was shifting position so that fabric caught against fabric; the vestigial scales of one of the black lake's blind eel-like fish caught the sun and reflected it, a gleaming silver serpent in the obsidian waters. She threw. The knife flew clean and true to target and sang as it struck home.

She straightened up. "Capercoy," she said. "Maybe Balkney. But I'd be surprised if you were Rinpen. What's on your mind?"

"Time," her watcher replied, and stepped away from the shadows at the rock-wall to show himself. Balkney. The Hangman. A Bench executioner, and welcome to the job; but he was no more personally unpleasant about it than the next man, so long as the next man was understood to be a Bench specialist. There were much worse ways to die than by Balkney's agency, and she had implemented some of them from time to time herself. Time. That was what Balkney had just said.

There was more to it than that, though, she was sure. She moved downrange to her targets to retrieve her knives without reply, to leave him plenty of space in which to speak.

"Specifically, the time that has elapsed between the death of the First Secretary at Chilleau and now. What can we do to speed the resolution of the issue?"

He'd tell her. This wasn't any sort of a casual conversation. Examining one blade, holding it up to the sun-stars in the sky—there was a minute nick in the edge, wasn't there?—Rafenkel wondered what was on Balkney's mind. "Go on."

Now he was beside her, and reached out for the knife she had been frowning at. Holding it up to the light himself. "Yes. It's sharp. It's a knife." He could be very unpleasant when he meant to be; now he was just being moody. He handed the knife back to her. "We have two problems with our instructions as they stand, as I see it. One, that it calls for revisitation of issues that do not need to be discussed. Haspirzak is willing to freely admit that it should not be the next First Judge. It therefore makes no sense to take the time to challenge Haspirzak against all comers."

He could say that. He was here for Haspirzak, to represent the Third Judge's interest and put forth the Third Judge's platform. He was right, too: Haspirzak was not in serious contention for the Selection; was it really necessary to go through a formal disqualification of a Judiciary that had never entered itself into competition in the first place?

"We've never done this before," she reminded him. "It's best to be careful, accordingly. History will judge. It's up to us to ensure that we find the best solution to a situation that is already deeply to be regretted without creating any unnecessary turmoil to sap our resources and trouble our citizenry."

"Which is exactly why I think we should reconsider," he said, agreeably enough, taking her arm to walk her to a stone bench beside the door of the air-lock that would lead them back into the research station, embedded in the living rock. He was not a tall man, and she was tall for a Dolgorukij; but "tall for a Dolgorukij female" meant about the same thing as "medium height, Standard," when applied to city people, and so he had to lower his head to maintain eye contact.

"I'm not in the least interested in proving to history that Haspirzak was really and truly not an option. I do want to be sure that some alternatives are at least addressed. It's not just Chilleau, one question. It's at least three."

And he had a point, there.

She could hear the soft plashing of oars; someone was out there in the darkness beyond the full-spectrums, lit only by the piped light from the surface. Zeman would be having a scull. There were no breezes here to disturb the surface of the water; she had seen Zeman now, and that scull seemed to glide upon glass.

"Chilleau at Chilleau now, Chilleau at Fontailloe, Chilleau at Chilleau later." Yes, she had heard the issues identified. "And, of course, Fontailloe at Fontailloe. Or nothing."

Balkney snorted. The sound carried over the still water to echo vaguely in the dark. The acoustics of this place were strange. Zeman would be able to hear the entire conversation; that was one of the reasons it was safe to be having it—a third party could witness to the exact nature of the conversation, and testify as to whether there was evidence of collusion or undue influence.

"The confederacy model. Yes. If you ask me that shouldn't be so much as discussed. But it's as you said. The verdict of history."

"So what do the others think?" Rafenkel asked casually, fitting her knife into its soft wrap alongside its fellows. They were beautiful knives. She was fond of them. Far from Emandisan steel, of course, but there was very little that could really compare.

"Tanifer spoke to me about it." The question clearly did not embarrass Balkney in the slightest. "Said that he'd discussed it with Nion and Rinpen. I talked to Capercoy. No one's spoken to Delleroy or Ivers, of course."

Because they weren't here. Well. It was hardly a conspiracy, then, if everybody was in on it. "Zeman?"

"I thought I'd stick around and wait for him. I like the idea of cutting out some iterations to save time, Rafe. I don't like the thought of not working out every real alternative, and that means time, and I can only stand the idea of taking more time if I can make it up somewhere."

If things went on much longer, Fleet would have to cede much more responsibility to the home defense fleets for police duty than

Fleet wanted to, because Fleet simply didn't have the resources to do all that needed to be done by way of patrol and containment, and even if Fleet managed to wrest the additional taxation privileges that it sought from the Bench it wouldn't solve the problem. Money couldn't create a disciplined recruit class overnight.

But Fleet was holding out against ceding any of its authority to the home defense fleets for reasons that Rafenkel knew to be excellent. Once give people the idea that they could patrol their own spheres of influence and keep their own peace, and they would be very reluctant to give that power up, and even more reluctant to continue to remit tax money to fund an external Fleet to do a job that they could do themselves.

There was the other consideration, of course, as well; the Combine had never quite adjusted to Bench-dictated equal rights for Sarvaw, and what was to stop the Combine's home defense fleet from finishing the job that Chuvishka Kospodar had so notoriously started, generations ago? The Bench meant one law for all people, at least where trade was concerned. Home defense fleets had their own stores to house. What was the phrase? Their own oxen to gore?

"No harm in at least speaking to Tirom about it." Brisinje's First Secretary was their official point of contact with the Bench for the purposes of this exercise; he would be coming down with Delleroy and Ivers, when she got here, and they could be started.

They could have been started already, but Ivers was for the Second Judge, who had been cruelly robbed of the Selection and there was nothing anybody could do about it. There was no honorable way in which they could decide issues between themselves without the wronged judge's representative on hand to follow the events and agreements, and speak for Chilleau's interest. "We could meet after third-meal. Clarify parameters. Be ready to go."

Balkney was gazing out over the black lake, now, at the bioluminescence in the water stirred and roiled by the oars of Zeman's scull. "Do you think she did it?"

Knives stowed, Rafenkel rolled the bundle and tied it closed with one hand. Practice. "Ivers?" Well, yes, obviously Ivers. "Could have. We all know that Verlaine's agenda would have been difficult to implement, especially where Fleet's concerned. But unless she had reason to believe that the penance was genuinely worse than the peccadillo, assassination seems too extreme. Fleet wouldn't have allowed any drastic measures. He'd have had to take it slowly."

"Interesting analysis," Balkney said, waving for Zeman to come to shore. People like Balkney were employed against sensitive targets—and dangerous ones. Like other Bench specialists. Like senior administrative officials? "Thank you. See you in common after third-meal, Rafe."

There hadn't been a Bench warrant on the First Secretary. How could there have been? And yet Chilleau's security system had been gotten past. That took a very sophisticated understanding of Security codes. Whether or not Jils Ivers had that level of in-depth knowledge Rafenkel didn't know, but she would have been surprised if Balkney didn't have what it would take. Balkney and Tanifer, to name the two most obvious.

Preconceptions and assumptions were the enemy; they would put out your eyes and blind you to the army that stood gathering in the young wheat until it was too late and the raiders were upon you. Rafenkel put hers away in the locked place in her mind that she kept for such enemies of analysis and went to wash and change before she took third-meal.

"Really?" Rukota said, impressed, and set a "yaohat" token down in Sperantz. The card-array was almost complete. Had Vogel noticed that with the placement of yaohat in the Sperantz slot, the way was clear for Rukota to put Caliform in Jabe, and take the hand with "forests"? "That was you, at Ankhor? I'm impressed."

He meant it, too. The Ankhor campaigns had been among the ugliest and unhappiest with which he had ever been associated. He'd been a much more junior officer then, of course.

Vogel nodded. He was a man of more or less usual height, with a grizzled iron-gray moustache and a battered campaign hat pushed well back on his head, whose relatively broad high forehead coupled with the deep set of his pale blue eyes pointed at a lineage somewhere down along the Glenglies group, class six hominid.

"Fleet had ten cruisers in reserve," Vogel said. "Port Carue had stealth atomics. We'd never have been able to stop it if both sides hadn't been equally convinced that the balance of power was in their hands."

"How d'you mean?" This was intriguing. Yes, he knew what Fleet had been holding; standing off on vector transit, due to arrive within hours if the cease-fire hadn't been declared. He hadn't heard about any stealth atomics, but come to think of it Fleet's cruiser array had never made it in to the official narratives either that he had ever noticed.

"Game theory." Vogel plucked a card out of his hand and put it down in Magenir.

Wait a minute, Rukota thought, alarmed. There were three, five, seven tokens containing water all around Magenir. If Vogel played anything with an earthquake in it he could sweep the board on a lahar.

"Each party believed they were negotiating from a position of strength. Neither party felt that they'd been forced to it by circumstances because both had secret weapons that they could easily have deployed. At the same time each side believed that the other really had no choice whether they knew it or not. Stable outcome."

He was in trouble. He was in serious trouble. He didn't have a single card that had containment anywhere in it. Could he get away with "delta" in Gamie? That would channel all the water away safely. He wasn't sure what else he could try. He set it down.

"Well, we were all just as glad to see it over." Many of the people he'd been with, at any rate. Yes, there had been some among them who had resented being deprived of a chance to work off a little steam. The only trouble with a successful Jurisdiction, Rukota decided, was that there was too much law and order in the world for people to have a good appreciation for how horrible chaos and conflict could be. They'd been lucky at Ankhor. There'd been a large civilian population in Port Carue, non-combatants, citizens and the trading community.

Even people who had held the civilian population responsible for the extremism of its government had found no way to blame the merchant community. For himself Rukota hadn't been able to ever quite figure out how some domestic laborer in a public school could be held responsible enough for the political intransigence of an oligarchy to deserve to die for being there.

Vogel frowned at his hand, suddenly, but it wasn't a worried frown. It was one of concentration. Rukota felt a sinking sensation in the pit of his stomach. No, it would be too unfair. But nobody had played "nibs," not yet, Vogel could have it in his hand, and if he did—

and if he put it in Sacroe—there would be almost no way to avoid a cataclysmic "worldfire," if that happened, and Vogel would win the game as well as the hand.

"It was a close one," Vogel admitted. There was a note of decision and determination in his voice. "But, yes, we pulled it off, because both sides were willing to avoid slaughtering the other if it could be done. Best basis for an entente, really, positive desire to not inflict tremendous losses on the other side. I think maybe I'll try playing—"

The talk-alert sounded at the door to the ready-room just in time. Vogel looked up toward the door with an expression of mild annoyance on his face, and played "belange" in Sacroe. Belange, and not nibs. Belange had gale force in it—why, if Rukota played his last remaining "severance" in Hellox he would have a near-nova, and he'd never even seen one played before, the odds against the combination were . . . the odds were—

They were more than he could calculate. "Step through," Rukota called, and put down his hand. "Are they ready for us in Secured Medical?"

The door opened; one of Koscuisko's people came through. Micmac Pyotr. Maybe Pyotr Micmac, Rukota decided, since he'd heard Koscuisko call the big black-skinned Skaltsparmal bond-involuntary "Pyotr" but never "Mister Pyotr," and Koscuisko called his bond-involuntaries by their names. Something to do with delicacy in the issue of reminding them of the detention facility in which they had been Bonded, Rukota understood, since a bond-involuntary took his formal name from the establishment at which he had been placed under governor for the thirty-year term of his sentence. Unless he was Nurail. Rukota didn't think there were any Pyotr Detention Facilities, but he couldn't recall having heard of a Micmac Detention Facility, either.

"Yes, General Rukota, thank you. Ship's chief medical officer to be waiting for General Rukota and Bench intelligence specialist Vogel in Secured Medical, sir, if the officer will follow me."

Well, he could finish the hand, or he could just go. Vogel might believe he was taking an easy escape from a losing position if he did that, but it didn't matter. He had seen the potential for a genuine near-nova. It was enough. He could die without regret, even if not happily.

"Shall we?" he asked; Vogel pushed back from the table, set his cap on straight, and almost saluted. Almost. Vogel knew. "After you," Vogel said.

Resisting the temptation to see what Vogel had been holding in his hand in reserve, Rukota led the way out of the room, following Pyotr and the two Security with him down the corridors. One bond-involuntary, Godsalt; one not, a woman, Smath, he thought.

Koscuisko was waiting for them when they got there. Secured Medical was in one of the most remote areas of the entire ship—not that a ship of even the *Ragnarok*'s significant size could have any remote places on it, especially when you'd been living there for as many years as many of the *Ragnarok*'s crew had been. Koscuisko didn't look happy. Why should he? Rukota couldn't imagine anybody being happy about going into a torture-chamber, and Koscuisko was the one who knew exactly what had gone on in there.

It was widely understood that Koscuisko's peculiar advantage in Inquisition lay in the combination of empathy and exquisite sadism, that was true—a culturally inculcated passion to be the master of all that he surveyed, coupled with the unpredictable psychological quirk that afflicted a small but select group of unfortunate souls. Koscuisko was a decent enough sort in other areas of his life for all that, and nobody had sent him down to Secured Medical since Rukota had come on board; so he had no particular problem with Koscuisko.

In fact, Rukota almost liked Koscuisko, if only by association. Koscuisko's troops were as solid as any Rukota had ever had the pleasure to associate with. Koscuisko didn't get the credit for that, no, of course not; but he did get credit for being an officer that honest troops respected and were fond of even when they couldn't exactly bring themselves to admire him.

"Specialist," Koscuisko said, and bowed. "General. We may go in, now." But he made no move to key the admit until Pyotr, standing behind Rukota in the corridor, coughed gently. The sound seemed to wake Koscuisko up, in some sense, and he turned to the panel beside the door with no visible sign of reluctance save for the white lines of his tensely compressed lips. Rukota didn't usually notice much about men's lips, but there was so little color in Koscuisko's face to begin with that the additional paleness of Koscuisko's mouth was hard to miss. This was harder for Koscuisko than he'd anticipated, perhaps.

The door slid open on its diagonal track. Koscuisko stepped through and waited—facing the far wall, which wasn't all that very far—until the female troop Pyotr had brought with them had closed the outer door and given the all-clear. "Secured, your Excellency."

He could see the rise and fall of Koscuisko's shoulders as Koscuisko took a deep breath, then keyed the admit. The inner door slid open, and there it was, Secured Medical. Rukota had seen one of these places once before in his life—it was an orientation item—but this was different. This had been one of the most frequently used such rooms in Fleet until Captain Lowden's death, and a person generally didn't expect to see the Ship's Engineer in the Inquisitor's seat, either.

Koscuisko had certainly not expected that. Rukota could tell by the half-a-step backward that Koscuisko took, raising one hand half-way in the classic gesture of suspicion and reproach and defensiveness. Wheatfields stood up and stepped off the little platform, a gently malicious smile not so much on his face as expressed in his entire body. "Nice to see you, Andrej," Wheatfields said. "I just thought I'd be present for your return to your old environs. You must have so many happy memories of this place."

But there was something else going on here as well. Rukota could almost smell it. He couldn't figure it out, but he could sense it. "Memories, at least," Koscuisko said, with no particular emotion that Rukota could identify in his voice. "You've re-arranged, I see."

The wall in front of the Inquisitor's chair had been completely covered, floor to ceiling, by stacked crates, perhaps two crates deep. The wall-panels behind which the instruments of torture were stored, the door at the far end of the room that led to the small cell where a prisoner under interrogation would be kept—all completely blocked off. Rukota didn't know what was in the crates but he knew he wouldn't be surprised if they were the heaviest things the Engineer could come up with.

Even the ceiling had an anomalous look, paneled with flatform storage in netting; no sign of the grid or any of the suspension points. Thorough. A person wouldn't know that this had ever been anything but a store-room except for the chair in the middle of it—a perfectly innocuous seat with padded arm-rests, comfortable, provided for the Inquisitor's use—and the aisle that had been cleared through to the right of the doorway to give access to the evidence locker. Just another anonymous panel in the wall, but one of the most secure places on board the *Ragnarok*.

"Do you like it?" Wheatfields asked, standing very close to Koscuisko in a casually threatening manner. "I'm sure we could arrange to forget you're down here, Andrej. Except that your damned Security would probably come looking for you," he added, looking at Pyotr over Koscuisko's head. Wheatfields was an extraordinarily tall man, fully an eight taller than Rukota himself. Rukota glanced back over his own shoulder, just in time to catch Pyotr's polite bow of acknowledgment. Wheatfields didn't like Koscuisko, but he was apparently unwilling to make Koscuisko's Security uncomfortable just to make the point.

"I could watch tapes to pass the time," Koscuisko said. His voice had turned chillingly cold. "I understand you have some. Thank you, Serge, it is kind of you to be here for me."

The attack seemed to be as effective as it was apparently unexpected. Wheatfields stepped back a pace, but it was almost as if he'd actually staggered. From what Rukota had gathered of the tribal knowledge of the *Ragnarok*, this was a rare moment of ascendancy, for Koscuisko; but Koscuisko didn't seem to have noticed.

Koscuisko turned to his right instead, stepping through the shallow aisle between boxes to the wall to code his secured-access admits. Rukota hesitated for a moment before deciding that noticing the possibility that Koscuisko had floored Wheatfields would only contribute to the awkwardness, and going after Koscuisko to watch over his shoulder.

The locker opened. There were two records inside that Rukota could see; Koscuisko lifted one out—top shelf, a small box, no larger than a modestly-sized meal-tray—and held it out for Rukota to take, not looking at him, before taking the second record out.

"Access modification," Koscuisko said. "On authority Andrej Ulexeievitch Koscuisko, Ship's Inquisitor, assigned to the Jurisdiction Fleet Ship *Ragnarok*. Confirm."

The record seemed to think about it for a moment. Rukota knew that what the record was doing was confirming Koscuisko's voice, the genetic information in the sweat of Koscuisko's hands, and scanning the central Judicial files for any hint that Andrej Ulexeievitch Koscuisko was no longer the appropriate authority. Finding none—

obviously enough—the record said "Confirmed" in its calm clear voice, and Koscuisko seemed to relax by some unquantifiable fraction.

"Access is granted for purpose of lawful investigation to the following named individuals. Please state your name and your rank. Karol Aphon Vogel." Koscuisko passed the record in his hands to Vogel, who took it.

"Bench intelligence specialist," Vogel confirmed. "Karol Aphon Vogel. Judicial ad-hoc investigation in process. File in record." Or, in other words, the record could check and make sure that Vogel was Vogel, but would not be expecting to find any other information; nor would the record release any to inquiries from its controller in Judicial systems. As far as anybody would be able to find out Vogel would still be exactly as disappeared as Rukota understood he'd been before he'd arrived on the *Ragnarok*, no more, no less.

And now it was his turn. He passed the record that Koscuisko had handed to him off to the nearest person—Smath, as it happened— took the genuine record from Vogel, and spoke.

"General Dierryk Rukota, Second Fleet, Ibliss Judiciary. On detail, assigned." Well, that was what his last status had been, at least— detailed on behalf of Pesadie Training Command to oversee a preliminary audit investigation. He couldn't help but wonder what the record would make of his claim, though.

"Identity confirmed. Status is not confirmed."

So he wouldn't find out. Oh, well. Maybe he didn't want to know.

"These two named and registered individuals are to have access to Secured Medical, by order and direction of Captain Jennet ap Rhiannon, Jurisdiction Fleet Ship *Ragnarok*, commanding. They are to have joint access only. No unaccompanied access is authorized."

Another intriguing question, there, but the record didn't seem to notice it. Koscuisko would have invoked ap Rhiannon's name and status as captain when he'd secured the forged record in the first place, however, so maybe that hurdle wasn't so very high. Because the record only said "Confirmed."

Koscuisko put the record back in its locker where it lived. The entire room was on record. It did not need to be anyplace in particular to talk to Ship's Security. "Give the Bench specialist the evidence, Smish," Koscuisko said. "Specialist Vogel. This piece of evidence is that which you wish to examine." It was marked, as well; Koscuisko's secure-code, *evidence*, bright and clear as its status-panel. "Serge, I need you to move some more of these boxes. Two can tell you where. Because Specialist Vogel will not begin his analysis until we are on record. Also I expect another chair will be required, and a table, and lights."

Rukota hadn't really thought about it, but Koscuisko was right. Vogel clearly couldn't be allowed to take the forged record out of this room. Koscuisko would lose control of his evidence; and this evidence was the foundation of the *Ragnarok*'s defense.

Without proof that the accusations against the *Ragnarok*'s Security were false—as demonstrated by the torture and confession and death, on record, of four people who were undeniably alive—it was back to an internal squabble about protocol and insubordination. An internal squabble that would require investigation, which meant Inquiry, which meant torture and killing of at least some of the *Ragnarok*'s crew; and the execution of its acting captain as well, if Fleet upheld a finding of mutinous intent.

"And I expect to see you damned in Hell forever, Andrej." But the tone of Wheatfields' voice didn't match the venom of his words; it was almost cheerful.

"You'll have plenty of company there, Serge. The Balancers will have to build a special arena, I expect. One can hear the news report already, Andrej Koscuisko has died, demand for visitor's passes to Hell swamps administration."

Wheatfields snorted and moved as if to go past Koscuisko and away, but did the most peculiar thing. He stopped on his way past, and put one hand to Koscuisko's shoulder.

"Adding arrant egomania to your already impressive list of personal shortcomings," Wheatfields said. "I'll send some people."

Koscuisko merely nodded, as if he was accepting a rebuke. Or expressing appreciation. For what? He hadn't taken Wheatfields' hand off at the wrist for touching him, either. Once Wheatfields had left Koscuisko spoke to Vogel. "I will ask Cousin Stanoczk to send people to attend you," Koscuisko said. "You will have no difficulty understanding why I do not wish to ask any of the ship's security to be here. If there is anything that you need please let me know."

"Very kind, your Excellency. I'm sure we'll be very well taken care of. No need to keep you."

Go away. Koscuisko was clearly just as happy to do just that. It was only the stray glance that Rukota chanced to intercept that clarified things in Rukota's mind; because the expression on Koscuisko's face, turning his head to look around him as he walked away, was one of a truly indescribable longing.

Koscuisko was suffering from being here, yes, but it was worse than that; because Koscuisko all-too-clearly almost wished that he was staying to ask somebody questions.

But Wheatfields already knew that, didn't he? That was why he'd been here. Koscuisko had guessed that Wheatfields knew; that was why Koscuisko had made so brutal a reference to the murder of Wheatfields' beloved, so many years ago. Wheels within wheels within wheels. It was dangerous to let people stay on one ship with one another for so long. When a Command had time to forge bonds of such intimacy between its crew there was no force in known Space that could tear it apart.

Now more than ever Rukota understood that the captain and crew of the *Ragnarok* was capable of anything, absolutely anything, and nothing that Fleet could do would stop them. It was a profoundly depressing thought.

Vogel pulled a packet of playing cards out of the chest-plaquet of his uniform. "While we're waiting?" Vogel asked, and handed the forged record to Rukota. "We can use the chair."

The arms for a surface, the seat for the playing-field. The floor had not been covered over. It was still the grim gray lattice of a torture cell, through which blood could drip and be washed away when it was all over and the body had been fed to the conversion furnaces. That the room was clean Rukota had no doubt. He still couldn't quite envision playing a game of cards on such a surface as that.

"You're on," he said. "Your deal or mine?"

CHAPTER SEVEN

Unexpected Developments

Early in Brisinje's morning the talk-alert sounded. Jils Ivers woke from a deep sleep and blinked twice at the darkness above her. "Yes."

Brisinje. A bed in a luxury guest suite. A very plush and ostentatious luxury guest suite, and one she would have enjoyed much more if it hadn't been for the hints she'd gotten that she was expected to require such expensive perquisites as due her, at least at Brisinje Judiciary.

There was nothing to stop a Bench specialist from enjoying luxury, of course, because a Bench specialist was as likely to be found in a crib that rented by the hour or a tiny sleeping-hex in a port or in a slums in a shack roofed over with waste packaging material as lolling around in a tubful of heated scented water in a suite the size of a city block with a view of the river worth millions. If she wanted to sample the life of an autocrat, however, she could always just visit Azanry, and see if she could wrangle an invitation to attend on Andrej Koscuisko's parents at Chelatring Side, in the mountains . . .

"Warning order," the talk-alert said. Padrake, Jils realized. "There's fast-meal on the table, Jils, get yourself dressed. We've got to move out before sunrise."

Traveling at night didn't present any real barriers to a determined observer; it simply reduced the odds of being accidentally observed by some casual passer-by. "With you shortly," she replied, and then

waited for the clear-tone on the talk-alert to sound before she got out
of bed.

She hadn't bothered to unpack most of her kit last night so it didn't
take much time to pack up and get dressed. Fast-meal was on the table
as Padrake had promised; the kilpers was hot and the cream was
buttery, just as she liked it.

When she'd retrieved her data-reader from its safe and opened up
the outermost door of the suite to step out into the very early morning
Padrake was there, sitting on a low stone bench in the atrium, waiting
for her.

"Slept well, I hope?" he asked with a wink, which she filed away for
future reference. "Arik's waiting for us, let's go."

Was he really? She wasn't sure she liked the sound of that. There
was a thin line between a First Secretary waiting because a meeting
had been scheduled or a late development had to be pursued and
reported on, and a First Secretary waiting because a Bench specialist
felt she outranked him and he could very well just wait.

There were two ground-cars waiting at the gate to the guest-
compound, and Arik Tirom was in the first one waiting—hands
folded in his lap, evidently meditating with his eyes closed. Someone
got out of the second car, saluted, got right back in; Security. Padrake
pointed; Jils went to join Arik Tirom in the first car, murmuring a
polite "Good-greeting, First Secretary," as she ducked her head to
climb in and sit down on the padded bench facing the rear of the
vehicle.

Tirom opened one eye and grinned at her. "If you say so, Specialist
Ivers. I call it altogether too early in the morning for any greeting to
be good. Nothing personal." It was a common complaint for the First
Secretary, apparently; because all Padrake said—respectfully enough,
Jils supposed—was "You've got just enough time for a short nap,
Arik," as he joined her on the bench in the ground-car.

By the tell-tales in the framework all around her Jils could see that
it was a high-security model of ground-car with the full range of
detection avoidance technologies on board, but perhaps the single
most important of those was the fact that it looked like a perfectly
innocuous, not too new, not too expensive, general-purpose ground-
car, from the outside at least.

That made things a little cramped on the inside of the car, but Jils couldn't make up her mind to be very much bothered by the heat and the pressure of Padrake's body, so close to hers. Her body knew his body, and remembered it fondly for its strength and grace and the abstract beauty of the masculine frame when it was unclothed.

She could feel her own flesh relaxing against his as against a familiar and comfortable support, a safe place; and had just gotten to the point of deciding whether or not she was going to start thinking about sleeping arrangements wherever they were going when the ground-car pulled to a stop and the doors slid open.

"Site secured," the ground-car's systems said. "Shuttle is on stand-by. Confirm departure in twelve."

The second ground-car was stopped as well, but she couldn't see any of the Security: quite possibly they were already emplaced. There were no hints of sunrise on the horizon—any horizon; the sky was a faintly glowing deep-napped charcoal gray, the smoke and ash in the upper atmosphere catching the lights from the burning launch-fields and diffusing it through the sky until it wasn't even possible to tell which direction the launch-fields were.

When a fire of that sort got large enough, it was frequently all that could be done to contain it. There was no way to actually extinguish an entire field of burning fuel-tanks without more resources than the Bench apparently had here at Brisinje—not with a city so close by. All they could do was to keep the surrounding areas from harm as well as they could, and let the fire burn out.

Most of the fuel-stores would have been safely bunkered in hardened compartments with significant thermal buffering, yes, of course. But thermal buffering was only good for a range of temperatures over a period of time, and if the fire too hot—or went on for too long—even thermal buffers could fail. It was unnecessary for her to remind herself that a sabotaged thermal buffer would fail much more quickly and efficiently.

The uniform glow in the sky and its unnaturally gray-black color gave the scene a very surreal cast. They had stopped on an old concrete apron at the riverside, in front of a seemingly rather dilapidated one-story building—quite small, one or two rooms if that, surely. There were weeds growing up between the cracks in the concrete and the apron.

But the bracket-lock on the door only looked old; that would never yield to a key code sequence, Jils thought, watching Padrake invoke the secures with his identity-chop. *That* bracket-lock was a fully functioning security spider, suspicious and conservative, that kept them waiting for several long moments before it grudgingly agreed that Padrake's chop was exactly what it claimed to be, and let its bolt slip.

That meant the defensive traps and alarms set around and within were temporarily deactivated, Jils knew. Or else the spider had decided that there was something just a whisper web-filament thin the wrong side of "all correct" about Padrake's chop and wanted them all inside where it could keep them until Port security could arrive.

Inside there had once been an office, with a squared-off inner office in the middle of the otherwise unpartitioned building; it looked a little bit like a public ground-transportation station, to Jils, and then she realized that that was not too far from its actual purpose. Padrake led the two of them, Jils and the First Secretary, around to the rear wall of the inner office, where the controls were; the shaft-car was waiting for them. Self-braking linear descent module.

A mine elevator, in principle, but a very well-appointed one with built-in seating and pleasant surfaces, freshly oxygenated air in circulation, all of the amenities. She checked the ceiling by force of habit as she stepped in: yes, there was the emergency escape hatch, right where it was supposed to be.

Padrake locked off the doors and keyed the program, and the elevator started to move. There was nowhere to go but down from their current level, though, so—Jils asked herself—was "elevator" really the right word? It would be when they were ready to come up again, yes, but who knew when that would be?

"It'll be fifteen or twenty," Padrake said to her, seating himself near the control panel. "Make yourself comfortable." Tirom had already done so, Jils noted; he'd made this trip before, obviously enough.

"Where are we going?" She knew the obvious answer. Padrake would know she knew. She trusted him to answer the right question.

"Chambers here are built on an old flood plain, Jils, a gigantic lahar runoff zone. But underneath the layer of mud deposit that went down when the Broken Crown mountains blew there are caverns in the rock that were there even before that happened. There's an abandoned research station."

How far down were they going? She didn't want to ask. If she stopped to think about it she'd get claustrophobic: but that explained the constant air circulation, right there. Claustrophobia. People could frequently succeed in ignoring the fact that they were encased in a tiny box descending at an unknown rate of speed for an unknown distance through layers of what had once been mud and rock and boiling water to spend an indeterminate period of time in an undisclosed location if they could feel what their most primitive brain would interpret as a breeze, in their faces.

A research station buried deep would have had limited contact with the surface; limited accessibility, and probably in-depth life science monitoring, so that there could be no off-the-record collusion between Bench specialists. As if there would be . . . but then such collusion would be all the more dangerous if it did happen—Jils reminded herself—because of just that presumption, that of course there would not be.

"And your role in this visit, First Secretary?" she asked.

Tirom had been listening quietly, with one hand resting on his knee and the other arm flung over the back of the empty seat next to him, across from where Jils sat on the corner angle adjacent to Padrake's left. He looked very comfortable. No issues with very deep places, or if there were any he was good enough at hiding them to fool Jils.

"Official Bench sponsorship, Dame Ivers, formal approval of predetermined scheme of procedure. I get to make a speech. Then I get out, and leave you and Padrake to do the job we need for you to do."

There were no view-ports in this car and she was just as glad of it. She couldn't see depth, speed of descent, time remaining, on the controls; Padrake's body was in the way. How long had they been traveling?

"You'll be getting regular reports, then, I expect?" Her normally precise time-sense did not feel quite trustworthy to her; she decided against trying to second-guess herself. Maybe there was something about traveling down rather than up or across that had a disorienting effect on her internal chronometer—at least where the gravity was not artificially generated. She hadn't been deep in a long time, not deep in the earth rather than deep in deep space.

And the deep she'd been hadn't been so deep as this, surely, it had taken her three hours to descend the cable-line into Cabinap, but that had been on her own power with a simple gravity-assist. More controlled. Safer. She and Karol—she cut off that line of thought and frowned, trying to concentrate on what Tirom was saying. She'd asked the question. The least she could do was pay attention to the answer.

"There's a central comm console, secured transmit, needless to say." Prudent and proper, just and judicious, Jils thought, irreverently. "The Bench needs you to be concentrating all of your special skills and qualifications on the one issue. Forget all about the rest of known Space just for now, Dame."

She'd gone into isolation to brainstorm solutions and model approaches before. She had to admit that this sounded like the most complete isolation she'd ever done. Even on vector in the middle of nowhere you could get a conversation of sorts going with someone, if you had the power and there was someone scanning frequency or waiting for a predetermined contact.

She couldn't think of anything intelligent to say; she lapsed into silence after a polite "Thank you, sir," and brooded. If they killed her they would leave her here. They might even simply leave her here, and let the "killing" part take care of itself.

The announcement of the Selection would be a wonderful time to release intelligence about the execution of Bench intelligence specialist Jils Ivers in connection with the investigation into the death of First Secretary Verlaine. It would be the truth, too, just not enough of it, but the investigation could be declared officially closed.

They would need to minimize the uncertainty in the environment, regardless of the final determination on a new First Judge. She would be a very tidy surrogate solution. She had until the Selection was decided, though.

She couldn't let her mind whirl like this. She had to put it away. She had a task facing her that she knew to be of more importance than her own life. Now was not the time to deny the Bench the best she had to offer just because it might include her own execution, for the good of the Judicial order.

"And we're here," Padrake said, reaching out to touch one of the controls. "It'll just be a moment for the doors. They'll be waiting for us in the theater, Arik, Jils, right, here we are, let's go."

The face of the car opened on a horizontal track to reveal a narrow, dimly-lit corridor of dressed rock, and an airlock at the end of it. Contamination measures, Jils decided. There were three airlocks in all, each combining a number of different techniques to keep the interior as free of pollutants as possible—light, subsonics, positive air pressure.

Three airlocks, and on the far end of them when the door opened to let them pass Jils saw a welcoming committee waiting for them, more Bench specialists than she had ever seen in one place before in her life. Not that that was so difficult a benchmark to exceed.

There were five of them waiting, Balkney in the lead; for a moment Jils was convinced that she had traveled through three airlocks for nothing—that she would be shot down here and now, and what a mess *that* would make, she'd seen it—before reason reasserted itself. They'd not shoot her in front of Brisinje's First Secretary. They'd wait.

"Gentles," the First Secretary said, and it occurred to Jils that apart from answering her question it was almost the first thing he'd said all trip. It was early. Maybe he was asleep. "You honor us. Is there a particular reason for this greeting party?"

There was a woman there with them, middling tall, dark blonde hair done up in a thick fat glossy braid, a face like a stereotypical pastoral worker of some sort—ruddy mouth, beautiful skin, dark arched eyebrows over dark brown eyes. Milkmaid, maybe. When she spoke, Jils knew in an instant that she was Combine, from the accent; and realized who the woman had to be. Rafenkel. Sant-Dasidar Judiciary. Was it her imagination, or did she see a hint of a bright red something hanging around the woman's neck beneath her duty-dress, something like the red halter of the Malcontent?

"It's an historic occasion," the woman said. "We don't initiate a convocation every day. We felt a little formality might be in order. The others are waiting for us in the theater."

In fact they'd never come together in Convocation before, or if they had it had never been recorded.

"Thank you, Dame Rafenkel," Tirom said, confirming Jils' assumption about the woman's identity. "After you."

Yes, the corridors were narrow and low-ceilinged, but they had room to walk two abreast. They'd have had to get heavy equipment into and out of the research station, Jils reminded herself. It wasn't far to another airlock, but one that opened onto a paved floor rather than one lined with sanitation fabric this time; and there was significantly more light.

"This way," Rafenkel said politely. The double doors of the theater were propped open to welcome them. As theaters went it was very small indeed, with seats in three tiers to accommodate a total of perhaps eighteen people all told. There was a table at the base of the theater, its lowest level, seven or eight steps down from the entry doors. Some chairs.

Capercoy, from the Fifth Judiciary at Cintaro, was seated at the table along with a sleepy-eyed man with glossy black hair whom she knew by reputation as Rinpen from Ibliss. Capercoy stood up, Rinpen went up the middle of the room to close the doors, Balkney ushered the First Secretary to a seat and sat down himself next to Tirom. Jils found a spot for herself and Padrake seemed to waver between several choices before he elected to place himself just in front of her, in the lowest tier of seats.

Once the doors were closed Capercoy spoke. "Thank you for coming, First Secretary. Welcome back, Delleroy; welcome, Ivers." *Why did they bother to secure the doors?* Jils wondered. Everybody was here. Nine Bench Specialists; one First Secretary. "You know the main purpose of our gathering, First Secretary, to present the Bench instruction to proceed and to establish the ground-rules. We've been talking about it and we think we want to change some of the ground-rules, so we want to place a revised agenda in front of you before we go on record."

She could see a subtle twitch in the uniform fabric across Padrake's shoulders. Surprise. Wariness. Nothing too obvious, but it was there for people who knew how to look at Padrake, and she did.

"Indeed," Tirom said, with commendable aplomb. "Do your fellows know about this?"

Capercoy glanced over in her direction, his golden-brown eyes touching first on Padrake's face and then on hers. Calm. Sure. Confident. "No, First Secretary, neither Delleroy nor Ivers have participated in this discussion. You'll remember, sir, that when the Bench decided on convocation it was with full knowledge that there was not much by way of an idea on how to proceed. But we had a plan."

"Which you wish to emend," Tirom agreed, perhaps to show that he had been listening. "What do you propose?"

"We take it as given that the most obvious solution is to find a way to select Chilleau Judiciary. If your counterpart at Chilleau had not been murdered it is almost certain that Chilleau would have taken the selection—" with a Bench specialist's characteristic care, Capercoy had elected to characterize the selection as "almost" certain, Jils noticed— "and in fact it's widely believed in some areas that Verlaine was killed in order to prevent that from happening."

Yes. Old news. "And if that's why Verlaine was killed it's a bad idea in principle to let anyone get the idea that it works." Rafenkel had seated herself opposite Padrake, on the other side of the room; she spoke calmly, reasonably, and she made a lot of sense. "Our first priority should be to see whether there's any way in which Chilleau could still be selected."

"We do the Bench a disservice if we artificially restrict our selection set," Capercoy continued, building on Rafenkel's point as smoothly as though they'd scripted it. "After discussion we've decided that we'd like to propose consideration of Chilleau's selection standing without challenge as our first step. Because if there is a way we don't need to spend weeks working to the least worst alternative. The best solution remains Chilleau, if it can be done. We are all agreed on it."

That would gratify the Second Judge to a significant extent if she could hear it, Jils knew, but she was unlikely to. If she ever did it would be only well after the convocation had concluded, announced its findings, and dissolved. Too bad.

"Does the Fifth Judge know about this?" Padrake demanded. "She can't have intended you to propose any such thing, Capercoy."

The Fifth Judge stood to gain the most from a consideration that excluded Chilleau Judiciary, and Capercoy was her representative.

Capercoy shook his head. "Of course not, Delleroy, we have communication security in effect. No, it wasn't in her instructions, anywhere. But she knows as well as anybody that we're here to make the best choice. If we can find a way we can all go home early. Your endorsement, First Secretary."

This was a waste of time. Wasn't it? Hadn't they come here exactly because Chilleau Judiciary could not be selected so soon after losing its senior administrative officer? Well, no, they hadn't. They were here because it was assumed that Verlaine's death put Chilleau out of the competition. Bench specialists didn't like to assume.

Padrake didn't like this proposal, either, she could hear it in his voice. "Wait one, Capercoy, we can't stop there. It's not enough to ask if Chilleau can be selected. Why not ask whether a Judge should be promoted at Fontailloe, instead? Their administrative apparatus is intact. Or why not select the Second Judge, but send her to Fontailloe while Chilleau recovers?"

Ridiculous. Fontailloe was out of consideration. It was an old, tried, venerated practice to exclude the previous incumbent's Judiciary from the selection for the new First Judge, and the very few times when an exception had been made—always for only the very best, the very most pressing reasons—the Bench had invariably learned to regret it all over again. It was a solid curb on the natural tendency of power centers to pull more and more and more into their gravitational fields. Corruption was all but inevitable. Abuse went without saying.

And yet Capercoy merely nodded. "All reasonably possible alternatives will be considered, Delleroy. I ask again for your endorsement, First Secretary, we need to be sure we know what we can't do before we turn to the question of what is not impossible, and seven out of nine of us are agreed. Ivers and Delleroy have not yet been polled."

"I'm surprised," Tirom said. "But I can see your point. There is an additional issue, however. We have already suffered serious losses to the infrastructure of the Bench while we have been trying to figure out how to handle the situation. What if you derive no different result from such preliminary arguments from those already argued and discarded?"

That had been the first line of scrimmage, after all, the Second Judge insisting that the selection go forward, the balance of the Bench declining to make any quick decisions. Well, most of the balance of the Bench, anyway—all of the Judiciaries that had been prepared to back Cintaro among them, and without a First Judge there was no tie-breaking vote to overbalance an even four-four split against Chilleau. Fontailloe didn't count. The First Judge was dead. And this was all the First Judge's fault, Jils thought resentfully, for dying so inconsiderately of a stroke in the first place.

"We've done an informal survey, First Secretary, and we believe that there are enough stipulations in place to address that issue. Ibliss will waive its place in the match. Supicor is willing to cede if it can't beat Cintaro. It was anticipated that Brisinje might be willing to cede as well. We can make up the time. And since those of us who've had a chance to discuss it are determined on seeing the test through, we will be testing those arguments along with the previously decided procedures if we have to. Your endorsement, First Secretary."

Tirom was backed into a corner, and he obviously knew it. "Very well, Capercoy. All present in favor of modifying the agreed-upon procedure along the lines proposed by Capercoy here in your presence and on your behalf will so signify by saying 'Yes.'"

Seven voices, all more or less determined, but all seven. Jils wasn't sure what she thought about it. She knew she wanted time to think before she would be ready to cast her vote; but her vote was not needed. The majority opinion was clear.

"So be it." Tirom stood up, with a grim expression on his face. "As it has been spoken, so it shall be done. Now. I should be getting back. Padrake, if you'll take me back to the elevator."

"We'll go with you," Capercoy said. Jils hardly heard him. They were going to start by arguing for Chilleau Judiciary. She'd thought she'd have days ahead of her, days to sit and observe the debate and not have to think about much of anything except whether the debate was fully and freely executed without intimidation, duress, improper influence, or evidence of collusion. That was out the airlock now as surely as Tirom would soon be.

Jils stood up and fetched her kit from under the seat as Padrake and Capercoy went away with Tirom. There was a woman she didn't think she'd met—young woman. It was hard to remember how young she'd been when she'd sworn her duty; young, ambitious, and almost too sure that there were answers and she would find them. She'd found them. But they'd been to the wrong questions.

"Dame Ivers?" the young woman said, offering her hand. "We haven't met. Ghel Nion. For the Seventh Judge at Supicor."

Ah. Yes. "Good to make your acquaintance, Dame," Jils said, returning the offered hand-clasp with a cordiality that she did not really feel. "Could I ask you to show me to quarters? I've got all of this unpacking to do." She hefted her kit, and Nion grinned.

"It's a convocation, Ivers, not a beach-party. How did you get a cabaña into that little package? Delighted. This way."

The Seventh Judge, at Supicor. Supicor had been the first of all the

Judiciaries, the original—a long, long time ago. Supicor that had given birth to Jurisdiction, nourished it, promulgated it across known Space as the Bench expanded and encountered other hominid cultures as it came. All hominid cultures could be traced on genetic markers back to Supicor, so either the Bench represented Supicor's second wave of expansion or they'd come to Supicor from somewhere and rebounded.

Genetic evidence suggested support for the "second wave" theory, but as far as Jils knew nobody except for the occasional zealot really cared. It had been a very long time ago. What mattered was where they were now, not where they had come from. Supicor was old and frayed and dingy, desperately poor, with only its story of cradling all hominids to sustain its pride. No more than that.

Just outside the door to the theater Jils had to stop herself, abruptly, to avoid knocking in to Rafenkel, who was just straightening up from leaning against the far wall of the corridor with her arms folded across her breast. Watching. The doors had been open; what had she been watching for?

"Tirom's got an escort," Rafenkel said to Nion. Nion was behind Jils; Jils couldn't see her face, but could guess that Nion was a little surprised to be confronted. "Only polite to give a fellow Bench specialist at least as much honor. Lead on, Nion, I'll bring up the rear and provide the travelogue."

Jils shrugged. "Just so long as I get to quarters," she agreed, hoping she didn't sound churlish. She was just tired. "Need to rinse my mouth." No, she needed a year off, and to discover who had killed First Secretary Verlaine and why, and where Karol Vogel was, and what it had been about Padrake's exact tone of voice that was bothering her ever so slightly at the back of her brain.

As if he'd been surprised, but not enough. As if he'd seen it coming. Could he have been in illicit communication with the Bench specialists here, before he had come down himself? He'd probably escorted them all down. That was true. He had been back and forth. He could have seen it coming. That was true. There was no need to invent complications where none existed.

"We'll get you taken care of," Nion said cheerfully. There was a note of annoyance at the back of her voice, but a very subtle one. Too early for Jils to begin to think about what it was or why it was there. "It'll be this way."

It was clearly between Nion and Rafenkel, one way or the other. "Combine?" Jils asked Rafenkel, following Nion down the corridor. "I understand that the Koscuisko familial corporation is particularly rich, this time of year."

Rafenkel grinned. Jils hadn't had time to form much of an opinion—apart from a baseline assessment, Bench intelligence specialist, good at her job or she'd be dead—but it was a good smile, cheerful and open and attractive. Something in the water in the Combine, maybe; every Combine national Jils had ever met had had an engaging smile.

"This or any other time, Dame Ivers. Is it true that you were a guest at Chelatring Side? The stories that they tell about the place. I don't know how you survived it."

Neither did Jils. The Dolgorukij notion of festive dining at the top echelons of the Koscuisko familial corporation had been almost more than she'd been able to take; and then to be expected to dance, within an hour of rising from the table—

"'Tongue cannot speak nor mind conceive the words to contain the horror,'" Jils quoted at Rafenkel, and smiled back. One of Padrake's. Rafenkel didn't seem to recognize it.

"We'll get you settled," Nion said. "And go find the others. You can tell us all about it."

Of course. How had she missed it? She was not to be allowed to speak privately with anybody. Not to wander in the corridors by herself. But was this to protect her against someone . . . or themselves against her?

Her temporarily cheerful mood destroyed Jils nodded, silently, and followed Nion through the halls to quarters.

CHAPTER EIGHT

Explosive Events

She didn't try much by way of small talk as Rafenkel and Nion escorted her through the narrow corridors to her billet. Looking for ambush at every turn—it was second nature—Jils admired the straightness of the hallway and the relative scarcity of either turnings or doors. There were relatively few places where one could lay in wait. Unless people were on fairly intimate terms with one another it would be difficult to actually pass, in these confined conduits, without going over or under each other. Somebody had taken all of the fire safety and evacuation management officers away and gotten them good and drunk, during the planning phases of this station.

Around one corner the corridor suddenly widened to more than twice its previous allowance; living quarters, Jils guessed. There were doors. Rafenkel stopped in front of one about halfway down the corridor and keyed the admit. "Home," Rafenkel said, with a flourishing gesture of one hand.

Jils went through and put her kit bag down on the little table that was there, thinking. If they took her they'd probably do for her, but then both women would have to be in on it; and the odds that one of them would change her mind about the propriety of the action at some later date would be high enough that Jils herself would not care for them.

Therefore neither Nion nor Rafenkel was likely to try to kill her right now. Was that why Rafenkel had waited—to protect Jils from Nion? Or had that been why Nion had offered to escort her, to give Jils a little security in Rafenkel's company? Rafenkel had not seemed surprised to see Nion, and had been able to see in. Nion had seemed a little startled to see Rafenkel. Tentative score, Rafenkel positive, Nion neutral, Ivers on the edge.

"What happens next?" Jils asked, looking around her. It was a small room with its own shower and toilet. The station had converters on its water supply, clearly enough, or else she was just mis-remembering about the generally unhealthy properties of centuries-old water in caves. Standard ventilation—she could put an alarm on that—a security locker, and someone had made the bed up for her, narrow though it was. That had been a charitable impulse. Was she going to have to tear the bed apart to check for silent assassins?

No. If someone was going to hide a bomb in her bed they would not have made the bed up. They would have let her do that, to lull her into a false sense of security. Someone had made up the bed. That was saying that there was no need to tear it apart. Maybe it was a complicated double-braid. Maybe there was a bomb. Maybe there was to be poison in her food, gas from the ventilator, a quick silent assault in a dark corridor.

Maybe she was surrendering to fear and paranoia. If someone was going to kill her they would, but they needed her right now for the convocation. She had to concentrate. She had a duty to perform.

"There's a schematic on the wall, there, but I wouldn't trust it," Rafenkel said. "Maybe it'll be different for you, but I can't seem to keep my directions straight down here. We've started to make signs." Some of which, Jils realized, they had passed on their way here, though she wouldn't have realized they were guideposts per se. "And the way the station is laid out, one wrong turn and you could be in for a long walk once you finally realize you're going in the wrong direction."

Rafenkel was fiddling with the schematic as she spoke, standing just to the inside of the door. When she had successfully invoked a route on the interactive map she stepped back and away, out of the room again. She had her back to Nion. But she kept between Nion and Jils, Jils noticed.

"So get yourself situated, and call in to the commons. There's rhyti. Cavene. Kilpers, someone said you drank kilpers—Delleroy, I think.

We'll come and fetch you. Better to get an escort until you've had a chance to familiarize, and if you want a laugh ask Zeman how far it is from the airlock to the laundry. Be ready to duck."

Waving cheerfully Rafenkel turned, and—taking Nion by the arm—headed back up the corridor in the direction from which they'd just come. Jils shut the door and secured it, thoughtfully. She didn't have any unpacking to do to speak of; she almost didn't bother securing the data she'd been carrying with her since she left Chilleau— there was nobody here but Bench specialists.

On the other hand not even a Bench specialist necessarily had a good reason to know what was in that data, and failing to secure data was a bad habit to get into. She locked it up and had a wash, changed her boots out for padding-socks and sat down on the bed to stare at the closed door for a while. Yes, Rafenkel had suggested she call for an escort. Jils wasn't sure she was interested. It was good to be alone, even if not very alone, even if only for a little while.

It wasn't to be left to her to decide. The crisp chime of the talk-alert startled her—it was an old style of signal, more confrontational in a sense than the newer generation whose parametrics adjusted for the number of people in the room and whether their rate of respiration indicated that they were sleeping or otherwise engaged, and adjusted frequency and volume accordingly. Sighing, Jils stood up to go to the door; the station's talk-alert was not so primitive as to wait for a manual toggle, however, although Jils could have wished it were. The signal came through once the talk-alert knew that it had gotten her attention.

"Jils." It was Balkney, Jils thought; she didn't know him very well, but she had worked with him before. "Got a flask of kilpers with your name on it, but the management doesn't want me carrying flasks through the corridors, they're afraid I'll spill things and spoil the rugs." Of which there were none, but that wouldn't stop Balkney. The man was ingenious. He could manage all sorts of impossible things; Jils had seen him do it. "Rinpen and Nion are coming out to collect you. Don't want you to get lost. See you soon."

Out. And all without waiting for a response. *Don't want you to get lost*, Balkney had said; but wasn't that exactly what she had at the back of her mind like an unclean dish-rag? Someone wanting her to get lost?

One way or the other she didn't feel like waiting passively for an escort. There was a perfectly good schematic on the wall. She studied it for a moment or two and opened the door just in time to not see anybody.

Somebody had been there. She could smell it. She didn't know who it was. Her mind was convinced that she had seen something out of the corner of her eye but it couldn't make up her mind which corner had processed the fleeting image. This *was* one of the shorter corridors; a person *could* disappear around a corner. Unless she selected one or the other end and sprinted, the odds of actually catching sight of anyone's back were too uncertain to make the trial worth the tariff.

Shutting her eyes she stilled her mind to let the fugitive impression process into retrievable memory in her brain. Scent. Something almost not heard at all about a footfall or the sound of fabric against fabric. She would find out who it was. There were voices, coming down the corridor; it took stern self-discipline to keep that fact apart from what her mind only almost remembered of what direction someone might have gone away in. She could afford no assumptions that if people were coming from one direction, any observer who might have been in the corridor had gone away in the other. She could afford to make no assumptions at all.

"—said to clear out. So she did, that's all. Then the judge got angry about it, but it was the judge who'd told her, so I'm not sure what the point was."

Not a voice Jils recognized, and so there was good odds it was Rinpen and not Nion. When the second person replied, Jils felt the satisfaction of a hypothesis confirmed.

"You see? There. That's just what's wrong with the Courts these days. A judge, of all people, and if a judge is surprised at what people make of her words—these people need keepers—"

It sounded like a complaint that was both traditional and familiar among Bench specialists, the incompetence of the supreme power under Law—the Judges who codified and interpreted the Law—to think their way out of a puzzle grid. Familiar: but disquieting. Surely this was not the time or place to be mocking the judges on whom the stability of the Bench relied . . . but on the other hand where better than here? There was no one around but Bench specialists. She was being too sensitive. Pressure valves were critical to their psychological health.

"You called for a transport?" the one who wasn't Nion called, pitching his voice to carry. Young to not-exactly-young man, brown hair, a face and features that called no attention to themselves whatever: now this, Jils thought with satisfaction, was a Bench specialist. Not one of those flashy models like Padrake Delleroy or Capercoy or Balkney.

"Moments ago. Your gratuity is in question. Rinpen, I expect?"

Nion made a quiet little face that gave her expression a very fleeting charm, apparently chagrinned. "Sorry, Ivers, it's either introduce you to people you've known for years or forget to introduce you. I once tried to introduce a judge to her own First Secretary. True story. But I'll deny it."

As a line of banter, it was successful, as far as it went. There didn't seem to be much genuine camaraderie in it, though. It should have carried an "and wasn't I embarrassed, too" scent to it rather than the faint whiff of "yes, and any really good Bench specialist would have done exactly the same in my place."

"How did you manage that?" Rinpen asked, apparently interested. Jils went along between the two of them, listening to Nion talk.

"Cintaro," Nion said, as if that explained everything. Rinpen laughed as though it did. Jils kept shut, concentrating on the route, waiting for it to deviate from the direction in which she expected it to be going.

"What a flopper," Rinpen said, after a moment in which it apparently became clear that Jils did not mean to react had elapsed. "Did you ever hear about that one case in Circuit, Ivers? The one with the three stud bulls and the—"

Yes, she had. It sounded absurd enough on the surface, and the judge's approach to a solution had certainly been unique and original. It had been unique enough to have stopped the situation from escalating. The judge had won that case, in Jils' estimation; and had never minded that she looked a little silly all the while.

"Yeah, I heard." Jils laid an extra layer of respectful appreciation on top of her meaning, just for the sake of being difficult. "Brilliant jurisprudence. Brilliant."

Nion looked at Jils a little sideways now, and Jils noted her expression approvingly. *You do know when you're being laughed at.*

"No need to tile that hearth, Ivers," Nion said. "You're here for

Chilleau. But Capercoy likes you. It won't be as if it was your own Judge who won, but he'll share the wealth, he's decent. Reasonable."

For a moment Jils didn't know what to think. For one, the Second Judge at Chilleau Judiciary was no more "her" judge in any sense than she was Chilleau's Bench specialist assigned—Bench specialists were based, but not assigned, precisely in order to avoid the development of particular interests. That was one of the things that made Padrake's level of intimacy with Secretary Tirom a little unusual.

But more than that, Nion's choice of adjectives could hardly be a coincidence. Reasonable people were corrupt. Unless Nion was trying to imply something about Capercoy it was in very poor taste to say any such thing, and if Nion was trying to do just that she'd better have evidence to back up her insinuations.

While Jils was trying to decide how to react Nion caught Jils' eye, and winked. Jils relaxed, only slightly mortified. What was meat for one Bench specialist was grain for another. Payback, that was all, no more and no less, and here they were at the end of the communal kitchen area where three Bench specialists were sitting on stools around the high sleek-metal surface of the work-table, waiting for them.

Simms Balkney was there with Rafenkel, looking very owlish—he had larger eyes than most people she knew, and very deep-set they were. Cadaverous skeletal structure, so far as his head went in any case, and the effect only got more pronounced as he grew older and the flesh slowly thinned across his face.

He had a cup of kilpers ready, and pushed it across the high broad chromed-steel table-top toward her. "Nice to see you, Jils," he said. "Things have been interesting at Second, I guess. Tell me about it. We're starving for gossip here, starving."

Now that Padrake was here, that would change. Jils could be confident of that. Karol's note had indicated that Balkney hadn't done the murder; that didn't mean he wouldn't murder her. The thought gave her a place to start as Nion and Rinpen joined them at the table with their own beverages of choice. Zeman was here, too, but Zeman was snacking on a cracker of some sort with nothing to drink at all.

"Not interesting enough, Balkney. For interesting we'd have to have developments, and this is going on slimmer than anything I've ever seen. It's ugly. I'm glad to be here—on vacation. I still haven't heard from Vogel, though."

Rafenkel drank her rhyti, looking at the blurry reflection of her face in the table-top.

Zeman looked at Balkney, who shrugged. "So far as I know nobody else has, either," Balkney said. "I heard he'd left for Gonebeyond, though. To take up with a woman he used to know."

A woman? That was absurd. Karol didn't know any women. Not in anything like a going-off-to-Gonebeyond sense of the term. She'd never even heard gossip about . . . oh. The Langsariks' Flag Captain. Walton Agenis.

It could be. Karol had cherished—or at least harbored—feelings for that woman, feelings that had been complicated by his sense of frustration over the failure of the amnesty he'd arranged. Jils wasn't sure Verlaine had ever forgiven Karol for his creative solution to that particular problem, but the issue was all academic, now.

"Mixed up with Malcontents, is what I heard," Rinpen admitted. Jils glanced over at Rafenkel quickly, curious to see if she would react to the suggestion; but Rafenkel gave no sign of finding it of any more than merely passing interest. "At least there were indications that some Malcontents were looking for him. I didn't think he even liked Dolgorukij. Maybe that was why they were looking for him."

She could explain that she had asked the Malcontent for help in finding out what had happened to Karol, whether he was living or was dead. That would entail a moderate amount of embarrassment, though, and maybe it was just as well to let people speculate on why the Malcontent might be interested in Karol's whereabouts. Karol needed more dark hints in his dossier to keep it interesting.

"Tell me what's been going on around here," she suggested, instead of bothering to explain. "What's our plan?"

"Well, we had one," Balkney said. "We even got started a little early. We weren't sure when you'd make it through and we all need to be back on the job, the other job, I mean." Keeping the peace. Assisting the judges. Carrying out the Bench's instructions. "But we weren't entirely satisfied. If we can rule out Fontailloe and Chilleau at the beginning some of us can leave right away. Or not, of course." And if they couldn't rule out either or both Judiciaries at the onset they'd be no further behind because of it.

"Tanifer is all for a break in tradition." It was a bit of a surprise to hear Rafenkel speak; she'd been quiet throughout, nursing her rhyti.

"Nion is pretty adamant about Chilleau's unfitness, aren't you, Nion? Maybe you should refocus your investigation, Jils."

In other words, maybe Nion had done it. That wasn't even funny. It was particularly unfunny because she'd thought along the same lines, and made sure that no Bench specialist had been anywhere near Chilleau at the time—no Bench specialist but her, that was. And maybe Karol, since nobody knew where he was and could therefore not say where he hadn't been.

"Oh, yes," Nion said, as if playing along. "I killed Verlaine because Chilleau was the only thing standing between Supicor and the Selection. Yes. Right." Was it her imagination—Jils asked herself—or was there a note of genuine resentment, there? "But we all know it wasn't you, Ivers. You'd have been set for life. Bench specialist presiding at Chilleau Judiciary with a First Judge in residence—you're the last person who could have wanted Verlaine dead."

No, the Second Judge was the last person. Second to the last person. Surely the last person who could have wanted Verlaine dead had been Verlaine himself. "I expect to reap my reward when the time comes," Jils retorted frostily. "But only if Supicor takes it. As we planned, Nion."

Still there was that odd undernote, an assumption that a Bench specialist had a personal stake in the Selection and could expect to reap a personal profit.

Balkney snorted into his flask of water. Or water-like whatever, he certainly seemed relaxed and comfortable enough, though Jils didn't smell alcohol or any other fragrant intoxicant. "Sorry you lost your post, in that case, Ivers," Balkney said. "When everybody knows it's Cintaro."

About whose Judge Nion and Rinpen had just been joking in less than complimentary terms. "I can neither affirm nor deny your assertion," Jils said. She needed to shut herself up and sleep. Fatigue and stress were eroding her faculties. There were no hidden motives to be adduced from two Bench specialists mocking a Judge. It was in poor taste, but that was all. "It'll be interesting to see what history makes of it, after the fact, when the First Judge is presiding at Chilleau Judiciary."

Bench specialists, suggesting that their peers were reasonable. But there was a point to be made there. Sooner or later reason would prevail. She had no reason to have assassinated Verlaine, and—if base motives were to be appealed to—every reason not to. She could only be guilty if there were undisclosed motives or a sincere conviction that Chilleau's proposed reform program would do more harm than good, and she trusted in the intelligence and common sense of her peers to conclude that such was not the case. All she had to do was wait.

It would help if she could find the way through to the identity of the murderer while she was waiting. For that she had to get through Convocation, and back to Chilleau.

A warning tone sounded across the station's internal comm; Nion looked up at the speaker in the ceiling. "They're back," she said. That would be Padrake and Capercoy, Jils assumed, back from escorting Secretary Tirom back to the surface. "Let's go. The sooner we can settle this whole problem the sooner we can all get back to the real world."

Jils' sentiments, almost exactly. Carrying her flask of kilpers Jils went with Balkney and Rafenkel, Nion and Zeman and Rinpen, to sit down and discuss where they would start to argue for the least worst solution to the chaos into which Verlaine's murder threatened to plunge all of Jurisdiction space.

Bond-involuntaries were criminals. So much was clearly understood by everybody in Fleet, with the possible exception of Andrej Koscuisko. They were no ordinary class of criminals, however; the Bond could only be imposed in cases of crimes against the Judicial order, which was generally held to apply to sabotage, persons vandalizing or otherwise damaging Bench property, some minor political dissidents, and—in recent years—Nurail.

It was a privilege extended only to people whose psychological profiles gave a reasonably good assurance that they could survive the ferocious stress that life under governance meant for a Security slave, or a service slave, because there were people under Bond in the service houses, but they never earned back the cost of their indoctrination and benefits package so there were fewer of them. They didn't last. Someone was always taking a bribe on the sly to let a patron alone with a service Bond for a few hours, and then professing shock and outrage when something happened.

It had happened to a service bond-involuntary in Port Burkhayden not very long ago, Robert knew. He knew because the service bond-involuntary had been his sister, and the officer had been sent ahead to make good the property damage before the officer's cousin Paval I'shenko Danzilar could file a grievance for delivery of damaged goods.

Fleet hadn't been making Bonds for very long—the technology had been slow to perfect, and there were the cost-benefit problems, of course. It was expensive to put a man under Bond because the governor itself was a sophisticated piece of deviltry, training and indoctrination took time and effort, men had to be taught to fight and fear and there were still altogether too many unfortunate accidents.

A man under Bond could kill himself if he could face the consequences both of making a sloppy job of it and of succeeding in ending his life but not in concealing the self-willed nature of his death. Failed suicide attempts were interpreted by governors as willful damage to valuable Fleet property and punished accordingly, and Robert couldn't remember what it had been like when his governor had started to cook off on him in port Burkhayden, but he knew it must have been impressively terrible because Chief Stildyne had been much kinder to him since, even when he wasn't thinking about it.

Success in killing oneself but failure to disguise the intentioned nature of the act meant that the Bench would cancel the waiver it held as a guarantee of good behavior against prosecution of your family and friends and their families and families' friends and their kye and their domestic poultry and the rodents behind the stove in the cook-house for crimes against the rule of Law and the Judicial order, and all of your suffering on their behalf to try to protect them would be for naught.

If you were Nurail that didn't so much matter because the Bench had already had your goods and chattel but they would still try to find somebody who could be made to repay the cost of your training, maintenance, and upkeep.

Not more than forty years, Standard. The Bench had not been making bond-involuntaries for longer than that. It had been only forty years ago since the Bench had begun to authorize some people, and not others, to inflict torture, as an attempt to control the use of torture as an instrument of State and bring the abuse of sentient creatures under the control of the rule of Law. It had been well intentioned, perhaps. The people who had built up the system of Inquiry had felt that it was humane and pitiful of them to do so. If they'd only been able to see where they'd been going . . .

There had been forty years for bond-involuntaries to learn how to manage with a governor, how to live to claim the prize that waited for them on the Day that their sentence was completed. On that day a bond-involuntary became a reborn soul with accumulated pay and benefits, a full pension with honors, exemption from all local taxes and tariffs wherever he wished to go and from most of the Bench assessments as well, free passage on Fleet transport on demand—so many perquisites and privileges that it hardly seemed possible to grasp. But Robert had seen it happen.

When he'd been on *Scylla*, one of Koscuisko's teams had pulled a narrow one through a narrower cleft, preventing some saboteurs from gaining control of one of her main battle cannon, saving the ship. Captain Irshah Parmin had petitioned for revocation of Bond in light of this signal service. Joslire had been dead by the time the petition had been approved, but three others of Robert's fellows had gone free.

Over forty years a culture of self-defense had developed from nothing. It was a culture of finger-code, and groupings, the unwritten but strictly observed convention that a bond-involuntary could not be teased or tormented with questions or demands that could place any man in conflict with himself and engage his governor—and one of those conventions was that bond-involuntaries were never to be quartered but with other bond-involuntaries, and their quarters were not to be under surveillance.

They were under thirty-two hour surveillance by definition. Ship's Security declined to intrude on what limited privacy they had, and there were penalties assessed any unbonded troops caught in bond-involuntary quarters unless as a party of three or more with at least one officer of the rank of Chief Warrant or higher—another provision intended to protect bond-involuntaries from more abuse or punishment than their lives were to them already, though it didn't always work out quite as well as that.

There were only six of them assigned to the *Ragnarok*. There were technically speaking quarters for twenty-five, but nobody knew of any ship with a full complement of bond-involuntaries and the fact that they were six gave them two que-bays, enough space for ten. The common areas could be connected. They were connected now.

Everybody was here except for Pyotr, and there was suspicion and confusion in the air.

"He wouldn't," Godsalt said flatly. "Makes no sense, to take us out from underneath that thing and then just have to put the screws down again. I don't care. I haven't got family."

Bonds didn't talk about their families. Not about their crimes, not about their experiences with the dancing-masters, not about where they'd come from or hoped to return to. Bond-involuntaries especially never talked about the future. It was too painful to fantasize about that out loud.

"So he knows," Hirsel argued back. Godsalt was tall and lean and limber in the conventional sense, but Hirsel was as curly-headed as a yearling. "Robert?"

He was responsible for finding things out, and just because he liked people and they generally seemed to like him back for whatever reasons of their own that they might have. Especially female people. He was the intelligence officer of the group, he supposed, but shouldn't that mean that he got custard for bribes?

Two liked custard, and when you wanted a favor you could generally obtain at least a hearing with the promise of a dish of custard to be delivered well out of Koscuisko's ken. Desmodontae did not digest milk sugars very effectively. She liked custards, but they gave her a belly-ache, and she and the officer had been squabbling over the issue almost since he had come to the *Ragnarok*, and Robert with him.

"Just after he came back," Robert confirmed. "Trips down to Intelligence, and couriers. Also no questions asked about stomach-powders. And she said something to me about my mother's brother's wife's family, so I think he was doing his research."

They generally gave him more credit than he thought he actually deserved as a Koscuisko expert. Just because he had known the officer for longer than any bond-involuntary still living in Fleet, because the only bond-involuntary that Koscuisko had known longer had been Joslire, who was dead.

Kerenko was Sarvaw, and Sarvaw was a kind of Dolgorukij. Kerenko should know if anybody did; but Kerenko was chewing his under-lip thoughtfully. "And there's a Malcontent involved. You never know what Malcontents are about. They're capable of anything."

This was something esoteric and private to the shared experience of Sarvaw and Aznir Dolgorukij that Robert did not understand at all. He had no difficulty understanding why Chief Stildyne was in so cheerful a mood since Cousin Stanoczk's courier had come on board, however. Two days ago. The officer's cousin had had a letter for Kerenko that Kerenko had received with astonished pleasure, read to himself and without his lips moving, and carried around in his bosom ever since.

"So this is the situation." It was Garrity's turn to speak. "He's been checking up on our families. He plans a leave on Emandis. Nobody understands what good he might think it will do to give us a taste of freedom if we were just going to have to go back, and we know he doesn't expect to be here for very much longer."

That was true. Koscuisko was here because he had evidence that would protect the *Ragnarok* against its enemies in Fleet, but once the *Ragnarok* had been exonerated by an audit inquiry Koscuisko could go home. Verlaine had freed Koscuisko, given him relief of Writ to be executed at Koscuisko's good pleasure. So Koscuisko was in the same situation as he had put them in, except backwards; he had come back from his home to rejoin his Command, and would be leaving Fleet to go back home, but not before he took care of business.

"So he's made a plan to steal us from the Bench. That cousin of his."

Robert could tell from the tone of Hirsel's voice that he was having a hard time getting used to a man who looked a lot like the officer but behaved so differently. He knew he was. Koscuisko's cousin was due to leave as soon as the *Ragnarok* dropped vector, though, so that was something.

"Are we going?" The Bench could not do more to his Megh than it had already; and she belonged to the Danzilar prince now, at any rate, who had decided to make of her a token of the contract he wanted between him and the people of Burkhayden, and would defend her accordingly. There were Nurail in Gonebeyond and rumors that the son of the war-leader of Darmon had escaped and was growing to manhood there, with all of the rest of his family dead. Maybe somewhere in Gonebeyond there was someone who remembered that Robert had had family. Megh would expect him to go. He would never see her again.

"That's to decide," Godsalt admitted. "Pyotr's twenty-four and some, less than five years short of reborn. I don't know what I would do in his place. But none of us really knows what's going on in the officer's mind, do we? And I'm not asking Chief."

There was nothing in Godsalt's brain to reinforce the respect due to rank, no reason they need call Koscuisko "the officer" and Stildyne "Chief" in quarters. But habit was a powerful force. And Koscuisko had warned them about giving themselves away; it would be too ungrateful to let all of that good work come to nothing. It was important to maintain appearances.

"I would." For what it was worth. "Whether it was six years or six weeks. I knew a man who embraced his death to be free." He hadn't actually been there when Joslire died, though. Koscuisko had had one of the others kiss Joslire on Robert's behalf. He'd heard about it from Code, who had come back to *Scylla* without the rest of his team. "I never doubted his decision."

Garrity stood up. It was almost time for him to report to Infirmary. Garrity was on sprains-and-strains in orthopedic, this fifth-week. Robert had never cared for that particular assignment; he had emotional associations with particular sorts of disjoints that were not to be quieted when there were too many near reminders.

"We'll hear about it before the end of his leave comes up," Garrity said. "So we've got a few days. But I'm glad we had a chance to synchronize. I couldn't believe what I thought he was thinking of. I should have just remembered that he's mad."

Robert nodded, and thumped Garrity in the shoulder in a friendly fashion as Garrity passed, to comfort him. Yes. Koscuisko was mad. Koscuisko was mad in this instance like a war-leader, who could imagine indescribable retreats when it came to saving the lives of those who had accepted his direction.

They hadn't been given any choice; a bond-involuntary had to accept direction, that was the whole point. That, and punishment. And still Koscuisko was quite correct to take them for people who had put their trust in him to direct and to guide them. There were contracts in a man's life that not even the Bench could break or regulate, unspoken and intangible; which reminded him for no particular reason that he owed Engineering an extra half-a-day's maintenance on the Wolnadi fighter for which his team was responsible.

The basic truth of the whole thing was simply that the Bench was about pain and fear and force, and there was no force in all of Jurisdiction that could stand against trust and faith and charity. That was the real reason that Koscuisko was so dangerous. All of this time the Bench had believed it was because the man had the truth-sense in him and could hear a person think, and the Bench had been wrong.

Robert took that simple truth down with him to the maintenance atmosphere and set it on a shelf while he changed into a cover-all, then carried it with him out to where the Wolnadi fighter stood in wait for the cleaning of some of its intake vents. It was a plain fact, no more and no less; but it was worthy of admiration still, breathtakingly seditious, categorically revolutionary, absolutely conservative, all at the same time, and he was proud of himself for having welcomed it.

"Of course it's not impregnable," Vogel said. Rukota couldn't see Vogel's exact expression, because of the goggles that Vogel was wearing. They'd borrowed some of the equipment from Koscuisko's surgery, though Rukota didn't think anybody had gotten around to telling Koscuisko that, yet. With luck the equipment would all be back in place, safe and sound and never the worse for wear, before Koscuisko noticed it was missing; and taking it to Secured Medical was simply moving it from one medical area to another, really, wasn't it?

"But there are good reasons to pretend it is. For one, the Bench expects every citizen to hold the Judicial process in the very highest respect, it certainly couldn't suggest that there could be any question at all about the integrity of its own employees. Particularly its elite."

Rukota could see the point, but it was a weak one, in his opinion. Leaning back in Koscuisko's chair he stared up at the ceiling. It had been two, nearly three days, and he was almost beside himself with boredom. Yes, Vogel was an interesting man. But Vogel was busy. Concentrating. And a Bench specialist, so he wasn't comfortable talking very much in the first place.

"For another—" Making a final adjustment, Vogel grunted in apparent satisfaction. The record lay on a portable table under a bright light; it bristled with wires and probes from Koscuisko's surgical set, and Vogel was using a scaling glove to move about within the record's interior, watching his progress on one of Koscuisko's monitors. All Rukota could see from where he sat was the plain box that housed the record.

"For another, the moment you mention any such thing people will start looking for it. It's human nature. Not their fault. And then if they get past one level of security they'll realize that there's another. And then another. It's just asking for trouble."

Not that anybody would believe that a record wasn't protected, not if they stopped to think about it. Rukota guessed that Vogel's point was along the lines of discouraging people from stopping to think about it. Records couldn't be had by just anybody, anyway; yes, there were powers of eights of them, but they were still a controlled-access commodity.

"Any hints yet on how this one was compromised?" Hour after hour watching Vogel sit perfectly still, moving his probes so carefully that Rukota couldn't see that he was even moving them at all. He'd watched over Vogel's shoulder for a good while, but that hadn't been able to hold his interest forever. The fact that he hadn't any idea what he was looking at—apart from the obvious, circuits, access nodes, input-output channels—hadn't helped him concentrate, either.

"Well." For a moment Rukota thought Vogel was trying to decide which version of "mind your own business" would best suit this particular circumstance. Vogel surprised him; completing an adjustment that had apparently distracted his attention, he began to talk.

"It's Pesadie's on-base record. There's not much question of that. Noycannir had access codes. They were inactive but not revoked which would make it easier to sneak one past the record. But these pieces of evidence had to be formally logged by someone with an active Writ, or else she had to have talked someone out of surrendering an open code. She had the open-and-close marker with her when she got there, I suspect, just a question of deciding what to fit in the space between them. I need to find where that code's hiding out. Once we find it, it can be analyzed, but until we do—no telling."

And it took as long as it did because records had complex and inter-related anti-tampering protocols, self-defense mechanisms in place. Also because Vogel wanted to avoid accidentally damaging any of the false evidence that had been read into this record, to preserve the best picture of how it had been done.

"Now, the warrant that was issued to me to execute wasn't

anything like a record in terms of its sophistication. But once I got suspicious and began to look at it I decided that the wear around the edges of the authorization chops wasn't quite normal. Looked as though they were perfectly ordinary Judicial chops, at first analysis, very well done. But by the third run-through there were some interesting anomalies in the layering. It's a signature of sorts. I'm wondering if the signature we find here will be the same."

"Any idea how much longer it's going to take?" This was a rude question, but Rukota was an artilleryman and it was armed transport that was supposed to be genteel if anybody was. No, it was the Combine home defense fleet that was supposed to be genteel. Beautiful manners, Dolgorukij, and such beautiful cheerful smiles that you almost had to smile back even as they rolled right over you—a Sarvaw had told him that. But she'd been an artilleryman herself, so a little attitude was to be expected.

Vogel shook his head. "I'm picking off the layers from the back to front till I can get at the internal auditor. Once I get through to that, I can see whether or not it recognizes some elements in common with the forgery on that warrant. One way or the other I should be able to talk it into disclosing the pedigree of the Writ that logged the core details of that false evidence, as well as the Writ that applied the shell. Reports say that the evidence was presented in good form, so there has to be a valid interrogation record buried in here someplace, and I want to know—where—it—came from."

Fair enough. Maybe he shouldn't be talking; it could distract Vogel. Vogel kept talking, though; talking to himself, maybe. "Forging a Judicial chop takes considerable technical sophistication. I couldn't do it. It was hard enough to catch the little nick in the edge that tipped me off. In a manner of speaking."

Soft, low-voiced, and apparently talking to the record as much as to Rukota. "There's this, and we were lucky, there's no other word for it. Sheer luck. If ap Rhiannon hadn't sent those troops home with Koscuisko, he might have gone off with Noycannir. We'd never have seen that record again. Maybe not Koscuisko, either, I heard that they found some ugly things in her baggage."

Somebody could have taken a short-cut of some sort, in other words. Not expecting the forged record to ever have to stand up under any kind of scrutiny. Rukota stifled a yawn; watching Vogel work was about as exciting as testing a maintenance atmosphere for leaks in its plasma field.

"But that clerk was from Chilleau Judiciary. And just very shortly after someone tried to get Koscuisko off on an unauthorized transit of some sort, Verlaine is killed. The security systems expertly compromised. Chilleau. Could be a coincidence."

If he stared too long at the ceiling, Rukota decided, he could begin to make out the shadows of equipment panels behind the false netted surface that the Engineer had in place. He didn't care to. It was hard enough to get clean when they left this place. He'd scrubbed the palms of his hands all but raw, after their first session. He didn't know how Vogel was taking it, but for himself his strategy was to avoid noticing anything that might remind him of where he was. He decided to study his thumb-nail for a while. He didn't have to worry about falling asleep by accident.

"Don't believe in coincidence, do we, sweetie? No. No, we don't."

Vogel's voice had changed. Rukota straightened up, intrigued. Not only had Vogel's voice changed, but something was different about the relationship of Vogel's body to the probe array—focus, perhaps. Vogel had been sitting there delicately playing a probe and talking about things just a moment ago. Now Vogel wasn't there at all—he was somewhere deep in that record-box, all of his attention directed at some single point with an unnerving concentration that seemed to intensify by the moment.

"Yes, that's right. We don't believe in coincidence. We're suspicious. We're paranoid. We're hostile and unpleasant, aren't we, girl? Yes. You're such a clever record. Show me what you've got. You can tell—"

Vogel stopped. His voice cut off abruptly in mid-phrase; the track of the probe on the screen that Rukota could just see from one side didn't waver. Vogel had frozen in place. As near as Rukota could tell Vogel wasn't even breathing. When Vogel spoke again it was in a perfectly normal tone of voice, but the word he said explained it all to Rukota, a little too well.

"Destructor."

It was a bomb.

The record wasn't a bomb, no, but it had been provided with a little cyborg intelligence that would put a bomb together from the materials provided in a record, if anything happened to set off its sequence. Two layers of normally inert microfoam here. A minute chip of an ordinarily harmless spacer-card there. A safely isolated impulse-generator way over there, where it could not possibly interfere with anything going on with the mechanical workings of the record, until some tiny crazed guardian rushed from pillar to post collecting bits and chips and rerouting circuitry—

Rukota dove for the open door between the chamber and the ready-room, to close it down. To contain the damage as much as possible. He and Vogel were on the wrong side of that door, but he wasn't going through by himself. He'd been given an assignment, to observe, he couldn't observe from the wrong side of a closed door. He had only Vogel's word that the record was going to explode—Vogel's word and his body language, and the tension that communicated between souls on a subconscious level and said get *out get out, get out, get out now, get out*—

"After you," Rukota said. The door was closing. He wasn't going to stand here and let it just close. Was he?

Vogel sprang like a tension-wire slipped out of true, up and away and through the closing door to crumple in a heap against the far wall of the small ready-room, the other side of the outside corridor. Rukota swung himself through the fast-narrowing aperture after Vogel, wheeling to one side, snatching his arm away just in time to prevent his hand from getting caught in the door and confusing it into opening wide all over again. Vogel was clawing his way to one side of the wall opposite Rukota—away from directly across from the door, well, that made sense —

It was quiet. Very quiet. Blissfully, peacefully quiet. He didn't want to distract it. It was wonderful. Quiet. No sound. No noise. Nothing. Tranquil.

Something jingled at him. He tried to scowl at it; nothing happened. Scowling was noise. He could hear the creaking sound of his numb muscles; he didn't want any disturbance. No. It was too nice just the way it was. Quiet. Quiet was the good way to be.

Where was he? He opened his eyes, but he couldn't see anything. Had he opened his eyes? Sometimes a person just thought he'd sat up, and gotten up, and gotten dressed and started to put his boots on and then the alert would go off again and a person would realize that he'd been dreaming. This was like no dreamscape Rukota had ever seen; it was a soft pearly white, absolutely uniform in tint and hue. When the atmosphere did that, a man couldn't tell eight from an eighth for visibility. No clue. But he'd heard his eyes open, the scrape of the inside of the lid against the surface, the clanging sound his eyelashes made knocking against each other as he dragged the upper past and away from the lower. Terrible racket. He'd never realized that his body was as loud as it was.

Something big and black suddenly swooped down upon him from somewhere in that pearly mist. It startled him. He couldn't move. What? What? He smelled—

He smelled the snow-edged tang of bottled atmosphere, and realized that he couldn't move because he'd not been breathing. It wasn't mist. It was fire suppressant foam. Someone was here with a mask. He still couldn't move. Protective gear, that was the answer, people in full environmental suits lifting him onto a litter. Air. He needed air. He wasn't getting enough air.

He could feel his muscles tense to take a breath, and something told him that it was a mistake but his body wasn't listening and then it hit him in the left side like a reverberation round and he recognized the sensation. Ribcage again, damn it. He hated cracked ribs. Single most aggravating injury a man could sustain, in Rukota's opinion. It had happened to him twice or three times before in his life and he was heartily sick of the experience. Muscles didn't seem to learn, though, they were still working, gasping for air.

Down the corridor—he presumed—then stop, and wait for the corridor to clear. Airlock, obviously. He could see walls, again. Here were his good friends in Security, at least he thought that was one of Koscuisko's people—Garrity? Into a mover and hurrying through the corridors hell-bent for Infirmary. It was still eerily quiet. He could hear the blood pulse in his jaw beneath his ear, a rushing sound like white noise, but it wasn't constant. Volume up; volume down. Volume up; volume down.

Then while they carried him down the corridor, just as they angled past a turning with impressive precision and commendable urgency, sound and sensation returned with equivalent suddenness and brutal force, taking his breath away all over again. Damn. That hurt. What had happened? He couldn't remember.

The litter-bearers slid the litter expertly onto the therapeutic bed in Infirmary's emergency room, and here was the scowling face of Koscuisko himself. Hospital whites, so that was good. Even in his duty whites Koscuisko's rank was lined through with crimson, however; there was no forgetting that this man was an Inquisitor, which made things just the littlest bit awkward for a man in Rukota's position of not knowing what position exactly he was in.

Koscuisko was an Inquisitor. Part of his reputation was that of knowing what you were thinking. Rukota had no idea what expression might be found on his face, but Koscuisko apparently read enough of the question in Rukota's eyes to answer it.

"An explosion in Secured Medical has destroyed a small area of Ship's Stores with unusual efficiency for so contained a blast. One assumes that there has been a problem with the forged record that you and Vogel were examining. Doctor Narion will attend to you. You are not bleeding and nothing appears to be broken but we will assume the worst until we can complete a scan. I must go and pick some pieces of the wall out of Vogel's cerebral cortex. More later."

Rukota listened very carefully, trying to be sure he could commit the speech to memory. There were large parts of it that made no sense to him. He needed to be able to retrieve those later, at which time he could examine them more carefully with better hope of determining the actual meaning of the words.

It sounded like Koscuisko had things under control. Rukota closed his eyes. When he opened them again there was another officer there, one he recognized as Doctor Narion—Koscuisko's soft-tissue specialist. "We're ready to go for scan," she said, "So we'll be able to tell you what your status is within an eight or so. All right? Yes. Good."

If she said so. He could hear, but things were a little fuzzy around their edges as though everybody in the room was drunk but him. There were good odds that in that case he was the one who was drunk, Rukota knew—or drugged, at minimum.

Fair enough, he told himself, and closed his eyes again.

CHAPTER NINE

Unthinkable Alternatives

Farilk's office was much smaller than Andrej's own, of course, but there was no sense of confinement—merely the security of a quiet, comfortable room. The chairs were set up carefully so that the one in which he had been invited to sit faced the door, so that one could be sure that it was closed. Andrej had never been seated in Farilk's chair before. It was very comfortable.

"As it happens Vogel had a pad of scar tissue on his scalp already," Andrej said, looking at the milky surface of the flask of rhyti in his hand. "And it was a small sort of a bomb. Damaged tissue, yes, but it's all insult and no bleeding. I put in a temporary plate. It'll metabolize itself away inside of two or three months."

He'd feared the damage to be much worse when they'd brought Vogel in, just yesterday. Farilk hadn't given him the least indication of needing an explanation for why Andrej had rescheduled his appointment; it was only Andrej's own discomfort that made him chatter on about it.

But he had noticed that he was chattering on about it, now. And that was not acceptable. It betrayed an acute case of nerves, and Farilk would simply sit quietly until he was ready to talk, and then he would have to make another appointment. He felt uncomfortable enough as it was, despite the chair. He didn't want to have to make another appointment.

"Scar tissue can come in very handy sometimes," Farilk said. "And there's definite value to not having to feel anything at the site of injury. Not feeling can also become an issue, of course. It's hard to know when to let scar tissue alone, isn't it?"

All right, Farilk wouldn't sit quietly and let Andrej talk. Maybe he wasn't interested in another appointment either. He had a fairly full case-load, between stress and sleep disturbances associated with the *Ragnarok*'s current status and recent adventures. And there were always issues arising on board. There were more than seven hundred souls on board of the *Ragnarok*. What would Farilk do if Two needed the assistance of a psychiatrist?

No, Farilk was just trying to help Andrej get over a difficult spot. That was all. He should accept the help when it was offered. Farilk was the professional, here.

"I have a survey of the literature conducted." He was going to lose track of that flask of rhyti, and drop it. Better to set it aside. "The experiences and police records of Fleet inquisitors returning to civilian life. Many of them I find form a relationship with the local civil authorities. In one instance on record there was a problem with the abuse of patients, but other indications in the personal history perhaps concealed the truth. You will laugh at me. I laugh at myself. I never imagined that I would have this difficulty."

Farilk dropped his eyes to his lap, considering, giving Andrej a moment to struggle with himself. "The first thing that must be done is to name the problem, your Excellency. This is helpful on many levels. On the most obvious it helps to reduce the possibility of a mistaken diagnosis, and consequent inappropriate treatment recommendations, on my part. On a less obvious but more meaningful level there is in many cultures the feeling that to name the thing gives us power over it."

Or gave the monster life. Names were difficult to predict, that way. "It is the absence in my life of torture." He could name it, if Farilk needed to hear that. He had spent enough time wrestling with it in his own mind before now. "I yearn for it. The pleasure that I had. The fact of taking pleasure was a horror to me. Now I thirst."

Farilk was not surprised; or, if he was, he hid it exceptionally well. He'd known Farilk for years. And although the talent was a product of habit and attention and learning how to read—and not the occult curse of some demon bestial or angelic—it was true more often than not that Andrej *did* know when a man was dissembling with him, or not.

"You still experience distress in the consideration of the requirements of Secured Medical, your Excellency?"

Farilk was just checking. Andrej stifled his temptation to leap to his feet and kiss Farilk on both cheeks, declare himself cured by virtue of overcoming his dread at last, and rushing out of the room to hang himself. Farilk was just establishing the clinical baseline. That was all.

"When Captain Lowden was alive and I was to go to seek confession on his direction I felt always the conflict between knowing what I was about to do and knowing that I was going to enjoy it. The passion that I feel in my heart when I remember frightens me. How long can I endure this before what is left to me of common decency is worn away at last?"

How long would it be before the savage hunger in his heart to hear the helpless cries of pain overpowered him, and betrayed a patient to the Inquisitor? Was Lowden to conquer him, was Lowden to continue to rule him, from beyond the borderlands of Death? Was it Lowden's vengeance against Andrej for his murder?

"Let's explore this, your Excellency."

No. Let us not. Let me go find a gun and shoot myself. Or—better— yes. Let us go down to Secured Medical, you and I, and I will provide you with all of the practical demonstration you can bear. "Yes?"

"You're accustomed to this stimulus, a very powerful one. Many others have failed to sustain the degree of stress you have been under. Your accommodation was extreme, but survival-oriented."

It was no such thing. It was the beast in the blood, the tyranny of his ancestors and the shame of his pretenses to decency. It had been no accommodation strategy. It had been the unfettering of an appetite so huge and powerful that he had had to struggle to restrain it, every time, every day, every hour. He had not always won. But if Farilk needed to believe that his delight in torture had been a psychological quirk evolved under pressure, if that was what Farilk needed to believe in order to continue to speak to him as though he was a human being—"I do not feel that I am surviving with any notable degree of success at this time, Doctor."

Farilk smiled, a bit painfully, at the formality of that title. "You are our staff expert on the mechanics of addiction, your Excellency. A thought experiment, and I only propose it to you now for you to conduct later at your leisure. Sometimes an addiction can be managed with smaller doses of a pharmacologically similar drug whose effect need not be as damaging."

Yes, and sometimes a very small amount of a related substance was enough to bring an addict's craving to the fore with newly redoubled savagery and force. "A thought experiment, you say."

Farilk nodded. "I mention this to you strictly in my capacity as your mental health partner, your Excellency. I don't know whether your personal experimentation has ever led you to take advantage of the services of a pain-worker. But the therapeutic value of a professional pain-worker's services is unquestioned," Farilk said, very firmly, as though to get it all out and said before Andrej could strike him across the face and stalk out. "A wide range of both physiological and psychological deficits can be very adequately addressed in selected individuals with the carefully controlled provision of extreme stimulus. The thought experiment that I propose to you is this, your Excellency, if you will entertain it."

He did feel like striking Farilk and stalking out. He wasn't sure what Farilk was getting at, not exactly, but whatever it was, it was deeply offensive. He was certain of that much.

Or it could be his emotional reaction to a threat, to a suggestion that terrified him. Either way Farilk was not going to continue unless Andrej agreed to hear him. Tiresome. As strict as any Protocol, but for much the same reasons, Andrej realized. Cooperation could not be forced. Temporary compliance could be obtained with fear and pain and the fear of pain, but people had to be tricked into cooperation, especially if it was to be in the service of their own torment. "I am listening."

Having said so, he was honor-bound to do so. No matter how violently his heart rejected what he thought Farilk was about to tell him.

"Imagine, if you will, your Excellency, that there is a person whose body will not respond to normal pleasurable sensation until it has been sensitized by the application of controlled stimulus. A person is suffering, your Excellency, and you are in a position to provide healing in a form that is unusual for you. You are going to treat this person who is in need of healing, but you are not going to harm her."

Farilk meant to make a sex professional of him. That was all this was about. Farilk meant to prostitute him to some silly girl who thought she wanted to be hit. No, of course Farilk meant to do no such thing; Andrej struggled to sit and listen while his mind and heart raged against the shocking suggestions that Farilk continued to propose, calmly, carefully, quietly.

"They are very glad to surrender their suffering to you because they are in need, so that you may take pleasure in it with their consent and their entire good-will, which is given to you freely and without coercion or duress. There are people who will intervene if the situation warrants it, and if at any time distress overpowers her she will stop the exercise."

Farilk stood up. "Would such a situation be the drug that helps manage the addiction? Or the irritation that makes withdrawal all the more difficult to bear? Which?"

Andrej admired his timing in more than one way: yes, the period for the interview was over—neither of them could bear too long spent in so intense a conversation—and also, yes, he had had all that he could bear to hear for the present, and he had to get away from here now. Right now. He couldn't even think of what Farilk had proposed to him. His mind was full of turmoil; he could not stop thinking— remembering—wishing. He had to get away.

"Think on it, please, your Excellency," Farilk said. Andrej stood up, dizzy. "And come back to see me in a few days. If I don't hear from you by next five I'll see about getting a place on your scheduler."

Because he was not to be permitted to let this lapse, now that he had raised the issue. That was only fair. That was only to be expected. He would himself find fault with Farilk if Farilk let any other soul come to him for assistance and then never come again, unless the problem solved itself, and this one was not going to solve itself unless someone should chance to honor him when he went to Emandis to visit Joslire's tablet by setting the memorial-hill slope on fire, and ending his life.

Therefore Andrej nodded, and choked out the appropriate response. "Yes, of course, Doctor. In a few days. Till then."

The door to Farilk's office opened as Andrej drew near, and he fled through it, so caught up in his own distress of spirit that he could not more than nod in response to the salute of the Intelligence technician that he passed in the corridor on his way out of Infirmary.

There were a limited number of places on this station that could reasonably be used for formal argument. It required a room large enough for one observer to sit in far enough away from the two disputants to be effectively ignored while still being close enough to hear and see; it had to have privacy—for concentration—and have observation capacity in place, for the historical record.

At the same time there were only nine of them, which meant that the most sessions that could possibly run concurrently was three. Three sites had been decided on, agreed upon, set up; one in the pantry, one in the main theater, and here. This was the one that Rafenkel liked best.

"Specialist Ivers, the Second Judge should be selected at Chilleau Judiciary; Specialist Delleroy, there should be no selection. Initial discussions. Specialist Rafenkel observing."

Her voice sounded oddly flattened to her in this little room, in some sense. It wasn't a room, exactly, perhaps; it was a floating observation station, eight-sided, tethered to the station on shore by a narrow causeway on pontoons. It hadn't been out on the lake earlier. They'd only gotten it set up over the past day, since Delleroy had arrived with Ivers.

Who were both waiting for her. "Call it," she said to Ivers. Ivers represented the status quo. The status quo, to the extent that it could reasonably be supported, was the default solution for the conservation of peace and order—if the mare hadn't foaled, there was no need to milk her.

"Even," Ivers said. Square-shouldered and cautious she sat there at the work-table opposite Delleroy, one hand loosely clenched on the table's surface. "Chilleau should be selected even though the First Secretary is dead."

All right. Rafenkel smiled—she'd have said odd, because of how odd the entire situation was. She toggled the random repeater and waited for a binary hit. Even. So Ivers got the first argument. There were advantages to going first; but advantages to hearing the other person's opening arguments first, too.

"You're open, Ivers," Rafenkel announced, just for formality's sake. Delleroy—slumped slantwise at his ease in his chair with his feet stretched well out—nodded his maned head in acknowledgement. Delleroy was all willow and brick where Ivers was an octave's growth of nut-bearing blackwood; a different sort of a tree entirely, but each with their own strength. Delleroy was prettier, but Ivers . . . what? She wasn't taller, darker, fairer, balder, anything that Rafenkel could think of just now.

All in all, Ivers really hadn't made much of an impression on a person at first meeting, no more than any other regiment of tactical cavalry might. No flash, no noise, no light reflecting off polished surfaces, just a quiet self-assured block of mortuary stone communicating a serene understanding of the fact that she would roll over you as though you weren't there, if need should be.

"Short meeting," Ivers said to Delleroy. Once the discussion started it was Rafenkel's business to become invisible unless something came up. "No contest that I can see, no contest at all. The Second Judge had already been identified as the dominant choice across all Judiciaries. We know what the citizenry want, we know who is preferred, confederacy wasn't on the options list and there is no reason to introduce it now. I'll take your tiles and we can all go take naps, Padrake."

Ivers held out her hand flat-palmed and precisely centered on the broad white line that divided the work-table into two symbolic spaces. There was a small stack of ceramic tiles in front of Delleroy; another at Ivers' elbow. Each of them represented one of the time-honored measures of the public welfare and prosperity of the common weal: incidence of violent crime, public compliance as measured by tax receipts and off-the-market economies, durable and perishable goods in pipeline. All of them issues that Bench specialists were accustomed to examine to make a determination on the health of any given system or situation; all of them measures of the effective rule of Law and the regulation of trade.

"Not so fast." Delleroy's tone of voice made it clear that he was no more serious about his theatrically exaggerated resentment than Ivers had been about her demand. Rafenkel didn't envy Delleroy the battle; she didn't know of anybody who would have chosen to defend the confederacy model, not with any other alternative available. "Let's just start at the beginning, here, Jils. Specialist Ivers. Sorry."

"All right, Delleroy," Ivers agreed. Reaching across the table, she muddled about with her fingers in his tile-array, and turned one up at random. "What have we got, here? Taxation base. How is the total tax burden of an enterprise in Haspirzak improved by not selecting the Second Judge? Instead of one central authority there will be nine, and each of them will inevitably develop its own procedures and requirements."

Ivers sat back, playing with the tile, turning it over and over again in her fingers. "Which means nine times as many people to go between and implement, lawyers and law courts and port authorities and the explosion of existing administrative structures into a whole new entrenched hierarchy more concerned with perpetuating its own survival and development than encouraging the free and fair exchange of goods and services."

Rafenkel let her breath out in a rush, leaning against the padded curve of the low-backed chair almost staggered. Delleroy straightened up in his seat for his own part, and if Rafenkel wasn't mistaken Delleroy winked at her. *Yes. It was an impressive rant, wasn't it? But that's our job, ranting impressively.*

"You are so cynical," Delleroy said, a note of humor in his voice that just barely escaped being blatantly affectionate. "But that's good. Cynical is good. We need cynical to examine all angles with open eyes. Chilleau doesn't have a chance of keeping the lid on inconsistent taxation. We select Chilleau, and what happens?"

Ivers raised an eyebrow and waited.

"I'll tell you what happens." Of course Delleroy would. The question had been rhetorical. "People see a First Judge selected at a Judiciary in which a senior officer was murdered, and no culprit brought to justice. They conclude that the law can be gotten 'round, and if murder won't be pursued and prosecuted, who's going to seriously bother with a little spot of fraud here and there?"

There was the most peculiar sound in the air on the Ivers side of the table, Rafenkel thought. A little bit like the nap on a velvet wall-hanging spontaneously surging from one side to the other with a low-voiced sound just out of the reach of Rafenkel's ears that communicated only menace. The sound of Ivers' hackles rising, and snarling as they came.

"Assuming of course," Ivers said cheerfully, giving Delleroy no satisfaction of a perceptible reaction, "that it is known to have been a murder. And that a culprit is not apprehended, guilty or not if need be. While the unwholesome effect on taxation and trade obtains with the confederation model whether the murder of Chilleau's First Secretary is ever solved or not, as it will be, without fail."

Delleroy raised one hand where it lay on the table and showed Ivers the palm of his hand: *peace.* "Of course," he said. "But we don't know when that'll happen, do we, with Chilleau's only Bench specialist available pulled off on to other assignments like this one? And if the murder is solved, the public perception remains of an administrative apparatus without an experienced head. Advantage will be taken."

Delleroy could rant with the best; Rafenkel considered it a privilege to be witness. He was only getting started, too, so much was evident as he continued. "Percentages skimmed off tax collections, ad-hoc and off-the-record taxes assessed or disguised as fees, proceeds to pay for Bench offices reduced because collections are being harvested and the Bench forced to raise taxes to pay for the agents to investigate what's gone wrong with tax collections."

It all sounded so reasonable when Delleroy said it. He had the rhetorical flourishes down in his body-language as well, leaning into his argument, leaning back to let his final bolt home. "If the Judge gets to keep all of her own taxes, it's in her best interest to maximize the efficiency of collections and minimize fraud—a much more manageable task at the individual Bench level. Enlightened self-interest."

Ivers, however, had known Delleroy—Rafenkel reminded herself—and was apparently at least partially immune to his persuasiveness. "Inequitable taxation," Ivers retorted. "Every Judge for herself and the devil take the hindmost. Influence brokering. Arms races. There must be a clearly identified and perceived central authority. Chilleau Judiciary, in fact."

One tax collector was better than nine, in other words. Rafenkel could see both sides of the argument, which surprised her a little bit.

"Selecting Chilleau means funding Fleet for civil order operations on a greatly expanded level," Delleroy warned. Not giving up. Ivers grinned. What, had Ivers been afraid that Delleroy was going to roll over?

"Not selecting Chilleau means funding Fleet for the same purpose, and for the formation of dedicated Bench detachments besides. More tax revenue requirements. It won't wash, Padrake. Delleroy."

He started to lift his hand to make a point, shut his mouth and closed his hand, glanced over to one side; then his face cleared and he leaned forward, both forearms on the table.

"Fleet detachments which can be funded out of revenues no longer required to support a central administration, sufficient to pay for Fleet agency enforcement of collection of existing taxes in a manner uniform Bench-wide. Confederation won't increase citizens' taxes. Confederation will be tax-neutral."

"While selecting Chilleau guarantees that existing Fleet resources, requiring no additional tax revenues, enforce the tax codes across all of Jurisdiction space, uniformly. You know it perfectly well. You son of a bitch."

The almost-too-apparent affection that Rafenkel had heard from Delleroy was there in equal measure in Ivers' voice. Ivers was pleased with Delleroy's stubbornness, Rafenkel decided. She *had* been afraid he'd fail to prosecute his case as vigorously as possible, in light of the previous association—and out of consideration for the challenges of her current position as well.

"So's your old man," Delleroy said. "I know nothing of the sort. So maybe confederation would increase administration costs of shipping. Benches responsible only for themselves will see their own best interest served in efficient and cost-effective management. They'll be working for themselves, not the First Judge."

Ivers' present situation was not enviable, Rafenkel knew. The easiest and most obvious solution to the problem of Verlaine's unsolved murder was to assassinate Ivers for the good of the Judicial order and declare her guilty after the fact. Specialist Nion had been talking a little too openly about related subjects; that was part of the reason that Rafenkel had decided to make it her business to see that Ivers and Nion weren't alone together.

"At the expense of the common weal, Delleroy, Bench against Bench and the citizens paying the price for power struggles at the upper echelons."

They were clearly only getting started on taxes, and before any tiles could pass they had to agree, Delleroy and Ivers, that the advantage lay with one argument or the other. If they could not agree she, Rafenkel, would rule that there was no advantage to either for that element, and take the tile out of play. Taxes clearly had a great deal of play left in it.

"Bench against Bench gives us unprecedented opportunities to test alternate strategies on a local level. The one that is most efficient will prevail, and other Benches will adopt it out of their own self-interest. Confederation will improve the common weal by driving out the best tax model for adoption."

Rafenkel settled her back against the padded seat of her chair and folded her arms across her chest.

It was going to be a long session.

Hours later and Ivers had taken the victory so far—one tile. Delleroy had finally conceded that it was entirely possible that confederation would result in a short-term increase in the tax burdens and potentially middle-term tax increases as well. He'd surrendered the tile only with a reconsideration marker on it, though. They were both stubborn. Rafenkel was impressed by the strength of the defense Delleroy was putting up for the choice of last resort; but she wasn't unhappy about it when the time came to take a break.

"No, with increased administrative infrastructure it becomes more—and not less—difficult for people to obtain medical care," Ivers was insisting, calmly. "Especially specialized medical care. How many Mayon surgical colleges are there, under Jurisdiction? Not more than fourteen—if you don't count Mayon."

That was a bit of a stretch, maybe. There were in sufficient plenty of surgical colleges, just few with the range and depth and breadth of Mayon's resources. Since that was Ivers' point, Rafenkel decided to let it go, on her own personal private score-board—and was just shifting in her seat to listen to Delleroy's rebuttal when something caught her eye, from outside the room. At the end of the floating path, yes, on the ancient shore on which the station had been built— Capercoy. Capercoy with one arm raised high overhead, waving—what? Oh. A pre-pack package.

"Yeah," Ivers said, before Rafenkel or Delleroy had a chance to react. "And I'm on kitchen with Capercoy today. He probably just wants to make sure he doesn't hog all of the fun for himself. Rafenkel, we'll pick up after mid-meal, all right?"

Rafenkel nodded. Breaks were part of their schedule; an element in the common knowledge of Bench specialists was the maximization of intellectual analysis by careful management, periods of focus and concentration balanced by periods of rest during which apparently random thoughts could be safely entertained. In which case they frequently turned out not to be random thoughts at all.

"Agreed," Rafenkel answered, and closed the record she was making of proceedings.

Ivers started out the door and down the floating path, across the still black waters; there was no light except for that marking the way or reflecting from the station. In the blackness of the cave Ivers seemed to be walking through the void of Space. Rafenkel frowned; and then reminded herself that Capercoy was waiting for Ivers. There was no need for her to hurry after Ivers and come up with some excuse to go with her to the kitchen. Capercoy would look after her.

Alone in the small glassed-in room with Delleroy, Rafenkel set her things in order while Delleroy stretched from toe to finger-tip and back again before he relaxed abruptly against the back of his chair once more, as though the sinews stringing his limbs together had suddenly been cut. "Long session," Delleroy said. "Tough argument."

He was right on both counts, so Rafenkel nodded. "You're really pushing it, aren't you?" It wasn't easy to remember that Delleroy was just the debtor's advocate, here, and charged with putting his assigned solution forward as vigorously as possible. He argued with such conviction. If she hadn't known better she would have concluded that he'd been thinking hard about it for a very long time.

"She'd respect nothing less," Delleroy said, with a decided nod. "I couldn't do any less. She'd know."

Yes, Delleroy and Ivers had history. But also yes, if Ivers suspected Delleroy of softening his attack for whatever reason she would lose respect for him. So would Rafenkel herself.

"Gotta respect your professionalism." She could give him that ungrudgingly. "I wouldn't want to be defending confederation."

Raising his head Delleroy gazed thoughtfully into the middle distance at the opposite side of the floating room. "That's what I thought at first," he said, in a tone of voice that Rafenkel could only characterize in her mind as one of reluctant confession. "But the more I think about it the more sense it makes. Will Cintaro accept the Second Judge? No. Cintaro wants it for herself. We can't go any of the

Fontailloe routes, not if we pay the least bit of attention to the past. None of the other Judiciaries have the support to take over the role, especially if Cintaro is not selected and must be dealt with. Confederation works for me, Rafenkel. It does."

He should save the persuasive speeches for people who could be moved by them, Rafenkel told herself. Still, he sounded sincere. "Confederation is anarchy." The Sixth Judge, Rafenkel's Judge, was willing to accept even Supicor in the role of First Judge rather than have no First Judge at all.

The Sixth Judge and her advisors foresaw no difficulties in resisting any undue demands on Supicor's part if it came to that, and Sant-Dasidar could afford to spend a little extra by way of common benefit tax money to Supicor for infrastructure restoration and management. "My Judge will demand *she* be Selected, before it comes to that."

Delleroy shrugged. "An interesting point, Rafenkel, because in the final analysis what can the Sixth Judge actually do? Call out the Fleet? No, Fleet is more than happy for any excuse it gets to preserve its autonomy by coming up with reasons why it oughtn't do as the Judge tells it. At least not right away. Not without careful consideration."

She had to laugh, because he was right. That was one reason why the Sixth Judge liked it at Sant-Dasidar: the Jurisdiction Fleet might withhold resources, but so long as she had the cooperation of the Dolgorukij Combine—a solid five-in-eight of the population, a good seven-in-eight of the Bench resources—she had a perfectly good fleet of her very own to direct at will.

It didn't seem quite right to let his claim go by without a challenge, though, no matter how true she thought it might be. "The Judge is the voice of the Law, and the rule of Law is the foundation of Jurisdiction. Not even Fleet can stand against the verdict of the Bench for long, not without destroying the basic assumptions of our social contract. You know it."

The Bench had no significant police force of its own, and if the Fleet disregarded the Bench it could do so with impunity, but without the legal and administrative framework of the Bench Fleet would find itself without supplies, without resources, without recruits—and challenged for local dominion by home defense fleets like that of the Combine, or the Emandis home defense fleet in Brisinje Judiciary.

Delleroy leaned one arm on the table's surface, sitting at an angle to the table to face her very directly. "I'll tell you what the foundation of the Bench is," he said, low-voiced and intent. "It's not the Judges. It's not the Fleet. It's not the clerks of Court of the planetary governments or system proxies, or any of those things. It's us. Plain and simple. We are the foundation of the rule of Law, Rafenkel, Bench specialists. It's us who run the Bench anyway. What difference can it make who calls herself First Judge? It's the Bench specialists assigned who do the real work."

That it was perfectly true in a limited sense did not mean that Delleroy had any business actually saying such a thing. "We're the hidden weapon of the Bench," she corrected, a little bit frostily. "And only a weapon or a tool. Mind your place."

"Come on." Delleroy's tone made it clear that he didn't have any patience just now for pious clichés. "You're the one who knows better than that, Rafenkel. It's our job, not the Judges' or the First Secretaries', to see what needs to be done and then make it happen. Why are we here in the first place? Because each one of those Judges knows that no solution we won't support can stand. How about the way we rewrote the rules, for an example? Whose idea was that, anyway?"

Changing the strategy for attacking the debate, he meant. Rafenkel frowned a bit, thinking. "I heard from Balkney. He heard from Capercoy and was about to talk to Zeman. I don't know. Does it matter?" It had been a good idea. She could understand his curiosity, but she hadn't bothered to ask, herself. She'd thought she'd find out as things went forward.

"Of course it doesn't." Delleroy stood up. "Time to eat. We're going to need our strength. That Ivers, she's a tough one."

Maybe Delleroy was right. Maybe the Bench did run on Bench specialists, rather than the Judges. There were many Judges and few Bench specialists—an enormous amount of power without well-defined limits in the hands of a small number of fanatically anonymous operatives, running things from behind the scenes. What was to stop them from simply taking the Law into their own hands and redefining it as they saw fit? What was to stop them from taking over?

Little things. Duty and honor, and the fact that their only excuse for what they sometimes had to do was that it was in the service of the greater good and the common weal. An historical understanding of the necessary fact that the moment people started to make up their own rules they lost their objectivity and began to act at cross purposes with one another, with inevitable negative consequences for the population.

Was Delleroy hinting that a Bench specialist had truly assassinated the First Secretary, and not some misguided Fleet high-level operative?

Would the Jurisdiction be in worse shape if it were being run by Bench specialists? There would still be Judges, and the rule of Law—but no one single presiding, unifying voice. If the Judiciary were to be run by Bench specialists, what was there to prevent some one Bench specialist from plotting against the others, and ultimately establishing an absolute autocracy?

What was to stop any one given Judge from doing just that if there was no recognized highest-level authority, under Delleroy's confederacy model? Had Delleroy actually been sounding her out on building an influence base for Brisinje, or for Padrake Delleroy, when confederacy came to the Jurisdiction?

Delleroy was deep. It would be like him to be trying something like that just to demonstrate how seriously he took his assigned argument for confederation. *What an operator*, Rafenkel thought, admiringly; and followed Delleroy out of the debate room to get her mid-meal in the kitchen with the others.

Dierryk Rukota looked down through the sound-proofed clearwall into the pit of the Engineering bridge, resentfully. He would much rather have been down there with Wheatfields right now, looking at simulated fire-patterns from weapons placement proposals. Much.

Instead he was up here on the observation deck that overlooked the Engineering bridge, which was entirely too crowded. First Officer. Intelligence officer, Two, she'd always made him nervous. Ship's surgeon with his arms crossed over his chest, chewing on the cuticle of his thumb irritably; and, of course, brevet captain Jennet ap Rhiannon, glaring eye-to-eye with Karol Vogel where he sat.

"And Koscuisko's auxiliary imager. And the micro-flints. And an entire store-room, Vogel, and very nearly did a number on my weaponer as well, and that's not even getting to the real damage you've done this ship."

Her weaponer? That would be him, Rukota realized, impressed.

He hadn't quite realized that Fleet warships ever carried weaponers for the ship as a whole, rather than the crew-member assigned the role on the Wolnadi fighters. Here he had thought that he was just an irresponsible stow-away having the time of his life.

"Captain ap Rhiannon." Vogel sounded tired, and a little out of temper. "I can only assure you again. It was an accident. I had as much invested—no, I didn't. But appearances to the contrary notwithstanding, it was not a deliberate act of sabotage. Would I have to have died, to convince you of that?"

Rukota could sympathize with Vogel's irritation. He had been very thoroughly bruised and rattled by the explosion, but was otherwise unharmed. Vogel hadn't gotten quite far enough from the blast-funnel that the open doorway made when the bomb had exploded, and had had several pieces of miscellaneous Secured Medical picked out of his brain along with fragments of bone.

Koscuisko hadn't known about the borrowed—now destroyed— surgical set when he'd been operating. A good thing for Vogel, too, Rukota decided, with a sideways glance at Koscuisko's thunderous scowl. He'd never seen Koscuisko in a really bad mood before.

Ap Rhiannon looked thoughtful. "Might have been a good start, Specialist. Because without that Record I don't know how I am going to protect this crew from Fleet, and that means that you may have cost me lives."

Vogel rubbed his forehead wearily, seeming not so much aggravated now as discouraged. "I can give testimony. I saw it. That should count for something. And we ran all of the checks, you can ask your weaponer, he was there."

Oh, no, you don't, Vogel, Rukota thought, and kept his gaze fixed firmly on the scene below. He could see the status-boards. He could see the forward scans. The *Ragnarok* was due to drop vector; ap Rhiannon liked to watch. Vogel was not going to drag him into this if Rukota could help it. Vogel was the Bench specialist here. He could just deal with Jennet ap Rhiannon —

"We know," Two said cheerfully. She had no other mode that Rukota had ever been able to determine. It was an artifact of her translator. Her normal conversational range was well out of reach for most hominid ears, and her vocal apparatus was not set up for Standard. "We saw you. Yes. Every precaution. And if it had been anybody but a Bench specialist we would have no doubt. You suffer from the reputation of your breed."

In a manner of speaking. Vogel rubbed his forehead idly, as though his head ached; it should, Rukota thought. The skin that covered it was halfway healed already, but the plate that Koscuisko had laid over the brain tissue to keep bone in place while it healed would not be fully metabolized for at least three months.

"I'm not in the habit of losing evidence," Vogel said. "It's just not what I do. I'm annoyed about this myself, I'll never live it down."

Not the way in which to introduce the subject of regret, perhaps, "living it down." Rukota cleared his throat to draw attention away from Vogel's choice of words. "Coming up on a drop, your Excellency," Rukota said. "Go to audio?"

Ap Rhiannon seemed to think about it, but nodded. Rukota opened the feed. Wheatfields was talking.

"Shave a few off lateral, it's a loose vector and we're hot. Calm it down, Tamer." The main display screen was a muted blank, but at odd intervals a person could begin to see a speck of black that seemed to fly out of the blank center and off-screen in an arc that was still so wide it didn't look curved at all, from Rukota's point of view. It was just a schematic, Rukota knew that. But it meant that they were nearing the exit vector they had targeted on entry.

"How many hours since we hit?" Vogel asked, sounding curious even past his basic apparently discouraged condition. "The man's a maniac."

Yes, they'd made a swift transit. Wheatfields had taken nearly two days off of the trip by keeping up his velocity as they hit the entry vector. There were limits to how useful that sort of risk could be— miscalculation could spike a ship onto a harmonic, and you might end up somewhere quite different from where you were going.

But the *Ragnarok* had been an experimental test bed, a proving-model, and Wheatfields had been its Ship's Engineer for as long as it had been a functioning hull. Engineers didn't usually take risks. That was what Command Branch was for.

"He may be a maniac but he never blew up Secured Medical. And he had cause to," ap Rhiannon retorted. Rukota didn't think her heart was in it, though. She was watching the power oscillation monitors from over Wheatfields' shoulder, several lengths removed.

As if Wheatfields knew that he was being watched, he reached for the exact read that ap Rhiannon appeared to be examining, to make an adjustment. The key to successful vector exit was a smooth approach with no sudden shifts in the ship's momentum to throw the figurative stream of vector space into an eddy that would take the ship down with it. Nobody knew what "down" might mean, on vector.

When ships snagged on something on an exit vector they were invariably torn to pieces by the shearing shifts in force, like a thin-skinned glass boat hitting a rapids. There was no particular reason why it had to be done slowly; just that the less time one allowed oneself to brake to exit velocity the higher the possibility that you weren't going to be able to smooth your speed down perfectly, and come out of it alive.

"Set the index, Fan. Conner, take us down another three on that lateral, I want those engines recalibrated as soon as we drop vector. Careful. Sarend? What are you reading?"

Wheatfields did know that he was being watched, of course, Rukota reminded himself; he knew perfectly well that there were people on his observation deck. It had just been the illusion of cause and effect, that was all.

"The debouch's shifted a bit, your Excellency, we'll have another twelve to sneak up on it. I've sent a report out to Local. I read seven point six four by eight. It's not perfect, but it'll do."

Now Wheatfields stood, which brought his head almost uncomfortably close to the edge of the observation deck's overhang. Wheatfields was an unusually tall man, even for a Chigan—Chigan ran tall and thin to the Jurisdiction Standard to begin with. "Not good enough," Wheatfields said, firmly. "Need I remind you that our captain is watching? Nothing less than exceptional will be accepted. Recalculate, Sarend, vector in six."

Rukota couldn't see the technician's face from where he stood, but he knew how to interpret that set to a woman's shoulders. She wasn't in the least put out by the rebuke because it hadn't been a rebuke, but a compliment. A reminder. *You're exceptional. Be yourself. Show your captain what you're made of.*

"Seven point eight six nine by eight, sir, respectfully apologizing for point one three one variation due to yaw on section five outboard two. Confirmed."

Looking up over his shoulder to catch ap Rhiannon's eye
Wheatfields smiled. Rukota wasn't sure he'd ever seen Wheatfields
do that, but he hadn't been on board for more than a few months.
"Thank you, Sarend, Tamer, Fan, Conner. Tamer. Acquire the exit
vector."

On the main screen those little black dots were flying less and less
quickly, their arcs more and more pronounced. A thin border of
accumulated black dots had begun to collect all around the perimeter
of the forward screens like snow falling on a warmed wind-screen.
The *Ragnarok* was shedding speed.

"Up on twelve," Tamer said. "Down eight. Down eight. Down
seventeen. Up six." It clearly meant something to Wheatfields'
people, if not to Rukota. He knew the general idea—minute
adjustments to impulse streams and main reactor core feeds, to
make equally minute adjustments in the *Ragnarok*'s precise velocity.
Strictly speaking it wasn't necessary to come off vector exactly as one
had entered it but in reverse. Pilots and engineers prided themselves
on backing off a vector—facing forward—none the less. Point of
honor. And least wear and tear on the equipment from vector shear,
that way.

"Drop vector in three," Wheatfields said. "Tamer, if you're going
to fix that shift, now is the time to do it. Shade it for me—perfect."

Those little black dots were whirling out of the center of the screen
as though they were bullets of black ink shot into a funnel, collecting
at the sides, piling up. Thicker. Darker. Denser, almost moment by
moment. Nothing was actually arching or collecting or congealing,
Rukota knew it was just a schematic: but one whose data
representations made an elegant and effective sort of a description of
a ship on an inbound spiral off a vector.

"There it is." Wheatfields turned back to his chair and sat down,
leaning well back with an expression of mild benevolent self-
satisfaction on his face. "Your Excellency. We have Brisinje
Jurisdiction, Emandis space. —There is a communication waiting for
you."

Ap Rhiannon keyed the transmit. "Thank you, Engineer,
beautifully done, smoothest yet. Very impressive."

And it was, too, but ap Rhiannon was still talking. "That'll be
Emandis Station telling me I can't have cannon. Route it through to

my office, please, and Vogel can come with me to explain why we need to add a replacement surgical set and related equipment to an already full manifest."

"My pleasure, Captain," Vogel said with a gentle bow. He was lying, Rukota was sure, but nobody cared. Together ap Rhiannon and Vogel left; and once they were gone Two hopped down off of the chair in which she had been perched and lifted her beautiful black velvet muzzle with its extraordinary array of very sharp white teeth in Koscuisko's direction and chattered with her mouth, stilling herself— as usual—before the translation was well begun, to wait. Looking up at Koscuisko expectantly. Not only was Two's dialect out of range, it was apparently significantly faster—or perhaps simply that much more efficient—than normal hominid speech.

"You have reviewed the record, Andrej," she said. "What do you think?"

Koscuisko didn't answer directly. He looked to Rukota instead. There was something going on behind Koscuisko's pale eyes that Rukota didn't understand, but knew he didn't like. "I think that Secured Medical has been thoroughly destroyed," Koscuisko said. "It will never be usable for its original purpose again. To that degree Vogel has done me a significant service."

The words were pretty. But there was tension in them. "For which I cannot take credit, your Excellency," Rukota said modestly. "Nor assign any to Vogel. Nothing that I heard or saw would lead me to suspect that he was up to no good." Except for theft of surgical apparatus, of course. That had been a little underhanded of them. "You saw the tapes, what's your professional opinion?"

Koscuisko shook his head, looking very discouraged all of a sudden. He sat down, brooding over the Engineering deck on the other side of the clear-wall. "There are no obvious signs of hidden intent, but Vogel is a Bench specialist and I would not expect to see any from such a man. I have seen him produce what amounted to a raw-pelted lie by inference and misdirection, and in a very serious matter, and I doubted my suspicions even when I knew that they were all but certain to be true."

That would have been an interesting thing to see, Rukota decided. What had happened at Burkhayden—where Koscuisko had last seen Vogel, by report of gossip—that could possibly have elicited such a remark? Or did Koscuisko have history with Vogel that went further back than that?

"But you have no suspicions in this case," Rukota urged, to cover the awkward silence.

Koscuisko shrugged, turning his attention back to Two—who was waiting patiently for her answer. "I have no evidence. Vogel blew it up. I have no reason to believe that Vogel had any ulterior motive that would lead him here with the intent of destroying the forged record. But it is so convenient for the Bench, and so inconvenient for the *Ragnarok*. You know that the captain means to make an announcement on all-ship?"

"Very soon," Two agreed, with a crisp nod that came only half-way through the first word of the translation. "She does not trust her crew. She cannot believe that they are fully aware of consequences. It is insecurity."

Ap Rhiannon? Insecure? Rukota could have laughed, at that, except that he could understand Two's point. He didn't like it. "See here, Koscuisko, what motive could Vogel have had? He's a Bench specialist. Dedicated to the rule of Law."

"Yes." Koscuisko sounded somber. He was simply not in a very good mood, it seemed. He hadn't been in a very good mood since he'd come back off leave with a forged record. "The rule of Law, and the maintenance of the Judicial order. Both of which receive a very hard blow from the knowledge that a record has been compromised in order to incriminate innocent people. How are you to feel if you discover after years of mourning that someone you loved might never have even confessed—never mind enduring what inhumane duress— at all, before he was put to death by torture?"

So Vogel might have destroyed the record because it was forged, because the injustice of condemning the *Ragnarok* as a mutineer and its crew to Inquiry was not as potentially grave a threat to justice as the introduction of proof that the record could be manipulated. "I'd be willing to swear to the sincerity of Vogel's claimed motive, your Excellency. I couldn't, of course, not under oath. But I'd be willing to."

Koscuisko nodded. "Vogel was interested in knowing whether there was a connection between two forged Judicial instruments. We can speculate therefore that Vogel did not himself create the forged instruments. But whether he was about to discover a link, and was prevented by the forger's self-defense mechanism; or had discovered a link—and destroyed the record in order to protect somebody, an accomplice, perhaps—I don't know. I'd like to have him under a speak-serum. But without the captain's permission I have no authority."

Ap Rhiannon didn't care. She'd said so. The real importance lay in the fact that the forged record had been destroyed. They were naked and defenseless, and ap Rhiannon was much more interested in finding clothing than in determining whether Vogel had stolen her trousers. Time enough for that when she'd covered her back, Rukota supposed.

He could hear the clear-tone for the allship, and the voice of the captain. "Jennet ap Rhiannon, for the Command and crew of the Jurisdiction Fleet Ship *Ragnarok*. We are approaching Emandis Station for resupply. Down-leave will be granted according to policy with the First Officer's approval."

Was it his imagination, or could he hear her taking a deep breath before she went on?

"A recent accident has seriously compromised evidence that this ship was holding pertinent to its Appeal against Pesadie Training Command for inappropriate charges in the death of acting captain Cowil Brem during evaluation exercise. While I remain determined to defend the honor of this ship and the loyalty of its crew until it is vindicated, I cannot conceal from you the fact that we have lost significant leverage."

That was an understatement if he had ever heard one. The crew could be under no illusions as to what it meant.

"I encourage you all to take advantage of the opportunity to take down-leave at Emandis Station to consider your personal options in light of this information. Jennet ap Rhiannon, away, here."

It was quiet on the observation deck. Two raised one wing to scratch behind her ear with the claw at the end of the second joint, thoughtfully.

Koscuisko shook his head.

"Leave now, or forever wed your destiny to mine. She is an incurable romantic underneath it all; someone clearly permitted her to watch the wrong entertainment in her off hours when she was a child. If she had access to entertainment. If she had off hours. If she ever was a child."

Rukota snorted. Crèche-bred and romance? "Well, I'm not going anywhere," he declared firmly. "She might just try to leave without me. And she needs me. The ship, I mean. Who'll look after her cannon? No. How about you?"

"There are deserts on Emandis," Two said, suddenly, as though the idea had only just occurred to her. "With fat and juicy thermal columns. The maintenance atmosphere is not the same." Nor did the Ship's Engineer care for her using his maintenance atmosphere for soaring; it tended to unnerve his technicians. Who knocked into things. That knocked into other things. Rukota had heard more than one story about it. "And you, Andrej?"

"I believe she would be just as pleased to leave without me," Koscuisko said. "We have never been particularly comfortable with one another. I do not mean to leave these crew with an inadequate surgery." Was that a jab—Rukota wondered—or did Koscuisko have something else on his mind?

Koscuisko kept talking. "And still I cannot come all of this way, and not speak to Joslire where he rests. Where Joslire has gone I cannot guess. His marker is here. I am simply going to have to risk it."

There seemed to be nothing more to say. Excusing himself with a polite nod Rukota went away. The last thing that he heard as the door closed behind him was Two's voice, Two's translator's voice. "And *Scylla* will be coming there as well, you have friends on *Scylla*, if I remember?"

But the door closed before he heard Koscuisko's reply, and it was none of his business anyway. He went out to his work-station near the docks in the maintenance atmosphere to check the manifest one last time, to be sure he hadn't forgotten anything on his wish-list for weaponry from Emandis Station.

CHAPTER TEN

Sharp Words

"Yes, I grant you that Delleroy surrendered most of his markers to Chilleau," Bench specialist Nion said. "It's not a persuasive argument, though, is it? Only proves that confederacy is even less good an idea. Nothing more."

Jils sat at the side of the room, listening, watching. After taking an active role in the debate with Padrake—an exercise which had taken six full sessions, each one of them intellectually and even physically exhausting—it was as good as a holiday to do nothing more complex than sit and listen.

"Then you should simply extend that line of reasoning." Rinpen's voice was admirably calm in the face of Nion's almost-sneering one, Jils felt. Surely the fact that what Nion was sneering at was the very idea of selecting Chilleau Judiciary in any way, shape, or form had nothing to do with Jils' own feelings of mild aggravation. Surely. "We have previously established that selecting the Second Judge at Chilleau right now is better than confederacy. Selecting Chilleau Judiciary right now is less prudent than waiting for her administration to regroup, with Ivers' very professional help."

Nion rolled a pale eye at Jils and all but lifted her lip. There was something wrong with Nion, Jils decided. Andrej Koscuisko was a blond man of fair complexion and very pale eyes whose hair—fine-textured as that of Dolgorukij men who lacked chin-beards tended to be—was always falling across his forehead. Nion was so fair of face as to be almost blue with it, however, and her eyes were almost as pale as Koscuisko's.

So how was it that elements of physiognomy that interested Jils in Koscuisko's face moved her to nothing more than dislike when presented in an even more extreme form in Nion? Her hair was as fine as filament-wire, all of the hair that fell to her waist still making up a single braid of no more than a thumb's thickness, tied up into a depressing little knot at the back of Nion's head. If it had been her, Jils decided, she would have gotten a weave, or cut her hair short. Something.

"Yes, of course. Specialist Ivers is undoubtedly a significant asset in Chilleau Judiciary's administration. I'm sure it's very nice, being Bench specialist at the First Judge's seat. You should get Tanifer talking, some time."

Nion, like Padrake, seemed to identify the specialist with the Judiciary a little more closely than Jils was accustomed to. Padrake at least knew better. Bench specialists were rotated precisely in order to avoid developing inappropriate relationships with any one Judge; her own long association with Chilleau had been mildly anomalous, but she hadn't spent all of her time at Chilleau even when she had made it her base of operations at Verlaine's request.

Padrake's apparent assumption that Jils was personally committed to the Second Judge's cause was all the more puzzling in light of his own experience. They had teamed with each other five years ago. He had only been at Brisinje for two years or so, she remembered him telling her—she thought. No. Five years. No. Two years. Which?

Shifting in her seat Jils swallowed back a sigh of exasperation. If anyone was in danger of identifying too closely with the agenda of any one particular Judge it was surely Padrake himself, on first-name terms with the First Secretary, and all. And these were not very comfortable chairs. They'd been brought in to the theater from one of the laboratory areas, light, flimsy things with a very thinly padded seat.

Why she shouldn't use the perfectly good seats that were already here in the theater room Jils did not know, but the procedures they had all agreed on called for the observer to be seated at right angles to the axis of discussion and not more than five eights distant from the table with the tiles, and none of the rather more comfortable chairs already here could be pulled off of their anchors and placed correctly.

Since Jils was observing, Nion could make all the acid comments she liked without fear of reprisals; Jils was here to listen. Firmly pushing her pique away from her mind Jils crossed her arms over her chest and leaned back in the chair, pushing off with one foot to tilt the seat toward the back wall and brace it there.

"But, and Ivers is much too well disciplined to mention this, Rinpen, she knows as well as anyone that Chilleau is compromised and corrupt. There are rumors that a record has been compromised, by a clerk of Court at Chilleau Judiciary—Verlaine's special pet, in fact. And more."

Balancing a chair between its two back legs and the wall could be delicate business. Jils used the opportunity it gave her to adjust and shift and cover her unhappy surprise. There was no doubt in her mind but that the Malcontent had controlled the information as carefully as possible, and the Malcontent was as good a secret service as Jils had ever seen. But secrets that were big enough couldn't be kept forever.

If Nion knew about the existence of the forged record, did that mean Nion knew that Jils had been there when the secret had been discovered? It could look bad. Sitting here in the theater of a research station she didn't know how deep beneath Brisinje it suddenly seemed to Jils that it almost certainly looked much worse than she had imagined, before.

"There's no such thing as a Judiciary that has never been compromised." Rinpen's retort was gallantly fielded, but a little weak. "Citizens under Jurisdiction have already shown their willingness to move past the difficulties in Chilleau's recent past. The Domitt Prison. The Nurail. Even with Cintaro making a persuasive case out of the Domitt, the selection was in Chilleau's favor."

Well argued, but his heart didn't seem to be in it. Whether or not he'd heard about a forged record, he knew that there was an issue, now. Jils shifted her weight in her chair, irritated. She could have said something—but not without interfering unnecessarily with the discussion. Nion knew that. Nion was taking advantage. Jils was beginning to not like Nion.

She was beginning to dislike her chair, as well; its variety of functional ceramic tube-and-brace construction might well be durable and inexpensive, but it didn't feel quite solid to Jils in some obscure sense. Maybe she was just blaming it for Nion.

"A forged record," Nion repeated, as it seemed to Jils maliciously. "In a Judiciary characterized by the close working relationship between the First Secretary and Bench specialist detailed. What do you think the common citizen will make of the existence of a forged record, under those circumstances? Of the judicial insistence that a Fleet warship that leveled stolen battle cannon against Fleet defensive fortifications has committed no crime, when the only possible interpretation is that mutiny is being hushed up for the sake of the Dolgorukij Combine's tender feelings about its ancestral aristocracy?"

This was going too far. Arching her back to push against the wall with her shoulders Jils opened her mouth to say something; Rinpen looked at her—clearly worried—and Jils settled the chair back into its leaning position, though not without effort. Maybe the entire station had settled, sited as it was on the shores of an ancient lake which might well be unstable, and which had certainly never suffered the indignity of a structure of any sort until quite recently.

Maybe the floor was uneven. The chair wobbled and was a little difficult to control, its structural tubing loose. Probably just needed an adjustment, Jils told herself. Her own attitude certainly did.

"Which Combine, and the Judiciary in which it is located, can be counted on to exert themselves to stabilize Chilleau to the maximum extent of their ability." Rinpen spoke slowly, as though he was sounding out his own argument as he spoke. He apparently found it persuasive, however, because his voice strengthened and grew more confident as he continued. Maybe he had just been afraid that she was going to attack Nion, Jils thought. It was a good idea. Nion clearly needed attacked, with her ghostly pale complexion and her watery and watering eyes and her teeth that looked like milk-teeth and which were just wrong in an adult jaw, and not much of a chin either.

"The Bench expects its First Judge to show tact and discretion when dealing with locally influential persons." Jils set aside her irritation for a moment to listen; she was interested in where Rinpen's argument might be going. "And respects attributes that are important in minimizing conflicts that can lead to police actions."

Rinpen was sounding so self-assured now that it was almost as if he'd rehearsed this speech. Maybe he'd anticipated Nion's attack. Jils took a deep breath to calm and center herself, frowning at the way the chair's frame wobbled beneath her.

"Within limits," Nion insisted. "A Bench which enjoys the public trust and confidence will be granted credit by the other Judiciaries and the rest of Jurisdiction space, and only within limits. Chilleau does not."

That was perfectly true, but only as far as Bench specialists and senior Bench staff went. Oh, and senior Fleet officers.

"Meal break," Jils said, with one eye on the station's master chronometer. "Please suspend your discussion until we reconvene, here, after mid-meal." She wasn't sure it was mid-meal. There was no sense of time in this station, not even with chronometers at hand. It could be dawn in Brisinje. It could be midnight. Here and now whatever it was it was time to go eat, so Jils leaned her head back to push off from the wall again and tilt her chair forward onto all four of its floor-points fore and aft.

The front floor-points of the chair came down on the carpeted floor of the theater with a sharp impact that startled Jils. She had just enough time to realize that the chair had not stopped tipping forward when its front bar had struck the floor before something sliced up between her body and her right arm, tearing the fabric of her uniform, tearing her flesh.

Ceramics, she told herself. The sharp edge of a shattered structural tube caught against one of her ribs, taking her breath away in a manner that was familiar but not any more welcome for that. Ceramics, and brittle with age. She should have thought twice about leaning back in the chair, she should have noticed herself noticing that the chair didn't feel quite right.

She had a good long time to reproach herself as she struggled for breath against the pain in her side. She didn't particularly want to breathe, not really—she knew that the moment she did the pain in her side would only be worse. But she did have to. She was not going to relinquish consciousness. There was more than just her failure to notice her own perceptions that was wrong, here.

Jils took a breath at last, and found a black-humored sort of satisfaction in the fact that it did in fact hurt worse than anything she could call immediately to mind. She knew she'd been hurt worse. She knew she had good reasons for not thinking about that. She lay on her back and panted shallowly, half-hearing Rinpen beside her. Nion must have gone for the medikit. Jils hoped Nion had gone for the medikit. She hoped Nion wouldn't try to use it on her.

"Can't leave you alone for a minute," someone said. It was Padrake, here, now. She was beginning to focus, but not particularly appreciating it. Padrake held a long jagged spear of crazed and shattered ceramic tubing up where Jils could see it; "Just missed sliding up into your abdominal cavity," Padrake said cheerfully. "Lucky you, Jils."

She didn't like the undertone of worry that she could hear in his voice. She knew how to read him. He was shocked, frightened, almost. She'd thought that something was wrong. Now she knew she'd been right, but that didn't make her any happier than breathing had.

"Lift," someone said—Zeman.

Jils appreciated the expert handling of the people who were moving her onto the gurney; she also appreciated the fact that nobody had given her any drugs yet. There was a heavy pad of medical compress laced around her now, to staunch the bleeding; that hurt too. They were going to have to move her; the sealers and the blood-fluid and the rest, all that would be in the little clinic. Jils began to wonder how badly she'd been injured. The idea was almost more than she could bear to contemplate—Bench intelligence specialist Jils Tarocca Ivers, to be assassinated by an old lab chair?

"Ivers," Zeman said. "Long bad graze, bleeding pretty good, scraped rib-bones. If the shard had slipped just a little we wouldn't be having this conversation. We need to give urgent care, but you'll be ambulatory again in about two hours. How about a dose of this or that?"

She hadn't been assassinated by a chair. That was what was wrong. Someone had watched her, seen her leaning back, had sabotaged her chair. Maybe not. Maybe she was imagining things. Maybe pain was making her paranoid. Paranoid was not necessarily a bad thing to be.

"Let me have one of this. And at least five of that." It was hard to choke out the words, because it hurt to breathe. More than that, though, part of her brain was desperate not to accept any drugs. It would be so easy, if she was drugged. She could have an idiopathic allergic reaction to a micro-fungus that had crept into the solution somehow. Her heart could absent-mindedly forget to beat. It wouldn't take much.

"Maybe a fraction of the other thing," Padrake suggested. Jils hadn't felt the dose go through; she could tell that she'd been dosed, though, because her thinking seemed to sharpen and focus all at once. Jils knew that Padrake was worried. He'd keep an eye out.

Nobody who wanted her dead for the good of the Judicial order could decently murder her by stealth anyway; executions had to be announced. *Jils Ivers, in the matter of the crime of assassination of a senior Bench official, it is my judgment and my decision that you are at fault and are appropriately to be punished therefore.* Announced and then acknowledged; no games with chairs that had gone unused for too long, no tricks with drugs would satisfy the jury of a Bench specialist's peers. She was probably safer right here, right now, than she had been since Verlaine had been murdered.

"Two fractions of the other thing." Jils held up two fingers to make her point, and then closed her eyes. Closing her eyes helped her concentrate on capturing her memories before they faded, before anesthetic drugs clouded her judgment.

While they moved her to the tiny medical unit Jils focused her mind, listening only to be sure she heard Padrake from time to time. The furniture had been here as long as the station had, though new equipment had been brought in to support the special needs of Convocation—secured communications transmission equipment, among other things.

The environment was stable, controlled humidity, minimal fluctuations. Structural tubing could fracture under stress, but there shouldn't have been the sorts of stresses that could lead to materials fatigue on such a level. She needed to have a look at that chair, what was left of it. She needed to have a look at the other chairs as well.

The shard had scraped up along her ribs to her armpit, or at least that was what it felt like. The pain was a dull ache, but they hadn't given her enough drugs to deprive her of consciousness. They'd known better than that. None of them would have wanted to lose consciousness in a situation like this. All of them were fully capable of having the same questions about the accident as she did, so how could any of them hope to get away with sabotage?

She was making assumptions based on expectations of common values that might not be universally common at all. How was she to know? Could she go up to Rinpen or Nion or Rafenkel and say "Pardon me for asking, but if you were going to assassinate me do you mind telling me how you'd go about it?"

Medical unit. Someone eased her arm up and away, someone cut her uniform blouse and exposed her side. She smelled a sterile field generator in action, felt a familiar prickling tingle traveling up her side as the quick-knit unit worked its way from point of entry to the endmost extent of the wound.

The transparent membrane would seal the wound and keep it clean while open for observation, and would gradually shrink toward its vertical midline over time, drawing the new skin back over the wound to heal without a scar. Or much of one. You could have the scar tissue peeled, and there'd be a new scar, but a fainter, thinner one. Two or three peels and there was no scar left to speak of, but it was a tedious process that Jils had never had patience for.

The quick-knit's resonation was exquisitely uncomfortable against newly scraped rib-bones. Jils set her teeth and waited; it would be over soon enough. She'd take a break, sleep for a few hours. If there was something to be found out about the chair she'd find out about it. If someone didn't want her to find out about the chair, she'd find that out too.

And then she was going to find a way out of here. She had no intention of sitting quietly and waiting to be killed. Under the new procedure, her role could be safely terminated at the front of the process. The longer she could keep Chilleau's bid alive the longer she would live; but if someone had just tried to kill her they clearly weren't waiting. Neither would she.

There had to be other ways to get to the surface than just the lift-car. There had to be. She would find them, because if she didn't find something to do soon, some way to take charge of her own destiny, something that would give her the illusion of control over her fate, she was going to go to pieces. If that happened she'd never know who'd killed Sindha Verlaine, and why.

"Timurcillium must be as close to untraceable as you can get," Rafenkel observed in as neutral a tone as possible. Ivers would already have noted that; it was hard to ignore. The chair had been carefully painted with an antiquing agent, something used extensively on the forged objets d'art market and otherwise mostly ignored because it was in everything—a component of packing materials.

For instance, the pre-pack packaging material, in an inerted form, could be pulverized and washed out with a mildly acidic solution to pull the substance out of its inerting matrix. And the packaging was pulverized in the kitchen after every meal service, and many of the things people mixed in their water yielded a mildly acidic solution. Kilpers was one of them.

"But only where the tubing meets the seat. And then only on one or two chairs," Ivers said, as if meditatively. They had found two other chairs in the theater treated in the same manner, the ceramic tubing carefully painted with timurcillium to create a line of weakness that would shear under sharp pressure and split off just such a spear as had nearly skewered Ivers. They were out in storage, now, tagged as hazardous, waiting for forensic examination.

They had all been grouped together, so that Ivers could easily have selected any one of them—or none at all. Ivers had been observing a debate. Someone had moved the chair that had been there for the observer, but whoever had done it had waited until the theater had gone off-monitor. Ivers might have selected a treated chair anyway. Ivers liked to lean her chair up against the wall, and the more comfortable chairs didn't tip.

"Target," Ivers said. "The chair only fails on impact. It's still load-bearing. And if it went when someone was just sitting on it, the knife-section of the tube wouldn't have enough momentum to do much damage. The only person likely to be actually hurt is the one who is letting her chair fall four-square to the floor again. Me."

Rafenkel could see the argument; it was clear enough. Why Ivers might have rigged the accident herself was a little less clear, but to look at Zeman he wasn't sure. Rinpen had been talking to Zeman. Rinpen had been talking to her, too, but she hadn't been able to buy the argument at all.

There was no need for Ivers to stage an attack to divert suspicion away from herself because, prior to the chair's collapse, there had been no other incidents in which Ivers had been suspected of anything—except for the problem of Verlaine's murder, of course, but the incident in that case did nothing to absolve Ivers of Verlaine's murder and everything to endorse suspicion of Ivers' guilt by making it clear that someone thought she might very well be guilty, and need killing.

"If there's anyone who could stunt that and stay off the record while they were doing it, it's probably a Bench specialist," Capercoy said, gently. He had a very agreeable accent, soft and warm and fuzzy around the edges with a bit of an occasional drawl to it that dropped the middle out of words from time to time, when it was least expected. "We're not likely to come up with an answer before Convocation is finished, Jils. The report's one thing; what we're going to do about it is another."

Ivers dropped her head, clearly struggling with frustration. Rafenkel could empathize. "If I thought it'd do any good to stand up on the table and solemnly swear that I had neither thought nor word nor deed in the killing of Sindha Verlaine, I'd do it," Ivers said. Her voice held little hope that Rafenkel could hear. "But nobody who already thinks differently would believe me. I wouldn't believe me, on principle."

Too true. It was part of the burden of the Bench specialist never to believe what anybody told them. "Look here," Rafenkel said. She'd had an idea. "Maybe nobody was trying to kill you. Maybe it was a well-intentioned warning. Clumsily executed, yes. In poor taste, yes. But nobody's killing anybody until the Selection is decided. We can't do that unless Chilleau is represented, at least for now."

Ivers nodded, looking very tired. She wore no visible bandaging, but her movements were a little awkward; it had to be wearing on her. A slice up the side was no joke, and if it hadn't been calculated to kill her the margin of error had been irresponsibly small.

"I was counting on that, Rafenkel. Thought I'd have a bit of a break. But then you decided to reroute the decision tree."

True enough, yet again. At the time Rafenkel had thought it likely to be welcome to Ivers—get her in, get her out of a vulnerable situation as quickly as possible. The trick with the chair could have been calculated to encourage her to disqualify Chilleau and escape, because if she was successful in defending the Second Judge's bid against Fontailloe's challenge, she was going to have to wait until the final decision had been made as to which Judiciary Chilleau would face in final debate. Was someone working on Ivers' nerves to persuade her to cut her losses, throw her own platform, and flee?

"All right, Jils," Capercoy said. "You're okay for the run. Cintaro will not accept the selection of Chilleau, not until the administrative issues are cleared up."

The gap left by Verlaine's murder, obviously. His successor could not hope to build the contacts and relationships of a lifetime in a single year. "And Fontailloe is simply not an option. Nobody believes otherwise except for Tanifer, and I'm not so sure even Tanifer does. So you'll be here till the end. And once Cintaro is selected, we can leave together."

Safety in numbers. She and Balkney had been trying to keep an eye on Ivers since Ivers got here. Balkney had apparently liked Ivers on the few occasions in the past that they had worked together; he was worried for her sake.

"Sant-Dasidar will endorse Cintaro if Chilleau is out," Rafenkel said. Capercoy was being very up-front and candid; she could do no less. Maybe full disclosure would reassure Ivers, at least a little bit. "But not otherwise. The Sixth Judge's story is that Chilleau is still the correct selection. She doesn't have to worry about Fleet giving her any problems."

Fleet had successfully maintained exclusive control over the practitioners the Bench needed to run its Protocols, and any attempts to wean the Bench from the Protocols was an attempt to destroy a primary element of Fleet's leverage in the time-honored power struggle between the Bench and the military chartered by the Bench to uphold the rule of Law and the Judicial order.

"Fleet giving who problems?" This was a voice from the doorway; the door had been left open—nobody was saying anything that everybody couldn't hear—but Rafenkel was a little startled, regardless. She hadn't heard Delleroy approach. "Not Brisinje. She'll have the Emandisan on 'em so fast, but we've never had any issues with Fleet, Jils. How are you, ready for the wars again?"

Ivers relaxed when Delleroy came into the room. She didn't slump or slouch; to the contrary, her shoulders seemed to have lifted by some degree, as though a weight on them had been lifted away. Balkney and the Widowmaker had been forced to marry, in the end, and Widowmaker had gone onto the inactive roster—at least in theory. Delleroy and Ivers were going to have to face a similar decision sooner or later. It was too clear—at least to Rafenkel—that they responded to each other on a dangerously trusting level.

"How'd it go with you?" Ivers asked, affection almost blatant in her voice. "Balkney chewed your skinny ass?"

Delleroy shook his head. "I'm not doing very well, Jils. But it's not my fault. Confederacy just doesn't have the chops."

"I'll remember you said that," Ivers said. "I may be able to use it. I'd better go, gentles, Tanifer and I are going to start our talk about Fontailloe, and why Chilleau is clearly the better choice."

Or not, from Fontailloe's point of view. "I'll walk you out," Delleroy said. "We've been busy. Want to know how that scrape is doing. Later, gentles."

Given the mutual feeling Delleroy and Ivers appeared to share, Rafenkel felt perfectly comfortable letting Delleroy do the escorting.

"Later," Capercoy replied, on Rafenkel's behalf as well as his own.

Rafenkel stood and stretched. She was going to be glad to get away from here herself, but not as glad as Balkney and Ivers alike, always supposing both of them lived that long.

Ap Rhiannon had asked him to come and review the surgical set requirements, but Andrej Koscuisko didn't think she had his surgical set on her mind. There had been trouble brewing between the two of them since he had returned to the *Ragnarok* to find her captain. It had only been a matter of time before an explosion occurred—one he had himself primed and ignited.

"The requisition is complete and correct in all material aspects, your Excellency," Andrej confirmed, setting his chop to the senior medical officer's certification of destruction of original issue. She was watching him as suspiciously as a scholar's assistant a too-confident intern, as though expecting the worst at any moment and more than ready to return grief for grief in generously compounded measure. "I hope there is no question of fault to be found with my stores and issues. The equipment was taken. Pure and simple."

She shook her head. Leaning well back in her chair in her office— the captain's office, that had been Lowden's before her—she put her feet up on the desk and squinted at the toe of her right boot. "Stolen, Koscuisko, no question. No. I've never had cause to doubt the professionalism and the attention to procedure and detail that you have nurtured in Infirmary."

That sounded like a compliment, and made Andrej nervous. "Very kind, your Excellency. Fully deserved, the praise of Section, with no merit accruing to me thereby. It is their doing."

Now she put her hand back to rest on the top edge of the chair's neck-support and gaze up at the ceiling. "Oh, but praise is due, your

Excellency, you lead by example and indirection. Bad example. What really impresses me is how well they do with you there to mislead them."

Well, that was a rebuke burnished and brilliant. He could appreciate it for what it was. "You're too kind." Of what did she intend to accuse him this time? There was so much. And yet he had an idea that he knew where she was going.

"Not at all, Doctor, I have no difficulty in recognizing superlative performance despite its unfortunate implications. This is a ship at war with its own Command, Koscuisko, we can't hope to survive without trust. I agreed to trust you to come on board and rejoin your crew, I respected your motives. I'm sorry to see you have extended no such trust to me."

Tricking a sheet of plain-form out from underneath a stack of flat-files she pushed it across the desk at him. Andrej took it. His personnel request to cover his planned leave at Emandis: all of his bond-involuntaries. Even Robert. Robert had known Joslire. Of all people Robert should be allowed to go, and gaze upon Joslire's memorial tablet.

"Explain to me, your Excellency, in what way have I disappointed you?" Andrej was genuinely confused. Surely Stoshi hadn't gone so far as to speak to the captain, before he'd left. That would have been— well, actually, something one might expect, from a Malcontent. "I have shared no confidences with anybody on board this ship with regards to my requested leave that I have withheld from my Command. At the same time one might be excused for having thought that his reasons for wishing to visit a man's memorial tablet might justly be considered personal."

She blew her breath out between clenched teeth, making a sort of a frustrated sound, rolling her eyes at him with transparent disgust. "If you say so. I'm not going to let whatever personal issue you might have with this office interfere with my professional duties toward this ship. You have reason to mistrust the captain of the *Ragnarok*. I can respect that."

Pulling her chop on its chain out from underneath her blouse she reached for the release and endorsed it, then passed it back. "For that reason, Koscuisko, you're going to Emandis on leave, and you're taking every bond-involuntary troop on my inventory with you. We are in more dangerous a situation than ever yet, we've lost our sole protection, such as it was, the record is gone, and nobody who trusts a Bench specialist to do what she wishes they would deserves to live. If letting you steal these troops is what it takes to get you off this ship then I say steal away, Doctor."

Oh, now he was getting angry. Had she no respect for the regard in which he held the people who had seen him through horrors of which she could have no immediate knowledge? "You have determined that with the record no longer available I seek the first opportunity to run away from my duty." That was what she had said. More or less. "It is true that I worry about my gentlemen. Somebody ought, and I am considerably obliged to them. To you not at all."

That was a little harsh. He was obliged to her for sending the wrong team of Security home to Azanry with him, months ago—an action born of what he had to admit was justified paranoia that had saved him from a plot to take his freedom, if not his life. And still what was missing between them was respect. She did not credit him with having feelings. Self-interest seemed to be as far as she would go in attributing motive to his actions.

"The feeling is mutual," ap Rhiannon retorted sharply. "You are by repute among the finest battle surgeons in Fleet, or at least you were when Lowden let you alone to do your job. I've seen you in Infirmary. You could be a significant strength to this Command, Koscuisko, and that's why I can't afford any ambiguity over why you're here. If that insults you I'm sorry."

She was angry herself, so much was obvious. She didn't seem to have noticed, however; her tone remained fairly level and her language moderately temperate. Maybe she was simply telling the truth. It was possible.

"I have said that I mean to stay with my Command, your Excellency, the ship is yours but Infirmary is mine. You do insult me, when you suggest that I am looking for ways out."

Not until the *Ragnarok*'s appeal had been heard and sustained. Verlaine was dead but the documentation Verlaine had signed and sent to him on Azanry was still legal and binding, fully executed; relief of Writ. He could go home and strive to live up to his son's inflated image, and dread the day when Anton would find out. He could be free, his family had half-forgiven him for quarreling with his father already, and he had much to do to repair the damage he had done to alliances and trading relationships when he had married Marana.

Until the *Ragnarok*'s appeal had been accepted, he would do none of those things. It was a point of honor. The crew of this ship had persistently treated him like a human being, as well as merely an officer, during all of the years that he had been here; it almost convinced him that he was one, and there was no sacrifice that he could make that would begin to balance out the gratitude he felt toward every soul who declined to spit or make a sign against spiritual contamination when he walked past them in the corridors.

"Would you just listen to yourself?" Her voice had sharpened; he had succeeded in annoying her past her self-discipline at last, as it seemed. "You're the inheriting son of the Koscuisko familial corporation. You have a clearly communicated abhorrence for your Inquisitorial function and an unfortunate history with Fleet Captain Lowden, deceased."

Leaning over her desk with her hands folded—as though to prevent herself from throwing something—she stared at him ferociously as she spoke on. "By any measure of rational evaluation, by any sane measure, you have more to lose than the entire crew of the *Ragnarok* combined, and you get insulted when I suggest that you cannot be relied upon because there is too large a gap between what you say and what anybody, anybody at all, can see with their own two eyes."

Well, if she put it that way Andrej supposed he could see her point. She was crèche-bred. She knew nothing of honor as Andrej understood it. Her entire life had been an indoctrination into the lowest common denominator of peoples' desires and convictions.

"For this reason you release the bond-involuntaries to go with me to see Joslire, because you wish to remove any obstacles in my path, so that I may leave."

She didn't answer; she didn't need to. He could see her endorsement in her eyes.

"You surprise me, Captain. Bond-involuntaries are valuable resources. To throw them away—just to be rid of me—"

"They're good troops." She was the captain. She could interrupt him. But she didn't do it the way Lowden had. She wasn't making a point about her rank, Andrej's subordinate status, about how careful

Andrej had to be to avoid provoking her into assessing sanctions against the bond-involuntaries. She was just interrupting. "I hate to lose them. Under any other circumstances I wouldn't allow it at any cost. Cost is the issue."

Well, that sounded reasonable; and she sounded calm enough, as she continued. "You've wanted to take them for a long time. You can do me much more damage by staying, and being unhappy about it, than taking six bond-involuntary troops. We'll need the Wolnadi crew and we won't be able to replace them, but they're not going to be needed for Inquiry while I'm in command of this ship, so take them and go and don't come back."

That wasn't likely to be a very long time, was it? *While I am in command of this ship*, she'd said. Once the *Ragnarok*'s appeal had been accepted, once the ship had been cleared of wrong-doing and restored to active status, ap Rhiannon's career was over. It wouldn't matter that the appeal had been upheld, then. She'd thrown it away the moment she'd decided on her course of action. It was too bad that she wouldn't let him respect her for it.

She'd given him an order. What was he going to do? He had a sudden temptation to refuse, just to be spiteful—but then all of his arranging would come to nothing. No. He had to get them away. He'd known when he'd performed the surgeries that to expect a man to bend his neck to a governor twice in his life was simply not to be entertained. Even if she meant to strand him on Emandis Station he had to go, so that the Bonds could get clear of Fleet before Fleet found out what he'd done with them.

Maybe it would be for the best if she *did* strand him; it would tend to support the idea that she had not known what he was doing. Nobody knew what he had been doing. He had told nobody. They were welcome to guess what they liked, and he knew very well that the guesses of his staff were not likely to have hit far from the mark, but he had said nothing.

"I will. Thank you." She could have held them on board. She could have kept some of them back as hostages for his good behavior. She was going to let them all go, and if it hadn't been for her explanation, he wouldn't have been able to believe it. She wasn't letting them go. She was sending them away, in order to be rid of him. "A final question, Captain, with your permission."

"Of course."

"If I should come back without them, your Excellency, will it be to find my boots and baggage on the loading docks?"

It was a challenge. They both knew it was. She only considered it, however; she did not rise to her feet and throw the half-empty flask of brutally red wine that was a constant feature of her desk at him.

After a moment of careful deliberation she replied. "I am willing to put up with a great deal from you, Koscuisko, to have your services for my crew. No. I won't throw you out. But I'll believe it when I see it."

They had exhausted all their available topics for conversation, Andrej decided. He bowed, doing his best to make it an honest salute.

"Very well, your Excellency. Thank you, and good-greeting."

"Enjoy your leave," she said, and turned away to study a report-scan as he left.

He'd find out soon enough whether she meant what she'd said, or not. But for now he had to go and tell Stildyne to muster his bond-involuntary troops to go with him to Emandis Station, to accompany him to Joslire's grave-site; it would be the last duty they would ever be called up on to perform. It was fitting that it should take place in a graveyard.

CHAPTER ELEVEN
Privileged Relationships

The captain's shallop was a small sturdy craft that would carry up to thirty-two souls in ease and relative comfort. It had come down to Emandis Station from the *Ragnarok* with half that number. When their errand was done, Stildyne would proceed down to Emandis itself—the port city of Jeltaria, in the arid zone between the sapphire sea of Genet and the thorny brown-black hills of the Minto range—to command Koscuisko's escort to the place where the memorial tablet of Joslire Ise-I'let stood over the dead man's ashes in the glittering white ground.

"Brachi, I'm nervous," Koscuisko said, staring up at the great rolling globe of Emandis in the sky above the depot station with a look of longing on his face such as Stildyne had seldom seen. "I have not seen him for all of this time. I wonder if I should not leave them behind, Joslire doesn't know them. Except for Robert. And you must come as well."

Robert St. Clare had known Curran, a man Stildyne himself had never met. Up until quite recently he had been half-convinced that he hated Koscuisko's Emandisan bond-involuntary for the affection with which Koscuisko remembered him.

But then he'd analyzed Koscuisko's back-sheath bit by minute bit on the thula during their trip from Azanry back to the *Ragnarok* after the assault on Koscuisko these weeks gone past, though. There was no way in which the catch could have slipped, no explanation for how the knife had fallen free and into Koscuisko's hand when he lay helpless at the mercy of his enemy. For Koscuisko's life, Stildyne could forgive the dead man the fact that Koscuisko loved him.

"No, it'll be all right," Stildyne said, still surprised when Koscuisko used his personal name. They'd had words about it. Cultural differences. Koscuisko was trying to observe Stildyne's preference, at the expense of his own behavioral expectations; staggering. The effort said more to Stildyne about the value that Koscuisko placed on him than the use of his personal name could touch, satisfying though that was. "They're Bonds. They might have been his shipmates if things had been different. You know how they look after one another."

It had been a good thing to say, apparently. Koscuisko seemed to relax all at once, and smiled very cheerfully. "A telling point," Koscuisko agreed. "Thank you. If we are not careful First Officer will leave without us, let's hurry."

Mendez' business was with the depot master. Emandis Station had declined to pre-clear for load-out without a personal visit. She was well within her rights to do so—it was munitions that the *Ragnarok* was after, and in significant quantity—but they were all unhappily suspicious that she was simply stalling for as long as she could. *Scylla* was in route, with three attendant corvettes. If Emandis Station held them here until *Scylla* arrived, and *Scylla* was unfriendly . . .

Scylla wouldn't lay a finger on them. The *Ragnarok*'s legal status was unresolved, but the fact that Captain ap Rhiannon had lodged a formal and acknowledged appeal was not in question. There were no Fleet intelligence groups at Emandis Station. Emandis Station was run by the Emandis home defense fleet, EHDS, as a semi-autonomous enterprise under contract to provision Fleet and license to obtain and store controlled items.

Fleet couldn't put an interrogations group down without permission. And Jennet ap Rhiannon had made herself clear on allship: they had nothing to hide or to explain; they would stay out of trouble, and trouble would stay away from them. If Fleet wanted to wrangle with the *Ragnarok*, it would need a pretext to do so, when it was in a home defense fleet depot. Their captain expected them all to refrain from supplying one.

Stildyne followed Koscuisko to the mover where Mendez sat

waiting, and they were off for the depot's administrative center. Emandisan Station was clean and bright and beautiful, standing several hours off of Emandis itself and rejoicing in a generated atmosphere—a very gracious grid—and all of the amenities for rest and recreation of crews in transit. It was a short ride down wide tree-lined lanes from the docking site to the depot master's office. Koscuisko said little, watching the planet high overhead; Mendez nothing at all.

The depot master's office when they got there was small but well-furnished, very clearly the workspace of a busy woman who had neither time nor patience for external rank-signals. The depot master rose to her feet as they were buzzed through to her office, nodding her head once in response to Mendez' formal greeting; but let Mendez know straightaway that there were to be some issues to resolve.

"Your Excellency," she said. She didn't sit down; she didn't suggest they sit, either. "I'm sorry you had this trip for nothing, sir. Emandis Station cannot release this stores manifest."

In fact First Officer had come in person because Emandis Station had already suggested that it could not release the requested stores. Jennet ap Rhiannon did not take "no" for an answer, unless it were in response to "Any problem with that?" Mendez was clearly not at all surprised at the depot master's claim; he folded his hands in front of him and protested: quietly, calmly, logically.

"Our requisitions are all Fleet-standard, Depot. And I need those stores. Especially the munitions. On what grounds do you decline to execute your mission and release these supplies?"

Now she sat down slowly, and invited Mendez to rest himself with a gesture of her hand. She wasn't Emandisan, Stildyne decided; so much was obvious. She was tall and almost blond and a little sun-burnt; all of the Emandisan that Stildyne had seen represented were slender people, not tall, dark-eyed and dark-complected. Singularly elegant and superlatively self-disciplined, which was not to say that the depot master wasn't.

"Release of replacement equipment must be accompanied by surrender of the equipment it is to replace, your Excellency, you know that." Polite, but inflexible. A civil servant from somewhere else in Brisinje, perhaps, responsible for the depot and very sure of her procedures. "You have failed to present appropriately endorsed waiver documents. Unless you carry them with you for surrender here and now I cannot release the munitions you demand."

Koscuisko hadn't been explicitly invited to sit down, but he did so, quietly and unobtrusively. Stildyne stood. The only time he sat down in the presence of his officer of assignment was when they were playing cards in quarters after shift. Or in the sauna. Or when Koscuisko came to his tiny cell of an office, which did not happen often.

"You are in receipt of a preliminary copy of our duly logged exception document," Mendez noted, mildly. "It's at the headquarters of the home defense fleet even now. We don't want to create any friction here, depot master, but we need our stores. My Captain doesn't want to see me back without them."

The *Ragnarok* needed guns. It was an experimental test-bed that had never been issued its full complement—or if the artillery had been issued it had never been delivered, much less installed. Maybe it was being held somewhere for the day when the *Ragnarok* would be formally commissioned as a ship of war. Or maybe someone had sold it off on the invisible market. That was how the *Ragnarok* had acquired the single battle cannon it could deploy, after all—they had liberated it from the invisible market, where it had been sitting in inventory as a case of deck-wipes.

The rest of the stores would be welcome, but as it was the ship could not defend itself against more than one or two of the warships in its weight class if Fleet decided to assert itself. Shooting their way out of Taisheki Station had been an act of mutiny—technically speaking, anyway.

"You know the exception report must be endorsed at Fleet headquarters level, your Excellency, the home defense fleet's authority in this instance is limited. I cannot in all good conscience release a primary equipment load of this level without more explicit instructions, First Officer, I trust you will forgive me. Will that be all? Your crew will be welcome to stand down for rest and recreation, of course, once your bond has been—excuse me."

One of the alerts on the depot master's desk had gone off, blinking at her with a brilliant blue urgency. Frowning, she keyed her receive; whoever it was, whatever it was, she started to say something as if angrily, glanced quickly at First Officer and Koscuisko sitting in her office, decided against saying a word. She didn't speak. She closed the comm with a sharp and irritated gesture and stood up, her chair rolling back to hit the wall behind her and bounce forward again in reaction to the vigor of her action.

"Excuse me," she repeated; and quit the room without another word. Very strange. Mendez looked back over his shoulder at Stildyne and Koscuisko alike, then put his hands to the arms of his chair, clearly preparing to leave.

"We'll have to consult the captain," Mendez said. "I don't care to go back without a loading schedule. No reason to put you through that, though, Andrej, you're already cleared for planetfall at Jeltaria. Why don't you and Stildyne just—"

The door to the depot master's office opened, and someone entirely different came in. An Emandisan. In the uniform of the home defense fleet; if Stildyne knew his rank markers, this was a senior officer, in the logistics branch. Stores and supplies. The officer seemed to hesitate, very slightly, as he passed the place where Koscuisko—who was looking a little confused, from Stildyne's angle on him—still sat in his chair; but continued toward the desk with such brisk dispatch that Stildyne decided he'd imagined it.

"We're in receipt of your requisition, your Excellency," the Emandisan said. His Standard was perfect. "Also of the exception document. I've been instructed to treat it as a fully endorsed Fleet instrument. We can begin to load out in five hours' time, will that be acceptable?"

First Officer settled back in his chair, warily, looking if anything even more uncertain than Koscuisko. "Very acceptable, and thank you. But this would seem to be a reversal of sorts. A man can't help but feel a little concerned, what's going on?"

It could be a trap, Stildyne supposed. Yet what could the Emandisan home defense fleet have against the *Ragnarok*? The quarrel ap Rhiannon had with the Fleet was just that—with the Jurisdiction Fleet. Home defense fleets tended to keep well clear of any Jurisdiction entanglements.

"Depot master Seprayan is a very conservative administrator," the Emandisan agreed. "Intelligence indicates however that it is not reasonable in this case to demand surrender of resources never issued. We will cover it with Fleet if we have to."

It sounded reasonable enough, if not for the fact that moments ago the depot master had been adamantly unreasonable about it. Taking a clearly determined breath Mendez challenged the reversal head-on. "To what do we owe this unusual accommodation, Mark Captain?"

Mark captain. That was right, Stildyne thought, impressed. He hadn't taken the spacing of the bands across the man's right shoulder into account.

"In all the history of Emandis there has never until now been an alien who has worn Emandisan steel," the mark captain said, looking at Koscuisko almost hungrily before focusing his attention back on Mendez. "As you may be aware, First Officer, a knife-fighter's five-knives are cultural artifacts that we consider to be of defining importance. A man was wronged. We owe it to his knives to make it up to him, any way we can, and an officer assigned to the Jurisdiction Fleet Ship *Ragnarok* is the lawful custodian of those knives; who can expect every cooperation from Emandis Station, accordingly."

Koscuisko had sat forward and was staring at his boots, with his hands folded in front of him and the knuckles showing white. Mendez eyed Koscuisko a little cautiously before he responded to this rather startling, if welcome, statement.

"I see, Mark Captain. Very well, we'll be glad to take advantage. Doctor Koscuisko has been cleared for transit to Emandis proper, to the city of Jeltaria. We were hoping for a local pilot."

There was an unusual sort of tension in the mark captain's voice as he replied. "The local pilot who was scheduled to perform that service has been delayed at Brisinje, your Excellency." He was talking to Koscuisko now, Stildyne realized, not Mendez at all, and Mendez outranked Koscuisko. But didn't seem to mind. "We have another man waiting. We're sorry. We understand how anxious you must be to meet your brother, and he you; but it can't be helped. He is a pilot first and a man with family second, as are we all."

Koscuisko's brother? Stildyne frowned. He hadn't realized that Koscuisko had any brothers in the Emandisan HDF. The Combine's home defense fleet, yes, Koscuisko's brother Lo, the next youngest after Meeka, older than Nikosha by some years. It wasn't impossible, of course, only one of Koscuisko's brothers—Nikosha, the youngest— had been there when Stildyne had accompanied Koscuisko to Chelatring Side to meet with Koscuisko's parents.

No, of course not Koscuisko's brother. Curran's brother. Ise-I'let's brother. Koscuisko wore Joslire Curran's knives. That clearly made Koscuisko family, in some sense: reasonable enough, Stildyne decided. Totally unexpected, but reasonable.

Koscuisko stood up, as though suddenly incapable of fully controlling his emotions. "I wish to be taken to the place as soon as possible," Koscuisko said. "I have been waiting since I found out we were coming here. I will hope we can still meet. But I can't wait. I need to go."

The mark captain nodded with grave and evident respect. "Of course, your Excellency, and it may yet be that Ise-I'let gets away from Brisinje before your ship leaves our station. In the mean time, First Officer—"

Mendez signaled his attention with politely raised eyebrows, and the mark captain continued.

"In the mean time, we invite your ship to enjoy the hospitality of Emandis Station until that time comes, whenever it should be."

That meant more than it seemed to, Stildyne realized. Once the load was complete the *Ragnarok* would typically have a limited period of time to clear the system: the Bench wanted no conflict between Fleet and civilians. Here and now the mark captain was indicating that the *Ragnarok* was welcome to remain in Emandisan space, for a little while at least.

It was as much as saying that the *Ragnarok* was to be offered the protection of the Emandisan home defense fleet. In light of the current tension between the *Ragnarok* and the rest of the Jurisdiction's Fleet, that was a particularly interesting privilege to have extended. Was it really just because Koscuisko had Joslire's knives, or was there something else going on?

The *Ragnarok* would get its commissioning issue of arms and munitions at last; Koscuisko would have a chance to sit with Joslire's people and mourn. If everything was actually to turn out to be as easy and as satisfying as that they would all be happy, the captain, the First Officer, the Ship's Engineer, Koscuisko, everybody. If.

But just in case the Emandisan didn't intend Koscuisko's knives to leave, Stildyne was going to be prepared to fight.

Grunting a little—her side hurt where she'd been injured, and the ventilation shaft was by no means sized for a traveler—Jils pulled herself head-and-shoulders out of the primary ventilator access and into the air-well to shine her lantern up into the blackness of the shaft above.

"Do you see anything?" Balkney asked, his hands around her ankles to anchor her and his voice muffled by the barrier of her own body in the vent-conduit. Jils scanned the sides of the air-well, playing the focused beam of the lantern from wall to wall of the naked rock shaft as far up the walls as the light would reach.

"There's a lot of rock." Just beneath her, though, she could see rungs fixed in the wall. The floor didn't look too far. She hoped that perspective did not deceive her; with only artificial light, the chances of confusing the eye with shades of gray were uncomfortably high. The rungs gave her a reference, though. They seemed to be about the same size in a flat two-dimensional comparison at the bottom of the air-well as within an arm's-reach beneath her. "Let loose of me, Balkney, I'm going down."

She felt the lifting away of his grip on her ankles, and wriggled forward. Awkward. Balkney could do it, maybe Capercoy; any of the women. Padrake would never fit through here, though, he had altogether too much shoulder.

Turning onto her back as she worked her way forward Jils took hold of the rung just above the access and pulled herself out, into the air-well. Balkney reached his hand out for the lantern as she began to climb down, leaning over the air-well from the vent-conduit shaft on his elbows to train the light on her route. Yes. Not very far down. If they had been on the surface the vent-access might have been the flat roof of a one-story building. Reaching the bottom Jils dusted her hands together, looking around.

"I don't see any other access," Balkney said, from above. He'd angled himself over to one side to shine the lantern up along the wall that rose into the darkness above the shaft, rung after rung, into obscurity.

Jils shuddered. She didn't want to think of how far down they were.

"What do you think?" He had the light. She was at the bottom of the air-well. He could back up into the shaft and lock the grill and leave her. She could try to climb out. Maybe if she did she'd fall. If she was lucky she'd fall from high enough to die on impact. That would be better than starving to death. There was no water here. What had she been thinking?

"Catch," Balkney said, and let the lantern drop. She had an emergency glim on her; he probably did as well. He might have stopped to let someone know where they were going, between his meeting with her in the kitchens after session and their rendezvous outside the generator station. If both of them disappeared someone might know where to look for them. She could hope. She hadn't really thought this through, impelled to the experiment after hours spent brooding over how deep they were and how unhappy it made her to think that there was only one way out.

Balkney was a sober married man, but he still climbed like a cat, jumping the last few feet to land sure-footed with his flexed knees more than equal to the force of the impact. He barely made a sound, when he landed. The air was still; sound didn't carry. Why was the air still? Maybe she just didn't feel its current. This was an air-well. There almost had to be some sort of an air current, whether passive or actively generated.

"I think it's a long way up," Balkney said, staring up into the gloom with his normally sharp face practically knife-edged in his concentration. "It was a long way down. Seemed to be. Hard to judge from inside a car. I'd want protection if I was going to try to climb that ladder. Assuming it goes anywhere else than another vent-shaft, of course."

"If this is the one, the schematic seems to imply it goes all the way up." There did have to be air-wells, almost necessarily. They were deep enough that the air would not refresh by normal exchange quickly enough to sustain human life where none had ever existed. A doorway into a lost world, and someone had put in an air-well? It was a guarantee of contamination. She hadn't decided what the station's founders might have been thinking, either, but she remembered why she'd wanted to get Balkney alone.

From the inside pocket of her blouse, she pulled the piece of paper she'd been carrying around with her for days. "While you're busy looking at things, Balkney, have a look at this."

He took the paper by one corner and held it up, shining the light from the lantern full on its surface. Frowning, but a frown that smoothed over into surprise—and then a kind of amused recognition. "Hah," Balkney said. "Well. Interesting. I found a bookmark in a text that turned up in my queue, myself. Didn't bring it, sorry." He handed the sketch back, the little drawing Karol had done, the Hangman. *Not guilty.* "I didn't connect it with Vogel at the time."

Balkney had said that he hadn't heard anything about Karol's whereabouts. He could easily have been lying, but that wasn't the way Balkney did it. Balkney didn't tell lies. He simply avoided making statements that were counter-factual in such a way as to facilitate whatever assumptions he didn't mind being made. And he'd made a positive statement of negative contact with Karol Vogel.

"So what'd yours say?" Jils asked, interested. The walls of the air-well seemed to be moving, drawing in on her, closing in. It was an intriguing effect, but not one that she particularly appreciated. "Here, you can tell me on the way out."

Moving slowly and deliberately she turned toward the rung-ladder on the wall, listening and waiting. It would be so easy to leave her here. He wouldn't have to lay a hand on her. And he was a Bench executioner; it was his job to make people disappear.

"It said Ivers didn't do it," Balkney said, his voice measured and thoughtful from the bottom of the shaft. He couldn't possibly be having reservations about his own position, could he? She climbed up past the access in order to swing into it feet-first, and back down the shaft on her belly as she had come. It hadn't been so long a trek from the corridor to the air-well, but it took longer to crawl than it would have taken to walk. Of course. She could see Balkney jump up lithely to take the first rung, and stayed to watch—just in case he was wondering if she had murder on her own mind.

"At least that's what I decided it meant. You tell me." She had to hurry backwards to give him room to get in. His boots were a little on the worn side of relatively new, Jils noted. Leather soles. The stitching would need attention in another few months.

What was she doing, getting distracted by shoe-leather? Leather soles didn't grip like some other materials, nor were they as quiet. Balkney hadn't intended on sneaking up on anybody or on having to dance if he did. Shouldn't she be listening to what he was saying?

"It was a peculiar piece of cutlery, with a solid line on the curved edge. Shadowing the blade, but not the edge. I thought it might be

Vogel's style, but it took me some time to decipher the message. Ivers is clean."

Backing down the vent-conduit shaft on her hands and knees Jils realized suddenly what Balkney wasn't saying. Battle-axe. The image caught her by surprise and she laughed, a short sort of a barking sound that startled her almost as much as it seemed to have startled Balkney.

"Right," she agreed, to let him know that everything was under control. "I understand." The edge was sharp and clear, no clean-up necessary. Battle-axe. It had been a long time since anybody had called her that. Balkney might be one of the few people left in service who would connect it to her.

Or Balkney could be making it up. He had nothing to show her; he'd said so. If he'd brought the sketch with him she'd have suspected that, too, and wondered if he'd fabricated the sketch in order to mislead her. For that Balkney would've had to know that she was going to find a doodle on a courier from Chilleau to Brisinje. That was stretching it. Unless he'd planted the doodle, but that was stretching it even further.

"So what's next?" she asked. Balkney hadn't said anything, busy working his way down the vent-shaft after her. All right, he knew she trusted him to a limited extent, she knew he trusted her. She could have left him at the bottom of the air-well just as easily as he could have left her there. "Something I need to know?"

He stopped moving in the shaft. "Nion," he said. "Has a new sort of way of thinking, a little like Delleroy and maybe Rinpen and possibly Tanifer. Privileged model."

So it hadn't been just her imagination. It was good to think that she hadn't just been seeing things, but not good to think that Padrake could have lost his focus to such an extent. "Why do you say that?"

Balkney had started to move again, but slowly. They were near the entrance to the shaft. "She spoke to me," Balkney said. Though Jils couldn't see his face, the tone of his voice made her think that he was trying to pick his words very carefully. "Maybe to some of the others, I'm not sure. About executing a Writ. She'd heard stories about me. She seemed a little too interested in some of them. Mosch, for one."

Bench intelligence specialist Elipse Mosch. She'd lost her way amid the lawless confusion of the Lettel uprising sixteen years ago, and started to behave like a warlord rather than a guardian of the Judicial order. Balkney had removed her for the good of the Bench and its citizens, but it hadn't been easy—or without controversy.

Some people still affected to believe that Mosch had been a Bench-sanctioned agent provocateur, but Balkney's point—Jils supposed—was that the hit had made his reputation, in the small secretive community of Bench specialists. Now Balkney wanted her to know that Nion might be looking for a target of opportunity whose acquisition might do the same for Nion.

"Whoever killed Verlaine is *mine*." She had no intention of meekly surrendering her revenge to bolster the reputation of a young Bench specialist. Showing her throat would be as good as a confession of guilt anyway. Reputations were to be earned by hard work and personal achievement; assassination was the easy way out, a short-cut. "I mean to have satisfaction."

They were back at the corridor, Balkney dropping out of the vent-shaft to land lightly on his feet beside her. His expression remained mild, but betrayed a little surprise. Yes. She supposed she *was* angry. "I won't be getting in your way," he said. "I've got a wife and children to think of. I think Capercoy is solid. Maybe Rafenkel. Just watch yourself."

It wasn't much to ask, and had been well intentioned. It wasn't his fault she was so keyed up. "Thanks," she said, and offered her hand. "I appreciate it. But how are we going to know about the air-well?"

Shifting the conversation back into neutral territory, careful to ensure that nothing was said that couldn't be safely overheard. Balkney nodded in apparent appreciation of the tactic and started down the corridor with a quick firm grasp of her hand.

"The question would be how deep it was capped off, if it's been capped. We could come back with a crawler, but those things are slow." Because the little mechanical climbers were very safe, and proceeded cautiously in order to successfully navigate difficult terrain. Vertical surfaces, for one, but the air-well had been dressed rock for at least a portion of its depth, and that would be relatively easy for a crawler to negotiate. "Maybe if we look at the station's life support protocols we'll find something."

That was an idea. If life support had a safety consideration hidden away somewhere in its library, it might tell them whether the original builders had made any allowances for a catastrophic failure of transport or ventilation. If she had built this data station, she would certainly have wanted to be sure about that, but these people had done some rather odd things. Light wells. And were those light wells wide enough for an adult hominid to ascend?

It was a welcome distraction from the issues on her mind, and looking for ways out helped her to manage her discomfort at being more or less trapped. There was only the one lift that anybody seemed to know of. If something happened to that—she supposed someone might climb the elevator shaft, but there was no way of knowing even if it was a straight line of ascent, and an accident could as easily have jammed the escape routes as anything else—

"After third-meal," she suggested. "In the maintenance area." This was not so large a station that it took very long to walk from place to place; they were coming back into the living area already. Balkney would have to go and observe Capercoy versus Rinpen on whether a new Judge should be raised from the subordinates available at Fontailloe. She was due to argue Chilleau against Zeman, with Padrake watching.

"See you, then," Balkney agreed, and turned off down a side corridor as they neared the kitchen. Jils stopped in mid-corridor, listening keenly to the sound of nobody near her, nobody at all. Padrake. Balkney had said that he thought Capercoy was solid, and Rafenkel probably. Nothing about Padrake. Was that odd?

Was that a data-point that contained information, or just noise? Had he not mentioned Padrake because he assumed Jils had come to her own conclusions, or had his remark been a little more deliberate than that?

Suspicion was a Bench specialist's friend, but it could become a liability if it was not carefully controlled. There was sometimes a thin line between healthy caution and paranoia. Jils meant to stay on the sane side of it, if she hadn't strayed too far already.

Putting the question in her mind away for the time being, Jils went though into the kitchen to take mid-meal and prepare her thoughts to challenge Zeman for the honor of Chilleau Judiciary.

The signs were not good. First Officer was pacing like an animal held in close confinement, her eyes fixed fiercely on some spot on the floor always three-eighths ahead of her no-longer-quite-flawlessly-shined boots, smoothing her light brown hair back across the rounded top of her narrow head with a gesture that stopped only barely short of clutching at hairs in sheer frustration. Caleigh Samons had seen this behavior before. First Officer was in danger of blowing her retard circuits past any hope of immediate recovery.

"Munitions packs. Expired propulsion recharges. Quantifiable rounds. Nothing else? Are you sure? A spare shallop, perhaps, for ap Rhiannon to use to send out for fresh sallets out of season?"

The depot master kept to her seat behind her desk, calm and imperturbable. She didn't seem unsympathetic; in fact she seemed quite aware that she was throwing propellant packs into the conversion furnaces, almost glad of the conflagration Caleigh feared would explode upon them soon.

"Well, battle cannon, First Officer, and a spares set for five Wolnadi fighters since the basic issue is more than ten years old. The *Ragnarok* asked for nothing less than a full munitions load, accordingly approved for release by Emandis Station's home defense fleet administration."

First Officer stopped at one side of the depot master's office to look into the watch-monitors. Loading docks. Container after container after container, munitions and stores and consumables and perishables and new boots for everyone, and—standing in the middle of a small clear space on the docks on one monitor—a very tall man and a very large bat.

He was easily twice as tall as the bat, and he wore uniform. Caleigh didn't think First Officer could actually discern the *Ragnarok*'s ship-mark on the man's shoulder, not on watch-monitor, not from here. There was no doubt of his identity, all the same: Serge of Wheatfields, Ship's Engineer, Jurisdiction Fleet Ship *Ragnarok*. And the Intelligence officer, assigned same.

First Officer Saligrep Linelly swore and spun on her heel to put the clearly irritating sight behind her. "Don't get me wrong, depot master," she said. "No intention of butting into your business, fully satisfied at all times in the past with the professionalism and performance of the Emandis Station depot. I just can't help wondering how ap Rhiannon rates. We wouldn't dare dump a requirements ticket as deep as that one had to be on you, not without adequate warning. And very good reasons. And negotiations with the supplier chain further on up."

The depot master nodded in solemn agreement, and closed her portfolio. "I appreciate that, your Excellency," she said. "And to be fair to the *Ragnarok* I can understand, abstractly at least, why they have to have so much right now. They never did get primary load, in all likelihood, it's never been formally commissioned as anything but a test bed. I told them to wait for Fleet clearance. I was over-ruled, First Officer."

And resented it, too, the depot master made no secret of that. There was no reason why she should. A person was welcome to feel as much resentment as she liked over incidents that could properly be resented, so long as a person didn't let it interfere with her duty.

"Over-ruled." First Officer sat down, a little heavily, and folded her hands across her belly, slumped in her seat. "In what way? By whom?"

"By the Emandis home defense fleet, your Excellency. Having apparently elected to accord the *Ragnarok*'s chief medical officer the status of an Emandisan knife-fighter, it is the duty of the Emandisan fleet to oblige him with defensive supplies as he sees fit."

First Officer let her hands drop to the sides of the chair, letting them hang dangling in mid-air. After a moment First Officer spoke, very calmly really, Caleigh thought. "The *Ragnarok*'s chief medical officer is not Emandisan, so far as I know."

The depot master nodded solemnly. "No. The *Ragnarok*'s chief medical officer is not Emandisan."

"He is in fact Dolgorukij, I believe," First Officer suggested; and the depot master nodded again. She was beginning to think about smiling, Caleigh thought; it was lurking in the corners of her eyes. It wasn't a malicious smile by any means, no, it was a cheerful supportive smile a-borning, *yes, you are right, it makes no sense.*

First Officer took a deep breath and seemed to be weighing her next words carefully, but said them all the same, and once she started to speak the words gained momentum and passion and life and brilliance until they shimmered in the air.

"He is in fact Andrej Koscuisko, Andrej-freaking-Shoeskoe, Andrej never learned in all of these years and about to get himself killed and his entire command with him Shoeskoe, Andrej how one poor crèche-bred brevet captain was expected to make a dent in his thick Dolgorukij skull Shoeskoe, Andrej Captain Irshah Parmin is really going to regret not having killed him when he had the chance Shoeskoe—"

"That's the man," the depot master agreed. "The first man from an alien bloodline to carry Emandisan steel in the history of Emandisan steel, and the history of Emandisan steel is the history of the Emandisan. So they tell me. Gone downplanet to visit some people he knows, I understand. To talk to someone he used to know, at the memorial site."

Of course. Joslire Curran. "Well, I heard," First Officer said, looking back over her right shoulder at Caleigh—who was glad she'd left her team outside the office, now, and not just because it wasn't over-large an office. "I heard that Koscuisko didn't even know it was Emandisan steel. Didn't have a clue. Carried five-knives for more than three years and never once wondered about them."

It was true. And of course it was hard to believe now that the story was out. Why should Koscuisko have wondered? Curran had provided them; only a man with considerably more ego than Andrej Koscuisko would have suspected that he'd been made bearer of a priceless artifact. Koscuisko's ego was perfectly healthy, but he had not been prone to delusions of grandeur in the time that Caleigh had known him.

"I was there," Caleigh said, in response to First Officer's implied invitation of a remark. "I saw it. It was Curran who made them sacred to Koscuisko. All of the rest about Emandisan steel, I don't think that ever meant as much to him as the fact that Curran's life's-blood was on those knives."

"You know, Koscuisko used to be under Irshah Parmin's command," First Officer said to the depot master, thoughtfully. "Maybe if we let the home defense fleet know that, we'd get clearance to draw from reserves. Worth a try, anyway, don't you think?"

No, the depot master didn't; she didn't seem to have much of an opinion either way. Caleigh knew what First Officer had on her mind, though. *He was ours before he went to the* Ragnarok, *and if having him is the key to Emandis Station's depot, well, we can arrange that. The captain wants to sit down for a talk with Koscuisko anyway.*

First Officer covered any potential awkwardness by standing up, talking on just as if the question had no answer. Perfectly true, in a manner of speaking. "Well. Thank you for your candor, depot master. We'll be in touch, and if you would go ahead and initiate load of what you can release to us we'd appreciate it. Crew's been anticipating extra shifts required to stow supplies all the way from Brisinje, hate to disappoint them."

This was something that the depot master clearly understood, and she seized it all the more happily for being a return to business as she was accustomed to it. "Very good, First Officer, slips four-eight and five-one, and as far away from the *Ragnarok* crew as possible. We can begin to load in about eight, your Excellency."

Not that there was much left to load on First Officer's manifest, not after the depot master had run it against stores available. Caleigh could find it in her to resent it a little bit herself. *Scylla* deserved the stores. What was the *Ragnarok* going to do with a munitions load, if it did not mean to defend itself against its own Fleet using its own Fleet's own resources, as it had at Taisheki?

Peculiar things had always happened around Koscuisko. Failure of Writ at the Domitt Prison. The Emandis home defense fleet shaking the whole purse of the depot out for Jennet ap Rhiannon to pick and chose what struck her fancy, because Andrej Koscuisko wore Emandisan steel.

The captain was going to have a thing or two to say to Caleigh's former officer of assignment, and she followed her First Officer out of the room with her sense of resignation warring with her presentiment of peculiarities yet to come in Andrej Koscuisko's wake.

CHAPTER TWELVE

Home is the hunter

In the depot master's office, Andrej had heard the Emandisan officer speak with increasing distress; and now as he stood on the landing field at Jeltaria his feelings of foreboding deepened into an anguished conviction that everything was to go wrong. Horribly wrong. Irreversibly wrong. Stoshi could have warned him; Stoshi had said nothing. Two could have tipped him off; had she actually tried to do so? Hadn't she told him that transport was arranged, and that he would be met?

Fool that he was, he had taken her to mean that there would be someone to make local arrangements. A guide. Someone who had contacted the family on his behalf and negotiated a meeting, someone who could tell him about Joslire's family and how things were and what he could expect. He'd been mistaken.

There was a welcoming party waiting for them, maidens with flowers, a cavalcade of ground-transport cars; and people. Well, people in the welcoming committee, yes, obviously enough; but people waiting for him as well, six people of them, waiting on a large golden carpet of beaten reed-fiber—local handicrafts. Pots of flowering plants.

Chairs, and attendants, and Andrej hadn't known what he was going to say to Joslire's people in the first place and could not call to mind even a single one of the ideas he might have had, under the stress of being so suddenly confronted by aged women of Joslire's family. They had to be. They could not be anybody else.

In the overcast hush of the waiting launch-field Andrej stepped down the loading ramp to take his place in the Security formation. Something caught his eye as he came forward; a twitch of a finger. Lek Kerenko. Finger-code, *the milk-maid's daughter*. Lek had been with him on Azanry, at the Matredonat, when he had outraged propriety and astonished his Marana by marrying her. It was a good point. A man capable of so brazen an act as he had committed at that time, and in that place, had no right to feel nervous just because a private pilgrimage had turned into a media event.

Stildyne marched them all across the thermal sheathing that blanketed the launch-field's surface; it wasn't a standard formation by any means—that would be six, and they were eight—but his gentlemen rose to the unusual occasion like the superlative soldiers that they were. There was a young officer waiting for them just short of the room-sized reed-mat; Andrej couldn't decipher her rank, but she made her function explicit at once.

"Your Excellency." Something seemed odd about her accent; Andrej realized that it was the fact that she didn't seem to have one, not that his ear could detect. Her Standard was flawless. "A very great honor, sir. If I might translate for his Excellency. My name is Piross, and I'm to make introductions, at his Excellency's will and good pleasure."

Security spread out with solemnly measured tread and posted themselves along the near edge of the reed mat and its sides, facing out. Facing away. Making the room defined by the reed-mat a private space. There was no breath of wind; the air was as still as though there was no such thing as a wind in Jeltaria, and the clouds were gray and thick and heavy with rain. They would not let the women of Joslire's family sit in the open in the rain, surely?

"My Intelligence officer said that I would meet with his surviving relatives," Andrej said to Piross. "If one of them is Joslire's mother I have not been warned, and fear an embarrassment. It is a terrible thing in my home-world to come face to face with a man's mother, and not demonstrate appropriate respect."

Piross nodded sharply, as if acknowledging an instruction. Covering for his confusion, Andrej thought, gratefully. "His mother's sister, your Excellency, and his father's mother. His eldest sister. The son of another of his mother's sisters, the son of one of his father's brothers, and the wife of his surviving brother, with her firstborn child."

The Emandisan officer at the depot had said Joslire's brother was not there. It was so strange to look at these people and see Joslire in their faces.

"What am I to do?" They were looking at him, those old women, hawk-eyed and merciless. *Where did you come from. Why are you here. What business can you have, you too-pale man, why are we troubled with your presence?*

"You give her the knife and show her your hand. She may prick your hand. She will give you back the knife. Then we'll all go to the orchard, and they'll open the gate for you."

Knife, what knife? Which knife? Of course he had brought them. They were Joslire's. "But which is the right one?" he asked in a low voice, trying to control his panic. That knife, perhaps. Of course it would be that knife. It could be no other, the one that he wore between his shoulderblades when he wore it at all, the one that he tended to wear even when he did not feel the need to go fully armed to a staff meeting. He didn't wait for her reply. He had enough to go on, and he was the son of the Koscuisko prince after all. He had generations of ritual bred into him.

"Mister Stildyne," Andrej said, unfastening the secures of his duty blouse. Black, because he was one of the *Ragnarok*'s Primes; it was a particular black whose use in uniform was restricted to officers of senior rank. Of course his under-blouse was clean, and in good repair. If it were otherwise he would have no choice but to be humiliated in public, and the Saints only knew in what broadcast and record and rebroadcast record, by appearing in disrespectfully slovenly dress.

Stildyne would never have let such a thing happen. Stildyne stood at Andrej's back to take Andrej's blouse; in his shirtsleeves Andrej stepped onto the reed-mat and crossed its padded surface to where the old women sat. They looked much older than he had at first taken them to be, once he was close enough to see; it was not the creasing of facial skin that spoke of the years, but the shining of the bones of the hand beneath the skin, the fingers thin as a bird's wing.

These women represented the blood that had been Joslire's life, and their dead—the missing generation, Joslire's brothers and sisters if he'd had any—had fallen victim to the same cruel treachery that had enslaved Joslire. Andrej knelt, because they were women and they were old and they were not to be asked to rise by a man who had any respect for his mother.

Down on both knees, he bowed his head, raising his hand to draw the knife. Flattening his palm Andrej considered it—this was the weapon that had taken Joslire's life—and presented it to the oldest of the women, who sat like an abbess with her hands to her thighs watching him closely with her dark eyes.

"Tell her that I have brought these back," Andrej said, not looking at Piross. "They have saved my life on at least one occasion, and freed Joslire from his. He should have them back. They belong to his family."

The translator spoke. The oldest woman leaned forward and drew Andrej's hand toward her with the knife still across its palm; seemed to squint at the scar on Andrej's palm—where Joslire had pushed that knife through, back to palm, and pinned his hand and Andrej's hand together—then picked it up.

Holding it to the cloud-diffused light of the sun at midheaven she turned it slowly from side to side, as if she were evaluating its condition; and then she spoke. Her voice was quavery with age, but firm and self-possessed for all that.

"Tell him he is mistaken," Piross said, from behind Andrej. "The knife does not follow the family, grandson, the family follows the knife."

The old woman leaned forward again as the translator was speaking, reaching out for Andrej. To touch his head, and give him benediction? Andrej bowed his head, but she was going for the back of his neck instead. The sheath. She sheathed the knife between his shoulder-blades, and it felt warm to the touch all along its length as if it had absorbed a day-long dose of full sunlight during its few moments naked beneath the cloudy Emandisan sky.

Then she stood up, and beckoned to Andrej to do the same. "Now we will go and meet the family," she said, through the translator. "But put on your costume, and bring your people. We want to be sure that your ancestors understand who you are, so that they'll know you when they see you, the next time."

What was he to do?

Grandson, she'd called him—or whatever she had called him, Piross had translated it that way, and Piross' command of Standard was excellent. Unchallengeable. What was expected of him, what—

Look to the second son. His mother's housemaster had told him that, early and often. In someone else's house look to the second son and guide on him. The first son is the inheriting son, and if you do as he does you may commit a mis-step. The worst thing that can happen to you if you look to the second son is that you gain a reputation for being over-careful to avoid giving offense, and there is hardly a thing as an excess of politeness where the inheriting son of a great house is concerned. Look to the second son and you will do honor to your father's name and your mother's nurture.

There was no second son here; there were only Joslire's cousins. Andrej turned his head to find one of them, to discover what he should be doing—lead? Follow? What?

One of Joslire's cousins caught Andrej's eye just as Piross started talking. "His Excellency is expected to walk behind the women of the family but ahead of its other men," she said. "You will not travel in the same cars."

Joslire's cousin seemed to acquire the scent of Andrej's confusion, all at once; he grinned, so broad and open and unguarded a smile— there in an instant and gone almost as quickly—that it struck Andrej to the heart. He'd seen that smile before. Not very often, but he'd seen it, and the pain that the reminder in the flesh brought home to him staggered him where he stood.

Stildyne was behind him, with his blouse; holding it to help Andrej dress himself, steadying Andrej at his back as he had been doing for all of these years. Andrej stood for a moment longer than was perhaps strictly necessary; Stildyne stood with him with Stildyne's hands to Andrej's shoulders as if in the act of smoothing the fabric to lie perfectly flat.

Hadn't the Emandisan officer suggested that Andrej's brother was hoping to meet him? Why hadn't he noticed? Because the reminders of this place, of how much he had learned from Joslire and how much lost when Joslire had claimed the Day, deprived him of his capacity for rational thought. He had to rethink his arrangements. How was he to make this work?

The cars would be waiting, and there were elderly women. Even if they had not been the knives' family, they would still be old women who had suffered much and who should not be kept waiting while one man brooded over his difficulties as if he were the only person here who'd had any in his life.

Straightening his spine Andrej nodded to Stildyne over his shoulder, and turned crisply on his heel to follow the women to the transport that was waiting—with a full police escort, name of all Saints—and the translator with them.

On Azanry, Koscuisko's planet of origin, burial places were great gleaming stoneworks let into the ground; Stildyne had seen pictures. Not everybody was buried in such splendor, of course not, but in the burial places of the old aristocratic families you could sometimes walk down row upon row of stone boxes underground before you reached that which had once held the founder of the line.

Dasidar himself was buried in the dead-house of the Autocrat's court, Dyraine of the Weavers beside him. There were tours available on remote. They had to recycle the space, in the older families; there wasn't room for everybody, any more. The first, the last, and four parents, and everybody else moved off into much smaller boxes that contained just bones in disarray. Dolgorukij funeral customs fascinated Stildyne. Many of the things about the Dolgorukij interested him; Koscuisko was as good as a hobby, that way.

This was no huge stone house of the dead, no anonymous envelope of residue from an industrial funeral. The transport cars drew up beside a long white wall, and through the gates Stildyne could see that the wall ran up the slope of a modest little hill on either side. There was a plantation of some sort. The translator had said orchard, hadn't she?

Stildyne got out of the car on one side while Koscuisko and the translator exited through the other. There were Security everywhere, Emandisan security. The port authority apparently took Koscuisko much more seriously than Koscuisko had expected, or Stildyne either. Stildyne didn't know yet whether or not there was going to be a fight about Koscuisko's knives, though the old woman's actions coupled with the translator's explanation did seem to imply that the knives were to be left with the officer.

Jeltaria was arid and dry, for all that it was on the banks of an inland sea. The apron in front of the gate was covered in crushed white rock that caught the light and sparkled in the clear air. The clouds had lifted a little, it was even warmer than before—Stildyne could feel himself sweat.

Curran's family were holding the gates. Koscuisko was to go through. The oldest woman said something; Stildyne looked to Koscuisko's translator. "Come into the orchard and meet your ancestors," the translator said.

There was all this police presence; would Koscuisko want his people to go in with him?

Koscuisko gave Stildyne the nod and Stildyne started the Security detachment through the gate, past Joslire's family. Nobody stopped Security, so it was clearly all right. Once they were through the two cousins closed the wooden gate, behind them; the oldest woman headed off down the main axis of the orchard, talking as she went. Koscuisko hurried to catch up, which meant Security hurried and Stildyne hurried and the translator hurried as well.

"There have been more than thirty-five generations of the knife in our family." The old woman, but the translator's voice was that of a young woman. It was a little confusing. "Not all of equal duration, of course. I will show you the first to take your knives into his hand. And then you may go and speak to your brother."

The orchard-garden was a regular matrix of white stone-graveled pathways and earth-boxes on the ground, four or five feet high, two or three times as long, half that length deep or wide. Each of the raised beds contained a tree with ripening fruit: yes, an orchard. The old woman was headed up the hillside at a determined pace with Koscuisko following after.

"What are these trees?" Koscuisko asked the translator; who translated the question for the old woman's benefit—just so she would know, Stildyne supposed—but answered it herself, not waiting for the old woman to do so.

"They're a slow-growing hardwood, your Excellency, a nut-bearing tree. The peculiarities of the Madic tree include the required proximity of juvenile as well as past-bearing trees for successful fructification to occur, and they are hungry for flesh, in the first years of their growing."

They weren't beautiful trees. They were looking more sinister to Stildyne by the moment, as a matter of fact; but vegetables had that effect on him in general. He'd never seen a tree but in pictures until he'd been a grown man of twenty, and even then it had been a tame tree in a zoological gardens. He could remember the first time he'd seen wild ones. The experience had been very unnerving.

"You feed them on the bodies of your dead," Koscuisko said. There was something in his voice that made Stildyne almost want to shudder, and it took a great deal to have an effect like that on a man who had to face Brachi Stildyne in the mirror every morning. "What is it of the tree that earns it so much honor?"

The old woman had led them to a place halfway up the slope of the little hill. The walls of the raised beds there were old and primitive, piled stones that had been gradually collapsing over who knew how many years; the tree that still stood there was long dead, bleached and scoured and polished by wind and dust and sun and time.

"This is the first man who ever kissed the knife that you now wear." The old woman was looking at Koscuisko, though it was the translator of course who put the words into plain Standard. "Touch his hand, grandson. Know your ancestor."

Taking Koscuisko's hand she climbed up the little rubble of the rock into the raised bed where the dead tree stood, and put Koscuisko's hand—Koscuisko's scarred hand—to the trunk of the tree. Koscuisko snatched his hand away as if out of the thermal exhaust of a conversion furnace.

"Holy Mother," Koscuisko said, but it was sometimes hard for Stildyne to decide whether he were swearing or praying. This was one of those times. "It sings." And carefully Koscuisko put his hand back to the dead trunk of the tree. "It is humming. Alive. Breathing."

The translator said nothing, but the old woman who had named herself Koscuisko's grandmother smiled as if she knew exactly what he had said. Maybe she did. There was no particular reason to assume that she couldn't understand the spoken word perfectly well, or well enough, even if she didn't actually speak it.

"We had no body to feed a tree when Joslire came back to the orchard," the old woman said. "There was only ash, and bits of bone. We worked it into the earth around the ancestor, so that Joslire would have the strength to find his way. Here he rests, Koscuisko of the others."

No tablet. No marker, no stone. Stildyne knew that Koscuisko had expected some object to look upon and call a grave, and there was none; only the dirt and debris around the base of an old tree, and little bits of something cinder-looking. Not what Koscuisko had expected, not at all. Stildyne wondered why. Koscuisko was a thorough man, he should have been better prepared; or was this a closely held secret, permitted to Emandisan families, not widely published in tourism documentation?

Koscuisko put his forehead to the trunk of the old—dead—tree, and was silent. The old woman nodded, as though she was satisfied about something.

"You do not need the translator to talk to your own brother," the old woman said—and the officer who Koscuisko did not need in order to communicate with Joslire Ise-I'let translated with evident care. "I leave you with your people. We do not allow others into our orchards, grandson. Use your time wisely."

Whatever that meant. Leave for Koscuisko to be here with off-worlders, perhaps, in the middle of a private family orchard. There were a lot of the trees here. Joslire's family had apparently been around for a long time.

The sound of old and young women walking away down those graveled paths was clearly audible in the orchard's stillness. When Stildyne could no longer hear their footsteps Koscuisko raised his head, and spoke.

"Gentles, I have something to say to you," Koscuisko said, to the tree trunk. "And there cannot be very much time." Turning away from the tree Koscuisko accepted the nearest helping hand—Robert's, as it happened—to climb down out of the raised bed, standing with his back to the containment wall.

"Brachi, I would ask you to forgive me if I believed that you did not know my purpose from the start, even if I did not dare to tell you. Perhaps you have heard from Lek that I was offered my freedom, on Azanry, gentles. The First Secretary at Chilleau Judiciary has granted relief of Writ."

Nobody stared. So they all knew, not surprisingly. Koscuisko nodded, as if accepting this as an answer. "Very good. It means I do not mean to stay for longer than I must, on board the *Ragnarok*. We stand here in the presence of a man I loved, and killed so that he could be free."

Clearly wasn't proposing that he kill them, Stildyne knew—or hoped. There would have been no reason for Koscuisko to take such risks to tinker with their governors if all he wanted to do was kill them.

"There is a small freighter at the launch-field where we came in, a respectable beast from the Khabardi shipyards. I know that you will be as shocked as I to hear that there are people even in the heart of Jurisdiction who have dealings with the outlaws of Gonebeyond space."

"Sending us away, are you?" Robert said suddenly, almost vehemently. "And why d'you assume that we'll just go? My duty was not of my choice, your Excellency, but it is my duty, and you should not insult us. After all."

After all that they had been through together. After all that they had learned from one another. After all that they had meant to one another.

Koscuisko shook his head. "I will tell you a secret, Robert, and you will understand. I could not live in Fleet without your help. All of your help," Koscuisko added, looking at Stildyne, right at him. "I will not be able to live in Fleet at all for very much longer." Koscuisko seemed clearly determined, but to be thinking twice even so. He took a deep breath, and continued.

"If you do not leave now someone in the future may be able to compel you to admit that I murdered Captain Lowden in Burkhayden, and set fire to the service house to burn the body so that he could not come back to it. I was not thinking very clearly at the time."

No, Stildyne thought. *You can't tell them that. You can't tell them. Nobody is supposed to know. I don't know. Nobody knows. How could you tell them*—and then he understood, even as Koscuisko spoke on.

"But now I have told you, and betrayed your trust by giving you a terrible secret. You will not dispute with me. You must go away. Please. There is little enough in Gonebeyond, but I am assured that there are neither governors, nor facilities that could impose them without killing if they tried."

Well, that was a comfort, wasn't it? Stildyne asked himself. Maybe it was. He'd worked with Bonds for almost his entire life in Fleet. He'd seen the things a governor could do, and at Burkhayden he was the man who had done them.

"If you can take the chances you've taken," Pyotr said, "We can have some too. The tax-collector also must pay taxes."

Koscuisko nodded. "And I can't make anybody go. I have no cause to believe I know what is in your hearts, because you have been prisoners in my presence all of these years. But here in the place of the dead I ask it of you. I have owed my life to Joslire. I have owed my life to you. My cousin has a place for you to go, in Gonebeyond. He says it will be deficient in the luxuries of life, but you will be free."

His cousin? So that as where Stanoczk had gotten himself off to, in such a hurry. Stildyne hadn't minded Stanoczk's precipitate departure, no, of course not.

"But you're not coming," Hirsel pointed out. "Have I got that part right?"

Stildyne could see sweat running down the side of Koscuisko's neck. It was uncomfortably warm, and close—but Koscuisko's face was pale.

"Good enough for us, but not for you? What kind of an offer is that?"

"The ship needs me." It was immediately obvious to Stildyne, and apparently to Koscuisko as well, that the suggestion was not to be accepted. Koscuisko raised both hands, palms outward, making hushing gestures. "It needs you too, but we have other Wolnadi crews, we can cope. We have no other neurosurgeon. You are not needed to work in Secured Medical. And also I mean to keep the truth hidden for as long as possible, there is Security on the vector."

"What's the plan, then?" Lek Kerenko asked, a little skeptically. "Better dead than Bonded, your Excellency, but if I can avoid both at the same time I will."

They'd all known Koscuisko was up to something. They'd all known. They must have wondered among themselves what it could be. What Koscuisko was offering could not but be fraught with danger and promised hardship; Koscuisko was clearly grateful to Lek for making the most positive response yet.

"And I mean both to be avoided, if there is any way that I can make it so. We are going to the service house, gentles, and in the early morning a car will come to take you to the launch field. I have sent you on an errand. The freighter has a cleared departure, and I will simply have to stay in bed until the ship has acquired its vector. Well into the morning. Nearly half-a-day, to be safe."

"What if we don't all go?" Godsalt asked, frowning. "Pyotr is so close to Reborn. Not to get personal, man."

"If you don't all go I will only have sent some of you. First Officer will not press the issue as long as he has the say about it." Which could not be very long, of course. That was part of what had been on Koscuisko's mind all along, clearly enough. "But I hope you may all decide. You will need each other. You are the only people who could understand what you have endured."

Pyotr was about to say something, but Hirsel put his hand to Pyotr's shoulder, Robert took a half a step back and caught Garrity's eye; Godsalt nodded. Lek shook his head as though he were discouraged, but he said nothing.

Koscuisko turned his back to them all and raised his head to stare up into the dead branches of the tree whose roots were dressed with the mortal remains of a man Koscuisko still loved. "I would wish to have you with me always if I could," Koscuisko said. "But my motive would be selfish, it would be for my sake and not yours. I don't know how I am to do without you."

It was at that moment that Stildyne understood that he was going to go with them. He didn't think Koscuisko realized it, yet; Stildyne had only just now seen the logic of it for himself. He couldn't unsee it. There was no acceptable alternative. Koscuisko loved these people. They'd need someone who understood their situation, someone who could stand between them and the rest of the world and smooth out the rough spots until they had had time to learn again what it was to be free.

When Koscuisko continued he had apparently found a new strength of determination, his voice strong and steady, if pitched low. "I only tell you this because I could not bear to send you away from me without at least once acknowledging how much I owe. I ask you to do this knowing that it is a risk and that life will not be easy, even if you get cleanly away. I have watched you suffer for these years. Please. Take the only chance that you may get to be away from suffering, at least of that particular sort."

In the still air Stildyne was half-convinced that he could actually hear himself sweat.

"Why aren't you coming? And tell us the truth of it. It's owed," Lek said suddenly.

Koscuisko looked back over his shoulder, but didn't turn around. "Six renegade bond-involuntaries lost in Gonebeyond are not worth the effort it would take to return them," Koscuisko said. His voice was harsh and hopeless. "I can't go. Fleet would have no choice but to report a kidnap or an absence without leave, and follow in force. There would be a bounty. There would be no disappearing, no new life."

Koscuisko had a point. Stildyne hadn't thought about it, because the course of action that Koscuisko had suggested was taking its own sweet time to sink in. They'd all known that Koscuisko was up to something, or he understood nothing of these men, and they were by definition intelligent men with the psychological resilience it demanded to be forced to become an instrument of torture, to live in fear of torture, and yet live. They were probably smarter than he was, with the possible exception of St. Clare.

"Thought of everything, he has," Robert said to Godsalt, who stood next to him. "It's like him. Here's what's left of Jos, though, you didn't know him, and I did. I didn't get to say good-bye to Joslire, either."

Koscuisko winced, and closed his eyes. But when he opened them again and turned around to face them, the expression on his face was resolute—almost cold. "Good-bye, Robert," Koscuisko said. "Thou hast been very good to me, and had little but abuse and care for thanks. I pray to all Saints that you will be free. Lek. Good-bye. I will explain your absence to my son."

There was a solid core of merciless determination in Koscuisko's nature; Stildyne had seen it once or twice before. It made him shudder now, too. There would be no turning Andrej Koscuisko from his purpose, regardless of the cost.

"Pyotr, good-bye, and thank you for the care that you have had of me. Godsalt. Good-bye, I will miss you, and so will Soft Tissue Displacement, I will have to answer to my staff for it. Hirsel, good-bye, and may you have better luck in the future than you have ever had in the past. Good-bye, Garrity, I can only hope that you can forgive me when I say that I hope I never see you again. Ever. After tonight."

Stildyne had never known another man who could make up his mind like Koscuisko. It had been one of the things that had intrigued him from the start, well before he'd realized that Koscuisko's opinion had begun to matter to him much more than it ought to have done. "Fall back," Stildyne suggested. "Give the officer some room."

Koscuisko turned his back again. One hand on the retaining wall of the raised bed to steady himself Koscuisko reached down, just at hip-height, and took up a handful of the earth that was there. What he did with it Stildyne didn't know; he was occupied in moving Security off to a respectful distance.

Koscuisko hadn't said good-bye to him. He wasn't going to get to say good-bye. He was going to have to just get up and go, and never see Koscuisko again. It was hard. But that was life. It was even funny that no one else appeared to have realized that Stildyne had no choice but to leave Koscuisko if he loved Koscuisko, and he had long since been forced to accept the awkward fact that he did.

Then, like fluid coloring when Koscuisko dripped a catalyst into a flask in his pharmacology lab, the air filled in an instant with a fine mist of soaking rain. There was no seeing Koscuisko at the tree; did Koscuisko know where they were, could he find them? It came on so suddenly that the scent of moisture followed after the drenching mist.

Stildyne wondered if he should send out a scouting party, but no, here was Koscuisko back again, walking slowly and contemplatively with his head bent to the ground and the rain coming in little rivulets across his face and shoulders. What was the hurry, after all? Stildyne asked himself. They had already been wet from the inside out, what sense was there in hurrying to avoid getting wet from the outside in? It wasn't as if the rain was cold. It was warm rain. It was almost exactly as hot as it had been before the rain had started.

The thick mist of rainfall obscured walls and boundaries and the skyline of the city in front of them. They were alone, for these few moments, all alone, with each other.

No one spoke. Moving at a meditative pace they walked in an appropriate formation out of the orchard into the street, and loaded into the ground-transport cars to go to the service house as Koscuisko had arranged.

The welcoming party was still waiting. Andrej couldn't face them, not just now. He was ashamed—there were old women and a young mother, he'd kept them waiting—but he had reached the utmost tolerance of his psychological resilience. He should have done more research. He had no one to blame but himself.

Even before he had realized the opportunity this would give him to send his gentlemen away, he had long dreamed of kneeling down at

Joslire's grave, in front of Joslire's marker, and telling the silent earth how much he missed his friend. There had been no grave. There had been no marker. He had trodden in his boots on sacred ground, and not known it. Yes, the tree sang of itself; but right now Andrej could find no comfort in that.

"Beg for me the pardon of these people," he said to the translator. "My heart is full. I can't speak, I'm not fit for company, and there are my gentlemen. Only one night. If it is disrespect of the dead—I don't know what I will do—"

She was every eighth the professional; there was no hint of surprise or disapproval on her face or in her voice. "It is understood," she assured him gravely. "His Excellency's accustomed practice. They are only making sure that you don't need to talk right now, sir."

It was all right. Or at least to be overlooked in dignified silence. In front of the family of the murdered man he was to go directly from the burial ground to the service house. He had done that on the night of Joslire's death, as he remembered, but they had stopped at the port's hospital first, to dress the wounds that the others had suffered—and to burn the body, sending it up in smoke.

Joslire had been there when Andrej had discovered that he had an appetite for torture. Joslire had kept him company, and given him comfort. Andrej hadn't realized how much difference it made. He'd been alone in Port Rudistal, watching the temperature gauge of the hospital's incinerators. Then there'd been the furnaces at the Domitt Prison—

Andrej shuddered. He was alone now. He had sent them away and they would go, even Robert whom he loved also. They would go because he bade them, and then he would be alone.

"I'd like to get the officer changed," Stildyne said, to the translator. It was a voice that put a hand to Andrej's shoulder to steady him. To comfort him, in a different way than Joslire's friendship had strengthened him, but Stildyne was a different man and Andrej owed him much more than he could possibly repay. "If it wouldn't give offense to the family."

The translator bowed politely one more time, but Andrej had remembered who he was; and crossed the wet concrete apron before the orchard gate to bow in turn to Joslire's family. The least honor he could do to them was to make his own excuses.

"I'm honored to see the place where his ancestors are." And that was true. "I need some time to settle my own mind. And I have wished my Security to have the opportunity to take recreation, and will be sending them back to the ship on an errand for me tomorrow. I ask to be forgiven."

If he didn't go with them, they couldn't go to the service house. Not under ordinary rules. And since he claimed to be sending them off in the morning this was their only chance to have a little fun.

The youngest woman spoke, her expression anxious, her baby fretful in her arms. "Does his Excellency leave in the morning?" she asked, in rather less fluent Standard than that of the translator. "Shona I wish to have the chance. Joslire was his brother."

This Andrej could promise honestly. It would be two or three days before the *Ragnarok*'s load-out was completed, and whether the *Ragnarok* would let him back on board at all was to be seen. "I mean to stay in port as long as I may be allowed," he said. "If all Saints are generous it will give us both the chance, your husband and I. Will it be possible to visit with your family, tomorrow?"

The translator spoke for him; the oldest woman smiled. There was a ghost there, too. "Required," the old woman said; the translator actually blushed as she said the words. "Transport will come for you, grandson. You have not seen your house. We have not seen you in your place."

She had just put him in his place, though, and decisively, if kindly enough. Yes, he would be forgiven if he went elsewhere tonight. No, he would not be forgiven if he failed to be a dutiful adopted son tomorrow. Even as heartsore as he was Andrej had to smile.

"I will prove that I can take instruction, and do my utmost to shadow in his place in such a way as may do honor to his memory," he promised. "Please excuse me now."

Security were loaded in the cars already, all except Stildyne; and there were Emandisan Port Authority security to protect his Security while they protected him. He hadn't been so flamboyantly secured in his life.

Sitting in the ground-car on the way to the city's public house, Andrej leaned back against the padded cradle of the seat and closed his eyes, listening to the pain that was in his heart and mind. Joslire was dead. It had been a mistake to come. It had reminded him, and Joslire was dead all over again, fresh dead, new dead, gone and gone and gone and gone. He'd forgotten how much it hurt. He'd thought he'd put the agony away. There had been the Domitt Prison; he had not had time. Had that been his error? Had he never truly mourned his friend Joslire?

Not a mistake. It was his second chance, to feel the loss as though it was just done and suffer for it without the need to master his emotions and turn his mind to work. "When we arrive," he said, knowing that Stildyne would be listening, "If you would make the arrangements, Brachi. I can't face the negotiations now. Convince them."

Arrival at a service house too often caused an uproar, and all manner of misunderstandings founded in his personal notoriety. He was the Ship's Inquisitor on board the Jurisdiction Fleet Ship *Ragnarok*; he clearly could not be offered any ordinary accommodation.

Pain-workers would be called for, and if he could convince the house-master that in fact he did not wish to reproduce in his intimate behavior the regrettable activities of his professional life, they were all too ready to conclude that he desired a beating. Once upon a time he had grown so weary of trying to make himself understood that he had agreed, *oh, very well*; it had not been a successful experiment.

The animal portion of his nature did not experience sharp sensation as pleasurable, and the professional portion of his nature could not be silenced from making a technical critique. The last thing he needed when he wished to engage was to be so forcibly reminded of exactly what he was in all of its grim horror, and things had simply not gone well at all.

He'd felt so sorry for the woman, he'd tipped her outrageously, but she'd known. He'd been able to tell. It was a part of his curse: he could tell. He had learned the lessons of patient interface too well, in school; and when people were distressed or suffering he could smell it like a drug.

"I'll see to it," Stildyne promised. "If you're going to sit up, do you want a game of cards, later on in the evening?"

Stildyne would do that for him. When Stildyne was done with his own enjoyment he would come and sit with Andrej in the officer's suite at a service house, and keep him company. Andrej thought about it, but shook his head.

"Thank, you, Brachi, but not this night." Stildyne would only remind him of the fact that there were men in a different area of the service house that he would never see again. Not dead; but going away from him regardless.

Which reminded him—"I didn't dare say anything." He owed Stildyne trust and confidence, and had showed him neither. "And Stoshi only finalized arrangements when he came on board. I do not ask if Stoshi said anything to you. I only ask your pardon for reserving my confidence. I believed it necessary."

"I should have guessed," Stildyne said. He sounded more than usually meditative, to Andrej; and meditation wasn't usually something he associated with Stildyne. "Only myself to blame. It's a useful reminder, of how things can be perfectly obvious in hindsight and to all intents and purposes invisible in plain sight all along."

Yes, Stildyne was right. "I'll have my supper," Andrej said. It was getting to be evening-time, by the sun. "It's nice to be alone, once in a while. Maybe they'll have something of interest for you."

Officers had orderlies, someone from Security detailed every night to stand outside their quarters and attend to whatever chore might need doing. Boots. Fetching supper. Playing cards with drunken officers. On board the *Ragnarok* he was never alone. Or never far from the company of another soul; it was not the same thing.

"We'll see," Stildyne promised, sounding a little amused. It wasn't as though he believed for one moment that Andrej didn't know— surely not. "Don't worry. I'll take care of everything."

"You always do," Andrej acknowledged. Then the ride was quiet until they reached the service house, and all went in.

"I don't blame the depot master," Captain Irshah Parmin said thoughtfully to his cup of bhan. "I'd be angry too. I've been angry. I never met a man who fried my breakfast ungreased like Koscuisko could, not ever in my life. An accomplished officer. Yes."

But it was clear enough to Caleigh that he was seriously unhappy. He had the Intelligence officer's report in cube in front of him; rumors, gossip, innuendo, report. From what he'd shared with them all—Ship's First, Intelligence, Doctor Weasel-Boy, Caleigh Samons— there was a very peculiar dynamic at work in Fleet these days; Koscuisko had been notorious almost from the beginning of his career, and now the stored-up anxieties of certain elements in Fleet appeared to be attaching themselves to Koscuisko, rather than to the woman who had done more to earn Fleet's resentment honestly and fairly.

Caleigh could feel the injustice of it, for ap Rhiannon's sake. Koscuisko had a reputation, but it wasn't difficult to acquire one in his line of work, especially with Verlaine doing his best to raise Koscuisko's profile by persecuting him relentlessly. It would have taken a much more subtle man than Koscuisko all of his faculties to avoid acquiring a name for himself in Fleet.

It was ap Rhiannon who had taken the *Ragnarok* and left Taisheki—Koscuisko merely executing his orders, by reliable report— and still people who should have known better, who did know better, affected to believe that Andrej Koscuisko was the cause and the ringleader of disaffection on board the *Ragnarok*.

"It's not your problem," First Officer reminded him. "Koscuisko was reassigned years ago. So you feel that you missed a chance with him. He's not yours to nurture and cultivate. It's no reflection on *Scylla*."

The captain laughed short and sharp and sudden, losing control of a moderate amount of bhan as he did so. "What, Jennet ap Rhiannon is going to develop Koscuisko's professional presentation? Don't make me laugh." Ignoring the fact that First Officer just had, Caleigh noted, but kept the thought to herself. She was here on sufferance. The captain only involved her at all because she'd been Koscuisko's chief of Security while Koscuisko had been here on *Scylla*. They had grief in common. "She couldn't professional deportment her way out of a—that's unfair. I take it back. They're well suited, now that I come to think of it."

Doctor Weasel-Boy sniggered, but everybody affected to ignore him. He kept shut. "You could just as easily turn quietly around and go back to Brisinje," First Officer pointed out. "Pick up a few stores for the sake of appearances. Now is not the time to make issues with Emandis Station."

The captain scowled. "Emandis Station has decided to make issues with Fleet, it seems to me," he observed, not unreasonably, in Caleigh's opinion. "Who's to say there has to be any trouble? He's a Fleet resource, I'm a former commander, I haven't seen him. Isn't it my bounden duty to try to get him to see the error of his ways?"

"Maybe you'll get lucky," Doctor Weasel-Boy suggested. "Maybe he'll try to talk some of your crew over, and he can be shot while escaping. Making lewd and unseemly suggestions to a senior Security warrant with intent to debauch. I know I would."

And had, on a fairly frequent basis, since he had come on board. It didn't really bother Caleigh, not all that much. She'd been dealing with the impact of her body on the opposite sex since she'd been six years shy of her maiden voyage. The other sex, too, but the women Caleigh had known had usually been significantly more subtle about things.

"Just go borrow him a bit, Chief," the captain said to her, not bothering to look at Weasel-Boy. "Leave his Security out of it, he frets about them. Tell him I'd like the favor of a word or two in my office. He'll understand. You won't have any trouble."

Yes, Koscuisko would understand—Koscuisko understood force and coercion much better than the average medical officer, force and coercion being his stock in trade. No, she wouldn't have any trouble with him if she could keep clear of his Security. "Shall I leave word at the desk for ap Rhiannon, sir?" There was no need to specify which desk; Intelligence knew where Koscuisko was expected to be.

Men who were subject to the threat of death had no business being predictable, but Koscuisko would always go first to a service house to turn his Security over to the service staff for a little of the sort of recreation that didn't usually come with much of a rest. She'd been to a service house with Koscuisko herself, on one memorable occasion. The man knew what he was doing with anatomy.

Irshah Parmin made a face, his lower lip thrust halfway to his chin. "N—I—yes. Yes. All right. The officer is paying a call on the Command and general staff of the Jurisdiction Fleet Ship *Scylla* at the request of a former commanding officer. Something like that, Salli, what do you think?"

First Officer didn't think much of it, by the looks of her, but apparently she could see the humor anyway. "Better than a ransom note," she admitted. "Try to stay away from any guns-for-surgeons suggestions, Chief. And you know Koscuisko as well as anybody here, after all."

Except for Code Pyatte, that was to say—the only bond-involuntary left on board who had been here while Koscuisko had. She'd better leave Code behind. Asking a bond-involuntary to kidnap a former officer of assignment would probably upset his equilibrium; the conflict could have an unpredictable effect on his governor, and Koscuisko would never forgive that. Never.

"Very good, your Excellency," Caleigh said. "With respect, sir, and only for the sake of clarification. Your instructions are to escort the chief medical officer of the Jurisdiction Fleet Ship *Ragnarok* to *Scylla* from wherever I find him in an Emandisan port, whether he likes it or not. Without being noticed by the Port Authority, if I can help it."

"You make it sound as though there was something unusual about it," the captain complained. "Yes, Chief, precise and correct, as always. Thank you."

Caleigh saluted with a bow. She was done here. Turning to leave, she heard Doctor Weasel-Boy speak up one more time. "I've got some good stuff for Dolgorukij," Doctor Weasel-Boy said. "If he doesn't want to talk to you when he gets here, I mean. I could help you with that. Maybe I should go with Chief Samons, your Excellency, much less chance of Koscuisko kicking up if he's unconscious, we'll find a big enough box—"

"Shut up and get out," the captain said. "Thank you, First Officer."

Caleigh had to hurry if she was to be far enough ahead of Weasel-Boy to be able to credibly ignore him if he called after her. She took long steps as quickly as she could without actually running, thinking all the while. She had her instructions. No harm was threatened or likely to befall him. Koscuisko was likely to be angry, but he wouldn't blame her personally.

There were people on board of *Scylla* who remembered Andrej Koscuisko. Where were they going to quarter him, if the captain decided to hang on to him for a few days? And would there be visiting hours? A sign-up sheet? Come and see the Inquisitor, very rare Dolgorukij senior officer, only one known in captivity?

The captain had Koscuisko's best interest at heart, if only in his own way. Koscuisko was unlikely to see it the captain's way.

But it would be good to see Koscuisko again. She'd seen a lot more of him at his worst than she had of other officers, and on balance she liked him anyway.

She wondered how she was going to get around his Security. He'd have sent his Bonds downstairs to recreate themselves, but Security Chief Stildyne was no slouch—

Koscuisko would have sent Stildyne off to find amusement, as well. She'd figure it out when she got there. The middle of second shift, on *Scylla*, so it was coming up evening in Port Jeltaria, it would be six-eights on toward morning already when they got there. She'd see what the situation was then.

Mulling her team composition over in her mind, Caleigh hurried away to her tiny office to issue a warning order for involuntary escort, senior officer, leaving immediately.

CHAPTER THIRTEEN

New Beginnings

"Privacy," Stildyne said firmly, with his back to the common-room. "That's what's wanted. Privacy, and dinner, and if a professional is wanted later one of them will call. Thank you. But no players. Just feed them and leave them alone."

The floor-manager looked confused, but Stildyne had left her no room for further protest. He knew that the Bonds had a great deal to think about. If he'd been Pyotr—only a few years away from an honorable retirement, and a future as a privileged citizen—what would he do?

He didn't know. And he couldn't guess. What the governor did to a bond-involuntary was all but unimaginable, to a free soul. It had only been in the past few days that Stildyne had begun to realize what Koscuisko had been seeing all along: that after all these years these men were strangers to him. He hadn't begun to know Robert or Lek or Garrity or Godsalt or Hirsel—or even Pyotr. He had known bond-involuntaries, respected them, valued them, but hadn't known the men at all.

The floor-manager nodded. "Very well, Chief. Dinner it is. I'll go put the order in, any dietary restrictions? Liquor?"

Why don't you ask them, Stildyne thought. He knew the answer. They were slaves; they had no competence to speak on their own behalf. That was his job. "Mister Kerenko?"

Turning back to call for Lek, Stildyne's eye had caught on one of the house staff coming out of a niche with an armload of linen. There were private cubicles arranged around the perimeter of the common-room, eight or ten of them. If Stildyne had to guess, it would be that the bed-linen would be as crisp tomorrow as it was right now. It would take a man with nerves of stalloy to sleep, after what Koscuisko had said to them.

Lek came forward, to the doorway in which Stildyne stood talking to the floor-manager in the corridor. "Chief."

"Lek, I'd like you to go with this woman to the kitchen, and make the pull. Mister Kerenko knows everybody's likes and dislikes, he'll be able to help you. I should go check on the officer, now, Lek, all right?"

Kerenko nodded and then bowed, and if Stildyne hadn't known he would not have guessed that Kerenko need no longer fear punishment for any minor failing, howsoever slight. On the other hand, although it was true, Kerenko didn't really know it yet either, perhaps. On a higher-function conscious level Kerenko knew, but Kerenko had undergone the same careful indoctrination as the others, operant conditioning, perfection or punishment.

Koscuisko had to realize that. Koscuisko had to know that he was sending Stildyne into Gonebeyond space with these men. He had to.

Koscuisko wasn't going to get away with it, not without at least saying good-bye. If Stildyne was never going to see Koscuisko again—and he couldn't really pretend that he was going to—he was going to demand the same consideration Koscuisko had extended to his gentles, that of having his departure acknowledged with regret.

He wasn't going to worry about Kerenko and the floor-manager. Bond-involuntaries knew how to act the part, and none of them were stupid. "Carry on," Stildyne said. "I'll see you all in the morning." The very early morning. He wasn't going to ask them. He was just going. It was for Koscuisko's sake, not for their sakes, that he was going; he had no intention of giving anybody any rash ideas about consensus.

Walking away—before anybody had a chance to challenge him on his promise, statement, insinuation—Stildyne made his way through the service corridors to the next-to-uppermost floor, where the senior officer's suite would be located. Service houses were standard built, standard run, regulated and taxed by Jurisdiction; there were a limited number of floor plans. He knew his way around a service house. So did Koscuisko.

Had he known all along that Koscuisko had killed Lowden, Stildyne wondered? Yes, he knew perfectly well what Robert St. Clare had done, and if Koscuisko hadn't convinced him and Karol Vogel alike that Robert himself had no idea, Stildyne would have killed Koscuisko's favorite at the first opportunity just to keep him from a death by slow torture and the consequent anguish that'd inflict on Koscuisko. He knew with equal perfection exactly what would, or at the very least could, happen to Koscuisko himself, if the story ever got out.

The story would get out. Koscuisko had told them all; no matter how careful they were, compromise was bound to occur, sooner or later. Koscuisko had told them in order to convince them to leave. Which led him back to the vexed question: did Koscuisko understand that Stildyne had no real choice but to leave as well?

No. If Koscuisko had, he would have said good-bye. He had not said good-bye. After all of this time Koscuisko didn't understand that loving him meant seeing to his needs and concerns first, and consulting Stildyne's own preferences fifth or sixth.

Yes, his preference would be to stay, where he could have Koscuisko's company—on a fairly intimate level—even if he could never have Koscuisko. But the bond-involuntary troops were not, for all the perfection of their discipline and the beauty of their martial competence and the strength of their character, grown men who could be simply sent way with their governors off line.

They had been trained and taught and conditioned to live within cruelly narrow boundaries. They would need help. They would need him. Koscuisko loved them; therefore Stildyne had no choice but to do what would be best for them.

Should he say something? Koscuisko would thank him for his sacrifice. Koscuisko might possibly embrace him—as a man, not as a lover—and tell him that his sacrifice was noble and admirable, when in fact it was neither, at its base. Koscuisko would be surprised. If he were not surprised, it would mean that Koscuisko had counted on Stildyne to exile himself in Gonebeyond for Koscuisko's sake, expected it, planned on it, decided it and never so much as mentioned it to Stildyne himself, taking the only gift that Stildyne had to give him for granted as his. Already his.

Koscuisko wouldn't do that to a bond-involuntary. But there was a chance that he would do that to Stildyne. Koscuisko had been raised to mastery, and could have no doubt after all these years that Stildyne was his man to direct and command.

Stildyne was just deciding that he could not take the chance of finding out when he opened up the door between the service corridor and the main passageway, and discovered the house-master and her assistant in the passageway arguing between themselves in muted but passionate tones.

"It'll never work," the assistant was saying. She was the short plump one, and Stildyne liked women plump when he had to choose among women. "The very idea, asking a customer to provide services. They say he's sensitive about it, too. He'll have us dismissed. We'll lose our pensions."

The house-master herself was not too very much taller, but she was much less generously padded, and the way she wore her red hair gave her something of a vaguely predatory air. "He's a doctor, here's a patient. And we'll just ask. We could lose our license if we can't provide services on demand, just as easily as—Chief Stildyne."

She changed her tone and her demeanor the moment she noticed him coming down the hall. "Is everything arranged to your satisfaction, Chief? The men decently put away for the evening?"

"No complaints." The assistant house-master had a document in her hand that looked vaguely familiar to Stildyne for some reason that he couldn't quite identify at first. It was just a document. A legal document. A medical record; yes, a doctor's order. A prescription. "May I see that?"

He'd surprised them, and they hadn't been very comfortable with whatever it was in the first place. It was the most natural thing in the world for Stildyne to reach out and pluck the doctor's order from the assistant's apparently sweaty grasp.

"Ah, no, Chief, if it's all the same, private document—really, I protest—"

Yes, it was a private document. Not as if he was going to say anything to anybody about it. He was leaving in the morning; he was going far far away and he wasn't coming back ever again. Of what possible interest was a doctor's order to him? It was a Fleet document, that was interesting. It was executed and authorized by Koscuisko's own Chief of Psychiatric, that was even more interesting.

One word, and Stildyne passed the document back. He understood. He understood more than he really wanted to, but that was his own fault. "Well, well. Caught with two cruiser-killers standing off, and your pain-worker's on vacation."

"Had to go home very suddenly, we haven't had time to find a back-up, it's not like it's a common specialty. And you know how strict the licensing authority can be—" the assistant started, a little crossly. The house-master trod on her assistant's foot with passion, and the assistant shut up.

"Medical requirement," the house-master said firmly. "These things aren't passed out like port freedoms, Chief, you know that. It's got to be hard enough for her to come here with something like this. I really don't want to contemplate the grief it'll give her to have come here hoping, and have to go away again—without."

There and then Stildyne decided that he wasn't going to say good-bye, in case it turned out that Koscuisko had been assuming he'd be going all along. It was a small risk, a slim chance, but the potential reassurance was not much greater than the possibility for disaster. Since he was going, he'd go with his illusions intact. And he wouldn't meet the Bonds in the morning as they left, either—that could intimidate them. Give them second thoughts, make them wary about whether they were being set up. Paranoia was an occupational hazard for a bond-involuntary.

He'd meet them on the field, on board the ship, where it would be obvious that he was going and everybody who had decided to come would have made that decision as freely as possible beforehand, without any spoken or unspoken influence from him.

For that he had to find the ship. This was a respectable port, but by no means a major mercantile hub; there was only the one launch-field. Koscuisko had said that it was a Khabardi freighter; he had all night, he could do it. What he needed was to find the ship with the Dolgorukij accent, and if it was wearing a red halter around its neck he would not be in the least surprised. There was the chance that Koscuisko's cousin Stanoczk would be coming with them to consider.

"Good luck trying," Stildyne said, sincerely. "I'd lean on the soul-in-need angle, if I were you. You'll be lucky if he doesn't throw you bodily out."

"But there's a chance?" the assistant asked eagerly, being apparently recovered from her trodden toe.

Stildyne nodded. "He's been approached before, but in different contexts. Twice as awkward that she's on the same ship, could be construed as fraternization, Captain frowns on that." So did Koscuisko. Koscuisko was prickly about relations between ranks, because of the power inequities that existed.

Koscuisko had explained it to Stildyne as proof that no man could exploit a bond-involuntary for selfish gratification and call himself a man—long before Stildyne had confessed to Koscuisko that he had done just that, in his past. A bond-involuntary was not in a position to give consent because a bond-involuntary could not refuse a superior officer anything. That was the reason they were exploited, though, of course—Stildyne had thought at the time that that should have been staggering clear to Koscuisko.

When Stildyne had told Koscuisko, when circumstances had made it necessary to make it plain to Koscuisko what Stildyne himself had done, Koscuisko had replied that Stildyne's previous abuse of bond-involuntaries was not as important as his current abstention from abuse. It was a nice thought. Stildyne believed that Koscuisko meant it.

Now he was going to find out whether it was true, now. He was going to Gonebeyond with people he'd had parties with for his personal amusement, before Koscuisko's time, when Lowden had expected it. Almost required it. He'd find out whether having *stopped* was important enough to make amends for having *done* in the first place when they got to Gonebeyond and those men came to realize that they were free and Stildyne was outnumbered.

"We must try," the house-master said. "We've a duty."

Stildyne nodded again. Yes. She did have a duty. Service houses were to maintain adequate staff to provide services as needed on request. A doctor's order was a particularly important request.

"Remember that he's a doctor, and you may be able to make it work," Stildyne said. "A woman is in pain. He won't like that. I've got things to attend to."

If he couldn't find the right ship on his own he would have no choice but to come back here and wait with the others. And he didn't know how much time he had, before someone came for the others, so if he didn't intend to be left behind he had better get started. He didn't have time to talk to Koscuisko anyway. Yes. That was right.

The house-master stepped up to the door to signal for admittance, and Stildyne slipped back into the service corridor and away before Koscuisko could catch him mooning about in the halls and ask him what he thought he was doing.

Andrej Koscuisko stood at the viewing-wall looking out across the low-roofed city of Jeltaria, toward the launch-field. He couldn't see individual craft, not from here; and he didn't want to take the chance of calling up a detail. It might seem suspicious, later.

There was no telling how long it would be possible to keep knowledge of the bond-involuntaries' departure from interested parties—or from parties that would interest themselves, parties that would become interested once they found out. If that happened too soon, they might track the craft, and intercept it before it reached the vector. It was four hours between Emandis Station and the dar-Nevan vector. He had checked. A fraction of a day, starting tomorrow morning; sighing, Andrej turned from the wall and touched off the view.

There were no actual windows in the officer's suite of most public-houses, for two reasons; one of them being the requirement to be able to get around, to get at the various rooms in the suite from all angles, and the other being the need for security. Not that it had done Lowden the least bit of good. Threat was anticipated from outside; that an assassin would approach through the public accesses, come to the front door—that was not included in the planning process.

To be fair there were no instances of officers being murdered by subordinate officers in service houses that Andrej had ever heard of. Now his gentlemen had all heard of it, though, and Stildyne as well. Where was Stildyne? Andrej wanted to talk to him; to beg his pardon for not having included him in planning at a much earlier stage, among other things. He could have used Stildyne's help. Even now there were probably things that Stildyne could think about that were beyond Andrej.

On the other hand they were at a service house and Stildyne had his appetites, just as any man might. Much less opportunity than some of the bond-involuntaries to find appropriate avenues on board ship, however. If Stildyne thought of something suddenly in the middle of the night, he would come and tell him. Andrej could be confident of that. He decided not to bother him. Among the staff here at the service house, Stildyne might have already found a genial young man of the general type that he preferred.

There was a signal at the door. His dinner, perhaps; without Stildyne to play cards with him, the evening was likely to drag a bit, but Andrej couldn't see calling for companionship. He had visited with Joslire in the graveyard, and sent his gentles away. He was going to be no kind of company at all.

"Step through," he called, because the door hadn't opened as it might if it was just house-staff with his meal or more towels or something of the sort. House staff would come through the service corridors anyway, wouldn't they? Was there a problem?

It was the house-master and her assistant. Andrej had been greeted by the house-master upon his arrival; now the house-master bowed very properly and took a deep breath and shot a glance at her assistant and spoke.

"Very sorry to disturb his Excellency, who has made his preference for solitude very clear. We have an unusual situation, sir, a problem. May we trouble his Excellency to entertain a situation report?"

They were already troubling him, as far as that went. But his dinner wasn't here. That they wanted him to do something for them was obvious; they would not have come to see him just to tell him about their lives and difficulties. "I will sit down," he said, and turned his back to go into the little sitting-room to the left of the suite's reception and dining area. "Yes, come."

Neither woman would cross the threshold into the sitting area, however, which rather amused him although it kept him on his feet out of baseline politeness. In his experience, women with red hair had not been characterized by reserve and shyness. The house-master was a red-head with a very pale complexion, and her teeth were not to the Jurisdiction standard—some cosmetic defect that she'd never bothered to address, clearly enough. Her teeth were a bit crowded at the front of her mouth, and put him in mind of a river-wolf, somehow.

"His Excellency is not the only soul from the *Ragnarok* to honor us this afternoon," the house-master said, from the doorway where she stood. "The port authority notified us, of course, and we've taken the usual measures to prepare to accommodate a cruiser-killer class warship. Two."

Scylla and *Ragnarok*, she meant, Andrej assumed. And she was probably not talking about the bond-involuntaries or Stildyne when she spoke of other *Ragnarok* crew. "And this has to do with me what, please?"

"With respect, sir, believe us, profound and sincere, and not wishing to give offense in the slightest. Your Excellency. There's a prescription here to be filled. And we can't provide. The only pain-worker we have on staff has had to take an emergency personal leave."

Pain-worker? They wanted him to beat somebody for them. There was something in him that leapt at the offered opportunity with savage delight, but Andrej had no intention of acknowledging that appetite.

"I'm on holiday, and I'm not interested. I give you the benefit of the doubt and trust that you do not mean to insult me. Good-greeting."

Get out. The house-master looked to her assistant; her assistant bit her lip, but seemed to think of something, all of a sudden.

"Yes, sir, of course, your Excellency. But it is a doctor's order, sir, and us unable to oblige. The patron is clearly in significant distress. Could you not consider it, your Excellency? Doctor?"

As if a doctor were required to inflict recreational beatings in a brothel. No. Services houses had pain-workers for that—trained professionals who had studied the careful management of intense physical sensation to elicit a pleasurable or ecstatic response, people as far removed from the genuine practice of Inquiry as an actor was from a murderer. As he was, from an honest man.

"Let me be blunt." Since they weren't taking the hint. "I have no experience in whatever is required. My expertise lies in far more destructive fields than any appropriate to a service house. I cannot oblige you. Good-greeting."

The house-master shook her head, her close-cropped hair catching the light as she did so. "The patron is fearfully nervous, sir. We understand completely if you don't care to become involved, it's an extreme imposition on our part to so much as suggest it, sir. But she's gotten this far, and if we turn her away, who knows when she'll have the opportunity? Or the nerve to take advantage of it? If you could just look at the order, your Excellency. It's more than awkward for us, a woman is suffering, and craves relief."

With a sigh of resignation Andrej put out his hand for the scrip that the house-master had in her own, and carried it over to sit down with it at the table and have a look. This entire interchange was offensive in the highest degree, but it was unquestionably a distraction.

The patient's name he did not recognize, but the authorizing physician was his own Chief of Psychiatric. "After careful evaluation a therapeutic exposure to traditional stimuli in a controlled atmosphere is recommended in order to confirm diagnosis by treatment. Appropriate access to a licensed pain-worker is therefore prescribed the named patient under the provisions of, billing code thus-and-such. By direction, Somerstrand Farilk, Chief of Psychiatric, Jurisdiction Fleet Ship *Ragnarok*."

No, it was not possible that Farilk had sent a patient here in order to encourage Andrej to consider the proposal that Farilk had made. If Farilk said that one of Two's under-technicians suffered from some psychological deficit that might be usefully addressed by a pain-worker, then it was so. Andrej had worked with his clinical staff for too long not to have an informed respect for each and every one of them.

They weren't on the *Ragnarok* because their professional qualifications were wanting. Fleet could, and did, integrate mediocrities successfully at every level of operation. They were on the *Ragnarok* because they wanted to be there, or couldn't fit in to the political environment of the Commands in which they had found themselves prior to their frequently involuntary transfer.

The house-master was right. A woman was suffering. How could they suggest that he venture into territory that lay well outside his area of actual expertise?

If he did not, they would send her back to the ship depressed and desperate, without comfort, as though unworthy of consideration because her need was outside the normal parameters of the Jurisdiction standard.

He'd taken extreme measures to relieve suffering before. She was not a bond-involuntary; but did she deserve less of his consideration because of that? Officers did not consort intimately with lower ranks, not on Jennet ap Rhiannon's *Ragnarok*. And yet he was not long for the *Ragnarok* one way or the other. Either the Selection would be decided, the *Ragnarok*'s appeal resolved, and he would be free to go home a civilian; or ap Rhiannon could just as easily refuse to let him back on board of his own ship, and solve in that way the problem she apparently had believing his commitment to the Command.

If he stayed here he would brood. He would pace, and struggle with a selfish instinct to seek out Stildyne for companionship and conversation, which could only embarrass Brachi if he were in bed with some blond. "I make no promises," he said. "And it is highly irregular. Show me to the place and I will see what I can do."

If it was true that he had accidentally been bound to St. Andrej Malcontent, rather than Filial Piety, at his naming, then he should consider the teaching of the Malcontent. The Malcontent had never cared whether a person's need was odd or unusual, acceptable or unacceptable. The Malcontent only cared whether people were fed and clothed, and had a dry place to sleep, and got whatever it was that they needed to understand the mystery of the Holy Mother's plan for them in this world.

He would try to do his duty to the Saint. He owed the Malcontent for many favors already; for the freedom of the bond-involuntary troops he loved, as just the latest example. He would go and talk to the patient, they would negotiate, and if the Holy Mother used him to bring peace to another soul—whether or not it was a Dolgorukij soul—it would be a small start on the very long journey that lay ahead of him, if he ever hoped to make reparation for crimes that could not be undone.

The signal came at the door very early in the morning, but nobody had slept. "Good-greeting," the floor manager said. "Your car is waiting."

Robert looked around him one last time: walls, benches, beds in rooms on one side or the other, littered with the remains of two large meals. Little drink. A man wanted to be sure he knew what he was doing, when he left the world as he knew it.

"Very good." In Chief Stildyne's absence Pyotr acted as their Chief. Pyotr had more years of service than Chief Stildyne did, and it was no particular secret that if he had not been a Security slave he would have made Chief Warrant years ago; First Officer had certainly never taken exception to anybody's tendency to treat Pyotr as though he were one. "Formation, gentlemen. Let's go."

It wouldn't do to keep the officer waiting. The officer wanted them out; he'd made that painfully clear. No last words or parting embrace, and still it was a wrench. He had followed Andrej Koscuisko all the way from Fleet Orientation Station Medical, and lucky for him, too.

It hadn't been his doing. Koscuisko had happened on a secret that Koscuisko hadn't been supposed to have, and it would have meant the end of young Robert had Koscuisko not got stubborn about it. All of these years. Nobody here knew what Koscuisko had done to save Robert's life.

Nobody alive knew Koscuisko better than he did, which was why he knew that there was no help for it, no help at all. Koscuisko wanted them gone. They'd go. It was the last time they'd ever do what Koscuisko wanted.

There hadn't been much left to discuss, last night—they'd got most of the chewing done before, as the implications of Koscuisko's surgeries became more and more clear. Koscuisko had always wanted rid of them, for their own sakes. He never would give himself the credit he'd earned honestly for doing what he could to protect them from the bullies of the world, and shield them from the horrors to which they'd been condemned.

Robert had written long speeches in his head to be delivered to Koscuisko once the Day had dawned and he was free to speak. They'd go unspoken, now, forever, and it was probably just as well, but it was a shame. He'd had some good lines in there. Pointed remarks about men who cherished guilt, which was after all a form of vanity that did not become a man. About men who cared for people by whom they would not accept being cared for without a fight. Things of that nature.

It was short of dawn; the air smelled sweetly of damp dust. It was already hot outside, or at least warm, and oppressive with humidity; the fog lay heavily around the streets and alleys that their transport passed on the way to the launch-field. Nobody spoke. Robert wondered if the others were disappointed that they hadn't had a chance to say good-bye to Stildyne. They knew more about Stildyne than Robert did—they'd all been here longer than he had, except for Godsalt, Godsalt was new. But even Robert had seen for himself the change that Koscuisko had wrought in Brachi Stildyne, and honored him for it.

Maybe it would have been too risky, too much of a compromise. Stildyne was going to have to explain to First Officer where his troops had gone. First Officer wasn't going to be interested in listening to Koscuisko about it. Stildyne was responsible to First Officer for keeping track of troops; he'd be in for an interesting interview.

It was a shame not to have a chance to take his hand, though. Koscuisko had been considerably harder on Stildyne than on any of the rest of them, and for Robert's part he appreciated how Stildyne had borne up under Koscuisko. Stildyne had been good to them. It was hard to go without saying good-bye.

It was hard to go. There was no future for them under Jurisdiction; Koscuisko was right about that. He was right about many things. When he was wrong about things, it was generally in holding a belief that there was no way around one thing or another. Robert had noticed this about him a long time ago.

It was hard to blame Koscuisko for the failing of his imagination, though, when it was so richly peopled with horrors that were real and not imagined at all. Koscuisko could be excused some shying away from consequences because Koscuisko had a so much better than average understanding of what those consequences were.

It only made it more impressive, in Robert's mind, that Koscuisko had made up his mind finally to hazard the really very seriously extreme consequences of declining to exercise his Writ again ever.

Those consequences made flight to Gonebeyond a rational strategy, and that made Robert annoyed at Koscuisko's insistence on not going with them; but he was done being annoyed with Koscuisko. There was no reasoning with the man when he had his attention fixed. The closest thing that Robert had ever known to the ferocity of Koscuisko's concentration was that of a professional herding dog, but he'd never observed as much to Koscuisko. People who weren't herding people couldn't be expected to understand.

The launch-field was brightly lit but uncertain in the outlines of its lanes and outbuildings because of the night-fog. The traffic control gate checked their report papers and waved them on through, party of six to report to Khabardi freighter *Kavkazki Pass* to receive cargo on instruction, his Excellency Andrej Ulexeievitch Koscuisko, Jurisdiction Fleet Ship *Ragnarok*. Very normal and unremarkable.

They left the ground-car that had brought them from the service house at the field transport barn and took a mover out onto the launch-field itself, heading for the material handling lanes where the freighter they were to board was to be found. Someone might eventually notice that they'd never called for transport back from the launch-field to the service house, but they were all bond-involuntaries under orders, and it would simply be assumed that they were doing as they had been instructed—as was in fact the case.

A Khabardi freighter was a Combine ship. Surely that would be suspicious after the fact, but Koscuisko did not seem to intend to attempt to conceal his complicity in their flight. How could he? Flight was impossible without his direct intervention, surely—oh, yes, they were technically speaking all on Safe, but Koscuisko's not-entirely-secret surgeries were bound to come out after this.

And it was Koscuisko's choice and Koscuisko's decision, Robert reminded himself, following Pyotr up into the belly of the beast, hearing Lek behind him. There was a man standing in the cargo bay of the ship waiting for them; nobody Robert knew.

"Pyotr Micmac?" the man said. He was a big man, big hands, knobby shoulders, deep voice. Accent. "Kazmer Daigule, I'm to be your pilot. How many are we taking on board?"

Someone had come into the doorway between the cargo bay and the interior of the ship as Daigule spoke; short, female, Robert thought. Pyotr looked past Daigule with mild curiosity but said only "There are six of us all told, pilot. When do we leave?"

"Come on, then, so that we can secure and clear. We're leaving as soon as we're locked and loaded, no time to waste, come on. You've got a pilot? Kerenko? Come with me, pilot."

Well, that was a familiar note in a welter of unreality—come on, hurry up, let's get going. Wait. Robert could understand that. He stood to one side as the others boarded—Godsalt, Hirsel, Garrity. It was an intelligent ship, this Khabardi; it sealed up promptly and efficiently, then said something in some Combine dialect or another that sounded almost like something Koscuisko said when he got impatient to be off.

"Clear," the woman said. "This way. We'll seal down here. Introductions and explanations once we're off." Since she was apparently one of the crew it was likely that she'd know if the loading ramp wasn't happy with the job that Robert and Garrity had done of securing it.

There were the universal telltales to consider—there was no room for linguistic misunderstandings where things like security doors for space flight were concerned—and the u-ts looked perfectly happy to Robert, so he followed the woman, and Garrity followed him, out of the cargo bay and up to the freighter's main access and into the front of the ship up by the wheelhouse. It was a small wheelhouse; freighters liked to use all available space for freight, not like a courier ship, not like that luxury model that had come to Pesadie to take Koscuisko home on leave.

"Get strapped in," she said, and went forward into the wheelhouse. Robert could hear her over the status-line that ran to all of the passenger shells, the little alcoves lining the corridor just short of the wheelhouse where people who weren't actively engaged in flying the ship were expected to secure themselves while the freighter made space.

Garrity took a place across the corridor from Robert. Robert could see his face in the dim light of the shell, but not his expression. Ducking his head out for a last quick look Robert counted, quickly. Six or seven passenger shells on a side, and his was the furthest from the wheelhouse. This freighter would carry fourteen to twenty souls, then, since there were usually two to four souls running loose even at launch to make sure everything came off as it was expected.

"Packages all loaded," Robert heard the woman say. "Ready for departure, Kaz."

The pilot switched the shells into braid, so that they could listen. They weren't on transmit, no, not in the shells; only the wheelhouse transmitted on approach and on departure.

"Launch control. Khabardi freighter *Kavkazki Pass* requests final clearance, outbound for dar-Nevan vector to Oma. Please confirm."

"We hear you, *Kavkazki Pass*. We'll have a clearance for you in just a moment. Did you have any last minute callers? The gate thinks someone might have come looking for you." Launch control sounded a little bored, actually. Clearly not very excited about anything that might be happening this time of morning, but the launch had been carefully timed, Robert realized. The second half of first shift, long enough in for people to have gotten all of their routine shift-initiation checks out of the way, but before they started to perk up and take an interest in their environment, looking for the end of their shift.

"Been and gone, Launch Control. Permission to initiate launch sequence."

"Transmitting clearance codes, *Kavkazki Pass*. Hope you enjoyed your stay, come again, and thank you for selecting Jeltaria Field for your in-transit requirements. Launch Control, away, here."

The freighter had started to move. There was a rolling tone, built in to the background noise, a subtle audio cue as to what the craft was doing—moving into launch position, angling for launch, launching. Robert knew that he wasn't actually hearing the sound of wheels against pavement or anything of the sort. A person's ear still strained to hear, and the rolling tone was provided for its psychological effect.

The pilot had switched his transmit off, but Robert could hear voices from the wheelhouse almost as easily—narrow corridor. As many paces. "Are we related?" Lek was saying.

The pilot replied, "I'm not your cousin, if that's what you mean. No. No more than any two Sarvaw, Kerenko, and our mutual cousin Maritzj here, she's Arakcheyek. Comm officer. Have you done the dar-Nevan vector before?"

"Not for years," Lek said. "Cousin Maritzj." It was hard to read from the sound of Lek's voice to an expression on his face; Robert couldn't quite figure out the tone of voice. The woman was a Malcontent? He hadn't known there were female Malcontents.

"We're going to angle for a spin that would drop us at Oma, but sharpen the approach in the last fractions. We're not supposed to know how to reach Gonebeyond from Emandis Station, but I've done it before. No worries."

The pitch and intensity of the rolling tone had changed. The freighter had reached its slot on the launch field; the tank had attached. He'd done this time and again since he'd started following Koscuisko—not often on a freighter, no, but often enough. This was different. This was the end. This was taking them away, and they would not be coming back here, ever.

"Yes," the pilot said, apparently in response to a question Robert hadn't heard. "Five tanks. People are used to Combine freighters taking the high road. We've got perishable cargo, or at least that's our story."

Five tanks. Robert was impressed. Five booster tanks from Jeltaria Field would get them up and through atmosphere and spank them smartly on their way to the vector, too, before falling away to land themselves quietly at depot for refueling. It meant the freighter would be using much less of its own fuel to get out of Emandis space. The idea filled Robert with a sudden nearly nostalgic sort of anxiety; who knew how far the freighter's fuel would have to carry them, to get to wherever they were going in Gonebeyond?

"Final clearance confirmed," the pilot said. "*Kavkazki Pass* away here. Good-greeting, Jeltaria, and we look forward to seeing you again, some time."

No shielding in known Space would damper the roar of five tanks lifting something as large as a Khabardi freighter from the ground. There would be no overhearing conversation for several minutes, now, so Robert closed his eyes and took a deep breath and tried not to worry about the fact that they were leaving the officer all alone, by himself, and only Chief Stildyne to keep after him for ever after.

When it got quiet, he knew that the tanks had detached, which meant they'd cleared atmosphere. They were outbound. No need to be strapped into shell any more.

The woman came down the corridor from the wheelhouse, talking as she went. "We'll leave Kaz and your man in the wheelhouse for now. Come along, I'll show you what I can about where we're going and what we expect to find there. Follow me. Common-room is just this way, a bit cramped right now but we needed all the space we could get for cargo."

That made sense. Robert unstrapped, and waited for the end of the line. Pyotr. Godsalt. Hirsel. Garrity across from Robert stepped out, but then stopped, looking back toward the wheelhouse with an expression of astonishment on his face.

"You heard the comm officer," Robert heard a familiar voice say. "Get a move on, man."

It was their Chief. Robert pushed away and out of his niche. Stildyne. As big as life and twice as ugly, which meant actually very ugly, since it was Stildyne. "What are you doing here?" Robert asked, feeling delighted but unable to understand why. "Who's minding the officer?"

"Koscuisko can take care of himself," Stildyne growled, but not too sincerely. "Unlike you. Get along, Robert. There's a briefing to be had."

Stildyne. Stildyne had come. Why? Why hadn't he told them? Had he been afraid that they'd decline to take him? Robert supposed they could have. But it was academic. Stildyne was here. Life would be easier, with their Chief to look after them.

Gladdened by the presence of a familiar note in the middle of all of this strange new music, Robert went after the others into the common room, to squeeze himself in between crates and boxes and listen to what the comm officer could tell them about what the future might hold for them, when they reached Gonebeyond.

A familiar sound in the outer room woke Andrej, and he took a moment—not moving—to collect his wits. Where was he, and what was he doing here? Unfamiliar bed, but familiar enough—a service house, the bedding a careful balance between luxury and practical attention to the commonsense requirements to clean and freshen on a daily basis. Or even more frequently. Someone in bed with him, what was that about? Oh. Yes. Her. She wasn't a house professional, or she wouldn't have taken the liberty of falling asleep in a patron's bed, not unless she'd been invited—or instructed—to do so.

Not a house professional. She'd come with a medical order, that was right. And he, he had agreed to see what he could do; and there they were. If he meant to take a status check he had better move quickly; Security were in the outer room, come to collect him for one reason or another or perhaps simply to see to his fast-meal—an intimacy Stildyne permitted himself to which Andrej took no exception. The woman lay on her side with her back to him, one arm tucked beneath her head; turning onto his side Andrej lifted the bedclothes away from her body.

There were ways around the Protocols. As soon as there had been Protocols established people had found ways around them; and there were strict limits on the degree of damage that a judicial officer was authorized to inflict directly or by proxy without evidence or confession. Wherever there were limits there were cheats, ways to hurt a man without harming him, without leaving evidence of abuse outside of Protocols. She was substantially unbruised, the skin unbroken; Andrej knew that he had been fierce with her, and could see very little evidence.

She'd been fierce with him as well, in her own way. Hearing Security behind him Andrej covered her over again, drawing the covers well up behind her head on the pillow; Stildyne might recognize her if she stirred, and that would be awkward.

It was awkward enough as it was. He was going home, he was leaving, she was a member of the same command as he but Jennet ap Rhiannon did not care for the fact that he was a member of her command at all and he certainly would not be, if the captain ever found out that he had spent the evening in a service house engaged in intimacies conventional and unconventional with one of Two's intelligence analysts.

Stildyne could step lightly when he wanted to, something that Andrej had always admired—it was no small thing to move so large a muscle mass so quietly; but something wasn't right.

He turned his head to look back over his shoulder toward the door. For a moment he relaxed, scolding himself; *there, you see, Andrej, nothing out of the ordinary, your chief of Security. Yes. That's all.*

Then he froze in the bed and stared in horror, because it was a chief of Security, but it was the wrong chief of Security, even if she was carrying a curt-robe in a completely harmless manner.

"Sorry to wake you, sir," she said. "Captain Irshah Parmin particularly requests the favor of an interview. If his Excellency would care to step into the next room to get dressed, please."

He held out his hand for the robe, wondering if he was dreaming. Caleigh Samons. He hadn't seen Caleigh Samons for how long? Not as though he didn't think about her, from time to time, because she was unquestionably one of the most desirable women he had ever met in his life, as well as being a thoroughly professional chief of Security.

In fact his fish, his masculine nature, portions of his anatomy better left unacknowledged in polite company, were greeting this sudden apparition with unseemly interest, even though they had been thoroughly exercised very recently. "What is the meaning of this intrusion?" he asked, because it was expected of him, surely. She couldn't possibly imagine that she could simply amble into his bedroom and demand that he get dressed without some protest on his part.

"Outside, if you please, sir," she repeated firmly, if still quietly. "We'd just as soon not create an alarm. No sense in embarrassing your gentlemen, your Excellency. This way."

His gentlemen. His Security. His bond-involuntaries assigned, whom she would presume to be sleeping off an evening of their own two levels down. If there was an alarm they would be expected to respond to it. What time was it? Had they left? Were they still here? Because if they were still here he couldn't let an alarm go off. It would destroy any chance of moving them quietly and unobtrusively to the launch-field. Someone would notice if they left suddenly.

And if they had left already, he couldn't afford anybody noticing that, either. The longer nobody noticed that they were gone, the longer they had to make for the vector undetected, innocent and uninteresting cargo of an innocent and uninteresting freighter. What was he going to do?

The woman rolled over in the bed, seeking his warmth. Andrej slid out and away from her carefully, doing his best to avoid waking her up. Samons stood to one side, watching the woman carefully; Andrej watched too, belting his robe around his waist, watched as she stretched and settled her head on the pillow and stilled back into a profound sleep again. Her eyes. Andrej was almost certain that she'd opened her eyes, but if she had she hadn't really seen anything; because she certainly closed them without any sign of alarm or surprise.

Hurrying through into the next room Andrej waited, impatiently, for Samons to close the communicating door. If the woman woke up, Samons might take it into her head to borrow them both for an interview with Captain Irshah Parmin; she'd said she didn't want an alarm—she clearly didn't want anybody realizing that she was taking him. He was being kidnapped. If the woman came too they would all find out that he'd been in bed with one of Two's people, and the woman would be humiliated, and much more harm than good was sure to come of it.

"Well," he said, quietly, so that she would know he didn't mean to kick up a fuss. "What have you done with Stildyne? He is not going to be happy, Chief, and I won't stand between the two of you. You will be on your own. I'm not happy either. I hope Captain Irshah Parmin has some very good reasons to share with ap Rhiannon, or there will be some serious irritation at Emandis Station."

He would normally have washed before he dressed, and had his fast-meal as well. He was hungry. He had had an unaccustomed amount of exercise, last night. Chief Samons might well remember his personal habits from the years that they had spent together on *Scylla*; if she did he could hope for fast-meal at some point, when she could manage it, but that point was clearly not to be now.

He turned his back on her to start to dress. She'd seen him stitchless often enough before, but a man had his pride, and it had also been several years—she might imagine him to be more impressive in his person than he actually was, and if so he had no intention of disabusing her of any flattering notions that she might be entertaining.

"All quiet in the service house," she said. "Special escort, we told the house security. They know *Scylla*'s ship-mark when they see it. I need us to be out of here before anybody comes knocking on your door with your morning rhyti, your Excellency, best all around."

Andrej accepted the trousers that she held out for him, stepping into the one leg and then the other, fastening his waistband over his under-blouse. "I've never heard of officers kidnapping each others' chief medical officers," he said, partially to keep the conversation going and partially because he couldn't quite believe what seemed to be happening. "Isn't this an act of piracy? I'm sure Irshah Parmin outranks ap Rhiannon within Fleet, but she *is* the captain of the *Ragnarok*, and I *am* medical resources assigned. He has no right."

"Can't be helped, sir." Andrej thought he remembered that tone in Samons' voice, thought he recognized it. "Command direction received. You know the captain's always been a little irrational on the subject of Koscuiskos. I'm sorry."

She handed him his boots, and he sat down. Yes. Captain Irshah Parmin had always been a little irrational on the subject of young Andrej Koscuisko, no longer quite as young as he used to be. Andrej had had good reason to be grateful for it, too. He'd known at the time that Irshah Parmin was being very patient with him; he hadn't understood until later, until he'd had to deal with Captain Lowden, how horrible his life and that of his bond-involuntaries assigned could have been had Irshah Parmin not made generous allowances for foolish young officers with no real understanding of their position in Fleet. Very generous allowances. Far more patient than Andrej himself would probably have been, had the roles been reversed.

That didn't make it all right for Irshah Parmin to send Security into Andrej's bedroom to take him off in the middle of the night and leave his own Security behind.

But in light of the fact that Andrej could not afford any disturbances that might interfere with the stealthy departure of his gentlemen or expose that departure prematurely, it couldn't hurt to concentrate on reserving judgment until he'd heard what Irshah Parmin had to say.

She shook out his duty blouse for him, very formally indeed. Andrej settled the shoulders and shot his cuffs and made up his mind to make the best of things, at least for now.

"Somebody's going to have to write a note to Stildyne for me," he said, and nodded, to signify that he was ready to go. "Because I'm not trying to explain this to him on my own. I give you fair warning."

"First Officer will apologize in person," she promised, with a bow. "If the captain won't, that is. Thank you, your Excellency, this way, and it is good to see you again."

Well, yes, it was.

There were people waiting in the corridor outside, nobody Andrej recognized, and all wearing *Scylla*'s ship-mark. No bond-involuntaries. He wondered if there were people that he knew, still on board *Scylla*.

"So tell me, who is running the Infirmary, these days?" he asked; and went off down the hall under Security escort, a detained man, to go and have a word with Irshah Parmin.

CHAPTER FOURTEEN

Reunions

Koscuisko was what seemed to Caleigh to be uncharacteristically quiet on the trip to the launch-field, and on the courier. He sat in the passenger-compartment, and then in the courier, with his face turned to the window. Not speaking. He'd asked a few general questions at the start, that was true; information gathering, and well done at that, but then he had lapsed into silence. She couldn't say exactly what she had expected from him but it wasn't stillness. She remembered him as having been a man moderately restless in spirit, always curious. Always inquiring.

It had been years since she had seen him last, though. He'd lost weight, or gained weight, or maybe his weight had shifted. He looked a deal older than she remembered him, but she remembered him as having looked very young, and he still didn't look quite his age in Standard years. Dolgorukij were a long-lived subspecies of hominid. They took that much longer to start to look mature in years, not as though Koscuisko was, not yet. How old was he? Somewhere in his thirties, she thought, but she couldn't remember.

When the courier came to rest in the maintenance atmosphere of *Scylla*, Koscuisko rose to his feet and left the passenger cabin as though he were returning to his duty post, and not come against his will under Security escort. Why not? Caleigh thought. There was only the one of him. It wasn't as if he could make an escape of whatever sort. Nodding to her mildly confused Security, Caleigh formed them up, and followed Koscuisko out onto the docks of the maintenance atmosphere.

Koscuisko paused for a moment on the loading apron, looking out past the cargo handling drones to Emandis Station and Emandis itself beyond; was he looking for the *Ragnarok*, Caleigh wondered? *Ragnarok* was there, but *Ragnarok* had taken the central loading slips, by right of first arrival. *Scylla* made do with one of Emandis Station's auxiliary docks, and Irshah Parmin was just as happy about that as he was about everything else that had to do with the *Ragnarok*. If Koscuisko was wondering about setting off a distance flare, an appeal to his people, he gave no sign of it.

Turning, Koscuisko started into the maintenance corridor, heading toward the captain's office. There were people in the halls who knew who Koscuisko was; Koscuisko gave no sign of noticing that either, but Caleigh knew that the news would be all over the ship within moments.

That was all right. They knew Koscuisko was here, but they didn't know why, nor did they realize that he was here under armed escort— though some of the crew might put things together. Koscuisko was not accompanied by his own Security escort but by one of *Scylla*'s, properly speaking Doctor Weasel-Boy's. There were words there for those with the learning to read the language.

Koscuisko knew where he was going, yes, and he made no attempt to divert in his progress toward his goal. When they reached the captain's office, though, he didn't signal; he went straight through, and if Caleigh hadn't given a quick warning from her point behind the detachment Koscuisko might have succeeded in surprising Irshah Parmin.

As it was, the captain looked startled when Caleigh saw him, following close on Koscuisko's heels. Koscuisko stopped a precise distance from the captain's desk and saluted, bowing, before he assumed a modified position of attention-wait and looked at the captain in silence. That was rude. Koscuisko should say something. But kidnapping him had been even more rude, and Irshah Parmin didn't seem much taken aback. The captain had been accustomed to Koscuisko being rude—just not on purpose. By accident, which was almost excusable, most of the time.

"Good-greeting," the captain said, standing up. "Thank you for coming. Apologies for the less than customary method of extending the invitation, Doctor, you know the First Officer I think? You won't know Doctor Lazarbee, our chief medical officer."

Koscuisko nodded to First Officer, but only just glanced at Doctor Weasel-Boy—didn't even nod. Caleigh suppressed a wince. Doctor Weasel-Boy was a man to sniff out a slight and cherish it; they were off to a good start, they were.

"First Officer," Koscuisko said. "Captain. If there is any precedent for making off with another command's resources by force of arms I have never heard of it, your Excellency. You must have very good reason for spitting in my captain's face."

His captain? Ap Rhiannon? Irshah Parmin frowned; Caleigh could feel herself flushing with annoyance. "His" captain, indeed. But it wasn't her argument. She'd been sent to bring Koscuisko; she had brought him. She was not here to argue with him on the relative merits of the two ship's captains.

"Turnabout's fair play." The captain sat down, slowly. "Care to be seated, Doctor? I'm worried about you. Ap Rhiannon's just the cosmetic code. But it's bad enough even so, I'd have thought you'd be anxious to get away."

Koscuisko sat, but he didn't relax. "I was anxious enough to get back to my ship. Why would I want to get away? I mean no disrespect, your Excellency, but you have your own chief medical officer—Doctor Lazarbee?—and I am posted to the *Ragnarok*."

The captain walked his fingers along the edge of his desk, contemplatively, before he answered. "Yes, well, in point of fact the *Ragnarok*'s annoyed me. Why can't I get my stores loads, I ask, and they tell me it's because the *Ragnarok* has a prior claim in. When I ask why Emandis Station is willing to release not only primes, but seconds and terces, to the *Ragnarok* they give me some inarticulate nonsense with the word 'Koscuisko' in it."

A muscle jumped, suddenly, in the side of Koscuisko's face, near the hinge of his jaw. A grin. "And you thought if you had the right stores-chop you could get some supplies transferred? Redirected? I don't see it happening, your Excellency."

Captain Irshah Parmin spread out the fingers of his hand in an expansive gesture. "We won't know until we try it, will we? I'm not asking for much. We'll send you back to the *Ragnarok* as soon as they notice you've gone missing. In return for a satisfactory conclusion to a dialog, of course."

He should just come out and say that he was worried about Koscuisko and wanted to make sure that Koscuisko had a chance to brief with *Scylla*'s Intelligence officer. He should just say that. But Koscuisko had set him off balance, Caleigh supposed, and Koscuisko had always been exceptionally good at annoying the captain. Or maybe he just didn't want to talk in front of Weasel-Boy.

"You probably shouldn't expect any immediate reaction." Koscuisko gave no sign of softening toward the captain's proposal, either explicit or implicit. Koscuisko had to know that Irshah Parmin hadn't borrowed him as a marker in a stores dispute. Irshah Parmin had just so much as said so, after all. "I was granted several days' down-leave, and expected to sequester myself with Joslire's family. You remember Joslire. He has a brother that I am anxious to meet."

"They'll have noticed you're missing by the time they want to leave, surely." Yes, Irshah Parmin remembered Joslire. He didn't react to Koscuisko's remarks, however, possibly because there was no answer for Koscuisko's not-very-indirect rebuke. "Tell you what, go and visit around for a bit, catch up on old acquaintances. Chief Samons will escort you."

As opposed to Doctor Weasel-Boy, that was to say. As *Scylla*'s posted chief medical officer, Weasel-Boy might have reasonably expected to have that responsibility, and Koscuisko was a bit of a celebrity of sorts in Fleet. Maybe that was why Irshah Parmin wanted Weasel-Boy kept out of Koscuisko's way. Or maybe it was just that without a Security escort there was nothing standing in Koscuisko's way should he decide to go down to the maintenance atmosphere, commandeer a crew, and leave; or at least attempt to send a distress call.

"You understand that I object to having been brought here, and to being kept here," Koscuisko said. "I put you on notice that the captain may not be as anxious for an exchange of hostages as you flatteringly suggest. And that you are keeping me from making the acquaintance of an Emandisan family to which I apparently belong, or who possibly belong to me, by virtue of Joslire's knives. There is apart from all that no arguing with you, your Excellency, and I should like my fast-meal, if I may."

"Oh, feed the man his breakfast," Doctor Weasel-Boy said, suddenly. "Priorities, after all. I'll hunt up Conner to take you through my infirmary, Koscuisko, Conner remembers you, can hardly stop talking about you in fact. Captain, if I may be excused."

Captain Irshah Parmin had turned his head to stare at Doctor Weasel-Boy with an expression of mild incredulity that was almost exactly the same with which Koscuisko was regarding his counterpart. Caleigh wanted to laugh, it was so perfect; but she was technically responsible to First Officer for Weasel-Boy, and managed to contain herself. Weasel-Boy was easy to alienate, and she already did so on a regular basis. It was best to avoid exacerbating the problem, if possible.

Irshah Parmin turned back to Koscuisko. "By all means, Doctor," the captain said. "I'll send First Officer to you in officer's mess." Where First Officer could have a heart-to-heart talk with Koscuisko, without Doctor Weasel-Boy in attendance. First Officer didn't care for Weasel-Boy. Nobody did. First Officer wouldn't want to share sensitive intelligence with Koscuisko in Weasel-Boy's company, in order to avoid raising any questions that she had no intention of answering about sources of information.

"Thank you, your Excellency," Koscuisko said, apparently reconciled to a few hours spent on *Scylla* now that he had registered his protest. It would be only a few hours, too, Caleigh was sure of it. Koscuisko's Security would wake up, Koscuisko's Chief of Security would form them up to go and fetch their officer, and then they'd find out that Koscuisko wasn't there. They wouldn't be keeping Koscuisko from Joslire's family for more than the forepart of the day.

Maybe she could go with Koscuisko when they returned him to Emandis, and meet those people herself. There were Security still on board who had known Joslire Curran, and one who had been there the night that Koscuisko had killed him.

"What's that about your new family, sir?" she asked, as she left the captain's office with Koscuisko and his escort. "And there's a brother?"

Koscuisko was annoyed, but his temper would improve once he'd been fed. It almost always had. "With wife and child," Koscuisko confirmed, heading down the hall toward the officer's mess. "Grandmother, elderly aunt, two cousins, older sister. Not much of a family resemblance, they all look Emandisan to me, but I've seen Joslire's grin and I never thought to see it again. There's an orchard."

If Koscuisko said so. She wasn't sure she'd ever seen a bond-involuntary grin; certainly never, outside Koscuisko's immediate company. She'd worried about whether Koscuisko's influence on bond-involuntaries would trip them up in the service of less sympathetic officers, but Koscuisko's successor Doctor Aldrai had been genially willing to ignore Security entirely and First Officer was having none of Weasel-Boy's periodic complaints of insolence or insubordination, perhaps because Weasel-Boy complained as or more frequently about other officers as about bond-involuntary Security assigned.

"I should wait to ask you for the details, sir." She needed to go round up some Security. Code was on sleep-shift, but Code wouldn't mind; Code might even be on his way to the officer's mess right now. Someone would have told him. "If you'll give me your parole of honor I'll go speak to the First Officer. While you're eating."

"Go and speak away, Chief," Koscuisko said. "I'm not going anywhere until I've had my rhyti. I hope there's decent rhyti. I remember what we used to have to put up with."

She was not in a position to judge. She didn't drink the stuff. She left Koscuisko to his fast-meal and went down to Security to collect the people who had worked with Koscuisko when he'd been here, and who might want to hear about Joslire Curran's family.

It was unquestionably the case that one officer's mess was very like another, and yet Andrej found himself almost uncomfortably aware that he was not on the *Ragnarok* as he ate his fast-meal. The rhyti was all wrong. He didn't know the Security. First Officer Linelly he remembered, of course; at the bottom of it all—he decided—what he liked least was the fact that they remembered him.

They seemed to have been fond of him, in some sense, and that was better than to be held in contempt, as the current chief medical officer apparently was. He hadn't heard anything one way or another about Doctor Lazarbee, not even to know what his clinical concentration was. There was no use pretending that Doctor Lazarbee hadn't heard of him, and that was the reason that being remembered was a problem.

When he had been among the crew of the Jurisdiction Fleet Ship *Scylla* there had been hope for him. He had not yet fallen into the depths at which Captain Lowden treated with Ship's Inquisitors. He had been a sinner, but not damned, and it was doubly painful to think back on his innocent self-assurance in those days knowing what he knew now about the fact that he was a man addicted.

If he'd had nothing but captains like Irshah Parmin, he might have found redemption, given time. He might have ended his service and gone home without a thirst so savage in his heart that he did not dare to name it. If only, if only, and yet he had only himself to blame. Hadn't Irshah Parmin tried to teach him, before it was too late?

Hadn't the captain greeted him with genuine sorrow on his return to *Scylla* from Rudistal, to tell him that he was to be transferred and that no bond-involuntaries assigned were to be allowed to follow him, with the single exception of Robert St. Clare—whom Irshah Parmin was not permitted to keep?

And yet he could not have kept silent and held his peace about the Domitt Prison. Even if he had known what ruin would come into his life, what atrocities he was bound to commit, what was to become of him, once he had looked upon the pitiful fuel to the furnace fires of the Domitt Prison he could not have said nothing, not without embracing a damnation even more detestable than that to which he was fairly condemned.

"Rumor has it that there was a warrant out," First Officer was saying. She'd cleared the room; it was just three of them, First Officer, the Intelligence officer—Bassin Emer—and Andrej Koscuisko. Fast-meal, but neither of them were eating. "And an assassination attempt, first at Burkhayden. Then on home ground. And definite undercurrents of unhappiness in some senior Fleet quarters. He's worried about you."

Irshah Parmin was a good captain. Perhaps that meant he took occasional liberties with ethical behavior, and doubtless he wouldn't mind if it turned out that ap Rhiannon wanted Andrej so much that she'd trade stores or munitions to have him back and argue the legal points later. That hadn't been why Irshah Parmin had sent Samons to kidnap him. Andrej was trying to respect the captain's charitable impulse, but it was hard to feel reasonable about anything with the freighter carrying his Bonds still short of the exit vector, by his reckoning.

"There was no assassination attempt at Burkhayden." He was in a position to know, though he wasn't going to tell. Robert had murdered the man who had brutalized his sister. He himself, Andrej Koscuisko, had killed Captain Lowden, and he should have done it very much the sooner than he had, too. There had been a warrant, that was true. But he couldn't verify the existence of a warrant without leading intelligent people to wonder about the assassination of Griers Verigson Lowden, officially on record as a Free Government terrorist attack.

How many other Free Government terrorist crimes had actually been Bench-sanctioned actions? There was a Free Government, he knew that; nothing he had ever heard or seen in his personal experiences as an Inquisitor would support its existence as anything more than a small, stubborn, desperate, only very loosely organized resistance movement.

If there was a grand plan and a command structure and an authority hierarchy, Andrej had never heard of any such thing first-hand from persons in a position to know. Maybe that was what was really dangerous about the Free Government, though. If it hadn't represented genuine population unrest, it wouldn't keep on cropping up spontaneously.

First Officer was watching him, waiting. Andrej frowned at himself, and refocused. "Assassination attempt on home ground, yes, but I have good reason to believe it was an isolated act. A deranged clerk of Court." There almost had to be conspiracy behind the forgery of the record, true enough; but he wasn't going to get into that. He certainly wasn't going in any direction that might lead an intelligent person like First Officer to conclude that the evidence of that conspiracy, the forged record, no longer existed. Had been destroyed under circumstances that were ambiguous, at best.

"And for the rest, the captain has never been very happy with me either. So there are no new issues there." His principle antagonist, First Secretary Verlaine, had declared truce, and sent him documents for relief of Writ. Verlaine was dead and he had told Specialist Ivers to hold the documentation until the *Ragnarok*'s appeal had been resolved, so there were complications—but no surprises. "There, we are done. May I go back to Jeltaria, now?"

He was tempted to add that his Security would be wondering where he'd got to, but he didn't want to raise the issue of Security in anybody's mind. The longer he could avoid people starting to wonder where his Security had got to the better, and for that he had to do what he could to prevent people from noticing that they were missing. They weren't missing. He knew exactly where they were, if only in a general sense. That was between him, and Security, and Chief Stildyne, though, and there was a thought, Stildyne would cover for Security. Stildyne was in on it. Stildyne knew that Andrej wanted those troops away.

How Stildyne felt about Andrej's plan was something Andrej had yet to discuss with him. He'd wanted to talk to Stildyne much earlier, and been prevented. He didn't think he was looking forward to the interview, but it was unquestionably owed. How could he, of all men, have exiled his own people to Gonebeyond, sent bond-involuntaries out on their own to make a new life in an environment about which they knew next to nothing?

After years of impressing on Stildyne how seriously Andrej took protecting his people, how could he send them away unprotected, abandoned them all with a wave of his hand and an it's-been-good-to-know-you? Stildyne would never accept such behavior without remark, rebuke, objection.

"Not my call, Andrej," First Officer said cheerfully. "I can't swear to Captain that you show evidence of understanding the gravity of the situation, and the peril in which you appear to be. Reflects badly on a man to have his subordinate officers murdered, he feels. Even if they're not his subordinate officers any more. You can't possibly expect him to believe ap Rhiannon is in a position to protect you."

No, indeed, especially given the fact that ap Rhiannon didn't like him. Or didn't trust him. Or something. Andrej poured himself another flask of rhyti, since there were no Security here to do it for him. "Cold as it may sound, Salli, it is no longer Captain Irshah Parmin's business. I'm very annoyed. I have people to see, down-planet."

He could almost hear Stildyne's voice, mocking and scornful. *Yes, sir, of course, sir, spend six years—twelve years—talking about how people ought to treat troops, and then decide that it's for other people. Right.* Almost, but not quite. There was something about the imagined sound of Stildyne's voice that puzzled him. He was missing something.

"I'll tell him. But he's pretty annoyed himself, I don't mind telling you. The depot's not stripped bare, exactly, but all of the sexiest goodies are gone, and you know how Irshah Parmin feels about home defense fleets to begin with."

Yes, he knew how Fleet felt about HDFs. They were useful political tools, sops to proud world-families or systems; they were cost-effective reserve resources that Fleet could, and did, deploy when it didn't want to spend its own money. They were a means to an end, a way to encourage continued investment in research and development that Fleet could direct and profit from, again without having to pay for it. But to the extent that they represented an exception to Fleet's otherwise absolute monopoly on the lawful use of force of arms, Fleet distrusted them all in principle, as opponents just waiting for a good excuse to cause trouble.

And if you expect me to accept this without an argument after all the years I've spent trying to figure out what you wanted from me you've got an over-rated reputation for psychological acuity, with respect, your Excellency.

What was it about the unusual tone of Stildyne's imaginary voice in his head? It sounded like Stildyne—half-disgusted, laying down the law—but Stildyne indistinct around the edges. Fuzzy. Distant. Half-way to the exit vector.

Andrej jumped to his feet as though the seat of his chair had suddenly bitten him in a very delicate place. Distant. Half-way to the exit vector. Stildyne had left, Stildyne had gone, Stildyne had exiled himself to Gonebeyond to take care of those troops—to stand between them and their conditioning, to ease them back into the life of free men. Stildyne. Gone.

Why hadn't he guessed it? Why hadn't he realized that once Stildyne knew, Stildyne would make exactly that decision?

Was it because he had gotten so used to Stildyne that he hadn't envisioned a life without him? Or was it—to his shame—that after all that Stildyne had done to be what Andrej wanted, Andrej still expected him to fall short of expectation?

"Something the matter?" First Officer asked carefully, dropping a napkin onto the table to soak up the rhyti Andrej had spilled when he'd stood up so suddenly.

"Nothing new." It was true. He hadn't foreseen it. He hadn't planned for it. He should have at least wondered, he should have tried harder to talk to Stildyne about it, and now Stildyne was gone and Andrej was ashamed.

There had to be a dancing-master. Reborn men were never simply abandoned to their freedom without the careful assistance of people who could teach them to be free again, the same people who had taught them to be slaves in the first place. What had he been thinking? "I am as immense an ass as I have ever been, Salli, and the captain is quite right to be annoyed with me. I should be locked up for my own safety, in the Saint Andrej Thick-Headed Refuge for the Hopelessly Oblivious."

He sat down again, slowly. Gone, without a word. Why should there have been one? Stildyne would assume that Andrej would speak if he had something to say. Andrej had not spoken. But Stildyne had gone anyway, true to the calling Stildyne had embraced, and he was in so much more trouble with his cousin Stanoczk than he had been before when he had been in enough trouble already for accepting Stildyne's service without acknowledging its motivation or ultimate source. Just because he disapproved in principle of men who enjoyed other men, when the man that they sought to enjoy was him.

Stildyne had never made anything like an improper advance, not after the first one. All of these years he had blamed Brachi Stildyne for being what he was; but Stildyne was an honest man who had changed and grown and sacrificed with no hope of reward—or even recognition—and now there was this.

"If you say so, of course." First Officer sounded a little bit dubious, but not disposed to pry. "Finished with your meal? There are people out there who are eager to see you, Andrej. Doctor Lazarbee has made himself unpopular. I'll just turn you over to Samons for the time being."

First Officer pushed herself away from table to stand up. Andrej folded his napkin and matched the gesture, gazing at the debris on his plate with a bowed head. "I'm sure Captain has only my best interest at heart," Andrej said. "A man doesn't care to be handled quite so casually. But I was unquestionably among the less responsive of his junior officers, and he was far more charitable to me than I could have deserved. I'm not minding seeing you again, Salli."

"Nor I you," First Officer said, and grinned; held out her hand with a sudden spontaneous gesture, and clasped his very warmly. "Come around after third-shift and you'll hear more than you probably need to know about Lazarbee. If Captain made allowances for you, you spoiled this ship for all but the very highest standard of medical administration ever after, and Weasel-Boy is not it."

That was kind of her, as well. There was nothing he could do at this moment to repair the injustice he had done to Brachi Stildyne except to dread what his cousin Stanoczk would have to say to him about it. The best he could do right here and right now was to keep people busy, keep them from wondering why there was no alarm from Emandis Station about officers gone missing from service houses.

The longer he could hold off the inevitable questions the better chance they had of successfully acquiring the dar-Nevan vector for Gonebeyond space. And no matter how careful the planning, there was always the possibility of an error—the chance of a mistake —

No, he wouldn't give it life by thinking about it. Andrej waved to the Security who stood outside the now-open door to the officer's mess, calling them in. "Tell me who is wearing green-sleeves on board of *Scylla*, in these days," he suggested. "And all of the gossip about Chief Samons. Before she gets back."

Where Caleigh Samons was concerned he needed all the help that he could get to fortify himself against her elegant lithe body, and her beautiful eyes, and the fact that she could probably break him into two pieces as easily as though he had not been Dolgorukij at all.

In Koscuisko's absence, Jennet ap Rhiannon had had the Chief of Psychiatric in, to represent Medical at her staff meeting. It was not a regularly scheduled staff meeting; ap Rhiannon was in undress uniform, and had lowered the horizon in the flask of strong red wine that she was drinking by an appreciable margin within the past hour. Rukota had to grant that she showed no signs whatever of being under the influence.

Different categories of hominid reacted differently to given intoxicants. If his suspicions about her genetic background were correct, she should be as vulnerable to that wine as anybody; perhaps that was why she drank so much of it—to keep up an habituated, if relative, immunity.

"She slept how long?" ap Rhiannon asked Doctor Farilk, with a tone of slightly outraged incredulity in her voice. "So she hadn't been to a service house for a while, what had she been doing all night to sleep till half-way to sundown? Why didn't they turn her out?"

"Your Excellency," Doctor Farilk said, gently. "With respect."

Yes, the woman had slept that long, she'd had a physically intense experience of whatever sort, perhaps the first opportunity she had had to sample a particular form of recreation that made no sense whatever to Rukota but neither did the idea that his wife loved him, out of all the men and women that so beautiful and intelligent a woman could have had for the asking, and yet it was true.

They hadn't turned her out of bed because she'd been sleeping in the officer's suite, and the house staff hadn't had any instruction to rouse her. For all the house staff had known, Koscuisko had intended to come back.

But above all, it was none of the captain's business, and an invasion of privacy to speculate. Ap Rhiannon rubbed her eyes with a weary gesture, and nodded. "Of course, Doctor Farilk. Please excuse my indelicacy."

That wasn't a word Rukota would have expected to hear, out of ap Rhiannon. He frowned. What was in that wine? Ap Rhiannon was still talking, though, and sounding enough like ap Rhiannon to allay any fears he might have had about drugs in her liquor.

"So *Scylla* sent troops to take Koscuisko away, and we have a witness who can attest to the ship's-mark, which the night staff also confirm. But she was asleep at the time, and by the time she woke up it was much later than she had expected. She found no Security from the *Ragnarok* on site. So she came back to report, and *Scylla* is probably wondering why nobody's sent for their chief medical officer back, yet."

Just exactly so. The night staff was also in a position to attest to the fact that Koscuisko had ordered transport for his people out to the launch-field, after which they'd not been seen again. Nor did Stildyne seem to be on the job, though nobody appeared to have seen him leave. They had left; so much was almost screamingly obvious.

Koscuisko had jacked the bond-involuntaries' governors and sent them away, and they'd either killed Stildyne or taken him with them. Rukota didn't think they would have murdered their Chief, but he had almost as much difficulty imagining them inviting Stildyne to come on a picnic with them to Gonebeyond—which was their only possible destination, under the circumstances.

"If somebody doesn't say something soon somebody is going to really wonder," First Officer Ralph Mendez observed. Rukota liked Mendez. Mendez was a very comfortable man to be alone with, in the sense that you could be with Mendez and completely alone at the same time. "We've got to make some noise, your Excellency."

"One of the best battle-surgeons in the inventory," Karol Vogel added, quietly, from where he sat at the far end of the table savoring some bean tea. "You'd almost think you didn't want him back. And if a ship doesn't want its battle surgeon it's because it doesn't think it's going to need one, which means no battle, which means conflict avoidance."

Which all added up to Gonebeyond space all over again, though Vogel wasn't so rude as to come right out and say so. The *Ragnarok* had no intention of being held at Emandis Station, however. Their escape from Taisheki had been narrow enough, and loss of life had been avoided by lucky accident alone. They weren't likely to have any such luck again, and they were still all one Fleet. Any casualties inflicted by one ship upon the other would be casualties inflicted upon themselves, in a very real sense.

"Koscuisko knows how I feel about him, Vogel," ap Rhiannon retorted. A lot of people didn't care for Inquisitors as a class, but Rukota didn't think that was ap Rhiannon's problem with the man. "He hasn't convinced me to trust him differently. He has more to lose than any twenty of the rest of us combined. He's better off well clear of *Ragnarok*, and *Ragnarok* is, consequently, better off well clear of him."

She did have a point. Rukota's very limited experience of Andrej Koscuisko had led him to conclude that Koscuisko was as stubborn as ap Rhiannon, and to suspect that the equivalence was an at least partial explanation for ap Rhiannon's distrust; but it was abstractly true that Koscuisko was to be a very important man in Combine affairs, and could buy even the Jurisdiction Fleet Ship *Ragnarok* for a garden-ornament, if he decided that he wanted one.

"There is a ship." It was Two. She'd been very quiet; Rukota had almost forgotten she was there. He was getting used to sitting with giant bats, perhaps. "One that is still several hours from acquiring the exit vector, unlike another ship similar in some ways that has almost reached the vector even now. If the captain determines that the ship is carrying contraband, she could very well go in pursuit of it."

"The *Ragnarok* leaves Emandis Station, *Scylla* will follow after it—" Rukota started to object. Two lifted up the flange of her wing for silence, and Rukota shut up.

"Emandis Station is not pleased to have *Scylla* borrowing other peoples' officers without prior clearance. It seems to communicate a lack of respect, I am told. And also Andrej wears five-knives. Emandis Station will not facilitate *Scylla*'s pursuit, from analysis. It is possible that *Scylla*'s departure might even be impeded. Shocking."

"So we can get out if we don't mind leaving Koscuisko," the Ship's Engineer said, with no little degree of self-satisfaction in his voice. "What's not to like?"

Disgusting. "Well, Koscuisko might have thoughts on the issue," Rukota pointed out. Koscuisko wasn't here. He had nobody to speak for him. It was almost too bad, how willing they seemed to be to leave Koscuisko to his own devices—except, of course, that a man with Koscuisko's money had a much wider range of devices available to him than the Jurisdiction Fleet Ship *Ragnarok*.

"I'd better go down," Vogel said to ap Rhiannon, letting Rukota's protest pass without comment. "It'll be expected. And we really can't have home defense fleets in open conflict with Fleet resources. Jils Ivers is at Brisinje; she and Koscuisko have history together, and I've got to get to Brisinje anyway. Maybe I can call on her for help."

Well, it wasn't anybody's history with Koscuisko that mattered so much as the almost irresistible temptation that something like this would present to the Emandisan fleet to take advantage of the situation to assert some autonomy. That was a problem for Bench specialists, though. Vogel was right enough about that.

Ap Rhiannon nodded. "Yes, thank you, Bench specialist. General Rukota will meet you on the docks to see you off." She waited until Vogel had gotten up and made his salute and gone away. Then ap Rhiannon leaned across the table and looked at Two. "That ship?" she asked. Two shook her vulpine velvet-pelted head with sharp decisive clarity.

"Of course not, your Excellency. But so long as we are chasing a ship as if it had bond-involuntaries on it, honest port authorities will be doing their best to clear the vector approach so that a fugitive may be safely fired upon. Distracting authorities from bothering to question any other ships that might be approaching the vector at this moment. We are to abandon Andrej; it seems the least that we can do."

Chase a ship, create a decoy. Leave Emandisan space. Get away. Ap Rhiannon sighed. "I'm not completely happy about that," she said.

"He is unquestionably a good surgeon. And he runs an efficient Infirmary. But better him than us."

Well, if that didn't restore his faith in ap Rhiannon's enlightened self-interest. Yes. The ship did profit from Koscuisko's medical skills. She had to cut her losses and run, though, and Rukota couldn't argue too much with that.

"I'll go make sure Vogel gets off," Rukota suggested. "Good-greeting, your Excellency. First Officer. Engineer. Two. Doctor Farilk."

He needed to find out what Farilk liked to drink, Rukota decided, on his way out of the room. He had an idea that Farilk's take on staff meetings might be very different indeed than what Rukota thought was happening in them; and there was a vector transit in their near future, with nothing to do between here and Gonebeyond but gossip about one another.

Caleigh Samons stood at attention-rest behind Andrej Koscuisko in the captain's office, trying hard to calculate how indebted she was to Koscuisko for giving her a spectator's ticket to a show such as she could scarcely have imagined. Three senior officers from the Emandisan home defense fleet. A Bench intelligence specialist. First Officer, Captain Irshah Parmin, Andrej Ulexeievitch Koscuisko, and even Weasel-Boy was here—though what his excuse might be she couldn't guess, and nobody else had bothered to ask.

"Fleet Captain, with all due respect. Emandis Station and the public mercantile ports of Emandis proper are the lawful responsiblity of the Emandis home defense fleet. You have breached a public trust by your ill-considered actions. In earlier years it would certainly have been considered a direct insult."

They had been called to the captain's office when the delegation from Emandis Station had docked; Koscuisko had been offered a chair, and had sat down. The Emandisan officers had similarly been offered chairs, and had declined to sit—one among them bowing gravely in Koscuisko's direction as they politely refused to be accommodated. Or accommodating.

Nobody had asked Weasel-Boy to sit and Caleigh wouldn't have known what to do if anybody had asked her; First Officer had taken her post behind the captain, to his left. First Officer's posture was perfect. Koscuisko's posture was respectful and attentive, but confused—if she still knew how to read Koscuisko.

"Provost Marshal Jenner." Irshah Parmin spread his hands out on his desk in a gesture of solicitation and propitiation, but it was a carefully controlled gesture—one that preserved the dignity of the office. "Surely that's stating things a bit strongly. Even your merchant ships have a right to police up their own crew, though I grant you that we failed to go through proper channels to notify you first."

"He's not your crew. He's the *Ragnarok*'s crew. And he's an Emandisan national besides. You sent a team of Security into a public service house, your Excellency, to grab a man out of bed and terrorize an innocent young woman—our apologies, your Excellency, for the reference," the provost marshal said to Koscuisko, as if an aside.

Then he faced back to where the captain sat waiting, clearly aware of the fact that the provost marshal wasn't finished with him yet. "And in front of a Bench intelligence specialist, Captain. We consider this a very serious affront. If there was a First Judge presiding you would not be so ready to violate the integrity of the Port Authority, I think."

Strong language. The Bench specialist referred to—a man of middling height with an iron-gray moustache and a fine physique, his battered old campaign hat tucked into the plaquet of his uniform, which looked so new as to create suspicion in Caleigh's mind that it had been made specially for the occasion—made a little gesture with pursed lips, glancing down and away from the provost marshal; as if finding the odor of the Emandisan's irritation a little high. He hadn't said much beyond the polite exchange of greetings, though he and Koscuisko apparently knew each other.

The captain gathered his hands into a carefully arranged clasp on his desk in front of him, and spoke to his thumbs with equal care. "If there were a First Judge presiding, the Emandis home defense fleet might be a little more cautious in its accusations, provost marshal. Koscuisko is a Bench resource, not an Emandisan national. No disrespect was intended toward the Emandis home defense fleet or the Port Authority or anything to do with Emandis Station. I failed to consider that a simple administrative act might be so interpreted."

He was telling the truth, too, Caleigh knew. First Officer had had reservations from the beginning. First Officer stood motionless and silent now, giving no sign of having any I-told-you-so sorts of thoughts. Caleigh had to admire her professionalism.

"Koscuisko carries five-knives," The Emandisan provost marshal had gone a little pale, in Caleigh's estimation. It was hard for her to tell, with Emandisan; they were darker-complected than many hominid sub-species, something like an average between the too-fair Dolgorukij and a Gilzirait as dark as the luminous shadow of an earth across the face of one of its moons.

She'd never learned to really interpret Joslire's expressions, but when he had been dying his skin had seemed the color of a shark's skin beneath the cold street-lights. "And five-knives are a cultural artifact of signal importance to our community. By virtue of the knives he is an Emandisan knife-fighter, and the operant term in this instance is 'Emandisan.' Furthermore he has family in port Jeltaria who have waited for a long time to talk about his relationship with his teacher."

Would that be Joslire, Caleigh wondered? And the provost marshal wasn't through with the captain yet—"We demand his immediate restoration, your Excellency. You have no right to hold an Emandisan citizen against his will, unless you accuse him of crimes against the Bench."

Koscuisko stirred; he put his head down, covering his face with one hand, elbow leaning upon the arm of his chair. Was that a quiver or a twitch she saw disturb the fabric of the duty-blouse across his broad back? Was he laughing?

Captain Irshah Parmin was not insensible to the humor of the situation, even if the Emandisan themselves betrayed no sign of being anything less than absolutely serious. "Well, he was a Bench resource first," the captain said. "Met his man Joslire in orientation, didn't he? So he belongs to Fleet first, and Emandis second. And he's got people of his own, I understand, but they're not complaining, so forget them."

The captain stood up. "While regretting having given offense, Provost Marshall, I repeat that we view this as a strictly internal Fleet matter. One in which the Emandisan home defense fleet should not interfere or attempt to intervene. Specialist Vogel?"

What the captain meant to ask or expected to hear from the Bench specialist were fated to remain forever unknown. Before he had a chance to more than say Vogel's name the talk-alert cleared its attention-tone, and the Intelligence officer's voice resounded throughout the room.

"With respect, your Excellency, and my apologies for the interruption, sir. The *Ragnarok* has cast off its freight-lines and is preparing to leave the docks. Stated destination, the dar-Nevan vector, to leave Emandis system for an undisclosed location."

Koscuisko put his hands to the arms of his chair and half-rose out of his seat, his shoulders practically radiating mistrustful fury—glaring at Specialist Vogel.

The Emandisan didn't look surprised. And neither did Specialist Vogel. That fact did not escape the notice of Captain Irshah Parmin, who raised his eyebrows at Vogel and growled. "What is this, Bench specialist?"

Vogel raised a loosely clenched fist to his mouth and coughed with polite diffidence. "Oh, yes. That. Some of the *Ragnarok*'s troops have gone missing, seven in all. The *Ragnarok*'s Intelligence officer has credible evidence that places them en route to the exit vector even now."

Caleigh did a quick mental calculation. It was nearing the end of third-shift in a very eventful day; she had borrowed Koscuisko from the service house this morning. Early this morning. Had they even been at the service house when she had done the thing? She'd been worried about Koscuisko's bond-involuntary security, and they hadn't even been in the service house at all.

Had that been why the house staff hadn't challenged her story more strenuously—because they knew that Koscuisko's Security had already left, or were leaving? Had they assumed that Caleigh's team had been replacements for Koscuisko's security, *Scylla* and *Ragnarok* taking turns to husband a valuable resource?

Koscuisko closed his eyes with a grimace that Caleigh could not interpret, and slumped back in his seat. The Emandisan provost marshal nodded.

"Requested clearance to go in pursuit," the provost marshal said. "Load-out was at a status break, so there wasn't much of an issue with terminating the load without completing the inventory, though it does leave the ship without its third redundancy in dry-goods. We're told that evidence puts the fugitive ship on an approach vector that could place them in Gonebeyond."

"There's a ship, is there?" the captain demanded, harshly. "Wait, let me guess. It's an Emandisan. No. Wait. A Combine ship."

"Neither, by report," Vogel replied, calmly and with measured regret in his voice. "Some fairly general-purpose rental fleet ship aroused suspicions when it logged an unusual angle of approach to the vector, and it doesn't seem to behave quite like a ship of its class with a standard-components propulsion system. I'm sorry, your Excellency, this must come as a blow, I've heard that you were close."

"Robert," Koscuisko said, as if he was agreeing with something that Vogel had suggested. "Robert, and Lek, and Pyotr—who would have thought—"

"Hah," Doctor Lazarbee said. Caleigh only just barely didn't jump; she'd forgotten he was in the room, but yes, here he was, coming forward to stand beside the chair in which Koscuisko sat. "So much for the Koscuisko mystique, eh? Put the rascals on Safe and they're out of here. Maybe it was a mistake to bring 'em, Koscuisko, reminded them of what sorts of things happen to your Security—stabbed, wasn't it?"

Koscuisko stood up from out of his chair altogether too quickly, pivoting on the heel of one foot as he came and pushing with the ball of the other to provide the impetus for his movement.

Caleigh saw the black-clothed arc of Koscuisko's right arm raised with swift but controlled power too late to intervene before his clenched fist made contact with the side of Weasel-Boy's jaw and sent him staggering backwards to fall over a chair in the captain's conference area and collapse.

Caleigh was impressed. Koscuisko had always been strongly left-dominant when she'd had the training of him. Stildyne had clearly been working closely with Koscuisko to balance out his available lines of attack.

"You released the *Ragnarok*?" the captain asked the Emandisan provost marshal. From the tone of his voice he already knew the answer. The provost marshal did not shrug—he was more polite than that—but the shrug was in the air regardless.

"Load-out terminated by request, inventory duly signed over, we have no reason to wish to detain a ship ready to depart," the provost marshal said. In the corner of the room Caleigh could see Doctor

Weasel-Boy struggling to rise before subsiding into a helpless crumple once again. Nobody seemed to be paying much attention.

"I have an unresolved issue with the *Ragnarok*," Irshah Parmin pointed out, very reasonably and calmly, Caleigh thought. "The ship is also under appeal of very serious charges, guilty of mutiny in form at best. If I let the *Ragnarok* depart from system with a full munitions load I fail in my duty to the Fleet and to the Bench. We leave immediately to intercept the *Ragnarok*, First Officer, mark and move."

Koscuisko sat back down, rubbing the knuckles of his right hand absent-mindedly, thanking Caleigh with a nod when she handed him a white-square to wipe his hand. His skin was bleeding. Just as well, really; blood cleaned a wound. "She's going without me," Koscuisko said to Vogel. "Damn her. And damn you, too, for letting her, that's my ship, Vogel, those are my people."

"We'll begin the disengage immediately, of course," the provost marshal said to Irshah Parmin. "If I recall correctly we're in the middle of the potable water cycle, though, we won't be able to shift until we can complete the cycle if we don't want to risk a major spill. Probably half a day, Fleet Captain."

"No, disengage now, if we wait half a day we'll never catch that ship, the *Ragnarok* can probably make the vector in half a day—"

It certainly made things convenient for the *Ragnarok*, Caleigh thought—Koscuisko's Security deciding to make a run for it. Too convenient? No, Koscuisko seemed genuinely rattled by Vogel's revelation. A lucky accident, then, for the *Ragnarok*.

"I'm sorry, Fleet Captain, but we must insist. We don't like to disengage mid-process at all, it's dangerous to try to stop mass load sequences once they've been initiated. Taking any shortcuts cannot be countenanced. No." The provost marshal sounded sincerely regretful, utterly serious. There wasn't the slightest hint of any gleeful cackling in his tone of voice, his expression, his body language.

"We'll start to cut *Scylla* loose as soon as possible, but it will be at least sixteen hours. Perhaps twenty. You are in the middle of your reloads sequence, but we won't have to handle too much by way of munitions recall, that will be a help."

Captain Irshah Parmin stood up and leaned over his desk. "So we don't have a chance. All right. Send some of your corvettes. Stop the

Ragnarok short of the exit vector. I wouldn't put it past her to take the entire ship into Gonebeyond on pretext—what a nightmare—"

The provost marshal shook his head. "I'm sorry," he said. "But it's an internal Fleet matter. We have no brief to intervene, and may not act on behalf of Fleet without direction from the Ninth Judge at Brisinje."

"Which direction I will forward as soon as possible," Vogel added, in a reassuring tone of voice. "I'm borrowing a courier from Emandis Station to take me to Brisinje immediately. I may even beat the *Ragnarok* to the vector, I don't know, though, the Engineer can shift that hull with admirable efficiency. Experimental technology, as I understand, it's got a great future from what I see of it."

"Infamous," the captain said, sitting back down. In the corner, Doctor Weasel-Boy was still waving his arms and legs around in the air, very much like a beetle on its back. "You're all in this together. Vogel. Provost Marshall. Koscuisko, for all I know. Well. If that's the way you're going to play it."

The provost marshal bowed with perfect respect and precision. *Yes. That's exactly the way we're going to play it.* The captain nodded in disgusted resignation and continued.

"Go to Brisinje, Bench specialist, tell First Secretary Tirom that we'll be held over here for a few days. Never mind sending the Emandisan fleet instructions, though, I don't want to encourage anybody to throw themselves away in Gonebeyond. Koscuisko. You're to be orphaned, it seems, and there are no Security resources on Emandis Station rated for specialty escort. After all, we had you picked up and packed off before anybody even noticed."

That was unnecessary, Caleigh thought. But the captain was angry, now, in a calm understated Irshah Parmin sort of a way. Koscuisko had done it again. "So, with apologies, Provost Marshall, we'll just keep him safe with us until Fleet can decide how to dispose of him. Koscuisko stays an internal Fleet matter. Will that be all?"

"Objecting once again in the strongest possible terms," the provost marshal said to Vogel. "To repeat. Emandisan national, and a uniquely privileged citizen. Fleet has no authority to detain Koscuisko or to place his knives in bondage. We will be unable to permit the *Scylla* to leave Emandis Station so long as Koscuisko remains on board, unless of his own free will."

Worse and worse and worse—almost absurdly so. "Do I get a say in this?" Koscuisko asked the captain.

"No."

"Just asking," Koscuisko replied politely, and seemed to relax in his chair. Koscuisko at least knew what was going to be happening to him, in the near term: nothing.

"Jils Ivers is at Brisinje," Vogel said to Koscuisko. "I'll see if she can be spared to mediate. If you think it might help."

"I'd be happy to see Dame Ivers again." No, there was still something else going on with Koscuisko, Caleigh decided. What was it? Something to do with Ivers, whoever she was?

"If you're quite finished, Koscuisko, you can clear out. Provost Marshall, go, Specialist Vogel, good-greeting. Intelligence, put the *Ragnarok* on monitor." Just so that the captain could cultivate his aggravation by watching the *Ragnarok* leave, Caleigh supposed. "First Officer. Send someone to pick up Doctor Lazarbee, would you? Very kind."

Fleet Captain Irshah Parmin didn't trouble himself over-much with things he couldn't help. This situation was one of those things.

But he was unquestionably as angry, in his calm resigned fashion, as Caleigh thought she had ever seen him in her life.

CHAPTER FIFTEEN

Intervention

"If Fontailloe can't seat the next First Judge from existing Judicial resources, then Fontailloe can't seat the Second Judge from Chilleau," Jils said firmly. "The issue remains the same."

"There may be no single judge at Fontailloe ready to assume the role of First Judge, true." Jeru Tanifer had grown old in the service of the Bench. What would become of Tanifer under the new administration at Fontailloe was anybody's guess. "All the more reason to provide on-site guidance during a difficult time."

"Fontailloe has to promote a judge either way," Nion said suddenly. Jils was startled to hear it. Nion was observing; she wasn't supposed to be engaging in the debate, in any sense. Turning her head toward the window Jils examined Nion's face in reflection— belligerent in expression. Tanifer had turned his head as well, but to look at Nion, apparently as surprised as Jils.

"Inappropriate interjection," Tanifer said reprovingly. "Ivers. Your call. The point is one that I might have brought into discussion. I'd rather not have to abstain from making it."

Nion's point was hardly one that hadn't occurred to people before, though. With one last long look at the reflection in the window— Nion, Tanifer, Ivers—Jils turned back to face Tanifer. "The point is in fair play," she agreed. "To return to your point. On-site guidance might be for the long-term good of Fontailloe, using the Second

Judge's experience as a resource to develop a newly promoted judge's confidence. Such an accommodation has not been felt necessary in the past, however. And who's to see to Chilleau if we move its Judge?"

Nion had folded her arms and was staring out the window with evident frustration and disgust. The only direction in which there was anything to see from the observation float was toward the station; the station's lights illuminated its walls, and the walkway between the shore and the float was lined with gleams. In every other direction there was nothing but black water, the cave's roof disappearing into the darkness, and the far shores of the lake out of sight.

It was night-time in Brisinje, Jils realized. No light from the surface shone through those light-wells to give any definition to the world outside the float. There was only the dark, and the station.

"A new First Judge from Fontailloe could be perceived as outside the Bench's entrenched interest," Tanifer said thoughtfully. "Promote at Fontailloe, send the new judge to Chilleau while Chilleau's new First Secretary comes up to speed."

"That's the worst of both worlds." It was a prescription for disaster, and Jils meant to write the dosage instructions out carefully. "Meanwhile you pull the Second Judge out of the Judiciary that she has made her home for an entire career and place her at the mercy of the First Secretary of the old First Judge, a man loyal to the memory of na Roqua den Tensa and accustomed to doing things the previous incumbent's way. There will be inevitable resentments if they feel they are having a Judge imposed on them, especially if she is just going to be there for a few years."

In fact, the only thing that Jils could think of that would be worse than sending the Second Judge to Fontailloe would be not declaring a new First Judge at all. Confederacy still took the prize for the single worst solution to the situation they were in, as far as Jils was concerned.

Tanifer sighed. "I need a personal functions break," he said. "Want anything from the kitchen? Coming with me?"

Jils declined with a polite wave of her hand. She didn't particularly need to stretch her legs just now; she'd save her break, she might want it later on in the session. They were three hours into this session, and it was the second day they'd been arguing. Two, three hours to go, and then they'd pick it up again after a sleep break.

Tanifer rose to his feet and left the room without looking at Nion; Jils stayed sat, running through their progress in her mind. She wasn't sure they were much closer to agreement than they had been days ago.

"Look at that," Nion said, suddenly. Jils pulled herself out of her concentration to see what Nion was talking about. Standing up from her observer's post, Nion took the six steps required to cross the room to stand at the outermost angle of the room, staring into the blackness; what did she see?

Jils didn't feel like standing up. She was tired, and her ribs hurt. Nion was an unpleasant person. Jils didn't like her. Her teeth were all wrong, baby teeth, baby teeth grown to adult size in an adult jaw to grotesque effect. Jils had to shake her head at herself; Nion's teeth were a part of her lineage, not a moral failing of any sort. But Jils still didn't feel like standing up. "Look at what?"

"That," Nion repeated, encouragingly, and pointed.

Wearily Jils rose to her feet—there wasn't any point to being gratuitously rude, after all—and went to stand beside Nion, a little behind Nion and to the left. It was a habit. It was just a habit. Most hominids were right-dominant. Their instinct was to turn to bring their right hands into play against an enemy standing to their left. It didn't work with Bench specialists, or with anybody else who had trained much in hand-to-hand; but it was still a default.

Facing away from the station into the darkness all Jils could see was the interior of the room, mirrored in the glass. "I'm not getting you," Jils said. "I don't see anything except for our reflections."

"While I see a traitor to the Bench." Nion took a step to the right, turning so that she and Jils faced each other. She had a hand-harpoon, a light little crossbow handarm-sized that could be folded flat and carried almost anywhere concealed in a sleeve or a boot. "And the person who will restore the honor of the service. You killed First Secretary Sindha Verlaine, Ivers. Die for it."

Nion fired. Jils feinted right—if Nion was right-handed it would be Nion's instinct to follow an attempted escape from right to left in her own frame of reference—and dropped to the ground with a push to the left, trying to move as much of her body out of the path of the harpoon as possible. Pocket-harpoons didn't have much range, by and large, and made up for the lack by carrying poison in the cutting edge of the barbel-headed point. Nion didn't have to deliver a traumatic wound to kill her, so Nion would—had—aimed for the body.

It was a very slim chance, but it was the only one Jils had. There was only one round to a pocket-harpoon. It had no target tracking system; part of the reason that the weapon could be successfully concealed was its lack of an intelligence of its own. If she could confuse Nion's aim enough, and move fast enough, she might escape a fatal cut. She reached out for Nion as she dropped, hoping to set Nion off balance; she got Nion's ankle, pulled it sharply, and Nion lost her footing and fell.

Had she been hit? Jils couldn't tell. She didn't have time to check, either. Nion would have used a fast-acting poison, one without a readily available antidote; Nion's best hope of having her act accepted as a killing for cause lay in being sure that the "killing" part of it was already accomplished before the question came up, because once Jils was dead the precise reason why she had been killed receded somewhat in importance. Jils knew how that worked.

She didn't feel a cut; the sharp pain in her scraped ribs when she hit the ground distracted her. If she hadn't been cut Nion would, necessarily, try to cut her again. From the moment Nion had drawn the weapon it had been Nion against Ivers to the death, and if Jils was going to die at the hands of someone with such unnatural teeth she was going to do her damnedest to take Nion down with her. Self-respect demanded nothing less.

Nion fell, and before Nion hit the ground Jils rolled away, curling her body into the space in which Nion had been standing to avoid the harpoon if it had not pierced her. It lay on the ground behind Jils; maybe it had sliced her as it passed, but if it hadn't, she wasn't about to lie still and wait for Nion to pick it up.

Nion had scrambled to her hands and knees, reaching for the harpoon. Jils kicked once to send it clattering away from them, and then again to connect with Nion's throat. Nion wasn't paying attention. Nion wanted the harpoon. Jils didn't have one.

She had a fraction of one second to think about her alternatives while Nion lay gasping for breath on the floor with her hand to her throat. Jils wasn't armed because they were all to have left their weapons on the surface. That was to her advantage. Nion was distracted by the loss of her harpoon.

Jils started to rise to grab a chair and see if she could break a tube out of the frame to serve as a bludgeon; started, but her ribs had other ideas and sent her back down to the floor with a gasp of surprised pain that was only intensified when Nion—having struggled to her feet, now, in the time that Jils had let escape her, handicapped by the pain from recently scored bone—kicked her in the ribs where the cut had been before stumbling across the room; for her harpoon, Jils supposed.

She couldn't breathe, and her ribs hurt like little she could call to her mind for comparison. It didn't matter. If she didn't do something she was much worse off than hurt, she was dead. She caught at the leg of the chair by the table, the one she'd been sitting in, and managed to push it into Nion's pathway as Nion turned on her with harpoon in hand like a knife.

It would work very well for a knife. All Nion had to do was to cut her, but Nion fell over the chair that Jils sent across her path of advance and crashed to the ground. Nion did not loose her hold on the harpoon.

Jils couldn't let Nion rise again, not if she was to have a chance, any chance at all. Staggering to her feet Jils put one foot down on Nion's hand to fix it in its place and dropped down heavily onto one knee, which landed in the middle of Nion's back. She was off balance; Nion almost threw her, fighting, snarling with an inarticulate cry of rage.

Jils smelled blood, and knew it wasn't hers. Nion had been cut by the harpoon, Nion was poisoned by her own weapon, but that wouldn't stop Nion from using the last few moments of her life to take Jils out with her, any more than it had stopped Jils even with less certitude of the coming end. Jils couldn't afford to gamble on whether she could get out and defensibly away from Nion before Nion got her. Not in her condition.

Jils took Nion's hand between her two hands, got Nion's jaw cradled into her left palm, and twisted. Something snapped. The body went still.

Now finally Jils could crawl away from Nion, so long as she kept to the other side of Nion from the hand that held the harpoon. Nion was not dead yet, though she would be losing consciousness quickly. But Nion was no longer capable of coordinated movement or directed action: Jils had broken Nion's neck. It was over. They didn't have the medical equipment here on station to stabilize so serious a compromise, and the poison on the harpoon would be doing its work as well.

Had Nion killed her? Had she been cut by the harpoon? Was the white-hot aching anguish in her side just the protest of her recently injured body?

She sat down at the table, her movements slow and clumsy. She tried to remember what the sequence of the attack had been to give herself a list of things to check, places to look for her death warrant incised upon her skin by the poisoned edge of a hand-harpoon. She couldn't remember. Was she dying already?

The door to the room burst open with a sudden furious force, and Padrake came through with fragments of structural beams decorating his shoulders. He had beautifully broad shoulders. Jils had always particularly admired them.

"Harpoons," Jils said to him, hearing the slurring at the edges of her own words. "One down. Don't know about self."

"Can you walk?" Padrake asked, his eyes moving from point to point as he took in the particulars of the scene.

Jils shook her head. "Not sure. But I don't want to fall into the water." There were others coming in behind Padrake. There was Tanifer, for one. Capercoy. Balkney. Rinpen. "Not confident of swimming."

She didn't want to breathe. It hurt to even think about swimming. "Medical," Padrake said firmly. "Sorry about this, Jils, please don't kill me—"

If he'd tried to take her up in to his arms to carry her, she would have. It was too absurd. His innate sense of self-preservation served him well; he shouldered her instead, one arm hooked around a thigh and the other supporting her shoulder. Being carried like a sack of spent-grains was marginally better than being carried off in a litter, Jils supposed.

She was very tired.

She concentrated on breathing past the pain in her side and was pleasantly surprised when she did not, in fact, die on her way to the station's tiny medical area.

⊕ ⊕ ⊕

In the past seven days Shona Ise-I'let had worked double shifts for material management and then recreated himself in the warehouse moving stores with cranes and auto-movers, sleeping when he had to and eating whenever he paused to think about it.

The launch-fields of Brisinje proper were still fully enveloped in the fires that had started days ago. A huge black stinking stain in the atmosphere had reached the brilliant clear blue skies of Imennou, the night-fog leaving sooty streaks on the white walls as it lifted in the morning. The flowers were dying, poisoned.

People who worked outside had to wear respirator masks and wash carefully as soon as they were indoors; people with respiratory illnesses were not to stir out-of-doors at all. The public services in Imennou were stretched to their limit to see to the welfare of such people, young and old alike.

If people couldn't get out-of-doors they couldn't get to the markets. If people couldn't get to the markets they began to run short of provisions. Provisions were beginning to thin, though there was still enough food—the local crops had been almost exhausted, but there were still areas the smoke had not reached, fields that continued to yield. Local transport could still sustain them.

One of the old quarters of Brisinje had been burned as well; there'd been a rumor that some of the saboteurs responsible for the destruction at the launch-field had been found, and a mob of frustrated, fearful people had gone in to take the very most primitive kind of revenge on guilty and innocent alike. There needed to be an answer. There needed to be a Selection. That a riot could light fires in Brisinje within eyeshot of Bench chambers was a horror too profound to be described.

Shona had worked—with Brisinje out of operation, all of the cargo handling had to be absorbed through smaller facilities well removed from the source of the disaster—but Shona had been counting, as well. Seven days. The *Ragnarok* had almost certainly left Emandis Station. He had no hope.

His family had met Andrej Koscuisko. They had taken him to where Joslire's ashes had been scattered into the sacred earth. Then they had heard nothing more of him. They had been told that Fleet had jurisdiction problems, that the Port Authority had lodged a complaint; but they'd not seen the man himself but the once.

Shona had resigned himself, almost. His crew, the others on board of the courier, had done what they could to help him along, alternating between attempting to distract him and leaving him strictly alone.

He could not honorably put his private thirst to meet the man to whom his brother had given the most precious thing on all Emandis above the fact that cargo had to move and trade continue or else the suffering caused by the burning launch-fields of Brisinje would extend far beyond the boundaries of Brisinje Jurisdiction. Could not. Wanted passionately to be able to, and worked as hard as he could to manage his piercing sense of deprivation—or at least to dull it, with fatigue.

Six days, and Shona was sitting in the launch controller's function room in front of three schemers, juggling alternate projections to find a launch sequence for ships of varying sizes that would maximize the weight that they could lift in the next thirty-two hours.

Things were relatively quiet; and in every quiet moment a man consulted the schemers on the question of re-arranging the launch sequences. There were always adjustments that could be made. There was always new information coming in. The entry lines were out on a courier coming in from Emandis Station; Shona heard the ship's identification without paying attention. He was tired.

Someone came and handed him a launch-ticket, and he sighed in resignation. *Priority redirect, depart for Brisinje immediately, and depart from there on arrival of passenger or passengers for Emandis Station as quickly as possible, all available means to be employed to speed the transit.*

He punched the orders into the nearest schemer, watching the ship's identification scroll across the reader while he waited for the schemer to calculate the delay that this would create for everybody else at Imennou. Yes, that was an elite Emandisan courier. Yes, it could clear in very little time. Yes, the crew was on site. Yes, he could bring it in to Brisinje, there were places you could put a courier down if you really had to—somebody really had to—

Wait. That was his courier. His ship. He was the pilot there, on the manifest. Courier pilot Shona Ise-I'let, in support of Bench specialist Vogel. Imennou to Brisinje to Emandis Station, special priority, departure—immediate.

Shona jumped to his feet and turned away from the schemers toward the room to shout out his discovery—his good fortune. They were all waiting for him, staring, smiling. He couldn't help smiling back. Koscuisko would be gone well before he could possibly get to Emandis Station, it was two days' transit—but he was going home. As much as he appreciated the need for extra help at Imennou, he wanted to get home, he'd been on one mission or another for too long. His baby would have forgotten what he looked like.

"You'd best go get some sleep, pilot," the shift leader said, her voice full of mischief. "You've got to ferry a Bench specialist to Brisinje. We don't dare put you on a priority mission with less than your full preparation cycle, do we?"

As if he was going to be able to sleep. Yes, he would be able to sleep, because he had to. No responsible pilot would attempt a difficult entry through Brisinje's local atmosphere with anything less than all his faculties, let alone a run to Emandis at top speed.

Could it be—might it be possible—was there any chance—

He couldn't afford to think about it. He smiled again—showing his teeth, almost rude, where Shona came from—and hurried out of the room, helped on his way by the cheers of the people who had been his companions for these days of desperation struggling to absorb the freight, process the inventories, get the cargoes to where they needed to be.

His family had at least met the man. His wife would tell him all about it. He was going home. He'd missed his chance, his one chance, the only chance that he might ever have—but he was going home. Joslire would understand.

His brother knew that necessity brought sacrifice better than any living man of Shona's acquaintance. With that comforting thought Shona sought his billet, and lay down, and chanted himself to sleep with the words in his mind. Home. Home. Home, home, home. He was going home.

"Leaving," Jils said with determination, forming the words with care. The painkillers were making her groggy, and she couldn't afford groggy. They could kill her much more easily that way. How many of the people here wanted her dead? Had Nion been the only one? Were they all just waiting for a chance?

Possibly. But to lapse into paranoia was to surrender her reason. She had to make up her mind to at least act as though she could trust anybody here, anybody at all. Padrake. She could trust Padrake. Surely Padrake knew her as well as anybody yet living—Balkney, she could trust him too, Karol had said so.

"Delleroy's contacted Tirom," Balkney assured her, not preventing her from standing up—exactly—but standing so close to her, in the tiny medical area, that there was no way in which she could attempt to straighten to her feet from her seated position without becoming much more intimate with Balkney than she had any intention of doing. For one thing, Jils was afraid of his wife. Any sane person would be.

People said that the Hangman was a cold, ruthless assassin, a man who could kill without his pulse changing—she didn't believe it. He'd been paired with his wife for quite a few years, now, and both of them still living, as well as the children.

She lay back down on the bed in frustrated resignation. All right, she was going to trust Balkney, but she was still shaken and weary, injured and in shock and full of all kinds of drugs. Antidotes, in case she'd been scratched. Pain medication. She wasn't sure what. Nion was dead, her corpse in a locker in a storage room; what they were going to do with it down here Jils couldn't imagine.

But she couldn't stay. It was not possible for her to continue to function in this environment. She had no intention of giving anyone another chance. The next assault would end it for her for certain; she was weak, now, and vulnerable.

"Apparently you're needed at Emandis Station, Ivers. Conflict between the home defense fleet and Fleet rapidly escalating toward critical mass, and you're the Bench specialist to defuse it, lucky you." Balkney had turned to the bedside chair to seat himself, once she lay back down. Once she surrendered. "You're to go up with Delleroy, he's to accompany you, represent the Ninth Judge, and so on. It's two days to Emandis Station, not much less with even a really good pilot. Plenty of time for you to rest up. Jils."

Balkney said her name with an unusual emphasis, almost as if it was something he'd still been deciding whether or not he was going to say it until it was actually spoken. He surprised her; he'd never used her personal name. "What?"

"You keep your eye on Delleroy. There's something that doesn't feel quite right to me, there. If you were my friend I'd be right here with you." And he was; and he was. "If you'd been my lover I wouldn't be letting you alone with anybody, not even a sober abstemious married man like me. Particularly with a sober abstemious married man whose primary role under Jurisdiction has been as an eraser of redundant lives. I'm not happy about this."

Well, that was just ridiculous. She knew Padrake; Balkney didn't. Padrake was actually doing his imitation of a man almost demented with worry and distraction, really. It could be hard to tell, sometimes, that was all.

"Since we are alone together," she suggested, feeling the cumulative effect of drugs and excitement, fatigue and pain slowly but certainly begin to overwhelm her. "I'm blaming any snoring on you. I'm gone, Balkney. Sorry. Can't help it."

"I'll be here."

His voice faded into a twilight as sudden as it was profound, and ceased to impart any meaning.

She'd just gotten past the initial disorientation of waking after having fallen asleep under the influence of drugs when she heard Padrake come into the room, singing out cheerfully. "Up and at them, Jils, we've got a lift to catch. They're waiting for us topside, let's go, are you okay to walk?"

"I'm tired," she replied, her eyes still closed. "Not crippled. Where are we going?"

Someone had a hand at her shoulder, helping her up. Her entire body still ached, and her ribs—oh, yes. That was right. Her ribs. That had been earlier. The hand at her shoulders didn't feel particularly Padrake-like; Jils opened her eyes just as Rafenkel turned away to reach for a flask of water.

"Topside," Padrake repeated. "We've got to go. Emandis Station needs you, courier on stand-by, Chilleau's sent someone to speak for the Second Judge in your absence. Ready?"

"Stims," Rafenkel murmured to Jils, showing her a small handful of pills that Rafenkel was holding in the palm of her hand. "Garden-variety, caffeine and ferridose. It's only been a few hours. And you can sleep on the courier."

Rafenkel said they were stims. They looked like the common run of freely used stimulants; could be poison, of course. But she'd settled her mind, as she'd slept, on the subject of paranoia. Wasn't going to give in to it.

"Thanks." She took the pills—they tasted like common stims, too, that bitter metallic tang that was intended to discourage over-use and prevent accidental ingestion—and drained the glass of water. Could be poison in the water as well. On the other hand at any moment there could be an earthquake—Brisinje was still geologically active—the entire cave could collapse, and she'd be just as dead.

She'd survived an assassination attempt, maybe two, and these were her peers—Bench specialists. Maybe Nion hadn't been quite up to speed, and made careless by arrogance. The fact remained that Nion had tried to kill her, and failed, and if anybody else meant to they'd have had plenty of chances by now, and she was not—was *not*—going to surrender to fear. "Who's come for Chilleau, Padrake?"

She pushed herself carefully up to her feet, feeling wobbly but intact. Her ribs hurt. She didn't mind them hurting. Pain was useful—it reminded a person that she was still alive. It could be a distraction—but if she was going to Emandis Station she'd be sleeping on the courier, as Rafenkel had suggested. Padrake would be there as well, wouldn't he? He'd said "we." So that was all right, then.

"I'm not actually sure that Chilleau sent him," Padrake admitted. "But Arik's checked, and the Second Judge will accept the substitution, under the circumstances. Let's go."

What circumstances were those, exactly? That of having been almost killed, and having no intention of whatever sort of staying in this dangerous-to-her environment for a moment longer? Or the circumstance of the Second Judge being disgusted with her for her failure to find out who had killed the First Secretary, frustration that was trending unquestionably toward a conviction that Jils had done it herself?

She wasn't interested in thinking about things. She settled herself in the lift and waited for her mind to clear. As the lift started signaling the end of trip—nearing surface, arriving, clearing atmosphere, opening doors—did it occur to her that, in the combined distraction of her physical state and her concerns and reservations, she couldn't remember what answer Padrake had made to her question about who it was that Chilleau had found to send here in her place.

"Who are we meeting?" she asked Padrake, who had been resting himself with his legs stretched out and his arms folded as his eyes closed. "Anybody I know?"

He opened his eyes with an expression of mild confusion. "It's sure that you know him," Padrake said. "Vogel. Missing for months, just turned up in Emandis, but his affidavits are apparently in order or Chilleau wouldn't have agreed. I'd like to get the story on that, but we're not going to have time, I'm afraid."

The lift had stopped and cleared. The doors slid open. Karol. In uniform, no less, but he had his old jacket and his equally as old or older campaign hat in his kit or her name was not Jils Tarocca Ivers.

And also First Secretary Arik Tirom, frowning anxiously, who moved forward to offer her his hand as she exited the lift with the apparent intention of assisting her. "Dame Ivers. Very unpleasant for you, Bench specialist, completely undeserved I'm sure it goes without saying."

They smelled. They both did, ever so subtly, of soot and smoke. The launch-fields were still burning, then.

"Thank you." She couldn't be rude to Brisinje's First Secretary—not without good reason; she didn't have it in her to be rude for the sake of being rude. Not like Nion. "Academic now, sir. Karol. Where've you been?"

No, that wasn't right, she should ask *how have you been*. She should. He looked a little worn around the edges, and twenty years younger at the same time. *How've you been, what do you mean by disappearing and strewing cryptic little sketches hither and yon, what do you think you're up to*? She couldn't. She'd gotten close to Karol, they'd worked very well together, she'd felt his disappearance as a personal loss and a professional handicap, and she was in pain and not in a very moderate state of mind.

"Plenty to tell you about that, Jils," Karol said. "But later. I came to ask you to go to Emandis Station. *Scylla*'s taken Andrej Koscuisko, Emandis claims him for a native son and objects to *Scylla*'s misappropriation of valuable cultural artifacts, and the *Ragnarok*'s left the system so *Scylla* doesn't know how it can let Koscuisko off the ship without losing face."

And as angry as she'd been at Karol for more than a year, as angry as she was at him right now, she had to step back in the privacy of her own mind to admire the succinctness with which he gave her situation, problem, background, and probable unfortunate outcome to be avoided, by implication. They were good together. As agents, never as lovers, but there were ways in which she was closer to him than she'd been to any lover.

Even Padrake? Padrake was standing behind her with his arms folded again, and the vibrations in the aether from the Padrake sector toward the Karol direction were not in particular warm and friendly. Best if she avoided any comparison of degrees of intimacy in her mind while she was standing between the two of them.

"I can get him out," she said. "But only if he'll come. All right. I'll see what I can do." She knew things about Koscuisko's exact legal status with respect to Fleet that no one else around here might know. Verlaine had known, Verlaine had obtained a grant of relief of Writ for Koscuisko, but Verlaine was dead. The clerk at Chilleau who had processed it and the Second Judge might remember, but they weren't here; no Fleet Captain would let himself be dictated to by any clerk of Court, and the Second Judge had other things on her mind. "Have you been briefed, Karol?"

"First Secretary's given me the brief-packet," Karol said. "The rest of it I'll have to figure out as we go along. Where are we?"

"Ask Balkney." Karol might not know who was part of Convocation. "So far all I'm really sure of is that everybody thinks confederation is a sub-optimal solution and Fontailloe is out of the question, either as a temporary home pending re-architecture of Chilleau's administration or as the base of a newly elevated First Judge. Balkney can tell you, though. I'm prejudiced."

You can trust Balkney. Maybe Capercoy; maybe Rafenkel, and nobody else that she cared to name. Karol had already made up his mind about that, though. She didn't add anything more, and Padrake spoke over her shoulders to the First Secretary.

"Two days there and two days back, Arik, if we're lucky. With Vogel coming on line we could lose a few days while he gets himself calibrated, but some of the disputation can be settled in the mean time. I'll be back inside of five days."

Jils looked at him—what did he mean, he'd be back? Padrake tilted his head down to meet her eyes, and seemed almost to blush.

"You're to go on to Chilleau, Jils, once we're done at Emandis

Station. The Second Judge doesn't care to interrupt the process a second time."

No, the Second Judge didn't care to have Jils represent her in Convocation, not if she had anybody—anybody at all—to use instead. That wasn't quite fair, though. Karol was as good as she could have hoped to be, his only handicap his lack of immersion in the problem and its possible solutions over the recent months.

And who knew? Maybe that wouldn't be a handicap after all. Maybe a man who had not been inside the problem would see the way clear to a best possible solution that would otherwise escape them. She could hope. Since she was to have no further opportunity to contribute to the process, hope was all that she was to be able to do.

She was going to Emandis Station to mediate between Fleet and the Emandis home defense fleet on the subject of Andrej Koscuisko. She was going in person, to signify the importance that the Bench put on pursuing good relations between the two—and perhaps because she had the authority to tell a Fleet Captain what to do, but only if she was actually there. She was going to remind both parties that the Bench was still the ultimate authority. And she was going because the Second Judge had dug up Karol Vogel from somewhere and sent him to replace her as quickly as possible.

"Very well," Jils agreed. "Let's get going. But you owe me an explanation, Vogel." For too many things to be mentioned here and now. He knew it, too, because he nodded. And then gave a little start, the way he did when a thought turned a corner in his mind and burst into the forefront of his consciousness, surprising him.

"Oh. There's one more thing. Koscuisko's angry at me. But it wasn't my fault. It was booby-trapped. Ask him about it."

What could that possibly be supposed to mean—but Karol hurried past her into the lift, and the First Secretary followed. To effect the introductions, Jils supposed, not really required but necessary for the sake of the formalities. History was watching. What would history make of this mid-process switch-out of the personnel?

As if it mattered. No Bench specialist was under any false impression as to what history might say about them, if they ever turned up in history at all. To an extent it was a failure to turn up on any sort of a public record, if you were a Bench specialist.

"Let's go, Jils," Padrake said softly, as though in sympathy with the turmoil in her mind. Karol turned up out of nowhere, with some vague protest about Koscuisko. Something booby-trapped? What could he possibly be talking about?

What else could he be talking about, except the Record, the forged record whose patently false evidence was to have formed the keystone of the *Ragnarok*'s defense of its crew against accusations of mutiny and murder?

She was cold. She could wait. *Ask Koscuisko*, Karol had said. She'd do that. She would. "Let's get out of here," she agreed with a nod, and led the way out of the block-house to where the ground cars were waiting to take them to the launch-field, and thence to Emandis Station.

This wasn't a convocation, Rafenkel told herself, disgusted. This was a circus. The chair collapsing under Ivers might have been a practical joke gone awry—might have been. Might. But Nion was dead, and while there was unquestionably a harpoon in evidence, who knew for sure where it had come from or who had attempted to deploy it?

If she had been Ivers and wished to kill Nion, she certainly wouldn't have used the harpoon herself. She would have shown it, let Nion take it away from her, and then killed Nion in self-defense. She would have. There were problems with that approach, of course.

"Specialist Vogel," First Secretary Tirom said. He had come as far as the airlock but was not, apparently, going to address them in the theater; this wasn't a formal visit on behalf of the Bench, but an administrative errand. "Some of you may already know him. Chilleau Judiciary has agreed to transfer its proxy to Specialist Vogel, in Specialist Ivers' absence."

The first problem would be that it was a risk. Nion was younger than Ivers was and Ivers had been recently injured. If that had been the plan it was unnecessarily hazardous, as well as unnecessarily complicated.

"I know Vogel," Balkney said. "Who's to speak for Brisinje, though, First Secretary?"

The larger problem lay in what Ivers' possible motive might have been. Rafenkel couldn't come up with any that satisfied her. Why would Ivers want to kill Nion? It was understood that under the circumstances such a frame might successfully hold, since it was easy—well, relatively easy—to understand why Nion might have wanted to kill Ivers. But Bench specialists didn't waste killings.

"Padrake's expected return date is in approximately five days," Tirom said. That would be two days out, one day to resolve the problem, two days back. "We're hoping his absence doesn't delay things. Vogel can speak for Chilleau."

"That isn't why I came, though," Vogel said, suddenly. Maybe not suddenly—no, his tone of voice was temperate and his body language perfectly calm and respectful—but it surprised Rafenkel; and Tirom as well, apparently.

Vogel nodded his head in response to Tirom's questioning look, and continued. "I'm glad to be here to speak for Chilleau Judiciary. But I was actually coming to introduce a new element into the deliberations. There are nine Judiciaries represented here, First Secretary, and yet nobody speaks for a developing market that stands in as much need of regulation of trade and preservation of civil order as any. Maybe more."

Tirom was staring. Rafenkel thought she might be staring too. She knew perfectly well what Vogel was saying; she just didn't quite believe it.

"Launch-fields are burning," Tirom said. "Cities are in a state of anarchy. Entire economies have been thrown into a state of chaos. And you want to talk to us about Gonebeyond space? There is no Tenth Judiciary, Vogel."

Vogel shook his head. "No, First Secretary, you're absolutely right, there is no Tenth Judiciary. But there will be. The Selection we make will define Judicial policy for the next twenty to sixty years." Depending upon the choice, and the individual chosen. "The new First Judge will have to deal with Gonebeyond. The previous incumbent's policy is no longer appropriate in that respect."

The previous incumbent, that would be Fontailloe. Tanifer, who stood toward the back of the small crowd at the airlock, looked thoughtful to Rafenkel—but made no remark. None was required. They all knew that Fontailloe's approach to Gonebeyond had been to ignore it.

"It's not a formal position," Balkney said to the First Secretary. "But Vogel's right, as well. We haven't been putting as much weight on that element as perhaps we should, in light of the population expansion in Gonebeyond."

Yes, it had come up, and no, they hadn't made a tile for it. They had too many problems within Jurisdiction space, right here, right now, to care much about Gonebeyond, which after all presented no challenge to Bench markets. Still, Vogel's point was well taken. Gonebeyond was a market. And the new First Judge was going to have to decide how to deal with it as things changed and developed over the years.

Tirom seemed reluctant to accept Balkney's remark—though it was clearly reasonable, and nobody objected to it. After a moment he nodded his head, slowly. "Very well," Tirom said. "And on behalf of the new First Judge, whoever she may be, thanks for raising the issue, Specialist Vogel. There should be no real delay to process, I hope. If all of the Judiciaries represented are willing to hear Vogel speak on behalf of Gonebeyond space Brisinje has no objection."

And again, nobody spoke, so nobody was objecting, either. The small detail of Supicor being unrepresented with Nion dead went either unremarked or discounted as overtaken by events.

"Thanks," Vogel said to Tirom, at least in part to end an uncertain silence in which nobody seemed willing to speak up. "We'll get right on it, First Secretary."

Go away now and leave us alone, we've got work to do. Well, maybe not so much *leave us alone* as *we'll get back to it.*

Whether Tirom took it in the former or the latter sense Rafenkel couldn't tell. There were no hints in his tone of voice or his expression; maybe that was the answer right there, though. In whichever sense Tirom interpreted Vogel's words, he was not obviously offended.

"Thank you as well, Specialist Vogel. The Bench appreciates your willingness to step in at this time of need. You know how to reach me if you need to—" they'd all just tested that, with the crisis created by Nion's assault and death—but it was something to say, Rafenkel supposed. "Till later, then. I'll see myself up, yes, thank you."

He had brought Security with him, waiting in the lift-car; but they all knew what he meant. Once the airlock had closed, once the telltale on the wall had reported that the lift-car had begun its ascent, Capercoy raised his voice. "Let's all gather in the theater," Capercoy suggested. "We probably need to brief Vogel. I wouldn't mind a briefing myself."

"Two eighths," Tanifer agreed. "Time for a beverage break. What'll you take, Vogel?"

This was actually not so much a polite request as a subtle signal, *I for one don't feel like I need to watch this man every moment.* There was more than one kind of baseline being established, here.

"Bean tea if you've got it." Vogel's response in turn was similarly coded, *and I don't mind not watching you fix my beverage.* "Kavene if you don't. Thanks."

Bean tea, indeed. Some Bench specialists had an exalted notion of what was available in small scientific research stations. It was a pretty safe bet that there were few enough sources of bean tea in Gonebeyond. Rafenkel shook her head, and went off to open up the theater.

CHAPTER SIXTEEN

Resets

"We're operating at a disadvantage here, Vogel," Rafenkel said frankly, once everybody had assembled. The theater was much the same as the last time Rafenkel had been here—the table at the end of the room, the three ranks of chairs in tiers, the secured communications console behind the table on the far wall. "So we're just going to have to do our best and let things fall out where they may. I'll start. The Sixth Judge is for Chilleau. She won't have Fontailloe. She'll take Cintaro if she can't have Chilleau, but she'd rather claim it for herself than admit a confederation."

This wasn't what anybody had planned; they had wanted something more formal, more professional. Nion had taken that away from them. It was a good thing she was dead.

Balkney sighed. "Ivers has kept Chilleau alive to date, we've been unable to disqualify the Second Judge and move on. Haspirzak is willing to accept Chilleau, but not Cintaro. Haspirzak believes that any other choice will bring chaos."

"And Ibliss is afraid that selecting Chilleau will bring chaos, and wants to go with Cintaro," Rinpen added, with dispassionate regret. Maybe it was good to sit down and lay things out in plain speech. They'd been talking around it so carefully, so much, that the situation hadn't been as clear as it might have been.

Now that she sat in the theater and listened, it seemed clear to

Rafenkel that there had been little real movement on anybody's part since they'd got here. If anything, peoples' opinions seemed more—and not less—polarized than she remembered them as having been, when they had begun.

"Supicor believes she has a chance as a compromise consolidation," Zeman said. Zeman was here for Eighth, not Seventh, but there was no one to speak for Seventh and Zeman had spent the most time with Nion in discussion to date. "Eighth just wants an answer. Any answer. She'd even go for confederacy if she had no choice, but that's Delleroy's position."

Vogel nodded. "I can speak for the Second Judge," he said. "Though I'm sure Jils has been doing a better job of it than I can. I can tell you with a fair degree of confidence that Verlaine wouldn't have accepted any solution that included Fontailloe, and he didn't like Cintaro either. To the extent that I'm representing Gonebeyond as well as Chilleau, I'm going to have to insist on that."

Strong language. Bench specialists usually didn't issue ultimata, not amongst themselves.

"What's your reasoning?" Capercoy asked. "Verlaine's dead."

Vogel nodded. "Dead, but I can still hear him clearly enough. More Judiciaries and more local authority, he'd say. And Fontailloe was to blame for making torture an instrument of State, he'd say, and Cintaro was right there with her."

If this was true, Verlaine had been much more radical in his thinking than anyone had guessed—or at least more so than Rafenkel suspected. "Explain," she suggested. "More Judiciaries?"

Vogel nodded again. "Yes, each with a reduced span of control. It's all a control issue at the heart of it, obviously enough. And when did we start getting in to Inquisition in a big way? Fontailloe felt that it was losing control. Feeling the lines of direction and administration beginning to slip. Jurisdiction's gotten too big for nine Judiciaries."

Which would explain Vogel's reference to a non-existence Tenth Judiciary, Rafenkel supposed.

Balkney shook his head, as though there was something in his ear that he was trying to dislodge. "We're not going to argue dead men's protocols, Vogel," Balkney said firmly. "What's your agenda?"

"Chilleau," Vogel replied calmly. "Behind Ivers all the way. With a sideline in the future of Gonebeyond space. Whoever takes the

Selection is going to be presiding over a crucial point in the history of the Bench. We're going to need a Judge with the flexibility to face a whole new set of challenges. It's not going to be like it's ever been before. Gonebeyond's too big to just send in the Fleet and hope for the best."

So Cintaro was out, from Vogel's point of view. Because Cintaro wanted more prisons and more emphasis on the Protocols, and Vogel's point—to the extent that Rafenkel thought she understood it—was, among other things, that to open a dialog with Gonebeyond would take a Judge who was capable of understanding what had forced people to flee in the first place. No administration identified with the maintenance or furtherance of Inquiry was going to get very far in persuading Gonebeyond to consider any sort of integration into Jurisdiction space.

"Well, we knew from the start that the default solution was Chilleau if it could be done," Tanifer said. "Ivers and I had been discussing whether the Second Judge could be moved to Fontailloe. Supicor, I think we can all agree that Supicor wasn't going anywhere. Am I right?"

Nobody disagreed, so Capercoy spoke. "Down to Fontailloe, Cintaro, Chilleau," Capercoy said. "If it's not Cintaro, the Judge will very possibly claim a degree of independence, with all that that means. If it is Cintaro we over-rule the clearly expressed majority opinion, and that means even more of the same."

Capercoy didn't finish the thought. He didn't have to. They all knew where it was going.

They couldn't pass over Chilleau Judiciary—her administration couldn't hold the Bench together—but they couldn't select Cintaro, who would elect to respond by turning her back on the rest of Jurisdiction space. There was one solution that acknowledged the weakness in Chilleau's administration and minimized the damage that would be caused by a Fifth Judge deciding to make her own rules—

"Forget Fontailloe," Rinpen said to Tanifer. "Fontailloe is not going to happen. If we all work Chilleau versus Cintaro we may have a solution by the time Delleroy gets back. We can't wait any longer than that. We don't dare."

Tanifer nodded. Rafenkel was almost certain she knew what he was thinking.

There would have to be a newly promoted Judge at Fontailloe no matter what; and if it turned out that the confederacy model was their least-worst choice there would be a new First Judge at Fontailloe. Because all of the Judges would be First Judges, in their own jurisdictions.

If they were to be forced to consider confederacy after all, after all the sport they'd had with Delleroy on the issue, she was never going to hear the end of it from him.

"Taken?" Padrake asked, coming forward into the wheelhouse where Jils stood looking over the pilot's shoulder at his schematics. Two days from Brisinje to Emandis Station; Karol had come in person—so the *Ragnarok* was at least two days gone. Koscuisko was two days detained. She wondered—no, she didn't—what sort of a mood he was going to be in when they got there.

"That's what it says," she agreed, passing the briefing sheet to Padrake. "They pulled him out of the service house between late supper and early breakfast. Did it so quietly that there were no alarms for his Security, except that his Security had apparently already left by the time it happened."

Padrake leaned up against the bulkhead to one side of the entryway into the wheelhouse, shaking his head as he scanned the brief. "Protest from the *Ragnarok* against unauthorized detention of personnel assigned. Counter-argument from *Scylla* for overdraw of Fleet resources at depot, but it's the EHDF that runs that depot, isn't it? And the *Ragnarok*'s left without him, so they can't be that upset that *Scylla*'s got him. A little bit insulting, that, wouldn't you say, Jils?"

"It's better not to make any assumptions where Koscuisko is concerned," Jils said, shaking her head. "He's got his own standards. Some of which I like, and some of which make no sense to me. You might want to be sure you come with me, when we get there, I've heard rumors about Koscuisko's vocabulary that we may find substantiated. We're going to need a record, a heat-resistant one—"

"With respect," the pilot said. It was the same pilot who had brought her here from Chilleau, and she'd been under the impression that Ise-I'let had been anxious to get home; what had happened? "If you'd clear the wheelhouse, Specialist Ivers, Specialist Delleroy. Vector transit to calculate, Specialists."

The pilot's voice was firm and clear, but there was tension in it that Jils didn't understand. Karol always got a little unhappy about his vector spins, though—not because there was ever anything wrong them, just because it was the way that he was. Maybe the pilot had already done his calculations when she'd joined him at Chilleau. It didn't really matter why. He wanted them out; they'd leave.

"Sorry, Ise-I'let," Padrake said, straightening up. "Gone directly. Jils. I'll be in my cabin. Got a little bit of a technical problem to chew on."

Right. "You go right ahead." No, she didn't need his company, not in the same room. The bed-cabins on a courier were small. She had work to do. "Let me know when you have a moment, though, courier pilot. I have a question. Thanks."

Out. He didn't have to say it; the word lay writ large across the tension in the fabric of his uniform across his back. Something was eating at him. It was a good idea to leave people alone when they were calculating vector spins; she followed Padrake out of the wheelhouse and through to the middle portion of the corridor, where the bed-cabins were. Padrake's was across the hall.

Padrake closed his door behind him, with one last concerned glance at her as he did; she winked at him—she wasn't going to be fussed over, no matter how much of a guilty pleasure it was—and went to the small locker in her bed-cabin to pull out the data she'd been carrying with her since she'd left Chilleau. She left the door open. She was tired of feeling enclosed.

She hadn't gotten very far with it before. She'd just kept on starting, realizing she couldn't recall a word she'd read, starting again. She started at the beginning one more time, re-reading those long dry bits of ships going one way, ships going another. Cargoes. Passengers. Fleet movements.

There'd been a battlewagon at Ygau, and Fleet presence at several other vectors besides—Burig, Ktank, Upos, Wellocks, Panthis. She found that she remembered more than she'd realized; and was just marveling, again, at the casualty rates that the Terek Vector assessed against its traffic when the pilot rapped with his knuckles on the frame of the open door to announce himself.

"You had a question, Dame Ivers?" The vector calculation seemed to have taken it out of him; he was pale, which was not in the least attractive on an Emandisan.

Jils had to pull herself up out of the traffic at Terek and think for a moment. Yes. She *had* wanted to ask the pilot. "Thank you, courier pilot. Personal curiosity. You ferried Specialist Vogel from Emandis Station?"

The pilot shook his head. "From Imennou, Specialist. We've been lending a hand at the launch-field there, trying to handle the overflow from Brisinje."

He wasn't going to volunteer any information: discreet young man. A good choice, for a courier pilot. She'd thought his name was familiar; why was that? "I was interested in whether you'd seen Specialist Vogel before. I'd found a piece of paper in the exercise wheel on the way from Chilleau that appeared to have come from him, but I hadn't realized at that time that he was anywhere in particular."

The pilot smiled, very easily, very engagingly. "Specialist Vogel told me that you would be wanting to know," he said. "Yes. I'd seen him before, but he'd been acting as a port inspector at the time. Some weeks ago, and it was at Panthis, I think."

Miserable tanner that he was. A port inspector. Karol didn't like port inspectors; he took advantage of the role to act out everything he found objectionable in the breed, and sometimes she thought he had a little too much fun doing it, too.

"I hope he didn't make things too difficult." Though if the pilot remembered Karol he was likely to have reason.

The pilot smiled again: but there was something hurt and hungry creeping into his face that made Jils anxious for his sake. "It was a memorable occasion, Dame. He pretended that there wasn't anything wrong with our documentation, and that he was furious about it. No chance to kick up. Free liquor at Panthis for as long as we care to drink, kind of him, you know there's always something wrong with the documentation."

Yes, she did. And she knew exactly how Karol had played it. "Something on your mind, pilot?"

"You and Specialist Delleroy." The words came out in a bit of a rush. "I do my best not to overhear conversations that are none of my business, Dame. But I'd resigned myself to the fact that Andrej Koscuisko was gone and I was not going to get to see him, after all."

It couldn't be that the courier pilot had been looking forward to catching a glimpse of Koscuisko the way a man went to a zoological garden to see a venomous snake—or a botanical gardens, for that matter, to wander in amongst the poisons. There was some personal reason behind Ise-I'let's interest, Jils was sure of it; and chose her words with care, accordingly.

"If it's confrontation you had in mind I'll have to warn you." Not as though it would surprise Koscuisko himself. She wouldn't be surprised if he'd got bored with it, *you inhumane monster, you killed my father—my brother—my wife—my child—my friend.*

She could almost hear Koscuisko's voice, cold and clear and as cutting as ice for all the soft edge of some of his characteristically Dolgorukij diphthongs: *Yes, yours and those of better men than you, what do you want from me? An apology? It would be hypocritical of me to tender one, I am in the abstract sense sorry for your loss, but I decline to attempt to pretend to you that I did not enjoy it. At least probably. You can't expect me to keep your murdered dead apart from all the others, there were simply too many of them. Now do get out of my way, and if you wish to pull a knife, you will have to clear it with my Security.*

She shook herself with a little scowl, annoyed—too easy by half. The pilot was waiting for her to finish her thought. "You'd be best advised not to initiate a confrontation on board of *Scylla*. He used to be their chief medical officer, at one time. They might take it amiss. That, and one *is* expected to wait one's turn in line, and it's a prodigious long one."

"He is at Emandis Station?"

Had he heard her at all? Was he even listening?

She nodded. "Yes, on *Scylla*. In protective custody, I gather. My job is to get him off the *Scylla* without provoking armed confrontation between the Emandis home defense fleet and Fleet, and I think I have just the approach, too." The EHDF, that reminded her. What had Karol told her? Emandis Station claimed Koscuisko for a native son?

The pieces fell into place. Ise-I'let. She should have remembered. Koscuisko had lost a man at port Rudistal, a bond-involuntary who had been with him since his earliest days at Fleet Orientation Station Medical. Joslire Curran had been an Emandisan knife-fighter; that meant five-knives.

And at the point of his death, under honorable circumstances in the performance of his duty and by his choice to spare the Bench the

expense of rehabilitating him, his legal status had reverted to that of
a free man with full citizenship—and his name to the one he had
carried before his condemnation. Ise-I'let. The courier pilot was
related to Koscuisko's man, and in all likelihood meant to demand the
return of the knives.

"Souls under Bond have no families," the pilot said. "No contacts,
no communications. Nothing. But I've asked everywhere I've had any
chance at all, and from what I've heard Koscuisko didn't just restore
our honor and our position when he killed Jos. He loved my brother.
I loved my brother. We have things in common. I thought I'd missed
my chance to talk to him."

That was all very well and good as far as it went, but Jils wasn't sure
it went far enough. Koscuisko had peculiarities—"Excuse me if I'm
speaking of things that I don't understand," Jils said, as gently as she
could. "Does Koscuisko want to speak to you?"

Koscuisko was on *Scylla*. How could she promise this earnest
young man that he'd have his chance when she had no idea whether
Koscuisko would be willing to engage in a conversation?

The pilot nodded. "I heard from my family, Dame. They met him
at the launch-field in Jeltaria, and took him to the orchard. Then the
Ragnarok left, and they believed he had gone with them. My wife and
child have never touched the holy steel."

He shut up abruptly, as if he had said too much. Five-knives, all
right, Jils decided. That was between Koscuisko and his man's family.
It was none of her business.

"Dolgorukij value kinship ties, as a general rule." Whether
Koscuisko did was anybody's guess, but in many ways he was a
traditionally conservative Dolgorukij—his family was among the
more conservative of the great families, among other things. "I think
you have a good chance of seeing him." On shipboard only, of course,
in case there was an issue about the knives and Koscuisko decided not
to give them up.

Where were Koscuisko's five-knives? On board the *Ragnarok*,
which would mean gone? She had the feeling that given the apparent
willingness of the Emandisan to get sticky about Koscuisko, the news
that the knives had left the system without their escort would not go
over well. Would Koscuisko have taken them with him to visit Joslire's
family? She could hope. Traditional, and ceremonial-minded.

"These days I have been struggling with it," the pilot admitted. "It will be a great thing in my life. Thank you, Dame Ivers."

It was little enough to have done. Jils waved him away cheerfully enough, then turned back to her data. Wait a minute. The pilot had said he'd seen Karol at Panthis? She went to the door and put her head out into the corridor.

"Ise-I'let. Sorry. Tell me again. How many are some weeks, and had you ever seen him before that?"

The pilot had turned around when she called to him, and stood now in the corridor, considering her question. "Well, Dame. Let me think. I started Brisinje to Ygau to Terek, lay over in Sashama, then through Burig to Wellocks. That would have been about the time the First Secretary died, I think. We heard the news coming off Wellocks to Terek again. Then we were had a mission to Upos from there, on to Panthis, where Specialist Vogel came on." And left her a message. "So that was just before we went back to Chilleau on standard courier. Three weeks before I carried you Chilleau to Brisinje, Dame."

It was hard to follow the pilot's line of thought, but Jils could see the reasoning—rehearsing his travels, *if this is six weeks ago I must be in Panthis*. If Karol had heard about the death and started his own investigation he would have had time. If Karol had done the murder, though—

Now the door to Padrake's bed-cabin opened to reveal Padrake standing in the doorway with his collar and cuffs undone, a stylus in his hand. "What's going on?" Padrake asked. "Garrile to Nabmedor, Fellau and Warbay and cold Boglynn shore?"

No, Wellocks to Burig to Upos, and—Jils shook her head, annoyed. It didn't matter. She'd only been interested in the one piece of information. The pilot apparently recognized the reference, because he grinned; and then he sang—very surprisingly, but in a very nice voice really, in a middle register. "'As a boy, then a man, then a master of men.' Jetorix, anyway. With respect, Specialist Delleroy."

"You just go on back to the wheelhouse, my lad," Padrake said, with his accent as rich and plummy as it got only when he was drunk or being silly. "I've business to transact with this fair maid blithe and bonny. Away with you, now."

A very appealing smile, the pilot had. He bowed and turned and closed the door between the wheelhouse and the corridor; Padrake straightened up—his head dangerously close to the lintel of the door, he was a tall man—and cleared his throat.

"And now, me proud beauty—how are you feeling?" His voice returned to its more normal speaking tone as he crossed the hall to follow her into her cabin.

"Tired and irate," she said, consideringly. "And sore. So don't you get any ideas, my man. There is a time and a place for everything. And this is neither."

"But I'm an intelligence specialist," he argued, closing the door. It was not a large bed-cabin. It was even smaller with two people in it. Between the bed, the table with the data, and the two of them, it was fairly well filled as spaces went. "It's my mission to collect and analyze information. Tired? In what way? Irate, about what? Sore, exactly where, exactly precisely where, exactly precisely and uniquely where?"

Tired of watching her back and wondering about everybody who crossed her path. Irate and angry that she'd been attacked, twice, she'd had to kill to save her life and she could never stop herself from wondering if there had been another way around the problem that she just hadn't seen in time. Nion hadn't deserved to die for ambition. Well, maybe she had, and any Bench specialist displaying stupidity deserved the same—Nion had been stupid, incautious, overbold, grand-standing—

"Mostly my ribs." She was tired. She could use a little recreation. She and Padrake had been lovers before, and if anything his hawk-hooded eyes, his leonine mane had grown more decorative over the past few years. He'd always been a very attractive man, and there was a good deal of him in the appropriate places in appropriate measure, too. "Here."

He started to move, but then drew back, as though he had suddenly thought of something. "Oh. Wait. Rafenkel gave these to me. I'm supposed to try to get you to take some, how about it?"

Painkillers. She took the mediflask and looked at its contents. "Fast-acting?"

"No, I don't think so, sorry, standard issue—Oh."

Yes. Oh. She opened up the mediflask and shook out the standard dose, one each, repeat on the third hour until asleep or stupefied, whichever came first. She usually had a good hour, maybe more, or—with the condition of her body to consider—maybe less.

Taking the mediflask into the tiny lavatory she swallowed the dose with a flask-full of water to help it dissolve; and then she joined Padrake again in the bed-cabin. Handsome Padrake. Attractive Padrake. Padrake whose body already knew things about hers, whose body hers knew and wanted, again. Maybe she'd never entirely stopped wanting him. That had been one of the reasons that she'd put distance between them in the first place, after all.

"Mostly here," she repeated, pointing. Padrake took his cue; he put his arms around her, one arm laid carefully across her shoulders so that the arm that went around her waist did so on the unhurt side.

"Not here," he said, and touched his fingers to the hollow of her back where her spine lay in its channels. "Not here." Where her uniform fell from the waist to the hip, smoothing the fabric with all due deliberation over her backside to make absolutely sure that nothing hurt there. "Not here either, I hope, Jils. Let me know."

He wouldn't hurt. She didn't have to worry about him. She knew the fragrance of his flesh, and the soft touch of his body-hair and the way the muscle of his back and shoulders felt beneath her fingertips. She knew the taste of Padrake's mouth, and he remembered how to kiss her, too, just the way she liked to be approached with lip and tongue. He knew. She remembered. It was good.

She laid aside her troubles with a contented sigh, and surrendered to the pleasures of a careful hour spent between lovers who had history to cushion their caresses.

Later—Jils didn't know how much later, but it was later, she was blissfully relaxed and boneless in the bed, and her ribs didn't hurt at all—later he left her, standing up to dress and go back to his own bed-cabin. There was only room in the bed for one and one-half people, and Jils had to sleep either on her back or on one side; it left little room for Padrake. And he hadn't taken any pain medication.

One eye half-open, too lazy and asleep to turn her head, Jils watched Padrake dress, admiring his back. Those beautiful shoulders. The taurian power of his neck, the way the muscle tapered—not too much, he had a figure, but not too extreme a waist—down to braid into the strong set of his hips. Yes. A fine figure of a man. She closed her eyes, smiling.

When she opened them again it was because she had heard

something, and might have been alarmed had she not seen Padrake's familiar back. Still dressing, apparently, she had dozed off for mere moments. She hadn't heard the clicktone of a scroller at all, she'd heard him fastening his trousers, or something. The data was on the table, he might have accidentally nudged it, what did it matter? He was dressing, she was asleep. She felt wonderful. Wonderful. Hadn't felt this good since she could remember when.

She closed her eyes again and didn't open them till hours had elapsed, Padrake long gone.

"Tell me," Andrej said gently, tossing a token onto the pile in the middle of the table. "I hope to hear that things go well with you, Code?"

Code Pyatte had been one of the bond-involuntaries assigned when Andrej had served on *Scylla*. He considered the tokens in his array and discarded, rather more sedately than Andrej had. "It's been quiet, your Excellency. Quiet is good. I mean in specific quarters, sir."

There were other bond-involuntaries here in the small cabin, none of whom Andrej knew, though they'd claimed to know of him. Technically speaking they were on watch; he'd been under confinement to quarters since he'd struck the chief medical officer. What was his name? Weasel-Boy? No. Lazarbee. It was hard to sit with Code and know that there was nothing Andrej could do for him; he couldn't even tell Code that Robert had escaped. Code was under Bond, and would suffer for hearing the information.

"I understand." He knew exactly what Code was saying. Captain Irshah Parmin had kept his chief medical officer clear of special assignments, and Secured Medical as empty as possible. Andrej hadn't understood how careful Irshah Parmin really was about that, either.

It was another area of the life of a Ship's Inquisitor in which Captain Lowden, late and emphatically unlamented, had opened Andrej's eyes and left him wishing he'd remained half-blind forever. "Morrisey, your call, I think. Your Doctor Aldrai has a good name in circles, from what I understand, one of our best burn specialists if I remember?"

The other bond-involuntaries were not as much at ease with him as Code was, and there wasn't anything that Andrej could do about that. He couldn't send them away, not when they wanted to be here.

Chief Samons had already let him know that their eagerness to pull the duty had not pleased Doctor Lazarbee.

Morrisey—that was Efitt Morrisey, Andrej had heard Code call her by that name but he didn't care to push her comfort boundaries by presuming intimacy—grabbed a token and let it fly, with a confused murmur, "This troop—ah—begging his Excellency's pardon—" that Andrej let pass without remark.

It was hard. He remembered too clearly how a bond-involuntary could suffer out of simple confusion. And there was nothing he could do except to be as calm as possible, and notice nothing.

"Aldrai was all right," Code said quietly, waiting for his team-mate to make the next move. "She was willing to stay on, too, she liked the company. It seems that Fleet had other ideas. There were officers who were particularly interested in coming to work for *Scylla*, as the gossip has it."

Four-handed spanners was not an intellectually challenging game, but it didn't have to be. Andrej had never been good at cards. Dice, bones, stones, rollers he could manage with adequate skill and sometimes a fair degree of luck; cards he could deal in a very ordinary way, on a good day.

It had made him popular in school. Many people who might otherwise have had reservations about socializing with Dolgorukij aristocrats had discovered themselves perfectly capable of trying to take his money in a cheerful and convivial fashion, once they'd made up their minds that there was no unfair advantage on either side.

Andrej considered Code's careful phrasing while he studied his array. Why would someone want to come to *Scylla*? The command was a good one, yes, but Brisinje was a quiet Judiciary, or had been before the troubles had broken out. Safe, quiet, uneventful. "Perhaps someone felt he needed a vacation," Andrej proposed, picking up a token. If he could get three more in the same family he'd win the hand, for the first time all day.

Code shook his head. "That would be a reasonable supposition," Code said, with a peculiar weight on the word "reasonable" that made Andrej's ears prick up. "The officer claims to have been sent on a mission, as it were. Worked closely with the Bench specialist in Brisinje in the past, by his report. You didn't want to give me that token, sir."

Code lay his tokens out in array. Five. Seven. Nine. Eleven. Reefers.

It was a relatively modest array, to be sure, but it was a complete one; and beat any array-in-progress by definition.

"Name of all Saints," Andrej swore, without much rancor. "Some octave I may beat you, Code, but it is not going to be at any time in the near future. Look at this, look, I could have had such a nice series, really, it grieves me deeply."

Out of the corner of his eye he saw Efitt Morrisey almost smile before she remembered who she was and sobered, quickly, with a side-long glance at Andrej to see if he had noticed. He'd noticed no such thing. Code collected tokens from the table, sorting them out into the starting array.

"Pulled strings, and got into a comfortable billet?" Andrej asked, after a moment's sad contemplation of the hand he might have had. "I wouldn't have connected a Bench specialist with any kind of reasonable people, myself."

He had to be careful with that, because although he and Code had been close to one another once, it had been five years, and a man did not lightly suggest that a bond-involuntary had cast aspersions on the integrity of a Bench specialist.

"Just what is said by some, sir," Code replied. Code was thinking, too. If it was hearsay he could report it so that the officer would know that it was being said. "Posted here from the *Galven* at Ygau, possibly eight months ago, sir. Willing and eager to do his Judicial duty, but the captain has had no calls of his own and declined others."

Andrej thought about this, somberly, looking at the tokens in his newly distributed array. An opportunist. Chief medical officers who were eager to do their Judicial duty were either willing to do whatever it took to further their careers—at the expense of truth and mercy—or else they were sadists, people who gloried in the inflicting of pain for its own sake. People like Andrej Ulexeievitch Koscuisko.

"Our captain has always been an extraordinarily stubborn man," Andrej said, by way of reassurance. "The more he's pressed, the more he digs in his heels. Such men are very good to find in command. *Scylla* is lucky to have him."

Importune chief medical officers aside, Captain Irshah Parmin was a conservative man, and no supporter of the Protocols past their point of usefulness—which ruled out most of the apparatus. He had protected Andrej. He had protected the bond-involuntaries. He would protect them still. And because of Captain Irshah Parmin, Code had never seen the *Ragnarok*, not from the inside, not when Lowden had been in command.

"I'll tell the officer that the officer said so," Code said, with a broad grin in his voice and his eyes, and a little smile on his face.

It was a rebuke—a loving rebuke, Andrej realized—and smiled back, delighted. Code was telling him that he should be more polite to the captain than he had been. It was true that he had not comported himself in the captain's presence as a man truly appreciative of all that Irshah Parmin had done for him. To be scolded by Code about it was wonderful.

There was a signal at the door; one of the other Bonds went to see what it was, engaging the talk-alert. The talk-alert was on muted standby in token of Andrej's status as a man in confinement; that way he didn't have to listen to the administrative chatter on board.

"Bench specialist Jils Ivers, your Excellency." It was Chief Samon's voice, and it was strained. "With pilot. To see you, sir."

As if he had any choice, but the troop at the door did him the courtesy of waiting to be told. Andrej nodded, and the troop opened the door. Specialist Ivers, well. He hadn't seen her since the *Ragnarok* had broken out of Taisheki Station, and sent her away on the Malcontent's thula.

The door slid open. There was Chief Samons. There was Specialist Ivers. Chief Samons was pale, though, and Ivers looked a little tense herself. Andrej stood up to greet her; she had been the bearer of very good news as well as very bad news, in his life, and there was something about her personality that he found very appealing, though he had never given much thought to exactly what it might be.

"Your Excellency," she said. "I hope I find you well, sir. May I introduce to you Joslire Ise-I'let's surviving brother."

She stood aside from the open doorway, and the man who had been behind her stepped forward. Andrej felt the skin across his shoulders prickle as though his uniform were full of static electricity. It was a young Emandisan of average height and build, and average appearance too for all Andrej knew, but there was his brother in that man's face, and Andrej had and still loved Joslire with gratitude for the enrichment of his life and companionship in evil hours, and sorrow for his loss.

"I have been very anxious to make your acquaintance," Andrej said, and could hear a tight sort of longing in his own voice. "I am Andrej Koscuisko, and I loved your brother. But he only ever called me by my name once in his life that I know of, and we are family now, the old woman said. Will you come and embrace me, for your brother's sake?"

Code had risen from the table when Andrej had stood up, as had the others—it being a concession on their part to sit down with him in the first place. Now Code drew his fellows out of the way, to the side of the room.

The Emandisan, Joslire's brother, advanced with an uncertain step. "Shona," he said. "Shona, your Excellency. Very glad—to meet you—very—"

An Emandisan, and in the uniform of the Emandisan home defense fleet, which Andrej could recognize by now; an apparently responsible person, and with a wife and child. For one moment he was overcome. In that moment Andrej took Joslire's brother to himself, and kissed him for his brother's sake, weeping. He hadn't expected to meet Joslire's brother after all. He hadn't been prepared for this.

But Emandisan were a people of dignity and sobriety. Releasing the man Andrej stood for as long as it took for him to fumble for a white-square and wipe his face; by the time he had thrust the dampened cloth away, both he and Joslire's brother had recovered themselves to a degree, howsoever temporarily.

"And what brings you, Dame Ivers?" Andrej asked, a little breathlessly. He was in control of his emotions. Yes. He was. He would not look at Shona Ise-I'let, or he would lose his composure. "Grateful as I am to you for bringing this man to me, you must have some other object as well, I am sure."

She stepped across the threshold and into the room, now, keeping her distance as if unwilling to interpose herself. "Even so, your Excellency. You are a situation, sir, single-handedly creating a point of contention between local and Fleet authorities no less potentially dangerous for its unexpected nature. I have to speak to the captain on your behalf."

She was serious about the danger of friction, but not about his fault. He could tell. "Take your time." He was not yet in control of his emotions; he had to pause and wrestle with them. "If Shona will humor me I have many things to say to him."

She nodded. "You'll have plenty of time, your Excellency. On our way to Chilleau for your documentation." She must have seen the sudden realization in his eyes because she grinned at him cheerfully, ruthlessly. Oh. Yes. Documentation.

The captain claimed him for Fleet; Ivers knew he was one thin brief away from being a civilian. Ivers didn't know that the record was to have protected the *Ragnarok* had been destroyed, and the *Ragnarok*'s best chance for vindication with it. "If I may leave my pilot with you, Chief, I need to join Specialist Delleroy. I don't mean to keep the captain waiting."

Chief Samons bowed; Ivers went out of the room. Chief Samons waved two of the bond-involuntaries after Ivers, on escort, Andrej supposed; and turned her attention to the pilot. Shona. Joslire's brother.

"Not wishing to intrude," she said. "We all know you were close, sir. But there's others. Permission to let them know."

Others who had known Joslire, like Code, desperate not to be noticed and sent away. How could he send Code away? Joslire had been his man, bound to him voluntarily of his own free will. *Be of Koscuisko, forever.* But Joslire had been Code's team-mate as well.

"You will not mind meeting others who also loved your brother?" Andrej asked, just to be sure. He didn't need his answer in so many words; he could read it in Shona's honest Emandisan face. Shona was not Joslire. Shona was not. But, oh, he looked like Joslire, in ways that went beyond his face and form. "By all means, Chief. Send to us the people who were here. And Code, if it isn't cruel to ask, Code will help me tell about the night when Joslire died."

It would be good to talk about Joslire with other people who remembered him. So long as he was to have his time alone with this Shona Andrej would share the wonder of Joslire's brother with an ungrudging heart, and be glad for Shona's sake.

CHAPTER SEVENTEEN

Vector Transit

Yes, one ship was very like another, and yes, she knew where she was going. *Scylla*'s security escort was politeness, not guidance. The last time she'd been on board one of Fleet's cruiserkiller-class warships it had been the *Ragnarok*; the *Ragnarok* was a substantially newer ship than *Scylla* was, and *Scylla*'s corridors looked just that little bit more worn by comparison.

Scylla had been to war, as well, and the *Ragnarok* never had. There was no such wear and weariness about the uniform or carriage of *Scylla*'s crew, however. In that at least *Scylla* and *Ragnarok* were similar; both crews seemed to have a sense of their identity as a Command, and to care for how they represented themselves to one another.

At the one critical turning, the Security pointed her toward the captain's office rather than toward the officer's mess; Jils nodded—as much to herself as anybody—and took the indicated route. They didn't expect too many people, all together. Who did they really need? The captain, his First Officer most like, and the representatives from the Emandisan Home Defense Fleet that Padrake had stopped to collect from Emandis proper as she came directly on to *Scylla* to have a word with Koscuisko, if possible, before negotiations were begun.

Koscuisko looked well. She hadn't really given him much of a chance to speak, however, not springing his man's brother on him the

918

way she'd done; nor was she sorry. The relationship between Koscuisko and Joslire Ise-I'let had been unusual enough to excite remark from its beginning, and it had only gotten more interesting when Koscuisko had taken Curran's life and inherited Emandisan steel.

Padrake was waiting for her in the captain's office when she arrived, Captain Irshah Parmin standing up to nod politely as she entered the room. He was not a tall man, and very broad-chested; most of the hair had gone from the top of his head and much of it seemed to have migrated to his eyebrows, giving him a very owlish look.

His First Officer was taller than he was, sturdily built, and looked vaguely annoyed; *Scylla*'s chief medical officer was there as well—the man had no neck to speak of—and something gave Jils the impression that it was the chief medical officer, and not the three Emandisan officers, who annoyed Saligrep Linelly, Ship's First Officer.

"You made good time," Jils said to Padrake, by way of greeting.

Padrake bowed to her with an expression of satisfaction on his face. "I've borrowed one of Emandis' couriers, I like flying with the Emandisan, they're the best. I'll be needing to leave as soon as we have a satisfactory resolution." Turning toward the captain—who was waiting—Padrake raised his voice, and got down to business.

"Since we are at this moment involved in very critical negotiations at Brisinje, your Excellency, the Ninth Judge hopes that we will be able to resolve this dispute in an expeditious manner. We've asked Specialist Ivers to accompany us because she has a particular past relationship with the officer and his Command—although that won't do us as much good as it might have done, since the *Ragnarok* has left the system."

"Was allowed to leave the system," the captain corrected, calmly. "Gentlemen. Would you care to be seated?" This was directed at the Emandisan officers; who declined with shakes of their heads. Jils wasn't about to sit down. She'd been sitting down all of this time. On the other hand, her ribs hurt. Padrake had been very careful, and her ribs still hurt.

He couldn't have received instruction from the Ninth Judge, though, so he was making that part up; but it was well within his brief. She wouldn't have brought the Judge into it, but Padrake was here specifically to represent her, since the dispute was within her jurisdiction. Everybody played fast and loose with attributions from time to time, when the situation called for it. Everybody.

Padrake kept to his feet, maintaining solidarity with the Emandisan officers. "These officers state that Andrej Koscuisko is an Emandisan national," he said to the captain, clearly by way of opening his argument. "You removed him under armed escort and in secret from an Emandisan port, in violation of police protocols. He should be returned because you should not have taken him. You further have no authority over him in his capacity as the custodian of Emandisan five-knives."

Padrake couldn't exactly call Koscuisko a knife-fighter. Koscuisko wasn't, not in the Emandisan sense. Someone who could fight with knives, yes, he had proved himself there—and she'd seen him.

"I regret the inadvertent impropriety I committed when I had him escorted to *Scylla*," the captain said, choosing his words with evident care. "I had not anticipated that my action, an internal Fleet redirect, would be interpreted as disregard of the Port Authority in any way. This was a failure of judgment on my part for which I am prepared to apologize."

One of the Emandisan officers nodded; they'd been over this ground before, as it seemed. The captain wasn't finished, though, and the Emandisan officer apparently knew it—they'd been over that as well, clearly enough. "However, Andrej Koscuisko is a Bench officer with a sworn duty to the Fleet. Whether the Emandis nation wishes to embrace him as their own is not at issue. He is a Fleet officer. Now that his command of assignment has left the system this is the only appropriate place for him to be."

Jils could see the argument. Unfortunately she was sure that the Emandisan could see its implications as clearly as she could; the unspoken "where he can be protected" was shimmering in the air. She was going to need to intervene before people got even more annoyed with one another than they were already.

"You're holding him against his will," one of the officers said. "In an environment in which he is exposed to insult." This was said with a meaningful glance in the direction of the unprepossessing person wearing the rank of chief medical officer coupled with *Scylla*'s ship-mark; there'd been friction, there, Jils surmised. "He is the custodian of the knives. There is enough residual hostility over the circumstances surrounding the unprecedented enslavement of the steel in the first place, your Excellency. We earnestly advise the minimization of anxiety over their present disposition. His family is waiting for him."

His family? Koscuisko's family was waiting for him—that was true enough—but nowhere near Emandis Station. Jils shook her head to clear it: she had to concentrate. And her ribs hurt.

"Permit me to intervene," she said, firmly. "Specialist Delleroy is here for the interest of the Bench; we can't afford conflict between Fleet and the EHDF, gentles, especially now when we are experiencing such increasing difficulty with keeping the peace. I was asked to come to represent Koscuisko's interest, though he didn't send for me. There's something you don't know, Captain, with respect."

It was something nobody knew but her, and Koscuisko, and maybe someone who had prepared the documentation. The Second Judge knew, if she hadn't forgotten under the strain of events. Verlaine knew, Verlaine had known, but Verlaine was dead.

Yes, they were all looking at her. She took a deep breath. She was going to have to shave a few curls off of the truth to make this work; was she going to be able to pull it off?

"Before his unexpected death First Secretary Verlaine sent me to Koscuisko when he was home on leave to offer him relief of Writ, in acknowledgement of some irregularities surrounding his renewal of his term of service with Fleet. Koscuisko has executed the documentation, and I have witnessed it. He requested a delay in filing while the legal status of the *Ragnarok* was in question—a matter of loyalty to his Command."

And the legalities surrounding the custody and placing-into-evidence of a record with forged evidence. But those were details whose disclosure was not required under the present circumstances, and which could only raise more questions than they answered.

"Koscuisko is a citizen again?" the chief medical officer said loudly—the adjective "brayed" sprang to Jils' mind, but she suppressed it sternly. "Then he's in violation for wearing the uniform, isn't he? Told you, your Excellency, there's something about your precious Ship's Inquisitor that just isn't what it ought to be."

Professional jealousy could be an ugly thing. It was particularly ugly in its immediate incarnation. The captain exchanged a quick—frustrated?—glance with his First Officer, but said nothing.

"Specialist Ivers, surely we can all agree that any such charge would be very poorly timed as far as the cause of political stability is concerned," one of the Emandisan officers said to her, very seriously.

She couldn't afford to let him continue; she was afraid that he'd say something that would be difficult to overlook, something that might come too close to appearing to be an overt threat. She held up her hand, and the officer fell silent.

"Koscuisko is not at this moment a citizen. It is only a question of filing, however. So you see that there is no need for you to offer Koscuisko a berth on *Scylla* pending a new assignment, your Excellency."

There was a wistful expression on the captain's face for one swiftly fleeting instant. It was gone so quickly that Jils wondered if she'd imagined it. "If you put it that way, Dame Ivers, I suppose not," the captain said. "Pity. We could have used him. Damn fine battle surgeon, I never saw a better one."

"Better rid of him, your Excellency," the chief medical officer said suddenly; Jils started—she hadn't exactly forgotten that he was there, but she certainly hadn't expected him to contribute to the conversation after the captain's wordless rebuff.

The First Officer looked either annoyed or disgusted, or maybe both, but let him talk.

"He's a disruptive element, he is. Encourages insubordinate behavior on the part of troops assigned. If I didn't already know that he can do no wrong in your eyes I'd have some issues to discuss at Captain's Mast, but I will content myself with pointing out his history of resisting his Judicial duty."

Captain Irshah Parmin stood up. "Disruptive," he said, with a sort of an almost affectionate disgust in his voice. "He's always been that. True enough. Specialist Ivers, if this is so, why did it require your personal intervention? You could have told us so. He hasn't mentioned it."

The captain was not suggesting that she'd made it up—not exactly. Padrake clearly had a slight touch of the uncertainties himself, however; and Padrake already knew that sending her personally was partially due to the sensitivity of the situation, and in larger part simply a face-saving approach to the fact that she had to be gotten away from Convocation before someone else decided to attack her.

"Koscuisko has no reason to mention the matter because it is in process, not complete. Until his ship of assignment left the system without him, he was probably content to wait out the appeal, and now that the ship has gone I am the only person at Chilleau who knows where I have put his documentation."

She'd had plenty of other things to think about when she'd gotten back to Chilleau Judiciary. Koscuisko had told her to put off filing the documentation. Whether he'd be willing now to take the freedom that Verlaine had offered him and go home was probably going to depend on how he felt about the legal status of the evidence that the *Ragnarok* held in custody; she'd talk with him once they were on their way to Chilleau. Away from here.

"If Koscuisko is in transitional status you cannot hold him, your Excellency. And we would not wish to, either." The Emandisan spokesman seemed to grasp what Jils was trying to do, and was apparently willing to put the face-saving solution forward. "We will provide you with transport to Chilleau. We'll need to call up a fresh crew, the one you're carrying has been on extended assignment. It will be a few hours. Captain?"

"I can release him to the protection of a Bench officer without prejudice to Fleet's interest," the captain conceded. "Will you be wanting anything else?"

A formal apology for the disrespect he'd shown when he'd had Koscuisko kidnapped, Jils supposed. He had said that he was sorry.

"Quite all right, your Excellency, professional respect, not the time to indulge too nice a sense of prerogative. Thank you." The point had been made, Jils had to admit. The Emandisan Home Defense Fleet had protested against the Fleet's behavior, and Fleet had had to stop and consider and make concessions. They could afford to let Koscuisko go, now. "We'll send you some fresh crew, Dame Ivers. The pilot is not going to want to be deprived."

Indeed not. Shona Ise-I'let and Andrej Koscuisko clearly had a lot to say to each other. If he'd been able to get off Brisinje days ago, when she'd arrived, maybe none of this would ever have happened. Oh, she would still have been attacked; and would still have killed her attacker, if she'd been lucky.

"I knew his brother as well, Provost Marshal," the captain said, his voice much more relaxed and genial now that the sticking point had been resolved. "No, not nearly as well as his fellow Security, but I'm curious. Would it be an imposition? I'd like to meet the man."

The Emandisan officer's expression was frankly and honestly appreciative. "There's a lot of balance to be restored with that family, your Excellency. I don't think it would be unwelcome in the least. You honor the memory, in fact."

Well, this was certainly tidy. Padrake was looking at her with peculiar intensity, as though he was trying to decide whether she had made it all up; but he was clearly sensitive to the mutually felt desire to get clear of this awkwardness as soon as possible, and turned his attention to Irshah Parmin.

"Very satisfactory solution," Padrake said. "On behalf of the Ninth Judge and First Secretary Arik Tirom alike I thank you both, Captain, Provost Marshal, for your willingness to meet halfway. I'll just go get my kit and be on my way. Got to get back, Specialist Ivers."

Yes. It was better if they didn't try to say good-bye in private, he'd be delayed again. She'd forgotten how easy it was to exploit his presence for the comfort of her body. She thought the success with which they had revived their terminated relationship had surprised them both equally; a reprise of the quarrels they'd had years ago was not required to prove the wisdom of leaving well enough alone and going on, grateful for a brief but not to be repeated interlude.

"Good speed, Specialist Delleroy. Show Vogel no mercy, he deserves none." Where had he been, and what had he been doing? Bench specialists didn't say good-bye. It was bad luck. "If you would like to come with me now, your Excellency, you can ask Koscuisko for yourself. About his relief of Writ."

Padrake had been on his way out; now he hesitated, and looked back over his shoulder at her. "And then you can see yourself to Infirmary, Specialist," Padrake said. "You've wounds to see to, and the finest facilities in Fleet right here. Doctor—Lazarbee? Yes, thank you, your Excellency, Doctor Lazarbee. I appeal to you to see that Specialist Ivers does not escape this ship without a thorough going-over."

She swallowed back a snort of fond irritation. There were drawbacks to being with people who knew one a little too well. Karol would almost certainly have left her to report herself—and she would have done it, too.

"As soon as I've spoken to Koscuisko, Specialist Delleroy," Jils promised. *Now get out, you tiresome person.* "Captain, First Officer, Provost Marshal. Shall we all go?"

The change of crew would leave the courier empty, but the data that she had on board was secured there. It was safe. She would go to Infirmary; she wouldn't mind a status check. It had only been two days. She felt as though it had been just two hours, suddenly; but that was the way of it—the body waited until after the crisis had passed to relax and start to mend, and that was what really hurt. Mending.

Well, six days between Brisinje and Chilleau to sleep, and then it would be back to the wars for her. A few hours to wait for fresh crew from Emandis Station, a visit to Infirmary; and then she would have nothing more to worry about beyond who had killed First Secretary Sindha Verlaine, and why.

Nobody could afford to trust anybody—that was one of the rules of a Bench specialist's life. The other side of the balance on that one, though, was that Bench specialists above all needed to be able to decide who they were going to trust amongst themselves. Erenja Rafenkel didn't know Karol Vogel; she didn't think she'd ever met the man. She trusted Capercoy and she trusted Balkney, as far as that went. Balkney trusted Vogel, and Balkney had more reason than most to be cautious about where he bestowed his trust.

It was two days after Vogel had come down with Brisinje's First Secretary to vouch for him; and Rafenkel was practicing her knives on the black beach of that obsidian lake, while Balkney retrieved knives and Vogel did nothing helpful whatever.

She could see the floater from here, the observation station on the lake in which Nion and Ivers had fought. Tanifer and Rinpen were there, arguing Fontailloe against a deferred Selection. Zeman was observing, Nion was dead, Delleroy and Ivers were gone—so with Balkney and Vogel and Capercoy all here interfering with her concentration, the full complement of Bench specialists in Convocation was accounted for.

"That's interesting," Capercoy said to Balkney as Rafenkel set up her array for her next round. "Because he told me that he'd heard it could only be Cintaro, in the end. He told the Fifth Judge that, too. She believed him."

There was more light in the observation float out on the lake than there was here on shore; Rafenkel doubted that anyone in that room would be able to see what any of them were doing very clearly. Capercoy stood with his back turned to the float even so. Capercoy's body had the kind of roundness to it that combined youth and muscle; toothsome, the effect, or maybe she'd just been down here for too long.

"Didn't tell me anything," Vogel said. "Of course I've been out of the country. But it does sound like something may be going in an interesting direction here. You say your Judge won't have Chilleau or Fontailloe, Cape?"

Delleroy had been busy, for a man who hadn't joined them until Ivers had arrived. Much of his work had apparently been done before anyone came down here, from what they were beginning to piece together. Told Balkney that it was almost certain to be Chilleau. Told Capercoy that there was no question about the Fifth Judge's eventual selection—what could he have hoped to gain? Division? Whose partisan was Delleroy, if it was not Brisinje's?

"She might have done before Delleroy got to her." Capercoy sounded sour about it, too. "Inappropriate influence. Told her that in light of the questions about Chilleau it was her duty to take the wheel and guide the Bench through the stormy seas into calm waters. Persuasive man. He had me, too."

If she thought about it she could find it in her heart to be offended, Rafenkel thought. Delleroy hadn't approached her with any inappropriate suggestions. Or had he? What was that he had been saying about who should be running the Bench? "If she won't accept Fontailloe or Chilleau we have a problem," Rafenkel said, just in case no one had noticed. "Because a lot of people feel it should be Chilleau. No matter what its First Secretary had proposed."

Vogel let his breath out in something that was halfway between a snort and a sigh. "Verlaine was a visionary," Vogel said. "The frustrating thing about that is that he was ahead of his time, but only just. I had a lot of respect for Verlaine. Not that we didn't have our differences."

"You know," Balkney said to her, walking a set of knives from the target back to where she stood with her weapons laid out in array on a podium in front of her. "Vogel seems to have told me that Ivers didn't do it. Vogel seems to have told Ivers that I didn't do it. I haven't heard Vogel say that he didn't do it. Where *have* you been? Not out of the country. Not for all this time."

"Well, not offing senior Bench officers, if that's what you mean," Vogel said scornfully. "But no. Not out of the country for quite all of this time. I thought I'd take a vacation, if you must know, and if Verlaine thought I was off on an errand so much the better, but he didn't send me."

"Vogel's got a woman in Gonebeyond," Capercoy said to her. "Wanton red-headed wench, as I understand." The way in which Capercoy chose to phrase his remark made her laugh; she missed her grouping. Balkney shook his head at her, sadly, and went to collect the knives for a do-over. She considered completing the partial grouping with him in it, but stayed her hand.

"I'll have you speak respectfully of Walton Agenis," Vogel warned, his voice light but careful enough to put them all on notice. He was serious about this. "I'd heard Verlaine talk about Gonebeyond in the abstract. Have you ever been? Interesting things happening, out that way."

Balkney brought Rafenkel back her knives. "Concentrate this time," Balkney said. *Between your shoulderblades*, Rafenkel thought, but she didn't say it.

"Well, that's nice," she said instead. "What does it have to do with the selection?" Two days, and Tanifer couldn't see his way clear to give up. It couldn't be Fontailloe. Even if there hadn't been history against it, Chilleau with a seasoned Judge and a new administration was to be preferred to Fontailloe with a seasoned administration and a new Judge.

"Someone's manipulating judicial documents," Vogel said. "You've heard the rumors, I'm sure. Manipulating judicial documents is only the first step toward manipulating Bench policy, even authority. I'd have stayed in Gonebeyond and been happy if Fleet had taken Verlaine out, but I don't think Fleet did it."

That meant Vogel thought Ivers did it? No. Not Ivers, not Balkney. "We're just not getting a piece, somewhere," Balkney said, stepping well clear of Rafenkel's line of fire. "Frustrating. I'm having that just-out-of-reach-solution feeling. I hate that."

"Analysis," Capercoy suggested. "Speculation only. Verlaine was killed to prevent him from implementing his proposed reforms, assumption one."

"Or that's just the obvious motive and it had nothing to do with Verlaine's reforms," Rafenkel said, weighing the knife in her hand. "The immediate effect is to put the selection on hold. Verlaine's reforms may still be adopted by the new First Judge, whoever she is. Verlaine's murder cripples Chilleau."

"With Cintaro the benefiting party," Capercoy agreed. "But Cintaro had made up her mind to not winning."

"You said that Delleroy talked to her," Vogel reminded Capercoy. "In what context was that?"

Capercoy was silent, thinking.

Rafenkel threw the knife. One. Good hit.

"Setting up Convocation." Capercoy spoke slowly, clearly concentrating. "She didn't have much of a mind about it before, willing to step into the breach but not about to defy the majority call. It could have been a subtle long-term plot, of course."

Balkney apparently didn't think so. "Cintaro wouldn't have been able to predict the convocation. If Cintaro had done it, she'd have laid claim to the title by default a lot sooner than this. Fleet's done its best to milk the Bench dry for privileges and tax revenues, but they'd have made their move if it had been a Fleet plot. Same reasoning."

This was the sort of random-fire exercise that could lead to breakthroughs or a dead wall. Rafenkel knew which one she felt they were heading for. "What else had been going on around there? Apart from the obvious. Verlaine's reforms were a threat. But he would have had to negotiate them."

"No, Bench specialists would have had to negotiate them," Balkney countered. "As always. It doesn't matter what the Judge gets up to, it's the Bench specialist who gets stuck with the work. That's the way of things."

Rafenkel's knife went wide of target again. Vogel made a show of moving carefully up-range; she ignored him. "Bench specialist privileged model," Rafenkel said, almost to herself. She hadn't thought about it, not like this. "What would we usually do? Step in, wouldn't we? Help the new incumbent out until he had his feet underneath him?"

"But Jils couldn't do it," Vogel said. "Especially after she discovered the body, she was the obvious suspect. And I was out of the country. Jils had a murder to solve. Chilleau would need help from someone else."

"Help or annexation." Capercoy sounded as though he wanted to be sick to his stomach. "Delleroy's due to move on, he's been here five years. Brisinje is quiet. Vogel was gone, and Ivers had worked with Delleroy before."

It was a huge and horrible accusation. And there was not a shred of evidence to support it. None. "So he's been preaching confederation because he's sure it'll fail?" Rafenkel asked, dubiously. "And doing it wrong, because I'm convinced?"

"Working with Cintaro so he can be the man to manage that," Balkney said. "The man of the hour. But it's all supposition. Doesn't change our immediate task."

He was looking at something. Turning her head, Rafenkel saw the debating party on its way out across the lighted causeway between the observation float and the shore. Since Nion's death they had all gone into the observation float together and left it as a group.

"Cintaro's determined," Capercoy said, one last time. Just in case they'd gotten distracted, Rafenkel supposed. "I don't know whether Delleroy could manage that. Maybe he can. But it'll come to shooting."

As ideas went, the suggestion that Padrake Delleroy, and perhaps some others who had been heard to speak to the issue of privilege and Bench specialists, was responsible for the death of Sindha Verlaine was new and terrible and too convincing to be summarily dismissed. But Balkney was right. They still had a primary mission that was independent of who had murdered Verlaine and why. They still owed Jurisdiction space a solution to the problem of Selection, the best solution they could find.

Delleroy would be back inside of three days. With Zeman and Tanifer and Rinpen out of debate, they could all gather in the kitchen. Vogel could regale them with stories of the Langsarik fleet in Gonebeyond. They could criticize each other's eating habits, and keep an eye out for pointed daggers falling from the ceiling or chairs splintering into spears or hand-harpoons appearing in the starchies where they had no business being.

"Let's eat," Rafenkel suggested. She took the knives Vogel returned to her and wrapped them up in their case for safe-keeping. Three days from now, and Padrake Delleroy might have some questions to answer.

In the particular Emandisan sub-culture in which Shona had been raised, the dead weren't much spoken of except as they served as anchors or reference-points in history and kinship; *in your great-grandfather's time*, or *she's your sister's daughter-in-law*. When a man needed the companionship and the advice of his dead, he went to the orchard and sat down beneath a tree and meditated.

Shona himself hadn't had that opportunity, no; the first years of his life had been spent in poverty and isolation. He could see, now that he was a man, how kith and kin and complete strangers had taken what quiet steps they could to better, soften, smooth the family's plight—even at risk of sanctions themselves, on occasion.

He had not been allowed to enter the family orchard until he had carried Joslire's ashes there and held the container while his grandmother had parceled Joslire out amongst the trees. To fruit, they needed minerals and organic compounds found in the remains of dead animals, and all of the trees had fruited in the following year.

It had been an additional sum of money, quite a substantial one, because the fruit from a family's orchard was held to impart some of the strength of the family itself, and sold at a premium comparable to proprietary pharmaceutical drugs. It had been just one more wonder in a year full of wonders, because before the year was out the government had fallen and the orchard walls had been restored at the administration's expense.

He'd been too young to understand what they meant to do to his brother when they had arrested Joslire. At that time he had been more immediately affected by the execution of his other brothers, his father, his uncles; later he'd understood that a clean killing had been merciful, compared to the imposition of the Bond. He remembered rather little about Joslire. Joslire had been away from home for most of Shona's life anyway; the discipline of the knife-fighter did not account for family ties.

But these people remembered his brother. It was more than just the chance to meet Andrej Koscuisko at last; more even than finding in Koscuisko no shimmering madman with an obscene appetite and the curse of the truth-sense upon him, no demonic spiritual entity whose glance could wither babies in their mother's womb, but an ordinary officer—perhaps an extraordinary officer, but an ordinary man—who felt his emotions keenly, and who had loved Shona's brother so much that he was prepared to love Shona as well for Joslire's sake. More than that.

There were people here who wanted to talk to him about Joslire. Officers; crew. The captain, the First Officer, the chief of Security. One of the bond-involuntaries on board had known Joslire and the others had heard about him. The medical technicians in Infirmary, where he had gone with Specialist Ivers at her suggestion possibly for just that reason, remembered Joslire. Some of it to be sure was just the natural instinct of good-hearted people to fondly reminisce about the dead, but that fond reminiscence was exactly what was left unspoken and private, among Emandisan.

When the time came to leave Shona was anxious to get away. He needed to be by himself for a little while to rest and store up all of the things he had been told, so that he could tell them in the orchard where his child could hear when his child was old enough. The provost marshal and the Port Authority's representatives had commended him to his duty and left; Koscuisko, Ivers, the new crew, they were all on board of the courier, and free of *Scylla*'s maintenance atmosphere at last.

It was a trip that Shona had made before—ferrying Specialist Delleroy—but this time it was not his responsibility to do the vector calculations, so he only went to the wheelhouse out of habit, really. And because his heart was too full to speak further with Koscuisko just now. The pilot that Emandis Station had sent was an older man, Nairob; Shona knew him, if not intimately, and greeted him with a cordial salute as he stepped across the threshold from the corridor.

"Pleasure to be carrying," Nairob said cheerfully, his hands on his boards as he ran his baseline calibration. They were clear of Emandis Station; "Four hours to the exit vector, and then Chilleau in four days after that. Enough time?"

Shona opened his mouth to confirm that supposition, but thought again. Four days from Emandis Station to Chilleau Judiciary meant shaving a little more than two days off the usual transit by taking Emandisan to Chilleau direct, which could only be done with a courier but was only seldom if ever attempted by larger craft—there was a risk involved.

Any time a man made a vector transit there was a risk, risk was a fact of life, but Chilleau direct—if the calculation went wrong they could be killed, yes, there was a chance, but they could be worse than killed. They could be lost. Lost, killed, it made little difference to most people, but Andrej Koscuisko was traveling on the courier this time— and Andrej Koscuisko was carrying five-knives.

They were Joslire's five-knives. If they were lost in a vector mishap it would be the end of a line of direct transmission that went back to the days of open-fire forging in the desert. Koscuisko was a man, but those knives were part of what it meant to be Emandisan. It had been a crime to ever have let them leave Emandis, a crime for which the government that had persecuted his family had been punished. To put the knives at risk would be worse than a crime: it would be a betrayal.

"No." He couldn't do that. It was no fault of Nairob's that he made the suggestion; Shona was personally notorious for taking slightly riskier approaches and getting away with it. Nairob was only doing as he not unreasonably expected Shona to have done in his place. "Let's take the slow transit just this once, Nairob. More time to talk. We've got knives on board."

The expression on Nairob's face changed from one of mild confusion to one of moderately horrified understanding. "Knives," Nairob said. "You're right, Shona. Six days it is. Dar-Nevan to Brisinje, to Chilleau via Anglerhaz."

Shona nodded. "We'll be bored," he said, with gratitude for Nairob's quick comprehension. "Or maybe your people will be bored. But we won't be sorry. Thanks, Nairob."

He knew where Koscuisko was—in Delleroy's bed-cabin; he knew where Specialist Ivers was, too. It was an unusual feeling to be a passenger on the courier rather than its pilot; but he was a passenger, and he was going to take advantage of the privilege to go and lie down. He had six days. He had time.

When he got home he was going to write down everything that he could remember, and then he'd go and tell it to the trees.

"I wasn't sure you'd go along," Ivers said. She didn't want to play cards; she claimed she had work to do and she probably did. She was who she was, after all, while Andrej himself wasn't. He was what he was, yes, but as to who he was—that remained open to debate. "I appreciate your willingness to contribute to a non-violent solution."

He shook his head. Unlike Specialist Ivers, he had nothing to do, nothing whatever; his personal effects were on board the *Ragnarok*, and who knew where the *Ragnarok* was? He wasn't sure he wanted to.

Scylla had provided him with appropriate uniform, clean linen; but as far as new translations of the corrupt and confusing text to the controversial "Apiary" section of the story of Dasidar and Dyraine went, *Scylla*'s on-boards had had nothing to offer. That was hardly surprising.

The work was still too raw and unpolished; the Autocrat had yet to authorize its release, nor would she until and unless a consensus could be reached on whether Dasidar had slept in the meadow in the summer sun dreaming of the sweetness of Dyraine's lips, or had simply broken open somebody's skep to rob the bees of honey to sweeten his drink.

Andrej had his own opinions. Stealing honey might well be less noble an occupation than dreaming of lost love, but Dasidar had been starving all throughout the "High-mountain-song," and a man who didn't have the sense to eat when he was starving fell a few pegs on the estimability scale, in Andrej's mind.

"I've no choice, really." He was sitting at the tiny work-table in his tiny bed-cabin with a recent issue of proceedings from a conference at the surgical college on Mayon. The controversy of the day was whether surgical interventions that remediated the results of simple aging were too obviously reasonable to be considered twice, or an affront against nature and religion and morality and the dignity of persons needing but unable to afford such interventions to address deficits resulting from poverty, illness, or trauma. Andrej was not much interested in it. "My ship's gone off without me. And Vogel has probably told you about the Record. So you see."

No, she didn't see. Vogel hadn't told her. In which case Andrej wondered whether he should have, but it was done now. "No, your Excellency." She didn't need to call him that; but it was the title appropriate to his civil rank, as well as the military or judicial rank he was ready to surrender. "Karol said something, but I wouldn't have connected it. Where did you find him, anyway?"

She was sitting opposite from him at the table, which was so small that their knees periodically touched. She was leaning just the slightest fraction of a little bit. The tech on *Scylla* had told him that Ivers had a genuinely nasty scrape all up on one side of her rib-cage, and scored bone hurt—especially ribs, because they were always moving when a person didn't expect them to be.

"It wasn't my idea. I don't think he likes me." Though Vogel liked him well enough, or disliked him little enough, to have covered up the murder Andrej had done at Port Burkhayden. If he started thinking about that, though, he might accidentally say something about it. "My cousin Stanoczk came with letters for me. Vogel arrived with him."

The Malcontent wouldn't be interested in the controversy at Mayon either. To a Malcontent the solution would have been obvious: let those who wished, and could afford it, purchase such services at a premium, to fund the surgeries for those whose need was not a matter of relative convenience and who could not otherwise afford to seek healing. There were ways in which life made sense from the Malcontent's point of view. *Let all souls under the Canopy of Heaven contribute what they can, and be provided what they need.*

"Did he say anything about where he'd been, or why he'd gone?"

Andrej thought about this. Could he answer it without compromising himself? "He told the captain that he had evidence of the subversion of the Judicial process to accomplish individually motivated acts of vengeance not sanctioned by Judge or required for the upholding of the Judicial order." Yes, that was right. Vogel had said that to ap Rhiannon. "Then my disgusting cousin told him that there was a Record that contained false evidence in the custody of the *Ragnarok*. He wanted a look at it."

She wasn't saying anything, waiting for him. He sighed. "Which he was granted. The Record blew up, Specialist Ivers. We lost one of the surgical imaging sets, which was annoying because you see nobody had mentioned to Medical that one was to be borrowed. The Record is gone. The *Ragnarok* is judicially naked. And ap Rhiannon does not like me either."

Was it just him, or did he sound as though he was whining? Yes. He was whining. He shook his head at his hand lying on top of the table, discouraged.

"That's good," Ivers said. "You're off the hook. Security has taken off for parts unknown, your ship has gone after them, and the record no longer requires the presence on board of a Judicial officer to preserve its legal integrity as evidence. You can go home."

Except that his Security had gone off to parts unknown and the *Ragnarok* had gone after them, and the ship had no Judicial officers on board to give legally valid evidence of what he knew about the motives and actions of the captain and its crew.

Oh, and the fact that he longed for the environment he had believed that he sought to escape, addicted to the pleasure that the beast intrinsic to his being had learned to take in the suffering of captive souls. He could go home and hang himself, and if he was lucky it would be before anybody offered to show Anton Andreievitch some tapes.

She apparently misinterpreted his abstraction, because she added a gently voiced "Does he remind you very much of Curran?"

He knew exactly what she meant, though it was hard not to smile at the turn her questioning had taken. "Joslire has been dead for many years." He had no wish to embarrass her. "I'd forgotten how much I missed him, and Shona—I beg your pardon, Courier Pilot Ise-I'let— is not so much like him in appearance as in manner. I know that Joslire is dead, and to see a man out of the corner of my eye who moves in the same way is disconcerting."

In fact there were ways in which he could have wished that he had never met Joslire's brother, because it freshened his awareness of bereavement. The pain was older now, though. The ache of it was familiar enough to almost be a comfort in itself. "And he is his own person, which is helpful. Also I have much to tell him about his brother and the debt I owe. Six weeks would not be enough time for that."

Six days in transit, the pilot had said. Andrej wondered whether the *Ragnarok* was off vector, wherever it had gone. He wondered if his people had arrived in Gonebeyond, and what welcome they had found there.

"When he approached me first I thought he meant to confront you," Ivers said, rubbing at the back of her neck with one hand. She was clearly weary, but was being difficult about medication. In that way she was like her compeer Vogel. These people simply lacked a basic respect for pain and its effects on their own bodies, and as a doctor Andrej could not approve. "Took me a moment to remember. And you did kill his brother, after all."

People did not need to keep reminding him. He knew what he had done. He had been there, she had not. "Begged him to stay," Andrej said, remembering. "The Captain had told me that he had petitioned for revocation of Bond. He might have come home a free man, and known his brother. He would not agree."

"Loved him, and killed him anyway?" she asked. "My apologies for the intrusion, your Excellency. I should get back to work."

Yes, it was an intrusion; yes, she owed him an apology. But on the other hand she had always been honest with him, as far as he knew, and had held up her end of it when he had asked her not to file the documents that would have taken him away from the *Ragnarok* so long as he could do it any good by staying there. He would tell her. Somebody needed to understand. No, somebody else; the Emandisan seemed to know all that there was, as it seemed to Andrej.

"Killed him because I loved him." He hadn't wanted to. He could have made Joslire stay. It had been in his power, even his authority, to do so. And had he denied Joslire for his own selfish reasons his shame would be even greater than it was already. "It was his wish. To have done less would have been to dishonor the service he had done me. Not despite, Specialist Ivers. Because."

She should understand that, if anybody could. On the other hand in her line of work perhaps one of the reasons for avoiding personal ties was precisely to avoid a conflict between duty and devotion. She nodded, as though accepting his assertion without necessarily understanding it; and left the table to go across the narrow corridor to her own bed-cabin. She had data to examine.

In a few hours they would be dropping off vector to make for Anglerhaz out of Brisinje space, and then to Chilleau. Shona was giving the crew a hand, in between talks, fleeing to one chore or another as the weight of memory and reminiscence overpowered him and Andrej alike, one in receipt and the other in transmission. Andrej wished that Robert could have been there. There were important ways in which Robert and Joslire had been as close, or even closer, than Joslire and Andrej, and there were things about their life outside of their officer's company that Andrej knew nothing about.

But that had gone as Andrej had desired it to do, and Stildyne had gone with them. With them they'd taken his last credible excuse for wishing to remain with the *Ragnarok*. There was nothing left for him on ship-board any longer but duty and honor and the welfare of people to whom he was indebted.

He had no way of following his ship, no way of rejoining the *Ragnarok* now. Ap Rhiannon had won. There was nothing left to him to do but to go home, and be damned.

Jils Ivers closed the door to her bed-cabin and sat down at the table, ignoring the aching of her body with grim determination. She was being sent back to Chilleau. She needed to get away from the claustrophobic intimacy of Convocation, but she had no prize to take back to Chilleau with her.

She'd headed off an unpleasant confrontation between Fleet and Emandis Station, yes, she was escorting Andrej Koscuisko to Chilleau Judiciary to be relieved of his Writ at last, but he wasn't entirely happy about that. Nothing had been solved. The *Ragnarok* was gone, not vindicated, and if she had been Jennet ap Rhiannon she would not be coming back at any time soon.

She had no news of the Selection, and was no closer to solving the problem of Verlaine's death than she had been when she had left Chilleau eighteen days ago. As a Bench specialist, she had learned early in her career that if she tried to judge her impact on the world in terms of success or failure she would fall into error; it was sometimes as important for the good of the Judicial order that she fail as that she succeed.

But she was tired, and losing hope. There had to be a solution to Verlaine's murder, but was she ever going to see through to find it? She'd failed. Had failed, was failing, and could not see anything ahead of her but failure in the future.

It wasn't a good feeling; nor was the sickening sense of futility and familiarity that she experienced when she opened up her locker and took out the data that she'd carried with her from Chilleau to Brisinje to Emandis Station, and now back to Chilleau again.

She'd at least put the first part of her analysis behind her. She'd scanned the first portion of this traffic record so many times that she almost felt she could write it from memory, now. Traffic incoming and outgoing at Wellocks, where the saboteur had successfully destroyed all of the records on site and only the presence of the Jurisdiction Fleet Ship *Shikander* had kept order for the crucial hours between the discovery of the destruction and the resumption of normal operations. At Burig. At Upos.

The traffic on all adjacent vectors, some of it just there to provide an index in magnitude of activity, some of it maybe holding information. Panthis. Ygau. Terek. The casualty rate on Terek before, during, and after, as aggressive young pilots in expensive couriers gambled their lives against bragging points for speed and daring and against each other, Pintabo and Mirag, Fleet's adjutant courier service, desperately poor family-owned ships trying to make delivery premiums, home defense fleet and Combine ships and—

Home defense fleet? Emandisan home defense fleet. Jils scrolled up eight and sixteen views on her data reader, confused. How could she have missed that? The pilot was identified, as well as the craft and its class and cargo; she'd come out with Ise-I'let on the courier. This courier. She would have noticed it on her way to Brisinje. Had she not gotten this far before Karol's note had distracted her?

It must have been. It wasn't the sort of thing a person would overlook. There it was, plain as day, Shona Ise-I'let had been on the Terek vector outbound from Chilleau the day after the murder had been discovered, a day and three-eighths after it had been done. A good pilot in a fast ship could get from Chilleau to Terek in so long if he pushed it, though it wasn't what the vector authority would assume.

Except she clearly remembered some of the ships further down the manifest, partially because one of them was named after a politician that Jils despised. She remembered that. She didn't remember having seen Ise-I'let's courier in the data. She had to have gone right past it.

She'd been over the same data at least three times, on her way to Brisinje, at intervals during her stay in Convocation, again on her way from Brisinje to Emandis Station. She hadn't missed it. She wouldn't have missed it. She was stressed and distracted and unhappy, but her brain hadn't stopped working, she'd have seen it and taken it up to ask Ise-I'let what he'd been doing—who he'd been doing it for, exactly—

Standing up suddenly Jils felt the pain in her ribs that reminded her of the fact that she'd sustained a painful if superficial wound even before Nion had tried to kill her. She had to fall back to lean against the wall to catch her breath. She hadn't seen it. So it had not been there. Someone had tampered with the data, but the data was protected, it had its own secures, who could have gotten the data to open itself to be read, let alone managed to insert a record without the data-reader itself realizing that something was wrong?

She'd kept the data in her locker at convocation. Anyone might have gotten access to it. Anyone. Nion, perhaps.

But she'd looked at the data on her way to Emandis Station, she'd been looking at the data when Ise-I'let had come back from the wheelhouse to talk to her, and if that line of information had been there then she would have put her finger to it and asked him then and there. She hadn't done that. So that line of information hadn't been there.

It had been added to her data between the time she had carried it on board, and now. There was only one person who could logically have done it, who had the skill and the specialized knowledge and the daring to do it, but Jils couldn't stand to think of what that meant.

There was a way to find out. Picking up the data reader she opened up her door and stepped into the corridor to signal at the opposite door, to see if Ise-I'let was in there talking to Koscuisko.

CHAPTER EIGHTEEN

Smoke and Clarity

Koscuisko had invited him in almost eagerly, and closed the door—out of respect for his privacy, Shona supposed, and was grateful. He wasn't sure how he felt being so close to the man in such a small space; whether it was knowing who Koscuisko was, or knowing that Koscuisko wore the knives, or what, Shona didn't know, but it was there. This man was to be watched and warded. He was dangerous. He meant no harm to Shona, of that Shona was convinced; but there it was. Koscuisko had the ghost of the wolf in him. Joslire must have seen it, Shona decided; and known that Koscuisko was fit to wear Emandisan steel.

"No," Koscuisko said. Koscuisko had a bottle on the table, two glasses; Shona had accepted the offer of a drink politely, but hadn't taken more than a few sips. Koscuisko's cortac brandy was a taste not commonly cultivated among Emandisan. The bloodlines lacked the ability to metabolize the poison in the drink. An Emandisan could share a sociable glass if he was very careful and took no more than a fraction of the flask, but if he forgot himself in a misguided fit of camaraderie after sunset, he would be deathly ill before the sun rose in the morning.

Koscuisko had to know that. Koscuisko did not press Shona to drink, and when Koscuisko poured for himself and tipped the bottle to top up Shona's drink he let the gesture go with a clink of glass to glass each time, and did not raise the level in Shona's glass by so much as one drop. It was only the ritual, for Koscuisko. Shona was content to sit and taste the brandy in small sips from time to time, and listen.

"No, we never really talked about that. I suppose I could have asked him, but I didn't want to ask him, because if I did he had to tell me. It didn't seem that it could possibly be something he would wish to discuss. When he mentioned any family it was too obvious that the memory gave him very great pain."

So all of this time Koscuisko had known that there had been family, but no more than that. Of course Joslire couldn't have explained to Koscuisko about the knives. It would have been as much as an admission that Joslire had put them on Koscuisko, and Joslire—as Koscuisko told the story—had enjoyed the joke of that until the very end.

"It's one man in a generation, your Excellency, chosen by aptitude and willingness and temperament, and endorsed by the ancestors. Those who have gone before had my brother singled out from the day he was born. So goes the story, at least." Koscuisko needed to understand. It was important. Shona felt an anguished ache in his heart that Koscuisko should understand, and wondered if the brandy was affecting his emotions.

"There are Malcontents, on Azanry," Koscuisko replied, in an encouraging and contemplative tone of voice. "The Holy Mother has marked them from the moment of their birth, because it goes without saying that no one would chose that path if there were any other. But it is between the soul and the Holy Mother. Sometimes it is clear that a man is for the Malcontent, but at other times it comes as a surprise to everyone."

Including the individual concerned? That did seem to be Koscuisko's point. "The knives themselves will not stay sheathed for a man they do not accept. He would have known when he first sheathed one against your body. If the knife did not jump out of the sheath, it meant that it had tasted your spirit and decided that you would carry it with honor."

Koscuisko looked concerned and wary at once, as though he wasn't sure of what he meant to say next. "I have wondered how I could carry them in that way," Koscuisko said. In what way? Shona wondered. With honor, perhaps? "To take them with me, everywhere I have gone, Shona. Everywhere. Many times have I decided I dishonor his gift and made up my mind to leave the knives behind. I do not wear them often on shipboard, but—other times—I want to have them there."

Koscuisko couldn't know what he was saying. He didn't know. The fact of the knives aside he was no more Emandisan than Shona was Aznir Dolgorukij. Shona took a deep breath to steady his voice. "May one ask whether his Excellency ever—used them. With respect. Sir."

For a moment Koscuisko looked confused, and Shona concentrated on not holding his breath. He couldn't imagine it. No one in custody of Emandisan steel could, not what Koscuisko was tasked to do. Then Koscuisko's face paled and he started back in his chair, and Shona knew that it was all right.

"May all Saints turn from me in my final hour if I could ever have done so mean a thing to Joslire." Koscuisko knew what Shona had meant. Exactly. "I am a sinner, Shona, a murderer of men and women and there have been those that I knew to be too young and killed anyway, as quickly as I could. Joslire's memory I have never soiled in that manner. They're the only clean things about me, and I do not wish to give them up."

Shona closed his eyes for one brief moment of relieved gratitude. Joslire had known what he was doing. It hadn't been a fluke, an accident of circumstances and opportunity.

"No one could dare to request them of you," Shona said. "They cannot be alienated from you, by law and the ethic of the holy steel. You don't need to be concerned about it. Trust me on this."

The talk-alert at the door signaled before Koscuisko could reply, and the doors opened without any polite interval to wait for an invitation. It was Dame Ivers, and she had a flat-panel data display with her—a reader of a sort that Shona recognized, from seeing Specialist Delleroy with them.

"You," Dame Ivers said to Shona, who stood up when she came in but who had no idea what might have excited her. "Ise-I'let. You were at Terek after Verlaine was killed?"

The question was unexpected; Shona had to think. When exactly had Chilleau's First Secretary died, been killed, when had he heard of it? Coming off of Wellocks at Terek, hadn't it been? "I'm not sure, Bench specialist," Shona admitted. "Is it important?"

"These are traffic records from Terek," she said, brandishing the data reader. "They say you were at Terek. They didn't say that before. The data's been compromised. I need to know if—"

There was a voice behind Specialist Ivers now, though, in the hall, and although Shona couldn't see who it was he recognized Nairob's accent.

"With your permission, Bench specialist. We're coming up on the vector debouchment, Dame, I'd like to ask for Ise-I'let's presence in the wheelhouse, if he can be spared."

Nairob would drop vector by himself if he had to; Shona had done it on more than one occasion. Prudent and responsible pilots backed each other up, however, and Shona was the one who had reminded Nairob that there were five-knives on board. Or were there? Koscuisko had not offered to let him see them—they'd been in company before, and it hadn't seemed to occur to Koscuisko since.

Shona hadn't thought about it either, until just now. Maybe Koscuisko didn't actually have the knives with him. Maybe the knives had left with the *Ragnarok*—but how could that be? He felt comfortable with Koscuisko. Koscuisko smelled like family. He had to be carrying the knives.

Specialist Ivers nodded—if a little reluctantly, as it seemed to Shona—and stepped aside. "Of course," she said. "There'll be time later. Please feel free, courier pilot."

So now of course he *did* have to leave the room and go with Nairob to the wheelhouse, wondering. Trying to remember. Where had he been? Terek? He'd picked up Specialist Delleroy at Ygau where Delleroy had been on board of JFS *Galven*, that was right. Delleroy had been working with Fleet and vector control to help contain the panic when they'd found out that the traffic offices had been sabotaged. That had been before anybody had heard about Verlaine's death.

As Shona crossed the threshold into the wheelhouse he heard Koscuisko suddenly raise his voice, behind him, in the corridor. "It's a bomb!" Koscuisko shouted. "All shields. Now!"

There was a sound of something falling to the floor on the other side of the corridor—as if from Specialist Ivers' bed-cabin—but Shona couldn't stop to think about it. All shields, Koscuisko had said. The nearest mechanism that could be used to engage the courier's blast containment defenses was on the outside wall, though, just outside the wheelhouse; Nairob was already at his console and looking up—alarmed, concerned—as Shona turned back to the corridor.

Nairob would have to make the vector drop by himself after all. Shona had to engage the blast shields, and once the wheelhouse was sealed off it would stay that way until the courier was boarded.

Half-a-step toward the open doorway to pull the plunger-rod and close the circuit, manually, but Koscuisko had reached and thrown and something sank into the outside wall facing the corridor, sank deep into the emergency containment access and quivered there, ringing with the force of its impact.

Shona started back on instinct—it was too close to his face, he reacted without thinking—and that reflexive recoil saved him from being crushed as the blast shields fell with brutal force and the speed of desperation.

Shona stood there staring at the now-sealed connecting door between the wheelhouse and the rest of the ship. All over the ship the blast walls would have fallen, sealing the courier off into nine separate life-sustainment zones, each quarantined from the others to minimize whatever damage might have befallen them. The rest of the crew would be wondering what had happened. Shona was wondering what had happened himself.

"Did he say a bomb?" Nairob asked. Shona shook himself out of his temporary paralysis and turned back to the boards. The knife. That was what he'd seen. Koscuisko had thrown the knife. That was how Koscuisko had engaged the blast shields. He'd seen it, and he hadn't seen it at all. What was going on?

"I'm not sure." He couldn't remember what he thought he'd heard Koscuisko say. He was shaken by the brutal suddenness of it, by the fear that gripped a man when the blast shields came down to know that something had gone terribly wrong and that their lives were at the mercy of luck and chance. "He may have said a bomb. I didn't see a bomb. Did you see a bomb?"

Nairob reached for a control on his console, scowling. "No. No sign of one in health monitoring, either. We'll drop vector and then we can try to figure it out. Check my calculations? I'd appreciate it."

Shona was good at vector calculations. It was a natural aptitude that had served him well in the past. "He seemed perfectly rational just now," Shona said, calling up the model. "There's no telling, I guess." He'd wondered if Koscuisko had the knives. Koscuisko did. Shona had seen one.

Was it still there, outside the wheelhouse, sunk deep into the structure of the ship? Did the emergency containment initiation sequence generate enough heat or other energy to damage the blade, to destroy the knife, to obliterate something that carried the lives and souls of all of its custodians with it, lost forever?

He was shaken to the pit of his stomach. His hand trembled as he picked out threads on the console to test the patterns of force that would work upon the courier as it dropped from vector transit back into normal space. Concentrate. The needful task now; speculation later. The knife. Koscuisko had thrown the knife. Shona had seen her. It had to be her. It couldn't possibly have been anything else.

Something knocked all at once against the sealed doorway between the wheelhouse and the corridor, as though the courier had been a gigantic melon that some huge hand had just slapped to hear how ripe it was by its resonance. *Tock.*

It felt like something hitting Shona in the head from all directions at once, sending him sprawling across his console while Nairob actually fell forward into the narrow space between the consoles and the viewing-port. One blow, one giant's fist, and then the alarm system on the inboard health monitors started up all at once orange and venomously green and red: the upper lining of the ship below the hull. The atmospheric integrity of the cargo bay. The power-plant where two of the crew were on duty while a third sat on the communications board.

Something had hit the courier, but from the inside out, and from the monitors responsible for the passenger cabins just outside the wheelhouse, from the corridor itself—there was nothing.

Nairob dragged himself to his feet, clambering up and over the console. "A bomb," Nairob said. "Do we have navigation? Do we have propulsion? Can we see?"

The view-ports were still registering, but the modeling projections had gone blank. There was nothing there. The consoles claimed that the courier was still at speed and on its course, some minor perturbations, nothing that couldn't be addressed; but the ship was blind.

There were no projected schematics, no visual summaries, no sense of whether the course that Nairob had scheduled would drop them where and when they were expected. Shona took a deep breath. It could be done on manual. Nairob had had the calculations done, and the ship could still tell them what they had to do to correct for what had just happened.

He'd never wanted to drop vector by hand, but once they'd got past this they would never have to do it for the first time ever again. They'd get past this. They would. The courier was a good piece of machinery, a very capable craft, and Nairob was good. *He* was good.

Koscuisko had given the knife to the ship to try to save them all. There was no report of any sort from the part of the ship in which Shona had left Koscuisko and Dame Ivers alike, and one of the skin-sensors thought that they might have begun to lose just the tiniest bit of atmosphere, which was just the tiniest bit more than they could afford.

"We need to get back on course," Shona said firmly, setting his console to rights and sitting down. "We don't have much time. We'll start the distress beacon once we're off the vector. Can you give me a calibration on the course deviation?"

They were going to bring this courier off vector safely whether or not there had been a bomb. There were six souls on board this ship, even if he didn't count Koscuisko and Ivers. He didn't dare include them, in his mind. He had to concentrate on the lives that they could save. There was nothing he could do about Koscuisko and Ivers until they could get help.

"It's slow," Nairob said. "But it's coming. Here. Deviation on linear acceleration, mark."

If he could not so much as bring lives that Koscuisko had tried to save to port, he would not dare to step into the family orchard, ever again.

Jils Ivers crawled over the debris of the bed-cabin wall painfully. The emergency sulfurs were glowing; the light gave everything a ghastly green-yellow hue, the shadows flat and deceptive. No depth perception: in the dim light she could make out nothing amidst the wreckage on the floor except for something rounded and lighter in color than its surroundings that could be the back of a man's head.

The relative positioning was right—Koscuisko had been between her and the door when the bomb had gone off—but she couldn't tell for sure. She was going to have to get to him somehow, and she hurt. Nothing was broken so far as she could tell—the joints that weren't working were refusing to work in a manner characteristic of a sprain or torn muscle, not a broken bone—but one of the other things that she knew from experience was that it frequently came as a surprise, later, to realize the extent of an injury.

She'd had a rough time of it, recently, the collapsing chair, Nion's harpoon, now this. Lovemaking with Padrake didn't count and she wasn't going to think about it now. "Koscuisko. Hey. You. Anders. Wake up. You've got explaining to do."

He hadn't gotten much done in the short space of time between his decision to seize the data reader and throw it across the corridor into her bed-cabin, and the explosion itself. If he had, she'd lost it in the haze that being blown sideways could cast over events immediately prior to a traumatic accident.

She hadn't gotten the exact reason why, but Koscuisko's conviction had been absolute. Between the two of them, they'd gotten the intervening doors closed, and they'd deployed the interior barrier wall, before they'd been interrupted. If they hadn't gotten those things accomplished, it might well have been a termination, not an interruption, so she was just as glad.

"You. Andrej. Up, and face the world. Wake up. Are you bleeding, can you tell?" It was slow going, crawling across the floor. She had to stop every few moments to catch her breath, but she was beginning to worry about Koscuisko because she couldn't see any movement in the rubble. There was very little of the barrier wall left; if he was underneath it, there would be digging to do.

The heap of rubble with the possibly blond head rumbled a bit like the ground in a seismic aftershock; subsided, buckled like the swell of a rising river, and said something in a language that Jils could identify as probably a Combine dialect of some sort, possibly High Aznir. She couldn't translate it, but if he felt anything like she felt, it was probably just as well.

"That's the ticket." She said it as cheerfully as she could manage, but she couldn't afford to relax yet. There was no telling. He was apparently alive, but in what sort of condition? "I hope your kit is somewhere you can find it. I've got a headache."

Slowly, the rubble on the floor hove up and fell away, and Koscuisko rolled over toward her to lie upon his back making small grunting sounds. Very disgusted grunting sounds. She could hear him shift against the debris on the floor, a little a time; he was testing, she realized it by the pattern of sound. Feet, knees, hips, hands, elbows, arms.

"Nothing feels splintered," he said, but his voice was very strained. "I don't think I'm bleeding. How do you find yourself, Bench specialist?"

"I can crawl fairly well." The inbred formality of the aristocratic class of Aznir struck her as more amusing than it probably actually was; they had just been blown up together, and he was calling her by title. "Just point me at the probable location. I want a drink of water."

No, she wanted his medical kit, because stimulants and painkillers seemed clearly the order of the day. "Far wall," Koscuisko gasped. "Farthest from the wheelhouse. I don't know what direction that is, right now. Regrets."

Yes, she had regrets too, and the fact that she was going to have to keep moving was worth a series all to itself. Koscuisko had been between her and the corridor. If she turned around and crawled the other way she should find the far wall, and the bed-cabins were small. They were lucky the bomb hadn't breached the hull. If Koscuisko hadn't gotten the blast shields deployed it might have done. What had Koscuisko used to set the sequence off? A knife?

"Bedding," Jils announced. "Fabric, anyway." So she was on the right track.

Koscuisko coughed. "Go left. Small trunk. Maybe destroyed." His voice was sounding stronger. Weren't there emergency stores in the hull somewhere? She was feeling better as well, but it was important not to take that as a sign that nothing was wrong. They were undoubtedly both in shock. That was in turn probably why she wanted water.

She took it slow and easy, and by the time she'd found Koscuisko's trunk Koscuisko had come dragging himself over the remains of walls and furnishings to join her and help her dig it out. A good third of the upper part of the case had been smashed in, but Koscuisko didn't seem to mind. Prying the trunk open with an effort visible even in the low sulfur-lights Koscuisko searched the interior, then grunted in evident satisfaction.

"Well done," Koscuisko said. "Thank you. Water?" His voice had the strained and gravelly sound of a man trying not to cough, because if he started he wouldn't be able to stop. Jils had done her coughing. She wished Koscuisko luck with the attempt.

There was no predicting some of the exact impacts of any one blast; this one had taken the doors off of the emergency stores that had filled one wall between bed-cabins on that side of the ship, but left the stores themselves more or less intact. She pulled out items as she located them, water, oxygen, the medical set. It was hard work even with Koscuisko to help her and she wasn't at her best just now. Koscuisko didn't seem to be bending his right hand or any of its fingers, but that could be a trick of the light.

"Enough," Koscuisko said, and lifted the seal on a water-flask. "Here. Take these." He had a small assortment of tablets, pills, capsules in his left hand, passing them to her awkwardly with the flask held between two fingers.

She accepted the offered medications, and the flask; but paused to toss them in the palm of her hand, weighing them up. "What's this?"

"Later." Koscuisko had turned back to his kit to sort out a set of drugs for his own use, washing them down with a second flask of water. She wondered why she was taking drugs in this form, but then she realized that the dose-styli were usually kept in the lid of the kit, and the lid was damaged. Maybe they were smashed. Maybe Koscuisko didn't trust them. "Shut up and drink."

Nobody had spoken so bluntly to her for a long time. It made her smile; Koscuisko was not to be questioned in his own field. It took her most of the flask to get the pills down one and two at a time, with her throat as raw from coughing as it was; when she had finished she sat still in her temporary resting place and closed her eyes to wait for something to happen. Was it getting cold? No. She was cold because she was in shock. There were emergency blankets in stores, perhaps, but she didn't have the energy to find them.

"What happened?" Koscuisko asked, after a while. "I can't quite remember. Do you?"

She thought about it, appreciating the fact that her body was beginning to not hurt as much and that she was feeling much warmer and that it seemed easier to breathe. Had he given her an altitude booster? "There was something in the data I wanted to ask Ise-I'let about. That started it."

"You came to ask him whether he'd been at Terek when—something." Koscuisko spoke slowly, but there was less and less slurring to the edges of his words as he spoke on. "Shona had to leave. You said that the data had been tampered with."

It was beginning to come back to her. "I'd have remembered it. Not the first time through, no, I might have missed it once, not made the connection. But I'd looked at that exact data at least three times. It wasn't there before."

"And it seemed to me self-evident that the data had been booby-trapped as well as tampered with," Koscuisko said, contemplatively. "I don't quite remember—let me think." He reached out for another flask of water; she passed it to him, remembering for herself while he drank and thought.

Yes. He'd been very definite. *It's a bomb*, he'd said, and torn the data-reader from her hands. Tossed it through the open door of her bed-cabin, closed the door on it, pushed her very vigorously into his own—she'd fallen across the table, she remembered—and thrown something, before he'd jumped into the room and closed the door and put his back to it to catch his breath before he'd suggested that she help him deploy the inside wall, with such convincing urgency that she had.

Then nothing had happened. Nothing. They'd been sealed into the small bed-cabin with nothing to do but stare at one another, since Koscuisko had thrown her data into the next room and there was to be no getting out of this until they'd dropped vector and called the vector traffic control. Koscuisko had had some explaining to do. That was what she'd been thinking when the bomb had gone off.

"I don't know if Vogel told you," Koscuisko said. "When he tried to coax the secret out of the record that Noycannir had brought to Chelatring Side, it blew up in his face, which fortunately had been similarly assaulted in the past so that there was scar tissue that protected him. When the record realized that someone was suspicious of it, it destroyed itself."

Koscuisko had told her at least part of that before, but maybe he didn't remember. She wasn't exactly sure what was new and what repeated, herself. "I hadn't tampered with the data-reader, though. It wouldn't have known I was suspicious unless it was carrying an ear, and a thinker as well."

Both relatively sophisticated organics. It was possible.

Koscuisko, however, shook his head. He had shifted himself to put his back to what was left of the bed, now, and in the yellow light his expression was very difficult to read. His voice sounded increasingly confident, though.

"You wanted to ask Shona something. The new data raised an issue in your mind. Therefore it was placed there to send you to Shona. Therefore once you and Shona stood together it would explode. It wasn't meant to destroy the courier, necessarily. It only had to kill the two of you."

No, he was reaching. That didn't make sense. She knew his reputation for making sometimes unnervingly precise intuitive deductions, reaching conclusions that seemed prescient or occult; she didn't believe this was any such thing. So there was a reason that Koscuisko thought as he did.

"Help me out on this," she suggested. "I'm not getting you. Data could be planted to incriminate Shona, or to mislead."

She thought he might have nodded. "I'll be honest with you, Dame Ivers, I'm not quite sure of that myself. But why would someone have wished to incriminate Shona? It is Bench specialists that he ferries, Specialist Delleroy, a great deal of the time. And if you were to ask me who my first guess was for a soul who could tamper with a data record, I might say 'any given Bench specialist.'"

Padrake. Koscuisko had no way of knowing where her suspicions lay; she hadn't shared the crucial timing with him. "Placing him at Terek at the wrong time would just lead to suspicion, though. And what if the next person who saw the data had no access to Ise-I'let?"

"You are to return to Chilleau, Specialist Ivers, you will not be using this data record. It will be wiped and reconfigured. But if Shona was in a position to place Delleroy at Terek he might have said something to you. You might find out independently. Then if you found that the data was not there you would surely suspect a flaw in the source record. As it was you brought it to Shona direct, as I recall? I have a headache."

She was getting sleepy. It wasn't Koscuisko's fault. He sounded a little drowsy himself, and maybe sleep wasn't such a bad idea. If they were to live, the rescuers would wake them up; if they were to die it was surely better to die in one's sleep, because if she stayed awake she'd be forced to confront how all the pieces trended toward a fit.

They didn't all mesh, no. She needed to sit down with Ise-I'let to see what he could tell her. They simply all fit around a missing piece in the puzzle she had been trying to solve for months now, the problem of who had killed Sindha Verlaine. There was still that hole in the center of the picture; but as she put things together, the outline of that missing information looked more and more like Padrake Delleroy.

"He always was good with his hands," she said sleepily, and then woke up with an embarrassed start to the implications of her own choice of words. Koscuisko wouldn't know. But she did. There was a problem. There had to be a problem.

She could find a way that it could not have been Padrake. She would, even if he had spent as much time as he could get alone with her. She'd thought it was because of old times, maybe to protect her—had he only been waiting for a chance to see the data all along, in order to subvert it? "But the record was a Judicial document. Where would he have—"

She shut herself up as she realized the connection she had made in her own mind, while she had not been watching. Koscuisko didn't seem to have noticed a lack of obvious connection between the two issues, the sabotaged data-reader and the forged record. Koscuisko was still thinking only along the lines of the idea that the same people had been responsible for putting bombs in both of them. Wasn't he?

"One of my gentlemen on *Scylla* said to me that their new chief medical officer had powerful friends, at the very highest levels. He even said the words 'Bench specialist.' This was the gossip network's explanation for the unexpected and unwelcome displacement of Doctor Aldrai in Doctor Lazarbee's favor. Both officers of course have custody of a Writ to Inquire, as do I—for now at least. If a man wanted a favor, he could provide a blanked record, and authenticate evidence that was not there. One with a Writ could then add to the evidence, but if there had been no evidence, the record might be convinced that no addition had been made. Conceivably."

No, Koscuisko was thinking back to the circumstances in which that damned record had been forged in the first place. The record hadn't been forged. It was an honest record. The evidence had been fabricated, and the record tricked into accepting it as original and authenticated data. Someone had authenticated the data, or the data shell, someone with an active Writ—unlike Mergau Noycannir, who didn't have access to records to carry around. Someone like the chief medical officer currently on board of the Jurisdiction Fleet Ship *Scylla*.

"Padrake seemed not to know him," Jils insisted, thinking back. "Where did he transfer from, did your Security tell you that?"

Her voice was more accusing, challenging, than she had intended. Koscuisko didn't seem to notice. He'd taken medication too. "I think Code said he'd come from the *Galven*, if that helps."

It did not. It didn't help at all. JFS *Galven* had been at Ygau when the traffic records had been attacked, apparently unsuccessfully, but now she knew. The traffic records at Ygau had been altered to remove one single entry: Padrake Delleroy coming from Chilleau, met by Shona Ise-I'let piloting the courier.

Padrake wouldn't have needed anybody's help to engineer an apparently failed attack on traffic records. So the favor he'd owed Lazarbee hadn't been that, but the provision of an authenticated record to be forged, a record that Padrake had provided to Mergau Noycannir for her own purposes—Padrake had no reason to wish Koscuisko dead, Padrake didn't care about Koscuisko one way or the other, why should he?

No. Padrake had provided the record in exchange for something else. Security codes. Noycannir had sold Chilleau's security codes to Padrake for the instrument of her revenge against Andrej Koscuisko, but he hadn't needed any but a very specific set. Koscuisko had killed Noycannir; Padrake had assassinated First Secretary Sindha Verlaine.

Why?

The room shook, suddenly; Koscuisko made a sound of startled pain, followed by a series of shallow gasping grunts. He was more hurt than he had seemed to be, possibly more hurt than he had realized. That was the way of it. And frequently it was the relatively minor injuries that really hurt.

"What's happening?" Koscuisko asked, his voice a little choked in his throat. The room hadn't stopped shaking; if it was what Jils thought it was, it was going to get worse, instead of better.

"We're dropping vector." That had to be it. "And if we're lucky we'll make it in one piece. Hang on. This may not be fun."

There was nothing to hang on to, but Koscuisko didn't argue back. Maybe he had other things to think about. She knew she did. First

Secretary Arik Tirom had said that Verlaine's proposed reforms would destroy the entire Bench if Chilleau became the seat of the new First Secretary. Padrake hadn't seemed to disagree. Padrake, and Nion, and who knew who else, had all seemed to believe that Bench specialists were the natural authorities under Jurisdiction, that Bench specialists should be running things.

Jils closed her eyes and concentrated, and if she wept she knew it was just pain. And that was all. What Padrake meant to do in Convocation she couldn't imagine; she was simply going to have to go back, and find out.

Things got quiet.

They were either off the vector or they were never getting off vector, because the ship was losing atmosphere and the oxygen generators wouldn't last forever. They could try to drop vector again, she supposed, but if they'd missed at Brisinje it could be another six or seven days before they reached a debouchment point. She didn't think they had that long. She concentrated on her problem to keep her mind way from grief and horror, because she needed all the focus she could get.

Padrake had killed Verlaine in order to prevent Chilleau Judiciary from being selected. That done, why would he stop at further shaping of the Bench's destiny? He believed that he was properly the man to shape the Bench's destiny, he and other Bench specialists—but only right-thinking Bench specialists, clearly enough.

He'd used favors from Doctor Lazarbee to get the codes he'd needed to get in and out of Chilleau, and if Koscuisko hadn't killed Noycannir, Padrake would almost certainly have had it done himself, and Jils couldn't believe that Lazarbee had much of a future.

Padrake would do what had to be done to keep Lazarbee quiet until the danger had passed, and then Lazarbee would meet with some unfortunate accident or another, or be accused of falsifying a record for personal gain, to the detriment of the rule of Law and the Judicial order.

It could be Karol. It could be. Koscuisko had said that the forged record had exploded when Karol had tried to find out its secrets, but who was to say that Karol hadn't destroyed it to prevent its secrets from ever being plumbed? Karol had disappeared, no one had heard from him; no one knew where he was. Karol. Karol could have done it.

No, he couldn't have. Karol had had no possible access to the data-reader. Karol could have killed Verlaine, but Karol could not have gotten past all of Chilleau Judiciary's Security to do it without leaving visual evidence or setting off the alarms. Karol's talents in security codes and bombs were respectable and solid, but well short of the genius class. That was Padrake Delleroy.

But Koscuisko had also said that Karol had come on board with a Malcontent. Koscuisko didn't trust Malcontents, but had absolute faith in them; Koscuisko was Dolgorukij, and could be wrong. But the Combine was a conservative economic power, and would have no interest in the destabilization of the Judicial order and the disruption of trade. But wasn't that just what Arik Tirom had claimed to fear would happen if Chilleau Judiciary took the Selection?

The Sixth Judge at Sant-Dasidar had endorsed Chilleau's candidacy with the Combine's full approval, but the Malcontent didn't answer to the Combine. The Malcontent answered only to its founder and patron saint, who had been dead for some time.

It wasn't outside the realm of possibility. The Malcontent had the resources to have engineered it all. It would mean that the Malcontent had risked Andrej Koscuisko's life; but only risked it, and it had been a madwoman from Chilleau Judiciary who had threatened it, so couldn't that have been part of the Malcontent's plan?

Karol wouldn't have set a bomb that could destroy the courier. There were other crew here beside her and Ise-I'let. Karol killed when he had to, they all had, but Karol did his best to minimize the collateral damages. It was a personal quirk of his. Or he could have set the bomb to destroy the courier knowing that she would believe by that token that it had not been him, if something went wrong and she survived.

He'd set that fire in the service house in Burkhayden the night he'd killed Captain Lowden, after all, to put a good face on the cover story. That had been something so uncharacteristic of Karol that she'd had problems with it ever since, and had half-convinced herself that he'd fled in shame and self-disgust.

No one had been killed in the fire. The gods looked after fools and drunkards, favored the oppressed; Karol could not have counted on that, though, not when he'd set the fire. Unlike him. Absolutely unlike him. Why had he done it?

He hadn't done it at all. That was why. Karol had brought Andrej Koscuisko in off of the streets that night and put him to bed at Center House, and gone back out. The story was that Karol had found Koscuisko wandering in the streets too drunk to speak, alone and unaccompanied. That was the story. Maybe it was true, at least that part of it.

Karol hadn't set any fires in Burkhayden that night. So Karol hadn't set any fires to cover up his murder of Lowden, so Karol hadn't murdered Lowden, whether or not it had been Lowden's name on the Warrant that Karol had been carrying and suddenly Jils was irrationally convinced that it had not been.

Karol had been in a sour mood from the beginning, at Burkhayden, and particularly sour about Lowden—and Koscuisko. It wouldn't have perturbed Karol out of the ordinary to have an assassination order on Lowden; Jils wouldn't have minded if the task had been hers to do, not apart from the basic unpleasantness involved.

Karol had been annoyed about Koscuisko. Not at Koscuisko; about Koscuisko. The warrant had been out for Koscuisko. Koscuisko had killed his captain. Karol knew it. Did Koscuisko? Had Koscuisko been so drunk that night that he didn't remember?

Because if he did—why hadn't Koscuisko called on the Malcontent to get him out of Jurisdiction altogether, knowing as Koscuisko did the penalty for such a crime? Had that been why Koscuisko had sent the bond-involuntaries ahead—

The room shook again, but only gently this time. It was enough to sharpen Jils' focus. She'd let herself get distracted, fantasizing.

"Voices," Koscuisko said.

Jils closed her eyes, her heart full of gratitude; it was a warm feeling, but it hurt. They had been found. They were rescued. They were going to be safe. She could hear the voices too; the impacts that they felt were the containment walls coming away, lifted out of the courier if they couldn't be re-stowed.

They'd cleared the vector. One of vector traffic control's emergency response ships had them in its maintenance atmosphere, and was coming through to see what might be left of them.

The voices were coming clearer, closer. From the direction of the wheelhouse, now, and Jils could hear Ise-I'let in the lead. "Through here. Look at this mess. We don't know—we lost our intership in the explosion, they'd be here, I think—"

"In here," Koscuisko called, then coughed. Jils could almost hear him swearing at himself for raising his voice, but it did the trick. In an instant the ruins of the little room were full of rescue workers, lights, Shona Ise-I'let, stumbling across the debris that lay knee-deep on the floor toward where Koscuisko sat with his back up against what was left of the bed.

"Alive," Ise-I'let gasped, almost sobbed. "Dame Ivers, sir, is she— did she—"

"Just here," Koscuisko assured the pilot, gesturing very carefully with his right hand. His right hand had swollen to twice its normal size, his wrist as thick as she imagined his knee might be; not a good thing, for a surgeon, but at least he had been in rest dress when it had happened. Loose cuffs. "Keeping me company. Get the litter. She's been injured."

As if he hadn't been. Koscuisko was a doctor, though, and apparently the rescue team responded to his authority as well; they carried the emergency patient transport over to where she was, and began to stabilize her body to be moved. It wasn't pleasant. She was still certain that she wasn't badly hurt, or not badly injured, but that didn't have a particular relation to the amount of pain it caused to move a muscle.

"Him next," she told the senior man. "Don't let him fool you. In worse shape than I am." But Koscuisko was talking to Ise-I'let, and not listening to her.

"I'm sorry," Ise-I'let was saying. "Sir. About the knife. She's gone. No trace of her."

"What's that?" Koscuisko asked. His words were a little indistinct because he had his face turned away from her, talking to the pilot. "Knife, what knife?"

Oh. Yes. She remembered. Koscuisko had thrown a knife, and brought the blast walls down to seal the ship. It had saved their lives. It had all happened very, very fast.

"We'll get Dame Ivers another one." Koscuisko was sounding increasingly groggy. They were rescued now; they were safe. He could let go. It was a common shock stress reaction, she'd done it many times herself. "Have it inscribed, perhaps."

The pilot shook his head. "No, sir, your knife. Her. Behind your back. I saw her. You threw the knife, your Excellency, don't you remember?"

Apparently not. Jils lay very still as the rescue team prepared to move her, listening to what was going on in order to distract her as much as possible from what was about to happen to her.

"She threw the knife," Koscuisko insisted. "I haven't thrown any knives. I'd know. I've been lying against it for however long it's been, Shona, I know the feel of an empty sheath and it is not. See for yourself. Go ahead, I have to—sit up—anyway—"

"Don't move," one of the rescue team said, suddenly and firmly. "Your Excellency. You know better than that, sir. Not a twitch. Unless you don't think we know what we're doing?"

It was a well-chosen challenge, one medical professional to another, and both accustomed to absolute and immediate obedience in their own areas. Koscuisko apparently surrendered.

"It's there," Koscuisko assured Ise-I'let. "It was Ivers who threw the knife. Trust me on this. You'll see." Koscuisko was doomed to embarrassment, because Koscuisko was wrong. He'd thrown the knife. She'd seen him. She remembered. She was wearing three knives, not five, though one was at her back.

She had much bigger problems to worry about, and if she was going to live she had to start in on them immediately. "Keep this quiet," she said to the closest rescuer, a woman who wore rank. "No report to Brisinje. Must reach Brisinje as soon as possible, secured mission. See to it. No word."

The officer nodded. "Very good, Bench specialist," the officer said. "You'll be on your way as soon as we can bring up a new courier. Medical team on stand-by."

There was nothing more that she could do for now. What had she been thinking, about Koscuisko? That all of the stress unwound on one at once when the pressure was taken off the line? It overwhelmed her in a wave. She was just tired and hurt enough to let it.

There was one tile on the table between Rafenkel and Vogel, and Rafenkel stared at it morosely. "Isn't there any way around this?" she asked. "Any way at all?"

Four days and then some since Vogel had arrived, since their focus had shifted from "anything but confederation" to "is there any way around confederation?" Not long enough. Rafenkel had observed the tiling debates; she had participated in the tiling debates. She could see what the future held in store as well as the next man—or better, from the point of view of her birth-culture, since she wasn't a man at all but a woman with inherently greater powers of foresight and reasoning.

"Setting aside the issue of crimes that may have been committed," Vogel said gently. "Even if we placed a team of Bench specialists at Chilleau to help. We're damned good but we're not perfect, at least I'm not. How long would it take for partisanship to come between us and the rule of Law? Inequities between Bench specialists at Chilleau running the Bench administration and other Bench specialists, tying Bench specialists to administrative tasks rather than what the Bench chartered us to do—we're better off with confederated Judiciaries than with Bench specialists trying to do a First Secretary's job."

He pushed the tile toward her. His role was to represent Chilleau; he was doing so a little oddly—arguing why they didn't dare—but the situation was even more odd than it had been. What Brisinje's First Secretary was going to make of it was anybody's guess.

She already had most of the other tiles; in terms of the short-term stability of the Bench, of crucial measures of quality of life for average citizens, confederation was better than chaos. And chaos was promised under any other circumstances that she could think of. First Secretary Verlaine could rise from the dead—but that would cause as many problems as it solved, surely.

"No, not quite yet," she said with an upraised hand, declining to accept the offered tile. She spoke for Sant-Dasidar, or at least she had come here in order to speak for Sant-Dasidar. Vogel had introduced Gonebeyond as an element into their joint deliberations. "I've got one last thing for you. The Combine. One of the single most aggressive economic forces under Jurisdiction, Vogel, and that's just because the Bench took their guns away."

In a manner of speaking. The Dolgorukij Combine had been its own thriving little empire when the Bench had made first contact, and had shown a brisk and blood-thirsty eagerness to absorb the Bench rather than the other way around. That was history. The Bench had demonstrated its overwhelmingly superior firepower and suggested that conquest was simply an inefficient form of trade, which the Bench's overlordship would enable the Combine to do better.

The Combine had cut its military forces back to its home defense fleet, the Bench had created Sant-Dasidar Judiciary to contain the Combine and the miscellaneous planetary systems that had been next on the shopping list of the Dolgorukij dire-wolf, and they'd sorted well enough together over the years. Until now.

Vogel was waiting for her to continue. "If we confederate, there is no curb on Sant-Dasidar's ambitions. The Judge is an honorable woman, but the Combine will be moving into Gonebeyond space, Vogel, you know it will. The last time the Dolgorukij landed to develop a market it was on Sarvaw."

Vogel gestured with the thumbs of his folded hands, as though they were nodding their heads—his thumbtips—in approval. "True enough," Vogel said. "But that's not to say good didn't come of it. Sarvaw forensics are among the best in known Space. All of those mass graves to practice on, and not all of that very old, as collective memories go. Ugh. Never liked those people. Present company excepted, no offense meant, Rafe."

She had to smile. "None taken. But if we lose a single prevailing voice we lose control of the Combine, at least the Combine in Gonebeyond. These are my people, Vogel. I'm telling you this as a native daughter. It is probably not a good idea to unleash the dogs. It's almost certainly a bad idea for Gonebeyond itself."

What he might have said in reply was interrupted, before he could get it out. The talk-alert. Zeman, in the theater, at the master communications console. With seven people they could run two sets of tile-debates, but that meant one person left over with nothing to do and everybody had gotten to feeling that they wanted to know where everybody was at all times.

"Station alert. Incoming from the surface, Specialist Delleroy, alone, confirmed. Arrival in five eighths."

Delleroy was back. Not a moment too soon. They had to announce a solution; they had to do it publicly and quickly. Any idle speculations about Delleroy's potential involvement in murder were just that, speculations. First things first.

They had to proceed carefully. If Delleroy was guilty of conspiracy to commit murder it would be a tenth level command termination, and she'd seen the tapes. Koscuisko could hold a man for eight days at the tenth level. The Bench would demand no less.

She hadn't shared the discussion she'd had with Vogel and the others with anybody who hadn't been there, three days ago; because it was just speculation and because she had no way of knowing who his accomplices might be, if any.

"We'll collect in the theater," Capercoy—who was observing—suggested. "The discussion is tabled on Gonebeyond versus Dolgorukij economic development. Ah, involuntary market development in Gonebeyond. Something like that."

Their procedure had gotten less formal over time as they'd learnt each others' strengths and weaknesses. It wasn't for any lack of sensitivity to the importance of the subject matter, no—quite the contrary.

"Be with you shortly," Balkney said over the all-station. "Going through the kitchen on the way there."

Good idea. "And Capercoy away here," Capercoy said.

Delleroy would have news from the outside. He could tell them what was going on. They could see how he reacted to the news that it was his position that seemed to have the most strength.

Maybe those reactions would tell them everything they needed to know about the suspicions that had arisen as to his role in the murder.

CHAPTER NINETEEN

Warring States

"Is that the lot?" Vogel asked Rafenkel as she carried the ninth tile-box into the theater. "Right." He shut the door. There was no particular reason to shut the door, but it was habit common to them all—Bench specialists closed doors. "I don't know where you're going to find room on that table, though."

It was seven shallow steps down from the upper level to the floor of the theater, seven wide and spacious, carpeted steps. They'd carried Ivers out of here after the incident with the chair perhaps as long as eight days ago and had had no difficulty getting the litter up and out into the corridor.

The table in the middle of the theater, on the lowest level of the floor, was stacked with tile-boxes already—some of them sealed and others not. The lab chairs that had been Ivers' downfall had been removed; there was no sense in taking any chances. The communications console depended from the far wall, opposite the double doors into the theater, and between it and the table stacked with boxes stood Padrake Delleroy.

He looked a little stressed to Rafenkel, and that was unusual. She didn't think she'd seen him so grimly determined ever before, and that was unusual too, because Jils Ivers was his friend and had been his lover, but Rafenkel didn't think that he'd been so visibly harried even after Ivers had fought with Nion and been forced to kill Nion to save her life.

"I spoke to the First Secretary before I came," Delleroy was saying to Balkney. "I was in a hurry, but he *is* the First Secretary, and he expected to be heard. We're asked to announce a decision within the day. He'll be coming down."

Rafenkel saw Delleroy's glance over his shoulder at the console board behind him. One of the schematics there would tell them when someone was coming, so that they could meet the party at the airlock. It was all part of station monitoring.

"How long have we got?" Balkney asked. "You got in what, six hours ago?"

"Yesterday," Delleroy replied, with a grimace. "It's taken me this long to brief and clear Chambers. There's so much going on. We have our work cut out for us."

She could understand that, Rafenkel thought. They all needed to get out of here and back to work. They were going to, too; maybe not as Delleroy had planned it—if he had planned anything—but they had to get back to the rule of Law and the Judicial order, while there was any of either left.

"Then Tirom's due any minute now," Vogel said. "Let's get started. Who goes first?"

Delleroy closed his eyes and spun around three times, stopping himself with one hand slapped decisively down atop a tile-box. "Here," Delleroy said. "Who's this one? Oh. Rafenkel."

Rafenkel shrugged. It really didn't matter. Sitting down at the table she opened up the box; there were the tiles she had taken, and the ones that had not been played. Plucking one out of its slot in the box she placed it, face down, into the scanner, and rested the middle finger of her right hand atop its surface while the scanner did its work, comparing her biometric profiles against the information encoded in the chip she'd used to seal it once it had been played.

"Rafenkel," the scanner announced. "Element four, the cost of infrastructure. Chilleau four. Confederacy three."

The scanner read to the communications console and the communications console was talking to a secured receiver under Arik Tirom's personal seal. Capercoy had brought flat-form and stylus, Rafenkel noted, and was marking a grid. She had to smile. Yes. A cross-check was always a good thing to have. She picked up the next tile.

"Rafenkel. Element two, the availability of goods and services for sale. Chilleau five. Cintaro two."

Not all of her tiles had been played; but there were still a number of them to get through. At least they wouldn't have to go through Nion's; Nion was dead, her voice stilled, her tiles inaccessible, and she hadn't been getting very far anyway.

"Rafenkel. Element six, civic involvement and ownership. Chilleau four. Fontailloe three."

Cintaro, Fontailloe, Chilleau, confederacy. It went on and on and on. "Tanifer. Element sixteen, productivity in manufacturing. Fontailloe six. Cintaro one."

When it was Capercoy's turn Vogel took over Capercoy's record-keeping, making little sums of tidy figures, setting running totals in tiny script off to one side. Rafenkel watched over his shoulder for a little while: Cintaro dropping rapidly in relation to everybody else, Fontailloe's position as a losing proposition more and more obvious by the tile, but Chilleau and Confederacy—too close to call, and alternating back and forth on almost every tile.

"Capercoy. Element fifteen, equitable tax burdens. Cintaro four. Chilleau three."

When Capercoy was finished and Rinpen was done Delleroy reached out for his own tile-box and pulled it toward himself, sitting down at the table with an air of confronting an anxiety-provoking task. He pulled out a tile. "Delleroy. Element twelve, effective population policing and management. Confederacy five, Chilleau two."

She thought she remembered that one. On the board behind Delleroy's back the telltales engaged to give notice; somebody was in the lift-car, coming down. She decided against disturbing anybody. It would only be an interruption. They were all tired. They needed to get this over and done with.

"Delleroy. Element eleven, the common weal. Confederacy six. Fontailloe one."

That sounded a little extreme; was it her imagination—Rafenkel wondered—or did Tanifer frown? Tanifer would remember, though, surely. Tanifer had been there when the tile had been judged and awarded. Who had proctored that discussion? Had it been Nion?

Balkney had noticed the comm console's message; he caught

Zeman's eye, and nodded toward the doors. Someone was going to have to leave to meet the lift-car and open the airlock, or risk a breach of atmosphere. Delleroy looked up sharply as Balkney and Zeman left the room and closed the door behind them, but he didn't seem to think about the First Secretary's impending arrival. He put another tile in the reader, and held it in its place with the tip of his middle finger.

"Nion," the scanner said. "Element two. Confederacy five, Fontailloe two."

Wait, Rafenkel thought.

Delleroy had picked up the next tile, putting it into the reader with a methodical sort of precision. "Delleroy. Element seven—"

No, the scanner had said Nion. She'd heard it. Rafenkel reached for the tile that Delleroy had just put down; he brushed her hand away with an impatient gesture that sent tiles flying. There were tiles all over the floor. Which one had just said Nion?

"Delleroy. Element seven. Chilleau seven, Confederacy zero." That wasn't right either. Delleroy didn't seem to have noticed. He went right on as though he hadn't heard, reaching for the next tile in his box—his tile-set, his, uniquely his, Padrake Delleroy's, the tiles he had won in debate with his peers. He had not argued for Chilleau but against it. She must have misheard. But she remembered no such polarized result from Delleroy's debate with Ivers; that had been one of the things she'd noted from the start—almost all of the spreads were within one or two points of each other.

She was frowning, watching Delleroy; he seemed to take notice, like a man hearing a message on time-delay. "What's wrong with these tiles?" he asked, his voice light and aggrieved. "I never won that from Jils. Has someone been tampering with these?"

"Nion," the scanner said. "Element—"

Delleroy sprang to his feet, backing away from the table toward comm console on the wall. "What kind of a trick is this?"

"Well, damn, Delleroy," Vogel said. "I was hoping you could tell us."

Silence. Delleroy stared, the fingers of his right hand twitching as though feeling for the butt of an absent weapon, coming to rest on the comm console behind his back instead. The contact seemed to calm him. "Explain yourself," he suggested. "You've gone in and what, altered the tile's secures? Changed the data? Is that what you've done? We're all waiting to hear, Vogel, tell us."

Vogel shook his head. "Sorry to disappoint," Vogel said. "I don't have the expertise. Feeling my way through the secures on these tile-boxes, that's about my limit. All I did was trade a few tiles between your cache and Nion's. Wanted to see what would happen when you tried to log someone else's tile into the scanner."

Delleroy had straightened up; his expression was contained, even confident. "I'm glad I don't have to be the one to tell Jils," he said. "That it was you. Trying to shape the future to your own liking, and what does it get you, after all?"

"It's a good effort." Vogel sounded almost admiring. "My cap's off to you, for that. But the evidence is in these tiles. Or are those booby-trapped, as well? That was a sweet job, on that record. Whoever did that was a genius, on my tally-board."

"Recess," Rafenkel said. "Time out. Share the story, you two. Why did the tile think Delleroy was Nion?"

"Because Delleroy told it he was Nion," Vogel said. "Or at least that'd be my guess. A genius, I tell you. But you'll come to a bad end yet, Delleroy, I'm sorry to say."

Rafenkel stood where she was, behind Capercoy—who had resumed his tallying when his tiles had been read—and listening, and trying to make sense of this. Capercoy had set his flat-form to one side and was beginning to stand up, slowly and carefully, not making any moves sudden enough to attract the attention of either Delleroy or Vogel.

Vogel had his back to them, including Tanifer; he wouldn't see Tanifer exchange an uneasy glance with Rinpen and start back up to the upper level of the theater. Delleroy could see that, though. Delleroy apparently did.

"Empty talk will get you nowhere, Vogel, this is all a diversionary tactic, isn't it? Something to distract us all from the holes in your story? Tell you what I'll do."

It was a confident, in-control, fully in command of the situation tone of voice, the sort that went with a folding of arms across the chest and a casual leaning back against the wall. Delleroy wasn't folding his arms across his chest, though. And he wasn't leaning back against the comm console, either. Comm console. Rafenkel frowned.

"Come on," she said. "The two of you. I don't know what your issues are, but I'm sure they can be more efficiently addressed than this."

Delleroy should step away from the comm console. Delleroy wasn't moving. She didn't know exactly what she didn't like about him being there, but she knew she didn't like it.

"What will you do?" Vogel challenged, seeming to ignore Rafenkel's attempted intervention. Rinpen had reached the opposite end of the room, and was opening up the doors as unobtrusively as possible.

"I wouldn't do that if I were you," Delleroy said. "I may need you to bear witness. Or do you have this pre-arranged amongst you all? Don't open that door."

Reluctantly Rinpen turned away from the door to put his back to the wall. "Just thinking, somebody should go after Balkney and Zeman," Rafenkel said. "If there's going to be a confrontation we should all be in on it at once, wouldn't you say? Delleroy?"

The doors to the theater opened as Rinpen spoke. Balkney and Zeman back after their errand, clearly enough; who was with them?

Brisinje's First Secretary, Arik Tirom; Bench specialist Jils Ivers. Glancing quickly at Delleroy to see how he was taking this unexpected appearance Rafenkel noted that the quality of his surprise seemed to be of a different order than just that Tirom was here before Delleroy had expected him to arrive. Vogel took advantage of the distraction to take half-a-step forward, apparently in order to close on Delleroy where he stood; Delleroy stopped Vogel with a word.

"Don't. It's not worth your life, Vogel. Jils, what are you doing here? I thought you were on your way to Chilleau."

Ivers was white in the face, limping badly as she came forward. There were other people behind Ivers and Tirom in the corridor, Rafenkel saw. Security.

"I don't think I need to get to Chilleau to resolve my problem." Ivers' voice was calm and controlled, but bitterly regretful. "On behalf of the Second Judge at Chilleau Judiciary I accuse you, Padrake Delleroy, of the murder of Sindha Verlaine, and of attempting to subvert thereby the Judicial order and the rule of Law."

Jils hadn't wanted the First Secretary to accompany her, but she knew that she was operating on fuel reserves that were running dangerously low. She couldn't spare the time it would have taken to dissuade him; perhaps it would be for the best after all, she'd decided. She had things to say to Padrake that he wasn't going to like hearing. Maybe Tirom's presence would help keep the situation under control. She was under no illusion that the simple act of bringing a squad of Security was enough to do that, where Bench specialists were involved.

When the doors to the lift-car opened at the bottom of the access shaft she took a position squarely in front of the others in the car, determined to gain and maintain control of the situation. They would know that she was coming. They would not know about the three squads of Security who had started down the air-well hours ago. The cable-car was a careful mover, but it was slow. According to the calculations she had reviewed, they would be arriving soon; but there was no way to tell how close they were without compromising the secrecy of their descent.

It was Balkney waiting for her there—Balkney, and Zeman. Balkney was startled to see her, and perhaps a little startled at her appearance as well. She could walk in the scaffold-boot, but not quickly. The brace they'd put on her shoulder was cumbersome and annoying, even if it didn't show underneath her uniform; but it was better than having her concentration interrupted by periodic bouts of intense pain every time she breathed too deeply or turned her head the wrong way.

"Where is everybody?" Jils asked, not moving out of the doorway of the car until she knew what she was walking into. "Where's Padrake?"

"Preliminary count, in the theater," Balkney replied, not asking the questions that were obvious to both of them—*what are you doing here, what's going on, what happened to you. Why do you want Delleroy.* "Left 'em all there. Zeman and I came out when we saw your signal."

Good. Everybody in one place; better chance of keeping this as clean as possible. It wasn't going to be clean. It was going to be ugly. It was going to be painful. She needed to get it done.

"Follow me," Jils said to the Security squad, because she didn't give orders to First Secretaries or to other Bench specialists when she could safely rely on their curiosity to motivate them to do what she wanted.

"We'll just be joining the rest in the theater. I have some tiles to tally myself."

She couldn't take the chance of saying anything more. The knowledge that she held within her was so painful as to be all but intolerable. She hadn't told Tirom what Delleroy had done. She didn't know how much of it had been Tirom's idea.

Balkney and Zeman followed without comment; was Balkney remembering what she'd told him, days ago? That Verlaine's assassin was hers? Karol had told her Balkney hadn't done it; now she knew who had, though she did not have evidence in hand. Evidence would come.

Koscuisko's injuries were not to be permanently disabling. The medical staff's initial evaluation on Koscuisko's right hand was guardedly positive. Koscuisko was the best there was. He would get answers and obtain evidence.

She was forgetting something; she knew she was. The doors to the theater were closed. She could hear voices, inside, angry voices raised against each other. The voice nearest the door sounded more cautious than angry. They wouldn't hear her if she signaled; so she simply opened up the door—it was awkward, but one of the Security helped her, once they understood what she was trying to do.

There they all were. Rinpen and Tanifer, by the door; Capercoy and Rafenkel on the middle tier standing to one side of the aisle, Karol closest to Padrake, Padrake with his back to the comm console. Padrake stared at her, apparently stunned; she stared back, looking for something in his face that would let her believe that she had been mistaken.

No such luck.

Karol began to move on Padrake; Padrake looked at Karol out of the corner of his eye. "Not worth your life," Padrake said. "Jils. I thought that you were in transit to Chilleau."

She'd just bet he did. Something had clearly been going on, Padrake was at bay; she could gather no hint about what it might be, beyond the obvious fact that Padrake and Karol seemed to be in opposition.

"I realized I didn't need to go back to Chilleau to resolve my problem." *Because you set a bomb in my data-reader, Padrake. Because you tried to kill me, and that gave me time to think about things from a whole new vector.* "It's overdue. On behalf of the Second Judge at Chilleau Judiciary, Padrake. You are guilty of the murder of Sindha Verlaine, and of attempting to subvert thereby the Judicial order and the rule of Law."

She could see the pain in his eyes as she spoke, and felt his wince like a knife in her own stomach. It had to be said now, openly, here. She didn't know how many of the people here were co-conspirators. Padrake would tell her, though. Koscuisko would leave Padrake no choice.

"Jils." She couldn't quite interpret the choked sound in his voice. "That's in rather poor taste, isn't it? Arik. Nice to see you again."

"Murder," Jils said. She wasn't going to let him defuse this situation. She wasn't going to let him talk his way around it, through it, over it, underneath it, out of it. "To the great despite of the common weal. Single-handedly throwing all of known Space into turmoil and confusion and civil anarchy. You. Padrake Delleroy."

She took a step down the shallow flight to the table in the middle of the room, behind which Padrake stood. Padrake laughed, but there was a little fear in it. She might be the only person here who could detect that note of deeply submerged panic, but she knew Padrake better than any of the others. Oh, she knew Padrake. She knew his laugh and his smell and the weight and warmth of his body in her bed, her body knew the comfort and security that his embrace had given her. She knew Padrake. She heard fear.

"I think the doctors need to adjust your medication, Jils," Padrake said. "You aren't making sense. What possible reason could you have for making such a wild accusation?"

The others weren't moving. Why was that? Were they waiting to hear what she had to say, before they cast their lots, who to believe?

"Preponderance of circumstantial evidence." She took another step, but stopped, reaching for the back of a chair to steady herself. He hadn't been entirely off target with his remark about medication. She had to be careful to focus what energy, what strength she had left on the crucial points. "The traffic records that were destroyed to draw attention away from the ones that were only slightly altered. Your relationship with the chief medical officer on *Galven*, and where Noycannir got the record."

It would make little sense to the others. They'd heard the rumors about a forged record, yes, but they couldn't have guessed at its significance—unless they were all much smarter than she was, and it was possible, of course. She doubted it.

Padrake knew exactly what she meant, but more than that, it was clear from the look on Padrake's face that he knew what she was saying. So the others would know that much. She had to keep on, she had to get it all out before she lost the threads.

"You let me believe you didn't know Lazarbee. You didn't know how much the pilot had told me. You weren't sure I'd notice that the traffic data had been tampered with. That was why you tried to blow up the whole ship."

"Jils!" It was a cry of honest anguish; she could hear it echo in her heart. "Jils, why would I have done such a thing as that? Even if. Even. If I had. Why would I have killed Sindha Verlaine?"

It wasn't the question she wanted to hear. She knew that, and was ashamed. The question she wanted to hear was "Jils, how could I ever try to harm you?" She had let herself go. She had lost her professional detachment. It was the others who answered for her; had they known all along?

"Well, you did tell us that Verlaine was the worst threat to the stability of the Bench that the Jurisdiction had ever faced," Balkney said, very gently.

"And that Bench specialists should be running the Bench," Rafenkel added. "We had a talk about it. Remember? Verlaine would have put an end to that idea."

"So what better solution all around than to remove an enemy of the Judicial order, and take his place at Chilleau while the administration struggled to recover?" Karol's question was rhetorical. Unfortunately. They made it all too clear. Altruism and self-interest, duty and honor muddled up with the lust for power and privilege—too much sense by half.

"This is beginning to sound suspiciously like a set-up job." Padrake spoke with aggressive bravado, but he was afraid. What was he afraid of? The truth? "What's your take on all of this, Arik? Don't tell me they've gotten to you, too."

The First Secretary. Jils had forgotten that he was there. Now he came forward. "It's perfectly true about Verlaine," he said. "You and I were in complete agreement about that, Padrake. You were out of contact for some days, around that time, and you told me exactly where you'd been. You don't usually seem to feel a need to do that. A man could wonder."

But we will find out, Jils thought; and knew what Padrake was afraid of. He was right to be afraid of Andrej Koscuisko. Any sane person would be—not of the man himself, not necessarily, but of what he could do. What he would do. What he was going to do to Padrake, because the evidence that existed was enough to go to the extreme levels of the Protocols even as it stood in light of the gravity of the accusation; and the Bench would want to know how deep and wide the contagion had spread. Padrake. The Bench would do that to Padrake. Padrake, whom she loved.

"You've all taken leave of your rational faculties," Padrake said firmly. "Or worse. I can't believe that you'd be in on a plot against me, Jils, not even to save yourself."

Padrake whom she loved, and who'd tried to murder her. That Padrake. Putting her hand to the holster at her side she drew her side-arm; she'd come prepared. She was in no condition to fight. "Nobody's plotting against you," she said, as calmly as she could. "It's you. Isn't it? Don't bother denying it, we'll have the truth of the matter soon enough."

Koscuisko, here. Would his sense of duty allow him to go home, with this unresolved? Could Koscuisko sacrifice the greater good of the Judicial order to his personal morality—put his wife and child above the chance that a lesser torturer would lose Padrake to death before the crucial question of co-conspirators had been answered in full?

And the inquiry would just spread and keep on spreading; and the Bench needed all of its resources, to concentrate on restoring order and the regulation of trade. Verlaine was dead; no number of collateral torture-killings could reverse that and set the Judiciary back to where it had been before.

If there were other Bench specialists involved, the Bench needed them to do their jobs. The Bench couldn't afford to throw any of them away, whether they'd been traitors to their sworn duty or not. It didn't matter what anybody had done, not now. It was what they did next that would make the difference.

"And if you think I'm going quietly to be drugged into self-incrimination you're insane, all of you." Padrake straightened up proudly as he said so, one hand at his side, but one hand touching lightly against the comm console behind him.

She knew exactly what Padrake was saying, if nobody else did. *Do I have a bomb? Maybe not, Jils. Can you take that chance, with Arik Tirom in the room? No. You have to kill me. And we both know it.*

He wouldn't. He couldn't possibly. There was no bomb. It was a bluff. He meant to escape the retributive punishment that he had earned. But there could be a bomb, and she—and Karol—were perhaps the only people here who knew that.

"Stand away," she warned, raising her side-arm. If there was a bomb she needed to make sure that he didn't touch a toggle with one last desperate gesture as he died. She could hear a commotion in the corridor behind her; the squads of Security that she'd sent down the air-well had arrived. One bomb; thirty-eight souls on station. "Hands to the front, Padrake, or I'll shoot."

He'd tried to kill her. He'd been willing to sacrifice the courier and its crew to protect himself. There was no guarantee that he might not decide to take them all with him, since he was going to die—more or less quickly. The game was up. He was discovered. There was no hope left for Padrake now.

"You couldn't hurt me, Jils," he said, but it was a challenge, calculated to make her angry. Angry enough to shoot him. His hand went out across the comm console behind him, his fingers searching for something on the board. "We love each other. I love you, Jils. Always loved. You couldn't—"

Hurt me.

She could hear Andrej Koscuisko's voice, explaining it to her. *Killed him because I loved him. Because. Not despite.*

She could see Karol moving, again, so smoothly that it was almost invisible; and knew that within moments Karol would be on Padrake, to subdue him. The room was full of Bench specialists. Once let Karol close with Padrake and they would all mob Padrake at once. Padrake would be taken alive. She couldn't let that happen.

She fired the round to strike him full in the chest at his left side, so that the reflex of his body would pull him away from the comm console. Her aim was off; she hit more of his chest than she'd needed to, stenciling patterns in blood and flesh against the back wall.

It was messy, but it worked. His body spun away from the console under the force of the impact, the walls and floor and furnishings drenched in an instant with the blood from the cavity in his chest. The uncoordinated flailing of his limbs was terrible to see. She couldn't bear to look, even though his face was turned toward the wall. How many fractions of consciousness left to a man, when blood ceased to carry oxygen to the brain?

Padrake's blood was all around him, the walls, his clothing, the floor. His body wriggled like a crushed insect's, and it was unspeakably grotesque to see him—beautiful Padrake—made over by her hand into an object of horror.

At least it did not go on for very long.

She didn't need to go down. She knew that he was dead. They didn't have the resuscitation equipment here that they would need to even try to salvage him, and when traumatic injury led to such a sudden massive loss of blood there was very little chance of any medical intervention succeeding even in the best of circumstances.

Always loved you, Jils. And the Hell of it was that he had very possibly been telling the truth about that, even though he had tried to kill her with a bomb—and who knew what his role had been in the earlier incidents, the one with Nion, the one with the chair?

She sat down in the nearest chair very suddenly. Crossing her arms on the back of the seat in front of her—her side-arm still grasped in her right hand—Jils began to weep.

Always loved you. Killed him because she loved him. It didn't change the fact that she had killed him, or that he was dead. She wished that somebody would do the same for her, right here, right now; but nobody had ever loved her as he had. And nobody ever would.

"Down the air-well?" She heard Balkney's voice as though in another room, and knew that he was speaking to the Security. "Well done. You need to get out as quickly as possible. We don't know what Delleroy may or may not have done."

Karol was beside her with a hand around her upper arm, carefully. "Let's go, Jils," Karol said. "We're evacuating. Now. First Secretary, tell her."

"Get up and get back to the lift-car, Ivers," Tirom said. "I'm not leaving without you. Come on. We need to leave. We need to leave immediately."

And abandon Padrake's body on the floor, there at the far end of the room? Let it lie there to rot without a word said over him, without a wish for a speedy passage, like vermin? Even vermin were cleaned up, cleared away, burned—how could she leave him here like an embarrassing lump of body-waste best left ignored and unacknowledged and forgotten —

She had to get the First Secretary out of here. She had to get them all out of here. Padrake knew bombs. There was no telling. He might well have been down here well before any of the others had arrived, under pretext of making necessary preparations.

Leaning heavily on Karol she stood up; she could hardly sense where her own arms and legs had gone, she moved clumsily, but she could move. Out of the theater with Padrake left behind like a soiled tissue. To the lift-car with Tirom and Karol, Rafenkel and Security, to make the ascent to the surface before some fail-safe device of Padrake's could explode and kill them all anyway.

She had done her duty. It could not touch the comfort she had taken in his body, but it was all she had.

This is your Captain speaking. There has been an announcement from Brisinje with respect to the selection of a new First Judge.

It was end-of-shift on *Scylla*, and Doctor Benal Lazarbee was on his way to quarters with a little something extra in his duty-blouse. He'd heard the announcement. Irshah Parmin had had all of the senior people on board to the officer's mess to hear the news, Ship's Primes, Security warrants, staff officers and all, promiscuously together. The man had no sense of propriety, but Lazarbee didn't care. Irshah Parmin was immaterial as of now, him and all the rest of his crew.

The Bench has determined that the rule of Law and the public weal is best served in the immediate future by operating on a confederacy model for the near term.

The message was being broadcast on all-ship three times a shift for four shifts, just to make sure that everybody had a chance to hear the news and meditate on its implications. As a senior officer his quarters would be blessedly quiet, however; and Lazarbee had plans for his peace and quiet, plans that involved the narcotics in his pocket and something that Delleroy had brought him on his last visit.

"Doctor Lazarbee!"

Someone was running after him through the corridor; moderately annoyed, Lazarbee turned around. One of the clinicians, one of the Old Guard, one of those tiresome people who were all too prone to tell tales of how it had been when they'd had Koscuisko as their CMO. "What is it, Galins?"

Once order has been restored and trade relations regularized the Bench will revisit this interim governmental model. All souls under Jurisdiction are urged to cooperate with the authorities to the maximum extent in their power in order to maintain the benefits of peace and justice for all.

Galins was in a state, so much was obvious; flushed in the face and sweating, speaking quickly, and a little out of breath. She'd been running hard. "Need you to release the secures on scheduled narcotics, your Excellency, we've got a pain management issue, and Doctor Phinny not on shift for another four eighths."

What business was it of Galins' if he'd ended his duty shift a little early, today? He was responsible for validating the narcotics inventory on a periodic basis; he'd signed off on the report and locked the stores. It wouldn't do at all for him to open the stores on his own codes again before the pilferage was discovered. "Galins, I've had a very long shift, and I'm tired. I'm returning to quarters. It'll have been four eighths by the time you get back to Infirmary, aren't you on duty? Better hurry."

No, he needed Phinny to open the stores; that way the reconciliation was Phinny's problem. All of the stores had been accounted for when Lazarbee had signed off on them, after all, there was his chop, to prove it. And a nice little present from himself to himself in his pocket to help while away the time, as soon as he could get to quarters.

Fleet will continue to work closely with Bench officers to ensure a smooth transition and protect the rights of citizens from disorder and anarchy. Your pay and benefits will not be affected by this decision, but will continue to accrue according to the contract you have made with the Bench.

Firmly ignoring the tiresome person behind him Lazarbee betook himself down the corridor toward quarters. Galins wasn't going to follow him. "Go take yourself off to polish my boots, or something," Lazarbee said to the orderly who waited at the door to his rooms.

Security. Another chapter of the Andrej Koscuisko Admirers club. "I want my privacy, for once."

We remain attached to the Ninth Judiciary, and depart Emandis Station for Brisinje shortly. This is your Captain, thanking you in advance for your flexibility, your professionalism, and your continued support of the rule of Law and the Judicial order.

Finally, he was in his sanctuary, and it was quiet. Stripping off his uniform blouse he poured himself a drink, and toasted the irony; the confederacy model after all, and Delleroy had been dead set against it from the beginning. Not as though it mattered. Delleroy would continue to deliver. A Bench specialist knew how handy a cooperative Writ could be, and made generous and tangible gestures of appreciation.

The chastral that Delleroy had brought him was illegal in and of itself because its therapeutic applications were too unreliable for practical use and silly people were always overdosing. Reasonable people understood how to manage chastral, though, and properly handled chastral provided a wonderfully satisfying experience. That was the other reason it was so expensive. Lazarbee had counted up the profit he would make free and clear on Delleroy's gift and decided that he truly deserved a little treat for himself by way of celebration.

The trick was to mix the stuff with a narcotic, and to have a reputable supplier. The narcotic served as a natural supplement that smoothed out chastral's rough edges, and a reputable supplier could be counted on not to adulterate her product with cheap synthetic imitations. Lazarbee himself used a reasonable amount of an inert starch, but he had a quality product, and it was the buyer who was to beware, after all.

Lazarbee opened up the box that Delleroy had brought him and smiled happily. His flask was half-full of drink; he dropped a beautifully formed crystalline lump of chastral into the liquor and poured the narcotic he'd taken from stores in on top. He was Ship's Inquisitor; under any other Command he would be free to prescribe himself whatever he liked, but Irshah Parmin was an uncooperative fellow who knew how to make himself tiresome and Lazarbee didn't like any of his subordinate staff enough to worry about the explanations they'd have to invent to cover the discrepancies. Who cared?

He let the chastral dissolve in solution while he peeled himself out of his boots and unfastened his waistband. Taking up the glassful of elixir he lay down on his back on his bed and sighed deeply and happily, taking a drink. This was going to be so good. He could feel the sensation creeping into his fingertips almost immediately, a tingling in his earlobes and his nose; and hastened to finish the glass, so as to have the full dose before the drug distracted him.

It was wonderful. The prickling in his extremities had progressed to the palms of his hands and the soles of his feet, and he couldn't help but shift uncomfortably as it took his genitals. All he had to do was wait. First there was the tingling; the alcohol helped to smooth that out. Then there would be a warming, and a sweet glowing sensation, and a swelling wave of rapture would take mind and body alike in its embrace and carry him away into the realm of the gods.

Delleroy had gotten his hands on some really good stuff. The prickling was more intense than he could remember ever having experienced before; and it seemed to be getting worse. Much worse. It wasn't prickling. It was burning. The pins and needles had turned to shards of glass dipped in acid, and his skin was melting, dripping off of subcutaneous tissue, soaking into muscle, eating away his bones—

No. It wasn't happening. It was just a stronger-than-usual reaction. There was no fire. There was no acid. All he had to do was wait. It would be worth it. He knew it would be. All he had to do was last this out, and he could smell the fragrance of resin and wet leaves perfuming the air. He breathed deeply, trying to focus, shaking with the intensity of his pain. Resin. Wet leaves.

Poison.

Delleroy was going to have a lot of explaining to do, trying to foist an inferior grade of chastral off on him as though it was worth money—this stuff was filthy with insecticide. A lot. A lot of explaining. A lot—

But the pain would not go away, and Lazarbee could not move. Security. Security would be back, the officer's orderly, with his third-meal. Eventually. He'd quit his shift early. He'd sent Security away.

The drug was not adulterated. The drug was poisoned. It wasn't a drug at all. It was just poison. Delleroy wanted to kill him. Why?

It was working, too. The narcotic paralyzed him, but did not stop the agony that was traveling up each nerve-fiber in his body to his spine and up the spinal column to his brain. He couldn't move. He couldn't speak. He could not even scream. Delleroy had killed him, but Delleroy was taking his own good time, and somehow that was the worst part about dying.

"No, Jils," Karol said, sounding like a man who was tired of the argument. "There really isn't any might-have-been there. Delleroy might have gotten away with fudging the tiles if you hadn't taken Nion out. But by the time he got back from Emandis Station it was pretty clear that the unimaginable was in fact the best solution we had for now."

The launch-fields of Brisinje lay in smoldering ruins; from where Jils Ivers stood with Karol on the wide white-scrubbed terrace of guest quarters, facing the river, she could see the towering clouds on the far horizon, the turquoise-colored mountains, the work crews in the river sieving the bottom clear of ash with divers. There were work-crews all over the city, washing and decontaminating as they went.

Traffic was far from normal—no heavy freight would move through the Ninth Judge's capital for some time to come—but passenger traffic could get in and out, small ships, couriers. There was one out on the improv field, waiting for Karol to fly Andrej Koscuisko to Chilleau to file his documents before the Second Judge, and then go home. Not Karol, of course. Karol was for Chilleau, since Chilleau was short a Bench specialist. Jils wasn't going back. Brisinje needed her. Padrake had done damage in this place; she meant to right the balance.

"If you'd have told me when I got here that there'd be no Selection I would have laughed." The announcement had been made months ago, not as though she was ever going to get used to it. It was the end of the Bench as they knew it, the confederation model after all, but if it was the uttermost failure of everything that she'd believed in and worked for all her life still the Bench had not fallen into chaos and anarchy. Not yet.

"There are a lot of things I'd never have predicted." Karol sounded amused, in a sad sort of a way. "All we can do is keep our eye on our duty and hope for the best."

There were going to be problems with Fleet. She just knew it. Already *Scylla* had tried to poach Koscuisko out of his hospital bed and back into his old berth as its chief medical officer, Doctor

Lazarbee having suffered an unforeseen accident involving excess quantities of the wrong sort of recreational drugs.

That Padrake had had other accomplices, even among surviving Bench specialists, was almost certain; but it didn't matter now. Nobody was going to have time or energy to corrupt the Confederation and subvert the rule of Law. Everybody had far too much work to do.

"Well, come and see me from time to time, Karol." Tirom had made her feel wanted here, as well as needed. Padrake's old office had been returned to a senior administrative official and one found for her in much more congenial quarters—hidden away in the under-corridors, far away from Tirom and the Judge alike.

Maybe they felt regretfully responsible about Padrake's role in the nightmare that Verlaine's murder had been making of her life. She didn't care what their reasons were. She liked it here. And she couldn't bring herself to like the thought of working with the Second Judge again, not after those months of arctic suspicion, disapproval, frustration.

"We'll see." He was turning his campaign hat around and around in his hands, as though committing the precise details of its sweat-band to memory. "I'll be getting out to the launch-field. Wouldn't do to keep Koscuisko waiting."

No, of course not. Jils had to smile. Koscuisko had been as restless as an imprisoned animal, a predator, thirsty for blood—but in a good way. He'd be wearing a cyborg brace on his right hand for some time yet to make absolutely sure of some of the reknits, but the medical facility had run out of excuses why he had to stay. The interns were all in mourning. Having a surgeon of Koscuisko's caliber captive in one's own rooms had been the chance of a lifetime, for Brisinje's teaching hospital; and they had exploited their access fully.

"Better get moving," Jils agreed. She had decided, lying in the ruins of the courier's bed-cabin, that Karol hadn't killed Captain Lowden—Koscuisko had. She hadn't said anything to either man about it. It somehow did not seem all that important. "But if you ever disappear into Gonebeyond again I'm coming after you. I promise."

He didn't seem to feel effectively threatened, which was a shame. "Later, Jils," he said, and embraced her briefly, fraternally, almost shyly.

She watched him go across the terrace back through the building, heading out to take a ground-car to the improv field where his courier waited. It wasn't an Emandis courier, this time, but something that the Combine had sent for Koscuisko's use; Karol would be piloting alone.

A Combine courier could almost fly itself. They were the best that there was to be had in Jurisdiction space. Karol was a good pilot, too, she knew that from experience.

If anybody could see Koscuisko safely to where he needed to be, it was Karol Vogel. With that reassuring thought, Jils turned away from watching the divers in the river to get back to the administration of Brisinje Judiciary.

EPILOGUE

Karol Vogel had things to do and people to see, but first he had to get Koscuisko back to Koscuisko's home ground. Koscuisko would have his hands full on Azanry, Karol was sure of it. Sant-Dasidar was doing as well as any of her sister Judiciaries and better than most; it was an artifact, perhaps, of the fact that the Dolgorukij had always understood hierarchy.

Half-way across the Anglerhaz vector to Chilleau from Brisinje Karol eased back on his record-checks and slumped against his clamshell, tired but satisfied. He'd land Koscuisko at Chilleau. The Second Judge would want him to get right on things; he'd already heard a few words on the subject, but under the circumstances he thought he could probably insist on ferrying Koscuisko on to Azanry himself. Good public relations. Respect for high-ranking civilian persons of importance.

Hearing movement from the direction of the doorway behind him Karol looked back over his shoulder at Koscuisko standing on the threshold with a lefrol in one hand and a somber expression on his face. People didn't usually smoke lefrols in wheel-houses; smoke carried particulate matter, which could get into the mechanisms. So could dust and dander, though, and that didn't stop people from sitting in wheel-houses shedding both like it was going out of style.

"Come on in," Karol said. "The water's fine."

Bending his head Koscuisko stepped forward to seat himself to

Karol's right, in the second-seat on the boards. It was a very nice courier, but it was Koscuisko's, after all. If Koscuisko wanted to smoke in his own wheelhouse it was between him and the wheelhouse. There was a dish for the ash, built in to the console; Koscuisko inhaled a deep draught of the smoke, and set the lefrol under the vapor-capture hood before he let his breath back out again.

"I have heard many interesting rumors about where you have been, Bench specialist," Koscuisko said, left hand to right wrist as though his fingers hurt. The cyborg bracing that crept around Koscuisko's right hand glinted dully in the low light of the wheelhouse, and made a clicking sound when it struck a hard surface. "Talk to me about Gonebeyond space."

Why should he? Because Koscuisko was trying to make conversation, that was why. And why not? He'd covered up Koscuisko's murder of Captain Lowden in Burkhayden; he'd declined to execute a Warrant for Koscuisko's life. He might as well talk to the man. That didn't mean he had to make things easy. "What've you heard?"

"I've heard that people go seeking Gonebeyond, but I've never quite understood what one is supposed to find there."

Koscuisko had arranged for six bond-involuntary troops to escape their Bonds for Gonebeyond space. Maybe he was anxious about it. Karol looked at the little ticket on the console that held the calculations for his vector transit from Aznir space, and shrugged his shoulders.

"Well, I've heard that it's depressing. Nobody there but refugees. No night life to speak of. Why do you ask?"

"I may have sent a surgical kit into Gonebeyond with no qualified user. It was irresponsible of me." It wasn't the answer Karol had expected, but if he, Karol, wasn't going to admit having been in Gonebeyond, why would Koscuisko confess to what he'd done with those Security troops? "There cannot be much by way of infrastructure in such a place."

"There isn't." Maybe if he made the first move he'd find out what was on Koscuisko's mind. "Doesn't matter much. People in Gonebeyond are living on borrowed time anyway." Because they were escapees, and usually from a threat or sentence of some sort. "The environment keeps the population down. Could be done on a budget, though, a hospital wouldn't need any geriatric care, and very little by way of pediatrics."

Reaching for his lefrol Koscuisko took a hit and set it back down. Karol reminded himself that he disapproved of mood-altering drugs in principle, and that was what a lefrol was, at its base—a delivery system for a psychoactive drug, one that could be physically addicting. Finally Koscuisko spoke. "I am in a position to do you a service, Vogel," Koscuisko said. "A significant savings in time and effort."

An intriguing claim. What did it mean? "I'm listening," Karol said. Naturally occurring, though, lefrols—the leaf was a native botanical of some sort. That made it a little different from taking pure forms of a drug, perhaps.

"I will not disguise from you. It will be significantly more awkward for me to disappear once I have returned to Azanry; and yet it must be done, in one way or another. I have business in Gonebeyond, Vogel, and since I expect you'll be going back, it would be just as convenient if I went with you, wouldn't it?"

Karol had to laugh. "Business, your Excellency? What business does the Koscuisko familial corporation have in Gonebeyond? There are no markets. There's practically no economy. It's hard enough to make a bare living in Gonebeyond, let alone a profit, and I should know, I've been there."

Koscuisko nodded. "Yes, but it is not as a member of my House that I must go. I have something to do. Apologies for some wrongs must be made in person, or they might as well not ever have been made at all, and I have much to say to my Chief of Security."

Chief of Security. Karol thought he remembered Koscuisko's Chief of Security. Seven people were being chased by the *Ragnarok* when the *Ragnarok* hit the Dar-Nevan vector, and only six of them were bond-involuntaries. "You're an idiot." And Karol didn't mind saying so. "Send a nice fruit basket. You've got a wife, and a boy-child."

"My wife will do very well without me, Vogel, and it is better for my son if he never knows his father. But if I should drop out of sight on some local excursion there must be investigations, and there will be blame. There is no help for it. Accidents are not allowed to befall the sons of princes."

Koscuisko was serious. Karol had a hard time believing it, but there was no mistaking the somber tone of Koscuisko's voice. Koscuisko was probably capable of lying to him, but Koscuisko had no reason to do so. "And if you and I disappear together, I'm to blame? I don't like it. Malcontents scare me."

Not so serious as not to smile at Karol's only modestly extravagant claim, but even his smile was sober and serious. "To hint that a Bench Specialist might be at fault would be disrespectful, Vogel. And my cousin Stanoczk has worked with you before, he will know better. It will be an unfortunate incident, but no more than that."

Too bad. Karol didn't think he would have minded the notoriety of being Koscuisko's killer, so long as he hadn't had to actually kill Koscuisko to gain it. "You can't possibly know what you're getting yourself into."

Still, Koscuisko was right about infrastructure, with especial reference to hospitals. His reputation as a torturer was so loud around him that Koscuisko's reputation as a battle surgeon tended to get lost in the noise, but it was there.

"I know that I sent people ahead, and that the ship to which I remain assigned followed. Trust me on this, Vogel, I mean to go into Gonebeyond, and find my ship and crew. Consider how much better my chances are of surviving for two days on end if I throw myself on your mercy for guidance and protection."

He wasn't the least bit interested. But Koscuisko was quite right about his chances of simply dropping off a vector in Gonebeyond and hoping to live for three shifts, even assuming that Koscuisko could even find his way into Gonebeyond without getting killed on the way.

The Malcontent might possibly oblige Koscuisko, if asked; so who did he want Koscuisko to be obliged to? The Malcontent? Or Bench Specialist Karol Aphon Vogel, who had things going in Gonebeyond, an economy to nourish, a community to build?

Karol thought about it for a moment before straightening up and keyed a communication transmit. "Chilleau," Karol said. "Karol Vogel here. Modified travel plans, will proceed to Azanry direct, please transmit." There were people who would protect Koscuisko because he was a doctor. Maybe it would work.

Koscuisko drew his lefrol out from underneath the vapor-capture hood and drank its pungent smoke deep into his lungs, the bracing on his hand casting strange low-relief shadows across his face.

"Bench specialist," Chilleau said. "Proceeding to Azanry direct, confirmed. We'll notify the Combine vectors, will there be anything else, sir?"

"Thanks, Chilleau. Vogel away, here." And that was that; it was done. Well, it wasn't done yet, but it was on its way to being done, and Koscuisko knew it, too, to look at him.

"Holy Mother," Koscuisko said, softly, prayerfully. "I will never see my family again."

And still he was clearly determined on his course. Karol heard regret in Koscuisko's voice, but no second thoughts. There were so many things he could say in response; the safest was the surest, however, so Karol shrugged his shoulders and stood up to stretch.

"You're going to be too busy to notice," Karol said, and went aft to the galley for something to drink.